short fiction

short fiction

An Anthology | Second Edition

Mark Levene & Rosemary Sullivan

OXFORD
UNIVERSITY PRESS

Oxford University Press is a department of the University of Oxford.
It furthers the University's objective of excellence in research, scholarship,
and education by publishing worldwide. Oxford is a registered trade mark of
Oxford University Press in the UK and in certain other countries.

Published in Canada by
Oxford University Press
8 Sampson Mews, Suite 204,
Don Mills, Ontario M3C 0H5 Canada

www.oupcanada.com

First Edition published in 2003

Library and Archives Canada Cataloguing in Publication

Short fiction (2015)
Short fiction : an anthology / edited by Mark Levene and Rosemary Sullivan.—Second edition.

Includes index.
ISBN 978-0-19-900936-7 (pbk.)

1. Short stories. 2. Short stories, Canadian (English). I. Levene, Mark, editor II. Sullivan, Rosemary, editor III. Title.

PN6120.2.S47 2015 808.83′1 C2014-907930-3

Cover art: Philip Koch, Rooms by the Sea, oil on panel, 14 × 21", 2013. philipkoch.org

Oxford University Press is committed to our environment.
Wherever possible, our books are printed on paper which comes from responsible sources.

Printed and bound in the United States of America
1 2 3 4 — 18 17 16 15

Contents

Preface

After a decade of pedagogical enthusiasm for *Short Fiction: An Anthology*, Oxford University Press asked us to prepare a second edition. This decision came at a particularly auspicious, even heady, time in the fortunes of contemporary short fiction. It seemed that from 2009 to 2014, few weeks went by without major literary journals heralding new work by an established writer or the refashioning of the form by a writer in early career. The reviews, for instance, of George Saunders's *Tenth of December* and Karen Russell's *Vampires in the Lemon Grove* may well have felt hyperbolic until one read even the opening pages of their remarkable stories. Their peers seem to comprise a battalion of inventive, courageous writers, among them Lynn Coady, Sarah Hall, Tessa Hadley, Junot Díaz, Chimamanda Ngozi Adichie, Anne Enright, Andrew Sullivan, and David Bezmozgis. In the nature of things sadly, only some could be included in this edition. In their writing many occupy the interzones of realism and surrealism, and many create a new demotic, arising from life in Haiti, Puerto Rico, the Cumbrian valleys, and the American suburbs. In a moment of rare symbiosis between private work and public recognition, the Swedish Academy awarded the 2013 Nobel Prize to Alice Munro, the first time a writer exclusively of short fiction was so honoured. The possibilities in the short story have come to seem infinite.

With this abundance, we have renewed our commitment to justice and restraint. We believe no contemporary anthology should be prescriptive; in being truthful to the experience of fiction, an anthology must keep the scholarly apparatus to a minimum. It should contain as many stories on as wide a variety of themes and from as many cultural perspectives as is possible. We hope our selection of stories offers the individual instructor the opportunity to examine the formal aspects of a story in the context of the genre's historical evolution as well as in terms of issues ranging from gender, race, and cultural identity to those of intimacy, sexuality, solitude, and spirituality.

The introduction suggests that there are many corridors through the book, each of which invites critical thinking about how stories are constructed, how they reflect cultural concerns, and how they affect readers. Everywhere our impulse has been to resist closing doors and to convey possibility and richness. In the course of our work, many people have been helpful. We would like to thank in particular Tamara Capar, Dave Ward, Michael Trussler, Ella Soper, and of course our families. There is also an unusual level of thanks: to Robert Stone for his presence and to Alice Munro, the presiding spirit over this volume and over the short story as it moves in its ellipses, precisions, and mysteries, its daunting control of time and place, toward what may be a new primacy among literary forms.

The Editors

PART I
Introduction

The House of Fiction

A good short story is a story that is not too long and which gives the reader the feeling he has undergone a memorable experience.

Martha Foley

It's the chamber music of literature and has the same kind of devotee.

Hortense Calisher

Always in the short story there is this sense of outlawed figures wandering about the fringes of society. . . . As a result there is in the short story at its most characteristic something we do not often find in the novel—an intense awareness of human loneliness.

Frank O'Connor

I want stories to startle and engage me within the first few sentences, and in their middle to widen or deepen or sharpen my knowledge of human activity, and to end by giving me a sensation of completed statement.

John Updike

Short stories are the way I live.

an undergraduate student

It is the black room at the centre of the house with all other rooms leading to and away from it.

Alice Munro

The modern short story may be defined as the distillation of an essence.

William Trevor

Unlike the novel a short story may be, for all purposes, essential.

Jorge Luis Borges

The reason for beginning this introduction with a small yet representative grouping of comments about the story is to emphasize the range but also the consistency of reaction the form inspires, from truisms to awe, and a sort of reverential confusion or submission to the story's unique magic. The first statement comes from the long-time editor of *Best American Short Stories* (a series that began in 1915), who decided to go with a soft, utterly open definition. Oddly, given the complexity of his own short fiction, John Updike does the same, except with a more discernible moral twist. Calisher, O'Connor, and Munro register the sweep of tone in all narrative: the lyrical, the dark, the lonely. The student quoted along with Trevor and Borges articulates something we all intuit: that there is a fundamental quality to the short story we might unguardedly but accurately call "essential," something about transience, mortality, artistic shaping, and the ways we read—how we align ourselves and our experience with narrative.

That word "essential" has often been used by short story editors, who comment that, difficult as the short story is to define, particularly to answer the vexed question, "How short is short?" stories have their deepest roots in human speech and oral tradition. It's fairly easy to spin back through the centuries to imagine stories about a hunt, a migration, or the danger of playing, say, with snakes. Because "she said, he said" is a narrative formula we encounter regularly—in a telephone conversation, for instance, or in a story we might submit to a magazine—we think we know what a short story is. It's an incident recounted by a friend or a family member that we wish, sometimes desperately, would be shorter. Sometimes it's a personal narrative we'd like to be longer, its spaces filled, its significance elaborated. (Of course, our own deeply compelling stories require the duration and the space of *War and Peace*.) Implicitly or explicitly, the stories in the collection are about telling. Woody Allen's "The Kugelmass Episode" hinges on the glorious comedy of telling and re-telling; Alice Munro's "Fits" depicts narrative as a social and personal necessity, the denial of which has terrible consequences. This ostensibly curious pairing of stories is an instance of the striking way many of the selections here play off of one another.

The short story genre is identified both as indigenous to the modern world—"a young art" and "a child of this century," as Elizabeth Bowen announced—and as being rooted in numerous historical forms. A broad chronological ancestry of the short story includes the creation myths of various cultures; Aesop's fables; certain kinds of sequences in the Old and New Testaments, such as the story of Cain and Abel and the parable of the virgins (The Book of Job is more like a novella); and separable units in classical literature—for example, in Petronius's *Satyricon* and Apuleius's *Metamorphoses* (*The Golden Ass*). The Middle Ages contributed the French *fabliaux* and, most importantly, two series of collected tales, Boccaccio's *Decameron* (c.1349–1351) and Chaucer's *Canterbury Tales* (1385–1400). One should also note here the legacy of *One Thousand and One Nights*. Among the many aspects of the modern short story that these tales anticipate is the fascinating and complex relation of part to whole, which is inescapable in thinking not only about a short story collection, but also about the peculiarly intense importance that details in an individual story take on. The connection between a narrative segment and the overall structure of the work becomes even closer in England during the seventeenth and eighteenth centuries, most notably in the digressions that punctuate Henry Fielding's sweeping novels *Tom Jones* and *Joseph Andrews*. Also resembling embryonic short stories are the types of prose narrative that emerged in the burgeoning periodical literature of the 1700s, among them Gothic and adventure stories and artistically rough but earnest morality tales.

Whether in 1613 Cervantes wrote short stories as we understand them now, or to what extent the original French *conte* is a reduced image of the post-Hawthorne and post-Poe short story, are intricate contextual issues better left to literary historians. More directly productive for inquiries into the textures and appeal of specific short stories and into the genre as a whole are the ghostly and supernatural spaces explored by a number of nineteenth-century writers in Germany, the United States, and Russia (and, to a lesser extent, England). The period between 1810 and 1842 was enormously important for the emergence of the short story as a distinctive form: Heinrich von Kleist's volumes of stories appeared in 1810 and 1811, the brothers Grimm produced their widely popular *Fairy Tales* in 1812, and E.T.A. Hoffmann's first collection was published in 1814. Rerouting these German models through American preoccupations, Washington Irving wrote "Rip Van Winkle" and "The Legend of Sleepy Hollow" (*The Sketch Book of Geoffrey Crayon, Gent.*, 1819–1820). Nathaniel Hawthorne's tales began appearing in *The Token*, then in his first collection, *Twice-Told Tales* (1837), the most brilliant and seminal volume in the as yet short history of the short story. Reviewing the expanded version in 1842, Edgar Allen Poe created a prescriptive theory for the short story based on the reader's psychology (which required the reader to digest the story at a single sitting to allow the tale's "unity of effect" its full impact) and wrote his own fascinating and influential stories, among them *Tales of the Grotesque and Arabesque* (1839), *The Fall of the House of Usher* (1839), and *The Murders in the Rue Morgue* (1841).

If, somehow, short stories had ended here, they would have simply been a version of the prose romance with its stress on archetypes and extreme states. In the "houses of fiction" they would have been floor after floor of "the black room(s)" Munro refers to above, moist from the fevers of their inhabitants, often bloody, often echoing frightening compulsions (the rooms and garden in "Rappaccini's Daughter," the creaking, collapsing Usher mansion/psyche). But the ordinary world is never to be shut out for long, certainly not by its artists. Among the writers responsible for shaping a type of short narrative grounded in more familiar settings and states of behaviour are Pushkin, Gogol, Turgenev, Tolstoy, Flaubert, and Melville. But the usual and correct emphasis in this late nineteenth-century transition from the fantastic to the realistic—as long as we remember that the transition is not absolute, that *all* good short stories are marked by a unique, coiled intensity—is on the work of Guy de Maupassant (1850–1893), Herman Melville (1819–1891), and ultimately that of Anton Chekhov (1860–1904). Described as a writer "who had escaped from tradition and authority" (Kate Chopin), Maupassant gravitated toward meticulously structured, definitive plots and almost chiselled physical detail. In "A Short History of the Short Story" (2006), William Boyd locates Melville's *The Piazza Tales* (1856) as the "first real exemplars of the short story's strange power." By age and temperament Chekhov was much closer to the emerging spirit of modernism. Felt to be a writer who helped change perceptions of the world, he often preferred a more diffuse structure for his deeply compassionate renderings of pain, loss, and hope. Along with brilliant, enigmatic endings, Chekhov positioned details to startle, to modify perspective, and to mark the very sharp, sometimes funny, joins between layers of human experience. He recreated the fundamental nature of a fictional character "as mood rather than as either symbolic projection or realistic depiction" and made plot "the expression of a complex inner state" (Charles E. May).

It's hardly surprising that with the attraction in all the arts at this time to depict states of consciousness, the English translation of Chekhov's stories in 1916 helped concentrate the impulse among writers, painters, and philosophers to "make it [that is, everything] new." This process was already taking a remarkable turn in the way

James Joyce was writing his short stories. Eventually and after painful difficulties with the publisher over the disturbing quality of their physical details, the stories appeared as *Dubliners* (1914). Written, he declared, as a composite "chapter in the moral history of his country," the stories seem overwhelmingly claustrophobic: the dark houses, the dusty rooms, all versions of one another, every frustrated life a dull echo of everyone else's. But far more than use of the "epiphany"—a moment of sudden and often disturbing realization or illumination that occurs in many of his stories—Joyce's genius was in directing us toward the untold, the absent, stories adjacent to the overt ones being told. In "The Sisters" the priest's story is interpreted or usurped, and at the end remains an inaccessible mystery. The power and the beauty of "The Dead" is that, whereas the cause of Lily's hostility to men is an implication that can have no development, Gretta's narrative breaks through the silence—and the marital role—to which it was confined, and transforms not only Gabriel's story about himself but also his language of strict categories and judgments. Joyce claimed that he wrote *Dubliners* in a style of "scrupulous meanness," which is certainly an apt phrase for the surface, for the direct experiences, of his characters. But the hidden or absent stories reflect a generosity, as well as a sense of the limits to what any of us can usually know. With these elusive narratives Joyce gives the recently renovated short story a further new direction—outward and inward, toward mystery and silence—at the same time as he twists and deepens the wholesale movement to internalize experience that modernism undertook, the monumental change, as Irving Howe conceives it, from the heroism of "deed to the heroism of consciousness." The covert stories of the priest and of Lily, the aunts and their niece, redirect us, as all stories do, back to the beginning, or in terms of this collection, to the epigraphs: Eliot's rose garden and Munro's roomy house, where time and space intersect, creating that commingling of possibility and impossibility we sense that only the short story conveys so perfectly.

While it is not the purpose of this introduction to overburden the stories themselves with an ostensibly exhaustive—therefore exhausting and dismissible—historical apparatus, a workable sense of the period that followed the publication and immediate impact of Chekhov's and Joyce's great stories is a significant part of the reading process. It is quite clear, for instance, that the 1920s became a boom time for the short story. Katherine Mansfield put her distinctive, allusive mark on the Chekhovian story; Isaac Babel published his collection *Red Cavalry* (1925), a technically adventurous grafting of lyricism and humour onto the harshness of Russian history; and D.H. Lawrence, fierce individualist that he was, created a fusion of inner and outer landscapes reminiscent of the American writers, Hawthorne in particular, whose stories so deeply attracted him. The twenties also saw the arrival of two other remarkable and very distinctive voices. In the countless stories he offered to a burgeoning magazine readership, F. Scott Fitzgerald produced an elegiac prose that seemed a mirror to the age. Ernest Hemingway, the more experimental writer, pressed implication and omission as far, it seemed, as they could go. (It turned out, however, that decades later, Raymond Carver and more recently Lydia Davis and George Saunders would press them even further.) Hemingway reduced dialogue and narrative detail to the point where every word feels surrounded by silence, a silence that infiltrates and challenges the reader's imagination.

Fitzgerald and Hemingway continued to write short stories through the 1930s (as did Elizabeth Bowen, Graham Greene, Frank O'Connor, and most brilliantly, William Faulkner), but the tenor of the world had changed. W.H. Auden called the thirties "a low, dishonest decade." A hyperbolic phrase, it still captures something of the brutal tawdriness attached to the ideologies that arrived with the Great Depression. Increased militarism and seismic pre–World War II events, notably the Spanish Civil War, began to dwarf the humanistic assumptions of the twenties, above all the confidence that language and narrative form could register the mysteries of the human psyche, what Virginia Woolf called its "myriad of impression." The thirties became a time for examining "the big picture" (as described in competing and blood-splattered visionary tracts, *Mein Kampf* and *The Communist Manifesto*), and big pictures do not, as a rule, lend themselves to short stories. A social context of faith and ideology is inhospitable to the glimpses, fragments, ambiguities, and underlying skepticism that make up the core of short fiction.

But it is inaccurate to imply that the decline of the short story was absolute. Although there were innumerable forgettable stories about the heroism of labour and class, many by skilled writers such as Langston Hughes and William Saroyan, some fascinating modifications of the genre appeared. In stories much later collected as *The Railway Accident and Other Stories* (1969), Edward Upward reintroduced the element of fable by way of Kafkaesque dream-states and an unusually oblique, enigmatic Marxism. In 1939 Jean Paul Sartre's collection *Le Mur* appeared, and Christopher Isherwood published *Goodbye to Berlin* (the Sally Bowles section became the perennially lucrative nightclub musical, *Cabaret*) which brilliantly ties personal experience to political experience and understatedly depicts the emergence of German fascism. Remarkable and significant as some short fiction of the thirties was, Hemingway's work through the decade is a rather unnerving representation of the age. In 1933 he published the wonderful *Winner Take Nothing* (which includes our selection, "A Clean, Well-Lighted Place"), in addition to some of his most meretricious writing, for instance his play "The Fifth Column" and appalling stories such as "The Denunciation" and "Night Before Battle."

It is a commonplace of literary history that the immediate postwar period was a time of retrenchment and exhaustion from the enormity of ideas, massacres, expectations, and dashed hopes. The Holocaust and the nuclear attacks on Japan were twin traumas of unprecedented scope and durability. Retreat from literary experiments and their underlying cultural assumptions was inevitable, and the modernist slogan "make it new" became "make it safe—and make it sad." Yet, numerous volumes of superb if restrained short stories appeared in the forties and early fifties, notably by English writers such as V.S. Pritchett, William Sansom, Angus Wilson, and Elizabeth Taylor, and in Germany by Heinrich Böll. But through the catalysts of ethnicity, regionalism, and a complex international prominence, American writers (Bernard Malamud, James Baldwin, Paul Bowles, Eudora Welty, Flannery O'Connor, J.D. Salinger, Grace Paley) redirected the lineage of the short story, paradoxically opening and modulating the form's inherent sense of the solitary. With the suburban fascinations of John Cheever and John Updike and the cultural clout of *The New Yorker*, the short story in the United States was heading toward its second magnificent flourishing, first in the postmodern fiction of John Hawkes, John Barth, and Robert Coover, then in the superb multifarious voices of Raymond Carver, Tobias Wolff, Louise Erdrich, Lorrie Moore, Rick Moody, and Sherman Alexie. But another movement was occurring simultaneously that was to reshape significantly how we read stories, particularly with reference to questions of cultural perspective.

In his seminal essay "Central and Eccentric Writing" (1974), the Mexican novelist Carlos Fuentes described the deep anxiety he felt starting out as a Latin American writer: "It is one thing to write from within a culture that deems itself central and another thing to write from the boundaries of eccentricity—an eccentricity defined by the central culture's claim to universality." As an adolescent reading the opening sentence of Jane Austen's novel *Pride and Prejudice*—"It is a truth universally acknowledged"—Fuentes felt chagrined. It was clear that British literature had "captured the logos" and that as a Mexican he was condemned forever to exile on the periphery of world literature. But then he discovered Emily Brontë, "the bearer of tragic oppositions, secret dreams. . . . outlawed loves." Hers was the voice of rebellion against the central culture's monopoly on power. Slowly he developed his own Mexican voice that melded his Aztec and Spanish roots with his love of world literature, perhaps best exemplified in *The Hydra Head* (1978), his novel about international espionage in which characters speak a code language borrowed from Shakespeare's *Hamlet*. Fuentes's search for national identity, embedded in a nationalism that was not aggressive but rather defensive, was duplicated in the many post-colonial literary movements that were taking place worldwide and that gave rise to new English-language writing in India, Africa, the Caribbean, Australia, New Zealand—in those cultures that had been relegated to the periphery of world power.

Perhaps the Canadian experience can serve as a paradigm, since Canadian writers also searched for a voice through much of the twentieth century. Early examples of the Canadian story were often simply imitations of British models, though there were exceptions, for instance by Robert Barr, Duncan Campbell Scott, and Sara Jeannette Duncan. Even more striking is the unique importance of the animal story, a form that Sir Charles G.D. Roberts took in fascinating directions. Later, Sinclair Ross, Raymond Knister, Hugh Garner, and especially Morley Callaghan wrote exceptional stories, but it would be decades before the magical alliance of the short story and Canadian literary life emerged. A complex factor in the transformation of the Canadian short story from meagreness to magnificence was the extraordinary role played by CBC Radio, or rather by the way producer and program organizer Robert Weaver conceived and actualized his role. Particularly through the programs *Book Time* and *Anthology*, which ran from 1953 to 1985, he did as much as any one person could to make the short story flourish. That the venue for this development in the country's literary history was radio is a testament, as Northrop Frye noted, to the unusual publicness of Canadian cultural life. That stories were read and heard as part of, or in counterpoint to, the texture of ordinary life points to the suggestions that follow about the intricate bonds between reader and story. Now, a mere list of superb Canadian short story writers, from Alice Munro and Mavis Gallant to Alistair MacLeod and Barbara Gowdy, would occupy several lines of print. And that list would be a reflection of the inclusiveness of the genre, giving place to immigrant writers such as Josef Škvorecky and Dionne Brand, and to Native writers like Thomas King and Beth Brant. No longer is the issue who gets to write but how rich, how powerfully persuasive the story is, how layered a relationship it creates with the reader.

But the marvellous drama of the Canadian short story also requires recognition of some significant facts about broader currents in literary history. There are cultures in which the short story has thrived, but where the monumental novel has not (Canada and Ireland, *Ulysses* and *Finnegans Wake* notwithstanding), and there are cultures (the United States, Russia, and to a lesser extent England) in which the two have developed in lockstep. William Trevor makes the marvellous point that "when the [Victorian] novel reared its head Ireland wasn't ready for it." Allowing for the dangers in generalizing about "national character," one can suggest that Canadian writers also weren't ready for the Dickensian narrative or the modernist novel that came afterward. Ireland's ongoing love for oral tradition and Canada's attraction to the hybrid and aversion to anything ideological and monolithic are likely factors in the strength of the short story in these two countries. In Russia and the United States, the short story provided—and provides—a spirit counter to that which the expansive and encyclopedic novel (*The Brothers Karamazov*, *Moby-Dick*, *Gravity's Rainbow*) attracts.

Describing his preference for "big books," the novelist Robert Stone, an enthusiast of big books and a wary writer of short stories, provides an evocative perspective on the connection between the fictional work and the reader's spatial and temporal zones of response: "I use the white space. I'm interested in precise meaning and in reverberation, in associative levels. What you're trying to do when you write is to crowd the reader out of his own space and occupy it with yours, in a good cause. You're trying to take over his sensibility and deliver an experience that moves from mere information." This process of habitation, with its suggestions of power and education, is how novels, particularly panoramic ones rooted in some modification of the realist tradition, establish their presence, their claim, on the reader's attention and expectation. But "crowding the reader out," occupying her experiential space with the narrative's dominion, is also a process that sharply distinguishes the novel from the short story. The tension between the imminence of the ending, of "closure," and the ways in which details delay the smooth rush toward the story's conclusion have increasingly seemed productive areas for theorists who are concerned with going beyond the modest claim that the short story is a story that is short. Following one element in Poe's analysis of the short story form, the critic Norman Friedman observes: "Because we can complete it at one sitting, the experience of closure in a story relates differently to our other life rhythms than reading a novel or a poem. It creates a rhythm of its own which is definite enough to displace our life rhythm until it is over. We can enter, move through, and leave the story without interruption, and thus we build the story world as we read, apart from the other claims on our attention."

Stone and Friedman, novelist and critic, fix their attitudes toward both the novel and the short story on the nature of emotional and imaginative displacement, on the premise that each form creates a total presence within the reader. The narrative arrives like a moving van and for an hour or a week fills the reader's space with furniture, subtle or brutal conversations, even perhaps a typhoon or a war. But it seems more reasonable to argue that the relative brevity of the story, along with the heightened claim on the reader's attention to detail and the imminence of the ending, produce something very different from complete displacement. If anything, there is a painful tension between the story's rhythm and our own "life rhythms," between presented, shaped narrative and our own jagged, graceless life stories. Short stories instill a profound ambivalence: they are complete (while underlining the incompleteness that comes from the internal stories only glimpsed), they are published in an almost lapidary way, they create a compulsion, evoke a necessity around concentrated or distilled event and perspective, and they cover a certain amount of moral space in a certain time, all while pressing the limits of implication. The English short story writer William Sansom exults that the story "should spread beyond its economy: short, it should be enormous." But brevity, even if it pushes a quantitative boundary (a story, say, or fifty pages), and the ever-present ending also announce an aesthetic fragility that intensifies even as it confirms the reader's common, everyday sense of transience. Our own narratives are never far from the foreground in reading a short story. We do not so much relinquish our stories as we keep them hovering around the margins of the very temporarily present ten or twenty or thirty pages by Lawrence or Lessing, Hemingway or Atwood, less in a straightforward process of personal identification and comparison—yes, that's exactly how it felt driving a stolen Mercedes across Montana (Ford, "Rock Springs"), or no, when I'm old I won't need a clean, well-lighted place (Hemingway)—than in a subtle, fluid balance of our own presences and absences with those of the written narrative.

We sense this intricate balance most when a story is published in a magazine; in fact, it is one of the many paradoxes about short fiction that the practicalities of magazine publication are so helpful to our developing a theoretical perspective on the genre. There are two losses to the short story genre from the steady reduction in the number of magazine outlets for writers. In 1919 there were at least six major venues in the United States; now there is really just one, *The New Yorker*, with short stories appearing periodically in *Esquire*, *Harper's*, and *The Atlantic Monthly*. (In Canada the situation has always been terrible.) The first loss is financial, making it virtually impossible for a short story writer to survive in the way F. Scott Fitzgerald did. The second loss is to the aesthetic and visceral nature of reading. When a story appears in a magazine, the imprint of those "life rhythms" that comes from our ordinary spaces is intensified, made even more provisional, by the magazine format, by flipping pages to find the next paragraph, by ads—since it is usually a *New Yorker* page—for a bracelet by Tiffany & Co. or breakfast at the Plaza Hotel. When the first version of Alice Munro's brilliant, multi-layered story "The Love of a Good Woman" appeared there, it occupied pages 102–141 of a December 1996 issue. It had a subtitle, "A murder, a mystery, a romance," and an opening photograph of a sheer nightgown. The text was surrounded by clever, sophisticated cartoons and ads for a National Gallery exhibition as well as for jazz CDs and a miraculous coffee maker. These elements are, in effect, "noise" for the reader, but noise that deepens the complex sense of harmonious isolation that exists between reader and story. When Munro's story became the opening part of the printed collection, this sensory flurry disappeared and was replaced by those white spaces which are as important a part of her narratives as the visible words and which the reader has to negotiate with a similar sense of precariousness and demand for attentiveness as that experienced in a magazine.

Short stories and modern life would seem to be made for one another. Reflecting on this intimacy, the South African writer Nadine Gordimer, as deft a creator of short fiction as of novels, noted as early as 1968: "The short story is a fragmented and restless form, a matter of hit or miss, and it is perhaps for this reason that it suits modern consciousness—which seems best expressed as flashes of fearful insight alternating with near-hypnotic states of indifference." For her, short stories are inherently truer "to the nature of whatever can be grasped of human reality." She states, "Each of us has a thousand lives and a novel gives a character only one. *For the sake of the form* . . . the quality of human life . . . is more like the flash of fireflies, in and out, now here, now there, in darkness. Short story writers see by the light of the flash; theirs is the art of the only thing one can be sure of—the present moment." Certainly a story such as the one that follows, Chekhov's "The Lady with the Dog," seems to contradict or at least to complicate Gordimer's assertion about the art of the present, but on the whole her sense of the interchange between artistic form and human experience feels right. But if it is right, why, when Barbara Kingsolver edited *The Best American Short Stories 2001*, weren't magazine editors pleading with writers for fistfuls of stories, and why were novels so heavy as to cause serious tendon damage so popular? She wonders:

> We Americans are such busy people you'd think we'd jump at the chance to have our literary wisdom served in doses that fit handily between taking the trash to the curb and waiting for the carpool. We should favour the short story and adore the poem. But we don't. Short story collections rarely sell half as well as novels; they are never blockbusters. They are hardly ever even block-denters.

One completely unprovable explanation for this paradox in 2001 and beyond is worth consideration. Perhaps the short story is too suitable, too much a reflection of our daily fragments. Perhaps we don't want to be reminded that although we have a "thousand lives," we live out at best only a couple of them. Perhaps we require the sort of complete habitation of our inner space that the novel can provide, preferring not the flash of fireflies but a large lighthouse. Sarah Hall, one of the luminaries in the Magical Year of the Short Story, 2013, announced like a punch: "Short Stories are often strong meat." Reading them is often "exquisitely unsettling" and requires "a certain amount of nerve and maturity." In the same week as Hall won The BBC National Short Story Award, Alice Munro was awarded the Nobel Prize for Literature. Jonathan Franzen's joy was ubiquitous: "We had to wait more than a century, but we finally have a Nobel for a pure short-story writer." As a year, 2013 was like the "marvelous clear jelly" Munro gorgeously imagines in "Material." Lydia Davis received the International Man Booker, which Munro had won in 2009; Lynn Coady was awarded the Scotiabank Giller Prize for her story collection, *Hellgoing*; Karen Russell published the dazzling *Vampires in the Lemon Grove*; and George Saunders pushed critical synonym-scrambling to the limit with *Tenth of December*, a collection which was very much a blockbuster.

Assuming that the differences in the impact of the short story between 2001 and 2013 (by way of the also notable 2009) were not simply weird, whirling, inexplicable accidents, the pattern-makers in us would at least like to identify dominant as well as covert factors. First and difficult not to notice, there was war, the always reliable force of transformation. Geoff Dyer, almost unparalleled in his ability to see, appraised the literature arising from the Afghan and Iraqi conflicts. "If there were ever a time when the human stories contained within historical events . . . could only be assimilated and comprehended when they had been processed by a novel . . . that time has passed." Consigning the "creaking machinery of the novel" to the past, writers of long-form reporting such as Lawrence Wright and Dexter Filkins have an uncluttered deftness in deploying story and character. Dyer's 2110 essay, "The Human Heart of the Matter," was widely read and influential. Between 2006 and 2011, the novel's stature as the prime expression of extreme human experience took a serious hit. Hybrid narratives unencumbered by literary baggage like Filkins's *The Forever War* (2008) seemed more fitting to the times. Of course, the same point, noted above, was and continues to be made about the short story, itself a consummate hybrid. Whatever degree of readjustment in literary hierarchies was occurring in the latter part of the decade, the short story was expanding its dominion. When Don DeLillo returned to varieties of terrorism beyond the smoke and debris of Lower Manhattan, it was within the short story and the publication of his first collection, *The Angel Esmeralda: Nine Stories* (2011). The pre-eminent artists in the form, Alice Munro and Lydia Davis, probably did not spend a lot of time on genre market reports; they just kept working, issuing respectively in 2009 the flinty self-questioning *Too Much Happiness* and the layered cool enigmas of *The Collected Stories*. Anyone looking at these stories (and their startling alliance with single narratives located and marketed on the Internet) must shrug away any vestigial notions of categorization. We are back within the language of the "essential," from which reflections on the short story never depart for long. In her essay on the form, Sarah Hall says, "At first glance normal-seeming events are taking place, but mundanity gives way to the peculiar, the perilous, the capricious. Short stories are manifestations, their own literary phenomena . . . The reader is left to decide what everything might mean, and in this way the form is inordinately respectful." Invoking "mystery" and "resonance," William Boyd turns the superb phrase, "a complexity of afterthought" to characterize the effect of great stories, and Christopher Ricks, one of the judges who awarded Davis the Man Booker International Prize, gives us "vigilance" as a prime quality. Vigilance, nerve, respect, exhilaration, fear: we are close to heart of the matter. And at street level, there are love blogs to the short story.

Two Stories and Reflections

ANTON CHEKHOV was born in 1860 in Taganrog. Despite the family's economic difficulties, he completed his local schooling and studied medicine at Moscow University, which he financed in part by selling short, humorous stories to magazines and newspapers. He practised as a physician only sporadically, devoting himself first to the short story, then in 1887 to the stage, an attachment that produced *The Seagull* (1896), *Uncle Vanya* (1899), *The Three Sisters* (1901), and *The Cherry Orchard*

(1904). Through the Moscow Art Theatre he met the actress Olga Knipper. They married in 1901, and he died from his tuberculosis in 1904, at forty-four years of age.

RAYMOND CARVER was born in 1938 in Clatskanie, Oregon, and raised in Yakima, Washington. He had a family when he was barely out of his teens and worked at a variety of jobs, including one at a sawmill in California with his father. He took a writing course at Chico State College with the novelist John Gardner. Because of the little time he could devote to writing, he chose poetry and short stories. He published his first story, "The Furious Seasons," in 1961, but his difficulties with finances and alcohol increased along with his artistic productivity. After his marriage broke up, he began living with the poet Tess Gallagher. Seen by critics as the foremost practitioner of "minimalism," Carver moved toward a more expansive prose, notably in *Cathedral* (1983). He died of cancer at fifty years of age.

There are numerous reasons for having these two stories and a brief, selective commentary on each precede the collection proper. Anton Chekhov and Raymond Carver were extraordinarily influential as short story writers in the ways they attended to beginnings and endings, to detail, and to the relationship between situation and states of mind. In their work the line between sadness and humour is astonishingly porous, an instance of the ambiguity we often sense in short stories. Superb as individual narratives, the two stories also have a unique attachment: Carver's story is about Chekhov. Reading a biography of the great Russian writer, therefore "reading" the final moments of Chekhov's life, Carver was in the position we all occupy as readers. He had to look around corners, fill in the spaces that had been left open by a story. He went on to make the mysteries of the event his own imagined story with its own mysteries, which in different ways is what we all do.

The Lady with the Dog

I

It was said that a new person had appeared on the seafront: a lady with a little dog. Dmitri Dmitritch Gurov, who had by then been a fortnight at Yalta, and so was fairly at home there, had begun to take an interest in new arrivals. Sitting in Verney's pavilion, he saw, walking on the seafront, a fair-haired young lady of medium height, wearing a béret; a white Pomeranian dog was running behind her.

And afterwards he met her in the public gardens and in the square several times a day. She was walking alone, always wearing the same béret, and always with the same white dog; no one knew who she was, and every one called her simply "the lady with the dog."

"If she is here alone without a husband or friends, it wouldn't be amiss to make her acquaintance," Gurov reflected.

He was under forty, but he had a daughter already twelve years old, and two sons at school. He had been married young, when he was a student in his second year, and by now his wife seemed half as old again as he. She was a tall, erect woman with dark eyebrows, staid and dignified, and, as she said of herself, intellectual. She read a great deal, used phonetic spelling, called her husband, not Dmitri, but Dimitri, and he secretly considered her unintelligent, narrow, inelegant, was afraid of her, and did not like to be at home. He had begun being unfaithful to her long ago—had been unfaithful to her often, and, probably on that account, almost always spoke ill of women, and when they were talked about in his presence, used to call them "the lower race."

It seemed to him that he had been so schooled by bitter experience that he might call them what he liked, and yet he could not get on for two days together without "the lower race." In the society of men he was bored and not himself, with them he was cold and uncommunicative; but when he was in the company of women he felt free, and knew what to say to them and how to behave; and he was at ease with them even when he was silent. In his appearance, in his character, in his whole nature, there was something attractive and elusive which allured women and disposed them in his favour; he knew that, and some force seemed to draw him, too, to them.

Experience often repeated, truly bitter experience, had taught him long ago that with decent people, especially Moscow people—always slow to move and irresolute—every intimacy, which at first so agreeably diversifies life and appears a light and charming adventure, inevitably grows into a regular problem of extreme intricacy, and in the long run the situation becomes unbearable. But at every fresh meeting with an interesting woman this experience seemed to slip out of his memory, and he was eager for life, and everything seemed simple and amusing.

One evening he was dining in the gardens, and the lady in the béret came up slowly to take the next table. Her expression, her gait, her dress, and the way she did her hair told him that she was a lady, that she was married, that she was in Yalta for the first time and alone, and that she was dull there. . . . The stories told of the immorality in such places as Yalta are to a great extent untrue; he despised them, and knew that such stories were for the most part made up by persons who would themselves have been glad to sin if they had been able; but when the lady sat down at the next table three paces from him, he remembered these tales of easy conquests, of trips to the mountains, and the tempting thought of a swift, fleeting love affair, a romance with an unknown woman, whose name he did not know, suddenly took possession of him.

He beckoned coaxingly to the Pomeranian, and when the dog came up to him he shook his finger at it. The Pomeranian growled: Gurov shook his finger at it again.

The lady looked at him and at once dropped her eyes.

"He doesn't bite," she said, and blushed.

"May I give him a bone?" he asked; and when she nodded he asked courteously, "Have you been long in Yalta?"

"Five days."

"And I have already dragged out a fortnight here."

There was a brief silence.

"Time goes fast, and yet it is so dull here!" she said, not looking at him.

"That's only the fashion to say it is dull here. A provincial will live in Belyov or Zhidra and not be dull, and when he comes here it's 'Oh, the dullness! Oh, the dust!' One would think he came from Grenada."

She laughed. Then both continued eating in silence, like strangers, but after dinner they walked side by side; and there sprang up between them the light jesting conversation of people who are free and satisfied, to whom it does not matter where they go or what they talk about. They walked and talked of the strange light on the sea: the water was of a soft warm lilac hue, and there was a golden streak from the moon upon it. They talked of how sultry it was after a hot day. Gurov told her that he came from Moscow, that he had taken his degree in Arts, but had a post in a bank; that he had trained as an opera singer, but had given it up, that he owned two houses in Moscow. . . . And from her he learned that she had grown up in Petersburg, but had lived in S—— since her marriage two years before, that she was staying another month in Yalta, and that her husband, who needed a holiday too, might perhaps come and fetch her. She was not sure whether her husband had a post in a Crown Department or under the Provincial Council—and was amused by her own ignorance. And Gurov learned, too, that she was called Anna Sergeyevna.

Afterwards he thought about her in his room at the hotel—thought she would certainly meet him next day; it would be sure to happen. As he got into bed he thought how lately she had been a girl at school, doing lessons like his own daughter; he recalled the diffidence, the angularity, that was still manifest in her laugh and her manner of talking with a stranger. This must have been the first time in her life she had been alone in surroundings in which she was followed, looked at, and spoken to merely from a secret motive which she could hardly fail to guess. He recalled her slender, delicate neck, her lovely grey eyes.

"There's something pathetic about her, anyway," he thought, and fell asleep.

II

A week had passed since they had made acquaintance. It was a holiday. It was sultry indoors, while in the street the wind whirled the dust round and round, and blew people's hats off. It was a thirsty day, and Gurov often went into the pavilion, and pressed Anna Sergeyevna to have syrup and water or an ice. One did not know what to do with oneself.

In the evening when the wind had dropped a little, they went out on the groyne to see the steamer come in. There were a great many people walking about the harbour; they had gathered to welcome someone, bringing bouquets. And two peculiarities of a well-dressed Yalta crowd were very conspicuous: the elderly ladies were dressed like young ones, and there were great numbers of generals.

Owing to the roughness of the sea, the steamer arrived late, after the sun had set, and it was a long time turning about before it reached the groyne. Anna Sergeyevna looked through her lorgnette at the steamer and the passengers as though looking for acquaintances, and when she turned to Gurov her eyes were shining. She talked a great deal and asked disconnected questions, forgetting next moment what she had asked; then she dropped her lorgnette in the crush.

The festive crowd began to disperse; it was too dark to see people's faces.

The wind had completely dropped, but Gurov and Anna Sergeyevna still stood as though waiting to see someone else come from the steamer. Anna Sergeyevna was silent now, and sniffed the flowers without looking at Gurov.

"The weather is better this evening," he said. "Where shall we go now? Shall we drive somewhere?"

She made no answer.

Then he looked at her intently, and all at once put his arm round her and kissed her on the lips, and breathed in the moisture and the fragrance of the flowers; and he immediately looked round him, anxiously wondering whether any one had seen them.

"Let us go to your hotel," he said softly. And both walked quickly.

The room was close and smelled of the scent she had bought at the Japanese shop. Gurov looked at her and thought: "What different people one meets in the world!" From the past he preserved memories of careless, good-natured women, who loved cheerfully and were grateful to him for the happiness he gave them, however brief it might be; and of women like his wife who loved without any genuine feeling, with superfluous phrases, affectedly, hysterically, with an expression that suggested that it was not love nor passion, but something more significant; and of two or three others, very beautiful, cold women, on whose faces he had caught a glimpse of a rapacious expression—an obstinate desire to snatch from life more than it could give, and these were capricious, unreflecting, domineering, unintelligent women not in their first youth, and when Gurov grew cold to them their beauty excited his hatred, and the lace on their linen seemed to him like scales.

But in this case there was still the diffidence, the angularity of inexperienced youth, an awkward feeling; and there was a sense of consternation as though someone had suddenly knocked at the door. The attitude of Anna Sergeyevna—"the lady with the dog"—to what had happened was somehow peculiar, very grave, as though it were her fall—so it seemed, and it was strange and inappropriate. Her face dropped and faded, and on both sides of it her long hair hung down mournfully; she mused in a dejected attitude like "the woman who was a sinner" in an old-fashioned picture.

"It's wrong," she said. "You will be the first to despise me now."

There was a watermelon on the table. Gurov cut himself a slice and began eating it without haste. There followed at least half an hour of silence.

Anna Sergeyevna was touching; there was about her the purity of a good, simple woman who had seen little of life. The solitary candle burning on the table threw a faint light on her face, yet it was clear that she was very unhappy.

"How could I despise you?" asked Gurov. "You don't know what you are saying."

"God forgive me," she said, and her eyes filled with tears. "It's awful."

"You seem to feel you need to be forgiven."

"Forgiven? No. I am a bad, low woman; I despise myself and don't attempt to justify myself. It's not my husband but myself I have deceived. And not only just now; I have been deceiving myself for a long time. My husband may be a good, honest man, but he is a flunky! I don't know what he does there, what his work is, but I know he is a flunky! I was twenty when I was married to him.

I have been tormented by curiosity; I wanted something better. 'There must be a different sort of life,' I said to myself. I wanted to live! To live, to live! . . . I was fired by curiosity . . . you don't understand it, but, I swear to God, I could not control myself; something happened to me: I could not be restrained. I told my husband I was ill, and came here. . . . And here I have been walking about as though I were dazed, like a mad creature; . . . and now I have become a vulgar, contemptible woman whom any one may despise."

Gurov felt bored already, listening to her. He was irritated by the naïve tone, by this remorse, so unexpected and inopportune; but for the tears in her eyes, he might have thought she was jesting or playing a part.

"I don't understand," he said softly. "What is it you want?"

She hid her face on his breast and pressed close to him.

"Believe me, believe me, I beseech you . . ." she said. "I love a pure, honest life, and sin is loathsome to me. I don't know what I am doing. Simple people say: 'The Evil One has beguiled me.' And I may say of myself now that the Evil One has beguiled me."

"Hush, hush! . . ." he muttered.

He looked at her fixed, scared eyes, kissed her, talked softly and affectionately, and by degrees she was comforted, and her gaiety returned; they both began laughing.

Afterwards when they went out there was not a soul on the seafront. The town with its cypresses had quite a deathlike air, but the sea still broke noisily on the shore; a single barge was rocking on the waves, and a lantern was blinking sleepily on it.

They found a cab and drove to Oreanda.

"I found out your surname in the hall just now: it was written on the board—Von Diderits," said Gurov. "Is your husband a German?"

"No; I believe his grandfather was a German, but he is an Orthodox Russian himself."

At Oreanda they sat on a seat not far from the church, looked down at the sea, and were silent. Yalta was hardly visible through the morning mist; white clouds stood motionless on the mountaintops. The leaves did not stir on the trees, grasshoppers chirruped, and the monotonous hollow sound of the sea rising up from below, spoke of the peace, of the eternal sleep awaiting us. So it must have sounded when there was no Yalta, no Oreanda here; so it sounds now, and it will sound as indifferently and monotonously when we are all no more. And in this constancy, in this complete indifference to the life and death of each of us, there lies hid, perhaps, a pledge of our eternal salvation, of the unceasing movement of life upon earth, of unceasing progress towards perfection. Sitting beside a young woman who in the dawn seemed so lovely, soothed and spellbound in these magical surroundings—the sea, mountains, clouds, the open sky—Gurov thought how in reality everything is beautiful in this world when one reflects: everything except what we think or do ourselves when we forget our human dignity and the higher aims of our existence.

A man walked up to them—probably a keeper—looked at them and walked away. And this detail seemed mysterious and beautiful, too. They saw a steamer come from Theodosia, with its lights out in the glow of dawn.

"There is dew on the grass," said Anna Sergeyevna, after a silence.

"Yes. It's time to go home."

They went back to the town.

Then they met every day at twelve o'clock on the seafront, lunched and dined together, went for walks, admired the sea. She complained that she slept badly, that her heart throbbed violently; asked the same questions, troubled now by jealousy and now by fear that he did not respect her sufficiently. And often in the square or gardens, when there was no one near them, he suddenly drew her to him and kissed her passionately. Complete idleness, these kisses in broad daylight while he looked round in dread of someone's seeing them, the heat, the smell of the sea, and the continual passing to and fro before him of idle, well-dressed, well-fed people, made a new man of him; he told Anna Sergeyevna how beautiful she was, how fascinating. He was impatiently passionate, he would not move a step away from her, while she was often pensive and continually urged him to confess that he did not respect her, did not love her in the least, and thought of her as nothing but a common woman. Rather late almost every evening they drove somewhere out of town, to Oreanda or to the waterfall; and the expedition was always a success, the scenery invariably impressed them as grand and beautiful.

They were expecting her husband to come, but a letter came from him, saying that there was something wrong with his eyes, and he entreated his wife to come home as quickly as possible. Anna Sergeyevna made haste to go.

"It's a good thing I am going away," she said to Gurov. "It's the finger of destiny!"

She went by coach and he went with her. They were driving the whole day. When she had got into a compartment of the express, and when the second bell had rung, she said:

"Let me look at you once more . . . look at you once again. That's right."

She did not shed tears, but was so sad that she seemed ill, and her face was quivering.

"I shall remember you . . . think of you," she said. "God be with you; be happy. Don't remember evil against me. We are parting forever—it must be so, for we ought never to have met. Well, God be with you."

The train moved off rapidly, its lights soon vanished from sight, and a minute later there was no sound of it, as though everything had conspired together to end as quickly as possible that sweet delirium, that madness. Left alone on the platform, and gazing into the dark distance, Gurov listened to the chirrup of the grasshoppers and the hum of the telegraph wires, feeling as though he had only just waked up. And he thought, musing, that there had been another episode or adventure in his life, and it, too, was at an end, and nothing was left of it but a memory. . . . He was moved, sad, and conscious of a slight remorse. This young woman whom he would never meet again had not been happy with him; he was genuinely warm and affectionate with her, but yet in his manner, his tone, and his caresses there had been a shade of light irony, the coarse condescension of a happy man who was, besides, almost twice her age. All the time she had called him kind, exceptional, lofty; obviously he had seemed to her different from what he really was, so he had unintentionally deceived her. . . .

Here at the station was already a scent of autumn; it was a cold evening. "It's time for me to go north," thought Gurov as he left the platform. "High time!"

III

At home in Moscow everything was in its winter routine; the stoves were heated, and in the morning it was still dark when the children were having breakfast and getting ready for school, and the nurse would light the lamp for a short time. The frosts had begun already. When the first snow has fallen, on the first day of sledge-driving it is pleasant to see the white earth, the white roofs, to draw soft, delicious breath, and the season brings back the days of one's youth. The old limes and birches, white with hoar-frost, have a good-natured expression; they are nearer to one's heart than cypresses and palms, and near them one doesn't want to be thinking of the sea and the mountains.

Gurov was Moscow born; he arrived in Moscow on a fine frosty day, and when he put on his fur coat and warm gloves, and walked along Petrovka, and when on Saturday evening he heard the ringing of the bells, his recent trip and the places he had seen lost all charm for him. Little by little he became absorbed in Moscow life, greedily read three newspapers a day, and declared he did not read the Moscow papers on principle! He already felt a longing to go to restaurants, clubs, dinner-parties, anniversary celebrations, and he felt flattered at entertaining distinguished lawyers and artists, and at playing cards with a professor at the doctors' club. He could already eat a whole plateful of salt fish and cabbage. . . .

In another month, he fancied, the image of Anna Sergeyevna would be shrouded in a mist in his memory, and only from time to time would visit him in his dreams with a touching smile as others did. But more than a month passed, real winter had come, and everything was still clear in his memory as though he had parted with Anna Sergeyevna only the day before. And his memories glowed more and more vividly. When in the evening stillness he heard from his study the voices of his children, preparing their lessons, or when he listened to a song or the organ at the restaurant, or the storm howled in the chimney, suddenly everything would rise up in his memory: what had happened on the groyne, and the early morning with the mist on the mountains, and the steamer coming from Theodosia, and the kisses. He would pace a long time about his room, remembering it all and smiling; then his memories passed into dreams, and in his fancy the past was mingled with what was to come. Anna Sergeyevna did not visit him in dreams, but followed him about everywhere like a shadow and haunted him. When he shut his eyes he saw her as though she were living before him, and she seemed to him lovelier, younger, tenderer than she was; and he imagined himself finer than he had been in Yalta. In the evenings she peeped out at him from the bookcase, from the fireplace, from the corner—he heard her breathing, the caressing rustle of her dress. In the street he watched the women, looking for someone like her.

He was tormented by an intense desire to confide his memories to someone. But in his home it was impossible to talk of his love, and he had no one outside; he could not talk to his tenants nor to anyone at the bank. And what had he to talk of? Had he been in love, then? Had there been anything beautiful, poetical, or edifying or simply interesting in his relations with Anna Sergeyevna? And there was nothing for him but to talk vaguely of love, of woman, and no one guessed what it meant; only his wife twitched her black eyebrows, and said: "The part of a lady-killer does not suit you at all, Dimitri."

One evening, coming out of the doctors' club with an official with whom he had been playing cards, he could not resist saying:

"If only you knew what a fascinating woman I made the acquaintance of in Yalta!"

The official got into his sledge and was driving away, but turned suddenly and shouted:

"Dmitri Dmitritch!"

"What?"

"You were right this evening: the sturgeon was a bit too strong!"

These words, so ordinary, for some reason moved Gurov to indignation, and struck him as degrading and unclean. What savage manners, what people! What senseless nights, what uninteresting, uneventful days! The rage for card-playing, the gluttony, the drunkenness, the continual talk always about the same thing. Useless pursuits and conversations always about the same things absorb the better part of one's time, the better part of one's strength, and in the end there is left a life grovelling and curtailed, worthless and trivial, and there is no escaping or getting away from it—just as though one were in a madhouse or a prison.

Gurov did not sleep all night, and was filled with indignation. And he had a headache all next day. And the next night he slept badly; he sat up in bed, thinking, or paced up and down his room. He was sick of his children, sick of the bank; he had no desire to go anywhere or to talk of anything.

In the holidays in December he prepared for a journey, and told his wife he was going to Petersburg to do something in the interests of a young friend—and he set off for S——. What for? He did not very well know himself. He wanted to see Anna Sergeyevna and to talk with her—to arrange a meeting if possible.

He reached S—— in the morning, and took the best room at the hotel, in which the floor was covered with grey army cloth, and on the table was an inkstand, grey with dust and adorned with a figure on horseback, with its hat in its hand and its head broken off. The hotel porter gave him the necessary information; Von Diderits lived in a house of his own in Old Gontcharny Street—it was not far from the hotel: he was rich and lived in good style, and had his own horses; every one in the town knew him. The porter pronounced the name "Dridirits."

Gurov went without haste to Old Gontcharny Street and found the house. Just opposite the house stretched a long grey fence adorned with nails.

"One would run away from a fence like that," thought Gurov, looking from the fence to the windows of the house and back again.

He considered: today was a holiday, and the husband would probably be at home. And in any case it would be tactless to go into the house and upset her. If he were to send her a note it might fall into her husband's hands, and then it might ruin everything. The best thing was to trust to chance. And he kept walking up and down the street by the fence, waiting for a chance. He saw a beggar go in at the gate and dogs fly at him; then an hour later he heard a piano, and the sounds were faint and indistinct. Probably it was Anna Sergeyevna playing. The front door suddenly opened, and an old woman came out, followed by the familiar white Pomeranian. Gurov was on the point of calling to the dog, but his heart began beating violently, and in his excitement he could not remember the dog's name.

He walked up and down, and loathed the grey fence more and more, and by now thought irritably that Anna Sergeyevna had forgotten him, and was perhaps already amusing herself with someone else, and that that was very natural in a young woman who had nothing to look at from morning till night but that confounded fence. He went back to his hotel room and sat for a long while on the sofa, not knowing what to do, then he had dinner and a long nap.

"How stupid and worrying it is!" he thought when he woke and looked at the dark windows: it was already evening. "Here I've had a good sleep for some reason. What shall I do in the night?"

He sat on the bed, which was covered by a cheap grey blanket, such as one sees in hospitals, and he taunted himself in his vexation:

"So much for the lady with the dog . . . so much for the adventure. . . . You're in a nice fix. . . ."

That morning at the station a poster in large letters had caught his eye. "The Geisha" was to be performed for the first time. He thought of this and went to the theatre.

"It's quite possible she may go to the first performance," he thought.

The theatre was full. As in all provincial theatres, there was a fog above the chandelier, the gallery was noisy and restless; in the front row the local dandies were standing up before the beginning of the performance, with their hands behind them; in the Governor's box the Governor's daughter, wearing a boa, was sitting in the front seat, while the Governor himself lurked modestly behind the curtain with only his hands visible; the orchestra was a long time tuning up; the stage curtain swayed. All the time the audience were coming in and taking their seats Gurov looked at them eagerly.

Anna Sergeyevna, too, came in. She sat down in the third row, and when Gurov looked at her his heart contracted, and he understood clearly that for him there was in the whole world no creature so near, so precious, and so important to him; she, this little woman, in no way remarkable, lost in a provincial crowd, with a vulgar lorgnette in her hand, filled his whole life now, was his sorrow and his joy, the one happiness that he now desired for himself, and to the sounds of the inferior orchestra, of the wretched provincial violins, he thought how lovely she was. He thought and dreamed.

A young man with small side-whiskers, tall and stooping, came in with Anna Sergeyevna and sat down beside her; he bent his head at every step and seemed to be continually bowing. Most likely this was the husband whom at Yalta, in a rush of bitter feeling, she had called a flunky. And there really was in his long figure, his side-whiskers, and the small bald patch on his head, something of the flunky's obsequiousness; his smile was sugary, and in his buttonhole there was some badge of distinction like the number on a waiter.

During the first interval the husband went away to smoke; she remained alone in her stall. Gurov, who was sitting in the stalls, too, went up to her and said in a trembling voice, with a forced smile.

"Good evening."

She glanced at him and turned pale, then glanced again with horror, unable to believe her eyes, and tightly gripped the fan and the lorgnette in her hands, evidently struggling with herself not to faint. Both were silent. She was sitting, he was standing, frightened by her confusion and not venturing to sit down beside her. The violins and the flute began tuning up. He felt suddenly frightened; it seemed as though all the people in the boxes were looking at them. She got up and went quickly to the door; he followed her, and both walked senselessly along passages, and up and down stairs, and figures in legal, scholastic, and civil service uniforms, all wearing badges, flitted before their eyes. They caught glimpses of ladies, of fur coats hanging on pegs; the draughts blew on them, bringing a smell of stale tobacco. And Gurov, whose heart was beating violently, thought:

"Oh, heavens! Why are these people here and this orchestra! . . ."

And at that instant he recalled how when he had seen Anna Sergeyevna off at the station he had thought that everything was over and they would never meet again. But how far they were still from the end!

On the narrow, gloomy staircase over which was written, "To the Amphitheatre," she stopped.

"How you have frightened me!" she said, breathing hard, still pale and overwhelmed. "Oh, how you have frightened me! I am half dead. Why have you come? Why?"

"But do understand, Anna, do understand . . ." he said hastily in a low voice. "I entreat you to understand. . . ."

She looked at him with dread, with entreaty, with love; she looked at him intently, to keep his features more distinctly in her memory.

"I am so unhappy," she went on, not heeding him. "I have thought of nothing but you all the time; I live only in the thought of you. And I wanted to forget, to forget you; but why, oh, why, have you come?"

On the landing above them two schoolboys were smoking and looking down, but that was nothing to Gurov; he drew Anna Sergeyevna to him, and began kissing her face, her cheeks, and her hands.

"What are you doing, what are you doing!" she cried in horror, pushing him away. "We are mad. Go away today; go away at once. . . . I beseech you by all that is sacred, I implore you. . . . There are people coming this way!"

Someone was coming up the stairs.

"You must go away," Anna Sergeyevna went on in a whisper. "Do you hear, Dmitri Dmitritch? I will come and see you in Moscow. I have never been happy; I am miserable now, and I never, never shall be happy, never! Don't make me suffer still more! I swear I'll come to Moscow. But now let us part. My precious, good, dear one, we must part!"

She pressed his hand and began rapidly going downstairs, looking around at him, and from her eyes he could see that she really was unhappy. Gurov stood for a little while, listened, then, when all sound had died away, he found his coat and left the theatre.

IV

And Anna Sergeyevna began coming to see him in Moscow. Once in two or three months she left S——, telling her husband that she was going to consult a doctor about an internal complaint—and her husband believed her, and did not believe her. In Moscow she stayed at the Slaviansky Bazaar hotel, and at once sent a man in a red cap to Gurov. Gurov went to see her, and no one knew of it.

Once he was going to see her in this way on a winter morning (the messenger had come the evening before when he was out). With him walked his daughter, whom he wanted to take to school: it was on the way. Snow was falling in big wet flakes.

"It's three degrees above freezing-point, and yet it is snowing," said Gurov to his daughter. "The thaw is only on the surface of the earth; there is quite a different temperature at a greater height in the atmosphere."

"And why are there no thunderstorms in the winter, Father?"

He explained that, too. He talked, thinking all the while that he was going to see *her*, and no living soul knew of it, and probably never would know. He had two lives: one, open, seen and known by all who cared to know, full of relative truth and of relative falsehood, exactly like the lives of his friends and acquaintances; and another life running its course in secret. And through some strange, perhaps accidental, conjunction of circumstances, everything that was essential, of interest and of value to him, everything in which he was sincere and did not deceive himself, everything that made the kernel of his life, was hidden from other people; and all that was false in him, the sheath in which he hid himself to conceal the truth—such, for instance, as his work in the bank, his discussions at the club, his "lower race," his presence with his wife at anniversary festivities—all that was open. And he judged of others by himself, not believing in what he saw, and always believing that every man had his real, most interesting life under the cover of secrecy and under the cover of night. All personal life rested on secrecy, and possibly it was partly on that account that civilized man was so nervously anxious that personal privacy should be respected.

After leaving his daughter at school, Gurov went on to the Slaviansky Bazaar. He took off his fur coat below, went upstairs, and softly knocked at the door. Anna Sergeyevna, wearing his favourite grey dress, exhausted by the journey and the suspense, had been expecting him since the evening before. She was pale; she looked at him, and did not smile, and he had hardly come in when she fell on his breast. Their kiss was slow and prolonged, as though they had not met for two years.

"Well, how are you getting on there?" he asked. "What news?"

"Wait; I'll tell you directly. . . . I can't talk."

She could not speak; she was crying. She turned away from him, and pressed her handkerchief to her eyes.

"Let her have her cry out. I'll sit down and wait," he thought, and he sat down in an armchair.

Then he rang and asked for tea to be brought to him, and while he drank his tea she remained standing at the window with her back to him. She was crying from emotion, from the miserable consciousness that their life was so hard for them; they could only meet in secret, hiding themselves from people, like thieves! Was not their life shattered?

"Come, do stop!" he said.

It was evident to him that this love of theirs would not soon be over, that he could not see the end of it. Anna Sergeyevna grew more and more attached to him. She adored him, and it was unthinkable to say to her that it was bound to have an end some day; besides, she would not have believed it!

He went up to her and took her by the shoulders to say something affectionate and cheering, and at that moment he saw himself in the looking-glass.

His hair was already beginning to turn grey. And it seemed strange to him that he had grown so much older, so much plainer during the last few years. The shoulders on which his hands rested were warm and quivering. He felt compassion for this life, still so warm and lovely, but probably already not far from beginning to fade and wither like his own. Why did she love him so much? He always seemed to women different from what he was, and they loved in him not himself, but the man created by their imagination, whom they had been eagerly seeking all their lives; and afterwards, when they noticed their mistake, they loved him all the same. And not one of them had been happy with him. Time passed, he had made their acquaintance, got on with them, parted, but he had never once loved; it was anything you like, but not love.

And only now when his head was grey he had fallen properly, really in love—for the first time in his life.

Anna Sergeyevna and he loved each other like people very close and akin, like husband and wife, like tender friends; it seemed to them that fate itself had meant them for one another, and they could not understand why he had a wife and she a husband; and it was as though they were a pair of birds of passage, caught and forced to live in different cages. They forgave each other for what they were ashamed of in their past, they forgave everything in the present, and felt that this love of theirs had changed them both.

In moments of depression in the past he had comforted himself with any arguments that came into his mind, but now he no longer cared for arguments; he felt profound compassion, he wanted to be sincere and tender. . . .

"Don't cry, my darling," he said. "You've had your cry; that's enough. . . . Let us talk now, let us think of some plan."

Then they spent a long while taking counsel together, talked of how to avoid the necessity for secrecy, for deception, for living in different towns and not seeing each other for long at a time. How could they be free from this intolerable bondage?

"How? How?" he asked, clutching his head. "How?"

And it seemed as though in a little while the solution would be found, and then a new and splendid life would begin; and it was clear to both of them that they had still a long, long road before them, and that the most complicated and difficult part of it was only just beginning.

1899

Reflection on "The Lady With the Dog"

In his tribute to the earlier Russian author and "one of the greatest stories ever written," Vladimir Nabokov composes his own brilliant opening: "Chekhov comes into the story. . . . without knocking. There is no dilly-dallying." An arresting phrase, it's also too modest. Chekhov's first sentence, like that of the best stories, is a creation from nothing. It announces not only selected specifics, but also that *these* specifics, from a choice of thousands, millions, are the ones to drive the story. The white space surrounding and following the title has been filled. The sense of both random and purposeful creativity, their bright newness, is underlined by the momentum of Chekhov's meticulous phrasing: "It was said that a new person had appeared on the seafront: a lady with a little dog." The words "it was said," reflect both the submerged narrative of gossip in the resort of Yalta and the narrator's particular and more humane authority. But having begun the story with subtle reiterations of beginnings—"an interest in new arrivals"—Chekhov quickly moves to a stress on endings that will shape the enigmatic nature of Gurov's emotional transitions as well as the actual conclusion of the story in the technical sense of its stopping on a specific page. Gurov's experience, much affected by his grim, pretentious Moscow wife, is that every initially "light and charming adventure" *ends* in pain and complexity. Nevertheless, extolling vitality and the enchanting encounters life offers, he pursues the timid and "angular" Anna (while terrorizing her fluff of a dog), and his abstract identification of her with all women as "the lower race" begins to alter.

In the brief second section of the story—there are four, ranging over a swath of time and moving from one location to another, creating a kind of diffuse, meandering structure that violates whatever principles of narrative unity existed in 1899—Chekhov's genius at positioning details takes hold of the way we perceive Gurov and this liaison. He is a man given to abrupt changes in mood and in the very nature of his language. Reminding himself again about the inevitable and unpleasant endings to his serial encounters with women, he thinks that when he "grew cold to them their beauty excited his hatred, and the lace on their linen seemed to him like scales." This terrible image makes it seem likely that Gurov will treat Anna very badly, but the movement, the rhythm, of a Chekhov story is that the expected moment does not occur and is replaced by something more oblique and puzzling, here by the watermelon Gurov slices into after they have made love and Anna has drooped and "faded" in her dejection and remorse. At the end of this unit of the story, after Anna has returned to the town of S—— and her "flunky" of a husband (she has begun to take on Gurov's harshness just as he will absorb her tenderness), he accuses himself of being deceptive and coarse with her. Chekhov made a magnificent choice with the watermelon. It marks the sudden shifts in emotional planes that will endow the conclusion—Gurov's affirmation of a "beginning"—with a lovely but fretful ambiguity. Being a consummate hedonist with pretences of delicacy, Gurov could not have been pictured hacking away at a large roast or picking chicken wings from a bucket. Moist and pliable, the watermelon is a perfect emblem of raw sensory experience that Gurov needs to transform, to transcend. But we also wonder whether the detail is an emblem for Anna herself, for the affair, a question that the story declines to answer.

Back in Moscow with the seasons changing, Gurov expects the affair to recede as both charm and memory, but instead of vanishing, Anna "seemed to him lovelier, younger, tenderer than she was; and he imagined himself finer than he had been in Yalta." When he tries circuitously to convey something about her powerful presence, an acquaintance unwittingly replicates the vulgarity of Gurov's watermelon response to Anna's guilt with a comment about the rankness of the sturgeon dinner at their club. Horrified, enraged, by this "degrading," dull repetitiveness, which is so much part of him, Gurov runs off to Anna and S——, where initially he encounters only greyness: a "grey army cloth" on the hotel floor, objects "grey with dust," and in front of Anna's house, "a long grey fence adorned with nails." That the sequence ends with sweet promises and declarations is a testament to the sad magic the lovers prompt in one another—seen sharply through the brief occupation of the story's perspective by two high school boys who, behind a veil of smoke, indifferently take in the pair on the theatre landing below them.

The final section is almost dizzying in the incomplete readings that it compels. Taking his daughter to school on the way to a rendezvous with Anna, who now has been visiting him in Moscow for months, Gurov concludes with distinct satisfaction that he has "two lives" (the notion of parallel or intersecting lives is at the heart of Joyce's "The Dead" and of Munro's recent stories): one public and overt, his job, marriage, etc.; the other secret and "essential." The first ambiguity is in the "disappearance" from his attention of the daughter with whom he is walking and speaking, the daughter he was so clearly reminded of when he first met Anna and her pet dog. The daughter becomes one of those startling absences short stories frequently hinge on. She is replaced by the image in the hotel room of Anna "wearing his favourite grey dress." The dress may be grey, but the narrative detail is blazing, carrying with it all the specificities of the hotel and of provincial life in her town of S——, and connecting as it soon does with Gurov's mirror perception of his greying hair. An upbeat possibility is that, like his later relative-in-ego, Gabriel Conroy in "The Dead," he has transformed social judgment (the grey fence) into a rich and immediate and generous sense of mortality that he finds echoed in Anna's gestures and words, that he still thinks the end will come, but has softened this conviction with gratitude for love. Shading but not really contradicting this possibility is the suspicion that, glimpsing again a perfectibility he had sensed in Yalta, Gurov has exchanged the rhetoric of the rakish skeptic for the rhetoric of lonely, fraught passion. The last word of the story is "beginning," but it seems interchangeable with "end."

Errand

CHEKHOV. On the evening of March 22, 1897, he went to dinner in Moscow with his friend and confidant Alexei Suvorin. This Suvorin was a very rich newspaper and book publisher, a reactionary, a self-made man whose father was a private at the battle of Borodino. Like Chekhov, he was the grandson of a serf.

They had that in common: each had peasant's blood in his veins. Otherwise, politically and temperamentally, they were miles apart. Nevertheless, Suvorin was one of Chekhov's few intimates, and Chekhov enjoyed his company.

Naturally, they went to the best restaurant in the city, a former town house called the Hermitage—a place where it could take hours, half the night even, to get through a ten-course meal that would, of course, include several wines, liqueurs, and coffee. Chekhov was impeccably dressed, as always—a dark suit and waistcoat, his usual pince-nez. He looked that night very much as he looks in the photographs taken of him during this period. He was relaxed, jovial. He shook hands with the maître d', and with a glance took in the large dining room. It was brilliantly illuminated by ornate chandeliers, the tables occupied by elegantly dressed men and women. Waiters came and went ceaselessly. He had just been seated across the table from Suvorin when suddenly, without warning, blood began gushing from his mouth. Suvorin and two waiters helped him to the gentlemen's room and tried to staunch the flow of blood with ice packs. Suvorin saw him back to his own hotel and had a bed prepared for Chekhov in one of the rooms of the suite. Later, after another hemorrhage, Chekhov allowed himself to be moved to a clinic that specialized in the treatment of tuberculosis and related respiratory infections. When Suvorin visited him there, Chekhov apologized for the "scandal" at the restaurant three nights earlier but continued to insist there was nothing seriously wrong. "He laughed and jested as usual," Suvorin noted in his diary, "while spitting blood into a large vessel."

Maria Chekhov, his younger sister, visited Chekhov in the clinic during the last days of March. The weather was miserable; a sleet storm was in progress, and frozen heaps of snow lay everywhere. It was hard for her to wave down a carriage to take her to the hospital. By the time she arrived she was filled with dread and anxiety.

"Anton Pavlovich lay on his back," Maria wrote in her *Memoirs*. "He was not allowed to speak. After greeting him, I went over to the table to hide my emotions." There, among bottles of champagne, jars of caviar, bouquets of flowers from well-wishers, she saw something that terrified her: a freehand drawing, obviously done by a specialist in these matters, of Chekhov's lungs. It was the kind of sketch a doctor often makes in order to show his patient what he thinks is taking place. The lungs were outlined in blue, but the upper parts were filled in with red. "I realized they were diseased," Maria wrote.

Leo Tolstoy was another visitor. The hospital staff were awed to find themselves in the presence of the country's greatest writer. The most famous man in Russia? Of course they had to let him in to see Chekhov, even though "nonessential" visitors were forbidden. With much obsequiousness on the part of the nurses and resident doctors, the bearded, fierce-looking old man was shown into Chekhov's room. Despite his low opinion of Chekhov's abilities as a playwright (Tolstoy felt the plays were static and lacking in any moral vision. "Where do your characters take you?" he once demanded of Chekhov. "From the sofa to the junk room and back"), Tolstoy liked Chekhov's short stories. Furthermore, and quite simply, he loved the man. He told Gorky, "What a beautiful, magnificent man: modest and quiet, like a girl. He even walks like a girl. He's simply wonderful." And Tolstoy wrote in his journal (everyone kept a journal or a diary in those days), "I am glad I love . . . Chekhov."

Tolstoy removed his woollen scarf and bearskin coat, then lowered himself into a chair next to Chekhov's bed. Never mind that Chekhov was taking medication and not permitted to talk, much less carry on a conversation. He had to listen, amazedly, as the Count began to discourse on his theories of the immortality of the soul. Concerning that visit, Chekhov later wrote, "Tolstoy assumes that all of us (humans and animals alike) will live on in a principle (such as reason or love) the essence and goals of which are a mystery to us. . . . I have no use for that kind of immortality. I don't understand it, and Lev Nikolayevich was astonished I didn't."

Nevertheless, Chekhov was impressed with the solicitude shown by Tolstoy's visit. But, unlike Tolstoy, Chekhov didn't believe in an afterlife and never had. He didn't believe in anything that couldn't be apprehended by one or more of his five senses. And as far as his outlook on life and writing went, he once told someone that he lacked "a political, religious, and philosophical world view. I change it every month, so I'll have to limit myself to the description of how my heroes love, marry, give birth, die, and how they speak."

Earlier, before his TB was diagnosed, Chekhov had remarked, "When a peasant has consumption, he says, "There's nothing I can do. I'll go off in the spring with the melting of the snows." (Chekhov himself died in the summer, during a heat wave.) But once Chekhov's own tuberculosis was discovered he continually tried to minimize the seriousness of his condition. To all appearances, it was as if he felt, right up to the end, that he might be able to throw off the disease as he would a lingering catarrh. Well into his final days, he spoke with seeming conviction of the possibility of an improvement. In fact, in a letter written shortly before his end, he went so far as to tell his sister that he was "putting on a bit of flesh" and felt much better now that he was in Badenweiler.

Badenweiler is a spa and resort city in the western area of the Black Forest, not far from Basel. The Vosges are visible from nearly anywhere in the city, and in those days the air was pure and invigorating. Russians had been going there for years to soak in the hot mineral baths and promenade on the boulevards. In June 1904, Chekhov went there to die.

Earlier that month, he'd made a difficult journey by train from Moscow to Berlin. He travelled with his wife, the actress Olga Knipper, a woman he'd met in 1898 during rehearsals for *The Seagull*. Her contemporaries describe her as an excellent actress. She was talented, pretty, and almost ten years younger than the playwright. Chekhov had been immediately attracted to her, but was slow to act on his feelings. As always, he preferred a flirtation to marriage. Finally, after a three-year courtship involving many separations, letters, and the inevitable misunderstandings, they were at last married, in a private ceremony in Moscow, on May 25, 1901. Chekhov was enormously happy. He called Olga his "pony," and sometimes "dog" or "puppy." He was also fond of addressing her as "little turkey" or simply as "my joy."

In Berlin, Chekhov consulted with a renowned specialist in pulmonary disorders, a Dr Karl Ewald. But, according to an eyewitness, after the doctor examined Chekhov he threw up his hands and left the room without a word. Chekhov was too far gone for help: this Dr Ewald was furious with himself for not being able to work miracles, and with Chekhov for being so ill.

A Russian journalist happened to visit the Chekhovs at their hotel and sent back this dispatch to his editor: "Chekhov's days are numbered. He seems mortally ill, is terribly thin, coughs all the time, gasps for breath at the slightest movement, and is running a high temperature." This same journalist saw the Chekhovs off at Potsdam Station when they boarded their train for Badenweiler. According to his account, "Chekhov had trouble making his way up the small staircase at the station. He had to sit down for several minutes to catch his breath." In fact, it was painful for Chekhov to move: his legs ached continually and his insides hurt. The disease had attacked his intestines and spinal cord. At this point he had less than a month to live. When Chekhov spoke of his condition now, it was, according to Olga, "with an almost reckless indifference."

Dr Schwöhrer was one of the many Badenweiler physicians who earned a good living by treating the well-to-do who came to the spa seeking relief from various maladies. Some of his patients were ill and infirm, others simply old and hypochondriacal. But Chekhov's was a special case: he was clearly beyond help and in his last days. He was also very famous. Even Dr Schwöhrer knew his name: he'd read some of Chekhov's stories in a German magazine. When he examined the writer early in June, he voiced his appreciation of Chekhov's art but kept his medical opinions to himself. Instead, he prescribed a diet of cocoa, oatmeal drenched in butter, and strawberry tea. This last was supposed to help Chekhov sleep at night.

On June 13, less than three weeks before he died, Chekhov wrote a letter to his mother in which he told her his health was on the mend. In it he said, "It's likely that I'll be completely cured in a week." Who knows why he said this? What could he have been thinking? He was a doctor himself, and he knew better. He was dying, it was as simple and as unavoidable as that. Nevertheless, he sat out on the balcony of his hotel room and read railway timetables. He asked for information on sailings of boats bound for Odessa from Marseilles. But he knew. At this stage he had to have known. Yet in one of the last letters he ever wrote he told his sister he was growing stronger by the day.

He no longer had any appetite for literary work, and hadn't for a long time. In fact, he had very nearly failed to complete *The Cherry Orchard* the year before. Writing that play was the hardest thing he'd ever done in his life. Toward the end, he was able to manage only six or seven lines a day. "I've started losing heart," he wrote Olga. "I feel I'm finished as a writer, and every sentence strikes me as worthless and of no use whatever." But he didn't stop. He finished his play in October 1903. It was the last thing he ever wrote, except for letters and a few entries in his notebook.

A little after midnight on July 2, 1904, Olga sent someone to fetch Dr Schwöhrer. It was an emergency: Chekhov was delirious. Two young Russians on holiday happened to have the adjacent room, and Olga hurried next door to explain what was happening. One of the youths was in his bed asleep, but the other was still awake, smoking and reading. He left the hotel at a run to find Dr Schwöhrer. "I can still hear the sound of the gravel under his shoes in the silence of that stifling July night," Olga wrote later on in her memoirs. Chekhov was hallucinating, talking about sailors, and there were snatches of something about the Japanese. "You don't put ice on an empty stomach," he said when she tried to place an ice pack on his chest.

Dr Schwöhrer arrived and unpacked his bag, all the while keeping his gaze fastened on Chekhov, who lay gasping in the bed. The sick man's pupils were dilated and his temples glistened with sweat. Dr Schwöhrer's face didn't register anything. He was not an emotional man, but he knew Chekhov's end was near. Still, he was a doctor, sworn to do his utmost, and Chekhov held on to life, however tenuously. Dr Schwöhrer prepared a hypodermic and administered an injection of camphor, something that was supposed to speed up the heart. But the injection didn't help—nothing, of course, could have helped. Nevertheless, the doctor made known to Olga his intention of sending for oxygen. Suddenly, Chekhov roused himself, became lucid, and said quietly, "What's the use? Before it arrives I'll be a corpse."

Dr Schwöhrer pulled on his big moustache and stared at Chekhov. The writer's cheeks were sunken and grey, his complexion waxen; his breath was raspy. Dr Schwöhrer knew the time could be reckoned in minutes. Without a word, without conferring with Olga, he went over to an alcove where there was a telephone on the wall. He read the instructions for using the device. If he activated it by holding his finger on a button and turning a handle on the side of the phone, he could reach the lower regions of the hotel—the kitchen. He picked up the receiver, held it to his ear, and did as the instructions told him. When someone finally answered, Dr Schwöhrer ordered a bottle of the hotel's best champagne. "How many glasses?" he was asked. "Three glasses!" the doctor shouted into the mouthpiece. "And hurry, do you hear?" It was one of those rare moments of inspiration that can easily enough be overlooked later on, because the action is so entirely appropriate it seems inevitable.

The champagne was brought to the door by a tired-looking young man whose blond hair was standing up. The trousers of his uniform were wrinkled, the creases gone, and in his haste he'd missed a loop while buttoning his jacket. His appearance was that of someone who'd been resting (slumped in a chair, say, dozing a little), when off in the distance the phone had clamoured in the early-morning hours—great God in heaven!—and the next thing he knew he was being shaken awake by a superior and told to deliver a bottle of Moët to room 211. "And hurry, do you hear?"

The young man entered the room carrying a silver ice bucket with the champagne in it and a silver tray with three cut-crystal glasses. He found a place on the table for the bucket and glasses, all the while craning his neck, trying to see into the other room, where someone panted ferociously for breath. It was a dreadful, harrowing sound, and the young man lowered his chin into his collar and turned away as the ratchety breathing worsened. Forgetting himself, he stared out the open window toward the darkened city. Then this big imposing man with a thick moustache pressed some coins into his hand—a large tip, by the feel of it—and suddenly the young man saw the door open. He took some steps and found himself on the landing, where he opened his hand and looked at the coins in amazement.

Methodically, the way he did everything, the doctor went about the business of working the cork out of the bottle. He did it in such a way as to minimize, as much as possible, the festive explosion. He poured three glasses and, out of habit, pushed the cork back into the neck of the bottle. He then took the glasses of champagne over to the bed. Olga momentarily released her grip on Chekhov's hand—a hand, she said later, that burned her fingers. She arranged another pillow behind his head. Then she put the cool glass of champagne against Chekhov's palm and made sure his fingers closed around the stem. They exchanged looks—Chekhov, Olga, Dr Schwöhrer. They didn't touch glasses. There was no toast. What on earth was there to drink to? To death? Chekhov summoned his remaining strength and said, "It's been so long since I've had champagne." He brought the glass to his lips and drank. In a minute or two Olga took the empty glass from his hand and set it on the nightstand. Then Chekhov turned onto his side. He closed his eyes and sighed. A minute later, his breathing stopped.

Dr Schwöhrer picked up Chekhov's hand from the bedsheet. He held his fingers to Chekhov's wrist and drew a gold watch from his vest pocket, opening the lid of the watch as he did so. The second hand on the watch moved slowly, very slowly. He let it move around the face of the watch three times while he waited for signs of a pulse. It was three o'clock in the morning and still sultry in the room. Badenweiler was in the grip of its worst heat wave in years. All the windows in both rooms stood open, but there was no sign of a breeze. A large, black-winged moth flew through a window and banged wildly against the electric lamp. Dr Schwöhrer let go of Chekhov's wrist. "It's over," he said. He closed the lid of his watch and returned it to his vest pocket.

At once Olga dried her eyes and set about composing herself. She thanked the doctor for coming. He asked if she wanted some medication—laudanum, perhaps, or a few drops of valerian. She shook her head. She did have one request, though: before the authorities were notified and the newspapers found out, before the time came when Chekhov was no longer in her keeping, she wanted to be alone with him for a while. Could the doctor help with this? Could he withhold, for a while anyway, news of what had just occurred?

Dr Schwöhrer stroked his moustache with the back of a finger. Why not? After all, what difference would it make to anyone whether this matter became known now or a few hours from now? The only detail that remained was to fill out a death certificate, and this could be done at his office later on in the morning, after he'd slept a few hours. Dr Schwöhrer nodded his agreement and prepared to leave. He murmured a few words of condolence. Olga inclined her head. "An honour," Dr Schwöhrer said. He picked up his bag and left the room and, for that matter, history.

It was at this moment that the cork popped out of the champagne bottle; foam spilled down onto the table. Olga went back to Chekhov's bedside. She sat on a footstool, holding his hand, from time to time stroking his face. "There were no human voices, no everyday sounds," she wrote. "There was only beauty, peace, and the grandeur of death."

She stayed with Chekhov until daybreak, when thrushes began to call from the garden below. Then came the sound of tables and chairs being moved about down there. Before long, voices carried up to her. It was then a knock sounded at the door. Of course she thought it must be an official of some sort—the medical examiner, say, or someone from the police who had questions to ask and forms for her to fill out, or maybe, just maybe, it could be Dr Schwöhrer returning with a mortician to render assistance in embalming and transporting Chekhov's remains back to Russia.

But, instead, it was the same blond young man who'd brought the champagne a few hours earlier. This time, however, his uniform trousers were neatly pressed, with stiff creases in front, and every button on his snug green jacket was fastened. He seemed quite another person. Not only was he wide awake but his plump cheeks were smooth-shaven, his hair was in place, and he appeared anxious to please. He was holding a porcelain vase with three long-stemmed yellow roses. He presented these to Olga with a smart click of his heels. She stepped back and let him into the room. He was there, he said, to collect the glasses, ice bucket, and tray, yes. But he also wanted to say that, because of the extreme heat, breakfast would be served in the garden this morning. He hoped this weather wasn't too bothersome; he apologized for it.

The woman seemed distracted. While he talked, she turned her eyes away and looked down at something in the carpet. She crossed her arms and held her elbows. Meanwhile, still holding his vase, waiting for a sign, the young man took in the details of the room. Bright sunlight flooded through the open windows. The room was tidy and seemed undisturbed, almost untouched. No garments were flung over chairs, no shoes, stockings, braces, or stays were in evidence, no open suitcases. In short, there was no clutter, nothing but the usual heavy pieces of hotel room furniture. Then, because the woman was still looking down, he looked down, too, and at once spied a cork near the toe of his shoe. The woman did not see it—she was looking somewhere else. The young man wanted to bend over and pick up the cork, but he was still holding the roses and was afraid of seeming to intrude even more by drawing any further attention to himself. Reluctantly, he left the cork where it was and raised his eyes. Everything was in order except for the uncorked, half-empty bottle of champagne that stood alongside two crystal glasses over on the little table. He cast his gaze about once more. Through an open door he saw that the third glass was in the bedroom, on the nightstand. But someone still occupied the bed! He couldn't see a face, but the figure under the covers lay perfectly motionless and quiet. He noted the figure and looked elsewhere. Then, for a reason he couldn't understand, a feeling of uneasiness took hold of him. He cleared his throat and moved his weight to the other leg. The woman still didn't look up or break her silence. The young man felt his cheeks grow warm. It occurred to him, quite without his having thought it through, that he should perhaps suggest an alternative to breakfast in the garden. He coughed, hoping to focus the woman's attention, but she didn't look at him. The distinguished foreign guests could, he said, take breakfast in their rooms this morning if they wished. The young man (his name hasn't survived, and it's likely he perished in the Great War) said he would be happy to bring up a tray. Two trays, he added, glancing uncertainly once again in the direction of the bedroom.

He fell silent and ran a finger around the inside of his collar. He didn't understand. He wasn't even sure the woman had been listening. He didn't know what else to do now; he was still holding the vase. The sweet odour of the roses filled his nostrils and inexplicably caused a pang of regret. The entire time he'd been waiting, the woman had apparently been lost in thought. It was as if all the while he'd been standing there, talking, shifting his weight, holding his flowers, she had been someplace else, somewhere far from Badenweiler. But now she came back to herself, and her face assumed another expression. She raised her eyes, looked at him, and then shook her head. She seemed to be struggling to understand what on earth this young man could be doing there in the room holding a vase with three yellow roses. Flowers? She hadn't ordered flowers.

The moment passed. She went over to her handbag and scooped up some coins. She drew out a number of banknotes as well. The young man touched his lips with his tongue; another large tip was forthcoming, but for what? What did she want him to do? He'd never before waited on such guests. He cleared his throat once more.

No breakfast, the woman said. Not yet, at any rate. Breakfast wasn't the important thing this morning. She required something else. She needed him to go out and bring back a mortician. Did he understand her? Herr Chekhov was dead, you see. *Comprenez-vous?* Young man? Anton Chekhov was dead. Now listen carefully to me, she said. She wanted him to go downstairs and ask someone at the front desk where he could go to find the most respected mortician in the city. Someone reliable, who took great pains in his work and whose manner was appropriately reserved. A mortician, in short, worthy of a great artist. Here, she said, and pressed the money on him. Tell them downstairs that I have specifically requested you to perform this duty for me. Are you listening? Do you understand what I'm saying to you?

The young man grappled to take in what she was saying. He chose not to look again in the direction of the other room. He had sensed that something was not right. He became aware of his heart beating rapidly under his jacket, and he felt perspiration break out on his forehead. He didn't know where he should turn his eyes. He wanted to put the vase down.

Please do this for me, the woman said. I'll remember you with gratitude. Tell them downstairs that I insist. Say that. But don't call any unnecessary attention to yourself or to the situation. Just say that this is necessary, that I request it—and that's all. Do your hear me? Nod if you understand. Above all, don't raise an alarm. Everything else, all the rest, the commotion—that'll come soon enough. The worst is over. Do we understand each other?

The young man's face had grown pale. He stood rigid, clasping the vase. He managed to nod his head.

After securing permission to leave the hotel he was to proceed quietly and resolutely, though without any unbecoming haste, to the mortician's. He was to behave exactly as if he were engaged on a very important errand, nothing more. He was engaged on an important errand, she said. And if it would help keep his movements purposeful he should imagine himself as someone moving down the busy sidewalk carrying in his arms a porcelain vase of roses that he had to deliver to an important man. (She spoke quietly, almost confidentially, as if to a relative or a friend.) He could even tell himself that the man he was going to see was expecting him, was perhaps impatient for him to arrive with his flowers. Nevertheless, the young man was not to become excited and run, or otherwise break his stride. Remember the vase he was carrying! He was to walk briskly, comporting himself at all times in as dignified a manner as possible. He should keep walking until he came to the mortician's house and stood before the door. He would then raise the brass knocker and let it fall, once, twice, three times. In a minute the mortician himself would answer.

This mortician would be in his forties, no doubt, or maybe early fifties—bald, solidly built, wearing steel-frame spectacles set very low on his nose. He would be modest, unassuming, a man who would ask only the most direct and necessary questions. An apron. Probably he would be wearing an apron. He might even be wiping his hands on a dark towel while he listened to what was being said. There'd be a faint whiff of formaldehyde on his clothes. But it was all right, and the young man shouldn't worry. He was nearly a grownup now and shouldn't be frightened or repelled by any of this. The mortician would hear him out. He was a man of restraint and bearing, this mortician, someone who could help allay people's fears in this situation, not increase them. Long ago he'd acquainted himself with death in all its various guises and forms; death held no surprises for him any longer, no hidden secrets. It was this man whose services were required this morning.

The mortician takes the vase of roses. Only once while the young man is speaking does the mortician betray the least flicker of interest, or indicate that he's heard anything out of the ordinary. But the one time the young man mentions the name of the deceased, the mortician's eyebrows rise just a little. Chekhov, you say? Just a minute, and I'll be with you.

Do you understand what I'm saying, Olga said to the young man. Leave the glasses. Don't worry about them. Forget about crystal wine glasses and such. Leave the room as it is. Everything is ready now. We're ready. Will you go?

But at that moment the young man was thinking of the cork still resting near the toe of his shoe. To retrieve it he would have to bend over, still gripping the vase. He would do this. He leaned over. Without looking down, he reached out and closed it into his hand.

1987

Reflection on "Errand"

Like "The Lady with the Dog," "Errand" is set in a sequence of rooms, but pivots on a series of adjacent moments. Carver's opening is tighter, more elliptical, but it also blends beginning with end. The first word, "Chekhov," is at once an invocation and a sudden entry into both the life the writer led and his death. The more we know about Chekhov, the more we bring to this startling first word of the story, the fuller this sense of the opening will be, and the more it will seem to reflect the process by which the story came to be written, which is itself a fascinating story. Carver recounts reading Henri Troyat's biography, *Chekhov*, and being particularly taken with one detail in the account of Chekhov's final moments: that, spontaneously and breaking all decorum and solemn sensibleness, the attending physician ordered a bottle of champagne. "This little piece of human business struck me as an extraordinary action. Before I really knew what I was going to do with it, or how I was going to proceed, I felt I had been launched into a short story of my own then and there." Carver wondered how the doctor actually got the champagne so late at night at a German spa. "The only thing that was clear to me was that I thought I saw an opportunity to pay homage . . . to Chekhov, the writer who has meant so much to me for such a long time." To "bring it off," to "do it rightly and honourably," Carver created a sort of internal duet for the story, the first historical, the second "poetic" and emphatically imagined. The first half of the story, ending with the doctor's magnificent gesture, is full of dates and historical figures; everyone, including the gravely ill Chekhov himself, scribbling away in diaries, memoirs, journals, and letters about the condition of the great writer, a specificity due to someone who actually lived somewhere beyond the page. There are notations in this historical sequence about the presence of waiters and bottles of champagne, details that will shift from a documentary-like background to the lovingly created foreground of the time surrounding the death.

Carver answered his own question about the champagne by having his Dr Schwöhrer read and follow the directions for using the telephone to call the kitchen. Between the injunction for the waiter to hurry and the appearance in the story and in the room of the "young man . . . carrying a silver ice bucket with the champagne in it and a silver tray with three cut-crystal glasses" is one of those brilliant white spaces of text that short story writers are so adept at using. Here the space is filled with the mysteriously accomplished transition from the biography Carver read to the unseen, undocumented elements of the story open to his imagination: the waiter himself, the cork that pops out of the unfinished bottle, and the language Olga, Chekhov's wife, uses to instruct the waiter and later to record that monumental hot July morning. Both look down at the floor, yet she does not see the cork; she is distracted but he does not yet know why; "the young man wanted to bend over and pick up the cork, but he was still holding the roses and was afraid of seeming to intrude even more by drawing any further attention to himself"; again, he does not know why. His sense of "uneasiness" and "regret" takes focus as Olga instructs him to proceed to a mortician "worthy of a great artist." Wonderfully, the instruction itself becomes a story, and the story becomes the present. The verbs rapidly alter: "He was engaged on an important errand" glides into a picture she draws of the mortician: "Probably he would be wearing an apron." Then the scene develops the intense reality of Chekhov's own fiction: "The mortician takes the vase of roses. Only once while the young man is speaking does the mortician betray the least flicker of interest," and that is to "the name of the deceased." That Olga becomes the writer is not a usurpation of his life and mystery as it is in Joyce's "The Sisters." After all, "Errand" is a story about continuations and symmetries, the most moving of which is our realization that Carver devoted the last of his stories to the end of Chekhov's life.

PART II

The Short Story

Nathaniel Hawthorne

1804–1864

Houses figure prominently in Nathaniel Hawthorne's fiction: *Mosses from an Old Manse, The House of the Seven Gables*, and most notably, "The Custom House," which opens his majestic drama of Puritan hauntings, *The Scarlet Letter*. But Hawthorne—who once considered himself "the obscurest man of letters in America"—would have been startled to know that in 2002 he had an unusual importance in George Bush's White House: that his story "The Birthmark" was the first homework assignment for the President's Council on Bioethics. D.H. Lawrence would have readily understood the choice of Hawthorne's story: "That blue-eyed darling Nathaniel knew disagreeable things in his inner soul. He was careful to send them out in disguise" (*Studies in Classic American Literature*). Disguised or not, he sent out what he knew in the form of Hester Prynne—"how her beauty shone out, and made a halo of the misfortune and ignominy in which she was enveloped"—and in the collisions of nature and artifice in "The Birthmark" (1843) and "Rappaccini's Daughter" (1844). His other tales of psychic enchantment include "Young Goodman Brown" (1835), and "The Artist of the Beautiful" (1844). Hawthorne was certainly the "darling" of his family. Born in Salem—he had one of the witch trial judges in his lineage—he was doted upon by his mother, his sisters, and his mother's family (his father died when Hawthorne was four). The first in his family to attend college, he graduated from Bowdoin in Maine in 1825, then returned to a twelve-year period of reclusive literary education in his "chamber under the eaves." This ended with the publication of *Twice-Told Tales* in 1837, the volume that initiated his career and, under Poe's scrutiny, the seriousness of the form. (Poe extensively reviewed the *Tales* and made them the basis for his theory of the short story.) After marrying in 1842, Hawthorne and his wife, [CMOS 6.23] Sophia, moved to Concord where he met Emerson and Thoreau and wrote *Mosses from an Old Manse* (1846). After the success of *The Scarlet Letter* (1850), he quickly composed *The House of the Seven Gables* (1851) and *The Blithedale Romance* (1852), based on his earlier, unsatisfying experiences at the utopian Brook Farm. When his former Bowdoin classmate, Franklin Pierce, was elected president of the United States, Hawthorne became the US consul in Liverpool until 1857. In Italy he became a friend of Robert Browning and wrote his last complete novel, *The Marble Faun* (1860), which, cryptic as it is, has "an uncanny light" (Kathryn Harrison).

Rappaccini's Daughter

From the Writings of Aubépine

We do not remember to have seen any translated specimens of the productions of M. de l'Aubépine; a fact the less to be wondered at, as his very name is unknown to many of his own countrymen, as well as to the student of foreign literature. As a writer, he seems to occupy an unfortunate position between the Transcendentalists (who, under one name or another, have their share in all the current literature of the world), and the great body of pen-and-ink men who address the intellect and sympathies of the multitude. If not too refined, at all events too remote, too shadowy and unsubstantial in his modes of development, to suit the taste of the latter class, and yet too popular to satisfy the spiritual or metaphysical requisitions of the former, he must necessarily find himself without an audience; except here and there an individual, or possibly an isolated clique. His writings, to do them justice, are not altogether destitute of fancy and originality; they might have won him greater reputation but for an inveterate love of allegory, which is apt to invest his plots and characters with the aspect of scenery and people in the clouds, and to steal away the human warmth out of his conceptions. His fictions are sometimes historical, sometimes of the present day, and sometimes, so far as can be discovered, have little or no reference either to time or space. In any case, he generally contents himself with a very slight embroidery of outward manners,—the faintest possible counterfeit of real life,—and endeavours to create an interest by some less obvious peculiarity of the subject. Occasionally, a breath of nature, a raindrop of pathos and tenderness, or a gleam of humour, will find its way into the midst of his fantastic imagery, and make us feel as if, after all, we were yet within the limits of our native earth. We will only add to this very cursory notice, that M. de l'Aubépine's productions, if the reader chance to take them in precisely the proper point of view, may amuse a leisure hour as well as those of a brighter man; if otherwise, they can hardly fail to look excessively like nonsense.

Our author is voluminous; he continues to write and publish with as much praiseworthy and indefatigable prolixity, as if his efforts were crowned with the brilliant success that so justly attends those of Eugene Sue. His first appearance was by a collection of stories, in a long series of volumes, entitled "*Contes deux fois racontées*." The titles of some of his more recent works (we quote from memory) are as follows:—"*Le Voyage Céleste à Chemin de Fer*," 3 tom. 1839. "*Le nouveau Père Adam et la nouvelle Mère Eve*," 2 tom. 1839. "*Roderic; ou le Serpent à l'estomac*," 2 tom. 1840. "*Le Culte du Feu*," a folio volume of ponderous research into the religion and ritual of the old Persian Ghebers, published in 1841. "*La Soirée du Chateau en Espagne*," 1 tom. 8 vo. 1842; and "*L'Artiste du Beau; ou le Papillon Mécanique*," 5 tom. 4 to. 1843. Our somewhat wearisome perusal of this startling catalogue of volumes has left behind it a certain personal affection and sympathy, though by no means admiration, for M. de l'Aubépine; and we would fain do the little in our power towards introducing him favourably to the American public. The ensuing tale is a translation of his "*Beatrice; ou la Belle Empoisonneuse*," recently published in "*La Revue Anti-Aristocratique*." This journal, edited by the Comte de Bearhaven, has, for some years past, led the defence of liberal principles and popular rights, with a faithfulness and ability worthy of all praise.

A young man, named Giovanni Guasconti, came, very long ago, from the more southern region of Italy, to pursue his studies at the University of Padua. Giovanni, who had but a scanty supply of gold ducats in his pocket, took lodgings in a high and gloomy chamber of an old edifice, which looked not unworthy to have been the palace of a Paduan noble, and which, in fact, exhibited over its entrance the armorial bearings of a family long since extinct. The young stranger, who was not unstudied in the great poem of his country, recollected that one of the ancestors of this family, and perhaps an occupant of this very mansion, had been pictured by Dante as a partaker of the immortal agonies of his Inferno. These reminiscences and associations, together with the tendency to heart-break natural to a young man for the first time out of his native sphere, caused Giovanni to sigh heavily, as he looked around the desolate and ill-furnished apartment.

"Holy Virgin, Signor," cried old dame Lisabetta, who, won by the youth's remarkable beauty of person, was kindly endeavouring to give the chamber a habitable air, "what a sigh was that to come out of a young man's heart! Do you find this old mansion gloomy? For the love of heaven, then, put your head out of the window, and you will see as bright sunshine as you have left in Naples."

Guasconti mechanically did as the old woman advised, but could not quite agree with her that the Paduan sunshine was as cheerful as that of southern Italy. Such as it was, however, it fell upon a garden beneath the window, and expended its fostering influences on a variety of plants, which seemed to have been cultivated with exceeding care.

"Does this garden belong to the house?" asked Giovanni.

"Heaven forbid, Signor!—unless it were fruitful of better pot-herbs than any that grow there now," answered old Lisabetta. "No; that garden is cultivated by the own hands of Signor Giacomo Rappaccini, the famous Doctor, who, I warrant him, has been heard of as far as Naples. It is said that he distils these plants into medicines that are as potent as a charm. Oftentimes you may see the Signor Doctor at work, and perchance the Signora his daughter, too, gathering the strange flowers that grow in the garden."

The old woman had now done what she could for the aspect of the chamber, and, commending the young man to the protection of the saints, took her departure.

Giovanni still found no better occupation than to look down into the garden beneath his window. From its appearance, he judged it to be one of those botanic gardens, which were of earlier date in Padua than elsewhere in Italy, or in the world. Or, not improbably, it might once have been the pleasure-place of an opulent family; for there was the ruin of a marble fountain in the centre, sculptured with rare art, but so woefully shattered that it was impossible to trace the original design from the chaos of remaining fragments. The water, however, continued to gush and sparkle into the sunbeams as cheerfully as ever. A little gurgling sound ascended to the young man's window, and made him feel as if the fountain were an immortal spirit, that sung its song unceasingly, and without heeding the vicissitudes around it; while one century embodied it in marble, and another scattered the perishable garniture on the soil. All about the pool into which the water subsided, grew various plants, that seemed to require a plentiful supply of moisture for the nourishment of gigantic leaves, and, in some instances, flowers gorgeously magnificent. There was one shrub in particular, set in a marble vase in the midst of the pool, that bore a profusion of purple blossoms, each of which had the lustre and richness of a gem; and the whole together made a show so resplendent that it seemed enough to illuminate the garden, even had there been no sunshine. Every portion of the soil was peopled with plants and herbs, which, if less beautiful, still bore tokens of assiduous care; as if all had their individual virtues, known to the scientific mind that fostered them. Some were placed in urns, rich with old carving, and others in common garden-pots; some crept serpent-like along the ground, or climbed on high, using whatever means of ascent was offered them. One plant had wreathed itself round a statue of Vertumnus, which was thus quite veiled and shrouded in a drapery of hanging foliage, so happily arranged that it might have served a sculptor for a study.

While Giovanni stood at the window, he heard a rustling behind a screen of leaves, and became aware that a person was at work in the garden. His figure soon emerged into view, and showed itself to be that of no common labourer, but a tall, emaciated, sallow, and sickly-looking man, dressed in a scholar's garb of black. He was beyond the middle term of life, with grey hair, a thin grey beard, and a face singularly marked with intellect and cultivation, but which could never, even in his more youthful days, have expressed much warmth of heart.

Nothing could exceed the intentness with which this scientific gardener examined every shrub which grew in his path; it seemed as if he was looking into their inmost nature, making observations in regard to their creative essence, and discovering why one leaf grew in this shape, and another in that, and wherefore such and such flowers differed among themselves in hue and perfume. Nevertheless, in spite of this deep intelligence on his part, there was no approach to intimacy between himself and these vegetable existences. On the contrary, he avoided their actual touch, or the direct inhaling of their odours, with a caution that impressed Giovanni most disagreeably; for the man's demeanour was that of one walking among malignant influences, such as savage beasts, or deadly snakes, or evil spirits, which, should he allow them one moment of licence, would wreak upon him some terrible fatality. It was strangely frightful to the young man's imagination, to see this air of insecurity in a person cultivating a garden, that most simple and innocent of human toils, and which had been alike the joy and labour of the unfallen parents of the race. Was this garden, then, the Eden of the present world?—and this man, with such a perception of harm in what his own hands caused to grow, was he the Adam?

The distrustful gardener, while plucking away the dead leaves or pruning the too luxuriant growth of the shrubs, defended his hands with a pair of thick gloves. Nor were these his only armour. When, in his walk through the garden, he came to the magnificent plant that hung its purple gems beside the marble fountain, he placed a kind of mask over his mouth and nostrils, as if all this beauty did but conceal a deadlier malice. But finding his task still too dangerous, he drew back, removed the mask, and called loudly, but in the infirm voice of a person affected with inward disease:

"Beatrice!—Beatrice!"

"Here am I, my father! What would you?" cried a rich and youthful voice from the window of the opposite house; a voice as rich as a tropical sunset, and which made Giovanni, though he knew not why, think of deep hues of purple or crimson, and of perfumes heavily delectable.—"Are you in the garden?"

"Yes, Beatrice," answered the gardener, "and I need your help."

Soon there emerged from under a sculptured portal the figure of a young girl, arrayed with as much richness of taste as the most splendid of the flowers, beautiful as the day, and with a bloom so deep and vivid that one shade more would have been too much. She looked redundant with life, health, and energy; all of which attributes were bound down and compressed, as it were, and girdled tensely, in their luxuriance, by her virgin zone. Yet Giovanni's fancy must have grown morbid, while he looked down into the garden; for the impression which the fair stranger made upon him was as if here were another flower, the human sister of those vegetables ones, as beautiful as they—more beautiful than the richest of them—but still to be touched only with a glove, nor to be approached without a mask. As Beatrice came down the garden path, it was observable that she handled and inhaled the odour of several of the plants, which her father had most sedulously avoided.

"Here, Beatrice," said the latter,—"see how many needful offices require to be done to our chief treasure. Yet, shattered as I am, my life might pay the penalty of approaching it so closely as circumstances demand. Henceforth, I fear, this plant must be consigned to your sole charge."

"And gladly will I undertake it," cried again the rich tones of the young lady, as she bent towards the magnificent plant, and opened her arms as if to embrace it. "Yes, my sister, my splendour, it shall be Beatrice's task to nurse and serve thee; and thou shalt reward her with thy kisses and perfumed breath, which to her is as the breath of life!"

Then, with all the tenderness in her manner that was so strikingly expressed in her words, she busied herself with such attentions as the plant seemed to require; and Giovanni, at his lofty window, rubbed his eyes, and almost doubted whether it were a girl tending her favourite flower, or one sister performing the duties of affection to another. The scene soon terminated. Whether Doctor Rappaccini had finished his labours in the garden, or that his watchful eye had caught the stranger's face, he now took his daughter's arm and retired. Night was already closing in; oppressive exhalations seemed to proceed from the plants, and steal upward past the open window; and Giovanni, closing the lattice, went to his couch, and dreamed of a rich flower and beautiful girl. Flower and maiden were different and yet the same, and fraught with some strange peril in either shape.

But there is an influence in the light of morning that tends to rectify whatever errors of fancy, or even of judgment, we may have incurred during the sun's decline, or among the shadows of the night, or in the less wholesome glow of moonshine. Giovanni's first movement on starting from sleep, was to throw open the window, and gaze down into the garden which his dreams had made so fertile of mysteries. He was surprised, and a little ashamed, to find how real and matter-of-fact an affair it proved to be, in the first rays of the sun, which gilded the dew-drops that hung upon leaf and blossom, and, while giving a brighter beauty to each rare flower, brought everything within the limits of ordinary experience. The young man rejoiced, that, in the heart of the barren city, he had the privilege of overlooking this spot of lovely and luxuriant vegetation. It would serve, he said to himself, as a symbolic language, to keep him in communion with Nature. Neither the sickly and thought-worn Doctor

Giacomo Rappaccini, it is true, nor his brilliant daughter, were now visible; so that Giovanni could not determine how much of the singularity which he attributed to both, was due to their own qualities, and how much to his wonder-working fancy. But he inclined to take a most rational view of the whole matter.

In the course of the day, he paid his respects to Signor Pietro Baglioni, professor of medicine in the University, a physician of eminent repute, to whom Giovanni had brought a letter of introduction. The Professor was an elderly personage, apparently of genial nature, and habits that might almost be called jovial; he kept the young man to dinner, and made himself very agreeable by the freedom and liveliness of his conversation, especially when warmed by a flask or two of Tuscan wine. Giovanni, conceiving that men of science, inhabitants of the same city, must needs be on familiar terms with one another, took an opportunity to mention the name of Doctor Rappaccini. But the Professor did not respond with so much cordiality as he had anticipated.

"Ill would it become a teacher of the divine art of medicine," said Professor Pietro Baglioni, in answer to a question of Giovanni, "to withhold due and well considered praise of a physician so eminently skilled as Rappaccini. But, on the other hand, I should answer it but scantily to my conscience, were I to permit a worthy youth like yourself, Signor Giovanni, the son of an ancient friend, to imbibe erroneous ideas respecting a man who might hereafter chance to hold your life and death in his hands. The truth is, our worshipful Doctor Rappaccini has as much science as any member of the faculty—with perhaps one single exception—in Padua, or all Italy. But there are certain grave objections to his professional character."

"And what are they?" asked the young man.

"Has my friend Giovanni any disease of body or heart, that he is so inquisitive about physicians?" said the Professor, with a smile. "But as for Rappaccini, it is said of him—and I, who know the man well, can answer for its truth—that he cares infinitely more for science than for mankind. His patients are interesting to him only as subjects for some new experiment. He would sacrifice human life, his own among the rest, or whatever else was dearest to him, for the sake of adding so much as a grain of mustard-seed to the great heap of his accumulated knowledge."

"Methinks he is an awful man, indeed," remarked Guasconti, mentally recalling the cold and purely intellectual aspect of Rappaccini. "And yet, worshipful Professor, is it not a noble spirit? Are there many men capable of so spiritual a love of science?"

"God forbid," answered the Professor, somewhat testily—"at least, unless they take sounder views of the healing art than those adopted by Rappaccini. It is his theory, that all medicinal virtues are comprised within those substances which we term vegetable poisons. These he cultivates with his own hands, and is said even to have produced new varieties of poison, more horribly deleterious than Nature, without the assistance of this learned person, would ever have plagued the world withal. That the Signor Doctor does less mischief than might be expected, with such dangerous substances, is undeniable. Now and then, it must be owned, he has effected—or seemed to effect—a marvellous cure. But, to tell you my private mind, Signor Giovanni, he should receive little credit for such instances of success—they being probably the work of chance—but should be held strictly accountable for his failures, which may justly be considered his own work."

The youth might have taken Baglioni's opinions with many grains of allowance, had he known that there was a professional warfare of long continuance between him and Doctor Rappaccini, in which the latter was generally thought to have gained the advantage. If the reader be inclined to judge for himself, we refer him to certain black-letter tracts on both sides, preserved in the medical department of the University of Padua.

"I know not, most learned Professor," returned Giovanni, after musing on what had been said of Rappaccini's exclusive zeal for science—"I know not how dearly this physician may love his art; but surely there is one object more dear to him. He has a daughter."

"Aha!" cried the Professor with a laugh. "So now our friend Giovanni's secret is out. You have heard of this daughter, whom all the young men in Padua are wild about, though not half a dozen have ever had the good hap to see her face. I know little of the Signora Beatrice, save that Rappaccini is said to have instructed her deeply in his science, and that, young and beautiful as fame reports her, she is already qualified to fill a professor's chair. Perchance her father destines her for mine! Other absurd rumours there be, not worth talking about, or listening to. So now, Signor Giovanni, drink off your glass of Lacryma."

Guasconti returned to his lodgings somewhat heated with the wine he had quaffed, and which caused his brain to swim with strange fantasies in reference to Doctor Rappaccini and the beautiful Beatrice. On his way, happening to pass by a florist's, he bought a fresh bouquet of flowers.

Ascending to his chamber, he seated himself near the window, but within the shadow thrown by the depth of the wall, so that he could look down into the garden with little risk of being discovered. All beneath his eye was a solitude. The strange plants were basking in the sunshine, and now and then nodding gently to one another, as if in acknowledgement of sympathy and kindred. In the midst, by the shattered fountain, grew the magnificent shrub, with its purple gems clustering all over it; they glowed in the air, and gleamed back again out of the depths of the pool, which thus seemed to overflow with coloured radiance from the rich reflection that was steeped in it. At first, as we have said, the garden was a solitude. Soon, however,—as Giovanni had half-hoped, half-feared, would be the case,—a figure appeared beneath the antique sculptured portal, and came down between the rows of plants, inhaling their various perfumes, as if she were one of those beings of old classic fable, that lived upon sweet odours. On again beholding Beatrice, the young man was even startled to perceive how much her beauty exceeded his recollection of it; so brilliant, so vivid was its character, that she glowed amid the sunlight, and, as Giovanni whispered to himself, positively illuminated the more shadowy intervals of the garden path. Her face being now more revealed than on the former occasion, he was struck by its expression of simplicity and sweetness; qualities that had not entered into his idea of her character, and which made him ask anew, what manner of mortal she might be. Nor did he fail again to observe, or imagine, an analogy between the beautiful girl and the gorgeous shrub that hung its gem-like flowers over the fountain; a resemblance which Beatrice seemed to have indulged a fantastic humour in heightening, both by the arrangement of her dress and the selection of its hues.

Approaching the shrub, she threw open her arms, as with a passionate ardour, and drew its branches into an intimate embrace; so intimate, that her features were hidden in its leafy bosom, and her glistening ringlets all intermingled with the flowers.

"Give me thy breath, my sister," exclaimed Beatrice; "for I am faint with common air! And give me this flower of thine, which I separate with gentlest fingers from the stem, and place it close beside my heart."

With these words, the beautiful daughter of Rappaccini plucked one of the richest blossoms of the shrub, and was about to fasten it in her bosom. But now, unless Giovanni's draughts of wine had bewildered his senses, a singular incident occurred. A small orange-coloured reptile, of the lizard or chameleon species, chanced to be creeping along the path, just at the feet of Beatrice. It appeared to Giovanni—but, at the distance from which he gazed, he could scarcely have seen anything so minute—it appeared to him, however, that a drop or two of moisture from the broken stem of the flower descended upon the lizard's head. For an instant, the reptile contorted itself violently, and then lay motionless in the sunshine. Beatrice observed this remarkable phenomenon, and crossed herself, sadly, but without surprise; nor did she therefore hesitate to arrange the fatal flower in her bosom. There it blushed, and almost glimmered with the dazzling effect of a precious stone, adding to her dress and aspect the one appropriate charm, which nothing else in the world could have supplied. But Giovanni, out of the shadow of his window, bent forward and shrank back, and murmured and trembled.

"Am I awake? Have I my senses?" said he to himself. "What is this being?—beautiful, shall I call her?—or inexpressibly terrible?"

Beatrice now strayed carelessly through the garden, approaching closer beneath Giovanni's window, so that he was compelled to thrust his head quite out of its concealment in order to gratify the intense and painful curiosity which she excited. At this moment, there came a beautiful insect over the garden wall; it had perhaps wandered through the city and found no flowers nor verdure among those antique haunts of men, until the heavy perfumes of Doctor Rappaccini's shrubs had lured it from afar. Without alighting on the flowers, this winged brightness seemed to be attracted by Beatrice, and lingered in the air and fluttered about her head. Now, here it could not be but that Giovanni Guasconti's eyes deceived him. Be that as it might, he fancied that while Beatrice was gazing at the insect with childish delight, it grew faint and fell at her feet;—its bright wings shivered; it was dead—from no cause that he could discern, unless it were the atmosphere of her breath. Again Beatrice crossed herself and sighed heavily, as she bent over the dead insect.

An impulsive movement of Giovanni drew her eyes to the window. There she beheld the beautiful head of the young man—rather a Grecian than an Italian head, with fair, regular features, and a glistening of gold among his ringlets—gazing down upon her like a being that hovered in midair. Scarcely knowing what he did, Giovanni threw down the bouquet which he had hitherto held in his hand.

"Signora," said he, "there are pure and healthful flowers. Wear them for the sake of Giovanni Guasconti!"

"Thanks, Signor," replied Beatrice, with her rich voice, that came forth as it were like a gush of music; and with a mirthful expression half childish and half woman-like. "I accept your gift, and would fain recompense it with this precious purple flower; but if I toss it into the air, it will not reach you. So Signor Guasconti must even content himself with my thanks."

She lifted the bouquet from the ground, and then as if inwardly ashamed at having stepped aside from her maidenly reserve to respond to a stranger's greeting, passed swiftly homeward through the garden. But, few as the moments were, it seemed to Giovanni when she was on the point of vanishing beneath the sculptured portal, that his beautiful bouquet was already beginning to wither in her grasp. It was an idle thought; there could be no possibility of distinguishing a faded flower from a fresh one at so great a distance.

For many days after this incident, the young man avoided the window that looked into Doctor Rappaccini's garden, as if something ugly and monstrous would have blasted his eyesight, had he been betrayed into a glance. He felt conscious of having put himself, to a certain extent, within the influence of an unintelligible power, by the communication which he had opened with Beatrice. The wisest course would have been, if his heart were in any real danger, to quit his lodgings and Padua itself, at once; the next wiser, to have accustomed himself, as far as possible, to the familiar and day-light view of Beatrice; thus bringing her rigidly and systematically within the limits of ordinary experience. Least of all, while avoiding her sight, ought Giovanni to have remained so near this extraordinary being, that the proximity and possibility even of intercourse, should give a kind of substance and reality to the wild vagaries which his imagination ran riot continually into producing. Guasconti had not a deep heart—or at all events, its depths were not sounded now—but he had a quick fancy, and an ardent southern temperament, which rose every instant to a higher fever-pitch. Whether or no Beatrice possessed those terrible attributes—that fatal breath—the affinity with those so beautiful and deadly flowers—which were indicated by what Giovanni had witnessed, she had at least instilled a fierce and subtle poison into his system. It was not love, although her rich beauty was a madness to him; nor horror, even while he fancied her spirit to be imbued with the same baneful essence that seemed to pervade her physical frame; but a wild offspring of both love and horror that had each parent in it, and burned like one and shivered like the other. Giovanni knew not what to dread; still less did he know what to hope; yet hope and dread kept a continual warfare in his breast, alternately vanquishing one another and starting up afresh to renew the contest. Blessed are all simple emotions, be they dark or bright! It is the lurid intermixture of the two that produces the illuminating blaze of the infernal regions.

Sometimes he endeavoured to assuage the fever of his spirit by a rapid walk through the streets of Padua, or beyond its gates; his footsteps kept time with the throbbings of his brain, so that the walk was apt to accelerate itself to a race. One day, he found himself arrested; his arm was seized by a portly personage who had turned back on recognizing the young man, and expended much breath in overtaking him.

"Signor Giovanni!—stay, my young friend!" cried he. "Have you forgotten me? That might well be the case, if I were as much altered as yourself."

It was Baglioni, whom Giovanni had avoided, ever since their first meeting, from a doubt that the Professor's sagacity would look too deeply into his secrets. Endeavouring to recover himself, he stared forth wildly from his inner world into the outer one, and spoke like a man in a dream:

"Yes, I am Giovanni Guasconti. You are Professor Pietro Baglioni. Now let me pass!"

"Not yet—not yet, Signor Giovanni Guasconti," said the Professor, smiling, but at the same time scrutinizing the youth with an earnest glance.—"What; did I grow up side by side with your father, and shall his son pass me like a stranger, in these old streets of Padua? Stand still, Signor Giovanni; for we must have a word or two, before we part."

"Speedily, then, most worshipful Professor, speedily!" said Giovanni, with feverish impatience. "Does not your worship see that I am in haste?"

Now, while he was speaking, there came a man in black along the street, stooping and moving feebly, like a person in inferior health. His face was all overspread with a most sickly and sallow hue, but yet so pervaded with an expression of piercing and active intellect, that an observer might easily have overlooked the merely physical attributes, and have seen only this wonderful energy. As he passed, this person exchanged a cold and distant salutation with Baglioni, but fixed his eyes upon Giovanni with an intentness that seemed to bring out whatever was within him worthy of notice. Nevertheless, there was a peculiar quietness in the look, as if taking merely a speculative, not a human, interest in the young man.

"It is Doctor Rappaccini!" whispered the Professor, when the stranger had passed.—"Has he ever seen your face before?"

"Not that I know," answered Giovanni, starting at the name.

"He *has* seen you!—he must have seen you!" said Baglioni, hastily. "For some purpose or other, this man of science is making a study of you. I know that look of his! It is the same that coldly illuminates his face, as he bends over a bird, a mouse, or a butterfly, which, in pursuance of some experiment, he has killed by the perfume of a flower;—a look as deep as Nature itself, but without Nature's warmth of love. Signor Giovanni, I will stake my life upon it, you are the subject of one of Rappaccini's experiments!"

"Will you make of fool of me?" cried Giovanni, passionately. "*That*, Signor Professor, were an untoward experiment."

"Patience, patience!" replied the imperturbable Professor.—"I tell thee, my poor Giovanni, that Rappaccini has a scientific interest in thee. Thou hast fallen into fearful hands! And the Signora Beatrice? What part does she act in this mystery?"

But Guasconti, finding Baglioni's pertinacity intolerable, here broke away, and was gone before the Professor could again seize his arm. He looked after the young man intently, and shook his head.

"This must not be," said Baglioni to himself. "The youth is the son of my old friend, and shall not come to any harm from which the arcana of medical science can preserve him. Besides, it is too insufferable an impertinence in Rappaccini, thus to snatch the lad out of my own hands, as I may say, and make use of him for his infernal experiments. This daughter of his! It shall be looked to. Perchance, most learned Rappaccini, I may foil you where you little dream of it!"

Meanwhile, Giovanni had pursued a circuitous route, and at length found himself at the door of his lodgings. As he crossed the threshold, he was met by old Lisabetta, who smirked and smiled, and was evidently desirous to attract his attention; vainly, however, as the ebullition of his feelings had momentarily subsided into a cold and dull vacuity. He turned his eyes full upon the withered face that was puckering itself into a smile, but seemed to behold it not. The old dame, therefore, laid her grasp upon his cloak.

"Signor!—Signor!" whispered she, still with a smile over the whole breadth of her visage, so that it looked not unlike a grotesque carving in wood, darkened by centuries—"Listen, Signor! There is a private entrance into the garden!"

"What do you say?" exclaimed Giovanni, turning quickly about, as if an inanimate thing should start into feverish life.—"A private entrance into Doctor Rappaccini's garden!"

"Hush! hush!—not so loud!" whispered Lisabetta, putting her hand over his mouth. "Yes; into the worshipful Doctor's garden, where you may see all his fine shrubbery. Many a young man in Padua would give gold to be admitted among those flowers."

Giovanni put a piece of gold into her hand.

"Show me the way," said he.

A surmise, probably excited by his conversation with Baglioni, crossed his mind, that this interposition of old Lisabetta might perchance be connected with the intrigue, whatever were its nature, in which the Professor seemed to suppose that Doctor Rappaccini was involving him. But such a suspicion, though it disturbed Giovanni, was inadequate to restrain him. The instant that he was aware of the possibility of approaching Beatrice, it seemed an absolute necessity of his existence to do so. It mattered not whether she were angel or demon; he was irrevocably within her sphere, and must obey the law that whirled him onward, in ever lessening circles, towards a result which he did not attempt to foreshadow. And yet, strange to say, there came across him a sudden doubt, whether this intense interest on his part were not delusory—whether it were really of so deep and positive a nature as to justify him in now thrusting himself into an incalculable position—whether it were not merely the fantasy of a young man's brain, only slightly, or not at all, connected with his heart!

He paused—hesitated—turned half about—but again went on. His withered guide led him along several obscure passages, and finally undid a door, through which, as it was opened, there came the sight and sound of rustling leaves with the broken sunshine glimmering among them. Giovanni stepped forth, and forcing himself through the entanglement of a shrub that wreathed its tendrils over the hidden entrance, he stood beneath his own window, in the open area of Doctor Rappaccini's garden.

How often is it the case, that, when impossibilities have come to pass, and dreams have condensed their misty substance into tangible realities, we find ourselves calm, and even coldly self-possessed, amid circumstances which it would have been a delirium of joy or agony to anticipate! Fate delights to thwart us thus. Passion will choose his own time to rush upon the scene, and lingers sluggishly behind, when an appropriate adjustment of events would seem to summon his appearance. So was it now with Giovanni. Day after day, his pulses had throbbed with feverish blood, at the improbable idea of an interview with Beatrice, and of standing with her, face to face, in this very garden, basking in the Oriental sunshine of her beauty, and snatching from her full gaze the mystery which he deemed the riddle of his own existence. But now there was a singular and untimely equanimity within his breast. He threw a glance around the garden to discover if Beatrice or her father were present, and perceiving that he was alone, began a critical observation of the plants.

The aspect of one and all of them dissatisfied him; their gorgeousness seemed fierce, passionate, and even unnatural. There was hardly an individual shrub which a wanderer, straying by himself through a forest, would not have been startled to find growing wild, as if an unearthly face had glared at him out of the thicket. Several, also, would have shocked a delicate instinct by an appearance of artificialness, indicating that there had been such commixture, and, as it were, adultery of various vegetable species, that the production was no longer of God's making, but the monstrous offspring of man's depraved fancy, glowing with only an evil mockery of beauty. They were probably the result of experiment, which, in one or two cases, had succeeded in mingling plants individually lovely into a compound possessing the questionable and ominous character that distinguished the whole growth of the garden. In fine, Giovanni recognized but two or three plants in the collection, and those of a kind that he well knew to be poisonous. While busy with these contemplations, he heard the rustling of a silken garment, and turning, beheld Beatrice emerging from beneath the sculptured portal.

Giovanni had not considered with himself what should be his deportment; whether he should apologize for his intrusion into the garden, or assume that he was there with the privity, at least, if not by the desire, of Doctor Rappaccini or his daughter. But Beatrice's manner placed him at his ease, though leaving him still in doubt by what agency he had gained admittance. She came lightly along the path, and met him near the broken fountain. There was surprise in her face, but brightened by a simple and kind expression of pleasure.

"You are a connoisseur in flowers, Signor," said Beatrice with a smile, alluding to the bouquet which he had flung her from the window. "It is no marvel, therefore, if the sight of my father's rare collection has tempted you to take a nearer view. If he were here, he could tell you many strange and interesting facts as to the nature and habits of these shrubs, for he has spent a lifetime in such studies, and this garden is his world."

"And yourself, lady"—observed Giovanni—"if fame says true—you, likewise, are deeply skilled in the virtues indicated by these rich blossoms, and these spicy perfumes. Would you deign to be my instructress, I should prove an apter scholar than if taught by Signor Rappaccini himself."

"Are there such idle rumours?" asked Beatrice, with the music of a pleasant laugh. "Do people say that I am skilled in my father's science of plants? What a jest is there! No; though I have grown up among these flowers, I know no more of them than their hues and perfume; and sometimes, methinks I would fain rid myself of even that small knowledge. There are many flowers here, and those not the least brilliant, that shock and offend me, when they meet my eye. But, pray, Signor, do not believe these stories about my science. Believe nothing of me save what you see with your own eyes."

"And must I believe all that I have seen with my own eyes?" asked Giovanni pointedly, while the recollection of former scenes made him shrink. "No, Signora, you demand too little of me. Bid me believe nothing, save what comes from your own lips."

It would appear that Beatrice understood him. There came a deep flush to her cheek; but she looked full into Giovanni's eyes, and responded to his gaze of uneasy suspicion with a queen-like haughtiness.

"I do so bid you, Signor!" she replied. "Forget whatever you may have fancied in regard to me. If true to the outward senses, still it may be false in its essence. But the words of Beatrice Rappaccini's lips are true from the depths of the heart outward. Those you may believe!"

A fervour glowed in her whole aspect, and beamed upon Giovanni's consciousness like the light of truth itself. But while she spoke, there was a fragrance in the atmosphere around her, rich and delightful, though evanescent, yet which the young man, from an indefinable reluctance, scarcely dared to draw into his lungs. It might be the odour of the flowers. Could it be Beatrice's breath, which thus embalmed her words with a strange richness, as if by steeping them in her heart? A faintness passed like a shadow over Giovanni, and flitted away; he seemed to gaze through the beautiful girl's eyes into her transparent soul, and felt no more doubt or fear.

The tinge of passion that had coloured Beatrice's manner vanished; she became gay, and appeared to derive a pure delight from her communication with the youth, not unlike what the maiden of a lonely island might have felt, conversing with a voyager from the civilized world. Evidently her experience of life had been confined within the limits of that garden. She talked now about matters as simple as the daylight or summer-clouds, and now asked questions in reference to the city, or Giovanni's distant home, his friends, his mother, and his sisters; questions indicating such seclusion, and such lack of familiarity with modes and forms, that Giovanni responded as if to an infant. Her spirit gushed out before him like a fresh rill, that was just catching its first glimpse of the sunlight, and wondering at the reflections of earth and sky which were flung into its bosom. There came thoughts, too, from a deep source, and fantasies of a gem-like brilliancy, as if diamonds and rubies sparkled upward among the bubbles of the fountain. Ever and anon, there gleamed across the young man's mind a sense of wonder, that he should be walking side by side with the being who had so wrought upon his imagination—whom he had idealized in such hues of terror—in whom he had positively witnessed such manifestations of dreadful attributes—that he should be conversing with Beatrice like a brother, and should find her so human and so maiden-like. But such reflections were only momentary; the effect of her character was too real, not to make itself familiar at once.

In this free intercourse, they had strayed through the garden, and now, after many turns among its avenues, were come to the shattered fountain, beside which grew the magnificent shrub with its treasury of glowing blossoms. A fragrance was diffused from it, which Giovanni recognized as identical with that which he had attributed to Beatrice's breath, but incomparably more powerful. As her eyes fell upon it, Giovanni beheld her press her hand to her bosom, as if her heart were throbbing suddenly and painfully.

"For the first time in my life," murmured she, addressing the shrub, "I had forgotten thee!"

"I remember, Signora," said Giovanni, "that you once promised to reward me with one of these living gems for the bouquet, which I had the happy boldness to fling to your feet. Permit me now to pluck it as a memorial of this interview."

He made a step towards the shrub, with extended hand. But Beatrice darted forward, uttering a shriek that went through his heart like a dagger. She caught his hand, and drew it back with the whole force of her slender figure. Giovanni felt her touch thrilling through his fibres.

"Touch it not!" exclaimed she, in a voice of agony. "Not for thy life! It is fatal!"

Then, hiding her face, she fled from him, and vanished beneath the sculptured portal. As Giovanni followed her with his eyes, he beheld the emaciated figure and pale intelligence of Doctor Rappaccini, who had been watching the scene, he knew not how long, within the shadow of the entrance.

No sooner was Guasconti alone in his chamber, than the image of Beatrice came back to his passionate musings, invested with all the witchery that had been gathering around it ever since his first glimpse of her, and now likewise imbued with a tender warmth of girlish womanhood. She was human: her nature was endowed with all gentle and feminine qualities; she was worthiest to be worshipped; she was capable, surely, on her part, of the height and heroism of love. Those tokens, which he had hitherto considered as proofs of a frightful peculiarity in her physical and moral system, were now either forgotten, or, by the subtle sophistry of passion, transmuted into a golden crown of enchantment, rendering Beatrice more admirable, by so much as she was the more unique. Whatever had looked ugly, was now beautiful; or, if incapable of such a change, it stole away and hid itself among those shapeless half-ideas, which throng the dim region beyond the daylight of our perfect consciousness. Thus did he spend the night, nor fell asleep, until the dawn had begun to awake the slumbering flowers in Doctor Rappaccini's garden, whither Giovanni's dreams doubtless led him. Up rose the sun in his due season, and flinging his beams upon the young man's eyelids, awoke him to a sense of pain. When thoroughly aroused, he became sensible of a burning and tingling agony in his hand—in his right hand—the very hand which Beatrice had grasped in her own, when he was on the point of plucking one of the gem-like flowers. On the back of that hand there was now a purple print, like that of four small fingers, and the likeness of a slender thumb upon his wrist.

Oh, how stubbornly does love—or even that cunning semblance of love which flourishes in the imagination, but strikes no depth of root into the heart—how stubbornly does it hold its faith, until the moment come, when it is doomed to vanish into thin mist! Giovanni wrapt a handkerchief about his hand, and wondered what evil thing had stung him, and soon forgot his pain in a reverie of Beatrice.

After the first interview, a second was in the inevitable course of what we call fate. A third; a fourth; and a meeting with Beatrice in the garden was no longer an incident in Giovanni's daily life, but the whole space in which he might be said to live; for the anticipation and memory of that ecstatic hour made up the remainder. Nor was it otherwise with the daughter of Rappaccini. She watched for the youth's appearance, and flew to his side with confidence as unreserved as if they had been playmates from early infancy—as if they were such playmates still. If, by any unwonted chance, he failed to come at the appointed moment, she stood beneath the window, and sent up the rich sweetness of her tones to float around him in his chamber, and echo and reverberate throughout his heart—"Giovanni! Giovanni! Why tarriest thou? Come down!"—And down he hastened into that Eden of poisonous flowers.

But, with all this intimate familiarity, there was still a reserve in Beatrice's demeanour, so rigidly and invariably sustained, that the idea of infringing it scarcely occurred to his imagination. By all appreciable signs, they loved; they had looked love, with eyes that conveyed the holy secret from the depths of one soul into the depths of the other, as if it were too sacred to be whispered by the way; they had even spoken love, in those gushes of passion when their spirits darted forth in articulated breath, like tongues of long-hidden flame; and yet there had been no seal of lips, no clasp of hands, nor any slightest caress, such as love claims and hallows. He had never touched one of the gleaming ringlets of her hair; her garment—so marked was the physical barrier between them—had never been waved against him by a breeze. On a few occasions when Giovanni had seemed tempted to overstep the limit, Beatrice grew so sad, so stern, and withal wore such a look of desolate separation, shuddering at itself, that not a spoken word was requisite to repel him. At such times, he was startled at the horrible suspicions that rose, monster-like, out of the caverns of his heart, and stared him in the face; his love grew thin and faint as the morning mist; his doubts alone had substance. But when Beatrice's face brightened again, after the momentary shadow, she was transformed at once from the mysterious, questionable being, whom he had watched with so much awe and horror; she was now the beautiful and unsophisticated girl, whom he felt that his spirit knew with a certainty beyond all other knowledge.

A considerable time had now passed since Giovanni's last meeting with Baglioni. One morning, however, he was disagreeably surprised by a visit from the Professor, whom he had scarcely thought of for whole weeks, and would willingly have forgotten still longer. Given up, as he had long been, to a pervading excitement, he could tolerate no companions, except upon condition of their perfect sympathy with his present state of feeling. Such sympathy was not to be expected from Professor Baglioni.

The visitor chatted carelessly, for a few moments, about the gossip of the city and the University, and then took up another topic.

"I have been reading an old classic author lately," said he, "and met with a story that strangely interested me. Possibly you may remember it. It is of an Indian prince, who sent a beautiful woman as a present to Alexander the Great. She was as lovely as the dawn, and gorgeous as the sunset; but what especially distinguished her was a certain rich perfume in her breath—richer than a garden of Persian roses. Alexander, as was natural to a youthful conqueror, fell in love at first sight with this magnificent stranger. But a certain sage physician, happening to be present, discovered a terrible secret in regard to her."

"And what was that?" asked Giovanni, turning his eyes downward to avoid those of the Professor.

"That this lovely woman," continued Baglioni, with emphasis, "had been nourished with poisons from her birth upward, until her whole nature was so imbued with them, that she herself had become the deadliest poison in existence. Poison was her element of life. With that rich perfume of her breath, she blasted the very air. Her love would have been poison!—her embrace death! Is not this a marvellous tale?"

"A childish fable," answered Giovanni, nervously starting from his chair. "I marvel how your worship finds time to read such nonsense, among your graver studies."

"By the bye," said the Professor, looking uneasily about him, "what singular fragrance is this in your apartment? Is it the perfume of your gloves? It is faint, but delicious, and yet, after all, by no means agreeable. Were I to breathe it long, methinks it would make me ill. It is like the breath of a flower—but I see no flowers in the chamber."

"Nor are there any," replied Giovanni, who had turned pale as the Professor spoke; "nor, I think, is there any fragrance, except in your worship's imagination. Odours, being a sort of element combined of the sensual and the spiritual, are apt to deceive us in this manner. The recollection of a perfume—the bare idea of it—may easily be mistaken for a present reality."

"Aye; but my sober imagination does not often play such tricks," said Baglioni; "and were I to fancy any kind of odour, it would be that of some vile apothecary drug, wherewith my fingers are likely enough to be imbued. Our worshipful friend Rappaccini, as I have heard, tinctures his medicaments with odours richer than those of Araby. Doubtless, likewise, the fair and learned Signora Beatrice would minister to her patients with draughts as sweet as a maiden's breath. But woe to him that sips them!"

Giovanni's face evinced many contending emotions. The tone in which the Professor alluded to the pure and lovely daughter of Rappaccini was a torture to his soul; and yet, the intimation of a view of her character, opposite to his own, gave instantaneous distinctness to a thousand dim suspicions, which now grinned at him like so many demons. But he strove hard to quell them, and to respond to Baglioni with a true lover's perfect faith.

"Signor Professor," said he, "you were my father's friend—perchance, too, it is your purpose to act a friendly part towards his son. I would fain feel nothing towards you, save respect and deference. But I pray you to observe, Signor, that there is one subject on which we must not speak. You know not the Signora

Beatrice. You cannot, therefore, estimate the wrong—the blasphemy, I may even say—that is offered to her character by a light or injurious word."

"Giovanni!—my poor Giovanni!" answered the Professor, with a calm expression of pity, "I know this wretched girl far better than yourself. You shall hear the truth in respect to the poisoner Rappaccini, and his poisonous daughter. Yes; poisonous as she is beautiful! Listen; for even should you do violence to my grey hairs, it shall not silence me. That old fable of the Indian woman has become a truth, by the deep and deadly science of Rappaccini, and in the person of the lovely Beatrice!"

Giovanni groaned and hid his face.

"Her father," continued Baglioni, "was not restrained by natural affection from offering up his child, in this horrible manner, as the victim of his insane zeal for science. For—let us do him justice—he is as true a man of science as ever distilled his own heart in an alembic. What, then, will be your fate? Beyond a doubt, you are selected as the material of some new experiment. Perhaps the result is to be death—perhaps a fate more awful still! Rappaccini, with what he calls the interest of science before his eyes, will hesitate at nothing."

"It is a dream!" muttered Giovanni to himself, "surely it is a dream!"

"But," resumed the Professor, "be of good cheer, son of my friend! It is not yet too late for the rescue. Possibly, we may even succeed in bringing back this miserable child within the limits of ordinary nature, from which her father's madness has estranged her. Behold this little silver vase! It was wrought by the hands of the renowned Benvenuto Cellini, and well worthy to be a love-gift to the fairest dame in Italy. But its contents are invaluable. One little sip of this antidote would have rendered the most virulent poisons of the Borgias innocuous. Doubt not that it will be as efficacious against those of Rappaccini. Bestow the vase, and the precious liquid within it, on your Beatrice, and hopefully await the result."

Baglioni laid a small, exquisitely wrought silver phial on the table, and withdrew, leaving what he had said to produce its effect upon the young man's mind.

"We will thwart Rappaccini yet!" thought he, chuckling to himself, as he descended the stairs. "But, let us confess the truth of him, he is a wonderful man!—a wonderful man indeed! A vile empiric, however, in his practice, and therefore not to be tolerated by those who respect the good old rules of the medical profession!"

Throughout Giovanni's whole acquaintance with Beatrice, he had occasionally, as we have said, been haunted by dark surmises as to her character. Yet, so thoroughly had she made herself felt by him as a simple, natural, most affectionate and guileless creature, that the image now held up by Professor Baglioni, looked as strange and incredible, as if it were not in accordance with his own original conception. True, there were ugly recollections connected with his first glimpses of the beautiful girl; he could not quite forget the bouquet that withered in her grasp, and the insect that perished amid the sunny air, by no ostensible agency, save the fragrance of her breath. These incidents, however, dissolving in the pure light of her character, had no longer the efficacy of facts, but were acknowledged as mistaken fantasies, by whatever testimony of the senses they might appear to be substantiated. There is something truer and more real, than what we can see with the eyes, and touch with the finger. On such better evidence, had Giovanni founded his confidence in Beatrice, though rather by the necessary force of her high attributes, than by any deep and generous faith, on his part. But, now, his spirit was incapable of sustaining itself at the height to which the early enthusiasm of passion had exalted it; he fell down, grovelling among earthly doubts, and defiled therewith the pure whiteness of Beatrice's image. Not that he gave her up; he did but distrust. He resolved to institute some decisive test that should satisfy him, once for all, whether there were those dreadful peculiarities in her physical nature, which could not be supposed to exist without some corresponding monstrosity of soul. His eyes, gazing down afar, might have deceived him as to the lizard, the insect, and the flowers. But if he could witness, at the distance of a few paces, the sudden blight of one fresh and healthful flower in Beatrice's hand, there would be room for no further question. With this idea, he hastened to the florist's, and purchased a bouquet that was still gemmed with the morning dew-drops.

It was now the customary hour of his daily interview with Beatrice. Before descending into the garden, Giovanni failed not to look at his figure in the mirror; a vanity to be expected in a beautiful young man, yet, as displaying itself at that troubled and feverish moment, the token of a certain shallowness of feeling and insincerity of character. He did gaze, however, and said to himself, that his features had never before possessed so rich a grace, nor his eyes such vivacity, nor his cheeks so warm a hue of superabundant life.

"At least," thought he, "her poison has not yet insinuated itself into my system. I am no flower to perish in her grasp!"

With that thought, he turned his eyes on the bouquet, which he had never once laid aside from his hand. A thrill of indefinable horror shot through his frame, on perceiving that those dewy flowers were already beginning to droop; they wore the aspect of things that had been fresh and lovely, yesterday. Giovanni grew white as marble, and stood motionless before the mirror, staring at his own reflection there, as at the likeness of something frightful. He remembered Baglioni's remark about the fragrance that seemed to pervade the chamber. It must have been the poison in his breath! Then he shuddered—shuddered at himself! Recovering from his stupor, he began to watch, with curious eye, a spider that was busily at work, hanging its web from the antique cornice of the apartment, crossing and re-crossing the artful system of interwoven lines, as vigorous and active a spider as ever dangled from an old ceiling. Giovanni bent towards the insect, and emitted a deep, long breath. The spider suddenly ceased its toil; the web vibrated with a tremor originating in the body of the small artisan. Again Giovanni sent forth a breath, deeper, longer, and imbued with a venomous feeling out of his heart; he knew not whether he were wicked or only desperate. The spider made a convulsive gripe with his limbs, and hung dead across the window.

"Accursed! Accursed!" muttered Giovanni, addressing himself. "Hast thou grown so poisonous, that this deadly insect perishes by thy breath?"

At that moment, a rich, sweet voice came floating up from the garden:—

"Giovanni! Giovanni! It is past the hour! Why tarriest thou! Come down!"

"Yes," muttered Giovanni again. "She is the only being whom my breath may not slay! Would that it might!"

He rushed down, and in an instant, was standing before the bright and loving eyes of Beatrice. A moment ago, his wrath and despair had been so fierce that he could have desired nothing so much as to wither her by a glance. But, with her actual presence, there came influences which had too real an existence to be at once shaken off; recollections of the delicate and benign power of her feminine nature, which had so often enveloped him in a religious calm; recollections of many a holy and passionate outgush of her heart, when the pure fountain had been unsealed from its depths, and made visible in its transparency to his mental eye; recollections which, had Giovanni known how to estimate them, would have assured him that all this ugly mystery was but an earthly illusion, and that, whatever mist of evil might seem to have gathered over her, the real Beatrice was a heavenly angel. Incapable as he was of such high faith, still her presence had not utterly lost its magic. Giovanni's rage was quelled into an aspect of sullen insensibility. Beatrice, with a quick spiritual sense, immediately felt that there was a gulf of blackness between them, which neither he nor she could pass. They walked on together, sad and silent, and came thus to the marble fountain, and to its pool of water on the ground, in the midst of which grew the shrub that bore gem-like blossoms. Giovanni was affrighted at the eager enjoyment—the appetite, as it were—with which he found himself inhaling the fragrance of the flowers.

"Beatrice," asked he abruptly, "whence came this shrub?"

"My father created it," answered she, with simplicity.

"Created it! created it!" repeated Giovanni. "What mean you, Beatrice?"

"He is a man fearfully acquainted with the secrets of nature," replied Beatrice; "and, at the hour when I first drew breath, this plant sprang from the soil, the offspring of his science, of his intellect, while I was but his earthly child. Approach it not!" continued she, observing with terror that Giovanni was drawing nearer to the shrub. "It has qualities that you little dream of. But I, dearest Giovanni,—I grew up and blossomed with the plant, and was nourished with its breath. It was my sister, and I loved it with a human affection: for alas! hast thou not suspected it? there was an awful doom."

Here Giovanni frowned so darkly upon her that Beatrice paused and trembled. But her faith in his tenderness reassured her, and made her blush that she had doubted for an instant.

"There was an awful doom," she continued,—"the effect of my father's fatal love of science—which estranged me from all society of my kind. Until Heaven sent thee, dearest Giovanni, Oh! how lonely was thy poor Beatrice!"

"Was it a hard doom?" asked Giovanni, fixing his eyes upon her.

"Only of late have I known how hard it was," answered she tenderly. "Oh, yes; but my heart was torpid, and therefore quiet."

Giovanni's rage broke forth from his sullen gloom like a lightning-flash out of a dark cloud.

"Accursed one!" cried he, with venomous scorn and anger. "And finding thy solitude wearisome, thou hast severed me, likewise, from all the warmth of life; and enticed me into thy region of unspeakable horror!"

"Giovanni!" exclaimed Beatrice, turning her large bright eyes upon his face. The force of his words had not found its way into her mind: she was merely thunder-struck.

"Yes, poisonous thing!" repeated Giovanni, beside himself with passion. "Thou hast done it! Thou hast blasted me! Thou hast filled my veins with poison! Thou hast made me as hateful, as ugly, as loathsome and deadly a creature as thyself,—a world's wonder of hideous monstrosity! Now—if our breath be happily as fatal to ourselves as to all others—let us join our lips in one kiss of unutterable hatred, and so die!"

"What has befallen me?" murmured Beatrice, with a low moan out of her heart. "Holy Virgin pity me, a poor heartbroken child!"

"Thou! Dost thou pray?" cried Giovanni, still with the same fiendish scorn. "Thy very prayers, as they come from thy lips, taint the atmosphere with death. Yes, yes; let us pray! Let us to church, and dip our fingers in the holy water at the portal! They that come after us will perish as by a pestilence. Let us sign crosses in the air! It will be scattering curses abroad in the likeness of holy symbols!"

"Giovanni," said Beatrice calmly, for her grief was beyond passion, "why dost thou join thyself with me thus in those terrible words? I, it is true, am the horrible thing thou namest me. But thou!—what hast thou to do, save with one other shudder at my hideous misery, to go forth out of the garden and mingle with thy race, and forget that there ever crawled on earth such a monster as poor Beatrice?"

"Dost thou pretend ignorance?" asked Giovanni, scowling upon her. "Behold! This power have I gained from the pure daughter of Rappaccini!"

There was a swarm of summer-insects flitting through the air, in search of the food promised by the flower-odours of the fatal garden. They circled round Giovanni's head, and were evidently attracted towards him by the same influence which had drawn them, for an instant, within the sphere of several of the shrubs. He sent forth a breath among them, and smiled bitterly at Beatrice, as at least a score of the insects fell dead upon the ground.

"I see it! I see it!" shrieked Beatrice. "It is my father's fatal science! No, no, Giovanni; it was not I! Never, never! I dreamed only to love thee, and be with thee a little time, and so to let thee pass away, leaving but thine image in mine heart. For, Giovanni—believe it—though my body be nourished with poison, my spirit is God's creature, and craves love as its daily food. But my father!—he has united us in this fearful sympathy. Yes; spurn me!—tread upon me!—kill me! Oh, what is death, after such words as thine? But it was not I! Not for a world of bliss would I have done it!"

Giovanni's passion had exhausted itself in its outburst from his lips. There now came across him a sense, mournful, and not without tenderness, of the intimate and peculiar relationship between Beatrice and himself. They stood, as it were, in an utter solitude, which would be made none the less solitary by the densest throng of human life. Ought not, then, the desert of humanity around them to press this insulated pair closer together? If they should be cruel to one another, who was there to be kind to them? Besides, thought Giovanni, might there not still be a hope of his returning within the limits of ordinary nature, and leading Beatrice—the redeemed Beatrice—by the hand? Oh, weak, and selfish, and unworthy spirit, that could dream of an earthly union and earthly happiness as possible, after such deep love had been so bitterly wronged as was Beatrice's love by Giovanni's blighting words! No, no; there could be no such hope. She must pass heavily, with that broken heart, across the borders of Time—she must bathe her hurts in some fount of Paradise, and forget her grief in the light of immortality—and *there* be well!

But Giovanni did not know it.

"Dear Beatrice," said he, approaching her, while she shrank away, as always at his approach, but now with a different impulse—"dearest Beatrice, our fate is not yet so desperate. Behold! There is a medicine, potent, as a wise physician has assured me, and almost divine in its efficacy. It is composed of ingredients the most opposite to those by which thy awful father has brought this calamity upon thee and me. It is distilled of blessed herbs. Shall we not quaff it together, and thus be purified from evil?"

"Give it me!" said Beatrice, extending her hand to receive the little silver phial which Giovanni took from his bosom. She added, with a peculiar emphasis: "I will drink—but do thou await the result."

She put Baglioni's antidote to her lips; and, at the same moment, the figure of Rappaccini emerged from the portal, and came slowly towards the marble fountain. As he drew near, the pale man of science seemed to gaze with a triumphant expression at the beautiful youth and maiden, as might an artist who should spend his life in achieving a picture or a group of statuary, and finally be satisfied with his success. He paused—his bent form grew erect with conscious power, he spread out his hands over them, in the attitude of a father imploring a blessing upon his children. But those were the same hands that had thrown poison into the stream of their lives! Giovanni trembled. Beatrice shuddered nervously, and pressed her hand upon her heart.

"My daughter," said Rappaccini, "thou art no longer lonely in the world! Pluck one of those precious gems from thy sister shrub, and bid thy bridegroom wear it in his bosom. It will not harm him now! My science, and the sympathy between thee and him, have so wrought within his system, that he now stands apart from common men, as thou dost, daughter of my pride and triumph, from ordinary women. Pass on, then, through the world, most dear to one another, and dreadful to all besides!"

"My father," said Beatrice, feebly—and still, as she spoke, she kept her hand upon her heart—"wherefore didst thou inflict this miserable doom upon thy child?"

"Miserable!" exclaimed Rappaccini. "What mean you, foolish girl? Dost thou deem it misery to be endowed with marvellous gifts, against which no power nor strength could avail an enemy? Misery, to be able to quell the mightiest with a breath? Misery, to be as terrible as thou art beautiful? Wouldst thou, then, have preferred the condition of a weak woman, exposed to all evil, and capable of none?"

"I would fain have been loved, not feared," murmured Beatrice, sinking down upon the ground.—" But now it matters not, I am going, father, where the evil, which thou hast striven to mingle with my being, will pass away like a dream—like the fragrance of these poisonous flowers, which will no longer taint my breath among the flowers of Eden. Farewell, Giovanni! Thy words of hatred are like lead within my heart—but they, too, will fall away as I ascend. Oh, was there not, from the first, more poison in thy nature than in mine?"

To Beatrice—so radically had her earthly part been wrought upon by Rappaccini's skill—as poison had been life, so the powerful antidote was death. And thus the poor victim of man's ingenuity and of thwarted nature, and of the fatality that attends all such efforts of perverted wisdom, perished there, at the feet of her father and Giovanni. Just at that moment, Professor Pietro Baglioni looked forth from the window, and called loudly, in a tone of triumph mixed with horror, to the thunder-stricken man of science:

"Rappaccini! Rappaccini! And is *this* the upshot of your experiment?"

1844

Edgar Allan Poe

1809–1849

Edgar Allan Poe's woefully abbreviated life was defined by the death of his parents when he was three, by an imaginative variety of excesses, and by a less various but powerful imagination. Born in Boston and taken in by John and Frances Allan after his parents' death, he attended schools in England (1815–1820), and later in Richmond, Virginia. He had to withdraw from the University of Virginia, and his unlikely placement at West Point, following several years in the US Army, ended with his dismissal. He worked erratically as a literary journalist in a variety of editorial positions in Baltimore, Philadelphia, and New York, but despite some success, was undone again by high-proof alcohol and, in the eyes of his contemporaries, meagre will. In 1836 he married his thirteen-year-old cousin, who died in 1847. In 1849 Poe was looking toward marriage with Elmira Royster Shelton, a childhood sweetheart turned wealthy widow, but the anticipatory celebration left him unconscious on a Baltimore street, and he died days afterwards. As both a writer and the first theorist of the short story, Poe's legacy—beyond that of perpetuating the portrait of the artist in Romantic torment—has been more long-lasting and productive than was his brief life. His meticulously wrought narratives made the psychosexual Gothic a perennial element of the genre, and his "ratiocinative" pieces, such as "The Purloined Letter" (1845), virtually created the detective story as a new form. While writers ranging from Baudelaire to Flannery O'Connor, Ian McEwan, and Stephen King are obviously Poe's children, his impact on literary criticism has also been profound. Whatever critical perspectives exist on short fiction are rooted in his fiercely intelligent, abstracted readings. Primarily through reviews, above all of Hawthorne's *Twice-Told Tales* in 1842, Poe scrutinized the nature of literary originality and design. His famous emphasis was on "unity of effect or impression," which can only be achieved within a sharply circumscribed period of time: "During the hour of perusal the soul of the reader is at the writer's control. There are no external or extrinsic influences—resulting from weariness or interruption." Profoundly debatable as this assertion is, Poe's brilliance was in aligning the power of narrative with the complex process of reading.

The Fall of the House of Usher

Son Coeur est un luth suspend;
Sitôt qu'on le touché il résonne.

De Béranger

During the whole of a dull, dark, and soundless day in the autumn of the year, when the clouds hung oppressively low in the heavens, I had been passing alone, on horseback, through a singularly dreary tract of country; and at length found myself, as the shades of the evening drew on, within view of the melancholy House of Usher. I know not how it was—but, with the first glimpse of the building, a sense of insufferable gloom pervaded my spirit. I say insufferable; for the feeling was unrelieved by any of that half-pleasurable, because poetic, sentiment, with which the mind usually receives even the sternest natural images of the desolate or terrible. I looked upon the scene before me—upon the mere house, and the simple landscape features of the domain—upon the bleak walls—upon the vacant eye-like windows—upon a few rank sedges—and upon a few white trunks of decayed trees—with an utter depression of soul which I can compare to no earthly sensation more properly than to the after-dream of the reveller upon opium—the bitter lapse into everyday life—the hideous dropping off of the veil. There was an iciness, a sinking, a sickening of the heart—an unredeemed dreariness of thought which no goading of the imagination could torture into aught of the sublime. What was it—I paused to think—what was it that so unnerved me in the contemplation of the House of Usher? It was a mystery all insoluble; nor could I grapple with the shadowy fancies that crowded upon me as I pondered. I was forced to fall back upon the unsatisfactory conclusion, that while, beyond doubt, there *are* combinations of very simple natural objects which have the power of thus affecting us, still the analysis of this power lies among considerations beyond our depth. It was possible, I reflected, that a mere different arrangement of the particulars of the scene, of the details of the picture, would be sufficient to modify, or perhaps to annihilate its capacity for sorrowful impression; and, acting upon this idea, I reined my horse to the precipitous brink of a black and lurid tarn that lay in unruffled lustre by the dwelling, and gazed down—but with a shudder even more thrilling than before—upon the remodelled and inverted images of the grey sedge, and the ghastly tree-stems, and the vacant and eye-like windows.

Nevertheless, in this mansion of gloom I now proposed to myself a sojourn of some weeks. Its proprietor, Roderick Usher, had been one of my boon companions in boyhood; but many years had elapsed since our last meeting. A letter, however, had lately reached me in a distant part of the country—a letter from him—which, in its wildly importunate nature, had admitted of no other than a personal reply. The MS gave evidence of nervous agitation. The writer spoke of acute bodily illness—of a mental disorder which oppressed him—and of an earnest desire to see me, as his best, and indeed his only personal friend, with a view of attempting, by the cheerfulness of my society, some alleviation of his malady. It was the manner in which all this, and much more, was said—it was the apparent *heart* that went with his request—which allowed me no room for hesitation; and I accordingly obeyed forthwith what I still considered a very singular summons.

Although, as boys, we had been even intimate associates, yet I really knew little of my friend. His reserve had been always excessive and habitual. I was aware, however, that his very ancient family had been noted, time out of mind, for a peculiar sensibility of temperament, displaying itself, through long ages, in many works of exalted art, and manifested, of late, in repeated deeds of munificent yet unobtrusive charity, as well as in a passionate devotion to the intricacies, perhaps even more than to the orthodox and easily recognizable beauties, of musical science. I had learned, too, the very remarkable fact, that the stem of the Usher race, all time-honoured as it was, had put forth, at no period, any enduring branch; in other words, that the entire family lay in the direct line of descent, and had always, with very trifling and very temporary variation, so lain. It was this deficiency, I considered, while running over in thought the perfect keeping of the character of the premises with the accredited character of the people, and while speculating upon the possible influence which the one, in the long lapse of centuries, might have exercised upon the other—it was this deficiency, perhaps, of collateral issue, and the consequent undeviating transmission, from sire to son, of the patrimony with the name, which had, at length, so identified the two as to merge the original title of the estate in the quaint and equivocal appellation of the "House of Usher"—an appellation which seemed to include, in the minds of the peasantry who used it, both the family and the family mansion.

I have said that the sole effect of my somewhat childish experiment—that of looking down within the tarn—had been to deepen the first singular impression. There can be no doubt that the consciousness of the rapid increase of my superstition—for why should I not so term it?—served mainly to accelerate the increase itself. Such, I have long known, is the paradoxical law of all sentiments having terror as a basis. And it might have been for this reason only, that, when I again uplifted my eyes to the house itself, from its image in the pool, there grew in my mind a strange fancy—a fancy so ridiculous, indeed, that I but mention it to show the vivid force of the sensations which oppressed me. I had so worked upon my imagination as really to believe that about the whole mansion and domain there hung an atmosphere peculiar to themselves and their immediate vicinity—an atmosphere which had no affinity with the air of heaven, but which had reeked up from the decayed trees, and the grey wall, and the silent tarn—a pestilent and mystic vapour, dull, sluggish, faintly discernible, and leaden-hued.

Shaking off from my spirit what *must* have been a dream, I scanned more narrowly the real aspect of the building. Its principal feature seemed to be that of an excessive antiquity. The discoloration of ages had been great. Minute fungi overspread the whole exterior, hanging in a fine tangled web-work from the eaves. Yet all this was apart from any extraordinary dilapidation. No portion of the masonry had fallen; and there appeared to be a wild inconsistency between its still perfect adaptation of parts, and the crumbling condition of the individual stones. In this there was much that reminded me of the specious totality of old woodwork which has rotted for long years in some neglected vault, with no disturbance from the breath of the external air. Beyond this indication of extensive decay, however, the fabric gave little token of instability. Perhaps the eye of a scrutinizing observer might have discovered a barely perceptible fissure, which, extending from the roof of the building in front, made its way down the wall in a zigzag direction, until it became lost in the sullen waters of the tarn.

Noticing these things, I rode over a short causeway to the house. A servant in waiting took my horse, and I entered the Gothic archway of the hall. A valet, of stealthy step, thence conducted me, in silence, through many dark and intricate passages in my progress to the *studio* of his master. Much that I encountered on the way contributed, I know not how, to heighten the vague sentiments of which I have already spoken. While the objects around me—while the carvings of the ceilings, the sombre tapestries of the walls, the ebon blackness of the floors, and the phantasmagoric armorial trophies which rattled as I strode, were but matters to which, or to such as which, I had been accustomed from my infancy—while I hesitated not to acknowledge how familiar was all this—I still wondered to find how unfamiliar were the fancies which ordinary images were stirring up. On one of the staircases, I met the physician of the family. His countenance, I thought, wore a mingled expression of low cunning and perplexity. He accosted me with trepidation and passed on. The valet now threw open a door and ushered me into the presence of his master.

The room in which I found myself was very large and lofty. The windows were long, narrow, and pointed, and at so vast a distance from the black oaken floor as to be altogether inaccessible from within. Feeble gleams of encrimsoned light made their way through the trellised panes, and served to render sufficiently distinct the more prominent objects around; the eye, however, struggled in vain to reach the remoter angles of the chamber, or the recesses of the vaulted and fretted ceiling. Dark draperies hung upon the walls. The general furniture was profuse, comfortless, antique, and tattered. Many books and musical instruments lay scattered about, but failed to give any vitality to the scene. I felt that I breathed an atmosphere of sorrow. An air of stern, deep, and irredeemable gloom hung over and pervaded all.

Upon my entrance, Usher arose from a sofa on which he had been lying at full length, and greeted me with a vivacious warmth which had much in it, I at first thought, of an overdone cordiality—of the constrained effort of the *ennuyé* man of the world. A glance, however, at his countenance, convinced me of his perfect sincerity. We sat down; and for some moments, while he spoke not, I gazed upon him with a feeling half of pity, half of awe. Surely, a man had never before so terribly altered, in so brief a period, as had Roderick Usher! It was with difficulty that I could bring myself to admit the identity of the wan being before me with the companion of my early boyhood. Yet the character of his face had been at all times remarkable. A cadaverousness of complexion; an eye large, liquid, and luminous beyond comparison; lips somewhat thin and very pallid, but of a surpassingly beautiful curve; a nose of a delicate Hebrew model, but with a breadth of nostril unusual in similar formations; a finely moulded chin, speaking, in its want of prominence, of a want of moral energy; hair of a more than web-like softness and tenuity; these features, with an inordinate expansion above the regions of the temple, made up altogether a countenance not easily to be forgotten. And now in the mere exaggeration of the prevailing character of these features, and of the expression they were wont to convey, lay so much of change that I doubted to whom I spoke. The now ghastly pallor of the skin, and the now miraculous lustre of the eye, above all things startled and even awed me. The silken hair, too, had been suffered to grow all unheeded, and as, in its wild gossamer texture, it floated rather than fell about the face, I could not, even with effort, connect its Arabesque expression with any idea of simple humanity.

In the manner of my friend I was at once struck with an incoherence—an inconsistency; and I soon found this to arise from a series of feeble and futile struggles to overcome an habitual trepidancy—an excessive nervous agitation. For something of this nature I had indeed been prepared, no less by his letter, than by reminiscences of certain boyish traits, and by conclusions deduced from his peculiar physical conformation and temperament. His action was alternately vivacious and sullen. His voice varied rapidly from a tremulous indecision (when the animal seemed utterly in abeyance) to that species of energetic concision—that abrupt, weighty, unhurried, and hollow-sounding enunciation—that leaden, self-balanced and perfectly modulated guttural utterance, which may be observed in the lost drunkard, or the irreclaimable eater of opium, during the period of his most intense excitement.

It was thus that he spoke of the object of my visit, of his earnest desire to see me, and of the solace he expected me to afford him. He entered, at some length, into what he conceived to be the nature of his malady. It was, he said, a constitutional and a family evil, and one for which he despaired to find a remedy—a mere nervous affection, he immediately added, which would undoubtedly soon pass off. It displayed itself in a host of unnatural sensations. Some of these, as he detailed them, interested and bewildered me; although, perhaps, the terms, and the general manner of the narration had their weight. He suffered much from morbid acuteness of the senses; the most insipid food was alone endurable; he could wear only garments of certain texture; the odours of all flowers were oppressive; his eyes were tortured by even a faint light; and there were but peculiar sounds, and these from stringed instruments, which did not inspire him with horror.

To an anomalous species of terror I found him a bounden slave. "I shall perish," said he, "I *must* perish in this deplorable folly. Thus, thus, and not otherwise, shall I be lost. I dread the events of the future, not in themselves, but in their results. I shudder at the thought of any, even the most trivial, incident, which may operate upon this intolerable agitation of soul. I have, indeed, no abhorrence of danger, except in its absolute effect—in terror. In this unnerved—in this pitiable condition—I feel that the period will sooner or later arrive when I must abandon life and reason together, in some struggle with the grim phantasm, FEAR."

I learned, moreover, at intervals, and through broken and equivocal hints, another singular feature of his mental condition. He was enchanted by certain superstitious impressions in regard to the dwelling which he tenanted, and whence, for many years, he had never ventured forth—in regard to an influence whose supposititious force was conveyed in terms too shadowy here to be restated—an influence which some peculiarities in the mere form and substance of his family mansion, had, by dint of long sufferance, he said, obtained over his spirit—an effect which the *physique* of the grey walls and turrets, and of the dim tarn into which they all looked down, had, at length, brought about upon the *morale* of his existence.

He admitted, however, although with hesitation, that much of the peculiar gloom which thus afflicted him could be traced to a more natural and far more palpable origin—to the severe and long-continued illness—indeed to the evidently approaching dissolution—of a tenderly beloved sister—his sole companion for long years—his last and only relative on earth. "Her decease," he said, with a bitterness which I can never forget, "would leave him (him the hopeless and the frail) the last of the ancient race of the Ushers." While he spoke, the lady Madeline (for so was she called) passed slowly though a remote portion of the apartment, and, without having noticed my presence, disappeared. I regarded her with an utter astonishment not unmingled with dread—and yet I found it impossible to account for such feelings. A sensation of stupor oppressed me, as my eyes followed her retreating steps. When a door, at length, closed upon her, my glance sought instinctively and eagerly the countenance of the brother— but he had buried his face in his hands, and I could only perceive that a far more than ordinary wanness had overspread the emaciated fingers through which trickled many passionate tears.

The disease of the lady Madeline had long baffled the skill of her physicians. A settled apathy, a gradual wasting away of the person, and frequent although transient affections of a partially cataleptical character, were the usual diagnosis. Hitherto she had steadily borne up against the pressure of her malady, and had not betaken herself finally to bed; but, on the closing in of the evening of my arrival at the house, she succumbed (as her brother told me at night with inexpressible agitation) to the prostrating power of the destroyer; and I learned that the glimpse I had obtained of her person would thus probably be the last I should obtain—that the lady, at least while living, would be seen by me no more.

For several days ensuing, her name was unmentioned by either Usher or myself: and during this period I was busied in earnest endeavours to alleviate the melancholy of my friend. We painted and read together; or I listened, as if in a dream, to the wild improvisations of his speaking guitar. And thus, as a closer and still closer intimacy admitted me more unreservedly into the recesses of his spirit, the more bitterly did I perceive the futility of all attempt at cheering a mind from which the darkness, as if an inherent positive quality, poured forth upon all objects of the moral and physical universe, in one unceasing radiation of gloom.

I shall ever bear about me a memory of the many solemn hours I thus spent alone with the master of the House of Usher. Yet I should fail in any attempt to convey an idea of the exact character of the studies, or of the occupations, in which he involved me, or led me the way. An excited and highly distempered ideality threw a sulphureous lustre over all. His long improvised dirges will ring forever in my ears. Among other things, I hold painfully in mind a certain singular perversion and amplification of the wild air of the last waltz of Von Weber. From the paintings over which his elaborate fancy brooded, and which grew, touch by touch, into vaguenesses at which I shuddered the more thrillingly, because I shuddered knowing not why;—from these paintings (vivid as their images now are before me) I would in vain endeavour to educe more than a small portion which should lie within the compass of merely written words. By the utter simplicity, by the nakedness of his designs, he arrested and overawed attention. If ever mortal painted an idea, that mortal was Roderick Usher. For me at least—in the circumstances then surrounding me—there arose out of the pure abstractions which the hypochondriac contrived to throw upon his canvas, an intensity of intolerable awe, no shadow of which felt I ever yet in the contemplation of the certainly glowing yet too concrete reveries of Fuseli.

One of the phantasmagoric conceptions of my friend, partaking not so rigidly of the spirit of abstraction, may be shadowed forth, although feebly, in words. A small picture presented the interior of an immensely long and rectangular vault or tunnel, with low walls, smooth, white, and without interruption or device. Certain accessory points of the design served well to convey the idea that this excavation lay at an exceeding depth below the surface of earth. No outlet was observed in any portion of its vast extent, and no torch, or other artificial source of light was discernible; yet a flood of intense rays rolled throughout, and bathed the whole in a ghastly and inappropriate splendour.

I have just spoken of that morbid condition of the auditory nerve which rendered all music intolerable to the sufferer, with the exception of certain effects of stringed instruments. It was, perhaps, the narrow limits to which he thus confined himself upon the guitar, which gave birth, in great measure, to the fantastic character of his performances. But the fervid *facility* of his *impromptus* could not be so accounted for. They must have been, and were, in the notes, as well as in the words of his wild fantasias (for he not unfrequently accompanied himself with rhymed verbal improvisations), the result of that intense mental collectedness and concentration to which I have previously alluded as observable only in particular moments of the highest artificial excitement. The words of one of these rhapsodies I have easily remembered. I was, perhaps, the more forcibly impressed with it, as he gave it, because, in the under or mystic current of its meaning, I fancied that I perceived, and for the first time, a full consciousness on the part of Usher, of the tottering of his lofty reason upon her throne. The verses, which were entitled "The Haunted Palace," ran very nearly, if not accurately, thus:

I.

In the greenest of our valleys,
   By good angels tenanted,
Once a fair and stately palace—
   Radiant palace—reared its head.
In the monarch Thought's dominion—
   It stood there!
Never seraph spread a pinion
   Over fabric half so fair.

II.

Banners yellow, glorious, golden,
   On its roof did float and flow;
(This—all this—was in the olden
   Time long ago)
And every gentle air that dallied,
   In that sweet day,
Along the ramparts plumed and pallid,
   A winged odour went away.

III.

Wanderers in that happy valley
   Through two luminous windows saw
Spirits moving musically
   To a lute's well-tunèd law,
Round about a throne, where sitting
   (Porphyrogene!)
In state his glory well befitting,
   The ruler of the realm was seen.

IV.

And all with pearl and ruby glowing
   Was the fair palace door,
Through which came flowing, flowing, flowing
   And sparkling evermore,
A troop of Echoes whose sweet duty
   Was but to sing,
In voices of surpassing beauty,
   The wit and wisdom of their king.

V.

But evil things, in robes of sorrow,
   Assailed the monarch's high estate;
(Ah, let us mourn, for never morrow
   Shall dawn upon him, desolate!)
And, round about his home, the glory
   That blushed and bloomed
Is but a dim-remembered story
   Of the old time entombed.

VI.

And travellers now within that valley,
Through the red-litten windows, see
Vast forms that move fantastically
To a discordant melody;
While, like a rapid ghastly river,
Through the pale door,
A hideous throng rush out forever,
And laugh—but smile no more.

I well remember that suggestions arising from this ballad, led us into a train of thought wherein there became manifest an opinion of Usher's which I mention not so much on account of its novelty, (for other men have thought thus,) as on account of the pertinacity with which he maintained it. This opinion, in its general form, was that of the sentience of all vegetable things. But, in his disordered fancy, the idea had assumed a more daring character, and trespassed, under certain conditions, upon the kingdom of inorganization. I lack words to express the full extent, or the earnest *abandon* of his persuasion. The belief, however, was connected (as I have previously hinted) with the grey stones of the home of his forefathers. The conditions of the sentience had been here, he imagined, fulfilled in the method of collocation of these stones—in the order of their management, as well as in that of the many *fungi* which overspread them, and of the decayed trees which stood around—above all, in the long undisturbed endurance of this arrangement, and in its reduplication in the still waters of the tarn. Its evidence—the evidence of the sentience—was to be seen, he said, (and I here started as he spoke,) in the gradual yet certain condensation of an atmosphere of their own about the waters and the walls. The result was discoverable, he added, in that silent, yet importunate and terrible influence which for centuries had moulded the destinies of his family, and which made *him* what I now saw him—what he was. Such opinions need no comment, and I will make none.

Our books—the books which, for years, had formed no small portion of the mental existence of the invalid—were, as might be supposed, in strict keeping with this character of phantasm. We pored together over such works as the Ververt et Chartreuse of Gresset; the Belphegor of Machiavelli; the Heaven and Hell of Swedenborg; the Subterranean Voyage of Nicholas Klimm by Holberg; the Chiromancy of Robert Flud, of Jean D'Indaginé, and of De la Chambre; the Journey into the Blue Distance of Tieck; and the City of the Sun of Campanella. One favourite volume was a small octavo edition of the *Directorium Inquisitorum*, by the Dominican Eymeric de Gironne; and there were passages in Pomponius Mela, about the old African Satyrs and Aegipans, over which Usher would sit dreaming for hours. His chief delight, however, was found in the perusal of an exceedingly rare and curious book in quarto Gothic—the manual of a forgotten church—the *Vigiliae Mortuorum secundum Chorum Ecclesiae Maguntinae*.

I could not help thinking of the wild ritual of this work, and of its probable influence upon the hypochondriac, when, one evening, having informed me abruptly that the lady Madeline was no more, he stated his intention of preserving her corpse for a fortnight, (previously to its final interment,) in one of the numerous vaults within the main walls of the building. The worldly reason, however, assigned for this singular proceeding, was one which I did not feel at liberty to dispute. The brother had been led to this resolution (so he told me) by consideration of the unusual character of the malady of the deceased, of certain obtrusive and eager inquiries on the part of her medical men, and of the remote and exposed situation of the burial-ground of the family. I will not deny that when I called to mind the sinister countenance of the person whom I met upon the staircase, on the day of my arrival at the house, I had no desire to oppose what I regarded as at best but a harmless, and by no means an unnatural, precaution.

At the request of Usher, I personally aided him in the arrangements for the temporary entombment. The body having been encoffined, we two alone bore it to its rest. The vault in which we placed it (and which had been so long unopened that our torches, half smothered in its oppressive atmosphere, gave us little opportunity for investigation) was small, damp, and entirely without means of admission for light; lying, at great depth, immediately beneath that portion of the building in which was my own sleeping apartment. It had been used, apparently, in remote feudal times, for the worst purposes of a donjon keep, and, in later days, as a place of deposit for powder, or some highly combustible substance, as a portion of its floor, and the whole interior of a long archway through which we reached it, were carefully sheathed with copper. The door, of massive iron, had been, also, similarly protected. Its immense weight caused an unusually sharp grating sound, as it moved upon its hinges.

Having deposited our mournful burden upon tressels within this region of horror, we partially turned aside the yet unscrewed lid of the coffin, and looked upon the face of the tenant. A striking similitude between the brother and sister now first arrested my attention; and Usher, divining, perhaps, my thoughts, murmured out some few words from which I learned that the deceased and himself had been twins, and that sympathies of a scarcely intelligible nature had always existed between them. Our glances, however, rested not long upon the dead—for we could not regard her unawed. The disease which had thus entombed the lady in the maturity of youth, had left, as usual in all maladies of a strictly cataleptical character, the mockery of a faint blush upon the bosom and the face, and that suspiciously lingering smile upon the lip which is so terrible in death. We replaced and screwed down the lid, and, having secured the door of iron, made our way, with toil, into the scarcely less gloomy apartments of the upper portion of the house.

And now, some days of bitter grief having elapsed, an observable change came over the features of the mental disorder of my friend. His ordinary manner had vanished. His ordinary occupations were neglected or forgotten. He roamed from chamber to chamber with hurried, unequal, and objectless step. The pallor of his countenance had assumed, if possible, a more ghastly hue—but the luminousness of his eye had utterly gone out. The once occasional huskiness of his tone was heard no more; and a tremulous quaver, as if of extreme terror, habitually characterized his utterance. There were times, indeed, when I thought his unceasingly agitated mind was labouring with some oppressive secret, to divulge which he struggled for the necessary courage. At times, again, I was obliged to resolve all into the mere inexplicable vagaries of madness, for I beheld him gazing upon vacancy for long hours, in an attitude of the profoundest attention, as if listening to some imaginary sound. It was no wonder that his condition terrified—that it infected me. I felt creeping upon me, by slow yet certain degrees, the wild influences of his own fantastic yet impressive superstitions.

It was, especially, upon retiring to bed late in the night of the seventh or eighth day after the placing of the lady Madeline within the donjon, that I experienced the full power of such feelings. Sleep came not near my couch—while the hours waned and waned away. I struggled to reason off the nervousness which had dominion over me. I endeavoured to believe that much, if not all of what I felt, was due to the bewildering influence of the gloomy furniture of the room—of the dark and tattered draperies, which, tortured into motion by the breath of a rising tempest, swayed fitfully to and fro upon the walls, and rustled uneasily about the decorations of the bed. But my efforts were fruitless. An irrepressible tremor gradually pervaded my frame; and, at length, there sat upon my very heart an incubus of utterly causeless alarm. Shaking this off with a gasp and a struggle, I uplifted myself upon the pillows, and, peering earnestly within the intense darkness of the chamber, hearkened—I know not why, except that an instinctive spirit prompted me—to certain low and indefinite sounds which came, through the pauses of the storm, at long intervals, I knew not whence. Overpowered by an intense sentiment of horror, unaccountable yet unendurable, I threw on my clothes with haste (for I felt that I should sleep no more during the night), and endeavoured to arouse myself from the pitiable condition into which I had fallen, by pacing rapidly to and fro through the apartment.

I had taken but few turns in this manner, when a light step on an adjoining staircase arrested my attention. I presently recognized it as that of Usher. In an instant afterward he rapped, with a gentle touch, at my door, and entered, bearing a lamp. His countenance was, as usual, cadaverously wan—but, moreover, there was a species of mad hilarity in his eyes—an evidently restrained *hysteria* in his whole demeanour. His air appalled me—but anything was preferable to the solitude which I had so long endured, and I even welcomed his presence as a relief.

"And you have not seen it?" he said abruptly, after having stared about him for some moments in silence—"you have not then seen it?—but, stay! you shall." Thus speaking, and having carefully shaded his lamp, he hurried to one of the casements, and threw it freely open to the storm.

The impetuous fury of the entering gust nearly lifted us from our feet. It was, indeed, a tempestuous yet sternly beautiful night, and one wildly singular in its terror and its beauty. A whirlwind had apparently collected its force in our vicinity; for there were frequent and violent alterations in the direction of the wind; and the exceeding density of the clouds (which hung so low as to press upon the turrets of the house) did not prevent our perceiving the lifelike velocity with which they flew careering from all points against each other, without passing away into the distance. I say that even their exceeding density did not prevent our perceiving this—yet we had no glimpse of the moon or stars—nor was there any flashing forth of the lightning. But the under surfaces of the huge masses of agitated vapour, as well as all terrestrial objects immediately around us, were glowing in the unnatural light of a faintly luminous and distinctly visible gaseous exhalation which hung about and enshrouded the mansion.

"You must not—you shall not behold this!" said I, shudderingly, to Usher, as I led him, with a gentle violence, from the window to a seat. "These appearances, which bewilder you, are merely electrical phenomena not uncommon—or it may be that they have their ghastly origin in the rank miasma of the tarn. Let us close this casement;—the air is chilling and dangerous to your frame. Here is one of your favourite romances. I will read, and you shall listen;—and so we will pass away this terrible night together."

The antique volume which I had taken up was the "Mad Trist" of Sir Launcelot Canning; but I had called it a favourite of Usher's more in sad jest than in earnest; for, in truth, there is little in its uncouth and unimaginative prolixity which could have had interest for the lofty and spiritual ideality of my friend. It was, however, the only book immediately at hand; and I indulged a vague hope that the excitement which now agitated the hypochondriac, might find relief (for the history of mental disorder is full of similar anomalies) even in the extremeness of the folly which I should read. Could I have judged, indeed, by the wild over-strained air of vivacity with which he hearkened, or apparently hearkened, to the words of the tale, I might well have congratulated myself upon the success of my design.

I had arrived at that well-known portion of the story where Ethelred, the hero of the Trist, having sought in vain for peaceable admission into the dwelling of the hermit, proceeds to make good an entrance by force. Here, it will be remembered, the words of the narrative run thus:

"And Ethelred, who was by nature of a doughty heart, and who was now mighty withal, on account of the powerfulness of the wine which he had drunken, waited no longer to hold parley with the hermit, who, in sooth, was of an obstinate and maliceful turn, but, feeling the rain upon his shoulders, and fearing the rising of the tempest, uplifted his mace outright, and, with blows, made quickly room in the plankings of the door for his gauntleted hand; and now pulling therewith sturdily, he so cracked, and ripped, and tore all asunder, that the noise of the dry and hollow-sounding wood alarumed and reverberated throughout the forest."

At the termination of this sentence I started, and for a moment, paused; for it appeared to me (although I at once concluded that my excited fancy had deceived me)—it appeared to me that, from some very remote portion of the mansion, there came, indistinctly, to my ears, what might have been, in its exact similarity of character, the echo (but a stifled and dull one certainly) of the very cracking and ripping sound which Sir Launcelot had so particularly described. It was, beyond doubt, the coincidence alone which had arrested my attention; for, amid the rattling of the sashes of the casements, and the ordinary commingled noises of the still increasing storm, the sound, in itself, had nothing, surely, which should have interested or disturbed me. I continued the story:

"But the good champion Ethelred, now entering within the door, was sore enraged and amazed to perceive no signal of the maliceful hermit; but, in the stead thereof, a dragon of a scaly and prodigious demeanour, and of a fiery tongue, which sate in guard before a palace of gold, with a floor of silver; and upon the wall there hung a shield of shining brass with this legend enwritten—

Who entereth herein, a conqueror hath bin;
Who slayeth the dragon, the shield he shall win;

And Ethelred uplifted his mace, and struck upon the head of the dragon, which fell before him, and gave up his pesty breath, with a shriek so horrid and harsh, and withal so piercing, that Ethelred had fain to close his ears with his hands against the dreadful noise of it, the like whereof was never before heard."

Here again I paused abruptly, and now with a feeling of wild amazement—for there could be no doubt whatever that, in this instance, I did actually hear (although from what direction it proceeded I found it impossible to say) a low and apparently distant, but harsh, protracted, and most unusual screaming or grating sound—the exact counterpart of what my fancy had already conjured up for the dragon's unnatural shriek as described by the romancer.

Oppressed, as I certainly was, upon the occurrence of the second and most extraordinary coincidence, by a thousand conflicting sensations, in which wonder and extreme terror were predominant, I still retained sufficient presence of mind to avoid exciting, by any observation, the sensitive nervousness of my companion. I was by no means certain that he had noticed the sounds in question; although, assuredly, a strange alteration had, during the last few minutes, taken place in his demeanour. From a position fronting my own, he had gradually brought round his chair, so as to sit with his face to the door of the chamber; and thus I could but partially perceive his features, although I saw that his lips trembled as if he were murmuring inaudibly. His head had dropped upon his breast—yet I knew that he was not asleep, from the wide and rigid opening of the eye as I caught a glance of it in profile. The motion of his body, too, was at variance with this idea—for he rocked from side to side with a gentle yet constant and uniform sway. Having rapidly taken notice of all this, I resumed the narrative of Sir Launcelot, which thus proceeded:

"And now, the champion, having escaped from the terrible fury of the dragon, bethinking himself of the brazen shield, and of the breaking up of the enchantment which was upon it, removed the carcass from out of the way before him, and approached valorously over the silver pavement of the castle to where the shield was upon the wall; which in sooth tarried not for his full coming, but fell down at his feet upon the silver floor, with a mighty great and terrible ringing sound."

No sooner had these syllables passed my lips, than—as if a shield of brass had indeed, at the moment, fallen heavily upon a floor of silver—I became aware of a distinct, hollow, metallic, and clangorous, yet apparently muffled reverberation.

Completely unnerved, I leaped to my feet; but the measured rocking movement of Usher was undisturbed. I rushed to the chair in which he sat. His eyes were bent fixedly before him, and throughout his whole countenance there reigned a stony rigidity. But, as I placed my hand upon his shoulder, there came a strong shudder over his whole person; a sickly smile quivered about his lips; and I saw that he spoke in a low, hurried, and gibbering murmur, as if unconscious of my presence. Bending closely over him, I at length drank in the hideous import of his words.

"Not hear it?—yes, I hear it, and *have* heard it. Long—long—long—many minutes, many hours, many days, have I heard it—yet I dared not—oh, pity me, miserable wretch that I am!—I *dared* not—I dared not speak! *We have put her living in the tomb*! Said I not that my senses were acute? I *now* tell you that I heard her first feeble movements in the hollow coffin. I heard them—many, many days ago—yet I dared not—*I dared not speak*! And now—tonight—Ethelred—ha! ha!—the breaking of the hermit's door, and the death-cry of the dragon, and the clangour of the shield! say, rather, the rending of her coffin, and the grating of the iron hinges of her prison, and her struggles within the coppered archway of the vault! Oh whither shall I fly? Will she not be here anon? Is she not hurrying to upbraid me for my haste? Have I not heard her footstep on the stair? Do I not distinguish that heavy and horrible beating of her heart? Madman!" here he sprang furiously to his feet, and shrieked out his syllables, as if in the effort he were giving up his soul—"MADMAN! I TELL YOU THAT SHE NOW STANDS WITHOUT THE DOOR!"

As if in the superhuman energy of his utterance there had been found the potency of a spell—the huge antique panels to which the speaker pointed, threw slowly back, upon the instant, their ponderous and ebony jaws. It was the work of the rushing gust—but then without those doors there DID stand the lofty and enshrouded figure of lady Madeline of Usher. There was blood upon her white robes, and the evidence of some bitter struggle upon every portion of her emaciated frame. For a moment she remained trembling and reeling to and fro upon the threshold, then, with a low moaning cry, fell heavily inward upon the person of her brother, and in her violent and now final death-agonies, bore him to the floor a corpse, and a victim to the terrors he had anticipated.

From that chamber, and from that mansion, I fled aghast. The storm was still abroad in all its wrath as I found myself crossing the old causeway. Suddenly there shot along the path a wild light, and I turned to see whence a gleam so unusual could have issued; for the vast house and its shadows were alone behind me. The radiance was that of the full, setting, and blood-red moon which now shone vividly through that once barely discernible fissure of which I have before spoken as extending from the roof of the building, in a zigzag direction, to the base. While I gazed, this fissure rapidly widened—there came a fierce breath of the whirlwind—the entire orb of the satellite burst at once upon my sight—my brain reeled as I saw the mighty walls rushing asunder—there was a long tumultuous shouting sound like the voice of a thousand waters—and the deep and dank tarn at my feet closed sullenly and silently over the fragments of the "HOUSE OF USHER."

1839

Gustave Flaubert

1821–1880

Gustave Flaubert is regarded as one of the supreme masters of the realistic novel. He viewed the novel as an artifact, which he constructed meticulously and patiently using, as he said, *le seul mot juste* ("the one precise word"). He detested the romantic vision of the inspired artist, insisting that "immersed in life you cannot see it clearly." At the age of twenty-eight he proclaimed his famous principle of artistic detachment: "You can portray wine, love, women, glory, on condition . . . of being neither a drinker, a lover, a husband, or a soldier." Flaubert was born in Rouen, France. The family lived on the hospital grounds of the Hôtel-Dieu, where his father was chief surgeon. The dissection room of the hospital looked directly onto the family garden, and one of Flaubert's childhood memories was of the innumerable times he and his sister climbed the trellis to gaze curiously on all the corpses laid out on tables. After a failed attempt to become a lawyer, Flaubert dedicated himself to writing, living with his widowed mother and niece in Croisset, near Rouen, and escaping each month to Paris. Despite suffering from a disease of the nerves (probably epilepsy), he was a great traveller—visiting Corsica, Egypt, Syria, Greece, Italy, and Morocco. Whenever abroad he lived the lifestyle of a sybarite. Detesting bourgeois respectability, he saw his vocation as the great "demoralizer"—he would tell the truth, no matter how ugly, without judging his characters or teaching his audience. In 1857, after five years of work, Flaubert published his masterpiece, *Madame Bovary*, the story of an adulterous, unhappy love affair of a provincial wife, Emma Bovary. (The novel is so much a fact of the French imagination that the noun *bovarysme* is used to denote a romantic or unreal conception of oneself, a quality that is exemplified by the book's protagonist.) The unsentimental depiction of adultery was condemned as offensive to morality and religion, and Flaubert was prosecuted, though not convicted. *Madame Bovary* was followed by *Salammbô* (1863), a novel set in ancient Carthage; *L'Éducation sentimentale* (1870) and *Trois contes* (1877), which includes the short story "Un coeur simple" ("A Simple Soul"). Flaubert's unfinished satire *Bouvard et Pécuchet* was published a year after he died at the age of fifty-nine. A voluminous correspondent, his letters were published in nine volumes in 1933.

A Simple Soul

I

For half a century the housewives of Pont-l'Évêque had envied Madame Aubain her servant Félicité. For a hundred francs a year, she cooked and did the housework, washed, ironed, mended, harnessed the horse, fattened the poultry, made the butter, and remained faithful to her mistress—although the latter was by no means an agreeable person.

Madame Aubain had married a comely youth without any money, who died in the beginning of 1809, leaving her with two young children and a number of debts. She sold all her property excepting the farm of Toucques and the farm of Geffosses, the income of which barely amounted to 5,000 francs; then she left her house in Saint-Melaine, and moved into a less pretentious one which had belonged to her ancestors and stood back of the marketplace. This house, with its slate-covered roof, was built between a passageway and a narrow street that led to the river. The interior was so unevenly graded that it caused people to stumble. A narrow hall separated the kitchen from the parlour, where Madame Aubain sat all day in a straw armchair near the window. Eight mahogany chairs stood in a row against the white wainscoting. An old piano, standing beneath a barometer, was covered with a pyramid of old books and boxes. On either side of the yellow marble mantelpiece, in Louis XV style, stood a tapestry armchair. The clock represented a temple of Vesta; and the whole room smelled musty, as it was on a lower level than the garden.

On the first floor was Madame's bedchamber, a large room papered in a flowered design and containing the portrait of Monsieur dressed in the costume of a dandy. It communicated with a smaller room, in which there were two little cribs, without any mattresses. Next, came the parlour (always closed), filled with furniture covered with sheets. Then a hall, which led to the study, where books and papers were piled on the shelves of a bookcase that enclosed three quarters of the big black desk. Two panels were entirely hidden under pen-and-ink sketches, gouache landscapes, and Audran engravings, relics of better times and vanished luxury. On the second floor, a garret window lighted Félicité's room, which looked out upon the meadows.

She arose at daybreak, in order to attend mass, and she worked without interruption until night; then, when dinner was over, the dishes cleared away and the door securely locked, she would bury the log under the ashes and fall asleep in front of the hearth with a rosary in her hand. Nobody could bargain with greater obstinacy, and as for cleanliness, the lustre on her brass saucepans was the envy and despair of other servants. She was most economical, and when she ate she would gather up crumbs with the tip of her finger, so that nothing should be wasted of the loaf of bread weighing twelve pounds which was baked especially for her and lasted three weeks.

Summer and winter she wore a dimity kerchief fastened in the back with a pin, a cap which concealed her hair, a red skirt, grey stockings, and an apron with a bib like those worn by hospital nurses.

Her face was thin and her voice shrill. When she was twenty-five, she looked forty. After she had passed fifty, nobody could tell her age; erect and silent always, she resembled a wooden figure working automatically.

II

Like every other woman, she had had an affair of the heart. Her father, who was a mason, was killed by falling from a scaffolding. Then her mother died and her sisters went their different ways; a farmer took her in, and while she was quite small, let her keep cows in the fields. She was clad in miserable rags, beaten for the slightest offence, and finally dismissed for a theft of thirty sous which she did not commit. She took service on another farm where she tended the poultry; and as she was well thought of by her master, her fellow workers soon grew jealous.

One evening in August (she was then eighteen years old), they persuaded her to accompany them to the fair at Colleville. She was immediately dazzled by the noise, the lights in the trees, the brightness of the dresses, the laces and gold crosses, and the crowd of people all hopping at the same time. She was standing modestly at a distance, when presently a young man of well-to-do appearance, who had been leaning on the pole of a wagon and smoking his pipe, approached her, and asked her for a dance. He treated her to cider and cake, bought her a silk shawl, and then, thinking she had guessed his purpose, offered to see her home. When they came to the end of a field he threw her down brutally. But she grew frightened and screamed, and he walked off.

One evening, on the road leading to Beaumont, she came upon a wagon loaded with hay, and when she overtook it, she recognized Théodore. He greeted her calmly, and asked her to forget what had happened between them, as it "was all the fault of the drink."

She did not know what to reply and wished to run away.

Presently he began to speak of the harvest and of the notables of the village; his father had left Colleville and bought the farm of Les Écots, so that now they would be neighbours. "Ah!" she exclaimed. He then added that his parents were looking around for a wife for him, but that he, himself, was not so anxious and preferred to wait for a girl who suited him. She hung her head. He then asked her whether she had ever thought of marrying. She replied, smilingly, that it was wrong of him to make fun of her. "Oh! no, I am in earnest," he said, and put his left arm around her waist while they sauntered along. The air was soft, the stars were bright, and the huge load of hay oscillated in front of them, drawn by four horses whose ponderous hoofs raised clouds of dust. Without a word from their driver they turned to the right. He kissed her again and she went home. The following week, Théodore obtained meetings.

They met in yards, behind walls, or under isolated trees. She was not ignorant, as girls of well-to-do families are—for the animals had instructed her;—but her reason and her instinct of honour kept her from falling. Her resistance exasperated Théodore's love and so in order to satisfy it (or perchance ingenuously), he offered to marry her. She would not believe him at first, so he made solemn promises. But, in a short time he mentioned a difficulty; the previous year, his parents had purchased a substitute for him; but any day he might be drafted and the prospect of serving in the army alarmed him greatly. To Félicité his cowardice appeared proof of his love for her, and her devotion to him grew stronger. When she met him, he would torture her with his fears and his entreaties. At last, he announced that he was going to the prefect himself for information, and would let her know everything on the following Sunday, between eleven o'clock and midnight.

When the time drew near, she ran to meet her lover.

But instead of Théodore one of his friends was at the meeting place.

He informed her that she would never see her sweetheart again; for, in order to escape the conscription, he had married a rich old woman, Madame Lehoussais, of Toucques.

The poor girl's sorrow was frightful. She threw herself on the ground, she cried and called on the Lord, and wandered around desolately until sunrise. Then she went back to the farm, declared her intention of leaving, and at the end of the month, after she had received her wages, she packed all her belongings in a handkerchief and started for Pont-l'Évêque.

In front of the inn, she met a woman wearing widow's weeds, and upon questioning her, learned that she was looking for a cook. The girl did not know very much, but appeared so willing and so modest in her requirements, that Madame Aubain finally said:

"Very well, I will give you a trial."

And half an hour later Félicité was installed in her house. At first she lived in constant anxiety that was caused by "the style of the household" and the memory of "Monsieur," that hovered over everything. Paul and Virginia, the one aged seven, and the other barely four, seemed made of some precious material; she carried them pig-a-back, and was greatly mortified when Madame Aubain forbade her to kiss them every other minute.

But in spite of all this, she was happy. The comfort of her new surroundings had obliterated her sadness. Every Thursday, friends of Madame Aubain dropped in for a game of cards, and it was Félicité's duty to prepare the table and heat the foot-warmers. They arrived at exactly eight o'clock and departed before eleven. Every Monday morning, the dealer in second-hand goods, who lived under the alleyway, spread out his wares on the sidewalk. Then the city would be filled with a buzzing of voices in which the neighing of horses, the bleating of lambs, the grunting of pigs, could be distinguished, mingled with the sharp sound of wheels on cobblestones. About twelve o'clock, when the market was in full swing, there appeared at the front door a tall, middle-aged peasant, with a hooked nose and a cap on the back of his head; it was Robelin, the farmer of Geffosses. Shortly afterwards came Liébard, the farmer of Toucques, short, rotund, and ruddy, wearing a grey jacket and spurred boots. Both men brought their landlady either chickens or cheese. Félicité would invariably thwart their ruses and they held her in great respect. At various times, Madame Aubain received a visit from the Marquis de Grémanville, one of her uncles, who was ruined and lived at Falaise on the remainder of his estates. He always came at dinnertime and brought an ugly poodle with him, whose paws soiled the furniture. In spite of his efforts to appear a man of breeding (he even went so far as to raise his hat every time he said "My deceased father"), his habits got the better of him, and he would fill his glass a little too often and relate broad stories. Félicité would show him out very politely and say: "You have had enough for this time, Monsieur de Grémanville! Hoping to see you again!" and would close the door.

She opened it gladly for Monsieur Bourais, a retired lawyer. His bald head and white cravat, the ruffling of his shirt, his flowing brown coat, the manner in which he took snuff, his whole person, in fact, produced in her the kind of awe which we feel when we see extraordinary persons. As he managed Madame's estates, he spent hours with her in Monsieur's study; he was in constant fear of being compromised, had a great regard for the magistracy and some pretensions to learning.

In order to facilitate the children's studies, he presented them with an engraved geography which represented various scenes of the world: cannibals with feather headdresses, a gorilla kidnapping a young girl, Arabs in the desert, a whale being harpooned, etc.

Paul explained the pictures to Félicité. And, in fact, this was her only literary education.

The children's studies were under the direction of a poor devil employed at the town hall, who sharpened his pocket knife on his boots and was famous for his penmanship.

When the weather was fine, they went to Geffosses. The house was built in the centre of the sloping yard; and the sea looked like a grey spot in the distance. Félicité would take slices of cold meat from the lunch basket and they would sit down and eat in a room next to the dairy. This room was all that remained of the cottage that had been torn down. The dilapidated wallpaper trembled in the drafts. Madame Aubain, overwhelmed by recollections, would hang her head, while the children were afraid to open their mouths. Then, "Why don't you go and play?" their mother would say; and they would scamper off.

Paul would go to the old barn, catch birds, throw stones into the pond, or pound the trunks of the trees with a stick till they resounded like drums. Virginia would feed the rabbits and run to pick the wild flowers in the fields, and her flying legs would disclose her little embroidered pantalettes. One autumn evening, they struck out for home through the meadows. The new moon illumined part of the sky and a mist hovered like a veil over the sinuosities of the river. Oxen, lying in the pastures, gazed mildly at the passing persons. In the third field, however, several of them got up and surrounded them. "Don't be afraid," cried Félicité; and murmuring a sort of lament she passed her hand over the back of the nearest ox; he turned away and the others followed. But when they came to the next pasture, they heard frightful bellowing.

It was a bull which was hidden from them by the fog. He advanced towards the two women, and Madame Aubain prepared to flee for her life. "No, no! not so fast," warned Félicité. Still they hurried on, for they could hear the noisy breathing of the bull close behind them. His hoofs pounded the grass like hammers, and presently he began to gallop! Félicité turned around and threw patches of grass in his eyes. He hung his head, shook his horns and bellowed with fury. Madame Aubain and the children, huddled at the end of the field, were trying to jump over the ditch. Félicité continued to back before the bull, blinding him with dirt, while she shouted to them to make haste.

Madame Aubain finally slid into the ditch, after shoving first Virginia and then Paul into it, and though she stumbled several times she managed, by dint of courage, to climb the other side of it.

The bull had driven Félicité up against a fence; the foam from his muzzle flew in her face and in another minute he would have disembowelled her. She had just time to slip between two bars and the huge animal, thwarted, paused.

For years, this occurrence was a topic of conversation in Pont-l'Évêque. But Félicité took no credit to herself, and probably never knew that she had been heroic.

Virginia occupied her thoughts solely, for the shock she had sustained gave her a nervous affliction and the physician, M. Poupart, prescribed the saltwater bathing at Trouville. In those days, Trouville was not greatly patronized. Madame Aubain gathered information, consulted Bourais, and made preparations as if they were going on an extended trip.

The baggage was sent the day before on Liébard's cart. On the following morning, he brought around two horses, one of which had a woman's saddle with a velveteen back to it, while on the crupper of the other was a rolled shawl that was to be used for a seat. Madame Aubain mounted the second horse, behind Liébard. Félicité took charge of the little girl, and Paul rode M. Lechaptois's donkey, which had been lent for the occasion on the condition that they should be careful of it. The road was so bad that it took two hours to cover the eight miles. The two horses sank knee-deep into the mud and stumbled into ditches; sometimes they had to jump over them. In certain places, Liébard's mare stopped abruptly. He waited patiently till she started again and talked of the people whose estates bordered the road, adding his own moral reflections to the outline of their histories. Thus, when they were passing through Toucques, and came to some windows draped with nasturtiums, he shrugged his shoulders—and said: "There's a woman, Madame Lehoussais, who, instead of taking a young man—" Félicité could not catch what followed; the horses began to trot, the donkey to gallop, and they turned into a lane; then a gate swung open, two farmhands appeared, and they all dismounted at the very threshold of the farmhouse.

Mother Liébard, when she caught sight of her mistress, was lavish with joyful demonstrations. She got up a lunch which comprised a leg of mutton, tripe, sausages, a chicken fricassée, sweet cider, a fruit tart, and some preserved prunes; then to all this the good woman added polite remarks about Madame, who appeared to be in better health, Mademoiselle, who had grown to be "superb," and Paul, who had become singularly sturdy; she spoke also of their deceased grandparents, whom the Liébards had known, for they had been in the service of the family for several generations.

Like its owners, the farm had an ancient appearance. The beams of the ceiling were mouldy, the walls black with smoke, and the windows grey with dust. The oak sideboard was filled with all sorts of utensils, plates, pitchers, tin bowls, wolf-traps. The children laughed when they saw a huge syringe. There was not a tree in the yard that did not have mushrooms growing around its foot, or a bunch of mistletoe hanging in its branches. Several of the trees had been blown down, but they had started to grow in the middle and all were laden with quantities of apples. The thatched roofs, which were of unequal thickness, looked like brown velvet and could resist the fiercest gales. But the wagon-shed was fast crumbling to ruins. Madame Aubain said that she would attend to it, and then gave orders to have the horses saddled.

It took another thirty minutes to reach Trouville. The little caravan dismounted in order to pass Les Ecores, a cliff that overhangs the bay, and a few minutes later, at the end of the dock, they entered the yard of the Golden Lamb, an inn kept by Mother David.

During the first few days, Virginia felt stronger, owing to the change of air and the action of the sea-baths. She took them in her little chemise, as she had no bathing suit, and afterwards her nurse dressed her in the cabin of a customs officer, which was used for that purpose by other bathers.

In the afternoon, they would take the donkey and go to the Roches-Noires, near Hennequeville. The path led at first through undulating grounds, and thence to a plateau, where pastures and tilled fields alternated. At the edge of the road, mingling with the brambles, grew holly bushes, and here and there stood large dead trees whose branches traced zigzags upon the blue sky.

Ordinarily, they rested in a field facing the ocean, with Deauville on their left, and Havre on their right. The sea glittered brightly in the sun and was as smooth as a mirror, and so calm that they could scarcely distinguish its murmur; sparrows chirped joyfully and the immense canopy of heaven spread over it all. Madame Aubain brought out her sewing, and Virginia amused herself by braiding reeds; Félicité wove lavender blossoms, while Paul was bored and wished to go home.

Sometimes they crossed the Toucques in a boat, and started to hunt for sea-shells. The outgoing tide exposed starfish and sea-urchins, and the children tried to catch the flakes of foam which the wind blew away. The sleepy waves lapping the sand unfurled themselves along the shore that extended as far as the eye could see, but where land began, it was limited by the downs which separated it from the "Swamp," a large meadow shaped like a hippodrome. When they went that way, Trouville, on the slope of a hill below, grew larger and larger as they advanced, and, with all its houses of unequal height, seemed to spread out before them in a sort of giddy confusion.

When the heat was too oppressive, they remained in their rooms. The dazzling sunlight cast bars of light between the shutters. Not a sound in the village, not a soul on the sidewalk. This silence intensified the tranquility of everything. In the distance, the hammers of some caulkers pounded the hull of a ship, and the sultry breeze brought them an odour of tar.

The principal diversion consisted in watching the return of the fishing-smacks.

As soon as they passed the beacons, they began to ply to windward. The sails came down on two of their three masts, and with their foresails swelled up like balloons they glided over the waves and anchored in the middle of the harbour. Then they crept up alongside of the dock and the sailors threw the quivering fish over the side of the boat; a line of carts was waiting for them, and women with white caps sprang forward to receive the baskets and embrace their menfolk.

One day, one of them spoke to Félicité, who, after a little while, returned to the house gleefully. She had found one of her sisters, and presently Nastasie Barette, wife of Léroux, made her appearance holding an infant in her arms, another child by the hand, while on her left was a little cabin-boy with his hands in his pockets and his cap on his ear.

At the end of fifteen minutes, Madame Aubain bade her go.

They always hung around the kitchen, or approached Félicité when she and the children were out walking. The husband, however, did not show himself.

Félicité developed a great fondness for them; she bought them a stove, some shirts, and a blanket; it was evident that they exploited her. Her foolishness annoyed Madame Aubain, who, moreover did not like the nephew's familiarity, for he called her son "thou";—and, as Virginia began to cough and the season was over, she decided to return to Pont-l'Évêque.

Monsieur Bourais assisted her in the choice of school. The one at Caen was considered the best. So Paul was sent away and bravely said goodbye to them all, for he was glad to go to live in a house where he could have boy companions.

Madame Aubain resigned herself to the separation from her son because it was unavoidable. Virginia brooded less and less over it. Félicité missed the noise he made, but soon a new occupation diverted her mind; beginning from Christmas, she accompanied the little girl to her catechism lesson every day.

III

After she had made a curtsy at the threshold, she would walk up the aisle between the double lines of chairs, open Madame Aubain's pew, sit down, and look around.

Girls and boys, the former on the right, the latter on the left-hand side of the church, filled the stalls of the choir; the priest stood beside the reading-desk; on one stained window of the side-aisle the Holy Ghost hovered over the Virgin; on another one, Mary knelt before the Child Jesus, and behind the altar, a wooden group represented Saint Michael felling the dragon.

The priest first read a condensed lesson of sacred history. Félicité encountered Paradise, the Flood, the Tower of Babel, the blazing cities, the dying nations, the shattered idols; and out of this she developed a great respect for the Almighty and a great fear of His wrath. Then, when she listened to the Passion, she wept. Why had they crucified Him who loved little children, nourished the people, made the blind see, and who out of humility, had wished to be born among the poor, in a stable? The sowings, the harvests, the wine presses, all those familiar things which the Scriptures mention, formed a part of her life; the word of God sanctified them; and she loved the lambs with increased tenderness for the sake of the Lamb, and the doves because of the Holy Ghost.

She found it hard, however, to think of the latter as a person, for was it not a bird, a flame, and sometimes only a breath? Perhaps it is its light that at night hovers over swamps, its breath that propels the clouds, its voice that renders church-bells harmonious. And Félicité worshipped devoutly, while enjoying the coolness and the stillness of the church.

As for the dogma, she could not understand it and did not even try. The priest discoursed, the children recited, and she went to sleep, only to awaken with a start when they were leaving the church and their wooden shoes clattered on the stone pavement.

In this way, she learned her catechism, her religious education having been neglected in her youth; and thenceforth she imitated all Virginia's religious practices, fasted when she did, and went to confession with her. At the Corpus-Christi Day they both decorated an altar.

She worried in advance over Virginia's first communion. She fussed about the shoes, the rosary, the book, and the gloves. With what nervousness she helped the mother dress the child!

During the entire ceremony, she felt anguished. Monsieur Bourais hid part of the choir from view, but directly in front of her, the flock of maidens, wearing white wreaths over their lowered veils, formed a snow-white field, and she recognized her darling by the slenderness of her neck and her devout attitude. The bell tinkled. All the heads bent and there was a silence. Then, at the peals of the organ the singers and the worshippers struck up the *Agnus Dei*; the boys' procession began; behind them came the girls. With clasped hands, they advanced step by step to the lighted altar, knelt at the first step, received one by one the Host, and returned to their seats in the same order. When Virginia's turn came, Félicité leaned forward to watch her, and through that imagination which springs from true affection, she at once became the child, whose face and dress became hers, whose heart beat in her bosom, and when Virginia opened her mouth and closed her lids, she did likewise and came very near fainting.

The following day, she presented herself early at the church so as to receive communion from the curé. She took it with the proper feeling, but did not experience the same delight as on the previous day.

Madame Aubain wished to make an accomplished girl of her daughter; and as Guyot could not teach English nor music, she decided to send her to the Ursulines at Honfleur.

The child made no objection, but Félicité sighed and thought Madame was heartless. Then, she thought that perhaps her mistress was right, as these things were beyond her sphere. Finally, one day, an old *fiacre* stopped in front of the door and a nun stepped out. Félicité put Virginia's luggage on top of the carriage, gave the coachman some instructions, and smuggled six jars of jam, a dozen pears, and a bunch of violets under the seat.

At the last minute, Virginia had a fit of sobbing; she embraced her mother again and again, while the latter kissed her on her forehead, and said: "Now, be brave, be brave!" The step was pulled up and the *fiacre* rumbled off.

Then Madame Aubain had a fainting spell, and that evening all her friends, including the two Lormeaus, Madame Lechaptois, the ladies Rochefeuille, Messieurs de Houppeville, and Bourais, called on her and tendered their sympathy.

At first the separation proved very painful to her. But her daughter wrote her three times a week and the other days she, herself, wrote to Virginia. Then she walked in the garden, read a little, and in this way managed to fill out the emptiness of the hours.

Each morning, out of habit, Félicité entered Virginia's room and gazed at the walls. She missed combing her hair, lacing her shoes, tucking her in her bed, and the bright face and little hand when they used to go out for a walk. In order to occupy herself she tried to make lace. But her clumsy fingers broke the threads; she had no heart for anything, lost her sleep, and "wasted away," as she put it.

In order to have some distraction, she asked leave to receive the visits of her nephew Victor.

He would come on Sunday, after church, with ruddy cheeks and bared chest, bringing with him the scent of the country. She would set the table and they would sit down opposite each other, and eat their dinner; she ate as little as possible, herself, to avoid any extra expense, but would stuff him so with food that he would finally go to sleep. At the first stroke of vespers she would wake him up, brush his trousers, tie his cravat and walk to church with him, leaning on his arm with maternal pride.

His parents always told him to get something out of her, either a package of brown sugar, or soap, or brandy, and sometimes even money. He brought her his clothes to mend, and she accepted the task gladly, because it meant another visit from him.

In August, his father took him on a coasting-vessel.

It was vacation time and the arrival of the children consoled Félicité. But Paul was capricious, and Virginia was growing too old to be thee-and-thou'd, a fact which seemed to produce a sort of embarrassment in their relations.

Victor went successively to Morlaix, to Dunkirk, and to Brighton; whenever he returned from a trip he would bring her a present. The first time it was a box of shells; the second, a coffee cup; the third, a big doll of gingerbread. He was growing handsome, had a good figure, a tiny moustache, kind eyes, and a little leather cap that sat jauntily on the back of his head. He amused his aunt by telling her stories mingled with nautical expressions.

One Monday, the 14th of July, 1819 (she never forgot the date), Victor announced that he had been engaged on a merchant-vessel and that in two days he would take the steamer at Honfleur and join his ship, which was going to start from Havre very soon. Perhaps he might be away two years.

The prospect of his departure filled Félicité with despair, and in order to bid him farewell, on Wednesday night, after Madame's dinner, she put on her pattens and trudged the four miles that separated Pont-l'Évêque from Honfleur.

When she reached the Calvary, instead of turning to the right, she turned to the left and lost herself in coal yards; she had to retrace her steps; some people she spoke to advised her to hasten. She walked helplessly around the harbour filled with vessels, and knocked against hawsers. Presently the ground sloped abruptly, lights flitted to and fro, and she thought all at once that she had gone mad when she saw some horses in the sky.

Others, on the edge of the dock, neighed at the sight of the ocean. A derrick pulled them up in the air and dumped them into a boat, where passengers were bustling about among barrels of cider, baskets of cheese, and bags of meal; chickens cackled, the captain swore, and a cabin-boy rested on the railing, apparently indifferent to his surroundings. Félicité, who did not recognize him, kept shouting: "Victor!" He suddenly raised his eyes, but while she was prepared to rush up to him, they withdrew the gang-plank.

The packet, towed by singing women, glided out of the harbour. Her hull squeaked and the heavy waves beat up against her sides. The sail had turned and nobody was visible;—and on the ocean, silvered by the light of the moon, the vessel formed a black spot that grew dimmer and dimmer, and finally disappeared.

When Félicité passed the Calvary again, she felt as if she must entrust that which was dearest to her to the Lord; and for a long while she prayed, with uplifted eyes and a face wet with tears. The city was sleeping; some customs officials were taking the air; and the water kept pouring through the holes of the dam with a deafening roar. The town clock struck two.

The parlour of the convent would not open until morning, and surely a delay would annoy Madame; so, in spite of her desire to see the other child, she went home. The maids of the inn were just arising when she reached Pont-l'Évêque.

So the poor boy would be on the ocean for months! His previous trips had not alarmed her. One can come back from England and Brittany; but America, the colonies, the islands, were all lost in an uncertain region at the very end of the world.

From that time on, Félicité thought solely of her nephew. On warm days she feared he would suffer from thirst, and when it stormed, she was afraid he would be struck by lightning. When she harkened to the wind that rattled in the chimney and dislodged the tiles on the roof, she imagined that he was being buffeted by the same storm, perched on top of a shattered mast, with his whole body bent backward and covered with sea-foam; or,—these were recollections of the engraved geography—he was being devoured by savages, or captured in a forest by apes, or dying on some lonely coast. She never mentioned her anxieties, however.

Madame Aubain worried about her daughter.

The sisters thought that Virginia was affectionate but delicate. The slightest emotion enervated her. She had to give up her piano lessons. Her mother insisted upon regular letters from the convent. One morning, when the postman failed to come, she grew impatient and began to pace to and fro, from her chair to the window. It was really extraordinary! No news since four days!

In order to console her mistress by her own example, Félicité said:

"Why, Madame, I haven't had any news for six months!—"

"From whom?—"

"Why—from my nephew."

"Oh, yes, your nephew!" And shrugging her shoulders, Madame Aubain continued to pace the floor as if to say: "I did not think of it.—Besides, I do not care, a cabin-boy, a pauper—but my daughter—what a difference! just think of it!—"

Félicité, although she had been reared roughly, was very indignant. Then she forgot about it.

It appeared quite natural to her that one should lose one's head about Virginia.

The two children were of equal importance; they were united in her heart and their fate was to be the same.

The chemist informed her that Victor's vessel had reached Havana. He had read the information in a newspaper.

Félicité imagined that Havana was a place where people did nothing but smoke, and that Victor walked around among negroes in a cloud of tobacco. Could a person, in case of need, return by land? How far was it from Pont-l'Évêque? In order to learn these things, she questioned Monsieur Bourais. He reached for his map and began some explanation concerning longitudes, and smiled with superiority at Félicité's bewilderment. At last, he took his pencil and pointed out an imperceptible black point in the scallops of an oval blotch, adding: "There it is." She bent over the map; the maze of coloured lines hurt her eyes without enlightening her; and when Bourais asked her what puzzled her, she requested him to show her the house Victor lived in. Bourais threw up his hands, sneezed, and then laughed uproariously; such ignorance delighted his soul; but Félicité failed to understand the cause of his mirth, she whose intelligence was so limited that she perhaps expected to see even the picture of her nephew!

It was two weeks later that Liébard came into the kitchen at market time, and handed her a letter from her brother-in-law. As neither of them could read, she called upon her mistress.

Madame Aubain, who was counting the stitches of her knitting, laid her work down beside her, opened the letter, started, and in a low tone and with a searching look said: "They tell you of misfortune. Your nephew—."

He had died. The letter told nothing more.

Félicité dropped on a chair, leaned her head against the back and closed her lids; presently they grew pink. Then, with drooping head, inert hands, and staring eyes she repeated at intervals:

"Poor little chap! poor little chap!"

Liébard watched her and sighed. Madame Aubain was trembling. She proposed to the girl to go to see her sister in Trouville. With a single motion, Félicité replied that it was not necessary. There was a silence. Old Liébard thought it about time for him to take leave.

Then Félicité uttered: "They have no sympathy, they do not care!"

Her head fell forward again, and from time to time, mechanically, she toyed with the long knitting-needles on the work-table.

Some women passed through the yard with a basket of wet clothes.

When she saw them through the window, she suddenly remembered her own wash; as she had soaked it the day before, she must go and rinse it now. So she arose and left the room.

Her tub and her board were on the bank of the Toucques. She threw a heap of clothes on the ground, rolled up her sleeves and grasped her bat; and her loud pounding could be heard in the neighbouring gardens. The meadows were empty, the breeze wrinkled the stream, at the bottom of which were long grasses that looked like the hair of corpses floating in the water. She restrained her sorrow and was very brave until night; but, when she had gone to her own room, she gave way to it, burying her face in the pillow and pressing her two fists against her temples.

A long while afterward, she learned through Victor's captain, the circumstances which surrounded his death. At the hospital they had bled him too much, treating him for yellow fever. Four doctors held him at one time. He died almost instantly, and the chief surgeon had said:

"Here goes another one!"

His parents had always treated him barbarously; she preferred not to see them again, and they made no advances, either from forgetfulness or out of innate hardness.

Virginia was growing weaker.

A cough, continual fever, oppressive breathing, and spots on her cheeks indicated some serious trouble. Monsieur Poupart had advised a sojourn in Provence. Madame Aubain decided that they would go, and she would have had her daughter come home at once, had it not been for the climate of Pont-l'Évêque.

She made an arrangement with a livery-stable man who drove her over to the convent every Tuesday. In the garden there was a terrace, from which the view extends to the Seine. Virginia walked in it, leaning on her mother's arm and treading the dead vine leaves. Sometimes the sun, shining through the clouds, made her blink her lids, when she gazed at the sails in the distance, and let her eyes roam over the horizon from the chateau of Tancarville to the lighthouses of Havre. Then they rested in the arbour. Her mother had bought a little cask of fine Malaga wine, and Virginia, laughing at the idea of becoming intoxicated, would drink a few drops of it, but never more.

Her strength returned. Autumn passed. Félicité began to reassure Madame Aubain. But, one evening, when she returned home after an errand, she met M. Boupart's coach in front of the door; M. Boupart himself was standing in the vestibule and Madame Aubain was tying the strings of her bonnet. "Give me my foot-warmer, my purse, and my gloves; and be quick about it," she said.

Virginia had congestion of the lungs; perhaps it was desperate. "Not yet," said the physician, and both got into the carriage, while the snow fell in thick flakes. It was almost night and very cold.

Félicité rushed to the church to light a candle. Then she ran after the coach which she overtook after an hour's chase, sprang up behind and held on to the straps. But suddenly a thought crossed her mind: "The yard had been left open; supposing that burglars got in!" And down she jumped.

The next morning, at daybreak, she called at the doctor's. He had been home, but had left again. Then she waited at the inn, thinking that strangers might bring her a letter. At last, at daylight she took the coach from Lisieux.

The convent was at the end of a steep and narrow street. When she arrived about at the middle of it, she heard strange noises, a funeral knell. "It must be for someone else," thought she; and she pulled the knocker violently.

After several minutes had elapsed, she heard footsteps, the door was half opened and a nun appeared. The good sister, with an air of compunction, told her that "she had just passed away." And at the same time the tolling of Saint- Léonard's increased.

Félicité reached the second floor. Already at the threshold, she caught sight of Virginia lying on her back, with clasped hands, her mouth open and her head thrown back, beneath a black crucifix inclined toward her, and stiff curtains which were less white than her face. Madame Aubain lay at the foot of the couch, clasping it with her arms and uttering groans of agony. The Mother Superior was standing on the right side of the bed. The three candles on the bureau made red blurs, and the windows were dimmed by the fog outside. The nuns carried Madame Aubain from the room.

For two nights, Félicité never left the corpse. She would repeat the same prayers, sprinkle holy water over the sheets, get up, come back to the bed and contemplate the body. At the end of the first vigil, she noticed that the face had taken on a yellow tinge, the lips grew blue, the nose grew pinched, the eyes were sunken. She kissed them several times and would not have been greatly astonished had Virginia opened them; to souls like these the supernatural is always quite simple. She washed her, wrapped her in a shroud, put her into the casket, laid a wreath of flowers on her head and arranged her curls. They were blonde and of an extraordinary length for her age. Félicité cut off a big lock and put half of it into her bosom, resolving never to part with it.

The body was taken to Pont-l'Évêque, according to Madame Aubain's wishes; she followed the hearse in a closed carriage.

After the ceremony it took three quarters of an hour to reach the cemetery. Paul, sobbing, headed the procession; Monsieur Bourais followed, and then came the principal inhabitants of the town, the women covered with black capes, and Félicité. The memory of her nephew, and the thought that she had not been able to render him these honours, made her doubly unhappy, and she felt as if he were being buried with Virginia.

Madame Aubain's grief was uncontrollable. At first she rebelled against God, thinking that he was unjust to have taken away her child—she who had never done anything wrong, and whose conscience was so pure! But no! she ought to have taken her south. Other doctors would have saved her. She accused herself, prayed to be able to join her child, and cried in the midst of her dreams. Of the latter, one more especially haunted her. Her husband, dressed like a sailor, had come back from a long voyage, and with tears in his eyes told her that he had received the order to take Virginia away. Then they both consulted about the hiding-place.

Once she came in from the garden, all upset. A moment before (and she showed the place), the father and daughter had appeared to her, one after the other; they did nothing but look at her.

During several months she remained inert in her room. Félicité scolded her gently; she must go on living for her son and also for the other one, for "her memory."

"Her memory!" replied Madame Aubain, as if she were just awakening, "Oh! yes, yes, you do not forget her!" This was an allusion to the cemetery where she had been expressly forbidden to go.

But Félicité went there every day. At four o'clock exactly, she would go through the town, climb the hill, open the gate and arrive at Virginia's tomb. It was a small column of pink marble with a flat stone at its base, and it was surrounded by a little plot enclosed by chains. The flower beds were bright with blossoms. Félicité watered their leaves, renewed the gravel, and knelt on the ground in order to till the earth properly. When Madame Aubain was able to visit the cemetery she felt very much relieved and consoled.

Years passed, all alike and marked by no other events than the return of the great church holidays: Easter, Assumption, All Saints' Day. Household happenings constituted the only data to which in later years they often referred. Thus, in 1825, workmen painted the vestibule; in 1827, a portion of the roof almost killed a man by falling into the yard. In the summer of 1828, it was Madame's turn to offer the hallowed bread; at the time, Bourais disappeared mysteriously; and the old acquaintances, Guyot, Hebard, Madame Lechaptois, Robelin, old Grémanville, paralyzed since a long time, passed away one by one. One night, the driver of the mail in Pont-l'Évêque announced the Revolution of July. A few days afterward a new sub-prefect was nominated, the Baron de Larsonnière, ex-consul in America, who, besides his wife, had his sister-in-law and her three grown daughters with him. They were often seen on their lawn, dressed in loose blouses, and they had a parrot and a negro servant. Madame Aubain received a call, which she returned promptly. As soon as she caught sight of them, Félicité would run and notify her mistress. But only one thing was capable of arousing her: a letter from her son.

He could not follow any profession as he was absorbed in drinking. His mother paid his debts and he made fresh ones; and the sighs that she heaved while she knitted at the window reached the ears of Félicité who was spinning in the kitchen.

They walked in the garden together, always speaking of Virginia, and asking each other if such and such a thing would have pleased her, and what she would probably have said on this or that occasion.

All her little belongings were put away in a closet of the room which held the two little beds. But Madame Aubain looked them over as little as possible. One summer day, however, she resided herself to the task and when she opened the closet the moths flew out.

Virginia's frocks were hung under a shelf where there were three dolls, some hoops, a doll-house, and a basin which she had used. Félicité and Madame Aubain also took out the skirts, the handkerchiefs, and the stockings and spread them on the beds, before putting them away again. The sun fell on the piteous things, disclosing their spots and creases formed by the motions of the body. The atmosphere was warm and blue, and a blackbird trilled in the garden; everything seemed to live in happiness. They found a little hat of soft brown plush, but it was entirely moth-eaten. Félicité asked for it. Their eyes met and filled with tears; at last the mistress opened her arms and the servant threw herself against her breast and they hugged each other, giving vent to their grief in a kiss which equalized them for a moment.

It was the first time that this had ever happened, for Madame Aubain was not of an expansive nature. Félicité was as grateful for it as if it had been some favour, and thenceforth loved her with animal-like devotion and a religious veneration.

Her kind-heartedness developed. When she heard the drums of a marching regiment passing through the street, she would stand in the doorway with a jug of cider and give the soldiers a drink. She nursed cholera victims. She protected Polish refugees, and one of them even declared that he wished to marry her. But they quarrelled, for one morning when she returned from the Angelus she found him in the kitchen coolly eating a dish which he had prepared for himself during her absence.

After the Polish refugees, came Colmiche, an old man who was credited with having committed frightful misdeeds in '93. He lived near the river in the ruins of a pig-sty. The urchins peeped at him through the cracks in the walls and threw stones that fell on his miserable bed, where he lay gasping with catarrh, with long hair, inflamed eyelids, and a tumour as big as his head on one arm.

She got him some linen, tried to clean his hovel, and dreamed of installing him in the bake-house without his being in Madame's way. When the tumour broke, she dressed it every day; sometimes she brought him some cake and placed him in the sun on a bundle of hay; and the poor old creature, trembling and drooling, would thank her in his broken voice, and put out his hands whenever she left him. Finally he died; and she had a mass said for the repose of his soul.

That day a great joy came to her: at dinnertime, Madame de Larsonnière's servant called with the parrot, the cage, and the perch and chain and lock. A note from the baroness told Madame Aubain that as her husband had been promoted to a prefecture, they were leaving that night, and she begged her to accept the bird as a remembrance and a token of her esteem.

For a long time the parrot had been on Félicité's mind, because he came from America, which reminded her of Victor, and she had approached the negro on the subject.

Once even, she had said: "How glad Madame would be to have him!"

The man had repeated this remark to his mistress who, not being able to keep the bird, took this means of getting rid of it.

IV

He was called Loulou. His body was green, his head blue, the tips of his wings were pink, and his breast was golden.

But he had the tiresome tricks of biting his perch, pulling his feathers out, scattering refuse, and spilling the water of his bath. Madame Aubain grew tired of him and gave him to Félicité for good.

She undertook his education, and soon he was able to repeat: "Pretty boy! Your servant, sir! I salute you, Marie!" His perch was placed near the door and several persons were astonished that he did not answer to the name of "Jacquot," for every parrot is called Jacquot. They called him a goose and a log, and these taunts were like so many dagger thrusts to Félicité. Strange stubbornness of the bird which would not talk when people watched him!

Nevertheless, he sought society; for on Sunday, when the ladies Rochefeuille, Monsieur de Houppeville and the new habitués, Onfroy, the chemist, Monsieur Varin, and Captain Mathieu, dropped in for their game of cards, he struck the window panes with his wings and made such a racket that it was impossible to talk.

Bourais's face must have appeared very funny to Loulou. As soon as he saw him he would begin to roar. His voice re-echoed in the yard, and the neighbours would come to the windows and begin to laugh, too; and in order that the parrot might not see him, Monsieur Bourais edged along the wall, pushed his hat over his eyes to hide his profile, and entered by the garden door, and the looks he gave the bird lacked affection. Loulou, having thrust his head into the butcher-boy's basket, received a slap, and from that time he always tried to nip his enemy. Fabu threatened to wring his neck, although he was not cruelly inclined, notwithstanding his big whiskers and tattooings. On the contrary, he rather liked the bird and, out of deviltry, tried to teach him oaths. Félicité, whom his manner alarmed, put Loulou in the kitchen, took off his chain, and let him walk all over the house.

When he went downstairs, he rested his beak on the steps, lifted his right foot and then his left one; but his mistress feared that such feats would give him vertigo. He became ill and was unable to eat. There was a small growth under his tongue like those chickens are sometimes afflicted with. Félicité pulled it off with her nails and cured him. One day, Paul was imprudent enough to blow the smoke of his cigar in his face; another time, Madame Lormeau was teasing him with the tip of her umbrella and he swallowed the tip. Finally he got lost.

She had put him on the grass to cool him and went away only for a second; when she returned, she found no parrot! She hunted among the bushes, on the bank of the river, and on the roofs, without paying any attention to Madame Aubain who screamed at her: "Take care! you must be insane!" Then she searched every garden in Pont-l'Évêque and stopped the passers-by to inquire of them: "Haven't you perhaps seen my parrot?" To those who had never seen the parrot, she described him minutely. Suddenly she thought she saw something green fluttering behind the mills at the foot of the hill. But when she was at the top of the hill she could not see it. A hod-carrier told her that he had just seen the bird in Saint-Melaine, in Mother Simon's store. She rushed to the place. The people did not know what she was talking about. At last she came home, exhausted, with her slippers worn to shreds, and despair in her heart. She sat down on the bench near Madame and was telling of her search when presently a light weight dropped on her shoulder—Loulou! What the deuce had he been doing? Perhaps he had just taken a little walk around town!

She did not easily forget her scare; in fact, she never got over it. In consequence of a cold, she caught a sore throat; and some time afterward she had an earache. Three years later she was stone deaf, and spoke in a very loud voice even in church. Although her sins might have been proclaimed throughout the diocese without any shame to herself, or ill effects to the community, the cure thought it advisable to receive her confession in the vestry room.

Imaginary buzzings also added to her bewilderment. Her mistress often said to her: "My goodness, how stupid you are!" and she would answer: "Yes, Madame," and look for something.

The narrow circle of her ideas grew more restricted than it already was; the bellowing of the oxen, the chime of the bells no longer reached her intelligence. All things moved silently, like ghosts. Only one noise penetrated her ears: the parrot's voice.

As if to divert her mind, he reproduced for her the tick-tack of the spit in the kitchen, the shrill cry of the fish-vendors, the saw of the carpenter who had a shop opposite, and when the doorbell rang, he would imitate Madame Aubain: "Félicité! go to the front door."

They held conversations together, Loulou repeating the three phrases of his repertory over and over, Félicité replying by words that had no greater meaning, but in which she poured out her feelings. In her isolation, the parrot was almost a son, a lover. He climbed upon her fingers, pecked at her lips, clung to her shawl, and when she rocked her head to and fro like a nurse, the big wings of her cap and the wings of the bird flapped in unison. When clouds gathered on the horizon and the thunder rumbled, Loulou would scream, perhaps because he remembered the storms in his native forests. The dripping of the rain would excite him to frenzy; he flapped around, struck the ceiling with his wings, upset everything, and would finally fly into the garden to play. Then he would come back into the room, light on one of the andirons, and hop around in order to get dry.

One morning during the terrible winter of 1837, when she had put him in front of the fireplace on account of the cold, she found him dead in his cage, hanging to the wire bars with his head down. He had probably died of congestion. But she believed that he had been poisoned, and although she had no proofs whatever, her suspicion rested on Fabu.

She wept so sorely that her mistress said: "Why don't you have him stuffed?"

She asked the advice of the chemist, who had always been kind to the bird.

He wrote to Havre for her. A certain man named Fellacher consented to do the work. But, as the diligence driver often lost parcels entrusted to him, Félicité resolved to take her pet to Honfleur herself.

Leafless apple trees lined the edges of the road. The ditches were covered with ice. The dogs on the neighbouring farms barked; and Félicité, with her hands beneath her cape, her little black sabots and her basket, trotted along nimbly in the middle of the sidewalk. She crossed the forest, passed by the Haut-Chêne, and reached Saint-Gatien.

Behind her, in a cloud of dust and impelled by the steep incline, a mailcoach drawn by galloping horses advanced like a whirlwind. When he saw a woman in the middle of the road, who did not get out of the way, the driver stood up in his seat and shouted to her and so did the postillion, while the four horses, which he could not hold back, accelerated their pace; the two leaders were almost upon her; with a jerk of the reins he threw them to one side, but, furious at the incident, he lifted his big whip and lashed her from her head to her feet with such violence that she fell to the ground unconscious.

Her first thought, when she recovered her senses, was to open the basket. Loulou was unharmed. She felt a sting on her right cheek; when she took her hand away it was red, for the blood was flowing.

She sat down on a pile of stones, and sopped her cheek with her handkerchief; then she ate a crust of bread she had put in her basket, and consoled herself by looking at the bird.

Arriving at the top of Ecquemanville, she saw the lights of Honfleur shining in the distance like so many stars; further on, the ocean spread out in a confused mass. Then a weakness came over her; the misery of her childhood, the disappointment of her first love, the departure of her nephew, the death of Virginia; all these things came back to her at once, and, rising like a swelling tide in her throat, almost choked her.

Then she wished to speak to the captain of the vessel, and without stating what she was sending, she gave him some instructions.

Fellacher kept the parrot a long time. He always promised that it would be ready for the following week; after six months he announced the shipment of a case, and that was the end of it. Really, it seemed as if Loulou would never come back to his home. "They have stolen him," thought Félicité.

Finally he arrived, sitting bolt upright on a branch which could be screwed into a mahogany pedestal, with his foot in the air, his head on one side, and in his beak a nut which the naturalist, from love of the sumptuous, had gilded. She put him in her room.

This place, to which only a chosen few were admitted, looked like a chapel and a second-hand shop, so filled was it with devotional and heterogeneous things. The door could not be opened easily on account of the presence of a large wardrobe. Opposite the window that looked out into the garden, a bull's-eye opened on the yard; a table was placed by the cot and held a washbasin, two combs, and a piece of blue soap in a broken saucer. On the walls were rosaries, medals, a number of Holy Virgins, and a holy-water basin made out of a coconut; on the bureau, which was covered with a napkin like an altar, stood the box of shells that Victor had given her; also a watering can and a balloon, writing books, the engraved geography, and a pair of shoes; on the nail which held the mirror, hung Virginia's little plush hat! Félicité carried this sort of respect so far that she even kept one of Monsieur's old coats. All the things which Madame Aubain discarded, Félicité begged for her own room. Thus, she had artificial flowers on the edge of the bureau, and the picture of the Comte d'Artois in the recess of the window. By means of a board, Loulou was set on a portion of the chimney which advanced into the room. Every morning when she awoke, she saw him in the dim light of dawn and recalled bygone days and the smallest details of insignificant actions, without any sense of bitterness or grief.

As she was unable to communicate with people, she lived in a sort of somnambulistic torpor. The processions of Corpus-Christi Day seemed to wake her up. She visited the neighbours to beg for candlesticks and mats so as to adorn the temporary altars in the street.

In church, she always gazed at the Holy Ghost, and noticed that there was something about him that resembled a parrot. The likeness appeared even more striking on a coloured picture by Espinal, representing the baptism of our Saviour. With his scarlet wings and emerald body, it was really the image of Loulou. Having bought the picture, she hung it near the one of the Comte d'Artois so that she could take them in at one glance.

They associated in her mind, the parrot becoming sanctified through the neighbourhood of the Holy Ghost, and the latter becoming more lifelike in her eyes, and more comprehensible. In all probability the Father had never chosen as messenger a dove, as the latter has no voice, but rather one of Loulou's ancestors. And Félicité said her prayers in front of the coloured picture, though from time to time she turned slightly toward the bird.

She desired very much to enter in the ranks of the "Daughters of the Virgin." But Madame Aubain dissuaded her from it.

A most important event occurred: Paul's marriage.

After being first a notary's clerk, then in business, then in the customs, and a tax collector, and having even applied for a position in the administration of woods and forests, he had at last, when he was thirty-six years old, by a divine inspiration, found his vocation: registrature! and he displayed such a high ability that an inspector had offered him his daughter and his influence.

Paul, who had become quite settled, brought his bride to visit his mother.

But she looked down upon the customs of Pont-l'Évêque, put on airs, and hurt Félicité's feelings. Madame Aubain felt relieved when she left.

The following week they learned of Monsieur Bourais's death in an inn. There were rumours of suicide, which were confirmed; doubts concerning his integrity arose. Madame Aubain looked over her accounts and soon discovered his numerous embezzlements; sales of wood which had been concealed from her, false receipts, etc. Furthermore, he had an illegitimate child, and entertained a friendship for "a person in Dozulé."

These base actions affected her very much. In March 1853, she developed a pain in her chest; her tongue looked as if it were coated with smoke, and the leeches they applied did not relieve her oppression; and on the ninth evening she died, being just seventy-two years old.

People thought that she was younger, because her hair, which she wore in bands framing her pale face, was brown. Few friends regretted her loss, for her manner was so haughty that she did not attract them. Félicité mourned for her as servants seldom mourn for their masters. The fact that Madame should die before herself perplexed her mind and seemed contrary to the order of things, and absolutely monstrous and inadmissible. Ten days later (the time to journey from Besançon), the heirs arrived. Her daughter-in-law ransacked the drawers, kept some of the furniture, and sold the rest; then they went back to their own home.

Madame's armchair, foot-warmer, work-table, the eight chairs, everything was gone! The places occupied by the pictures formed yellow squares on the walls. They had taken the two little beds, and the wardrobe had been emptied of Virginia's belongings! Félicité went upstairs, overcome with grief.

The following day a sign was posted on the door; the chemist screamed in her ear that the house was for sale.

For moment she tottered, and had to sit down.

What hurt her most was to give up her room,—so nice for poor Loulou! She looked at him in despair and implored the Holy Ghost, and it was this way that she contracted the idolatrous habit of saying her prayers kneeling in front of the bird. Sometimes the sun fell through the window on his glass eye, and lighted a great spark in it which sent Félicité int o ecstasy.

Her mistress had left her an income of three hundred and eighty francs. The garden supplied her with vegetables. As for clothes, she had enough to last her till the end of her days, and she economized on the light by going to bed at dusk.

She rarely went out, in order to avoid passing in front of the second-hand dealer's shop where there was some of the old furniture. Since her fainting spell, she dragged her leg, and as her strength was failing rapidly, old Mother Simon, who had lost her money in the grocery business, came every morning to chop the wood and pump the water.

Her eyesight grew dim. She did not open the shutters after that. Many years passed. But the house did not sell or rent. Fearing that she would be put out, Félicité did not ask for repairs. The laths of the roof were rotting away, and during one whole winter her bolster was wet. After Easter she spat blood.

Then Mother Simon went for a doctor. Félicité wished to know what her complaint was. But, being too deaf to hear, she caught only one word: "Pneumonia." She was familiar with it and gently answered:—"Ah! like Madame," thinking it quite natural that she should follow her mistress.

The time for the altars in the street drew near.

The first one was always erected at the foot of the hill, the second in front of the post office, and the third in the middle of the street. This position occasioned some rivalry among the women and they finally decided upon Madame Aubain's yard.

Félicité's fever grew worse. She was sorry that she could not do anything for the altar. If she could, at least, have contributed something toward it! Then she thought of the parrot. Her neighbours objected that it would not be proper. But the curé gave his consent and she was so grateful for it that she begged him to accept after her death, her only treasure, Loulou. From Tuesday until Saturday, the day before the event, she coughed more frequently. In the evening her face was contracted, her lips stuck to her gums and she began to vomit; and on the following day, she felt so low that she called for a priest.

Three neighbours surrounded her when the dominie administered the Extreme Unction. Afterwards she said that she wished to speak to Fabu.

He arrived in his Sunday clothes, very ill at ease among the funereal surroundings.

"Forgive me," she said, making an effort to extend her arm, "I believed it was you who killed him!"

What did such accusations mean? Suspect a man like him of murder! And Fabu became excited and was about to make trouble.

"Don't you see she is not in her right mind?"

From time to time Félicité spoke to shadows. The women left and Mother Simon sat down to breakfast.

A little later, she took Loulou and holding him up to Félicité: "Say goodbye to him, now!" she commanded.

Although he was not a corpse, he was eaten up by worms; one of his wings was broken and the wadding was coming out of his body. But Félicité was blind now, and she took him and laid him against her cheek. Then Mother Simon removed him in order to set him on the altar.

V

The grass exhaled an odour of summer; flies buzzed in the air, the sun shone on the river and warmed the slated roof. Old Mother Simon had returned to Félicité and was peacefully falling asleep.

The ringing of bells woke her; the people were coming out of church. Félicité's delirium subsided. By thinking of the procession, she was able to see it as if she had taken part in it. All the schoolchildren, the singers, and the firemen walked on the sidewalks, while in the middle of the street came first the custodian of the church with his halberd, then the beadle with a large cross, the teacher in charge of the boys, and a sister escorting the little girls; three of the smallest ones, with curly heads, threw rose leaves into the air; the deacon with outstretched arms conducted the music; and two incense-bearers turned with each step they took toward the Holy Sacrament, which was carried by M. le Curé, attired in his handsome chasuble and walking under a canopy of red velvet supported by four men. A crowd of people followed, jammed between the walls of the houses hung with white sheets; at last the procession arrived at the foot of the hill.

A cold sweat broke out on Félicité's forehead. Mother Simon wiped it away with a cloth, saying inwardly that some day she would have to go through the same thing herself.

The murmur of the crowd grew louder, was very distinct for a moment and then died away. A volley of musketry shook the window panes. It was the postillions saluting the Sacrament. Félicité rolled her eyes and said as loudly as she could:

"Is he all right?" meaning the parrot.

Her death agony began. A rattle that grew more and more rapid shook her body. Froth appeared at the corners of her mouth, and her whole frame trembled. In a little while could be heard the music of the bass horns, the clear voices of the children and the man's deeper notes. At intervals all was still, and their shoes sounded like a herd of cattle passing over the grass.

The clergy appeared in the yard. Mother Simon climbed on a chair to reach the bull's-eye, and in this manner could see the altar. It was covered with a lace cloth and draped with green wreaths. In the middle stood a little frame containing relics; at the corners were two little orange trees, and all along the edge were silver candlesticks, porcelain vases containing sunflowers, lilies, peonies, and tufts of hydrangeas. This mound of bright colours descended diagonally from the first floor to the carpet that covered the sidewalk. Rare objects arrested one's eye. A golden sugar-bowl was crowned with violets, earrings set with Alençon stones were displayed on green moss, and two Chinese screens with their bright landscapes were near by. Loulou, hidden beneath roses, showed nothing but his blue head which looked like a piece of lapis lazuli.

The singers, the canopy-bearers, and the children lined up against the sides of the yard. Slowly the priest ascended the steps and placed his shining sun on the lace cloth. Everybody knelt. There was deep silence; and the censers slipping on their chains were swung high in the air. A blue vapour rose in Félicité's room. She opened her nostrils and inhaled it with a mystic sensuousness; then she closed her lids. Her lips smiled. The beats of her heart grew fainter and fainter, and vaguer, like a fountain giving out, like an echo dying away;—and when she exhaled her last breath, she thought she saw in the half-opened heavens a gigantic parrot hovering above her head.

1877

Henry James

1843–1916

The term "Jamesian" is synonymous with complex narrative structures and meticulously sustained perspectives, with fine etchings of fine sensibilities, with the "international theme" of American and European expectations, with morally intricate stories developed from actual dinner party anecdotes. The more easily fatigued of James's readers associate his transatlantic fiction with a kind of oceanic syntax, with seemingly endless waves of observation and nuance. But James straddled not only continents, but also the seismic shift from the nineteenth to the twentieth century. He was eighteen when the American Civil War erupted, and his principal literary mentor was George Eliot, yet he became central to the emergence of modernism, through his criticism and through his major works, *The Wings of the Dove* (1902), *The Ambassadors* (1903), and *The Golden Bowl* (1904). But in its brilliant creation of perspective, its exquisite rendering of the enigmas of a child's knowledge and innocence, *What Maisie Knew* (1897) may be the perfect jewel in his collection. The first novelist to write self-consciously about the novel as an art form, James set out to create an analytical framework for the novel analogous to Shelley's *Defence of Poetry* (1821), to elevate prose narrative and rescue it from previous writers' sense of apology and rambling purposes. His philosopher father had counselled vagueness, whereas James pursued "solidity of specification."

The James family was wealthy and culturally eccentric. Born in New York, as were his brother, William, and sister, Alice, Henry studied with a small army of tutors, and then attended schools in Geneva and Paris. He entered Harvard Law School in 1862, but withdrew soon after, and, in opposition to his father's notion that art was too specific and narrow an undertaking, turned to writing. He published his first story, "A Tragedy of Error," in 1864, in the *North American Review*, and by 1868 had published a number of stories and a prodigious quantity of reviews. He was acquainted with numerous prominent writers, including Turgenev, Flaubert, and de Maupassant. For periods of time he devoted himself to "short lengths," to focusing his "small circular frame upon as many different spots as possible." James's theatrical ambitions were destroyed by both audiences and critics, but he transferred his sense of the dramatic and the visual to the short story and to the longer form, the novella, what he called "the blest nouvelle." James lived in England from 1875 until his death, becoming a British citizen in 1915.

Europe

I

"Our feeling is, you know, that Becky *should* go." That earnest little remark comes back to me, even after long years, as the first note of something that began, for my observation, the day I went with my sister-in-law to take leave of her good friends. It's a memory of the American time, which revives so at present—under some touch that doesn't signify—that it rounds itself off as an anecdote. That walk to say good-bye was the beginning; and the end, so far as I enjoyed a view of it, was not till long after; yet even the end also appears to me now as of the old days. I went, in those days, on occasion, to see my sister-in-law, in whose affairs, on my brother's death, I had had to take a helpful hand. I continued to go indeed after these little matters were straightened out, for the pleasure, periodically, of the impression—the change to the almost pastoral sweetness of the good Boston suburb from the loud longitudinal New York. It was another world, with other manners, a different tone, a different taste; a savour nowhere so mild, yet so distinct, as in the square white house—with the pair of elms, like gigantic wheat-sheaves, in front, the rustic orchard not far behind, the old-fashioned door-lights, the big blue-and-white jars on the porch, the straight bricked walk from the high gate—that enshrined the extraordinary merit of Mrs Rimmle and her three daughters.

These ladies were so much of the place and the place so much of themselves that from the first of their being revealed to me I felt that nothing else at Brookbridge much mattered. They were what, for me, at any rate, Brookbridge had most to give: I mean in the way of what it was naturally strongest in, the thing we called in New York the New England expression, the air of Puritanism reclaimed and refined. The Rimmles had brought this down to a wonderful delicacy. They struck me even then—all four almost equally—as very ancient and very earnest, and I think theirs must have been the house in all the world in which "culture" first came to the aid of morning calls. The head of the family was the widow of a great public character—as public characters were understood at Brookbridge—whose speeches on anniversaries formed a part of the body of national eloquence spouted in the New England schools by little boys covetous of the most marked, though perhaps the easiest, distinction. He was reported to have been celebrated, and in such fine declamatory connections that he seemed to gesticulate even from the tomb. He was understood to have made, in his wife's company, the tour of Europe at a date not immensely removed from that of the battle of Waterloo. What was the age then of the bland firm antique Mrs Rimmle at a period of her being first revealed to me? That's a point I'm not in a position to determine—I remember mainly that I was young enough to regard her as having reached the limit. And yet the limit for Mrs Rimmle must have been prodigiously extended; the scale of its extension is in fact the very moral of this reminiscence. She was old, and her daughters were old, but I was destined to know them all as older. It was only by comparison and habit that—however much I recede—Rebecca, Maria, and Jane were the "young ladies."

I think it was felt that, though their mother's life, after thirty years of widowhood, had had a grand backward stretch, her blandness and firmness—and this in spite of her extreme physical fraility—would be proof against any surrender not overwhelmingly justified by time. It had appeared, years before, at a crisis of which the waves had not even yet quite subsided, a surrender not justified by anything nameable, that she should go to Europe with her daughters and for her health. Her health was supposed to require constant support; but when it had at that period tried conclusions with the idea of Europe it was not the idea of Europe that had been insidious enough to prevail. She hadn't gone, and Becky, Maria, and

Jane hadn't gone, and this was long ago. They still merely floated in the air of the visit achieved, with such introductions and such acclamations, in the early part of the century; they still, with fond glances at the sunny parlour-walls, only referred, in conversation, to divers pictorial and other reminders of it. The Miss Rimmles had quite been brought up on it, but Becky, as the most literary, had most mastered the subject. There were framed letters—tributes to their eminent father—suspended among the mementoes, and of two or three of these, the most foreign and complimentary, Becky had executed translations that figured beside the text. She knew already, through this and other illumination, so much about Europe that it was hard to believe for her in that limit of adventure which consisted only of her having been twice to Philadelphia. The others hadn't been to Philadelphia, but there was a legend that Jane had been to Saratoga. Becky was a short stout fair person with round serious eyes, a high forehead, the sweetest neatest enunciation, and a miniature of her father—"done in Rome"—worn as a breastpin. She had written the life, she had edited the speeches, of the original of this ornament, and now at last, beyond the seas, she was really to tread in his footsteps.

Fine old Mrs Rimmle, in the sunny parlour and with a certain austerity of cap and chair—though with a gay new "front" that looked like rusty brown plush—had had so unusually good a winter that the question of her sparing two members of her family for an absence had been threshed as fine, I could feel, as even under that Puritan roof, any case of conscience had ever been threshed. They were to make their dash while the coast, as it were, was clear, and each of the daughters had tried—heroically, angelically, and for the sake of each of her sisters—not to be one of the two. What I encountered that first time was an opportunity to concur with enthusiasm in the general idea that Becky's wonderful preparation would be wasted if she were the one to stay with their mother. Their talk of Becky's preparation (they had a sly old-maidish humour that was as mild as milk) might have been of some mixture, for application somewhere, that she kept in a precious bottle. It had been settled at all events that, armed with this concoction and borne aloft by their introductions, she and Jane were to start. They were wonderful on their introductions, which proceeded naturally from their mother and were addressed to the charming families that in vague generations had so admired vague Mr Rimmle. Jane, I found at Brookbridge, had to be described, for want of other description, as the pretty one, but it wouldn't have served to identify her unless you had seen the others. *Her* preparation was only this figment of her prettiness—only, that is, unless one took into account something that, on the spot, I silently divined: the lifelong secret passionate ache of her little rebellious desire. They were all growing old in the yearning to go, but Jane's yearning was sharpest. She struggled with it as people at Brookbridge mostly struggled with what they liked, but fate, by threatening to prevent what she *dis*liked and what was therefore a duty—which was to stay at home instead of Maria—had bewildered her, I judged, not a little. It was she who, in the words I have quoted, mentioned to me Becky's case and Becky's affinity as the clearest of all. Her mother moreover had on the general subject still more to say.

"I positively desire, I really quite insist that they shall go," the old lady explained to us from her stiff chair. "We've talked about it so often, and they've had from me so clear an account—I've amused them again and again with it—of what's to be seen and enjoyed. If they've had hitherto too many duties to leave, the time seems to have come to recognize that there are also many duties to *seek*. Wherever we go we find them—I always remind the girls of that. There's a duty that calls them to those wonderful countries, just as it called, at the right time, their father and myself—if it be only that of laying-up for the years to come the same store of remarkable impressions, the same wealth of knowledge and food for conversation as, since my return, I've found myself so happy to possess." Mrs Rimmle spoke of her return as of something of the year before last, but the future of her daughters was somehow, by a different law, to be on the scale of great vistas, of endless after-tastes. I think that, without my being quite ready to say it, even this first impression of her was somewhat upsetting; there was a large placid perversity, a grim secrecy of intention, in her estimate of the ages.

"Well, I'm so glad you don't delay it longer," I said to Miss Becky before we withdrew. "And whoever should go," I continued in the spirit of the sympathy with which the good sisters had already inspired me, "I quite feel, with your family, you know, that *you* should. But of course I hold that every one should." I suppose I wished to attenuate my solemnity; there was, however, something in it I couldn't help. It must have been a faint foreknowledge.

"Have you been a great deal yourself?" Miss Jane, I remembered, enquired.

"Not so much but that I hope to go a good deal more. So perhaps we shall meet," I encouragingly suggested.

I recall something—something in the nature of susceptibility to encouragement—that this brought into the more expressive brown eyes to which Miss Jane mainly owed it that she was the pretty one. "Where, do you think?"

I tried to think, "Well, on the Italian lakes—Como, Bellaggio, Lugano." I liked to say the names to them.

"'Sublime, but neither bleak nor bare—not misty are the mountains there!'" Miss Jane softly breathed, while her sister looked at her as if her acquaintance with the poetry of the subject made her the most interesting feature of the scene she evoked.

But Miss Becky presently turned to me. "Do you know everything—?"

"Everything?"

"In Europe."

"Oh yes," I laughed, "and one or two things even in America."

The sisters seemed to me furtively to look at each other. "Well, you'll have to be quick—to meet *us*," Miss Jane resumed.

"But surely when you're once there you'll stay on."

"Stay on?"—they murmured it simultaneously and with the oddest vibration of dread as well as of desire. It was as if they had been in presence of a danger and yet wished me, who "knew everything," to torment them with still more of it.

Well, I did my best. "I mean it will never do to cut it short."

"No, that's just what I keep saying," said brilliant Jane. "It would be better in that case not to go."

"Oh, don't talk about not going—at this time!" It was none of my business, but I felt shocked and impatient.

"No, not at *this* time!" broke in Miss Maria, who, very red in the face, had joined us. Poor Miss Maria was known as the flushed one; but she was not flushed—she only had an unfortunate surface. The third day after this was to see them embark.

Miss Becky, however, desired as little as any one to be in any way extravagant. "It's only the thought of our mother," she explained.

I looked a moment at the old lady, with whom my sister-in-law was engaged. "Well—your mother's magnificent."

"*Isn't* she magnificent?"—they eagerly took it up.

She *was*—I could reiterate it with sincerity, though I perhaps mentally drew the line when Miss Maria again risked, as a fresh ejaculation: "I think she's better than Europe!"

"Maria!" they both, at this, exclaimed with a strange emphasis: it was as if they feared she had suddenly turned cynical over the deep domestic drama of their casting of lots. The innocent laugh with which she answered them gave the measure of her cynicism.

We separated at last, and my eyes met Mrs Rimmle's as I held for an instant her aged hand. It was doubtless only my fancy that her calm cold look quietly accused me of something. Of what *could* it accuse me? Only, I thought, of thinking.

II

I left Brookbridge the next day, and for some time after that had no occasion to hear from my kinswoman; but when she finally wrote there was a passage in her letter that affected me more than all the rest. "Do you know the poor Rimmles never, after all, 'went'? The old lady, at the eleventh hour, broke down; everything broke down, and all of *them* on top of it, so that the dear things are with us still. Mrs Rimmle, the night after our call, had, in the most unexpected manner, a turn for the worse—something in the nature (though they're rather mysterious about it) of a seizure; Becky and Jane felt it—dear devoted stupid angels that they are—heartless to leave her at such a moment, and Europe's indefinitely postponed. However, they think they're still going—or think they think it—when she's better. They also think—or *think* they think—that she *will* be better. I certainly pray she may." So did I—quite fervently. I was conscious of a real pang—I didn't know how much they had made me care.

Late that winter my sister-in-law spent a week in New York; when almost my first enquiry on meeting her was about the health of Mrs Rimmle.

"Oh she's rather bad—she really is, you know. It's not surprising that at her age she should be infirm."

"Then what the deuce *is* her age?"

"I can't tell you to a year—but she's immensely old."

"That of course I saw," I replied—"unless you literally mean so old that the records have been lost."

My sister-in-law thought. "Well, I believe she wasn't positively young when she married. She lost three or four children before these women were born."

We surveyed together a little, on this, the "dark backward." "And they were born, I gather, *after* the famous tour? Well then, as the famous tour was a manner to celebrate—wasn't it?—the restoration of the Bourbons—" I considered, I gasped. "My dear child, what on earth do you make her out?"

My relative, with her Brookbridge habit, transferred her share of the question to the moral plane—turned it forth to wander, by implication at least, in the sandy desert of responsibility. "Well, you know, we all immensely admire her."

"You can't admire her more than I do. She's awful."

My converser looked at me with a certain fear. "She's *really* ill."

"Too ill to get better?"

"Oh no—we hope not. Because then they'll be able to go."

"And *will* they go if she should?"

"Oh the moment they should be quite satisfied. I mean *really*," she added.

I'm afraid I laughed at her—the Brookbridge "really" was a thing so by itself. "But if she shouldn't get better?" I went on.

"Oh don't speak of it! They want so to go."

"It's a pity they're so infernally good," I mused.

"No—don't say that. It's what keeps them up."

"Yes, but isn't it what keeps *her* up too?"

My visitor looked grave. "Would you like them to kill her?"

I don't know that I was then prepared to say I should—though I believe I came very near it. But later on I burst all bounds, for the subject grew and grew. I went again before the good sisters ever did—I mean I went to Europe. I think I went twice, with a brief interval, before my fate again brought round for me a couple of days at Brookbridge. I had been there repeatedly, in the previous time, without making the acquaintance of the Rimmles; but now that I had had the revelation I couldn't have it too much, and the first request I preferred was to be taken again to see them. I remember well indeed the scruple I felt—the real delicacy—about betraying that *I* had, in the pride of my power, since our other meeting, stood, as their phrase went, among romantic scenes; but they were themselves the first to speak of it, and what moreover came home to me was that the coming and going of their friends in general—Brookbridge itself having even at that period one foot in Europe—was such as to place constantly before them the pleasure that was only postponed. They were thrown back after all on what the situation, under a final analysis, had most to give—the sense that, as every one kindly said to them and they kindly said to every one, Europe would keep. Every one felt for them so deeply that their own kindness in alleviating every one's feelings was really what came out most. Mrs Rimmle was still in her stiff chair and in the sunny parlour, but if *she* made no scruple of introducing the Italian lakes my heart sank to observe that she dealt with them, as a topic, not in the least in the leave-taking manner in which Falstaff babbled of green fields.

I'm not sure that after this my pretexts for a day or two with my sister-in-law weren't apt to be a mere cover for another glimpse of these particulars: I at any rate never went to Brookbridge without an irrepressible eagerness for our customary call. A long time seems to me thus to have passed, with glimpses and lapses, considerable impatience, and still more pity. Our visits indeed grew shorter, for, as my companion said, they were more and more of a strain. It finally struck me that the good sisters even shrank from me a little as from one who penetrated their consciousness in spite of himself. It was as if they knew where I thought they ought to be, and were moved to deprecate at last, by a systematic silence of that hemisphere, the criminality I fain would fix on them. They were full instead—as with the instinct of throwing dust in my eyes—of little pathetic hypocrisies about Brookbridge interests and delights. I dare say that as time went on my deeper sense of their situation came practically to rest on my companion's report of it. I certainly think I recollect every word we ever exchanged about them, even if I've lost the thread of the special occasions. The impression they made on me after each interval always broke out with extravagance as I walked away with her.

"*She* may be as old as she likes—I don't care. It's the fearful age the 'girls' are reaching that constitutes the scandal. One shouldn't pry into such matters, I know; but the years and the changes are really going. They're all growing old together—it will presently be too late; and their mother meanwhile perches over them like a vulture—what shall I call it?—calculating. Is she waiting for them successively to drop off? She'll survive them each and all. There's something too remorseless in it."

"Yes, but what do you want her to do? If the poor thing can't die she *can't*. Do you want her to take poison or to open a blood-vessel? I dare say she'd prefer to go."

"I beg your pardon," I must have replied; "you daren't say anything of the sort. If she'd prefer to go she *would* go. She'd feel the propriety, the decency, the necessity of going. She just prefers *not* to go. She prefers to stay and keep up the tension, and her calling them 'girls' and talking of the good time they'll still have is the mere conscious mischief of a subtle old witch. They won't have *any* time—there isn't any time to have! I mean there's, on her own part, no real loss of measure or of perspective in it. She *knows* she's a hundred and ten, and she takes a cruel pride in it."

My sister-in-law differed with me about this; she held that the old woman's attitude was an honest one and that her magnificent vitality, so great in spite of her infirmities, made it inevitable she should attribute youth to persons who had come into the world so much later. "Then suppose she should die?"—so my fellow student of the case always put it to me.

"Do you mean while her daughters are away? There's not the least fear of that—not even if at the very moment of their departure she should be *in extremis*. They'd find her all right on their return."

"But think how they'd feel not to have been with her?"

"That's only, I repeat, on the unsound assumption. If they'd only go tomorrow—literally make a good rush for it—they'll be with her when they come back. That will give them plenty of time." I'm afraid I even heartlessly added that if she *should*, against every probability, pass away in their absence they wouldn't have to come back at all—which would be just the compensation proper to their long privation. And then Maria would come out to join the two others, and they would be—though but for the too scanty remnant of their career—as merry as the day is long.

I remained ready, somehow, pending the fulfillment of that vision, to sacrifice Maria; it was only over the urgency of the case for the others respectively that I found myself balancing. Sometimes it was for Becky I thought the tragedy deepest—sometimes, and in quite a different manner, I thought it most dire for Jane. It was Jane after all who had most sense of life. I seemed in fact dimly to descry in Jane a sense—as yet undescribed by herself or by any one—of all sorts of queer things. Why didn't *she* go? I used desperately to ask; why didn't she make a bold personal dash for it, strike up a partnership with some one or other of the travelling spinsters in whom Brookbridge more and more abounded? Well, there came a flash for me at a particular point of the grey middle desert: my correspondent was able to let me know that poor Jane at last *had* sailed. She had gone of a sudden—I liked my sister-in-law's view of suddenness—with the kind Hathaways, who had made an irresistible grab at her and lifted her off her feet. They were going for the summer and for Mr Hathaway's health, so that the opportunity was perfect and it was impossible not to be glad that something very like physical force had finally prevailed. This was the general feeling at Brookbridge, and I might imagine what Brookbridge had been brought to from the fact that, at the very moment she was hustled off, the doctor, called to her mother at the peep of dawn, had considered that *he* at least must stay. There had been real alarm—greater than ever before; it actually did seem as if this time the end had come. But it was Becky, strange to say, who, though fully recognizing the nature of the crisis, had kept the situation in hand and insisted upon action. This, I remember, brought back to me a discomfort with which I had been familiar from the first. One of the two had sailed, and I was sorry it wasn't the other. But if it had been the other I should have been equally sorry.

I saw with my eyes that very autumn what a fool Jane would have been if she had again backed out. Her mother had of course survived the peril of which I had heard, profiting by it indeed as she had profited by every other; she was sufficiently better again to have come downstairs. It was there that, as usual, I found her, but with a difference of effect produced somehow by the absence of one of the girls. It was as if, for the others, though they hadn't gone to Europe, Europe had come to them: Jane's letters had been so frequent and so beyond even what could have been hoped. It was the first time, however, that I perceived on the old woman's part a certain failure of lucidity. Jane's flight was clearly the great fact with her, but she spoke of it as if the fruit had now been plucked and the parenthesis closed. I don't know what sinking sense of still further physical duration I gathered, as a menace, from this first hint of her confusion of mind.

"My daughter has been; my daughter has been—" She kept saying it, but didn't say where; that seemed unnecessary, and she only repeated the words to her visitors with a face that was all puckers and yet now, save in so far as it expressed an ineffaceable complacency, all blankness. I think she rather wanted us to know how little she had stood in the way. It added to something—I scarce knew what—that I found myself desiring to extract privately from Becky. As our visit was to be of the shortest my opportunity—for one of the young ladies always came to the door with us—was at hand. Mrs Rimmle, as we took leave, again sounded her phrase, but she added this time: "I'm so glad she's going to have always—"

I knew so well what she meant that, as she again dropped, looking at me queerly and becoming momentarily dim, I could help her out. "Going to have what *you* have?"

"Yes, yes—my privilege. Wonderful experience," she mumbled. She bowed to me a little as if I would understand. "She has things to tell."

I turned, slightly at a loss, to Becky. "She has then already arrived?"

Becky was at that moment looking a little strangely at her mother, who answered my question. "She reached New York this morning—she comes on today."

"Oh then—!" But I let the matter pass as I met Becky's eye—I saw there was a hitch somewhere. It was not she but Maria who came out with us; on which I cleared up the question of their sister's reappearance.

"Oh no, not tonight," Maria smiled; "that's only the way mother puts it. We shall see her about the end of November—the Hathaways are so indulgent. They kindly extend their tour."

"For *her* sake? How sweet of them!" my sister-in-law exclaimed.

I can see our friend's plain mild old face take on a deeper mildness, even though a higher colour, in the light of the open door. "Yes, it's for Jane they prolong it. And do you know what they write?" She gave us time, but it was too great a responsibility to guess. "Why, that it has brought her out."

"Oh, I knew it *would*!" my companion sympathetically sighed.

Maria put it more strongly still. "They say we wouldn't know her."

This sounded a little awful, but it was after all what I had expected.

III

My correspondent in Brookbridge came to me that Christmas, with my niece, to spend a week; and the arrangement had of course been prefaced by an exchange of letters, the first of which from my sister-in-law scarce took space for acceptance of my invitation before going on to say: "The Hathaways are back—but without Miss Jane!" She presented in a few words the situation thus created at Brookbridge, but was not yet, I gathered, fully in possession of the other one—the situation created in "Europe" by the presence there of that lady. The two together, however that might be, demanded, I quickly felt, all my attention, and perhaps my impatience to receive my relative was a little sharpened by my desire for the whole story. I had it at last, by the Christmas fire, and I may say without reserve that it gave me all I could have hoped for. I listened eagerly, after which I produced the comment: "Then she simply refused—"

"To budge from Florence? Simply. She had it out there with the poor Hathaways, who felt responsible for her safety, pledged to restore her to her mother's, to her sisters' hands, and showed herself in a light, they mention under their breath, that made their dear old hair stand on end. Do you know what, when they first got back, they said of her—at least it was *his* phrase—to two or three people?"

I thought for a moment. "That she had 'tasted blood'?"

My visitor fairly admired me. "How clever of you to guess! It's exactly what he did say. She appeared—she continues to appear, it seems—in a new character."

I wondered a little. "But that's exactly—don't you remember?—what Miss Maria reported to us from them; that we 'wouldn't know her.'"

My sister-in-law perfectly remembered. "Oh yes—she broke out from the first. But when they left her she was worse."

"Worse?"

"Well, different—different from anything she ever *had* been or—for that matter—had had a chance to be." My reporter hung fire a moment, but presently faced me. "Rather strange and free and obstreperous."

"Obstreperous?" I wondered again.

"Peculiarly so, I inferred, on the question of not coming away. She wouldn't hear of it and, when they spoke of her mother, said she had given her mother up. She had thought she should like Europe, but didn't know she should like it so much. They had been fools to bring her if they expected to take her away. She was going to see what she could—she hadn't yet seen half. The end of it at any rate was that they had to leave her alone."

I seemed to see it all—to see even the scared Hathaways. "So she *is* alone?"

"She told them, poor thing, it appears, and in a tone they'll never forget, that she was in any case quite old enough to be. She cried—she quite went on—over not having come sooner. That's why the only way for her," my companion mused, "*is*, I suppose, to stay. They wanted to put her with some people or other—to find some American family. But she says she's on her own feet."

"And she's still in Florence?"

"No—I believe she was to travel. She's bent on the East."

I burst out laughing. "Magnificent Jane! It's most interesting. Only I feel that I distinctly *should* 'know' her. To my sense, always, I must tell you, she had it in her."

My relative was silent a little. "So it now appears Becky always felt."

"And yet pushed her off? Magnificent Becky!"

My companion met my eyes a moment. "You don't know the queerest part. I mean the way it has *most* brought her out."

I turned it over; I felt I should like to know—to that degree indeed that, oddly enough, I jocosely disguised my eagerness. "You don't mean she has taken to drink?"

My visitor had a dignity—and yet had to have a freedom. "She has taken to flirting."

I expressed disappointment. "Oh she took to *that* long ago. Yes," I declared at my kinswoman's stare, "she positively flirted—with me!"

The stare perhaps sharpened. "Then you flirted with *her*?"

"How else could I have been as sure as I wanted to be? But has she means?"

"Means to flirt?"—my friend looked an instant as if she spoke literally. "I don't understand about the means—though of course they have something. But I have my impression," she went on. "I think that Becky—" It seemed almost too grave to say.

But *I* had no doubts. "That Becky's backing her?"

She brought it out. "Financing her."

"Stupendous Becky! So that morally then—"

"Becky's quite in sympathy. But isn't it too odd?" my sister-in-law asked.

"Not in the least. Didn't we know, as regards Jane, that Europe was to bring her out? Well, it has also brought out Rebecca."

"It has indeed!" my companion indulgently sighed. "So what would it do if she were there?"

"I should like immensely to see. And we *shall* see."

"Do you believe then she'll still go?"

"Certainly. She *must*."

But my friend shook it off. "She won't."

"She shall!" I retorted with a laugh. But the next moment I said: "And what does the old woman say?"

"To Jane's behaviour? Not a word—never speaks of it. She talks now much less than she used—only seems to wait. But it's my belief she thinks."

"And—do you mean—knows?"

"Yes, knows she's abandoned. In her silence there she takes it in."

"It's her way of making Jane pay?" At this, somehow, I felt more serious. "Oh dear, dear—she'll disinherit her!"

When in the following June I went on to return my sister-in-law's visit the first object that met my eyes in her little white parlour was a figure that, to my stupefaction, presented itself for the moment as that of Mrs Rimmle. I had gone to my room after arriving and had come down when dressed; the apparition I speak of had arisen in the interval. Its ambiguous character lasted, however, but a second or two—I had taken Becky for her mother because I knew no one but her mother of that extreme age. Becky's age was quite startling; it had made a great stride, though, strangely enough, irrecoverably seated as she now was in it, she had a wizened brightness that I had scarcely yet seen in her. I remember indulging on this occasion in two silent observations: one on the article of my not having hitherto been conscious of her full resemblance to the old lady, and the other to the effect that, as I had said to my sister-in-law at Christmas, "Europe," even as reaching her only through Jane's sensibilities, had really at last brought her out. She was in fact "out" in a manner of which this encounter offered to my eyes a unique example: it was the single hour, often as I had been at Brookbridge, of my meeting her elsewhere than in her mother's drawing-room. I surmise that, besides being adjusted to her more marked time of life, the garments she wore abroad, and in particular her little plain bonnet, presented points of resemblance to the close sable sheath and the quaint old headgear that, in the white house behind the elms, I had from far back associated with the eternal image in the stiff chair. Of course I immediately spoke of Jane, showing an interest and asking for news; on which she answered me with a smile, but not at all as I had expected.

"*Those* are not really the things you want to know—where she is, whom she's with, how she manages, and where she's going next—oh, no!" And the admirable woman gave a laugh that was somehow both light and sad—sad, in particular, with a strange long weariness. "What you do want to know is when she's coming back."

I shook my head very kindly, but out of a wealth of experience that, I flattered myself, was equal to Miss Becky's. "I do know it. Never."

Miss Becky exchanged with me at this a long deep look. "Never."

We had, in silence, a little luminous talk about it, at the end of which she seemed to have told me the most interesting things. "And how's your mother?" I then enquired.

She hesitated, but finally spoke with the same serenity. "My mother's all right. You see she's not alive."

"Oh Becky!" my sister-in-law pleadingly interjected.

But Becky only addressed herself to me. "Come and see if she is. *I* think she isn't—but Maria perhaps isn't so clear. Come at all events and judge and tell me."

It was a new note, and I was a little bewildered. "Ah, but I'm not a doctor!"

"No, thank God—you're not. That's why I ask you." And now she said good-bye.

I kept her hand a moment. "*You're* more alive than ever!"

"I'm very tired." She took it with the same smile, but for Becky it was much to say.

IV

"Not alive," the next day, was certainly what Mrs Rimmle looked when, arriving in pursuit of my promise, I found her, with Miss Maria, in her usual place. Though wasted and shrunken she still occupied her high-backed chair with a visible theory of erectness, and her intensely aged face—combined with something dauntless that belonged to her very presence and that was effective even in this extremity—might have been that of some immemorial sovereign, of indistinguishable sex, brought forth to be shown to people in disproof of the rumour of extinction. Mummified and open-eyed she looked at me, but I had no impression that she made me out. I had come this time without my sister-in-law, who had frankly pleaded to me—which also, for a daughter of Brookbridge, was saying much—that the house had grown too painful. Poor Miss Maria excused Miss Becky on the score of her not being well—and that, it struck me, was saying most of all. The absence of the others gave the occasion a different note; but I talked with Miss Maria for five minutes and recognized that—save for her saying, of her own movement, anything about Jane—she now spoke as if her mother had lost hearing or sense, in fact both, alluding freely and distinctly, though indeed favourably, to her condition. "She has expected your visit and much enjoys it," my entertainer said, while the old woman, soundless and motionless, simply fixed me without expression. Of course there was little to keep me; but I became aware as I rose to go that there was more than I had supposed.

On my approaching her to take leave Mrs Rimmle gave signs of consciousness. "Have you heard about Jane?"

I hesitated, feeling a responsibility, and appealed for direction to Maria's face. But Maria's face was troubled, was turned altogether to her mother's. "About her life in Europe?" I then rather helplessly asked.

The old lady fronted me on this in a manner that made me feel silly. "Her life?"—and her voice, with this second effort, came out stronger. "Her death, if you please."

"Her death?" I echoed, before I could stop myself, with the accent of deprecation.

Miss Maria uttered a vague sound of pain, and I felt her turn away, but the marvel of her mother's little unquenched spark still held me. "Jane's dead. We've heard," said Mrs Rimmle. "We've heard from—where is it we've heard from?" She had quite revived—she appealed to her daughter.

The poor old girl, crimson, rallied to her duty. "From Europe."

Mrs Rimmle made at us both a little grim inclination of the head. "From Europe." I responded, in silence, by a deflection from every rigour, and, still holding me, she went on: "And now Rebecca's going."

She had gathered by this time such emphasis to say it that again, before I could help myself, I vibrated in reply. "To Europe—now?" It was as if for an instant she had made me believe it.

She only stared at me, however, from her wizened mask; then her eyes followed my companion. "Has she gone?"

"Not yet, mother." Maria tried to treat it as a joke, but her smile was embarrassed and dim.

"Then where is she?"

"She's lying down."

The old woman kept up her hard queer gaze, but directing it after a minute at me. "She's going."

"Oh, some day!" I foolishly laughed; and on this I got to the door, where I separated from my younger hostess, who came no further.

Only, as I held the door open, she said to me under cover of it and very quietly: "It's poor mother's idea."

I saw—it was her idea. Mine was—for some time after this, even after I had returned to New York and to my usual occupations—that I should never again see Becky. I had seen her for the last time, I believed, under my sister-in-law's roof, and in the autumn it was given to me to hear from that fellow admirer that she had succumbed at last to the situation. The day of the call I have just described had been a date in the process of her slow shrinkage—it was literally the first time she had, as they said at Brookbridge, given up. She had been ill for years, but the other state of health in the contemplation of which she had spent so much of her life had left her till too late no margin for heeding it. The power of attention came at last simply in the form of the discovery that it *was* too late; on which, naturally, she had given up more and more. I had heard indeed, for weeks before, by letter, how Brookbridge had watched her do so; in consequence of which the end found me in a manner prepared. Yet in spite of my preparation there remained with me a soreness, and when I was next—it was some six months later—on the scene of her martyrdom I fear I replied with an almost rabid negative to the question put to me in due course by my kinswoman. "Call on them? Never again!"

I went none the less the very next day. Everything was the same in the sunny parlour—everything that most mattered, I mean: the centenarian mummy in the high chair and the tributes, in the little frames on the walls, to the celebrity of its late husband. Only Maria Rimmle was different; if Becky, on my last seeing her, had looked as old as her mother, Maria—save that she moved about—looked older.

I remember she moved about, but I scarce remember what she said; and indeed what was there to say? When I risked a question, however, she found a reply.

"But *now* at least—?" I tried to put it to her suggestively.

At first she was vague, "'Now'?"

"Won't Miss Jane come back?"

Oh, the headshake she gave me! "Never." It positively pictured to me, for the instant, a well-preserved woman, a rich ripe *seconde jeunesse* by the Arno.

"Then that's only to make more sure of your finally joining her."

Maria Rimmle repeated her headshake. "Never."

We stood so a moment bleakly face to face; I could think of no attenuation that would be particularly happy. But while I tried I heard a hoarse gasp that fortunately relieved me—a signal strange and at first formless from the occupant of the high-backed chair. "Mother wants to speak to you," Maria then said.

So it appeared from the drop of the old woman's jaw, the expression of her mouth opened as if for the emission of sound. It was somehow difficult for me to seem to sympathize without hypocrisy, but, so far as a step nearer could do that, I invited communication. "Have you heard where Becky's gone?" the wonderful witch's white lips then extraordinarily asked.

It drew from Maria, as on my previous visits, an uncontrollable groan, and this in turn made me take time to consider. As I considered, however, I had an inspiration. "To Europe?"

I must have adorned it with a strange grimace, but my inspiration had been right. "To Europe," said Mrs Rimmle.

1899

Kate Chopin

1851–1904

Kate Chopin was born in St Louis, Missouri. Her father was a successful merchant who had emigrated from Ireland, and her mother was a prominent member of the French-Creole community. Her father died in a train accident on the inaugural journey of the Pacific Railroad when she was a young child. At the age of nineteen she married Oscar Chopin, a cotton factor for plantation owners, with whom she had six children. Taking up writing after the death of her husband, she published her first work, a poem, in the Chicago periodical *America* in 1889. In her first novel she addressed the radical themes of women's emancipation and the issue of marital fidelity and divorce, themes she would continue to explore throughout her career. She is best known for her 1899 novel *The Awakening*, an account of a young married woman whose life is irrevocably changed when she finds herself attracted to a young Creole man. With its theme of sexual liberation the novel was considered scandalous and even pornographic, and Chopin was publicly denounced as immoral and perverse. So extreme was the critical abuse that she slowly abandoned writing. She died of a cerebral hemorrhage at the age of fifty-three. She was rediscovered by the reading public when her complete works were reissued in two volumes in 1969.

Beyond the Bayou

The bayou curved like a crescent around the point of land on which La Folle's cabin stood. Between the stream and the hut lay a big abandoned field, where cattle were pastured when the bayou supplied them with water enough. Through the woods that spread back into unknown regions the woman had drawn an imaginary line, and past this circle she never stepped. This was the form of her only mania.

She was now a large, gaunt black woman, past thirty-five. Her real name was Jacqueline, but every one on the plantation called her La Folle, because in childhood she had been frightened literally "out of her senses," and had never wholly regained them.

It was when there had been skirmishing and sharpshooting all day in the woods. Evening was near when P'tit Maître, black with powder and crimson with blood, had staggered into the cabin of Jacqueline's mother, his pursuers close at his heels. The sight had stunned her childish reason.

She dwelt alone in her solitary cabin, for the rest of the quarters had long since been removed beyond her sight and knowledge. She had more physical strength than most men, and made her patch of cotton and corn and tobacco like the best of them. But of the world beyond the bayou she had long known nothing, save what her morbid fancy conceived.

People at Bellissime had grown used to her and her way, and they thought nothing of it. Even when "Old Mis' " died, they did not wonder that La Folle had not crossed the bayou, but had stood upon her side of it, wailing and lamenting.

P'tit Maître was now the owner of Bellissime. He was a middle-aged man, with a family of beautiful daughters about him, and a little son whom La Folle loved as if he had been her own. She called him Chéri, and so did every one else because she did.

None of the girls had ever been to her what Chéri was. They had each and all loved to be with her, and to listen to her wondrous stories of things that always happened "yonda, beyon' de bayou."

But none of them had stroked her black hand quite as Chéri did, nor rested their heads against her knee so confidingly, nor fallen asleep in her arms as he used to do. For Chéri hardly did such things now, since he had become the proud possessor of a gun, and had had his black curls cut off.

That summer—the summer Chéri gave La Folle two black curls tied with a knot of red ribbon—the water ran so low in the bayou that even the little children at Bellissime were able to cross it on foot, and the cattle were sent to pasture down by the river. La Folle was sorry when they were gone, for she loved these dumb companions well, and liked to feel that they were there, and to hear them browsing by night up to her own inclosure.

It was Saturday afternoon, when the fields were deserted. The men had flocked to a neighbouring village to do their week's trading, and the women were occupied with household affairs,—La Folle as well as the others. It was then she mended and washed her handful of clothes, scoured her house, and did her baking.

In this last employment she never forgot Chéri. Today she had fashioned croquignoles of the most fantastic and alluring shapes for him. So when she saw the boy come trudging across the old field with his gleaming little new rifle on his shoulder, she called out gaily to him, "Chéri! Chéri!"

But Chéri did not need the summons, for he was coming straight to her. His pockets all bulged out with almonds and raisins and an orange that he had secured for her from the very fine dinner which had been given that day up at his father's house.

He was a sunny-faced youngster of ten. When he had emptied his pockets, La Folle patted his round red cheek, wiped his soiled hands on her apron, and smoothed his hair. Then she watched him as, with his cakes in his hand, he crossed her strip of cotton back of the cabin, and disappeared into the wood.

He had boasted of the things he was going to do with his gun out there.

"You think they got plenty deer in the wood, La Folle?" he had inquired, with the calculating air of an experienced hunter.

"*Non, non!*" the woman laughed. "Don't you look fo' no deer, Chéri. Dat's too big. But you bring La Folle one good fat squirrel fo' her dinner tomorrow, an' she goin' be satisfi'."

"One squirrel ain't a bite. I'll bring you mo' 'an one, La Folle," he had boasted pompously as he went away.

When the woman, an hour later, heard the report of the boy's rifle close to the wood's edge, she would have thought nothing of it if a sharp cry of distress had not followed the sound.

She withdrew her arms from the tub of suds in which they had been plunged, dried them upon her apron, and as quickly as her trembling limbs would bear her, hurried to the spot whence the ominous report had come.

It was as she feared. There she found Chéri stretched upon the ground, with his rifle beside him. He moaned piteously:—

"I'm dead, La Folle! I'm dead! I'm gone!"

"*Non, non!*" she exclaimed resolutely, as she knelt beside him. "Put you' arm 'roun' La Folle's nake, Chéri. Dat's nuttin'; dat goin' be nuttin'." She lifted him in her powerful arms.

Chéri had carried his gun muzzle-downward. He had stumbled,—he did not know how. He only knew that he had a ball lodged somewhere in his leg, and he thought that his end was at hand. Now, with his head upon the woman's shoulder, he moaned and wept with pain and fright.

"Oh, La Folle! La Folle! it hurt so bad! I can' stan' it, La Folle!"

"Don't cry, *mon bébé, mon bébé, mon Chéri*!" the woman spoke soothingly as she covered the ground with long strides. "La Folle goin' mine you; Doctor Bonfils goin' come make *mon Chéri* well again."

She had reached the abandoned field. As she crossed it with her precious burden, she looked constantly and restlessly from side to side. A terrible fear was upon her,—the fear of the world beyond the bayou, the morbid and insane dread she had been under since childhood.

When she was at the bayou's edge she stood there, and shouted for help as if a life depended upon it:—

"Oh, P'tit Maître! P'tit Maître! Venez donc! Au secours! Au secours!"

No voice responded. Chéri's hot tears were scalding her neck. She called for each and every one upon the place, and still no answer came.

She shouted, she wailed; but whether her voice remained unheard or unheeded, no reply came to her frenzied cries. And all the while Chéri moaned and wept and entreated to be taken home to his mother.

La Folle gave a last despairing look around her. Extreme terror was upon her. She clasped the child close against her breast, where he could feel her heart beat like a muffled hammer. Then shutting her eyes, she ran suddenly down the shallow bank of the bayou, and never stopped till she had climbed the opposite shore.

She stood there quivering an instant as she opened her eyes. Then she plunged into the footpath through the trees.

She spoke no more to Chéri, but muttered constantly, "Bon Dieu, ayez pitié La Folle! Bon Dieu, ayez pitié moi!"

Instinct seemed to guide her. When the pathway spread clear and smooth enough before her, she again closed her eyes tightly against the sight of that unknown and terrifying world.

A child, playing in some weeds, caught sight of her as she neared the quarters. The little one uttered a cry of dismay.

"La Folle!" she screamed, in her piercing treble. "La Folle done cross de bayer!"

Quickly the cry passed down the line of cabins.

"Yonda, La Folle done cross de bayou!"

Children, old men, old women, young ones with infants in their arms, flocked to doors and windows to see this awe-inspiring spectacle. Most of them shuddered with superstitious dread of what it might portend. "She totin' Chéri!" some of them shouted.

Some of the more daring gathered about her, and followed at her heels, only to fall back with new terror when she turned her distorted face upon them. Her eyes were bloodshot and the saliva had gathered in a white foam on her black lips.

Some one had run ahead of her to where P'tit Maître sat with his family and guests upon the gallery.

"P'tit Maître! La Folle done cross de bayou! Look her! Look her yonda totin' Chéri!" This startling intimation was the first which they had of the woman's approach.

She was now near at hand. She walked with long strides. Her eyes were fixed desperately before her, and she breathed heavily, as a tired ox.

At the foot of the stairway, which she could not have mounted, she laid the boy in his father's arms. Then the world that had looked red to La Folle suddenly turned black,—like that day she had seen powder and blood.

She reeled for an instant. Before a sustaining arm could reach her, she fell heavily to the ground.

When La Folle regained consciousness, she was at home again, in her own cabin and upon her own bed. The moon rays, streaming in through the open door and windows, gave what light was needed to the old black mammy who stood at the table concocting a tisane of fragrant herbs. It was very late.

Others who had come, and found that the stupor clung to her, had gone again. P'tit Maître had been there, and with him Doctor Bonfils, who said that La Folle might die.

But death had passed her by. The voice was very clear and steady with which she spoke to Tante Lizette, brewing her tisane there in a corner.

"Ef you will give one good drink tisane, Tante Lizette, I b'lieve I'm goin' sleep, me."

And she did sleep; so soundly, so healthfully, that old Lizette without compunction stole softly away, to creep back through the moonlit fields to her own cabin in the new quarters.

The first touch of the cool grey morning awoke La Folle. She arose, calmly, as if no tempest had shaken and threatened her existence but yesterday.

She donned her new blue cottonade and white apron, for she remembered that this was Sunday. When she had made for herself a cup of strong black coffee, and drunk it with relish, she quitted the cabin and walked across the old familiar field to the bayou's edge again.

She did not stop there as she had always done before, but crossed with a long, steady stride as if she had done this all her life.

When she had made her way through the brush and scrub cottonwood trees that lined the opposite bank, she found herself upon the border of a field where the white, bursting cotton, with the dew upon it, gleamed for acres and acres like frosted silver in the early dawn.

La Folle drew a long, deep breath as she gazed across the country. She walked slowly and uncertainly, like one who hardly knows how, looking about her as she went.

The cabins, that yesterday had sent a clamour of voices to pursue her, were quiet now. No one was yet astir at Bellissime. Only the birds that darted here and there from hedges were awake, and singing their matins.

When La Folle came to the broad stretch of velvety lawn that surrounded the house, she moved slowly and with delight over the springy turf, that was delicious beneath her tread.

She stopped to find whence came those perfumes that were assailing her senses with memories from a time far gone.

There they were, stealing up to her from the thousand blue violets that peeped out from green, luxuriant beds. There they were, showering down from the big waxen bells of the magnolias far above her head, and from the jessamine clumps around her.

There were roses, too, without number. To right and left palms spread in broad and graceful curves. It all looked like enchantment beneath the sparkling sheen of dew.

When La Folle had slowly and cautiously mounted the many steps that led up to the veranda, she turned to look back at the perilous ascent she had made. Then she caught sight of the river, bending like a silver bow at the foot of Bellissime. Exultation possessed her soul.

La Folle rapped softly upon a door near at hand. Chéri's mother soon cautiously opened it. Quickly and cleverly she dissembled the astonishment she felt at seeing La Folle.

"Ah, La Folle! Is it you, so early?"

"*Oui*, madame. I come ax how my po' li'le Chéri to, 's mo'nin'."

"He is feeling easier, thank you, La Folle. Dr Bonfils says it will be nothing serious. He's sleeping now. Will you come back when he awakes?"

"*Non*, madame. I'm goin' wait yair tell Chéri wake up." La Folle seated herself upon the topmost step of the veranda.

A look of wonder and deep content crept into her face as she watched for the first time the sun rise upon the new, the beautiful world beyond the bayou.

1894

Joseph Conrad

1857–1924

That Joseph Conrad was a strange man—throwing a newborn son's baby clothes out a train window—and a unique writer (to extrapolate from Frederic Jameson, perhaps the first and only "pre-postmodernist") is not exactly hot literary news. But the permutations of his extraordinariness seem endlessly exciting and endlessly frightening, since this Polish-born writer was bent on eroding differences, not on a social or political level, but between barbarism and civilization, between the organic and the inanimate, between, it almost seems, space and time itself. If it had been possible, Conrad would have collapsed the more impervious and absolute dualities of his life: Poland and England, Dostoevsky and James. Given his deep epistemological radicalism, Conrad's blurring of genres is hardly surprising; as Gail Fraser admirably describes, "story," "tale," and "novel," have an unstable position in Conrad's narrative lexicon. He had enormous respect for the literary possibilities of short fiction and perhaps even more for the opportunities it presented for popular, and therefore financial, success. Just as important was the issue of cultural success. He saw these literary possibilities realized in such figures as Maupassant, Flaubert, and Turgenev. Masters of short narrative, to Conrad they were compelling figures of achievement and sophistication.

The road to Conrad's approximations of the literary gentleman was tumultuous, his decisions en route often deeply courageous. Born Josef Teodor Konrad Korzeniowski, he was orphaned at age twelve, his mother dying from the brutal conditions of the family's political exile in northern Russia, his father—a translator, a poet, and a devout Polish nationalist—dying four years later. At seventeen

"Conrad" set out for Marseilles and a career first in the French merchant service, then in the British merchant navy. Perpetually addicted to various "destructive elements," he was involved in gun-running exploits for the Spanish Carlists and made his now legendary voyage along the Congo in 1890. Just before, he began writing *Almayer's Folly* (1895)—in English, creating an astonishing precedent for the linguistic transformations of subsequent writers such as Beckett, Koestler, and Nabokov. When the novel was accepted for publication in 1894, Conrad brought his maritime life to an end. He married Jessie George and, despite a tangled, oppressive domestic life, wrote a series of remarkable novels and short stories, among them "Heart of Darkness" (1899), *Lord Jim* (1900), *Typhoon and Other Stories* (1903), *Chance* (1913), and *Victory* (1915). *Nostromo* (1904) is probably even more consummately modernist than is *Ulysses*, and *The Secret Agent* (1907) the most complete expression of irony since Swift's *A Modest Proposal*.

An Outpost of Progress

I

There were two white men in charge of the trading station. Kayerts, the chief, was short and fat; Carlier, the assistant, was tall, with a large head and a very broad trunk perched upon a long pair of thin legs. The third man on the staff was a Sierra Leone nigger, who maintained that his name was Henry Price. However, for some reason or other, the natives down the river had given him the name of Makola, and it stuck to him through all his wanderings about the country. He spoke English and French with a warbling accent, wrote a beautiful hand, understood bookkeeping, and cherished in his innermost heart the worship of evil spirits. His wife was a negress from Loanda, very large and very noisy. Three children rolled about in sunshine before the door of his low, shed-like dwelling. Makola, taciturn and impenetrable, despised the two white men. He had charge of a small clay storehouse with a dried-grass roof, and pretended to keep a correct account of beads, cotton cloth, red kerchiefs, brass wire, and other trade goods it contained. Besides the storehouse and Makola's hut, there was only one large building in the cleared ground of the station. It was built neatly of reeds, with a veranda on all the four sides. There were three rooms in it. The one in the middle was the living room, and had two rough tables and a few stools in it. The other two were the bedrooms for the white men. Each had a bedstead and a mosquito net for all furniture. The plank floor was littered with the belongings of the white men: open half-empty boxes, torn wearing apparel, old boots; all the things dirty, and all the things broken, that accumulate mysteriously round untidy men. There was also another dwelling-place some distance away from the buildings. In it, under a tall cross much out of the perpendicular, slept the man who had seen the beginning of all this; who had planned and had watched the construction of this outpost of progress. He had been, at home, an unsuccessful painter who, weary of pursuing fame on an empty stomach, had gone out there through high protections. He had been the first chief of that station. Makola had watched the energetic artist die of fever in the just finished house with his usual kind of "I told you so" indifference. Then, for a time, he dwelt alone with his family, his account books, and the Evil Spirit that rules the lands under the equator. He got on very well with his god. Perhaps he had propitiated him by a promise of more white men to play with, by and by. At any rate the director of the Great Trading Company, coming up in a steamer that resembled an enormous sardine box with a flat-roofed shed erected on it, found the station in good order, and Makola as usual quietly diligent. The director had the cross put up over the first agent's grave, and appointed Kayerts to the post. Carlier was told off as second in charge. The director was a man ruthless and efficient, who at times, but very imperceptibly, indulged in grim humour. He made a speech to Kayerts and Carlier, pointing out to them the promising aspect of their station. The nearest trading-post was about three hundred miles away. It was an exceptional opportunity for them to distinguish themselves and to earn percentages on the trade. This appointment was a favour done to beginners. Kayerts was moved almost to tears by his director's kindness. He would, he said, by doing his best, try to justify the flattering confidence, etc., etc. Kayerts had been in the Administration of the Telegraphs, and knew how to express himself correctly. Carlier, an ex-non-commissioned officer of cavalry in an army guaranteed from harm by several European Powers, was less impressed. If there were commissions to get, so much the better; and, trailing a sulky glance over the river, the forests, the impenetrable bush that seemed to cut off the station from the rest of the world, he muttered between his teeth, "We shall see, very soon."

Next day, some bales of cotton goods and a few cases of provisions having been thrown on shore, the sardine-box steamer went off, not to return for another six months. On the deck the director touched his cap to the two agents, who stood on the bank waving their hats, and turning to an old servant of the Company on his passage to headquarters, said, "Look at those two imbeciles. They must be mad at home to send me such specimens. I told those fellows to plant a vegetable garden, build new storehouses and fences, and construct a landing stage. I bet nothing will be done! They won't know how to begin. I always thought the station on this river useless, and they just fit the station!"

"They will form themselves there," said the old stager with a quiet smile.

"At any rate, I am rid of them for six months," retorted the director.

The two men watched the steamer round the bend, then, ascending arm in arm the slope of the bank, returned to the station. They had been in this vast and dark country only a very short time, and as yet always in the midst of other white men, under the eye and guidance of their superiors. And now, dull as they were to the subtle influences of surroundings, they felt themselves very much alone, when suddenly left unassisted to face the wilderness; a wilderness rendered more strange, more incomprehensible by the mysterious glimpses of the vigorous life it contained. They were two perfectly insignificant and incapable individuals, whose existence is only rendered possible through the high organization of civilized crowds. Few men realize that their life, the very essence of their character, their capabilities and their audacities, are only the expression of their belief in the safety of their surroundings. The courage, the composure, the confidence; the emotions and principles; every great and every insignificant thought belongs not to the individual but to the crowd: to the crowd that believes blindly in the irresistible force of its institutions and of its morals, in the power of its police and of its opinion. But the contact with pure unmitigated savagery, with primitive nature and primitive man, brings sudden and profound trouble into the heart. To the sentiment of being alone of one's kind, to the clear perception of the loneliness of one's thoughts, of one's sensations—to the negation of the habitual, which is safe, there is added the affirmation of the unusual, which is dangerous; a suggestion of things vague, uncontrollable, and repulsive, whose discomposing intrusion excites the imagination and tries the civilized nerves of the foolish and the wise alike.

Kayerts and Carlier walked arm in arm, drawing close to one another as children do in the dark; and they had the same, not altogether unpleasant, sense of danger which one half suspects to be imaginary. They chatted persistently in familiar tones. "Our station is prettily situated," said one. The other assented with enthusiasm, enlarging volubly on the beauties of the situation. Then they passed near the grave. "Poor devil!" said Kayerts. "He died of fever, didn't he?" muttered Carlier, stopping short. "Why," retorted Kayerts, with indignation, "I've been told that the fellow exposed himself recklessly to the sun. The climate here, everybody says, is not at all worse than at home, as long as you keep out of the sun. Do you hear that, Carlier? I am chief here, and my orders are that you should not expose yourself to the sun!" He assumed his superiority jocularly, but his meaning was serious. The idea that he would, perhaps, have to bury Carlier and remain alone, gave him an inward shiver. He felt suddenly that this Carlier was more precious to him here, in the centre of Africa, than a brother could be anywhere else. Carlier, entering into the spirit of the thing, made a military salute and answered in a brisk tone, "Your orders shall be attended to, chief!" Then he burst out laughing, slapped Kayerts on the back and shouted, "We shall let life run easily here! Just sit still and gather in the ivory those savages will bring. This country has its good points, after all!" They both laughed loudly while Carlier thought: That poor Kayerts; he is so fat and unhealthy. It would be awful if I had to bury him here. He is a man I respect. . . . Before they reached the veranda of their house they called one another "my dear fellow."

The first day they were very active, pottering about with hammers and nails and red calico, to put up curtains, make their house habitable and pretty; resolved to settle down comfortably to their new life. For them an impossible task. To grapple effectually with even purely material problems requires more serenity of mind and more lofty courage than people generally imagine. No two beings could have been more unfitted for such a struggle. Society, not from any tenderness, but because of its strange needs, had taken care of those two men, forbidding them all independent thought, all initiative, all departure from routine; and forbidding it under pain of death. They could only live on condition of being machines. And now, released from the fostering care of men with pens behind their ears, or of men with gold lace on the sleeves, they were like those lifelong prisoners who, liberated after many years, do not know what use to make of their freedom. They did not know what use to make of their faculties, being both, through want of practice, incapable of independent thought.

At the end of two months Kayerts often would say, "If it was not for my Melie, you wouldn't catch me here." Melie was his daughter. He had thrown up his post in the Administration of the Telegraphs, though he had been for seventeen years perfectly happy there, to earn a dowry for his girl. His wife was dead, and the child was being brought up by his sisters. He regretted the streets, the pavements, the cafés, his friends of many years; all the things he used to see, day after day; all the thoughts suggested by familiar things—the thoughts effortless, monotonous, and soothing of a Government clerk; he regretted all the gossip, the small enmities, the mild venom, and the little jokes of Government offices. "If I had had a decent brother-in-law," Carlier would remark, "a fellow with a heart, I would not be here." He had left the army and had made himself so obnoxious to his family by his laziness and impudence, that an exasperated brother-in-law had made superhuman efforts to procure him an appointment in the Company as a second-class agent. Having not a penny in the world he was compelled to accept this means of livelihood as soon as it became quite clear to him that there was nothing more to squeeze out of his relations. He, like Kayerts, regretted his old life. He regretted the clink of sabre and spurs on a fine afternoon, the barrack-room witticisms, the girls of garrison towns; but, besides, he had also a sense of grievance. He was evidently a much ill-used man. This made him moody, at times. But the two men got on well together in the fellowship of their stupidity and laziness. Together they did nothing, absolutely nothing, and enjoyed the sense of the idleness for which they were paid. And in time they came to feel something resembling affection for one another.

They lived like blind men in a large room, aware only of what came in contact with them (and of that only imperfectly), but unable to see the general aspect of things. The river, the forest, all the great land throbbing with life, were like a great emptiness. Even the brilliant sunshine disclosed nothing intelligible. Things appeared and disappeared before their eyes in an unconnected and aimless kind of way. The river seemed to come from nowhere and flow nowhither. It flowed through a void. Out of that void, at times, came canoes, and men with spears in their hands would suddenly crowd the yard of the station. They were naked, glossy black, ornamented with snowy shells and glistening brass wire, perfect of limb. They made an uncouth babbling noise when they spoke, moved in a stately manner, and sent quick, wild glances out of their startled, never-resting eyes. Those warriors would squat in long rows, four or more deep, before the veranda, while their chiefs bargained for hours with Makola over an elephant tusk. Kayerts sat on his chair and looked down on the proceedings, understanding nothing. He stared at them with his round blue eyes, called out to Carlier, "Here, look! look at that fellow there—and that other one, to the left. Did you ever see such a face? Oh, the funny brute!"

Carlier, smoking native tobacco in a short wooden pipe, would swagger up twirling his moustaches, and surveying the warriors with haughty indulgence, would say—

"Fine animals. Brought any bone? Yes? It's not any too soon. Look at the muscles of that fellow—third from the end. I wouldn't care to get a punch on the nose from him. Fine arms, but legs no good below the knee. Couldn't make cavalry men of them." And after glancing down complacently at his own shanks, he always concluded: "Pah! Don't they stink! You. Makola! Take that herd over to the fetish" (the storehouse was in every station called the fetish, perhaps because of the spirit of civilization it contained) "and give them up some of the rubbish you keep there. I'd rather see it full of bone than full of rags."

Kayerts approved.

"Yes, yes! Go and finish that palaver over there, Mr Makola. I will come round when you are ready, to weigh the tusk. We must be careful." Then turning to his companion: "This is the tribe that lives down the river; they are rather aromatic. I remember, they had been once before here. D'ye hear that row? What a fellow has got to put up with in this dog of a country! My head is split."

Such profitable visits were rare. For days the two pioneers of trade and progress would look on their empty courtyard in the vibrating brilliance of vertical sunshine. Below the high bank, the silent river flowed on glittering and steady. On the sands in the middle of the stream, hippos and alligators sunned themselves side by side. And stretching away in all directions, surrounding the insignificant cleared spot of the trading post, immense forests, hiding fateful complications of fantastic life, lay in the eloquent silence of mute greatness. The two men understood nothing, cared for nothing but for the passage of days that separated them from the steamer's return. Their predecessor had left some torn books. They took up these wrecks of novels, and, as they had never read anything of the kind before, they were surprised and amused. Then during long days there were interminable and silly discussions about plots and personages. In the centre of Africa they made acquaintance of Richelieu and d'Artagnan, of Hawk's Eye and of Father Goriot, and of many other people. All these imaginary personages became subjects for gossip as if they had been living friends. They discounted their virtues, suspected their motives, decried their successes; were scandalized at their duplicity or were doubtful about their courage. The accounts of crimes filled them with indignation, while tender or pathetic passages moved them deeply. Carlier cleared his throat and said in a soldierly voice, "What nonsense!" Kayerts, his round eyes suffused with tears, his fat cheeks quivering, rubbed his bald head, and declared, "This is a splendid book. I had no idea there were such clever fellows in the world." They also found some old copies of a home paper. That print discussed what it was pleased to call "Our Colonial Expansion" in high-flown language. It spoke much of the rights and duties of civilization, of the sacredness of the civilizing work, and extolled the merits of those who went about bringing light, and faith and commerce to the dark places of the earth. Carlier and Kayerts read, wondered, and began to think better of themselves. Carlier said one evening, waving his hand about, "In a hundred years, there will be perhaps a town here. Quays, and warehouses, and barracks, and—and—billiard rooms. Civilization, my boy, and virtue—and all. And then, chaps will read that two good fellows, Kayerts and Carlier, were the first civilized men to live in this very spot!" Kayerts nodded, "Yes, it is a consolation to think that." They seemed to forget their dead predecessor; but, early one day, Carlier went out and replanted the cross firmly. "It used to make me squint whenever I walked that way," he explained to Kayerts over the morning coffee. "It made me squint, leaning over so much. So I just planted it upright. And solid, I promise you! I suspended myself with both hands to the crosspiece. Not a move. Oh, I did that properly."

At times Gobila came to see them. Gobila was the chief of the neighbouring villages. He was a grey-headed savage, thin and black, with a white cloth round his loins and a mangy panther skin hanging over his back. He came up with long strides of his skeleton legs, swinging a staff as tall as himself, and, entering the common room of the station, would squat on his heels to the left of the door. There he sat, watching Kayerts, and now and then making a speech which the other did not understand. Kayerts, without interrupting his occupation, would from time to time say in a friendly manner: "How goes it, you old image?" and they would smile at one another. The two whites had a liking for that old and incomprehensible creature, and called him Father Gobila. Gobila's manner was paternal, and he seemed really to love all white men. They all appeared to him very young, indistinguishably alike (except for stature), and he knew that they were all brothers, and also immortal. The death of the artist, who was the first white man whom he knew intimately, did not disturb this belief, because he was firmly convinced that the white stranger had pretended to die and got himself buried for some mysterious purpose of his own, into which it was useless to inquire. Perhaps it was his way of going home to his own country? At any rate, these were his brothers, and he transferred his absurd affection to them. They returned it in a way. Carlier slapped him on the back, and recklessly struck off matches for his amusement. Kayerts was always ready to let him have a sniff of the ammonia bottle. In short, they behaved just like that other white creature that had hidden itself in a hole in the ground. Gobila considered them attentively. Perhaps they were the same being with the other—or one of them was. He couldn't decide—clear up that mystery; but he remained always very friendly. In consequence of that friendship the women of Gobila's village walked in single file through the reedy grass, bringing every morning to the station, fowls, and sweet potatoes, and palm wine, and sometimes a goat. The Company never provisions the stations fully, and the agents required those local supplies to live. They had them through the good will of Gobila, and lived well. Now and then one of them had a bout of fever, and the other nursed him with gentle devotion. They did not think much of it. It left them weaker, and their appearance changed for the worse. Carlier was hollow-eyed and irritable. Kayerts showed a drawn, flabby face above the rotundity of his stomach, which gave him a weird aspect. But being constantly together, they did not notice the change that took place gradually in their appearance, and also in their dispositions.

Five months passed in that way.

Then, one morning, as Kayerts and Carlier, lounging in their chairs under the veranda, talked about the approaching visit of the steamer, a knot of armed men came out of the forest and advanced towards the station. They were strangers to that part of the country. They were tall, slight, draped classically from neck to heel in blue fringed cloths, and carried percussion muskets over their bare right shoulders. Makola showed signs of excitement, and ran out of the storehouse (where he spent all his days) to meet these visitors. They came into the courtyard and looked about them with steady, scornful glances. Their leader, a powerful and determined-looking negro with bloodshot eyes, stood in front of the veranda and made a long speech. He gesticulated much, and ceased very suddenly.

There was something in his intonation, in the sounds of the long sentences he used, that startled the two whites. It was like a reminiscence of something not exactly familiar, and yet resembling the speech of civilized men. It sounded like one of those impossible languages which sometimes we hear in our dreams.

"What lingo is that?" said the amazed Carlier. "In the first moment I fancied the fellow was going to speak French. Anyway, it is a different kind of gibberish to what we ever heard."

"Yes," replied Kayerts. "Hey, Makola, what does he say? Where do they come from? Who are they?"

But Makola, who seemed to be standing on hot bricks, answered hurriedly, "I don't know. They come from very far. Perhaps Mrs Price will understand. They are perhaps bad men."

The leader, after waiting for a while, said something sharply to Makola, who shook his head. Then the man, after looking round, noticed Makola's hut and walked over there. The next moment Mrs Makola was heard speaking with great volubility. The other strangers—they were six in all—strolled about with an air of ease, put their heads through the door of the store-room, congregated round the grave, pointed understandingly at the cross, and generally made themselves at home.

"I don't like those chaps—and, I say, Kayerts, they must be from the coast; they've got firearms," observed the sagacious Carlier.

Kayerts also did not like those chaps. They both, for the first time, became aware that they lived in conditions where the unusual may be dangerous, and that there was no power on earth outside of themselves to stand between them and the unusual. They became uneasy, went in and loaded their revolvers. Kayerts said, "We must order Makola to tell them to go away before dark."

The strangers left in the afternoon, after eating a meal prepared for them by Mrs Makola. The immense woman was excited, and talked much with the visitors. She rattled away shrilly, pointing here and there at the forests and at the river. Makola sat apart and watched. At times he got up and whispered to his wife. He accompanied the strangers across the ravine at the back of the station-ground, and returned slowly looking very thoughtful. When questioned by the white men he was very strange, seemed not to understand, seemed to have forgotten French—seemed to have forgotten how to speak altogether. Kayerts and Carlier agreed that the nigger had had too much palm wine.

There was some talk about keeping a watch in turn, but in the evening everything seemed so quiet and peaceful that they retired as usual. All night they were disturbed by a lot of drumming in the villages. A deep, rapid roll near by would be followed by another far off—then all ceased. Soon short appeals would rattle out here and there, then all mingle together, increase, become vigorous and sustained, would spread out over the forest, roll through the night, unbroken and ceaseless, near and far, as if the whole land had been one immense drum booming out steadily an appeal to heaven. And through the deep and tremendous noise sudden yells that resembled snatches of songs from a madhouse darted shrill and high in discordant jets of sound which seemed to rush far above the earth and drive all peace from under the stars.

Carlier and Kayerts slept badly. They both thought they had heard shots fired during the night—but they could not agree as to the direction. In the morning Makola was gone somewhere. He returned about noon with one of yesterday's strangers, and eluded all Kayerts' attempts to close with him: had become deaf apparently. Kayerts wondered. Carlier, who had been fishing off the bank, came back and remarked while he showed his catch, "The niggers seem to be in a deuce of a stir; I wonder what's up. I saw about fifteen canoes cross the river during the two hours I was there fishing." Kayerts, worried, said, "Isn't this Makola very queer today?" Carlier advised, "Keep all our men together in case of some trouble."

II

There were ten station men who had been left by the Director. Those fellows, having engaged themselves to the Company for six months (without having any idea of a month in particular and only a very faint notion of time in general), had been serving the cause of progress for upwards of two years. Belonging to a tribe from a very distant part of the land of darkness and sorrow, they did not run away, naturally supposing that as wandering strangers they would be killed by the inhabitants of the country; in which they were right. They lived in straw huts on the slope of a ravine overgrown with reedy grass, just behind the station buildings. They were not happy, regretting the festive incantations, the sorceries, the human sacrifices of their own land; where they also had parents, brothers, sisters, admired chiefs, respected magicians, loved friends, and other ties supposed generally to be human. Besides, the rice rations served out by the Company did not agree with them, being a food unknown to their land, and to which they could not get used. Consequently they were unhealthy and miserable. Had they been of any other tribe they would have made up their minds to die—for nothing is easier to certain savages than suicide—and so have escaped from the puzzling difficulties of existence. But belonging, as they did, to a warlike tribe with filed teeth, they had more grit, and went on stupidly living through disease and sorrow. They did very little work, and had lost their splendid physique. Carlier and Kayerts doctored them assiduously without being able to bring them back into condition again. They were mustered every morning and told off to different tasks—grass-cutting, fence-building, tree-felling, etc., etc., which no power on earth could induce them to execute efficiently. The two whites had practically very little control over them.

In the afternoon Makola came over to the big house and found Kayerts watching three heavy columns of smoke rising above the forests. "What is that?" asked Kayerts. "Some villages burn," answered Makola, who seemed to have regained his wits. Then he said abruptly: "We have got very little ivory; bad six months' trading. Do you like get a little more ivory?"

"Yes," said Kayerts, eagerly. He thought of percentages which were low.

"Those men who came yesterday are traders from Loanda who have got more ivory than they can carry home. Shall I buy? I know their camp."

"Certainly," said Kayerts. "What are those traders?"

"Bad fellows," said Makola, indifferently. "They fight with people, and catch women and children. They are bad men, and got guns. There is a great disturbance in the country. Do you want ivory?"

"Yes," said Kayerts. Makola said nothing for a while. Then: "Those workmen of ours are no good at all," he muttered, looking round. "Station in very bad order, sir. Director will growl. Better get a fine lot of ivory, then he say nothing."

"I can't help it; the men won't work," said Kayerts. "When will you get that ivory?"

"Very soon," said Makola. "Perhaps tonight. You leave it to me, and keep indoors, sir. I think you had better give some palm wine to our men to make a dance this evening. Enjoy themselves. Work better tomorrow. There's plenty of palm wine—gone a little sour."

Kayerts said "yes," and Makola, with his own hands carried big calabashes to the door of his hut. They stood there till the evening, and Mrs Makola looked into every one. The men got them at sunset. When Kayerts and Carlier retired, a big bonfire was flaring before the men's huts. They could hear their shouts and drumming. Some men from Gobila's village had joined the station hands, and the entertainment was a great success.

In the middle of the night, Carlier waking suddenly, heard a man shout loudly; then a shot was fired. Only one. Carlier ran out and met Kayerts on the veranda. They were both startled. As they went across the yard to call Makola, they saw shadows moving in the night. One of them cried, "Don't shoot! It's me, Price." Then Makola appeared close to them. "Go back, go back, please," he urged, "you spoil all." "There are strange men about," said Carlier. "Never mind; I know," said Makola. Then he whispered, "All right. Bring ivory. Say nothing! I know my business." The two white men reluctantly went back to the house, but did not sleep. They heard footsteps, whispers, some groans. It seemed as if a lot of men came in, dumped heavy things on the ground, squabbled a long time, then went away. They lay on their hard beds and thought: "This Makola is invaluable." In the morning Carlier came out, very sleepy, and pulled at the cord of the big bell. The station hands mustered every morning to the sound of the bell. That morning nobody came. Kayerts turned out also, yawning. Across the yard they saw Makola come out of his hut, a tin basin of soapy water in his hand. Makola, a civilized nigger, was very neat in his person. He threw the soapsuds skilfully over a wretched little yellow cur he had, then turning his face to the agent's house, he shouted from the distance. "All the men gone last night!"

They heard him plainly, but in their surprise they both yelled out together: "What?" Then they stared at each other. "We are in a proper fix now," growled Carlier. "It's incredible!" muttered Kayerts. "I will go to the huts and see," said Carlier, striding off. Makola coming up found Kayerts standing alone.

"I can hardly believe it," said Kayerts, tearfully. "We took care of them as if they had been our children."

"They went with the coast people," said Makola after a moment of hesitation.

"What do I care with whom they went—the ungrateful brutes!" exclaimed the other. Then with sudden suspicion, and looking hard at Makola, he added: "What do you know about it?"

Makola moved his shoulders, looking down on the ground. "What do I know? I think only. Will you come and look at the ivory I've got there? It is a fine lot. You never saw such."

He moved towards the store. Kayerts followed him mechanically, thinking about the incredible desertion of the men. On the ground before the door of the fetish lay six splendid tusks.

"What did you give for it?" asked Kayerts, after surveying the lot with satisfaction.

"No regular trade," said Makola."They brought the ivory and gave it to me. I told them to take what they most wanted in the station. It is a beautiful lot. No station can show such tusks. Those traders wanted carriers badly, and our men were no good here. No trade, no entry in books; all correct."

Kayerts nearly burst with indignation. "Why!" he shouted, "I believe you have sold our men for these tusks!" Makola stood impassive and silent. "I—I—will—I," stuttered Kayerts. "You fiend!" he yelled out.

"I did the best for you and the Company," said Makola, imperturbably. "Why you shout so much? Look at this tusk."

"I dismiss you! I will report you—I won't look at the tusk. I forbid you to touch them. I order you to throw them into the river. You—you!"

"You very red, Mr Kayerts. If you are so irritable in the sun, you will get a fever and die—like the first chief!" pronounced Makola impressively.

They stood still, contemplating one another with intense eyes, as if they had been looking with effort across immense distances. Kayerts shivered. Makola had meant no more than he said, but his words seemed to Kayerts full of ominous menace! He turned sharply and went away to the house. Makola retired into the bosom of his family; and the tusks, left lying before the store, looked very large and valuable in the sunshine.

Carlier came back on the veranda. "They're all gone, hey?" asked Kayerts from the far end of the common room in a muffled voice. "You did not find anybody?"

"Oh, yes," said Carlier, "I found one of Gobila's people lying dead before the huts—shot through the body. We heard that shot last night."

Kayerts came out quickly. He found his companion staring grimly over the yard at the tusks, away by the store. They both sat in silence for a while. Then Kayerts related his conversation with Makola. Carlier said nothing. At the mid-day meal they ate very little. They hardly exchanged a word that day. A great silence seemed to lie heavily over the station and press on their lips. Makola did not open the store; he spent the day playing with his children. He lay full-length on a mat outside his door, and the youngsters sat on his chest and clambered all over him. It was a touching picture. Mrs Makola was busy cooking all day as usual. The white men made a somewhat better meal in the evening. Afterwards, Carlier smoking his pipe strolled over to the store; he stood for a long time over the tusks, touched one or two with his foot, even tried to lift the largest one by its small end. He came back to his chief, who had not stirred from the veranda, threw himself in the chair and said—

"I can see it! They were pounced upon while they slept heavily after drinking all that palm wine you've allowed Makola to give them. A put-up job! See? The worst is, some of Gobila's people were there, and got carried off too, no doubt. The least drunk woke up, and got shot for his sobriety. This is a funny country. What will you do now?"

"We can't touch it, of course," said Kayerts.

"Of course not," answered Carlier.

"Slavery is an awful thing," stammered out Kayerts in an unsteady voice.

"Frightful—the sufferings," grunted Carlier with conviction.

They believed their words. Everybody shows respectful deference to certain sounds that he and his fellows can make. But about feelings people really know nothing. We talk with indignation or enthusiasm; we talk about oppression, cruelty, crime, devotion, self-sacrifice, virtue, and we know nothing real beyond the words. Nobody knows what suffering or sacrifice mean—except, perhaps the victims of the mysterious purpose of these illusions.

Next morning they saw Makola very busy setting up in the yard the big scales used for weighing ivory. By and by Carlier said: "What's that filthy scoundrel up to?" and lounged out into the yard. Kayerts followed. They stood watching. Makola took no notice. When the balance was swung true, he tried to lift a tusk into the scale. It was too heavy. He looked up helplessly without a word, and for a minute they stood round that balance as mute and still as three statues. Suddenly Carlier said: "Catch hold of the other end, Makola—you beast!" and together they swung the tusk up. Kayerts trembled in every limb. He muttered, "I say! O! I say!" and putting his hand in his pocket found there a dirty bit of paper and the stump of a pencil. He turned his back on the others, as if about to do something tricky, and noted stealthily the weights which Carlier shouted out to him with unnecessary loudness. When all was over Makola whispered to himself: "The sun's very strong here for the tusks." Carlier said to Kayerts in a careless tone: "I say, chief, I might just as well give him a lift with this lot into the store."

As they were going back to the house Kayerts observed with a sigh: "It had to be done." And Carlier said: "It's deplorable, but, the men being Company's men the ivory is Company's ivory. We must look after it." "I will report to the Director, of course," said Kayerts. "Of course; let him decide," approved Carlier.

At midday they made a hearty meal. Kayerts sighed from time to time. Whenever they mentioned Makola's name they always added to it an opprobrious epithet. It eased their conscience. Makola gave himself a half-holiday, and bathed his children in the river. No one from Gobila's villages came near the station that day. No one came the next day, and the next, nor for a whole week. Gobila's people might have been dead and buried for any sign of life they gave. But they were only mourning for those they had lost by the witchcraft of white men, who had brought wicked people into their country. The wicked people were gone, but fear remained. Fear always remains. A man may destroy everything within himself, love and hate and belief, and even doubt; but as long as he clings to life he cannot destroy fear: the fear, subtle, indestructible, and terrible, that pervades his being; that tinges his thoughts; that lurks in his heart; that watches on his lips the struggle of his last breath. In his fear, the mild old Gobila offered extra human sacrifices to all the Evil Spirits that had taken possession of his white friends. His heart was heavy. Some warriors spoke about burning and killing, but the cautious old savage dissuaded them. Who could foresee the woe those mysterious creatures, if irritated, might bring? They should be left alone. Perhaps in time they would disappear into the earth as the first one had disappeared. His people must keep away from them, and hope for the best.

Kayerts and Carlier did not disappear, but remained above on this earth, that, somehow, they fancied had become bigger and very empty. It was not the absolute and dumb solitude of the post that impressed them so much as an inarticulate feeling that something from within them was gone, something that worked for their safety, and had kept the wilderness from interfering with their hearts. The images of home; the memory of people like them, of men that thought and felt as they used to think and feel, receded into distances made indistinct by the glare of unclouded sunshine. And out of the great silence of the surrounding wilderness, its very hopelessness and savagery seemed to approach them nearer, to draw them gently, to look upon them, to envelop them with a solicitude irresistible, familiar, and disgusting.

Days lengthened into weeks, then into months. Gobila's people drummed and yelled to every new moon, as of yore, but kept away from the station. Makola and Carlier tried once in a canoe to open communications, but were received with a shower of arrows, and had to fly back to the station for dear life. That attempt set the country up and down the river into an uproar that could be very distinctly heard for days. The steamer was late. At first they spoke of delay jauntily, then anxiously, then gloomily. The matter was becoming serious. Stores were running short. Carlier cast his lines off the bank, but the river was low, and the fish kept out in the stream. They dared not stroll far away from the station to shoot. Moreover, there was no game in the impenetrable forest. Once Carlier shot a hippo in the river. They had no boat to secure it, and it sank. When it floated up it drifted away, and Gobila's people secured the carcass. It was the occasion for a national holiday, but Carlier had a fit of rage over it and talked about the necessity of exterminating all the niggers before the country could be made habitable. Kayerts mooned about silently; spent hours looking at the portrait of his Melie. It represented a little girl with long bleached tresses and a rather sour face. His legs were much swollen, and he could hardly walk. Carlier, undermined by fever, could not swagger any more, but kept tottering about, still with a devil-may-care air, as became a man who remembered his crack regiment. He had become hoarse, sarcastic, and inclined to say unpleasant things. He called it, "being frank with you." They had long ago reckoned their percentages on trade, including in them that last deal of "this infamous Makola." They had also concluded not to say anything about it. Kayerts hesitated at first—was afraid of the Director.

"He has seen worse things done on the quiet," maintained Carlier, with a hoarse laugh. "Trust him! He won't thank you if you blab. He is no better than you or me. Who will talk if we hold our tongues? There is nobody here."

That was the root of the trouble! There was nobody there; and being left there alone with their weakness, they became daily more like a pair of accomplices than like a couple of devoted friends. They had heard nothing from home for eight months. Every evening they said, "Tomorrow we shall see the steamer." But one of the Company's steamers had been wrecked, and the Director was busy with the other, relieving very distant and important stations on the main river. He thought that the useless station, and the useless men, could wait. Meantime Kayerts and Carlier lived on rice boiled without salt, and cursed the Company, all Africa, and the day they were born. One must have lived on such diet to discover what ghastly trouble the necessity of swallowing one's food may become. There was literally nothing else in the station but rice and coffee; they drank the coffee without sugar. The last fifteen lumps Kayerts had solemnly locked away in his box, together with a half-bottle of Cognâc, "in case of sickness," he explained. Carlier approved. "When one is sick," he said, "any little extra like that is cheering."

They waited. Rank grass began to sprout over the courtyard. The bell never rang now. Days passed, silent, exasperating, and slow. When the two men spoke, they snarled; and their silences were bitter, as if tinged by the bitterness of their thoughts.

One day after a lunch of boiled rice, Carlier put down his cup untasted, and said: "Hang it all! Let's have a decent cup of coffee for once. Bring out that sugar, Kayerts!"

"For the sick," muttered Kayerts, without looking up.

"For the sick," mocked Carlier. "Bosh! . . . Well! I am sick."

"You are no more sick than I am, and I go without," said Kayerts in a peaceful tone.

"Come! out with that sugar, you stingy old slave-dealer."

Kayerts looked up quickly. Carlier was smiling with marked insolence. And suddenly it seemed to Kayerts that he had never seen that man before. Who was he? He knew nothing about him. What was he capable of? There was a surprising flash of violent emotion within him, as if in the presence of something undreamt of, dangerous, and final. But he managed to pronounce with composure—

"That joke is in very bad taste. Don't repeat it."

"Joke!" said Carlier, hitching himself forward on his seat. "I am hungry—I am sick—I don't joke! I hate hypocrites. You are a hypocrite. You are a slave-dealer. I am a slave-dealer. There's nothing but slave-dealers in this cursed country. I mean to have sugar in my coffee today, anyhow!"

"I forbid you to speak to me in that way," said Kayerts with a fair show of resolution.

"You!—What?" shouted Carlier, jumping up.

Kayerts stood up also. "I am your chief," he began, trying to master the shakiness of his voice.

"What?" yelled the other. "Who's chief? There's no chief here. There's nothing here: there's nothing but you and I. Fetch the sugar—you pot-bellied ass."

"Hold your tongue. Go out of this room," screamed Kayerts."I dismiss you—you scoundrel!"

Carlier swung a stool. All at once he looked dangerously in earnest. "You flabby, good-for-nothing civilian—take that!" he howled.

Kayerts dropped under the table, and the stool struck the grass inner wall of the room. Then, as Carlier was trying to upset the table, Kayerts in desperation made a blind rush, head low, like a cornered pig would do, and overturning his friend, bolted along the veranda, and into his room. He locked the door, snatched his revolver, and stood panting. In less than a minute Carlier was kicking at the door furiously, howling, "If you don't bring out that sugar, I will shoot you at sight, like a dog. Now then—one—two—three. You won't? I will show you who's the master."

Kayerts thought the door would fall in, and scrambled through the square hole that served for a window in his room. There was then the whole breadth of the house between them. But the other was apparently not strong enough to break in the door, and Kayerts heard him running round. Then he also began to run laboriously on his swollen legs. He ran as quickly as he could, grasping the revolver, and unable yet to understand what was happening to him. He saw in succession Makola's house, the store, the river, the ravine, and the low bushes; and he saw all those things again as he ran for the second time round the house. Then again they flashed past him. That morning he could not have walked a yard without a groan.

And now he ran. He ran fast enough to keep out of sight of the other man.

Then as, weak and desperate, he thought, "Before I finish the next round I shall die," he heard the other man stumble heavily, then stop. He stopped also. He had the back and Carlier the front of the house, as before. He heard him drop into a chair cursing, and suddenly his own legs gave way, and he slid down into a sitting posture with his back to the wall. His mouth was as dry as a cinder, and his face was wet with perspiration—and tears. What was it all about? He thought it must be a horrible illusion; he thought he was dreaming; he thought he was going mad! After a while he collected his senses. What did they quarrel about? That sugar! How absurd! He would give it to him—didn't want it himself. And he began scrambling to his feet with a sudden feeling of security. But before he had fairly stood upright, a common-sense reflection occurred to him and drove him back into despair. He thought: "If I give way now to that brute of a soldier, he will begin this horror again tomorrow—and the day after—every day—raise other pretensions, trample on me, torture me, make me his slave—and I will be lost! Lost! The steamer may not come for days—may never come." He shook so that he had to sit down on the floor again. He shivered forlornly. He felt he could not, would not move any more. He was completely distracted by the sudden perception that the position was without issue—that death and life had in a moment become equally difficult and terrible.

All at once he heard the other push his chair back; and he leaped to his feet with extreme facility. He listened and got confused. Must run again! Right or left? He heard footsteps. He darted to the left, grasping his revolver, and at the very same instant, as it seemed to him, they came into violent collision. Both shouted with surprise. A loud explosion took place between them; a roar of red fire, thick smoke; and Kayerts, deafened and blinded, rushed back thinking: "I am hit—it's all over." He expected the other to come round—to gloat over his agony. He caught hold of an upright of the roof—"All over!" Then he heard a crashing fall on the other side of the house, as if somebody had tumbled headlong over a chair—then silence. Nothing more happened. He did not die. Only his shoulder felt as if it had been badly wrenched, and he had lost his revolver. He was disarmed and helpless! He waited for his fate. The other man made no sound. It was a stratagem. He was stalking him now! Along what side? Perhaps he was taking aim this very minute!

After a few moments of an agony frightful and absurd, he decided to go and meet his doom. He was prepared for every surrender. He turned the corner, steadying himself with one hand on the wall; made a few paces, and nearly swooned. He had seen on the floor, protruding past the other corner, a pair of turned-up feet. A pair of white naked feet in red slippers. He felt deadly sick, and stood for a time in profound darkness. Then Makola appeared before him, saying quietly: "Come along, Mr Kayerts. He is dead." He burst into tears of gratitude; a loud, sobbing fit of crying. After a time he found himself sitting in a chair and looking at Carlier, who lay stretched on his back. Makola was kneeling over the body.

"Is this your revolver?" asked Makola, getting up.

"Yes," said Kayerts; then he added very quickly, "He ran after me to shoot me—you saw!"

"Yes, I saw," said Makola. "There is only one revolver; where's his?"

"Don't know," whispered Kayerts in a voice that had become suddenly very faint.

"I will go and look for it," said the other, gently. He made the round along the veranda, while Kayerts sat still and looked at the corpse. Makola came back empty-handed, stood in deep thought, then stepped quietly into the dead man's room, and came out directly with the revolver, which he held up before Kayerts. Kayerts shut his eyes. Everything was going round. He found life more terrible and difficult than death. He had shot an unarmed man.

After meditating for a while, Makola said softly, pointing at the dead man who lay there with his right eye blown out—

"He died of fever." Kayerts looked at him with a stony stare. "Yes," repeated Makola, thoughtfully, stepping over the corpse, I think he died of fever. Bury him tomorrow."

And he went away slowly to his expectant wife, leaving the two white men alone on the veranda.

Night came, and Kayerts sat unmoving on his chair. He sat quiet as if he had taken a dose of opium. The violence of the emotions he had passed through produced a feeling of exhausted serenity. He had plumbed in one short afternoon the depths of horror and despair, and now found repose in the conviction that life had no more secrets for him: neither had death! He sat by the corpse thinking; thinking very actively, thinking very new thoughts. He seemed to have broken loose from himself altogether. His old thoughts, convictions, likes and dislikes, things he respected and things he abhorred, appeared in their true light at last! Appeared contemptible and childish, false and ridiculous. He revelled in his new wisdom while he sat by the man he had killed. He argued with himself about all things under heaven with that kind of wrong-headed lucidity which may be observed in some lunatics. Incidentally he reflected that the fellow dead there had been a noxious beast anyway; that men died every day in thousands; perhaps in hundreds of thousands—who could tell?—and that in the number, that one death could not possibly make any difference; couldn't have any importance, at least to a thinking creature. He, Kayerts, was a thinking creature. He had been all his life, till that moment, a believer in a lot of nonsense like the rest of mankind—who are fools; but now he thought! He knew! He was at peace; he was familiar with the highest wisdom! Then he tried to imagine himself dead, and Carlier sitting in his chair watching him; and his attempt met with such unexpected success, that in a very few moments he became not at all sure who was dead and who was alive. This extraordinary achievement of his fancy startled him, however, and by a clever and timely effort of mind he saved himself just in time from becoming Carlier. His heart thumped, and he felt hot all over at the thought of that danger. Carlier! What a beastly thing! To compose his now disturbed nerves—and no wonder!—he tried to whistle a little. Then, suddenly, he fell asleep, or thought he had slept; but at any rate there was a fog, and somebody had whistled in the fog.

He stood up. The day had come, and a heavy mist had descended upon the land: the mist penetrating, enveloping, and silent; the morning mist of tropical lands; the mist that clings and kills; the mist white and deadly, immaculate and poisonous. He stood up, saw the body, and threw his arms above his head with a cry like that of a man who, waking from a trance, finds himself immured forever in a tomb. "*Help! . . . My god!*"

A shriek inhuman, vibrating and sudden, pierced like a sharp dart the white shroud of that land of sorrow. Three short, impatient screeches followed, and then, for a time, the fog-wreaths rolled on, undisturbed, through a formidable silence. Then many more shrieks, rapid and piercing, like the yells of some exasperated and ruthless creature, rent the air. Progress was calling to Kayerts from the river. Progress and civilization and all the virtues. Society was calling to its accomplished child to come, to be taken care of, to be instructed, to be judged, to be condemned; it called him to return to that rubbish heap from which he had wandered away, so that justice could be done.

Kayerts heard and understood. He stumbled out of the veranda, leaving the other man quite alone for the first time since they had been thrown there together. He groped his way through the fog, calling in his ignorance upon the invisible heaven to undo its work. Makola flitted by in the mist, shouting as he ran—

"Steamer! Steamer! They can't see. They whistle for the station. I go ring the bell. Go down to the landing, sir. I ring."

He disappeared. Kayerts stood still. He looked upwards; the fog rolled low over his head. He looked round like a man who has lost his way; and he saw a dark smudge, a cross-shaped stain, upon the shifting purity of the mist. As he began to stumble towards it, the station bell rang in a tumultuous peal its answer to the impatient clamour of the steamer.

The Managing Director of the Great Civilizing Company (since we know that civilization follows trade) landed first, and incontinently lost sight of the steamer. The fog down by the river was exceedingly dense; above, at the station, the bell rang unceasing and brazen.

The Director shouted loudly to the steamer:

"There is nobody down to meet us; there may be something wrong, though they are ringing. You had better come, too!"

And he began to toil up the steep bank. The captain and the engine-driver of the boat followed behind. As they scrambled up the fog thinned, and they could see their Director a good way ahead. Suddenly they saw him start forward, calling to them over his shoulder:— "Run! Run to the house! I've found one of them. Run, look for the other!"

He had found one of them! And even he, the man of varied and startling experience, was somewhat discomposed by the manner of this finding. He stood and fumbled in his pockets (for a knife) while he faced Kayerts, who was hanging by a leather strap from the cross. He had evidently climbed the grave, which was high and narrow, and after tying the end of the strap to the arm, had swung himself off. His toes were only a couple of inches above the ground; his arms hung stiffly down; he seemed to be standing rigidly at attention, but with one purple cheek playfully posed on the shoulder. And, irreverently, he was putting out a swollen tongue at his Managing Director.

1896

Charles G.D. Roberts

1860–1943

Sir Charles George Douglas Roberts was born in Douglas, New Brunswick, and grew up in Sackville, where his father served as rector of St Ann's Church. Roberts studied at the University of New Brunswick, receiving his BA in 1879 and his MA in 1881, and then worked as a schoolteacher, as an editor of the Toronto periodical *The Week*, and as a professor at King's College, Nova Scotia. During this time he established himself as a writer of considerable talent, publishing his first collection of poetry, *Orion and Other Poems*, in 1880 and his first volume of animal stories, *Earth's Enigmas*, in 1896. In 1897 he moved to New York City, leaving his family in Fredericton, never to live with them again. He lived in New York for ten years, working on his own writing and editing *The Illustrated American*. Between 1907 and 1925 he lived and travelled in Europe. He wrote prose and poetry during this time—publishing *Poems* (1901, 1907) and *New Poems* (1919)—lectured throughout Europe, and also served in World War I. He returned to live in Toronto in 1925.

Roberts's influence on Canadian literature was immense. He was one of the group known as the "Confederation Poets," who were among the first to devote themselves to depicting the Canadian landscape in their work, and has been called the father of Canadian literature for the influence he had on other writers of his generation. But in addition to his poetry, Roberts wrote a great deal of prose, including works of fiction and non-fiction. He is credited as having invented (with Ernest Thompson Seton) the modern animal story. He claimed that animals are not governed only by instinct but rather by "something directly akin to reason," and often elected to tell his story from the animal's perspective. In the forty years following the publication of *Earth's Enigmas*, Roberts wrote over a dozen collections of animal stories. In 1890 he was named a fellow of the Royal Society of Canada and was knighted in 1935.

When Twilight Falls on the Stump Lots

The wet, chill first of the spring, its blackness made tender by the lilac wash of the afterglow, lay upon the high, open stretches of the stump lots. The winter-whitened stumps, the sparse patches of juniper and bay just budding, the rough-mossed hillocks, the harsh boulders here and there up-thrusting from the soil, the swampy hollows wherein a coarse grass began to show green, all seemed anointed, as it were, to an ecstasy of peace by the chrism of that paradisal colour. Against the lucid immensity of the April sky the thin tops of five or six soaring ram-pikes aspired like violet flames. Along the skirts of the stump lots a fir wood reared a ragged-crested wall of black against the red amber of the horizon.

Late that afternoon, beside a juniper thicket not far from the centre of the stump lots, a young black and white cow had given birth to her first calf. The little animal had been licked assiduously by the mother's caressing tongue till its colour began to show of a rich dark red. Now it had struggled to its feet, and, with its disproportionately long, thick legs braced wide apart, was beginning to nurse. Its blunt wet muzzle and thick lips tugged eagerly, but somewhat blunderingly as yet, at the unaccustomed teats; and its tail lifted, twitching with delight, as the first warm streams of mother milk went down its throat. It was a pathetically awkward, unlovely little figure, not yet advanced to that youngling winsomeness which is the heritage, to some degree and at some period, of the infancy of all the kindreds that breathe upon the earth. But to the young mother's eyes it was the most beautiful of things. With her head twisted far around, she nosed and licked its heaving flanks as it nursed; and between deep, ecstatic breathings she uttered in her throat low murmurs, unspeakably tender, of encouragement and caress. The delicate but pervading flood of sunset colour had the effect of blending the ruddy-hued calf into the tones of the landscape; but the cow's insistent blotches of black and white stood out sharply, refusing to harmonize. The drench of violet light was of no avail to soften their staring contrasts. They made her vividly conspicuous across the whole breadth of the stump lots, to eyes that watched her from the forest coverts.

The eyes that watched her—long, fixedly, hungrily—were small and red. They belonged to a lank she-bear, whose gaunt flanks and rusty coat proclaimed a season of famine in the wilderness. She could not see the calf, which was hidden by a hillock and some juniper scrub; but its presence was very legibly conveyed to her by the mother's solicitous watchfulness. After a motionless scrutiny from behind the screen of fir branches, the lean bear stole noiselessly forth from the shadows into the great wash of violet light. Step by step, and very slowly, with the patience that endures because confident of its object, she crept toward that oasis of mothering joy in the vast emptiness of the stump lots. Now crouching, now crawling, turning to this side and to that, taking advantage of every hollow, every thicket, every hillock, every aggressive stump, her craft succeeded in eluding even the wild and menacing watchfulness of the young mother's eyes.

The spring had been a trying one for the lank she-bear. Her den, in a dry tract of hemlock wood some furlongs back from the stump lots, was a snug little cave under the uprooted base of a lone pine, which had somehow grown up among the alien hemlocks only to draw down upon itself at last, by its superior height, the fury of a passing hurricane. The winter had contributed but scanty snowfall to cover the bear in her sleep; and the March thaws, unseasonably early and ardent, had called her forth to activity weeks too soon. Then frosts had come with belated severity, sealing away the budding tubers, which are the bear's chief dependence for spring diet; and worst of all, a long stretch of interval meadow by the neighbouring river, which had once been rich in groundnuts, had been ploughed up the previous spring and subjected to the producing of oats and corn. When she was feeling the pinch of meagre rations, and when the fat which a liberal autumn of blueberries had laid up about her ribs was getting as shrunken as the last snow in the thickets, she gave birth to two hairless and hungry little cubs. They were very blind, and ridiculously small to be born of so big a mother; and having so much growth to make during the next few months, their appetites were immeasurable. They tumbled, and squealed, and tugged at their mother's teats, and grew astonishingly, and made huge haste to cover their bodies with fur of a soft and silken black; and all this vitality of theirs made a strenuous demand upon their mother's milk. There were no more bee-trees left in the neighbourhood. The long wanderings which she was forced to take in her search for roots and tubers were in themselves a drain upon her nursing powers. At last, reluctant though she was to attract the hostile notice of the settlement, she found herself forced to hunt on the borders of the sheep pastures. Before all else in life was it important to her that these two tumbling little ones in the den should not go hungry. Their eyes were open now—small and dark and whimsical, their ears quaintly large and inquiring for their roguish little faces. Had she not been driven by the unkind season to so much hunting and foraging, she would have passed near all her time rapturously in the den under the pine root, fondling those two soft miracles of her world.

With the killing of three lambs—at widely scattered points, so as to mislead retaliation—things grew a little easier for the harassed bear; and presently she grew bolder in tampering with the creatures under man's protection. With one swift, secret blow of her mighty paw she struck down a young ewe which had strayed within reach of her hiding-place. Dragging her prey deep into the woods, she fared well upon it for some days, and was happy with her growing cubs. It was just when she had begun to feel the fasting which came upon the exhaustion of this store that, in a hungry hour, she sighted the conspicuous markings of the black and white cow.

It is altogether unusual for the black bear of the eastern woods to attack any quarry so large as a cow, unless under the spur of fierce hunger or fierce rage. The she-bear was powerful beyond her fellows. She had the strongest possible incentive to bold hunting, and she had lately grown confident beyond her wont. Nevertheless, when she began her careful stalking of this big game which she coveted, she had no definite intention of forcing a battle with the cow. She had observed that cows, accustomed to the protection of man, would at times leave their calves asleep and stray off some distance in their pasturing. She had even seen calves left all by themselves in a field, from morning till night, and had wondered at such negligence in their mothers. Now she had a confident idea that sooner or later the calf would lie down to sleep, and the young mother roam a little wide in search of the scant young grass. Very softly, very self-effacingly, she crept nearer step by step, following up the wind, till at last, undiscovered, she was crouching behind a thick patch of juniper, on the slope of a little hollow not ten paces distant from the cow and the calf.

By this time the tender violet light was fading to a greyness over hillock and hollow; and with the deepening of the twilight the faint breeze, which had been breathing from the northward, shifted suddenly and came in slow, warm pulsations out of the south. At the same time the calf, having nursed sufficiently, and feeling his baby legs tired of the weight they had not yet learned to carry, laid himself down. On this the cow shifted her position. She turned half round, and lifted her head high. As she did so a scent of peril was borne in upon her fine nostrils. She recognized it instantly. With a snort of anger she sniffed again; then stamped a challenge with her fore hoofs, and levelled the lance-points of her horns toward the menace. The next moment her eyes, made keen by the fear of love, detected the black outline of the bear's head through the coarse screen of the juniper. Without a second's hesitation, she flung up her tail, gave a short bellow, and charged.

The moment she saw herself detected, the bear rose upon her hindquarters; nevertheless she was in a measure surprised by the sudden blind fury of the attack. Nimbly she swerved to avoid it, aiming at the same time a stroke with her mighty forearm, which, if it had found its mark, would have smashed her adversary's neck. But as she struck out, in the act of shifting her position, a depression of the ground threw her off her balance. The next instant one sharp horn caught her slantingly in the flank, ripping its way upward and inward, while the mad impact threw her upon her back.

Grappling, she had her assailant's head and shoulders in a trap, and her gigantic claws cut through the flesh and sinew like knives; but at the desperate disadvantage of her position she could inflict no disabling blow. The cow, on the other hand, though mutilated and streaming with blood, kept pounding with her whole massive weight, and with short tremendous shocks crushing the breath from her foe's ribs.

Presently, wrenching herself free, the cow drew off for another battering charge; and as she did so the bear hurled herself violently down the slope, and gained her feet behind a dense thicket of bay shrub. The cow, with one eye blinded and the other obscured by blood, glared around for her in vain, then, in a panic of mother terror, plunged back to her calf.

Snatching at the respite, the bear crouched down, craving that invisibility which is the most faithful shield of the furtive kindred. Painfully, and leaving a drenched red trail behind her, she crept off from the disastrous neighbourhood. Soon the deepening twilight sheltered her. But she could not make haste; and she knew that death was close upon her.

Once within the woods, she struggled straight toward the den that held her young. She hungered to die licking them. But destiny is as implacable as iron to the wilderness people, and even this was denied her. Just a half score of paces from the lair in the pine root, her hour descended upon her. There was a sudden redder and fuller gush upon the trail; the last light of longing faded out of her eyes; and she lay down upon her side.

The merry little cubs within the den were beginning to expect her, and getting restless. As the night wore on, and no mother came, they ceased to be merry. By morning they were shivering with hunger and desolate fear. But the doom of the ancient wood was less harsh than its wont, and spared them some days of starving anguish; for about noon a pair of foxes discovered the dead mother, astutely estimated the situation, and then, with the boldness of good appetite, made their way into the unguarded den.

As for the red calf, its fortune was ordinary. Its mother, for all her wounds, was able to nurse and cherish it through the night; and with morning came a searcher from the farm and took it, with the bleeding mother, safely back to the settlement. There it was tended and fattened, and within a few weeks found its way to the cool marble slabs of a city market.

1902

Sara Jeannette Duncan

1861–1922

Born in Brantford, Canada West (Ontario), Sara Jeanette Duncan attended Toronto Normal School but soon gave up teaching for a career as a journalist. She got her start professionally at the age of twenty-three when she travelled to New Orleans with the intention of writing and selling freelance articles on the Cotton Centennial of 1884. One of the first female Canadian journalists, she worked as an editorial writer and book reviewer for the *Washington Post* (1885–1886), and as a columnist for the *Toronto Globe* (1886–1887) and the *Montreal Star* (1887–1888). Aspiring to become a novelist, she set off in 1888 with a fellow journalist on a world tour. In India she met and married Everard Cotes, a museum entomologist, and they lived in India for most of the next three decades. She produced her first book, *A Social Departure: How Orthodocia and I Went Round the World by Ourselves*, in 1890.

Despite being a prolific author—she went on to publish more than twenty books—Duncan is recognized today chiefly for two of her works: *The Imperialist* (1904), which is considered one of the most sophisticated and penetrating novels written in Canada before World War I; and *The Pool in the Desert* (1903), a collection of short stories about India and Anglo-Indians. These are powerful satires of the suffocating colonial world that Duncan found herself in. A subtle subtext is her preoccupation with the issue of female independence.

The Pool in the Desert

I knew Anna Chichele and Judy Harbottle so well, and they figured so vividly at one time against the rather empty landscape of life in a frontier station, that my affection for one of them used to seem little more, or less, than a variant upon my affection for the other. That recollection, however, bears examination badly; Judy was much the better sort, and it is Judy's part in it that draws me into telling the story. Conveying Judy is what I tremble at: her part was simple. Looking back—and not so very far—her part has the relief of high comedy with the proximity of tears; but looking closely, I find that it is mostly Judy, and what she did is entirely second, in my untarnished picture, to what she was. Still I do not think I can dissuade myself from putting it down.

They would, of course, inevitably have found each other sooner or later, Mrs Harbottle and Mrs Chichele, but it was I who actually introduced them; my palmy veranda in Rawul Pindi, where the tea-cups used to assemble, was the scene of it. I presided behind my samovar over the early formalities that were almost at once to drop from their friendship, like the sheath of some bursting flower. I deliberately brought them together, so the birth was not accidental, and my interest in it quite legitimately maternal. We always had tea in the veranda in Rawul Pindi, the drawing-room was painted blue, blue for thirty feet up to the whitewashed cotton ceiling; nothing of any value in the way of a human relation, I am sure, could have originated there. The veranda was spacious and open, their mutual observation had room and freedom; I watched it to and fro. I had not long to wait for my reward; the beautiful candour I expected between them was not ten minutes in coming. For the sake of it I had taken some trouble, but when I perceived it revealing I went and sat down beside Judy's husband, Robert Harbottle, and talked about Pharaoh's split hoof. It was only fair; and when next day I got their impressions of one another, I felt single-minded and deserving.

I knew it would be a satisfactory sort of thing to do, but perhaps it was rather more for Judy's sake than for Anna's that I did it. Mrs Harbottle was only twenty-seven then and Robert a major, but he had brought her to India out of an episode too colour-flushed to tone with English hedges; their marriage had come, in short, of his divorce, and as too natural a consequence. In India it is well known that the eye becomes accustomed to primitive pigments and high lights; the aesthetic consideration, if nothing else, demanded Robert's exchange. He was lucky to get a Piffer regiment, and the Twelfth were lucky to get him; we were all lucky, I thought, to get Judy. It was an opinion, of course, a good deal challenged, even in Rawul Pindi, where it was thought, especially in the beginning, that acquiescence was the most the Harbottles could hope for. That is not enough in India; cordiality is the common right. I could not have Judy preserving her atmosphere at our tea parties and gymkhanas. Not that there were two minds among us about "the case"; it was a preposterous case, sentimentally undignified, from some points of view deplorable. I chose to reserve my point of view, from which I saw it, on Judy's behalf, merely quixotic, preferring on Robert's just to close my eyes. There is no doubt that his first wife was odious to a degree which it is simply pleasanter not to recount, but her malignity must almost have amounted to a sense of humour. Her detestation of her cousin Judy Thynne dated much further back than Robert's attachment. That began in Paris, where Judy, a young widow, was developing a real vein at Julian's. I am entirely convinced that there was nothing, as people say, "in it," Judy had not a thought at that time that was not based on Chinese white and permeated with good-fellowship; but there was a good deal of it, and no doubt the turgid imagination of the first Mrs Harbottle dealt with it honestly enough. At all events, she saw her opportunity, and the depths of her indifference to Robert bubbled up venomously into the suit. That it was undefended was the senseless mystery; decency ordained that he and Judy should have made a fight, even in the hope that it would be a losing one. The reason it had to be a losing one—the reason so immensely criticized—was that the petitioning lady obstinately refused to bring her action against any other set of circumstances than those to which, I have no doubt, Judy contributed every indiscretion. It is hard to imagine Robert Harbottle refusing her any sort of justification that the law demands short of beating her, but her malice would accept nothing of which the account did not go for final settlement to Judy Thynne. If her husband wanted his liberty, he should have it, she declared, at that price and no other. Major Harbottle did indeed deeply long for his liberty, and his interesting friend, Mrs Thynne, had, one can only say, the most vivid commiseration for his bondage. Whatever chance they had of winning, to win would be, for the end they had at heart, to lose, so they simply abstained, as it were, from comment upon the detestable procedure which terminated in the rule absolute. I have often wondered whether the whole business would not have been more defensible if there had been on Judy's part any emotional spring for the leap they made. I offer my conviction that there was none, that she was only extravagantly affected by the ideals of the Quarter—it is a transporting atmosphere—and held a view of comradeship which permitted the reversal of the modern situation filled by a blameless correspondent. Robert, of course, was tremendously in love with her; but my theory is that she married him as the logical outcome of her sacrifice and by no means the smallest part of it.

It was all quite unimaginable, as so many things are, but the upshot of it brought Judy to Rawul Pindi, as I have said, where I for one thought her mistake insignificant compared with her value. It would have been great, her value, anywhere; in the middle of the Punjab it was incalculable. To explain why would be to explain British India, but I hope it will appear; and I am quite willing, remember, to take the responsibility if it does not.

Somers Chichele, Anna's son, it is absurd to think, must have been about fifteen then, reflecting at Winchester with the other "men" upon the comparative merits of tinned sardines and jam roll, and whether a packet of real Egyptians was not worth the sacrifice of either. His father was colonel of the Twelfth; his mother was still charming. It was the year before Dick Forsyth came down from the neighbourhood of Sheikhbudin with a brevet and a good deal of personal damage. I mention him because he proved Anna's charm in the only conclusive way before the eyes of us all; and the station, I remember, was edified to observe that if Mrs Chichele came out of the matter "straight"—one relapses so easily into the simple definitions of those parts—which she undoubtedly did, she owed it in no small degree to Judy Harbottle. This one feels to be hardly a legitimate reference, but it is something tangible to lay hold upon in trying to describe the web of volitions which began to weave itself between the two that afternoon on my veranda and which afterward became so strong a bond. I was delighted with the thing; its simplicity and sincerity stood out among our conventional little compromises at friendship like an ideal. She and Judy had the assurance of one another; they made upon one another the finest and often the most unconscionable demands. One met them walking at odd hours in queer places, of which I imagine they were not much aware. They would turn deliberately off the Maidan and away from the bandstand to be rid of our irrelevant bows; they did their duty by the rest of us, but the most egregious among us, the Deputy-Commissioner for selection, could see that he hardly counted. I thought I understood, but that may have been my fatuity; certainly when their husbands inquired what on earth they had been talking of, it usually transpired that they had found an infinite amount to say about nothing. It was a little worrying to hear Colonel Chichele and Major Harbottle describe their wives as "pals," but the fact could not be denied, and after all we were in the Punjab. They were pals too, but the terms were different.

People discussed it according to their lights, and girls said in pretty wonderment that Mrs Harbottle and Mrs Chichele were like men, they never kissed each other. I think Judy prescribed these conditions. Anna was far more a person who did as the world told her. But it was a poor negation to describe all that they never did; there was no common little convention of attachment that did not seem to be tacitly omitted between them. I hope one did not too cynically observe that they offered these to their husbands instead; the redeeming observation was their husbands' complete satisfaction. This they maintained to the end. In the natural order of things Robert Harbottle should have paid heavily for interfering as he did in Paris between a woman and what she was entitled to live for. As a matter of fact he never paid anything at all; I doubt whether he ever knew himself a debtor. Judy kept her temperament under like a current and swam with the tides of the surface, taking refreshing dips only now and then which one traced in her eyes and her hair when she and Robert came back from leave. That sort of thing is lost in the sands of India, but it makes an oasis as it travels, and it sometimes seemed to me a curious pity that she and Anna should sit in the shade of it together, while Robert and Peter Chichele, their titular companions, blundered on in the desert. But after all, if you are born blind—and the men were both immensely liked, and the shooting was good.

Ten years later Somers joined. The Twelfth were at Peshawur. Robert Harbottle was Lieutenant-Colonel by that time and had the regiment. Distinction had incrusted, in the Indian way, upon Peter Chichele, its former colonel; he was General Commanding the District and KCB. So we were all still together in Peshawur. It was great luck for the Chicheles, Sir Peter's having the district, though his father's old regiment would have made it pleasant enough for the boy in any case. He came to us, I mean, of course, to two or three of us, with the interest that hangs about a victim of circumstances; we understood that he wasn't a "born soldier." Anna had told me on the contrary that he was a sacrifice to family tradition made inevitable by the General's unfortunate investments. Bellona's bridegroom was not a role he fancied, though he would make a kind of compromise as best man; he would agree, she said, to be a war correspondent and write picturesque specials for the London halfpenny press. There was the humour of the poor boy's despair in it, but she conveyed it, I remember, in exactly the same tone with which she had said to me years before that he wanted to drive a milk-cart. She carried quite her half of the family tradition, though she could talk of sacrifice and make her eyes wistful, contemplating for Somers the limitations of the drill-book and the camp of exercise, proclaiming and insisting upon what she would have done if she could only have chosen for him. Anna Chichele saw things that way. With more than a passable sense of all that was involved, if she could have made her son an artist in life or a commander-in-chief, if she could have given him the seeing eye or the Order of the Star of India, she would not have hesitated for an instant. Judy, with her single mind, cried out, almost at sight of him, upon them both, I mean both Anna and Sir Peter. Not that the boy carried his condemnation badly, or even obviously; I venture that no one noticed it in the mess; but it was naturally plain to those of us who were under the same. He had put in his two years with a British regiment at Meerut—they nurse subalterns that way for the Indian army—and his eyes no longer played with the tinsel vision of India; they looked instead into the arid stretch beyond. This preoccupation conveyed to the Surgeon-Major's wife the suggestion that Mr Chichele was the victim of a hopeless attachment. Mrs Harbottle made no such mistake; she saw simply, I imagine, the beginnings of her own hunger and thirst in him, looking back as she told us across a decade of dusty sunsets to remember them. The decade was there, close to the memory of all of us; we put, from Judy herself downward, an absurd amount of confidence in it.

She looked so well the night she met him. It was English mail day; she depended a great deal upon her letters, and I suppose somebody had written her a word that brought her that happy, still excitement that is the inner mystery of words. He went straight to her with some speech about his mother having given him leave, and for twenty minutes she patronized him on a sofa as his mother would not have dreamed of doing.

Anna Chichele, from the other side of the room, smiled on the pair.

"I depend on you and Judy to be good to him while we are away," she said. She and Sir Peter were going on leave at the end of the week to Scotland, as usual, for the shooting.

Following her glance I felt incapable of the proportion she assigned me. "I will see after his socks with pleasure," I said. "I think, don't you, we may leave the rest to Judy?"

Her eyes remained upon the boy, and I saw the passion rise in them, at which I turned mine elsewhere. Who can look unperturbed upon such a privacy of nature as that?

"Poor old Judy!" she went on. "She never would be bothered with him in all his dear hobble-dehoy time; she resented his claims, the unreasonable creature, used to limit me to three anecdotes a week; and now she has him on her hands, if you like. See the pretty air of deference in the way he listens to her! He has nice manners, the villain, if he is a Chichele!"

"Oh, you have improved Sir Peter's," I said kindly.

"I do hope Judy will think him worth while. I can't quite expect that he will be up to her, bless him, she is so much cleverer, isn't she, than any of us? But if she will just be herself with him it will make such a difference."

The other two crossed the room to us at that, and Judy gaily made Somers over to his mother, trailing off to find Robert in the billiard room.

"Well, what has Mrs Harbottle been telling you?" Anna asked him.

The young man's eye followed Judy, his hand went musingly to his moustache.

"She was telling me," he said, "that people in India were sepulchres of themselves, but that now and then one came who could roll away another's stone."

"It sounds promising," said Lady Chichele to me.

"It sounds cryptic," I laughed to Somers, but I saw that he had the key.

I can not say that I attended diligently to Mr Chichele's socks, but the part corresponding was freely assigned me. After his people went I saw him often. He pretended to find qualities in my tea, implied that he found them in my talk. As a matter of fact it was my inquiring attitude that he loved, the knowledge that there was no detail that he could give me about himself, his impressions and experiences, that was unlikely to interest me. I would not for the world imply that he was egotistical or complacent, absolutely the reverse, but he possessed an articulate soul which found its happiness in expression, and I liked to listen. I feel that these are complicated words to explain a very simple relation, and I pause to wonder what is left to me if I wished to describe his commerce with Mrs Harbottle. Luckily there is an alternative; one needn't do it. I wish I had somewhere on paper Judy's own account of it at this period, however. It is a thing she would have enjoyed writing and more enjoyed communicating, at this period.

There was a grave reticence in his talk about her which amused me in the beginning. Mrs Harbottle had been for ten years important enough to us all, but her serious significance, the light and the beauty in her, had plainly been reserved for the discovery of this sensitive and intelligent person not very long from Sandhurst and exactly twenty-six. I was barely allowed a familiar reference, and anything approaching a flippancy was met with penetrating silence. I was almost rebuked for lightly suggesting that she must occasionally find herself bored in Peshawur.

"I think not anywhere," said Mr Chichele; "Mrs Harbottle is one of the few people who sound the privilege of living."

This to me, who had counted Mrs Harbottle's yawns on so many occasions! It became presently necessary to be careful, tactful, in one's implications about Mrs Harbottle, and to recognize a certain distinction in the fact that one was the only person with whom Mr Chichele discussed her at all.

The day came when we talked of Robert; it was bound to come in the progress of understanding and affectionate colloquy which had his wife for inspiration. I was familiar, of course, with Somers's opinion that the Colonel was an awfully good sort; that had been among the preliminaries and become understood as the base of all references. And I liked Robert Harbottle very well myself. When his adjutant called him a born leader of men, however, I felt compelled to look at the statement consideringly.

"In a tight place," I said—dear me, what expressions had the freedom of our little frontier drawing-rooms!—"I would as soon depend on him as anybody. But as for leadership—"

"He is such a good fellow that nobody here does justice to his soldierly qualities," said Mr Chichele, "except Mrs Harbottle."

"Has she been telling you about them?" I inquired.

"Well," he hesitated, "she told me about the Mulla Nulla affair. She is rather proud of that. Any woman would be."

"Poor dear Judy!" I mused.

Somers said nothing, but looked at me, removing his cigarette, as if my words would be the better of explanation.

"She has taken refuge in them—in Bob Harbottle's soldierly qualities—ever since she married him," I continued.

"Taken refuge," he repeated, coldly, but at my uncompromising glance his eyes fell.

"Well?" I said.

"You mean—"

"Oh, I mean what I say," I laughed. "Your cigarette has gone out—have another."

"I think her devotion to him splendid."

"Quite splendid. Have you seen the things he brought her from the Simla Art Exhibition? He said they were nice bits of colour, and she has hung them in the drawing-room, where she will have to look at them every day. Let us admire her—dear Judy."

"Oh," he said, with a fine air of detachment, "do you think they are so necessary, those agreements?"

"Well," I replied, "we see that they are not indispensable. More sugar? I have only given you one lump. And we know, at all events," I added, unguardedly, "that she could never have had an illusion about him."

The young man looked up quickly. "Is that story true?" he asked.

"There was a story, but most of us have forgotten it. Who told you?"

"The doctor."

"The Surgeon-Major," I said, "has an accurate memory and a sense of proportion. As I suppose you were bound to get it from somebody, I am glad you got it from him."

I was not prepared to go on, and saw with some relief that Somers was not either. His silence, as he smoked, seemed to me deliberate; and I had oddly enough at this moment for the first time the impression that he was a man and not a boy. Then the Harbottles themselves joined us, very cheery after a gallop from the Wazir-Bagh. We talked of old times, old friendships, good swords that were broken, names that had carried far, and Somers effaced himself in the perfect manner of the British subaltern. It was a long, pleasant gossip, and I thought Judy seemed rather glad to let her husband dictate its level, which, of course, he did. I noticed when the three rode away together that the Colonel was beginning to sit down rather solidly on his big New Zealander; and I watched the dusk come over from the foot-hills for a long time thinking more kindly than I had spoken of Robert Harbottle.

I have often wondered how far happiness is contributed to a temperament like Judy Harbottle's, and how far it creates its own; but I doubt whether, on either count, she found as much in any other winter of her life except perhaps the remote ones by the Seine. Those ardent hours of hers, when everything she said was touched with the flame of her individuality, came oftener; she suddenly cleaned up her palate and began to translate in one study after another the language of the frontier country, that spoke only in stones and in shadows under the stones and in sunlight over them. There is nothing in the Academy of this year, at all events, that I would exchange for the one she gave me. She lived her physical life at a pace which carried us all along with her; she hunted and drove and danced and dined with such sincere intention as convinced us all that in hunting and driving and dancing and dining there were satisfactions that had been somehow overlooked. The Surgeon-Major's wife said it was delightful to meet Mrs Harbottle, she seemed to enjoy everything so thoroughly; the Surgeon-Major looked at her critically and asked her if she were quite sure she hadn't a night temperature. He was a Scotchman. One night Colonel Harbottle, hearing her give away the last extra, charged her with renewing her youth.

"No, Bob," she said, "only imitating it."

Ah, that question of her youth. It was so near her—still, she told me once, she heard the beat of its flying, and the pulse in her veins answered the false signal. That was afterward, when she told the truth. She was not so happy when she indulged herself otherwise. As when she asked one to remember that she was a middle-aged woman, with middle-aged thoughts and satisfactions.

"I am now really happiest," she declared, "when the Commissioner takes me in to dinner, when the General Commanding leads me to the dance."

She did her best to make it an honest conviction. I offered her a recent success not crowned by the Academy, and she put it down on the table. "By and by," she said. "At present I am reading Pascal and Bossuet." Well, she was reading Pascal and Bossuet. She grieved aloud that most of our activities in India were so indomitably youthful, owing to the accident that most of us were always so young. "There is no dignified distraction in this country," she complained, "for respectable ladies nearing forty." She seemed to like to make these declarations in the presence of Somers Chichele, who would look at her with a little queer smile—a bad translation, I imagine, of what he felt.

She gave herself so generously to her seniors that somebody said Mrs Harbottle's girdle was hung with brass hats. It seems flippant to add that her complexion was as honest as the day, but the fact is that the year before Judy had felt compelled, like the rest of us, to repair just a little the ravages of the climate. If she had never done it one would not have looked twice at the absurdity when she said of the powder-puff in the dressing room, "I have raised that thing to the level of an immorality," and sailed in to dance with an uncompromising expression and a face uncompromised. I have not spoken of her beauty; for one thing it was not always there, and there were people who would deny it altogether, or whose considered comment was, "I wouldn't call her plain." They, of course, were people in whom she declined to be interested, but even for those of us who could evoke some demonstration of her vivid self her face would not always light in correspondence. When it did there was none that I liked better to look at; and I envied Somers Chichele his way to make it the pale, shining thing that would hold him lifted, in return, for hours together, with I know not what mystic power of a moon upon the tide. And he? Oh, he was dark and delicate, by nature simple, sincere, delightfully intelligent. His common title to charm was the rather sweet seriousness that rested on his upper lip, and a certain winning gratification in his attention; but he had a subtler one in his eyes, which must be always seeking and smiling over what they found; those eyes of perpetual inquiry for the exquisite which ask so little help to create it. A personality to button up in a uniform, good heavens!

As I begin to think of them together I remember how the maternal note appeared in her talk about him.

"His youth is pathetic," she told me, "but there is nothing that he does not understand."

"Don't apologize, Judy!" I said. We were so brusque on the frontier. Besides, the matter still suffered a jocular presentment. Mrs Harbottle and Mr Chichele were still "great friends"; we could still put them next each other at our dinner parties without the feeling that it would be "marked." There was still nothing unusual in the fact that when Mrs Harbottle was there Mr Chichele might be taken for granted. We were so broad-minded also, on the frontier.

It grew more obvious, the maternal note. I began positively to dread it, almost as much, I imagine, as Somers did. She took her privileges all in Anna's name, she exercised her authority quite as Lady Chichele's proxy. She went to the very limit. "Anna Chichele," she said actually in his presence, "is a fortunate woman. She has all kinds of cleverness, and she has her tall son. I have only one little talent, and I have no tall son." Now it was not in nature that she could have had a son as tall as Somers, nor was that desire in her eyes. All civilization implies a good deal of farce, but this was a poor refuge, a cheap device; I was glad when it fell away from her sincerity, when the day came on which she looked into my fire and said simply, "An attachment like ours has no terms."

"I wonder," I said.

"For what comes and goes," she went on dreamily, "how could there be a formula?"

"Look here, Judy," I said, "you know me very well. What if the flesh leaps with the spirit?"

She looked at me, very white. "Oh no," she said, "no."

I waited, but there seemed nothing more that she could say; and in the silence the futile negative seemed to wander round the room repeating itself like an echo, "Oh no, no." I poked the fire presently to drown the sound of it. Judy sat still, with her feet crossed and her hands thrust into the pockets of her coat, staring into the coals.

"Can you live independently, satisfied with your interests and occupations?" she demanded at last. "Yes, I know you can. I can't. I must exist more than half in other people. It is what they think and feel that matters to me, just as much as what I think and feel. The best of life is in that communication."

"It has always been a passion with you, Judy," I replied. "I can imagine how much you miss—"

"Whom?"

"Anna Chichele," I said softly.

She got up and walked about the room, fixing here and there an intent regard upon things which she did not see. "Oh, I do," she said at one point, with the effect of pulling herself together. She took another turn or two, and then finding herself near the door she went out. I felt as profoundly humiliated for her as if she had staggered.

The next night was one of those that stand out so vividly, for no reason that one can identify, in one's memory. We were dining with the Harbottles, a small party, for a tourist they had with them. Judy and I and Somers and the traveller had drifted out into the veranda, where the scent of Japanese lilies came and went on the spring wind to trouble the souls of any taken unawares. There was a brightness beyond the foot-hills where the moon was coming, and I remembered how one tall clump swayed out against it, and seemed in passionate perfume to lay a burden on the breast. Judy moved away from it and sat clasping her knees on the edge of the veranda. Somers, when his eyes were not upon her, looked always at the lily.

Even the spirit of the globe-trotter was stirred, and he said, "I think you Anglo-Indians live in a kind of little paradise."

There was an instant's silence, and then Judy turned her face into the lamp-light from the drawing-room. "With everything but the essentials," she said.

We stayed late; Mr Chichele and ourselves were the last to go. Judy walked with us along the moonlit drive to the gate, which is so unnecessary a luxury in India that the servants always leave it open. She swung the stiff halves together.

"Now," she said, "it is shut."

"And I," said Somers Chichele, softly and quickly, "am on the other side."

Even over that depth she could flash him a smile. "It is the business of my life," she gave him in return, "to keep this gate shut." I felt as if they had forgotten us. Somers mounted and rode off without a word; we were walking in a different direction. Looking back, I saw Judy leaning immovable on the gate, while Somers turned in his saddle, apparently to repeat the form of lifting his hat. And all about them stretched the stones of Kabul valley, vague and formless in the tide of the moonlight . . .

Next day a note from Mrs Harbottle informed me that she had gone to Bombay for a fortnight. In a postscript she wrote, "I shall wait for the Chicheles there, and come back with them." I remember reflecting that if she could not induce herself to take passage to England in the ship that brought them, it seemed the right thing to do.

She did come back with them. I met the party at the station. I knew Somers would meet them, and it seemed to me, so imminent did disaster loom, that someone else should be there, someone to offer a covering movement or a flank support wherever it might be most needed. And among all our smiling faces disaster did come, or the cold premonition of it. We were all perfect, but Somers's lip trembled. Deprived for a fortnight he was eager for the draft, and he was only twenty-six. His lips trembled, and there, under the flickering station-lamps, suddenly stood that of which there never could be again any denial, for those of us who saw.

Did we make, I wonder, even a pretense of disguising the consternation that sprang up among us, like an armed thing, ready to kill any further suggestion of the truth? I don't know. Anna Chichele's unfinished sentence dropped as if someone had given her a blow upon the mouth. Coolies were piling the luggage into a hired carriage at the edge of the platform. She walked mechanically after them, and would have stepped in with it but for the sight of her own gleaming landau drawn up within a yard or two, and the General waiting. We all got home somehow, taking it with us, and I gave Lady Chichele twenty-four hours to come to me with her face all one question and her heart all one fear. She came in twelve.

"Have you seen it—long?" Prepared as I was her directness was demoralizing.

"It isn't a mortal disease."

"Oh, for Heaven's sake—"

"Well, not with certainty, for more than a month."

She made a little spasmodic movement with her hands, then dropped them pitifully. "Couldn't you do *any*thing?"

I looked at her, and she said at once, "No, of course you couldn't."

For a moment or two I took my share of the heavy sense of it, my trivial share, which yet was an experience sufficiently exciting. "I am afraid it will have to be faced," I said.

"What will happen?" Anna cried. "Oh, what will happen?"

"Why not the usual thing?" Lady Chichele looked up quickly as if at a reminder. "The ambiguous attachment of the country," I went on, limping but courageous, "half declared, half admitted, that leads vaguely nowhere, and finally perishes as the man's life enriches itself—the thing we have seen so often."

"Whatever Judy is capable of it won't be the usual thing. You know that."

I had to confess in silence that I did.

"It flashed at me—the difference in her—in Bombay." She pressed her lips together and then went on unsteadily. "In her eyes, her voice. She was mannered, extravagant, elaborate. With me! All the way up I wondered and worried. But I never thought—" She stopped; her voice simply shook itself into silence. I called a servant.

"I am going to give you a good stiff peg," I said. I apologize for the "peg," but not for the whisky and soda. It is a beverage on the frontier, of which the vulgarity is lost in the value. While it was coming I tried to talk of other things, but she would only nod absently in the pauses.

"Last night we dined with him, it was guest night at the mess, and she was there. I watched her, and she knew it. I don't know whether she tried, but anyway, she failed. The covenant between them was written on her forehead whenever she looked at him, though that was seldom. She dared not look at him. And the little conversation they had—you would have laughed—it was a comedy of stutters. The facile Mrs Harbottle!"

"You do well to be angry, naturally," I said; "but it would be fatal to let yourself go, Anna."

"Angry? Oh, I am *sick*. The misery of it! The terror of it! If it were anybody but Judy! Can't you imagine the passion of a temperament like that in a woman who has all these years been feeding on herself? I tell you she will take him from my very arms. And he will go—to I dare not imagine what catastrophe! Who can prevent it? Who can prevent it?"

"There is you," I said.

Lady Chichele laughed hysterically. "I think you ought to say, 'There are you.' I—what can I do? Do you realize that it's *Judy*? My friend—my other self? Do you think we can drag all that out of it? Do you think a tie like that can be broken by an accident—by a misfortune? With it all I *adore* Judy Harbottle. I love her, as I have always loved her, and—it's damnable, but I don't know whether, whatever happened, I wouldn't go on loving her."

"Finish your peg," I said. She was sobbing.

"Where I blame myself most," she went on, "is for not seeing in him all that makes him mature to her—that makes her forget the absurd difference between them, and take him simply and sincerely as I know she does, as the contemporary of her soul if not of her body. I saw none of that. Could I, as his mother? Would he show it to me? I though him just a charming boy, clever, too, of course, with nice instincts and well plucked; we were always proud of that, with his delicate physique. Just a boy! I haven't yet stopped thinking how different he looks without his curls. And I thought she would be just kind and gracious and delightful to him because he was my son."

"There, of course," I said, "is the only chance."

"Where—what?"

"He is your son."

"Would you have me appeal to her? Do you know I don't think I could?"

"Dear me, no. Your case must present itself. It must spring upon her and grow before her out of your silence, and if you can manage it, your confidence. There is a great deal, after all, remember, to hold her in that. I can't somehow imagine her failing you. Otherwise—"

Lady Chichele and I exchanged a glance of candid admission.

"Otherwise she would be capable of sacrificing everything—everything. Of gathering her life into an hour. I know. And do you know if the thing were less impossible, less grotesque, I should not be so much afraid? I mean that the *absolute* indefensibility of it might bring her a recklessness and a momentum which might—"

"Send her over the verge," I said. "Well, go home and ask her to dinner."

There was a good deal more to say, of course, than I have thought proper to put down here, but before Anna went I saw that she was keyed up to the heroic part. This was none the less to her credit because it was the only part, the dictation of a sense of expediency that despaired while it dictated. The noble thing was her capacity to take it, and, amid all that warred in her, to carry it out on the brave high lines of her inspiration. It seemed a literal inspiration, so perfectly calculated that it was hard not to think sometimes, when one saw them together, that Anna had been lulled into a simple resumption of the old relation. Then from the least thing possible—the lift of an eyelid—it flashed upon one that between these two every moment was dramatic, and one took up the word with a curious sense of detachment and futility, but with one's heart beating like a trip-hammer with the mad excitement of it. The acute thing was the splendid sincerity of Judy Harbottle's response. For days she was profoundly on her guard, then suddenly she seemed to become practically, vividly aware of what I must go on calling the great chance, and passionately to fling herself upon it. It was the strangest co-operation without a word or a sign to show it conscious—a playing together for stakes that could not be admitted, a thing to hang upon breathless. It was there between them—the tenable ground of what they were to each other: they occupied it with almost an equal eye upon the tide that threatened, while I from my mainland tower also made an anguished calculation of the chances. I think in spite of the menace, they found real beatitudes; so keenly did they set about the business that it brought them moments finer than any they could count in the years that were behind them, the flat and colourless years that were gone. Once or twice the wild idea even visited me that it was, after all, the projection of his mother in Somers that had so seized Judy Harbottle, and that the original was all that was needed to help the happy process of detachment. Somers himself at the time was a good deal away on escort duty: they had a clear field.

I can not tell exactly when—between Mrs Harbottle and myself—it became a matter for reference more or less overt, I mean her defined problem, the thing that went about between her and the sun. It will be imagined that it did not come up like the weather; indeed, it was hardly ever to be envisaged and never to be held; but it was always there, and out of our joint consciousness it would sometimes leap and pass, without shape or face. It might slip between two sentences, or it might remain, a dogging shadow, for an hour. Or a week would go by while, with a strong hand, she held it out of sight altogether and talked of Anna—always of Anna. Her eyes shone with the things she told me then: she seemed to keep herself under the influence of them as if they had the power of narcotics. At the end of a time like this she turned to me in the door as she was going and stood silent, as if she could neither go nor stay. I had been able to make nothing of her that afternoon: she had seemed preoccupied with the pattern of the carpet which she traced continually with her riding crop, and finally I, too, had relapsed. She sat haggard, with the fight forever in her eyes, and the day seemed to sombre about her in her corner. When she turned in the door, I looked up with sudden prescience of a crisis.

"Don't jump," she said, "it was only to tell you that I have persuaded Robert to apply for furlough. Eighteen months. From the first of April. Don't touch me." I suppose I made a movement towards her. Certainly I wanted to throw my arms about her; with the instinct, I suppose, to steady her in her great resolution.

"At the end of that time, as you know, he will be retired. I had some trouble, he is so keen on the regiment, but I think—I have succeeded. You might mention it to Anna."

"Haven't you?" sprang past my lips.

"I can't. It would be like taking an oath to tell her, and—I can't take an oath to go. But I mean to."

"There is nothing to be said," I brought out, feeling indeed that there was not. "But I congratulate you, Judy."

"No, there is nothing to be said. And you congratulate me, no doubt!"

She stood for a moment quivering in the isolation she made for herself; and I felt a primitive angry revolt against the delicate trafficking of souls that could end in such ravage and disaster. The price was too heavy; I would have denuded her, at the moment, of all that had led her into this, and turned her out a clod with fine shoulders like fifty other women in Peshawur. Then, perhaps, because I held myself silent and remote and she had no emotion of fear from me, she did not immediately go.

"It will beat itself away, I suppose, like the rest of the unreasonable pain of the world," she said at last; and that, of course, brought me to her side. "Things will go back to their proportions. This," she touched an open rose, "will claim its beauty again. And life will become—perhaps—what it was before." Still I found nothing to say, I could only put my arm in hers and walk with her to the edge of the veranda where the syce was holding her horse. She stroked the animal's neck. "Everything in me answered him," she informed me, with the grave intelligence of a patient who relates a symptom past. As she took the reins she turned to me again. "His spirit came to mine like a homing bird," she said, and in her smile even the pale reflection of happiness was sweet and stirring. It left me hanging in imagination over the source and the stream, a little blessed in the mere understanding.

Too much blessed for confidence, or any safe feeling that the source was bound. Rather I saw it leaping over every obstacle, flashing to its destiny. As I drove to the Club the next day I decided that I would not tell Anna Chichele of Colonel Harbottle's projected furlough. If to Judy telling her would be like taking an oath that they would go, to me it would at least be like assuming sponsorship for their intention. That would be heavy indeed. From the first of April—we were then in March. Anna would hear it soon enough from the General, would see it soon enough, almost, in the *Gazette*, when it would have passed into irrecoverable fact. So I went by her with locked lips, kept out of the way of those eyes of the mother that asked and asked, and would have seen clear to any depth, any hiding-place of knowledge like that. As I pulled up at the Club I saw Colonel Harbottle talking concernedly to the wife of our Second-in-Command, and was reminded that I had not heard for some days how Major Watkins was going on. So I, too, approached Mrs Watkins in her victoria to ask. Robert Harbottle kindly forestalled her reply. "Hard luck, isn't it? Watkins has been ordered home at once. Just settled into their new house, too—last of the kit came up from Calcutta yesterday, didn't it, Mrs Watkins? But it's sound to go—Peshawur is the worst hole in Asia to shake off dysentery in."

We agreed upon this and discussed the sale-list of her new furniture that Mrs Watkins would have to send round the station, and considered the chances of a trooper—to the Watkinses with two children and not a penny but his pay it did make it easier not to have to go by a liner—and Colonel Harbottle and I were half-way to the reading-room before the significance of Major Watkins's sick leave flashed upon me.

"But this," I cried, "will make a difference to your plans. You won't—"

"Be able to ask for that furlough Judy wants. Rather not. I'm afraid she's disappointed—she was tremendously set on going—but it doesn't matter tuppence to me."

I sought out Mrs Harbottle, at the end of the room. She looked radiant; she sat on the edge of the table and swung a light-hearted heel. She was talking to people who in themselves were a witness to high spirits, Captain the Hon. Freddy Gisborne, Mrs Flamboys.

At sight of me her face clouded, fell suddenly into the old weary lines. It made me feel somehow a little sick; I went back to my cart and drove home.

For more than a week I did not see her except when I met her riding with Somers Chichele along the peach-bordered road that leads to the Wazir-Bagh. The trees were all in blossom and made a picture that might well catch dreaming hearts into a beatitude that would correspond. The air was full of spring and the scent of violets, those wonderful Peshawur violets that grow in great clumps, tall and double. Gracious clouds came and trailed across the frontier barrier; blue as an idyll it rose about us; the city smiled in her gardens.

She had it all in her face, poor Judy, all the spring softness and more, the morning she came, intensely controlled, to announce her defeat. I was in the drawing-room doing the flowers; I put them down to look at her. The wonderful telegram from Simla arrived—that was the wonderful part—at the same time; I remembered how the red, white, and blue turban of the telegraph peon bobbed up behind her shoulder in the veranda. I signed and laid it on the table; I suppose it seemed hardly likely that anything could be important enough to interfere at the moment with my impression of what love, unbounded and victorious, could do with a face I thought I knew. Love sat there careless of the issue, full of delight. Love proclaimed that between him and Judith Harbottle it was all over—she had met him, alas, in too narrow a place—and I marvelled at the paradox with which he softened every curve and underlined every vivid note of personality in token that it had just begun. He sat there in great serenity, and though I knew that somewhere behind lurked a vanquished woman, I saw her through such a radiance that I could not be sure of seeing her at all . . .

She went back to the very first of it; she seemed herself intensely interested in the facts; and there is no use in pretending that, while she talked, the moral consideration was at all present with me either; it wasn't. Her extremity was the thing that absorbed us; she even, in tender thoughtfulness, diagnosed it from its definite beautiful beginning.

"It was there, in my heart, when I woke one morning, exquisite and strange, the assurance of a gift. How had it come there, while I slept? I assure you when I closed my eyes it did not exist for me . . . Yes, of course, I had seen him, but only somewhere at dinner . . . As the day went on it changed—it turned into a clear pool, into a flower. And I—think of my not understanding! I was pleased with it! For a long time, for days, I never dreamed that it could be anything but a little secret joy. Then, suddenly—oh, I had not been perceiving enough!—it was in all my veins, a tide, an efflorescence, a thing of my very life.

"Then—it was a little late—I understood, and since—

"I began by hating it—being furious, furious—and afraid, too. Sometimes it was like a low cloud, hovering and travelling always with me, sometimes like a beast of prey that went a little way off and sat looking at me . . .

"I have—done my best. But there is nothing to do, to kill, to abolish. How can I say, 'I will not let you in,' when it is already there? How can I assume indifference when this thing is imposed upon every moment of my day? And it has grown so sweet—the longing—that—isn't it strange?—I could more willingly give him up than the desire of him. That seems impossible to part with as life itself."

She sat reflective for a moment, and I saw her eyes slowly fill.

"Don't—don't *cry*, Judy," I faltered, wanting to horribly, myself.

She smiled them dry.

"Not now. But I am giving myself, I suppose, to many tears."

"God help you," I said. What else was there to say?

"There is no such person," she replied, gaily. "There is only a blessed devil."

"Then you go all the way—to the logical conclusion?"

She hardly hesitated. "To the logical conclusion. What poor words!"

"May I ask—when?"

"I should like to tell you that quite definitely, and I think I can. The English mail leaves tonight."

"And you have arranged to take it?"

"We have arranged nothing. Do you know"—she smiled as if at the fresh colours of an idyll—"we have not even come to the admission? There has been between us no word, no vision. Ah, we have gone in bonds, and dumb! Hours we have had, exquisite hours of the spirit, but never a moment of the heart, a moment confessed. It was mine to give—that moment, and he has waited—I know—wondering whether perhaps it would ever come. And today—we are going for a ride today, and I do not think we shall come back."

"O Judy," I cried, catching at her sleeve, "he is only a boy!"

"There were times when I thought that conclusive. Now the misery of it has gone to sleep; don't waken it. It pleases me to believe that the years are a convention. I never had any dignity, you know, and I seem to have missed the moral deliverance. I only want—oh, you know what I want. Why don't you open your telegram?"

I had been folding and fingering the brown envelope as if it had been a scrap of waste-paper.

"It is probably from Mrs Watkins about the victoria," I said, feeling its profound irrelevance. "I wired an offer to her in Bombay. However"—and I read the telegram, the little solving telegram from Army Headquarters. I turned my back on her to read it again, and then I replaced it very carefully and put it in my pocket. It was a moment to take hold of with both hands, crying on all one's gods for steadiness.

"How white you look!" said Mrs Harbottle, with concern. "Not bad news?"

"On the contrary, excellent news. Judy, will you stay to lunch?"

She looked at me, hesitating. "Won't it seem rather a compromise on your part? When you ought to be rousing the city—"

"I don't intend to rouse the city," I said.

"I have given you the chance."

"Thank you," I said, grimly, "but the only real favour you can do me is to stay and lunch." It was then just on one.

"I'll stay," she said, "if you will promise not to make any sort of effort. I shouldn't mind, but it would distress you."

"I promise absolutely," I said, and ironical joy rose up in me, and the telegram burned in my pocket.

She would talk of it, though I found it hard to let her go on, knowing and knowing and knowing as I did that for that day at least it could not be. There was very little about herself that she wanted to tell me; she was there confessed a woman whom joy had overcome; it was understood that we both accepted that situation. But in the details which she asked me to take charge of it was plain that she also kept a watchful eye upon fate—matters of business.

We were in the drawing-room. The little round clock in its Armritsar case marked half-past three. Judy put down her coffee cup and rose to go. As she glanced at the clock the light deepened in her eyes, and I, with her hand in mine, felt like an agent of the Destroyer—for it was half-past three—consumed myself with fear lest the blow had miscarried. Then as we stood, suddenly, the sounds of hoofs at a gallop on the drive, and my husband threw himself off at the door and tore through the hall to his room; and in the certainty that overwhelmed me even Judy, for an instant, stood dim and remote.

"Major Jim seems to be in a hurry," said Mrs Harbottle, lightly, "I have always liked your husband. I wonder whether he will say tomorrow that he always liked me."

"Dear Judy, I don't think he will be occupied with you tomorrow."

"Oh, surely, just a little, if I go tonight."

"You won't go tonight."

She looked at me helplessly. I felt as if I were insisting upon her abasement instead of her salvation. "I wish—"

"You're not going—you're not! You can't! Look!"

I pulled it out of my pocket and thrust it at her—the telegram. It came, against every regulation, from my good friend the Deputy Adjutant-General, in Simla, and it read, "*Row Khurram 12th probably ordered front three hours' time.*"

Her face changed—how my heart leaped to see it change!—and that took command there which will command trampling, even in the women of the camp, at news like this.

"What luck that Bob couldn't take his furlough!" she exclaimed, single-thoughted. "But you have known this for hours"—there was even something of the Colonel's wife, authority, incisiveness. "Why didn't you tell me? Ah—I see."

I stood before her abashed, and that was ridiculous, while she measured me as if I presented in myself the woman I took her to be. "It wasn't like that," she said. I had to defend myself. "Judy," I said, "if you weren't in honour bound to Anna, how could I know that you would be in honour bound to the regiment? There was a train at three."

"I beg to assure you that you have overcalculated," said Mrs Harbottle. Her eyes were hard and proud. "And I am not sure"—a deep red swept over her face, a man's blush—"in the light of this I am not sure that I am not honour bound to Anna."

We had reached the veranda, and at her signal her coachman drove quickly up. "You have kept me here three hours when there was the whole of Bob's kit to see to," she said, as she flung herself in; "you might have thought of that."

It was a more than usually tedious campaign, and Colonel Robert Harbottle was ambushed and shot in a place where one must believe pure boredom induced him to take his men. The incident was relieved, the newspapers said—and they are seldom so clever in finding relief for such incidents—by the dash and courage shown by Lieutenant Chichele, who, in one of those feats which it has lately been the fashion to criticize, carried the mortally wounded body of his Colonel out of range at conspicuous risk of depriving the Queen of another officer. I helped Judy with her silent packing; she had forgiven me long before that; and she settled almost at once into the flat in Chelsea which has since been credited with so delightful an atmosphere, went back straight into her own world. I have always kept her first letters about it, always shall. For months after, while the expedition still raged after snipers and rifle-thieves, I discussed with Lady Chichele the probable outcome of it all. I have sometimes felt ashamed of leaping as straight as I did with Anna to what we thought the inevitable. I based no calculation on all Mrs Harbottle had gone back to, just as I had based no calculation on her ten years' companionship in arms when I kept her from the three o'clock train. This last was a retrospection in which Anna naturally could not join me; she never knew, poor dear, how fortunate as to its moment was the campaign she deplored, and nothing to this day can have disturbed her conviction that the bond she was at such magnificent pains to strengthen, held against the strain, as long, happily, as the supreme need existed. "How right you were!" she often said. "She did, after all, love me best, dear, wonderful Judy!" Her distress about poor Robert Harbottle was genuine enough, but one could not be surprised at a certain ambiguity; one tear for Robert, so to speak, and two for her boy. It could hardly be, for him, a marriage after his mother's heart. And she laid down with some emphasis that Somers was brilliantly entitled to all he was likely to get—which was natural, too . . .

I had been from the beginning so much "in it" that Anna showed me, a year later, though I don't believe she liked doing it, the letter in part of which Mrs Harbottle shall finally excuse herself.

"Somers will give you this," I read, "and with it take back your son. You will not find, I know, anything grotesque in the charming enthusiasm with which he has offered his life to me; you understand too well, you are too kind. And you wonder that I can so render up a dear thing which I might keep and would once have taken, think how sweet in the desert is the pool, and how barren was the prospect from Balclutha."

It was like her to abandon in pride a happiness that asked so much less humiliation; I don't know why, but it was like her. And of course, when one thought of it, she had consulted all sorts of high expediencies. But I sat silent with remembrance, quieting a pang in my heart, trying not to calculate how much it had cost Judy Harbottle to take her second chance.

1903

Stephen Crane

1871–1900

From the start of his writing life Stephen Crane's aesthetic was clear: "The nearer the writer gets to life the greater he becomes as an artist." Crane had already haunted and absorbed the darker zones of New York City and out of his own pocket published the relentlessly naturalistic *Maggie: A Girl of the Streets* (1893), which had no popular success. But as the American novelist Robert Stone notes with amusement in his introduction to *The Red Badge of Courage* (1895), the closest Crane had come to anything "strenuous" was his semester as catcher for the Syracuse University baseball team. When he came to write the novel, "life" became synonymous with the utter magic of creativity. Drawing from his young but boundless imaginative resources and a friend's series of magazines about the Civil War, Crane wrote the dazzling, visceral narrative of Henry Fleming at war. "Perhaps," says Stone, "there are earlier novels that have so combined psychological intimacy with dense external detail. Few since have done it so simply and surely and eloquently." With the success of this novel, Crane more than made up for the insularity of his Newark upbringing and Syracuse education and became more than a little like his young soldier. As a journalist he reported on the Greco-Turkish and Spanish-American wars for the New York *World* and the New York *Journal*, and went on to publish a total of fourteen books—a prodigious number given his uncertain health and finances. In 1898 he moved to England with his companion, Cora Taylor, met Joseph Conrad and H.G. Wells, along with other important literary figures, and died in Germany—his death another appalling statistic in the history of tuberculosis. But along with *The Red Badge of Courage*, Crane's abiding works, registered in his highly visual and charged impressionistic style, are the story collections *The Open Boat and Other Tales of Adventure* (1898), *The Monster and Other Stories* (1899), and *Wounds in the Rain* (1900).

The Open Boat

A Tale Intended to be after the Fact: Being the Experience of Four Men from the Sunk Steamer "Commodore"

I

None of them knew the colour of the sky. Their eyes glanced level, and were fastened upon the waves that swept toward them. These waves were of the hue of slate, save for the tops, which were of foaming white, and all of the men knew the colours of the sea. The horizon narrowed and widened, and dipped and rose, and at all times its edge was jagged with waves that seemed thrust up in points like rocks.

Many a man ought to have a bathtub larger than the boat which here rode upon the sea. These waves were most wrongfully and barbarously abrupt and tall, and each froth-top was a problem in small-boat navigation.

The cook squatted in the bottom, and looked with both eyes at the six inches of gunwale which separated him from the ocean. His sleeves were rolled over his fat forearms, and the two flaps of his unbuttoned vest dangled as he bent to bail out the boat. Often he said, "Gawd! that was a narrow clip." As he remarked it he invariably gazed eastward over the broken sea.

The oiler, steering with one of the two oars in the boat, sometimes raised himself suddenly to keep clear of water that swirled in over the stern. It was a thin little oar, and it seemed often ready to snap.

The correspondent, pulling at the other oar, watched the waves and wondered why he was there.

The injured captain, lying in the bow, was at this time buried in that profound dejection and indifference that comes, temporarily at least, to even the bravest and most enduring when, willy-nilly, the firm fails, the army loses, the ship goes down. The mind of the master of a vessel is rooted deep in the timbers of her, though he command for a day or a decade; and this captain had on him the stern impression of a scene in the greys of dawn of seven turned faces, and later a stump of a topmast with a white ball on it, that slashed to and fro at the waves, went low and lower, and down. Thereafter there was something strange in his voice. Although steady, it was deep with mourning, and of a quality beyond oration or tears.

"Keep 'er a little more south, Billie," said he.

"A little more south, sir," said the oiler in the stern.

A seat in this boat was not unlike a seat upon a bucking bronco, and, by the same token, a bronco is not much smaller. The craft pranced and reared and plunged like an animal. As each wave came, and she rose for it, she seemed like a horse making at a fence outrageously high. The manner of her scramble over these walls of water is a mystic thing, and, moreover, at the top of them were ordinarily these problems in white water, the foam racing down from the summit of each wave, requiring a new leap, and a leap from the air. Then, after scornfully bumping a crest, she would slide and race and splash down a long incline, and arrive bobbing and nodding in front of the next menace.

A singular disadvantage of the sea lies in the fact that, after successfully surmounting one wave, you discover that there is another behind it, just as important and just as nervously anxious to do something effective in the way of swamping boats. In a ten-foot dinghy one can get an idea of the resources of the sea in the line of waves that is not probable to the average experience, which is never at sea in a dinghy. As each slaty wall of water approached, it shut all else from the view of the men in the boat, and it was not difficult to imagine that this particular wave was the final outburst of the ocean, the last effort of the grim water. There was a terrible grace in the move of the waves, and they came in silence, save for the snarling of the crests.

In the wan light the faces of the men must have been grey. Their eyes must have glinted in strange ways as they gazed steadily astern. Viewed from a balcony, the whole thing would, doubtless, have been weirdly picturesque. But the men in the boat had no time to see it, and if they had had leisure, there were other things to occupy their minds. The sun swung steadily up the sky, and they knew it was broad day because the colour of the sea changed from slate to emerald-green streaked with amber lights, and the foam was like tumbling snow. The process of the breaking day was unknown to them. They were aware only of this effect upon the colour of the waves that rolled toward them.

In disjointed sentences the cook and the correspondent argued as to the difference between a life-saving station and a house of refuge. The cook had said: "There's a house of refuge just north of the Mosquito Inlet Light, and as soon as they see us they'll come off in their boat and pick us up."

"As soon as who see us?" said the correspondent.

"The crew," said the cook.

"Houses of refuge don't have crews," said the correspondent. "As I understand them, they are only places where clothes and grub are stored for the benefit of shipwrecked people. They don't carry crews."

"Oh, yes, they do," said the cook.

"No, they don't," said the correspondent.

"Well, we're not there yet, anyhow," said the oiler in the stern.

"Well," said the cook, "perhaps it's not a house of refuge that I'm thinking of as being near Mosquito Inlet Light; perhaps it's a life-saving station."

"We're not there yet," said the oiler in the stern.

II

As the boat bounced from the top of each wave the wind tore through the hair of the hatless men, and as the craft plopped her stern down again the spray slashed past them. The crest of each of these waves was a hill, from the top of which the men surveyed for a moment a broad, tumultuous expanse, shining and wind-riven. It was probably splendid, it was probably glorious, this play of the free sea, wild with lights of emerald and white and amber.

"Bully good thing it's an on-shore wind," said the cook. "If not, where would we be? Wouldn't have a show."

"That's right," said the correspondent.

The busy oiler nodded his assent.

Then the captain, in the bow, chuckled in a way that expressed humour, contempt, tragedy, all in one. "Do you think we've got much of a show now, boys?" said he.

Whereupon the three were silent, save for a trifle of hemming and hawing. To express any particular optimism at this time they felt to be childish and stupid, but they all doubtless possessed this sense of the situation in their minds. A young man thinks doggedly at such times. On the other hand, the ethics of their condition was decidedly against any open suggestion of hopelessness. So they were silent.

"Oh, well," said the captain, soothing his children, "we'll get ashore all right."

But there was that in his tone which made them think; so the oiler quoth, "Yes! if this wind holds."

The cook was bailing. "Yes! if we don't catch hell in the surf."

Canton-flannel gulls flew near and far. Sometimes they sat down on the sea, near patches of brown seaweed that rolled over the waves with a movement like carpets on a line in a gale. The birds sat comfortably in groups, and they were envied by some in the dinghy, for the wrath of the sea was no more to them than it was to a covey of prairie-chickens a thousand miles inland. Often they came very close and stared at the men with black, bead-like eyes. At these times they were uncanny and sinister in their unblinking scrutiny, and the men hooted angrily at them, telling them to be gone. One came, and evidently decided to alight on the top of the captain's head. The bird flew parallel to the boat, and did not circle, but made short sidelong jumps in the air in chicken fashion. His black eyes were wistfully fixed upon the captain's head. "Ugly brute," said the oiler to the bird. "You look as if you were made with a jackknife." The cook and the correspondent swore darkly at the creature. The captain naturally wished to knock it away with the end of the heavy painter, but he did not dare do it, because anything resembling an emphatic gesture would have capsized this freighted boat; and so, with his open hand, the captain gently and carefully waved the gull away. After it had been discouraged from the pursuit the captain breathed easier on account of his hair, and others breathed easier because the bird struck their minds at this time as being somehow gruesome and ominous.

In the meantime the oiler and the correspondent rowed; and also they rowed. They sat together in the same seat, and each rowed an oar. Then the oiler took both oars; then the correspondent took both oars; then the oiler; then the correspondent. They rowed and they rowed. The very ticklish part of the business was when the time came for the reclining one in the stern to take his turn with the oars. By the very last star of truth, it is easier to steal eggs from under a hen than it was to change seats in the dinghy. First the man in the stern slid his hand along the thwart and moved with care, as if he were of Sèvres. Then the man in the rowing-seat slid his hand along the other thwart. It was all done with the most extraordinary care. As the two sidled past each other, the whole party kept watchful eyes on the coming wave, and the captain cried: "Look out, now! Steady, there!"

The brown mats of seaweed that appeared from time to time were like islands, bits of earth. They were travelling, apparently, neither one way nor the other. They were, to all intents, stationary. They informed the men in the boat that it was making progress slowly toward the land.

The captain, rearing cautiously in the bow after the dinghy soared on a great swell, said that he had seen the lighthouse at Mosquito Inlet. Presently the cook remarked that he had seen it. The correspondent was at the oars then, and for some reason he too wished to look at the lighthouse; but his back was toward the far shore, and the waves were important, and for some time he could not seize an opportunity to turn his head. But at last there came a wave more gentle than the others, and when at the crest of it he swiftly scoured the western horizon.

"See it?" said the captain.

"No," said the correspondent, slowly; "I didn't see anything."

"Look again," said the captain. He pointed. "It's exactly in that direction."

At the top of another wave the correspondent did as he was bid, and this time his eyes chanced on a small, still thing on the edge of the swaying horizon. It was precisely like the point of a pin. It took an anxious eye to find a lighthouse so tiny.

"Think we'll make it, Captain?"

"If this wind holds and the boat don't swamp, we can't do much else," said the captain.

The little boat, lifted by each towering sea and splashed viciously by the crests, made progress that in the absence of seaweed was not apparent to those in her. She seemed just a wee thing wallowing miraculously, top up, at the mercy of five oceans. Occasionally a great spread of water, like white flames, swarmed into her.

"Bail her, cook," said the captain, serenely.

"All right, Captain," said the cheerful cook.

III

It would be difficult to describe the subtle brotherhood of men that was here established on the seas. No one said that it was so. No one mentioned it. But it dwelt in the boat, and each man felt it warm him. They were a captain, an oiler, a cook, and a correspondent, and they were friends—friends in a more curiously iron-bound degree than may be common. The hurt captain, lying against the water-jar in the bow, spoke always in a low voice and calmly; but he could never command a more ready and swiftly obedient crew than the motley three of the dinghy. It was more than a mere recognition of what was best for the common safety. There was surely in it a quality that was personal and heartfelt. And after this devotion to the commander of the boat, there was this comradeship, that the correspondent, for instance, who had been taught to be cynical of men, knew even at the time was the best experience of his life. But no one said that it was so. No one mentioned it.

"I wish we had a sail," remarked the captain. "We might try my overcoat on the end of an oar, and give you two boys a chance to rest." So the cook and the correspondent held the mast and spread wide the overcoat; the oiler steered; and the little boat make good way with her new rig. Sometimes the oiler had to scull sharply to keep a sea from breaking into the boat, but otherwise sailing was a success.

Meanwhile the lighthouse had been growing slowly larger. It had now almost assumed colour, and appeared like a little grey shadow on the sky. The man at the oars could not be prevented from turning his head rather often to try for a glimpse of this little grey shadow.

At last, from the top of each wave, the men in the tossing boat could see land. Even as the lighthouse was an upright shadow on the sky, this land seemed but a long black shadow on the sea. It certainly was thinner than paper. "We must be about opposite New Smyrna," said the cook, who had coasted this shore often in schooners. "Captain, by the way, I believe they abandoned that life-saving station there about a year ago."

"Did they?" said the captain.

The wind slowly died away. The cook and the correspondent were not now obliged to slave in order to hold high the oar; but the waves continued their old impetuous swooping at the dinghy, and the little craft, no longer under way, struggled woundily over them. The oiler or the correspondent took the oars again.

Shipwrecks are *apropos* of nothing. If men could only train for them and have them occur when the men had reached pink condition, there would be less drowning at sea. Of the four in the dinghy none had slept any time worth mentioning for two days and two nights previous to embarking in the dinghy, and in the excitement of clambering about the deck of a foundering ship they had also forgotten to eat heartily.

For these reasons, and for others, neither the oiler nor the correspondent was fond of rowing at this time. The correspondent wondered ingenuously how in the name of all that was sane could there be people who thought it amusing to row a boat. It was not an amusement; it was a diabolical punishment, and even a genius of mental aberrations could never conclude that it was anything but a horror to the muscles and a crime against the back. He mentioned to the boat in general how the amusement of rowing struck him, and the weary-faced oiler smiled in full sympathy. Previously to the foundering, by the way, the oiler had worked double watch in the engine room of the ship.

"Take her easy now, boys," said the captain. "Don't spend yourselves. If we have to run a surf you'll need all your strength, because we'll sure have to swim for it. Take your time."

Slowly the land arose from the sea. From a black line it became a line of black and a line of white—trees and sand. Finally the captain said that he could make out a house on the shore. "That's the house of refuge, sure," said the cook. "They'll see us before long, and come out after us."

The distant lighthouse reared high. "The keeper ought to be able to make us out now, if he's looking through a glass," said the captain. "He'll notify the lifesaving people."

"None of those other boats could have got ashore to give word of the wreck," said the oiler, in a low voice, "else the lifeboat would be out hunting us."

Slowly and beautifully the land loomed out of the sea. The wind came again. It had veered from the northeast to the southeast. Finally a new sound struck the ears of the men in the boat. It was the low thunder of the surf on the shore. "We'll never be able to make the lighthouse now," said the captain. "Swing her head a little more north, Billie."

"A little more north, sir," said the oiler.

Whereupon the little boat turned her nose once more down the wind, and all but the oarsman watched the shore grow. Under the influence of this expansion doubt and direful apprehension were leaving the minds of the men. The management of the boat was still most absorbing, but it could not prevent a quiet cheerfulness. In an hour, perhaps, they would be ashore.

Their backbones had become thoroughly used to balancing in the boat, and they now rode this wild colt of a dinghy like circus men. The correspondent thought that he had been drenched to the skin, but happening to feel in the top pocket of coat, he found therein eight cigars. Four of them were soaked with seawater; four were perfectly scatheless. After a search, somebody produced three dry matches; and thereupon the four waifs rode in their little boat and, with an assurance of an impending rescue shining in their eyes, puffed at the big cigars, and judged well and ill of all men. Everybody took a drink of water.

IV

"Cook," remarked the captain, "there don't seem to be any signs of life about your house of refuge."

"No," replied the cook. "Funny they don't see us!"

A broad stretch of lowly coast lay before the eyes of the men. It was of low dunes topped with dark vegetation. The roar of the surf was plain, and sometimes they could see the white lip of a wave as it spun up the beach. A tiny house was blocked out black upon the sky. Southward, the slim lighthouse lifted its little grey length.

Tide, wind, and waves were swinging the dinghy northward. "Funny they don't see us," said the men.

The surf's roar was here dulled, but its tone was nevertheless thunderous and mighty. As the boat swam over the great rollers the men sat listening to this roar. "We'll swamp sure," said everybody.

It is fair to say here that there was not a life-saving station within twenty miles in either direction; but the men did not know this fact, and in consequence they made dark and opprobrious remarks concerning the eyesight of the nation's life-savers. Four scowling men sat in the dinghy, and surpassed records in the invention of epithets.

"Funny they don't see us."

The light-heartedness of a former time had completely faded. To their sharpened minds it was easy to conjure pictures of all kinds of incompetency and blindness and, indeed, cowardice. There was the shore of the populous land, and it was bitter and bitter to them that from it came no sign.

"Well," said the captain, ultimately, "I suppose we'll have to make a try for ourselves. If we stay out here too long, we'll none of us have strength left to swim after the boat swamps."

And so the oiler, who was at the oars, turned the boat straight for the shore. There was a sudden tightening of muscles. There was some thinking.

"If we don't all get ashore," said the captain,—"if we don't all get ashore, I suppose you fellows know where to send news of my finish?"

They then briefly exchanged some addresses and admonitions. As for the reflections of the men, there was a great deal of rage in them. Perchance they might be formulated thus: "If I am going to be drowned—if I am going to be drowned—if I am going to be drowned, why, in the name of the seven mad gods who rule the sea, was I allowed to come thus far and contemplate sand and trees? Was I brought here merely to have my nose dragged away as I was about to nibble the sacred cheese of life? It is preposterous! If this old ninny-woman, Fate, cannot do better than this, she should be deprived of the management of men's fortunes. She is an old hen who knows not her intention. If she has decided to drown me, why did she not do it in the beginning, and save me all this trouble? The whole affair is absurd . . . But no; she cannot mean to drown me. She dare not drown me. She cannot drown me. Not after all this work!" Afterward the man might have had an impulse to shake his fist at the clouds. "Just you drown me, now, and then hear what I call you!"

The billows that came at this time were more formidable. They seemed always just about to break and roll over the little boat in a turmoil of foam. There was a preparatory and long growl in the speech of them. No mind unused to the sea would have concluded that the dinghy could ascend these sheer heights in time. The shore was still afar. The oiler was a wily surfman. "Boys," he said swiftly, "she won't live three minutes more, and we're too far out to swim. Shall I take her to sea again, Captain?"

"Yes; go ahead!" said the captain.

This oiler, by a series of quick miracles and fast and steady oarsmanship, turned the boat in the middle of the surf and took her safely to sea again.

There was a considerable silence as the boat bumped over the furrowed sea to deeper water. Then somebody in gloom spoke: "Well, anyhow, they must have seen us from the shore by now."

The gulls went in slanting flight up the wind toward the grey, desolate east. A squall, marked by dingy clouds, and clouds brick-red, like smoke from a burning building, appeared from the southeast.

"What do you think of those life-saving people? Ain't they peaches?"

"Funny they haven't seen us."

"Maybe they think we're out here for sport! Maybe they think we're fishin." Maybe they think we're damned fools."

It was a long afternoon. A changed tide tried to force them southward, but wind and wave said northward. Far ahead, where coastline, sea, and sky formed their mighty angle, there were little dots which seemed to indicate a city on the shore.

"St Augustine?"

The captain shook his head. "Too near Mosquito Inlet."

And the oiler rowed, and then the correspondent rowed; then the oiler rowed. It was weary business. The human back can become the seat of more aches and pains than are registered in books for the composite anatomy of a regiment. It is a limited area, but it can become the theatre of innumerable muscular conflicts, tangles, wrenches, knots, and other comforts.

"Did you ever like to row, Billie?" asked the correspondent.

"No," said the oiler; "hang it!"

When one exchanged the rowing-seat for a place at the bottom of the boat, he suffered a bodily depression that caused him to be careless of everything save an obligation to wiggle one finger. There was cold seawater swashing to and fro in the boat, and he lay in it. His head, pillowed on a thwart, was within an inch of the swirl of a wave-crest, and sometimes a particularly obstreperous sea came inboard and drenched him once more. But these matters did not annoy him. It is almost certain that if the boat had capsized he would have tumbled comfortably out upon the ocean as if he felt sure that it was a great, soft mattress.

"Look! There's a man on the shore!"

"Where?"

"There! See 'im? See 'im?"

"Yes, sure! He's walking along."

"Now he's stopped. Look! He's facing us!"

"He's waving at us!"

"So he is! By thunder!"

"Ah, now we're all right! Now we're all right! There'll be a boat out here for us in half an hour."

"He's going on. He's running. He's going up to that house there."

The remote beach seemed lower than the sea, and it required a searching glance to discern the little black figure. The captain saw a floating stick, and they rowed to it. A bath towel was by some weird chance in the boat, and tying this on the stick, the captain waved it. The oarsman did not dare turn his head, so he was obliged to ask questions.

"What's he doing now?"

"He's standing still again. He's looking, I think . . . There he goes again—toward the house . . . Now he's stopped again."

"Is he waving at us?"

"No, not now; he was, though."

"Look! There comes another man!"

"He's running."

"Look at him go, would you!"

"Why, he's on a bicycle. Now he's met the other man. They're both waving at us. Look!"

"There comes something up the beach."

"What the devil is that thing?"

"Why, it looks like a boat."

"Why, certainly, it's a boat."

"No; it's on wheels."

"Yes, so it is. Well, that must be the lifeboat. They drag them along shore on a wagon."

"That's the life boat, sure."

"No, by ———, it's—it's an omnibus."

"I tell you it's a lifeboat."

"It is not! It's an omnibus. I can see it plain. See? One of these big hotel omnibuses."

"By thunder, you're right. It's an omnibus, sure as fate. What do you suppose they are doing with an omnibus? Maybe they are going around collecting the life-crew, hey?"

"That's it, likely. Look! There's a fellow waving a little black flag. He's standing on the steps of the omnibus. There come those other two fellows. Now they're all talking together. Look at the fellow with the flag. Maybe he ain't waving it!"

"That ain't a flag, is it? That's his coat. Why, certainly, that's his coat."

"So it is; it's his coat. He's taken it off and is waving it around his head. But would you look at him swing it!"

"Oh, say, there isn't any life-saving station there. That's just a winter-resort hotel omnibus that has brought over some of the boarders to see us drown."

"What's that idiot with the coat mean? What's he signalling, anyhow?

"It looks as if he were trying to tell us to go north. There must be a life-saving station up there."

"No; he thinks we're fishing. Just giving us a merry hand. See? Ah, there, Willie!"

"Well, I wish I could make something out of those signals. What do you suppose he means?"

"He don't mean anything; he's just playing."

"Well, if he'd just signal us to try the surf again, or to go to sea and wait, or go north, or go south, or go to hell, there would be some reason in it. But look at him! He just stands there and keeps his coat revolving like a wheel. The ass!"

"There come more people."

"Now there's quite a mob. Look! Isn't that a boat?"

"Where? Oh, I see where you mean. No, that's no boat."

"That fellow is still waving his coat."

"He must think we like to see him do that. Why don't he quit it? It don't mean anything."

"I don't know. I think he is trying to make us go north. It must be that there's a life-saving station there somewhere."

"Say, he ain't tired yet. Look at 'im wave!"

"Wonder how long he can keep that up. He's been revolving his coat ever since he caught sight of us. He's an idiot. Why aren't they getting men to bring a boat out? A fishing-boat—one of those big yawls—could come out here all right. Why don't he do something?"

"Oh, it's all right now."

"They'll have a boat out here for us in less than no time, now that they've seen us."

A faint yellow tone came into the sky over the low land. The shadows on the sea slowly deepened. The wind bore coldness with it, and the men began to shiver.

"Holy smoke!" said one, allowing his voice to express his impious mood, "if we keep on monkeying out here! If we've got to flounder out here all night!"

"Oh, we'll never have to stay here all night! Don't you worry. They've seen us now, and it won't be long before they'll come chasing out after us."

The shore grew dusky. The man waving a coat blended gradually into this gloom, and it swallowed in the same manner the omnibus and the group of people. The spray, when it dashed uproariously over the side, made the voyagers shrink and swear like men who were being branded.

"I'd like to catch the chump who waved the coat. I feel like soaking him one, just for luck."

"Why? What did he do?"

"Oh, nothing, but then he seemed so damned cheerful."

In the meantime the oiler rowed, and then the correspondent rowed, and then the oiler rowed. Grey-faced and bowed forward, they mechanically, turn by turn, plied the leaden oars. The form of the lighthouse had vanished from the southern horizon, but finally a pale star appeared, just lifting from the sea. The streaked saffron in the west passed before the all-merging darkness, and the sea to the east was black. The land had vanished, and was expressed only by the low and drear thunder of the surf.

"If I am going to be drowned—if I am going to be drowned—if I am going to be drowned, why, in the name of the seven mad gods who rule the sea, was I allowed to come thus far and contemplate sand and trees? Was I brought here merely to have my nose dragged away as I was about to nibble the sacred cheese of life?"

The patient captain, drooped over the water-jar, was sometimes obliged to speak to the oarsman.

"Keep her head up! Keep her head up!"

"Keep her head up, sir." The voices were weary and low.

This was surely a quiet evening. All save the oarsman lay heavily and listlessly in the boat's bottom. As for him, his eyes were just capable of noting the tall black waves that swept forward in a most sinister silence, save for an occasional subdued growl of a crest.

The cook's head was on a thwart, and he looked without interest at the water under his nose. He was deep in other scenes. Finally he spoke. "Billie," he murmured dreamfully, "what kind of pie do you like best?"

V

"Pie!" said the oiler and the correspondent, agitatedly. "Don't talk about those things, blast you!"

"Well," said the cook, "I was just thinking about ham sandwiches, and—"

A night on the sea in an open boat is a long night. As darkness settled finally, the shine of the light, lifting from the sea in the south, changed to full gold. On the northern horizon a new light appeared, a small bluish gleam on the edge of the waters. These two lights were the furniture of the world. Otherwise there was nothing but waves.

Two men huddled in the stern, and distances were so magnificent in the dinghy that the rower was enabled to keep his feet partly warm by thrusting them under his companions. Their legs indeed extended far under the rowing-seat until they touched the feet of the captain forward. Sometimes, despite the efforts of the tired oarsman, a wave came piling into the boat, an icy wave of the night, and the chilling water soaked them anew. They would twist their bodies for a moment and groan, and sleep the dead sleep once more, while the water in the boat gurgled about them as the craft rocked.

The plan of the oiler and the correspondent was for one to row until he lost the ability, and then arouse the other from his seawater couch in the bottom of the boat.

The oiler plied the oars until his head drooped forward and the overpowering sleep blinded him; and he rowed yet afterward. Then he touched a man in the bottom of the boat, and called his name. "Will you spell me for a little while?" he said meekly.

"Sure, Billie," said the correspondent, awaking and dragging himself to a sitting position. They exchanged places carefully, and the oiler, cuddling down in the seawater at the cook's side, seemed to go to sleep instantly.

The particular violence of the sea had ceased. The waves came without snarling. The obligation of the man at the oars was to keep the boat headed so that the tilt of the rollers would not capsize her, and to preserve her from filling when the crests rushed past. The black waves were silent and hard to be seen in the darkness. Often one was almost upon the boat before the oarsman was aware.

In a low voice the correspondent addressed the captain. He was not sure that the captain was awake, although this iron man seemed to be always awake. "Captain, shall I keep her making for that light north, sir?"

The same steady voice answered him. "Yes. Keep it about two points off the port bow."

The cook had tied a life-belt around himself in order to get even the warmth which this clumsy cork contrivance could donate, and he seemed almost stove-like when a rower, whose teeth invariably chattered wildly as soon as he ceased his labour, dropped down to sleep.

The correspondent, as he rowed, looked down at the two men sleeping under foot. The cook's arm was around the oiler's shoulders, and, with their fragmentary clothing and haggard faces, they were the babes of the sea—a grotesque rendering of the old babes in the wood.

Later he must have grown stupid at his work, for suddenly there was a growling of water, and a crest came with a roar and a swash into the boat, and it was a wonder that it did not set the cook afloat in his life-belt. The cook continued to sleep, but the oiler sat up, blinking his eyes and shaking with the new cold.

"Oh, I'm awful sorry, Billie," said the correspondent, contritely.

"That's all right, old boy," said the oiler, and lay down again and was asleep.

Presently it seemed that even the captain dozed, and the correspondent thought that he was the one man afloat on all the oceans. The wind had a voice as it came over the waves, and it was sadder than the end.

There was a long, loud swishing astern of the boat, and a gleaming trail of phosphorescence, like blue flame, was furrowed on the black waters. It might have been made by a monstrous knife.

Then there came a stillness, while the correspondent breathed with the open mouth and looked at the sea.

Suddenly there was another swish and another long flash of bluish light, and this time it was alongside the boat, and might almost have been reached with an oar. The correspondent saw an enormous fin speed like a shadow through the water, hurling the crystalline spray and leaving the long glowing trail.

The correspondent looked over his shoulder at the captain. His face was hidden, and he seemed to be asleep. He looked at the babes of the sea. They certainly were asleep. So, being bereft of sympathy, he leaned a little way to one side and swore softly into the sea.

But the thing did not then leave the vicinity of the boat. Ahead or astern, on one side or the other, at intervals long or short, fled the long sparkling streak, and there was to be heard the whiroo of the dark fin. The speed and power of the thing was greatly to be admired. It cut the water like a gigantic and keen projectile.

The presence of this biding thing did not affect the man with the same horror that it would if he had been a picnicker. He simply looked at the sea dully and swore in an undertone.

Nevertheless, it is true that he did not wish to be alone with the thing. He wished one of his companions to awake by chance and keep him company with it. But the captain hung motionless over the water-jar, and the oiler and the cook in the bottom of the boat were plunged in slumber.

VI

"If I am going to be drowned—if I am going to be drowned—if I am going to be drowned, why, in the name of the seven mad gods who rule the sea, was I allowed to come thus far and contemplate sand and trees?"

During this dismal night, it may be remarked that a man would conclude that it was really the intention of the seven mad gods to drown him, despite the abominable injustice of it. For it was certainly an abominable injustice to drown a man who had worked so hard, so hard. The man felt it would be a crime most unnatural. Other people had drowned at sea since galleys swarmed with painted sails, but still—

When it occurs to a man that nature does not regard him as important, and that she feels she would not maim the universe by disposing of him, he at first wishes to throw bricks at the temple, and he hates deeply the fact that there are no bricks and no temples. Any visible expression of nature would surely be pelleted with his jeers.

Then, if there be no tangible thing to hoot, he feels, perhaps, the desire to confront a personification and indulge in pleas, bowed to one knee, and with hands supplicant, saying, "Yes, but I love myself."

A high cold star on a winter's night is the word he feels that she says to him. Thereafter he knows the pathos of his situation.

The men in the dinghy had not discussed these matters, but each had, no doubt, reflected upon them in silence and according to his mind. There was seldom any expression upon their faces save the general one of complete weariness. Speech was devoted to the business of the boat.

To chime the notes of his emotion, a verse mysteriously entered the correspondent's head. He had even forgotten that he had forgotten this verse, but it suddenly was in his mind.

A soldier of the Legion lay dying in Algiers;
There was lack of woman's nursing, there was dearth of woman's tears;
But a comrade stood beside him, and he took that comrade's hand,
And he said, "I never more shall see my own, my native land."

In his childhood the correspondent had been made acquainted with the fact that a soldier of the Legion lay dying in Algiers, but he had never regarded it as important. Myriads of his school-fellows had informed him of the soldier's plight, but the dinning had naturally ended by making him perfectly indifferent. He had never considered it his affair that a soldier of the Legion lay dying in Algiers, nor had it appeared to him as a matter for sorrow. It was less to him than the breaking of a pencil's point.

Now, however, it quaintly came to him as a human, living thing. It was no longer merely a picture of a few throes in the breast of a poet, meanwhile drinking tea and warming his feet at the grate; it was an actuality—stern, mournful, and fine.

The correspondent plainly saw the soldier. He lay on the sand with his feet out straight and still. While his pale left hand was upon his chest in an attempt to thwart the going of his life, the blood came between his fingers. In the far Algerian distance, a city of low square forms was set against the sky that was faint with the last sunset hues. The correspondent, plying the oars and dreaming of the slow and slower movements of the lips of the solider, was moved by a profound and perfectly impersonal comprehension. He was sorry for the soldier of the Legion who lay dying in Algiers.

The thing which had followed the boat and waited had evidently grown bored at the delay. There was no longer to be heard the slash of the cutwater, and there was no longer the flame of the long trail. The light in the north still glimmered, but it was apparently no nearer to the boat. Sometimes the boom of the surf rang in the correspondent's ears, and he turned the craft seaward then and rowed harder. Southward, some one had evidently built a watch-fire on the beach. It was too low and too far to be seen, but it made a shimmering, roseate reflection upon the bluff back of it, and this could be discerned from the boat. The wind came stronger, and sometimes a wave suddenly raged out like a mountain cat, and there was to be seen the sheen and sparkle of a broken crest.

The captain, in the bow, moved on his water-jar and sat erect. "Pretty long night," he observed to the correspondent. He looked at the shore. "Those life-saving people take their time."

"Did you see that shark playing around?"

"Yes, I saw him. He was a big fellow, all right."

"Wish I had known you were awake."

Later the correspondent spoke into the bottom of the boat.

"Billie!" There was a slow and gradual disentanglement. "Billie, will you spell me?"

"Sure," said the oiler.

As soon as the correspondent touched the cold, comfortable seawater in the bottom of the boat and had huddled close to the cook's life-belt he was deep in sleep, despite the fact that his teeth played all the popular airs. This sleep was so good to him that it was but a moment before he heard a voice call his name in a tone that demonstrated the last stages of exhaustion. "Will you spell me?"

"Sure, Billie."

The light in the north had mysteriously vanished, but the correspondent took his course from the wide-awake captain.

Later in the night they took the boat farther out to sea, and the captain directed the cook to take one oar at the stern and keep the boat facing the seas. He was to call out if he should hear the thunder of the surf. This plan enabled the oiler and the correspondent to get respite together. "We'll give those boys a chance to get into shape again," said the captain. They curled down and, after a few preliminary chatterings and trembles, slept once more the dead sleep. Neither knew they had bequeathed to the cook the company of another shark, or perhaps the same shark.

As the boat caroused on the waves, spray occasionally bumped over the side and gave them a fresh soaking, but this had no power to break their repose. The ominous slash of the wind and the water affected them as it would have affected mummies.

"Boys," said the cook, with the notes of every reluctance in his voice, "she's drifted pretty close. I guess one of you had better take her to sea again." The correspondent, aroused, heard the crash of the toppled crests.

As he was rowing, the captain gave him some whisky and water, and this steadied the chills out of him. "If I ever get ashore and anybody shows me even a photograph of an oar—"

At last there was a short conversation.

"Billie! . . . Billie, will you spell me?"

"Sure," said the oiler.

VII

When the correspondent again opened his eyes, the sea and the sky were each of the grey hue of the dawning. Later, carmine and gold was painted upon the waters. The morning appeared finally, in its splendour, with a sky of pure blue, and the sunlight flamed on the tips of the waves.

On the distant dunes were set many little black cottages, and a tall white windmill reared above them. No man, nor dog, nor bicycle appeared on the beach. The cottages might have formed a deserted village.

The voyagers scanned the shore. A conference was held in the boat. "Well," said the captain, "if no help is coming, we might better try a run through the surf right away. If we stay out here much longer we will be too weak to do anything for ourselves at all." The others silently acquiesced in this reasoning. The boat was headed for the beach. The correspondent wondered if none ever ascended the tall windtower, and if then they never looked seaward. This tower was a giant, standing with its back to the plight of the ants. It represented in a degree, to the correspondent, the serenity of nature amid the struggles of the individual—nature in the wind, and nature in the vision of men. She did not seem cruel to him then, nor beneficent, nor treacherous, nor wise. But she was indifferent, flatly indifferent. It is, perhaps, plausible that a man in this situation, impressed with the unconcern of the universe, should see the innumerable flaws of his life and have them taste wickedly in his mind and wish for another chance. A distinction between right and wrong seems absurdly clear to him, then, in this new ignorance of the grave-edge, and he understands that if he were given another opportunity he would mend his conduct and his words, and be better and brighter during an introduction or at a tea.

"Now, boys," said the captain, "she is going to swamp sure. All we can do is to work her in as far as possible, and then when she swamps, pile out and scramble for the beach. Keep cool now, and don't jump until she swamps sure."

The oiler took the oars. Over his shoulders he scanned the surf. "Captain," he said, "I think I'd better bring her about, and keep her head-on to the seas, and back her in."

"All right, Billie," said the captain. "Back her in." The oiler swung the boat then, and, seated in the stern, the cook and the correspondent were obliged to look over their shoulders to contemplate the lonely and indifferent shore.

The monstrous inshore rollers heaved the boat high until the men were again enabled to see the white sheets of water scudding up the slanted beach. "We won't get in very close," said the captain. Each time a man could wrest his attention from the rollers, he turned his glance toward the shore, and in the expression of the eyes during this contemplation there was a singular quality. The correspondent, observing the others, knew that they were not afraid, but the full meaning of their glances was shrouded.

As for himself, he was too tired to grapple fundamentally with the fact. He tried to coerce his mind into thinking of it, but the mind was dominated at this time by the muscles, and the muscles said they did not care. It merely occurred to him that if he should drown it would be a shame.

There were no hurried words, no pallor, no plain agitation. The men simply looked at the shore. "Now, remember to get well clear of the boat when you jump," said the captain.

Seaward the crest of a roller suddenly fell with a thunderous crash, and the long white comber came roaring down upon the boat.

"Steady now," said the captain. The men were silent. They turned their eyes from the shore to the comber and waited. The boat slid up the incline, leaped at the furious top, bounced over it, and swung down the long back of the wave. Some water had been shipped, and the cook bailed it out.

But the next crest crashed also. The tumbling, boiling flood of white water caught the boat and whirled it almost perpendicular. Water swarmed in from all sides. The correspondent had his hands on the gunwale at this time, and when the water entered at that place he swiftly withdrew his fingers, as if he objected to wetting them.

The little boat, drunken with this weight of water, reeled and snuggled deeper into the sea.

"Bail her out cook! Bail her out!" said the captain.

"All right, Captain," said the cook.

"Now, boys, the next one will do for us sure," said the oiler. "Mind to jump clear of the boat."

The third wave moved forward, huge, furious, implacable. It fairly swallowed the dinghy, and almost simultaneously the men tumbled into the sea. A piece of life-belt had lain in the bottom of the boat, and as the correspondent went overboard he held this to his chest with his left hand.

The January water was icy, and he reflected immediately that it was colder than he had expected to find it off the coast of Florida. This appeared to his dazed mind as a fact important enough to be noted at the time. The coldness of the water was sad; it was tragic. This fact was somehow mixed and confused with his opinion of his own situation so tha it seemed almost a proper reason for tears. The water was cold.

When he came to the surface he was conscious of little but the noisy water. Afterward he saw his companions in the sea. The oiler was ahead in the race. He was swimming strongly and rapidly. Off to the correspondent's left, the cook's great white and corked back bulged out of the water; and in the rear the captain was hanging with his one good hand to the keel of the overturned dinghy.

There is a certain immovable quality to a shore, and the correspondent wondered at it amid the confusion of the sea.

It seemed also very attractive; but the correspondent knew that it was a long journey, and he paddled leisurely. The piece of life-preserver lay under him, and sometimes he whirled down the incline of a wave as if he were on a hand-sled.

But finally he arrived at a place in the sea where travel was beset with difficulty. He did not pause swimming to inquire what manner of current had caught him, but there his progress ceased. The shore was set before him like a bit of scenery on a stage, and he looked at it, and understood with his eyes each detail of it.

As the cook passed, much farther to the left, the captain was calling to him, "Turn over on your back, cook! Turn over on your back and use the oar."

"All right, sir." The cook turned on his back, and, paddling with an oar, went ahead as if he were a canoe.

Presently the boat also passed to the left of the correspondent, with the captain clinging with one hand to the keel. He would have appeared like a man raising himself to look over a board fence if it were not for the extraordinary gymnastics of the boat. The correspondent marvelled that the captain could still hold to it.

They passed on nearer to shore,—the oiler, the cook, the captain,—and following them went the water-jar, bouncing gaily over the seas.

The correspondent remained in the grip of this strange new enemy, a current. The shore, with its white slope of sand and its green bluff, topped with little silent cottages, was spread like a picture before him. It was very near to him then, but he was impressed as one who, in a gallery, looks at a scene from Brittany or Algiers.

He thought: "I am going to drown? Can it be possible? Can it be possible? Can it be possible?" Perhaps an individual must consider his own death to be the final phenomenon of nature.

But later a wave perhaps whirled him out of this small deadly current, for he found suddenly that he could again make progress toward the shore. Later still he was aware that the captain, clinging with one hand to the keel of the dinghy, had his face turned away from the shore and toward him, and was calling his name. "Come to the boat! Come to the boat!"

In his struggle to reach the captain and the boat, he reflected that when one gets properly wearied drowning must really be a comfortable arrangement—a cessation of hostilities accompanied by a large degree of relief; and he was glad of it, for the main thing in his mind for some moments had been horror of the temporary agony; he did not wish to be hurt.

Presently he saw a man running along the shore. He was undressing with most remarkable speed. Coat, trousers, shirt, everything flew magically off him.

"Come to the boat!" called the captain.

"All right, Captain." As the correspondent paddled, he saw the captain let himself down to bottom and leave the boat. Then the correspondent performed his one little marvel of voyage. A large wave caught him and flung him with ease and supreme speed completely over the boat and far beyond it. It struck him even then as an event in gymnastics and a true miracle of the sea. An overturned boat in the surf is not a plaything to a swimming man.

The correspondent arrived in water that reached only to his waist, but his condition did not enable him to stand for more than a moment. Each wave knocked him into a heap, and the undertow pulled at him.

Then he saw the man who had been running and undressing, and undressing and running, come bounding into the water. He dragged ashore the cook, and then waded toward the captain; but the captain waved him away and sent him to the correspondent. He was naked—naked as a tree in winter; but a halo was about the head, and he shone like a saint. He gave a strong pull, and a long drag, and a bully heave at the correspondent's hand. The correspondent, schooled in the minor formulae, said, "Thanks, old man." But suddenly the man cried, "What's that?" He pointed a swift finger. The correspondent said, "Go."

In the shallows, face downward, lay the oiler. His forehead touched sand that was periodically, between each wave, clear of the sea.

The correspondent did not know all that transpired afterward. When he achieved safe ground he fell, striking the sand with each particular part of his body. It was as if he had dropped from a roof, but the thud was grateful to him.

It seems that instantly the beach was populated with men with blankets, clothes, and flasks, and women with coffee-pots and all the remedies sacred to their minds. The welcome of the land to the men from the sea was warm and generous; but a still and dripping shape was carried slowly up the beach, and the land's welcome for it could only be the different and sinister hospitality of the grave.

When it came night, the white waves paced to and fro in the moonlight, and the wind brought the sound of the great sea's voice to the men on shore, and they felt that they could then be interpreters.

1898

James Joyce

1882–1941

The basic details of James Joyce's life have become one of the stories central to the modern age: a devout mother and a Parnellite father with a good voice rather than a vocation; erratic attendance and distinguished academic achievement at several Jesuit schools; a degree from University College, Dublin; life with the Galway-born Nora (his common-law wife—until 1931, when they married) in Trieste, Zurich, and later, in Paris, from 1920 until the German invasion; then an early death from a bleeding ulcer. Though Joyce did not live in Ireland for most of his adult life, the country, its religion, and its politics (and Joyce's reactions to and against them) feature largely in his books, making his biographical details more than usually interesting to the reader. His mother's Catholicism and his exposure to fire-and-brimstone sermons, and his father's fervent support of Charles Stewart Parnell, the leader of the Home Rule Party (which campaigned for Irish nationalism) were two of the greatest influences on his life and writing. Yet his choices were often in opposition to movements and fashions: at university he championed the work of Henrik Ibsen and criticized the proponents of the Celtic literary revival (which involved such literary figures as Yeats and Synge). Finally he left Ireland for the freedom that Europe seemed to offer, teaching and writing in near poverty for many years. His fame grew and his genius was recognized, his career helped along by Ezra Pound and the editor Harriet Weaver, who helped him personally and financially. He attracted a circle of aspiring writers and admirers of literature while living in Paris in the 1920s and 1930s and working on *Finnegans Wake* (1939). He and Nora left France in 1940, and he died in early 1941, in Zurich.

Out of these elements Joyce reconstituted, if not quite "the uncreated conscience of [his] race"—as Stephen Daedalus vows to do at the end of the largely autobiographical *A Portrait of the Artist as a Young Man* (1916)—then certainly the very nature of prose fiction. Joyce became the same kind of father—a literary figure both to revere and to measure oneself against—to subsequent writers as Dante and Shakespeare had been to him. In *Ulysses* (1922) and *Finnegans Wake* (1939) he expanded all conceivable parameters of the novel, just as in *Dubliners* (1914), which was rooted in the earlier writing of his terse, poetic "epiphanies," Joyce forged the modern short story by directing the individual piece toward absences, hints, and layered narrative, and the collection itself toward symmetry and completion. Two stories are included here to provide a sense of how they are simultaneously discrete narrative units and part of a larger whole.

An Encounter

It was Joe Dillon who introduced the Wild West to us. He had a little library made up of old numbers of *The Union Jack*, *Pluck* and *The Halfpenny Marvel*. Every evening after school we met in his back garden and arranged Indian battles. He and his fat young brother Leo the idler held the loft of the stable while we tried to carry it by storm; or we fought a pitched battle on the grass. But, however well we fought, we never won siege or battle and all our bouts ended with Joe Dillon's war dance of victory. His parents went to eight-o'clock mass every morning in Gardiner Street and the peaceful odour of Mrs Dillon was prevalent in the hall of the house. But he played too fiercely for us who were younger and more timid. He looked like some kind of an Indian when he capered round the garden, an old tea-cosy on his head, beating a tin with his fist and yelling:

—Ya! yaka, yaka, yaka!

Everyone was incredulous when it was reported that he had a vocation for the priesthood. Nevertheless it was true.

A spirit of unruliness diffused itself among us and, under its influence, differences of culture and constitution were waived. We banded ourselves together, some boldly, some in jest and some almost in fear: and of the number of these latter, the reluctant Indians who were afraid to seem studious or lacking in robustness, I was one. The adventures related in the literature of the Wild West were remote from my nature but, at least, they opened doors of escape. I liked better some American detective stories which were traversed from time to time by unkempt fierce and beautiful girls. Though there was nothing wrong in these stories and though their intention was sometimes literary they were circulated secretly at school. One day when Father Butler was hearing the four pages of Roman History clumsy Leo Dillon was discovered with a copy of *The Halfpenny Marvel.*

—This page or this page? This page? Now, Dillon, up! *Hardly had the day* … Go on! What day? *Hardly had the day dawned* … Have you studied it? What have you there in your pocket?

Everyone's heart palpitated as Leo Dillon handed up the paper and everyone assumed an innocent face. Father Butler turned over the pages, frowning.

—What is this rubbish? he said. *The Apache Chief!* Is this what you read instead of studying your Roman History? Let me not find any more of this wretched stuff in this college. The man who wrote it, I suppose, was some wretched scribbler that writes these things for a drink. I'm surprised at boys like you, educated, reading such stuff. I could understand it if you were … National School boys. Now, Dillon, I advise you strongly, get at your work or …

This rebuke during the sober hours of school paled much of the glory of the Wild West for me and the confused puffy face of Leo Dillon awakened one of my consciences. But when the restraining influence of the school was at a distance I began to hunger again for wild sensations, for the escape which those chronicles of disorder alone seemed to offer me. The mimic warfare of the evening became at last as wearisome to me as the routine of school in the morning because I wanted real adventures to happen to myself. But real adventures, I reflected, do not happen to people who remain at home: they must be sought abroad.

The summer holidays were near at hand when I made up my mind to break out of the weariness of school-life for one day at least. With Leo Dillon and a boy named Mahony I planned a day's miching. Each of us saved up sixpence. We were to meet at ten in the morning on the Canal Bridge. Mahony's big sister was to write an excuse for him and Leo Dillon was to tell his brother to say he was sick. We arranged to go along the Wharf Road until we came to the ships, then to cross in the ferryboat and walk out to see the Pigeon House. Leo Dillon was afraid we might meet Father Butler or someone out of the college; but Mahony asked, very sensibly, what would Father Butler be doing out at the Pigeon House. We were reassured: and I brought the first stage of the plot to an end by collecting sixpence from the other two, at the same time showing them my own sixpence. When we were making the last arrangements on the eve we were all vaguely excited. We shook hands, laughing, and Mahony said:

—Till to-morrow, mates.

That night I slept badly. In the morning I was first-comer to the bridge as I lived nearest. I hid my books in the long grass near the ashpit at the end of the garden where nobody ever came and hurried along the canal bank. It was a mild sunny morning in the first week of June. I sat up on the coping of the bridge admiring my frail canvas shoes which I had diligently pipeclayed overnight and watching the docile horses pulling a tram-load of business people up the hill. All the branches of the tall trees which lined the mall were gay with little light green leaves and the sunlight slanted through them on to the water. The granite stone of the bridge was beginning to be warm and I began to pat it with my hands in time to an air in my head. I was very happy.

When I had been sitting there for five or ten minutes I saw Mahony's grey suit approaching. He came up the hill, smiling, and clambered up beside me on the bridge. While we were waiting he brought out the catapult which bulged from his inner pocket and explained some improvements which he had made in it. I asked him why he had brought it and he told me he had brought it to have some gas with the birds. Mahony used slang freely, and spoke of Father Butler as Bunsen Burner. We waited on for a quarter of an hour more but still there was no sign of Leo Dillon. Mahony, at last, jumped down and said:

—Come along. I knew Fatty'd funk it.

—And his sixpence . . . ? I said.

—That's forfeit, said Mahony. And so much the better for us—a bob and a tanner instead of a bob.

We walked along the North Strand Road till we came to the Vitriol Works and then turned to the right along the Wharf Road. Mahony began to play the Indian as soon as we were out of public sight. He chased a crowd of ragged girls, brandishing his unloaded catapult and, when two ragged boys began, out of chivalry, to fling stones at us, he proposed that we should charge them. I objected that the boys were too small, and so we walked on, the ragged troop screaming after us: *Swaddlers! Swaddlers!* thinking that we were Protestants because Mahony, who was dark-complexioned, wore the silver badge of a cricket club in his cap. When we came to the Smoothing Iron we arranged a siege; but it was a failure because you must have at least three. We revenged ourselves on Leo Dillon by saying what a funk he was and guessing how many he would get at three o'clock from Mr Ryan.

We came then near the river. We spent a long time walking about the noisy streets flanked by high stone walls, watching the working of cranes and engines and often being shouted at for our immobility by the drivers of groaning carts. It was noon when we reached the quays and, as all the labourers seemed to be eating their lunches, we bought two big currant buns and sat down to eat them on some metal piping beside the river. We pleased ourselves with the spectacle of Dublin's commerce—the barges signalled from far away by their curls of woolly smoke, the brown fishing fleet beyond Ringsend, the big white sailing-vessel which was being discharged on the opposite quay. Mahony said it would be right skit to run away to sea on one of those big ships and even I, looking at the high masts, saw, or imagined, the geography which had been scantily dosed to me at school gradually taking substance under my eyes. School and home seemed to recede from us and their influences upon us seemed to wane.

We crossed the Liffey in the ferryboat, paying our toll to be transported in the company of two labourers and a little Jew with a bag. We were serious to the point of solemnity, but once during the short voyage our eyes met and we laughed. When we landed we watched the discharging of the graceful threemaster which we had observed from the other quay. Some bystander said that she was a Norwegian vessel. I went to the stern and tried to decipher the legend upon it but, failing to do so, I came back and examined the foreign sailors to see had any of them green eyes for I had some confused notion. . . . The sailors' eyes were blue and grey and even black. The only sailor whose eyes could have been called green was a tall man who amused the crowd on the quay by calling out cheerfully every time the planks fell:

—All right! All right!

When we were tired of this sight we wandered slowly into Ringsend. The day had grown sultry, and in the windows of the grocers' shops musty biscuits lay bleaching. We bought some biscuits and chocolate which we ate sedulously as we wandered through the squalid streets where the families of the fishermen live. We could find no dairy and so we went into a huckster's shop and bought a bottle of raspberry lemonade each. Refreshed by this, Mahony chased a cat down a lane, but the cat escaped into a wide field. We both felt rather tired and when we reached the field we made at once for a sloping bank over the ridge of which we could see the Dodder.

It was too late and we were too tired to carry out our project of visiting the Pigeon House. We had to be home before four o'clock lest our adventure should be discovered. Mahony looked regretfully at his catapult and I had to suggest going home by train before he regained any cheerfulness. The sun went in behind some clouds and left us to our jaded thoughts and the crumbs of our provisions.

There was nobody but ourselves in the field. When we had lain on the bank for some time without speaking I saw a man approaching from the far end of the field. I watched him lazily as I chewed one of those green stems on which girls tell fortunes. He came along by the bank slowly. He walked with one hand upon his hip and in the other hand he held a stick with which he tapped the turf lightly. He was shabbily dressed in a suit of greenish-black and wore what we used to call a jerry hat with a high crown. He seemed to be fairly old for his moustache was ashen-grey. When he passed at our feet he glanced up at us quickly and then continued his way. We followed him with our eyes and saw that when he had gone on for perhaps fifty paces he turned about and began to retrace his steps. He walked towards us very slowly, always tapping the ground with his stick, so slowly that I thought he was looking for something in the grass.

He stopped when he came level with us and bade us good-day. We answered him and he sat down beside us on the slope slowly and with great care. He began to talk of the weather, saying that it would be a very hot summer and adding that the seasons had changed greatly since he was a boy—a long time ago. He said that the happiest time of one's life was undoubtedly one's schoolboy days and that he would give anything to be young again. While he expressed these sentiments which bored us a little we kept silent. Then he began to talk of school and of books. He asked us whether we had read the poetry of Thomas Moore or the works of Sir Walter Scott and Lord Lytton. I pretended that I had read every book he mentioned so that in the end he said:

—Ah, I can see you are a bookworm like myself. Now, he added, pointing to Mahony who was regarding us with open eyes, he is different; he goes in for games.

He said he had all Sir Walter Scott's works and all Lord Lytton's works at home and never tired of reading them. Of course, he said, there were some of Lord Lytton's works which boys couldn't read. Mahony asked why couldn't boys read them—a question which agitated and pained me because I was afraid the man would think I was as stupid as Mahony. The man, however, only smiled. I saw that he had great gaps in his mouth between his yellow teeth. Then he asked us which of us had the most sweethearts. Mahony mentioned lightly that he had three totties. The man asked me how many had I. I answered that I had none. He did not believe me and said he was sure I must have one. I was silent.

—Tell us, said Mahony pertly to the man, how many have you yourself?

The man smiled as before and said that when he was our age he had lots of sweethearts.

—Every boy, he said, has a little sweetheart.

His attitude on this point struck me as strangely liberal in a man of his age. In my heart I thought that what he said about boys and sweethearts was reasonable. But I disliked the words in his mouth and I wondered why he shivered once or twice as if he feared something or felt a sudden chill. As he proceeded I noticed that his accent was good. He began to speak to us about girls, saying what nice soft hair they had and how soft their hands were and how all girls were not so good as they seemed to be if one only knew. There was nothing he liked, he said, so much as looking at a nice young girl, at her nice white hands and her beautiful soft hair. He gave me the impression that he was repeating something which he had learned by heart or that, magnetised by some words of his own speech, his mind was slowly circling round and round in the same orbit. At times he spoke as if he were simply alluding to some fact that everybody knew, and at times he lowered his voice and spoke mysteriously as if he were telling us something secret which he did not wish others to overhear. He repeated his phrases over and over again, varying them and surrounding them with his monotonous voice. I continued to gaze towards the foot of the slope, listening to him.

After a long while his monologue paused. He stood up slowly, saying that he had to leave us for a minute or so, a few minutes, and, without changing the direction of my gaze, I saw him walking slowly away from us towards the near end of the field. We remained silent when he had gone. After a silence of a few minutes I heard Mahony exclaim:

—I say! Look what he's doing!

As I neither answered nor raised my eyes Mahony exclaimed again:

—I say . . . He's a queer old josser!

—In case he asks us for our names, I said, let you be Murphy and I'll be Smith.

We said nothing further to each other. I was still considering whether I would go away or not when the man came back and sat down beside us again. Hardly had he sat down when Mahony, catching sight of the cat which had escaped him, sprang up and pursued her across the field. The man and I watched the chase. The cat escaped once more and Mahony began to throw stones at the wall she had escaladed. Desisting from this, he began to wander about the far end of the field, aimlessly.

After an interval the man spoke to me. He said that my friend was a very rough boy and asked did he get whipped often at school. I was going to reply indignantly that we were not National School boys to be *whipped*, as he called it; but I remained silent. He began to speak on the subject of chastising boys. His mind, as if magnetised again by his speech, seemed to circle slowly round and round its new centre. He said that when boys were that kind they ought to be whipped and well whipped. When a boy was rough and unruly there was nothing would do him any good but a good sound whipping. A slap on the hand or a box on the ear was no good: what he wanted was to get a nice warm whipping. I was surprised at this sentiment and involuntarily glanced up at his face. As I did so I met the gaze of a pair of bottle-green eyes peering at me from under a twitching forehead. I turned my eyes away again.

The man continued his monologue. He seemed to have forgotten his recent liberalism. He said that if ever he found a boy talking to girls or having a girl for a sweetheart he would whip him and whip him; and that would teach him not to be talking to girls. And if a boy had a girl for a sweetheart and told lies about it then he would give him such a whipping as no boy ever got in this world. He said that there was nothing in this world he would like so well as that. He described to me how he would whip such a boy as if he were unfolding some elaborate mystery. He would love that, he said, better than anything in this world; and his voice, as he led me monotonously through the mystery, grew almost affectionate and seemed to plead with me that I should understand him.

I waited till his monologue paused again. Then I stood up abruptly. Lest I should betray my agitation I delayed a few moments pretending to fix my shoe properly and then, saying that I was obliged to go, I bade him good-day. I went up the slope calmly but my heart was beating quickly with fear that he would seize me by the ankles. When I reached the top of the slope I turned round and, without looking at him, called loudly across the field:

—Murphy!

My voice had an accent of forced bravery in it and I was ashamed of my paltry stratagem. I had to call the name again before Mahony saw me and hallooed in answer. How my heart beat as he came running across the field to me! He ran as if to bring me aid. And I was penitent; for in my heart I had always despised him a little.

1914

The Dead

Lily, the caretaker's daughter, was literally run off her feet. Hardly had she brought one gentleman into the little pantry behind the office on the ground floor and helped him off with his overcoat than the wheezy hall door bell clanged again and she had to scamper along the bare hallway to let in another guest. It was well for her she had not to attend to the ladies also. But Miss Kate and Miss Julia had thought of that and had converted the bathroom upstairs into a ladies' dressing room. Miss Kate and Miss Julia were there, gossiping and laughing and fussing, walking after each other to the head of the stairs, peering down over the banisters and calling down to Lily to ask her who had come.

It was always a great affair, the Misses Morkan's annual dance. Everybody who knew them came to it, members of the family, old friends of the family, the members of Julia's choir, any of Kate's pupils that were grown up enough and even some of Mary Jane's pupils too. Never once had it fallen flat. For years and years it had gone off in splendid style as long as anyone could remember; ever since Kate and Julia, after the death of their brother Pat, had left the house in Stoney Batter and taken Mary Jane, their only niece, to live with them in the dark gaunt house on Usher's Island, the upper part of which they had rented from Mr Fulham, the corn-factor on the ground floor. That was a good thirty years ago if it was a day. Mary Jane, who was then a little girl in short clothes, was now the main prop of the household for she had the organ in Haddington Road. She had been through the Academy and gave a pupils' concert every year in the upper room of the Antient Concert Rooms. Many of her pupils belonged to better-class families on the Kingstown and Dalkey line. Old as they were, her aunts also did their share. Julia, though she was quite grey, was still the leading soprano in Adam and Eve's, and Kate, being too feeble to go about much, gave music lessons to beginners on the old square piano in the back room. Lily, the caretaker's daughter, did housemaid's work for them. Though their life was modest they believed in eating well; the best of everything: diamond-bone sirloins, three-shilling tea, and the best bottled stout. But Lily seldom made a mistake in the orders so that she got on well with her three mistresses. They were fussy, that was all. But the only thing they would not stand was back answers.

Of course they had good reason to be fussy on such a night. And then it was long after ten o'clock and yet there was no sign of Gabriel and his wife. Besides they were dreadfully afraid that Freddy Malins might turn up screwed. They would not wish for worlds that any of Mary Jane's pupils should see him under the influence; and when he was like that it was sometimes very hard to manage him. Freddy Malins always came late but they wondered what could be keeping Gabriel: and that was what brought them every two minutes to the banisters to ask Lily had Gabriel or Freddy come.

—O, Mr Conroy, said Lily to Gabriel when she opened the door for him, Miss Kate and Miss Julia thought you were never coming. Good-night, Mrs Conroy.

—I'll engage they did, said Gabriel, but they forget that my wife here takes three mortal hours to dress herself.

He stood on the mat, scraping the snow from his galoshes, while Lily led his wife to the foot of the stairs and called out:

—Miss Kate, here's Mrs Conroy.

Kate and Julia came toddling down the dark stair at once. Both of them kissed Gabriel's wife, said she must be perished alive and asked was Gabriel with her.

—Here I am as right as the mail, Aunt Kate! Go on up. I'll follow, called out Gabriel from the dark.

He continued scraping his feet vigorously while the three women went upstairs, laughing, to the ladies' dressing room. A light fringe of snow lay like a cape on the shoulders of his overcoat and like toecaps on the toes of his galoshes; and, as the buttons of his overcoat slipped with a squeaking noise through the snow-stiffened frieze, a cold fragrant air from out-of-doors escaped from crevices and folds.

—Is it snowing again, Mr Conroy? asked Lily.

She had preceded him into the panty to help him off with his overcoat. Gabriel smiled at the three syllables she had given his surname and glanced at her. She was a slim, growing girl, pale in complexion and with hay-coloured hair. The gas in the pantry made her look still paler. Gabriel had known her when she was a child and used to sit on the lowest step nursing a rag doll.

—Yes, Lily, he answered, and I think we're in for a night of it.

He looked up at the pantry ceiling, which was shaking with the stamping and shuffling of feet on the floor above, listened for a moment to the piano, and then glanced at the girl, who was folding his overcoat carefully at the end of a shelf.

—Tell me, Lily, he said in a friendly tone, do you still go to school?

—O no, sir, she answered. I'm done schooling this year and more.

—O, then, said Gabriel gaily, I suppose we'll be going to your wedding one of these fine days with your young man, eh?

The girl glanced back at him over her shoulder and said with great bitterness:

—The men that is now is only all palaver and what they can get out of you.

Gabriel coloured as if he felt he had made a mistake and, without looking at her, kicked off his galoshes and flicked actively with his muffler at his patent-leather shoes.

He was a stout tallish young man. The high colour of his cheeks pushed upwards even to his forehead where it scattered itself in a few formless patches of pale red; and on his hairless face there scintillated restlessly the polished lenses and the bright gilt rims of the glasses which screened his delicate and restless eyes. His glossy black hair was parted in the middle and brushed in a long curve behind his ears where it curled slightly beneath the groove left by his hat.

When he had flicked lustre into his shoes he stood up and pulled his waistcoat down more tightly on his plump body. Then he took a coin rapidly from his pocket.

—O Lily, he said, thrusting it into her hands, it's Christmastime, isn't it? Just . . . here's a little. . . .

He walked rapidly towards the door.

—O no, sir! cried the girl, following him. Really, sir, I wouldn't take it.

—Christmastime! Christmastime! said Gabriel, almost trotting to the stairs and waving his hand to her in deprecation.

The girl, seeing that he had gained the stairs, called out after him:

—Well, thank you, sir.

He waited outside the drawing room door until the waltz should be finished, listening to the skirts that swept against it and to the shuffling of feet. He was still discomposed by the girl's bitter and sudden retort. It had cast a gloom over him which he tried to dispel by arranging his cuffs and the bows of his tie. Then he took from his waistcoat pocket a little paper and glanced at the headings he had made for his speech. He was undecided about the lines from Robert Browning for he feared they would be above the heads of his hearers. Some quotation that they could recognize from Shakespeare or from the Melodies would be better. The indelicate clacking of the men's heels and the shuffling of their soles reminded him that their grade of culture differed from his. He would only make himself ridiculous by quoting poetry to them which they could not understand. They would think that he was airing his superior education. He would fail with them just as he had failed with the girl in the pantry. He had taken up a wrong tone. His whole speech was a mistake from first to last, an utter failure.

Just then his aunts and his wife came out of the ladies' dressing room. His aunts were two plainly dressed old women. Aunt Julia was an inch or so the taller. Her hair, drawn low over the tops of her ears, was grey; and grey also, with darker shadows, was her large flaccid face. Though she was stout in build and stood erect her slow eyes and parted lips gave her the appearance of a woman who did not know where she was or where she was going. Aunt Kate was more vivacious. Her face, healthier than her sister's, was all puckers and creases, like a shrivelled red apple, and her hair, braided in the same old-fashioned way, had not lost its ripe nut colour.

They both kissed Gabriel frankly. He was their favourite nephew, the son of their dead elder sister, Ellen, who had married T.J. Conroy of the Port and Docks.

—Gretta tells me you're not going to take a cab back to Monkstown tonight, Gabriel, said Aunt Kate.

—No, said Gabriel, turning to his wife, we had quite enough of that last year, hadn't we? Don't you remember, Aunt Kate, what a cold Gretta got out of it? Cab windows rattling all the way, and the east wind blowing in after we passed Merrion. Very jolly it was. Gretta caught a dreadful cold.

Aunt Kate frowned severely and nodded her head at every word.

—Quite right, Gabriel, quite right, she said. You can't be too careful.

—But as for Gretta there, said Gabriel, she'd walk home in the snow if she were let.

Mrs Conroy laughed.

—Don't mind him, Aunt Kate, she said. He's really an awful bother, what with green shades for Tom's eyes at night and making him do the dumb-bells, and forcing Eva to eat the stirabout. The poor child! And she simply hates the sight of it! . . . O, but you'll never guess what he makes me wear now!

She broke out into a peal of laughter and glanced at her husband, whose admiring and happy eyes had been wandering from her dress to her face and hair. The two aunts laughed heartily too, for Gabriel's solicitude was a standing joke with them.

—Galoshes! said Mrs Conroy. That's the latest. Whenever it's wet underfoot I must put on my galoshes. Tonight even he wanted me to put them on, but I wouldn't. The next thing he'll buy me will be a diving suit.

Gabriel laughed nervously and patted his tie reassuringly while Aunt Kate nearly doubled herself, so heartily did she enjoy the joke. The smile soon faded from Aunt Julia's face and her mirthless eyes were directed towards her nephew's face. After a pause she asked:

—And what are galoshes, Gabriel?

—Galoshes, Julia! exclaimed her sister. Goodness me, don't you know what galoshes are? You wear them over your . . . over your boots, Gretta, isn't it?

—Yes, said Mrs Conroy. Guttapercha things. We both have a pair now. Gabriel says everyone wears them on the continent.

—O, on the continent, murmured Aunt Julia, nodding her head slowly.

Gabriel knitted his brows and said, as if he were slightly angered:

—It's nothing very wonderful but Gretta thinks it very funny because she says the word reminds her of Christy Minstrels.

—But tell me, Gabriel, said Aunt Kate, with brisk tact. Of course, you've seen about the room. Gretta was saying . . .

—O, the room is all right, replied Gabriel. I've taken one in the Gresham.

—To be sure, said Aunt Kate, by far the best thing to do. And the children, Gretta, you're not anxious about them?

—O, for one night, said Mrs Conroy. Besides, Bessie will look after them.

—To be sure, said Aunt Kate again. What a comfort it is to have a girl like that, one you can depend on! There's that Lily, I'm sure I don't know what has come over her lately. She's not the girl she was at all.

Gabriel was about to ask his aunt some questions on this point but she broke off suddenly to gaze after her sister who had wandered down the stairs and was craning her neck over the banisters.

—Now, I ask you, she said, almost testily, where is Julia going? Julia! Julia! Where are you going?

Julia, who had gone halfway down one flight, came back and announced blandly:

—Here's Freddy.

At the same moment a clapping of hands and a final flourish of the pianist told that the waltz had ended. The drawing room door was opened from within and some couples came out. Aunt Kate drew Gabriel aside hurriedly and whispered into his ear:

—Slip down, Gabriel, like a good fellow and see if he's all right, and don't let him up if he's screwed. I'm sure he's screwed. I'm sure he is.

Gabriel went to the stairs and listened over the banisters. He could hear two persons talking in the pantry. Then he recognized Freddy Malins' laugh. He went down the stairs noisily.

It's such a relief, said Aunt Kate to Mrs Conroy, that Gabriel is here. I always feel easier in mind when he's here. . . . Julia, there's Miss Daly and Miss Power will take some refreshment. Thanks for your beautiful waltz, Miss Daly. It made lovely time.

A tall wizen-faced man, with a stiff grizzled moustache and swarthy skin, who was passing out with his partner said:

—And may we have some refreshment, too, Miss Morkan?

—Julia, said Aunt Kate summarily, and here's Mr Browne and Miss Furlong. Take them in, Julia, with Miss Daly and Miss Power.

—I'm the man for the ladies, said Mr Browne, pursing his lips until his moustache bristled and smiling in all his wrinkles. You know, Miss Morkan, the reason they are so fond of me is—

He did not finish his sentence, but, seeing that Aunt Kate was out of earshot, at once led the three young ladies into the back room. The middle of the room was occupied by two square tables placed end to end, and on these Aunt Julia and the caretaker were straightening and smoothing a large cloth. On the sideboard were arrayed dishes and plates, and glasses and bundles of knives and forks and spoons. The top of the closed square piano served also as a sideboard for viands and sweets. At a smaller sideboard in one corner two young men were standing, drinking hop-bitters.

Mr Browne led his charges thither and invited them all, in jest, to some ladies' punch, hot, strong, and sweet. As they said they never took anything strong he opened three bottles of lemonade for them. Then he asked one of the young men to move aside, and, taking hold of the decanter, filled out for himself a goodly measure of whisky. The young men eyed him respectfully while he took a trial sip.

—God help me, he said, smiling, it's the doctor's orders.

His wizened face broke into a broader smile, and the three young ladies laughed in musical echo to his pleasantry, swaying their bodies to and fro, with nervous jerks of their shoulders. The boldest said:

—O, now, Mr Browne, I'm sure the doctor never ordered anything of the kind.

Mr Browne took another sip of his whisky and said, with sidling mimicry:

—Well, you see, I'm like the famous Mrs Cassidy, who is reported to have said: *Now, Mary Grimes, if I don't take it, make me take it, for I feel I want it.*

His hot face had leaned forward a little too confidentially and he had assumed a very low Dublin accent so that the young ladies, with one instinct, received his speech in silence. Miss Furlong, who was one of Mary Jane's pupils, asked Miss Daly what was the name of the pretty waltz she had played; and Mr Browne, seeing that he was ignored, turned promptly to the two young men who were more appreciative.

A red-faced young woman, dressed in pansy, came into the room, excitedly clapping her hands and crying:

—Quadrilles! Quadrilles!

Close on her heels came Aunt Kate, crying:

—Two gentlemen and three ladies, Mary Jane!

—O, here's Mr Bergin and Mr Kerrigan, said Mary Jane. Mr Kerrigan, will you take Miss Powers? Miss Furlong, may I get you a partner, Mr Bergin. O, that'll just do now.

—Three ladies, Mary Jane, said Aunt Kate.

The two young gentlemen asked the ladies if they might have the pleasure, and Mary Jane turned to Miss Daly.

—O, Miss Daly, you're really awfully good, after playing for the last two dances, but really we're so short of ladies tonight.

—I don't mind in the least, Miss Morkan.

—But I've a nice partner for you, Mr Bartell D'Arcy, the tenor. I'll get him to sing later on. All Dublin is raving about him.

—Lovely voice, lovely voice! said Aunt Kate.

As the piano had twice begun the prelude to the first figure Mary Jane led her recruits quickly from the room. They had hardly gone when Aunt Julia wandered slowly into the room, looking behind her at something.

—What is the matter, Julia? asked Aunt Kate anxiously. Who is it?

Julia, who was carrying in a column of table-napkins, turned to her sister and said, simply, as if the question had surprised her:

—It's only Freddy, Kate, and Gabriel with him.

In fact right behind her Gabriel could be seen piloting Freddy Malins across the landing. The latter, a young man of about forty, was of Gabriel's size and build, with very round shoulders. His face was fleshy and pallid, touched with colour only at the thick hanging lobes of his ears and at the wide wings of his nose. He had coarse features, a blunt nose, and convex and receding brow, tumid and protruded lips. His heavy-lidded eyes and the disorder of his scanty hair made him look sleepy. He was laughing heartily in a high key at a story which he had been telling Gabriel on the stairs and at the same time rubbing the knuckles of his left fist backwards and forwards into his left eye.

—Good evening, Freddy, said Aunt Julia.

Freddy Malins bade the Misses Morkan good evening in what seemed an offhand fashion by reason of the habitual catch in his voice and then, seeing that Mr Browne was grinning at him from the sideboard, crossed the room on rather shaky legs and began to repeat in an undertone the story he had just told to Gabriel.

—He's not so bad, is he? said Aunt Kate to Gabriel.

Gabriel's brows were dark but he raised them quickly and answered:

—O no, hardly noticeable.

—Now, isn't he a terrible fellow! she said. And his poor mother made him take the pledge on New Year's Eve. But come on, Gabriel, into the drawing room.

Before leaving the room with Gabriel she signalled to Mr Browne by frowning and shaking her forefinger in warning to and fro. Mr Browne nodded in answer and, when she had gone, said to Freddy Malins:

—Now, then, Teddy, I'm going to fill you out a good glass of lemonade just to buck you up.

Freddy Malins, who was nearing the climax of his story, waved the offer aside impatiently but Mr Browne, having first called Freddy Malins' attention to a disarray in his dress, filled out and handed him a full glass of lemonade. Freddy Malins' left hand accepted the glass mechanically, his right hand being engaged in the mechanical readjustment of his dress. Mr Browne, whose face was once more wrinkling with mirth, poured out for himself a glass of whisky while Freddy Malins exploded, before he had well reached the climax of his story, in a kink of high-pitched bronchitic laughter and, setting down his untasted and overflowing glass, began to rub the knuckles of his left fist backwards and forwards into his left eye, repeating words of his last phrase as well as his fit of laugher would allow him.

Gabriel could not listen while Mary Jane was playing her Academy piece, full of runs and difficult passages, to the hushed drawing room. He liked music but the piece she was playing had no melody for him and he doubted whether it had any melody for the other listeners, though they had begged Mary Jane to play something. Four young men, who had come from the refreshment room to stand in the doorway at the sound of the piano, had gone away quietly in couples after a few minutes. The only persons who seemed to follow the music were Mary Jane herself, her hands racing along the keyboard or lifted from it at the pauses like those of a priestess in momentary imprecation, and Aunt Jane standing at her elbow to turn the page.

Gabriel's eyes, irritated by the floor, which glittered with beeswax under the heavy chandelier, wandered to the wall above the piano. A picture of the balcony scene in *Romeo and Juliet* hung there and beside it was a picture of the two murdered princes in the Tower which Aunt Julia had worked in red, blue, and brown wools when she was a girl. Probably in the school they had gone to as girls that kind of work had been taught, for one year his mother had worked for him as a birthday present a waistcoat of purple tabinet, with little foxes' heads upon it, lined with brown satin and having round mulberry buttons. It was strange that his mother had had no musical talent though Aunt Kate used to call her the brains carrier of the Morkan family. Both she and Julia had always seemed a little proud of their serious and matronly sister. Her photograph stood before the pierglass. She held an open book on her knees and was pointing out something in it to Constantine who, dressed in a man-o'-war suit, lay at her feet. It was she who had chosen the names for her sons for she was very sensible of the dignity of family life. Thanks to her, Constantine was now senior curate in Balbriggan and, thanks to her, Gabriel himself had taken his degree in the Royal University. A shadow passed over his face as he remembered her sullen opposition to his marriage. Some slighting phrases she had used still rankled in his memory; she had once spoken of Gretta as being country cute and that was not true of Gretta at all. It was Gretta who had nursed her during all her last long illness in their house at Monkstown.

He knew that Mary Jane must be near the end of piece for she was playing again the opening melody with runs of scales after every bar and while he waited for the end the resentment had died down in his heart. The piece ended with a trill of octaves in the treble and a final deep octave in the bass. Great applause greeted Mary Jane as, blushing and rolling up her music nervously, she escaped from the room. The most vigorous clapping came from the four young men in the doorway who had gone away to the refreshment room at the beginning of the piece but had come back when the piano had stopped.

Lancers were arranged. Gabriel found himself partnered with Miss Ivors. She was a frank-mannered talkative young lady, with a freckled face and prominent brown eyes. She did not wear a low-cut bodice and the large brooch which was fixed in the front of her collar bore on it an Irish device.

When they had taken their places she said abruptly:

—I have a crow to pluck with you.

—With me? said Gabriel.

She nodded her head gravely.

—What is it? asked Gabriel, smiling at her solemn manner.

—Who is G.C.? answered Miss Ivors, turning her eyes upon him.

Gabriel coloured and was about to knit his brows, as if he did not understand, when she said bluntly:

—O, innocent Amy! I have found out that you write for *The Daily Express*. Now, aren't you ashamed of yourself?

—Why should I be ashamed of myself? asked Gabriel, blinking his eyes and trying to smile.

—Well, I'm ashamed of you, said Miss Ivors frankly. To say you'd write for a rag like that. I didn't think you were a West Briton.

A look of perplexity appeared on Gabriel's face. It was true that he wrote a literary column every Wednesday in *The Daily Express*, for which he was paid fifteen shillings. But that did not make him a West Briton surely. The books he received for review were almost more welcome than the paltry cheque. He loved to feel the covers and turn over the pages of newly printed books. Nearly every day when his teaching in the college was ended he used to wander down the quays to the second-hand booksellers, to Hickey's on Bachelor's Walk, to Webb's or Massey's on Aston's Quay, or to O'Clohissey's in the bystreet. He did not know how to meet her charge. He wanted to say literature was above politics. But they were friends of many years' standing and their careers had been parallel, first at the University and then as teachers: he could not risk a grandiose phrase with her. He continued blinking his eyes and trying to smile and murmured lamely that he saw nothing political in writing reviews of books.

When their turn to cross had come he was still perplexed and inattentive. Miss Ivors promptly took his hand in a warm grasp and said in a friendly tone:

—Of course, I was only joking. Come, we cross now.

When they were together again she spoke of the University question and Gabriel felt more at ease. A friend of hers had shown her his review of Browning's poems. That was how she had found out the secret: but she liked the review immensely. Then she said suddenly:

—O, Mr Conroy, will you come for an excursion to the Aran Isles this summer? We're going to stay there a whole month. It will be splendid out in the Atlantic. You ought to come. Mr Clancy is coming, and Mr Kilkelly and Kathleen Kearney. It would be splendid for Gretta too if she'd come. She's from Connacht, isn't she?

—Her people are, said Gabriel shortly.

—But you will come, won't you? said Miss Ivors, laying her warm hand eagerly on his arm.

—The fact is, said Gabriel, I have already arranged to go—

—Go where? asked Miss Ivors.

—Well, you know, every year I go for a cycling tour with some fellows and so—

—But where? asked Miss Ivors.

—Well, we usually go to France or Belgium or perhaps Germany, said Gabriel awkwardly.

—And why do you go to France and Belgium, said Miss Ivors, instead of visiting your own land?

—Well, said Gabriel, it's partly to keep in touch with the languages and partly for a change.

—And haven't you your own language to keep in touch with—Irish? asked Miss Ivors.

—Well, said Gabriel, if it comes to that, you know, Irish is not my language.

Their neighbours had turned to listen to the cross-examination. Gabriel glanced right and left nervously and tried to keep his good humour under the ordeal which was making a blush invade his forehead.

—And haven't you your own land to visit, continued Miss Ivors, that you know nothing of, your own people, and your own country?

—O, to tell you the truth, retorted Gabriel suddenly, I'm sick of my own country, sick of it!

—Why? asked Miss Ivors.

Gabriel did not answer for his retort had heated him.

—Why? repeated Miss Ivors.

They had to go visiting together and, as he had not answered her, Miss Ivors said warmly:

—Of course, you've no answer.

Gabriel tried to cover his agitation by taking part in the dance with great energy. He avoided her eyes for he had seen a sour expression on her face. But when they met in the long chain he was surprised to feel his hand firmly pressed. She looked at him from under her brows for a moment quizzically until he smiled. Then, just as the chain was about to start again, she stood on tiptoe and whispered into his ear:

—West Briton!

When the lancers were over Gabriel went away to a remote corner of the room where Freddy Malins' mother was sitting. She was a stout feeble old woman with white hair. Her voice had a catch in it like her son's and she stuttered slightly. She had been told that Freddy had come and that he was nearly all right. Gabriel asked her whether she had had a good crossing. She lived with a married daughter in Glasgow and came to Dublin on a visit once a year. She answered placidly that she had had a beautiful crossing and that the captain had been most attentive to her. She spoke also of the beautiful house her daughter kept in Glasgow, and of all the nice friends they had there. While her tongue rambled on Gabriel tried to banish from his mind all memory of the unpleasant incident with Miss Ivors. Of course the girl or woman, or whatever she was, was an enthusiast but there was a time for all things. Perhaps he ought not to have answered her like that. But she had no right to call him a West Briton before people, even in joke. She had tried to make him ridiculous before people, heckling him and staring at him with her rabbit's eyes.

He saw his wife making her way towards him through the waltzing couples. When she reached him she said into his ear:

—Gabriel, Aunt Kate wants to know won't you carve the goose as usual. Miss Daly will carve the ham and I'll do the pudding.

—All right, said Gabriel.

—She's sending in the younger ones first as soon as this waltz is over so that we'll have the table to ourselves.

—Were you dancing? asked Gabriel.

—Of course I was. Didn't you see me? What words had you with Molly Ivors?

—No words. Why? Did she say so?

—Something like that. I'm trying to get that Mr D'Arcy to sing. He's full of conceit, I think.

—There were no words, said Gabriel moodily, only she wanted me to go for a trip to the west of Ireland and I said I wouldn't.

His wife clasped her hands excitedly and gave a little jump.

—O, do go, Gabriel, she cried. I'd love to see Galway again.

—You can go if you like, said Gabriel coldly.

She looked at him for a moment, then turned to Mrs Malins and said:

—There's a nice husband for you, Mrs Malins.

While she was threading her way back across the room Mrs Malins, without adverting to the interruption, went on to tell Gabriel what beautiful places there were in Scotland and beautiful scenery. Her son-in-law brought them every year to the lakes and they used to go fishing. Her son-in-law was a splendid fisher. One day he caught a fish, a beautiful big big fish, and the man in the hotel boiled it for their dinner.

Gabriel hardly heard what she said. Now that supper was coming near he began to think again about his speech and about the quotation. When he saw Freddy Malins coming across the room to visit his mother Gabriel left the chair free for him and retired into the embrasure of the window. The room had already cleared and from the back room came the clatter of plates and knives. Those who still remained in the drawing room seemed tired of dancing and were conversing quietly in little groups. Gabriel's warm trembling fingers tapped the cold pane of the window. How cool it must be outside! How pleasant it would be to walk out alone, first along by the river and then through the park! The snow would by lying on the branches of the trees and forming a bright cap on the top of the Wellington Monument. How much more pleasant it would be there than at the supper table!

He ran over the headings of his speech: Irish hospitality, sad memories, the Three Graces, Paris, the quotation from Browning. He repeated to himself a phrase he had written in his review: *One feels that one is listening to a thought-tormented music.* Miss Ivors had praised the review. Was she sincere? Had she really any life of her own behind all her propagandism? There had never been any ill-feeling between them until that night. It unnerved him to think that she would be at the supper table, looking up at him while he spoke with her critical quizzing eyes. Perhaps she would not be sorry to see him fail in his speech. An idea came into his mind and gave him courage. He would say, alluding to Aunt Kate and Aunt Julia: *Ladies and Gentlemen, the generation which is now on the wane among us may have had its faults but for my part I think it had certain qualities of hospitality, of humour, of humanity, which the new and very serious and hypereducated generation that is growing up around us seems to me to lack.* Very good: that was one for Miss Ivors. What did he care that his aunts were only two ignorant old women?

A murmur in the room attracted his attention. Mr Browne was advancing from the door, gallantly escorting Aunt Julia, who leaned upon his arm, smiling and hanging her head. An irregular musketry of applause escorted her also as far as the piano and then, as Mary Jane seated herself on the stool, and Aunt Julia, no longer smiling, half turned so as to pitch her voice fairly into the room, gradually ceased. Gabriel recognized the prelude. It was that of an old song of Aunt Julia's—*Arrayed for the Bridal.* Her voice, strong and clear in tone, attacked with great spirit the runs which embellish the air and though she sang very rapidly she did not miss even the smallest of the grace notes. To follow the voice, without looking at the singer's face, was to feel and share the excitement of swift and secure flight. Gabriel applauded loudly with all the others at the close of the song and loud applause was borne in from the invisible supper table. It sounded so genuine that a little colour struggled into Aunt Julia's face as she bent to replace in the music stand the old leather-bound songbook that had her initials on the cover. Freddy Malins, who had listened with his head perched sideways to hear her better, was still applauding when everyone else had ceased and talking animatedly to his mother who nodded her head gravely and slowly in acquiescence. At last, when he could clap no more, he stood up suddenly and hurried across the room to Aunt Julia whose hand he seized and held in both his hands, shaking it when words failed him or the catch in his voice proved too much for him.

—I was just telling my mother, he said, I never heard you sing so well, never. No, I never heard your voice so good as it is tonight. Now! Would you believe that now? That's the truth. Upon my word and honour that's the truth. I never heard your voice sound so fresh and so . . . so clear and fresh, never.

Aunt Julia smiled broadly and murmured something about compliments as she released her hand from his grasp. Mr Browne extended his open hand towards her and said to those who were near him in a manner of a showman introducing a prodigy to an audience:

—Miss Julia Morkan, my latest discovery!

He was laughing very heartily at this himself when Freddy Malins turned to him and said:

—Well, Browne, if you're serious you might make a worse discovery. All I can say is I never heard her sing half so well as long as I am coming here. And that's the honest truth.

—Neither did I, said Mr Browne. I think her voice has greatly improved.

Aunt Julia shrugged her shoulders and said with meek pride:

—Thirty years ago I hadn't a bad voice as voices go.

—I often told Julia, said Aunt Kate emphatically, that she was simply thrown away in that choir. But she never would be said by me.

She turned as if to appeal to the good sense of the others against a refractory child while Aunt Julia gazed in front of her, a vague smile of reminiscence playing on her face.

—No, continued Aunt Kate, she wouldn't be said or led by anyone, slaving there in that choir night and day, night and day. Six o'clock on Christmas morning! And all for what?

—Well, isn't it for the honour of God, Aunt Kate? asked Mary Jane, twisting round on the piano-stool and smiling.

Aunt Kate turned fiercely on her niece and said:

—I know all about the honour of God, Mary Jane, but I think it's not at all honourable for the pope to turn out the women out of the choirs that have slaved there all their lives and put little whipper-snappers of boys over their heads. I suppose it is for the good of the Church if the pope does it. But it's not just, Mary Jane, and it's not right.

She had worked herself into a passion and would have continued in defence of her sister for it was a sore subject with her but Mary Jane, seeing that all the dancers had come back, intervened pacifically:

—Now, Aunt Kate, you're giving scandal to Mr Browne who is of the other persuasion.

Aunt Kate turned to Mr Browne, who was grinning at this allusion to his religion, and said hastily:

—O, I don't question the pope's being right. I'm only a stupid old woman and I wouldn't presume to do such a thing. But there's such a thing as common everyday politeness and gratitude. And if I were in Julia's place I'd tell that Father Healy straight up to his face . . .

—And besides, Aunt Kate, said Mary Jane, we really are all hungry and when we are hungry we are all very quarrelsome.

—And when we are thirsty we are also quarrelsome, added Mr Browne.

—So that we had better go to supper, said Mary Jane, and finish the discussion afterwards.

On the landing outside the drawing room Gabriel found his wife and Mary Jane trying to persuade Miss Ivors to stay for supper. But Miss Ivors, who had put on her hat and was buttoning her cloak, would not stay. She did not feel in the least hungry and she had already overstayed her time.

—But only for ten minutes, Molly, said Mrs Conroy. That won't delay you.

—To take a pick itself, said Mary Jane, after all your dancing.

—I really couldn't, said Miss Ivors.

—I am afraid you didn't enjoy yourself at all, said Mary Jane hopelessly.

—Ever so much, I assure you, said Miss Ivors, but you really must let me run off now.

—But how can you get home? asked Mrs Conroy.

—O, it's only two steps up the quay.

Gabriel hesitated a moment and said:

—If you will allow me, Miss Ivors, I'll see you home if you really are obliged to go.

But Miss Ivors broke away from them.

—I won't hear of it, she cried. For goodness sake go in to your suppers and don't mind me. I'm quite well able to take care of myself.

—Well, you're the comical girl, Molly, said Mrs Conroy frankly.

—*Beannacht libh*, cried Miss Ivors, with a laugh, as she ran down the staircase.

Mary Jane gazed after her, a moody puzzled expression on her face, while Mrs Conroy leaned over the banisters to listen for the hall door. Gabriel asked himself was he the cause of her abrupt departure. But she did not seem to be in ill humour: she had gone away laughing. He stared blankly down the staircase.

At that moment Aunt Kate came toddling out of the supper room, almost wringing her hands in despair.

—Where is Gabriel? she cried. Where on earth is Gabriel? There's everyone waiting in there, stage to let, and nobody to carve the goose!

—Here I am, Aunt Kate! cried Gabriel, with sudden animation, ready to carve a flock of geese, if necessary.

A fat brown goose lay at one end of the table and at the other end, on a bed of creased paper strewn with sprigs of parsley, lay a great ham, stripped of its outer skin and peppered over with crust crumbs, a neat paper frill round its shin and beside this was a round of spiced beef. Between these rival ends ran parallel lines of side-dishes: two little minsters of jelly, red and yellow; a shallow dish full of blocks of blancmange and red jam, a large green leaf-shaped dish with a stalk-shaped handle, on which lay bunches of purple raisins and peeled almonds, a companion dish on which lay a solid rectangle of Smyrna figs, a dish of custard topped with grated nutmeg, a small bowl full of chocolates and sweets wrapped in gold and silver papers, and a glass vase in which stood some tall celery stalks. In the centre of the table there stood, as sentries to a fruit-stand which upheld a pyramid of oranges and American apples, two squat old-fashioned decanters of cut glass, one containing port and the other dark sherry. On the closed square piano a pudding in a huge yellow dish lay in waiting and behind it were three squads of bottles of stout and ale and minerals, drawn up according to the colours of their uniforms, the first two black, with brown and red labels, the third and smallest squad white, with transverse green sashes.

Gabriel took his seat boldly at the head of the table and, having looked to the edge of the carver, plunged his fork firmly into the goose. He felt quite at ease now for he was an expert carver and liked nothing better than to find himself at the head of a well-laden table.

—Miss Furlong, what shall I send you? he asked. A wing or a slice of the breast?

—Just a small slice of the breast.

—Miss Higgins, what for you?

—O, anything at all, Mr Conroy.

While Gabriel and Miss Daly exchanged plates of goose and plates of ham and spiced beef Lily went from guest to guest with a dish of hot floury potatoes wrapped in a white napkin. This was Mary Jane's idea and she had also suggested apple sauce for the goose but Aunt Kate had said that plain roast goose without apple sauce had always been good enough for her and she hoped she might never eat worse. Mary Jane waited on her pupils and saw that they got the best slices and Aunt Kate and Aunt Julia opened and carried across from the piano bottles of stout and ale for the gentlemen and bottles of minerals for the ladies. There was a great deal of confusion and laughter and noise, the noise of orders and counter-orders, of knives and forks, of corks and glass-stoppers. Gabriel began to carve second helpings as soon as he had finished the first round without serving himself. Everyone protested loudly so that he compromised by taking a long draught of stout for he had found the carving hard work. Mary Jane settled down quietly to her supper but Aunt Kate and Aunt Julia were still toddling round the table, walking on each other's heels, getting in each other's way, and giving each other unheeded orders. Mr Browne begged of them to sit down and eat their suppers and so did Gabriel but they said there was time enough so that, at last, Freddy Malins stood up and, capturing Aunt Kate, plumped her down on her chair amid general laughter.

When everyone had been well served Gabriel said, smiling:

—Now, if anyone wants a little more of what vulgar people call stuffing let him or her speak.

A chorus of voices invited him to begin his own supper and Lily came forward with three potatoes which she had reserved for him.

—Very well, said Gabriel amiably, as he took another preparatory draught, kindly forget my existence, ladies and gentlemen, for a few minutes.

He set to his supper and took no part in the conversation with which the table covered Lily's removal of the plates. The subject of talk was the opera company which was then at the Theatre Royal. Mr Bartell D'Arcy, the tenor, a dark-complexioned young man with a smart moustache, praised very highly the leading contralto of the company but Miss Furlong thought she had a rather vulgar style of production. Freddy Malins said there was a negro chieftain singing in the second part of the Gaiety pantomime who had one of the finest tenor voices he had ever heard.

—Have you heard him? he asked Mr Bartell D'Arcy across the table.

—No, answered Mr Bartell D'Arcy carelessly.

—Because, Freddy Malins explained, now I'd be curious to hear your opinion of him. I think he has a grand voice.

—It takes Teddy to find out the really good things, said Mr Browne familiarly to the table.

—And why couldn't he have a voice too? asked Freddy Malins sharply. Is it because he's only a black?

Nobody answered this question and Mary Jane led the table back to the legitimate opera. One of her pupils had given her a pass for *Mignon*. Of course it was very fine, she said, but it made her think of poor Georgina Burns. Mr Browne could go back farther still, to the old Italian companies that used to come to Dublin—Tietjens, Ilma de Murzka, Campanini, the great Trebelli, Giuglini, Ravelli, Aramburo. Those were the days, he said, when there was something like singing to be heard in Dublin. He told too of how the top gallery of the old Royal used to be packed night after night, of how one night an Italian tenor had sung five encores to *Let Me Like a Soldier Fall*, introducing a high C every time, and of how the gallery boys would sometimes in their enthusiasm unyoke the horses from the carriage of some great *prima donna* and pull her themselves through the streets to her hotel. Why did they never play the grand old operas now, he asked, *Dinorah*, *Lucrezia Borgia*? Because they could not get the voices to sing them: that was why.

—O, well, said Mr Bartell D'Arcy, I presume there are as good singers today as there were then.

—Where are they? asked Mr Browne defiantly.

—In London, Paris, Milan, said Mr Bartell D'Arcy warmly. I suppose Caruso, for example, is quite as good, if not better than any of the men you have mentioned.

—Maybe so, said Mr Browne. But I may tell you I doubt it strongly.

—O, I'd give anything to hear Caruso sing, said Mary Jane.

—For me, said Aunt Kate, who had been picking a bone, there was only one tenor. To please me, I mean. But I suppose none of you ever heard of him.

—Who was he, Miss Morkan? asked Mr Bartell D'Arcy politely.

—His name, said Aunt Kate, was Parkinson. I heard him when he was in his prime and I think he had then the purest tenor voice that was ever put into a man's throat.

—Strange, said Mr Bartell D'Arcy. I never even heard of him.

—Yes, yes, Miss Morkan is right, said Mr Browne. I remember hearing of old Parkinson but he's too far back for me.

—A beautiful pure sweet mellow English tenor, said Aunt Kate with enthusiasm.

Gabriel having finished, the huge pudding was transferred to the table. The clatter of forks and spoons began again. Gabriel's wife served out spoonfuls of the pudding and passed the plates down the table. Midway down they were held up by Mary Jane, who replenished them with raspberry or orange jelly or with blancmange and jam. The pudding was of Aunt Julia's making and she received praises for it from all quarters. She herself said that it was not quite brown enough.

—Well, I hope, Miss Morkan, said Mr Browne, that I'm brown enough for you because, you know, I'm all brown.

All the gentlemen, except Gabriel, ate some of the pudding out of compliment to Aunt Julia. As Gabriel never ate sweets the celery had been left for him. Freddy Malins also took a stalk of celery and ate it with his pudding. He had been told that celery was a capital thing for the blood and he was just then under doctor's care. Mrs Malins, who had been silent all through the supper, said that her son was going down to Mount Melleray in a week or so. The table then spoke of Mount Melleray, how bracing the air was down there, how hospitable the monks were, and how they never asked for a penny-piece from their guests.

—And do you mean to say, asked Mr Browne incredulously, that a chap can go down there and put up there as if it were a hotel and live on the fat of the land and then come away without paying a farthing?

—O, most people give some donation to the monastery when they leave, said Mary Jane.

—I wish we had an institution like that in our Church, said Mr Browne candidly.

He was astonished to hear that the monks never spoke, got up at two in the morning, and slept in their coffins. He asked what they did it for.

—That's the rule of the order, said Aunt Kate firmly.

—Yes, but why? asked Mr Browne.

Aunt Kate repeated that it was the rule, that was all. Mr Browne still seemed not to understand. Freddy Malins explained to him, as best he could, that the monks were trying to make up for the sins committed by all the sinners in the outside world. The explanation was not very clear for Mr Browne grinned and said:

—I like that idea very much but wouldn't a comfortable spring bed do them as well as a coffin?

—The coffin, said Mary Jane, is to remind them of their last end.

As the subject had grown lugubrious it was buried in a silence of the table during which Mrs Malins could be heard saying to her neighbour in an indistinct undertone:

—They are very good men, the monks, very pious men.

The raisins and almonds and figs and apples and oranges and chocolates and sweets were now passed about the table and Aunt Julia invited all the guests to have either port or sherry. At first Mr Bartell D'Arcy refused to take either but one of his neighbours nudged him whispering something to him upon which he allowed his glass to be filled. Gradually as the last glasses were being filled the conversation ceased. A pause followed, broken only by the noise of the wine and by unsettlings of chairs. The Misses Morkan, all three, looked down at the tablecloth. Someone coughed once or twice and then a few gentlemen patted the table gently as a signal for silence. The silence came and Gabriel pushed back his chair and stood up.

The patting at once grew louder in encouragement and then ceased altogether. Gabriel leaned his ten trembling fingers on the tablecloth and smiled nervously at the company. Meeting a row of upturned faces he raised his eyes to the chandelier. The piano was playing a waltz tune and he could hear the skirts sweeping against the drawing room door. People, perhaps, were standing in the snow on the quay outside, gazing up at the lighted windows and listening to the waltz music. The air was pure there. In the distance lay the park where the trees were weighted with snow. The Wellington Monument wore a gleaming cap of snow that flashed westward over the white field of Fifteen Acres.

He began:

—Ladies and Gentlemen.

—It has fallen to my lot this evening, as in years past, to perform a very pleasing task but a task for which I am afraid my poor powers as a speaker are all too inadequate.

—No, no! said Mr Browne.

—But, however that may be, I can only ask you tonight to take the will for the deed and to lend me your attention for a few moments while I endeavour to express to you in words what my feelings are on this occasion.

—Ladies and Gentlemen. It is not the first time that we have gathered together under this hospitable roof, around this hospitable board. It is not the first time that we have been the recipients—or perhaps, I had better say, the victims—of the hospitality of certain good ladies.

He made a circle in the air with his arm and paused. Everyone laughed or smiled at Aunt Kate and Aunt Julia and Mary Jane who all turned crimson with pleasure. Gabriel went on more boldly:

—I feel more strongly with every recurring year that our country has no tradition which does it so much honour and which it should guard so jealously as that of its hospitality. It is a tradition that is unique as far as my experience goes (and I have visited not a few places abroad) among the modern nations. Some would say, perhaps, that with us it is rather a failing than anything to be boasted of. But granted even that, it is, to my mind, a princely failing, and one that I trust will long be cultivated among us. Of one thing, at least, I am sure. As long as this one roof shelters the good ladies aforesaid—and I wish from my heart it may do so for many and many a long year to come—the tradition of genuine warm-hearted courteous Irish hospitality, which our forefathers have handed down to us and which we in turn must hand down to our descendants, is still alive among us.

A hearty murmur of assent ran round the table. It shot through Gabriel's mind that Miss Ivors was not there and that she had gone away discourteously: and he said with confidence in himself:

—Ladies and Gentlemen.

—A new generation is growing up in our midst, a generation actuated by new ideas and new principles. It is serious and enthusiastic for these new ideas and its enthusiasm, even when it is misdirected, is, I believe, in the main sincere. But we are living in a skeptical and, if I may use the phrase, a thought-tormented age: and sometimes I fear that this new generation, educated or hypereducated as it is, will lack those qualities of humanity, of hospitality, of kindly humour which belonged to an older day. Listening tonight to the names of all those great singers of the past it seemed to me, I must confess, that we were living in a less spacious age. Those days might, without exaggeration, be called spacious days: and if they are gone beyond recall let us hope, at least, that in gatherings such as this we shall still speak of them with pride and affection, still cherish in our hearts the memory of those dead and gone great ones whose fame the world will not willingly let die.

—Hear, hear! said Mr Browne loudly.

—But yet, continued Gabriel, his voice falling into softer inflection, there are always in gatherings such as this sadder thoughts that will recur to our minds: thoughts of the past, of youth, of changes, of absent faces that we miss here tonight. Our path through life is strewn with many such sad memories: and were we to brood upon them always we could not find the heart to go on bravely with our work among the living. We have all of us living duties and living affections which claim, and rightly claim, our strenuous endeavours.

—Therefore, I will not linger on the past. I will not let any gloomy moralizing intrude upon us here tonight. Here we are gathered together for a brief moment from the bustle and rush of our everyday routine. We are met here as friends, in the spirit of good-fellowship, as colleagues, also to a certain extent, in the true spirit of *camaraderie*, and as the guests of—what shall I call them?—the Three Graces of the Dublin musical world.

The table burst into applause and laughter at this sally. Aunt Julia vainly asked each of her neighbours in turn to tell her what Gabriel had said.

—He says we are the Three Graces, Aunt Julia, said Mary Jane.

Aunt Julia did not understand but she looked up, smiling, at Gabriel, who continued in the same vein:

—Ladies and Gentlemen.

—I will not attempt to play tonight the part that Paris played on another occasion. I will not attempt to choose between them. The task would be an invidious one and one beyond my poor powers. For when I view them in turn, whether it be our chief hostess herself, whose good heart, whose too good heart, has become a byword with all who know her, or her sister, who seems to be gifted with perennial youth and whose singing must have been a surprise and a revelation to us all tonight, or, last but not least, when I consider our youngest hostess, talented, cheerful, hard-working and the best of nieces, I confess, Ladies and Gentlemen, that I do not know to which of them I should award the prize.

Gabriel glanced down at his aunts and, seeing the large smile on Aunt Julia's face and the tears which had risen to Aunt Kate's eyes, hastened to his close. He raised his glass of port gallantly, while every member of the company fingered a glass expectantly, and said loudly:

—Let us toast them all three together. Let us drink to their health, wealth, long life, happiness, and prosperity and may they long continue to hold the proud and self-won position which they hold in their profession and the position of honour and affection which they hold in our hearts.

All the guests stood up, glass in hand, and, turning towards the three seated ladies, sang in unison, with Mr Browne as leader.

For they are jolly gay fellows,
For they are jolly gay fellows,
For they are jolly gay fellows,
Which nobody can deny.

Aunt Kate was making frank use of her handkerchief and even Aunt Julia seemed moved. Freddy Malins beat time with his pudding-fork and the singers turned towards one another, as if in melodious conference, while they sang, with emphasis:

Unless he tells a lie,
Unless he tells a lie.

Then, turning once more towards their hostesses, they sang:

For they are jolly gay fellows,
For they are jolly gay fellows,
For they are jolly gay fellows,
Which nobody can deny.

The acclamation which followed was taken up beyond the door of the supper room by many of the other guests and renewed time after time, Freddy Malins acting as officer with his fork on high.

The piercing morning air came into the hall where they were standing so that Aunt Kate said:

—Close the door, somebody. Mrs Malins will get her death of cold.

—Browne is out there, Aunt Kate, said Mary Jane.

—Browne is everywhere, said Aunt Kate, lowering her voice.

Mary Jane laughed at her tone.

—Really, she said archly, he is very attentive.

—He has been laid on here like the gas, said Aunt Kate in the same tone, all during the Christmas.

She laughed herself this time good-humouredly and then added quickly:

—But tell him to come in, Mary Jane, and close the door. I hope to goodness he didn't hear me.

At that moment the hall door was opened and Mr Browne came in from the doorstep, laughing as if his heart would break. He was dressed in a long green overcoat with mock astrakhan cuffs and collar and wore on his head an oval fur cap. He pointed down the snow-covered quay from where the sound of shrill prolonged whistling was borne in.

—Teddy will have all the cabs in Dublin out, he said.

Gabriel advanced from the little pantry behind the office, struggling into his overcoat and, looking round the hall, said:

—Gretta not down yet?

—She's getting on her things, Gabriel, said Aunt Kate.

—Who's playing up there? asked Gabriel.

—Nobody. They're all gone.

—O no, Aunt Kate, said Mary Jane. Bartell D'Arcy and Miss O'Callaghan aren't gone yet.

—Someone is strumming at the piano, anyhow, said Gabriel.

May Jane glanced at Gabriel and Mr Browne and said with a shiver:

—It makes me feel cold to look at you two gentlemen muffled up like that. I wouldn't like to face your journey home at this hour.

—I'd like nothing better this minute, said Mr Browne stoutly, than a rattling fine walk in the country or a fast drive with a good spanking goer between the shafts.

—We used to have a very good horse and trap at home, said Aunt Julia sadly.

—The never-to-be-forgotten Johnny, said Mary Jane, laughing.

Aunt Kate and Gabriel laughed too.

—Why, what was wonderful about Johnny? asked Mr Browne.

—The late lamented Patrick Morkan, our grandfather, that is, explained Gabriel, commonly known in his later years as the old gentleman, was a glueboiler.

—O, now, Gabriel, said Aunt Kate, laughing, he had a starch mill.

—Well, glue or starch, said Gabriel, the old gentleman had a horse by the name of Johnny. And Johnny used to work in the old gentleman's mill, walking round and round in order to drive the mill. That was all very well; but now comes the tragic part about Johnny. One fine day the old gentleman thought he'd like to drive out with the quality to a military review in the park.

—The Lord have mercy on his soul, said Aunt Kate compassionately.

—Amen, said Gabriel. So the old gentleman, as I said, harnessed Johnny and put on his very best tall hat and his very best stock collar and drove out in grand style from his ancestral mansion somewhere near Back Lane, I think.

Everyone laughed, even Mrs Malins, at Gabriel's manner and Aunt Kate said:

—O now, Gabriel, he didn't live in Back Lane, really. Only the mill was there.

—Out from the mansion of his forefathers, continued Gabriel, he drove with Johnny. And everything went on beautifully until Johnny came in sight of King Billy's statue: and whether he fell in love with the horse King Billy sits on or whether he thought he was back again in the mill, anyhow he began to walk around the statue.

Gabriel paced in a circle round the hall in his galoshes amid the laughter of the others.

—Round and round he went, said Gabriel, and the old gentleman, who was very pompous old gentleman, was highly indignant. *Go on, sir! What do you mean, sir? Johnny! Johnny! Most extraordinary conduct! Can't understand the horse!*

The peals of laughter which followed Gabriel's imitation of the incident were interrupted by a resounding knock at the hall door. Mary Jane ran to open it and let in Freddy Malins, with his hat well back on his head and his shoulders humped with cold, was puffing and steaming after his exertions.

—I could only get one cab, he said.

—O, we'll find another along the quay, said Gabriel.

—Yes, said Aunt Kate. Better not keep Mrs Malins standing in the draught.

Mrs Malins was helped down the front steps by her son and Mr Browne and, after many manoeuvres, hoisted into the cab. Freddy Malins clambered in after her and spent a long time settling her on the seat, Mr Browne helping him with advice. At last she was settled comfortably and Freddy Malins invited Mr Browne into the cab. There was a good deal of confused talk, and then Mr Browne got into the cab. The cabman settled his rug over his knees, and bent down for the address. The confusion grew greater and the cabman was directed differently by Freddy Malins and Mr Browne, each of whom had his head out through a window of the cab. The difficulty was to know where to drop Mr Browne along the route and Aunt Kate, Aunt Julia, and Mary Jane helped the discussion from the doorstep with cross-directions and contradictions and abundance of laughter. As for Freddy Malins he was speechless with laughter. He popped his head in and out of the window every moment, to the great danger of his hat, and told his mother how the discussion was progressing till at last Mr Browne shouted to the bewildered cabman above the din of everybody's laughter:

—Do you know Trinity College?

—Yes, sir, said the cabman.

—Well, drive bang up against Trinity College gates, said Mr Browne, and then we'll tell you where to go. You understand now?

—Yes, said the cabman.

—Make like a bird for Trinity College.

—Right, sir, cried the cabman.

The horse was whipped up and the cab rattled off along the quay amid a chorus of laughter and adieus.

Gabriel had not gone to the door with the others. He was in a dark part of the hall gazing up the staircase. A woman was standing near the top of the first flight, in the shadow also. He could not see her face but he could see the terracotta and salmon-pink panels of her skirt which the shadow made appear black and white. It was his wife. She was leaning on the banisters, listening to something. Gabriel was surprised at her stillness and strained his ear to listen also. But he could hear little save the noise of laughter and dispute on the front steps, a few chords struck on the piano, and a few notes of a man's voice singing.

He stood still in the gloom of the hall, trying to catch the air that the voice was singing and gazing up at his wife. There was grace and mystery in her attitude as if she were a symbol of something. He asked himself what is a woman standing on the stairs in the shadow, listening to distant music, a symbol of. If he were a painter he would paint her in that attitude. Her blue felt hat would show off the bronze of her hair against the darkness and the dark panels of her skirt would show off the light ones. *Distant Music* he would call the picture if he were a painter.

The hall door was closed; and Aunt Kate, Aunt Julia, and Mary Jane came down the hall, still laughing.

—Well, isn't Freddy terrible? said Mary Jane. He's really terrible.

Gabriel said nothing but pointed up the stairs towards where his wife was standing. Now that the hall door was closed the voice and the piano could be heard more clearly. Gabriel held up his hand for them to be silent. The song seemed to be in the old Irish tonality and the singer seemed uncertain both of his words and of his voice. The voice, made plaintive by distance and by the singer's hoarseness, faintly illuminated the cadence of the air with words expressing grief:

O, the rain falls on my heavy locks
And the dew wets my skin,
My babe lies cold . . .

—O, exclaimed Mary Jane. It's Bartell D'Arcy singing and he wouldn't sing all the night. O, I'll get him to sing a song before he goes.

—O do, Mary Jane, said Aunt Kate.

Mary Jane brushed past the others and ran to the staircase but before she reached it the singing stopped and the piano was closed abruptly.

—O, what a pity! she cried. Is he coming down, Gretta?

Gabriel heard his wife answer yes and saw her come down towards them. A few steps behind her were Mr Bartell D'Arcy and Miss O'Callaghan.

—O, Mr D'Arcy, cried Mary Jane, it's downright mean of you to break off like that when we were all in raptures listening to you.

—I have been at him all the evening, said Miss O'Callaghan, and Mrs Conroy too and he told us he had a dreadful cold and couldn't sing.

—O, Mr D'Arcy, said Aunt Kate, now that was a great fib to tell.

—Can't you see that I'm as hoarse as a crow? said Mr D'Arcy roughly.

He went into the pantry hastily and put on his overcoat. The others, taken aback by his rude speech, could find nothing to say. Aunt Kate wrinkled her brows and made signs to the others to drop the subject. Mr D'Arcy stood swathing his neck carefully and frowning.

—It's the weather, said Aunt Julia, after a pause.

—Yes, everybody has colds, said Aunt Kate readily, everybody.

—They say, said Mary Jane, we haven't had snow like it for thirty years; and I read this morning in the newspapers that the snow is general all over Ireland.

—I love the look of snow, said Aunt Julia sadly.

—So do I, said Miss O'Callaghan. I think Christmas is never really Christmas unless we have the snow on the ground.

—But poor Mr D'Arcy doesn't like the snow, said Aunt Kate, smiling.

Mr D'Arcy came from the pantry, fully swathed and buttoned, and in a repentant tone told them the history of his cold. Everyone gave him advice and said it was a great pity and urged him to be very careful of his throat in the night air. Gabriel watched his wife who did not join in the conversation. She was standing right under the dusty fanlight and the flame of the gas lit up the rich bronze of her hair which he had seen her drying at the fire a few days before. She was in the same attitude and seemed unaware of the talk about her. At last she turned towards them and Gabriel saw that there was colour in her cheeks and that her eyes were shining. A sudden tide of joy went leaping out of his heart.

—Mr D'Arcy, she said, what is the name of that song you were singing?

—It's called *The Lass of Aughrim*, said Mr D'Arcy, but I couldn't remember it properly. Why? Do you know it?

—*The Lass of Aughrim*, she repeated. I couldn't think of the name.

—It's a very nice air, said Mary Jane. I'm sorry you were not in voice tonight.

—Now, Mary Jane, said Aunt Kate, don't annoy Mr D'Arcy. I won't have him annoyed.

Seeing that all were ready to start she shepherded them to the door where good-night was said:

—Well, good-night, Aunt Kate, and thanks for the pleasant evening.

—Good-night, Gabriel. Good-night, Gretta!

—Good-night, Aunt Kate, and thanks ever so much. Good-night, Aunt Julia.

—O, good-night, Gretta, I didn't see you.

—Good-night, Mr D'Arcy. Good-night, Miss O'Callaghan.

—Good-night, Miss Morkan.

—Good-night, again.

—Good-night, all. Safe home.

—Good-night. Good-night.

The morning was still dark. A dull yellow light brooded over the houses and the river; and the sky seemed to be descending. It was slushy underfoot; and only streaks and patches of snow lay on the roofs, on the parapets of the quay, and on the area railings. The lamps were still burning redly in the murky air and, across the river, the palace of the Four Courts stood out menacingly against the heavy sky.

She was walking on before him with Mr Bartell D'Arcy, her shoes in a brown parcel tucked under one arm and her hands holding her skirt up from the slush. She had no longer any grace of attitude but Gabriel's eyes were still bright with happiness. The blood went bounding along his veins; and the thoughts went rioting through his brain, proud, joyful, tender, valorous.

She was walking on before him so lightly and so erect that he longed to run after her noiselessly, catch her by the shoulders and say something foolish and affectionate into her ear. She seemed to him so frail that he longed to defend her against something and then to be alone with her. Moments of their secret life together burst like stars upon his memory. A heliotrope envelope was lying beside his breakfast-cup and he was caressing it with his hand. Birds were twittering in the ivy and the sunny web of the curtain was shimmering along the floor: he could not eat for happiness. They were standing on the crowded platform and he was placing a ticket inside the warm palm of her glove. He was standing with her in the cold, looking in through a grated window at a man making bottles in a roaring furnace. It was very cold. Her face, fragrant in the cold air, was quite close to his; and suddenly she called out to the man at the furnace:

—Is the fire hot, sir?

But the man could not hear her with the noise of the furnace. It was just as well. He might have answered rudely.

A wave of yet more tender joy escaped from his heart and went coursing in warm flood along his arteries. Like the tender fires of stars moments of their life together, that no one knew of or would ever know of, broke upon and illumined his memory. He longed to recall to her those moments, to make her forget the years of their dull existence together and remember only their moments of ecstasy. For the years, he felt, had not quenched his soul or hers. Their children, his writing, her household cares had not quenched all their souls' tender fire. In one letter that he had written to her then he had said: *Why is it that words like these seem to me so dull and cold? Is it because there is no word tender enough to be your name?*

Like distant music these words that he had written years before were borne towards him from the past. He longed to be alone with her. When the others had gone away, when he and she were in their room in the hotel, then they would be alone together. He would call her softly:

—Gretta!

Perhaps she would not hear at once: she would be undressing. Them something in his voice would strike her. She would turn and look at him. . . .

At the corner of Winetavern Street they met a cab. He was glad of its rattling noise as it saved him from conversation. She was looking out of the window and seemed tired. The others spoke only a few words, pointing out some building or street. The horse galloped along wearily under murky morning sky, dragging his old rattling box after his heels, and Gabriel was again in a cab with her, galloping to catch the boat, galloping to their honeymoon.

As the cab drove across O'Connell Bridge Miss O'Callaghan said:

—They say you never cross O'Connell Bridge without seeing a white horse.

—I see a white man this time, said Gabriel.

—Where? asked Mr Bartell D'Arcy.

Gabriel pointed to the statue, on which lay patches of snow. Then he nodded familiarly to it and waved his hand.

—Good-night, Dan, he said gaily.

When the cab drew up before the hotel Gabriel jumped out and, in spite of Mr Bartell D'Arcy's protest, paid the driver. He gave the man a shilling over his fare. The man saluted and said:

—A prosperous New Year to you, sir.

—The same to you, said Gabriel cordially.

She leaned for a moment on his arm in getting out of the cab and while standing at the curbstone, bidding the others good-night. She leaned lightly on his arm, as lightly as when she had danced with him a few hours before. He had felt proud and happy then, happy that she was his, proud of her grace and wifely carriage. But now, after the kindling again of so many memories, the first touch of her body, musical and strange and perfumed, sent through him a keen pang of lust. Under cover of her silence he pressed her arm closely to his side; and, as they stood at the hotel door, he felt that they had escaped from their lives and duties, escaped from home and friends and run away together with wild and radiant hearts to a new adventure.

An old man was dozing in a great hooded chair in the hall. He lit a candle in the office and went before them to the stairs. They followed him in silence, their feet falling in soft thuds on the thickly carpeted stairs. She mounted the stairs behind the porter, her head bowed in the ascent, her frail shoulders curved as with a burden, her skirt girt tightly about her. He could have flung his arms about her hips and held her still for his arms were trembling with desire to seize her and only the stress of his nails against the palms of his hands held the wild impulse of his body in check. The porter halted on the stairs to settle his guttering candle. They halted too on the steps below him. In the silence Gabriel could hear the falling of the molten wax into the tray and the thumping of his own heart against his ribs.

The porter led them along a corridor and opened a door. Then he set his unstable candle down on a toilet-table and asked at what hour they were to be called in the morning.

—Eight, said Gabriel.

The porter pointed to the tap of the electric light and began a muttered apology but Gabriel cut him short.

—We don't want any light. We have light enough from the street. And I say, he added, pointing to the candle, you might remove that handsome article, like a good man.

The porter took up his candle again, but slowly for he was surprised by such a novel idea. Then he mumbled good-night and went out. Gabriel shot the lock to.

A ghostly light from the street lamp lay in a long shaft from one window to the door. Gabriel threw his overcoat and hat on a couch and crossed the room towards the window. He looked down into the street in order that his emotion might calm a little. Then he turned and leaned against the chest of drawers with his back to the light. She had taken off her hat and cloak and was standing before a large swinging mirror, unhooking her waist. Gabriel paused for a few moments, watching her, and then said:

—Gretta!

She turned away from the mirror slowly and walked along the shaft of light towards him. Her face looked so serious and weary that the words would not pass Gabriel's lips. No, it was not the moment yet.

—You looked tired, he said.

—I am a little, she answered.

—You don't feel ill or weak?

—No, tired: that's all.

She went on to the window and stood there, looking out. Gabriel waited again and then, fearing that diffidence was about to conquer him, he said abruptly:

—By the way, Gretta!

—What is it?

—You know that poor fellow Malins? he said quickly.

—Yes. What about him?

—Well, poor fellow, he's a decent sort of chap after all, continued Gabriel in a false voice. He gave me back that sovereign I lent him and I didn't expect it really. It's a pity he wouldn't keep away from that Browne, because he's not a bad fellow at heart.

He was trembling now with annoyance. Why did she seem so abstracted? He did not know how he could begin. Was she annoyed, too, about something? If she would only turn to him or come to him of her own accord! To take her as she was would be brutal. No, he must see some ardour in her eyes first. He longed to be master of her strange mood.

—When did you lend him the pound? she asked, after a pause.

Gabriel strove to restrain himself from breaking out into brutal language about the sottish Malins and his pound. He longed to cry to her from his soul, to crush her body against his, to overmaster her. But he said:

—O, at Christmas, when he opened that little Christmas-card shop in Henry Street.

He was in such a fever of rage and desire that he did not hear her come from the window. She stood before him for an instant, looking at him strangely. Then, suddenly raising herself on tiptoe and resting her hands lightly on his shoulders, she kissed him.

—You are a very generous person, Gabriel, she said.

Gabriel, trembling with delight at her sudden kiss and at the quaintness of her phrase, put his hands on her hair and began smoothing it back, scarcely touching it with his fingers. The washing had made it fine and brilliant. His heart was brimming over with happiness. Just when he was wishing for it she had come to him of her own accord. Perhaps her thoughts had been running with his. Perhaps she had felt the impetuous desire that was in him and then the yielding mood had come upon her. Now that she had fallen to him so easily he wondered why he had been so diffident.

He stood, holding her head between his hands. Then, slipping one arm swiftly about her body and drawing her towards him, he said softly:

—Gretta dear, what are you thinking about?

She did not answer nor yield wholly to his arm. He said again, softly:

—Tell me what it is, Gretta. I think I know what is the matter. Do I know?

She did not answer at once. Then she said in an outburst of tears:

—O, I am thinking about that song, *The Lass of Aughrim*.

She broke loose from him and ran to the bed and, throwing her arms across the bed-rail, hid her face. Gabriel stood stock-still for a moment in astonishment and then followed her. As he passed in the way of the cheval-glass he caught sight of himself in full length, his broad, well-filled shirt-front, the face whose expression always puzzled him when he saw it in a mirror, and his glimmering gilt-rimmed eyeglasses. He halted a few paces from her and said:

—What about the song? Why does that make you cry?

She raised her head from her arms and dried her eyes with the back of her hand like a child. A kinder note than he had intended went into his voice.

—Why, Gretta? he asked.

—I am thinking about a person long ago who used to sing that song.

—And who was the person long ago? asked Gabriel, smiling.

—It was a person I used to know in Galway when I was living with my grandmother, she said.

The smile passed away from Gabriel's face. A dull anger began to gather again at the back of his mind and the dull fires of his lust began to glow angrily in his veins.

—Someone you were in love with? he asked ironically.

—It was a young boy I used to know, she answered, named Michael Furey. He used to sing that song, *The Lass of Aughrim*. He was very delicate.

Gabriel was silent. He did not wish her to think that he was interested in this delicate boy.

—I can see him so plainly, she said after a moment. Such eyes as he had: big dark eyes! And such an expression in them—an expression!

—O then, you were in love with him? said Gabriel.

—I used to go out walking with him, she said, when I was in Galway.

A thought flew across Gabriel's mind.

—Perhaps that was why you wanted to go to Galway with that Ivors girl? he said coldly.

She looked at him and asked in surprise:

—What for?

Her eyes made Gabriel feel awkward. He shrugged his shoulders and said:

—How do I know? To see him perhaps.

She looked away from him along the shaft of light towards the window in silence.

—He is dead, she said at length. He died when he was only seventeen. Isn't it a terrible thing to die so young as that?

—What was he? asked Gabriel, still ironically.

—He was in the gasworks, she said.

Gabriel felt humiliated by the failure of his irony and by the evocation of this figure from the dead, a boy in the gasworks. While he had been full of memories of their secret life together, full of tenderness and joy and desire, she had been comparing him in her mind with another. A shameful consciousness of his own person assailed him. He saw himself as a ludicrous figure, acting as a pennyboy for his aunts, a nervous well-meaning sentimentalist, orating to vulgarians and idealizing his own clownish lusts, the pitiable fatuous fellow he had caught a glimpse of in the mirror. Instinctively he turned his back more to the light lest she might see the shame that burned upon his forehead.

He tried to keep up his tone of cold interrogation but his voice when he spoke was humble and indifferent.

—I suppose you were in love with this Michael Furey, Gretta, he said.

—I was great with him at that time, she said.

Her voice was veiled and sad. Gabriel, feeling now how vain it would be to try to lead her whither he had purposed, caressed one of her hands and said, also sadly:

—And what did he die of so young, Gretta? Consumption, was it?

—I think he died for me, she answered.

A vague terror seized Gabriel at this answer as if, at that hour when he had hoped to triumph, some impalpable and vindictive being was coming against him, gathering forces against him in his vague world. But he shook himself free of it with an effort of reason and continued to caress her hand. He did not question her again for he felt that she would tell him of herself. Her hand was warm and moist: it did not respond to his touch but he continued to caress it just as he had caressed her first letter to him that spring morning.

—It was in the winter, she said, about the beginning of the winter when I was going to leave my grandmother's and come up here to the convent. And he was ill at the time in his lodgings in Galway and wouldn't be let out and his people in Oughterard were written to. He was in decline, they said, or something like that. I never knew rightly.

She paused for a moment and sighed.

—Poor fellow, she said. He was very fond of me and he was such a gentle boy. We used to go out together, walking, you know, Gabriel, like the way they do in the country. He was going to study singing only for his health. He had a very good voice, poor Michael Furey.

—Well; and then? asked Gabriel.

—And then when it came to the time for me to leave Galway and come up to the convent he was much worse and I wouldn't be let see him so I wrote a letter saying I was going up to Dublin and would be back in the summer and hoping he would be better then.

She paused for a moment to get her voice under control and then went on:

—Then the night before I left I was in my grandmother's house in Nun's Island, packing up, and I heard gravel thrown up against the window. The window was so wet I couldn't see so I ran downstairs as I was and slipped out the back into the garden and there was the poor fellow at the end of the garden, shivering.

—And did you not tell him to go back? asked Gabriel.

—I implored of him to go home at once and told him he would get his death in the rain. But he said he did not want to live. I can see his eyes as well as well! He was standing at the end of the wall where there was a tree.

—And did he go home? asked Gabriel.

—Yes, he went home. And when I was only a week in the convent he died and he was buried in Oughterard where his people came from. O, the day I heard that, that he was dead!

She stopped, choking with sobs, and, overcome by emotion, flung herself face downward on the bed, sobbing in the quilt. Gabriel held her hand for a moment longer, irresolutely, and then, shy of intruding on her grief, let it fall gently and walked quietly to the window.

She was fast asleep.

Gabriel, leaning on his elbow, looked for a few moments unresentfully on her tangled hair and half-open mouth, listening to her deep-drawn breath. So she had had that romance in her life: a man had died for her sake. It hardly pained him now to think how poor a part he, her husband, had played in her life. He watched her while she slept as though he and she had never lived together as man and wife. His curious eyes rested long upon her face and on her hair: and, as he thought of what she must have been then, in that time of her first girlish beauty, a strange friendly pity for her entered his soul. He did not like to say even to himself that her face was no longer beautiful but he knew that it was no longer the face for which Michael Furey had braved death.

Perhaps she had not told him all the story. His eyes moved to the chair over which she had thrown some of her clothes. A petticoat string dangled to the floor. One boot stood upright, its limp upper fallen down: the fellow of it lay upon its side. He wondered at his riot of emotions of an hour before. From what had it proceeded? From his aunt's supper, from his own foolish speech, from the wine and dancing, the merry-making when saying good-night in the hall, the pleasure of the walk along the river in the snow. Poor Aunt Julia! She, too, would soon be a shade with the shade of Patrick Morkan and his horse. He had caught that haggard look upon her face for a moment when she was singing *Arrayed for the Bridal*. Soon, perhaps, he would be sitting in that same drawing room, dressed in black, his silk hat on his knees. The blinds would be drawn down and Aunt Kate would be sitting beside him, crying and blowing her nose and telling him how Julia had died. He would cast about in his mind for some words that might console her, and would find only lame and useless ones. Yes, yes: that would happen very soon.

The air of the room chilled his shoulders. He stretched himself cautiously along under the sheets and lay down beside his wife. One by one they were all becoming shades. Better pass boldly into that other world, in the full glory of some passion, than fade and wither dismally with age. He thought of how she who lay beside him had locked in her heart for so many years that image of her lover's eyes when he had told her that he did not wish to live.

Generous tears filled Gabriel's eyes. He had never felt like that himself towards any woman but he knew that such a feeling must be love. The tears gathered more thickly in his eyes and in the partial darkness he imagined he saw the form of a young man standing under a dripping tree. Other forms were near. His soul had approached that region where dwell the vast hosts of the dead. He was conscious of, but could not apprehend, their wayward and flickering existence. His own identity was fading out into a grey impalpable world: the solid world itself which these dead had one time reared and lived in was dissolving and dwindling.

A few light taps upon the pane made him turn to the window. It had begun to snow again. He watched sleepily the flakes, silver and dark, falling obliquely against the lamplight. The time had come for him to set out on his journey westward. Yes, the newspapers were right: snow was general all over Ireland. It was falling on every part of the dark central plain, on the treeless hills, falling softly upon the Bog of Allen and, farther westward, softly falling into the dark mutinous Shannon waves. It was falling, too, upon every part of the lonely churchyard on the hill where Michael Furey lay buried. It lay thickly drifted on the crooked crosses and headstones, on the spears of the little gate, on the barren thorns. His soul swooned slowly as he heard the snow falling faintly through the universe and faintly falling, like the descent of their last end, upon all the living and the dead.

1914

Franz Kafka

1883–1924

W.H. Auden's perspective is compelling: "Had one to name the author who comes closest to bearing the same kind of relation to our age as Dante, Shakespeare, and Goethe bore to theirs, Kafka is the first one would think of." This most tender, uncertain of writers and his brutish but introspective age have a paradoxical commonality: through a floating dread and guilt that come to definition only through the random impositions of bureaucracies, through a series of impenetrable tyrannies, through a sense of the fragmentary as the very core of personal, social, and artistic existence. Unlike the other great modernists, Kafka embraces "incompletion" (John Updike's word) as the response to every riddle the world presented him with, from the presence of the unyielding Father and the absence of an immanent God, to the terrifying promise literature presents to the anxious and undeserving. Little of his work was published in the short time he was alive. The novels are unstable, protean structures, and many of the stories exist with alternative fragments; he asked—unpersuasively—his friend and editor, Max Brod, to destroy the manuscripts after his death. Kafka's personal ties were similarly unfinished: he broke three marriage engagements (two to Felice Bauer); and his happy relationship with Dora Dymant, a young Jewish socialist who helped him toward an easier attachment to Jewish culture, was cut short by his death from tuberculosis. Although he became the archetype of existential suffering for later readers, Kafka did, in fact, operate effectively within the demands of ordinary life: as a student he was successful, eventually receiving the degree of Doctor of Law from the German University in Prague, and for over a decade he was employed by an insurance company. But it is the writing that defines; his fitful, tormented, yet exultant art makes Kafka seem, in Updike's reverential view, "the last holy water, and the supreme fabulist of modern man's cosmic predicament."

Before the Law

Before the law stands a doorkeeper. To this doorkeeper there comes a man from the country and prays for admittance to the Law. But the doorkeeper says that he cannot grant admittance at the moment. The man thinks it over and then asks if he will be allowed in later. "It is possible," says the doorkeeper, "but not at the moment." Since the gate stands open, as usual, and the doorkeeper steps to one side, the man stoops to peer through the gateway into the interior. Observing that, the doorkeeper laughs and says: "If you are so drawn to it, just try to go in despite my veto. But take note: I am powerful. And I am only the least of the doorkeepers. From hall to hall there is one doorkeeper after another, each more powerful than the last. The third doorkeeper is already so terrible that even I cannot bear to look at him." These are difficulties the man from the country has not expected; the Law, he thinks, should surely be accessible at all times and to everyone, but as he now takes a closer look at the doorkeeper in his fur coat, with his big sharp nose and long, thin, black Tartar beard, he decides that it is better to wait until he gets permission to enter. The doorkeeper gives him a stool and lets him sit down at one side of the door. There he sits for days and years. He makes many attempts to be admitted, and wearies the doorkeeper by his importunity. The doorkeeper frequently has little interviews with him, asking him questions about his home and many other things, but the questions are put indifferently, as great lords put them, and always finish with the statement that he cannot be let in yet. The man, who has furnished himself with many things for his journey, sacrifices all he has, however valuable, to bribe the doorkeeper. The doorkeeper accepts everything, but always with the remark: "I am only taking it to keep you from thinking you have omitted anything." During these many years the man fixes his attention almost continuously on the doorkeeper. He forgets the other doorkeepers, and this first one seems to him the sole obstacle preventing access to the Law. He curses his bad luck, in his early years boldly and loudly; later, as he grows old, he only grumbles to himself. He becomes childish, and since in his yearlong contemplation of the doorkeeper he has come to know even the fleas in his fur collar, he begs the fleas as well to help him and to change the doorkeeper's mind. At length his eyesight begins to fail, and he does not know whether the world is really darker or whether his eyes are only deceiving him. Yet in his darkness he is now aware of a radiance that streams inextinguishably from the gateway of the Law. Now he has not very long to live. Before he dies, all his experiences in these long years gather themselves in his head to one point, a question he has not yet asked the doorkeeper. He waves him nearer, since he can no longer raise his stiffening body. The doorkeeper has to bend low toward him, for the difference in height between them has altered much to the man's disadvantage. "What do you want to know now?" asks the doorkeeper; "you are insatiable." "Everyone strives to reach the Law," says the man, "so how does it happen that for all these many years no one but myself has ever begged for admittance?" The doorkeeper recognizes that the man has reached his end, and, to let his failing senses catch the words, roars in his ear: "No one else could ever be admitted here, since this gate was made only for you. I am now going to shut it."

1915
translated by Willa and Edwin Muir

D.H. Lawrence

1885–1930

He still seems a force of nature. During his brief twenty years of artistic passion, in a barrage of novels, stories, poems, paintings, and letters, Lawrence created astonishing images: of enervating industrialism, of bloodless intellectuality, of the deformed bonds between men and women, but also of lovely marriage places and of the uncanny alliance between people and vegetation and animals. Part of our sense of his overwhelming energy and continuing presence comes, too, from his turbulent, fascinating biography—his tidal wave of a marriage, his explosive friendships, his vexed childhood. Born in Nottinghamshire to a coal miner father and a genteel mother, a former schoolteacher with high ambitions for her son, David Herbert Lawrence absorbed intensity early, from his parents' disharmony as well as from his own ill health. He taught for four years, also publishing two novels during this time, *The White Peacock* in 1911 and *The Trespasser* in 1912. Also in 1912 he ran off with the wife of one of his professors at Nottingham University College. One of the most tumultuous marriages in literary history—it was formalized in 1914 after Frieda's divorce—was underway. Lawrence's other marriage, between the psyche and language, took shape at the same time as *Sons and Lovers* (1913). Although still a sequential narrative, in it Lawrence is moving toward a new perception of character, one fundamental to an art he always considered personally and socially transformative, even messianic. "You mustn't look in my novel," he later wrote about *Women in Love* (1920), "for the old stable ego of the character. There is another ego, according to whose action the individual is unrecognizable." Lawrence announced that his "theme is carbon"—essential being—and created an incantatory prose and a narrative rhythm to articulate it—what Mark Shorer calls "a drama of primal compulsions, a psychic symbolization." Lawrence's ability to register the "carbon" of a culture as well as an individual is astonishingly evident in his *Etruscan Places* (1932), unique as travel writing in its beauty and vividness. One might wonder whether the short story would be suitable to Lawrence's style, but, among his dozen or so collections are some of the most brilliant stories in the language, such as "The Prussian Officer," "The Horse Dealer's Daughter," and "The Woman Who Rode Away." His genius for both physical and emotional detail, for sudden shifts in awareness, is as powerful in a brief compass as it is on a broader canvas. The Lawrences themselves also had very little time, living in England under the shadow of the war (a situation made more difficult by Frieda's German ancestry), then travelling (Italy, Australia, Mexico, New Mexico) in search of sun and like-minded souls. Tuberculosis brought the frenzy, the hope, and the image-making to an end in Vence, near Nice. Among his other works are *Studies in Classic American Literature* (1923), *St Mawr* (1925), *Lady Chatterley's Lover* (1928), and *The Man Who Died* (1929).

The Prussian Officer

I

They had marched more than thirty kilometres since dawn, along the white, hot road where occasional thickets of trees threw a moment of shade, then out into the glare again. On either hand, the valley, wide and shallow, glittered with heat; dark green patches of rye, pale young corn, fallow and meadow and black pine woods spread in a dull, hot diagram under a glistening sky. But right in front the mountains ranged across, pale blue and very still, snow gleaming gently out of the deep atmosphere. And towards the mountains, on and on, the regiment marched between the rye fields and the meadows, between the scraggy fruit trees set regularly on either side the high road. The burnished, dark green rye threw off a suffocating heat, the mountains drew gradually nearer and more distinct. While the feet of the soldiers grew hotter, sweat ran through their hair under their helmets, and their knapsacks could burn no more in contact with their shoulders, but seemed instead to give off a cold, prickly sensation.

He walked on and on in silence, staring at the mountains ahead, that rose sheer out of the land, and stood fold behind fold, half earth, half heaven, the heaven, the barrier with slits of soft snow, in the pale, bluish peaks.

He could now walk almost without pain. At the start, he had determined not to limp. It had made him sick to take the first steps, and during the first mile or so, he had compressed his breath, and the cold drops of sweat had stood on his forehead. But he had walked it off. What were they after all but bruises! He had looked at them, as he was getting up: deep bruises on the backs of his thighs. And since he had made his first step in the morning, he had been conscious of them, till now he had a tight, hot place in his chest, with suppressing the pain, and holding himself in. There seemed no air when he breathed. But he walked almost lightly.

The Captain's hand had trembled at taking his coffee at dawn: his orderly saw it again. And he saw the fine figure of the Captain wheeling on horseback at the farmhouse ahead, a handsome figure in pale blue uniform with facings of scarlet, and the metal gleaming on the black helmet and the sword-scabbard, and dark streaks of sweat coming on the silky bay horse. The orderly felt he was connected with that figure moving so suddenly on horseback: he followed it like a shadow, mute and inevitable and damned by it. And the officer was always aware of the tramp of the company behind, the march of his orderly among the men.

The Captain was a tall man of about forty, grey at the temples. He had a handsome, finely knit figure, and was one of the best horsemen in the West. His orderly, having to rub him down, admired the amazing riding-muscles of his loins.

For the rest, the orderly scarcely noticed the officer any more than he noticed himself. It was rarely he saw his master's face: he did not look at it. The Captain had reddish-brown, stiff hair, that he wore short upon his skull. His moustache was also cut short and bristly over a full, brutal mouth. His face was rather rugged, the cheeks thin. Perhaps the man was the more handsome for the deep lines in his face, the irritable tension of his brow, which gave him the look of a man who fights with life. His fair eyebrows stood bushy over light blue eyes that were always flashing with cold fire.

He was a Prussian aristocrat, haughty and overbearing. But his mother had been a Polish Countess. Having made too many gambling debts when he was young, he had ruined his prospects in the Army, and remained an infantry captain. He had never married: his position did not allow it, and no woman had ever moved him to it. His time he spent riding—occasionally he rode one of his own horses at the races—and at the officers' club. Now and then he took himself a mistress. But after such an event, he returned to duty with his brow still more tense, his eyes still more hostile and irritable. With the men, however, he was merely impersonal, though a devil when roused; so that, on the whole, they feared him, but had no great aversion from him. They accepted him as the inevitable.

To his orderly he was at first cold and just and indifferent: he did not fuss over trifles. So that his servant knew practically nothing about him, except just what orders he would give, and how he wanted them obeyed. That was quite simple. Then the change gradually came.

The orderly was a youth of about twenty-two, of medium height, and well built. He had strong, heavy limbs, was swarthy, with a soft, black, young moustache. There was something altogether warm and young about him. He had firmly marked eyebrows over dark, expressionless eyes, that seemed never to have thought, only to have received life direct through his senses, and acted straight from instinct.

Gradually the officer had become aware of his servant's young, vigorous, unconscious presence about him. He could not get away from the sense of the youth's person, while he was in attendance. It was like a warm flame upon the older man's tense, rigid body, that had become almost unliving, fixed. There was something so free and self-contained about him, and something in the young fellow's movement, that made the officer aware of him. And this irritated the Prussian. He did not choose to be touched into life by his servant. He might easily have changed his man, but he did not. He now very rarely looked direct at his orderly, but kept his face averted, as if to avoid seeing him. And yet as the young soldier moved unthinking about the apartment, the elder watched him, and would notice the movement of his strong young shoulders under the blue cloth, the bend of his neck. And it irritated him. To see the soldier's young, brown, shapely peasant's hand grasp the loaf or the wine bottle sent a flash of hate or of anger through the elder man's blood. It was not that the youth was clumsy: it was rather the blind, instinctive sureness of movement of an unhampered young animal that irritated the officer to such a degree.

Once, when a bottle of wine had gone over, and the red gushed out on to the tablecloth, the officer had started with an oath, and his eyes, bluey like fire, had held those of the confused youth for a moment. It was a shock for the young soldier. He felt something sink deeper, deeper into his soul, where nothing had ever gone before. It left him rather blank and wondering. Some of his natural completeness in himself was gone, a little uneasiness took its place. And from that time an undiscovered feeling had held between the two men.

Henceforward the orderly was afraid of really meeting his master. His sub-consciousness remembered those steely blue eyes and the harsh brows, and did not intend to meet them again. So he always stared past his master, and avoided him. Also, in a little anxiety, he waited for the three months to have gone, when his time would be up. He began to feel a constraint in the Captain's presence, and the soldier even more than the officer wanted to be left alone, in his neutrality as servant.

He had served the Captain for more than a year, and knew his duty. This he performed easily, as if it were natural to him. The officer and his commands he took for granted, as he took the sun and the rain, and he served as a matter of course. It did not implicate him personally.

But now if he were going to be forced into a personal interchange with his master he would be like a wild thing caught, he felt he must get away.

But the influence of the young soldier's being had penetrated through the officer's stiffened discipline, and perturbed the man in him. He, however, was a gentleman, with long, fine hands and cultivated movements, and was not going to allow such a thing as the stirring of his innate self. He was a man of passionate temper, who had always kept himself suppressed. Occasionally there had been a duel, an outburst before the soldiers. He knew himself to be always on the point of breaking out. But he kept himself hard to the idea of the Service. Whereas the young solider seemed to live out his warm, full nature, to give it off in his very movements, which had a certain zest, such as wild animals have in free movement. And this irritated the officer more and more.

In spite of himself, the Captain could not regain his neutrality of feeling towards his orderly. Nor could he leave the man alone. In spite of himself, he watched him, gave him sharp orders, tried to take up as much of his time as possible. Sometimes he flew into a rage with the younger soldier, and bullied him. Then the orderly shut himself off, as it were out of earshot, and waited, with sullen, flushed face, for the end of the noise. The words never pierced to his intelligence, he made himself, protectively, impervious to the feelings of his master.

He had a scar on his left thumb, a deep seam going across the knuckle. The officer had long suffered from it, and wanted to do something to it. Still it was there, ugly and brutal on the young, brown hand. At last the Captain's reserve gave way. One day, as the orderly was smoothing out the tablecloth, the officer pinned down his thumb with a pencil, asking:

"How did you come by that?"

The young man winced and drew back at attention.

"A wood axe, Herr Hauptmann," he answered.

The officer waited for further explanation. None came. The orderly went about his duties. The elder man was sullenly angry. His servant avoided him. And the next day he had to use all his willpower to avoid seeing the scarred thumb. He wanted to get hold of it and—A hot flame ran in his blood.

He knew his servant would soon be free, and would be glad. As yet, the soldier had held himself off from the elder man. The Captain grew madly irritable. He could not rest when the soldier was away, and when he was present, he glared at him with tormented eyes. He hated those fine, black brows over the unmeaning, dark eyes, he was infuriated by the free movement of the handsome limbs, which no military discipline could make stiff. And he became harsh and cruelly bullying, using contempt and satire. The young soldier only grew more mute and expressionless.

"What cattle were you bred by, that you can't keep straight eyes? Look me in the eyes when I speak to you."

And the soldier turned his dark eyes to the other's face, but there was no sight in them: he stared with the slightest possible cast, holding back his sight, perceiving the blue of his master's eyes, but receiving no look from them. And the elder man went pale, and his reddish eyebrows twitched. He gave his order, barrenly.

Once he flung a heavy military glove into the young soldier's face. Then he had the satisfaction of seeing the black eyes flare up into his own, like a blaze when straw is thrown on a fire. And he had laughed with a little tremor and a sneer.

But there were only two months more. The youth instinctively tried to keep himself intact: he tried to serve the officer as if the latter were an abstract authority and not a man. All his instinct was to avoid personal contact, even definite hate. But in spite of himself the hate grew, responsive to the officer's passion. However, he put it in the background. When he had left the Army he could dare acknowledge it. By nature he was active, and had many friends. He thought what amazing good fellows they were. But, without knowing it, he was alone. Now this solitariness was intensified. It would carry him through his term. But the officer seemed to be going irritably insane, and the youth was deeply frightened.

The soldier had a sweetheart, a girl from the mountains, independent and primitive. The two walked together, rather silently. He went with her, not to talk, but to have his arm around her, and for the physical contact. This eased him, made it easier for him to ignore the Captain; for he could rest with her held fast against his chest. And she, in some unspoken fashion, was there for him. They loved each other.

The Captain perceived it, and was mad with irritation. He kept the young man engaged all the evenings long, and took pleasure in the dark look that came on his face. Occasionally, the eyes of the two men met, those of the younger sullen and dark, doggedly unalterable, those of the elder sneering with restless contempt.

The officer tried hard not to admit the passion that had got hold of him. He would not know that his feeling for his orderly was anything but that of a man incensed by his stupid, perverse servant. So, keeping quite justified and conventional in his consciousness, he let the other thing run on. His nerves, however, were suffering. At last he slung the end of a belt in servant's face. When he saw the youth start back, the pain-tears in his eyes and the blood on his mouth, he had felt at once a thrill of deep pleasure and shame.

But this, he acknowledged to himself, was a thing he had never done before. The fellow was too exasperating. His own nerves must be going to pieces. He went away for some days with a woman.

It was a mockery of pleasure. He simply did not want the woman. But he stayed on for his time. At the end of it, he came back in an agony of irritation, torment, and misery. He rode all the evening, then came straight in to supper. His orderly was out. The officer sat with his long, fine hands lying on the table, perfectly still, and all his blood seemed to be corroding.

At last his servant entered. He watched the strong, easy young figure, the fine eyebrows, the thick black hair. In a week's time the youth had got back his old well-being. The hands of the officer twitched and seemed to be full of mad flame. The young man stood at attention, unmoving, shut off.

The meal went in silence. But the orderly seemed eager. He made a clatter with the dishes.

"Are you in a hurry?" asked the officer, watching the intent, warm face of his servant. The other did not reply.

"Will you answer my question?" said the Captain.

"Yes, sir," replied the orderly, standing with his pile of deep Army plates. The Captain waited, looked at him, then asked again:

"Are you in a hurry?"

"Yes, sir," came the answer, that sent a flash through the listener.

"For what?"

"I was going out, sir."

"I want you this evening."

There was a moment's hesitation. The officer had a curious stiffness of countenance.

"Yes, sir," replied the servant, in his throat.

"I want you tomorrow evening also—in fact, you may consider your evenings occupied, unless I give you leave."

The mouth with the young moustache set close.

"Yes, sir," answered the orderly, loosening his lips for a moment.

He again turned to the door.

"And why have you a piece of pencil in your ear?"

The orderly hesitated, then continued on his way without answering. He set the plates in a pile outside the door, took the stump of pencil from his ear, and put it in his pocket. He had been copying a verse for his sweetheart's birthday card. He returned to finish clearing the table. The officer's eyes were dancing, he had a little, eager smile.

"Why have you a piece of pencil in your ear?" he asked.

The orderly took his hands full of dishes. His master was standing near the great green stove, a little smile on his face, his chin thrust forward. When the young soldier saw him his heart suddenly ran hot. He felt blind. Instead of answering, he turned dazedly to the door. As he was crouching to set down the dishes, he was pitched forward by a kick from behind. The pots went in a stream down the stairs, he clung to the pillar of the banisters. And as he was rising he was kicked heavily again, and again, so that he clung sickly to the post for some moments. His master had gone swiftly into the room and closed the door. The maid-servant downstairs looked up the staircase and made a mocking face at the crockery disaster.

The officer's heart was plunging. He poured himself a glass of wine, part of which he spilled on the floor, and gulped the remainder, leaning against the cool, green stove. He heard his man collecting the dishes from the stairs. Pale, as if intoxicated, he waited. The servant entered again. The Captain's heart gave a pang, as of pleasure, seeing the young fellow bewildered and uncertain on his feet, with pain.

"Schöner!" he said.

The soldier was a little slower in coming to attention.

"Yes, sir!"

The youth stood before him, with pathetic young moustache, and fine eyebrows very distinct on his forehead of dark marble.

"I asked you a question."

"Yes, sir."

The officer's tone bit like acid.

"Why had you a pencil in your ear?"

Again the servant's heart ran hot, and he could not breathe. With dark, strained eyes, he looked at the officer, as if fascinated. And he stood there sturdily planted, unconscious. The withering smile came into the Captain's eyes, and he lifted his foot.

"I—I forgot it—sir," panted the soldier, his dark eyes fixed on the other man's dancing blue ones.

"What was it doing there?"

He saw the young man's breast heaving as he made an effort for words.

"I had been writing."

"Writing what?"

Again the soldier looked him up and down. The officer could hear him panting. The smile came into the blue eyes. The soldier worked his dry throat, but could not speak. Suddenly the smile lit like a flame on the officer's face, and a kick came heavily against the orderly's thigh. The youth moved a pace sideways. His face went dead, with two black, staring eyes.

"Well?" said the officer.

The orderly's mouth had gone dry, and his tongue rubbed in it as on dry brown-paper. He worked his throat. The officer raised his foot. The servant went stiff.

"Some poetry, sir," came the crackling, unrecognizable sound of his voice.

"Poetry, what poetry?" asked the Captain, with a sickly smile.

Again there was the working in the throat. The Captain's heart had suddenly gone down heavily, and he stood sick and tired.

"For my girl, sir," he heard the dry, inhuman sound.

"Oh!" he said, turning away. "Clear the table."

"Click!" went the soldier's throat; then again, "click!" and then the half-articulate:

"Yes, sir."

The young soldier was gone, looking old, and walking heavily.

The officer, left alone, held himself rigid, to prevent himself from thinking. His instinct warned him that he must not think. Deep inside him was the intense gratification of his passion, still working powerfully. Then there was a counter-action, a horrible breaking down of something inside him, a whole agony of reaction. He stood there for an hour motionless, a chaos of sensations, but rigid with a will to keep blank his consciousness, to prevent his mind grasping. And he held himself so until the worst of the stress had passed, when he began to drink, drank himself to an intoxication, till he slept obliterated. When he woke in the morning he was shaken to the base of his nature. But he had fought off the realization of what he had done. He had prevented his mind from taking it in, had suppressed it along with his instincts, and the conscious man had nothing to do with it. He felt only as after a bout of intoxication, weak, but the affair itself all dim and not to be recovered. Of the drunkenness of his passion he successfully refused remembrance. And when his orderly appeared with coffee, the officer assumed the same self he had had the morning before. He refused the event of the past night—denied it had ever been—and was successful in his denial. He had not done any such thing—not he himself. Whatever there might be lay at the door of a stupid, insubordinate servant.

The orderly had gone about in a stupor all the evening. He drank some beer because he was parched, but not much, the alcohol made his feeling come back, and he could not bear it. He was dulled, as if nine-tenths of the ordinary man in him were inert. He crawled about disfigured. Still, when he thought of the kicks, he went sick, and when he thought of the threat of more kicking, in the room afterwards, his heart went hot and faint, and he panted, remembering the one that had come. He had been forced to say, "For my girl." He was much too done even to want to cry. His mouth hung slightly open, like an idiot's. He felt vacant, and wasted. So, he wandered at his work, painfully, and very slowly and clumsily, fumbling blindly with the brushes, and finding it difficult, when he sat down, to summon the energy to move again. His limbs, his jaw, were slack and nerveless. But he was very tired. He got to bed at last, and slept inert, relaxed, in a sleep that was rather stupor than slumber, a dead night of stupefaction shot through with gleams of anguish.

In the morning were the manoeuvres. But he woke even before the bugle sounded. The painful ache in his chest, the dryness of his throat, the awful steady feeling of misery made his eyes come awake and dreary at once. He knew, without thinking, what had happened. And he knew that the day had come again, when he must go on with his round. The last bit of darkness was being pushed out of the room. He would have to move his inert body and go on. He was so young, and had known so little trouble, that he was bewildered. He only wished it would stay night, so that he could lie still, covered up by the darkness. And yet nothing would prevent the day from coming, nothing would save him from having to get up and saddle the Captain's horse, and make the Captain's coffee. It was there, inevitable. And then, he thought, it was impossible. Yet they would not leave him free. He must go and take the coffee to the Captain. He was too stunned to understand it. He only knew it was inevitable—inevitable, however long he lay inert.

At last, after heaving at himself, for he seemed to be a mass of inertia, he got up. But he had to force every one of his movements from behind, with his will. He felt lost, and dazed, and helpless. Then he clutched hold of the bed, the pain was so keen. And looking at his thighs, he saw the darker bruises on his swarthy flesh and he knew that, if he pressed one of his fingers on one of the bruises, he should faint. But he did not want to faint—he did not want anybody to know. No one should ever know. It was between him and the Captain. There were only the two people in the world now—himself and the Captain.

Slowly, economically, he got dressed and forced himself to walk. Everything was obscure, except just what he had his hands on. But he managed to get through his work. The very pain revived his dull senses. The worst remained yet. He took the tray and went up to the Captain's room. The officer, pale and heavy, sat at the table. The orderly, as he saluted, felt himself put out of existence. He stood still for a moment submitting to his own nullification—then he gathered himself, seemed to regain himself, and then the Captain began to grow vague, unreal, and the younger soldier's heart beat up. He clung to this situation—that the Captain did not exist—so that he himself might live. But when he saw his officer's hand tremble as he took the coffee, he felt everything falling shattered. And he went away, feeling as if he himself were coming to pieces, disintegrated. And when the Captain was there on horseback, giving orders, while he himself stood, with rifle and knapsack, sick with pain, he felt as if he must shut his eyes—as if he must shut his eyes on everything. It was only the long agony of marching with a parched throat that filled him with one single, sleep-heavy intention: to save himself.

II

He was getting used even to his parched throat. That the snowy peaks were radiant among the sky, that the whity-green glacier-river twisted through its pale shoals, in the valley below, seemed almost supernatural. But he was going mad with fever and thirst. He plodded on uncomplaining. He did not want to speak, not to anybody. There were two gulls, like flakes of water and snow, over the river. The scent of green rye soaked in sunshine came like a sickness. And the march continued, monotonously, almost like a bad sleep.

At the next farmhouse, which stood low and broad near the high road, tubs of water had been put out. The soldiers clustered round to drink. They took off their helmets, and the steam mounted from their wet hair. The Captain sat on horseback, watching. He needed to see his orderly. His helmet threw a dark shadow over his light, fierce eyes, but his moustache and mouth and chin were distinct in the sunshine. The orderly must move under the presence of the figure of the horseman. It was not that he was afraid, or cowed. It was as if he was disembowelled, made empty, like an empty shell. He felt himself as nothing, a shadow creeping under the sunshine. And, thirsty as he was, he could scarcely drink, feeling the Captain near him. He would not take off his helmet to wipe his wet hair. He wanted to stay in shadow, not to be forced into consciousness. Starting, he saw the light heel of the officer prick the belly of the horse; the Captain cantered away, and he himself could relapse into vacancy.

Nothing, however, could give him back his living place in the hot, bright morning. He felt like a gap among it all. Whereas the Captain was prouder, overriding. A hot flash went through the young servant's body. The Captain was firmer and prouder with life, he himself was empty as a shadow. Again the flash went through him, dazing him out. But his heart ran a little firmer.

The company turned up the hill, to make a loop for the return. Below, from among the trees, the farm-bell clanged. He saw the labourers, mowing barefoot at the thick grass, leave off their work and go downhill, their scythes hanging over their shoulders, like long, bright claws curving down behind them. They seemed like dream-people, as if they had no relation to himself. He felt as in a blackish dream: as if all the other things were there and had form, but he himself was only consciousness, a gap that could think and perceive.

The soldiers were tramping silently up the glaring hillside. Gradually his head began to revolve, slowly, rhythmically. Sometimes it was dark before his eyes, as if he saw this world through a smoked glass, frail shadows and unreal. It gave him a pain in his head to walk.

The air was too scented, it gave no breath. All the lush green-stuff seemed to be issuing its sap, till the air was deathly, sickly with the smell of greenness. There was the perfume of clover, like pure honey and bees. Then there grew a faint acrid tang—they were near the beeches; and then a queer clattering noise, and a suffocating, hideous smell; they were passing a flock of sheep, a shepherd in a black smock, holding his crook. Why should the sheep huddle together under this fierce sun? He felt that the shepherd would not see him, though he could see the shepherd.

At last there was the halt. They stacked rifles in a conical stack, put down their kit in a scattered circle around it, and dispersed a little, sitting on a small knoll high on the hillside. The chatter began. The soldiers were steaming with heat, but were lively. He sat still, seeing the blue mountains rising upon the land, twenty kilometres away. There was a blue fold in the ranges, then out of that, at the foot, the broad, pale bed of the river, stretches of whity-green water between pinkish-grey shoals among the dark pine woods. There it was, spread out a long way off. And it seemed to come downhill, the river. There was a raft being steered, a mile away. It was a strange country. Nearer, a red-roofed, broad farm with white base and square dots of windows crouched beside the wall of beech foliage on the wood's edge. There were long strips of rye and clover and pale green corn. And just at his feet, below the knoll, was a darkish bog, where globe flowers stood breathless still on their slim stalks. And some of the pale gold bubbles were burst, and a broken fragment hung in the air. He thought he was going to sleep.

Suddenly something moved into this coloured mirage before his eyes. The Captain, a small, light-blue and scarlet figure, was trotting evenly between the strips of corn, along the level brow of the hill. And the man making flag-signals was coming on. Proud and sure moved the horseman's figure, the quick, bright thing, in which was concentrated all the light of this morning, which for the rest lay a fragile, shining shadow. Submissive, apathetic, the young soldier sat and stared. But as the horse slowed to a walk, coming up the last steep path, the great flash flared over the body and soul of the orderly. He sat waiting. The back of his head felt as if it were weighted with a heavy piece of fire. He did not want to eat. His hands trembled slightly as he moved them. Meanwhile the officer on horseback was approaching slowly and proudly. The tension grew in the orderly's soul. Then again, seeing the Captain ease himself on the saddle, the flash blazed through him.

The Captain looked at the patch of light blue and scarlet, and dark heads, scattered closely on the hillside. It pleased him. The command pleased him. And he was feeling proud. His orderly was among them in common subjection. The officer rose a little on his stirrups to look. The young soldier sat with averted, dumb face. The Captain relaxed on his seat. His slim-legged, beautiful horse, brown as a beech nut, walked proudly uphill. The Captain passed into the zone of the company's atmosphere: a hot smell of men, of sweat, of leather. He knew it very well. After a word with the lieutenant, he went a few paces higher, and sat there, a dominant figure, his sweat-marked horse swishing its tail, while he looked down on his men, on his orderly, a nonentity among the crowd.

The young soldier's heart was like fire in his chest, and he breathed with difficulty. The officer, looking downhill, saw three of the young soldiers, two pails of water between them, staggering across a sunny green field. A table had been set up under a tree, and there the slim lieutenant stood, importantly busy. Then the Captain summoned himself to an act of courage. He called his orderly.

The flame leapt into the young soldier's throat as he heard the command, and he rose blindly, stifled. He saluted, standing below the officer. He did not look up. But there was the flicker in the Captain's voice.

"Go to the inn and fetch me . . ." the officer gave his commands. "Quick!" he added.

At the last word, the heart of the servant leapt with a flash, and he felt the strength come over his body. But he turned in mechanical obedience, and set off at a heavy run downhill, looking almost like a bear, his trousers bagging over his military boots. And the others watched this blind, plunging run all the way.

But it was only the outside of the orderly's body that was obeying so humbly and mechanically. Inside had gradually accumulated a core into which all the energy of that young life was compact and concentrated. He executed his commission, and plodded quickly back uphill. There was a pain in his head, as he walked, that made him twist his features unknowingly. But hard there in the centre of his chest was himself, himself, firm, and not to be plucked to pieces.

The captain had gone up into the wood. The orderly plodded through the hot, powerfully smelling zone of the company's atmosphere. He had a curious mass of energy inside him now. The Captain was less real than himself. He approached the green entrance to the wood. There, in the half-shade, he saw the horse standing, the sunshine and the flickering shadow of leaves dancing over his brown body. There was a clearing where timber had lately been felled. Here, in the gold-green shade beside the brilliant cup of sunshine, stood two figures, blue and pink, the bits of pink showing out plainly. The Captain was talking to his lieutenant.

The orderly stood on the edge of the bright clearing, where great trunks of trees, stripped and glistening, lay stretched like naked, brown-skinned bodies. Chips of wood littered the trampled floor, like splashed light, and the bases of the felled trees stood here and there, with their raw, level tops. Beyond was the brilliant, sunlit green of a beech.

"Then I will ride forward," the orderly heard his Captain say. The lieutenant saluted and strode away. He himself went forward. A hot flash passed through his belly, as he tramped towards his officer.

The Captain watched the rather heavy figure of the young soldier stumble forward, and his veins, too, ran hot. This was to be man to man between them. He yielded before the solid, stumbling figure with bent head. The orderly stooped and put the food on a level-sawn tree-base. The Captain watched the glistening, sun-inflamed, naked hands. He wanted to speak to the young soldier, but could not. The servant propped a bottle against his thigh, pressed open the cork, and poured out the beer into the mug. He kept his head bent. The Captain accepted the mug.

"Hot!" he said, as if amiably.

The flame sprang out of the orderly's heart, nearly suffocating him.

"Yes, sir." he replied between shut teeth.

And he heard the sound of the Captain's drinking, and he clenched his fists, such a strong torment came into his wrists. Then came the faint clang of the closing of the pot-lid. He looked up. The Captain was watching him. He glanced swiftly away. Then he saw the officer stoop and take a piece of bread from the tree-base. Again the flash of flame went through the young soldier, seeing the stiff body stoop beneath him, and his hands jerked. He looked away. He could feel the officer was nervous. The bread fell as it was being broken. The officer ate the other piece. The two men stood tense and still, the master laboriously chewing his bread, the servant staring with averted face, his fist clenched.

Then the young soldier started. The officer had pressed open the lid of the mug again. The orderly watched the lid of the mug, and the white hand that clenched the handle, as if he were fascinated. It was raised. The youth followed it with his eyes. And then he saw the thin, strong throat of the elder man moving up and down as he drank, the strong jaw working. And the instinct which had been jerking at the young man's wrists suddenly jerked free. He jumped, feeling as if it were rent in two by a strong flame.

The spur of the officer caught in a tree-root, he went down backwards with a crash, the middle of his back thudding sickeningly against a sharp-edged tree-base, the pot flying away. And in a second the orderly, with serious, earnest young face, and under-lip between his teeth, had got his knee in the officer's chest and was pressing the chin backward over the farther edge of the tree-stump, pressing, with all his heart behind in a passion of relief, the tension of his wrists exquisite with relief. And with the base of his palms he shoved at the chin, with all his might. And it was pleasant, too, to have that chin, that hard jaw already slightly rough with beard, in his hands. He did not relax one hair's breadth, but, all the force of all his blood exulting in his thrust, he shoved back the head of the other man, till there was a little "cluck" and a crunching sensation. Then he felt as if his head went to vapour. Heavy convulsions shook the body of the officer, frightening and horrifying the young soldier. Yet it pleased him, too, to repress them. It pleased him to keep his hands pressing back the chin, to feel the chest of the other man yield in expiration to the weight of his strong, young knees, to feel the hard twitchings of the prostrate body jerking his own whole frame, which was pressed down on it.

But it went still. He could look into the nostrils of the other man, the eyes he could scarcely see. How curiously the mouth was pushed out, exaggerating the full lips, and the moustache bristling up from them. Then, with a start, he noticed the nostrils gradually filled with blood. The red brimmed, hesitated, ran over, and went in a thin trickle down the face to the eyes.

It shocked and distressed him. Slowly, he got up. The body twitched and sprawled there, inert. He stood and looked at it in silence. It was a pity *it* was broken. It represented more than the thing which had kicked and bullied him. He was afraid to look at the eyes. They were hideous now, only the whites showing, and the blood running to them. The face of the orderly was drawn with horror at the sight. Well, it was so. In his heart he was satisfied. He had hated the face of the Captain. It was extinguished now. There was a heavy relief in the orderly's soul. That was as it should be. But he could not bear to see the long, military body lying broken over the tree-base, the line fingers crisped. He wanted to hide it away.

Quickly, busily, he gathered it up and pushed it under the felled tree-trunks, which rested their beautiful, smooth length either end on logs. The face was horrible with blood. He covered it with the helmet. Then he pushed the limbs straight and decent, and brushed the dead leaves off the fine cloth of the uniform. So, it lay quite still in the shadow under there. A little strip of sunshine ran along the breast, from a chink between the logs. The orderly sat by it for a few moments. Here his own life also ended.

Then, through his daze, he heard the lieutenant, in a loud voice, explaining to the men outside the wood, that they were to suppose the bridge on the river below was held by the enemy. Now they were to march to the attack in such and such a manner. The lieutenant had no gift of expression. The orderly, listening from habit, got muddled. And when the lieutenant began it all again he ceased to hear.

He knew he must go. He stood up. It surprised him that the leaves were glittering in the sun, and the chips of wood reflecting white from the ground. For him a change had come over the world. But for the rest it had not—all seemed the same. Only he had left it. And he could not go back. It was his duty to return with the beer-pot and the bottle. He could not. He had left all that. The lieutenant was still hoarsely explaining. He must go, or they would overtake him. And he could not bear contact with anyone now.

He drew his fingers over his eyes, trying to find out where he was. Then he turned away. He saw the horse standing in the path. He went up to it and mounted. It hurt him to sit in the saddle. The pain of keeping his seat occupied him as they cantered through the wood. He would not have minded anything, but he could not get away from the sense of being divided from the others. The path led out of the trees. On the edge of the wood he pulled up and stood watching. There in the spacious sunshine of the valley soldiers were moving in a little swarm. Every now and then, a man harrowing on a strip of fallow shouted to his oxen, at the turn. The village and the white-towered church was small in the sunshine. And he no longer belonged to it—he sat there, beyond, like a man outside in the dark. He had gone out from everyday life into the unknown, and he could not, he even did not want to go back.

Turning from the sun-blazing valley, he rode deep into the wood. Tree-trunks, like people standing grey and still, took no notice as he went. A doe, herself a moving bit of sunshine and shadow, went running through the flecked shade. There were bright green rents in the foliage. Then it was all pine wood, dark and cool. And he was sick with pain, he had an intolerable great pulse in his head, and he was sick. He had never been ill in his life. He felt lost, quite dazed with all this.

Trying to get down from the horse, he fell, astonished at the pain and his lack of balance. The horse shifted uneasily. He jerked its bridle and sent it cantering jerkily away. It was his last connection with the rest of things.

But he only wanted to lie down and not be disturbed. Stumbling through the trees, he came on a quiet place where beeches and pine trees grew on a slope. Immediately he had lain down and closed his eyes, his consciousness went racing on without him. A big pulse of sickness beat in him as if it throbbed through the whole earth. He was burning with dry heat. But he was too busy, too tearingly active in the incoherent race of delirium to observe.

III

He came to with a start. His mouth was dry and hard, his heart beat heavily, but he had not the energy to get up. His heart beat heavily. Where was he?—the barracks—at home? There was something knocking. And, making an effort, he looked round—trees, and litter of greenery, and reddish, bright, still pieces of sunshine on the floor. He did not believe he was himself, he did not believe what he saw. Something was knocking. He made a struggle towards consciousness, but relapsed. Then he struggled again. And gradually his surroundings fell into relationship with himself. He knew, and a great pang of fear went through his heart. Somebody was knocking. He could see the heavy, black rags of a fir tree overhead. Then everything went black. Yet he did not believe he had closed his eyes. He had not. Out of the blackness sight slowly emerged again. And someone was knocking. Quickly, he saw the blood-disfigured face of his Captain, which he hated. And he held himself still with horror. Yet, deep inside him, he knew that it was so, the Captain should be dead. But the physical delirium got hold of him. Someone was knocking. He lay perfectly still, as if dead, with fear. And he went unconscious.

When he opened his eyes again, he started, seeing something creeping swiftly up a tree-trunk. It was a little bird. And the bird was whistling overhead. Tap-tap-tap—it was the small, quick bird rapping the tree-trunk with its beak, as if its head were a little round hammer. He watched it curiously. It shifted sharply, in its creeping fashion. Then, like a mouse, it slid down the bare trunk. Its swift creeping sent a flash of revulsion through him. He raised his head. It felt a great weight. Then, the little bird ran out of the shadow across a still patch of sunshine, its little head bobbing swiftly, its white legs twinkling brightly for a moment. How neat it was in its build, so compact, with pieces of white on its wings. There were several of them. They were so pretty—but they crept like swift, erratic mice, running here and there among the beech-mast.

He lay down again exhausted, and his consciousness lapsed. He had a horror of the little creeping birds. All his blood seemed to be darting and creeping in his head. And yet he could not move.

He came to with a further ache of exhaustion. There was the pain in his head, and the horrible sickness, and his inability to move. He had never been ill in his life. He did not know where he was or what he was. Probably he had got sunstroke.

Or what else?—he had silenced the Captain for ever—some time ago—oh, a long time ago. There had been blood on his face, and his eyes had turned upwards. It was all right, somehow. It was peace. But now he had got beyond himself. He had never been here before. Was it life, or not life? He was by himself. They were in a big, bright place, those others, and he was outside. The town, all the country, a big bright place of light: and he was outside, here, in the darkened open beyond, where each thing existed alone. But they would all have to come out there sometime, those others. Little, and left behind him, they all were. There had been father and mother and sweetheart. What did they all matter? This was the open land.

He sat up. Something scuffled. It was a little, brown squirrel running in lovely, undulating bounds over the floor, its red tail completing the undulation of its body—and then, as it sat up, furling and unfurling. He watched it, pleased. It ran on again, friskily, enjoying itself. It flew wildly at another squirrel, and they were chasing each other, and making little scolding, chattering noises. The soldier wanted to speak to them. But only a hoarse sound came out of his throat. The squirrels burst away—they flew up the trees. And then he saw the one peeping round at him, halfway up a tree-trunk. A start of fear went through him, though, in so far as he was conscious, he was amused. It still stayed, its little, keen face staring at him halfway up the tree-trunk, its little ears pricked up, its clawey little hands clinging to the bark, its white breast reared. He started from it in panic.

Struggling to his feet, he lurched away. He went on walking, walking, looking for something—for a drink. His brain felt hot and inflamed for want of water. He stumbled on. Then he did not know anything. He went unconscious as he walked. Yet he stumbled on, his mouth open.

When, to his dumb wonder, he opened his eyes on the world again, he no longer tried to remember what it was. There was thick, golden light behind golden-green glitterings, and tall, grey-purple shafts, and darkness further off, surrounding him, growing deeper. He was conscious of a sense of arrival. He was amid the reality, on the real, dark bottom. But there was the thirst burning in his brain. He felt lighter, not so heavy. He supposed it was newness. The air was muttering with thunder. He thought he was walking wonderfully swiftly and was coming straight to relief—or was it water?

Suddenly he stood still with fear. There was a tremendous flare of gold, immense—just a few dark trunks like bars between him and it. All the young level wheat was burnished gold glaring on its silky green. A woman, full-skirted, a black cloth on her head for head-dress, was passing like a block of shadow through the glistening, green corn, into the full glare. There was a farm, too, pale blue in shadow, and the timber black. And there was a church spire, nearly fused away in the gold. The woman moved on, away from him. He had no language with which to speak to her. She was the bright, solid unreality. She would make a noise of words that would confuse him, and her eyes would look at him without seeing him. She was crossing there to the other side. He stood against a tree.

When at last he turned, looking down the long, bare grove whose flat bed was already filling dark, he saw the mountains in a wonder-light, not far away, and radiant. Behind the soft, grey ridge of the nearest range the further mountains stood golden and pale grey, the snow all radiant like pure, soft gold. So still, gleaming in the sky, fashioned pure out of the ore of the sky, they shone in their silence. He stood and looked at them, his face illuminated. And like the golden, lustrous gleaming of the snow he felt his own thirst bright in him. He stood and gazed, leaning against a tree. And then everything slid way into space.

During the night the lightning fluttered perpetually, making the whole sky white. He must have walked again. The world hung livid round him for moments, fields a level sheen of grey-green light, trees in dark bulk, and the range of clouds black across a white sky. Then the darkness fell like a shutter, and the night was whole. A faint flutter of a half-revealed world, that could not quite leap out of the darkness!—Then there again stood a sweep of pallor for the land, dark shapes looming, a range of clouds hanging overhead. The world was a ghostly shadow, thrown for a moment upon the pure darkness, which returned ever whole and complete.

And the mere delirium of sickness and fever went on inside him—his brain opening and shutting like the night—then sometimes convulsions of terror from something with great eyes that stared round a tree—then the long agony of the march, and the sun decomposing his blood—then the pang of hate for the Captain, followed by a pang of tenderness and ease. But everything was distorted, born of an ache and resolving into an ache.

In the morning he came definitely awake. Then his brain flamed with the sole horror of thirstiness! The sun was on his face, the dew was steaming from his wet clothes. Like one possessed, he got up. There, straight in front of him, blue and cool and tender, the mountains ranged across the pale edge of the morning sky. He wanted them—he wanted them alone—he wanted to leave himself and be identified with them. They did not move, they were still and soft, with white, gentle markings of snow. He stood still, mad with suffering, his hands crisping and clutching. Then he was twisting in a paroxysm on the grass.

He lay still, in a kind of dream of anguish. His thirst seemed to have separated itself from him, and to stand apart, a single demand. Then the pain he felt was another single self. Then there was the clog of his body, another separate thing. He was divided among all kinds of separate things. There was some strange, agonized connection between them, but they were drawing further apart. Then they would all split. The sun, drilling down on him, was drilling through the bond. Then they would all fall, fall through the everlasting lapse of space. Then again, his consciousness reasserted itself. He roused on to his elbow and stared at the gleaming mountains. There they ranked, all still and wonderful between earth and heaven. He stared till his eyes went black, and the mountains, as they stood in their beauty, so clean and cool, seemed to have it, that which was lost in him.

IV

When the soldiers found him, three hours later, he was lying with his face over his arms, his black hair giving off heat under the sun. But he was still alive. Seeing the open, black mouth the young soldiers dropped him in horror.

He died in the hospital at night, without having seen again.

The doctors saw the bruises on his legs, behind, and were silent.

The bodies of the two men lay together, side by side, in the mortuary, the one white and slender, but laid rigidly at rest, the other looking as if every moment it must rouse into life again, so young and unused, from slumber.

1914

Katherine Mansfield

1888–1923

The daughter of a Wellington, New Zealand, banker, Kathleen Mansfield Beauchamp (her birth name) was intent on a musical career after her years at Queen's College, London. But, supported by a parental grant, she embraced turn-of-the-century literary intensity perhaps too literally: she married, left her husband after several days, became pregnant by another man, had a miscarriage in Germany, and divorced. But her relationship and eventual marriage to the critic J. Middleton Murry proved personally and artistically enlivening. The two met in 1911, the same year she published her first collection of stories, *In a German Pension*. Together with D.H. Lawrence, who ultimately turned his venom on Mansfield, she edited the magazine *Signature* (1915), and she began to devote herself to the short story, considering it an art form congenial to depicting glimpses and moods. "The short story," she declared, "by reason of its aesthetics, is not and is not intended to be, the medium either for the exploration or long-term development of character. Character cannot be *more than shown—it is there for use, the use is dramatic. Foreshortening is not only unavoidable, it is right*" (emphasis in original). Often regarded as the first English author in whose work Chekhov's influence is strongly evident, Mansfield became the master of those epistemic openings—"And then, after six years, she saw him again"—the sudden creations out of nothing that help define the unique compulsion of the genre. Her most notable collections are *Bliss and Other Stories* (1920), *The Garden Party and Other Stories* (1922), and *The Dove's Nest and Other Stories* (1923). She is known, more darkly, as the model for the character Gudrun in Lawrence's *Women in Love* (1920). Her tuberculosis became fatal when she was thirty-five.

The Garden Party

And after all the weather was ideal. They could not have had a more perfect day for a garden party if they had ordered it. Windless, warm, the sky without a cloud. Only the blue was veiled with a haze of light gold, as it is sometimes in early summer. The gardener had been up since dawn, mowing the lawns and sweeping them, until the grass and the dark flat rosettes where the daisy plants had been seemed to shine. As for the roses, you could not help feeling they understood that roses are the only flowers that impress people at garden parties; the only flowers that everybody is certain of knowing. Hundreds, yes, literally hundreds, had come out in a single night; the green bushes bowed down as though they had been visited by archangels.

Breakfast was not yet over before the men came to put up the marquee.

"Where do you want the marquee put, mother?"

"My dear child, it's no use asking me. I'm determined to leave everything to you children this year. Forget I am your mother. Treat me as an honoured guest."

But Meg could not possibly go and supervise the men. She had washed her hair before breakfast, and she sat drinking her coffee in a green turban, with a dark wet curl stamped on each cheek. Jose, the butterfly, always came down in a silk petticoat and a kimono jacket.

"You'll have to go, Laura, you're the artistic one."

Away Laura flew, still holding her piece of bread-and-butter. It's so delicious to have an excuse for eating out of doors, and besides, she loved having to arrange things; she always felt she could do it so much better than anybody else.

Four men in their shirt-sleeves stood grouped together on the garden path. They carried staves covered with rolls of canvas, and they had big tool-bags slung on their backs. They looked impressive. Laura wished now that she was not holding that piece of bread-and-butter, but there was nowhere to put it, and she couldn't possibly throw it away. She blushed and tried to look severe and even a little bit short-sighted as she came up to them.

"Good morning," she said, copying her mother's voice. But that sounded so fearfully affected that she was ashamed, and stammered like a little girl, "Oh—er—have you come—is it about the marquee?"

"That's right, miss," said the tallest of the men, a lanky, freckled fellow, and he shifted his tool-bag, knocked back his straw hat, and smiled down at her. "That's about it."

His smile was so easy, so friendly, that Laura recovered. What nice eyes he had, small, but such a dark blue! And now she looked at the others, they were smiling too. "Cheer up, we won't bite," their smile seemed to say. How very nice workmen were! And what a beautiful morning! She mustn't mention the morning; she must be businesslike. The marquee.

"Well, what about the lily-lawn? Would that do?"

And she pointed to the lily-lawn with the hand that didn't hold the bread-and-butter. They turned, they stared in the direction. A little fat chap thrust out his under-lip, and the tall fellow frowned.

"I don't fancy it," said he. "Not conspicuous enough. You see, with a thing like a marquee," and he turned to Laura in his easy way, "you want to put it somewhere where it'll give you a bang slap in the eye, if you follow me."

Laura's upbringing made her wonder for a moment whether it was quite respectful of a workman to talk to her of bangs slap in the eye. But she did quite follow him.

"A corner of the tennis court," she suggested. "But the band's going to be in one corner."

"H'm, going to have a band, are you?" said another of the workmen. He was pale. He had a haggard look as his dark eyes scanned the tennis court. What was he thinking?

"Only a very small band," said Laura gently. Perhaps he wouldn't mind so much if the band was quite small. But the tall fellow interrupted.

"Look here, miss, that's the place. Against those rose trees. Over there. That'll do fine."

Against the karakas. Then the karaka trees would be hidden. And they were so lovely, with their broad, gleaming leaves, and their clusters of yellow fruit. They were like trees you imagined growing up on a desert island, proud, solitary, lifting their leaves and fruits to the sun in a kind of silent splendour. Must they be hidden by a marquee?

They must. Already the men had shouldered their staves and were making for the place. Only the tall fellow was left. He bent down, pinched a sprig of lavender, put his thumb and forefinger to his nose and snuffed up the smell. When Laura saw the gesture she forgot all about the karakas in her wonder of him caring for things like that—caring for the smell of lavender. How many men that she knew would have done such a thing. Oh, how extraordinarily nice workmen were, she thought. Why couldn't she have workmen for friends rather than the silly boys she danced with and who came to Sunday night supper? She would get on much better with men like these.

It's all the fault, she decided, as the tall fellow drew something on the back of an envelope, something that was to be looped up or left to hang, of these absurd class distinctions. Well, for her part, she didn't feel them. Not a bit, not an atom.... And now there came the chock-chock of wooden hammers. Some one whistled, some one sang out, "Are you right there, matey?" "Matey!" The friendliness of it, the—the— Just to prove how happy she was, just to show the tall fellow how at home she felt, and how she despised stupid conventions, Laura took a big bite of her bread-and-butter as she stared at the little drawing. She felt just like a work-girl.

"Laura, Laura, where are you? Telephone, Laura!" a voice cried from the house.

"Coming!" Away she skimmed, over the lawn, up the path, up the steps, across the veranda, and into the porch. In the hall her father and Laurie were brushing their hats ready to go to the office.

"I say, Laura," said Laurie very fast, "you might just give a squiz at my coat before this afternoon. See if it wants pressing."

"I will," said she. Suddenly she couldn't stop herself. She ran at Laurie and gave him a small, quick squeeze. "Oh, I do love parties, don't you?" gasped Laura.

"Ra-ther," said Laurie's warm, boyish voice, and he squeezed his sister too, and gave her a gentle push. "Dash off to the telephone, old girl."

The telephone. "Yes, yes; oh yes. Kitty? Good morning, dear. Come to lunch? Do, dear. Delighted of course. It will only be a very scratch meal—just the sandwich crusts and broken meringue-shells and what's left over. Yes, isn't it a perfect morning? Your white? Oh, I certainly should. One moment—hold the line. Mother's calling." And Laura sat back. "What, mother? Can't hear."

Mrs Sheridan's voice floated down the stairs. "Tell her to wear that sweet hat she had on last Sunday."

"Mother says you're to wear that *sweet* hat you had on last Sunday. Good. One o'clock. Bye-bye."

Laura put back the receiver, flung her arms over her head, took a deep breath, stretched, and let them fall. "Huh," she sighed, and the moment after the sigh she sat up quickly. She was still, listening. All the doors in the house seemed to be open. The house was alive with soft, quick steps and running voices. The green baize door that led to the kitchen regions swung open and shut with a muffled thud. And now there came a long, chuckling absurd sound. It was the heavy piano being moved on its stiff casters. But the air! If you stopped to notice, was the air always like this? Little faint winds were playing chase in at the tops of the windows, out at the doors. And there were two tiny spots of sun, one on the inkpot. Especially the one on the inkpot lid. It was quite warm. A warm little silver star. She could have kissed it.

The front door bell pealed, and there sounded the rustle of Sadie's print skirt on the stairs. A man's voice murmured; Sadie answered, careless, "I'm sure I don't know. Wait. I'll ask Mrs Sheridan."

"What is it, Sadie?" Laura came into the hall.

"It's the florist, Miss Laura."

It was, indeed. There, just inside the door, stood a wide, shallow tray full of pots of pink lilies. No other kind. Nothing but lilies—canna lilies, big pink flowers, wide open, radiant, almost frighteningly alive on bright crimson stems.

"O-oh, Sadie!" said Laura, and the sound was like a little moan. She crouched down as if to warm herself at that blaze of lilies; she felt they were in her fingers, on her lips, growing in her breast.

"It's some mistake," she said faintly. "Nobody ever ordered so many. Sadie, go and find mother."

But at that moment Mrs Sheridan joined them.

"It's quite right," she said calmly. "Yes, I ordered them. Aren't they lovely?" She pressed Laura's arm. "I was passing the shop yesterday, and I saw them in the window, and I suddenly thought for once in my life I shall have enough canna lilies. The garden party will be a good excuse."

"But I thought you said you didn't mean to interfere," said Laura. Sadie had gone. The florist's man was still outside at his van. She put her arm round her mother's neck and gently, very gently, she bit her mother's ear.

"My darling child, you wouldn't like a logical mother, would you? Don't do that. Here's the man."

He carried more lilies still, another whole tray.

"Bank them up, just inside the door, on both sides of the porch, please," said Mrs Sheridan. "Don't you agree, Laura?"

"Oh, I *do*, mother."

In the drawing room Meg, Jose, and good little Hans had at last succeeded in moving the piano.

"Now, if we put this chesterfield against the wall and move everything out of the room except the chairs, don't you think?"

"Quite."

"Hans, move these tables into the smoking room, and bring a sweeper to take these marks off the carpet and—one moment, Hans—" Jose loved giving orders to the servants, and they loved obeying her. She always made them feel they were taking part in some drama. "Tell Mother and Miss Laura to come here at once."

"Very good, Miss Jose."

She turned to Meg. "I want to hear what the piano sounds like, just in case I'm asked to sing this afternoon. Let's try over 'This Life is Weary.'"

Pom! Ta-ta-ta *Tee*-ta! The piano burst out so passionately that Jose's face changed. She clasped her hands. She looked mournfully and enigmatically at her mother and Laura as they came in.

This Life is *Wee*-ary,
A Tear—a Sigh.
A Love that *Chan*-ges,
This Life is *Wee*-ary,
A Tear—a Sigh.
A Love that *Chan*-ges,

And then . . . Good-bye!

But at the word "Good-bye," and although the piano sounded more desperate than ever, her face broke into a brilliant, dreadfully unsympathetic smile.

"Aren't I in good voice, mummy?" she beamed.

This Life is *Wee*-ary,
Hope comes to Die.

A Dream—a *Wa*-kening.

But now Sadie interrupted them. "What is it, Sadie?"

"If you please, m'm, cook says have you got the flags for the sandwiches?"

"The flags for the sandwiches, Sadie?" echoed Mrs Sheridan dreamily. And the children knew by her face that she hadn't got them. "Let me see." And she said to Sadie firmly, "Tell cook I'll let her have them in ten minutes."

Sadie went.

"Now, Laura," said her mother quickly, "come with me into the smoking room. I've got the names somewhere on the back of an envelope. You'll have to write them out for me. Meg, go upstairs this minute and take that wet thing off your head. Jose, run and finish dressing this instant. Do you hear me, children, or shall I have to tell your father when he comes home tonight? And—and, Jose, pacify cook if you do go into the kitchen, will you? I'm terrified of her this morning."

The envelope was found at last behind the dining-room clock, though how it had got there Mrs Sheridan could not imagine.

"One of you children must have stolen it out of my bag, because I remember vividly—cream cheese and lemon curd. Have you done that?"

"Yes."

"Egg and—" Mrs Sheridan held the envelope away from her. "It looks like mice. It can't be mice, can it?"

"Olive, pet," said Laura, looking over her shoulder.

"Yes, of course, olive. What a horrible combination it sounds. Egg and olive."

They were finished at last, and Laura took them off to the kitchen. She found Jose there pacifying the cook, who did not look at all terrifying. "I have never seen such exquisite sandwiches," said Jose's rapturous voice. "How many kinds did you say there were, cook? Fifteen?"

"Fifteen, Miss Jose."

"Well, cook, I congratulate you."

Cook swept up crusts with the long sandwich knife, and smiled broadly.

"Godber's has come," announced Sadie, issuing out of the pantry. She had seen the man pass the window.

That meant that cream puffs had come. Godber's were famous for their cream puffs. Nobody ever thought of making them at home.

"Bring them in and put them on the table, my girl," ordered cook.

Sadie brought them in and went back to the door. Of course Laura and Jose were far too grown-up to really care about such things. All the same they couldn't help agreeing that the puffs looked very attractive. Very. Cook began arranging them, shaking off the extra icing sugar.

"Don't they carry one back to all one's parties?" said Laura.

"I suppose they do," said practical Jose, who never liked to be carried back. "They look beautifully light and feathery, I must say."

"Have one each, my dears," said cook in her comfortable voice. "Yer ma won't know."

Oh, impossible. Fancy cream puffs so soon after breakfast. The very idea made one shudder. All the same, two minutes later Jose and Laura were licking their fingers with that absorbed inward look that only comes from whipped cream.

"Let's go into the garden, out by the back way," suggested Laura. "I want to see how the men are getting on with the marquee. They're such awfully nice men."

But the back door was blocked by cook, Sadie, Godber's man, and Hans.

Something had happened.

"Tuk-tuk-tuk," clucked cook like an agitated hen. Sadie had her hand clapped to her cheek as though she had a toothache. Hans's face was screwed up in the effort to understand. Only Godber's man seemed to be enjoying himself; it was his story.

"What's the matter? What happened?"

"There's been a horrible accident," said cook. "A man killed."

"A man killed! Where? How? When?"

But Godber's man wasn't going to have his story snatched from under his very nose.

"Know those little cottages just below here, miss?" Know them? Of course, she knew them. "Well, there's a young chap living there, name of Scott, a carter. His horse shied at a traction-engine, corner of Hawke Street this morning, and he was thrown out on the back of his head. Killed."

"Dead!" Laura stared at Godber's man.

"Dead when they picked him up," said Godber's man with relish. "They were taking the body home as I come up here." And he said to the cook, "He's left a wife and five little ones."

"Jose, come here." Laura caught hold of her sister's sleeve and dragged her through the kitchen to the other side of the green baize door. There she paused and leaned against it. "Jose!" she said, horrified, "however are we going to stop everything?"

"Stop everything, Laura!" cried Jose in astonishment. "What do you mean?"

"Stop the garden party, of course." Why did Jose pretend?

But Jose was still more amazed. "Stop the garden party? My dear Laura, don't be so absurd. Of course we can't do anything of the kind. Nobody expects us to. Don't be so extravagant."

"But we can't possibly have a garden party with a man dead just outside the front gate."

That really was extravagant, for the little cottages were in a lane to themselves at the very bottom of a steep rise that led up to the house. A broad road ran between them. True, they were far too near. They were the greatest possible eyesore, and they had no right to be in that neighbourhood at all. They were little mean dwellings painted a chocolate brown. In the garden patches there was nothing but cabbage stalks, sick hens, and tomato cans. The very smoke coming out of their chimneys was poverty-stricken. Little rags and shreds of smoke, so unlike the great silvery plumes that uncurled from the Sheridans' chimneys. Washer-women lived in the lane and sweeps and a cobbler, and a man whose house-front was studded all over with minute birdcages. Children swarmed. When the Sheridans were little they were forbidden to set foot there because of the revolting language and of what they might catch. But since they were grown up, Laura and Laurie on their prowls sometimes walked through. It was disgusting and sordid. They came out with a shudder. But still one must go everywhere; one must see everything. So through they went.

"And just think of what the band would sound like to that poor woman," said Laura.

"Oh, Laura!" Jose began to be seriously annoyed. "If you're going to stop a band playing every time some one has an accident, you'll lead a very strenuous life. I'm every bit as sorry about it as you. I feel just as sympathetic." Her eyes hardened. She looked at her sister just as she used to when they were little and fighting together. "You won't bring a drunken workman back to life by being sentimental," she said softly.

"Drunk! Who said he was drunk?" Laura turned furiously on Jose. She said just as they had used to say on those occasions, "I'm going straight up to tell mother."

"Do, dear," cooed Jose.

"Mother, can I come into your room?" Laura turned the big glass doorknob.

"Of course, child. Why, what's the matter? What's given you such a colour?" And Mrs Sheridan turned round from her dressing-table. She was trying on a new hat.

"Mother, a man's been killed," began Laura.

"*Not* in the garden?" interrupted her mother.

"No, no!"

"Oh, what a fright you gave me!" Mrs Sheridan sighed with relief, and took off the big hat and held it on her knees.

"But listen, mother," said Laura. Breathless, half-choking, she told the dreadful story. "Of course, we can't have our party, can we?" she pleaded. "The band and everybody arriving. They'd hear us, mother; they're nearly neighbours!"

To Laura's astonishment her mother behaved just like Jose; it was harder to bear because she seemed amused. She refused to take Laura seriously.

"But, my dear child, use your common sense. It's only by accident we've heard of it. If some one had died there normally—and I can't understand how they keep alive in those poky little holes—we should still be having our party, shouldn't we?"

Laura had to say "yes" to that, but she felt it was all wrong. She sat down on her mother's sofa and pinched the cushion frill.

"Mother, isn't it really terribly heartless of us?" she asked.

"Darling!" Mrs Sheridan got up and came over to her, carrying the hat. Before Laura could stop her she had popped it on. "My child!" said her mother, "the hat is yours. It's made for you. It's much too young for me. I have never seen you look such a picture. Look at yourself!" And she held up her hand-mirror.

"But, mother," Laura began again. She couldn't look at herself; she turned aside.

This time Mrs Sheridan lost patience just as Jose had done.

"You are being very absurd, Laura," she said coldly. "People like that don't expect sacrifices from us. And it's not very sympathetic to spoil everybody's enjoyment as you're doing now."

"I don't understand," said Laura, and she walked quickly out of the room into her own bedroom. There, quite by chance, the first thing she saw was this charming girl in the mirror, in her black hat trimmed with gold daisies, and a long black velvet ribbon. Never had she imagined she could look like that. Is mother right? she thought. And now she hoped her mother was right. Am I being extravagant? Perhaps it was extravagant. Just for a moment she had another glimpse of that poor woman and those little children, and the body being carried into the house. But it all seemed blurred, unreal, like a picture in the newspaper. I'll remember it again after the party's over, she decided. And somehow that seemed quite the best plan. . . .

Lunch was over by half-past one. By half-past two they were all ready for the fray. The green-coated band had arrived and was established in a corner of the tennis court.

"My dear!" trilled Kitty Maitland, "aren't they too like frogs for words? You ought to have arranged them round the pond with the conductor in the middle on a leaf."

Laurie arrived and hailed them on his way to dress. At the sight of him Laura remembered the accident again. She wanted to tell him. If Laurie agreed with the others, then it was bound to be all right. And she followed him into the hall.

"Laurie!"

"Hallo!" He was halfway upstairs, but when he turned round and saw Laura he suddenly puffed out his cheeks and goggled his eyes at her. "My word, Laura! You do look stunning," said Laurie.

"What an absolutely topping hat!"

Laura said faintly "Is it?" and smiled up at Laurie, and didn't tell him after all.

Soon after that people began coming in streams. The band struck up; the hired waiters ran from the house to the marquee. Wherever you looked there were couples strolling, bending to the flowers, greeting, moving on over the lawn. They were like bright birds that had alighted in the Sheridans' garden for this one afternoon, on their way to—where? Ah, what happiness it is to be with people who all are happy, to press hands, press cheeks, smile into eyes.

"Darling Laura, how well you look!"

"What a becoming hat, child!"

"Laura, you look quite Spanish. I've never seen you look so striking."

And Laura, glowing, answered softly, "Have you had tea? Won't you have an ice? The passion-fruit ices really are rather special." She ran to her father and begged him. "Daddy darling, can't the band have something to drink?"

And the perfect afternoon slowly ripened, slowly faded, slowly its petals closed.

"Never a more delightful garden party . . ." "The greatest success . . ." "Quite the most . . ."

Laura helped her mother with the good-byes. They stood side by side on the porch till it was all over.

"All over, all over, thank heaven," said Mrs Sheridan. "Round up the others, Laura. Let's go and have some fresh coffee. I'm exhausted. Yes, it's been very successful. But oh, these parties, these parties! Why will you children insist on giving parties!" And they all of them sat down in the deserted marquee.

"Have a sandwich, daddy dear. I wrote the flag."

"Thanks." Mr Sheridan took a bite and the sandwich was gone. He took another. "I suppose you didn't hear of a beastly accident that happened today?" he said.

"My dear," said Mrs Sheridan, holding up her hand, "we did. It nearly ruined the party. Laura insisted we should put it off."

"Oh, mother!" Laura didn't want to be teased about it.

"It was a horrible affair all the same," said Mr Sheridan. "The chap was married too. Lived just below in the lane, and leaves a wife and half a dozen kiddies, so they say."

An awkward little silence fell. Mrs Sheridan fidgeted with her cup. Really, it was very tactless of father . . .

Suddenly she looked up. There on the table were all those sandwiches, cakes, puffs, all uneaten, all going to be wasted. She had one of her brilliant ideas.

"I know," she said. "Let's make up a basket. Let's send that poor creature some of this perfectly good food. At any rate, it will be the greatest treat for the children. Don't you agree? And she's sure to have neighbours calling in and so on. What a point to have it all ready prepared. Laura!" She jumped up. "Get me the big basket out of the stairs cupboard."

"But, mother, do you really think it's a good idea?" said Laura.

Again, how curious, she seemed to be different from them all. To take scraps from their party. Would the poor woman really like that?

"Of course! What's the matter with you today? An hour or two ago you were insisting on us being sympathetic, and now—"

Oh well! Laura ran for the basket. It was filled, it was heaped by her mother.

"Take it yourself, darling," said she. "Run down just as you are. No, wait, take the arum lilies too. People of that class are so impressed by arum lilies."

"The stems will ruin her lace frock," said practical Jose.

So they would. Just in time. "Only the basket, then. And, Laura!"—her mother followed her out of the marquee—"don't on any account—"

"What, mother?"

No, better not put such ideas into the child's head! "Nothing! Run along."

It was just growing dusky as Laura shut their garden gates. A big dog ran by like a shadow. The road gleamed white, and down below in the hollow the little cottages were in deep shade. How quiet it seemed after the afternoon. Here she was going down the hill to somewhere where a man lay dead, and she couldn't realize it. Why couldn't she? She stopped a minute. And it seemed to her that kisses, voices, tinkling spoons, laughter, the smell of crushed grass were somehow inside her. She had no room for anything else. How strange! She looked up at the pale sky, and all she thought was, "Yes, it was the most successful party."

Now the broad road was crossed. The lane began, smoky and dark. Women in shawls and men's tweed caps hurried by. Men hung over the palings; the children played in the doorways. A low hum came from the mean little cottages. In some of them there was a flicker of light, and a shadow, crab-like, moved across the window. Laura bent her head and hurried on. She wished now she had put on a coat. How her frock shone! And the big hat with the velvet streamer—if only it was another hat! Were the people looking at her? They must be. It was a mistake to have come; she knew all along it was a mistake. Should she go back even now?

No, too late. This was the house. It must be. A dark knot of people stood outside. Beside the gate an old, old woman with a crutch sat in a chair, watching. She had her feet on a newspaper. The voices stopped as Laura drew near. The group parted. It was as though she was expected, as though they had known she was coming here.

Laura was terribly nervous. Tossing the velvet ribbon over her shoulder, she said to a woman standing by, "Is this Mrs Scott's house?" and the woman, smiling queerly, said, "It is, my lass."

Oh, to be away from this! She actually said, "Help me, God," as she walked up the tiny path and knocked. To be away from those staring eyes, or to be covered up in anything, one of those women's shawls even. I'll just leave the basket and go, she decided. I shan't even wait for it to be emptied.

Then the door opened. A little woman in black showed in the gloom.

Laura said, "Are you Mrs Scott?" But to her horror the woman answered, "Walk in, please, miss," and she was shut in the passage.

"No," said Laura, "I don't want to come in. I only want to leave this basket. Mother sent—"

The little woman in the gloomy passage seemed not to have heard her. "Step this way, please, miss," she said in an oily voice, and Laura followed her.

She found herself in a wretched little low kitchen, lighted by a smoky lamp. There was a woman sitting before the fire.

"Em," said the little creature who had let her in. "Em! It's a young lady." She turned to Laura. She said meaningly, "I'm 'er sister, miss. You'll excuse 'er, won't you?"

"Oh, but of course!" said Laura. "Please, please don't disturb her. I—I only want to leave—"

But at that moment the woman at the fire turned round. Her face, puffed up, red, with swollen eyes and swollen lips, looked terrible. She seemed as though she couldn't understand why Laura was there. What did it mean? Why was this stranger standing in the kitchen with a basket? What was it all about? And the poor face puckered up again.

"All right, my dear," said the other. "I'll thenk the young lady."

And again she began, "You'll excuse her, miss, I'm sure," and her face, swollen too, tried an oily smile.

Laura only wanted to get out, to get away. She was back in the passage. The door opened. She walked straight through into the bedroom where the dead man was lying.

"You'd like a look at 'im, wouldn't you?" said Em's sister, and she brushed past Laura over to the bed. "Don't be afraid, my lass,"—and now her voice sounded fond and sly, and fondly she drew down the sheet—" 'e looks a picture. There's nothing to show. Come along, my dear."

Laura came.

There lay a young man, fast asleep—sleeping so soundly, so deeply, that he was far, far away from them both. Oh, so remote, so peaceful. He was dreaming. Never wake him up again. His head was sunk in the pillows, his eyes were closed; they were blind under the closed eyelids. He was given up to his dream. What did garden parties and baskets and lace frocks matter to him? He was far from all those things. He was wonderful, beautiful. While they were laughing and while the band was playing, this marvel had come to the lane. Happy . . . happy . . . All is well, said that sleeping face. This is just as it should be. I am content.

But all the same you had to cry, and she couldn't go out of the room without saying something to him. Laura gave a loud childish sob.

"Forgive my hat," she said.

And this time she didn't wait for Em's sister. She found her way out of the door, down the path, past all those dark people. At the corner of the lane she met Laurie.

He stepped out of the shadow. "Is that you, Laura?"

"Yes."

"Mother was getting anxious. Was it all right?"

"Yes, quite. Oh, Laurie!" She took his arm, she pressed up against him.

"I say, you're not crying, are you?" asked her brother.

Laura shook her head. She was.

Laurie put his arm round her shoulder. "Don't cry," he said in his warm, loving voice. "Was it awful?"

"No," sobbed Laura. "It was simply marvellous. But, Laurie—" She stopped, she looked at her brother. "Isn't life," she stammered, "isn't life—" but what life was she couldn't explain. No matter. He quite understood.

"*Isn't* it, darling?" said Laurie.

1921

Bruno Schulz

1892–1942

The manner of Bruno Schulz's death in his hometown of Drohobycz (then Poland, now Ukraine) will always remain tied to his part in the world, his short life, and his abbreviated volume of work. The intense individuality of his drawings and stories carried over to his assassination. Unlike the fate of millions of Jews, his was intensely personal. Protected by one Gestapo officer (for whom he was painting home murals), Schulz was murdered by the German's rival, whose own protectee had himself been shot. "I have killed your Jew," the reported conversation went, "All right, now I will go and kill your Jew." There remains some uncertainty about the historical accuracy of this story, but it will always evoke Schulz's deep belief in the "mythicisation of reality" which informed every level and form of his artistry. But for him, the relation of myth and world meant luminous transcendence, not, as that day in 1942 has given us, an epigrammatic parable of monstrosity. What remains of his work, however, is magical in its humane inventiveness; Schulz is one of the few masters of short fiction to align "the verbal and the visual" (David Goldbarb). As a student in Drohobycz and in frequent periods of recovery from illness, he was pulled by the power of images in paintings and in literature. He studied architecture at the Polytechni in Liviv and for a short period in Vienna. Goldfarb reports that he "painted in oils," and his "first exhibition of graphic works took place in 1922, in Warsaw." For economic reasons he taught at a private Jewish high school in town; the job entailed instruction in drawing, but a former student recalls that Schulz chose to tell stories, leaving the visual to occupy layers in his private imagination. He published his first collection, *The Street of Crocodiles* (in Polish *The Cinnamon Shops*) in 1934, and his second, *Sanatorium under the Sign of the Hourglass*, in 1937. Their startling imagery and surreal dimension coupled with Schulz's personal fate have made him a mythic presence among later writers. He has a habit of appearing in various guises in recent novels, most notably in Cynthia Ozick's *The Messiah of Stockholm*. One mystery about Schulz is the fate and nature of a lost novel called *The Messiah*, a title and an absence reminiscent of Kafka, Schulz's primary literary ancestor.

Sanatorium Under the Sign of the Hourglass

The journey was long. The train, which ran only once a week on that forgotten branch line, carried no more than a few passengers. Never before had I seen such archaic coaches; withdrawn from other lines long before, they were spacious as living rooms, dark, and with many recesses. Corridors crossed the empty compartments at various angles; labyrinthine and cold, they exuded an air of strange and frightening neglect. I moved from coach to coach, looking for a comfortable corner. Drafts were everywhere: cold currents of air shooting through the interiors, piercing the whole train from end to end. Here and there a few people sat on the floor, surrounded by their bundles, not daring to occupy the empty seats. Besides, those high, convex oilcloth-covered seats were cold as ice and sticky with age. At the deserted stations no passengers boarded the train. Without a whistle, without a groan, the train would slowly start again, as if lost in meditation.

For a time I had the company of a man in a ragged railway man's uniform—silent, engrossed in his thoughts. He pressed a handkerchief to his swollen, aching face. Later even he disappeared, having slipped out unobserved at some stop. He left behind him the mark of his body in the straw that lay on the floor, and a shabby black suitcase he had forgotten.

Wading in straw and rubbish, I walked shakily from coach to coach. The open doors of the compartments were swinging in the drafts. There was not a single passenger left on the train. At last, I met a conductor, in the black uniform of that line. He was wrapping a thick scarf around his neck and collecting his things—a lantern, an official logbook.

"We are nearly there, sir," he said, looking at me with washed-out eyes.

The train was coming slowly to a halt, without puffing, without rattling, as if, together with the last breath of steam, life were slowly escaping from it. We stopped. Everything was empty and still, with no station buildings in sight. The conductor showed me the direction of the Sanatorium. Carrying my suitcase, I started walking along a narrow white road toward the dark trees of a park. With some curiosity, I looked at the landscape. The road along which I was walking led up to the brow of a gentle hill, from which a wide expanse of country could be seen. The day was uniformly gray, extinguished, without contrasts. And perhaps under the influence of that heavy and colorless aura, the great basin of the valley, in which a vast wooded landscape was arranged like theatrical scenery, seemed very dark. The rows of trees, one behind the other, ever grayer and more distant, descended the gentle slopes to the left and right. The whole landscape, somber and grave, seemed almost imperceptibly to float, to shift slightly like a sky full of billowing, stealthily moving clouds. The fluid strips and bands of forest seemed to rustle and grow with rustling like a tide that swells gradually toward the shore. The rising white road wound itself dramatically through the darkness of that woody terrain. I broke a twig from a roadside tree. The leaves were dark, almost black. It was a strangely charged blackness, deep and benevolent, like restful sleep. All the different shades of gray in the landscape derived from that one color. It was the color of a cloudy summer dusk in our part of the country, when the landscape has become saturated with water after a long period of rain and exudes a feeling of self-denial, a resigned and ultimate numbness that does not need the consolation of color.

It was completely dark among the trees of the parkland. I groped my way blindly on a carpet of soft needles. When the trees thinned, the planks of a footbridge resounded under my feet. Beyond it, against the blackness of the trees, loomed the gray walls of the many-windowed hotel that advertised itself as the Sanatorium. The double glass door of the entrance stood open. The little footbridge, with shaky handrails made of birch branches, led straight to it.

In the hallway there was semidarkness and a solemn silence. I moved on tiptoe from door to door, trying to see the numbers on them. Rounding a corner, I at last met a chambermaid. She had run out of a room, as if having torn herself from someone's importuning arms, and was breathless and excited. She could hardly understand what I was saying. I had to repeat it. She was fidgeting helplessly.

Had my telegram reached them? She spread her arms, her eyes moved sideways. She was only awaiting an opportunity to leap back behind the half-opened door, at which she kept squinting.

"I have come a long way. I booked a room here by telegram," I said with some impatience. "Whom shall I see about it?"

She did not know. "Perhaps you could wait in the restaurant," she babbled. "Everybody is asleep just now. When the doctor gets up, I shall announce you."

"They are asleep? But it is daytime, not night."

"Here everybody is asleep all the time. Didn't you know?" she said, looking at me with interest now. "Besides, it is never night here," she added coyly.

She had obviously given up the idea of escape, for she was now picking fussily at the lace of her apron. I left her there and entered the half-lit restaurant. There were some tables, and a large buffet ran the length of one wall. I was now feeling a little hungry and was pleased to see some pastries and a cake on the buffet.

I placed my suitcase on one of the tables. They were all unoccupied. I clapped my hands. No response. I looked into the next room, which was larger and brighter. That room had a wide window or loggia overlooking the landscape I already knew, which, framed by the window, seemed like a constant reminder of mourning, suggestive of deep sorrow and resignation. On some of the tables stood the remains of recent meals, uncorked bottles, half-empty glasses. Here and there lay the tips, not yet picked up by the waiters. I returned to the buffet and looked at the pastries and cake. They looked most appetizing. I wondered whether I should help myself; I suddenly felt extremely greedy. There was a particular kind of apple flan that made my mouth water. I was about to lift a piece of it with a silver knife when I felt somebody behind me. The chambermaid had entered the room in her soft slippers and was touching my back lightly.

"The doctor will see you now," she said, looking at her fingernails.

She stood facing me and, conscious of the magnetism of her wriggling hips, did not turn away. She provoked me, increasing and decreasing the distance between our bodies as, having left the restaurant, we passed many numbered doors. The passage became ever darker. In almost complete darkness, she brushed against me fleetingly.

"Here is the doctor's door," she whispered. "Please go in."

Dr. Gotard was standing in the middle of the room to receive me. He was a short, broad-shouldered man with a dark beard.

"We received your telegram yesterday," he said. "We sent our carriage to the station, but you must have arrived by another train. Unfortunately, the railway connections are not very good. Are you well?"

"Is my father alive?" I asked, staring anxiously into his calm face.

"Yes, of course," he answered, calmly meeting my questioning eyes. "That is, within the limits imposed by the situation," he added, half-closing his eyes. "You know as well as I that from the point of view of your home, from the perspective of your own country, your father is dead. This cannot be entirely remedied. That death throws a certain shadow on his existence here."

"But does Father himself know it, does he guess?" I asked him in a whisper.

He shook his head with deep conviction. "Don't worry," he said in a low voice. "None of our patients know it, or can guess. The whole secret of the operation," he added, ready to demonstrate its mechanism on his fingers, "is that we have put back the clock. Here we are always late by a certain interval of time of which we cannot define the length. The whole thing is a matter of simple relativity. Here your father's death, the death that has already struck him in your country, has not occurred yet."

"In that case," I said, "my father must be on his deathbed or about to die."

"You don't understand me," he said in a tone of tolerant impatience. "Here we reactivate time past, with all its possibilities, therefore also including the possibility of a recovery." He looked at me with a smile, stroking his beard. "But now you probably want to see your father. According to your request, we have reserved for you the other bed in your father's room. I shall take you there."

When we were out in the dark passage, Dr. Gotard spoke in a whisper. I noticed that he was wearing felt slippers, like the chambermaid. "We allow our patients to sleep long hours to spare their vitality. Besides, there is nothing better to do."

At last, we stopped in front of one of the doors, and he put a finger to his lips. "Enter quietly. Your father is asleep. Settle down to sleep, too. This is the best thing for you to do. Goodbye for now."

"Good-bye," I whispered, my heart beating fast.

I pressed the handle, and the door opened, like unresisting lips that part in sleep. I went in. The room was almost empty, gray and bare.

Under a small window, my father was lying on an ordinary wooden bed, covered by a pile of bedding, fast asleep. His breathing extracted layers of snoring from the depths of his breast. The whole room seemed to be lined with snores from floor to ceiling, and yet new layers were being added all the time. With deep emotion, I looked at Father's thin, emaciated face, now completely engrossed in the activity of snoring—a remote, trancelike face, which, having left its earthly aspect, was confessing its existence somewhere on a distant shore by solemnly telling its minutes.

There was no second bed in the room. Piercingly cold air blew in through the window. The stove had not been lit.

They don't seem to care much for patients here, I thought. To expose such a sick man to such drafts! And no one seems to do any cleaning here, either. A thick layer of dust covered the floor and the bedside table, on which stood medicine bottles and a cup of cold coffee. Stacks of pastries in the restaurant, yet they give the patients black coffee instead of anything more nourishing! But perhaps this is a detail compared with the benefits of having the clock put back.

I slowly undressed and climbed onto Father's bed. He did not wake up, but his snoring, having probably been pitched too high, fell an octave lower, forsaking its high declamatory tone. It became, as it were, more private, for his own use. I tucked Father in under his eiderdown, to protect him as much as possible from the drafts in the room. Soon I fell asleep by his side.

II

The room was in twilight when I woke up. Father was dressed and sitting at the table drinking tea, dunking sugar-coated biscuits in it. He was wearing a black suit of English cloth, which he had had made only the previous summer. His tie was rather loose.

Seeing that I was awake, he said with a pleasant smile on his pale face, "I am extremely pleased that you have come, Joseph. It was a real surprise! I feel so lonely here. But I suppose one should not complain in my situation. I have been through worse things, and if one were to itemize them all—but never mind. Imagine, on my very first day here they served an excellent fillet of beef with mushrooms. It was a hell of a piece of meat, Joseph. I must warn you most emphatically—beware if they should ever serve you fillet of beef! I can still feel the fire in my stomach. And the diarrhea—I could hardly cope with it. But I must tell you a piece of news," he continued. "Don't laugh. I have rented premises for a shop here. Yes, I have. And I congratulate myself for having had that bright idea. I have been bored most terribly, I must say. You cannot imagine the boredom. And so I at least have a pleasant occupation. Don't imagine anything grand. Nothing of the kind. A much more modest place than our old store. It is a booth compared with the previous one. Back home I would be ashamed of such a stall, but here, where we have had to give up so many of our pretensions—don't you agree, Joseph?" He laughed bitterly. "And so one manages somehow to live."

The wrong word—I was embarrassed by Father's confusion when he realized that he had used it.

"I see you are sleepy," he continued after a while. "Go back to sleep, and then you can visit me in the shop if you want. I am going there now to see how things are. You cannot imagine how difficult it has been to get credit, how mistrustful they are here of old merchants, of merchants with a reputable past. Do you recall the optician's shop in the market square? Well, our shop is right next door to it. There is still no sign over it, but you will find your way, I am sure. You can't miss it."

"Are you going out without a coat?" I asked anxiously.

"They have forgotten to pack it. Imagine, I could not find it in my trunk. But I don't really need it. That mild climate, that sweet air—"

"Please take my coat, Father," I insisted. "You must."

But Father was already putting on his hat. He waved to me and slipped out of the room.

I did not feel sleepy anymore. I felt rested and hungry. With pleasant anticipation I thought of the buffet. I dressed, wondering how many pastries to sample. I decided to start with the apple flan but did not forget the sponge cake with orange peel, which had caught my eye, too. I stood in front of the mirror to fix my tie, but the surface was like bottle glass: it secreted my reflection somewhere in its depth, and only an opaque blur was visible. I tried in vain to adjust the distance—approaching the mirror, then retreating from it—but no reflection would emerge from the silvery, fluid mist. I must ask for another looking glass, I thought, and left the room.

The corridor was completely dark. In one corner a tiny gas lamp flickered with a bluish flame, intensifying the impression of solemn silence. In that labyrinth of rooms, archways, and niches, I had difficulty remembering which door led to the restaurant.

I'll go out, I thought with sudden decision. I'll eat in the town. There must be a good café somewhere.

Beyond the gate, I plunged into the heavy, damp, sweet air of that peculiar climate. The grayness of the aura had become somewhat deeper; now it seemed to me that I was seeing daylight through mourning crepe.

I feasted my eyes on the velvety, succulent blackness of the darkest spots, on passages of dull grays and ashen, muted tones—that nocturne of a landscape. Waves of air fluttered softly around my face. They smelled of the sickly sweetness of stale rainwater.

And again that perpetual rustle of black forests—dull chords disturbing space beyond the limits of audibility! I was in the backyard of the Sanatorium. I turned to look at the rear of the main building, which was shaped like a horseshoe around a courtyard. All the windows were shuttered in black. The Sanatorium was in deep sleep. I went out by a gate in an iron fence. Nearby stood a dog kennel of extraordinary size, empty. Again I was engulfed and embraced by the black trees. Then it became somewhat lighter, and I saw outlines of houses between the trees. A few more steps and I found myself in a large town square.

What a strange, misleading resemblance it bore to the central square of our native city! How similar, in fact, are all the market squares in the world! Almost identical houses and shops!

The pavements were nearly empty. The mournful semidarkness of an undefined time descended from a sky of an indeterminable grayness. I could easily read all the shop signs and posters, yet it would not have surprised me to learn that it was the middle of the night. Only some of the shops were open. Others, their iron shutters pulled halfway down, were being hurriedly closed. A heady, rich, and inebriating air seemed to obscure some parts of the view, to wash away like a wet sponge some of the houses, a streetlamp, a section of signboard. At times it was difficult to keep one's eyes open, overcome as one was by a strange indolence or sleepiness. I began to look for the optician's shop that my father had mentioned. He had spoken of it as of something I knew, and he seemed to assume that I was familiar with local conditions. Didn't he remember that I had just come here for the first time? No doubt his mind was confused. Yet what could one expect of Father, who was only half-real, who lived a relative and conditional life, circumscribed by so many limitations! I cannot deny that much goodwill was needed to believe in his kind of existence. What he experienced was a pitiful substitute for life, depending on the indulgence of others, on a *consensus omnium* from which he drew his faint strength. It was clear that only by the solidarity of forbearance, by a communal averting of eyes from the obvious and shocking shortcomings of his condition, could this pitiful semblance of life maintain itself, for however short a moment, within the tissue of reality. The slightest doubt could undermine it, the faintest breeze of skepticism destroy it. Could Dr. Gotard's Sanatorium provide for Father this hothouse atmosphere of friendly indulgence and guard him from the cold winds of sober analysis? It was astonishing that in this insecure and questionable state of affairs, Father was capable of behaving so admirably.

I was glad when I saw a shop window full of cakes and pastries. My appetite revived. I opened the glass door, with the inscription "Ices" on it, and entered the dark interior. It smelled of coffee and vanilla. From the depths of the shop a girl appeared, her face misted over by dusk, and took my order. At last, after waiting so long, I could eat my fill of excellent doughnuts, which I dipped in my coffee. Surrounded by the dancing arabesques of dusk, I devoured pastries one after another, feeling darkness creep under my eyelids and stealthily fill me with its warm pulsations, its thousand delicate touches. In the end, only the window shone, like a gray rectangle, in the otherwise complete darkness. I knocked with my spoon on the tabletop, but in vain; no one appeared to take money for my refreshment. I left a silver coin on the table and walked out into the street.

In the bookshop next door, the light was still on. The shop assistants were busy sorting books. I asked for my father's shop. "It is next door to ours," one of them explained. A helpful boy even went with me to the door, to show me the way.

Father's shop had a glass pane in the door, the display window was not ready and was covered with a gray paper. On entering, I was astonished to see that the shop was full of customers. My father was standing behind the counter and adding a long row of figures on an invoice, repeatedly licking his pencil. The man for whom the invoice was being prepared was leaning over the counter and moving his index finger down the column of figures, counting softly. The rest of the customers looked on in silence.

My father gave me a look from over his spectacles and, marking his place on the invoice, said, "There is a letter for you. It is on the desk among all the papers." He went back to his sums. Meanwhile, the shop assistants were taking pieces of cloth bought by the customers, wrapping them in paper, and tying them with string. The shelves were only half-filled with cloth; some of them were still empty.

"Why don't you sit down, Father?" I asked softly, going behind the counter. "You don't take enough care of yourself, although you are very sick."

Father lifted his hand, as if wanting to reject my pleas, and did not stop counting. He looked very pale. It was obvious that only the excitement of his feverish activity sustained him and postponed the moment of complete collapse.

I went up to the desk and found not a letter but a parcel. A few days earlier, I had written to a bookshop about a pornographic book, and here it was already. They had found my address, or rather, Father's address, although he had only just opened a new shop here that had neither a name nor a signboard! What amazing efficiency in collecting information, what astounding delivery methods! And what incredible speed!

"You may read it in the office at the back," said my father, looking at me with displeasure. "As you can see, there is no room here."

The room behind the shop was still empty. Through a glass door some light filtered in from the shop. On the walls the shop assistants' overcoats hung from hooks. I opened the parcel and, by the faint light from the door, read the enclosed letter.

The letter informed me that the book I had ordered was unfortunately out of stock. They would look out for it, although the result of the search was uncertain; meanwhile, they were sending me, without obligation, a certain object, which, they were sure, would interest me. There followed a complicated description of a folding telescope with great refractive power and many other virtues. Interested, I took the instrument out of the wrapping. It was made of black oilcloth or canvas and was folded into the shape of a flattened accordion. I have always had a weakness for telescopes. I began to unfold the pleats of the instrument. Stiffened with thin rods, it rose under my fingers until it almost filled the room; a kind of enormous bellows, a labyrinth of black chambers, a long complex of camera obscuras, one within another. It looked, too, like a long-bodied model automobile made of patent leather, a theatrical prop, its lightweight paper and stiff canvas imitating the bulkiness of reality. I looked into the black funnel of the instrument and saw deep inside the vague outline of the back of the Sanatorium. Intrigued, I put my head deeper into the rear chamber of the apparatus. I could now see in my field of vision the maid walking along the darkened corridor of the Sanatorium, carrying a tray. She turned round and smiled. "Can you see me?" I asked myself. An overwhelming drowsiness misted my eyes. I was sitting, as it were, in the rear chamber of the telescope as if in the back seat of a limousine. A light touch on a lever and the apparatus began to rustle like a paper butterfly; I felt that it was moving and turning toward the door.

Like a large black caterpillar, the telescope crept into the lighted shop—an enormous paper arthropod with two imitation headlights on the front. The customers clustered together, retreating before this blind paper dragon; the shop assistants flung open the door to the street, and I rode slowly in my paper car amid rows of onlookers, who followed with scandalized eyes my truly outrageous exit.

III

That is how one lives in this town, and how time goes by. The greater part of the day is spent in sleeping—and not only in bed. No one is very particular when it comes to sleep. At any place, at any time, one is ready for a quiet snooze: with one's head propped on a restaurant table, in a horse-drawn cab, even standing up when, out for a walk, one looks into the hall of an apartment house for a moment and succumbs to the irrepressible need for sleep.

Waking up, still dazed and shaky, one continues the interrupted conversation or the wearisome walk, carries on complicated discussions without beginning or end. In this way, whole chunks of time are casually lost somewhere; control over the continuity of the day is loosened until it finally ceases to matter; and the framework of uninterrupted chronology that one has been disciplined to notice every day is given up without regret. The compulsive readiness to account for the passage of time, the scrupulous penny-wise habit of reporting on the used-up hours—the pride and ambition of our economic system—are forsaken. Those cardinal virtues, which in the past one never dared to question, have long ago been abandoned.

A few examples will illustrate this state of affairs. At a certain time of day or night—a hardly perceptible difference in the color of the sky allows one to tell which it is—I wake up in twilight at the railings of the footbridge leading to the Sanatorium. Overpowered by sleep, I must have wandered unconsciously for a long time all over the town before, mortally tired, I dragged myself to the bridge. I cannot say whether Dr. Gotard accompanied me on that walk, but now he stands in front of me, finishing a long tirade and drawing conclusions. Carried away by his own eloquence, he slips his hand under my arm and leads me somewhere. I walk on, with him, and even before we have crossed the bridge, I am asleep again. Through my closed eyelids I can vaguely see the Doctor's expressive gestures, the smile under his black beard, and I try to understand, without success, his ultimate point—which he must have triumphantly revealed, for he now stands with arms outstretched. We have been walking side by side for I don't know how long, engrossed in a conversation at cross-purposes, when all of a sudden I wake up completely. Dr. Gotard has gone; it is quite dark, but only because my eyes are shut. When I open them, I find that I am in our room and don't know how I got there.

An even more dramatic example: at lunchtime, I enter a restaurant in town, which is full and very noisy. Whom do I meet in the middle of it, at a table sagging under the weight of dishes? My father. All eyes are on him, while he, animated, almost ecstatic with pleasure, his diamond tiepin shining, turns in all directions, making fulsome conversation with everybody at once. With false bravado, which I observe with the greatest misgivings, he keeps ordering new dishes, which are then stacked on the table. He gathers them around him with glee, chewing and speaking at the same time, he mimes his great satisfaction with this feast and follows with adoring eyes Adam, the waiter, to whom, with an ingratiating smile, he gives more orders. And when the waiter, waving his napkin, rushes to get them, Father turns to the company and calls them to witness the irresistible charm of Adam, the Ganymede.

"A boy in a million," Father exclaims with a happy smile, half-closing his eyes, "a ministering angel! You must agree, gentlemen, that he is a charmer!"

I leave in disgust, unnoticed by Father. Had he been put there by the management of the restaurant in order to amuse the guests, he could not behave in a more ostentatious way. My head heavy with drowsiness, I stumble through the streets toward the Sanatorium. On a pillar box I rest my head and take a short siesta. At last, groping in darkness, I find the gate and go in. Our room is dark. I press the light switch, but there is no current. A cold draft comes from the window. The bed creaks in the darkness.

My father lifts his head from the pillows and says, "Ah, Joseph, Joseph! I have been lying here for two days without any attention. The bells are out of order, no one has been to see me, and my own son has left me, a very sick man, to run after girls in the town. Look how my heart is thumping!"

How do I reconcile all this? Has Father been sitting in the restaurant, driven there by an unhealthy greed, or has he been lying in bed feeling very ill? Are there two fathers? Nothing of the kind. The problem is the quick decomposition of time no longer watched with incessant vigilance.

We all know that time, this undisciplined element, holds itself within bounds but precariously, thanks to unceasing cultivation, meticulous care, and a continuous regulation and correction of its excesses. Free of this vigilance, it immediately begins to do tricks, run wild, play irresponsible practical jokes, and indulge in crazy clowning. The incongruity of our private times becomes evident. My father's time and my own no longer coincide.

Incidentally, the accusation that my father has made is completely groundless. I have not been chasing after girls. Swaying like a drunkard from one bout of sleep to another, I can hardly pay attention, even in my more wakeful moments, to the local ladies.

Moreover, the chronic darkness in the streets does not allow me to see faces clearly. What I have been able to observe—being a young man who still has a certain amount of interest in such things—is the peculiar way in which these girls walk.

Heedless of obstacles, obeying only some inner rhythm, each one walks in an inexorably straight line, as if along a thread that she seems to unwind from an invisible skein. This linear trot is full of mincing accuracy and measured grace. Each girl seems to carry inside her an individual rule, wound tight like a spring.

Walking thus, straight ahead, with concentration and dignity, they seem to have only one worry—not to break the rule, not to make any mistake, not to stray either to the right or to the left. And then it becomes clear to me that what they so conscientiously carry within themselves is an idée fixe of their own excellence, which the strength of their conviction almost transforms into reality. It is risked anticipation, without any guarantee: an untouchable dogma, held high, impervious to doubt.

What imperfections and blemishes, what retroussé or flat noses, what freckles or spots are smuggled under the bold flag of that fiction! There is no ugliness or vulgarity that cannot be lifted up to a fictional heaven of perfection by the flight of such a belief.

Sanctified by it, bodies become distinctly more beautiful, and feet, already shapely and graceful in their spotless footwear, speak eloquently, their fluid, shiny pacing monologue explaining the greatness of an idea that the closed faces are too proud to express. The girls keep their hands in the pockets of their short, tight jackets. In the cafes and in the theater, they cross their legs, uncovered to the knee, and hold them in provocative silence.

So much for one of the peculiarities of this town. I have already mentioned the black vegetation of the region. A certain kind of black fern deserves special mention: enormous bunches of it in vases are in the windows of every apartment here, and every public place. The fern is almost the symbol of mourning, the town's funeral crest.

IV

Conditions in the Sanatorium are becoming daily more insufferable. It has to be admitted that we have fallen into a trap. Since my arrival, when a semblance of hospitable care was displayed for the newcomer, the management of the Sanatorium has not taken the trouble to give us even the illusion of any kind of professional supervision. We are simply left to our own devices. Nobody caters to our needs. I have noticed, for instance, that the wires of the electric bells have been cut just behind the doors and lead nowhere. There is no service. The corridors are dark and silent by day and by night. I have a strong suspicion that we are the only guests in this Sanatorium and that the mysterious or discreet looks with which the chambermaid closes the doors of the rooms on entering or leaving are simply mystification.

I sometimes feel a strong desire to open each door wide and leave it ajar, so that the miserable intrigue in which we have got ourselves involved can be exposed.

And yet I am not quite convinced that my suspicions are justified. Sometimes, late at night, I meet Dr. Gotard in a corridor, hurrying somewhere in a white coverall, with an enema bottle in his hand, preceded by the chambermaid. It would be difficult to stop him then and demand an explanation.

Were it not for the restaurant and pastry shop in town, one might starve to death. So far, I have not succeeded in getting a second bed for our room. There is no question of the sheets being changed.

One has to admit that the general neglect of civilized habits has affected both of us, too. To get into bed dressed and with shoes on was once, for me—a civilized person—unthinkable. Yet now, when I return home late, sleep drunk, the room is in semidarkness and the curtains at the window billow in a cold breeze. Half-dazed, I tumble onto the bed and bury myself in the eiderdown. Thus I sleep for irregular stretches of time, for days or weeks, wandering through empty landscapes of sleep, always on the way, always on the steep roads of respiration, sometimes sliding lightly and gracefully from gentle slopes, then climbing laboriously up the cliffs of snoring. At their summit I embrace the horizons of the rocky and empty desert of sleep. At some point, somewhere on the sharp turn of a snore, I wake up half-conscious and feel the body of my father at the foot of the bed. He lies there curled up, small as a kitten. I fall asleep again, with my mouth open, and the vast panorama of mountain landscape glides past me majestically.

In the shop, my father displays an energetic activity, transacting business and straining all his capacities to attract customers. His cheeks are flushed with animation, his eyes shine. In the Sanatorium he is very sick, as sick as during his last weeks at home. It is obvious that the end must be imminent. In a weak voice he addresses me: "You should look into the store more often, Joseph. The shop assistants are robbing us. You can see that I am no longer equal to the task. I have been lying here sick for weeks, and the shop is being neglected, left to run itself. Was there any mail from home?"

I begin to regret this whole undertaking. Perhaps we were misled by skillful advertising when we decided to send Father here. Time put back—it sounded good, but what does it come to in reality? Does anyone here get time at its full value, a true time, time cut off from a fresh bolt of cloth, smelling of newness and dye? Quite the contrary. It is used-up time, worn out by other people, a shabby time full of holes, like a sieve.

No wonder. It is time, as it were, regurgitated—if I may be forgiven this expression: secondhand time. God help us all!

And then there is the matter of the highly improper manipulation of time. The shameful tricks, the penetration of time's mechanism from behind, the hazardous fingering of its wicked secrets! Sometimes one feels like banging the table and exclaiming, "Enough of this! Keep off time, time is untouchable, one must not provoke it! Isn't it enough for you to have space? Space is for human beings, you can swing about in space, turn somersaults, fall down, jump from star to star, but for goodness' sake, don't tamper with time!"

On the other hand, can I be expected to give notice to Dr. Gotard? However miserable Father's existence, I am able to see him, to be with him, to talk to him. In fact, I should be infinitely grateful to Dr. Gotard.

Several times, I have wanted to speak openly to Dr. Gotard, but he is elusive. He has just gone to the restaurant, says the chambermaid. I turn to go there, when she runs after me to say that she was wrong, that Dr. Gotard is in the operating theater. Hurrying upstairs, I wonder what kind of operations can be performed here; I enter the anteroom and am told to wait. Dr. Gotard will be with me in a moment, he had just finished the operation, he is washing his hands. I can almost visualize him: short, taking long steps, his coat open, hurrying through a succession of hospital wards. After a while, what am I told? Dr. Gotard had not been there at all, no operation has been performed there for many years. Dr. Gotard is asleep in his room, his black beard sticking up into the air. The room fills with his snores as if with clouds that lift him in his bed, ever higher and higher—a great pathetic ascension on waves of snores and voluminous bedding.

Even stranger things happen here—things that I try to conceal from myself and that are quite fantastic in their absurdity. Whenever I leave our room, I have the impression that someone who has been standing behind the door moves quickly away and turns a corner. Or somebody seems to be walking in front of me, not looking back. It is not a nurse. I know who it is! "Mother!" I exclaim, in a voice trembling with excitement, and my mother turns her face to me and looks at me for a moment with a pleading smile. Where am I? What is happening here? What maze have I become entangled in?

V

I don't know why—it may be the time of year—but the days are growing more severe in color, darker and blacker. It seems as if one were looking at the world through black glasses.

The landscape is now like the bottom of an enormous aquarium full of watery ink. Trees, people, and houses merge, swaying like underwater plants against the background of the inky deep.

Packs of black dogs are often seen in the vicinity of the Sanatorium. Of all shapes and sizes, they run at dusk along the roads and paths, engrossed in their own affairs, silent, tense, and alert.

They run in twos and threes, with outstretched necks, their ears pricked up, whining softly in plaintive tones that escape from their throats as if against their will—signals of the highest nervousness. Absorbed in running, hurrying, always on their way somewhere, always pursuing some mysterious goal, they hardly notice the passersby. Occasionally one shoots out a glance while running past, and then the black and intelligent eyes are full of a rage contained only by haste. At times the dogs even rush at one's feet, succumbing to their anger, with heads held low and ominous snarls, but soon think better of it and turn away.

Nothing is to be done about this plague of dogs, but why does the management of the Sanatorium keep an enormous Alsatian on a chain—a terror of a beast, a werewolf of truly demoniacal ferocity? I shiver with fear whenever I pass his kennel, by which he stands immobile on his short chain, a halo of matted hair bristling around his head, bewhiskered and bearded, his powerful jaws displaying the whole apparatus of his long teeth. He does not bark, but his wild face contorts at the sight of a human being. He stiffens with an expression of boundless fury and, slowly raising his horrible muzzle, breaks into a low, fervent, convulsive howl that comes from the very depths of his hatred—a howl of despair and lament of his temporary impotence.

My father walks past the beast with indifference whenever we go out together. As for myself, I am deeply shaken when confronted by the dog's impotent hatred. I am now some two heads taller than Father who, small and thin, trots at my side with the mincing gait of a very old man.

Approaching the city square one day, we noticed an extraordinary commotion. Crowds of people filled the streets. We heard the incredible news that an enemy army had entered the town.

In consternation, people exchanged alarmist and contradictory news that was hard to credit. A war not preceded by diplomatic activity? A war amid blissful peace? A war against whom and for what reason? We were told that the enemy incursion gave heart to a group of discontented townspeople, who have come out in the open, armed, to terrorize the peaceful inhabitants. We noticed, in fact, a group of these activists, in black civilian clothing with white straps across their breasts, advancing in silence, their guns at the ready. The crowd fell back on to the pavements, as they marched by, flashing from under their hats ironic dark looks, in which there was a touch of superiority, a glimmer of malicious and perverse enjoyment, as if they could hardly stop themselves from bursting into laughter. Some of them were recognized by the crowd, but the exclamations of relief were at once stilled by the sight of rifle barrels. They passed by, not challenging anybody. All the streets filled at once with a frightened, grimly silent crowd. A dull hubbub floated over the city. We seemed to hear a distant rumble of artillery and the rattle of gun carriages.

"I must get to the shop," said my father, pale but determined. "You need not come with me," he added. "You will be in my way. Go back to the Sanatorium."

The pull of cowardice made me obey him. I saw my father trying to squeeze himself through the compact wall of bodies in the crowd and lost sight of him.

I broke into a run along side streets and alleys, and hurried toward the upper part of the town. I realized that by going uphill I might be able to avoid the center, now packed solid by people.

Farther up, the crowd thinned and at last completely disappeared. I walked quietly along empty streets to the municipal park. Streetlamps were lit there and burned with a dark bluish flame, the color of asphodels, the flowers of mourning. Each light was surrounded by a swarm of dancing june bugs, heavy as bullets, carried on their slanting flight by vibrating wings. The fallen were struggling clumsily in the sand, their backs arched, hunched beneath the hard shields under which they were trying to fold the delicate membranes of their wings. On grassy plots and paths people were walking along, engrossed in carefree conversation.

The trees at the far end of the park drooped into the courtyards of houses that were built on lower ground on the other side of the park wall. I strolled along that wall on the park side, where it reached only to my breast; on the other side, it fell in escarpments to the level of courtyards. In one place, a ramp of firm soil rose from the courtyards to the top of the wall. There I crossed the wall without difficulty and squeezed between houses into a street. As I had expected, I found myself almost facing the Sanatorium; its back was outlined clearly in a black frame of trees. As usual, I opened the gate in the iron fence and saw from a distance the watchdog at his post. As usual, I shivered with aversion and wished to pass by him as quickly as possible, so as not to have to listen to his howl of hatred; but I suddenly noticed that he was unchained and was circling toward the courtyard, barking hollowly and trying to cut me off.

Rigid with fright, I retreated and, instinctively looking for shelter, crept into a small arbor, sure that all my efforts to evade the beast would be in vain. The shaggy animal was leaping toward me, his muzzle already pushing into the arbor. I was trapped. Horror-struck, I then saw that the dog was on a long chain that he had unwound to its full length, and that the inside of the arbor was beyond the reach of his claws. Sick with fear, I was too weak to feel any relief. Reeling, almost fainting, I raised my eyes. I had never before seen the beast from so near, and only now did I see him clearly. How great is the power of prejudice! How powerful the hold of fear! How blind had I been! It was not a dog, it was a man. A chained man, whom, by a simplifying metaphoric wholesale error, I had taken for a dog. I don't want to be misunderstood. He was a dog, certainly, but a dog in human shape. The quality of a dog is an inner quality and can be manifested as well in human as in animal shape. He who was standing in front of me in the entrance to the arbor, his jaws wide open, his teeth bared in a terrible growl, was a man of middle height, with a black beard. His face was yellow, bony; his eyes were black, evil, and unhappy. Judging by his black suit and the shape of his beard, one might take him for an intellectual or a scholar. He might have been Dr. Gotard's unsuccessful elder brother. But that first impression was false. The large hands stained with glue, the two brutal and cynical furrows running down from his nostrils and disappearing into his beard, the vulgar horizontal wrinkles on the low forehead quickly dispelled that first impression. He looked more like a bookbinder, a tub-thumper, a vocal party member—a violent man, given to dark, sudden passions. And it was this—the passionate depth, the convulsive bristling of all his fibres, the mad fury of his barking when the end of a stick was pointed at him—that made him a hundred percent dog.

If I tried to escape through the back of the arbor, I thought, I would completely elude his reach and could walk along a side path to the gate of the Sanatorium. I was about to put my leg over the railing when I suddenly stopped. I felt it would be too cruel simply to go away and leave the dog behind, possessed by his helpless and boundless fury. I could imagine his terrible disappointment, his inexpressible pain as I escaped from his trap, free once and for all from his clutches. I decided to stay.

I stepped forward and said quietly, "Please calm down. I shall unchain you."

His face, distorted by spasms of growling, became whole again, smooth and almost human. I went up to him without fear and unfastened the buckle of his collar. We walked side by side. The bookbinder was wearing a decent black suit but had bare feet. I tried to talk to him, but a confused babble was all I heard in reply. Only his eyes, black and eloquent, expressed a wild spurt of gratitude, of submission, which filled me with awe. Whenever he stumbled on a stone or a clod of earth, the shock made his face shrivel and contract with fear, and that expression was followed by one of rage. I would then bring him to order with a harsh comradely rebuke. I even patted him on the back. An astonished, suspicious, unbelieving smile tried to form on his face. Ah, how hard to bear was this terrible friendship! How frightening was this uncanny sympathy! How could I get rid of this man striding along with me, his eyes expressing his total submission, following the slightest changes in my face? I could not show impatience.

I pulled out my wallet and said in a matter-of-fact tone, "You probably need some money. I will lend you some with pleasure." But at the sight of my wallet his look became so unexpectedly wild that I put it away again as quickly as I could. For quite some time afterward, he could not calm himself and his features continued to be distorted by more spasms of growling. No, I could not stand this any longer. Anything, but not this. Matters were already confused and entangled enough.

I then noticed the glare of fire over the town: my father was somewhere in the thick of a revolution or in a burning shop. Dr. Gotard was unavailable. And to cap it all, my mother had appeared, incognito, on that mysterious errand! These were the elements of some great and obscure intrigue, which was hemming me in. I must escape, I thought, escape at any cost. Anywhere. I must drop this horrible friendship with a bookbinder who smells of dog and who is watching me all the time. We were now standing in front of the Sanatorium.

"Come to my room, please," I said with a polite gesture. Civilized gestures fascinated him, soothed his wildness. I let him enter my room first and gave him a chair.

"I'll go to the restaurant and get some brandy," I said.

He got up, terrified, and wanted to follow me.

I calmed his fears with gentle firmness. "You will sit here and wait for me," I said in a deep, sonorous voice, which concealed fear. He sat down again with a tentative smile.

I went out and walked slowly along the corridor, then downstairs and across the hall leading to the entrance door; I passed the gate, strode across the courtyard, banged the iron gate shut, and only then began to run, breathlessly, my heart thumping, my temples throbbing, along the dark avenue leading to the railway station.

Images raced through my head, each more horrible than the next. The impatience of the monster dog; his fear and despair when he realized that I had cheated him; another attack of fury, another bout of rage breaking out with unchecked force. My father's return to the Sanatorium, his unsuspecting knock at the door, and his confrontation with the terrible beast.

Luckily, in fact, Father was no longer alive; he could not really be reached, I thought with relief, and saw in front of me the black row of railway carriages ready to depart.

I got into one of them, and the train, as if it had been waiting for me, slowly started to move, without a whistle.

Through the window the great valley, filled with dark rustling forests—against which the walls of the Sanatorium seemed white—moved and turned slowly once again. Farewell, Father. Farewell, town that I shall never see again.

Since then, I have traveled continuously. I have made my home in that train, and everybody puts up with me as I wander from coach to coach. The compartments, enormous as rooms, are full of rubbish and straw, and cold drafts pierce them on gray, colorless days.

My suit became torn and ragged. I have been given the shabby uniform of a railway man. My face is bandaged with a dirty rag, because one of my cheeks is swollen. I sit on the straw, dozing, and when hungry, I stand in the corridor outside a second-class compartment and sing. People throw small coins into my hat: a black railway-man's hat, its visor half-torn away.

1937

F. Scott Fitzgerald

1896–1940

The disjunction in Francis Scott Key Fitzgerald's family background was the reverse of D.H. Lawrence's: in "Scotty's" case, paternal gentility and maternal (potato-famine Irish) rawness. Born in St Paul, Minnesota, Fitzgerald approached his education, first at a distinguished prep school, then at Princeton, with the determination to match social success with his good looks. Almost non-existent academic achievement forced him to leave university, but in 1916 he returned to Princeton, where, under the influence of Edmund Wilson, he read voluminously and wrote the draft of a novel, *The Romantic Egoist*, later published as his first, enormously successful work, *This Side of Paradise* (1920). During a spell in the army he met the rebellious Zelda Sayre (from a conservative family in Montgomery, Alabama), in his rapturous view "daring, beautiful, and golden—a top girl." After their marriage, the Fitzgerald mixture of talent, beauty, and boundless need became heady and toxic: high social frenzy in New York, Paris, and the Riviera; compulsive overspending creating the need to write for money; and the suspicion that genuine artistic success would elude him. In the early twenties, besides *The Beautiful and the Damned* (1922), he published story after story, mostly in the *Saturday Evening Post*, collected in *Flappers and Philosophers* (1921) and *Tales of the Jazz Age* (1922). He briefly transmuted his personal fascination with loss and corruption into *The Great Gatsby* (1925—the same year as Hemingway's *In Our Time*), but alcohol, depression, and Zelda's deepening mental abyss proved catastrophic. Despite a break in the downward spiral of his career and personal life in 1937—he wrote screenplays for Metro-Goldwyn-Mayer, and was able to pay some debts—the Fitzgerald decline was irreversible. His final novel, *The Last Tycoon* (1941), was unfinished at his death, and his social and literary reputation was in shreds. Fitzgerald has been so thoroughly identified with the boozy moods of the "Jazz Age" that his superb articulations as a modernist, above all in the densely historical *Tender Is the Night* (1934), have been blurred. Although his style, as in "Babylon Revisited," is more expansive and ostensibly more traditional than Hemingway's, it registers the frailties of the self, loss, and the lack of American "repose" with overwhelming power.

Babylon Revisited

I

"And where's Mr Campbell?" Charlie asked.

"Gone to Switzerland. Mr Campbell's a pretty sick man, Mr Wales."

"I'm sorry to hear that. And George Hardt?" Charlie inquired.

"Back in America, gone to work."

"And where is the Snow Bird?"

"He was in here last week. Anyway, his friend, Mr Schaeffer, is in Paris."

Two familiar names from the long list of a year and a half ago. Charlie scribbled an address in his notebook and tore out the page.

"If you see Mr Schaeffer, give him this," he said. "It's my brother-in-law's address. I haven't settled on a hotel yet."

He was not really disappointed to find Paris was so empty. But the stillness in the Ritz bar was strange and portentous. It was not an American bar any more—he felt polite in it, and not as if he owned it. It had gone back into France. He felt the stillness from the moment he got out of the taxi and saw the doorman, usually in a frenzy of activity at this hour, gossiping with a *chasseur* by the servants' entrance.

Passing through the corridor, he heard only a single, bored voice in the once-clamorous women's room. When he turned into the bar he travelled the twenty feet of green carpet with his eyes fixed straight ahead by old habit; and then, with his foot firmly on the rail, he turned and surveyed the room, encountering only a single pair of eyes that fluttered up from a newspaper in the corner. Charlie asked for the head barman, Paul, who in the latter days of the bull market had come to work in his own custom-built car—disembarking, however, with due nicety at the nearest corner. But Paul was at his country house today and Alix giving him information.

"No, no more," Charlie said, "I'm going slow these days."

Alix congratulated him: "You were going pretty strong a couple of years ago."

"I'll stick to it all right," Charlie assured him. "I've stuck to it for over a year and half now."

"How do you find conditions in America?"

"I haven't been to America for months. I'm in business in Prague, representing a couple of concerns there. They don't know about me down there."

Alix smiled.

"Remember the night of George Hardt's bachelor dinner here?" said Charlie. "By the way, what's become of Claude Fessenden?"

Alix lowered his voice confidentially: "He's in Paris, but he doesn't come here any more. Paul doesn't allow it. He ran up a bill of thirty thousand francs, charging all his drinks and his lunches, and usually his dinner, for more than a year. And when Paul finally told him he had to pay, he gave him a bad cheque."

Alix shook his head sadly.

"I don't understand it, such a dandy fellow. Now he's all bloated up—" He made a plump apple of his hands.

Charlie watched a group of strident queens installing themselves in a corner.

"Nothing affects them," he thought. "Stocks rise and fall, people loaf or work, but they go on forever." The place oppressed him. He called for the dice and shook with Alix for the drink.

"Here for long, Mr Wales?"

"I'm here for four or five days to see my little girl."

"Oh-h! You have a little girl?"

Outside, the fire-red, gas-blue, ghost-green signs shone smokily through the tranquil rain. It was late afternoon and the streets were in movement; the bistros gleamed. At the corner of the Boulevard des Capucines he took a taxi. The Place de la Concorde moved by in pink majesty; they crossed the logical Seine, and Charlie felt the sudden provincial quality of the Left Bank.

Charlie directed his taxi to the Avenue de l'Opera, which was out of his way. But he wanted to see the blue hour spread over the magnificent façade, and imagine that the cab horns, playing endlessly the first few bars of *Le Plus que lent*, were the trumpets of the Second Empire. They were closing the iron grille in front of Brentano's Book-store, and people were already at dinner behind the trim little bourgeois hedge of Duval's. He had never eaten at a really cheap restaurant in Paris. Five-course dinner, four francs fifty, eighteen cents, wine included. For some odd reason he wished that he had.

As they rolled on to the Left Bank and he felt its sudden provincialism, he thought, "I spoiled this city for myself. I didn't realize it, but the days came along one after another, and then two years were gone, and everything was gone, and I was gone."

He was thirty-five, and good to look at. The Irish mobility of his face was sobered by a deep wrinkle between his eyes. As he rang his brother-in-law's bell in the Rue Palatine, the wrinkle deepened till it pulled down his brows; he felt a cramping sensation in his belly. From behind the maid who opened the door darted a lovely little girl of nine who shrieked "Daddy!" and flew up, struggling like a fish, into his arms. She pulled his head around by one ear and set her cheek against his.

"My old pie," he said.

"Oh, daddy, daddy, daddy, daddy, dads, dads, dads!"

She drew him into the salon, where the family waited, a boy and a girl his daughter's age, his sister-in-law and her husband. He greeted Marion with his voice pitched carefully to avoid either feigned enthusiasm or dislike, but the response was more frankly tepid, though she minimized her expression of unalterable distrust by directing her regard toward his child. The two men clasped hands in a friendly way and Lincoln Peters rested his for a moment on Charlie's shoulder.

The room was warm and comfortably American. The three children moved intimately about, playing through the yellow oblongs that led to other rooms; the cheer of six o'clock spoke in the eager smacks of the fire and the sounds of French activity in the kitchen. But Charlie did not relax; his heart sat up rigidly in his body and he drew confidence from his daughter, who from time to time came close to him, holding in her arms the doll he had brought.

"Really extremely well," he declared in answer to Lincoln's question. "There's a lot of business there that isn't moving at all, but we're doing even better than ever. In fact, damn well. I'm bringing my sister over from America next month to keep house for me. My income last year was bigger than it was when I had money. You see, the Czechs—"

His boasting was for a specific purpose; but after a moment, seeing a faint restiveness in Lincoln's eye, he changed the subject:

"Those are fine children of yours, well brought up, good manners."

"We think Honoria's a great little girl too."

Marion Peters came back from the kitchen. She was a tall woman with worried eyes, who had once possessed a fresh American loveliness. Charlie had never been sensitive to it and was always surprised when people spoke of how pretty she had been. From the first there had been an instinctive antipathy between them.

"Well, how do you find Honoria?" she asked.

"Wonderful. I was astonished how much she's grown in ten months. All the children are looking well."

"We haven't had a doctor for a year. How do you like being back in Paris?"

"It seems very funny to see so few Americans around."

"I'm delighted," Marion said vehemently. "Now at least you can go into a store without their assuming you're a millionaire. We've suffered like everybody, but on the whole it's a good deal pleasanter."

"But it was nice while it lasted," Charlie said. "We were sort of royalty, almost infallible, with a sort of magic around us. In the bar this afternoon"—he stumbled, seeing his mistake—"there wasn't a man I knew."

She looked at him keenly. "I should think you'd have had enough of bars."

"I only stayed a minute. I take one drink every afternoon, and no more."

"Don't you want a cocktail before dinner?" Lincoln asked.

"I take only one drink every afternoon, and I've had that."

"I hope you keep to it," said Marion.

Her dislike was evident in the coldness with which she spoke, but Charlie only smiled; he had larger plans. Her very aggressiveness gave him an advantage, and he knew enough to wait. He wanted them to initiate the discussion of what they knew had brought him to Paris.

At dinner he couldn't decide whether Honoria was most like him or her mother. Fortunate if she didn't combine the traits of both that had brought them to disaster. A great wave of protectiveness went over him. He thought he knew what to do for her. He believed in character; he wanted to jump back a whole generation and trust in character again as the eternally valuable element. Everything else wore out.

He left soon after dinner, but not to go home. He was curious to see Paris by night with clearer and more judicious eyes than those of other days. He bought a *strapontin* for the Casino and watched Josephine Baker go through her chocolate arabesques.

After an hour he left and strolled toward Montmartre, up the Rue Pigalle in the Place Blanche. The rain had stopped and there were a few people in evening clothes disembarking from taxis in front of cabarets, and *cocottes* prowling singly or in pairs, and many Negroes. He passed a lighted door from which issued music, and stopped with the sense of familiarity; it was Bricktop's, where he had parted with so many hours and so much money. A few doors farther on he found another ancient rendezvous and incautiously put his head inside. Immediately an eager orchestra burst into sound, a pair of professional dancers leaped to their feet and a maître d'hôtel swooped toward him, crying, "Crowd just arriving, sir!" But he withdrew quickly.

"You have to be damn drunk," he thought.

Zelli's was closed, the bleak and sinister cheap hotels surrounding it were dark; up in the Rue Blanche there was more light and a local, colloquial French crowd. The Poet's Cave had disappeared, but the two great mouths of the Café of Heaven and the Café of Hell still yawned—even devoured, as he watched, the meager contents of a tourist bus—a German, a Japanese, and an American couple who glanced at him with frightened eyes.

So much for the effort and ingenuity of Montmartre. All the catering to vice and waste was on an utterly childish scale, and he suddenly realized the meaning of the word "dissipate"—to dissipate into thin air; to make nothing out of something. In the little hours of the night every move from place to place was an enormous human jump, an increase of paying for the privilege of slower and slower motion.

He remembered thousand-franc notes given to an orchestra for playing a single number, hundred-franc notes tossed to a doorman for calling a cab.

But it hadn't been given for nothing.

It had been given, even the most wildly squandered sum, as an offering to destiny that he might not remember the things most worth remembering, the things that now he would always remember—his child taken from his control, his wife escaped to a grave in Vermont.

In the glare of a *brasserie* a woman spoke to him. He bought her some eggs and coffee, and then, eluding her encouraging stare, gave her a twenty-franc note and took a taxi to his hotel.

II

He woke upon a fine fall day—football weather. The depression of yesterday was gone and he liked the people on the streets. At noon he sat opposite Honoria at Le

Grand Vatel, the only restaurant he could think of not reminiscent of champagne dinners and long luncheons that began at two and ended in a blurred and vague twilight.

"Now, how about vegetables? Oughtn't you to have some vegetables?"

"Well, yes."

"Here's *épinards* and *chou-fleur* and *carrots* and *haricots*."

"I'd like *chou-fleur*."

"Wouldn't you like to have two vegetables?"

"I usually only have one at lunch."

The waiter was pretending to be inordinately fond of children. "*Qu'elle est mignonne la petite! Elle parle exactement comme une Française.*"

"How about dessert? Shall we wait and see?"

The waiter disappeared. Honoria looked at her father expectantly.

"What are we going to do?"

"First, we're going to that toy store in the Rue Saint-Honoré and buy you anything you like. And then we're going to the vaudeville at the Empire."

She hesitated. "I like it about the vaudeville, but not the toy store."

"Why not?"

"Well, you brought me this doll." She had it with her. "And I've got lots of things. And we're not rich any more, are we?"

"We never were. But today you are to have anything you want."

"All right," she agreed resignedly.

When there had been her mother and a French nurse he had been inclined to be strict; now he extended himself, reached out for a new tolerance; he must be both parents to her and not shut any of her out of communication.

"I want to get to know you," he said gravely. "First let me introduce myself. My name is Charles J. Wales, of Prague."

"Oh, daddy!" her voice cracked with laughter.

"And who are you, please?" he persisted, and she accepted a rôle immediately: "Honoria Wales, Rue Palatine, Paris."

"Married or single?"

"No, not married. Single."

He indicated the doll. "But I see you have a child, madame."

Unwilling to disinherit it, she took it to her heart and thought quickly: "Yes, I've been married, but I'm not married now. My husband is dead."

He went on quickly, "And the child's name?"

"Simone. That's after my best friend at school."

"I'm very pleased that you're doing so well at school."

"I'm third this month," she boasted. "Elsie"—that was her cousin—"is only about eighteenth, and Richard is about at the bottom."

"You like Richard and Elsie don't you?"

"Oh, yes. I like Richard quite well and I like her all right."

Cautiously and casually he asked: "And Aunt Marion and Uncle Lincoln—which do you like best?"

"Oh, Uncle Lincoln, I guess."

He was increasingly aware of her presence. As they came in, a murmur of ". . . adorable" followed them, and now the people at the next table bent all their silences upon her, staring as if she were something no more conscious than a flower.

"Why don't I live with you?" she asked suddenly. "Because mamma's dead?"

"You must stay here and learn more French. It would have been hard for daddy to take care of you so well."

"I don't really need much taking care of any more. I do everything for myself."

Going out of the restaurant, a man and a woman unexpectedly hailed him.

"Well, the old Wales!"

"Hello there, Lorraine. . . . Dunc."

Sudden ghosts out of the past: Duncan Schaeffer, a friend from college. Lorraine Quarrles, a lovely, pale blonde of thirty; one of a crowd who had helped them make months into days in the lavish times of three years ago.

"My husband couldn't come this year," she said, in answer to his question. "We're poor as hell. So he gave me two hundred a month and told me I could do my worst on that. . . . This your little girl?"

"What about coming back and sitting down?" Duncan asked.

"Can't do it." He was glad for an excuse. As always, he felt Lorraine's passionate, provocative attraction, but his own rhythm was different now.

"Well, how about dinner?" she asked.

"I'm not free. Give me your address and let me call you."

"Charlie, I believe you're sober," she said judicially. "I honestly believe he's sober, Dunc. Pinch him and see if he's sober."

Charlie indicated Honoria with his head. They both laughed.

"What's your address?" said Duncan skeptically.

He hesitated, unwilling to give the name of his hotel.

"I'm not settled yet. I'd better call you. We're going to see the vaudeville at the Empire."

"There! That's what I want to do," Lorraine said." I want to see some clowns and acrobats and jugglers. That's just what we'll do, Dunc."

"We've got to do an errand first," said Charlie. "Perhaps we'll see you there."

"All right, you snob. . . . Good-by, beautiful little girl."

"Good-by."

Honoria bobbed politely.

Somehow, an unwelcome encounter. They liked him because he was functioning, because he was serious; they wanted to see him, because he was stronger than they were now, because they wanted to draw a certain sustenance from his strength.

At the Empire, Honoria proudly refused to sit upon her father's folded coat. She was already an individual with a code of her own, and Charlie was more and more absorbed by the desire of putting a little of himself into her before she crystallized utterly. It was hopeless to try to know her in so short a time.

Between the acts they came upon Duncan and Lorraine in the lobby where the band was playing.

"Have a drink?"

"All right, but not up at the bar. We'll take a table."

"The perfect father."

Listening abstractedly to Lorraine, Charlie watched Honoria's eyes leave their table, and he followed them wistfully about the room, wondering what they saw. He met her glance and she smiled.

"I liked that lemonade," she said.

What had she said? What had he expected? Going home in a taxi afterward, he pulled her over until her head rested against his chest.

"Darling, do you ever think about your mother?"

"Yes, sometimes," she answered vaguely.

"I don't want you to forget her. Have you got a picture of her?"

"Yes, I think so. Anyhow, Aunt Marion has. Why don't you want me to forget her?"

"She loved you very much."

"I loved her too."

They were silent for moment.

"Daddy, I want to come and live with you," she said suddenly.

His heart leaped; he had wanted it to come like this.

"Aren't you perfectly happy?"

"Yes, but I love you better than anybody. And you love me better than anybody, don't you, now that mummy's dead?"

"Of course I do. But you won't always like me best, honey. You'll grow up and meet somebody your own age and go marry him and forget you ever had a daddy."

"Yes, that's true," she agreed tranquilly.

He didn't go in. He was coming back at nine o'clock and he wanted to keep himself fresh and new for the thing he must say then.

"When you're safe inside, just show yourself in that window."

"All right. Good-by, dads, dads, dads, dads."

He waited in the dark street until she appeared, all warm and glowing, in the window above and kissed her fingers out into the night.

III

They were waiting. Marion sat behind the coffee service in a dignified black dinner dress that just faintly suggested mourning. Lincoln was walking up and down with the animation of one who had already been talking. They were as anxious as he was to get into the question. He opened it almost immediately:

"I suppose you know what I want to see you about—why I really came to Paris."

Marion played with the black stars on her necklace and frowned.

"I'm awfully anxious to have a home," he continued. "And I'm awfully anxious to have Honoria in it. I appreciate your taking in Honoria for her mother's sake, but things have changed now"—he hesitated and then continued more forcibly—"changed radically with me, and I want to ask you to reconsider the matter. It would be silly for me to deny that about three years ago I was acting badly—"

Marion looked up at him with hard eyes.

"—but all that's over. As I told you, I haven't had more than a drink a day for over a year, and I take that drink deliberately, so that the idea of alcohol won't get too big in my imagination. You see the idea?"

"No," said Marion succinctly.

"It's a sort of stunt I set myself. It keeps the matter in proportion."

"I get you," said Lincoln. "You don't want to admit it's got any attraction for you."

"Something like that. Sometimes I forget and don't take it. But I try to take it. Anyway, I couldn't afford to drink in my position. The people I represent are more than satisfied with what I've done, and I'm bringing my sister over from Burlington to keep house for me, and I want awfully to have Honoria too. You know that even when her mother and I weren't getting along well we never let anything that happened touch Honoria. I know she's fond of me and I know I'm able to take care of her and—well, there you are. How do you feel about it?"

He knew that now he would have to take a beating. It would last an hour or two hours, and it would be difficult, but if he modulated his inevitable resentment to the chastened attitude of the reformed sinner, he might win his point in the end.

Keep your temper, he told himself. You don't want to be justified. You want Honoria.

Lincoln spoke first: "We've been talking it over ever since we got your letter last month. We're happy to have Honoria here. She's a dear little thing, and we're glad to be able to help her, but of course that isn't the question—"

Marion interrupted suddenly. "How long are you going to stay sober, Charlie?" she asked.

"Permanently, I hope."

"How can anybody count on that?"

"You know I never did drink heavily until I gave up business and came over here with nothing to do. Then Helen and I began to run around with—"

"Please leave Helen out of it. I can't bear to hear you talk about her like that."

He stared at her grimly; he had never been certain how fond of each other the sisters were in life.

"My drinking only lasted about a year and a half—from the time we came over until I—collapsed."

"It was time enough."

"It was time enough," he agreed.

"My duty is entirely to Helen," she said. "I try to think what she would have wanted me to do. Frankly, from the night you did that terrible thing you haven't really existed for me. I can't help that. She was my sister."

"Yes."

"When she was dying she asked me to look out for Honoria. If you hadn't been in a sanitarium then, it might have helped matters."

He had no answer.

"I'll never in my life be able to forget that morning when Helen knocked at my door, soaked to the skin and shivering and said you'd locked her out."

Charlie gripped the sides of his chair. This was more difficult than he expected; he wanted to launch out into a long expostulation and explanation, but he only said: "The night I locked her out—" and she interrupted, "I don't feel up to going over that again."

After a moment's silence Lincoln said: "We're getting off the subject. You want Marion to set aside her legal guardianship and give you Honoria. I think the main point for her is whether she has confidence in you or not."

"I don't blame Marion," Charlie said slowly, "but I think she can have entire confidence in me. I had a good record up to three years ago. Of course, it's within human possibilities I might go wrong any time. But if we wait much longer I'll lose Honoria's childhood and my chance for a home." He shook his head, "I'll simply lose her, don't you see?"

"Yes, I see," said Lincoln.

"Why didn't you think of all this before?" Marion asked.

"I suppose I did, from time to time, but Helen and I were getting along badly. When I consented to the guardianship, I was flat on my back in a sanitarium and the market had cleaned me out. I knew I'd acted badly, and I thought if it would bring any peace to Helen, I'd agree to anything. But now it's different. I'm functioning, I'm behaving damn well, so far as—"

"Please don't swear at me," Marion said.

He looked at her, startled. With each remark the force of her dislike became more and more apparent. She had built up all her fear of life into one wall and faced it toward him. This trivial reproof was possibly the result of some trouble with the cook several hours before. Charlie became increasingly alarmed at leaving Honoria in this atmosphere of hostility against himself; sooner or later it would come out, in a word here, a shake of the head there, and some of that distrust would be irrevocably implanted on Honoria. But he pulled his temper down out of his face and shut it up inside him; he had won a point, for Lincoln realized the absurdity of Marion's remark and asked her lightly since when she had objected to the word "damn."

"Another thing," Charlie said: "I'm able to give her certain advantages now. I'm going to take a French governess to Prague with me. I've got a lease on a new apartment—"

He stopped, realizing that he was blundering. They couldn't be expected to accept with equanimity the fact that his income was again twice as large as their own.

"I suppose you can give her more luxuries than we can," said Marion. "When you were throwing away money we were living along watching every ten francs. . . . I suppose you'll start doing it again."

"Oh, no," he said. "I've learned. I worked hard for ten years, you know—until I got lucky in the market, like so many people. Terribly lucky. It won't happen again."

There was a long silence. All of them felt their nerves straining, and for the first time in a year Charlie wanted a drink. He was sure now that Lincoln Peters wanted him to have his child.

Marion shuddered suddenly; part of her saw that Charlie's feet were planted on the earth now, and her own maternal feeling recognized the naturalness of his desire; but she had lived for a long time with a prejudice—a prejudice founded on a curious disbelief in her sister's happiness, and which, in the shock of one terrible night, had turned to hatred for him. It had all happened at a point in her life where the discouragement of ill health and adverse circumstances made it necessary for her to believe in tangible villainy and a tangible villain.

"I can't help what I think!" she cried out suddenly. "How much you were responsible for Helen's death, I don't know. It's something you'll have to square with your own conscience."

An electric current of agony surged through him; for a moment he was almost on his feet, an unuttered sound echoing from his throat. He hung on to himself for a moment, another moment.

"Hold on there," said Lincoln uncomfortably. "I never thought you were responsible for that."

"Helen died of heart trouble," Charlie said dully.

"Yes, heart trouble." Marion spoke as if the phrase had another meaning for her.

Then, in the flatness that followed her outburst, she saw him plainly and she knew he had somehow arrived at control over the situation. Glancing at her husband, she found no help from him, and as abruptly as if it were a matter of no importance, she threw up the sponge.

"Do what you like!" she cried, springing up from her chair. "She's your child. I'm not the person to stand in your way. I think if it were my child I'd rather see her—" She managed to check herself. "You two decide it. I can't stand this. I'm sick. I'm going to bed."

She hurried from the room; after a moment Lincoln said:

"This has been a hard day for her. You know how strongly she feels—" His voice was almost apologetic: "When a woman gets an idea in her head."

"Of course."

"It's going to be all right. I think she sees now that you—can provide for the child, and so we can't very well stand in your way or Honoria's way."

"Thank you, Lincoln."

"I'd better go along and see how she is."

"I'm going."

He was still trembling when he reached the street, but a walk down the Rue Bonaparte to the quais set him up, and as he crossed the Seine, fresh and new by the quai lamps, he felt exultant. But back in his room he couldn't sleep. The image of Helen haunted him. Helen whom he had loved so until they had senselessly begun to abuse each other's love, tear it into shreds. On that terrible February night that Marion remembered so vividly, a slow quarrel had gone on for hours. There was a scene at the Florida, and then he attempted to take her home, and then she kissed young Webb at a table; after that there was what she had hysterically said. When he arrived home alone he turned the key in the lock in wild anger. How could he know she would arrive an hour later alone, that there would be a snowstorm in which she wandered about in slippers, too confused to find a taxi? Then the aftermath, her escaping pneumonia by a miracle, and all the attendant horror. They were "reconciled," but that was the beginning of the end, and Marion, who had seen with her own eyes and who imagined it to be one of many scenes from her sister's martyrdom, never forgot.

Going over it again brought Helen nearer, and in the white, soft light that steals upon half sleep near morning he found himself talking to her again. She said that he was perfectly right about Honoria and that she wanted Honoria to be with him. She said she was glad he was being good and doing better. She said a lot of other things—very friendly things—but she was in a swing in a white dress, and swinging faster and faster all the time, so that at the end he could not hear clearly all that she said.

IV

He woke up feeling happy. The door of the world was open again. He made plans, vistas, futures for Honoria and himself, but suddenly he grew sad, remembering all the plans he and Helen had made. She had not planned to die. The present was the thing—work to do and someone to love. But not to love too much, for he knew the injury that a father can do to a daughter or a mother to a son by attaching them too closely: afterward, out in the world, the child would seek in the marriage partner the same blind tenderness and, failing probably to find it, turn against love and life.

It was another bright, crisp day. He called Lincoln Peters at the bank where he worked and asked if he could count on taking Honoria when he left for Prague. Lincoln agreed that there was no reason for delay. One thing—the legal guardianship. Marion wanted to retain that a while longer. She was upset by the whole matter, and it would oil things if she felt that the situation was still in her control for another year. Charlie agreed, wanting only the tangible, visible child.

Then the question of a governess. Charlie sat in a gloomy agency and talked to a cross Béarnaise and to a buxom Breton peasant, neither of whom he could have endured. There were others whom he would see tomorrow.

He lunched with Lincoln Peters at Griffons, trying to keep down his exultation.

"There's nothing quite like your own child," Lincoln said. "But you understand how Marion feels too."

"She's forgotten how hard I worked for seven years there," Charlie said. "She just remembers one night."

"There's another thing." Lincoln hesitated. "While you and Helen were tearing around Europe throwing money away, we were just getting along. I didn't touch any of the prosperity because I never got ahead enough to carry anything but my insurance. I think Marion felt there was some kind of injustice in it—you not even working toward the end, and getting richer and richer."

"It went just as quick as it came," said Charlie.

"Yes, a lot of it stayed in the hands of chasseurs and saxophone players and maîtres d'hôtel—well, the big party's over now. I just said that to explain Marion's feelings about those crazy years. If you drop in about six o'clock tonight before Marion's too tired, we'll settle the details on the spot."

Back at his hotel, Charlie found a pneumatique that had been redirected from the Ritz bar where Charlie had left his address for the purpose of finding a certain man.

> DEAR CHARLIE: You were so strange when we saw you the other day that I wondered if I did something to offend you. If so, I'm not conscious of it. In fact, I have thought about you too much for the last year, and it's always been in the back of my mind that I might see you if I came over here. We *did* have such good times that crazy spring, like the night you and I stole the butcher's tricycle, and the time we tried to call on the president and you had the old derby rim and the wire cane. Everybody seems so old lately, but I don't feel old a bit. Couldn't we get together some time today for old time's sake? I've got a vile hang-over for the moment, but will be feeling better this afternoon and will look for you about five in the sweatshop at the Ritz.
>
> *Always devotedly,*
>
> *LORRAINE.*

His first feeling was one of awe that he had actually, in his mature years, stolen a tricycle and pedalled Lorraine all over the Étoile between the small hours and dawn. In retrospect it was a nightmare. Locking out Helen didn't fit in with any other act of his life, but the tricycle incident did—it was one of many. How many weeks or months of dissipation to arrive at the condition of utter irresponsibility?

He tried to picture how Lorraine had appeared to him then—very attractive; Helen was unhappy about it, though she said nothing. Yesterday, in the restaurant, Lorraine had seemed trite, blurred, worn away. He emphatically did not want to see her, and he was glad Alix had not given away his hotel address. It was a relief to think, instead, of Honoria, to think of Sundays spent with her and of saying good morning to her and of knowing she was there in his house at night, drawing her breath in the darkness.

At five he took a taxi and bought presents for all the Peters—a piquant cloth doll, a box of Roman soldiers, flowers for Marion, big linen handkerchiefs for Lincoln.

He saw, when he arrived in the apartment, that Marion had accepted the inevitable. She greeted him now as though he were a recalcitrant member of the family, rather than a menacing outsider. Honoria had been told she was going; Charlie was glad to see that her tact made her conceal her excessive happiness. Only on his lap did she whisper her delight and the question "When?" before she slipped away with the other children.

He and Marion were alone for a minute in the room, and on an impulse he spoke out boldly:

"Family quarrels are bitter things. They don't go according to any rules. They're not aches or wounds; they're more like splits in the skin that won't heal because there's not enough material. I wish you and I could be on better terms."

"Some things are hard to forget," she answered. "It's a question of confidence." There was no answer to this and presently she asked, "When do you propose to take her?"

"As soon as I can get a governess. I hoped the day after tomorrow."

"That's impossible. I've got to get her things in shape. Not before Saturday."

He yielded. Coming back into the room, Lincoln offered him a drink.

"I'll take my daily whisky," he said.

It was warm here, it was a home, people together by a fire. The children felt very safe and important; the mother and father were serious, watchful. They had things to do for the children more important than his visit here. A spoonful of medicine was, after all, more important than the strained relations between Marion and himself. They were not dull people, but they were very much in the grip of life and circumstances. He wondered if he couldn't do something to get Lincoln out of his rut at the bank.

A long peal at the doorbell; the *bonne à tout faire* passed through and went down the corridor. The door opened upon another long ring, and then voices, and the three in the salon looked up expectantly; Richard moved to bring the corridor within his range of vision, and Marion rose. Then the maid came back along the corridor, closely followed by the voices, which developed under the light into Duncan Schaeffer and Lorraine Quarrles.

They were gay, they were hilarious, they were roaring with laughter. For a moment Charlie was astounded; unable to understand how they ferreted out the Peters' address.

They both slid down another cascade of laughter. Anxious and at a loss, Charlie shook hands with them quickly and presented them to Lincoln and Marion. Marion nodded, scarcely speaking. She had drawn back a step toward the fire; her little girl stood beside her, and Marion put an arm about her shoulder.

With growing annoyance at the intrusion, Charlie waited for them to explain themselves. After some concentration Duncan said: "We came to invite you out to dinner. Lorraine and I insist that all this shishi, cagey business 'bout your address got to stop."

Charlie came closer to them, as if to force them backward down the corridor.

"Sorry, but I can't. Tell me where you'll be and I'll phone you in half an hour."

This made no impression. Lorraine sat down suddenly on the side of a chair, and focusing her eyes on Richard, cried, "Oh, what a nice little boy! Come here, little boy." Richard glanced at his mother, but did not move. With a perceptible shrug of her shoulders, Lorraine turned back to Charlie:

"Come and dine. Sure your cousins won' mine. See you so sel'om. Or solemn."

"I can't," said Charlie sharply. "You two have dinner and I'll phone you."

Her voice became suddenly unpleasant. "All right, we'll go. But I remember once when you hammered on my door at four a.m. I was enough of a good sport to give you a drink. Come on, Dunc."

Still in slow motion, with blurred, angry faces, with uncertain feet, they retired along the corridor.

"Good night," Charlie said.

"Good night!" responded Lorraine emphatically.

When he went back into the salon Marion had not moved, only now her son was standing in the circle of her other arm. Lincoln was still swinging Honoria back and forth like a pendulum from side to side.

"What an outrage!" Charlie broke out. "What an absolute outrage!"

Neither of them answered. Charlie dropped into an armchair, picked up his drink, set it down again and said:

"People I haven't seen for two years having the colossal nerve—"

He broke off. Marion had made the sound "Oh!" in one swift, furious breath, turned her body from him with a jerk and left the room.

Lincoln set down Honoria carefully.

"You children go in and start your soup," he said, and when they obeyed, he said to Charlie:

"Marion's not well and she can't stand shocks. That kind of people make her really physically sick."

"I didn't tell them to come here. They wormed your name out of somebody. They deliberately—"

"Well, it's too bad. It doesn't help matters. Excuse me a minute."

Left alone, Charlie sat tense in his chair. In the next room he could hear the children eating, talking in monosyllables, already oblivious to the scene between their elders. He heard a murmur of conversation from a farther room and then the ticking bell of a telephone receiver picked up, and in a panic he moved to the other side of the room and out of earshot.

In a minute Lincoln came back. "Look here, Charlie. I think we'd better call off dinner for tonight. Marion's in bad shape."

"Is she angry with me?"

"Sort of," he said, almost roughly. "She's not strong and—"

"You mean she's changed her mind about Honoria?"

"She's pretty bitter right now. I don't know. You phone me at the bank tomorrow."

"I wish you'd explain to her I never dreamed these people would come here. I'm just as sore as you are."

"I couldn't explain anything to her now."

Charlie got up. He took his coat and hat and started down the corridor. Then he opened the door of the dining room and said in a strange voice, "Good night, children."

Honoria rose and ran around the table to hug him.

"Good night, sweetheart," he said vaguely, and then trying to make his voice more tender, trying to conciliate something, "Good night, dear children."

V

Charlie went directly to the Ritz bar with the furious idea of finding Lorraine and Duncan, but they were not there, and he realized that in any case there was nothing he could do. He had not touched his drink at the Peters', and now he ordered a whisky-and-soda. Paul came over to say hello.

"It's a great change," he said sadly. "We do about half the business we did. So many fellows I hear about back in the States lost everything, maybe not in the first crash, but then in the second. Your friend George Hardt lost every cent, I hear. Are you back in the States?"

"No, I'm in business in Prague."

"I heard that you lost a lot in the crash."

"I did," and he added grimly, "but I lost everything I wanted in the boom."

"Selling short."

"Something like that."

Again the memory of those days swept over him like a nightmare—the people they met travelling; then people who couldn't add a row of figures or speak a coherent sentence. The little man Helen had consented to dance with at the ship's party, who had insulted her ten feet from the table; the women and girls carried screaming with drink or drugs out of public places—

—The men who locked their wives out in the snow, because the snow of twenty-nine wasn't real snow. If you didn't want it to be snow, you just paid some money.

He went to the phone and called the Peters' apartment; Lincoln answered.

"I called up because this thing is on my mind. Has Marion said anything definite?"

"Marion's sick," Lincoln answered shortly. "I know this thing isn't altogether your fault, but I can't have her go to pieces about it. I'm afraid we'll have to let it slide for six months; I can't take the chance of working her up to this state again."

"I see."

"I'm sorry, Charlie."

He went back to his table. His whisky glass was empty, but he shook his head when Alix looked at it questioningly. There wasn't much he could do now except send Honoria some things; he would send her a lot of things tomorrow. He thought rather angrily that this was just money—he had given so many people money. . . .

"No, no more," he said to the waiter. "What do I owe you?"

He would come back some day; they couldn't make him pay forever. But he wanted his child, and nothing was much good now, beside that fact. He wasn't young any more, with a lot of nice thoughts and dreams to have by himself. He was absolutely sure Helen wouldn't have wanted him to be so alone.

1931

William Faulkner

1897–1962

Like many American writers, William Faulkner populates his fiction with ghosts, most obviously those of slavery, the Civil War, and families in decline—the Sartorises, the Compsons, and underneath them, the Falkners—the original spelling of the family name. Faulkner's army of ghosts includes the very nature of the nineteenth-century South in its public losses and passions as it chokes the modern instinct toward introspection and solitary awareness. Dead at the end of Faulkner's first wholly distinctive novel, *The Sound and the Fury* (1929), Quentin Compson in *Absalom, Absalom!* (1936) becomes, through listening to the other narrators, the repository, the "barracks," for all the voices of the past that make the present a transit zone for their repetition and reconstruction. In its multivocal stories of loss, this novel, the greatest of Faulkner's achievements, approaches the dark, wondrous textures of ancient tragedy. Throughout his life and fiction Faulkner himself kept revisiting and transmuting the narrative of his great-grandfather in his incarnations as plantation owner, soldier, and novelist. But Faulkner could not escape being a child of the new century, with its own generation-defining war and aftermath. He enlisted in the Royal Canadian Air Force in 1918 (he didn't meet the height requirements of the American military) and then absorbed the postwar literary atmosphere of New Orleans around Sherwood Anderson. The highly self-conscious *Soldier's Pay* (1926) and the more satiric *Mosquitoes* (1927) were preparatory exercises in modern narrative. Rooted again in Oxford, Mississippi, (where Faulkner lived as a child after his birth in New Albany) he opened shop as "sole owner and proprietor" of Yoknapatawpha County (which bears a resemblance to his real-life county, Lafayette) with the publication of *Sartoris* and *The Sound and the Fury*, both in 1929. The next years of his life comprise one of the great periods of individual writing in literary history. Money was a persistent issue, however, though the magazine appetite for short stories proved highly lucrative for Faulkner, as it did for Fitzgerald. His major critical attention to the form was in declaring *Go Down, Moses* (1942) a novel, not a collection of stories; his arguments provide a sense of the rich complexity in the relation of part to whole in such a composite volume. Shortly after the publication of his *Collected Stories* in 1950, Faulkner was awarded the Nobel Prize. Given the nature of his life, there is something profoundly right in the conjunction of a hunting trip, a bout of prolonged drinking, and the delivery of a Nobel Prize address which was read as a majestic, sonorous tribute to "love and honour and pity and pride and compassion and sacrifice."

Pantaloon in Black

He stood in the worn, faded, clean overalls which Mannie herself had washed only a week ago, and heard the first clod strike the pine box. Soon he had one of the shovels himself, which in his hands (he was better than six feet and weighed better than two hundred pounds) resembled the toy shovel a child plays with at the shore, its half cubic foot of flung dirt no more than the light gout of sand the child's shovel would have flung.

Another member of his sawmill gang touched his arm and said, "Lemme have hit, Rider."

He didn't even falter. He released one hand in midstroke and flung it backward, striking the other across the chest, jolting him back a step, and restored the hand to the moving shovel, flinging the dirt with that effortless fury so that the mound seemed to be rising of its own volition, not built up from above but thrusting visibly upward out of the earth itself, until at last the grave, save for its rawness, resembled any other, marked off without order about the barren plot by shards of pottery and broken bottles and old brick and other objects insignificant to sight but actually of a profound meaning and fatal to touch, which no white man could have read. Then he straightened up and with one hand flung the shovel quivering upright in the mound like a javelin and turned and began to walk away, walking on even when an old woman came out of the meagre clump of his kin and friends and a few old people who had known him and his dead wife both since they were born, and grasped his forearm. She was his aunt. She had raised him. He could not remember his parents at all.

"Whar you gwine?" she said.

"Ah'm goan home," he said.

"You don't wants ter go back dar by yoself. You needs to eat. You come on home and eat."

"Ah'm goan home," he repeated, walking out from under her hand, his forearm like iron, as if the weight on it were no more than that of a fly, the other members of the mill gang whose head he was giving way quietly to let him pass. But before he reached the fence one of them overtook him; he did not need to be told it was his aunt's messenger.

"Wait, Rider," the other said. "We gots a jug in de bushes—" Then the other said what he had not intended to say, what he had never conceived of saying in circumstances like these, even though everybody knew it—the dead who either will not or cannot quit the earth yet, although the flesh they once lived in has been returned to it—let the preachers tell and reiterate and affirm how they left it not only without regret but with joy, mounting toward glory: "You don't wants ter go back dar. She be wawkin yit."

He didn't pause, glancing down at the other, his eyes red at the inner corners in his high, slightly back-tilted head. "Lemme alone, Acey," he said. "Doan mess wid me now," and went on, stepping over the three-strand wire fence without even breaking his stride, and crossed the road and entered the woods. It was middle dusk when he emerged from them and crossed the last field, stepping over that fence too in one stride, into the lane. It was empty at this hour of Sunday evening—no family in wagon, no rider, no walkers churchward to speak to him and carefully refrain from looking after him when he had passed—the pale, powder-light, powder-dry dust of August from which the long week's marks of hoof and wheel had been blotted by the strolling and unhurried Sunday shoes, with somewhere beneath them, vanished but not gone, fixed and held in the annealing dust, the narrow, splay-toed prints of his wife's bare feet where on Saturday afternoon she would walk to the commissary to buy their next week's supplies while he took his bath; himself, his own prints, setting the period now as he strode on, moving almost as fast as a smaller man could have trotted, his body breasting the air her body had vacated, his eyes touching the objects—post and tree and field and house and hill—her eyes had lost.

The house was the last one in the lane, not his but rented from the local white landowner. But the rent was paid promptly in advance, and even in just six months he had refloored the porch and rebuilt and reroofed the kitchen, doing the work himself on Saturday afternoon and Sunday with his wife helping him, and bought the stove. Because he made good money: sawmilling ever since he began to get his growth at fifteen and sixteen and now, at twenty-four, head of the timber gang itself because the gang he headed moved a third again as much timber between sunup and sundown as any other, handling himself at times out of the vanity of his own strength logs which ordinarily two men would have handled with cant hooks; never without work even in the old days when he had not actually needed the money, when a lot of what he wanted, needed perhaps, didn't cost money—the women bright and dark and for all purposes nameless he didn't need to buy, and it didn't matter to him what he wore, and there was always food for him at any hour of day or night in the house of his aunt who didn't even want to take the two dollars he gave her each Saturday. So there had been only the Saturday and Sunday dice and whisky that had to be paid for until that day six months ago when he saw Mannie, whom he had known all his life, for the first time and said to himself: "Ah'm thu wid all dat," and they married and he rented the cabin from Carothers Edmonds and built a fire on the hearth on their wedding night as the tale told how Uncle Lucas Beauchamp, Edmonds' oldest tenant, had done on his forty-five years ago and which had burned ever since. And he would rise and dress and eat his breakfast by lamplight to walk the four miles to the mill by sunup, and exactly one hour after sundown he would enter the house again, five days a week, until Saturday. Then the first hour would not have passed noon when he would mount the steps and knock, not on post or door frame but on the underside of the gallery roof itself, and enter and ring the bright cascade of silver dollars on to the scrubbed table in the kitchen where his dinner simmered on the stove and the galvanized tub of hot water and the baking-powder can of soft soap and the towel made of scalded flour sacks sewn together and his clean overalls and shirt waited, and Mannie would gather up the money and walk the half-mile to the commissary and buy their next week's supplies and bank the rest of the money in Edmonds' safe and return and they would eat once again without haste or hurry after five days—the sidemeat, the greens, the cornbread, the buttermilk from the well house, the cake which she baked every Saturday now that she had a stove to bake in.

But when he put his hand on the gate it seemed to him suddenly that there was nothing beyond it. The house had never been his anyway, but now even the new planks and sills and shingles, the hearth and stove and bed were all a part of the memory of somebody else, so that he stopped in the half-open gate and said aloud, as though he had gone to sleep in one place and then waked suddenly to find himself in another: "Whut's Ah doin hyar?" before he went on.

Then he saw the dog. He had forgotten it. He remembered neither seeing nor hearing it since it began to howl just before dawn yesterday—a big dog, a hound with a strain of mastiff from somewhere (he had told Mannie a month after they married: "Ah needs a big dawg. You's de onliest least thing whut ever kep up wid me one day, leff alone for weeks.") coming out from beneath the gallery and approaching, not running but seeming rather to drift across the dusk until it stood lightly against his leg, its head raised until the tips of his fingers just touched it, facing the house and making no sound; whereupon, as if the animal controlled it, had lain guardian before it during his absence and only this instant relinquished, the shell of planks and shingles facing him solidified, filled, and for the moment he believed that he could not possibly enter it.

"But Ah needs to eat," he said. "Us bofe needs to eat," he said, moving on though the dog did not follow until he turned and cursed it. "Come on hyar!" he said. "Whut you skeered of? She lacked you too, same as me."

They mounted the steps and crossed the porch and entered the house—the dusk-filled single room where all those six months were now crammed and crowded into one instant of time until there was no space left for air to breathe, crammed and crowded about the hearth where the fire which was to have lasted to the end of them, in front of which in the days before he was able to buy the stove he would enter after his four-mile walk from the mill and find her, the shape of her narrow back and haunches squatting, one narrow spread hand shielding her face from the blaze over which the other hand held the skillet, had already fallen to a dry, light soilure of dead ashes when the sun rose yesterday—and himself standing there while the last of light died about the strong and indomitable beating of his heart and the deep steady arch and collapse of his chest which walking fast over the rough going of woods and fields had not increased and standing still in the quiet and fading room had not slowed down.

Then the dog left him. The light pressure went off his flank; he heard the click and hiss of its claws on the wooden floor as it surged away, and the thought at first that it was fleeing. But it stopped just outside the front door, where he could see it now and the upfling of its head as the howl began; and then he saw her too.

She was standing in the kitchen door, looking at him. He didn't move. He didn't breathe or speak until he knew his voice would be all right, his face fixed too not to alarm her.

"Mannie," he said. "Hit's awright. Ah ain't afraid."

Then he took a step toward her, slow, not even raising his hand yet, and stopped. Then he took another step. But this time as soon as he moved she began to fade. He stopped at once, not breathing again, motionless, willing his eyes to see that she had stopped too. But she had not stopped. She was fading, going. "Wait," he said, talking as sweet as he had ever heard his voice speak to a woman: "Den lemme go wid you, honey." But she was going. She was going fast now; he could actually feel between them the insuperable barrier of that very strength which could handle alone a log which would have taken any two other men to handle, of the blood and bones and flesh too strong, invincible for life, having learned, at least once with his own eyes, how tough, even in sudden violent death, not a young man's bones and flesh perhaps but the will of that bone and flesh to remain alive, actually was.

Then she was gone. He walked through the door where she had been standing and went to the stove. He did not light the lamp. He needed no light. He had set the stove up himself and built the shelves for the dishes, from among which he took two plates by feel and from the pot, sitting cold on the cold stove, he ladled on to the plates the food which his aunt had brought yesterday and of which he had eaten yesterday, though now he did not remember when he had eaten it nor what it was, and carried plates to the scrubbed bare table beneath the single small fading window and drew two chairs up and sat down, waiting again until he knew his voice would be what he wanted it to be.

"Come on hyar now," he said roughly. "Come on hyar and eat yo supper. Ah ain't gonter have no . . ." and ceased, looking down at his plate, breathing the strong, deep pants, his chest arching and collapsing until he stopped it presently and held himself motionless for perhaps a half minute, and raised a spoonful of the cold and glutinous pease to his mouth. The congealed and lifeless mass seemed to bounce on contact with his lips. Not even warmed from mouth-heat, pease and spoon spattered and rang upon the plate; his chair crashed backward and he was standing, feeling the muscles of his jaw beginning to drag his mouth open, tugging upward the top half of his head. But he stopped that too before it became sound, holding himself again while he rapidly scraped the food from his plate on to the other and took it up and left the kitchen, crossed the other room and the gallery and set the plate on the bottom step and went on toward the gate.

The dog was not there but it overtook him within the first half-mile. There was a moon then, their two shadows flitting broken and intermittent among the trees or slanted long and intact across the slope of pasture or old abandoned fields upon the hills, the man moving almost as fast as a horse could have covered that ground, altering his course each time a lighted window came in sight, the dog trotting at heel while their shadows shortened to the moon's curve until at last they trod them and the last far lamp had vanished and the shadows began to lengthen on the other hand, keeping to heel even when a rabbit burst from almost beneath the man's foot, then lying in the grey of dawn beside the man's prone body, beside the laboured heave and collapse of the chest, the loud harsh snoring which sounded, not like groans of pain, but like someone engaged without arms in prolonged single combat.

When he reached the mill there was nobody there but the fireman, an older man just turning from the woodpile, watching quietly as he crossed the clearing, striding as if he were going to walk not only through the boiler shed but through (or over) the boiler too, the overalls which had been clean yesterday now draggled and soiled and drenched to the knees with dew, the cloth cap flung on to the side of his head, hanging peak downward over his ear as he always wore it, the whites of his eyes rimmed with red and with something urgent and strained about them.

"Whar yo bucket?" he said. But before the fireman could answer he had stepped past him and lifted the polished lard pail down from a nail in a post. "Ah just wants a biscuit," he said.

"Eat hit all," the fireman said. "Ah'll eat outen de yuthers' buckets at dinner. Den you gawn home and go bed. You don't looks good."

"Ah ain't come hyar to look," he said, sitting on the ground, his back against the post, the open pail between his knees, cramming the food into his mouth with his hands, wolfing it—pease again, also gelid and cold, a fragment of yesterday's Sunday fried chicken, a few rough chunks of this morning's fried sidemeat, a biscuit the size of a child's cap—indiscriminate, tasteless. The rest of the crew was gathering now, the voices and sounds of movement outside the boiler shed. Presently the white foreman rode into the clearing on a horse. Rider did not look up; setting the empty pail aside, rising, looking at no one, he went to the branch and lay on his stomach and lowered his face to the water, drawing the water into himself with the same deep, strong, troubled inhalations that he had snored with, or as when he had stood in the empty house at dusk yesterday, trying to get air.

Then the trucks were rolling. The air pulsed with the rapid beating of the exhaust and the whine and clang of the saw, the trucks rolling one by one up to the skidway as he mounted them in turn, to stand balanced on the load he freed, knocking the chocks out and casting loose the shackle chains and with his cant hook squaring the sticks of cypress and gum and oak one by one to the incline and holding them until the next two men of his gang were ready to receive and guide them, until the discharge of each truck became one long rumbling roar punctuated by grunting shouts and, as the morning grew and the sweat came, chanted phrases of song tossed back and forth. He did not sing with them. He rarely ever did, and this morning might have been no different from any other—himself man-height again above the heads which carefully refrained from looking at him, stripped to the waist now, the shirt removed and the overalls knotted about his hips by the suspender straps, his upper body bare except for the handkerchief about his neck and the cap clapped and clinging somehow over his right ear, the mounting sun sweat-glinted steel-blue on the midnight-coloured bunch and slip of muscles, until the whistle blew for noon and he said to the two men at the head of the skidway: "Look out. Git out de way," and rode the log down the incline, balanced erect in short rapid backward-running steps above the headlong thunder.

His aunt's husband was waiting for him, an old man as tall as he was, but lean, almost frail, carrying a tin pail in one hand and a covered plate in the other. They too sat in the shade beside the branch a short distance from where the others were opening their dinner pails. The bucket contained a fruit jar of buttermilk packed in a clean damp towsack. The covered dish was a peach pie, still warm.

"She baked hit fer you dis mawnin," the uncle said. "She say fer you to come home."

He didn't answer, bent forward a little, his elbows on his knees, holding the pie in both hands, wolfing at it, the syrupy filling smearing and trickling down his chin, blinking rapidly as he chewed, the whites of his eyes covered a little more by the creeping red.

"Ah went to yo house last night, but you want dar. She sont me. She wants you ter come on home. She kept de lamp burnin' all last night for you."

"Ah'm awright," he said.

"You ain't awright. De Lawd guv, and He tuck away. Put yo faith and trust in Him. And she kin help you."

"Whut faith and trust?" he said. "Whut Mannie ever done ter Him? Whut He wanter come messin' wid me and—"

"Hush!" the old man said. "Hush!"

Then the trucks were rolling again. Then he could stop needing to invent to himself reasons for his breathing, until after a while he began to believe he had forgot about breathing since now he could not hear it himself above the steady thunder of the rolling logs; whereupon as soon as he found himself believing he had forgotten it, he knew that he had not, so that, instead of tipping the final log on to the skidway, he stood up and cast his cant hook away as if it were a burnt match, and in the dying reverberation of the last log's rumbling descent he vaulted down between the two slanted tracks of the skid, facing the log which still lay on the truck. He had done it before—taken a log from the truck with his hands, balanced, and turned with it and tossed it on to the skidway, but never with a stick of this size. So that in a complete cessation of all sound save the pulse of the exhaust and the light free-running whine of the disengaged saw, since every eye there, even that of the white foreman, was upon him, he nudged the log to the edge of the truckframe and squatted and set his palms against the underside of it. For a time there was no movement at all. It was as if the unrational and inanimate wood had invested, mesmerized the man with some of its own primal inertia.

Then a voice said quietly: "He got hit. Hit's off de truck," and they saw the crack and gap of air, watching the infinitesimal straightening of the braced legs until the knees locked, the movement mounting infinitesimally through the belly's insuck, the arch of the chest, the neck cords, lifting the lip from the white clench of teeth in passing, drawing the whole head backward and only the bloodshot fixity of the eyes impervious to it, moving on up the arms and the straightening elbows until the balanced log was higher than his head.

"Only he ain't gonter turn wid dat un," the same voice said. "And when he try to put hit back on de truck, hit gonter kill him."

But none of them moved. Then—there was no gathering of supreme effort—the log seemed to leap suddenly backward over his head of its own volition, spinning, crashing, and thundering down the incline. He turned and stepped over the slanting track in one stride and walked through them as they gave way and went on across the clearing toward the woods even though the foreman called after him: "Rider!" and again: "You, Rider!"

At sundown he and the dog were in the river swamp four miles away—another clearing, itself not much larger than a room, a hut, a hovel partly of planks and partly of canvas, an unshaven white man standing in the door beside which a shotgun leaned, watching him as he approached, his hand extended with four silver dollars on the palm. "Ah wants a jug," he said.

"A jug?" the white man said. "You mean a pint. This is Monday. Ain't you all running this week?"

"Ah laid off," he said. "Whar's my jug?" waiting, looking at nothing apparently, blinking his bloodshot eyes rapidly in his high, slightly back-tilted head, then turning, the jug hanging from his crooked middle finger against his leg, at which moment the white man looked suddenly and sharply at his eyes as though seeing them for the first time—the eyes which had been strained and urgent this morning and which now seemed to be without vision too and in which no white showed at all—and said:

"Here. Gimme that jug. You don't need no gallon. I'm going to give you that pint, give it to you. Then you get out of here and stay out. Don't come back until—"

Then the white man reached and grasped the jug, whereupon the other swung it behind him, sweeping his other arm up and out so that it struck the white man across the chest.

"Look, white folks," he said. "Hit's mine. Ah done paid you."

The white man cursed him. "No you ain't. Here's your money. Put that jug down, nigger."

"Hit's mine," he said, his voice quiet, gentle even, his face quiet save for the rapid blinking of the red eyes. "Ah done paid for hit." Turning his back on the man and the gun both, he recrossed the clearing to where the dog waited beside the path to come to heel again. They moved rapidly on between the close walls of impenetrable cane-stalks which gave a sort of blondness to the twilight and possessed something of that oppression, that lack of room to breathe in, which the walls of his house had had. But this time, instead of fleeing it, he stopped and raised the jug and drew the cob stopper from the fierce dusk-reek of uncured alcohol and drank, gulping the liquid solid and cold as ice water, without either taste or heat until he lowered the jug and the air got in.

"Hah," he said. "Dat's right. Try me. Try me, big boy. Ah gots something hyar now dat kin whup you."

And, once free of the bottom's unbreathing blackness, there was the moon again. His long shadow and that of the lifted jug slanted away as he drank and then held the jug poised, gulping the silver air into his throat until he could breathe again, speaking to the jug: "Come on now. You always claims you's a better man den me. Come on now. Prove hit," and drank again, swallowing the chill liquid tamed of taste or heat either while the swallowing lasted, feeling it flow solid and cold with fire past and then enveloping the strong steady panting of his lungs until they ran suddenly free as his moving body did in the silver solid wall of air he breasted, and he was all right, his striding shadow and the trotting one of the dog travelling swift as those two clouds along the hill, the long cast of his motionless shadow and that of the lifted jug slanting across the slope as he watched the tall frail figure of his aunt's husband toiling up the hill.

"Dey tole me at de mill you wuz gone," the old man said. "Ah knowed whar to look. Come home, son. Dat ar can't help you."

"Hit done already hope me," he said. "Ah'm awready home. Ah'm snakebit now and pizen can't hawm me."

"Den stop and see her. Leff her look at you. Dat's all she axes: just leff her look at you—" But he was already moving. "Wait," the old man cried. "Wait!"

"You can't keep up," he said, speaking into the silver air, breasting aside the silver solid air which began to flow past him almost as fast as it would have flowed past a moving horse; the faint frail voice was already lost in the night's infinitude, his shadow and that of the dog scudding the free miles, the deep strong panting of his chest running free as air now because he was all right.

Then, drinking, he discovered suddenly that no more liquid was entering his mouth; swallowing, it was no longer passing down his throat, throat and mouth filled now with a solid and unmoving column which, without any reflex of revulsion, sprang columnar and intact and still retaining the shape of his gullet, outward glinting in the moonlight, to vanish into the myriad murmur of the dewed grass. He drank again; again his throat merely filled solidly until two icy rills ran from his mouth-corners; again the intact column sprang silvering, glinting, while he panted the chill of air into his throat, the jug poised before his mouth while he spoke to it:

"Awright. Ah'm gwy try you again. Soon as you makes up yo mind to stay whar Ah puts you Ah'll leff you alone."

He drank again, filling his gullet for the third time and for the third time lowered the jug one instant ahead of the bright intact repetition, panting, indrawing the cool of air until he could breathe. He stoppered the cob carefully back into the jug and stood with the deep strong panting of his chest, blinking, the long cast of his motionless and solitary shadow slanting away across the hill and beyond, across the mazy infinitude of all the night-bound earth.

"Awright," he said. "Ah just misread de sign wrong. Hit's done done me all de help Ah needs. Ah'm awright now. Ah doan needs no mo of hit."

He could see the lamp in the window as he crossed the pasture, passing the black-and-silver yawn of the sandy ditch where he had played as a boy with empty snuff-tins and rusted harness buckles and fragments of trace-chain and now and then an actual wheel, the garden patch where he had hoed in the spring days while his aunt stood sentry over him from the kitchen window, crossing the grassless yard in whose dust he had sprawled and crept before he learned to walk, and entered the house, the room, the light itself, his head backtilted a little, the jug hanging from his crooked finger against his knee.

"Unc Alec say you wanter see me," he said.

"Not just to see you," his aunt said. "To come home, whar we kin help you."

"Ah'm awright," he said. "Ah doan needs no help."

"No," she said. She rose from the chair and came and grasped his arm as she had grasped it yesterday beside the grave; again, as on yesterday, the forearm like iron under the hand. "No! When Alec come back and tole me how you had wawked off de mill and de sun not half down, Ah knowed why and whar. And dat can't help you."

"Hit done awready hope me. Ah'm awright now."

"Don't lie to me," she said. "You ain't never lied to me. Don't lie to me now."

Then he said it. It was his own voice, speaking quietly out of the tremendous panting of his chest which would presently begin to strain at the walls of this room too. But he would be gone in a moment.

"Nome," he said. "Hit ain't done me no good."

"And hit can't! Can't nothing help you but Him. Ax Him! Tole Him about hit! He wants to hyar you and help you!"

"Efn He God, Ah don't needs to tole Him. Efn He God, He awready know hit. Awright. Hyar Ah is. Leff Him come down hyar and do me some good."

"On yo knees!" she cried. "On yo knees and ax Him!" But it was not his knees on the floor: it was his feet, and for a space he could hear her feet too on the planks of the hall behind him and her voice crying after him from the door: "Spoot! Spoot!"—crying after him across the moon-dappled yard the name he had gone by in childhood and adolescence, before the men he worked with and the bright dark nameless women he had taken in course and forgotten until he saw Mannie that day and said, "Ah'm thu wid all dat," began to call him Rider.

It was just after midnight when he reached the mill again. The dog was gone now. This time he could not remember when nor where. At first he seemed to remember hurling the empty jug at it. But later the jug was still in his hand and it was not empty, although each time he drank now the two icy tunnels streamed from his mouth-corners, sopping his shirt and overalls until he walked constantly in the fierce chill of the liquid tamed now of flavour and heat and odour too even when the swallowing stopped.

"Sides," he said, "Ah wouldn't th'ow nothin at him. Ah mout kick him efn he needed hit and was close enough. But Ah wouldn't ruint no dawg chunkin' hit."

It was still in his hand when he entered the clearing and paused among the mute soaring of the moon-blond lumber stacks, standing in the middle of the now unimpeded shadow which he was treading again now as he had trod it last night, swaying a little, blinking about him at the stacked lumber, the skidway, the piled logs waiting for tomorrow, the boiler shed all quiet and blanched in the moon: and then it was all right. He was moving again. But he was not moving, he was drinking, the liquid cold and swift and tasteless and requiring no swallowing, so that he could not tell if it were going down inside or outside; but it was all right. And now he was moving, the jug gone now and he didn't know the when or where of that either, crossing the clearing, entering the boiler shed and through it, crossing the junctureless trepan of time's back-loop to the door of the tool-room, the faint glow of the lantern beyond the plankjoints, the surge and fall of a shadow between the light and the wall, the mutter of voices, the mute click and scutter of the dice, his hand loud on the barred door, his voice loud too: "Open hit. Hit's me. Ah'm snakebit and bound to die."

Then he was inside. They were the same faces—three members of his timber gang, three or four others of the mill crew, the white night-watchman with the heavy pistol in his hip pocket and the small heap of coins and worn banknotes on the floor before him; himself standing over the kneeling and squatting cycle, swaying a little, blinking, the deadened muscles of his face shaped into smiling while the white man stared at him. "Make room, gamblers," he said. "Ah'm snakebit and de pizen can't hawm me."

"You're drunk," the watchman said. "Get out of here. One of you niggers open that door and get him out of here."

"Dass awright, boss man," he said, his voice equable, almost deferential, his face still fixed in the faint rigid smiling beneath the blinking of the red eyes; "Ah ain't drunk. Ah just can't wawk straight fer dis hyar money weighin' me down."

Now he was kneeling too, the other six dollars of his last week's pay on the floor before him, blinking, still smiling at the face of the white man opposite, then still smiling, watching the dice pass from hand to hand around the circle as the watchman covered the bets, watching the soiled and palm-worn money in front of the white man gradually increase, watching the white man cast and win two doubled bets in succession, then lose one for twenty-five cents, the dice coming to him at last, the cupped snug clicking of them in his fist.

"Shoots a dollar," he said, and cast and watched the white man pick up the dice and flip them back to him. "Ah'm snakebit," he said. "Ah kin pass wid anything," and cast, and this time one of the others flipped the dice back. "Ah lets hit lay," he said, and cast, and moved as the white man moved, catching the white man's wrist before the hand reached the dice, the two of them squatting, facing each other above the dice and the money, his left hand grasping the white man's wrist, his face still fixed in the rigid and deadened smiling, his voice still almost deferential: "Ah kin pass even wid miss-outs. But dese hyar yuther boys—" until the hand sprang open and the second pair of dice clattered on to the floor beside the other two, and the white man wrenched it free and sprang up and back and reached the hand backward toward the pocket where the pistol was.

The razor hung between his shoulder blades from a loop of cotton string round his neck beneath his shirt. The same motion of the hand which brought the razor forward over his shoulder flipped the blade open and freed it from the cord, the blade opening on until the back edge of it lay across the knuckles of his fist, his thumb pressing the handle into his closing fingers, so that in the instant before the half-drawn pistol exploded he actually struck at the white man's throat not with the blade but with a sweeping blow of his fist, following through in the same motion so that not even the first jet of blood touched his hand or arm.

After it was over (it didn't take long; they found the prisoner on the following day, hanging from the bell rope in a negro schoolhouse about two miles from the sawmill, and the coroner had pronounced his verdict of death at the hands of a person or persons unknown and surrendered the body to its next of kin all within five minutes) the sheriff 's deputy who had been officially in charge of the business was telling his wife about it. It was in the kitchen; his wife was cooking supper, and the deputy had been up and in motion ever since the jail delivery shortly after midnight and he had covered considerable ground since, and he was spent now from lack of sleep and hurried food at hurried and curious hours and, sitting in a chair beside the stove, a little hysterical too.

"Them damn niggers," he said. "I swear to Godfrey, it's a wonder we have as little trouble with them as we do. Because why? Because they ain't human. They look like a man and they walk on their hind legs like a man, and they can talk and you can understand them and you think they understand you, at least now and then. But when it comes to the normal human feelings and sentiments of human beings, they might just as well be a damn herd of wild buffaloes. Now you take this one today—"

"I wish you would," his wife said harshly, a stout woman, handsome once, greying now and with a neck definitely too short, who looked not harried at all but choleric. Also she had attended a club rook party that afternoon and had won the first, the fifty-cent, prize until another member had insisted on a recount of the scores and the ultimate throwing out of one entire game. "Take him out of my kitchen, anyway. You sheriffs! Sitting around that courthouse all day long talking. It's no wonder two or three men can walk in and take prisoners out from under your noses. They would take your chairs and desks and window sills too if you ever got your backsides and feet off of them that long."

"It's more of them Birdsongs than just two or three," the deputy said. "There's forty-two active votes in that connection. Me and Mayfield taken the poll-list and counted them up one day. But listen—" The wife turned from the stove, carrying a dish. The deputy snatched his feet rapidly out of the way as she passed him and went on into the dining room. The deputy raised his voice a little. "His wife dies on him. All right. But does he grieve? He's the biggest man at the funeral. Grabs a shovel before they even got the box into the grave, I heard tell, and starts throwing dirt onto her faster than a slip scraper could. But that's all right—"

His wife came back. He moved his feet again. "—maybe that's the way he felt about her. There ain't any law against that, long as he never officiated at the deceasing too. But here the next day he's the first man at the mill except the fireman, getting there before the fireman had his fire going; five minutes earlier and he could even helped the fireman wake Birdsong up so he could go home and go back to bed again or even cut Birdsong's throat then and saved everybody trouble. So he comes to work, the first man on the job, when McAndrews would have given him the day off and paid him his time too, when McAndrews and everybody else expected him to take the day off, when any white man would have took the day off no matter how he felt about his wife, when even a little child would have had sense enough to take a holiday when he could still get paid too. But not him. The first man there, jumping from one truck to another before the whistle quit blowing even, snatching up ten-foot cypress logs by himself and throwing them around like matches. And then, just when everybody has decided that that's the way to take him, that that's the way he want to be took, he walks off the job in the middle of the afternoon without by-your-leave or thank you or good-by to McAndrews or nobody else, gets himself a whole gallon of bust-skull white-mule whisky, comes straight back to the mill to the same crap game where Birdsong has been running crooked dice on them mill niggers for fifteen years, goes straight to the same game where he has been peacefully losing a probably steady average ninety-nine per cent of his pay ever since he got big enough to read the spots on them miss-outs, and cuts Birdsong's throat clean to the neckbone five minutes later.

"So me and Mayfield go out there. Not that we expect to do any good, as he had probably passed Jackson, Tennessee, about daylight; and besides the simplest way to find him would be just to stay close behind them Birdsong boys. So it's just by the merest pure chance that we go by his house; I don't even remember why now; and there he is. Sitting behind the door with razor open on one knee and his shotgun on the other? No. Asleep. A big pot of pease set clean on the stove, and him laying in the back yard asleep in the broad sun with just his head under the edge of the porch and a dog that looked like a cross between a bear and a Polled Angus steer yelling fire and murder from the back door. And he wakes up and says, 'Awright, white folks. Ah done it. Jest don't lock me up,' and Mayfield says, 'Mr Birdsong's kinfolks ain't going to either. You'll have plenty of fresh air when they get a hold of you,' and he says, 'Ah done it. Jest don't lock me up'—advising, instructing the sheriff not to lock him up; he done it all right and it's too bad, but don't cut him off from the fresh air. So we loaded him into the car, when here come the old woman—his ma or aunt or something—panting up the road at a dog-trot, wanting to come with us, and Mayfield trying to tell her what might happen maybe to her too if them Birdsong kin catches us before we can get him locked up, only she is coming anyway and, like Mayfield says, her being in the car might be a good thing if the Birdsongs did happen to run into us, because interference with the law can't be condoned even if the Birdsong connection did carry that beat for Mayfield last summer. So we brought her along too and got him to town and into the jail all right and turned him over to Ketcham and Ketcham taken him on upstairs and the old woman coming too, telling Ketcham, 'Ah tried to raise him right. He was a good boy. He ain't ever been in no trouble till now. He will suffer for what he done. But don't let the white folks git him,' and Ketcham says, 'You and him ought to thought of that before he started barbering white men without using no lather,' and locked them both up in the cell because he felt like Mayfield did, that her being there might be a good influence on the Birdsong boys if anything started if he should run for sheriff when Mayfield's term was out. So he come on back downstairs and pretty soon the chain gang come in and he thought things had settled down for a while when all of a sudden he begun to hear the yelling, not howling: yelling, though there wasn't no words in it, and he grabbed his pistol and run back upstairs and into the room where the chain gang was, where he could see through the door bars into the cell where that nigger had done tore that iron cot clean out of the floor it was bolted to and was standing in the middle of the cell, holding the cot over his head like it was a baby's cradle, yelling, and the old woman sitting hunched into the corner and the nigger says to her, 'Ah ain't going to hurt you,' and throws the cot against the wall and comes and grabs holt of that steel door and rips it out of the wall—bricks, hinges and all—and walks out into the big room, toting the door over his head as if it were a gauze wire window screen, saying, 'It's awright. Ah ain't tryin' to git away.'

"Ketcham could have shot him right there, but like he figured, if it wasn't going to be the law, then the Birdsong boys ought to have first lick at him. So Ketcham don't shoot. Instead he jumps in behind where the chain-gang niggers were kind of backed off from that steel door, hollering, 'Grab him! Throw him down!' except they hang back at first until Ketcham gets up to where he can kick the ones he can reach, batting at the others with the flat of the pistol until they rush him. And Ketcham says for a good minute he would grab them up as they come in and fling them clean across the room like they was rag dolls, still saying, 'Ah ain't tryin' to git out, Ah ain't tryin' to git out,' until at last they pulled him down, a big mass of nigger arms and heads and legs boiling around on the floor and even then Ketcham says every now and then a nigger would come flying out and go sailing through the air across the room, spraddled like a flying squirrel and his eyes sticking out in front of him like the headlights on a car, until at last they had him down and Ketcham went in and begun peeling away niggers until he could see him laying there under the pile of niggers, laughing, with tears big as glass marbles popping out of his eyes and running across his face and down past his ears and making a kind of popping sound on the floor like somebody dropping bird eggs, laughing and laughing and saying, 'Hit look lack Ah just can't quit thinking. Look lack Ah just can't quit.' And what do you think of that?"

"I think if you eat any supper in this house you'll do it in the next five minutes," his wife said from the dining room. "I'm going to clear this table then and I'm going to the picture show."

1940

Jorge Luis Borges

1899–1986

Jorge Luis Borges was born in Buenos Aires, Argentina, where his father was a lawyer and a teacher of psychology and his mother a translator. Because his grandmother was English, much of his early reading was in that language. He began writing in Spanish and English when he was six, and had a translation of an Oscar Wilde story published in a Buenos Aires newspaper when he was nine. As a child he played almost exclusively with his younger sister Norah, acting out stories and playing with imaginary friends. When he was fifteen his family moved to Switzerland, where he studied at College Calvin from 1914 to 1918. During this time he was exposed to a variety of writing, including Valéry, Rimbaud, and Whitman. His classes were in French, and he taught himself German and Italian. Between 1918 and 1921, Borges lived with his family in Spain. He published his first poem in the magazine *Grecia* and became involved with the avant-garde ultraísta group of poets. Returning to Buenos Aires in 1921, he began to write the poems and the prose fables that made him famous, including the short story collections *Ficciones* (1945) and *El aleph* (1949). He wrote in relative obscurity until, in 1961, he was awarded the Prix Formentor—the International Publishers Prize—an honour he shared with Samuel Beckett. The award made him internationally famous. He became director of the National Library in Buenos Aires, and spent time as a visiting professor and guest lecturer at numerous American universities. His enormous erudition and his grasp of world literature are fundamental to the power of his art.

The Library of Babel

By this art you may contemplate the variation of the 23 letters. . . .

Anatomy of Melancholy, Pt 2, Sec. II, Mem. IV

The Universe (which others call the Library) is composed of an indefinite, perhaps infinite number of hexagonal galleries. In the centre of each gallery is a ventilation shaft, bounded by a low railing. From any hexagon one can see the floors above and below—one after another, endlessly. The arrangement of the galleries is always the same: Twenty bookshelves, five to each side, line four of the hexagon's six sides; the height of the bookshelves, floor to ceiling, is hardly greater than the height of a normal librarian. One of the hexagon's free sides opens into a narrow sort of vestibule, which in turn opens onto another gallery, identical to the first—identical in fact to all. To the left and right of the vestibule are two tiny compartments. One is for sleeping, upright; the other, for satisfying one's physical necessities. Through this space, too, there passes a spiral staircase, which winds upward and downward into the remotest distance. In the vestibule there is a mirror, which faithfully duplicates appearances. Men often infer from this mirror that the Library is not infinite—if it were, what need would there be for that illusory replication? I prefer to dream that burnished surfaces are a figuration and promise of the infinite. . . . Light is provided by certain spherical fruits that bear the name "bulbs." There are two of these bulbs in each hexagon, set crosswise. The light they give is insufficient, and unceasing.

Like all the men of the Library, in my younger days I travelled; I have journeyed in quest of a book, perhaps the catalogue of catalogues. Now that my eyes can hardly make out what I myself have written, I am preparing to die, a few leagues from the hexagon where I was born. When I am dead, compassionate hands will throw me over the railing; my tomb will be the unfathomable air, my body will sink for ages, and will decay and dissolve in the wind engendered by my fall, which shall be infinite. I declare that the Library is endless. Idealists argue that the hexagonal rooms are the necessary shape of absolute space, or at least of our *perception* of space. They argue that a triangular or pentagonal chamber is inconceivable. (Mystics claim that their ecstasies reveal to them a circular chamber containing an enormous circular book with a continuous spine that goes completely around the walls. But their testimony is suspect, their words obscure. That cyclical book is God.) Let it suffice for the moment that I repeat the classic dictum: *The Library is a sphere whose exact centre is any hexagon and whose circumference is unattainable.*

Each wall of each hexagon is furnished with five bookshelves; each bookshelf holds thirty-two books identical in format; each book contains four hundred ten pages; each page, forty lines; each line, approximately eighty black letters. There are also letters on the front cover of each book; those letters neither indicate nor prefigure what the pages inside will say. I am aware that that lack of correspondence once struck men as mysterious. Before summarizing the solution of the mystery (whose discovery, in spite of its tragic consequences, is perhaps the most important event in all history), I wish to recall a few axioms.

First: *The Library has existed AB AETERNITATE.* That truth, whose immediate corollary is the future eternity of the world, no rational mind can doubt. Man, the imperfect librarian, may be the work of chance or of malevolent demiurges; the universe, with its elegant appointments—its bookshelves, its enigmatic books, its indefatigable staircases for the traveller, and its water closets for the seated librarian—can only be the handiwork of a god. In order to grasp the distance that separates the human and the divine, one has only to compare these crude trembling symbols which my fallible hand scrawls on the cover of a book with the organic letters inside—neat, delicate, deep black, and inimitably symmetrical.

Second: *There are twenty-five orthographic symbols.*[1] That discovery enabled mankind, three hundred years ago, to formulate a general theory of the Library and thereby satisfactorily solve the riddle that no conjecture had been able to divine—the formless and chaotic nature of virtually all books. One book, which my father

[1]The original manuscript has neither numbers nor capital letters; punctuation is limited to the comma and the period. Those two marks, the space, and the twenty-two letters of the alphabet are the twenty-five sufficient symbols that our unknown author is referring to. [Ed note.]

once saw in a hexagon in circuit 15–94, consisted of the letters MCV perversely repeated from the first line to the last. Another (much consulted in this zone) is a mere labyrinth of letters whose penultimate page contains the phrase *O Time thy pyramids*. This much is known: For every rational line or forthright statement there are leagues of senseless cacophony, verbal nonsense, and incoherency. (I know of one semibarbarous zone whose librarians repudiate the "vain and superstitious habit" of trying to find sense in books, equating such a quest with attempting to find meaning in dreams or in the chaotic lines of the palm of one's hand. . . . They will acknowledge that the inventors of writing imitated the twenty-five natural symbols, but contend that that adoption was fortuitous, coincidental, and that books in themselves have no meaning. That argument, as we shall see, is not entirely fallacious.)

For many years it was believed that those impenetrable books were in ancient or far-distant languages. It is true that the most ancient peoples, the first librarians, employed a language quite different from the one we speak today; it is true that a few miles to the right, our language devolves into dialect and that ninety floors above, it becomes incomprehensible. All of that, I repeat, is true—but four hundred ten pages of unvarying MCVs cannot belong to any language, however dialectal or primitive it may be. Some have suggested that each letter influences the next, and that the value of MCV on page 71, line 3, is not the value of the same series on another line of another page, but that vague thesis has not met with any great acceptance. Others have mentioned the possibility of codes; that conjecture has been universally accepted, though not in the sense in which its originators formulated it.

Some five hundred years ago, the chief of one of the upper hexagons[2] came across a book as jumbled as all the others, but containing almost two pages of homogeneous lines. He showed his find to a travelling decipherer, who told him that the lines were written in Portuguese; others said it was Yiddish. Within the century experts had determined what the language actually was: a Samoyed Lithuanian dialect of Guaraní, with inflections from classical Arabic. The content was also determined: the rudiments of combinatory analysis, illustrated with examples of endlessly repeating variations. Those examples allowed a librarian of genius to discover the fundamental law of the Library. This philosopher observed that all books, however different from one another they might be, consist of identical elements: the space, the period, the comma, and the twenty-two letters of the alphabet. He also posited a fact which all travellers have since confirmed: *In all the Library, there are no two identical books*. From those incontrovertible premises, the librarian deducted that the Library is "total"—perfect, complete, and whole—and that its bookshelves contain all possible combinations of the twenty-two orthographic symbols (a number which, though unimaginably vast, is not infinite)—that is, all that is able to be expressed, in every language. *All*—the detailed history of the future, the autobiographies of the archangels, the faithful catalogue of the Library, thousands and thousands of false catalogues, the proof of the falsity of those false catalogues, a proof

[2]In earlier times, there was one man for every three hexagons. Suicide and diseases of the lung have played havoc with that proportion. An unspeakably melancholy memory: I have sometimes travelled for nights on end, down corridors and polished staircases, without coming across a single librarian.

of the falsity of the *true* catalogue, the gnostic gospel of Basilides, the commentary upon that gospel, the commentary on the commentary on that gospel, the true story of your death, the translation of every book into every language, the interpolations of every book into all books, the treatise Bede could have written (but did not) on the mythology of the Saxon people, the lost books of Tacitus.

When it was announced that the Library contained all books, the first reaction was unbounded joy. All men felt themselves the possessors of an intact and secret treasure. There was no personal problem, no world problem, whose eloquent solution did not exist—somewhere in some hexagon. The universe was justified; the universe suddenly became congruent with the unlimited width and breadth of humankind's hope. At that period there was much talk of The Vindications—books of *apologiae* and prophecies that would vindicate for all time the actions of every person in the universe and that held wondrous arcana for men's futures. Thousands of greedy individuals abandoned their sweet native hexagons and rushed downstairs, upstairs, spurred by the vain desire to find their Vindication. These pilgrims squabbled in the narrow corridors, muttered dark imprecations, strangled one another on the divine staircases, threw deceiving volumes down ventilation shafts, were themselves hurled to their deaths by men of distant regions. Others went insane. . . . The Vindications do exist (I have seen two of them, which refer to persons in the future, persons perhaps not imaginary), but those who went in quest of them failed to recall that the chance of a man's finding his own Vindication, or some perfidious version of his own, can be calculated to be zero.

At that same period there was also hope that the fundamental mysteries of mankind—the origin of the Library and of time—might be revealed. In all likelihood those profound mysteries can indeed be explained in words; if the language of the philosophers is not sufficient, then the multiform Library must surely have produced the extraordinary language that is required, together with the words and grammar of that language. For four centuries, men have been scouring the hexagons. . . . There are official searchers, the "inquisitors." I have seen them about their tasks: they arrive exhausted at some hexagon, they talk about a staircase that nearly killed them . . . rungs were missing . . . they speak with the librarian about galleries and staircases, and, once in a while, they take up the nearest book and leaf through it, searching for disgraceful or dishonourable words. Clearly, no one expects to discover anything.

That unbridled hopefulness was succeeded, naturally enough, by a similarly disproportionate depression. The certainty that some bookshelf in some hexagon contained precious books, yet that those precious books were forever out of reach, was almost unbearable. One blasphemous sect proposed that the searches be discontinued and that all men shuffle letters and symbols until those canonical books, through some improbable stroke of chance, had been constructed. The authorities were forced to issue strict orders. The sect disappeared, but in my childhood I have seen old men who for long periods would hide in the latrines with metal discs and a forbidden dice cup, feebly mimicking the divine disorder.

Others, going about it in the opposite way, thought the first thing to do was eliminate all worthless books. They would invade the hexagons, show credentials that were not always false, leaf disgustedly through a volume, and condemn entire walls of books. It is to their hygienic, ascetic rage that we lay the senseless loss of millions of volumes. Their name is execrated today, but those who grieve over the "treasures" destroyed in that frenzy overlook two widely acknowledged facts: One, that the Library is so huge that any reduction by human hands must be infinitesimal. And two, that each book is unique and irreplaceable, but (since the Library is total) there are always several hundred thousand imperfect facsimiles—books that differ by no more than a single letter, or a comma. Despite general opinion, I daresay that the consequences of the depredations committed by the Purifiers have been exaggerated by the horror those same fanatics inspired. They were spurred on by the holy zeal to reach—someday, through unrelenting effort—the books of the Crimson Hexagon—books smaller than natural books, books omnipotent, illustrated, and magical.

We also have knowledge of another superstition from that period: belief in what was termed the Book-Man. On some shelf in some hexagon, it was argued, there must exist a book that is the cipher and perfect compendium of *all other books*, and some librarian must have examined that book; this librarian is analogous to a god. In the language of this zone there are still vestiges of the sect that worshiped that distant librarian. Many have gone in search of Him. For a hundred years, men beat every possible path—and every path in vain. How was one to locate the idolized secret hexagon that sheltered Him? Someone proposed searching by regression: To locate book *A*, first consult book *B*, which tells where book *A* can be found; to locate book *B*, first consult book *C*, and so on, to infinity. . . . It is in ventures such as these that I have squandered and spent my years. I cannot think it unlikely that there is such a total book[3] on some shelf in the universe. I pray to the unknown gods that some man—even a single man, tens of centuries ago—has perused and read that book. If the honour and wisdom and joy of such a reading are not to be my own, then let them be for others. Let heaven exist, though my own place be in hell. Let me be tortured and battered and annihilated, but let there be one instant, one creature, wherein thy enormous Library may find its justification.

Infidels claim that the rule in the Library is not "sense," but "nonsense," and that "rationality" (even humble, pure coherence) is an almost miraculous exception. They speak, I know, of "the feverish Library whose random volumes constantly threaten to transmogrify into others, so that they affirm all things, deny all things, and confound and confuse all things, like some mad and hallucinating deity." Those words, which not only proclaim disorder but exemplify it as well, prove, as all can see, the infidels' deplorable taste and desperate ignorance. For while the Library contains all verbal structures, all the variations allowed by the twenty-five orthographic symbols, it includes not a single absolute piece of nonsense. It would be pointless to observe that the finest volume of all the many hexagons that I myself administer is titled *Combed Thunder*, while another is title *The Plaster Cramp*, and another, *Axaxaxas mlö*. Those phrases, at first apparently incoherent, are undoubtedly susceptible to cryptographic or allegorical "reading"; that reading,

[3]I repeat: In order for a book to exist, it is sufficient that it be *possible*. Only the impossible is excluded. For example, no book is also a staircase, though there are no doubt books that discuss and deny and prove that possibility, and others whose structure corresponds to that of a staircase.

that justification of the words' order and existence, is itself verbal and, *ex hypothesi*, already contained somewhere in the Library. There is no combination of characters one can make—*dhcmrlchtdj*, for example—that the divine Library has not foreseen and that in one or more of its secret tongues does not hide a terrible significance. There is no syllable one can speak that is not filled with tenderness and terror, that is not, in one of those languages, the mighty name of a god. To speak is to commit tautologies. This pointless, verbose epistle already exists in one of the thirty volumes of the five bookshelves in one of the countless hexagons—as does its refutation. (A number *n* of the possible languages employ the same vocabulary; in some of them, the *symbol* "library" possesses the correct definition "everlasting, ubiquitous system of hexagonal galleries," while a library—the thing—is a loaf of bread or a pyramid or something else, and the six words that define it themselves have other definitions. You who read me—are you certain you understand my language?)

Methodical composition distracts me from the present condition of humanity. The certainty that everything has already been written annuls us, or renders us phantasmal. I know districts in which the young people prostrate themselves before books and like savages kiss their pages, though they cannot read a letter. Epidemics, heretical discords, pilgrimages that inevitably degenerate into brigandage have decimated the population. I believe I mentioned the suicides, which are more and more frequent every year. I am perhaps misled by old age and fear, but I suspect that the human species—the *only* species—teeters at the verge of extinction, yet that the Library—enlightened, solitary, infinite, perfectly unmoving, armed with precious volumes, pointless, incorruptible, and secret . . . will endure.

I have just written the word "infinite." I have not included that adjective out of mere rhetorical habit; I hereby state that it is not illogical to think that the world is infinite. Those who believe it to have limits hypothesize that in some remote place or places the corridors and staircases and hexagons may, inconceivably, end—which is absurd. And yet those who picture the world as unlimited forget that the number of possible books is *not*. I will be bold enough to suggest this solution to the ancient problem: *The Library is unlimited but periodic*. If an eternal traveller should journey in any direction, he would find after untold centuries that the same volumes are repeated in the same disorder— which, repeated, becomes order: the Order. My solitude is cheered by that elegant hope.[4]

MAR DEL PLATA 1941

1941

translated by Andrew Hurley

---

[4]Letizia Alvarez de Toledo has observed that the vast Library is pointless; strictly speaking, all that is required is a *single volume*, of the common size, printed in nine- or ten-point type, that would consist of an infinite number of infinitely thin pages. (In the early seventeenth century, Cavalieri stated that every solid body is the superposition of an infinite number of planes.) Using that silken *vademecum* would not be easy: each apparent page would open into other similar pages; the inconceivable middle page would have no "back."

Ernest Hemingway

1899–1961

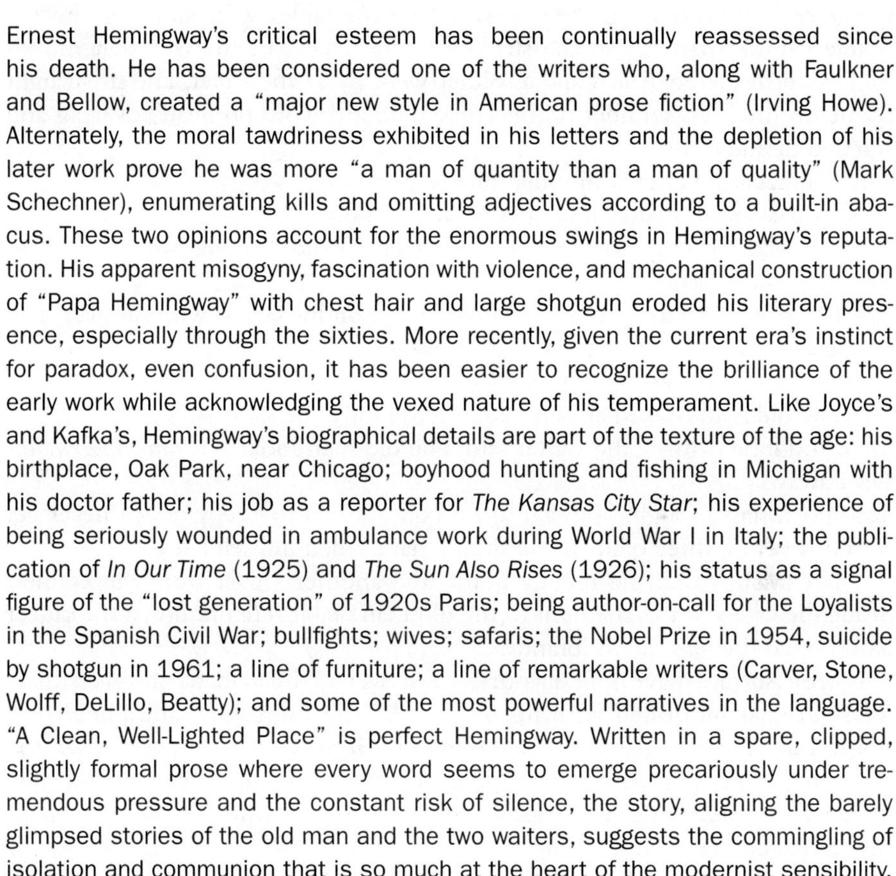

Ernest Hemingway's critical esteem has been continually reassessed since his death. He has been considered one of the writers who, along with Faulkner and Bellow, created a "major new style in American prose fiction" (Irving Howe). Alternately, the moral tawdriness exhibited in his letters and the depletion of his later work prove he was more "a man of quantity than a man of quality" (Mark Schechner), enumerating kills and omitting adjectives according to a built-in abacus. These two opinions account for the enormous swings in Hemingway's reputation. His apparent misogyny, fascination with violence, and mechanical construction of "Papa Hemingway" with chest hair and large shotgun eroded his literary presence, especially through the sixties. More recently, given the current era's instinct for paradox, even confusion, it has been easier to recognize the brilliance of the early work while acknowledging the vexed nature of his temperament. Like Joyce's and Kafka's, Hemingway's biographical details are part of the texture of the age: his birthplace, Oak Park, near Chicago; boyhood hunting and fishing in Michigan with his doctor father; his job as a reporter for *The Kansas City Star*; his experience of being seriously wounded in ambulance work during World War I in Italy; the publication of *In Our Time* (1925) and *The Sun Also Rises* (1926); his status as a signal figure of the "lost generation" of 1920s Paris; being author-on-call for the Loyalists in the Spanish Civil War; bullfights; wives; safaris; the Nobel Prize in 1954, suicide by shotgun in 1961; a line of furniture; a line of remarkable writers (Carver, Stone, Wolff, DeLillo, Beatty); and some of the most powerful narratives in the language. "A Clean, Well-Lighted Place" is perfect Hemingway. Written in a spare, clipped, slightly formal prose where every word seems to emerge precariously under tremendous pressure and the constant risk of silence, the story, aligning the barely glimpsed stories of the old man and the two waiters, suggests the commingling of isolation and communion that is so much at the heart of the modernist sensibility.

A Clean, Well-Lighted Place

It was late and everyone had left the café except an old man who sat in the shadow the leaves of the tree made against the electric light. In the daytime the street was dusty, but at night the dew settled the dust and the old man liked to sit late because he was deaf and now at night it was quiet and he felt the difference. The two waiters inside the café knew the old man was a little drunk, and while he was a good client they knew that if he became too drunk he would leave without paying, so they kept watch on him.

"Last week he tried to commit suicide," one waiter said.

"Why?"

"He was in despair."

"What about?"

"Nothing."

"How do you know it was nothing?"

"He has plenty of money."

They sat together at a table that was close against the wall near the door of the café and looked at the terrace where the tables were all empty except where the old man sat in the shadow of the leaves of the tree that moved slightly in the wind. A girl and a soldier went by in the street. The street light shone on the brass number on his collar. The girl wore no head covering and hurried beside him.

"The guard will pick him up," one waiter said.

"What does it matter if he gets what he's after?"

"He had better get off the street now. The guard will get him. They went by five minutes ago."

The old man sitting in the shadow rapped on his saucer with his glass. The younger waiter went over to him.

"What do you want?"

The old man looked at him. "Another brandy," he said.

"You'll be drunk," the waiter said. The old man looked at him. The waiter went away.

"He'll stay all night," he said to his colleague. "I'm sleepy now. I never get into bed before three o'clock. He should have killed himself last week."

The waiter took the brandy bottle and another saucer from the counter inside the café and marched out to the old man's table. He put down the saucer and poured the glass full of brandy.

"You should have killed yourself last week," he said to the deaf man. The old man motioned with his finger. "A little more," he said. The waiter poured on into the glass so that the brandy slopped over and ran down the stem into the top saucer of the pile. "Thank you," the old man said. The waiter took the bottle back inside the café. He sat down at the table with his colleague again.

"He's drunk now," he said.

"He's drunk every night."

"What did he want to kill himself for?"

"How should I know."

"How did he do it?"

"He hung himself with a rope."

"Who cut him down?"

"His niece."

"Why did they do it?"

"Fear for his soul."

"How much money has he got?"

"He's got plenty."

"He must be eighty years old."

"Anyway I should say he was eighty."

"I wish he would go home. I never get to bed before three o'clock. What kind of hour is that to go to bed?"

"He stays up because he likes it."

"He's lonely. I'm not lonely. I have a wife waiting in bed for me."

"He had a wife once too."

"A wife would be no good to him now."

"You can't tell. He might be better with a wife."

"His niece looks after him."

"I know. You said she cut him down."

"I wouldn't want to be that old. An old man is a nasty thing."

"Not always. This old man is clean. He drinks without spilling. Even now, drunk. Look at him."

"I don't want to look at him. I wish he would go home. He has no regard for those who must work."

The old man looked from his glass across the square, then over at the waiters.

"Another brandy," he said, pointing to his glass. The waiter who was in a hurry came over.

"Finished," he said, speaking with that omission of syntax stupid people employ when talking to drunken people or foreigners. "No more tonight. Close now."

"Another," said the old man.

"No. Finished." The waiter wiped the edge of the table with a towel and shook his head.

The old man stood up, slowly counted the saucers, took a leather coin purse from his pocket and paid for the drinks, leaving half a peseta tip.

The waiter watched him go down the street, a very old man walking unsteadily but with dignity.

"Why didn't you let him stay and drink?" the unhurried waiter asked. They were putting up the shutters. "It is not half-past two."

"I want to go home to bed."

"What is an hour?"

"More to me than to him."

"An hour is the same."

"You talk like an old man yourself. He can buy a bottle and drink at home."

"It's not the same."

"No, it is not," agreed the waiter with a wife. He did not wish to be unjust. He was only in a hurry.

"And you? You have no fear of going home before your usual hour?"

"Are you trying to insult me?"

"No, hombre, only to make a joke."

"No," the waiter who was in a hurry said, rising from pulling down the metal shutters. "I have confidence. I am all confidence."

"You have youth, confidence, and a job," the older waiter said. "You have everything."

"And what do you lack?"

"Everything but work."

"You have everything I have."

"No. I have never had confidence and I am not young."

"Come on. Stop talking nonsense and lock up."

"I am of those who like to stay late at the café," the older waiter said. "With all those who do not want to go to bed. With all those who need a light for the night."

"I want to go home and into bed."

"We are of two different kinds," the older waiter said. He was now dressed to go home. "It is not only a question of youth and confidence although those things are very beautiful. Each night I am reluctant to close up because there may be someone who needs the café."

"Hombre, there are bodegas open all night long."

"You do not understand. This is a clean and pleasant café. It is well lighted. The light is very good and also, now, there are shadows of the leaves."

"Good night," said the younger waiter.

"Good night," the other said. Turning off the electric light he continued the conversation with himself. It is the light of course but it is necessary that the place be clean and pleasant. You do not want music. Certainly you do not want music. Nor can you stand before a bar with dignity although that is all that is provided for these hours. What did he fear? It was not fear or dread. It was a nothing that he knew too well. It was all a nothing and a man was nothing too. It was only that and light was all it needed and a certain cleanness and order. Some lived in it and never felt it but he knew it all was nada y pues nada y nada y pues nada. Our nada who art in nada, nada be thy name thy kingdom nada thy will be nada in nada as it is in nada. Give us this nada our daily nada and nada us our nada as we nada our nadas and nada us not into nada but deliver us from nada; pues nada. Hail nothing full of nothing, nothing is with thee. He smiled and stood before a bar with a shining steam pressure coffee machine.

"What's yours?" asked the barman.

"Nada."

"Otro loco mas," said the barman and turned away.

"A little cup," said the waiter.

The barman poured it for him.

"The light is very bright and pleasant but the bar is unpolished," the waiter said.

The barman looked at him but did not answer. It was too late at night for conversation.

"You want another copita?" the barman asked.

"No, thank you," said the waiter and went out. He disliked bars and bodegas. A clean, well-lighted café was a very different thing. Now, without thinking further, he would go home to his room. He would lie in the bed and finally, with daylight, he would go to sleep. After all, he said to himself, it is probably only insomnia. Many must have it.

1930

Samuel Beckett

1906–1989

In his biography of James Joyce, Richard Ellmann describes Samuel Beckett visiting the other Irishman in Paris, their conversations weighty silences punctuated by complex philosophical declarations. In their own work the older Dubliner moved toward the linguistic omnivorousness of *Finnegans Wake*, the younger toward weaving the thinnest membrane between language and silence, between inhalation and exhalation. Born into a middle-class Protestant family, Beckett succinctly recalled, "I had little talent for happiness," which, unlike his talent for words and their erosion, he had no inclination to develop. He graduated from Trinity College, Dublin, in 1927, and the next year made his way to Paris, met and championed Joyce, and shortly afterwards published a volume of poetry, *Whoroscope* (1930), and in 1931 a critical scrutiny of Proust. He wandered through Europe, but in 1937 settled more decidedly in Paris, where he fought for the Resistance during the war, and wrote his terse ambivalences in French, then translated them into English. He published his first story, "Assumption," in *transition* (1929), and continued to write short fiction for sixty years; the last story, "Stirrings Still," written for his long-time Grove Press publisher, Barney Rosset, was issued a year before Beckett's death. Considering how often Beckett turned to the form and how closely the stories are tied to the plays and novels, it is very odd that his short fiction should be so rarely anthologized, or even noticed outside the sphere of professional Beckett studies. Yet, in their hybridity, the stories reflect the essential paradoxes of the form: the porousness of what is present and what is absent and their inherent sense of transience and of consummate artistic control. In "Imagination Dead Imagine" (1965) he collapses the parameters of grammar, of external and internal, of geometry and time; the story is at once perfectly transparent and perfectly opaque. Perhaps Beckett is so identified with *Waiting for Godot* (1955) and *Endgame* (1958) and the great trilogy of novels—in other words, so identified with the spirit and the time of the Theatre of the Absurd—that the more enigmatic and isolating short fiction might seem tangential. In 1969 he was awarded the Nobel Prize, for all his "white speck[s] lost in whiteness" ("Imagination Dead Imagine").

Imagination Dead Imagine

No trace anywhere of life, you say, pah, no difficulty there, imagination not dead yet, yes, dead, good, imagination dead imagine. Islands, waters, azure, verdure, one glimpse and vanished, endlessly, omit. Till all white in the whiteness the rotunda. No way in, go in, measure. Diameter three feet, three feet from ground to summit of the vault. Two diameters at right angles AB CD divide the white ground into two semicircles ACB BDA. Lying on the ground two white bodies, each in its semicircle. White too the vault and the round wall eighteen inches high from which it springs. Go back out, a plain rotunda, all white in the whiteness, go back in, rap, solid throughout, a ring as in the imagination the ring of bone. The light that makes all so white no visible source, all shines with the same white shine, ground, wall, vault, bodies, no shadow. Strong heat, surfaces hot but not burning to the touch, bodies sweating. Go back out, move back, the little fabric vanishes, ascend, it vanishes, all white in the whiteness, descend, go back in. Emptiness, silence, heat, whiteness, wait, the light goes down, all grows dark together, ground, wall, vault, bodies, say twenty seconds, all the greys, the light goes out, all vanishes. At the same time the temperature goes down, to reach its minimum, say freezing-point, at the same instant that the black is reached, which may seem strange. Wait, more or less long, light and heat come back, all grows white and hot together, ground, wall, vault, bodies, say twenty seconds, all the greys, till the initial level is reached whence the fall began. More or less long, for there may intervene, experience shows, between end of fall and beginning of rise, pauses of varying length, from the fraction of the second to what would have seemed, in other times, other places, an eternity. Same remark for the other pause, between end of rise and beginning of fall. The extremes, as long as they last, are perfectly stable, which in the case of the temperature may seem strange, in the beginning. It is possible too, experience shows, for rise and fall to stop short at any point and mark a pause, more or less long, before resuming, or reversing, the rise now fall, the fall rise, these in their turn to be completed, or to stop short and mark a pause, more or less long, before resuming, or again reversing, and so on, till finally one or the other extreme is reached. Such variations of rise and fall, combining in countless rhythms, commonly attend the passage from white and heat to black and cold, and vice versa. The extremes alone are stable as is stressed by the vibration to be observed when a pause occurs at some intermediate stage, no matter what its level and duration. Then all vibrates, ground, wall, vault, bodies, ashen or leaden or between the two, as may be. But on the whole, experience shows, such uncertain passage is not common. And most often, when the light begins to fail, and along with it the heat, the movement continues unbroken until, in the space of some twenty seconds, pitch black is reached and at the same instant say freezing-point. Same remark for the reverse movement, towards heat and whiteness. Next most frequent is the fall or rise with pauses of varying length in these feverish greys, without at any moment reversal of the movement. But whatever its uncertainties the return sooner or later to a temporary calm seems assured, for the moment, in the black dark or the great whiteness, with attendant temperature, world still proof against enduring tumult. Rediscovered miraculously after what absence in perfect voids it is no longer quite the same, from this point of view, but there is no other. Externally all is as before and the sighting of the little fabric quite as much a matter of chance, its whiteness merging in the surrounding whiteness. But go in and now briefer lulls and never twice the same storm. Light and heat remain linked as though supplied by the same source of which still no trace. Still on the ground, bent in three, the head against the wall at B, the arse against the wall at A, the knees against the wall between B and C, the feet against the wall between C and A, that is to say inscribed in the semicircle ACB, merging in the white ground were it not for the long hair of strangely imperfect whiteness, the white body of a woman finally. Similarly inscribed in the other semicircle, against the wall his head at A, his arse at B, his knees between A and D, his feet between D and B, the partner. On their right sides therefore both and back to back head to arse. Hold a mirror to their lips, it mists. With their left hands they hold their left legs a little below the knee, with their right hands their left arms a little above the elbow. In this agitated light, its great white calm now so rare and brief, inspection is not easy. Sweat and mirror notwithstanding they might well pass for inanimate but for the left eyes which at incalculable intervals suddenly open wide and gaze in unblinking exposure long beyond what is humanly possible. Piercing pale blue the effect is striking, in the beginning. Never the two gazes together except once, when the beginning of one overlapped the end of the other, for about ten seconds. Neither fat nor thin, big nor small, the bodies seem whole and in fairly good condition, to judge by the surfaces exposed to view. The faces too, assuming the two sides of a piece, seem to want nothing essential. Between their absolute stillness and the convulsive light the contrast is striking, in the beginning, for one who still remembers having been struck by the contrary. It is clear however, from a thousand little signs too long to imagine, that they are not sleeping. Only murmur ah, no more, in this silence, and at the same instant for the eye of prey the infinitesimal shudder instantaneously suppressed. Leave them there, sweating and icy, there is better elsewhere. No, life ends and no, there is nothing elsewhere, and no question now of ever finding again that white speck lost in whiteness, to see if they still lie still in the stress of that storm, or of a worse storm, or in the black dark for good, or the great whiteness unchanging, and if not what they are doing.

1966

Richard Wright

1908–1960

"The day *Native Son* appeared [in 1940] American culture was changed forever. No matter how much qualifying the book might later need, it made impossible a repetition of the old lies . . . Richard Wright's novel brought out into the open, as no one ever had before, the hatred, fear, and violence that have crippled and may yet destroy our culture" (Irving Howe). The circumstances of Wright's early life on a Mississippi plantation were not auspicious for the possibility of Irving Howe's famous account of *Native Son*'s publication or subsequent dinners with the postwar Parisian intelligentsia, Sartre and de Beauvoir, Koestler and Camus. The grandson of four grandparents born in slavery, Wright was abandoned by his father who chose to depart, followed by his mother's absence through disease and paralysis. When Wright was ten, his uncle was murdered, and a constrained, unquiet life with his fundamentalist grandmother followed. But in an important sense the various fears and menaces Wright encountered were the underside of his fascination with language, particularly language as social and personal weaponry, which he learned from H.L. Mencken. Violence made *Native Son* as inevitable as it was unlikely, a novel Ira Wells sees at the core of the literature of "domestic terror." Wright left the South in 1927 for Chicago where he joined the Communist Party, a strained affiliation punctuated and virtually terminated by witnessing the trial of a comrade that duplicated the Moscow Purges. Afterwards, "I went into the dark Chicago streets and walked home through the cold, filled with a sense of sadness. Once again I told myself that I must learn to stand alone" (*The God That Failed*). This determination involved moving to New York, finishing *Native Son*, and dealing, not always clearly, with the startling success of the novel that made Wright the most notable, admired, and—because of its terrible subject—feared Black writer in the United States. *Black Boy* (1945), his autobiography, maintained his remarkable literary and financial success, but driven by racial tensions over the Wrights' "mixed" marriage, the family migrated to Paris, where both the company and the culture moved him in the direction of existential thinking and toward the publication, in 1948, of the Camus-rooted *The Outsider* (1953). But in the last years of his life dreadfully abbreviated by a heart attack, Wright's readership had at best mixed responses to his post–*Native Son* work. The novel had also overshadowed his deftness and power as a short story writer. In its coiled narratives, *Uncle Tom's Children* predates *Native Son*, but the stories now most fully representative of Wright's ability in the tighter genre are the posthumously published *Eight Men* (1961). From "The Man Who Was Almost a Man" to the concluding "The Man Who Went to Chicago," Wright's naturalistic dialogue, rather than being dated, has a local permanence, an edgy register for the interplay of the humour and the gravity of race and maleness.

The Man Who Was Almost a Man

Dave struck out across the fields, looking homeward through paling light. Whut's the use talkin wid em niggers in the field? Anyhow, his mother was putting supper on the table. Them niggers can't understand nothing. One of these days he was going to get a gun and practice shooting, then they couldn't talk to him as though he were a little boy. He slowed, looking at the ground. Shucks, Ah ain scareda them even ef they are biggern me! Aw, Ah know whut Ahma do. Ahm going by ol Joe's sto n git that Sears Roebuck catlog n look at them guns. Mebbe Ma will lemme buy one when she gits mah pay from ol man Hawkins. Ahma beg her t gimme some money. Ahm ol ernough to hava gun. Ahm seventeen. Almost a man. He strode, feeling his long loose-jointed limbs. Shucks, a man oughta hava little gun aftah he done worked hard all day.

He came in sight of Joe's store. A yellow lantern glowed on the front porch. He mounted steps and went through the screen door, hearing it bang behind him. There was a strong smell of coal oil and mackerel fish. He felt very confident until he saw fat Joe walk in through the rear door, then his courage began to ooze.

"Howdy, Dave! Whutcha want?"

"How yuh, Mistah Joe? Aw, Ah don wanna buy nothing. Ah jus wanted t see ef yuhd lemme look at tha catlog erwhile."

"Sure! You wanna see it here?"

"Nawsuh. Ah wants t take it home wid me. Ah'll bring it back termorrow when Ah come in from the fiels."

"You plannin on buying something?"

"Yessuh."

"Your ma lettin you have your own money now?"

"Shucks. Mistah Joe, Ahm gittin t be a man like anybody else!"

Joe laughed and wiped his greasy white face with a red bandanna.

"Whut you plannin on buyin?"

Dave looked at the floor, scratched his head, scratched his thigh, and smiled. Then he looked up shyly.

"Ah'll tell yuh, Mistah Joe, ef yuh promise yuh won't tell."

"I promise."

"Waal, Ahma buy a gun."

"A gun? What you want with a gun?"

"Ah wanna keep it."

"You ain't nothing but a boy. You don't need a gun."

"Aw, lemme have the catlog, Mistah Joe. Ah'll bring it back."

Joe walked through the rear door. Dave was elated. He looked around at barrels of sugar and flour. He heard Joe coming back. He craned his neck to see if he were bringing the book. Yeah, he's got it. Gawddog, he's got it!

"Here, but be sure you bring it back. It's the only one I got."

"Sho, Mistah Joe."

"Say, if you wanna buy a gun, why don't you buy one from me? I gotta gun to sell."

"Will it shoot?"

"Sure it'll shoot."

"Whut kind is it?"

"Oh, it's kinda old . . . a left-hand Wheeler. A pistol. A big one."

"Is it got bullets in it?"

"It's loaded."

"Kin Ah see it?"

"Where's your money?"

"What yuh wan fer it?"

"I'll let you have it for two dollars."

"Just two dollahs? Shucks, Ah could buy tha when Ah git mah pay."

"I'll have it here when you want it."

"Awright, suh. Ah be in fer it."

He went through the door, hearing it slam again behind him. Ahma git some money from Ma n buy me a gun! Only two dollahs! He tucked the thick catalogue under his arm and hurried.

"Where yuh been, boy?" His mother held a steaming dish of black-eyed peas.

"Aw, Ma, Ah jus stopped down the road t talk wid the boys."

"Yuh know bettah t keep suppah waitin."

He sat down, resting the catalogue on the edge of the table.

"Yuh git up from there and git to the well n wash yosef! Ah ain feedin no hogs in mah house!"

She grabbed his shoulder and pushed him. He stumbled out of the room, then came back to get the catalogue.

"Whut this?"

"Aw, Ma, it's jusa catlog."

"Who yuh git it from?"

"From Joe, down at the sto."

"Waal, thas good. We kin use it in the outhouse."

"Naw, Ma." He grabbed for it. "Gimme ma catlog, Ma."

She held onto it and glared at him.

"Quit hollerin at me! Whut's wrong wid yuh? Yuh crazy?"

"But Ma, please. It ain mine! It's Joe's! He tol me t bring it back t im termorrow."

She gave up the book. He stumbled down the back steps, hugging the thick book under his arm. When he had splashed water on his face and hands, he groped back to the kitchen and fumbled in a corner for the towel. He bumped into a chair; it clattered to the floor. The catalogue sprawled at his feet. When he had dried his eyes he snatched up the book and held it again under his arm. His mother stood watching him.

"Now, ef yuh gonna act a fool over that ol book, Ah'll take it n burn it up."

"Naw, Ma, please."

"Waal, set down n be still!"

He sat down and drew the oil lamp close. He thumbed page after page, unaware of the food his mother set on the table. His father came in. Then his small brother.

"Whutcha got there, Dave?" his father asked.

"Jusa catlog," he answered, not looking up.

"Yeah, here they is!" His eyes glowed at blue-and-black revolvers. He glanced up, feeling sudden guilt. His father was watching him. He eased the book under the table and rested it on his knees. After the blessing was asked, he ate. He scooped up peas and swallowed fat meat without chewing. Buttermilk helped to wash it down. He did not want to mention money before his father. He would do much better by cornering his mother when she was alone. He looked at his father uneasily out of the edge of his eye.

"Boy, how come yuh don quit foolin wid tha book n eat yo suppah?"

"Yessuh."

"How you n ol man Hawkins gitten erlong?"

"Suh?"

"Can't yuh hear? Why don yuh lissen? Ah ast yu how wuz yuh n ol man Hawkins gittin erlong?"

"Oh, swell, Pa. Ah plows mo lan than anybody over there."

"Waal, yuh oughta keep you mind on whut yuh doin."

"Yessuh."

He poured his plate full of molasses and sopped it up slowly with a chunk of cornbread. When his father and brother had left the kitchen, he still sat and looked again at the guns in the catalogue, longing to muster courage enough to present his case to his mother. Lawd, ef Ah only had tha pretty one! He could almost feel the slickness of the weapon with his fingers. If he had a gun like that he would polish it and keep it shining so it would never rust. N Ah'd keep it loaded, by Gawd!

"Ma?" His voice was hesitant.

"Hunh?"

"Ol man Hawkins give yuh mah money yit?"

"Yeah, but ain no usa yuh thinking bout throwin nona it erway. Ahm keeping tha money sos yuh kin have cloes t go to school this winter."

He rose and went to her side with the open catalogue in his palms. She was washing dishes, her head bent low over a pan. Shyly he raised the book. When he spoke, his voice was husky, faint.

"Ma, Gawd knows Ah wans one of these."

"One of whut?" she asked, not raising her eyes.

"One of these," he said again, not daring even to point. She glanced up at the page, then at him with wide eyes.

"Nigger, is yuh gone plumb crazy?"

"Aw, Ma—"

"Git outta here! Don yuh talk t me bout no gun! Yuh a fool!"

"Ma, Ah kin buy one fer two dollahs."

"Not ef Ah knows it, yuh ain!"

"But yuh promised me one—"

"Ah don care what Ah promised! Yuh ain nothing but a boy yit!"

"Ma, ef yuh lemme buy one Ah'll *never* ast yuh fer nothing no mo."

"Ah tol yuh t git outta here! Yuh ain gonna toucha penny of tha money fer no gun! Thas how come Ah has Mistah Hawkins t pay yo wages t me, cause Ah knows yuh ain got no sense."

"But, Ma, we needa gun. Pa ain got no gun. We needa gun in the house. Yuh kin never tell whut might happen."

"Now don yuh try to maka fool oulta me, boy! Ef we did hava gun, yuh wouldn't have it!"

He laid the catalogue down and slipped his arm around her waist.

"Aw, Ma, Ah done worked hard alla summer n ain ast yuh fer nothing, is Ah, now?"

"Thas whut yuh spose t do!"

"But Ma, Ah wans a gun. Yuh kin lemme have two dollahs outta mah money. Please, Ma. I kin give it to Pa. . . . Please, Ma! Ah loves yuh, Ma."

When she spoke her voice came soft and low.

"What yu wan wida gun, Dave? Yuh don need no gun. Yuh'll git in trouble. N ef yo pa jus thought Ah let yuh have money t buy a gun he'd hava fit."

"Ah'll hide it, Ma. It ain but two dollahs."

"Lawd, chil, whut's wrong wid yuh?"

"Ain nothin wrong. Ma. Ahm almos a man now. Ah wans a gun."

"Who gonna sell yuh a gun?"

"Ol Joe at the sto."

"N it don cos but two dollahs?"

"Thas all, Ma. Jus two dollahs. Please, Ma."

She was stacking the plates away; her hands moved slowly, reflectively. Dave kept an anxious silence. Finally, she turned to him.

"Ah'll let yuh git tha gun ef yuh promise me one thing."

"What's tha, Ma?"

"Yuh bring it straight back t me, yuh hear? It be fer Pa."

"Yessum! Lemme go now, Ma."

She stooped, turned slightly to one side, raised the hem of her dress, rolled down the top of her stocking, and came up with a slender wad of bills.

"Here," she said. "Lawd knows yuh don need no gun. But yer pa does. Yuh bring it right back t me, yuh hear? Ahma put it up. Now ef yuh don, Ahma have yuh pa lick yuh so hard yuh won fergit it."

"Yessum."

He took the money, ran down the steps, and across the yard.

"Dave! Yuuuuuh Daaaaave!"

He heard, but he was not going to stop now. "Now, Lawd!"

The first movement he made the following morning was to reach under his pillow for the gun. In the gray light of dawn he held it loosely, feeling a sense of power. Could kill a man with a gun like this. Kill anybody, black or white. And if he were holding his gun in his hand, nobody could run over him; they would have to respect him. It was a big gun, with a long barrel and a heavy handle. He raised and lowered it in his hand, marveling at its weight.

He had not come straight home with it as his mother had asked; instead he had stayed out in the fields, holding the weapon in his hand, aiming it now and then at some imaginary foe. But he had not fired it; he had been afraid that his father might hear. Also he was not sure he knew how to fire it.

To avoid surrendering the pistol he had not come into the house until he knew that they were all asleep. When his mother had tiptoed to his bedside late that night and demanded the gun, he had first played possum; then he had told her that the gun was hidden outdoors, that he would bring it to her in the morning. Now he lay turning it slowly in his hands. He broke it, took out the cartridges, felt them, and then put them back.

He slid out of bed, got a long strip of old flannel from a trunk, wrapped the gun in it, and tied it to his naked thigh while it was still loaded. He did not go in to breakfast. Even though it was not yet daylight, he started for Jim Hawkins' plantation. Just as the sun was rising he reached the barns where the mules and plows were kept.

"Hey! That you, Dave?"

He turned. Jim Hawkins stood eying him suspiciously.

"What're yuh doing here so early?"

"Ah didn't know Ah wuz gittin up so early, Mistah Hawkins. Ah was fixin t hitch up ol Jenny n take her t the fiels."

"Good. Since you' re so early, how about plowing that stretch down by the woods?"

"Suits me, Mistah Hawkins."

"O.K. Go to it!"

He hitched Jenny to a plow and started across the fields. Hot dog! This is was just what he wanted. If he could get down by the woods, he could shoot his gun and nobody would hear. He walked behind the plow, hearing the traces creaking, feeling the gun tied tight to his thigh.

When he reached the woods, he plowed two whole rows before he decided to take out the gun. Finally, he stopped, looked in all directions, then untied the gun and held it in his hand. He turned to the mule and smiled.

"Know whut this is, Jenny? Naw, yuh wouldn know! Yuhs jusa ol mule! Anyhow, this is a gun, n it kin shoot, by Gawd!"

He held the gun at arm's length. Whut t hell, Ahma shoot this thing! He looked at Jenny again.

"Lissen here, Jenny! When Ah pull this ol trigger, Ah don wan yuh t run n acka fool now!"

Jenny stood with head down, her short ears pricked straight. Dave walked off about twenty feet, held the gun far out from him at arm's length, and turned his head. Hell, he told himself, Ah ain afraid. The gun felt loose in his fingers; he waved it wildly for a moment. Then he shut his eyes and tightened his forefinger. Boom! A report half deafened him and he thought his right hand was torn from his arm. He heard Jenny whinnying and galloping over the field, and he found himself on his knees squeezing his fingers hard between his legs. His hand was numb; he jammed it into his mouth, trying to warm it, trying to stop the pain. The gun lay at his feet. He did not quite know what had happened. He stood up and stared at the gun as though it were a living thing. He gritted his teeth and kicked the gun. Yuh almos broke mah arm! He turned to look for Jenny; she was far over the fields, tossing her head and kicking wildly.

"Hol on there, ol mule!"

When he caught up with her she stood trembling, walling her big white eyes at him. The plow was far away; the traces had broken. Then Dave stopped short, looking, not believing. Jenny was bleeding. Her left side was red and wet with blood. He went closer. Lawd, have mercy! Wondah did Ah shoot this mule? He grabbed for Jenny's mane. She flinched, snorted, whirled, tossing her head.

"Hol on now! Hol on."

Then he saw the hole in Jenny's side, right between the ribs. It was round, wet, red. A crimson stream streaked down the front leg, flowing fast. Good Gawd! Ah wuzn't shootin at tha mule. He felt panic. He knew he had to stop that blood, or Jenny would bleed to death. He had never seen so much blood in all his life. He chased the mule for half a mile, trying to catch her. Finally she stopped, breathing hard, stumpy tail half arched. He caught her mane and led her back to where the plow and gun lay. Then he stopped and grabbed handfuls of damp black earlh and tried to plug the bullet hole. Jenny shuddered, whinnied, and broke from him.

"Hol onl Hol on now!"

He tried to plug it again, but blood came anyhow. His fingers were hot and sticky. He rubbed dirt into his palms, trying to dry them. Then again he attempted to plug the bullet hole, but Jenny shied away, kicking her heels high. He stood helpless. He had to do something. He ran at Jenny; she dodged him. He watched a red stream of blood flow down Jenny's leg and form a bright pool at her feet.

"Jenny . . . Jenny," he called weakly.

His lips trembled. She's bleeding t death! He looked in the direction of home, wanting to go back, wanting to get help. But he saw the pistol lying in the damp black clay. He had a queer feeling that if he only did something, this would not be; Jenny would not be there bleeding to death.

When he went to her this time, she did not move. She stood with sleepy, dreamy eyes; and when he touched her she gave a low-pitched whinny and knelt to the ground, her front knees slopping in blood.

"Jenny . . . Jenny . . ." he whispered.

For a long time she held her neck erect; then her head sank, slowly. Her ribs swelled with a mighty heave and she went over.

Dave's stomach felt empty, very empty. He picked up the gun and held it gingerly between his thumb and forefinger. He buried it at the foot of a tree. He took a stick to cover the pool of blood with dirt—but what was the use? There was Jenny lying with her mouth open and her eyes walled and glassy. He could not tell Jim Hawkins he had shot his mule. But he had to tell something. Yeah, Ah'll tell em Jenny started gittin wil n fell on the joint of the plow . . . But that would hardly happen to a mule. He walked across the field slowly, head down.

It was sunset. Two of Jim Hawkins' men were over near the edge of the woods digging a hole in which to bury Jenny. Dave was surrounded by a knot of people, all of whom were looking down at the dead mule.

"I don't see how in the world it happened," said Jim Hawkins for the tenth time.

The crowd parted and Dave's mother, father, and small brother pushed into the center.

"Where Dave?" his mother called.

"There he is," said Jim Hawkins.

His mother grabbed him.

"Whut happened, Dave? Whut yuh done?"

"Nothin."

"C mon, boy, talk," his father said.

Dave took a deep breath and told the story he knew nobody believed.

"Waal," he drawled. "Ah brung ol Jenny down here sos Ah could do mah plowin. Ah plowed bout two rows, just like yuh see." He stopped and pointed at the long rows of upturned earth." Then somethin musta been wrong wid ol Jenny. She wouldn ack right a-tall. She started snortin n kickin her heels. Ah tried t hol her, but she pulled erway, rearin n goin in. Then when the point of the plow was stickin up in the air, she swung erroun n twisted herself back on it. . . . She stuck herself n started t bleed. N fo Ah could do anything, she wuz dead."

"Did you ever hear of anything like that in all your life?" asked Jim Hawkins.

There were white and black standing in the crowd. They murmured. Dave's mother came close to him and looked hard into his face. "Tell the truth, Dave," she said.

"Looks like a bullet hole to me," said one man.

"Dave, whut yuh do wid the gun?" his mother asked.

The crowd surged in, looking at him. He jammed his hands into his pockets, shook his head slowly from left to right, and backed away. His eyes were wide and painful.

"Did he hava gun?" asked Jim Hawkins.

"By Gawd, Ah tal yuh tha wuz a gun wound," said a man, slapping his thigh.

His father caught his shoulders and shook him till his teeth rattled.

"Tell whut happened, yuh rascal! Tell whut. . . ."

Dave looked at Jenny's stiff legs and began to cry.

"Whut yuh do wid tha gun?" his mother asked.

"What wuz he doin wida gun?" his father asked.

"Come on and tell the truth," said Hawkins. "Ain't nobody going to hurt you. . . ."

His mother crowded close to him.

"Did yuh shoot tha mule, Dave?"

Dave cried, seeing blurred white and black faces.

"Ahh ddinn gggo tt sshooot hher. . . . Ah ssswear ffo Gawd Ahh ddin. . . . Ah wuz a-tryin t sssee ef the old gggun would sshoot—"

"Where yuh git the gun from?" his father asked.

"Ah got it from Joe, at the sto."

"Where yuh git the money?"

"Ma give it t me."

"He kept worry in me, Bub. Ah had t. Ah tol im t bring the gun right back t me . . .. It was fer yuh, the gun."

"But how yuh happen to shoot that mule?" asked Jim Hawkins.

"Ah wuzn shoo tin at the mule, Mistah Hawkins. The gun jumped when Ah pulled the trigger. . . . N fo Ah knowed any thin Jenny was there a-bleedin."

Somebody in the crowd laughed. Jim Hawkins walked close to Dave and looked into his face.

"Well, looks like you have bought you a mule, Dave."

"Ah swear fo Gawd, Ah didn go t kill the mule, Mistah Hawkins!"

"But you killed her!"

All the crowd was laughing now. They stood on tiptoe and poked heads over one another's shoulders.

"Well, boy, looks like yuh done bought a dead mule! Hahaha!"

"Ain tha ershame."

"Hohohohoho."

Dave stood, head down, twisting his feet in the dirt.

"Well, you needn't worry about it, Bob," said Jim Hawkins to Dave's father. "Just let the boy keep on working and pay me two dollars a month."

"Whut yuh wan fer yo mule, Mistah Hawkins?"

Jim Hawkins screwed up his eyes.

"Fifty dollars."

"Whut yuh do wid tha gun?" Dave's father demanded.

Dave said nothing.

"Yuh wan me t take a tree n beat yuh till yuh talk!"

"Nawsuh!"

"Whut yuh do wid it?"

"Ah throwed it erway."

"Where?"

"Ah . . . Ah throwed it in the creek."

"Waal, c mon home. N firs thing in the mawnin git to tha creek n fin tha gun."

"Yessuh."

"Whut yuh pay fer it?"

"Two dollahs."

"Take tha gun n git yo money back n carry it to Mistah Hawkins, yuh hear? N don fergit Ahma lam you black bottom good fer this! Now march yosef on home, suh!"

Dave turned and walked slowly. He heard people laughing. Dave glared, his eyes welling with tears. Hot anger bubbled in him. Then he swallowed and stumbled on.

That night Dave did not sleep. He was glad that he had gotten out of killing the mule so easily, but he was hurt. Something hot seemed to turn over inside him each time he remembered how they had laughed. He tossed on his bed, feeling his hard pillow. N Pa says he's gonna beat me. . . . He remembered other beatings, and his back quivered. Naw, naw, Ah sho don wan im t beat me tha way no mo. Dam em all! Nobody ever gave him anything. All he did was work. They treat me like a mule, n then they beat me. He grilled his teeth. N Ma had t tell on me.

Well, if he had to, he would take old man Hawkins that two dollars. But that meant selling the gun. And he wanted to keep that gun. Fifty dollars for a dead mule.

He turned over, thinking how he had fired the gun. He had an itch to fire it again. Ef other men kin shoota gun, by Gawd, Ah kin! He was still, listening. Mebbe they all sleepin now. The house was still. He heard the soft breathing of his brother. Yes, now! He would go down and get that gun and see if he could fire it! He eased out of bed and slipped into overalls.

The moon was bright. He ran almost all the way to the edge of the woods. He stumbled over the ground, looking for the spot where he had buried the gun. Yeah, here it is. Like a hungry dog scratching for a bone, he pawed it up. He puffed his black cheeks and blew dirt from the trigger and barrel. He broke it and found four cartridges unshot. He looked around; the fields were filled with silence and moonlight. He clutched the gun stiff and hard in his fingers. But, as soon as he wanted to pull the trigger; he shut his eyes and turned his head. Naw, Ah can't shoot wid mah eyes closed n mah head turned. With effort he held his eyes open; then he squeezed. *Blooooo!* He was stiff, not breathing. The gun was still in his hands. Dammit, he'd done it! He fired again. *Blooooom!* He smiled. *Blooooom! Blooooom! Click, click.* There! It was empty. If anybody could shoot a gun, he could. He put the gun into his hip pocket and started across the fields.

When he reached the top of a ridge he stood straight and proud in the moonlight, looking at Jim Hawkins' big white house, feeling the gun sagging in his pocket. Lawd, ef Ah had just one mo bullet Ah'd taka shot at tha house. Ah'd like t scare ol man Hawkins jusa little . . . . Jusa enough t let im know Dave Saunders is a man.

To his left the road curved, miming to the tracks of the Illinois Central. He jerked his head, listening. From far off came a faint *hooooh-hoooof; hooooh-hoooof*.... He stood rigid. Two dollahs a mont. Les see now.... Tha means it'll take bout two years. Shucks! Ah'll be dam!

He started down the road, toward the tracks. Yeah, here she comes! He stood beside the track and held himself stiffly. Here she comes, erroun the ben.... C mon, yuh slow poke! C mon! He had his hand on his gun; something quivered in his stomach. Then the train thundered past, the gray and brown box cars rumbling and clinking. He gripped the gun tightly; then he jerked his hand out of his pocket. Ah betcha Bill wouldn't do it! Ah betcha.... The cars slid past, steel grinding upon steel. Ahm ridin yuh ternight, so hep me Gawd! He was hot all over. He hesitated just a moment; then he grabbed, pulled atop of a car, and lay flat. He felt his pocket; the gun was still there. Ahead the long rails were glinting in the moonlight, stretching away, away to somewhere, somewhere where he could be a man....

1961

Sinclair Ross

1908–1996

James Sinclair Ross was born on a homestead near Prince Albert, Saskatchewan. After the breakup of his parents' marriage, he lived with his mother and two siblings on a series of prairie farms, where his mother worked as a housekeeper. At sixteen he dropped out of school and took a job as a clerk with the Union Bank of Canada, which later became part of the Royal Bank, in Abbey, Saskatchewan. Banking became his career, and he spent forty years in the profession, working first in a number of small towns on the prairies, then moving to Winnipeg in 1933, and then, after four years of service in the Royal Canadian Ordinance Corps during World War II, in Montreal. After his retirement in 1968, Ross travelled to Europe. He settled for a time in Athens, and then moved to Spain, where he spent ten years in Barcelona and Malaga, before returning to Vancouver in 1980.

Ross is the author of four novels and eighteen stories published between 1934 and 1974. His best writing deals with the tragic history of the 1930s Depression and drought, with beleaguered prairie farms and towns as a backdrop. His evocation of prairie landscapes and themes inspired many western Canadian writers, including Lorna Crozier and Margaret Laurence. Especially influential is the 1941 novel *As for Me and My House*, now considered a classic of Canadian fiction, though it was overlooked in Canada until it was republished in 1957. It is a gripping narrative about an adulterous love affair, which also chronicles the enormous difficulty of practising art in 1930s Canada. The themes of loneliness, alienation, and repression that run through his work have been seen by some critics as an expression of Ross's own solitude and his homosexuality, which he did not discuss until the final years of his life. His short story collection *The Lamp at Noon and Other Stories* (1968), in which "The Painted Door" was first published, explores the psychological effects of a hostile prairie environment on the small communities and farms of his native province. "The Painted Door" was made into a film by the National Film Board of Canada in 1984.

The Painted Door

Straight across the hills it was five miles from John's farm to his father's. But in winter, with the roads impassable, a team had to make a wide detour and skirt the hills, so that from five the distance was more than treble to seventeen.

"I think I'll walk," John said at breakfast to his wife. "The drifts in the hills wouldn't hold a horse, but they'll carry me all right. If I leave early I can spend a few hours helping him with his chores, and still be back by suppertime."

She went to the window, and thawing a clear place in the frost with her breath, stood looking across the snow-swept farmyard to the huddle of stables and sheds. "There was a double wheel around the moon last night," she countered presently. "You said yourself we could expect a storm. It isn't right to leave me here alone. Surely I'm as important as your father."

He glanced up uneasily, then drinking off his coffee tried to reassure her. "But there's nothing to be afraid of—even supposing it does start to storm. You won't need to go near the stable. Everything's fed and watered now to last till night. I'll be back at the latest by seven or eight."

She went on blowing against the frosted pane, carefully elongating the clear place until it was oval-shaped and symmetrical. He watched her a moment or two longer, then more insistently repeated, "I say you won't need to go near the stable. Everything's fed and watered, and I'll see that there's plenty of wood in. That will be all right, won't it?"

"Yes—of course—I heard you—" It was a curiously cold voice now, as if the words were chilled by their contact with the frosted pane. "Plenty to eat—plenty of wood to keep me warm—what more could a woman ask for?"

"But he's an old man—living there all alone. What is it, Ann? You're not like yourself this morning."

She shook her head without turning. "Pay no attention to me. Seven years a farmer's wife—it's time I was used to staying alone."

Slowly the clear space on the glass enlarged: oval, then round, then oval again. The sun was risen above the frost mists now, so keen and hard a glitter on the snow that instead of warmth its rays seemed shedding cold. One of the two-year-old colts that had cantered away when John turned the horses out for water stood covered with rime at the stable door again, head down and body hunched, each breath a little plume of steam against the frosty air. She shivered, but did not turn. In the clear, bitter light the long white miles of prairie landscape seemed a region alien to life. Even the distant farmsteads she could see served only to intensify a sense of isolation. Scattered across the face of so vast and bleak a wilderness it was difficult to conceive them as a testimony of human hardihood and endurance. Rather they seemed futile, lost, to cower before the implacability of snow-swept earth and clear pale sun-chilled sky.

And when at last she turned from the window there was a brooding stillness in her face as if she had recognized this mastery of snow and cold. It troubled John. "If you're really afraid," he yielded, "I won't go today. Lately it's been so cold, that's all. I just wanted to make sure he's all right in case we do have a storm."

"I know—I'm not really afraid." She was putting in a fire now, and he could no longer see her face. "Pay no attention. It's ten miles there and back, so you'd better get started."

"You ought to know by now I wouldn't stay away," he tried to brighten her. "No matter how it stormed. Before we were married—remember? Twice a week I never missed and we had some bad blizzards that winter too."

He was a slow, unambitious man, content with his farm and cattle, naively proud of Ann. He had been bewildered by it once, her caring for a dull-witted fellow like him; then assured at last of her affection he had relaxed against it gratefully, unsuspecting it might ever be less constant than his own. Even now, listening to the restless brooding in her voice, he felt only a quick, unformulated kind of pride that after seven years his absence for a day should still concern her. While she, his trust and earnestness controlling her again:

"I know. It's just that sometimes when you're away I get lonely. . . . There's a long cold tramp in front of you. You'll let me fix a scarf around your face."

He nodded. "And on my way I'll drop in at Steven's place. Maybe he'll come over tonight for a game of cards. You haven't seen anybody but me for the last two weeks."

She glanced up sharply, then busied herself clearing the table. "It will mean another two miles if you do. You're going to be cold and tired enough as it is. When you're gone I think I'll paint the kitchen woodwork. White this time—you remember we got the paint last fall. It's going to make the room a lot lighter. I'll be too busy to find the day long."

"I will though," he insisted, "and if a storm gets up you'll feel safer, knowing that he's coming. That's what you need, maybe—someone to talk to besides me."

She stood at the stove motionless a moment, then turned to him uneasily. "Will you shave then, John—now—before you go?"

He glanced at her questioningly, and avoiding his eyes she tried to explain, "I mean—he may be here before you're back—and you won't have a chance then."

"But it's only Steven—we're not going anywhere."

"He'll be shaved, though—that's what I mean—and I'd like you too to spend a little time on yourself."

He stood up, stroking the heavy stubble on his chin. "Maybe I should—only it softens up the skin too much. Especially when I've got to face the wind."

She nodded and began to help him dress, bringing heavy socks and a big woollen sweater from the bedroom, wrapping a scarf around his face and forehead. "I'll tell Steven to come early," he said, as he went out. "In time for supper. Likely there'll be chores for me to do, so if I'm not back by six don't wait."

From the bedroom window she watched him nearly a mile along the road. The fire had gone down when at last she turned away, and already through the house there was an encroaching chill. A blaze sprang up again when the draughts were opened, but as she went on clearing the table her movements were furtive and constrained. It was the silence weighing upon her—the frozen silence of the bitter fields and sun-chilled sky—lurking outside as if alive, relentlessly in wait, mile-deep between her now and John. She listened to it, suddenly tense, motionless. The fire crackled and the clock ticked. Always it was there. "I'm a fool," she whispered, rattling the dishes in defiance, going back to the stove to put in another fire. "Warm and safe—I'm a fool. It's a good chance when he's away to paint. The day will go quickly. I won't have time to brood."

Since November now the paint had been waiting warmer weather. The frost on the walls on a day like this would crack and peel it as it dried, but she needed something to keep her hands occupied, something to stave off the gathering cold and loneliness. "First of all," she said aloud, opening the paint and mixing it with a little turpentine, "I must get the house warmer. Fill up the stove and open the oven door so that all the heat comes out. Wad something along the windowsills to keep out the draughts. Then I'll feel brighter. It's the cold that depresses."

She moved briskly, performing each little task with careful and exaggerated absorption, binding her thoughts to it, making it a screen between herself and the surrounding snow and silence. But when the stove was filled and the windows sealed it was more difficult again. Above the quiet, steady swishing of her brush against the bedroom door the clock began to tick. Suddenly her movements became precise, deliberate, her posture self-conscious, as if someone had entered the room and were watching her. It was the silence again, aggressive, hovering. The fire spit and crackled at it. Still it was there. "I'm a fool," she repeated. "All farmers' wives have to stay alone. I mustn't give in this way. I mustn't brood. A few hours now and they'll be here."

The sound of her voice reassured her. She went on: "I'll get them a good supper—and for coffee after cards bake some of the little cakes with raisins that he likes. . . . Just three of us, so I'll watch, and let John play. It's better with four, but at least we can talk. That's all I need—someone to talk to. John never talks. He's stronger—doesn't need to. But he likes Steven—no matter what the neighbours say. Maybe he'll have him come again, and some other young people too. It's what we need, both of us, to help keep young ourselves. . . . And then before we know it we'll be into March. It's cold still in March sometimes, but you never mind the same. At least you're beginning to think about spring."

She began to think about it now. Thoughts that outstripped her words, that left her alone again with herself and the ever-lurking silence. Eager and hopeful first, then clenched, rebellious, lonely. Windows open, sun and thawing earth again, the urge of growing, living things. Then the days that began in the morning at half-past four and lasted till ten at night; the meals at which John gulped his food and scarcely spoke a word; the brute-tired stupid eyes he turned on her if ever she mentioned town or visiting.

For spring was drudgery again. John never hired a man to help him. He wanted a mortgage-free farm; then a new house and pretty clothes for her. Sometimes, because with the best of crops it was going to take so long to pay off anyway, she wondered whether they mightn't better let the mortgage wait a little. Before they were worn out, before their best years were gone. It was something of life she wanted, not just a house and furniture; something of John, not pretty clothes when she would be too old to wear them. But John of course couldn't understand. To him it seemed only right that she should have the clothes—only right that he, fit for nothing else, should slave away fifteen hours a day to give them to her. There was in his devotion a baffling, insurmountable humility that made him feel the need of sacrifice. And when his muscles ached, when his feet dragged stolidly with weariness, then it seemed that in some measure at least he was making amends for his big hulking body and simple mind. Year after year their lives went on in the same little groove. He drove his horses in the field; she milked cows and hoed potatoes. By dint of his drudgery he saved a few months' wages, added a few dollars more each fall to his payments on the mortgage; but the only real difference that it all made was to deprive her of his companionship, to make him a little duller, older, uglier than he might otherwise have been. He never saw their lives objectively. To him it was not what he actually accomplished by means of the sacrifice that mattered, but the sacrifice itself, the gesture—something done for her sake.

And she, understanding, kept her silence. In such a gesture, however futile, there was a graciousness not to be shattered lightly. "John," she would begin sometimes, "you're doing too much. Get a man to help you—just for a month—" but smiling down at her he would answer simply, "I don't mind. Look at the hands on me. They're made for work." While in his voice there would be a stalwart ring to tell her that by her thoughtfulness she had made him only the more resolved to serve her, to prove his devotion and fidelity.

They were useless, such thoughts. She knew. It was his very devotion that made them useless, that forbade her to rebel. Yet over and over, sometimes hunched still before their bleakness, sometimes her brush making swift sharp strokes to pace the chafe and rancour that they brought, she persisted in them.

This now, the winter, was their slack season. She could sleep sometimes till eight, and John till seven. They could linger over their meals a little, read, play cards, go visiting the neighbours. It was the time to relax, to indulge and enjoy themselves; but instead, fretful and impatient, they kept on waiting for the spring. They were compelled now, not by labour, but by the spirit of labour. A spirit that pervaded their lives and brought with idleness a sense of guilt. Sometimes they did sleep late, sometimes they did play cards, but always uneasily, always reproached by the thought of more important things that might be done. When John got up at five to attend to the fire he wanted to stay up and go out to the stable. When he sat down to a meal he hurried his food and pushed his chair away again, from habit, from sheer work-instinct, even though it was only to put more wood on the stove, or go down cellar to cut up beets and turnips for the cows.

And anyway, sometimes she asked herself, why sit trying to talk with a man who never talked? Why talk when there was nothing to talk about but crops and cattle, the weather and the neighbours? The neighbours, too—why go visiting them when still it was the same—crops and cattle, the weather and the other neighbours? Why go to the dances in the schoolhouse to sit among the older women, one of them now, married seven years, or to waltz with the work-bent, tired old farmers to a squeaky fiddle tune? Once she had danced with Steven six or seven times in the evening, and they had talked about it for as many months. It was easier to stay at home. John never danced or enjoyed himself. He was always uncomfortable in his good suit and shoes. He didn't like shaving in the cold weather oftener than once or twice a week. It was easier to stay at home, to stand at the window staring out across the bitter fields, to count the days and look forward to another spring.

But now, alone with herself in the winter silence, she saw the spring for what it really was. This spring—next spring—all the springs and summers still to come. While they grew old, while their bodies warped, while their minds kept shrivelling dry and empty like their lives. "I mustn't," she said aloud again. "I married him—and he's a good man. I mustn't keep on this way. It will be noon before long, and then time to think about supper. . . . Maybe he'll come early—and as soon as John is finished at the stable we can all play cards."

It was getting cold again, and she left her painting to put in more wood. But this time the warmth spread slowly. She pushed a mat up to the outside door, and went back to the window to pat down the woollen shirt that was wadded along the sill. Then she paced a few times round the room, then poked the fire and rattled the stove lids, then paced again. The fire crackled, the clock ticked. The silence now seemed more intense than ever, seemed to have reached a pitch where it faintly moaned. She began to pace on tiptoe, listening, her shoulders drawn together, not realizing for a while that it was the wind she heard, thin-strained and whimpering through the eaves.

Then she wheeled to the window, and with quick short breaths thawed the frost to see again. The glitter was gone. Across the drifts sped swift and snakelike little tongues of snow. She could not follow them, where they sprang from, or where they disappeared. It was as if all across the yard the snow were shivering awake—roused by the warnings of the wind to hold itself in readiness for the impending storm. The sky had become a sombre, whitish grey. It, too, as if in readiness, had shifted and lay close to earth. Before her as she watched a mane of powdery snow reared up breast-high against the darker background of the stable, tossed for a moment angrily, and then subsided again as if whipped down to obedience and restraint. But another followed, more reckless and impatient than the first. Another reeled and dashed itself against the window where she watched. Then ominously for a while there were only the angry little snakes of snow. The wind rose, creaking the troughs that were wired beneath the eaves. In the distance, sky and prairie now were merged into one another linelessly. All round her it was gathering; already in its press and whimpering there strummed a boding of eventual fury. Again she saw a mane of snow spring up, so dense and high this time that all the sheds and stables were obscured. Then others followed, whirling fiercely out of hand; and, when at last they cleared, the stables seemed in dimmer outline than before. It was the snow beginning, long lancet shafts of it, straight from the north, borne almost level by the straining wind. "He'll be there soon," she whispered, "and coming home it will be in his back. He'll leave again right away. He saw the double wheel—he knows the kind of storm there'll be."

She went back to her painting. For a while it was easier, all her thoughts half-anxious ones of John in the blizzard, struggling his way across the hills; but petulantly again she soon began, "I knew we were going to have a storm—I told him so—but it doesn't matter what I say. Big stubborn fool—he goes his own way anyway. It doesn't matter what becomes of me. In a storm like this he'll never get home. He won't even try. And while he sits keeping his father company I can look after his stable for him, go ploughing through snowdrifts up to my knees—nearly frozen—"

Not that she meant or believed her words. It was just an effort to convince herself that she did have a grievance, to justify her rebellious thoughts, to prove John responsible for her unhappiness. She was young still, eager for excitement and distractions; and John's steadfastness rebuked her vanity, made her complaints seem weak and trivial. She went on, fretfully, "If he'd listen to me sometimes and not be so stubborn we wouldn't still be living in a house like this. Seven years in two rooms—seven years and never a new stick of furniture. . . . There—as if another coat of paint could make it different anyway."

She cleaned her brush, filled up the stove again, and went back to the window. There was a void white moment that she thought must be frost formed on the windowpane; then, like a fitful shadow through the whirling snow, she recognized the stable roof. It was incredible. The sudden, maniac raging of the storm struck from her face all its pettishness. Her eyes glazed with fear a little; her lips blanched. "If he starts for home now," she whispered silently—"But he won't—he knows I'm safe—he knows Steven's coming. Across the hills he would never dare."

She turned to the stove, holding out her hands to the warmth. Around her now there seemed a constant sway and tremor, as if the air were vibrating with the shudderings of the walls. She stood quite still, listening. Sometimes the wind struck with sharp, savage blows. Sometimes it bore down in a sustained, minute-long blast, silent with effort and intensity; then with a foiled shriek of threat wheeled away to gather and assault again. Always the eave-troughs creaked and sawed. She stared towards the window again, then detecting the morbid trend of her thoughts, prepared fresh coffee and forced herself to drink a few mouthfuls. "He would never dare," she whispered again. "He wouldn't leave the old man anyway in such a storm. Safe in here—there's nothing for me to keep worrying about. It's after one already. I'll do my baking now, and then it will be time to get supper ready for Steven."

Soon, however, she began to doubt whether Steven would come. In such a storm even a mile was enough to make a man hesitate. Especially Steven, who was hardly the one to face a blizzard for the sake of someone else's chores. He had a stable of his own to look after anyway. It would be only natural for him to think that when the storm blew up John had turned again for home. Another man would have—would have put his wife first.

But she felt little dread or uneasiness at the prospect of spending the night alone. It was the first time she had been left like this on her own resources, and her reaction, now that she could face and appraise her situation calmly, was gradually to feel it a kind of adventure and responsibility. It stimulated her. Before nightfall she must go to the stable and feed everything. Wrap up in some of John's clothes—take a ball of string in her hand, one end tied to the door, so that no matter how blinding the storm she could at least find her way back to the house. She had heard of people having to do that. It appealed to her now because suddenly it made life dramatic. She had not felt the storm yet, only watched it for a minute through the window.

It took nearly an hour to find enough string, to choose the right socks and sweaters. Long before it was time to start out she tried on John's clothes, changing and rechanging, striding around the room to make sure there would be play enough for pitching hay and struggling over snowdrifts; then she took them off again, and for a while busied herself baking the little cakes with raisins that he liked.

Night came early. Just for a moment on the doorstep she shrank back, uncertain. The slow dimming of the light clutched her with an illogical sense of abandonment. It was like the covert withdrawal of an ally, leaving the alien miles unleashed and unrestrained. Watching the hurricane of writhing snow rage past the little house she forced herself, "They'll never stand the night unless I get them fed. It's nearly dark already, and I've work to last an hour."

Timidly, unwinding a little of the string, she crept out from the shelter of the doorway. A gust of wind spun her forward a few yards, then plunged her headlong against a drift that in the dense white whirl lay invisible across her path. For nearly a minute she huddled still, breathless and dazed. The snow was in her mouth and nostrils, inside her scarf and up her sleeves. As she tried to straighten a smothering scud flung itself against her face, cutting off her breath a second time. The wind struck from all sides, blustering and furious. It was as if the storm had discovered her, as if all its forces were concentrated upon her extinction. Seized with panic suddenly she threshed out a moment with her arms, then stumbled back and sprawled her length across the drift.

But this time she regained her feet quickly, roused by the whip and batter of the storm to retaliative anger. For a moment her impulse was to face the wind and strike back blow for blow; then, as suddenly as it had come, her frantic strength gave way to limpness and exhaustion. Suddenly, a comprehension so clear and terrifying that it struck all thoughts of the stable from her mind, she realized in such a storm her puniness. And the realization gave her new strength, stilled this time to a desperate persistence. Just for a moment the wind held her, numb and swaying in its vise; then slowly, buckled far forward, she groped her way again towards the house.

Inside, leaning against the door, she stood tense and still a while. It was almost dark now. The top of the stove glowed a deep, dull red. Heedless of the storm, self-absorbed and self-satisfied, the clock ticked on like a glib little idiot. "He shouldn't have gone," she whispered silently. "He saw the double wheel—he knew. He shouldn't have left me here alone."

For so fierce now, so insane and dominant did the blizzard seem, that she could not credit the safety of the house. The warmth and lull around her was not real yet, not to be relied upon. She was still at the mercy of the storm. Only her body pressing hard like this against the door was staving it off. She didn't dare move.

She didn't dare ease the ache and strain. "He shouldn't have gone," she repeated, thinking of the stable again, reproached by her helplessness. "They'll freeze in their stalls—and I can't reach them. He'll say it's all my fault. He won't believe I tried."

Then Steven came. Quickly, startled to quietness and control, she let him in and lit the lamp. He stared at her a moment, then flinging off his cap crossed to where she stood by the table and seized her arms. "You're so white—what's wrong? Look at me—" It was like him in such little situations to be masterful. "You should have known better—for a while I thought I wasn't going to make it here myself—"

"I was afraid you wouldn't come—John left early, and there was the stable—"

But the storm had unnerved her, and suddenly at the assurance of his touch and voice the fear that had been gripping her gave way to an hysteria of relief. Scarcely aware of herself she seized his arm and sobbed against it. He remained still a moment unyielding, then slipped his other arm around her shoulder. It was comforting and she relaxed against it, hushed by a sudden sense of lull and safety. Her shoulders trembled with the easing of the strain, then fell limp and still. "You're shivering,"—he drew her gently towards the stove. "It's all right—nothing to be afraid of. I'm going to see to the stable."

It was a quiet, sympathetic voice, yet with an undertone of insolence, a kind of mockery even, that made her draw away quickly and busy herself putting in a fire. With his lips drawn in a little smile he watched her till she looked at him again. The smile too was insolent, but at the same time companionable; Steven's smile, and therefore difficult to reprove. It lit up his lean, still-boyish face with a peculiar kind of arrogance; features and smile that were different from John's, from other men's—wilful and derisive, yet naively so—as if it were less the difference itself he was conscious of, than the long-accustomed privilege that thereby fell his due. He was erect, tall, square-shouldered. His hair was dark and trim, his lips curved soft and full. While John, she made the comparison swiftly, was thickset, heavy-jowled, and stooped. He always stood before her helpless, a kind of humility and wonderment in his attitude. And Steven now smiled on her appraisingly with the worldly-wise assurance of one for whom a woman holds neither mystery nor illusion.

"It was good of you to come, Steven," she responded, the words running into a sudden, empty laugh. "Such a storm to face—I suppose I should feel flattered."

For his presumption, his misunderstanding of what had been only a momentary weakness, instead of angering quickened her, roused from latency and long disuse all the instincts and resources of her femininity. She felt eager, challenged. Something was at hand that hitherto had always eluded her, even in the early days with John, something vital, beckoning, meaningful. She didn't understand, but she knew. The texture of the moment was satisfyingly dreamlike: an incredibility perceived as such, yet acquiesced in. She was John's wife—she knew—but also she knew that Steven standing here was different from John. There was no thought or motive, no understanding of herself as the knowledge persisted. Wary and poised round a sudden little core of blind excitement she evaded him, "But it's nearly dark—hadn't you better hurry if you're going to do the chores? Don't trouble—I can get them off myself—"

An hour later when he returned from the stable she was in another dress, hair rearranged, a little flush of colour in her face. Pouring warm water for him from the kettle into the basin she said evenly, "By the time you're washed supper will be ready. John said we weren't to wait for him."

He looked at her a moment, "You don't mean you're expecting John tonight? The way it's blowing—"

"Of course." As she spoke she could feel the colour deepening in her face. "We're going to play cards. He was the one that suggested it."

He went on washing, and then as they took their places at the table, resumed, "So John's coming. When are you expecting him?"

"He said it might be seven o'clock—or a little later." Conversation with Steven at other times had always been brisk and natural, but now all at once she found it strained. "He may have work to do for his father. That's what he said when he left. Why do you ask, Steven?"

"I was just wondering—it's a rough night."

"You don't know John. It would take more than a storm to stop him."

She glanced up again and he was smiling at her. The same insolence, the same little twist of mockery and appraisal. It made her flinch, and ask herself why she was pretending to expect John—why there should be this instinct of defence to force her. This time, instead of poise and excitement, it brought a reminder that she had changed her dress and rearranged her hair. It crushed in a sudden silence, through which she heard the whistling wind again, and the creaking saw of the eaves. Neither spoke now. There was something strange, almost frightening, about this Steven and his quiet, unrelenting smile; but strangest of all was the familiarity: the Steven she had never seen or encountered, and yet had always known, always expected, always waited for. It was less Steven himself that she felt than his inevitability. Just as she had felt the snow, the silence and the storm. She kept her eyes lowered, on the window past his shoulder, on the stove, but his smile now seemed to exist apart from him, to merge and hover with the silence. She clinked a cup—listened to the whistle of the storm—always it was there. He began to speak, but her mind missed the meaning of his words. Swiftly she was making comparisons again; his face so different to John's, so handsome and young and clean-shaven. Swiftly, helplessly, feeling the imperceptible and relentless ascendancy that thereby he was gaining over her, sensing sudden menace in this new, more vital life, even as she felt drawn towards it.

The lamp between them flickered as an onslaught of the storm sent shudderings through the room. She rose to build up the fire again and he followed her. For a long time they stood close to the stove, their arms almost touching. Once as the blizzard creaked the house she spun around sharply, fancying it was John at the door; but quietly he intercepted her. "Not tonight—you might as well make up your mind to it. Across the hills in a storm like this—it would be suicide to try."

Her lips trembled suddenly in an effort to answer, to parry the certainty in his voice, then set thin and bloodless. She was afraid now. Afraid of his face so different from John's—of his smile, of her own helplessness to rebuke it. Afraid of the storm, isolating her here alone with him. They tried to play cards, but she kept starting up at every creak and shiver of the walls. "It's too rough a night," he repeated. "Even for John. Just relax a few minutes—stop worrying and pay a little attention to me."

But in his tone there was a contradiction to his words. For it implied that she was not worrying—that her only concern was lest it really might be John at the door.

And the implication persisted. He filled up the stove for her, shuffled the cards—won—shuffled—still it was there. She tried to respond to his conversation, to think of the game, but helplessly into her cards instead she began to ask, Was he right? Was that why he smiled? Why he seemed to wait, expectant and assured?

The clock ticked, the fire crackled. Always it was there. Furtively for a moment she watched him as he deliberated over his hand. John, even in the days before they were married, had never looked like that. Only this morning she had asked him to shave. Because Steven was coming—because she had been afraid to see them side by side—because deep within herself she had known even then. The same knowledge, furtive and forbidden, that was flaunted now in Steven's smile. "You look cold," he said at last, dropping his cards and rising from the table. "We're not playing, anyway. Come over to the stove for a few minutes and get warm."

"But first I think we'll hang blankets over the door. When there's a blizzard like this we always do." It seemed that in sane, commonplace activity there might be release, a moment or two in which to recover herself. "John has nails to put them on. They keep out a little of the draught."

He stood on a chair for her, and hung the blankets that she had carried from the bedroom. Then for a moment they stood silent, watching the blankets sway and tremble before the blade of wind that spurted around the jamb. "I forgot," she said at last, "that I painted the bedroom door. At the top there, see—I've smeared the blankets."

He glanced at her curiously, and went back to the stove. She followed him, trying to imagine the hills in such a storm, wondering whether John would come. "A man couldn't live in it," suddenly he answered her thoughts, lowering the oven door and drawing up their chairs one on each side of it. "He knows you're safe. It isn't likely that he'd leave his father, anyway."

"The wind will be in his back," she persisted. "The winter before we were married—all the blizzards that we had that year—and he never missed—"

"Blizzards like this one? Up in the hills he wouldn't be able to keep his direction for a hundred yards. Listen to it a minute and ask yourself."

His voice seemed softer, kindlier now. She met his smile a moment, its assured little twist of appraisal, then for a long time sat silent, tense, careful again to avoid his eyes.

Everything now seemed to depend on this. It was the same as a few hours ago when she braced the door against the storm. He was watching her, smiling. She dared not move, unclench her hands, or raise her eyes. The flames crackled, the clock ticked. The storm wrenched the walls as if to make them buckle in. So rigid and desperate were all her muscles set, withstanding, that the room around her seemed to swim and reel. So rigid and strained that for relief at last, despite herself, she raised her head and met his eyes again.

Intending that it should be for only an instant, just to breathe again, to ease the tension that had grown unbearable—but in his smile now, instead of the insolent appraisal that she feared, there seemed a kind of warmth and sympathy. An understanding that quickened and encouraged her—that made her wonder why but a moment ago she had been afraid. It was as if the storm had lulled, as if she had suddenly found calm and shelter.

Or perhaps, the thought seized her, perhaps instead of his smile it was she who had changed. She who, in the long, wind-creaked silence, had emerged from the increment of codes and loyalties to her real, unfettered self. She who now felt his air of appraisal as nothing more than understanding of the unfulfilled woman that until this moment had lain within her brooding and unadmitted, reproved out of consciousness by the insistence of an outgrown, routine fidelity.

For there had always been Steven. She understood now. Seven years—almost as long as John—ever since the night they first danced together.

The lamp was burning dry, and through the dimming light, isolated in the fastness of silence and storm, they watched each other. Her face was white and struggling still. His was handsome, clean-shaven, young. Her eyes were fanatic, believing desperately, fixed upon him as if to exclude all else, as if to find justification. His were cool, bland, drooped a little with expectancy. The light kept dimming, gathering the shadows round them, hushed, conspiratorial. He was smiling still. Her hands again were clenched up white and hard.

"But he always came," she persisted. "The wildest, coldest nights—even such a night as this. There was never a storm—"

"Never a storm like this one." There was a quietness in his smile now, a kind of simplicity almost, as if to reassure her. "You were out in it yourself for a few minutes. He'd have it for five miles, across the hills. . . . I'd think twice myself, on such a night before risking even one."

Long after he was asleep she lay listening to the storm. As a check on the draught up the chimney they had left one of the stovelids partly off, and through the open bedroom door she could see the flickering of flame and shadow on the kitchen wall. They leaped and sank fantastically. The longer she watched the more alive they seemed to be. There was one great shadow that struggled towards her threateningly, massive and black and engulfing all the room. Again and again it advanced, about to spring, but each time a little whip of light subdued it to its place among the others on the wall. Yet though it never reached her still she cowered, feeling that gathered there was all the frozen wilderness, its heart of terror and invincibility.

Then she dozed a while, and the shadow was John. Interminably he advanced. The whips of light still flickered and coiled, but now suddenly they were the swift little snakes that this afternoon she had watched twist and shiver across the snow. And they too were advancing. They writhed and vanished and came again. She lay still, paralyzed. He was over her now, so close that she could have touched him. Already it seemed that a deadly tightening hand was on her throat. She tried to scream but her lips were locked. Steven beside her slept on heedlessly.

Until suddenly as she lay staring up at him a gleam of light revealed his face. And in it was not a trace of threat or anger—only calm, and stonelike hopelessness.

That was like John. He began to withdraw, and frantically she tried to call him back. "It isn't true—not really true—listen, John—" but the words clung frozen to her lips. Already there was only the shriek of wind again, the sawing eaves, the leap and twist of shadow on the wall.

She sat up, startled now and awake. And so real had he seemed there, standing close to her, so vivid the sudden age and sorrow in his face, that at first she could not make herself understand she had been only dreaming. Against the conviction of his presence in the room it was necessary to insist over and over that he must still be with his father on the other side of the hills. Watching the shadows she had fallen asleep. It was only her mind, her imagination, distorted to a nightmare by the illogical and unadmitted dread of his return. But he wouldn't come. Steven was right. In such a storm he would never try. They were safe, alone. No one would ever know. It was only fear, morbid and irrational; only the sense of guilt that even her new-found and challenged womanhood could not entirely quell.

She knew now. She had not let herself understand or acknowledge it as guilt before, but gradually through the wind-torn silence of the night his face compelled her. The face that had watched her from the darkness with its stonelike sorrow—the face that was really John—John more than his features of mere flesh and bone could ever be.

She wept silently. The fitful gleam of light began to sink. On the ceiling and wall at last there was only a faint dull flickering glow. The little house shuddered and quailed, and a chill crept in again. Without wakening Steven she slipped out to build up the fire. It was burned to a few spent embers now, and the wood she put on seemed a long time catching light. The wind swirled through the blankets they had hung around the door, and then, hollow and moaning, roared up the chimney again, as if against its will drawn back to serve still longer with the onrush of the storm.

For a long time she crouched over the stove, listening. Earlier in the evening, with the lamp lit and the fire crackling, the house had seemed a stand against the wilderness, a refuge of feeble walls wherein persisted the elements of human meaning and survival. Now, in the cold, creaking darkness, it was strangely extinct, looted by the storm and abandoned again. She lifted the stove lid and fanned the embers till at last a swift little tongue of flame began to lick around the wood. Then she replaced the lid, extending her hands, and as if frozen in that attitude stood waiting.

It was not long now. After a few minutes she closed the draughts, and as the flames whirled back upon each other, beating against the top of the stove and sending out flickers of light again, a warmth surged up to relax her stiffened limbs. But shivering and numb it had been easier. The bodily well-being that the warmth induced gave play to an ever more insistent mental suffering. She remembered the shadow that was John. She saw him bent towards her, then retreating, his features pale and overcast with unaccusing grief. She relived their seven years together and, in retrospect, found them to be years of worth and dignity. Until crushed by it all at last, seized by a sudden need to suffer and atone, she crossed to where the draught was bitter, and for a long time stood unflinching on the icy floor.

The storm was close here. Even through the blankets she could feel a sift of snow against her face. The eaves sawed, the walls creaked, and the wind was like a wolf in howling flight.

And yet, suddenly she asked herself, hadn't there been other storms, other blizzards? And through the worst of them hadn't he always reached her?

Clutched by the thought she stood rooted a minute. It was hard now to understand how she could have so deceived herself—how a moment of passion could have quieted within her not only conscience, but reason and discretion too. John always came. There could never be a storm to stop him. He was strong, inured to the cold. He had crossed the hills since his boyhood, knew every creek-bed and gully. It was madness to go on like this—to wait. While there was still time she must waken Steven, and hurry him away.

But in the bedroom again, standing at Steven's side, she hesitated. In his detachment from it all, in his quiet, even breathing, there was such sanity, such realism. For him nothing had happened; nothing would. If she wakened him he would only laugh and tell her to listen to the storm. Already it was long past midnight; either John had lost his way or not set out at all. And she knew that in his devotion there was nothing foolhardy. He would never risk a storm beyond his endurance, never permit himself a sacrifice likely to endanger her lot or future. They were both safe. No one would ever know. She must control herself—be sane like Steven.

For comfort she let her hand rest a while on Steven's shoulder. It would be easier were he awake now, with her, sharing her guilt; but gradually as she watched his handsome face in the glimmering light she came to understand that for him no guilt existed. Just as there had been no passion, no conflict. Nothing but the sane appraisal of their situation, nothing but the expectant little smile, and the arrogance of features that were different from John's. She winced deeply, remembering how she had fixed her eyes on those features, how she had tried to believe that so handsome and young, so different from John's, they must in themselves be her justification.

In the flickering light they were still young, still handsome. No longer her justification—she knew now—John was the man—but wistfully still, wondering sharply at their power and tyranny, she touched them a moment with her fingertips again.

She could not blame him. There had been no passion, no guilt; therefore there could be no responsibility. Looking down at him as he slept, half-smiling still, his lips relaxed in the conscienceless complacency of his achievement, she understood that thus he was revealed in his entirety—all there ever was or ever could be. John was the man. With him lay all the future. For tonight, slowly and contritely through the day and years to come, she would try to make amends.

Then she stole back to the kitchen, and without thought, impelled by overwhelming need again, returned to the door where the draught was bitter still. Gradually towards morning the storm began to spend itself. Its terror blast became a feeble, worn-out moan. The leap of light and shadow sank, and a chill crept in again. Always the eaves creaked, tortured with wordless prophecy. Heedless of it all the clock ticked on in idiot content.

They found him the next day, less than a mile from home. Drifting with the storm he had run against his own pasture fence and overcome had frozen there, erect still, both hands clasping fast the wire.

"He was south of here," they said wonderingly when she told them how he had come across the hills. "Straight south—you'd wonder how he could have missed the buildings. It was the wind last night, coming every way at once. He shouldn't have tried. There was a double wheel around the moon."

She looked past them a moment, then as if to herself said simply, "If you knew him, though—John would try."

It was later, when they had left her a while to be alone with him, that she knelt and touched his hand. Her eyes dimmed, it was still such a strong and patient hand; then, transfixed, they suddenly grew wide and clear. On the palm, white even against its frozen whiteness, was a little smear of paint.

1968

Sheila Watson

1909–1998

Sheila Martin Doherty was born in New Westminster, British Columbia, the daughter of a doctor who served as superintendent of the Provincial Mental Hospital; the family lived on the grounds of the hospital. As a child she attended convent school, then went on to study at the University of British Columbia, receiving her BA in 1931 and her MA in 1933. For a number of years she taught school in small towns across BC, Including Dog Creek, Duncan, and Mission City; her first novel, the semiautobiographical *Deep Hollow Creek*, was written during this time, though it was not published until 1992. Set in the Cariboo region of the BC Interior, this brooding, poetic novel describes a young teacher and the community she finds herself in. In 1957 Watson began Ph.D. studies at the University of Toronto, under the direction of Marshall McLuhan. She was a professor at the University of Alberta from 1961 to 1975, and, with her husband, poet and playwright Wilfrid Watson, was very involved in the Edmonton literary community.

Watson was fascinated by the isolation and austere beauty of the land and its impact on the developing human character. Her best known book is *The Double Hook* (1959), an experimental novel that is elliptical and densely imagistic, reminiscent of William Faulkner's *As I Lay Dying*. Like *Deep Hollow Creek*, *The Double Hook* is set in BC's Cariboo country, and derives much of its power from the enigmatic beauty of a landscape that is at once real and symbolic. *The Double Hook* is an allegory of redemption: the main character attempts to escape his fate only to discover that forgiveness must be found in the community he has sought to flee. Many consider *The Double Hook* to be a masterpiece, an essential book in the Canadian canon, and the first Canadian postmodern novel. Watson also published two collections of short stories, *Four Stories* (1979) and *Five Stories* (1984).

Antigone

My father ruled a kingdom on the right bank of the river. He ruled it with a firm hand and a stout heart though he was often more troubled than Moses, who was simply trying to bring a stubborn and moody people under God's yoke. My father ruled men who thought they were gods or the instruments of gods or, at very least, god-afflicted and god-pursued. He ruled Atlas who held up the sky, and Hermes who went on endless messages, and Helen who'd been hatched from an egg, and Pan the gardener, and Kallisto the bear, and too many others to mention by name. Yet my father had no thunderbolt, no trident, no helmet or darkness. His subjects were delivered bound into his hands. He merely watched over them as the hundred-handed ones watched over the dethroned Titans so that they wouldn't bother Hellas again.

Despite the care which my father took to maintain an atmosphere of sober common sense in his whole establishment, there were occasional outbursts of self-indulgence which he could not control. For instance, I have seen Helen walking naked down the narrow cement path under the chestnut trees for no better reason, I suppose, than that the day was hot and the white flowers themselves lay naked and expectant in the sunlight. And I have seen Atlas forget the sky while he sat eating the dirt which held him up. These were things which I was not supposed to see.

If my father had been as sensible through and through as he was thought to be, he would have packed me off to boarding school when I was old enough to be disciplined by men. Instead he kept me at home with my two cousins who, except for the accident of birth, might as well have been my sisters. Today I imagine people concerned with our welfare would take such an environment into account. At the time I speak of most people thought us fortunate—especially the girls whose father's affairs had come to an unhappy issue. I don't like to revive old scandal and I wouldn't except to deny it; but it takes only a few impertinent newcomers in any community to force open cupboards which have been decently sealed by time. However, my father was so busy setting his kingdom to rights that he let weeds grow up in his own garden.

As I said, if my father had had all his wits about him he would have sent me to boarding school—and Antigone and Ismene too. I might have fallen in love with the headmaster's daughter and Antigone might have learned that no human being can be right always. She might have found out besides that from the seeds of eternal justice grow madder flowers than any which Pan grew in the gardens of my father's kingdom.

Between the kingdom which my father ruled and the wilderness flows a river. It is this river which I am crossing now. Antigone is with me.

How often can we cross the same river, Antigone asks.

Her persistence annoys me. Besides, Heraklitos made nonsense of her question years ago. He saw a river too—the Inachos, the Kephissos, the Lethaios. The name doesn't matter. He said: See how quickly the water flows. However agile a man is, however nimbly he swims, or runs, or flies, the water slips away before him. See, even as he sets down his foot the water is displaced by the stream which crowds along in the shadow of its flight.

But after all, Antigone says, one must admit that it is the same kind of water. The oolichans run in it as they ran last year and the year before. The gulls cry above the same bank. Boats drift towards the Delta and circle back against the current to gather up the catch.

At any rate, I tell her, we're standing on a new bridge. We are standing so high that the smell of mud and river weeds passes under us out to the straits. The unbroken curve of the bridge protects the eye from details of river life. The bridge is foolproof as a clinic's passport to happiness.

The old bridge still spans the river, but the cat-walk with its cracks and knot-holes, with its gap between planking and handrail has been torn down. The centre arch still grinds open to let boats up and down the river, but a child can no longer be walked on it or swung out on it beyond the water-gauge at the very centre of the flood.

I've known men who scorned any kind of bridge, Antigone says. Men have walked into the water, she says, or, impatient, have jumped from the bridge into the river below.

But these, I say, didn't really want to cross the river. They went Persephone's way, cradled in the current's arms, down the long halls under the pink feet of the gulls, under the booms and towlines, under the soft bellies of the fish.

Antigone looks at me.

There's no coming back, she says, if one goes far enough.

I know she's going to speak of her own misery and I won't listen. Only a god has the right to say: Look what I suffer. Only a god should say: What more ought I to have done for you that I have not done?

Once in winter, she says, a man walked over the river.

Taking advantage of nature, I remind her, since the river had never frozen before.

Yet he escaped from the penitentiary, she says. He escaped from the guards walking round the walls or standing with their guns in the sentry-houses at the four corners of the enclosure. He escaped.

Not without risk, I say. He had to test the strength of the ice himself. Yet safer perhaps than if he had crossed by the old bridge where he might have slipped through a knot-hole or tumbled out through the railing.

He did escape, she persists, and lived forever on the far side of the river in the Alaska tea and bulrushes. For where, she asks, can a man go farther then to the outermost edge of the world?

The habitable world, as I've said, is on the right bank of the river. Here is the market with its market stalls—the coops of hens, the long-tongued geese, the haltered calf, the bearded goat, the shoving pigs, and the empty bodies of cows and sheep and rabbits hanging on iron hooks. My father's kingdom provides asylum in the suburbs. Near it are the convent, the churches, and the penitentiary. Above these on the hill the cemetery looks down on the people and on the river itself.

It is a world spread flat, tipped up into the sky so that men and women bend forward, walking as men walk when they board a ship at high tide. This is the world I feel with my feet. It is the world I see with my eyes.

I remember standing once with Antigone and Ismene in the square just outside the gates of my father's kingdom. Here from a bust set high on a cairn the stone eyes of Simon Fraser look from his stone face over the river that he found.

It is the head that counts, Ismene said.

It's no better than an urn, Antigone said, one of the urns we see when we climb to the cemetery above.

And all I could think was that I didn't want an urn, only a flat green grave with a chain about it.

A chain won't keep out the dogs, Antigone said.

But his soul could swing on it, Ismene said, like a bird blown on a branch in the wind.

And I remembered Antigone's saying: The cat drags its belly on the ground and the rat sharpens its tooth in the ivy.

I should have loved Ismene, but I didn't. It was Antigone I loved. I should have loved Ismene because, although she walked the flat world with us, she managed somehow to see it round.

The earth is an oblate spheroid, she'd say. And I knew that she saw it there before her comprehensible and whole like a tangerine spiked through and held in place while it rotated on the axis of one of Nurse's steel sock needles. The earth was a tangerine and she saw the skin peeled off and the world parcelled out into neat segments, each segment sweet and fragrant in its own skin.

It's the head that counts, she said.

In her own head she made diagrams to live by, cut and fashioned after the eternal patterns spied out by Plato as he rummaged about in the sewing basket of the gods.

I should have loved Ismene. She would live now in some pre-fabricated and perfect chrysolite by some paradigm which made love round and whole. She would simply live and leave destruction in the purgatorial ditches outside her own walled paradise.

Antigone is different. She sees the world flat as I do and feels it tip beneath her feet. She has walked in the market and seen the living animals penned and the dead hanging stiff on their hooks. Yet she defies what she sees with a defiance which is almost denial. Like Atlas she tries to keep the vaulted sky from crushing the flat earth. Like Hermes she brings a message that there is life if one can escape to it in the brush and bulrushes in some dim Hades beyond the river. It is defiance not belief and I tell her that this time we walk the bridge to a walled cave where we can deny death no longer.

Yet she asks her question still. And standing there I tell her that Heraklitos has made nonsense of her question. I should have loved Ismene for she would have taught me what Plato meant when he said in all earnest that the union of the soul with the body is in no way better than dissolution. I expect that she understood things which Antigone is too proud to see.

I turn away from her and flatten my elbows on the high wall of the bridge. I look back at my father's kingdom. I see the terraces rolling down from the red-brick buildings with their barred windows. I remember hands shaking the bars and hear fingers tearing up paper and stuffing it through the meshes. Diktynna, mother of nets and high leaping fear. O Artemis, mistress of wild beasts and wild men.

The inmates are beginning to come out on the screened verandas. They pace up and down in straight lines or stand silent like figures which appear at the same time each day from some depths inside a clock.

On the upper terrace Pan the gardener is shifting sprinklers with a hooked stick. His face is shadowed by the brim of his hat. He moves as economically as an animal between the beds of lobelia and geranium. It is high noon.

Antigone has cut out a piece of sod and has scooped out a grave. The body lies in a coffin in the shade of the magnolia tree. Antigone and I are standing. Ismene is sitting between two low angled branches of the monkey puzzle tree. Her lap is filled with daisies. She slits the stem of one daisy and pulls the stem of another through it. She is making a chain for her neck and a crown for her hair.

Antigone reaches for a branch of the magnolia. It is almost beyond her grip. The buds flame above her. She stands on a small fire of daisies which smoulder in the roots of the grass.

I see the magnolia buds. They brood above me, whiteness feathered on whiteness. I see Antigone's face turned to the light. I hear the living birds call to the sun. I speak private poetry to myself: Between four trumpeting angels at the four corners of the earth a bride stands before the altar in a gown as white as snow.

Yet I must have been speaking aloud because Antigone challenges me: You're mistaken. It's the winds the angels hold, the four winds of the earth. After the just are taken to paradise the winds will destroy the earth. It's a funeral, she says, not a wedding.

She looks towards the building.

Someone is coming down the path from the matron's house, she says.

I notice that she has pulled one of the magnolia blossoms from the branch. I take it from her. It is streaked with brown where her hands have bruised it. The sparrow which she has decided to bury lies on its back. Its feet are clenched tight against the feathers of its breast. I put the flower in the box with it.

Someone is coming down the path. She is wearing a blue cotton dress. Her cropped head is bent. She walks slowly carrying something in a napkin.

It's Kallisto the bear, I say. Let's hurry. What will my father say if he sees us talking to one of his patients?

If we live here with him, Antigone says, what can he expect? If he spends his life trying to tame people he can't complain if you behave as if they were tame. What would your father think, she says, if he saw us digging in the Institution lawn?

Pan comes closer. I glower at him. There's no use speaking to him. He's deaf and dumb.

Listen, I say to Antigone, my father's not unreasonable. Kallisto thinks she's a bear and he thinks he's a bear tamer, that's all. As for the lawn, I say quoting my father without conviction, a man must have order among his own if he is to keep order in the state.

Kallisto has come up to see us. She is smiling and laughing to herself. She gives me her bundle.

Fish, she says.

I open the napkin.

Pink fish sandwiches, I say.

For the party, she says.

But it isn't a party, Antigone says. It's a funeral.

For the funeral breakfast, I say.

Ismene is twisting two chains of daisies into a rope. Pan has stopped pulling the sprinkler about. He is standing beside Ismene resting himself on his hooked stick. Kallisto squats down beside her. Ismene turns away, preoccupied, but she can't turn far because of Pan's legs.

Father said we never should
Play with madmen in the wood.

I look at Antigone.

It's my funeral, she says.

I go over to Ismene and gather up a handful of loose daisies from her lap. The sun reaches through the shadow of the magnolia tree.

It's my funeral, Antigone says. She moves possessively toward the body.

An ant is crawling into the bundle of sandwiches which I've put on the ground. A file of ants is marching on the sparrow's box.

I go over and drop daisies on the bird's stiff body. My voice speaks ritual words: Deliver me, O Lord, from everlasting death on this dreadful day. I tremble and am afraid.

The voice of a people comforts me. I look at Antigone. I look her in the eye.

It had better be a proper funeral then, I say.

Kallisto is crouched forward on her hands. Tears are running down her cheeks and she is licking them away with her tongue.

My voice rises again: I said in the midst of my days, I shall not see—

Antigone just stands there. She looks frightened, but her eyes defy me with their assertion.

It's my funeral, she says. It's my bird. I was the one who wanted to bury it.

She is looking for reason. She will say something which sounds eternally right.

Things have to be buried, she says. They can't be left lying around anyhow for people to see.

Birds shouldn't die, I tell her. They have wings. Cats and rats haven't wings.

Stop crying, she says to Kallisto. It's only a bird.

It has a bride's flower in its hand, Kallisto says.

We shall rise again, I mutter, but we shall not all be changed.

Antigone does not seem to hear me.

Behold, I say in a voice she must hear, in a moment, in the twinkling of an eye, the trumpet shall sound.

Ismene turns to Kallisto and throws the daisy chain about her neck.

Shall a virgin forget her adorning or a bride the ornament of her breast?

Kallisto is lifting her arms towards the tree.

The bridegroom has come, she says, white as a fall of snow. He stands above me in a great ring of fire.

Antigone looks at me now.

Let's cover the bird up, she says. Your father will punish us all for making a disturbance.

He has on his garment, Kallisto says, and on his thigh is written King of Kings.

I look at the tree. If I could see with Kallisto's eyes I wouldn't be afraid of death, or punishment, or the penitentiary guards. I wouldn't be afraid of my father's belt or his honing strap or his bedroom slipper. I wouldn't be afraid of falling into the river through a knot-hole in the bridge.

But, as I look, I see the buds falling like burning lamps and I hear the sparrow twittering in its box: Woe, woe, woe because of the three trumpets which are yet to sound.

Kallisto is on her knees. She is growling like a bear. She lumbers over to the sandwiches and mauls them with her paw.

Ismene stands alone for Pan the gardener has gone.

Antigone is fitting a turf in place above the coffin. I go over and press the edge of the turf with my feet. Ismene has caught me by the hand.

Go away, Antigone says.

I see my father coming down the path. He has an attendant with him. In front of them walks Pan holding the sprinkler hook like a spear.

What are you doing here? my father asks.

Burying a bird, Antigone says.

Here? my father asks again.

Where else could I bury it? Antigone says.

My father looks at her.

This ground is public property, he says. No single person has any right to an inch of it.

I've taken six inches, Antigone says. Will you dig up the bird again?

Some of his subjects my father restrained since they were moved to throw themselves from high places or to tear one another to bits from jealousy or rage. Others who disturbed the public peace he taught to walk in the airing courts or to work in the kitchen or the garden.

If men live at all, my father said, it is because discipline saves their life for them.

From Antigone he simply turned away.

1979

Tillie Olsen

1912/13–2007

Tillie Lerner was born in Mead or Omaha or Wahoo, Nebraska, in 1912 or 1913. The uncertainty of these first markers in her life was quickly absorbed by the certainty of constant financial struggle; even as a child she laboured at sub-subsistence jobs and the more fruitful care of the other children in the family. But a concomitant necessity in her world marked by the Depression and the iniquities of the thirties was a passionate and resilient political engagement (her parents had seen and suffered the 1905 installment of the Russian Revolution). In 1931 she joined the Young Communist League, a choice that would come to haunt her family twenty years later during the McCarthy storm and constrain her ability to hold a job. The literary work that emerges only intermittently in the thirties was that of a writer whose private, imaginative existence could only shadow her life as mother, wife, friend, political comrade, and wage-earner. "It was not a time that my writing self could be first." During a retreat to nurse her lungs, she wrote a significant amount of a novel, *Yonnondio*, a section of which brought her a book contract and a modest but stable income. It came at the cost, however, of separation from her then only daughter. Elsewhere in this anthology we note Mavis Gallant's pronouncement, "I've arranged matters so that I would be free to write. It's what I like doing." Had such arrangements been possible, Tillie Lerner would not have made them. Karla came home from her grandparents' and the book contract shriveled, but as family urgencies eased, her shadow stories began taking shape. An early version of "I Stand Here Ironing" drew a Stanford Creative Writing Fellowship in 1955–1956, and the collection in which it is the core, *Tell Me a Riddle*, was finally issued in 1962. In 1978, she published *Silences*, about the burdens faced by women writers. She died at age ninety-four, leaving a large family and few separate volumes, but countless entries in books such as this one. There readers can take on her spare, elegiac prose, which is on the verge of shattering into anguish and seared by the hot iron of inescapability.

I Stand Here Ironing

I stand here ironing, and what you asked me moves tormented back and forth with the iron.

"I wish you would manage the time to come in and talk with me about your daughter. I'm sure you can help me understand her. She's a youngster who needs help and whom I'm deeply interested in helping."

"Who needs help." . . . Even if I came, what good would it do? You think because I am her mother I have a key, or that in some way you could use me as a key? She has lived for nineteen years. There is all that life that has happened outside of me, beyond me.

And when is there time to remember, to sift, to weigh, to estimate, to total? I will start and there will be an interruption and I will have to gather it all together again. Or I will become engulfed with all I did or did not do, with what should have been and what cannot be helped.

She was a beautiful baby. The first and only one of our five that was beautiful at birth. You do not guess how new and uneasy her tenancy in her now-loveliness. You did not know her all those years she was thought homely, or see her poring over her baby pictures, making me tell her over and over how beautiful she had been—and would be. I would tell her—and was now, to the seeing eye. But the seeing eyes were few or nonexistent. Including mine.

I nursed her. They feel that's important nowadays. I nursed all the children, but with her, with all the fierce rigidity of first motherhood, I did like the books then said. Though her cries battered me to trembling and my breasts ached with swollenness, I waited till the clock decreed.

Why do I put that first? I do not even know if it matters, or if it explains anything.

She was a beautiful baby. She blew shining bubbles of sound. She loved motion, loved light, loved color and music and textures. She would lie on the floor in her blue overalls patting the surface so hard in ecstasy her hands and feet would blur. She was a miracle to me, but when she was eight months old I had to leave her daytimes with the woman downstairs to whom she was no miracle at all, for I worked or looked for work and for Emily's father, who "could no longer endure" (he wrote in his good-bye note) "sharing want with us."

I was nineteen. It was the pre-relief, pre-WPA world of the depression. I would start running as soon as I got off the streetcar, running up the stairs. The place smelling sour, and awake or asleep to startle awake, when she saw me she would break into a dogged weeping that could not be comforted, a weeping I can hear yet.

After a while I found a job hashing at night so I could be with her days, and it was better. But it came to where I had to bring her to his family and leave her.

It took a long time to raise the money for her fare back. Then she got chicken pox and I had to wait longer. When she finally came, I hardly knew her, walking quick and nervous like her father, looking like her father, thin, and dressed in a shoddy red that yellowed her skin and glared at the pockmarks. All the baby loveliness gone.

She was two. Old enough for nursery school they said, and I did not know then what I know now—the fatigue of the long day, and the lacerations of group life in the kinds of nurseries that are only parking places for children.

Except that it would have made no difference if I had known. It was the only place there was. It was the only way we could be together, the only way I could hold a job.

And even without knowing. I knew. I knew the teacher that was evil because all these years it has curdled into my memory, the little boy hunched in the corner, her rasp, "why aren't you outside, because Alvin hits you? that's no reason, go out, scaredy." I knew Emily hated it even if she did not clutch and implore "don't go Mommy" like the other children, mornings.

She always had a reason why we should stay home. Momma, you look sick. Momma, I feel sick. Momma, the teachers aren't there today, they're sick. Momma, we can't go, there was a fire there last night. Momma, it's a holiday today, no school, they told me.

But never a direct protest, never rebellion. I think of our others in their three-, four-year-oldness—the explosions, the tempers, the denunciations, the demands—and I feel suddenly ill. I put the iron down. What in me demanded that goodness in her? And what was the cost, the cost to her of such goodness!

The old man living in the back once said in his gentle way: "You should smile at Emily more when you look at her." What *was* in my face when I looked at her? I loved her. There were all the acts of love.

It was only with the others I remembered what he said, and it was the face of joy, and not of care or tightness or worry I turned to them—too late for Emily. She does not smile easily, let alone almost always as her brothers and sisters do. Her face is closed and sombre, but when she wants, how fluid. You must have seen it in her pantomimes, you spoke of her rare gift for comedy on the stage that rouses a laughter out of the audience so dear they applaud and applaud and do not want to let her go.

Where does it come from, that comedy? There was none of it in her when she came back to me that second time, after I had had to send her away again. She had a new daddy now to learn to love, and I think perhaps it was a better time.

Except when we left her alone nights, telling ourselves she was old enough.

"Can't you go some other time, Mommy, like tomorrow?" she would ask. "Will it be just a little while you'll be gone? Do you promise?"

The time we came back, the front door open, the clock on the floor in the hall. She rigid awoke. "It wasn't just a little while. I didn't cry. Three times I called you, just three times, and then I ran downstairs to open the door so you could come faster. The clock talked loud. I threw it away, it scared me what it talked."

She said the clock talked loud again that night I went to the hospital to have Susan. She was delirious with the fever that comes before red measles, but she was fully conscious all the week I was gone and the week after we were home when she could not come near the new baby or me.

She did not get well. She stayed skeleton thin, not wanting to eat, and night after night she had nightmares. She would call for me, and I would rouse from exhaustion to sleepily call back: "You're all right, darling, go to sleep, it's just a dream," and if she still called, in a sterner voice, "Now go to sleep, Emily, there's nothing to hurt you." Twice, only twice, when I had to get up for Susan anyhow, I went in to sit with her.

Now when it is too late (as if she would let me hold and comfort her like I do the others) I get lip and go to her at once at her moan or restless stirring. "Are you awake, Emily? Can I get you something?" And the answer is always the same: "No. I'm all right, go back to sleep, Mother."

They persuaded me at the clinic to send her away to a convalescent home in the country where "she can have the kind of food and care you can't manage for her, and you'll be free to concentrate on the new baby." They still send children to that place. I see pictures on the society page of sleek young women planning affairs to raise money for it, or dancing at the affairs, or decorating Easter eggs or filling Christmas stockings for the children.

They never have a picture of the children so I do not know if the girls still wear those gigantic red bows and the ravaged looks on the every other Sunday when parents can come to visit "unless otherwise notified"—as we were notified the first six weeks.

Oh it is a handsome place, green lawns and tall trees and fluted flower beds. High up on the balconies of each cottage the children stand, the girls in their red bows and white dresses, the boys in white suits and giant red ties. The parents stand below shrieking up to be heard and the children shriek down to be heard, and between them the invisible wall "Not To Be Contaminated by Parental Germs or Physical Affection."

There was a tiny girl who always stood hand in hand with Emily. Her parents never came. One visit she was gone. "They moved her to Rose Cottage" Emily shouted in explanation. "They don't like you to love anybody here."

She wrote once a week, the labored writing of a seven-year-old. "I am fine. How is the baby. If I write my leter nicly I will have a star. Love." There never was a star. We wrote every other day, letters she could never hold or keep but only hear read—once. "We simply do not have room for children to keep any personal possessions," they patiently explained when we pieced one Sunday's shrieking together to plead how much it would mean to Emily, who loved so to keep things, to be allowed to keep her letters and cards.

Each visit she looked frailer. "She isn't eating," they told us.

(They had runny eggs for breakfast or mush with lumps, Emily said later. I'd hold it in my mouth and not swallow. Nothing ever tasted good, just when they had chicken.)

It took us eight months to get her released home, and only the fact that she gained back so little of her seven lost pounds convinced the social worker.

I used to try to hold and love her after she came back, but her body would stay stiff, and after a while she'd push away. She ate little. Food sickened her, and I think much of life too. Oh she had physical lightness and brightness, twinkling by on skates, bouncing like a ball up and down up and down over the jump rope, skimming over the hill: but these were momentary.

She fretted about her appearance, thin and dark and foreign-looking at a time when every little girl was supposed to look or thought she should look a chubby blond replica of Shirley Temple. The doorbell sometimes rang for her, but no one seemed to come and play in the house or be a best friend. Maybe because we moved so much.

There was a boy she loved painfully through two school semesters. Months later she told me how she had taken pennies from my purse to buy him candy. "Licorice was his favorite and I brought him some every day, but he still liked Jennifer better'n me. Why, Mommy?" The kind of question for which there is no answer.

School was a worry to her. She was not glib or quick in a world where glibness and quickness were easily confused with ability to learn. To her overworked and exasperated teachers she was an overconscientious "slow learner" who kept trying to catch up and was absent entirely too often.

I let her be absent, though sometimes the illness was imaginary. How different from my now-strictness about attendance with the others. I wasn't working. We had a new baby, I was home anyhow. Sometimes, after Susan grew old enough, I would keep her home from school, too, to have them all together.

Mostly Emily had asthma, and her breathing, harsh and labored, would fill the house with a curiously tranquil sound. I would bring the two old dresser mirrors and her boxes of collections to her bed. She would select beads and single earrings, bottle tops and shells, dried flowers and pebbles, old postcards and scraps, all sorts of oddments: then she and Susan would play Kingdom, setting up landscapes and furniture, peopling them with action.

Those were the only times of peaceful companionship between her and Susan. I have edged away from it, that poisonous feeling between them, that terrible balancing of hurts and needs I had to do between the two, and did so badly, those earlier years.

Oh there are conflicts between the others too, each one human, needing, demanding, hurting, taking—but only between Emily and Susan, no, Emily toward Susan that corroding resentment. It seems so obvious on the surface, yet it is not obvious. Susan, the second child, Susan, golden- and curly-haired and chubby, quick and articulate and assured, everything in appearance and manner Emily was not; Susan, not able to resist Emily's precious things, losing or sometimes clumsily breaking them: Susan telling jokes and riddles to company for applause while Emily sat silent (to say to me later: that was *my* riddle, Mother, I told it to Susan); Susan, who for all the five years' difference in age was just a year behind Emily in developing physically.

I am glad for that slow physical development that widened the difference between her and her contemporaries, though she suffered over it. She was too vulnerable for that terrible world of youthful competition, of preening and parading, of constant measuring of yourself against every other, of envy, "If I had that copper hair," "If I had that skin. . . ." She tormented herself enough about not looking like the others, there was enough of the unsureness, the having to be conscious of words before you speak, the constant caring—what are they thinking of me? without having it all magnified by the merciless physical drives.

Ronnie is calling. He is wet and I change him. It is rare there is such a cry now. That time of motherhood is almost behind me when the ear is not one's own but must always be racked and listening for the child cry, the child call. We sit for a while and I hold him, looking out over the city spread in charcoal with its soft aisles of light. "*Shoogily*," he breathes and curls closer. I carry him back to bed, asleep. *Shoogily.* A funny word, a family word, inherited from Emily, invented by her to say: *comfort.*

In this and other ways she leaves her seal, I say aloud. And startle at my saying it. What do I mean? What did I start to gather together, to try and make coherent? I was at the terrible, growing years. War years. I do not remember them well. I was working, there were four smaller ones now, there was not time for her. She had to help be a mother, and housekeeper, and shopper. She had to set her seal. Mornings of crisis and near hysteria trying to get lunches packed, hair combed, coats and shoes found, everyone to school or Child Care on time, the baby ready for transportation. And always the paper scribbled on by a smaller one, the book looked at by Susan then mislaid, the homework not done. Running out to that huge school where she was one, she was lost, she was a drop: suffering over her unpreparedness, stammering and unsure in her classes.

There was so little time left at night after the kids were bedded down. She would struggle over books, always eating (it was in those years she developed her enormous appetite that is legendary in our family) and I would be ironing, or preparing food for the next day, or writing V-mail to Bill, or tending the baby. Sometimes, to make me laugh, or out of her despair, she would imitate happenings or types at school.

I think I said once: "Why don't you do something like this in the school amateur show?" One morning she phoned me at work, hardly understandable through the weeping: "Mother, I did it. I won, I won; they gave me first prize: they clapped and clapped and wouldn't let me go."

Now suddenly she was Somebody, and as imprisoned in her difference as she had been in her anonymity.

She began to be asked to perform at other high schools, even in colleges, then at city and statewide affairs. The first one we went to, I only recognized her that first moment when thin, shy, she almost drowned herself into the curtains. Then: Was this Emily? The control, the command, the convulsing and deadly clowning, the spell, then the roaring, stamping audience, unwilling to let this rare and precious laughter out of their lives.

Afterwards: You ought to do something about her with a gift like that—but without money or knowing how, what does one do? We have left it all to her, and the gift has as often eddied inside, clogged and clotted, as been used and growing.

She is coming. She runs up the stairs two at a time with her light graceful step, and I know she is happy tonight. Whatever it was that occasioned your call did not happen today.

"Aren't you ever going to finish the ironing, Mother? Whistler painted his mother in a rocker. I'd have to paint mine standing over an ironing board." This is one of her communicative nights and she tells me everything and nothing as she fixes herself a plate of food out of the icebox.

She is so lovely. Why did you want me to come in at all? Why were you concerned? She will find her way.

She starts up the stairs to bed. "Don't get *me* up with the rest in the morning." "But I thought you were having midterms." "Oh, those," she comes back in, kisses me, and says quite lightly, "in a couple of years when we'll all be atom-dead they won't matter a bit."

She has said it before. She *believes* it. But because I have been dredging the past, and all that compounds a human being is so heavy and meaningful in me, I cannot endure it tonight.

I will never total it all. I will never come in to say: She was a child seldom smiled at. Her father left me before she was a year old. I had to work her first six years when there was work, or I sent her home and to his relatives. There were years she had care she hated. She was dark and thin and foreign-looking in a world where the prestige went to blondness and curly hair and dimples; she was slow where glibness was prized. She was a child of anxious, not proud, love. We were poor and could not afford for her the soil of easy growth. I was a young mother, I was a distracted mother. There were the other children pushing up, demanding. Her younger sister seemed all that she was not. There were years she did not let me touch her. She kept too much in herself, her life was such she had to keep too much in herself. My wisdom came too late. She has much to her and probably little will come of it. She is a child of her age, of depression, of war, of fear.

Let her be. So all that is in her will not bloom—but in how many does it? There is still enough left to live by. Only help her to know—help make it so there is cause for her to know—that she is more than this dress on the ironing board, helpless before the iron.

1961

Albert Camus

1913–1960

Camus and Orwell died at almost the same age, just over forty-six years old. In 1950 and 1960 their deaths were a source of intense but still general sadness. They were both integral to their times in a way rare for writers. They were good men who clarified terrible history. But they have become a pairing often invoked in the post-9/11 world, the regret over their early deaths turning into a longing for their continued presence as sensibilities and as writers of essays, novels, and reflections that provide, if not a key to our current turmoils, then at least the possibility of a sane perspective. Having respected each other from a distance, they would not, one feels, be disappointed at this new Anglo-French partnership of humane indispensability. Susan Sontag has famously said of Camus, "no modern writer that I can think of, except Camus, has aroused love. His death in 1960 was felt as a personal loss by the whole literate world." Despite being born into a desperately poor family in Algiers, through the intercession of perceptive teachers and an astute uncle, Camus pursued highly intellectual reading with the same passion he devoted to football and swimming (Conor Cruise O'Brien). He attended the University of Algiers, worked within the Communist Party for three or four years, wrote his play *Caligula*, and began the two books responsible for his subsequent fame in Paris, *Le Mythe de Sisyphe* and *L'Etranger*. (In a 1946 letter, Samuel Beckett says to a friend: "Try and read it [*L'Etranger*], I think it is important.") Camus's departure from Algiers to France was followed by the country's fall to the Germans, and early on Camus was engaged in the Resistance, about which he remained reticent, his sense of ego muted by the need to do justice to others. He wrote for and edited to great effect the journal of the Resistance, *Combat*, and after the war became one of the luminaries among the Parisian intellectual "mandarins" (Sartre, de Beauvoir, Malraux, Koestler). Until about 1948 Camus's relationship with Sartre was generally warm, shaped by their mutual love of the theatre and spiced by their pursuits of the same women. But they came to a severe clash over the nature of postwar Communism as represented by the Soviet Union, with Sartre on the side of a revolutionary future, Camus articulating what was seen to be a mawkish humanism. This perception grew during the Algerian War, when Camus was expected—and declined—to express crystalline support for the Algerian nationalists. After publishing his *Algerian Chronicles*, only recently issued in English, Camus took on a public silence. But his posthumous voice has a strong Algerian inflection. When he died in a French sports car on a pastoral road, Camus had with him the partial manuscript of a novel rooted in his childhood in Algiers. In 1995 his daughter and son issued the book as *The First Man*, a companion to the stories in *Exile and the Kingdom* about the vexed morality of Algerian political engagement. Although Camus published comparatively few stories, these have tremendous power in layering conditions of exile, from the desert and from a common humanity.

The Guest

The schoolmaster was watching the two men climb toward him. One was on horseback, the other on foot. They had not yet tackled the abrupt rise leading to the schoolhouse built on the hillside. They were toiling onward, making slow progress in the snow, among the stones, on the vast expanse of the high, deserted plateau. From time to time the horse stumbled. Without hearing anything yet, he could see the breath issuing from the horse's nostrils. One of the men, at least, knew the region. They were following the trail although it had disappeared days ago under a layer of dirty white snow. The schoolmaster calculated that it would take them half an hour to get onto the hill. It was cold; he went back into the school to get a sweater.

He crossed the empty, frigid classroom. On the blackboard the four rivers of France, drawn with four different colored chalks, had been flowing toward their estuaries for the past three days. Snow had suddenly fallen in mid-October after eight months of drought without the transition of rain, and the twenty pupils, more or less, who lived in the villages scattered over the plateau had stopped coming. With fair weather they would return. Daru now heated only the single room that was his lodging, adjoining the classroom and giving also onto the plateau to the east. Like the class windows, his window looked to the south too. On that side the school was a few kilometers from the point where the plateau began to slope toward the south. In clear weather could be seen the purple mass of the mountain range where the gap opened onto the desert.

Somewhat warmed, Daru returned to the window from which he had first seen the two men. They were no longer visible. Hence they must have tackled the rise. The sky was not so dark, for the snow had stopped falling during the night. The morning had opened with a dirty light which had scarcely become brighter as the ceiling of clouds lifted. At two in the afternoon it seemed as if the day were merely beginning. But still this was better than those three days when the thick snow was falling amidst unbroken darkness with little gusts of wind that rattled the double door of the classroom. Then Daru had spent long hours in his room, leaving it only to go to the shed and feed the chickens or get some coal. Fortunately the delivery truck from Tadjid, the nearest village to the north, had brought his supplies two days before the blizzard. It would return in forty-eight hours.

Besides, he had enough to resist a siege, for the little room was cluttered with bags of wheat that the administration left as a stock to distribute to those of his pupils whose families had suffered from the drought. Actually they had all been victims because they were all poor. Every day Daru would distribute a ration to the children. They had missed it, he knew, during these bad days. Possibly one of the fathers or big brothers would come this afternoon and he could supply them with grain. It was just a matter of carrying them over to the next harvest. Now shiploads of wheat were arriving from France and the worst was over. But it would be hard to forget that poverty, that army of ragged ghosts wandering in the sunlight, the plateaus burned to a cinder month after month, the earth shriveled up little by little, literally scorched, every stone bursting into dust under one's foot. The sheep had died then by thousands and even a few men, here and there, sometimes without anyone's knowing.

In contrast with such poverty, he who lived almost like a monk in his remote schoolhouse, nonetheless satisfied with the little he had and with the rough life, had felt like a lord with his whitewashed walls, his narrow couch, his unpainted shelves, his well, and his weekly provision of water and food. And suddenly this snow, without warning, without the foretaste of rain. This is the way the region was, cruel to live in, even without men —who didn't help matters either. But Daru had been born here. Everywhere else, he felt exiled.

He stepped out onto the terrace in front of the schoolhouse. The two men were now halfway up the slope. He recognized the horseman as Balducci, the old gendarme he had known for a long time. Balducci was holding on the end of a rope an Arab who was walking behind him with hands bound and head lowered. The gendarme waved a greeting to which Daru did not reply, lost as he was in contemplation of the Arab dressed in a faded blue jellaba, his feet in sandals but covered with socks of heavy raw wool, his head surmounted by a narrow, short *chèche.* They were approaching. Balducci was holding back his horse in order not to hurt the Arab, and the group was advancing slowly.

Within earshot, Balducci shouted: "One hour to do the three kilometers from El Arneur!" Daru did not answer. Short and square in his thick sweater, he watched them climb. Not once had the Arab raised his head. "Hello," said Daru when they got up onto the terrace. "Come in and warm up." Balducci painfully got down from his horse without letting go the rope. From under his bristling mustache he smiled at the schoolmaster. His little dark eyes, deep-set under a tanned forehead, and his mouth surrounded with wrinkles made him look attentive and studious. Daru took the bridle, led the horse to the shed, and came back to the two men, who were now waiting for him in the school. He led them into his room. "I am going to heat up the classroom," he said. "We'll be more comfortable there." When he entered the room again, Balducci was on the couch. He had undone the rope tying him to the Arab, who had squatted near the stove. His hands still bound, the *chèche* pushed back on his head, he was looking toward the window. At first Daru noticed only his huge lips, fat, smooth, almost Negroid; yet his nose was straight, his eyes were dark and full of fever. The *chèche* revealed an obstinate forehead and, under the weathered skin now rather discolored by the cold, the whole face had a restless and rebellious look that struck Daru when the Arab, turning his face toward him, looked him straight in the eyes. "Go into the other room," said the schoolmaster, "and I'll make you some mint tea." "Thanks," Balducci said. "What a chore! How I long for retirement." And addressing his prisoner in Arabic: "Come on, you." The Arab got up and, slowly, holding his bound wrists in front of him, went into the classroom.

With the tea, Daru brought a chair. But Balducci was already enthroned on the nearest pupil's desk and the Arab had squatted against the teacher's platform facing the stove, which stood between the desk and the window. When he held out the glass of tea to the prisoner, Daru hesitated at the sight of his bound hands. "He might perhaps be untied." "Sure," said Balducci. "That was for the trip." He started to get to his feet. But Daru, setting the glass on the floor, had knelt beside the Arab.

Without saying anything, the Arab watched him with his feverish eyes. Once his hands were free, he rubbed his swollen wrists against each other, took the glass of tea, and sucked up the burning liquid in swift little sips.

"Good," said Daru. "And where are you headed?"

Balducci withdrew his mustache from the tea. "Here, son."

"Odd pupils! And you're spending the night?"

"No. I'm going back to El Ameur. And you will deliver this fellow to Tinguit. He is expected at police headquarters."

Balducci was looking at Daru with a friendly little smile.

"What's this story?" asked the schoolmaster. "Are you pulling my leg?"

"No, son. Those are the orders."

"The orders? I'm not . . ." Daru hesitated, not wanting to hurt the old Corsican. "I mean, that's not my job."

"What! What's the meaning of that? In wartime people do all kinds of jobs."

"Then I'll wait for the declaration of war!"

Balducci nodded.

"O.K. But the orders exist and they concern you too. Things are brewing, it appears. There is talk of a forthcoming revolt. We are mobilized, in a way."

Daru still had his obstinate look.

"Listen, son," Balducci said. "I like you and you must understand. There's only a dozen of us at El Ameur to patrol throughout the whole territory of a small department and I must get back in a hurry. I was told to hand this guy over to you and return without delay. He couldn't be kept there. His village was beginning to stir; they wanted to take him back. You must take him to Tinguit tomorrow before the day is over. Twenty kilometers shouldn't faze a husky fellow like you. After that, all will be over. You'll come back to your pupils and your comfortable life."

Behind the wall the horse could be heard snorting and pawing the earth. Daru was looking out the window. Decidedly, the weather was clearing and the light was increasing over the snowy plateau. When all the snow was melted, the sun would take over again and once more would burn the fields of stone. For days, still, the unchanging sky would shed its dry light on the solitary expanse where nothing had any connection with man.

"After all," he said, turning around toward Balducci, "what did he do?" And, before the gendarme had opened his mouth, he asked: "Does he speak French?"

"No, not a word. We had been looking for him for a month, but they were hiding him. He killed his cousin."

"Is he against us?"

"I don't think so. But you can never be sure."

"Why did he kill?"

"A family squabble, I think. One owed the other grain, it seems. It's not at all clear. In short, he killed his cousin with a billhook. You know, like a sheep, *kreezk!*"

Balducci made the gesture of drawing a blade across his throat and the Arab, his attention attracted, watched him with a sort of misery. Daru felt a sudden wrath against the man, against all men with their rotten spite, their tireless hates, their blood lust.

But the kettle was singing on the stove. He served Balducci more tea, hesitated, then served the Arab again, who, a second time, drank avidly. His raised arms made the jellaba fall open and the schoolmaster saw his thin, muscular chest.

"Thanks, kid," Balducci said. "And now, I'm off."

He got up and went toward the Arab, taking a small rope from his pocket.

"What are you doing?" Daru asked dryly.

Balducci, disconcerted, showed him the rope.

"Don't bother."

The old gendarme hesitated. "It's up to you. Of course, you are armed?"

"I have my shotgun."

"Where?"

"In the trunk."

"You ought to have it near your bed."

"Why? I have nothing to fear."

"You're crazy, son. If there's an uprising, no one is safe, we're all in the same boat."

"I'll defend myself. I'll have time to see them coming."

Balducci began to laugh, then suddenly the mustache covered the white teeth.

"You'll have time? O.K. That's just what I was saying. You have always been a little cracked. That's why I like you, my son was like that."

At the same time he took out his revolver and put it on the desk.

"Keep it; I don't need two weapons from here to El Ameur."

The revolver shone against the black paint of the table. When the gendarme turned toward him, the schoolmaster caught the smell of leather and horseflesh.

"Listen, Balducci," Daru said suddenly, "every bit of this disgusts me, and first of all your fellow here. But I won't hand him over. Fight, yes, if I have to. But not that."

The old gendarme stood in front of him and looked at him severely.

"You're being a fool," he said slowly. "I don't like it either. You don't get used to putting a rope on a man even after years of it, and you're even ashamed—yes, ashamed. But you can't let them have their way."

"I won't hand him over," Daru said again.

"It's an order, son, and I repeat it."

"That's right. Repeat to them what I've said to you: I won't hand him over."

Balducci made a visible effort to reflect. He looked at the Arab and at Daru. At last he decided.

"No, I won't tell them anything. If you want to drop us, go ahead; I'll not denounce you. I have an order to deliver the prisoner and I'm doing so. And now you'll just sign this paper for me."

"There's no need. I'll not deny that you left him with me."

"Don't be mean with me. I know you'll tell the truth. You're from hereabouts and you are a man. But you must sign, that's the rule."

Daru opened his drawer, took out a little square bottle of purple ink, the red wooden penholder with the "sergeant-major" pen he used for making models of penmanship, and signed. The gendarme carefully folded the paper and put it into his wallet. Then he moved toward the door.

"I'll see you off," Daru said.

"No," said Balducci. "There's no use being polite. You insulted me."

He looked at the Arab, motionless in the same spot, sniffed peevishly, and turned away toward the door. "Good-by, son," he said. The door shut behind him. Balducci appeared suddenly outside the window and then disappeared. His footsteps were muffled by the snow. The horse stirred on the other side of the wall and several chickens fluttered in fright. A moment later Balducci reappeared outside the window leading the horse by the bridle. He walked toward the little rise without turning around and disappeared from sight with the horse following him. A big stone could be heard bouncing down. Daru walked back toward the prisoner, who, without stirring, never took his eyes off him. "Wait," the schoolmaster said in Arabic and went toward the bedroom. As he was going through the, door, he had a second thought, went to the desk, took the revolver, and stuck it in his pocket. Then, without looking back, he went into his room.

For some time he lay on his couch watching the sky gradually close over, listening to the silence. It was this silence that had seemed painful to him during the first days here, after the war. He had requested a post in the little town at the base of the foothills separating the upper plateaus from the desert. There, rocky walls, green and black to the north, pink and lavender to the south, marked the frontier of eternal summer. He had been named to a post farther north, on the plateau itself. In the beginning, the solitude and the silence had been hard for him on these wastelands peopled only by stones. Occasionally, furrows suggested cultivation, but they had been dug to uncover a certain kind of stone good for building. The only plowing here was to harvest rocks. Elsewhere a thin layer of soil accumulated in the hollows would be scraped out to enrich paltry village gardens. This is the way it was: bare rock covered three quarters of the region. Towns sprang up, flourished, then disappeared; men came by, loved one another or fought bitterly, then died. No one in this desert, neither he nor his guest, mattered. And yet, outside this desert neither of them, Daru knew, could have really lived.

When he got up, no noise came from the classroom. He was amused at the unmixed joy he derived from the mere thought that the Arab might have fled and that he would be alone with no decision to make. But the prisoner was there. He had merely stretched out between the stove and the desk. With eyes open, he was staring at the ceiling. In that position, his thick lips were particularly noticeable, giving him a pouting look. "Come," said Daru. The Arab got up and followed him. In the bedroom, the schoolmaster pointed to a chair near the table under the window. The Arab sat down without taking his eyes off Daru.

"Are you hungry?"

"Yes," the prisoner said.

Daru set the table for two. He took flour and oil, shaped a cake in a frying-pan, and lighted the little stove that functioned on bottled gas. While the cake was cooking, he went out to the shed to get cheese, eggs, dates, and condensed milk diluted with water, and beat up the eggs into an omelette. In one of his motions he knocked against the revolver stuck in his right pocket. He set the bowl down, went into the classroom, and put the revolver in his desk drawer. When he came back to the room, night was falling. He put on the light and served the Arab. "Eat," he said. The Arab took a piece of the cake, lifted it eagerly to his mouth, and stopped short.

"And you?" he asked.

"After you. I'll eat too."

The thick lips opened slightly. The Arab hesitated, then bit into the cake determinedly.

The meal over, the Arab looked at the schoolmaster. "Are you the judge?"

"No, I'm simply keeping you until tomorrow."

"Why do you eat with me?"

"I'm hungry."

The Arab fell silent. Daru got up and went out. He brought back a folding bed from the shed, set it up between the table and the stove, perpendicular to his own bed. From a large suitcase which, upright in a comer, served as a shelf for papers, he took two blankets and arranged them on the camp bed. Then he stopped, felt useless, and sat down on his bed. There was nothing more to do or to get ready. He had to look at this man. He looked at him, therefore, trying to imagine his face bursting with rage. He couldn't do so. He could see nothing but the dark yet shining eyes and the animal mouth.

"Why did you kill him?" he asked in a voice whose hostile tone surprised him.

The Arab looked away.

"He ran away. I ran after him."

He raised his eyes to Daru again and they were full of a sort of woeful interrogation. "Now what will they do to me?"

"Are you afraid?"

He stiffened, turning his eyes away.

"Are you sorry?"

The Arab stared at him openmouthed. Obviously he did not understand. Daru's annoyance was growing. At the same time he felt awkward and self-conscious with his big body wedged between the two beds.

"Lie down there," he said impatiently. "That's your bed."

The Arab didn't move. He called to Daru:

"Tell me!"

The schoolmaster looked at him.

"Is the gendarme coming back tomorrow?"

"I don't know."

"Are you coming with us?"

"I don't know. Why?"

The prisoner got up and stretched out on top of the blankets, his feet toward the window. The light from the electric bulb shone straight into his eyes and he closed them at once.

"Why?" Daru repeated, standing beside the bed.

The Arab opened his eyes under the blinding light and looked at him, trying not to blink.

"Come with us," he said.

In the middle of the night, Daru was still not asleep. He had gone to bed after undressing completely; he generally slept naked. But when he suddenly realized that he had nothing on, he hesitated. He felt vulnerable and the temptation came to him to put his clothes back on. Then he shrugged his shoulders; after all, he wasn't a child and, if need be, he could break his adversary in two. From his bed he could observe him, lying on his back, still motionless with his eyes closed under the harsh light. When Daru turned out the light, the darkness seemed to coagulate all of a sudden. Little by little, the night came back to life in the window where the starless sky was stirring gently. The schoolmaster soon made out the body lying at his feet. The Arab still did not move, but his eyes seemed open. A faint wind was prowling around the schoolhouse. Perhaps it would drive away the clouds and the sun would reappear.

During the night the wind increased. The hens fluttered a little and then were silent. The Arab turned over on his side with his back to Daru, who thought he heard him moan. Then he listened for his guest's breathing, become heavier and more regular. He listened to that breath so close to him and mused without being able to go to sleep. In this room where he had been sleeping alone for a year, this presence bothered him. But it bothered him also by imposing on him a sort of brotherhood he knew well but refused to accept in the present circumstances. Men who share the same rooms, soldiers or prisoners, develop a strange alliance as if, having cast off their armor with their clothing, they fraternized every evening, over and above their differences, in the ancient community of dream and fatigue. But Daru shook himself; he didn't like such musings, and it was essential to sleep.

A little later, however, when the Arab stirred slightly, the schoolmaster was still not asleep. When the prisoner made a second move, he stiffened, on the alert. The Arab was lifting himself slowly on his arms with almost the motion of a sleepwalker. Seated upright in bed, he waited motionless without turning his head toward Daru, as if he were listening attentively. Daru did not stir; it has just occurred to him that the revolver was still in the drawer of his desk. It was better to act at once. Yet he continued to observe the prisoner, who, with the same slithery motion, put his feet on the ground, waited again, then began to stand up slowly. Daru was about to call out to him when the Arab began to walk, in a quite natural but extraordinary silent way. He was heading toward the door at the end of the room that opened into the shed. He lifted the latch with precaution and went out, pushing the door behind him without shutting it. Dara had not stirred. "He is running away," he merely thought. "Good riddance!" Yet he listened attentively. The hens were not fluttering; the guest must be on the plateau. A faint sound of water reached him, and he didn't know what it was until the Arab again stood framed in the doorway, closed the door carefully, and came back to bed without a sound. Then Daru turned his back on him and fell asleep. Still later he seemed, from the depths of his sleep, to hear furtive steps around the school house. "I'm dreaming! I'm dreaming!" he repeated to himself. And he went on sleeping.

When he awoke, the sky was clear; the loose window let in a cold, pure air. The Arab was asleep, hunched up under the blankets now, his mouth open, utterly relaxed. But when Daru shook him, he started dreadfully, staring at Daru with wild eyes as if he had never seen him and such a frightened expression that the schoolmaster stepped back. "Don't be afraid. It's me. You must eat." The Arab nodded his head and said yes. Calm had returned to his face, but his expression was vacant and listless.

The Arab, leaning over the cement floor of the shed, was washing his teeth with two fingers. Daru looked at him and said: "Come." He went back into the room ahead of the prisoner. He slipped a hunting-jacket on over his sweater and put on walking-shoes. Standing, he waited until the Arab had put on his *chèche* and sandals. They went into the classroom and the schoolmaster pointed to the exit, saying: "Go ahead." The fellow didn't budge. "I'm coming," said Daru. The Arab went out. Daru went back into the room and made a package of pieces of rusk, dates, and sugar. In the classroom, before going out, he hesitated a second in front of his desk, then crossed the threshold and locked the door. "That's the way," he said. He started toward the east, followed by the prisoner. But, a short distance from the schoolhouse, he thought he heard a slight sound behind them. He retraced his steps and examined the surroundings of the house; there was no one there. The Arab watched him without seeming to understand. "Come on," said Daru.

They walked for an hour and rested beside a sharp peak of limestone. The snow was melting faster and faster and the sun was drinking up the puddles at once, rapidly cleaning the plateau, which gradually dried and vibrated like the air itself. When they resumed walking, the ground rang under their feet. From time to time a bird rent the space in front of them with a joyful cry. Daru breathed in deeply the fresh morning light. He felt a sort of rapture before the vast familiar expanse, now almost entirely yellow under its dome of blue sky. They walked an hour more, descending toward the south. They reached a level height made up of crumbly rocks. From there on, the plateau sloped down, eastward, toward a low plain where there were a few spindly trees and, to the south, toward outcroppings of rock that gave the landscape a chaotic look.

Daru surveyed the two directions. There was nothing but the sky on the horizon. Not a man could be seen. He turned toward the Arab, who was looking at him blankly. Daru held out the package to him. "Take it," he said. "There are dates, bread, and sugar. You can hold out for two days. Here are a thousand francs too." The Arab took the package and the money but kept his full hands at chest level as if he didn't know what to do with what was being given to him. "Now look," the schoolmaster said as he pointed in the direction of the east, "there's the way to Tinguit. You have a two-hour walk. At Tinguit you'll find the administration and the police. They are expecting you." The Arab looked toward the east, still holding the package and the money against his chest. Daru took his elbow and turned him rather roughly toward the touch. At the foot of the height on which they stood could be seen a faint path. "That's the trail across the plateau. In a day's walk from here you'll find pasturelands and the first nomads. They'll take you in and shelter you according to their law." The Arab had now turned toward Daru and a sort of panic was visible in his expression. "Listen," he said. Daru shook his head: "No, be quiet. Now I'm leaving you." He turned his back on him, took two long steps in the direction of the school, looked hesitantly at the motionless Arab, and started off again. For a few minutes he heard nothing but his own step resounding on the cold ground and did not turn his head. A moment later, however, he turned around. The Arab was still there on the edge of the hill, his arms hanging now, and he was looking at the schoolmaster. Daru felt something rise in his throat. But he swore with impatience, waved vaguely, and started off again. He had already gone some distance when he again stopped and looked. There was no longer anyone on the hill.

Daru hesitated. The sun was now rather high in the sky and was beginning to beat down on his head. The schoolmaster retraced his steps, at first somewhat uncertainly, then with decision. When he reached the little hill, he was bathed in sweat. He climbed it as fast as he could and stopped, out of breath, at the top. The rock-fields to the south stood out sharply against the blue sky, but on the plain to the east a steamy heat was already rising. And in that slight haze, Daru, with heavy heart, made out the Arab walking slowly on the road to prison.

A little later, standing before the window of the classroom, the schoolmaster was watching the clear light bathing the whole surface of the plateau, but he hardly saw it. Behind him on the blackboard, among the winding French rivers, sprawled the clumsily chalked-up words he had just read: "You handed over our brother. You will pay for this." Daru looked at the sky, the plateau, and, beyond, the invisible lands stretching all the way to the sea. In this vast landscape he had loved so much, he was alone.

1957

Doris Lessing

1919–2013

Few writers have been so entwined with the extreme currents and changes in twentieth-century culture as Doris Lessing, and few have had so immediate, so extensive, an impact on their readers. She is a writer within whose circumference—to draw upon Northrop Frye's conception—readers have grown up, or at least aged in complexity. For many, their lives would have been very different without *The Golden Notebook* or stories such as "To Room 19" and "A Man and Two Women." Born in Persia (now Iran), she grew up in Rhodesia (now Zimbabwe), ended her formal education in Salisbury (now Harare) at fourteen, and in 1949, after two marriages, left for England with a son and the manuscript of her first novel, *The Grass Is Singing*, published in 1950 to high praise and expectation. Largely self-taught, she brings a formidable intelligence and a sense of partnership in "the great tradition" of English social fiction to the dominant elements of the age: colonialism, racism, communism, apocalypsism—all informed by the urgencies of gender and the calibrations of personal assertion. Among her most compelling works—besides *The Golden Notebook* (1962) and the *Children of Violence* series—are *Briefing for a Descent into Hell* (1971) and *Memoirs of a Survivor* (1974), both expressions of the sort of inner extremity articulated by the psychiatrist R.D. Laing. Her attachment to Sufism underlies her sometimes inaccessible and chilly excursions into science fiction, but she is at her best negotiating the zones of private need and political belief, as in *The Good Terrorist* (1985). Throughout her career, Lessing has moved emphatically from novel to short story, the latter particularly hospitable to her often brutal explorations of personal laceration.

A Man and Two Women

Stella's friends, the Bradfords, had taken a cheap cottage in Essex for the summer, and she was going down to visit them. She wanted to see them, but there was no doubt there was something of a let-down (and for them too) in the English cottage. Last summer Stella had been wandering with her husband around Italy; had seen the English couple at a café table, and found them sympathetic. They all liked each other, and the four went about for some weeks, sharing meals, hotels, trips. Back in London the friendship had not, as might have been expected, fallen off. Then Stella's husband departed abroad, as he often did, and Stella saw Jack and Dorothy by herself. There were a great many people she might have seen, but it was the Bradfords she saw most often, two or three times a week, at their flat or hers. They were at ease with each other. Why were they? Well, for one thing they were all artists in different ways. Stella designed wallpapers and materials; she had a name for it.

The Bradfords were *real* artists. He painted, she drew. They had lived mostly out of England in cheap places around the Mediterranean. Both from the North of England, they had met at art school, married at twenty, had taken flight from England, then returned to it, needing it, then off again: and so on, for years, in the rhythm of so many of their kind, needing, hating, loving England. There had been seasons of real poverty, while they lived on pasta or bread or rice, and wine and fruit and sunshine, in Majorca, southern Spain, Italy, North Africa.

A French critic had seen Jack's work, and suddenly he was successful. His show in Paris, then one in London, made money; and now he charged in the hundreds where a year or so ago he charged ten or twenty guineas. This had deepened his contempt for the values of the markets. For a while Stella thought that this was the bond between the Bradfords and herself. They were so very much, as she was, of the new generation of artists (and poets and playwrights and novelists) who had one thing in common, a cool derision about the racket. They were so very unlike (they felt) the older generation with their societies and their lunches and their salons and their cliques: their atmosphere of connivance with the snobberies of success. Stella, too, had been successful by a fluke. Not that she did not consider herself talented; it was that others as talented were unfêted, and unbought. When she was with the Bradfords and other fellow-spirits, they would talk about the racket, using each other as yardsticks or fellow-consciences about how much to give in, what to give, how to use without being used, how to enjoy without becoming dependent on enjoyment.

Of course Dorothy Bradford was not able to talk in quite the same way, since she had not been "discovered"; she had not "broken through." A few people with discrimination bought her unusual delicate drawings, which had a strength that was hard to understand unless one knew Dorothy herself. But she was not at all, as Jack was, a great success. There was a strain here, in the marriage, nothing much, it was kept in check by their scorn for their arbitrary rewards of "the racket." But it was there, nevertheless.

Stella's husband had said: "Well, I can understand that, it's like me and you—you're creative, whatever that may mean, I'm just a bloody TV journalist." There was no bitterness in this. He was a good journalist, and besides he sometimes got the chance to make a good small film. All the same, there was that between him and Stella, just as there was between Jack and his wife.

After a time Stella saw something else in her kinship with the couple. It was that the Bradfords had a close bond, bred of having spent so many years together in foreign places, dependent on each other because of their poverty. It had been a real love marriage, one could see it by looking at them. It was now. And Stella's marriage was a real marriage. She understood she enjoyed being with the Bradfords because the two couples were equal in this. Both marriages were those of strong, passionate, talented individuals; they shared a battling quality that strengthened them, not weakened them.

The reason why it had taken Stella so long to understand this was that the Bradfords had made her think about her own marriage, which was what she was beginning to take for granted, sometimes even found exhausting. She had understood, through them, how lucky she was in her husband; how lucky they all were. No marital miseries; nothing of (what they saw so often in friends) one partner in a marriage victim to the other, resenting the other; no claiming of outsiders as sympathizers or allies in an unequal battle.

There had been a plan for these four people to go off again to Italy or Spain, but then Stella's husband departed, and Dorothy got pregnant. So there was the cottage in Essex instead, a bad second-choice, but better, they all felt, to deal with a new baby on home ground, at least for the first year. Stella, telephoned by Jack (on Dorothy's particular insistence, he said) offered and received commiserations on its being only Essex and not Majorca or Italy. She also received sympathy because her husband had been expected back this weekend, but had wired to say he wouldn't be back for another month, probably—there was trouble in Venezuela. Stella wasn't really forlorn; she didn't mind living alone, since she was always supported by knowing her man would be back. Besides, if she herself were offered the chance of a month's "trouble" in Venezuela, she wouldn't hesitate, so it wasn't fair . . . fairness characterized their relationship. All the same, it was nice that she could drop down (or up) to the Bradfords, people with whom she could always be herself, neither more nor less.

She left London at midday by train, armed with food unobtainable in Essex: salamis, cheeses, spices, wine. The sun shone, but it wasn't particularly warm. She hoped there would be heating in the cottage, July or not.

The train was empty. The little station seemed stranded in a green nowhere. She got out, cumbered by bags full of food. A porter and a stationmaster examined, then came to succour her. She was a tallish, fair woman, rather ample; her soft hair, drawn back, escaped in tendrils, and she had great helpless-looking blue eyes. She wore a dress made in one of the materials she had designed. Enormous green leaves laid hands all over her body, and fluttered about her knees. She stood smiling, accustomed to men running to wait on her, enjoying them enjoying her. She walked with them to the barrier where Jack waited, appreciating the scene. He was a smallish man, compact, dark. He wore a blue-green summer shirt, and smoked a pipe and smiled, watching. The two men delivered her into the hands of the third, and departed, whistling, to their duties.

Jack and Stella kissed, then pressed their cheeks together.

"Good," he said, "food," relieving her of the parcels.

"What's it like here, shopping?"

"Vegetables all right, I suppose."

Jack was still Northern in this: he seemed brusque, to strangers; he wasn't shy, he simply hadn't been brought up to enjoy words. Now he put his arm briefly around Stella's waist, and said: "Marvellous, Stell, marvellous." They walked on, pleased with each other. Stella had with Jack, her husband had with Dorothy, these moments, when they said to each other wordlessly: If I were not married to my husband, if you were not married to your wife, how delightful it would be to be married to you. These moments were not the least of the pleasures of this four-sided friendship.

"Are you liking it down here?"

"It's what we bargained for."

There was more than his usual shortness in this, and she glanced at him to find him frowning. They were walking to the car, parked under a tree.

"How's the baby?"

"Little bleeder never sleeps, he's wearing us out, but he's fine."

The baby was six weeks old. Having the baby was a definite achievement: getting it safely conceived and born had taken a couple of years. Dorothy, like most independent women, had had divided thoughts about a baby. Besides, she was over thirty and complained she was set in her ways. All this—the difficulties, Dorothy's hesitations, had added up to an atmosphere which Dorothy herself described as "like wondering if some damned horse is going to take the fence." Dorothy would talk, while she was pregnant, in a soft staccato voice: Perhaps I don't really want a baby at all? Perhaps I'm not fitted to be a mother? Perhaps . . . and if so . . . and how . . .

She said: "Until recently Jack and I were always with people who took it for granted that getting pregnant was a disaster, and now suddenly all the people we know have young children and baby-sitters and . . . perhaps . . . if . . ."

Jack said: "You'll feel better when it's born."

Once Stella had heard him say, after one of Dorothy's long-troubled dialogues with herself: "Now that's enough, that's enough Dorothy." He had silenced her, taking the responsibility.

They reached the car, got in. It was a second-hand job recently bought. "They" (being the Press, the enemy generally) "wait for us" (being artists or writers who have made money) "to buy flashy cars." They had discussed it, decided that *not* to buy an expensive car if they felt like it would be allowing themselves to be bullied; but bought a second-hand one after all. Jack wasn't going to give *them* so much satisfaction, apparently.

"Actually we could have walked," he said, as they shot down a narrow lane, "but with these groceries, it's just as well."

"If the baby's giving you a tough time, there can't be much time for cooking." Dorothy was a wonderful cook. But now again there was something in the air as he said: "Food's definitely not too good just now. You can cook supper, Stell, we could do with a good feed."

Now Dorothy hated anyone in her kitchen, except, for certain specified jobs, her husband; and this was surprising.

"The truth is, Dorothy's worn out," he went on, and now Stella understood he was warning her.

"Well, it is tiring," said Stella soothingly.

"You were like that?"

Like that was saying a good more than just worn out, or tired, and Stella understood that Jack was really uneasy. She said, plaintively humorous: "You two always expect me to remember things that happened a hundred years ago, let me think. . . ."

She had been married when she was eighteen, got pregnant at once. Her husband had left her. Soon she had married Philip, who also had a small child from a former marriage. These two children—her daughter, seventeen, his son, twenty—had grown up together.

She remembered herself at nineteen, alone, with a small baby. "Well, I was alone," she said, "that makes a difference. I remember I was exhausted. Yes, I was definitely irritable and unreasonable."

"Yes," said Jack, with a brief reluctant look at her.

"All right, don't worry," she said, replying aloud as she often did to things Jack had not said aloud.

"Good," he said.

Stella thought of how she had seen Dorothy, in the hospital room, with the new baby. She had sat up in bed, in a pretty bed-jacket, the baby beside her in a basket. He was restless. Jack stood between basket and bed, one large hand on his son's stomach. "Now, you just shut up, little bleeder," he had said, as he grumbled. Then he had picked him up, as if he'd been doing it always, held him against his shoulder, and, as Dorothy held her arms out, had put the baby into them. "Want your mother, then? Don't blame you."

That scene, the ease of it, the way the two parents were together, had, for Stella, made nonsense of all the months of Dorothy's self-questioning. As for Dorothy, she had said, parodying the expected words but meaning them: "He's the most beautiful baby ever born. I can't imagine why I didn't have him before."

"There's the cottage," said Jack. Ahead of them was a small labourer's cottage, among full green trees, surrounded by green grass. It was painted white, had four sparkling windows. Next to it a long shed or structure that turned out to be a greenhouse.

"The man grew tomatoes," said Jack, "fine studio now."

The car came to rest under another tree.

"Can I just drop in to the studio?"

"Help yourself." Stella walked into the long, glass-roofed shed. In London Jack and Dorothy shared a studio. They had shared huts, sheds, any suitable building, all around the Mediterranean. They always worked side by side. Dorothy's end was tidy, exquisite, Jack's lumbered with great canvases, and he worked in a clutter.

Now Stella looked to see if this friendly arrangement continued, but as Jack came in behind her he said: "Dorothy's not set herself up yet, I miss her, I can tell you."

The greenhouse was still partly one: trestles with plants stood along the ends. It was lush and warm.

"As hot as hell when the sun's really going, it makes up. And Dorothy brings Paul in sometimes, so he can get used to a decent climate young."

Dorothy came in, at the far end, without the baby. She had recovered her figure. She was a small dark woman, with neat, delicate limbs. Her face was white, with scarlet rather irregular lips, and black glossy brows, a little crooked. So while she was not pretty, she was lively and dramatic-looking. She and Stella had their moments together, when they got pleasure from contrasting their differences, one woman so big and soft and blonde, the other so dark and vivacious.

Dorothy came forward through the shafts of sunlight, stopped, and said: "Stella, I'm glad you've come." Then forward again, to a few steps off, where she stood looking at them. "You two look good together," she said, frowning. There was something heavy and over-emphasized about both statements, and Stella said: "I was wondering what Jack had been up to?"

"Very good, I think," said Dorothy, coming to look at the new canvas on the easel. It was of sunlit rocks, brown and smooth, with blue sky, blue water, and people swimming in spangles of light. When Jack was in the south he painted pictures that his wife described as "dirt and grime and misery"—which was how they both described their joint childhood background. When he was in England he painted scenes like these.

"Like it!—it's good, isn't it?" said Dorothy.

"Very much," said Stella. She always took pleasure from the contrast between Jack's outward self—the small, self-contained little man who could have vanished in a moment into a crowd of factory workers in, perhaps, Manchester, and the sensuous bright pictures like these.

"And you?" asked Stella.

"Having a baby's killed everything creative in me—quite different from being pregnant," said Dorothy, but not complaining of it. She had worked like a demon while she was pregnant.

"Have a heart," said Jack, "he's only just got himself born."

"Well, I don't care," said Dorothy. "That's the funny thing, I *don't* care." She said this flat, indifferent. She seemed to be looking at them both again from a small troubled distance. "You two look good together," she said, and again there was the small jar.

"Well, how about some tea?" said Jack, and Dorothy said at once: "I made it when I heard the car. I thought better inside, it's not really hot in the sun." She led the way out of the greenhouse, her white linen dress dissolving in lozenges of yellow light from the glass panes above, so that Stella was reminded of the white limbs of Jack's swimmers disintegrating under sunlight in his new picture. The work of these two people was always reminding one of each other, or each other's work, and in all kinds of ways: they were so much married, so close.

The time it took to cross the space of rough grass to the door of the little house was enough to show Dorothy was right: it was really chilly in the sun. Inside two electric heaters made up for it. There had been two little rooms downstairs, but they had been knocked into one fine low-ceilinged room, stone-floored, whitewashed. A tea table, covered with a purple checked cloth stood waiting near a window where flowering bushes and trees showed through clean panes. Charming. They adjusted the heaters and arranged themselves so they could admire the English countryside through the glass. Stella looked for the baby; Dorothy said: "In the pram at the back." Then she asked: "Did yours cry a lot?"

Stella laughed and said again: "I'll try to remember."

"We expect you to guide and direct, with all your experience," said Jack.

"As far as I can remember, she was a little demon for about three months, for no reason I could see, then suddenly she became civilized."

"Roll on the three months," said Jack.

"Six weeks to go," said Dorothy, handling teacups in a languid indifferent manner Stella found new in her.

"Finding it tough going?"

"I've never felt better in my life," said Dorothy at once, as if being accused.

"You look fine."

She looked a bit tired, nothing much; Stella couldn't see what reason there was for Jack to warn her. Unless he meant the languor, a look of self-absorption? Her vivacity, a friendly aggressiveness that was the expression of her lively intelligence, was dimmed. She sat leaning back in a deep armchair, letting Jack manage things, smiling vaguely.

"I'll bring him in in a minute," she remarked, listening to the silence from the sunlit garden at the back.

"Leave him," said Jack. "He's quiet seldom enough. Relax, woman, and have a cigarette."

He lit a cigarette for her, and she took it in the same vague way, and sat breathing out smoke, her eyes half-closed.

"Have you heard from Philip?" she asked, not from politeness, but with sudden insistence.

"Of course she has, she got a wire," said Jack.

"I want to know how she feels," said Dorothy. "How do you feel, Stell?" She was listening for the baby all the time.

"Feel about what?"

"About his not coming back?"

"But he is coming back, it's only a month," said Stella, and heard, with surprise, that her voice sounded edgy.

"You see?" said Dorothy to Jack, meaning the words, not the edge on them.

At this evidence that she and Philip had been discussed, Stella felt, first, pleasure: because it was pleasurable to be understood by two such good friends; then she felt discomfort, remembering Jack's warning.

"See what?" she asked Dorothy, smiling.

"That's enough now," said Jack to his wife in a flash of stubborn anger, which continued the conversation that had taken place.

Dorothy took direction from her husband, and kept quiet a moment, then seemed impelled to continue: "I've been thinking it must be nice, having your husband go off and then come back. Do you realize Jack and I haven't been separated since we married? That's over ten years. Don't you think there's something awful in two grown people stuck together all the time like Siamese twins?" This ended in a wail of genuine appeal to Stella.

"No, I think it's marvellous."

"But you don't mind being alone so much?"

"It's not *so* much, it's two or three months in a year. Well, of course I mind. But I enjoy being alone, really. But I'd enjoy it too if we were together all the time. I envy you two." Stella was surprised to find her eyes wet with self-pity because she had to be without her husband another month.

"And what does he think?" demanded Dorothy. "What does Philip think?"

Stella said: "Well, I think he likes getting away from time to time—yes. He likes intimacy, he enjoys it, but it doesn't come as easily to him as it does to me." She had never said this before because she had never thought about it. She was annoyed with herself that she had had to wait for Dorothy to prompt her. Yet she knew that getting annoyed was what she must not do, with the state Dorothy was in, whatever it was. She glanced at Jack for guidance, but he was determinedly busy on his pipe.

"Well, I'm like Philip," announced Dorothy. "Yes, I'd love it if Jack went off sometimes. I think I'm being stifled being shut up with Jack day and night, year in, year out."

"Thanks," said Jack, short but good-humoured.

"No, but I mean it. There's something humiliating about two adult people never for one second out of each other's sight."

"Well," said Jack, "when Paul's a bit bigger, you buzz off for a month or so and you'll appreciate me when you get back."

"It's not that I don't appreciate you, it's not that at all," said Dorothy, insistent, almost strident, apparently fevered with restlessness. Her languor had quite gone, and her limbs jerked and moved. And now the baby, as if he had been prompted by his father's mentioning him, let out a cry. Jack got up, forestalling his wife, saying: "I'll get him."

Dorothy sat, listening for her husband's movements with the baby, until he came back, which he did, supporting the infant sprawled against his shoulder with a competent hand. He sat down, let his son slide on to this chest, and said: "There now, you shut up and leave us in peace a bit longer." The baby was looking up into his face with the astonished expression of the newly born, and Dorothy sat smiling at both of them. Stella understood that her restlessness, her repeated curtailed movements, meant that she longed—more, needed—to have the child in her arms, have its body against hers. And Jack seemed to feel this, because Stella could have sworn it was not a conscious decision that made him rise and slide the infant into his wife's arms. Her flesh, her needs, had spoken direct to him without words, and he had risen at once to give her what she wanted. This silent instinctive conversation between husband and wife made Stella miss her own husband violently, and with resentment against fate that kept them apart so often. She ached for Philip.

Meanwhile, Dorothy, now the baby was sprawled softly against her chest, the small feet in her hand, seemed to have lapsed into good humour. And Stella, watching, remembered something she really had forgotten: the close, fierce physical tie between herself and her daughter when she had been a tiny baby. She saw this bond in the way Dorothy stroked the small head that trembled on its neck as the baby looked up into his mother's face. Why, she remembered it was like being in love, having a new baby. All kinds of forgotten or unused instincts woke in Stella. She lit a cigarette, took herself in hand; set herself to enjoy the other woman's love affair with her baby instead of envying her.

The sun, dropping into the trees, struck the windowpanes; and there was a dazzle and a flashing of yellow and white light into the room, particularly over Dorothy in her white dress and the baby. Again Stella was reminded of Jack's picture of the white-limbed swimmers in sun-dissolving water. Dorothy shielded the baby's eyes with her hand and remarked dreamily: "This is better than any man, isn't it, Stell? Isn't it better than any man?"

"Well—no," said Stella laughing. "No, not for long."

"If you say so, you should know . . . but I can't imagine ever . . . tell me, Stell, does your Philip have affairs when he's away?"

"For God's sake!" said Jack, angry. But he checked himself.

"Yes, I am sure he does."

"Do you mind?" asked Dorothy, loving the baby's feet with her enclosing palm.

And now Stella was forced to remember, to think about having minded, minding, coming to terms, and the ways in which she now did not mind.

"I don't think about it," she said.

"Well I don't think I'd mind," said Dorothy.

"Thanks for letting me know," said Jack, short despite himself. Then he made himself laugh.

"And, you, do you have affairs while Philip's away?"

"Sometimes. Not really."

"Do you know, Jack was unfaithful to me this week," remarked Dorothy, smiling at the baby.

"That's *enough*," said Jack, really angry.

"No it isn't enough, it isn't. Because what's awful is, I don't care."

"Well, why should you care, in the circumstances?" Jack turned to Stella. "There's a silly bitch Lady Edith lives across that field. She got all excited, real live artists living down her lane. Well, Dorothy was lucky, she had an excuse in the baby, but I had to go to her silly party. Booze flowing in rivers, and the most incredible people—you know. If you read about them in a novel you'd never believe . . . but I can't remember much after about twelve."

"Do you know what happened?" said Dorothy. "I was feeding the baby, it was terribly early. Jack sat straight up in bed and said: 'Jesus, Dorothy, I've just remembered, I screwed that silly bitch Lady Edith on her brocade sofa.' "

Stella laughed. Jack let out a snort of laughter. Dorothy laughed, an unscrupulous chuckle of appreciation. Then she said seriously: "But that's the point, Stella—the thing is, I don't care a tuppenny damn."

"But why should you?" asked Stella.

"But it's the first time he ever has, and surely I should have minded?"

"Don't you be too sure of that," said Jack, energetically puffing his pipe. "Don't be too sure." But it was only for form's sake, and Dorothy knew it, and said: "Surely I should have cared, Stell?"

"No. You'd have cared if you and Jack weren't so marvellous together. Just as I'd care if Philip and I weren't . . ." Tears came running down her face. She let them. These were her good friends; and, besides, instinct told her tears weren't a bad thing, with Dorothy in this mood. She said, sniffing: "When Philip gets home, we always have a flaming bloody row in the first day or two, about something unimportant, but what it's really about, and we know it, is that I'm jealous of any affair he's had and vice versa. Then we go to bed and make up." She wept, bitterly, thinking of this happiness, postponed for a month, to be succeeded by the delightful battle of their day-to-day living.

"Oh, Stella," said Jack." Stell . . ." He got up, fished out a handkerchief, dabbed her eyes for her. "There, love, he'll be back soon."

"Yes, I know. It's just that you two are so good together and whenever I'm with you I miss Philip."

"Well, I suppose we're good together?" said Dorothy, sounding surprised. Jack, bending over Stella with his back to his wife, made a warning grimace, then stood up and turned, commanding the situation. "It's nearly six. You'd better feed Paul. Stella's going to cook supper."

"Is she, how nice," said Dorothy. "There's everything in the kitchen, Stella, how lovely to be looked after."

"I'll show you our mansion," said Jack.

Upstairs were two small white rooms. One was the bedroom, with their things and the baby's in it. The other was an overflow room, jammed with stuff. Jack picked up a large leather folder off the spare bed and said: "Look at these, Stell." He stood at the window, back to her, his thumb at work in his pipe-bowl, looking into the garden. Stella sat on the bed, opened the folder and at once exclaimed: "When did she do these?"

"The last three months she was pregnant. Never seen anything like it, she just turned them out one after the other."

There were a couple of hundred pencil drawings, all of two bodies in every kind of balance, tension, relationship. The two bodies were Jack's and Dorothy's, mostly unclothed, but not all. The drawings startled, not only because they marked a real jump forward in Dorothy's achievement, but because of their bold sensuousness. They were a kind of chant, or exaltation about the marriage. The instinctive closeness, the harmony of Jack and Dorothy, visible in every movement they made towards or away from each other, visible even when they were not together, was celebrated here with a frank, calm triumph.

"Some of them are pretty strong," said Jack, the Northern working-class boy reviving in him for a moment's puritanism.

But Stella laughed, because the prudishness masked pride: some of the drawings were indecent.

In the last few of the series the woman's body was swollen in pregnancy. They showed her trust in her husband, whose body, commanding hers, stood or lay in positions of strength and confidence. In the very last Dorothy stood turned away from her husband, her two hands supporting her big belly, and Jack's hands were protective on her shoulders.

"They are marvellous," said Stella.

"They are, aren't they."

Stella looked, laughing, and with love, towards Jack; for she saw that his showing her the drawings was not only pride in his wife's talent; but that he was using this way of telling Stella not to take Dorothy's mood too seriously. And to cheer himself up. She said, impulsively: "Well, that's all right then, isn't it."

"What?—Oh yes, I see what you mean, yes, I think it's all right."

"Do you know what?" said Stella, lowering her voice, "I think Dorothy's guilty because she feels unfaithful to you."

"*What?*"

"No, I mean, with the baby, and that's what it's all about."

He turned to face her, troubled, then slowly smiling. There was the same rich unscrupulous quality of appreciation in that smile as there had been in Dorothy's laugh over her husband and Lady Edith. "You think so?" They laughed together, irrepressibly and loudly.

"What's the joke?" shouted Dorothy.

"I'm laughing because your drawings are so good," shouted Stella.

"Yes, they are, aren't they?" But Dorothy's voice changed to flat incredulity: "The trouble is, I can't imagine how I ever did them, I can't imagine ever being able to do it again."

"Downstairs," said Jack to Stella, and they went down to find Dorothy nursing the baby. He nursed with his whole being, all of him in movement. He was wrestling with the breast, thumping Dorothy's plump pretty breast with his fists. Jack stood looking down at the two of them, grinning. Dorothy reminded Stella of a cat, half-closing her yellow eyes to stare over the kittens at work on her side, while she stretched out a paw where claws sheathed and unsheathed themselves, making a small rip-rip-rip on the carpet she lay on.

"You're a savage creature," said Stella laughing.

Dorothy raised her small vivid face and smiled. "Yes, I am," she said, and looked at the two of them calm, and from a distance, over the head of her energetic baby.

Stella cooked supper in a stone kitchen, with a heater brought by Jack to make it tolerable. She used the good food she had brought with her, taking trouble. It took some time, then the three ate slowly over a big wooden table. The baby was not asleep. He grumbled for some minutes on a cushion on the floor, then his father held him briefly, before passing him over, as he had done earlier, in response to his mother's need to have him close.

"I'm supposed to let him cry," remarked Dorothy. "But why should he? If he were an Arab or an African baby he'd be plastered to my back."

"And very nice too," said Jack. "I think they come out too soon into the light of day, they should just stay inside for about eighteen months, much better all round."

"Have a heart," said Dorothy and Stella together, and they all laughed; but Dorothy added, quite serious: "Yes, I've been thinking so, too."

This good nature lasted through the long meal. The light went cool and thin outside; and inside they let the summer dusk deepen, without lamps.

"I've got to go quite soon," said Stella, with regret.

"Oh, no, you've got to stay!" said Dorothy, strident. It was sudden, the return of the woman who made Jack and Dorothy tense themselves to take strain.

"We all thought Philip was coming, the children will be back tomorrow night, they've been on holiday."

"Then stay till tomorrow, I *want* you," said Dorothy, petulant.

"But I can't," said Stella.

"I never thought I'd want another woman around, cooking in my kitchen, looking after me, but I do," said Dorothy, apparently about to cry.

"Well, love, you'll have to put up with me," said Jack.

"Would you mind, Stell?"

"Mind *what*?" asked Stella, cautious.

"Do you find Jack attractive?"

"Very."

"Well, I know you do. Jack, do you find Stella attractive?"

"Try me," said Jack, grinning; but at the same time signalling warnings to Stella.

"Well then!" said Dorothy.

"A *ménage à trois*?" asked Stella, laughing. "And how about my Philip, where does he fit in?"

"Well, if it comes to that, I wouldn't mind Philip myself," said Dorothy, knitting her sharp black brows and frowning.

"I don't blame you," said Stella, thinking of her handsome husband.

"Just for a month, till he comes back," said Dorothy. "I tell you what, we'll abandon this silly cottage, we must have been mad to stick ourselves away in England in the first place. The three of us'll just pack up and go off to Spain or Italy with the baby."

"And what else?" inquired Jack, good-natured at all costs, using his pipe as a safety-valve.

"Yes, I've decided I approve of polygamy," announced Dorothy. She had opened her dress and the baby was nursing again, quietly this time, relaxed against her. She stroked his head, softly, softly, while her voice rose and insisted at the other two people: "I never understood it before, but I do now. I'll be the senior wife, and you two can look after me."

"Any other plans?" inquired Jack, angry now. "You just drop in from time to time to watch Stella and me have a go, is that it? Or are you going to tell us when we can go off and do it, give us your gracious permission?"

"Oh, I don't care what you do, that's the point," said Dorothy, sighing, sounding forlorn, however.

Jack and Stella, careful not to look at each other, sat waiting.

"I read something in the newspaper yesterday, it struck me," said Dorothy, conversational. "A man and two women living together—here, in England.

They are both his wives, they consider themselves his wives. The senior wife has a baby, and the younger wife sleeps with him—well, that's what it looked like, reading between the lines."

"You'd better stop reading between lines," said Jack. "It's not doing you any good."

"No, I'd like it," insisted Dorothy. "I think our marriages are silly. Africans and people like that, they know better, they've got some sense."

"I can just see you if I did make love to Stella," said Jack.

"Yes!" said Stella, with a short laugh which, against her will, was resentful.

"But I wouldn't mind," said Dorothy, and burst into tears.

"Now, Dorothy, that's enough," said Jack. He got up, took the baby, whose sucking was mechanical now, and said: "Now listen, you're going right upstairs and you're going to sleep. This little stinker's full as a tick, he'll be asleep for hours, that's my bet."

"I don't feel sleepy," said Dorothy, sobbing.

"I'll give you a sleeping pill, then."

Then started a search for sleeping pills. None to be found.

"That's just like us," wailed Dorothy, "we don't even have a sleeping pill in the place. . . . Stella, I wish you'd stay, I really do, why can't you?"

"Stella's going in just a minute, I'm taking her to the station," said Jack. He poured some Scotch into a glass, handed it to his wife and said: "Now drink that, love, and let's have an end of it. I'm getting fed-up." He sounded fed-up.

Dorothy obediently drank the Scotch, got unsteadily from her chair and went slowly upstairs. "Don't let him cry," she demanded, as she disappeared.

"Oh, you silly bitch," he shouted after her, "when have I let him cry? Here, you hold on a minute," he said to Stella, handing her the baby. He ran upstairs.

Stella held the baby. This was almost for the first time, since she sensed how much another woman's holding her child made Dorothy's fierce new possessiveness uneasy. She looked down at the small, sleepy, red face and said softly: "Well, you're causing a lot of trouble, aren't you?"

Jack shouted from upstairs: "Come up a minute, Stell." She went up, with the baby. Dorothy was tucked up in bed, drowsy from the Scotch, the bedside light turned away from her. She looked at the baby, but Jack took it from Stella.

"Jack says I'm a silly bitch," said Dorothy, apologetic, to Stella.

"Well, never mind, you'll feel different soon."

"I suppose so, if you say so. All right, I *am* going to sleep," said Dorothy, in a stubborn, sad little voice. She turned over, away from them. In the last flare of her hysteria she said: "Why don't you two walk to the station together, it's a lovely night."

"We're going to," said Jack, "don't worry."

She let out a weak giggle, but did not turn. Jack carefully deposited the now sleeping baby in the bed, about a foot from Dorothy. Who suddenly wriggled over until her small, defiant white back was in contact with the blanketed bundle that was her son.

Jack raised his eyebrows at Stella: but Stella was looking at mother and baby, the nerves of her memory filling her with sweet warmth. What right had this woman, who was in possession of such delight, to torment her husband, to torment her friends, as she had been doing—what right had she to rely on their decency as she did?

Surprised by these thoughts, she walked away downstairs, and stood at the door into the garden, her eyes shut, holding herself rigid against tears.

She felt a warmth on her bare arm—Jack's hand. She opened her eyes to see him bending towards her, concerned.

"It'd serve Dorothy right if I did drag you off into the bushes. . . ."

"Wouldn't have to drag me," she said; and while the words had the measure of facetiousness the situation demanded, she felt his seriousness envelop them both in danger.

The warmth of his hand slid across her back, and she turned towards him under its pressure. They stood together, cheeks touching, scents of skin and hair mixing with the smells of warmed grass and leaves.

She thought: What is going to happen now will blow Dorothy and Jack and that baby sky-high: it's the end of my marriage. I'm going to blow everything to bits—there was almost uncontrollable pleasure in it.

She saw Dorothy, Jack, the baby, her husband, the two half-grown children, all dispersed, all spinning downwards through the sky like bits of debris after an explosion.

Jack's mouth was moving along her cheek towards her mouth, dissolving her whole self in delight. She saw, against closed lids, the bundled baby upstairs, and pulled back from the situation, exclaiming energetically: "Damn Dorothy, damn her, damn her, I'd like to kill her. . . ."

And he, exploding into reaction, said in a low furious rage: "Damn you both! I'd like to wring both your bloody necks. . . ."

Their faces were a foot's distance from each other, their eyes staring hostility. She thought that if she had not had the vision of the helpless baby they would now be in each other's arms—generating tenderness and desire like a couple of dynamos, she said to herself, trembling with dry anger.

"I'm going to miss my train if I don't go," she said.

"I'll get your coat," he said, and went in, leaving her defenceless against the emptiness of the garden.

When he came out, he slid the coat around her without touching her, and said: "Come on, I'll take you by car." He walked away in front of her to the car, and she followed meekly over rough lawn. It really was a lovely night.

1963

Mavis Gallant

1922–2014

"I've arranged matters," Mavis Gallant has said with characteristic precision, "so that I would be free to write. It's what I like doing." The fierce purity of her pursuit of imaginative freedom has its roots in an unyielding instinct for "personal independence." The veteran of seventeen schools, including a Jansenist convent school, Gallant left her mother and stepfather in New York and, at age eighteen and virtually penniless, returned to Montreal where she worked for the *Montreal Standard* and was given the corroding task of writing captions for pictures of Holocaust victims. She married, then in 1950 left by herself for a life that has been spent mainly in Paris, a life devoted to English prose and a severe (she insists, Canadian) perspective on human experience in the middle of the twentieth century. From the start, her inclination has been to write about the displaced and the marginalized, a realm initially peopled by refugees in Montreal, Madrid, and Paris, then expanded to include the tyrannies exerted over children and women. She is the consummate anatomist of postwar experience, of the "small possibilities" for fascism in ordinary people. In keeping with the margins of society and politics, she has avoided a conventional realism. Her prose shades from the densely epigrammatic to the comically surreal, and even her volumes have an unusual cast, with stories migrating from one collection to another, some published years after they were written. Masterful in all from the shortest to the longest narrative forms, Gallant is a social satirist whose capacity for concentrated venom seems as limitless as the humanity of so many of the figures in her stories is limited. She came to create an almost military syntax, in which the second part of a sentence undermines or even negates the first. But there are brilliant, often lyrical exceptions to the confines she has established for her fiction. *From the Fifteenth District* (1979), with its social range of complex—and sympathetic—women, is a deeply compassionate volume, and as Janice Kulyk Keefer has said, the Linnet Muir sequence in *Home Truths*, particularly the two stories that follow, is "arguably her finest creation." These stories have an elegiac passion and a wry but pained sense of humanity. For once, characters' memories are creative and not a source of delusion. Much of Gallant's characteristic metaphor-making has been in the service of sharp, startling restrictions: "They stared at each other, as if they were strangers in a crush somewhere and her earring had caught on his coat" ("New Year's Eve"). But with Linnet, the past allows her to brush (*frôler*) against beauty as well as disease. "Two persons descend the street, stepping carefully. The child, reminded every day to keep her hands still, gesticulates wildly—there is a flash of a red mitten. I will never overtake this pair. Their voices are lost in snow."

In Youth Is Pleasure

My father died, then my grandmother; my mother was left, but we did not get on. I was probably disagreeable with anyone who felt entitled to give me instructions and advice. We seldom lived under the same roof, which was just as well. She had found me civil and amusing until I was ten, at which time I was said to have become pert and obstinate. She was impulsive, generous, in some ways better than most other people, but without any feeling for cause and effect; this made her at the least unpredictable and at the most a serious element of danger. I was fascinated by her, though she worried me; then all at once I lost interest. I was fifteen when this happened. I would forget to answer her letters and even to open them. It was not rejection or anything so violent as dislike but a simple indifference I cannot account for. It was much the way I would be later with men I fell out of love with, but I was too young to know that then. As for my mother, whatever I thought, felt, said, wrote, and wore had always been a positive source of exasperation. From time to time she attempted to alter the form, the outward shape at least, of the creature she thought she was modeling, but at last she came to the conclusion there must be something wrong with the clay. Her final unexpected upsurge of attention coincided with my abrupt unconcern: One may well have been the reason for the other.

It took the form of digging into my diaries and notebooks and it yielded, among other documents, a two-year-old poem, Kiplingesque in its rhythms, entitled "Why I Am a Socialist." The first words of the first line were "You ask . . . ," then came a long answer. But it was not an answer to anything she'd wondered. Like all mothers—at least, all I have known—she was obsessed with the entirely private and possibly trivial matter of a daughter's virginity. Why I was a Socialist she rightly conceded to be none of her business. Still, she must have felt she had to say something, and the something was "You had better be clever, because you will never be pretty." My response was to take—take, not grab—the poem from her and tear it up. No voices were raised. I never mentioned the incident to anyone. That is how it was. We became, presently, mutually unconcerned. My detachment was put down to the coldness of my nature, hers to the exhaustion of trying to bring me up. It must have been a relief to her when, in the first half of Hitler's war, I slipped quietly and finally out of her life. I was now eighteen, and completely on my own. By "on my own" I don't mean a show of independence with Papa-Mama footing the bills: I mean that I was solely responsible for my economic survival and that no living person felt any duty toward me.

On a bright morning in June I arrived in Montreal, where I'd been born, from New York, where I had been living and going to school. My luggage was a small suitcase and an Edwardian picnic hamper—a preposterous piece of baggage my father had brought from England some twenty years before; it had been with me since childhood, when his death turned my life into a helpless migration. In my purse was a birth certificate and five American dollars, my total fortune, the parting gift of a Canadian actress in New York, who had taken me to see *Mayerling* before I got on the train. She was kind and good and terribly hard up, and she had no idea that apart from some loose change I had nothing more. The birth certificate, which testified I was Linnet Muir, daughter of Angus and of Charlotte, was my right of passage. I did not own a passport and possibly never had seen one. In those days there was almost no such thing as a "Canadian." You were Canadian-born, and a British subject, too, and you had a third label with no consular reality, like the racial tag that on Soviet passports will make a German of someone who has never been to Germany. In Canada you were also whatever your father happened to be, which in my case was English. He was half Scot, but English by birth, by mother, by instinct. I did not feel a scrap British or English, but I was not an American either. In American schools I had refused to salute the flag. My denial of that curiously Fascist-looking celebration, with the right arm stuck straight out, and my silence when the others intoned the trusting ". . . and justice for all" had never been thought offensive, only stubborn. Americans then were accustomed to gratitude from foreigners but did not demand it; they quite innocently could not imagine any country fit to live in except their own. If I could not recognize it, too bad for me. Besides, I was not a refugee—just someone from the backwoods. "You got schools in Canada?" I had been asked. "You got radios?" And once, from a teacher, "What do they major in up there? Basket weaving?"

My travel costume was a white pique jacket and skirt that must have been crumpled and soot-flecked, for I had sat up all night. I was reading, I think, a novel by Sylvia Townsend Warner. My hair was thick and long. I wore my grandmother's wedding ring, which was too large, and which I would lose before long. I desperately wanted to look more than my age, which I had already started to give out as twenty-one. I was traveling light; my picnic hamper contained the poems and journals I had judged fit to accompany me into my new, unfettered existence, and some books I feared I might not find again in clerical Quebec—Zinoviev and Lenin's *Against the Stream*, and a few beige pamphlets from the Little Lenin Library, purchased secondhand in New York. I had a picture of Mayakovsky torn out of *Cloud in Trousers* and one of Paddy Finucane, the Irish RAF fighter pilot, who was killed the following summer. I had not met either of these men, but I approved of them both very much. I had abandoned my beloved but cumbersome anthologies of American and English verse, confident that I had whatever I needed by heart. I knew every word of Stephen Vincent Benet's "Litany for Dictatorships" and "Notes to Be Left in a Cornerstone," and the other one that begins:

> They shot the Socialists at half-past five
> In the name of victorious Austria. . . .

I could begin anywhere and rush on in my mind to the end. "Notes . . ." was the New York I knew I would never have again, for there could be no journeying backward; the words "but I walked it young" were already a gate shut on a part of my life. The suitcase held only the fewest possible summer clothes. Everything else had been deposited at the various war-relief agencies of New York. In those days I made symbols out of everything, and I must have thought that by leaving a tartan skirt somewhere I was shedding past time. I remember one of those wartime agencies well because it was full of Canadian matrons. They wore pearl earrings like the Duchess of Kent's and seemed to be practicing her tiny smile. Brooches pinned to their cashmere cardigans carried some daft message about the Empire. I heard one of them exclaiming, "You don't expect me, a Britisher, to drink tea made with tea bags!" Good plain girls from the little German towns of Ontario, christened probably Wilma, Jean, and Irma, they had flowing eighteenth-century names like Georgiana and Arabella now. And the Americans, who came in with their arms full of every stitch they could spare, would urge them, the Canadian matrons, to stand fast on the cliffs, to fight the fight, to slug the enemy on the landing fields, to belt him one on the beaches, to keep going with whatever iron rations they could scrape up in Bronxville and Scarsdale; and the Canadians half shut their eyes and tipped their heads back like Gertrude Lawrence and said in thrilling Benita Hume accents that they would do that—indeed they would. I recorded "They're all trained nurses, actually. The Canadian ones have a good reputation. They managed to marry these American doctors."

Canada had been in Hitler's war from the very beginning, but America was still uneasily at peace. Recruiting had already begun; I had seen a departure from New York for Camp Stewart in Georgia, and some of the recruits' mothers crying and even screaming and trying to run alongside the train. The recruits were going off to drill with broomsticks because there weren't enough guns; they still wore old-fashioned headgear and were paid twenty-one dollars a month. There was a song about it: "For twenty-one dollars a day, once a month." As my own train crossed the border to Canada I expected to sense at once an air of calm and grit and dedication, but the only changes were from prosperous to shabby, from painted to unpainted, from smiling to dour. I was entering a poorer and a curiously empty country, where the faces of the people gave nothing away. The crossing was my sea change. I silently recited the vow I had been preparing for weeks: that I would never be helpless again and that I would not let anyone make a decision on my behalf.

When I got down from the train at Windsor station, a man sidled over to me. He had a cap on his head and a bitter Celtic face, with deep indentations along his cheeks, as if his back teeth were pulled. I thought he was asking a direction. He repeated his question, which was obscene. My arms were pinned by the weight of my hamper and suitcase. He brushed the back of his hand over my breasts, called me a name, and edged away. The murderous rage I felt and the revulsion that followed were old friends. They had for years been my reaction to what my diaries called "their hypocrisy." "They" was a world of sly and mumbling people, all of them older than myself. I must have substituted "hypocrisy" for every sort of aggression, because fright was a luxury I could not afford. What distressed me was my helplessness—I who had sworn only a few hours earlier that I'd not be vulnerable again. The man's gaunt face, his drunken breath, the flat voice which I assigned to the graduate of some Christian Brothers teaching establishment haunted me for a long time after that. "The man at Windsor station" would lurk in the windowless corridors of my nightmares; he would be the passenger, the only passenger, on a dark tram. The first sight of a city must be the measure for all second looks.

But it was not my first sight. I'd had ten years of it here—the first ten. After that, and before New York (in one sense, my deliverance), there had been a long spell of grief and shadow in an Ontario city, a place full of mean judgments and grudging minds, of paranoid Protestants and slovenly Catholics. To this day I cannot bear the sight of brick houses, or of a certain kind of empty treeless street on a Sunday afternoon. My memory of Montreal took shape while I was there. It was not a random jumble of rooms and summers and my mother singing "We've Come to See Miss Jenny Jones," but the faithful record of the true survivor. I retained, I rebuilt a superior civilization. In that drowned world, Sherbrooke Street seemed to be glittering and white; the vision of a house upon that street was so painful that I was obliged to banish it from the memorial. The small hot rooms of a summer cottage became enormous and cool. If I say that Cleopatra floated down the Chateauguay River, that the Winter Palace was stormed on

Sherbrooke Street, that Trafalgar was fought on Lake St. Louis, I mean it naturally; they were the natural backgrounds of my exile and fidelity. I saw now at the far end of Windsor station—more foreign, echoing, and mysterious than any American station could be—a statue of Lord Mount Stephen, the founder of the Canadian Pacific, which everyone took to be a memorial to Edward VII. Angus, Charlotte, and the smaller Linnet had truly been: This was my proof; once upon a time my instructions had been to make my way to Windsor station should I ever be lost and to stand at the foot of Edward VII and wait for someone to find me.

I have forgotten to say that no one in Canada knew I was there. I looked up the number of the woman who had once been my nurse, but she had no telephone. I found her in a city directory, and with complete faith that "O. Carette" was indeed Olivia and that she would recall and welcome me I took a taxi to the east end of the city—the French end, the poor end. I was so sure of her that I did not ask the driver to wait (to take me where?) but dismissed him and climbed two flights of dark brown stairs inside a house that must have been built soon after Waterloo. That it was Olivia who came to the door, that the small gray-haired creature I recalled as dark and towering had to look up at me, that she unhesitatingly offered me shelter all seem as simple now as when I broke my fiver to settle the taxi. Believing that I was dead, having paid for years of Masses for the repose of my heretic soul, almost the first thing she said to me was "*Tu vis?*" I understood "*Tu es ici?*" We straightened it out later. She held both my hands and cried and called me *belle et grande*. "*Grande*" was good, for among American girls I'd seemed a shrimp. I did not see what there was to cry for; I was here. I was as naturally selfish with Olivia as if her sole reason for being was me. I stayed with her for a while and left when her affection for me made her possessive, and I think I neglected her. On her deathbed she told one of her daughters, the reliable one, to keep an eye on me forever. Olivia was the only person in the world who did not believe I could look after myself. Where she and I were concerned I remained under six.

Now, at no moment of this remarkable day did I feel anxious or worried or forlorn. The man at Windsor station could not really affect my view of the future. I had seen some of the worst of life, but I had no way of judging it or of knowing what the worst could be. I had a sensation of loud, ruthless power, like an enormous waterfall. The past, the part I would rather not have lived, became small and remote, a dark pinpoint. My only weapons until now had been secrecy and insolence. I had stopped running away from schools and situations when I finally understood that by becoming a name in a file, by attracting attention, I would merely prolong my stay in prison—I mean, the prison of childhood itself. My rebellions then consisted only in causing people who were physically larger and legally sovereign to lose their self-control, to become bleached with anger, to shake with such temper that they broke cups and glasses and bumped into chairs. From the malleable, sunny child Olivia said she remembered, I had become, according to later chronicles, cold, snobbish, and presumptuous. "You need an iron hand, Linnet." I can still hear that melancholy voice, which belonged to a friend of my mother's. "If anybody ever marries you he'd better have an iron hand." After today I would never need to hear this, or anything approaching it, for the rest of my life.

And so that June morning and the drive thought empty, sunlit, wartime streets are even now like a roll of drums in the mind. My life was my own revolution—the tyrants deposed, the constitution wrenched from unwilling hands; I was, all by myself, the liberated crowd setting the palace on fire; I was the flags, the trees, the bannered windows, the flower-decked trains. The singing and the skyrockets of the 1848 I so trustingly believed would emerge out of the war were me, no one but me; and, as in the lyrical first days of any revolution, as in the first days of any love affair, there wasn't the whisper of a voice to tell me, "You might compromise."

If making virtue of necessity has ever had a meaning it must be here: for I was independent *inevitably*. There were good-hearted Americans who knew a bit of my story—as much as I wanted anyone to know—and who hoped I would swim and not drown, but from the moment I embarked on my journey I went on the dark side of the moon. "You seemed so sure of yourself," they would tell me, still troubled, long after this. In the cool journals I kept I noted that my survival meant nothing in the capitalist system; I was one of those not considered to be worth helping, saving, or even investigating. Thinking with care, I see this was true. What could I have turned into in another place? Why, a librarian at Omsk or a file clerk at Tomsk. Well, it hadn't happened that way; I had my private revolution and I settled in with Olivia in Montreal. Sink or swim? Of course I swam. Jobs were for the having; you could pick them up off the ground. Working for a living meant just what it says—a brisk necessity. It would be the least important fragment of my life until I had what I wanted. The cheek of it, I think now: Penniless, sleeping in a shed room behind the kitchen of Olivia's cold-water flat, still I pointed across the wooden balustrade in a long open office where I was being considered for employment and said, "But I won't sit there." Girls were "there," penned in like sheep. I did not think men better than women—only that they did more interesting work and got more money for it. In my journals I called other girls "Coolies." I did not know if life made them bearers or if they had been born with a natural gift for giving in. "Coolie" must have been the secret expression of one of my deepest fears. I see now that I had an immense conceit: I thought I occupied a world other people could scarcely envision, let alone attain. It involved giddy risks and changes, stepping off the edge blindfolded, one's hand on nothing more than a birth certificate and a five-dollar bill. At this time of sitting in judgment I was earning nine dollars a week (until I was told by someone that the local minimum wage was twelve, on which I left for greener fields) and washing my white pique skirt at night and ironing at dawn, and coming home at all hours so I could pretend to Olivia I had dined. Part of this impermeable sureness that I needn't waver or doubt came out of my having lived in New York. The first time I ever heard people laughing in a cinema was there. I can still remember the wonder and excitement and amazement I felt. I was just under fourteen and I had never heard people expressing their feelings in a public place in my life. The easy reactions, the way a poignant moment caught them, held them still—all that was new. I had come there straight from Ontario, where the reaction to a love scene was a kind of unhappy giggling, while the image of a kitten or a baby induced a long flat "Aaaah," followed by shamed silence. You could imagine them blushing in the dark for having said that—just that "Aaaah." When I heard that open American laughter I thought I could be like these people too, but had been told not to be by everyone, beginning with Olivia: "*Pas si fort*" was something she repeated to me so often when I was small that my father had made a tease out of it, called "Passy four." From a tease it became oppressive too: "For the love of God, Linnet, passy four." What were these new people? Were they soft, too easily got at? I wondered that even then. Would a dictator have a field day here? Were they, as Canadian opinion had it, vulgar? Perhaps the notion of vulgarity came out of some incapacity on the part of the refined. Whatever they were, they couldn't all be daft; if they weren't I probably wasn't either. I supposed I stood as good a chance of being miserable here as anywhere, but at least I would not have to pretend to be someone else.

Now, of course there is much to be said on the other side: People who do not display what they feel have practical advantages. They can go away to be killed as if they didn't mind; they can see their sons off to war without a blink. Their upbringing is intended for a crisis. When it comes, they behave themselves. But it is murder in everyday life—truly murder. The dead of heart and spirit litter the landscape. Still, keeping a straight face makes life tolerable under stress. It makes *public* life tolerable—that is all I am saying; because in private people still got drunk, went after each other with bottles and knives, rang the police to complain that neighbors were sending poison gas over the transom, abandoned infant children and aged parents, wrote letters to newspapers in favor of corporal punishment, with inventive suggestions. When I came back to Canada that June, at least one thing had been settled: I knew that it was all right for people to laugh and cry and even to make asses of themselves. I had actually known people like that, had lived with them, and they were fine, mostly—not crazy at all. That was where a lot of my confidence came from when I began my journey into a new life and a dream past.

My father's death had been kept from me. I did not know its exact circumstances or even the date. He died when I was ten. At thirteen I was still expected to believe a fable about his being in England. I kept waiting for him to send for me, for my life was deeply wretched and I took it for granted he knew. Finally I began to suspect that death and silence can be one. How to be sure? Head-on questions got me nowhere. I had to create a situation in which some adult (not my mother, who was far too sharp) would lose all restraint and hurl the truth at me. It was easy: I was an artist at this. What I had not foreseen was the verbal violence of the scene or the effect it might have. The storm that seemed to break in my head, my need to maintain the pose of indifference ("What are you telling me that for? What makes you think I care?") were such a strain that I had physical reactions, like stigmata, which doctors would hopelessly treat on and off for years and which vanished when I became independent. The other change was that if anyone asked about my father I said, "Oh, he died." Now, in Montreal, I could confront the free adult world of falsehood and evasion on an equal footing, they would be forced to talk to me as they did to each other. Making appointments to meet my father's friends—Mr. Archie McEwen, Mr. Stephen Ross-Colby, Mt. Quentin Keller—I left my adult name, "Miss Muir." These were the men who eight, nine, ten years ago had asked, "Do you like your school?"—not knowing what else to say to children. I had curtsied to them and said, "Good night." I think what I wanted was special information about despair, but I should have known that would be taboo in a place where "like" and "don't like" were heavy emotional statements.

Archie McEwen, my father's best friend, or the man I mistook for that, kept me standing in his office on St. James Street West, he standing too, with his hands behind his back, and he said the following—not reconstructed or approximate but recalled, like "The religions of ancient Greece and Rome are extinct." or "O come, let us sing unto the Lord":

"Of course, Angus was a very sick man. I saw him walking along Sherbrooke Street. He must have just come out of hospital. He couldn't walk upright. He was using a stick. Inching along. His hair had turned gray. Nobody knew where Charlotte had got to, and we'd heard you were dead. He obviously wasn't long for this world either. He had too many troubles for any one man. I crossed the street because I didn't have the heart to shake hands with him. I felt terrible."

Savage? Reasonable? You can't tell, with those minds. Some recent threat had scared them. The Depression was too close, just at their heels. Archie McEwen did not ask where I was staying or where I had been for the last eight years; in fact, he asked only two questions. In response to the first I said, "She is married."

There came a gleam of interest—distant, amused: "So she decided to marry him, did she?"

My mother was highly visible; she had no secrets except unexpected ones. My father had nothing but. When he asked, "Would you like to spend a year in England with your Aunt Dorothy?" I had no idea what he meant and I still don't. His only brother, Thomas, who was killed in 1918, had not been married, he'd had no sisters, that anyone knew. Those English mysteries used to be common. People came out to Canada because they did not want to think about the Thomases and Dorothys anymore. Angus was a solemn man, not much of a smiler. My mother, on the other hand—I won't begin to describe her; it would never end—smiled, talked, charmed anyone she didn't happen to be related to, swam in scandal like a partisan among the people. She made herself the central figure in loud, spectacular dramas which she played with the houselights on; you could see the audience too. That was her mistake; they kept their reactions, like their lovemaking, in the dark. You can imagine what she must have been in this world where everything was hushed, muffled, disguised: She must have seemed all they had by way of excitement, give or take a few elections and wars. It sounds like a story about the old and stale, but she and my father had been quite young eight and ten years before. The dying man creeping along Sherbrooke Street was thirty-two. First it was light chatter, then darker gossip, and then it went too far (*he* was ill and he couldn't hide it; *she* had a lover and didn't try); then suddenly it became tragic, and open tragedy was disallowed. And so Mr. Archie McEwen could stand in his office and without a trace of feeling on his narrow Lowland face—not unlike my father's in shape—he could say, "I crossed the street."

Stephen Ross-Colby, a bachelor, my father's painter chum: The smell of his studio on St. Mark Street was the smell of a personal myth. I said timidly, "Do you happen to have anything of his—a drawing or anything?" I was humble because I was on a private, personal terrain of vocation that made me shy even of the dead.

He said, "No, nothing. You could ask around. She junked a lot of his stuff and he junked the rest when he thought he wouldn't survive. You might try . . ." He gave me a name or two. "It was all small stuff," said Ross-Colby. "He didn't do anything big." He hurried me out of the studio for a cup of coffee in a crowded place—the Honey Dew on St. Catherine Street, it must have been. Perhaps in the privacy of his studio I might have heard him thinking. Years after that he would try to call me "Lynn," which I never was, and himself "Steve." He'd come into his own as an artist by then, selling wash drawings of Canadian war graves, sun-splashed, wisteria mauve, lime green, with drifts of blossom across the name of the regiment; gained a reputation among the heartbroken women who bought these impersonations, had them framed—the only picture in the house. He painted the war memorial at Caen. ("Their name liveth forever.") His stones weren't stones but mauve bubbles—that is all I have against them. They floated off the page. My objection wasn't to "He didn't do anything big" but to Ross-Colby's way of turning the dead into thistledown. He said, much later, of that meeting, "I felt like a bastard, but I was broke, and I was afraid you'd put the bite on me."

Let me distribute demerits equally and tell about my father's literary Jewish friend, Mr. Quentin Keller. He was older than the others, perhaps by some twelve years. He had a whispery voice and a long pale face and a daughter older than I. "Bossy Wendy" I used to call her when, forced by her parents as I was by mine, Bossy Wendy had to take a whole afternoon of me. She had a room full of extraordinary toys, a miniature kitchen in which everything worked, of which all I recall her saying is "Don't touch." Wendy Keller had left Smith after her freshman year to marry the elder son of a Danish baron. Her father said to me, "There is only one thing you need to know and that is that your father was a gentleman."

Jackass was what I thought. Yes, Mr. Quentin Keller was a jackass. But he was a literary one, for he had once written a play called *Forbearance*, in which I'd had a role. I had bounded across the stage like a tennis ball, into the arms of a young woman dressed up like an old one, and cried my one line: "Here I am, Granny!" Of course, he did not make his living fiddling about with amateur theatricals; thanks to our meeting I had a good look at the inside of a conservative architect's private office—that was about all it brought me.

What were they so afraid of, I wondered. I had not yet seen that I was in a false position where they were concerned; being "Miss Muir" had not made equals of us but lent distance. I thought they had read my true passport, the invisible one we all carry, but I had neither the wealth nor the influence a provincial society requires to make a passport valid. My credentials were lopsided: The important half of the scales was still in the air. I needed enormous collateral security—fame, an alliance with a Powerful family, the power of money itself. I remember how Archie McEwen, trying to place me in some sensible context, to give me a voucher so he could take me home and show me to his wife, perhaps, asked his second question: "Who inherited the—?"

"The what, Mr. McEwen?"

He had not, of course, read "Why I Am a Socialist." I did not believe in inherited property. "Who inherited the—?" Would not cross my mind again for another ten years, and then it would be a drawer quickly opened and shut before demons could escape. To all three men the last eight years were like minutes; to me they had been several lives. Some of my confidence left me then. It came down to "Next time I'll know better," but would that be enough? I had been buffeted until now by other people's moods, principles, whims, tantrums; I had survived, but perhaps I had failed to grow some outer skin it was now too late to acquire. Olivia thought that; she was the only one. Olivia knew more about the limits of nerve than I did. Her knowledge came out of the clean, swept, orderly poverty that used to be tucked away in the corners of cities. It didn't spill out then, or give anyone a bad conscience. Nobody took its picture. Anyway, Olivia would not have sat for such a portrait. The fringed green rug she put over the treadle sewing machine was part of a personal fortune. On her mantelpiece stood a copper statuette of Voltaire in an armchair. It must have come down to her from some robustly anticlerical ancestor. "Who is he?" she said to me. "You've been to school in a foreign country." "A governor of New France," I replied. She knew Voltaire was the name of a bad man and she'd have thrown the figurine out, and it would have made one treasure less in the house. Olivia's maiden name was Ouvrardville, which was good in Quebec, but only really good if you were one of the rich ones. Because of her maiden name she did not want anyone ever to know she had worked for a family; she impressed this on me delicately—it was like trying to understand what a dragonfly wanted to tell. In the old days she had gone home every weekend, taking me with her if my parents felt my company was going to make Sunday a very long day. Now I understood what the weekends were about: Her daughters, Berthe and Marguerite, for whose sake she worked, were home from their convent schools Saturday and Sunday and had to be chaperoned. Her relatives pretended not to notice that Olivia was poor or even that she was widowed, for which she seemed grateful. The result of all this elegant sham was that Olivia did not say, "I was afraid you'd put the bite on me," or keep me standing. She dried her tears and asked if there was a trunk to follow. No? She made a pot of tea and spread a starched cloth on the kitchen table and we sat down to a breakfast of toast and honey. The honey tin was a ten-pounder decorated with bees the size of hornets. Lifting it for her, I remarked, "*C'est collant*," a word out of a frozen language that started to thaw when Olivia said, "*Tu vis?*"

On the advice of her confessor, who was to be my rival from now on, Olivia refused to tell me whatever she guessed or knew, and she was far too dignified to hint. Putting together the three men's woolly stories, I arrived at something about tuberculosis of the spine and a butchery of an operation. He started back to England to die there but either changed his mind or was too ill to begin the journey; at Quebec City, where he was to have taken ship, he shot himself in a public park at five o'clock in the morning. That was one version; another was that he died at sea and the gun was found in his luggage. The revolver figured in all three accounts. It was an officer's weapon from the Kaiser's war, that had belonged to his brother. Angus kept it at the back of a small drawer in the tall chest used for men's clothes and known in Canada as a highboy. In front of the revolver was a pigskin stud box and a pile of ironed handkerchiefs. Just describing that drawer dates it. How I happen to know the revolver was loaded and how I learned never to point a gun even in play is another story. I can tell you that I never again in my life looked inside a drawer that did not belong to me.

I know a woman whose father died, she thinks, in a concentration camp. Or was he shot in a schoolyard? Or hanged and thrown in a ditch? Were the ashes that arrived from some eastern plain his or another prisoner's? She invents different deaths. Her inventions have become her conversation at dinner parties. She takes on a child's voice and says, "My father died at Buchenwald." She chooses and rejects elements of the last act; one avoids mentioning death, shooting, capital punishment, cremation, deportation, even fathers. Her inventions are not thought neurotic or exhibitionist but something sanctioned by history. Peacetime casualties are not like that. They are lightning bolts out of a sunny sky that strike only one house. All around the ashy ruin lilacs blossom, leaves gleam. Speculation in public about the disaster would be indecent. Nothing remains but a silent, recurring puzzlement to the survivors: Why here and not there? Why this and not that? Before July was out I had settled his fate in my mind and I never varied: I thought he had died of homesickness; sickness for England was the consumption, the gun, the everything. "Everything" had to take it all in, for people in Canada then did not speak of irrational endings to life, and newspapers did not print that kind of news: This was because of the spiritual tragedy for Catholic families, and because the act had long been considered a criminal one in British law. If Catholic feelings were spared it gave the impression no one but Protestants ever went over the edge, which was unfair; and so the possibility was eliminated, and people came to a natural end in a running car in a closed garage, hanging from a rafter in the barn, in an icy lake with a canoe left to drift empty. Once I had made up my mind, the whole story somehow became none of my business: I had looked in a drawer that did not belong to me. More, if I was to live my own life I had to let go. I wrote in my journal that "they" had got him but would not get me, and after that there was scarcely ever a mention.

My dream past evaporated. Montreal, in memory, was a leafy citadel where I knew every tree. In reality I recognized nearly nothing and had to start from scratch. Sherbrooke Street had been the dream street, pure white. It was the avenue poor Angus descended leaning on a walking stick. It was a moat I was not allowed to cross alone; it was lined with gigantic spreading trees through which light fell like a rain of coins. One day, standing at a corner, waiting for the light to change, I understood that the Sherbrooke Street of my exile—my Mecca, my Jerusalem—was this. It had to be: There could not be two. It was *only* this. The limitless green where in a perpetual spring I had been taken to play was the campus of McGill University. A house, whose beauty had brought tears to my sleep, to which in sleep I'd returned to find it inhabited by ugly strangers, gypsies, was a narrow stone thing with a shop on the ground floor and offices above—if that was it, for there were several like it. Through the bare panes of what might have been the sitting room, with its deep private window seats, I saw neon strip-lighting along a ceiling. Reality, as always, was narrow and dull. And yet what dramatic things had taken place on this very corner: Once Satan had approached me—furry dark skin, claws, red eyes, the lot. He urged me to cross the street and I did, in front of a car that braked in time. I explained, "The Devil told me to." I had no idea until then that my parents did not believe what I was taught in my convent school. (Satan is not bilingual, by the way; he speaks Quebec French.) My parents had no God and therefore no Fallen Angel. I was scolded for lying, which was a thing my father detested, and which my mother regularly did but never forgave in others.

Why these two nonbelievers wanted a strong religious education for me is one of the mysteries. (Even in loss of faith they were unalike, for he was ex-Anglican and she was ex-Lutheran and that is not your same atheist—no, not at all.) "To make you tolerant" was a lame excuse, as was "French," for I spoke fluent French with Olivia, and I could read in two languages before I was four. Discipline might have been one reason—God knows, the nuns provided plenty of that—but according to Olivia I did not need any. It cannot have been for the quality of the teaching, which was lamentable. I suspect that it was something like sending a dog to a trainer (they were passionate in their concern for animals, especially dogs), but I am not certain it ever brought me to heel. The first of my schools, the worst, the darkest, was on Sherbrooke Street too. When I heard, years later, it had been demolished, it was like the burial of a witch. I had remembered it penitentiary size, but what I found myself looking at one day was simply a very large stone house. A crocodile of little girls emerged from the front gate and proceeded along the street—white-faced, black-clad, eyes cast down. I knew there were bored, fidgety, anxious, and probably hungry. I should have felt pity, but at eighteen all that came to me was thankfulness that I had been correct about one thing throughout my youth, which I now considered ended: Time had been on my side, faithfully, and unless you died you were always bound to escape.

1975

Voices Lost in Snow

Halfway between our two great wars, parents whose own early years had been shaped with Edwardian firmness were apt to lend a tone of finality to quite simple remarks: "Because I say so" was the answer to "Why?" and a child's response to "What did I just tell you?" could seldom be anything but "Not to"—not to say, do, touch, remove, go out, argue, reject, eat, pick up, open, shout, appear to sulk, appear to be cross. Dark riddles filled the corners of life because no enlightenment was thought required. Asking questions was "being tiresome," while persistent curiosity got one nowhere, at least nowhere of interest. How much has changed? Observe the drift of words descending from adult to child—the fall of personal questions, observations, unnecessary instructions. Before long the listener seems blanketed. He must hear the voice as authority muffled, a hum through snow. The tone has changed—it may be coaxing, even plaintive—but the words have barely altered. They still claim the ancient right-of-way through a young life.

"Well, old cock," said my father's friend Archie McEwen, meeting him one Saturday in Montreal. "How's Charlotte taking life in the country?" Apparently no had expected my mother to accept the country in winter.

"Well, old cock," I repeated to a country neighbor, Mr. Bainwood. "How's life?" What do you suppose it meant to me, other than a kind of weather vane? Mr. Bainwood thought it over, then came round to our house and complained to my mother.

"It isn't blasphemy," she said, not letting him have much satisfaction from the complaint. Still, I had to apologize. "I'm sorry" was a ritual habit with even less meaning than "old cock." "Never say that again," my mother said after he had gone.

"Why not?"

"Because I've just told you not to."

"What does it mean?"

"Nothing."

It must have been after yet another "Nothing" that one summer's day I ran screaming around a garden, tore the heads off tulips, and—no, let another voice finish it, the only authentic voices I have belong to the dead: ". . . then she *ate* them."

It was my father's custom if he took me with him to visit a friend on Saturdays not to say where we were going. He was more taciturn than any man I have known since, but that wasn't all of it; being young, I was the last person to whom anyone owed an explanation. These Saturdays have turned into one whitish afternoon, a windless snowfall, a steep street. Two persons descend the street, stepping carefully. The child, reminded every day to keep her hands still, gesticulates wildly—there is the flash of a red mitten. I will never overtake this pair. Their voices are lost in snow.

We were living in what used to be called the country and is now a suburb of Montreal. On Saturdays my father and I came in together by train. I went to the doctor, the dentist, to my German lesson. After that I had to get back to Windsor station by myself and on time. My father gave me a boy's watch so that the dial would be good and large. I remember the No. 83 streetcar trundling downhill and myself, wondering if the watch was slow, asking strangers to tell me the hour. Inevitably—how could it have been otherwise?—after his death, which would not be long in coming, I would dream that someone important had taken a train without me. My route to the meeting place—deviated, betrayed by stopped clocks—was always downhill. As soon as I was old enough to understand from my reading of myths and legends that this journey was a pursuit of darkness, its terminal point a sunless underworld, the dream vanished.

Sometimes I would be taken along to lunch with one or another of my father's friends. He would meet the friend at Pauzé's for oysters or at Drury's or the Windsor Grill. The friend would more often than not be Scottish- or English-sounding, and they would talk as if I were invisible, as Archie McEwen had done, and eat what I thought of as English food—grilled kidneys, sweetbreads—which I was too finicky to touch. Both my parents had been made wretched as children by having food forced on them and so that particular torture was never inflicted on me. However, the manner in which I ate was subject to precise attention. My father disapproved of the North American custom that he called "spearing" (knife laid on the plate, fork in the right hand). My mother's eye was out for a straight back, invisible chewing, small mouthfuls, immobile silence during the interminable adult loafing over dessert. My mother did not care for food. If we were alone together, she would sit smoking and reading, sipping black coffee, her elbows used as props—a posture that would have called for instant banishment had I so much as tried it. Being constantly observed and corrected was like having a fly buzzing around one's plate. At Pauzé's, the only child, perhaps the only female, I sat up to an oak counter and ate oysters quite neatly, not knowing exactly what they were and certainly not that they were alive. They were served as in "The Walrus and the Carpenter," with bread and butter, pepper and vinegar. Dessert was a chocolate biscuit—plates of them stood at intervals along the counter. When my father and I ate alone, I was not required to say much, nor could I expect a great deal in the way of response. After I had been addressing him for minutes, sometimes he would suddenly come to life and I would know he had been elsewhere. "Of course I've been listening," he would protest, and he would repeat by way of proof the last few words of whatever it was I'd been saying. He was seldom present. I don't know where my father spent his waking life: just elsewhere.

What was he doing alone with a child? Where was his wife? In the country, reading. She read one book after another without looking up, without scraping away the frost on the windows. "The Russians, you know, the Russians," she said to her mother and me, glancing around in the drugged way adolescent readers have. "They put salt on the windowsills in winter." Yes, so they did, in the nineteenth century, in the boyhood of Turgenev, of Tolstoy. The salt absorbed the moisture between two sets of windows sealed shut for half the year. She must have been in a Russian country house at that moment, surrounded by a large Russian family, living out vast Russian complications. The flat white fields beyond her imaginary windows were like the flat white fields she would have observed if only she had looked out. She was myopic; the pupil when she had been reading seemed to be the whole of the eye. What age was she then? Twenty-seven, twenty-eight. Her husband had removed her to the country; now that they were there he seldom spoke. How young she seems to me now—half twenty-eight in perception and feeling, but with a husband, a child, a house, a life, an illiterate maid from the village whose life she confidently interfered with and mismanaged, a small zoo of animals she alternately cherished and forgot; and she was the daughter of such a sensible, truthful, pessimistic woman—pessimistic in the way women become when they settle for what actually exists.

Our rooms were not Russian—they were aired every day and the salt became a great nuisance, blowing in on the floor.

"There, Charlotte, what did I tell you?" my grandmother said. This grandmother did not care for dreams or for children. If I sensed the first, I had no hint of the latter. Out of decency she kept it quiet, at least in a child's presence. She had the reputation, shared with a long-vanished nurse named Olivia, of being able to "do anything" with me, which merely meant an ability to provoke from a child behaviour convenient for adults. It was she who taught me to eat in the Continental way, with both hands in sight at all times upon the table, and who made me sit at meals with books under my arms so I would learn not to stick out my elbows. I remember having accepted this nonsense from her without a trace of resentment. Like Olivia, she could make the most pointless sort of training seem a natural way of life. (I think that as discipline goes this must be the most dangerous form of all.) She was one of three godparents I had—the important one. It is impossible for me to enter the mind of this agnostic who taught me prayers, who had already shed every remnant of belief when she committed me at the font. I know that she married late and reluctantly; she would have preferred a life of solitude and independence, next to impossible for a woman in her time. She had the positive voice of the born teacher, sharp manners, quick blue eyes, and the square, massive figure common to both lines of her ancestry—the west of France, the north of Germany. When she said "There, Charlotte, what did I tell you?" without obtaining an answer, it summed up mother and daughter both.

My father's friend Malcolm Withmore was the second godparent. He quarreled with my mother when she said something flippant about Mussolini, disappeared, died in Europe some years later, though perhaps not fighting for Franco, as my mother had it. She often rewrote other people's lives, providing them with suitable and harmonious endings. In her version of events you were supposed to die as you'd lived. He would write sometimes, asking me, "Have you been confirmed yet?" He had never really held a place and could not by dying leave a gap. The third godparent was a young woman named Georgie Henderson. She was my mother's choice, for a long time her confidante, partisan, and close sympathizer. Something happened, and they stopped seeing each other. Georgie was not her real name—it was Edna May. One of the reasons she had fallen out with my mother was that I had not been called Edna May too. Apparently, this had been promised.

Without saying where we were going, my father took me along to visit Georgie one Saturday afternoon.

"You didn't say you were bringing Linnet" was how she greeted him. We stood in the passage of a long, hot, high-ceilinged apartment, treading snow water into the rug.

He said, "Well, she is your godchild, and she has been ill."

My godmother shut the front door and leaned her back against it. It is in this surprisingly dramatic pose that I recall her. It would be unfair to repeat what I think I saw then, for she and I were to meet again once, only once, many years after this, and I might substitute a lined face for a smooth one and tough, large-knuckled hands for fingers that may have been delicate. One has to allow elbowroom in the account of a rival: "She must have had something" is how it generally goes, long after the initial "What can he see in her? He must be deaf and blind." Georgie, explained by my mother as being the natural daughter of Sarah Bernhardt and a stork, is only a shadow, a tracing, with long arms and legs and one of those slightly puggy faces with pulled-up eyes.

Her voice remains—the husky Virginia-tobacco whisper I associate with so many women of that generation, my parents' friends; it must have come of age in English Montreal around 1920, when girls began to cut their hair and to smoke. In middle life the voice would slide from low to harsh, and develop a chronic cough. For the moment it was fascinating to me—opposite in pitch and speed from my mother's, which was slightly too high and apt to break off, like that of a singer unable to sustain a long note.

It was true that I had been ill, but I don't think my godmother made much of it that afternoon, other than saying, "It's all very well to talk about that now, but I was certainly never told much, and as for that doctor, you ought to just hear what Ward thinks." Out of this whispered jumble my mother stood accused—of many transgressions, certainly, but chiefly of having discarded Dr Ward Mackey, everyone's doctor and a family friend. At the time of my birth my mother had all at once decided she liked Ward Mackey better than anyone else and had asked him to choose a name for me. He could not think of one, or, rather, thought of too many, and finally consulted his own mother. She had always longed for a daughter, so that she could call her after the heroine of a novel by, I believe, Marie Corelli. The legend so often repeated to me goes on to tell that when I was seven weeks old my father suddenly asked, "What did you say her name was?"

"*Votre fille a frôlé la phtisie,*" the new doctor had said, the one who had now replaced Dr. Mackey. The new doctor was known to me as Uncle Raoul, though we were not related. This manner of declaring my brush with consumption was worlds away from Ward Mackey's "subject to bilious attacks." Mackey's objections to Uncle Raoul were neither envious nor personal, for Mackey was the sort of bachelor who could console himself with golf. The Protestant in him truly believed those other doctors to be poorly trained and superstitious, capable of recommending the pulling of teeth to cure tonsillitis, and of letting their patients cough to death or perish from septicemia just through Catholic fatalism.

What parent could fail to gasp and marvel at Uncle Raoul's announcement? Any but either of mine. My mother could invent and produce better dramas any day; as for my father, his French wasn't all that good and he had to have it explained. Once he understood that I had grazed the edge of tuberculosis, he made his decision to remove us all to the country, which he had been wanting a reason to do for some time. He was, I think, attempting to isolate his wife, but by taking her out of the city he exposed her to a danger that, being English, he had never dreamed of: This was the heart-stopping cry of the steam train at night, sweeping across a frozen river, clattering on the ties of a wooden bridge. From our separate rooms my mother and I heard the unrivaled summons, the long, urgent, uniquely North American beckoning. She would follow and so would I, but separately, years and desires and destinations apart. I think that women once pledged in such a manner are more steadfast than men.

"*Frôler*" was the charmed word in that winter's story; it was a hand brushing the edge of folded silk, a leaf escaping a spiderweb. Being caught in the web would have meant staying in bed day and night in a place even worse than a convent school. Charlotte and Angus, whose lives had once seemed so enchanted, so fortunate and free that I could not imagine lesser persons so much as eating the same kind of toast for breakfast, had to share their lives with me, whether they wanted to or not—thanks to Uncle Raoul, who always supposed me to be their principal delight. I had been standing on one foot for months now, midway between "*frôler*" and "falling into," propped up by a psychosomatic guardian angel. Of course I could not stand that way forever; inevitably my health improved and before long I was declared out of danger and then restored—to the relief and pleasure of all except the patient.

"I'd like to see more of you than eyes and nose," said my godmother. "Take off your things." I offer this as an example of unnecessary instruction. Would anyone over the age of three prepare to spend the afternoon in a stifling room wrapped like a mummy in outdoor clothes? "She's smaller than she looks," Georgie remarked, as I began to emerge. This authentic godmother observation drives me to my only refuge, the insistence that she must have had something—he could not have been completely deaf and blind. Divested of hat, scarf, coat, overshoes, and leggings, grasping the handkerchief pressed in my hand so I would not interrupt later by asking for one, responding to my father's muttered "Fix your hair," struck by the command because it was he who had told me not to use "fix" in that sense, I was finally able to sit down next to him on a white sofa. My godmother occupied its twin. A low table stood between, bearing a decanter and glasses and a pile of magazines and, of course, Georgie's ashtrays; I think she smoked even more than my mother did.

On one of these sofas, during an earlier visit with my mother and father, the backs of my darling feet had left a smudge of shoe polish. It may have been the last occasion when my mother and Georgie were ever together. Directed to stop humming and kicking, and perhaps bored with the conversation in which I was not expected to join, I had soon started up again.

"It doesn't matter," my godmother said, though you could tell she minded.

"Sit up," my father said to me.

"I am sitting up. What do you think I'm doing?" This was not answering but answering back; it is not an expression I ever heard from my father, but I am certain it stood like a stalled truck in Georgie's mind. She wore the look people put on when they are thinking, Now what are you spineless parents going to do about that?

"Oh, for God's sake, she's only a child," said my mother, as though that had ever been an excuse for anything.

Soon after the sofa-kicking incident she and Georgie moved into the hibernation known as "not speaking." This, the lingering condition of half my mother's friendships, usually followed her having said the very thing no one wanted to hear, such as "Who wants to be called Edna May, anyway?"

Once more in the hot pale room where there was nothing to do and nothing for children, I offended my godmother again, by pretending I had never seen her before. The spot I had kicked was pointed out to me, though, owing to new slipcovers, real evidence was missing. My father was proud of my quite surprising memory, of its long backward reach and the minutiae of detail I could describe. My failure now to shine in a domain where I was naturally gifted, that did not require lessons or create litter and noise, must have annoyed him. I also see that my guileless-seeming needling of my godmother was a close adaptation of how my mother could be, and I attribute it to a child's instinctive loyalty to the absent one. Giving me up, my godmother placed a silver dish of mint wafers where I could reach them—white, pink, and green, overlapping—and suggested I look at a magazine. Whatever the magazine was, I had probably seen it, for my mother subscribed to everything then. I may have turned the pages anyway, in case at home something had been censored for children. I felt and am certain I have not invented Georgie's disappointment at not seeing Angus alone. She disliked Charlotte now, and so I supposed he came to call by himself, having no quarrel of his own; he was still close to the slighted Ward Mackey.

My father and Georgie talked for a while—she using people's initials instead of their names, which my mother would not have done—and they drank what must have been sherry, if I think of the shape of the decanter. Then we left and went down to the street in a wood-paneled elevator that had sconce lights, as in a room. The end of the afternoon had a particular shade of color then, which is not tinted by distance or enhancement but has to do with how streets were lighted. Lamps were still gas, and their soft gradual blooming at dusk made the sky turn a peacock blue that slowly deepened to marine, then indigo. This uneven light falling in blurred pools gave the snow it touched a quality of phosphorescence, beyond which were night shadows in which no one lurked. There were few cars, little sound. A fresh snowfall would lie in the streets in a way that seemed natural. Sidewalks were dangerous, casually sanded; even on busy streets you found traces of the icy slides children's feet had made. The reddish brown of the stone houses, the curve and slope of the streets, the constantly changing sky were satisfactory in a way that I now realize must have been aesthetically comfortable. This is what I saw when I read "city" in a book; I had no means of knowing that "city" one day would also mean drab, filthy, flat, or that city blocks could turn into dull squares without mystery.

We crossed Sherbrooke Street, starting down to catch our train. My father walked everywhere in all weathers. Already mined, colonized by an enemy prepared to destroy what it fed on, fighting it with every wrong weapon, squandering strength he should have been storing, stifling pain in silence rather than speaking up while there might have been time, he gave an impression of sternness that was a shield against suffering. One day we heard a mob roaring four syllables over and over, and we turned and went down a different street. That sound was starkly terrifying, something a child might liken to the baying of wolves.

"What is it?"

"Howie Morenz."

"Who is it? Are they chasing him"

"No, they like him," he said of the hockey player admired to the point of dementia. He seemed to stretch, as if trying to keep every bone in his body from touching a nerve; a look of helplessness such as I had never seen on a grown person gripped his face and he said this strange thing: "Crowds eat me. Noise eats me." The kind of physical pain that makes one seem rat's prey is summed up in my memory of this.

When we came abreast of the Ritz-Carlton after leaving Georgie's apartment, my father paused. The lights within at that time of day were golden and warm. If I barely knew what "hotel" meant, never having stayed in one, I connected the lights with other snowy afternoons, with stupefying adult conversation (Oh, those shut-in velvet-draped unaired low-voice problems!) compensated for by creamy bitter hot chocolate poured out of a pink-and-white china pot.

"You missed your gootay," he suddenly remembered. Established by my grandmother, "*goûter*" was the family word for tea. He often transformed French words, like putty, into shapes he could grasp. No, Georgie had not provided a *gotûer,* other than the mint wafers, but it was not her fault—I had not been announced. Perhaps if I had not been so disagreeable with her, he might have proposed hot chocolate now, though I knew better than to ask. He merely pulled my scarf up over my nose and mouth, as if recalling something Uncle Raoul had advised. Breathing inside knitted wool was delicious—warm, moist, pungent when one had been sucking on mint candies, as now. He said, "You didn't enjoy your visit much."

"Not very," through red wool.

"No matter," he said. "You needn't see Georgie again unless you want to," and we walked on. He must have been smarting, for he liked me to be admired. When I was not being admired I was supposed to keep quiet. "You needn't see Georgie again" was also a private decision about himself. He was barely thirty-one and had a full winter to live after this one—little more. Why? "Because I say so." The answer seems to speak out of the lights, the stones, the snow; out of the crucial second when inner and outer forces join, and the environment becomes part of the enemy too.

Ward Mackey used to mention me as "Angus's precocious pain in the neck," which is better than nothing. Long after that afternoon, when I was about twenty, Mackey said to me, "Georgie didn't play her cards well where he was concerned. There was a point where if she had just made one smart move she could have had him. Not for long, of course, but none of us knew that."

What cards, I wonder. The cards have another meaning for me—they mean a trip, a death, a letter, tomorrow, next year. I saw only one move that Saturday: My father placed a card faceup on the table and watched to see what Georgie made of it. She shrugged, let it rest. There she sits, looking puggy but capable, Angus waiting, the precocious pain in the neck turning pages, hoping to find something in the *National Geographic* harmful for children. I brush in my memory against the spiderweb: What if she had picked it up, remarking in her smoky voice, "Yes, I can use that"? It was a low card, the kind that only a born gambler would risk as part of a long-term strategy. She would never have weakened a hand that way; she was not gambling but building. He took the card back and dropped his hand, and their long intermittent game came to an end. The card must have been the eight of clubs—"a female child."

1976

Nadine Gordimer

1923–2014

Nadine Gordimer was born in Springs, a small gold-mining town in Transvaal, South Africa. The daughter of Jewish immigrants to that country, she was educated at a convent school, and studied for a year at the University of Witwatersrand, Johannesburg. From an early age Gordimer was determined to be a writer: she published her first story at fourteen, and she credits the books she read in her youth with developing her ability to question the environment of white privilege in which she was raised and the racist oppression that South African Blacks experienced. Her novels and short fiction, beginning with her first published volume, *Face to Face* (1949), explore, through careful depiction of the day-to-day lives of both white and Black South Africans, the many dimensions and varied consequences of racial segregation and apartheid. Her leftist views on apartheid ensured that life was not easy for her or her second husband, a refugee from Nazi Germany. Though her books are internationally acclaimed, three of them were banned in her own country. But despite the hostility that she faced as a white novelist fiercely opposed to apartheid, Gordimer chose to remain in South Africa, feeling that she had a part to play, both as a writer and as an activist. A prolific writer, she has published over a dozen novels, numerous collections of short fiction, and several works of non-fiction, as well as television plays and documentaries. With apartheid finally ended, Gordimer turned her attention to examining the damage done to society and personal relations. Her post-apartheid novel *The House Gun* (1998), focuses on an affluent white couple whose son is accused of murder; it examines the legacy of violence and the use and misuse of freedom, demonstrating that peace can be as perilous as war. Gordimer has lectured and taught writing at a number of American universities, including Harvard, Princeton, and Columbia. She won the Booker Prize in 1974 and the Nobel Prize for Literature in 1991. Her last novel was *No Time Like the Present* (2012).

Is There Nowhere Else Where We Can Meet?

It was a cool grey morning and the air was like smoke. In that reversal of the elements that sometimes takes place, the grey, soft, muffled sky moved like the sea on a silent day.

The coat collar pressed rough against her neck and her cheeks were softly cold as if they had been washed in ice water. She breathed gently with the air; on the left a strip of veld fire curled silently, flameless. Overhead a dove purred. She went on over the flat straw grass, following the trees, now on, now off the path. Away ahead, over the scribble of twigs, the sloping lines of black and platinum grass—all merging, tones but no colour, like an etching—was the horizon, the shore at which cloud lapped.

Damp burnt grass puffed black, faint dust from beneath her feet. She could hear herself swallow.

A long way off she saw a figure with something red on its head, and she drew from it the sense of balance she had felt at the particular placing of the dot of a figure in a picture. She was here; someone was over there. . . . Then the red dot was gone, lost in the curve of the trees. She changed her bag and parcel from one arm to the other and felt the morning, palpable, deeply cold and clinging against her eyes.

She came to the end of a direct stretch of path and turned with it round a dark-fringed pine and a shrub, now delicately boned, that she remembered hung with bunches of white flowers like crystals in the summer. There was a Native in a red woollen cap standing at the next clump of trees, where the path crossed a ditch and was bordered by white-splashed stones. She had pulled a little sheath of pine needles, three in a twist of thin brown tissue, and as she walked she ran them against her thumb. Down; smooth and stiff. Up; catching in gentle resistance as the minute serrations snagged at the skin. He was standing with his back toward her, looking along the way he had come; she pricked the ball of her thumb with the needle-ends. His one trouser leg was torn off above the knee, and the back of the naked leg and half-turned heel showed the peculiarly dead, powdery black of cold. She was nearer to him now, but she knew he did not hear her coming over the damp dust of the path. She was level with him, passing him; and he turned slowly and looked beyond her, without a flicker of interest, as a cow sees you go.

The eyes were red, as if he had not slept for a long time, and the strong smell of old sweat burned at her nostrils. Once past, she wanted to cough, but a pang of guilt at the red-weary eyes stopped her. And he had only a filthy rag—part of an old shirt?—without sleeves and frayed away into a great gap from underarm to waist. It lifted in the currents of cold as she passed. She had dropped the neat trio of pine needles somewhere, she did not know at what moment, so now, remembering something from childhood, she lifted her hand to her face and sniffed: yes, it was as she remembered, not as chemists pretend it in the bath salts, but a dusty green scent, vegetable rather than flower. It was clean, unhuman. Slightly sticky too; tacky on her fingers. She must wash them as soon as she got there. Unless her hands were quite clean, she could not lose consciousness of them, they obtruded upon her.

She felt a thudding through the ground like the sound of a hare running in fear and she was going to turn around and then he was there in front of her, so startling, so utterly unexpected, panting right into her face. He stood dead still and she stood dead still. Every vestige of control, of sense, of thought, went out of her as a room plunges into dark at the failure of power and she found herself whimpering like an idiot or a child. Animal sounds came out of her throat. She gibbered. For a moment it was Fear itself that had her by the arms, the legs, the throat; not fear of the man, of any single menace he might present, but Fear, absolute, abstract. If the earth had opened up in fire at her feet, if a wild beast had opened its terrible mouth to receive her, she could not have been reduced to less than she was now.

There was a chest heaving through the tear in front of her; a face panting; beneath the red hairy woolen cap the yellowish-red eyes holding her in distrust. One foot, cracked from exposure until it looked like broken wood, moved, only to restore balance in the dizziness that follows running, but any move seemed toward her and she tried to scream and the awfulness of dreams came true and nothing would come out. She wanted to throw the handbag and the parcel at him, and as she fumbled crazily for them she heard him draw a deep, hoarse breath and he grabbed out at her and—ah! It came. His hand clutched her shoulder.

Now she fought with him and she trembled with strength as they struggled. The dust puffed round her shoes and his scuffling toes. The smell of him choked her.—It was an old pyjama jacket, not a shirt—His face was sullen and there was a pink place where the skin had been grazed off. He sniffed desperately, out of breath. Her teeth chattered, wildly she battered him with her head, broke away, but he snatched at the skirt of her coat and jerked her back. Her face swung up and she saw the waves of a grey sky and a crane breasting them, beautiful as the figurehead of a ship. She staggered for balance and the handbag and parcel fell. At once he was upon them, and she wheeled about; but as she was about to fall on her knees to get there first, a sudden relief, like a rush of tears, came to her and instead, she ran. She ran and ran, stumbling wildly off through the stalks of dead grass, turning over her heels against hard winter tussocks, blundering through trees and bushes. The young mimosas closed in, lowering a thicket of twigs right to the ground, but she tore herself through, feeling the dust in her eyes and the scaly twigs hooking at her hair. There was a ditch, knee-high in blackjacks; like pins responding to a magnet they fastened along her legs, but on the other side there was a fence and then the road. . . . She clawed at the fence—her hands were capable of nothing—and tried to drag herself between the wires, but her coat got caught on a barb, and she was imprisoned there, bent in half, whilst waves of terror swept over her in heat and trembling. At last the wire tore through its hold on the cloth; wobbling, frantic, she climbed over the fence.

And she was out. She was out on the road. A little way on there were houses, with gardens, postboxes, a child's swing. A small dog sat at a gate. She could hear a faint hum, as of life, of talk somewhere, or perhaps telephone wires.

She was trembling so that she could not stand. She had to keep on walking, quickly, down the road. It was quiet and grey, like the morning. And cool. Now she could feel the cold air round her mouth and between her brows, where the skin stood out in sweat. And in the cold wetness that soaked down beneath her armpits and between her buttocks. Her heart thumped slowly and stiffly. Yes, the wind was cold; she was suddenly cold, damp-cold, all through. She raised her hand, still fluttering uncontrollably, and smoothed her hair; it was wet at the hairline. She guided her hand into her pocket and found a handkerchief to blow her nose.

There was the gate of the first house, before her.

She thought of the woman coming to the door, of the explanations, of the woman's face, and the police. Why did I fight, she thought suddenly. What did I fight for? Why didn't I give him the money and let him go? His red eyes, and the smell and those cracks in his feet, fissures, erosion. She shuddered. The cold of the morning flowed into her.

She turned away from the gate and went down the road slowly, like an invalid, beginning to pick the blackjacks from her stockings.

1952

Josef Škvorecký

1924–2012

Josef Škvorecký was born in Náchod, Bohemia, then a province of Czechoslovakia. He received his Ph.D. from Charles University, Prague, in 1951, and then worked as a teacher and translator before joining the Prague magazine *World Literature* as an editor. When his first novel, *Zbabelci* (later translated as *The Cowards*) was published in 1958, he was fired from his job as an editor and the novel was banned. Over the next ten years Škvorecký continued to write novels and short fiction, and even collaborated with such notable filmmakers as Milos Forman to write film scripts. Among the works he produced during this period are the novella *The Bass Saxophone* (1967), which celebrates his love of jazz as a revolutionary force for freedom, and *Miss Silver's Past* (1969), a mystery with a subtext of censorship in a totalitarian regime. In 1968, after the Soviet invasion of Czechoslovakia, he emigrated to North America with his wife, the novelist Zdena Salivarová. After spending a year in the US, Škvorecký took a teaching position at the University of Toronto. The couple settled in Toronto and established Sixty-Eight Publishers with the mandate of publishing Czech and Slovak literature banned in their homeland. Škvorecký has written and edited over fifty books, including mysteries, short story collections, historical novels, novels of adolescence, portraits of exiles, as well as film and literary criticism; most of his books have been translated into English. His novel *The Engineer of Human Souls* (1977), a searing depiction of post–World War II Czechoslovakia that draws on his own experience as a young person living under Nazism and then Stalinist Communism, received a Governor General's Award. In 2000, he published *When Eve Was Naked: A Journey through Life*, a fictionalized autobiography that comprises a series of stories arranged chronologically to emulate the evolution of Škvorecký's own life. Many of the stories are narrated by Danny Smirický, Škvorecký's fictional alter ego, who also appears in a number of other novels. The book offers a unique insight into the life of a writer whom critics consider, along with Milan Kundera and Václav Havel, one of the most important dissident writers to have emerged from the Communist era in Czechoslovakia. In 1990, the new president of the Czech Republic, Václav Havel, awarded Škvorecký the Order of the White Lion for his achievements as a writer and his contributions to the preservation of Czech literature.

panta rei

You can't step in the same river twice.

—*Heraclitus*

In those days, I was only a baby fascist while my father was a big fascist, although he didn't think of himself like that. That's today's simplified way of putting it; in the old days these things were more complicated. I was a little bourgeois boy in velvet pants, with a polka-dot handkerchief tied under my chin, and I'd taunt Voženil: "Bolshevik, Bolshevik!" as I munched on my frankfurter. Voženil waited to see if I'd leave him a morsel, and when I didn't he called me "you pen-pushing greedy-gut" and I paid him back with "you Bolshevik." Each of us brought it from home: me with my velvet pants and suspenders decorated with airplanes and locomotives, Voženil with his big loud mouth that always gave off the sweet smell of bread (he never brushed his teeth), clodhoppers passed down from an older brother, dirty words which I never used because I knew from home that you weren't supposed to. Still, my father was a big, strong fascist, even though he didn't think of himself in that way. He marched in processions sporting a cane because he had a limp inherited from the First World War, and he wore a silver-grey shirt. I boasted about him to schoolmates and was very proud of him when I stood on the sidewalk with my mother, who held me by the hand, and we watched him striding down the street, we watched him scowl and sing and shout.

Once, however, I saw him weep, and I couldn't believe my own eyes. That was the time the Conservative leader Dr Kramář died. Dad's large, meaty mouth which ground away at dinnertime like a millstone now collapsed into a crooked curve resembling the tragic semicircle painted on the lips of the great comedian George Voskovec (described by Dad as a drawing-room Bolshevik and agent of Moscow), tears rolled down his smooth-shaven cheeks, tears as big as the pearls in Mother's necklace but glassy, transparent and damp. Dad sat in the cool, darkened drawing room, with its violet wallpaper, black piano, and black furniture; only the gilded face of the grandfather clock glowed in the dusk. Tears as big as pearls, as big as drops of autumn rain kept dropping off Dad's vest. Facing him sat Mrs Zkoumal, editor of *Národní Listy*, dressed in a black silk gown, her red hair upswept into a mikado. Her elegant hands, with red-enamelled nails that extended a good centimetre beyond the fingertips, kept kneading a black-bordered handkerchief.

She moaned: "What a man! What a mind! A real giant! What a Czech! They don't come any finer! And they kept hounding him all his life! Bolsheviks, the Beneš crowd, clericals, the Castle, all of them! All of them are guilty! They hounded him to his grave! To deprive the nation of such a man! But they'll soon enough see what they have wrought!"

I didn't understand what was going on, while I sat in a chair in a black velvet suit, my feet dangling high above the floor, Mother next to me, also wearing black, not weeping but looking sad. But then she always looked sad. I gazed in fascination at that red-gold-rust-coloured mikado hairdo of Madam Editor, at her eyebrows as thin as a thread and arched like Gothic vaults in the church, her slender legs in silk stockings visible way past the knees because Madam Editor had her legs crossed and though her gown was a mourning gown it was also stylish, as could be expected from a youthful star on the *Národní Listy* editorial staff.

That was the first time I saw—and heard—Madam Editor.

Then a couple of years quickly went by and a lot happened. The Germans sent Dad to a concentration camp, because he took his nationalist convictions seriously. They took away our apartment and Mother moved us to Grandpa's house in the country.

One evening after the war, when I was already grown up, and had exchanged my velvet shorts for stylish close-cut trousers and played tenor sax in a jazz band, a man came to see us one evening and handed Mother a crumpled letter which Dad had given him in Oranienburg. Mother read it and started crying; she cried on and on—from that day on she turned even sadder and in the end she stopped talking, only sat and stared. Then they took her to an insane asylum.

That man told us how he and Dad slept in the same bunk and helped each other as well as they could, though they also argued. They argued on account of bolshevism. Dad believed that the Czech nation would come to its senses after the war—meaning that the National Democratic party would take over the government—and he became furious when the man maintained that Comrade Stalin would see to it that things turned out differently. Dad was altogether naive. He even behaved insolently toward the SS troopers, and so in the end they did away with him.

After they took Mother to the Asylum, Grandpa had a stroke and they kicked us out of the house. I moved to Prague, started to play tenor sax in Zetka's jazz band and became friends with Miss Julie Nedochodil, whose dad was a deputy of the Catholic Populist party. Not sensing anything wrong, he let me sublet a room in his beautiful modernist villa.

At his house I met Madam Editor for the second time.

She no longer wore a short gown, a red mikado hairdo, nor long red claws on her fingers. She was dressed in a shapeless grey outfit, her feet were modestly ensconced in low-heeled shoes, her hair was set in nondescript waves and on her bosom—which was hard to make out under the guileless blouse—a gold cross. She was sitting in the dining room, where the conversation centered on materialism and spiritualism. She kept casting devout glances at Franciscan Father Urbanec and held forth:

"Such obvious nonsense," she said. "How can anybody believe such things? This world, this fascinating universe filled with heavenly wonders, this body of mine, all those amazing miracles of creation which proclaim the glory of the Creator—can this be nothing but dead, uncreative, motionless matter?"

Father Urbanec kept nodding his head while his hand nestled a cut-glass goblet in which a little puddle of yellow wine from the Teplá cloister rolled gently from side to side like a spoonful of honey. In the rays of the sun, filtered through the greenery of Papa Nedochodil's lush garden, it emanated a golden glow into the dining room. Father Urbanec was responsible for guiding converts and Madam Editor was his sheep. She converted totally. She switched from the banned *Národní Listy* to the still tolerated *Lidová Demokracie*. She took her son out of public high school and enrolled him in the archbishop's school in Dejvice. She also launched a battle for the soul of her husband, and managed to return him to the pale of the Church in the nick of time, as he lay on his deathbed. Before this long-suffering agnostic breathed his last, the rite of a church wedding was performed with the assistance of Father Urbanec, so that after fifteen years of civil cohabitation their marriage became sanctified before God. The place of Dr Kramář in her heart was taken over by Father Urbanec. She even chose him as her confessor, and on the first Friday of every month pestered him with her sins, which she committed mainly in thought, less frequently in speech, and hardly ever in action. She joined the Society of Perpetual Veneration of the Consecrated Host, and also the Eucharistic Society of Saint Cypriana for reclaiming young women as novices. She also became a leader of Catholic Girl Scouts. She thus became—or rather, remained—a fighter against bolshevism, albeit under a new flag.

From that day on, I saw her quite often. She was a constant visitor at Papa Nedochodil's, picking his brains for political ideas. She took a critical stance toward me, because I favoured wild neckties and striped socks and on Sundays, instead of going to church, I blew hot licks in a popular dance joint in Vinohrady and elsewhere. She also criticized the virtually Bolshevik opinions of Pavel Nedochodil, a boy whom his family considered something of a failure and who entered the Young Communist Movement. She feared for our souls; performed heroic apostolic labours left and right. She managed to bring Julie to the verge of tears when that attractive Catholic girl bought herself a two-piece swimsuit; she got Madam Nedochodil to cancel her subscription to *Kino*; and she exerted such strong influence over Papa Nedochodil that he stopped reading detective stories. She radiated sanctity and deep faith.

Then a miracle happened to Slovakia: two shepherd children in Malá Fatra had a vision of the Virgin Mary. Madam Editor took off at once in search of miracle and news story. She went in the company of journalists, consisting of cynics from the communist *Rudé Právo* and sensation-seekers from *Svobodné Slovo*.

They came back a week later.

"You should have seen the cars, Doctor!" she reported to a gathering that was headed by Papa Nedochodil and Father Urbanec and that also included Julie with a somewhat uncatholically low-cut dress, and myself, sporting a specially selected Bikini-Nagasaki necktie.

"Bumper-to-bumper traffic for miles! We had to get out and walk, and only our newspaper passes got us through the throngs. We reached the little hill where they had put up a small, simple altar and at a quarter to three they brought the two children. The Virgin was supposed to appear at four, the hour of Christ's death. The children knelt and prayed, and that whole throng of hundreds and thousands knelt and prayed with them. Oh, Doctor! I've never experienced such a blissful feeling in my life! And then at four the children started to talk and we heard them asking questions and answering—we didn't see nor hear the Virgin but felt that she was there with us! And then a priest took the children away and as for myself—I can tell you, Doctor, I feel that I was present at a miracle!"

There was talk of visions and miracles, of Fatima, La Salette, Bernadette, stigmata, the holy shroud of Turin, and in the end, as usual, the conversation passed to the subject of communism and communists. Madam Editor recounted her experiences in this regard:

"It's a moral morass, Doctor! Those people lack the most basic moral sense! I am ashamed to talk about it, I really feel myself blushing—but I have to tell you what sort of people they are! Just imagine, Doctor! We spent the night in Bratislava in the Winston Hotel and the editors from *Rudé Právo*—well, you can imagine how they joked about the miracle! They blasphemed in a way I wouldn't care to repeat. Right after dinner I went to my room—and . . . I really don't know if I can say it with Julie sitting right here. . . ."

She nodded her head in the direction of the half-bared bosom of my companion, who responded with a grimace.

"But I'll say it straight out, so that all of you get the picture of that crowd. Just imagine, one of the *Rudé Právo* editors—a widower with two children—followed me and grabbed me upstairs in the hall—of course, he smelled like a brewery—and he wanted—no, I'm too ashamed—he wanted me—well, he wanted me to do his bidding! Doctor! Forgive me for saying it, under normal conditions such a thing would never pass my lips, I just want you to know with what sort of element we have the honour of dealing. And he made me a marriage proposal! But first he wanted . . . well, Doctor, that's bolshevism for you! In the afternoon, they witness an unforgettable moment on Malá Fatra and just a few hours later they're back in gutter. . . ."

Then came February.

Disaster.

They threw Papa Nedochodil out of Parliament and Madam Editor off the paper.

They gave her a job in a factory.

I was thrown off the faculty. I had to make a living playing the saxophone.

Pater Urbanec went to prison.

At first, Madam Editor came to see us almost every day seeking encouragement. Everything in the factory offended her. Vulgar jokes, immoral talk, coarse and dull work. "It's so mechanical, Doctor, so mechanical! There is absolutely no need for thought! And all my life I've worked with my mind!"

She was being broken into the job by an oldish foreman, a widower, who called her "girl" and made indecent proposals to her, such as inviting her out to the movies or to dances. Let's live a little, he'd say to her.

The Editor's horror knew no bounds.

Then Julie's older sister Tereza married a Protestant. Madam Editor kept wringing her hands and spent a week in churches (after work), kneeling and praying for poor Terezinka.

Some time later, I was sent to jail for two weeks for committing light physical damage, under the influence of alcohol, upon a certain youth who kept pawing Julie in places of her body that were out of bounds. When I got out, Madam Editor warned me that alcohol is bad for the health and arouses animal instincts, though in my case its effect was rather the opposite.

Strangely enough, I noticed that she didn't say a word about the soul or about morality.

Half a year later, Communist Youth member Pavel Nedochodil was elected as the Party's candidate. Madam Editor—whose visits to Papa Nedochodil had become much rarer—came one evening, and seemed to take the news in stride. For a while, she chatted about nothing in particular and then got on the subject of the factory, the need to understand those people, who actually aren't a bad sort, it's true they use immoral expressions but this is due to the fact that they had been deprived of a good education.

She didn't add "during the first, bourgeois republic," the standard phrase used by *Rudé Právo*, because she didn't dare go quite that far in the presence of Papa Nedochodil. I noticed that she wore a new dress, modestly high in front but at the same time quite close-fitting so that her bosom clearly outlined the space intended for it. Whatever she was like, Madam Editor certainly aroused sinful ideas. She also wore nylon stockings with black seams and white highheeled shoes. She told us that the foreman—that widower—heehee—kept hinting that the two of them ought to get hitched—he says—heehee—he needs a good woman. He says a man without a woman is no man at all. Of course, she doesn't take any of that too seriously. But on her birthday he bought her—heehee—a handbag. An awful one, of course. He's got real lowbrow taste. She didn't want to accept it, but he insisted and yesterday he even brought her—heehee—a bouquet of forget-me-nots . . .

After that, she stopped coming to Papa Nedochodil.

We heard various rumours.

We learned that she had moved in with that foreman and lived with him in one nest, as the expression goes.

And that she was getting active in the revolutionary workers' movement.

After that—well, after that there was no longer any interest in her at Papa Nedochodil's house.

Some more time passed, and in general I was getting along fine. I played tenor sax, and even had some female admirers.

I had a few smashing suits hanging in my closet, found a luxurious sublet on Rajský Hill in a villa of a former composer of hit songs for the Tyláček operetta company (who had made a timely switch to military marches and workers' choruses). I broke up with Miss Julie Nedochodil, who went on to marry a refrigerator repairman; and all in all, socialism suited me just fine.

One Sunday afternoon, in summer, as we were playing for a huge crowd in the Fučík Park of Rest Relaxation, my throat was getting parched and during our break I got into line in front of a watermelon stand.

The attendant kept slicing the watery spheres with a rusty knife and slid the section down a bare plank, where swarms of flies gaily copulated in the pink juice.

"Comrade!" I heard someone in back of me say, "Comrade! You ought to cover those boards with something, at least some wrapping paper! This is terribly unhygienic! And as a food handler you ought to wear a white coat! Not a sweaty shirt . . . It's not fair to your fellow comrades, comrade, to give them spoiled goods for their honestly earned money!"

I turned around.

My eyes nearly popped out of my head. I beheld a large, shining, five-point red star on the lapel of a modest yet elegant tailored dress.

In the dress stood Madam Editor.

I was sporting a jazzy white jacket and the hitch from my tenor sax was lopped around my neck.

I thought it wiser to remain anonymous.

1997

Flannery O'Connor

1925–1964

There are few, if any, writers as funny and as frightening as Flannery O'Connor, who grafted Gothic on to the folksy humour of her "good country people," a process driven by her especially dark version of Catholicism. The overall title for her work could be "Sin, Redemption, More Sin, and Less Redemption." As The Misfit in "A Good Man is Hard to Find" explains with awful clarity: "I call myself The Misfit . . . because I can't make what all I done wrong fit what all I gone through in punishment." Or as O'Connor explained: "writers who see by the light of their Christian faith will have . . . the sharpest eyes for the grotesque, for the perverse, and for the unacceptable." Her eyes were very sharp for the misworkings of grace and the relentlessness of cruelty, perceptions recorded in an almost hallucinatory precision of language. Some of this skill was honed at the University of Iowa's Writers' Workshop where she earned an MFA in 1947, two years after graduating from Georgia State College for Women. For two years she lived in New York, but lupus brought her back to the family's Georgia farm (she had been born in Savannah) where she raised peafowls and wrote two novels, *Wise Blood* (1952) and *The Violent Bear It Away* (1960), as well as those startling, violent stories that are among the most powerful in the language. O'Connor posthumously received the National Book Award in 1972 for her *Complete Stories*.

Revelation

The doctor's waiting room, which was very small, was almost full when the Turpins entered and Mrs Turpin, who was very large, made it look even smaller by her presence. She stood looming at the head of the magazine table set in the centre of it, a living demonstration that the room was inadequate and ridiculous. Her little bright black eyes took in all the patients as she sized up the seating situation. There was one vacant chair and a place on a sofa occupied by a blond child in a dirty romper who should have been told to move over and make room for the lady. He was five or six, but Mrs Turpin saw at once that no one was going to tell him to move over. He was slumped down in the seat, his arms idle at his sides and his eyes idle in his head; his nose ran unchecked.

Mrs Turpin put a firm hand on Claud's shoulder and said in a voice that included anyone who wanted to listen, "Claud, you sit in that chair there," and gave him a push down into the vacant one. Claud was florid and bald and sturdy, somewhat shorter than Mrs Turpin, but he sat down as if he were accustomed to doing what she told him to.

Mrs Turpin remained standing. The only man in the room besides Claud was a lean stringy old fellow with a rusty hand spread out on each knee, whose eyes were closed as if he were asleep or dead or pretending to be so as not to get up and offer her his seat. Her gaze settled agreeably on a well-dressed grey-haired lady whose eyes met hers and whose expression said: if that child belonged to me, he would have some manners and move over—there's plenty of room there for you and him too.

Claud looked up with a sigh and made as if to rise.

"Sit down," Mrs Turpin said. "You know you're not supposed to stand on that leg. He has an ulcer on his leg," she explained.

Claud lifted his foot onto the magazine table and rolled his trouser leg up to reveal a purple swelling on a plump marble-white calf.

"My!" the pleasant lady said. "How did you do that?"

"A cow kicked him," Mrs Turpin said.

"Goodness!" said the lady.

Claud rolled his trouser leg down.

"Maybe the little boy would move over," the lady suggested, but the child did not stir.

"Somebody will be leaving in a minute," Mrs Turpin said. She could not understand why the doctor—with as much money as they made charging five dollars a day to just stick their head in the hospital door and look at you—couldn't afford a decent-sized waiting room. This one was hardly bigger than a garage. The table was cluttered with limp-looking magazines and at one end of it there was a big green glass ashtray full of cigarette butts and cotton wads with little blood spots on them. If she had anything to do with the running of the place, that would have been emptied every so often. There were no chairs against the wall at the head of the room. It had a rectangular-shaped panel in it that permitted a view of the office where the nurse came and went and the secretary listened to the radio. A plastic fern in a gold pot sat in the opening and trailed its fronds down almost to the floor. The radio was softly playing gospel music.

Just then the inner door opened and a nurse with the highest stack of yellow hair Mrs Turpin had ever seen put her face in the crack and called for the next patient. The woman sitting beside Claud grasped the two arms of her chair and hoisted herself up; she pulled her dress free from her legs and lumbered through the door where the nurse had disappeared.

Mrs Turpin eased into the vacant chair, which held her tight as a corset. "I wish I could reduce," she said, and rolled her eyes and gave a comic sigh.

"Oh, *you* aren't fat," the stylish lady said.

"Ooooo I am too," Mrs Turpin said. "Claud he eats all he wants to and never weighs over one hundred and seventy-five pounds, but me I just look at something good to eat and I gain some weight," and her stomach and shoulders shook with laughter. "You can eat all you want to, can't you, Claud?" she asked, turning to him.

Claud only grinned.

"Well, as long as you have such a good disposition," the stylish lady said, "I don't think it makes a bit of difference what size you are. You just can't beat a good disposition."

Next to her was a fat girl of eighteen or nineteen, scowling into a thick blue book which Mrs Turpin saw was entitled *Human Development*. The girl raised her head and directed her scowl at Mrs Turpin as if she did not like her looks. She appeared annoyed that anyone should speak while she tried to read. The poor girl's face was blue with acne and Mrs Turpin thought how pitiful it was to have a face like that at that age. She gave the girl a friendly smile but the girl only scowled the harder. Mrs Turpin herself was fat but she had always had good skin, and, though she was forty-seven years old, there was not a wrinkle in her face except around her eyes from laughing too much.

Next to the ugly girl was the child, still in exactly the same position, and next to him was a thin leathery old woman in a cotton print dress. She and Claud had three sacks of chicken feed in their pump house that was in the same print. She had seen from the first that the child belonged with the old woman. She could tell by the way they sat—kind of vacant and white-trashy, as if they would sit there until Doomsday if nobody called and told them to get up. And at right angles but next to the well-dressed pleasant lady was a lank-faced woman who was certainly the child's mother. She had on a yellow sweat shirt and wine-coloured slacks, both gritty-looking, and the rims of her lips were stained with snuff. Her dirty yellow hair was tied behind with a little piece of red paper ribbon. Worse than niggers any day, Mrs Turpin thought.

The gospel hymn playing was, "When I looked up and He looked down," and Mrs Turpin, who knew it, supplied the last line mentally, "And wona these days I know I'll we-eara crown."

Without appearing to, Mrs Turpin always noticed people's feet. The well-dressed lady had on red and grey suede shoes to match her dress. Mrs Turpin had on her good black patent leather pumps. The ugly girl had on Girl Scout shoes and heavy socks. The old woman had on tennis shoes and the white-trashy mother had on what appeared to be bedroom slippers, black straw with gold braid threaded through them—exactly what you would have expected her to have on.

Sometimes at night when she couldn't go to sleep, Mrs Turpin would occupy herself with the question of who she would have chosen to be if she couldn't have been herself. If Jesus had said to her before he made her, "There's only two places available for you. You can either be a nigger or white trash," what would she have said? "Please, Jesus, please," she would have said, "just let me wait until there's another place available," and he would have said, "No, you have to go right now and I have only those two places so make up your mind." She would have wiggled and squirmed and begged and pleaded but it would have been no use and finally she would have said, "All right, make me a nigger then—but that don't mean a trashy one." And he would have made her a neat clean respectable Negro woman, herself but black.

Next to the child's mother was a red-headed youngish woman, reading one of the magazines and working a piece of chewing gum, hell for leather, as Claud would say. Mrs Turpin could not see the woman's feet. She was not white-trash, just common. Sometimes Mrs Turpin occupied herself at night naming the classes of people. On the bottom of the heap were most coloured people, not the kind she would have been if she had been one, but most of them; then next to them—not above, just away from—were the white-trash; then above them were the home-owners, and above them the home-and-land owners, to which she and Claud belonged. Above she and Claud were people with a lot of money and much bigger houses and much more land. But here the complexity of it would begin to bear in on her, for some of the people with a lot of money were common and ought to be below she and Claud and some of the people who had good blood had lost their money and had to rent and then there were coloured people who owned their homes and land as well. There was a coloured dentist in town who had two red Lincolns and a swimming pool and a farm with registered white-face cattle on it. Usually by the time she had fallen asleep all the classes of people were moiling and roiling around in her head, and she would dream they were all crammed in together in a box car, being ridden off to be put in a gas oven.

"That's a beautiful clock," she said and nodded to her right. It was a big wall clock, the face encased in a brass sunburst.

"Yes, it's very pretty," the stylish lady said agreeably. "And right on the dot too," she added, glancing at her watch.

The ugly girl beside her cast an eye upward at the clock, smirked, then looked directly at Mrs Turpin and smirked again. Then she returned her eyes to her book. She was obviously the lady's daughter because, although they didn't look anything alike as to disposition, they both had the same shape of face, and the same blue eyes. On the lady they sparkled pleasantly but in the girl's seared face they appeared alternately to smoulder and to blaze.

What if Jesus had said, "All right, you can be white-trash or a nigger or ugly"!

Mrs Turpin felt an awful pity for the girl, though she thought it was one thing to be ugly and another to act ugly.

The woman with the snuff-stained lips turned around in her chair and looked up at the clock. Then she turned back and appeared to look a little to the side of Mrs Turpin. There was a cast in one of her eyes. "You want to know wher you can get you one of them ther clocks?" she asked in a loud voice.

"No, I already have a nice clock," Mrs Turpin said. Once somebody like her got a leg in the conversation, she would be all over it.

"You can get you one with green stamps," the woman said. "That's most likely wher he got hisn. Save you up enough, you can get most anythang. I got me some joo'ry."

Ought to have got you a wash rag and some soap, Mrs Turpin thought.

"I get contour sheets with mine," the pleasant lady said.

The daughter slammed her book shut. She looked straight in front of her, directly through Mrs Turpin and on through the yellow curtain and the plate glass window which made the wall behind her. The girl's eyes seemed lit all of a sudden with a peculiar light, an unnatural light like night road signs give. Mrs Turpin turned her head to see if there was anything going on outside that she should see, but she could not see anything. Figures passing cast only a pale shadow through the curtain. There was no reason the girl should single her out for her ugly looks.

"Miss Finley," the nurse said, cracking the door. The gum-chewing woman got up and passed in front of her and Claud and went into the office. She had on red high-heeled shoes.

Directly across the table, the ugly girl's eyes were fixed on Mrs Turpin as if she had some very special reason for disliking her.

"This is wonderful weather, isn't it?" the girl's mother said.

"It's good weather for cotton if you can get the niggers to pick it," Mrs Turpin said, "but niggers don't want to pick cotton any more. You can't get the white folks to pick it and now you can't get the niggers—because they got to be right up there with the white folks."

"They gonna *try* anyways," the white-trash woman said, leaning forward.

"Do you have one of those cotton-picking machines?" the pleasant lady asked.

"No," Mrs Turpin said, "they leave half the cotton in the field. We don't have much cotton anyway. If you want to make it farming now, you have to have a little of everything. We got a couple of acres of cotton and a few hogs and chickens and just enough white-face that Claud can look after them himself."

"One thang I don't want," the white-trash woman said, wiping her mouth with the back of her hands. "Hogs. Nasty stinking things, a-gruntin and a-rootin all over the place."

Mrs Turpin gave her the merest edge of her attention. "Our hogs are not dirty and they don't stink," she said. "They're cleaner than some children I've seen. Their feet never touch the ground. We have a pig-parlour—that's where you raise them on concrete," she explained to the pleasant lady, "and Claud scoots them down with the hose every afternoon and washes off the floor." Cleaner by far than that child right there, she thought. Poor nasty little thing. He had not moved except to put the thumb of his dirty hand into his mouth.

The woman turned her face away from Mrs Turpin. "I know I wouldn't scoot down no hog with no hose," she said to the wall.

You wouldn't have no hog to scoot down, Mrs Turpin said to herself.

"A-gruntin and a-rootin and a-groanin," the woman muttered.

"We got a little of everything," Mrs Turpin said to the pleasant lady. "It's no use in having more than you can handle yourself with help like it is. We found enough niggers to pick our cotton this year but Claud he has to go after them and take them home again in the evening. They can't walk that half a mile. No they can't. I tell you," she said and laughed merrily, "I sure am tired of buttering up niggers, but you got to love em if you want em to work for you. When they come in the morning, I run out and I say, "Hi yawl this morning?" and when Claud drives them off to the field I just wave to beat the band and they just wave back." And she waved her hands rapidly to illustrate.

"Like you read out of the same book," the lady said, showing she understood perfectly.

"Child, yes, "Mrs Turpin said. "And when they come in from the field, I run out with a bucket of icewater. That's the way it's going to be from now on," she said. "You may as well face it."

"One thang I know," the white-trash woman said. "Two thangs I ain't going to do: love no niggers or scoot down no hog with no hose." And she let out a bark of contempt.

The look that Mrs Turpin and the pleasant lady exchanged indicated they both understood that you had to *have* certain things before you could *know* certain things. But every time Mrs Turpin exchanged a look with the lady, she was aware that the ugly girl's peculiar eyes were still on her, and she had trouble bringing her attention back to the conversation.

"When you got something," she said, "you got to look after it." And when you ain't got a thing but breath and britches, she added to herself, you can afford to come to town every morning and just sit on the Court House coping and spit.

A grotesque revolving shadow passed across the curtain behind her and was thrown palely on the opposite wall. Then a bicycle clattered down against the outside of the building. The door opened and a coloured boy glided in with a tray from the drug store. It had two large red and white paper cups on it with tops on them. He was a tall, very black boy in discoloured white pants and a green nylon shirt. He was chewing gum slowly, as if to music. He set the tray down in the office opening next to the fern and stuck his head through to look for the secretary. She was not in there. He rested his arms on the ledge and waited, his narrow bottom stuck out, swaying slowly to the left and right. He raised a hand over his head and scratched the base of his skull.

"You can see that button there, boy?" Mrs Turpin said. "You can punch that and she'll come. She's probably in the back somewhere."

"Is thas right?" the boy said agreeably, as if he had never seen the button before. He leaned to the right and put his finger on it. "She sometime out," he said and twisted around to face his audience, his elbows behind him on the counter. The nurse appeared and he twisted back again. She handed him a dollar and he rooted in his pocket and made the change and counted it out to her. She gave him fifteen cents for a tip and he went away with the empty tray. The heavy door swung so slowly and closed at length with the sound of suction. For a moment no one spoke.

"They ought to send all them niggers back to Africa," the white-trash woman said. "That's wher they come from in the first place."

"Oh, I couldn't do without my good coloured friends," the pleasant lady said.

"There's a heap of things worse than a nigger," Mrs Turpin agreed. "It's all kinds of them just like it's all kinds of us."

"Yes, and it takes all kinds to make the world go round," the lady said in her musical voice.

As she said it, the raw-complexioned girl snapped her teeth together. Her lower lip turned downwards and inside out, revealing the pale pink inside of her mouth. After a second it rolled back up. It was the ugliest face Mrs Turpin had ever seen anyone make and for a moment she was certain that the girl had made it at her. She was looking at her as if she had known and disliked her all her life—all of Mrs Turpin's life, it seemed too, not just all the girl's life. Why, girl, I don't even know you, Mrs Turpin said silently.

She forced her attention back to the discussion. "It wouldn't be practical to send them back to Africa," she said. "They wouldn't want to go. They got it too good here."

"Wouldn't be what they wanted—if I had anythang to do with it," the woman said.

"It wouldn't be a way in the world you could get all the niggers back over there," Mrs Turpin said. "They'd be hiding out and lying down and turning sick on you and wailing and hollering and raring and pitching. It wouldn't be a way in the world to get them over there."

"They got over here," the trashy woman said. "Get back like they got over."

"It wasn't so many of them then," Mrs Turpin explained.

The woman looked at Mrs Turpin as if here was an idiot indeed but Mrs Turpin was not bothered by the look, considering where it came from.

"Nooo," she said, "they're going to stay here where they can go to New York and marry white folks and improve their colour. That's what they all want to do, every one of them, improve their colour."

"You know what comes of that, don't you?" Claud asked.

"No, Claud, what?" Mrs Turpin said.

Claud's eyes twinkled. "White-faced niggers," he said with never a smile.

Everybody in the office laughed except the white-trash and the ugly girl. The girl gripped the book in her lap with white fingers. The trashy woman looked around her from face to face as if she thought they were all idiots. The old woman in the feed sack dress continued to gaze expressionless across the floor at the high-top shoes of the man opposite her, the one who had been pretending to be asleep when the Turpins came in. He was laughing heartily, his hands still spread out on his knees. The child had fallen to the side and was lying now almost face down in the old woman's lap.

While they recovered from their laughter, the nasal chorus on the radio kept the room from silence.

"You go to blank blank
And I'll go to mine
But we'll all blank along
To-geth-ther,
And all along the blank
We'll hep each other out
Smile-ling in any kind of
Weath-ther!"

Mrs Turpin didn't catch every word but she caught enough to agree with the spirit of the song and it turned her thoughts sober. To help anybody out that needed it was her philosophy of life. She never spared herself when she found somebody in need, whether they were white or black, trash or decent. And of all she had to be thankful for, she was most thankful that this was so. If Jesus had said, "You can be high society and have all the money you want and be thin and svelte-like, but you can't be a good woman with it," she would have had to say, "Well don't make me that then. Make me a good woman and it don't matter what else, how fat or how ugly or how poor!" Her heart rose. He had not made her a nigger or white-trash or ugly! He had made her herself and given her a little of everything. Jesus, thank you! she said. Thank you thank you thank you!

Whenever she counted her blessings she felt as buoyant as if she weighed one hundred and twenty-five pounds instead of one hundred and eighty.

"What's wrong with your little boy?" the pleasant lady asked the white-trashy woman.

"He has an ulcer," the woman said proudly. "He ain't give me a minute's peace since he was born. Him and her are just alike," she said, nodding at the old woman, who was running her leathery fingers through the child's pale hair. "Look like I can't get nothing down them two but Co' Cola and candy."

That's all you try to get down em, Mrs Turpin said to herself. Too lazy to light the fire. There was nothing you could tell her about people like them that she didn't know already. And it was not just that they didn't have anything. Because if you gave them everything, in two weeks it would all be broken or filthy or they would have chopped it up for lightwood. She knew all this from her own experience. Help them you must, but help them you couldn't.

All at once the ugly girl turned her lips inside out again. Her eyes were fixed like two drills on Mrs Turpin. This time there was no mistaking that there was something urgent behind them.

Girl, Mrs Turpin exclaimed silently, I haven't done a thing to you! The girl might be confusing her with somebody else. There was no need to sit by and let herself be intimidated. "You must be in college," she said boldly, looking directly at the girl. "I see you reading a book there."

The girl continued to stare and pointedly did not answer.

Her mother blushed at this rudeness. "The lady asked you a question, Mary Grace," she said under her breath.

"I have ears," Mary Grace said.

The poor mother blushed again. "Mary Grace goes to Wellesley College," she explained. She twisted one of the buttons on her dress. "In Massachusetts," she added with a grimace. "And in the summer she just keeps right on studying. Just reads all the time, a real bookworm. She's done real well at Wellesley; she's taking English and Math and History and Psychology and Social Studies," she rattled on, "and I think it's too much. I think she ought to get out and have fun."

The girl looked as if she would like to hurl them all through the plate glass window.

"Way up north," Mrs Turpin murmured and thought, well, it hasn't done much for her manners.

"I'd almost rather to have him sick," the white-trash woman said, wrenching the attention back to herself. "He's so mean when he ain't. Look like some children just take natural to meanness. It's some gets bad when they get sick but he was the opposite. Took sick and turned good. He don't give me no trouble now. It's me waitin to see the doctor," she said.

If I was going to send anybody back to Africa, Mrs Turpin thought, it would be your kind, woman. "Yes, indeed," she said aloud, but looking up at the ceiling, "it's a heap of things worse than a nigger." And dirtier than a hog, she added to herself.

"I think people with bad dispositions are more to be pitied than anyone on earth," the pleasant lady said in a voice that was decidedly thin.

"I thank the Lord he has blessed me with a good one," Mrs Turpin said. "The day has never dawned that I couldn't find something to laugh at."

"Not since she married me anyways," Claud said with a comical straight face.

Everybody laughed except the girl and the white-trash.

Mrs Turpin's stomach shook. "He's such a caution," she said, "that I can't help but laugh at him."

The girl made a loud ugly noise through her teeth.

Her mother's mouth grew thin and straight. "I think the worst thing in the world," she said, "is an ungrateful person. To have everything and not appreciate it. I know a girl," she said, "who has parents who would give her anything, a little brother who loves her dearly, who is getting a good education, who wears the best clothes, but who can never say a kind word to anyone, who never smiles, who just criticizes and complains all day long."

"Is she too old to paddle?" Claud asked.

The girl's face was almost purple.

"Yes," the lady said, "I'm afraid there's nothing to do but leave her to her folly. Someday she'll wake up and it'll be too late."

"It never hurt anyone to smile," Mrs Turpin said. "It just makes you feel better all over."

"Of course," the lady said sadly, "but there are just some people you can't tell anything to. They can't take criticism."

"If it's one thing I am," Mrs Turpin said with feeling, "it's grateful. When I think who all I could have been besides myself and what all I got, a little of everything, and a good disposition besides, I just feel like shouting, "Thank you, Jesus, for making everything the way it is!" It could have been different!" For one thing, somebody else could have got Claud. At the thought of this, she was flooded with gratitude and a terrible pang of joy ran through her. "Oh thank you, Jesus, Jesus, thank you!" she cried aloud.

The book struck her directly over her left eye. It struck almost at the same instant that she realized the girl was about to hurl it. Before she could utter a sound, the raw face came crashing across the table toward her, howling. The girl's fingers sank like clamps into the soft flesh of her neck. She heard the mother cry out and Claud shout, "Whoa!" There was an instant when she was certain that she was about to be in an earthquake.

All at once her vision narrowed and she saw everything as if it were happening in a small room far away, or as if she were looking at it through the wrong end of a telescope. Claud's face crumpled and fell out of sight. The nurse ran in, then out, then in again. Then the gangling figure of the doctor rushed out of the inner door. Magazines flew this way and that as the table turned over. The girl fell with a thud and Mrs Turpin's vision suddenly reversed itself and she saw everything large instead of small. The eyes of the white-trashy woman were staring hugely at the floor. There the girl, held down on one side by the nurse and on the other by her mother, was wrenching and turning in their grasp. The doctor was kneeling astride her, trying to hold her arm down. He managed after a second to sink a long needle into it.

Mrs Turpin felt entirely hollow except for her heart which swung from side to side as if it were agitated in a great empty drum of flesh.

"Somebody that's not busy call for the ambulance," the doctor said in the offhand voice young doctors adopt for terrible occasions.

Mrs Turpin could not have moved a finger. The old man who had been sitting next to her skipped nimbly into the office and made the call, for the secretary still seemed to be gone.

"Claud!" Mrs Turpin called.

He was not in his chair. She knew she must jump up and find him but she felt like someone trying to catch a train in a dream, when everything moves in slow motion and the faster you try to run the slower you go.

"Here I am," a suffocated voice, very unlike Claud's, said.

He was doubled up in the corner on the floor, pale as paper, holding his leg. She waned to get up and go to him but she could not move. Instead, her gaze was drawn slowly downward to the churning face on the floor, which she could see over the doctor's shoulder.

The girl's eyes stopped rolling and focused on her. They seemed a much lighter blue than before, as if a door that had been tightly closed behind them was now open to admit light and air.

Mrs Turpin's head cleared and her power of motion returned. She leaned forward until she was looking directly into the fierce brilliant eyes. There was no doubt in her mind that the girl did know her, knew her in some intense and personal way, beyond time and place and condition. "What you got to say to me?" she asked hoarsely and held her breath, waiting, as for a revelation.

The girl raised her head. Her gaze locked with Mrs Turpin's. "Go back to hell where you came from, you old warthog," she whispered. Her voice was low but clear. Her eyes burned for a moment as if she saw with pleasure that her message had struck its target.

Mrs Turpin sank back in her chair.

After a moment the girl's eyes closed and she turned her head wearily to the side.

The doctor rose and handed the nurse the empty syringe. He leaned over and put hands for a moment on the mother's shoulders, which were shaking. She was sitting on the floor, her lips pressed together, holding Mary Grace's hand in her lap. The girl's fingers were gripped like a baby's around her thumb. "Go on to the hospital," he said. "I'll call and make the arrangements."

"Now let's see that neck," he said in a jovial voice to Mrs Turpin. He began to inspect her neck with his first two fingers. Two little moon-shaped lines like pink fish bones were indented over her windpipe. There was the beginning of an angry red swelling above her eye. His fingers passed over this also.

"Lea'me be," she said thickly and shook him off. "See about Claud. She kicked him."

"I'll see about him in a minute," he said and felt her pulse. He was a thin grey-haired man, given to pleasantries. "Go home and have yourself a vacation the rest of the day," he said and patted her on the shoulder.

Quit your pattin me, Mrs Turpin growled to herself.

"And put an ice pack over the eye," he said. Then he went and squatted down beside Claud and looked at his leg. After a moment he pulled him up and Claud limped after him into the office.

Until the ambulance came, the only sounds in the room were the tremulous moans of the girl's mother, who continued to sit on the floor. The white-trash woman did not take her eyes off the girl. Mrs Turpin looked straight ahead at nothing. Presently the ambulance drew up, a long dark shadow, behind the curtain. The attendants came in and set the stretcher down beside the girl and lifted her expertly onto it and carried her out. The nurse helped the mother gather up her things. The shadow of the ambulance moved slightly away and the nurse came back in the office.

"That ther girl is going to be a lunatic, ain't she?" the white-trash woman asked the nurse, but the nurse kept on to the back and never answered her.

"Yes, she's going to be a lunatic," the white-trash woman said to the rest of them.

"Po' critter," the old woman murmured. The child's face was still in her lap. His eyes looked idly out over her knees. He had not moved during the disturbance except to draw one leg up under him.

"I thank Gawd," the white-trash woman said fervently, "I ain't a lunatic."

Claud came limping out and the Turpins went home.

As their pickup truck turned into their own dirt road and made the crest of the hill, Mrs Turpin gripped the window ledge and looked out suspiciously. The land sloped gracefully down through a field dotted with lavender weeds and at the start of the rise their small yellow frame house, with its little flower beds spread out around it like a fancy apron, sat primly in its accustomed place between two giant hickory trees. She would not have been startled to see a burnt wound between two blackened chimneys.

Neither of them felt like eating so they put on their house clothes and lowered the shade in the bedroom and lay down, Claud with his leg on a pillow and herself with a damp washcloth over her eye. The instant she was flat on her back, the image of a razor-backed hog with warts on its face and horns coming out behind its ears snorted into her head. She moaned, a low quiet moan.

"I am not," she said tearfully, "a warthog. From hell." But the denial had no force. The girl's eyes and her words, even the tone of her voice, low but clear, directed only to her, brooked no repudiation. She had been singled out for the message, though there was trash in the room to whom it might justly have been applied. The full force of this fact struck her only now. There was a woman there who was neglecting her own child but she had been overlooked. The message had been given to Ruby Turpin, a respectable, hard-working, church-going woman. The tears dried. Her eyes began to burn instead with wrath.

She rose on her elbow and the washcloth fell into her hand. Claud was lying on his back, snoring. She wanted to tell him what the girl had said. At the same time, she did not wish to put the image of herself as a wart hog from hell into his mind.

"Hey, Claud," she muttered and pushed his shoulder.

Claud opened one pale baby blue eye.

She looked into it warily. He did not think about anything. He just went his way.

"Wha, whasit?" he said and closed the eye again.

"Nothing," she said. "Does your leg pain you?"

"Hurts like hell," Claud said.

"It'll quit terreckly," she said and lay back down. In a moment Claud was snoring again. For the rest of the afternoon they lay there. Claud slept. She scowled at the ceiling. Occasionally she raised her fist and made a small stabbing motion over her chest as if she was defending her innocence to invisible guests who were like the comforters of Job, reasonable-seeming but wrong.

About five-thirty Claud stirred. "Got to go after those niggers," he sighed, not moving.

She was looking straight up as if there were unintelligible handwriting on the ceiling. The protuberance over her eye had turned a greenish blue. "Listen here," she said.

"What?"

"Kiss me."

Claud leaned over and kissed her loudly on the mouth. He pinched her side and their hands interlocked. Her expression of ferocious concentration did not change. Claud got up, groaning and growling, and limped off. She continued to study the ceiling.

She did not get up until she heard the pickup truck coming back with the Negroes. Then she rose and thrust her feet in her brown oxfords, which she did not bother to lace, and stumped out onto the back porch and got her red plastic bucket. She emptied a tray of ice cubes into it and filled it half full of water and went out into the back yard. Every afternoon after Claud brought the hands in, one of the boys helped him put out hay and the rest waited in the back of the truck until he was ready to take them home. The truck was parked in the shade under one of the hickory trees.

"Hi yawl this evening?" Mrs Turpin asked grimly, appearing with the bucket and the dipper. There were three women and a boy in the truck.

"Us doin nicely," the oldest woman said. "Hi you doin?" and her gaze struck immediately on the dark lump on Mrs Turpin's forehead. "You done fell down, ain't you?" she asked in a solicitous voice. The old woman was dark and almost toothless. She had on an old felt hat of Claud's set back on her head. The other two women were younger and lighter and they both had new bright green sun hats. One of them had hers on her head; the other had taken hers off and the boy was grinning beneath it.

Mrs Turpin set the bucket down on the floor of the truck. "Yawl hep yourselves," she said. She looked around to make sure Claud had gone. "No. I didn't fall down," she said, folding her arms. "It was something worse than that."

"Ain't nothing bad happen to you!" the old woman said. She said it as if they all knew Mrs Turpin was protected in some special way by Divine Providence. "You just had you a little fall."

"We were in town at the doctor's office for where the cow kicked Mr Turpin," Mrs Turpin said in a flat tone that indicated they could leave off their foolishness. "And there was this girl there. A big fat girl with her face all broke out. I could look at that girl and tell she was peculiar but I couldn't tell how. And me and her mama were just talking and going along and all of sudden WHAM! She throws this big book she was reading at me and . . ."

"Naw!" the old woman cried out.

"And then she jumps over the table and commences to choke me."

"Naw!" they all exclaimed, "naw!"

"Hi come she do that?" the old woman asked. "What ail her?"

Mrs Turpin only glared in front of her.

"Somethin ail her," the old woman said.

"They carried her off in an ambulance," Mrs Turpin continued, "but before she went she was rolling on the floor and they were trying to hold her down to give her a shot and she said something to me." She paused. "You know what she said to me?"

"What she say?" they asked.

"She said," Mrs Turpin began, and stopped, her face very dark and heavy. The sun was getting whiter and whiter, blanching the sky overhead so that the leaves of the hickory tree were black in the face of it. She could not bring forth the words. "Something real ugly," she muttered.

"She sho shouldn't said nothin ugly to you," the old woman said. "You so sweet. You the sweetest lady I know."

"She pretty too," the one with the hat on said.

"And stout," the other one said. "I never knowed no sweeter white lady."

"That's the truth befo' Jesus," the old woman said. "Amen! You des as sweet and pretty as you can be."

Mrs Turpin knew just exactly how much Negro flattery was worth and it added to her rage. "She said," she began again and finished this time with a fierce rush of breath, "that I was an old warthog from hell."

There was an astounded silence.

"Where she at?" the youngest woman cried in a piercing voice.

"Lemme see her. I'll kill her!"

"I'll kill her with you!" the other one cried.

"She b'long in the sylum," the old woman said emphatically. "You the sweetest white lady I know."

"She pretty too," the other two said. "Stout as she can be and sweet. Jesus satisfied with her!"

"Deed he is," the old woman declared.

Idiots! Mrs Turpin growled to herself. You could never say anything intelligent to a nigger. You could talk at them but not with them. "Yawl ain't drunk your water," she said shortly. "Leave the bucket in the truck when you're finished with it. I got more to do than just stand around and pass the time of day," and she moved off and into the house.

She stood for a moment in the middle of the kitchen. The dark protuberance over her eye looked like a miniature tornado cloud which might any moment sweep across the horizon of her brow. Her lower lip protruded dangerously. She squared her massive shoulders. Then she marched into the front of the house and out the side door and started down the road to the pig parlour. She had the look of a woman going single-handed, weaponless, into battle.

The sun was a deep yellow now like a harvest moon and was riding westward very fast over the far tree line as if it meant to reach the hogs before she did. The road was rutted and she kicked several good-sized stones out of her path as she strode along. The pig parlour was on a little knoll at the end of a lane that ran off from the side of the barn. It was a square of concrete as large as a small room, with a board fence about four feet high around it. The concrete floor sloped slightly so that the hog wash could drain off into a trench where it was carried to the field for fertilizer. Claud was standing on the outside, on the edge of the concrete, hanging onto the top board, hosing down the floor inside. The hose was connected to the faucet of a water trough nearby.

Mrs Turpin climbed up beside him and glowered down at the hogs inside. There were seven long-snouted bristly shoats in it—tan with liver-coloured spots—and an old sow a few weeks off from farrowing. She was lying on her side grunting. The shoats were running about shaking themselves like idiot children, their little slit pig eyes searching the floor for anything left. She had read that pigs were the most intelligent animal. She doubted it. They were supposed to be smarter than dogs. There had even been a pig astronaut. He had performed his assignment perfectly but died of a heart attack afterwards because they left him in his electric suit, sitting upright throughout his examination when naturally a hog should be on all fours.

A-gruntin and a-rootin and a-groanin.

"Gimme that hose," she said, yanking it away from Claud. "Go on and carry them niggers home and then get off that leg."

"You look like you might have swallowed a mad dog," Claud observed, but he got down and limped off. He paid no attention to her humours.

Until he was out of earshot, Mrs Turpin stood on the side of the pen, holding the hose and pointing the stream of water at the hind quarters of any shoat that looked as if it might try to lie down. When he had had time to get over the hill, she turned her head slightly and her wrathful eyes scanned the path. He was nowhere in sight. She turned back again and seemed to gather herself up. Her shoulders rose and she drew in her breath.

"What do you send me a message like that for?" she said in a low fierce voice, barely above a whisper but with the force of a shout in its concentrated fury. "How am I a hog and me both? How am I saved and from hell too?" Her free fist was knotted and with the other she gripped the hose, blindly pointing the stream of water in and out of the eye of the old sow whose outraged squeal she did not hear.

The pig parlour commanded a view of the back pasture where their twenty beef cows were gathered around the hay-bales Claud and the boy had put out.

The freshly cut pasture sloped down to the highway. Across it was their cotton field and beyond that a dark green dusty wood which they owned as well. The sun was behind the wood, very red, looking over the paling of trees like a farmer inspecting his own hogs.

"Why me?" she rumbled. "It's no trash around here, black or white, that I haven't given to. And break my back to the bone every day working. And do for the church."

She appeared to be the right size woman to command the arena before her. "How am I a hog?" she demanded. "Exactly how am I like them?" and she jabbed the stream of water at the shoats. "There was plenty of trash there. It didn't have to be me."

"If you like trash better, go get yourself some trash then," she railed. "You could have made me trash. Or a nigger. If trash is what you wanted why didn't you make me trash?" She shook her fist with the hose in it and a watery snake appeared momentarily in the air. "I could quit working and take it easy and be filthy," she growled. "Lounge about the sidewalks all day drinking root beer. Dip snuff and spit in every puddle and have it all over my face. I could be nasty.

"Or you could have made me a nigger. It's too late for me to be a nigger," she said with deep sarcasm, "but I could act like one. Lay down in the middle of the road and stop traffic. Roll on the ground."

In the deepening light everything was taking on a mysterious hue. The pasture was growing a peculiar glassy green and the streak of highway had turned lavender. She braced herself for a final assault and this time her voice rolled out over the pasture. "Go on," she yelled, "call me a hog! Call me a hog again. From hell. Call me a warthog from hell. Put that bottom rail on top. There'll still be a top and bottom!"

A garbled echo returned to her.

A final surge of fury shook her and she roared, "Who do you think you are?"

The colour of everything, field and crimson sky, burned for a moment with a transparent intensity. The question carried over the pasture and across the highway and the cotton field and returned to her clearly like an answer from beyond the wood.

She opened her mouth but no sound came out of it.

A tiny truck, Claud's, appeared on the highway, heading rapidly out of sight. Its gears scraped thinly. It looked like a child's toy. At any moment a bigger truck might smash into it and scatter Claud's and the niggers' brains all over the road.

Mrs Turpin stood there, her gaze fixed on the highway, all her muscles rigid, until in five or six minutes the truck reappeared, returning. She waited until it had had time to turn into their own road. Then like a monumental statue coming to life, she bent her head slowly and gazed, as if through the very heart of mystery, down into the big parlour at the hogs. They had settled all in one corner around the old sow who was grunting softly. A red glow suffused them. They appeared to pant with a secret life.

Until the sun slipped finally behind the tree line, Mrs Turpin remained there with her gaze bent to them as if she were absorbing some abysmal life-giving knowledge. At last she lifted her head. There was only a purple streak in the sky, cutting through a field of crimson and leading, like an extension of the highway, into the descending dusk. She raised her hands from the side of the pen in a gesture hieratic and profound. A visionary light settled in her eyes. She saw the streak as a vast swinging bridge extending upward from the earth through a field of living fire. Upon it a vast horde of souls were rumbling toward heaven. There were whole companies of white-trash, clean for the first time in their lives, and bands of black niggers in white robes, and battalions of freaks and lunatics shouting and clapping and leaping like frogs. And bringing up the end of the procession was a tribe of people whom she recognized at once as those who, like herself and Claud, had always had a little of everything and the God-given wit to use it right. She leaned forward to observe them closer. They were marching behind the others with great dignity, accountable as they had always been for good order and common sense and respectable behaviour. They alone were on key. Yet she could see by their shocked and altered faces that even their virtues were being burned away. She lowered her hands and gripped the rail of the hog pen, her eyes small but fixed unblinkingly on what lay ahead. In a moment the vision faded but she remained where she was, immobile.

At length she got down and turned off the faucet and made her slow way on the darkening path to the house. In the woods around her the invisible cricket choruses had struck up, but what she heard were the voices of the souls climbing upward into the starry field and shouting hallelujah.

1964

John Berger

b. 1926

In his edition of Berger's essays, Geoff Dyer, Berger's similarly polymathic student and intellectual heir, points to the centrality of the piece on Joyce's *Ulysses*, which Berger initially read when he was fourteen years old. In "The First and Last Recipe: *Ulysses*," we see Berger's "refusal to separate the two concerns that have dominated his life and work: the enduring mystery of great art and the lived experience of the oppressed." The essay, given its own section in the book, celebrates Joyce's truly "adult" and deeply human demand borne of the Dublin streets that he and his book "keep the company of the unimportant, those forever off stage." The link between Joyce's "low company" and the rapid emergence of Berger's humane Marxism (which developed when Berger was still a young man) is unmistakable. But Joyce melded the richness of ordinary life with the "prodigious erudition" that since 1922 has produced many thousands of Liffian migraines. Simply to glance at the list of books Berger has written (it takes a while) may produce an equivalent expectation of Learning's intimidation. But Berger reverses the Joycean duality: the company is often very high, in person or intellectual reach—Picasso, Monet, the nature of photography, the secrets of animals—but the prose is crystalline, invariably accessible. Another arc from Joyce to Berger is the fascination with seeing (even counting Berger's books that contain "seeing" or "looking" in the title takes a while). "Parallax," seeing things differently from a change in angle of perception, seems to underlie what became Berger's perennial investigation of "the Cubist moment." In *Ways of Seeing*, the companion book to the immensely successful 1972 BBC television series, he says: "Seeing comes before words . . . It is seeing which establishes our place in the surrounding world; we explain that world with words, but words can never undo the fact that we are surrounded by it." He studied painting at the Chelsea School of Art, turned toward art criticism, giving it a Marxist inflection in the mode of Walter Benjamin, and began writing novels. *G.*, a perhaps overly designed narrative, won the Booker Prize in 1972. In his severe acceptance speech, Berger expressed a degree of pleasure that some of the money would go to give voice to migrant workers in Europe. He famously declared too that half the prize money was destined for the London-based Black Panther Movement to make up at least in part for the exploitation of West Indians by men such as the one whose name adorns the Booker Prize. A less aggressive political trajectory of Berger's work led to a trilogy of works, including the often beautiful, elegiac composite of genres *Pig Earth*, about the frailty of rural French life. Berger wrote, bore witness, lived the difficult existence of the labourers, and has remained in a village in the Alps. Like D.H. Lawrence before him, he found England intolerable. Unlike Lawrence, however, he is not usually associated with the short story, which makes his luminous visual power largely inaccessible to readers. But his chiseled prose and deft angulations of seeing make the form wonderfully natural to him.

Islington

The borough of Islington has, during the last twenty-five years, become fashionable. In the fifties and sixties, the name Islington, when pronounced in central London or in the north-western suburbs, conjured up a remote and faintly suspect district. It is interesting to note how poor and therefore uneasy districts, even when they are geographically near a city centre, are pushed, in the immigration of those who are prospering, further away that they really are. Harlem in New York is an obvious example. For Londoners today Islington is far closer than it used to be.

When it was still remote, forty years ago, Hubert bought a small terraced house there, with a narrow back garden that sloped down to a canal. At that time he and his wife were teaching part-time in art schools and had no money to spare. The house, however, was cheap, dirt cheap.

They've moved to Islington! a friend told me at the time. And this news was like a late autumn afternoon when the daylight hours are becoming noticeably shorter. There was something of a foreclosure about it.

Soon afterwards, I went to live abroad. Occasionally over the years and on visits to London, I saw Hubert at the house of a common friend, but I never visited—until three days ago—his house in Islington. He and I had been students together at the same London art school in 1943. He was studying Textile Design and I was studying Painting, but there were certain classes we attended together: Life Drawing, History of Architecture, Human Anatomy.

He made an impression on me because of his fastidious persistence. He invariably wore a tie. He looked like a nineteenth-century bookbinder. He tended to be in a state of sad shock provoked by recurring modern stupidities, and his nails were always clean. I wore a long black Romantic overcoat and looked like a coachman—also of the nineteenth century. I drew with the blackest charcoal I could find, and to find any at all during the war wasn't easy—who had time in '41 or '42 to be burning charcoal? Sometimes I filched a stick from the teacher's supply; two kinds of theft were justifiable: Food for the hungry, Basic Materials for the artist.

The two of us were undoubtedly suspicious of one another. Hubert must have thought I was over-demonstrative and indiscreet to the point of exhibitionism; he seemed to me to be a tight-lipped elitist.

Nevertheless we listened to one another and would sometimes drink a beer together or share an apple. We were both aware that we were each considered by most of the other students to be deranged. Deranged because of our commitment to working at every possible moment. Practically nothing distracted us. Hubert drew from the model with the attentive restrained movements of a violinist tuning his instrument; I drew like a kitchen boy slapping tomatoes and cheese on to pizzas waiting to be put into the oven. Our approaches were very different. Nevertheless during the breaks every hour, when the model took a rest, we were the only two who stayed in the studio and went on working. Hubert often improved his drawing, bringing it to a kind of equanimity. I usually ruined mine.

Three days ago, after I had rung the bell of the house in Islington, he came to the front door with a beaming smile. His left arm was raised about his head in a gesture which was something between a welcome, a salute, and a cavalry officer's sign to his men to advance. Nobody could be less military that Hubert. Nevertheless he is a commander.

His face was gaunt and so meticulously shaved it looked sore. He was wearing a pair of baggy corduroy trousers with a wide black leather belt that hung loose, almost at the level of his trouser pockets.

Perfect timing, he said, the water has just boiled. Whereupon he waited for me to make some remark.

It's been a long time, I said.

By now we were at the top of the first short flight of stairs.

What kind of tea would you prefer: Earl Grey, Darjeeling or Green Leaf?

Green Leaf.

It's the healthiest, he said, it's what I drink every day.

The drawing room was full of rugs, cushions, objects, footrests, porcelain, dried flowers, collections, engravings, crystal decanters, pictures. It was hard to imagine anything new, anything new larger than a postcard, finding a home there, for there was no space. It was equally hard to imagine throwing a piece out to make more space, for everything had been found and chosen and placed over the years with the same love and attention. There was not a sea shell, a candlestick, a clock, a stool that stood out or appeared awkward. He indicated that I should sit in a Regency chair by the fireplace.

I enquired who had painted an abstract watercolour hanging near the door.

That's one of Gwen's, Hubert said. I've always liked it.

Gwen, his wife, a teacher of engraving, died twelve years ago. She was withdrawn, small, wore brogue shoes and looked like a lepidopterist. If she had held up her hand in the air anywhere—even on a wartime London bus—I would have expected a butterfly to land on it.

Hubert poured from a silver teapot into a Derbyshire cup on a table by the door and navigated around the many pieces of furniture across the room to deliver it to me. I wondered whether for him each room in the house had a navigation chart, like seas do. On the ground floor I had noticed the dining room was equally encumbered.

I made some cucumber sandwiches, if you would like one? he asked.

Thank you very much.

I had an aunt, he said, who maintained there were two golden rules about invitations to tea. One is that cucumber sandwiches and sponge cake are obligatory items, and the second is that guests have to insist upon leaving, and succeed in doing so, before six o'clock . . .

I heard the ticking of a pendulum clock on the shelf behind me. There were at least four clocks in the room.

I want to ask you a question about our art-school days, I said. Do you remember a girl, the same year as us, who was studying Theatre Costume? She went around a lot with Colette.

Colette! replied Hubert, I wonder what has become of her? She used to come in with a new dress every week, remember? Often with the pins still in it.

She used to stay with Colette in her rooms in Guildford Place, I said. The rooms were on the first floor, overlooking Coram's Fields. She was short, snub-nosed, had large eyes, was a little plump. Not at all talkative.

Coram's Fields, said Hubert. I saw a painting of them in a show the other day. By a young painter called Arturo di Stefano. Kids on a hot, hot day by a swimming pool playing with the water. Full of eternity—if I may so put it—childhood!

No swimming pool there then, I said. Just a boarded-up bandstand, and the tall trees that looked down at us in the morning when we looked out of the window.

I don't think I was ever at Colette's place, Hubert said.

Do you see whom I'm thinking about though?

Was it Pauline who had an affair with Joe, the farmer?

No, no, dark hair, short dark hair! Very white teeth. A bit stand-offish, walked around with her nose in the air.

You're not thinking of Jeanne with the two n's to her name?

Jeanne was tall! This one was small, roundish, tiny. She used to go home for weekends to somewhere smart like Newbury. Was it Newbury? Anyway, she loved horses.

Why do you need to know her name?

I've been trying for a long time to remember her name, and it keeps escaping me.

Was it Priscilla?

It was a very common name, that's what's so strange.

Probably she got married, most art students got married in those days and then her family name would have changed.

I only want her first name.

Are you trying to trace her whereabouts today?

On Mondays in June she came with strawberries from the countryside and would hand them round the whole class.

She may be dead, don't forget!

There are only a few people today whom I can consult, that's why I came to you.

True, unfortunately true. We are not so many. What was her work like?

Dull. Yet as soon as she came into a room you knew she had a sense of style. She shone. She said nothing and she shone.

I've always maintained that style is the inheritance of a number of talents. A single talent, however great, does not yield a sense of style. Did I take one of my pills? I'm talking too much.

I didn't see you do so.

I wish I could place her for you. I'm afraid I can't. She's gone.

Nobody wore hats in those days, and she did! She wore a hat as if she was going to the races! Askew on the back of her head.

He said nothing. I let him think. And the silence continued. Hubert had always been prone to silences—as if life hung by a thread and foolish talking might snap it. In the silence I could feel that, since Gwen's death, the standards the two of them had established and maintained here had in no way changed. What this room *liked* was still the same.

Let's go upstairs, he finally said, and I'll show you St Paul's, a splendid view of St Paul's from the balcony of my bedroom.

We took the stairs slowly. He held himself very upright. On the first landing he stopped and said: This terrace was built in the 1840s and the houses were destined for clerks who worked in the City. Poor man's Georgian, as you can see. And it didn't work out. Within a generation they had all been turned into lodging houses, with one or a couple of tenants living on each floor. And so it remained for a hundred years. When we arrived, forty years ago, the houses on the other side of the street didn't even have electricity. Only gas and paraffin lamps.

The wall of the staircase we were climbing was hung with sketches for textiles and framed samples of precious fabrics, some of them Persian-looking.

Before we bought this house it was a brothel, serving the lorry drivers who delivered goods to London from the North. Come into the bathroom. See that mirror with the mermaids? The tenants left it in the bedroom downstairs and Gwen insisted upon keeping it. Sometimes I see Beatrice in it, Gwen would say laughing, Beatrice waving at me! Beatrice was a whore and her name is scratched on one of the window panes in the drawing room.

As Hubert straightened the mirror on the bathroom wall, I caught a glimpse of his face in the glass and was reminded of him as a young man. Perhaps something to do with the glass being speckled and darkened, so that the expression in his eyes was by contrast more sparkling.

When we moved in we had no money, so we told ourselves it might take as long to make a house as it takes to make a garden. We restored it room by room, there are seven, floor by floor, year by year.

On the top floor, Hubert led me across his bedroom towards the French windows which gave on to a terrace.

Mind the geraniums! he said. I keep them out here to water them every morning.

They smell so strong!

Bloody cranesbill, he said, or in Latin: *Geraniu, sanguineum.*

I picked one of the leaves and sniffed it. It reminded me of her hair.

During the war ordinary soap was scarce, and there were no shampoos, unless you bought them on the black market. So newly washed hair smelt of itself. I remember her washing her hair in the morning after getting out of bed. It was summer and warm, and the windows were open. She washed it in an enamel handbasin which she filled with water from an enamel jug. There was no hot water in Colette's flat. Then she came back, with a towel wrapped round her head and nothing else on, lay down on the bed beside me and waited until her hair dried.

St Paul's, Hubert said, there's nothing else to match it! And built in record time, only thirty-five years! Work began nine years after the Great Fire of London in 1666, and it was finished in 1710. Christopher Wren was still around to see his masterpiece inaugurated.

He was reciting, almost word for word, what we had been obliged to learn by heart in the History of Architecture class. We were also obliged to go and draw the cathedral. It had survived many air raids unscathed, and had become a great patriotic monument. Churchill was filmed speaking in front of it. And when I drew its architectural details, I added Spitfire fighters in the sky behind!

The first time it was neither she nor I who made a choice. I had come to visit Colette after an evening class. We ate some soup. The three of us talked and it grew late. There was an air-raid warning. We switched off the lights and opened a window to watch the searchlights raking the sky above the trees in Coram's Fields. The raiders didn't seem especially near.

Sleep here, Colette proposed. It's better than going out. We can all sleep in this bed, it's large enough for four.

Which is what we did. Colette slept against the wall, she in the middle, and I on the outside. We took off most of our clothes but not all.

When we woke up, Colette was making toast and pouring cups of tea, and she and I were entangled together, legs and arms interlaced. We were not surprised by this, for both of us were aware of something more surprising: during the night each of us had put to sleep the other's sex, not by satisfying it, or by denying it, but by following a different desire which even today it's hard to name. No clinical descriptions fit. Perhaps it could only have happened in London during the spring of 1943. We found in each other's arms a way of leaving together, a transport elsewhere. We arranged ourselves, fitted ourselves together as if we were making a sleigh or a skateboard. (Only skateboards didn't yet exist.) Our destination wasn't important. Any departure was to an erogenous zone. What mattered was the distance we put behind us. We fed each other distance with every lick. Wherever our skins touched there was the promise of an horizon.

I stepped back into Hubert's bedroom, and noticed that it was different from the rest of the house. There was a double bed in the corner, but Gwen had never slept up here. This room was provisional—as though during the last decade Hubert had been camping here. The walls were entirely covered with images of plants and flowers—unframed prints, drawings, photographs, pages torn from books—and they were placed so close together that they looked almost like a wallpaper. Many were attached by drawing pins, and they made me think that he was constantly rearranging them. Except for the slippers under the bed and the collection of medicines on the bedside table, it looked like a student's room.

He noticed my interest and he pointed to a drawing, perhaps one of his own: Strange flower, no? Like the breast of a tiny thrush in full song! It originally came from Brazil. In English it's known as Birthwort. In Latin: *Aristolochia elegans*. Somewhere Lévi-Strauss says something about the Latin name of a plant. He says the Latin name personalises it. Birthwort is merely a species. *Aristolochia elegans* is a person, singular and unique. If you had this flower in your garden and it happened to die, you could mourn for it with its Latin name. Which you wouldn't do, if you knew it as Birthwort.

I was standing by the French windows. Shall I shut them? I asked.

Yes, do.

You always sleep with the windows shut?

Funny you should ask that, for recently it has been something of a problem. Before it was simple—I left them open all night. Now, before I go to bed, I open them. The house is so narrow it tends to be stuffy as soon as all the windows are shut. The other night I thought of the clerks who lived here when the house was new. Compared to us, they had very little space in their lives. Cramped offices, cramped horse-buses, cramped streets, cramped rooms. Then, come the small hours, before it's light, I get out of bed again and I go and shut the windows, so that when the street wakes up in the morning it's quiet.

You sleep late?

I wake up early, very early. I think I shut the windows because I need a kind of protection at the beginning of each new day. For some time now I've needed calm in the morning so I can face it. Every day you have to decide to be invincible.

I understand.

I doubt it, John. I'm a solitary man. Come, I'll show you the garden.

I had never before seen a garden like this one. It was full of bushes, flowers, shrubs, each flourishing, yet planted so close together it was impossible for a stranger to imagine finding a way between them. A single path led down to the canal and it was so tight one could only go down it walking sideways. Yet the density of the foliage was not like that of a jungle, but like the density of a closed book, which has to be read page by page. I spotted Michaelmas daisies, Winter jasmine, powder-puff hollyhocks and, bordering the path, Ribbon Grass known as Lady's Laces, and a citronella plant whose leaves, shaped like tongues, were growing in such a way, and had placed themselves in such an arrangement, that each was accommodated within the other's space. Each had found a position beside, or under, or over, or between, or around, its neighbouring leaves that allowed it to receive some light, to bend with the wind, to probe in its natural direction. And the whole impenetrable garden was like this.

There was nothing here when we came, said Hubert, not even grass. It had been used for years as a dump for all the houses along the terrace. A dump behind the brothel. Old baths, a gas stove, smashed prams, rotten rabbit-hutches. Try some of these grapes.

He stepped up to a vine growing against a brick wall that separated the garden from the neighbour's. Over each bunch of grapes he had placed a plastic bag to prevent the birds from eating them. He inserted his long hand inside one of these bags and, with his fingers, detached a few small white grapes, the colour of cloudy honey, and placed them on the palm of my hand.

The next time I went to Colette's flat in Guildford Place it was understood from the start that I would spend the night there. Colette slept on another bed in the second room. I took off all my clothes and she put on her loose embroidered nightdress. We discovered the same thing as last time. Once put together, we could leave. We travelled from bone to bone, from continent to continent. Sometimes we spoke. Not sentences, not endearments. The names of parts and places. Tibia and Timbuktu, Labia and Lapland, Earhole and Oasis. The names of the parts became pet names, the names of the places, passwords. We weren't dreaming. We simply became the Vasco da Gama of our two bodies. We paid the closest attention to each other's sleep, we never forgot one another. When she was deeply asleep her breathing was like surf. You took me to the bottom, she told me one morning.

We did not become lovers, we were scarcely friends, and we had little in common. I was not interested in horses, and she wasn't interested in the Freedom Press. When our paths crossed in the art school we had nothing to say to each other. This didn't worry us. We exchanged light kisses—on the shoulder or the back of the neck, never on the mouth—and we continued on our separate ways, like an elderly couple who happened to be working in the same school. As soon as it became dark, whenever we could, we met to do the same thing: to pass the whole night in each other's arms and, like this, to leave, to go elsewhere. Repeatedly.

Hubert was attaching an armful of stems with yellow flowers to a trellis with several lengths of raffia, his hands still trembling a little.

It's getting chilly, he said, let's go inside.

He shut and locked the door behind us.

This is my workroom—he nodded towards a large wooden bench with a chair in front of it—this week I'm putting seeds from the garden into little packets, each one properly labelled with its common and Latin names. Occasionally I have to look the Latin one up in the herbarium, my memory isn't what it was, though I'm happy to say I don't have to do it often.

What are these packets for? I asked.

I send them away. Every autumn I do the same. See these here. Love-in-a-mist. *Nigella damascena.* Two dozen packets.

You mean you sell them?

I give them away.

So many! You've got hundreds of packets!

There's an organisation which calls itself "Thrive," and they distribute seeds to people in need—old people's homes, orphanages, reception centres, transit camps—so that there are flowers in places where usually there would be none. It doesn't make much difference, of course, I realise that, but at least it's something. And for me, now, it's a way of sharing the pleasures of the garden. It's a satisfaction.

My recidivist erections were at first a distraction but once she had named them—we'll call them London! she said—they took their place and became no more urgent than—or as urgent as—the damp fern smell of her sweat, her rounded knees, or the curly black hairs in her arsehole. Everything under the blankets took us elsewhere. And elsewhere, we discovered the size of life. In daylight life often seemed small. For example, when drawing plaster casts of Roman statues in the Antique class, it seemed very small. Under the blankets she fingered the soles of my feet with her toes and sighed "Damascus." I combed her hair with my teeth and hissed "Scalp." Then as these or other gestures of ours became longer and slower and we succumbed to a single sleep, our two bodies took account of the unimaginable distances they offered one another and we left. In the morning we said nothing. We couldn't make sentences. Either she would go and wash her hair, or I would go to the window at the foot of the bed and look out across Coram's Fields and she would throw me my trousers.

My real problem, said Hubert, is in the drawers over there.

He pulled out a metal drawer which slid noiselessly towards us. Double imperial size, designed for storing architectural plans. The drawer was full of small abstract sketches and watercolours which gave the impression they were derived from places. Perhaps microscopic places, perhaps galactic. Paths. Localities. Openings. Obstacles. All drawn with fluid washes and meandering lines. Hubert gave the drawer a soft push and it slid back on its rails. He pulled out another—there were a dozen such drawers—which, this time, contained drawings. Intricately drawn with a hard pencil, full of scudding movements, such as you see in clouds and running water.

What am I to do with them? he asked.

They are Gwen's?

He nodded.

If I leave them here, he said, they'll be thrown away after my death. If I make a selection and keep only what seem to me to be the very best, what do I do with the others? Burn them? Give them to an art school or a library? They are not interested. When she was alive, Gwen never made a name for herself. She was simply passionate about drawing, about "capturing it" as she put it. She drew almost every day. She herself threw a lot away. What's in these drawers is what she wanted to keep.

He pulled out a third drawer, hesitated, and then selected with his slightly trembling hand a gouache and held it up.

Beautiful, I said.

What am I to do? I keep on putting it off. And if I do nothing, they'll all be thrown out.

You must put them in envelopes, I said.

Envelopes?

Yes. You sort them. You invent any system you like. By year, by colour, by preference, by size, by mood. And on each of the big envelopes you write her name and the category you've established. It'll take time. Not a single one must be misplaced. And in each envelope you put the drawings in order; you write a number very lightly on the back of each one.

An order according to what?

I don't know. You'll find out. There are drawings which look as if they should come first, and there's always a last drawing, isn't there? The order will take care of itself.

And what difference do you think these envelopes are going to make?

Who can tell? In any case they'll be better off.

You mean the drawings?

Yes. They'll be better off.

The clocks in the drawing room upstairs were chiming.

I must be off, I said.

He led me towards the front door. And after opening it, turning round, he looked at me quizzically.

Wasn't her name Audrey?

Audrey! Of course it was Audrey!

Funny little thing she was, said Hubert. She left I think after a couple of terms, which is why I couldn't place her straight away. She wasn't with us for long. And she wore hats, you're right.

He smiled distantly, for he could see I was pleased. We said our goodbyes.

The nameless desire Audrey and I shared came to an end as inexplicably as it had begun: inexplicably only because neither of us sought an explanation. The last time we slept together (and although I forgot her name, I can remember without the slightest hesitation that it was the month of June and her feet were dusty from wearing sandals all day long) she got into bed first, and I climbed on to the windowsill to detach the wooden frame of the blackout curtain, so that I could open the window and let in more air. Outside there was moonlight and all the trees around Coram's Fields were distinctly visible. I took in their every detail with a pleasure which included an anticipation because, in a minute or two, we would both, before setting out on the night's journey, be touching every detail of the other's body.

I slithered into bed beside her, and without a word she turned her back on me. There are a hundred ways of turning the back in bed. Most are inviting, some are languid. There is a way, though, that unmistakably announces refusal. Her shoulder blades became like armour plate.

I missed her too much to go to sleep, and she, I guessed, was pretending to sleep. I might have argued with her or started to kiss the back of her neck. Yet this was not our style. Bit by bit my perplexity slipped away and I felt thankful. I turned my own back and lay there cradling a gratitude for all that had happened in the bed with broken springs. At this moment a bomb fell. It was close by; we heard the windows shattering on the other side of the Fields and, further away, shouts. Neither of us spoke. Her shoulder blades relaxed. Her hand looked for mine, and we both lay there grateful.

Next morning when I left she didn't so much as glance up from her coffee bowl. She was staring into it as if she had decided, a few minutes before, that this was what she must do and that the future of our two lives depended upon it.

Hubert stood there in the doorway, left arm raised about his head, making a sign for the mounted troops to disperse. His face was fragile and invincible. It was getting dark.

I'll take your tip about the envelopes, he called after me.

I walked alone down the road past the other terraced houses.

You called me many names in your sleep, Audrey said as she took my arm, and my favourite was Oslo.

Oslo! I repeated, as we turned into Upper Street. The way her head now rested on my shoulder told me she was dead.

You said it rhymed with First Snow, she said.

2005

Gabriel García Márquez

1928–2014

Gabriel García Márquez was born in 1928 in Aracataca, a town in the coastal district of northern Colombia. Because of his parents' poverty his maternal grandparents raised him. The year he was born was marked by a strike against the American-owned United Fruit Company. In the town of Aracataca, government soldiers killed over one hundred workers, a tragedy known as the banana massacre; García Márquez would later write about this incident in his fiction. At the age of twelve he was sent to the Liceo Nacional, a school for gifted students run by the Jesuits, and then he studied law at the National University of Bogotá and the University of Cartagena. In 1948 he began writing a daily column for the Cartagena newspaper *El Universal*, and, in 1950, decided to abandon the study of law to devote himself full time to writing. He worked for several newspapers in the early 1950s; he joined the staff of the Bogotá newspaper *El Espectador* in 1954 as a writer of stories and film reviews and briefly became their European correspondent. Though he had begun writing stories in the 1940s, his first novella, *La Hojarasca* (*Leaf Storm*) was not published until 1955. In 1958 he married his childhood sweetheart, Mercedes Barcha, and within the year the couple moved to Cuba where he worked for *Prensa Latina* in Havana, before moving to New York and later, Mexico. Because of his close friendship with Fidel Castro he would be denied re-entry into the US until 1971. Although he had produced two novels and a collection of stories, his work did not get much attention until the publication of *Cien años de soledad* (*One Hundred Years of Solitude*) in 1967, which brought him international fame and numerous prizes. The novel describes the history of the fictional town of Macondo, where the fantastic and improbable exist comfortably beside the ordinary. Though it was the Cuban writer Alejo Carpentier who first used the term magic realism (*"lo real maravilloso"*) to describe the way Latin American writers seamlessly mixed elements of the fantastic and the mythological with realism in fiction, it was García Márquez's novel that gave the literary term common currency. In the 1970s García Márquez moved his family to Barcelona. They returned to Colombia in the early 1980s but, accused by the Conservative government of aiding the leftist guerillas, he was forced to seek political asylum in Mexico, where he died in April 2014. In 1982 he was awarded the Nobel Prize for Literature. After *One Hundred Years of Solitude*, García Márquez published another four novels and a collection of stories, as well as screenplays and works of journalism. In 1996, he wrote *Noticia de un secuestro* (*News of a Kidnapping*), a dramatic non-fiction account of a string of high-profile kidnappings that occurred in 1990 during Colombia's brutal drug wars. *Vivir para contarla* (*Live to Tell It*), the first volume of his memoirs, was published in 2002.

The Handsomest Drowned Man in the World

A Tale for Children

The first children who saw the dark and slinky bulge approaching through the sea let themselves think it was an enemy ship. Then they saw it had no flags or masts and they thought it was a whale. But when it washed up on the beach, they removed the clumps of seaweed, the jellyfish tentacles, and the remains of fish and flotsam, and only then did they see that it was a drowned man.

They had been playing with him all afternoon, burying him in the sand and digging him up again, when someone chanced to see them and spread the alarm in the village. The men who carried him to the nearest house noticed that he weighed more than any dead man they had ever known, almost as much as a horse, and they said to each other that maybe he'd been floating too long and the water had got into his bones. When they laid him on the floor they said he'd been taller than all other men because there was barely room for him in the house, but they thought that maybe the ability to keep on growing after death was part of the nature of certain drowned men. He had the smell of the sea about him and only his shape gave one to suppose that it was the corpse of a human being, because the skin was covered with a crust of mud and scales.

They did not even have to clean off his face to know that the dead man was a stranger. The village was made up of only twenty-odd wooden houses that had stone courtyards with no flowers and which were spread about on the end of a desertlike cape. There was so little land that mothers always went about with the fear that the wind would carry off their children and the few dead that the years had caused among them had to be thrown off the cliffs. But the sea was calm and bountiful and all the men fit into seven boats. So when they found the drowned man they simply had to look at one another to see that they were all there.

That night they did not go out to work at sea. While the men went to find out if anyone was missing in neighbouring villages, the women stayed behind to care for the drowned man. They took the mud off with grass swabs, they removed the underwater stones entangled in his hair, and they scraped the crust off with tools used for scaling fish. As they were doing that they noticed that the vegetation on him came from faraway oceans and deep water and that his clothes were in tatters, as if he had sailed through labyrinths of coral. They noticed too that he bore his death with pride, for he did not have the lonely look of other drowned men who came out of the sea or that haggard, needy look of men who drowned in rivers. But only when they finished cleaning him off did they become aware of the kind of man he was and it left them breathless. Not only was he the tallest, strongest, most virile, and best built man they had ever seen, but even though they were looking at him there was no room for him in their imagination.

They could not find a bed in the village large enough to lay him on nor was there a table solid enough to use for his wake. The tallest men's holiday pants would not fit him, not the fattest ones' Sunday shirts, nor the shoes of the one with the biggest feet. Fascinated by his huge size and his beauty, the women then decided to make him some pants from a large piece of sail and a shirt from some bridal brabant linen so that he could continue through his death with dignity. As they sewed, sitting in a circle and gazing at the corpse between stitches, it seemed to them that the wind had never been so steady nor the sea so restless as on that night and they supposed that the change had something to do with the dead man. They thought that if that magnificent man had lived in the village, his house would have had the widest doors, the highest ceiling, and the strongest floor, his bedstead would have been made from a midship frame held together by iron bolts, and his wife would have been the happiest woman. They thought that he would have had so much authority that he could have drawn fish out of the sea by calling their names and that he would have put so much work into his land that springs would have burst forth from among the rocks so that he would have been able to plant flowers on the cliffs. They secretly compared him to their own men, thinking that for all their lives theirs were incapable of doing what he could do in one night, and they ended up dismissing them deep in their hearts as the weakest, meanest, and most useless creatures on earth. They were wandering through that maze of fantasy when the oldest woman, who as the oldest had looked upon the drowned man with more compassion than passion, sighed:

"He has the face of someone called Esteban."

It was true. Most of them had only to take another look at him to see that he could not have any other name. The more stubborn among them, who were the youngest, still lived for a few hours with the illusion that when they put his clothes on and he lay among the flowers in patent leather shoes his name might be Lautaro. But it was a vain illusion. There had not been enough canvas, the poorly cut and worse sewn pants were too tight, and the hidden strength of his heart popped the buttons on his shirt. After midnight the whistling of the wind died down and the sea fell into its Wednesday drowsiness. The silence put an end to any last doubts: he was Esteban. The women who had dressed him, who had combed his hair, had cut his nails and shaved him were unable to hold back a shudder of pity when they had to resign themselves to his being dragged along the ground. It was then that they understood how unhappy he must have been with that huge body since it bothered him even after death. They could see him in life, condemned to going through doors sideways, cracking his head on crossbeams, remaining on his feet during visits, not knowing what to do with his soft, pink, sea-lion hands while the lady of the house looked for her most resistant chair and begged him, frightened to death, sit here, Esteban, please, and he, leaning against the wall, smiling, don't bother, ma'am, I'm fine where I am, his heels raw and his back roasted from having done the same thing so many times whenever he paid a visit, don't bother, ma'am, I'm fine where I am, just to avoid the embarrassment of breaking up the chair, and never knowing perhaps that the ones who said don't go, Esteban, at least wait till the coffee's ready, were the ones who later on would whisper the big boob finally left, how nice, the handsome fool has gone. That was what the women were thinking beside the body a little before dawn. Later, when they covered his face with a handkerchief so that the light would not bother him, he looked so forever dead, so defenceless, so much like their men that the first furrows of tears opened in their hearts. It was one of the younger ones who began the weeping. The others, coming to, went from sighs to wails, and the more they sobbed the more they felt like weeping, because the drowned man was becoming all the more Esteban for them, and so they wept so much, for he was the most destitute, most peaceful, and most obliging man on earth, poor Esteban. So when the men returned with the news that the drowned man was not from the neighbouring villages either, the women felt an opening of jubilation in the midst of their tears.

"Praise the Lord," they sighed, "he's ours!"

The men thought the fuss was only womanish frivolity. Fatigued because of the difficult nighttime inquiries, all they wanted was to get rid of the bother of the newcomer once and for all before the sun grew strong on that arid, windless day. They improvised a litter with the remains of foremasts and gaffs, tying it together with rigging so that it would bear the weight of the body until they reached the cliffs. They wanted to tie the anchor from a cargo ship to him so that he would sink easily into the deepest waves, where fish are blind and divers die of nostalgia, and bad currents would not bring him back to shore, as had happened with other bodies. But the more they hurried, the more the women thought of ways to waste time. They walked about like startled hens, pecking with the sea charms on their breasts, some interfering on one side to put a scapular of the good wind on the drowned man, some on the other side to put a wrist compass on him, and after a great deal of *get away from there, woman, stay out of the way, look, you almost made me fall on top of the dead man*, the men began to feel mistrust in their livers and started grumbling about why so many main-altar decorations for a stranger, because no matter how many nails and holy-water jars he had on him, the sharks would chew him all the same, but the women kept piling on their junk relics, running back and forth, stumbling, while they released in sighs what they did not in tears, so that the men finally exploded with *since when has there ever been such a fuss over a drifting corpse, a drowned nobody, a piece of cold Wednesday meat.* One of the women, mortified by so much lack of care, then removed the handkerchief from the dead man's face and the men were left breathless too.

He was Esteban. It was not necessary to repeat it for them to recognize him. If they had been told Sir Walter Raleigh, even they might have been impressed with his gringo accent, the macaw on his shoulder, his cannibal-killing blunderbuss, but there could be only one Esteban in the world and there he was, stretched out like a sperm whale, shoeless, wearing the pants of an undersized child, and with those stony nails that had to be cut with a knife. They only had to take the handkerchief off his face to see that he was ashamed, that it was not his fault that he was so big or so heavy or so handsome, and if he had known that this was going to happen, he would have looked for a more discreet place to drown in, seriously, I even would have tied the anchor off a galleon around my neck and staggered off a cliff like someone who doesn't like things in order not to be upsetting people now with this Wednesday dead body, as you people say, in order not to be bothering anyone with this filthy piece of cold meat that doesn't have anything to do with me. There was so much truth in his manner that even the most mistrustful men, the ones who felt the bitterness of endless nights at sea fearing that their women would tire of dreaming about them and begin to dream of drowned men, even they and others who were harder still shuddered in the marrow of their bones at Esteban's sincerity.

That was how they came to hold the most splendid funeral they could conceive of for an abandoned drowned man. Some women who had gone to get flowers in the neighbouring villages returned with other women who could not believe what they had been told, and those women went back for more flowers when they saw the dead man, and they brought more and more until there were so many flowers and so many people that it was hard to walk about. At the final moment it pained them to return him to the waters as an orphan and they chose a father and mother from among the best people, and aunts and uncles and cousins, so that through him all the inhabitants of the village became kinsmen. Some sailors who heard the weeping from a distance went off course and people heard of one who had himself tied to the mainmast, remembering ancient fables about sirens. While they fought for the privilege of carrying him on their shoulders along the steep escarpment by the cliffs, men and women became aware for the first time of the desolation of their streets, the dryness of their courtyards, the narrowness of their dreams as they faced the splendour and beauty of their drowned man. They let him go without an anchor so that he could come back if he wished and whenever he wished, and they all held their breath for the fraction of centuries the body took to fall into the abyss. They did not need to look at one another to realize that they were no longer all present, that they would never be. But they also knew that everything would be different from then on, that their houses would have wider doors, higher ceilings, and stronger floors so that Esteban's memory could go everywhere without bumping into beams and so that no one in the future would dare whisper the big boob finally died, too bad, the handsome fool has finally died, because they were going to paint their house fronts gay colours to make Esteban's memory eternal and they were going to break their backs digging for springs among the stones and planting flowers on the cliffs so that in future years at dawn the passengers on great liners would awaken, suffocated by the smell of gardens on the high seas, and the captain would have to come down from the bridge in his dress uniform, with his astrolabe, his pole star, and his row of war medals and, pointing to the promontory of roses on the horizon, he would say in fourteen languages, look there, where the wind is so peaceful now that it's gone to sleep beneath the beds, over there, where the sun's so bright that the sunflowers don't know which way to turn, yes, over there, that's Esteban's village.

1955
translated by Gregory Rabassa

William Trevor

b. 1928

William Trevor considers himself "a late starter as a writer," having published his first book, the novel *A Standard of Behaviour*, in 1958. Since then about twenty-five books have appeared: novels, plays, and a body of elegantly painful stories that include (so far) the lapidary, excruciating *After Rain* (1996) and *Collected Stories* (2009). For all the critical and popular success of his novels, Trevor describes being exasperated, even horrified, when a story defies his preference for glimpses and omissions and demands expansion into the longer form: "I think of myself as a short story writer who also writes novels." But before he was fully either of these, he was a teacher, an advertising copywriter in London, and for sixteen years a sculptor. Until the late fifties, this protean life reflected his early years as an unhappy part of an unhappy Protestant family in a series of moves from one town in Ireland to another. When his sculpture became too abstract—"Some part of me missed people"—he began honing a narrative form thoroughly hospitable to a sense of missing: people missing their innocence, their moment, their chance at clarity, their very lives. "I believe in not quite knowing," Trevor says. "I write out of curiosity and bewilderment. . . . I am still bewildered about the world." What he returns to are the lacerations caused by deception but also by honesty, a depth of sadness to which he devotes a gracious, highly visual purity of style that is its own sort of resolution and generosity. Born in County Cork, Trevor and his wife, Jane, have lived mainly in Dorset. For him the English are "rather strange people," and he reserves his harshest writing for their urban incarnations.

The Piano Tuner's Wives

Violet married the piano tuner when he was a young man. Belle married him when he was old.

There was a little more to it than that, because in choosing Violet to be his wife the piano tuner had rejected Belle, which was something everyone remembered when the second wedding was announced. "Well, she got the ruins of him anyway," a farmer of the neighbourhood remarked, speaking without vindictiveness, stating a fact as he saw it. Others saw it similarly, though most of them would have put the matter differently.

The piano tuner's hair was white and one of his knees became more arthritic with each damp winter that passed. He had once been svelte but was no longer so, and he was blinder than on the day he married Violet—a Thursday in 1951, June 7th. The shadows he lived among now had less shape and less density than those of 1951.

"I will," he responded in the small Protestant church of St Colman, standing almost exactly as he had stood on that other afternoon. And Belle, in her fifty-ninth year, repeated the words her one-time rival had spoken before this altar also. A decent interval had elapsed; no one in the church considered that the memory of Violet had not been honoured, that her passing had not been distressfully mourned. ". . . and with all my worldly goods I thee endow," the piano tuner stated, while his new wife thought she would like to be standing beside him in white instead of suitable wine-red. She had not attended the first wedding, although she had been invited. She'd kept herself occupied that day, whitewashing the chicken shed, but even so she'd wept. And tears or not, she was more beautiful—and younger by almost five years—than the bride who so vividly occupied her thoughts as she battled with her jealousy. Yet he had preferred Violet—or the prospect of the house that would one day become hers, Belle told herself bitterly in the chicken shed, and the little bit of money there was, an easement in a blind man's existence. How understandable, she was reminded later on, whenever she saw Violet guiding him as they walked, whenever she thought of Violet making everything work for him, giving him a life. Well, so could she have.

As they left the church the music was by Bach, the organ played by someone else today, for usually it was his task. Groups formed in the small graveyard that was scattered around the small grey building, where the piano tuner's father and mother were buried, with ancestors on his father's side from previous generations. There would be tea and a few drinks for any of the wedding guests who cared to make the journey to the house, two miles away, but some said goodbye now, wishing the pair happiness. The piano tuner shook hands that were familiar to him, seeing in his mental eye faces that his first wife had described for him. It was the depth of summer, as in 1951, the sun warm on his forehead and his cheeks, and on his body through the heavy wedding clothes. All his life he had known this graveyard, had first felt the letters on the stones as a child, spelling out to his mother the names of his father's family. He and Violet had not had children themselves, though they'd have liked them. He was her child, it had been said, a statement that was an irritation for Belle whenever she heard it. She would have given him children, of that she felt certain.

"I'm due to visit you next month," the old bridegroom reminded a woman whose hand still lay in his, the owner of a Steinway, the only one among all the pianos he tuned. She played it beautifully. He asked her to whenever he tuned it, assuring her that to hear was fee enough. But she always insisted on paying what was owing.

"Monday the third I think it is."

"Yes, it is, Julia."

She called him Mr Dromgould: he had a way about him that did not encourage familiarity in others. Often when people spoke of him he was referred to as the piano tuner, this reminder of his profession reflecting the respect accorded to the possessor of a gift. Owen Francis Dromgould his full name was.

"Well, we had a good day for it," the new young clergyman of the parish remarked. "They said maybe showers but sure they got it wrong.

"The sky—?"

"Oh, cloudless, Mr Dromgould, cloudless."

"Well, that's nice. And you'll come on over to the house, I hope?"

"He must, of course," Belle pressed, then hurried through the gathering in the graveyard to reiterate the invitation, for she was determined to have a party.

Some time later, when the new marriage had settled into a routine, people wondered if the piano tuner would begin to think about retiring. With a bad knee, and being sightless in old age, he would readily have been forgiven in the houses and the convents and the school halls where he applied his skill. Leisure was his due, the good fortune of company as his years slipped by no more than he deserved. But when, occasionally, this was put to him by the loquacious or the inquisitive he denied that anything of the kind was in his thoughts, that he considered only the visitation of death as bringing any kind of end. The truth was, he would be lost without his work, without his travelling about, his arrival every six months or so in one of the small towns to which he had offered his services for so long. No, no, he promised, they'd still see the white Vauxhall turning in at a farm gate or parked for half an hour in a convent play-yard, or drawn up on a verge while he ate his lunchtime sandwiches, his tea poured out of a Thermos by his wife.

It was Violet who had brought most of this activity about. When they married he was still living with his mother in the gate-lodge of Barnagorm House. He had begun to tune pianos—the two in Barnagorm House, another in the town of Barnagorm, and one in a farmhouse he walked to four miles away. In those days he was a charity because he was blind, was now and again asked to repair the sea-grass seats of stools or chairs, which was an ability he had acquired, or to play at some function or other the violin his mother had bought him in his childhood. But when Violet married him she changed his life. She moved into the gate-lodge, she and his mother not always agreeing but managing to live together none the less. She possessed a car, which meant she could drive him to wherever she discovered a piano, usually long neglected. She drove to houses as far away as forty miles. She fixed his charges, taking the consumption of petrol and wear and tear to the car into account. Efficiently she kept an address book and marked in a diary the date of each next tuning. She recorded a considerable improvement in earnings, and saw that there was more to be made from the playing of the violin than had hitherto been realized: Country-and-Western evenings in lonely public houses, the crossroads platform dances of summer—a practice that in 1951 had not entirely died out. Owen Dromgould delighted in his violin and would play it anywhere, for profit or not. But Violet was keen on the profit.

So the first marriage busily progressed, and when eventually Violet inherited her father's house she took her husband to live there. Once a farmhouse, it was no longer so, the possession of the land that gave it this title having long ago been lost through the fondness for strong drink that for generations had dogged the family but had not reached Violet herself.

"Now, tell me what's there," her husband requested often in their early years, and Violet told him about the house she had brought him to, remotely situated on the edge of the mountains that were blue in certain lights, standing back a bit from a bend in a lane. She described the nooks in the rooms, the wooden window shutters he could hear her pulling over and latching when wind from the east caused a draught that disturbed the fire in the room once called the parlour. She described the pattern of the carpet on the single flight of stairs, the blue-and-white porcelain knobs of the kitchen cupboards, the front door that was never opened. He loved to listen. His mother, who had never entirely come to terms with his affliction, had been impatient. His father, a stableman at Barnagorm House who'd died after a fall, he had never known. "Lean as a greyhound," Violet described his father from a photograph that remained.

She conjured up the big, cold hall of Barnagorm House. "What we walk around on the way to the stairs is a table with a peacock on it. An enormous silvery bird with bits of coloured glass set in the splay of its wings to represent the splendour of the feathers. Greens and blues," she said when he asked the colour, and yes, she was certain it was only glass, not jewels, because once, when he was doing his best with the badly flawed grand in the drawing-room, she had been told that. The stairs were on a curve, he knew from going up and down them so often to the Chappell in the nursery. The first landing was dark as a tunnel, Violet said, with two sofas, one at each end, and rows of unsmiling portraits half lost in the shadows of the walls.

"We're passing Doocey's now," Violet would say. "Father Feely's getting petrol at the pumps." Esso it was at Doocey's, and he knew how the word was written because he'd asked and had been told. Two different colours were employed; the shape of the design had been compared with shapes he could feel. He saw, through Violet's eyes, the gaunt façade of the McKirdys' house on the outskirts of Oghill. He saw the pallid face of the stationer in Kiliath. He saw his mother's eyes closed in death, her hands crossed on her breast. He saw the mountains, blue on some days, misted away to grey on others. "A primrose isn't flamboyant," Violet said. "More like straw or country butter, with a spot of colour in the middle." And he would nod, and know. Soft blue like smoke, she said about the mountains; the spot in the middle more orange than red. He knew no more about smoke than what she had told him also, but he could tell those sounds. He knew what red was, he insisted, because of the sound; orange because you could taste it. He could see red in the Esso sign and the orange spot in the primrose. "Straw" and "country butter" helped him, and when Violet called Mr Whitten gnarled it was enough. A certain Mother Superior was austere. Anna Craigie was fanciful about the eyes. Thomas in the sawmills was a streel. Bat Conlon had the forehead of the Merricks' retriever, which was stroked every time the Merricks' Broadwood was attended to.

Between one woman and the next, the piano tuner had managed without anyone, fetched by the possessors of pianos and driven to their houses, assisted in his shopping and his housekeeping. He felt he had become a nuisance to people, and knew that Violet would not have wanted that. Nor would she have wanted the business she built up for him to be neglected because she was no longer there. She was proud that he played the organ in St Colman's Church. "Don't ever stop doing that," she whispered some time before she whispered her last few words, and so he went alone to the church. It was on a Sunday, when two years almost had passed, that the romance with Belle began.

Since the time of her rejection Belle had been unable to shake off her jealousy, resentful because she had looks and Violet hadn't, bitter because it seemed to her that the punishment of blindness was a punishment for her too. For what else but a punishment could you call the dark the sightless lived in? And what else but a punishment was it that darkness should be thrown over her beauty? Yet there had been no sin to punish and they would have been a handsome couple, she and Owen Dromgould. An act of grace it would have been, her beauty given to a man who did not know that it was there.

It was because her misfortune did not cease to nag at her that Belle remained unmarried. She assisted her father first and then her brother in the family shop, making out tickets for the clocks and watches that were left in for repair, noting the details for the engraving of sports trophies. She served behind the single counter, the Christmas season her busy time, glassware and weather indicators the most popular wedding gifts, cigarette lighters and inexpensive jewellery for lesser occasions. In time, clocks and watches required only the fitting of a battery, and so the gift side of the business was expanded. But while that time passed there was no man in the town who lived up to the one who had been taken from her.

Belle had been born above the shop, and when house and shop became her brother's she continued to live there. Her brother's children were born, but there was still room for her, and her position in the shop itself was not usurped. It was she who kept the chickens at the back, who always had been in charge of them, given the responsibility on her tenth birthday: that, too, continued. That she lived with a disappointment had long ago become part of her, had made her what she was for her nieces and her nephew. It was in her eyes, some people noted, even lent her beauty a quality that enhanced it. When the romance began with the man who had once rejected her, her brother and his wife considered she was making a mistake, but did not say so, only laughingly asked if she intended taking the chickens with her.

That Sunday they stood talking in the graveyard when the handful of other parishioners had gone. "Come and I'll show you the graves," he said, and led the way, knowing exactly where he was going, stepping on to the grass and feeling the first gravestone with his fingers. His grandmother, he said, on his father's side, and for a moment Belle wanted to feel the incised letters herself instead of looking at them. They both knew, as they moved among the graves, that the parishioners who'd gone home were very much aware of the two who had been left behind. On Sundays, ever since Violet's death, he had walked to and from his house, unless it happened to be raining, in which case the man who drove old Mrs Purtill to church took him home also. "Would you like a walk, Belle?" he asked when he had shown her his family graves. She said she would.

Belle didn't take the chickens with her when she became a wife. She said she'd had enough of chickens. Afterwards she regretted that, because every time she did anything in the house that had been Violet's she felt it had been done by Violet before her. When she cut up meat for a stew, standing with the light falling on the board that Violet had used, and on the knife, she felt herself a follower. She diced carrots, hoping that Violet had sliced them. She bought new wooden spoons because Violet's had shrivelled away so. She painted the upright rails of the banisters. She painted the inside of the front door that was never opened. She disposed of the stacks of women's magazines, years old, that she found in an upstairs cupboard. She threw away a frying-pan because she considered it unhygienic. She ordered new vinyl for the kitchen floor. But she kept the flowerbeds at the back weeded in case anyone coming to the house might say she was letting the place become rundown.

There was always this dichotomy: what to keep up, what to change. Was she giving in to Violet when she tended her flowerbeds? Was she giving in to pettiness when she threw away a frying-pan and three wooden spoons? Whatever Belle did she afterwards doubted herself. The dumpy figure of Violet, grey-haired as she had been in the end, her eyes gone small in the plumpness of her face, seemed irritatingly to command. And the unseeing husband they shared, softly playing his violin in one room or another, did not know that his first wife had dressed badly, did not know she had thickened and become sloppy, did not know she had been an unclean cook. That Belle was the one who was alive, that she was offered all a man's affection, that she plundered his other woman's possessions and occupied her bedroom and drove her car, should have been enough. It should have been everything, but as time went on it seemed to Belle to be scarcely anything at all. He had become set in ways that had been allowed and hallowed in a marriage of nearly forty years: that was what was always there.

A year after the wedding, as the couple sat one lunchtime in the car which Belle had drawn into the gateway to a field, he said:

"You'd tell me if it was too much for you?"

"Too much, Owen?"

"Driving all over the country. Having to get me in and out. Having to sit there listening."

"It's not too much."

"You're good the way you've patience."

"I don't think I'm good at all."

"I knew you were in church that Sunday. I could smell the perfume you had on. Even at the organ I could smell it."

"I'll never forget that Sunday."

"I loved you when you let me show you the graves."

"I loved you before that."

"I don't want to tire you out, with all the traipsing about after pianos. I could let it go, you know."

He would do that for her, her thought was as he spoke. He wasn't much for a woman, he had said another time: a blind man moving on towards the end of his days. He confessed that when first he wanted to marry her he hadn't put it to her for more than two months, knowing better than she what she'd be letting herself in for if she said yes. "What's that Belle look like these days?" he had asked Violet a few years ago, and Violet hadn't answered at first. Then apparently she'd said: "Belle still looks a girl."

"I wouldn't want you to stop your work. Not ever, Owen."

"You're all heart, my love. Don't say you're not good."

"It gets me out and about too, you know. More than ever in my life. Down all those avenues to houses I didn't know were there. Towns I've never been to. People I never knew. It was restricted before."

The word slipped out, but it didn't matter. He did not reply that he understood about restriction, for that was not his style. When they were getting to know one another, after that Sunday by the church, he said he'd often thought of her in her brother's jeweller's shop, wrapping up what was purchased there, as she had wrapped for him the watch he bought for one of Violet's birthdays. He'd thought of her putting up the grilles over the windows in the evenings and locking the shop door, and then going upstairs to sit with her brother's family. When they were married she told him more: how most of the days of her life had been spent, only her chickens her own. "Smart in her clothes," Violet had added when she said the woman he'd rejected still looked a girl.

There hadn't been any kind of honeymoon, but a few months after he had wondered if travelling about was too much for her he took Belle away to a seaside resort where he and Violet had many times spent a week. They stayed in the same boarding-house, the Sans Souci, and walked on the long, empty strand and in lanes where larks scuttered in and out of the fuchsia, and on the cliffs. They drank in Malley's public house. They lay in autumn sunshine on the dunes.

"You're good to have thought of it." Belle smiled at him, pleased because he wanted her to be happy.

"Set us up for the winter, Belle."

She knew it wasn't easy for him. They had come to this place because he knew no other; he was aware before they set out of the complication that might develop in his emotions when they arrived. She had seen that in his face, a stoicism that was there for her. Privately, he bore the guilt of betrayal, stirred up by the smell of the sea and seaweed. The voices in the boarding-house were the voices Violet had heard. For Violet, too, the scent of honeysuckle had lingered into October. It was Violet who first said a week in the autumn sun would set them up for winter: that showed in him, also, a moment after he spoke the words.

"I'll tell you what we'll do," he said. "When we're back we'll get you the television, Belle."

"Oh, but you—"

"You'd tell me."

They were walking near the lighthouse on the cape when he said that. He would have offered the television to Violet, but Violet must have said she wouldn't be bothered with the thing. It would never be turned on, she had probably argued; you only got silliness on it anyway.

"You're good to me," Belle said instead.

"Ah no, no."

When they were close enough to the lighthouse he called out and a man called back from a window. "Hold on a minute," the man said, and by the time he opened the door he must have guessed that the wife he'd known had died. "You'll take a drop?" he offered when they were inside, when the death and the remarriage had been mentioned. Whisky was poured, and Belle felt that the three glasses lifted in salutation were an honouring of her, although this was not said. It rained on the way back to the boarding-house, the last evening of the holiday.

"Nice for the winter," he said as she drove the next day through rain that didn't cease. "The television."

When it came, it was installed in the small room that once was called the parlour, next to the kitchen. This was where mostly they sat, where the radio was. A fortnight after the arrival of the television set Belle acquired a small black sheepdog that a farmer didn't want because it was afraid of sheep. This dog became hers and was always called hers. She fed it and looked after it. She got it used to travelling with them in the car. She gave it a new name, Maggie, which it answered to in time.

But even with the dog and the television, with additions and disposals in the house, with being so sincerely assured that she was loved, with being told she was good, nothing changed for Belle. The woman who for so long had taken her husband's arm, who had guided him into rooms of houses where he coaxed pianos back to life, still claimed existence. Not as a tiresome ghost, some unforgiving spectre uncertainly there, but as if some part of her had been left in the man she'd loved.

Sensitive in ways that other people weren't, Owen Dromgould continued to sense his second wife's unease. She knew he did. It was why he had offered to give up his work, why he'd taken her to Violet's seashore and borne there the guilt of his betrayal, why there was a television set now, and a sheepdog. He had guessed why she'd re-covered the kitchen floor. Proudly he had raised his glass to her in the company of a man who had known Violet. Proudly, he had sat with her in the diningroom of the boarding-house and in Malley's public house.

Belle made herself remember all that. She made herself see the bottle of John Jameson taken from the cupboard in the lighthouse, and hear the boardinghouse voices. He understood, he did his best to comfort her; his affection was in everything he did. But Violet would have told him which leaves were on the turn. Violet would have reported that the tide was going out or coming in. Too late Belle realized that. Violet had been his blind man's vision. Violet had left her no room to breathe.

One day, coming away from the house that was the most distant they visited, the first time Belle had been there, he said:

"Did you ever see a room as sombre as that one? Is it the holy pictures that do it?"

Belle backed the car and straightened it, then edged it through a gateway that, thirty years ago, hadn't been made wide enough.

"Sombre?" she said on a lane like a riverbed, steering around the potholes as best she could.

"We used to wonder could it be they didn't want anything colourful in the way of wallpaper in case it wasn't respectful to the pictures."

Belle didn't comment on that. She eased the Vauxhall out onto the tarred road and drove in silence over a stretch of bogland. Vividly she saw the holy pictures in the room where Mrs Grenaghan's piano was: Virgin and Child, Sacred Heart, St Catherine with her lily, the Virgin on her own, Jesus in glory. They hung against nondescript brown; there were statues on the mantelpiece and on a corner shelf. Mrs Grenaghan had brought tea and biscuits to that small, melancholy room, speaking in a hushed tone as if the holiness demanded that.

"What pictures?" Belle asked, not turning her head, although she might have, for there was no other traffic and the bog road was straight.

"Aren't the pictures still in there? Holy pictures all over the place?"

"They must have taken them down."

"What's there then?"

Belle went a little faster. She said a fox had come from nowhere, over to the left. It was standing still, she said, the way foxes do.

"You want to pull up and watch him, Belle?"

"No. No, he's moved on now. Was it Mrs Grenaghan's daughter who played that piano?"

"Oh, it was. And she hasn't seen that girl in years. We used to say the holy pictures maybe drove her away. What's on the walls now?"

"A striped paper." And Belle added: "There's a photograph of the daughter on the mantelpiece."

Some time later, on another day, when he referred to one of the sisters at the convent in Meena as having cheeks as flushed as an eating apple, Belle said that the nun was chalky white these days, her face pulled down and sunken. "She has an illness so," he said.

Suddenly more confident, not caring what people thought, Belle rooted out Violet's plants from the flowerbeds at the back, and grassed the flowerbeds over. She told her husband of a change at Doocey's garage: Texaco sold instead of Esso. She described the Texaco logo, the big red star and how the letters of the word were arranged. She avoided stopping at Doocey's in case a conversation took place there, in case Doocey were asked if Esso had let him down, or what. "Well, no, I wouldn't call it silvery exactly," Belle said about the peacock in the hall of Barnagorm house. "If they cleaned it up I'd say it's brass underneath." Upstairs, the sofas at each end of the landing had new loose covers, bunches of different-coloured chrysanthemums on them. "Well no, not *lean*, I wouldn't call him that," Belle said with the photograph of her husband's father in her hand. "A sturdy face, I'd say." A schoolteacher whose teeth were once described as gusty had false teeth now, less of a mouthful, her smile sedate. Time had apparently drenched the bright white of the McKirdys' façade, almost a grey you'd call it. "Forget-me-not blue," Belle said one day, speaking of the mountains that were blue when the weather brought that colour out. "You'd hardly credit it." And it was never again said in the piano tuner's house that the blue of the mountains was the subtle blue of smoke.

Owen Dromgould had run his fingers over the bark of trees. He could tell the difference in the outline of their leaves; he could tell the thorns of gorse and bramble. He knew birds from their song, dogs from their bark, cats from the touch of them on his legs. There were the letters on the gravestones, the stops of the organ, his violin. He could see red, berries on holly and cotoneaster. He could smell lavender and thyme.

All that could not be taken from him. And it didn't matter if, overnight, the colour had worn off the kitchen knobs. It didn't matter if the china light-shade in the kitchen had a crack he hadn't heard about before. What mattered was damage done to something as fragile as a dream.

The wife he had first chosen had dressed drably: from silence and inflexions—more than from words—he learned that now. Her grey hair straggled to her shoulders, her back was a little humped. He poked his way about, and they were two old people when they went out on their rounds, older than they were in their ageless happiness. She wouldn't have hurt a fly, she wasn't a person you could be jealous of, yet of course it was hard on a new wife to be haunted by happiness, to be challenged by the simplicities there had been. He had given himself to two women; he hadn't withdrawn himself from the first, he didn't from the second.

Each house that contained a piano brought forth its contradictions. The pearls old Mrs Purtill wore were opals, the pallid skin of the stationer in Kiliath was freckled, the two lines of oaks above Oghill were surely beeches? "Of course, of course," Owen Dromgould agreed, since it was fair that he should do so. Belle could not be blamed for making her claim, and claims could not be made without damage or destruction. Belle would win in the end because the living always do. And that seemed fair also, since Violet had won in the beginning and had had the better years.

1997

Chinua Achebe

1930–2013

For Africans everywhere in the world, Achebe, in his passion and power, is akin to Mandela. Achebe is also one of those rare writers (Harriet Beecher Stowe, George

Orwell) who have had a direct, even verifiable, effect on prevailing attitudes, an effect not only undermining but also creative. Appalled at the abstract, proprietary, and colonially shaded representations of Africans in far too many Western novels, Achebe wrote his first novel, *Things Fall Apart* (1958), which "pioneered the fusion of Ibo folklore and idioms with the Western novel" (Maya Jaggi). Translated into a least fifty languages, celebrated on its fiftieth anniversary, the novel is at the heart of the many meanings of African—and beyond that, racial—liberation. But Achebe also became a renowned and fearsome polemicist. In his 1975 lecture at the University of Massachusetts, Amherst, he took on received opinion about a cornerstone of the modernist canon, Conrad's *Heart of Darkness*. He argued famously, then and now, that Conrad's creation of black stagehands, "clapping" their "hands" and "stamping" their "feet" [Conrad's words] around the pulsing "heart of darkness" negates the book's stature as "a great work of art." Along with vexing prevailing readerly perceptions of Conrad, the lecture also put the critical community in the direction of grappling with the strong current of attraction among modernists to the primal elements of immediate life as well as history. Achebe went on to write voluminously in a variety of genres, notably the tetralogy that includes *Arrow of God* (1964) and the short story collections, *The Sacrificial Egg and Other Stories* (1962) and *Girls at War* (1972). "Civil Peace," from the latter collection, draws on his love for Ibo oral traditions and revulsion at tribal violence. Born in eastern Nigeria, he worked in the Nigerian Broadcasting Corporation. During the Civil War, he served in the Biafran government. With the disastrous collapse of the Biafran attempt at independence, he began a distinguished career in teaching that initially alternated between positions in the United States and Nigeria. But after a terrible car accident near Lagos which paralyzed him, Achebe remained permanently in America. He taught for fifteen years at Bard College, then relocated to Brown University. He died in Boston. Six years prior to his death, Achebe was awarded the Man Booker International Prize.

Civil Peace

Jonathan Iwegbu counted himself extraordinarily lucky. "Happy survival!" meant so much more to him than just a current fashion of greeting old friends in the first hazy days of peace. It went deep to his heart. He had come out of the war with five inestimable blessings—his head, his wife Maria's head, and the heads of three out of their four children. As a bonus he also had his old bicycle—a miracle too but naturally not to be compared to the safety of five human heads.

The bicycle had a little history of its own. One day at the height of the war it was commandeered "for urgent military action." Hard as its loss would have been to him he would still have let it go without a thought had he not had some doubts about the genuineness of the officer. It wasn't his disreputable rags, nor the toes peeping out of one blue and one brown canvas shoes, nor yet the two stars of his rank done obviously in a hurry in biro, that troubled Jonathan; many good and heroic soldiers looked the same or worse. It was rather a certain lack of grip and firmness in his manner. So Jonathan, suspecting he might be amenable to influence, rummaged in his raffia bag and produced the two pounds with which he had been going to buy firewood which his wife, Maria, retailed to camp officials for extra stock-fish and corn meal, and got his bicycle back. That night he buried it in the little clearing in the bush where the dead of the camp, including his own youngest son, were buried. When he dug it up again a year later after the surrender all it needed was a little palm-oil greasing. "Nothing puzzles God," he said in wonder.

He put it to immediate use as a taxi and accumulated a small pile of Biafran money ferrying camp officials and their families across the four-mile stretch to the nearest tarred road. His standard charge per trip was six pounds and those who had the money were only glad to be rid of some of it in this way. At the end of a fortnight he had made a small fortune of one hundred and fifteen pounds.

Then he made the journey to Enugu and found another miracle waiting for him. It was unbelievable. He rubbed his eyes and looked again and it was still standing there before him. But, needless to say, even that monumental blessing must be accounted also totally inferior to the five heads in the family. This newest miracle was his little house in Ogui Overside. Indeed nothing puzzles God! Only two houses away a huge concrete edifice some wealthy contractor had put up just before the war was a mountain of rubble. And here was Jonathan's little zinc house of no regrets built with mud blocks quite intact! Of course the doors and windows were missing and five sheets off the roof. But what was that? And anyhow he had returned to Enugu early enough to pick up bits of old zinc and wood and soggy sheets of cardboard lying around the neighbourhood before thousands more came out of their forest holes looking for the same things. He got a destitute carpenter with one old hammer, a blunt plane, and a few bent and rusty nails in his tool bag to turn this assortment of wood, paper, and metal into door and window shutters for five Nigerian shillings or fifty Biafran pounds. He paid the pounds, and moved in with his overjoyed family carrying five heads on their shoulders.

His children picked mangoes near the military cemetery and sold them to soldiers' wives for a few pennies—real pennies this time—and his wife started making breakfast akara balls for neighbours in a hurry to start life again. With his family earnings he took his bicycle to the villages around and bought fresh palm-wine which he mixed generously in his rooms with the water which had recently started running again in the public tap down the road, and opened up a bar for soldiers and other lucky people with good money.

At first he went daily, then every other day, and finally once a week, to the offices of the Coal Corporation where he used to be a miner, to find out what was what. The only thing he did find out in the end was that that little house of his was even a greater blessing than he had thought. Some of his fellow ex-miners who had nowhere to return at the end of the day's waiting just slept outside the doors of the offices and cooked what meal they could scrounge together in Bournvita tins. As the weeks lengthened and still nobody could say what was what Jonathan discontinued his weekly visits altogether and faced his palm-wine bar.

But nothing puzzles God. Came the day of the windfall when after five days of endless scuffles in queues and counter-queues in the sun outside the Treasury he had twenty pounds counted into his palms as ex-gratia award for the rebel money he had turned in. It was like Christmas for him and for many others like him when the payments began. They called it (since few could manage its proper official name) *egg-rasher*.

As soon as the pound notes were placed in his palm Jonathan simply closed it tight over them and buried fist and money inside his trouser pocket. He had to be extra careful because he had seen a man a couple of days earlier collapse into near-madness in an instant before that oceanic crowd because no sooner had he got his twenty pounds than some heartless ruffian picked it off him. Though it was not right that a man in such an extremity of agony should be blamed yet many in the queues that day were able to remark quietly on the victim's carelessness, especially after he pulled out the innards of his pocket and revealed a hole in it big enough to pass a thief's head. But of course he had insisted that the money had been in the other pocket, pulling it out too to show its comparative wholeness. So one had to be careful.

Jonathan soon transferred the money to his left hand and pocket so as to leave his right free for shaking hands should the need arise, though by fixing his gaze at such an elevation as to miss all approaching human faces he made sure that the need did not arise, until he got home.

He was normally a heavy sleeper but that night he heard all the neighbourhood noises die down one after another. Even the night watchman who knocked the hour on some metal somewhere in the distance had fallen silent after knocking one o'clock. That must have been the last thought in Jonathan's mind before he was finally carried away himself. He couldn't have been gone for long, though, when he was violently awakened again.

"Who is knocking?" whispered his wife lying beside him on the floor.

"I don't know," he whispered back breathlessly.

The second time the knocking came it was so loud and imperious that the rickety old door could have fallen down.

"Who is knocking?" he asked then, his voice parched and trembling.

"Na tief-man and him people," came the cool reply. "Make you hopen de door." This was followed by the heaviest knocking of all.

Maria was the first to raise the alarm, then he followed and all their children.

"Police-o! Thieves-o! Neighbours-o! Police-o! We are lost! We are dead! Neighbours, are you asleep? Wake up! Police-o!"

This went on for a long time and then stopped suddenly. Perhaps they had scared the thief away. There was total silence. But only for a short while.

"You done finish?" asked the voice outside. "Make we help you small. Oya, everybody!"

"Police-o! Thief-man-o! Neighbours-o! we done loss-o! Police-o! . . ."

There were at least five other voices besides the leader's.

Jonathan and his family were now completely paralysed by terror. Maria and the children sobbed inaudibly like lost souls. Jonathan groaned continuously.

The silence that followed the thieves' alarm vibrated horribly. Jonathan all but begged their leader to speak again and be done with it.

"My frien," said he at long last, "we don try our best for call dem but I tink say dem all done sleep-o . . . So wetin we go do now? Sometaim you wan call soja? Or you wan make we call dem for you? Soja better pass police. No be so?"

"Na so!" replied his men. Jonathan thought he heard even more voices now than before and groaned heavily. His legs were sagging under him and his throat felt like sandpaper.

"My frien, why you no de talk again. I de ask you say you wan make we call soja?"

"No."

"Awrighto. Now make we talk business. We no be bad tief. We no like for make trouble. Trouble done finish. War done finish and all the katakata wey de for inside. No Civil War again. This time na Civil Peace. No be so?"

"Na so!" answered the horrible chorus.

"What do you want from me? I am a poor man. Everything I had went with this war. Why do you come to me? You know people who have money. We . . ."

"Awright! We know say you no get plenty money. But we sef no get even anini. So derefore make you open dis window and give us one hundred pound and we go commot. Orderwise we de come for inside now to show you guitar-boy like dis . . ."

A volley of automatic fire rang through the sky. Maria and the children began to weep aloud again.

"Ah, missisi de cry again. No need for dat. We done talk say we na good tief. We just take our small money and go nwayorly. No molest. Abi we de molest?"

"At all!" sang the chorus.

"My friends," began Jonathan hoarsely. "I hear what you say and I thank you. If I had one hundred pounds . . ."

"Lookia my frien, no be play we come play for your house. If we make mistake and step for inside you no go like am-o. So derefore . . ."

"To God who made me; if you come inside and find one hundred pounds, take it and shoot me and shoot my wife and children. I swear to God. The only money I have in this life is this twenty pounds *egg-rasher* they gave me today . . ."

"OK. Time de go. Make you open dis window and bring the twenty pound. We go manage am like dat."

There were now loud murmurs of dissent among the chorus: "Na lie de man de lie; e get plenty money . . . Make we go inside and search properly well . . . Wetin be twenty pound? . . ."

"Shurrup!" rang the leader's voice like a lone shot in the sky and silenced the murmuring at once. "Are you dere? Bring the money quick!"

"I am coming," said Jonathan fumbling in the darkness with the key of the small wooden box he kept by his side on the mat.

At the first sign of light as neighbours and others assembled to commiserate with him he was already strapping his five-gallon demijohn to his bicycle carrier and his wife, sweating in the open fire, was turning over akara balls in a wide clay bowl of boiling oil. In the comer his eldest son was rinsing out dregs of yesterday's palm-wine from old beer bottles.

"I count it as nothing," he told his sympathizers, his eyes on the rope he was tying. "What is *egg-rasher*? Did I depend on it last week? Or is it greater than other things that went with the war? I say, let *egg-rasher* perish in the flames! Let it go where everything else has gone. Nothing puzzles God."

1971

Toni Morrison

b. 1931

Toni Morrison was born Chloe Anthony Wofford in Lorain, Ohio. Her parents had moved from the South to escape racism, but Lorain was not a refuge from racist discrimination—when Toni was a child the family's house was set on fire by their landlord to encourage them to leave. She graduated from Lorain high school in 1949 and went on to get her BA from Howard University in 1953 and her MA from Cornell University in 1955. She taught at Texas Southern University and Howard University from 1955 to 1964, and then worked as an editor at Random House from 1965 to 1984, acting as mentor to many young African-American writers, such as Gayl Jones and Toni Cade Bambara. During this time she also worked on her own writing; her first novel, *The Bluest Eye* (1970), established her reputation as an important American writer, while her next novels, *Sula* (1973) and *Song of Solomon* (1977), were critical and commercial successes. Many of her novels are based on real stories of Black experience in the United States. For instance, *Beloved* (1987), which won the Pulitzer Prize, was influenced by accounts of Margaret Garner, a nineteenth-century slave who fled the South with her children and who, when threatened with recapture, tried to kill her children rather than return them to slavery. But though they record the tragic history and troubling persistence of racism in America, the novels remain profoundly affirmative. Morrison combines many traditions in her writing, including African-American oral tradition, magic realism, folklore, and myth. In addition to her fiction, she has published non-fiction, including *Playing in the Dark: Whiteness and the Literary Imagination* (1992), a collection of essays that examine the role race assumes in the reader/writer relationship. In 1993 she was awarded the Nobel Prize for Literature. She has been Robert F. Goheen Professor of the Humanities at Princeton University and in 2012 was awaded the Presidential Medal of Freedom. Among her recent works are the novels, *A Mercy* (2008) and *Home* (2012).

Recitatif

My mother danced all night and Roberta's was sick. That's why we were taken to St Bonny's. People want to put their arms around you when you tell them you were in a shelter, but it really wasn't bad. No big long room with one hundred beds like Bellevue. There were four to a room, and when Roberta and me came, there was a shortage of state kids, so we were the only ones assigned to 406 and could go from bed to bed if we wanted to. And we wanted to, too. We changed beds every night and for the whole four months we were there we never picked one out as our own permanent bed.

It didn't start out that way. The minute I walked in and the Big Bozo introduced us, I got sick to my stomach. It was one thing to be taken out of your own bed early in the morning—it was something else to be stuck in a strange place with a girl from a whole other race. And Mary, that's my mother, she was right. Every now and then she would stop dancing long enough to tell me something important and one of the things she said was that they never washed their hair and they smelled funny. Roberta sure did. Smell funny, I mean. So when the Big Bozo (nobody ever called her Mrs Itkin, just like nobody ever said St Bonaventure)—when she said, "Twyla, this is Roberta. Roberta, this is Twyla. Make each other welcome," I said, "My mother won't like you putting me in here."

"Good," said Bozo. "Maybe then she'll come and take you home."

How's that for mean? If Roberta had laughed I would have killed her, but she didn't. She just walked over to the window and stood with her back to us.

"Turn around," said the Bozo. "Don't be rude. Now Twyla. Roberta. When you hear a loud buzzer, that's the call for dinner. Come down to the first floor. Any fights and no movie." And then, just to make sure we knew what we would be missing, "*The Wizard of Oz*."

Roberta must have thought I meant that my mother would be mad about my being put in the shelter. Not about rooming with her, because as soon as Bozo left she came over to me and said, "Is your mother sick too?"

"No," I said. "She just likes to dance all night."

"Oh." She nodded her head and I liked the way she understood things so fast. So for the moment it didn't matter that we looked like salt and pepper standing there and that's what the other kids called us sometimes. We were eight years old and got F's all the time. Me because I couldn't remember what I read or what the teacher said. And Roberta because she couldn't read at all and didn't even listen to the teacher. She wasn't good at anything except jacks, at which she was a killer: pow scoop pow scoop pow scoop.

We didn't like each other all that much at first, but nobody else wanted to play with us because we weren't real orphans with beautiful dead parents in the sky. We were dumped. Even the New York City Puerto Ricans and the upstate Indians ignored us. All kinds of kids were in there, black ones, white ones, even two Koreans. The food was good, though. At least I thought so. Roberta hated it and left whole pieces of things on her plate: Spam, Salisbury steak—even Jell-O with fruit cocktail in it, and she didn't care if I ate what she wouldn't. Mary's idea of supper was popcorn and a can of Yoo-Hoo. Hot mashed potatoes and two weenies was like Thanksgiving for me.

It really wasn't bad, St Bonny's. The big girls on the second floor pushed us around now and then. But that was all. They wore lipstick and eyebrow pencil and wobbled their knees while they watched TV. Fifteen, sixteen, even, some of them were. They were put-out girls, scared runaways most of them. Poor little girls who fought their uncles off but looked tough to us, and mean. God, did they look mean. The staff tried to keep them separate from the younger children, but sometimes they caught us watching them in the orchard where they played radios and danced with each other. They'd light out after us and pull our hair or twist our arms. We were scared of them, Roberta and me, but neither of us wanted the other one to know it. So we got a good list of dirty names we could shout back when we ran from them through the orchard. I used to dream a lot and almost always the orchard was there. Two acres, four maybe, of these little apple trees. Hundreds of them. Empty and crooked like beggar women when I first came to St Bonny's but fat with flowers when I left. I don't know why I dreamt about that orchard so much. Nothing really happened there. Nothing all that important, I mean. Just the big girls dancing and playing the radio. Roberta and me watching. Maggie fell down there once. The kitchen woman with legs like parentheses. And the big girls laughed at her. We should have helped her up, I know, but we were scared of those girls with lipstick and eyebrow pencil. Maggie couldn't talk. The kids said she had her tongue cut out, but I think she was just born that way: mute. She was old and sandy-coloured and she worked in the kitchen. I don't know if she was nice or not. I just remember her legs like parentheses and how she rocked when she walked. She worked from early in the morning till two o'clock, and if she was late, if she had too much cleaning and didn't get out till two-fifteen or so, she'd cut through the orchard so she wouldn't miss her bus and have to wait another hour. She wore this really stupid little hat—a kid's hat with ear flaps—and she wasn't much taller than we were. A really awful little hat. Even for a mute, it was dumb—dressing like a kid and never saying anything at all.

"But what about if somebody tries to kill her?" I used to wonder about that. "Or what if she wants to cry? Can she cry?"

"Sure," Roberta said. "But just tears. No sounds come out."

"She can't scream?"

"Nope. Nothing."

"Can she hear?"

"I guess."

"Let's call her," I said. And we did.

"Dummy! Dummy!" She never turned her head.

"Bow legs! Bow legs!" Nothing. She just rocked on, the chin straps of her baby-boy hat swaying from side to side. I think we were wrong. I think she could hear and didn't let on. And it shames me even now to think there was somebody in there after all who heard us call her those names and couldn't tell on us.

We got along all right, Roberta and me. Changed beds every night, got F's in civics and communication skills and gym. The Bozo was disappointed in us, she said. Out of 130 of us state cases, 90 were under twelve. Almost all were real orphans with beautiful dead parents in the sky. We were the only ones dumped and the only ones with F's in three classes including gym. So we got along—what with her leaving whole pieces of things on her plate and being nice about not asking questions.

I think it was the day before Maggie fell down that we found out our mothers were coming to visit us on the same Sunday. We had been at the shelter twenty-eight days (Roberta twenty-eight and a half) and this was their first visit with us. Our mothers would come at ten o'clock in time for chapel, then lunch with us in the teachers' lounge. I thought if my dancing mother met her sick mother it might be good for her. And Roberta thought her sick mother would get a big bang out of a dancing one. We got excited about it and curled each other's hair. After breakfast we sat on the bed watching the road from the window. Roberta's socks were still wet. She washed them the night before and put them on the radiator to dry. They hadn't, but she put them on anyway because their tops were so pretty—scalloped in pink. Each of us had a purple construction-paper basket that we had made in craft class. Mine had a yellow crayon rabbit on it. Roberta's had eggs with wiggly lines of colour. Inside were cellophane grass and just the jelly beans because I'd eaten the two marshmallow eggs they gave us. The Bog Bozo came herself to get us. Smiling she told us we looked very nice and to come downstairs. We were so surprised by the smile we'd never seen before, neither of us moved.

"Don't you want to see your mommies?"

I stood up first and spilled the jelly beans all over the floor. Bozo's smile disappeared while we scrambled to get the candy up off the floor and put it back in the grass.

She escorted us downstairs to the first floor, where the other girls were lining up to file into the chapel. A bunch of grown-ups stood to one side. Viewers mostly. The old biddies who wanted servants and the fags who wanted company looking for children they might want to adopt. Once in a while a grandmother. Almost never anybody young or anybody whose face wouldn't scare you in the night. Because if any of the real orphans had young relatives they wouldn't be orphans. I saw Mary right away. She had on those green slacks I hated and hated even more now because didn't she know we were going to chapel? And that fur jacket with the pocket linings so ripped she had to pull to get her hands out of them. But her face was pretty—like always—and she smiled and waved like she was the little girl looking for her mother, not me.

I walked slowly, trying not to drop the jelly beans and hoping the paper handle would hold. I had to use my last Chiclet because by the time I finished cutting everything out, all the Elmer's was gone. I am left-handed and the scissors never worked for me. It didn't matter, though; I might just as well have chewed the gum. Mary dropped to her knees and grabbed me, mashing the basket, the jelly beans, and the grass into her ratty fur jacket.

"Twyla, baby. Twyla, baby!"

I could have killed her. Already I heard the big girls in the orchard the next time saying, "Twyyyyyla, baby!" But I couldn't stay mad at Mary while she was smiling and hugging me and smelling of Lady Esther dusting powder. I wanted to stay buried in her fur all day.

To tell the truth I forgot about Roberta. Mary and I got in line for the traipse into chapel and I was feeling proud because she looked so beautiful even in those ugly green slacks that made her behind stick out. A pretty mother on earth is better than a beautiful dead one in the sky even if she did leave you alone to go dancing.

I felt a tap on my shoulder, turned, and saw Roberta smiling. I smiled back, but not too much lest somebody think this visit was the biggest thing that ever happened in my life. Then Roberta said, "Mother, I want you to meet my roommate, Twyla. And that's Twyla's mother."

I looked up it seemed for miles. She was big. Bigger than any man and on her chest was the biggest cross I'd ever seen. I swear it was six inches long each way. And in the crook of her arm was the biggest Bible ever made.

Mary, simpleminded as ever, grinned and tried to yank her hand out of the pocket with the raggedy lining—to shake hands, I guess. Roberta's mother looked down at me and then looked down at Mary too. She didn't say anything, just grabbed Roberta with her Bible-free hand and stepped out of line, walking quickly to the rear of it. Mary was still grinning because she's not too swift when it comes to what's really going on. Then this light bulb goes off in her head and she says "That bitch!" really loud and us almost in the chapel now. Organ music whining; the Bonny Angels singing sweetly. Everybody in the world turned around to look. And Mary would have kept it up—kept calling her names if I hadn't squeezed her hands as hard as I could. That helped a little, but she still twitched and crossed and uncrossed her legs all through service. Even groaned a couple of times. Why did I think she would come there and act right? Slacks. No hat like the grandmothers and viewers, and groaning all the while. When we stood for hymns she kept her mouth shut. Wouldn't even look at the words on the page. She actually reached in her purse for a mirror to check her lipstick. All I could think of was that she really needed to be killed. The sermon lasted a year, and I knew the real orphans were looking smug again.

We were supposed to have lunch in the teachers' lounge, but Mary didn't bring anything, so we picked fur and cellophane grass off the mashed jelly beans and ate them. I could have killed her. I sneaked a look at Roberta. Her mother had brought chicken legs and ham sandwiches and oranges and a whole box of chocolate-covered grahams. Roberta drank milk from a thermos while her mother read the Bible to her.

Things are not right. The wrong food is always with the wrong people. Maybe that's why I got into waitress work later—to match up the right people with the right food. Roberta just let those chicken legs sit there, but she did bring a stack of grahams up to me later when the visit was over. I think she was sorry that her mother would not shake my mother's hand. And I liked that and I liked the fact that she didn't say a word about Mary groaning all the way through the service and not bringing any lunch.

Roberta left in May when the apple trees were heavy and white. On her last day we went to the orchard to watch the big girls smoke and dance by the radio. It didn't matter that they said, "Twyyyyyla, baby." We sat on the ground and breathed. Lady Esther. Apple blossoms. I still go soft when I smell one or the other. Roberta was going home. The big cross and the big Bible was coming to get her and she seemed sort of glad and sort of not. I thought I would die in that room of four beds without her and I knew Bozo had plans to move some other dumped kid in there with me. Roberta promised to write every day, which was really sweet of her because she couldn't read a lick so how could she write anybody? I would have drawn pictures and sent them to her but she never gave me her address. Little by little she faded. Her wet socks with the pink scalloped tops and her big serious-looking eyes—that's all I could catch when I tried to bring her to mind.

I was working behind the counter at the Howard Johnson's on the Thruway just before the Kingston exit. Not a bad job. Kind of a long ride from Newburgh, but okay once I got there. Mine was the second night shift, eleven to seven. Very light until a Greyhound checked in for breakfast around six-thirty. At that hour the sun was all the way clear of the hills behind the restaurant. The place looked better at night—more like shelter—but I loved it when the sun broke in, even if it did show all the cracks in the vinyl and the speckled floor looked dirty no matter what the mop boy did.

It was August and a bus crowd was just unloading. They would stand around a long while: going to the john, and looking at gifts and junk-for-sale machines, reluctant to sit down so soon. Even to eat. I was trying to fill the coffeepots and get them all situated on the electric burners when I saw her. She was sitting in a booth smoking a cigarette with two guys smothered in head and facial hair. Her own hair was so big and wild I could hardly see her face. But the eyes. I would know them anywhere. She had on a powder-blue halter and shorts outfit and earrings the size of bracelets. Talk about lipstick and eyebrow pencil. She made the big girls look like nuns. I couldn't get off the counter until seven o'clock, but I kept watching the booth in case they got up to leave before that. My replacement was on time for a change, so I counted and stacked my receipts as fast as I could and signed off. I walked over to the booth, smiling and wondering if she would remember me. Or even if she wanted to remember me. Maybe she didn't want to be reminded of St Bonny's or to have anybody know she was ever there. I know I never talked about it to anybody.

I put my hands in my apron pockets and leaned against the back of the booth facing them.

"Roberta? Roberta Fisk?"

She looked up. "Yeah?"

"Twyla."

She squinted for a second and then said, "Wow."

"Remember me?"

"Sure. Hey. Wow."

"It's been a while," I said, and gave a smile to the two hairy guys.

"Yeah. Wow. You work here?"

"Yeah," I said. "I live in Newburgh."

"Newburgh? No kidding?" She laughed then, a private laugh that included guys but only the guys, and they laughed with her. What could I do but laugh too and wonder why I was standing there with my knees showing out from that uniform. Without looking I could see the blue-and-white triangle on my head, my hair shapeless in a net, my ankles thick in white oxfords. Nothing could have been less sheer than my stockings. There was this silence that came down right after I laughed. A silence it was her turn to fill up. With introductions, maybe, to her boyfriends or an invitation to sit down and have a Coke. Instead she lit a cigarette off the one she'd just finished and said, "We're on our way to the Coast. He's got an appointment with Hendrix." She gestured casually toward the boy next to her.

"Hendrix? Fantastic," I said. "Really fantastic. What's she doing now?"

Roberta coughed on her cigarette and the two guys rolled their eyes up at the ceiling.

"Hendrix. Jimi Hendrix, asshole. He's only the biggest—Oh, wow. Forget it."

I was dismissed without anyone saying good-bye, so I thought I would do it for her.

"How's your mother?" I asked. Her grin cracked her whole face. She swallowed. "Fine," she said. "How's yours?"

"Pretty as a picture," I said and turned away. The backs of my knees were damp. Howard Johnson's really was a dump in the sunlight.

James is as comfortable as a house slipper. He liked my cooking and I liked his big loud family. They have lived in Newburgh all of their lives and talk about it the way people do who have always known a home. His grandmother has a porch swing older than his father and when they talk about streets and avenues and buildings they call them names they no longer have. They still call the A&P Rico's because it stands on property once a mom-and-pop store owned by Mr Rico. And they call the new community college Town Hall because it once was. My mother-in-law puts up jelly and cucumbers and buys butter wrapped in cloth from a dairy. James and his father talk about fishing and baseball and I can see them all together on the Hudson in a raggedy skiff. Half the population of Newburgh is on welfare now, but to my husband's family it was still some upstate paradise of a time long past. A time of ice houses and vegetable wagons, coal furnaces and children weeding gardens. When our son was born my mother-in-law gave me the crib blanket that had been hers.

But the town they remembered had changed. Something quick was in the air. Magnificent old houses, so ruined they had become shelter for squatters and rent risks, were bought and renovated. Smart IBM people moved out of their suburbs back into the city and put shutters up and herb gardens in their backyards. A brochure came in the mail announcing the opening of a Food Emporium. Gourmet food, it said—and listed items the rich IBM crowd would want. It was located in a new mall at the edge of town and I drove out to shop there one day—just to see. It was late in June. After the tulips were gone and the Queen Elizabeth roses were open everywhere. I trailed my cart along the aisle tossing in smoked oysters and Robert's sauce and things I knew would sit in my cupboard for years. Only when I found some Klondike ice cream bars did I feel less guilty about spending James's fireman's salary so foolishly. My father-in-law ate them with the same gusto little Joseph did.

Waiting in the checkout line I heard a voice say, "Twyla!"

The classical music piped over the aisles had affected me and the woman leaning toward me was dressed to kill. Diamonds on her hand, a smart white summer dress. "I'm Mrs Benson," I said.

"Ho. Ho. The Big Bozo," she sang.

For a split second I didn't know what she was talking about. She had a bunch of asparagus and two cartons of fancy water.

"Roberta!"

"Right."

"For heaven's sake. Roberta."

"You look great," she said.

"So do you. Where are you? Here? In Newburgh?"

"Yes. Over in Annandale."

I was opening my mouth to say more when the cashier called my attention to her empty counter.

"Meet you outside." Roberta pointed her finger and went into the express line.

I placed the groceries and kept myself from glancing around to check Roberta's progress. I remembered Howard Johnson's and looking for a chance to speak only to be greeted with a stingy "wow." But she was waiting for me and her huge hair was sleek now, smooth around a small, nicely shaped head. Shoes, dress, everything lovely and summery and rich. I was dying to know what happened to her, how she got from Jimi Hendrix to Annandale, a neighbourhood full of doctors and IBM executives. Easy, I thought. Everything is so easy for them. They think they own the world.

"How long," I asked her. "How long have you been here?"

"A year. I got married to a man who lives here. And you, you're married too, right? Benson, you said."

"Yeah. James Benson."

"And is he nice?"

"Oh, is he nice?"

"Well, is he?" Roberta's eyes were steady as though she really meant the question and wanted an answer.

"He's wonderful, Roberta. Wonderful."

"So you're happy."

"Very."

"That's good," she said and nodded her head. "I always hoped you'd be happy. Any kids? I know you have kids."

"One. A boy. How about you?"

"Four."

"Four?"

She laughed. "Stepkids. He's a widower."

"Oh."

"Got a minute? Let's have a coffee."

I thought about the Klondikes melting and the inconvenience of going all the way to my car and putting the bags in the trunk. Served me right for buying all that stuff I didn't need. Roberta was ahead of me.

"Put them in my car. It's right here."

And then I saw the dark blue limousine.

"You married a Chinaman?"

"No." She laughed. "He's the driver."

"Oh, my. If the Big Bozo could see you now."

We both giggled. Really giggled. Suddenly, in just a pulse beat, twenty years disappeared and all of it came rushing back. The big girls (whom we called gar girls—Roberta's misheard word for the evil stone faces described in a civics class) there dancing in the orchard, the ploppy mashed potatoes, the double weenies, the Spam with pineapple. We went into the coffee shop holding on to one another and I tried to think why we were glad to see each other this time and not before. Once, twelve years ago, we passed like strangers. A black girl and a white girl meeting in a Howard Johnson's on the road and having nothing to say. One in a blue-and-white triangle waitress hat, the other on her way to see Hendrix. Now we were behaving like sisters separated for much too long. Those four short months were nothing in time. Maybe it was the thing itself. Just being there, together. Two little girls who knew what nobody else in the world knew—how not to ask questions. How to believe what had to be believed. There was politeness in that reluctance and generosity as well. Is your mother sick too? No, she dances all night. Oh—and an understanding nod.

We sat in a booth by the window and fell into recollection like veterans.

"Did you ever learn to read?"

"Watch." She picked up the menu. "Special of the day. Cream of corn soup. Entrees. Two dots and a wriggly line. Quiche. Chef salad, scallops . . ."

I was laughing and applauding when the waitress came up.

"Remember the Easter baskets?"

"And how we tried to *introduce* them?"

"Your mother with that cross like two telephone poles."

"And yours with those tight slacks."

We laughed so loudly heads turned and made the laughter hard to suppress.

"What happened to the Jimi Hendrix date?"

Roberta made a blow-out sound with her lips.

"When he died I thought about you."

"Oh, you heard about him finally?"

"Finally. Come on, I was a small-town country waitress."

"And I was a small-town country dropout. God, were we wild. I still don't know how I got out of there alive."

"But you did."

"I did. I really did. Now I'm Mrs Kenneth Norton."

"Sounds like a mouthful."

"It is."

"Servants and all?"

Roberta held up two fingers.

"Ow! What does he do?"

"Computers and stuff. What do I know?"

"I don't remember a hell of a lot from those days, but Lord, St Bonny's is as clear as daylight. Remember Maggie? The day she fell down and those gar girls laughed at her?"

Roberta looked up from her salad and stared at me. "Maggie didn't fall," she said.

"Yes, she did. You remember."

"No, Twyla. They knocked her down. Those girls pushed her down and tore her clothes. In the orchard."

"I don't—that's not what happened."

"Sure it is. In the orchard. Remember how scared we were?"

"Wait a minute. I don't remember any of that."

"And Bozo was fired."

"You're crazy. She was there when I left. You left before me."

"I went back. You weren't there when they fired Bozo."

"What?"

"Twice. Once for a year when I was about ten, another for two months when I was fourteen. That's when I ran away."

"You ran away from St Bonny's?"

"I had to. What do you want? Me dancing in that orchard?"

"Are you sure about Maggie?"

"Of course I'm sure. You've blocked it, Twyla. It happened. Those girls had behaviour problems, you know."

"Didn't they, though. But why can't I remember the Maggie thing?"

"Believe me. It happened. And we were there."

"Who did you room with when you went back?" I asked her as if I would know her. The Maggie thing was troubling me.

"Creeps. They tickled themselves in the night."

My ears were itching and I wanted to go home suddenly. This was all very well but she couldn't just comb her hair, wash her face, and pretend everything was hunky-dory. After the Howard Johnson's snub. And no apology. Nothing.

"Were you on dope or what that time at Howard Johnson's?" I tried to make my voice sound friendlier than I felt.

"Maybe, a little. I never did drugs much. Why?"

"I don't know, you acted sort of like you didn't want to know me then."

"Oh, Twyla, you know how it was in those days: black—white. You know how everything was."

But I didn't know. I thought it was just the opposite. Busloads of blacks and whites came into Howard Johnson's together. They roamed together then: students, musicians, lovers, protesters. You got to see everything at Howard Johnson's, and blacks were very friendly with whites in those days. But sitting there with nothing on my plate but two hard tomato wedges wondering about the melting Klondikes it seemed childish remembering the slight. We went to her car and, with the help of the driver, got my stuff into my station wagon.

"We'll keep in touch this time," she said.

"Sure," I said. "Sure. Give me a call."

"I will," she said, and then, just as I was sliding behind the wheel, she leaned into the window. "By the way. Your mother. Did she ever stop dancing?"

I shook my head. "No. Never."

Roberta nodded.

"And yours? Did she ever get well?"

She smiled a tiny sad smile. "No. She never did. Look, call me, okay?"

"Okay," I said, but I knew I wouldn't. Roberta had messed up my past somehow with that business about Maggie. I wouldn't forget a thing like that. Would I?

Strife came to us that fall. At least that's what the paper called it. Strife. Racial strife. The word made me think of a bird—a big shrieking bird out of 1,000,000,000 BC. Flapping its wings and cawing. Its eye with no lid always bearing down on you. All day it screeched and at night it slept on the rooftops. It woke you in the morning, and from the *Today* show to the eleven o'clock news it kept you an awful company. I couldn't figure it out from one day to the next. I knew I was supposed to feel something strong, but I didn't know what, and James wasn't any help. Joseph was on the list of kids to be transferred from the junior high school to another one at some far-out-of-the-way place and I thought it was a good thing until I heard it was a bad thing. I mean I didn't know. All the schools seemed dumps to me, and the fact that one was nicer looking didn't hold much weight. But the papers were full of it and then the kids began to get jumpy. In August, mind you. Schools weren't even open yet. I thought Joseph might be frightened to go over there, but he didn't seem scared so I forgot about it, until I found myself driving along Hudson Street out there by the school they were trying to integrate and saw a line of women marching. And who do you suppose was in line, big as life, holding a sign in front of her bigger than her mother's cross? MOTHERS HAVE RIGHTS TOO! it said.

I drove on and then changed my mind. I circled the block, slowed down, and honked my horn.

Roberta looked over and when she saw me she waved. I didn't wave back, but I didn't move either. She handed her sign to another woman and came over to where I was parked.

"Hi."

"What are you doing?"

"Picketing. What's it look like?"

"What for?"

"What do you mean, "What for?" They want to take my kids and send them out of the neighbourhood. They don't want to go."

"So what if they go to another school? My boy's being bussed too, and I don't mind. Why should you?"

"It's not about us, Twyla. Me and you. It's about our kids."

"What's more *us* than that?"

"Well, it is a free country."

"Not yet, but it will be."

"What the hell does that mean? I'm not doing anything to you."

"You really think that?"

"I know it."

"I wonder what made me think you were different."

"I wonder what made me think you were different."

"Look at them," I said. "Just look. Who do they think they are? Swarming all over the place like they own it. And now they think they can decide where my child goes to school. Look at them, Roberta. They're Bozos."

Roberta turned around and looked at the women. Almost all of them were standing still now, waiting. Some were even edging toward us. Roberta looked at me out of some refrigerator behind her eyes. "No, they're not. They're just mothers."

"And what am I? Swiss cheese?"

"I used to curl your hair."

"I hated your hands in my hair."

The women were moving. Our faces looked mean to them of course and they looked as though they could not wait to throw themselves in front of a police car or, better yet, into my car and drag me away by my ankles. Now they surrounded my car and gently, gently began to rock it. I swayed back and forth like a sideways yo-yo. Automatically I reached for Roberta, like the old days in the orchard when they saw us watching them and we had to get out of there, and if one of us fell the other pulled her up and if one of us was caught the other stayed to kick and scratch, and neither would leave the other behind. My arm shot out of the car window but no receiving hand was there. Roberta was looking at me sway from side to side in the car and her face was still. My purse slid from the car seat down under the dashboard. The four policemen who had been drinking Tab in their car finally got the message and strolled over, forcing their way through the women. Quietly, firmly they spoke. "Okay, ladies. Back in line or off the streets."

Some of them went away willingly; others had to be urged away from the car doors and the hood. Roberta didn't move. She was looking steadily at me. I was fumbling to turn on the ignition, which wouldn't catch because the gear-shift was still in drive. The seats of the car were a mess because the swaying had thrown my grocery coupons all over and my purse was sprawled on the floor.

"Maybe I am different now, Twyla. But you're not. You're the same little state kid who kicked a poor old black lady when she was down on the ground. You kicked a black lady and you have the nerve to call me a bigot."

The coupons were everywhere and the guts of my purse were bunched under the dashboard. What was she saying? Black? Maggie wasn't black.

"She wasn't black," I said.

"Like hell she wasn't, and you kicked her. We both did. You kicked a black lady who couldn't even scream."

"Liar!"

"You're the liar! Why don't you just go on home and leave us alone, huh?"

She turned away and I skidded away from the curb.

The next morning I went into the garage and cut the side out of the carton our portable TV had come in. It wasn't nearly big enough, but after a while I had a decent sign: red spray-painted letters on a white background—AND SO DO

CHILDREN****. I meant just to go down to the school and tack it up somewhere so those cows on the picket line across the street could see it, but when I got there, some ten or so others had already assembled—protesting the cows across the street. Police permits and everything. I got in line and we strutted in time on our side while Roberta's group strutted on theirs. That first day we were all dignified, pretending the other side didn't exist. The second day there was name calling and finger gestures. But that was about all. People changed signs from time to time, but Roberta never did and neither did I. Actually my sign didn't make sense without Roberta's. "And so do children what?" one of the women on my side asked me. Have rights, I said, as though it was obvious.

Roberta didn't acknowledge my presence in any way, and I got to thinking maybe she didn't know I was there. I began to pace myself in the line, jostling people one minute and lagging behind the next, so Roberta and I could reach the end of our respective lines at the same time and there would be a moment in our turn when we would face each other. Still, I couldn't tell whether she saw me and knew my sign was for her. The next day I went early before we were scheduled to assemble. I waited until she got there before I exposed my new creation. As soon as she hoisted her MOTHERS HAVE RIGHTS TOO I began to wave my new one, which said, HOW WOULD YOU KNOW? I know she saw that one, but I had gotten addicted now. My signs got crazier each day, and the women on my side decided that I was a kook. They couldn't make heads or tails out of my brilliant screaming posters.

I brought a painted sign in queenly red with huge black letters that said, IS YOUR MOTHER WELL? Roberta took her lunch break and didn't come back for the rest of the day or any day after. Two days later I stopped going too and couldn't have been missed because nobody understood my signs anyway.

It was a nasty six weeks. Classes were suspended and Joseph didn't go to anybody's school until October. The children—everybody's children—soon got bored with that extended vacation they thought was going to be so great. They looked at TV until their eyes flattened. I spent a couple of mornings tutoring my son, as the other mothers said we should. Twice I opened a text from last year that he had never turned in. Twice he yawned in my face. Other mothers organized living room sessions so the kids would keep up. None of the kids could concentrate, so they drifted back to *The Price Is Right* and *The Brady Bunch*. When the school finally opened there were fights once or twice and some sirens roared through the streets every once in a while. There were a lot of photographers from Albany. And just when ABC was about to send up a news crew, the kids settled down like nothing in the world had happened. Joseph hung my HOW WOULD YOU KNOW? sign in his bedroom. I don't know what became of AND SO DO CHILDREN****. I think my father-in-law cleaned some fish on it. He was always puttering around in our garage. Each of his five children lived in Newburgh, and he acted as though he had five extra homes.

I couldn't help looking for Roberta when Joseph graduated from high school, but I didn't see her. It didn't trouble me much what she had said to me in the car. I mean the kicking part. I know I didn't do that, I couldn't do that. But I was puzzled by her telling me Maggie was black. When I thought about it I actually couldn't be certain. She wasn't pitch-black, I knew, or I would have remembered that. What I remembered was the kiddie hat and the semicircle legs. I tried to reassure myself about the race thing for a long time until it dawned on me that the truth was already there, and Roberta knew it. I didn't kick her; I didn't join in with the gar girls and kick that lady, but I sure did want to. We watched and never tried to help her and never called for help. Maggie was my dancing mother. Deaf, I thought, and dumb. Nobody inside. Nobody who would hear you if you cried in the night. Nobody who could tell you anything important that you could use. Rocking, dancing, swaying as she walked. And when the gar girls pushed her down and started roughhousing, I knew she wouldn't scream, couldn't—just like me—and I was glad about that.

We decided not to have a tree, because Christmas would be at my mother-in-law's house, so why have a tree at both places? Joseph was at SUNY New Paltz and we had to economize, we said. But at the last minute, I changed my mind. Nothing could be that bad. So I rushed around town looking for a tree, something small but wide. By the time I found a place, it was snowing and very late. I dawdled like it was the most important purchase in the world and the tree man was fed up with me. Finally I chose one and had it tied onto the trunk of the car. I drove away slowly because the sand trucks were not out yet and the streets could be murder at the beginning of a snowfall. Downtown the streets were wide and rather empty except for a cluster of people coming out of the Newburgh Hotel. The one hotel in town that wasn't built out of cardboard and Plexiglas. A party, probably. The men huddled in the snow were dressed in tails and the women had on furs. Shiny things glittered from underneath their coats. It made me tired to look at them. Tired, tired, tired. On the next corner was a small diner with loops and loops of paper bells in the window. I stopped the car and went in. Just for a cup of coffee and twenty minutes of peace before I went home and tried to finish everything before Christmas Eve.

"Twyla?"

There she was. In a silvery evening gown and dark fur coat. A man and another woman were with her, the man fumbling for change to put in the cigarette machine. The woman was humming and tapping on the counter with her fingernails. They all looked a little drunk.

"Well. It's you."

"How are you?"

I shrugged. "Pretty good. Frazzled. Christmas and all."

"Regular?" called the woman from the counter.

"Fine," Roberta called back and then, "Wait for me in the car."

She slipped into the booth beside me. "I have to tell you something, Twyla. I made up my mind if I ever saw you again, I'd tell you."

"I'd just as soon not hear anything, Roberta. It doesn't matter now, anyway."

"No," she said. "Not about that."

"Don't be long," said the woman. She carried two regulars to go and the man peeled his cigarette pack as they left.

"It's about St Bonny's and Maggie."

"Oh, please."

"Listen to me. I really did think she was black. I didn't make that up. I really thought so. But now I can't be sure. I just remembered her as old, so old. And because she couldn't talk—well, you know, I thought she was crazy. She'd been brought up in an institution like my mother was and like I thought I would be too. And you were right. We didn't kick her. It was the gar girls. Only them. But, well, I wanted to. I really wanted them to hurt her. I said we did it, too. You and me, but that's not true. And I don't want you to carry that around. It was just that I wanted to do it so bad that day—wanting to is doing it."

Her eyes were watery from the drinks she'd had, I guess. I know it's that way with me. One glass of wine and I start bawling over the littlest thing.

"We were kids, Roberta."

"Yeah, Yeah. I know, just kids."

"Eight."

"Eight."

"And lonely."

"Scared, too."

She wiped her cheeks with the heel of her hand and smiled. "Well, that's all I wanted to say."

I nodded and couldn't think of any way to fill the silence that went from the diner past the paper bells on out into the snow. It was heavy now. I thought I'd better wait for the sand trucks before starting home.

"Thanks, Roberta."

"Sure."

"Did I tell you? My mother, she never did stop dancing."

"Yes. You told me. And mine, she never got well." Roberta lifted her hand from the tabletop and covered her face with her palms. When she took them away she really was crying. "Oh, shit, Twyla. Shit, shit, shit. What the hell happened to Maggie?"

1983

Alice Munro

b. 1931

Munro has never been a writer with an eye on the distance between her origin (in Wingham, Huron County in Ontario) and Mount Parnassus and how best to get there. Even when she found herself in the realm of artistic grandeur with the award for the 2013 Nobel Prize in Literature, her modesty and lack of ego were more apparent than sonorous pronouncements about language and humanity. "This is a wonderful thing for me and a wonderful thing for the short story," she said with stunning understatement. We cannot know how differently she felt, if at all, about her life's work because of the recognition; we do know that during her first public interview in 1971, she said something that has been a living, shaping presence in her writing: "With me it has something to do with the fight against death, the feeling that we lose *everything every day* [my emphasis], and writing is a way of convincing yourself that you're doing something about this. You're not really, because the writing does not last much longer than you do." As recently as *Too Much Happiness* (2009), Munro has returned (in two stories) explicitly to this early but relentless perspective. Likely it is a variation on the social and personal admonition rooted in Wingham, "Who Do You Think You Are?," whose potency Munro has transformed, over forty years, into layers of skepticism and invention. Fascinated by "secret worlds" and by "gaps" ("I like gaps, all my stories have gaps"), Munro has published fourteen collections of stories, the first five exhibiting a striking alternation in mood. One exults in the immense possibilities of invention; in the next the texture is darker, the edges sharper, between the imagination and the world from which it draws. *The Progress of Love*, with the profoundly disquieting "Fits" at its centre, marks a redirection and an opening in Munro's explorations of invention and fact, toward the elongated social histories and dramas about knowing and possibility in *Open Secrets* (1994), *The Love of a Good Woman* (1998), and *Hateship, Friendship, Courtship, Loveship, Marriage* (2001). These collections drew from Richard Ford the marvelous perception of "Munro's freedom . . . from the hammerlock of any story's chosen formal features," her freedom to slip between points of view, alter verb tense and "apparent unities." But her most recent volumes, more or less coinciding with announcements about closing down her writing life, are more honed and reveal another dimension to her freedom: the freedom to reprise ideas and even the wording of specific passages from her earlier work, as she does with the 1971 interview about writing and permanence. Munro has always been a more unsettling writer than many of her readers have allowed themselves to accept. In fact, her stories ask the hardest questions: about happiness, about one's real life, and perhaps hardest of all, about what difference one's choices and accidents make. Munro has nerves of steel, like some other great ones, Joyce for instance, on or near Mount Parnassus. By returning to and refashioning crucial perspectives, such as what had been the magical intersections in characters' lives (Munro has often said that we have more than our apparent life), now darkened in the corrosive "Dimensions" (*Too Much Happiness*), she is not easy on herself. Munro is asking difficult and painful questions of her decades of work. We suspect that the answer, as it was for Del in *Lives of Girls and Women*, is "yes," an assent, even if an ambiguous one.

Fits

The two people who died were in their early sixties. They were both tall and well built, and carried a few pounds of extra weight. He was grey-haired, with a square, rather flat face. A broad nose kept him from looking perfectly dignified and handsome. Her hair was blonde, a silvery blonde that does not strike you as artificial anymore—though you know it is not natural—because so many women of that age have acquired it. On Boxing Day, when they dropped over to have a drink with Peg and Robert, she wore a pale-grey dress with a fine, shiny stripe in it, grey stockings, and grey shoes. She drank gin-and-tonic. He wore brown slacks and a cream-coloured sweater, and drank rye-and-water. They had recently come back from a trip to Mexico. He had tried parachute riding. She hadn't wanted to. They had gone to see a place in Yucatán—it looked like a well—where virgins were supposed to have been flung down, in the hope of good harvests.

"Actually, though, that's just a nineteenth-century notion," she said. "That's just the nineteenth-century notion of being so preoccupied with virginity. The truth probably is that they threw people down sort of indiscriminately. Girls or men or old people or whoever they could get their hands on. So not being a virgin would be no guarantee of safety!"

Across the room, Peg's two sons—the older one, Clayton, who was a virgin, and the younger one, Kevin, who was not—watched this breezy-talking silvery-blonde woman with stern, bored expressions. She had said that she used to be a high-school English teacher. Clayton remarked afterward that he knew the type.

Robert and Peg have been married for nearly five years. Robert was never married before, but Peg married for the first time when she was eighteen. Her two boys were born while she and her husband lived with his parents on a farm. Her husband had a job driving trucks of livestock to the Canada Packers Abattoir in Toronto. Other truck-driving jobs followed, taking him farther and farther away. Peg and the boys moved to Gilmore, and she got a job working in Kuiper's store, which was called the Gilmore Arcade. Her husband ended up in the Arctic, driving trucks to oil rigs across the frozen Beaufort Sea. She got a divorce.

Robert's family owned the Gilmore Arcade but had never lived in Gilmore. His mother and sisters would not have believed you could survive a week in such a place. Robert's father had bought the store, and two other stores in nearby towns, shortly after the Second World War. He hired local managers, and drove up from Toronto a few times during the year to see how things were getting on.

For a long time, Robert did not take much interest in his father's various businesses. He took a degree in civil engineering, and had some idea of doing work in underdeveloped countries. He got a job in Peru, travelled through South America, gave up engineering for a while to work on a ranch in British Columbia. When his father became ill, it was necessary for him to come back to Toronto. He worked for the Provincial Department of Highways, in an engineering job that was not a very good one for a man of his age. He was thinking of getting a teaching degree and maybe going up North to teach Indians, changing his life completely, once his father died. He was getting close to forty then, and having his third major affair with a married woman.

Now and then, he drove up to Gilmore and the other towns to keep an eye on the stores. Once, he brought Lee with him, this third—and, as it turned out, his last—married woman. She brought a picnic lunch, drank Pimm's No. 1 in the car, and treated the whole trip as a merry excursion, a foray into hillbilly country. She had counted on making love in the open fields, and was incensed to find they were all full of cattle or uncomfortable cornstalks.

Robert's father died, and Robert did change his life, but instead of becoming a teacher and heading for the wilderness, he came to live in Gilmore to manage the stores himself. He married Peg.

It was entirely by accident that Peg was the one who found them.

On Sunday evening, the farm woman who sold the Kuipers their eggs knocked on the door.

"I hope you don't mind me bringing these tonight instead of tomorrow morning," she said. "I have to take my daughter-in-law to Kitchener to have her ultrasound. I brought the Weebles theirs too, but I guess they're not home. I wonder if you'd mind if I left them here with you? I have to leave early in the morning. She was going to drive herself but I didn't think that was such a good idea. She's nearly five months but still vomiting. Tell them they can just pay me next time."

"No problem," said Robert. "No trouble at all. We can just run over with them in the morning. No problem at all!" Robert is a stocky, athletic-looking man, with curly, greying hair and bright brown eyes. His friendliness and obligingness are often emphatic, so that people might get the feeling of being buffeted from all sides. This is a manner that serves him well in Gilmore, where assurances are supposed to be repeated, and in fact much of conversation is repetition, a sort of dance of good intentions, without surprises. Just occasionally, talking to people, he feels something else, an obstruction, and isn't sure what it is (malice, stubbornness?) but it's like a rock at the bottom of a river when you're swimming—the clear water lifts you over it.

For a Gilmore person, Peg is reserved. She came up to the woman and relieved her of the eggs she was holding, while Robert went on assuring her it was no trouble and asking about the daughter-in-law's pregnancy. Peg smiled as she would smile in the store when she gave you your change—a quick transactional smile, nothing personal. She is a small slim woman with a cap of soft brown hair, freckles, and a scrubbed, youthful look. She wears pleated skirts, fresh neat blouses buttoned to the throat, pale sweaters, sometimes a black ribbon tie. She moves gracefully and makes very little noise. Robert once told her he had never met anyone so self-contained as she was. (His women have usually been talkative, stylishly effective, though careless about some of the details, tense, lively, "interesting.")

Peg said she didn't know what he meant.

He started to explain what a self-contained person was like. At that time, he had a very faulty comprehension of Gilmore vocabulary—he could still make mistakes about it—and he took too seriously the limits that were usually observed in daily exchanges.

"I know what the words mean," Peg said, smiling. "I just don't understand how you mean it about me."

Of course she knew what the words meant. Peg took courses, a different course each winter, choosing from what was offered at the local high school. She took a course on the History of Art, one on Great Civilizations of the East, one on Discoveries and Explorations Through the Ages. She went to class one night a week, even if she was very tired or had a cold. She wrote tests and prepared papers. Sometimes Robert would find a page covered with her small neat handwriting on top of the refrigerator or the dresser in their room.

Therefore we see that the importance of Prince Henry the Navigator was in the inspiration and encouragement of other explorers for Portugal, even though he did not go on voyages himself.

He was moved by her earnest statements, her painfully careful small handwriting, and angry that she never got more than a B-plus for these papers she worked so hard at.

"I don't do it for the marks," Peg said. Her cheekbones reddened under the freckles, as if she was making some kind of personal confession. "I do it for the enjoyment."

Robert was up before dawn on Monday morning, standing at the kitchen counter drinking his coffee, looking out at the fields covered with snow. The sky was clear, and the temperatures had dropped. It was going to be one of the bright, cold, hard January days that comes after weeks of west wind, of blowing and falling snow. Creeks, rivers, ponds frozen over, Lake Huron frozen over as far as you could see. Perhaps all the way this year. That had happened, though rarely.

He had to drive to Keneally, to the Kuiper store there. Ice on the roof was causing water underneath to back up and leak through the ceiling. He would have to chop up the ice and get the roof clear. It would take him at least half the day.

All the repair work and upkeep on the store and on this house is done by Robert himself. He has learned to do plumbing and wiring. He enjoys the feeling that he can manage it. He enjoys the difficulty, and the difficulty of winter, here. Not much more than a hundred miles from Toronto, it is a different country. The snowbelt. Coming up here to live was not unlike heading into the wilderness, after all. Blizzards still isolate the towns and villages. Winter comes down hard on the country, settles down just the way the two-mile-high ice did thousands of years ago. People live within the winter in a way outsiders do not understand. They are watchful, provident, fatigued, exhilarated.

A thing he likes about this house is the back view, over the open country. That makes up for the straggling dead-end street without trees or sidewalks. The street was opened up after the war, when it was taken for granted that everybody would be using cars, not walking anywhere. And so they did. The houses are fairly close to the street and to each other, and when everybody who lives in the houses is home, cars take up nearly all the space where sidewalks, boulevards, shade trees might have been.

Robert, of course, was willing to buy another house. He assumed they would do that. There were—there are—fine old houses for sale in Gilmore, at prices that are a joke, by city standards. Peg said she couldn't see herself living in those places. He offered to build her a new house in the subdivision on the other side of town. She didn't want that either. She wanted to stay in this house, which was the first house she and the boys had lived in on their own. So Robert bought it—she was only renting—and built on the master bedroom and another bathroom, and made a television room in the basement. He got some help from Kevin, less from Clayton. The house still looked, from the street, like the house he had parked in front of the first time he drove Peg home from work. One and a half storeys high, with a steep roof and a living-room window divided into square panes like the window on a Christmas card. White aluminum siding, narrow black shutters, black trim. Back in Toronto, he had thought of Peg living in this house. He had thought of her patterned, limited, serious, and desirable life.

He noticed the Weebles' eggs sitting on the counter. He thought of taking them over. But it was too early. The door would be locked. He didn't want to wake them. Peg could take the eggs when she left to open up the store. He took the Magic Marker that was sitting on the ledge under her reminder pad, and wrote on a paper towel, *Don't forget eggs to W's. Love, Robert.* These eggs were no cheaper than the ones you bought at the supermarket. It was just that Robert liked getting them from a farm. And they were brown. Peg said city people all had a thing about brown eggs—they thought brown eggs were more natural somehow, like brown sugar.

When he backed his car out, he saw that the Weebles' car was in their carport. So they were home from wherever they had been last night. Then he saw that the snow thrown up across the front of their driveway by the town snowplow had not been cleared. The plow must have gone by during the night. But he himself hadn't had to shovel any snow; there hadn't been any fresh snow overnight and the plow hadn't been out. The snow was from yesterday. They couldn't have been out last night. Unless they were walking. The sidewalks were not cleared, except along the main street and the school streets, and it was difficult to walk along the narrowed streets with their banks of snow, but, being new to town, they might have set out not realizing that.

He didn't look closely enough to see if there were footprints.

He pictured what happened. First from the constable's report, then from Peg's.

Peg came out of the house at about twenty after eight. Clayton had already gone off to school, and Kevin, getting over an ear infection, was down in the basement room playing a Billy Idol tape and watching a game show on television. Peg had not forgotten the eggs. She got into her car and turned on the engine to warm it up, then walked out to the street, stepped over the Weebles' uncleared snow, and went up their driveway to the side door. She was wearing her white knitted scarf and tam and her lilac-coloured, down-filled coat. Those coats made most of the women in Gilmore look like barrels, but Peg looked all right, being so slender.

The houses on the street were originally of only three designs. But by now most of them had been so altered, with new windows, porches, wings, and decks, that it was hard to find true mates anymore. The Weebles' house had been built as a mirror image of the Kuipers', but the front window had been changed, its Christmas-card panes taken out, and the roof had been lifted, so that there was a large upstairs window overlooking the street. The siding was pale green and the trim white, and there were no shutters.

The side door opened into a utility room, just as Peg's door did at home. She knocked lightly at first, thinking that they would be in the kitchen, which was only a few steps up from the utility room. She had noticed the car, of course, and wondered if they had got home late and were sleeping in. (She hadn't thought yet about the snow's not having been shovelled, and the fact that the plow hadn't been past in the night. That was something that occurred to her later on when she got into her own car and backed it out.) She knocked louder and louder. Her face was stinging already in the bright cold. She tried the door and found that it wasn't locked. She opened it and stepped into shelter and called.

The little room was dark. There was no light to speak of coming down from the kitchen, and there was a bamboo curtain over the side door. She set the eggs on the clothes dryer, and was going to leave them there. Then she thought she had better take them up into the kitchen, in case the Weebles wanted eggs for breakfast and had run out. They wouldn't think of looking in the utility room.

(This, in fact, was Robert's explanation to himself. She didn't say all that, but he forgot she didn't. She just said, "I thought I might as well take them up to the kitchen.")

The kitchen had those same bamboo curtains over the sink window and over the breakfast-nook windows, which meant that though the room faced east, like the Kuipers' kitchen, and though the sun was fully up by this time, not much light could get in. The day hadn't begun here.

But the house was warm. Perhaps they'd got up a while ago and turned up the thermostat, then gone back to bed. Perhaps they left it up all night—though they had seemed to Peg to be thriftier than that. She set the eggs on the counter by the sink. The layout of the kitchen was almost exactly the same as her own. She noticed a few dishes stacked, rinsed, but not washed, as if they'd had something to eat before they went to bed.

She called again from the living-room doorway.

The living room was perfectly tidy. It looked to Peg somehow too perfectly tidy, but that—as she said to Robert—was probably the way the living room of a retired couple was bound to look to a woman used to having children around. Peg had never in her life had as much tidiness around her she as might have liked, having gone from a family home where there were six children to her inlaws' crowded farmhouse, which was crowded further with her own babies. She had told Robert a story about once asking for a beautiful bar of soap for Christmas, pink soap with a raised design of roses on it. She got it, and she used to hide it after every use so that it wouldn't get cracked and mouldy in the cracks, the way soap always did in that house. She was grown up at that time, or thought she was.

She had stamped the snow off her boots in the utility room. Nevertheless she hesitated to walk across the clean, pale-beige living-room carpet. She called again. She used the Weebles' first names, which she barely knew. Walter and Nora. They had moved in last April, and since then they had been away on two trips, so she didn't feel she knew them at all well, but it seemed silly to be calling, "Mr and Mrs Weeble. Are you up yet, Mr and Mrs Weeble?"

No answer.

They had an open staircase going up from the living room, just as Peg and Robert did. Peg walked now across the clean, pale carpet to the foot of the stairs, which were carpeted in the same material. She started to climb. She did not call again.

She must have known then or she would have called. It would be the normal thing to do, to keep calling the closer you got to where people might be sleeping. To warn them. They might be deeply asleep. Drunk. That wasn't the custom of the Weebles, so far as anybody knew, but nobody knew them that well. Retired people. Early retirement. He had been an accountant; she had been a teacher. They had lived in Hamilton. They had chosen Gilmore because Walter Weeble used to have an aunt and uncle here, whom he visited as a child. Both dead now, the aunt and uncle, but the place must have held pleasant memories for him. And it was cheap; this was surely a cheaper house than they could have afforded. They meant to spend their money travelling. No children.

She didn't call; she didn't halt again. She climbed the stairs and didn't look around as she came up; she faced straight ahead. Ahead was the bathroom, with the door open. It was clean and empty.

She turned at the top of the stairs toward the Weebles' bedroom. She had never been upstairs in this house before, but she knew where that would be. It would be the extended room at the front, with the wide window overlooking the street.

The door was open.

Peg came downstairs and left the house by the kitchen, the utility room, the side door. Her footprints showed on the carpet and on the linoleum tiles, and outside on the snow. She closed the door after herself. Her car had been running all this time and was sitting in its own little cloud of steam. She got in and backed out and drove to the police station in the Town Hall.

"It's a bitter cold morning, Peg," the constable said.

"Yes, it is."

"So what can I do for you?"

Robert got more, from Karen.

Karen Adams was the clerk in the Gilmore Arcade. She was a young married woman, solidly built, usually good-humoured, alert without particularly seeming to be so, efficient without a lot of bustle. She got along well with customers; she got along with Peg and Robert. She had known Peg longer, of course. She defended her against people who said Peg had got her nose in the air since she married rich. Karen said Peg hadn't changed from what she always was. But after today she said, "I always believed Peg and me to be friends, but now I'm not so sure."

Karen started work at ten. She arrived a little before that and asked if there had been many customers in yet, and Peg said no, nobody.

"I don't wonder," Karen said. "It's too cold. If there was any wind, it'd be murder."

Peg had made coffee. They had a new coffeemaker, Robert's Christmas present to the store. They used to have to get takeouts from the bakery up the street.

"Isn't this thing marvellous?" Karen said as she got her coffee.

Peg said yes. She was wiping up some marks on the floor.

"Oh-oh," said Karen. "Was that me or you?"

"I think it was me," Peg said.

"So I didn't think anything of it," Karen said later. "I thought she must've tracked some mud. I didn't stop to think, Where would you get down to mud with all this snow on the ground?"

After a while, a customer came in, and it was Celia Simms, and she had heard. Karen was at the cash, and Peg was at the back, checking some invoices. Celia told Karen. She didn't know much; she didn't know how it had been done or that Peg was involved.

Karen shouted to the back of the store. "Peg! Peg! Something terrible has happened, and it's your next-door neighbours!"

Peg called back, "I know."

Celia lifted her eyebrows at Karen—she was one of those who didn't like Peg's attitude—and Karen loyally turned aside and waited till Celia went out of the store. Then she hurried to the back, making the hangers jingle on the racks.

"Both the Weebles are shot dead, Peg. Did you know that?"

Peg said, "Yes. I found them."

"You did! When did you?"

"This morning, just before I came in to work."

"They were murdered!"

"It was a murder-suicide," Peg said. "He shot her and then he shot himself. That's what happened."

"When she told me that," Karen said, "I started to shake. I shook all over and I couldn't stop myself." Telling Robert this, she shook again, to demonstrate, and pushed her hands up inside the sleeves of her blue plush jogging suit.

"So I said, 'What did you do when you found them,' and she said, 'I went and told the police.' I said, 'Did you scream, or what?' I said didn't her legs buckle, because I know mine would've. I can't imagine how I would've got myself out of there. She said she didn't remember much about getting out, but she did remember closing the door, the outside door, and thinking, Make sure that's closed in case some dog could get in. Isn't that awful? She was right, but it's awful to think of. Do you think she's in shock?"

"No," Robert said. "I think she's all right."

This conversation was taking place at the back of the store in the afternoon, when Peg had gone out to get a sandwich.

"She had not said one word to me. Nothing. I said, 'How come you never said a word about this, Peg,' and she said, 'I knew you'd find out pretty soon.' I said yes, but she could've told me. 'I'm sorry,' she says. 'I'm sorry.' Just like she's apologizing for some little thing like using my coffee mug. Only, Peg would never do that."

Robert had finished what he was doing at the Keneally store around noon, and decided to drive back to Gilmore before getting anything to eat. There was a highway diner just outside of town, on the way in from Keneally, and he thought that he would stop there. A few truckers and travellers were usually eating in the diner, but most of the trade was local—farmers on the way home, business and working men who had driven out from town. Robert liked this place, and he had entered it today with a feeling of buoyant expectation. He was hungry from his work in the cold air, and aware of the brilliance of the day, with the snow on the fields looking sculpted, dazzling, as permanent as marble. He had the sense he had fairly often in Gilmore, the sense of walking onto an informal stage, where a rambling, agreeable play was in progress. And he knew his lines—or knew, at least, that his improvisations would not fail. His whole life in Gilmore sometimes seemed to have this quality, but if he ever tried to describe it that way, it would sound as if it was an artificial life, something contrived, not entirely serious. And the very opposite was true. So when he met somebody from his old life, as he sometimes did when he went to Toronto, and was asked how he liked living in Gilmore, he would say, "I can't tell you how much I like it!" which was exactly the truth.

"Why didn't you get in touch with me?"

"You were up on the roof."

"You could have called the store and told Ellie. She would have told me."

"What good would that have done?"

"I could at least have come home."

He had come straight from the diner to the store, without eating what he had ordered. He did not think he would find Peg in any state of collapse—he knew her well enough for that—but he did think she would want to go home, let him fix her a drink, spend some time telling him about it.

She didn't want that. She wanted to go up the street to the bakery to get her usual lunch—a roll with ham and cheese.

"I let Karen go out to eat, but I haven't had time. Should I bring one back for you? If you didn't eat at the diner, I might as well."

When she brought him the sandwich, he sat and ate it at the desk where she had been doing invoices. She put fresh coffee and water into the coffeemaker.

"I can't imagine how we got along without this thing."

He looked at Peg's lilac-coloured coat hanging beside Karen's red coat on the washroom door. On the lilac coat there was a long crusty smear of reddish brown paint, down to the hemline.

Of course that wasn't paint. But on her coat? How did she get blood on her coat? She must have brushed up against them in that room. She must have got close.

Then he remembered the talk in the diner, and realized she wouldn't have needed to get that close. She could have got blood from the door frame. The constable had been in the diner, and he said there was blood everywhere, and not just blood.

"He shouldn't ever have used a shotgun for that kind of business," one of the men at the diner said.

Somebody else said, "Maybe a shotgun was all he had."

It was busy in the store most of the afternoon. People on the street, in the bakery and the café and the bank and the Post Office, talking. People wanted to talk face to face. They had to get out and do it, in spite of the cold. Talking on the phone was not enough.

What had gone on at first, Robert gathered, was that people had got on the phone, just phoned anybody they could think of who might not have heard. Karen had phoned her friend Shirley, who was at home in bed with the flu, and her mother, who was in the hospital with a broken hip. It turned out her mother knew already—the whole hospital knew. And Shirley said, "My sister beat you to it."

It was true that people valued and looked forward to the moment of breaking the news—Karen was annoyed at Shirley's sister, who didn't work and could get to the phone whenever she wanted to—but there was real kindness and consideration behind this impulse, as well. Robert thought so. "I knew she wouldn't want not to know," Karen said, and that was true. Nobody would want not to know. To go out into the street, not knowing. To go around doing all the usual daily things, not knowing. He himself felt troubled, even slightly humiliated, to think that he hadn't known; Peg hadn't let him know.

Talk ran backward from the events of the morning. Where were the Weebles seen, and in what harmlessness and innocence, and how close to the moment when everything was changed?

She had stood in line at the Bank of Montreal on Friday afternoon.

He had got a haircut on Saturday morning.

They were together, buying groceries, in the IGA on Friday evening at about eight o'clock.

What did they buy? A good supply? Specials, advertised bargains, more than enough to last for a couple of days?

More than enough. A bag of potatoes, for one thing.

Then reasons. The talk turned to reasons. Naturally. There had been no theories put forward in the diner. Nobody knew the reason, nobody could imagine. But by the end of the afternoon there were too many explanations to choose from.

Financial problems. He had been mixed up in some bad investment scheme in Hamilton. Some wild money-making deal that had fallen through. All their money was gone and they would have to live out the rest of their lives on the old-age pension.

They had owed money on their income taxes. Being an accountant, he thought he knew how to fix things, but he had been found out. He would be exposed, perhaps charged, shamed publicly, left poor. Even if it was only cheating the government, it would still be a disgrace when that kind of thing came out.

Was it a lot of money?

Certainly. A lot.

It was not money at all. They were ill. One of them or both of them. Cancer. Crippling arthritis. Alzheimer's disease. Recurrent mental problems. It was health, not money. It was suffering and helplessness they feared, not poverty.

A division of opinion became evident between men and women. It was nearly always the men who believed and insisted that the trouble had been money, and it was the women who talked of illness. Who would kill themselves just because they were poor, said some women scornfully. Or even because they might go to jail? It was always a woman too who suggested unhappiness in the marriage, who hinted at the drama of a discovered infidelity or the memory of an old one.

Robert listened to all these explanations but did not believe any of them. Loss of money, cancer, Alzheimer's disease. Equally plausible, these seemed to him, equally hollow and useless. What happened was that he believed each of them for about five minutes, no longer. If he could have believed one of them, hung on to it, it would have been as if something had taken its claws out of his chest and permitted him to breathe.

("They weren't Gilmore people, not really," a woman said to him in the bank. Then she looked embarrassed. "I don't mean like you.")

Peg kept busy getting some children's sweaters, mitts, snowsuits ready for the January sale. People came up to her when she was marking the tags, and she said, "Can I help you," so that they were placed right away in the position of being customers, and had to say that there was something they were looking for. The Arcade carried ladies' and children's clothes, sheets, towels, knitting wool, kitchenware, bulk candy, magazines, mugs, artificial flowers, and plenty of other things besides, so it was not hard to think of something.

What was it they were really looking for? Surely not much in the way of details, description. Very few people actually want that, or will admit they do, in a greedy and straightforward way. They want it, they don't want it. They start asking, they stop themselves. They listen and they back away. Perhaps they wanted from Peg just some kind of acknowledgement, some word or look that would send them away, saying, "Peg Kuiper is absolutely shattered. I saw Peg Kuiper. She didn't say much but you could tell she was absolutely shattered."

Some people tried to talk to her, anyway.

"Wasn't that terrible what happened down by you?"

"Yes, it was."

"You must have known them a little bit, living next door."

"Not really. We hardly knew them at all."

"You never noticed anything that would've led you to think this could've happened?"

"We never noticed anything at all."

Robert pictured the Weebles getting into and out of their car in the driveway. That was where he had most often seen them. He recalled their Boxing Day visit. Her grey legs made him think of a nun. Her mention of virginity had embarrassed Peg and the boys. She reminded Robert a little of the kind of woman he used to know. Her husband was less talkative, though not shy. They talked about Mexican food, which it seemed the husband had not liked. He did not like eating in restaurants.

Peg had said, "Oh, men never do!"

That surprised Robert, who asked her afterward did that mean she wanted to eat out more often?

"I just said that to take her side. I thought he was glaring at her a bit."

Was he glaring? Robert had not noticed. The man seemed too self-controlled to glare at his wife in public. Too well disposed, on the whole, perhaps in some way too indolent, to glare at anybody anywhere.

But it wasn't like Peg to exaggerate.

Bits of information kept arriving. The maiden name of Nora Weeble. Driscoll. Nora Driscoll. Someone knew a woman who had taught at the same school with her in Hamilton. Well-liked as a teacher, a fashionable dresser, she had some trouble keeping order. She had taken a French Conversation course, and a course in French cooking.

Some women here had asked her if she'd be interested in starting a book club, and she had said yes.

He had been more of a joiner in Hamilton than he was here. The Rotary Club. The Lions Club. Perhaps it had been for business reasons.

They were not churchgoers, as far as anybody knew, not in either place.

(Robert was right about the reasons. In Gilmore everything becomes known, sooner or later. Secrecy and confidentiality are seen to be against the public interest. There is a network of people who are married to or related to the people who work in the offices where all the records are kept.

There was no investment scheme, in Hamilton or anywhere else. No income-tax investigation. No problem about money. No cancer, tricky heart, high blood pressure. She had consulted the doctor about headaches, but the doctor did not think they were migraines, or anything serious.

At the funeral on Thursday, the United Church minister, who usually took up the slack in the cases of no known affiliation, spoke about the pressures and tensions of modern life but gave no more specific clues. Some people were disappointed, as if they expected him to do that—or thought that he might at least mention the dangers of falling away from faith and church membership, the sin of despair. Other people thought that saying anything more than he did say would have been in bad taste.)

Another person who thought Peg should have let him know was Kevin. He was waiting for them when they got home. He was still wearing his pyjamas.

Why hadn't she come back to the house instead of driving to the police station? Why hadn't she called to him? She could have come back and phoned. Kevin could have phoned. At the very least, she could have called him from the store.

He had been down in basement all morning, watching television. He hadn't heard the police come; he hadn't seen them go in or out. He had not known anything about what was going on until his girlfriend, Shanna, phoned him from school at lunch hour.

"She said they took the bodies out in garbage bags."

"How would she know?" said Clayton. "I thought she was at school."

"Somebody told her."

"She got that from television."

"She *said* they took them out in garbage bags."

"Shanna is a cretin. She is only good for one thing."

"Some people aren't good for anything."

Clayton was sixteen, Kevin fourteen. Two years apart in age but three years apart at school, because Clayton was accelerated and Kevin was not.

"Cut it out," Peg said. She had brought up some spaghetti sauce from the freezer and was thawing it in the double boiler. "Clayton. Kevin. Get busy and make me some salad."

Kevin said, "I'm sick. I might contaminate it."

He picked up the tablecloth and wrapped it around his shoulders like a shawl.

"Do we have to eat off that?" Clayton said. "Now he's got his crud on it?"

Peg said to Robert, "Are we having wine?"

Saturday and Sundays nights they usually had wine, but tonight Robert had not thought about it. He went down to the basement to get it. When he came back, Peg was sliding spaghetti into the cooker and Kevin had discarded the tablecloth. Clayton was making the salad. Clayton was small-boned, like his mother, and fiercely driven. A star runner, a demon examination writer.

Kevin was prowling around the kitchen, getting in the way, talking to Peg. Kevin was taller already than Clayton or Peg, perhaps taller than Robert. He had large shoulders and skinny legs and black hair that he wore in the nearest thing he dared to a Mohawk cut—Shanna cut it for him. His pale skin often broke out in pimples. Girls didn't seem to mind.

"So was there?" Kevin said. "Was there blood and guck all over?"

"Ghoul," said Clayton.

"Those were human beings, Kevin," Robert said.

"Were," said Kevin. "I know they *were* human beings. I mixed their drinks on Boxing Day. She drank gin and he drank rye. They were human beings then, but all they are now is chemicals. Mom? What did you see first? Shanna said there was blood and guck even out in the hallway."

"He's brutalized from all the TV he watches," Clayton said. "He thinks it was some video. He can't tell real blood from video blood."

"Mom? Was it splashed?"

Robert has a rule about letting Peg deal with her sons unless she asks for his help. But this time he said, "Kevin, you know it's about time you shut up."

"He can't help it," Clayton said. "Being ghoulish."

"You too, Clayton. You too."

But after a moment Clayton said, "Mom?" Did you scream?"

"No," said Peg thoughtfully. "I didn't. I guess because there wasn't anybody to hear me. So I didn't."

"I might have heard you," said Kevin, cautiously trying a comeback.

"You had the television on."

"I didn't have the sound on. I had my tape on. I might have heard you through the tape if you screamed loud enough."

Peg lifted a strand of the spaghetti to try it. Robert was watching her, from time to time. He would have said he was watching to see if she was in any kind of trouble, if she seemed numb, or strange, or showed a quiver, if she dropped things or made the pots clatter. But in fact he was watching her just because there was no sign of such difficulty and because he knew there wouldn't be. She was preparing an ordinary meal, listening to the boys in her usual mildly censorious but unruffled way. The only thing more apparent than usual to Robert was her gracefulness, lightness, quickness, and ease around the kitchen.

Her tone to her sons, under its severity, seemed shockingly serene.

"Kevin, go and get some clothes on, if you want to eat at the table."

"I can eat in my pyjamas."

"No."

"I can eat in bed."

"Not spaghetti, you can't."

While they were washing up the pots and pans together—Clayton had gone for his run and Kevin was talking to Shanna on the phone—Peg told Robert her part of the story. He didn't ask her to, in so many words. He started off with "So when you went over, the door wasn't locked?" and she began to tell him.

"You don't mind talking about it?" Robert said.

"I knew you'd want to know."

She told him she knew what was wrong—at least, she knew that something was terribly wrong—before she started up the stairs.

"Were you frightened?"

"No. I didn't think about it like that—being frightened."

"There could have been somebody up there with a gun."

"No. I knew there wasn't. I knew there wasn't anybody but me alive in the house. Then I saw his leg, I saw his leg stretched out into the hall, and I knew then, but I had to go on in and make sure."

Robert said, "I understand that."

"It wasn't the foot he had taken the shoe off that was out there. He took the shoe off his other foot, so he could use that foot to pull the trigger when he shot himself. That was how he did it."

Robert knew all about that already, from the talk in the diner.

"So," said Peg. "That's really about all."

She shook dishwater from her hands, dried them, and, with a critical look, began rubbing in lotion.

Clayton came in at the side door. He stamped the snow from his shoes and ran up the steps.

"You should see the cars," he said. "Stupid cars all crawling along this street. Then they have to turn around at the end and crawl back. I wish they'd get stuck. I stood out there and gave them dirty looks, but I started to freeze so I had to come in."

"It's natural," Robert said. "It seems stupid but it's natural. They can't believe it, so they want to see where it happened."

"I don't see their problem," Clayton said. "I don't see why they can't believe it. Mom could believe it all right. Mom wasn't surprised."

"Well, of course I was," Peg said, and this was the first time Robert had noticed any sort of edge to her voice. "Of course I was surprised, Clayton. Just because I didn't break out screaming."

"You weren't surprised they could do it."

"I hardly knew them. We hardly knew the Weebles."

"I guess they had a fight," said Clayton.

"We don't know that," Peg said, stubbornly working lotion into her skin. "We don't know if they had a fight, or what."

"When you and Dad used to have those fights?" Clayton said. "Remember, after we first moved to town? When he would be home? Over by the car wash? When you used to have those fights, you know what I used to think? I used to think one of you was going to come and kill me with a knife."

"That's not true," said Peg.

"It is true. I did."

Peg sat down at the table and covered her mouth with her hands. Clayton's mouth twitched. He couldn't seem to stop it, so he turned it into a little, taunting, twitching smile.

"That's what I used to lie in bed and think."

"Clayton. We would never either one of us ever have hurt you."

Robert believed that it was time he said something.

"What this is like," he said, "it's like an earthquake or a volcano. It's that kind of happening. It's a kind of fit. People can take a fit like the earth takes a fit. But it only happens once in a long while. It's a freak occurrence."

"Earthquakes and volcanoes aren't freaks," said Clayton, with a certain dry pleasure. "If you want to call that a fit, you'd have to call it a periodic fit. Such as people have, married people have."

"We don't," said Robert. He looked at Peg as if waiting for her to agree with him.

But Peg was looking at Clayton. She who always seemed pale and silky and assenting, but hard to follow as a watermark in fine paper, looked dried out, chalky, her outlines fixed in steady, helpless, unapologetic pain.

"No," said Clayton. "No, not you."

Robert told them that he was going for a walk. When he got outside, he saw that Clayton was right. There were cars nosing along the street, turning at the end, nosing their way back again. Getting a look. Inside those cars were just the same people, probably the very same people, he had been talking to during the afternoon. But now they seemed joined to their cars, making some new kind of monster that came poking around in a brutally curious way.

To avoid them, he went down a short dead-end street that branched off theirs. No houses had ever been built on this street, so it was not plowed. But the snow was hard, and easy to walk on. He didn't notice how easy it was to walk on until he realized that he had gone beyond the end of the street and up a slope, which was not a slope of land at all, but a drift of snow. The drift neatly covered the fence that usually separated the street from the field. He had walked over the fence without knowing what he was doing. The snow was that hard.

He walked here and there, testing. The crust took his weight without a whisper of a crack. It was the same everywhere. You could walk over the snowy fields as if you were walking on cement. (This morning, looking at the snow, hadn't he though of marble?) But this paving was not flat. It rose and dipped in a way that had not much to do with the contours of the ground underneath. The snow created its own landscape, which was sweeping, in a grand and arbitrary style.

Instead of walking around on the plowed streets of town, he could walk over the fields. He could cut across to the diner on the highway, which stayed open until midnight. He would have a cup of coffee there, turn around, and walk home.

One night, about six months before Robert married Peg, he and Lee were sitting drinking in his apartment. They were having an argument about whether it was permissible, or sickening, to have your family initial on your silverware. All of a sudden, the argument split open—Robert couldn't remember how, but it split open, and they found themselves saying the cruellest things to each other that they could imagine. Their voices changed from the raised pitch and speed of argument, and they spoke quietly with a subtle loathing.

"You always make me think of a dog," Lee said. "You always make me think of one of those dogs that push up on people and paw them, with their big disgusting tongues hanging out. You're so eager. All your friendliness and eagerness—that's really aggression. I'm not the only one who thinks this about you. A lot of people avoid you. They can't stand you. You'd be surprised. You push and paw in that eager pathetic way, but you have a calculating look. That's why I don't care if I hurt you."

"Maybe I should tell you one of the things I don't like, then," said Robert reasonably. "It's the way you laugh. On the phone particularly. You laugh at the end of practically every sentence. I used to think it was a nervous tic, but it always annoyed me. And I've figured out why. You're always telling somebody about what a raw deal you're getting somewhere or some unkind thing a person said to you—that's about two-thirds of your horrendously boring self-centred conversation. And then you laugh. Ha-ha, you can take it, you don't expect anything better. That laugh is sick."

After some more of this, they started to laugh themselves, Robert and Lee, but it was not the laughter of a breakthrough into reconciliation; they did not fall upon each other in relief, crying, "What rot, I didn't mean it, did you mean it?" ("No, of course not, of course I didn't mean it.") They laughed in recognition of their extremity, just as they might have laughed at another time, in the middle of quite different, astoundingly tender declarations. They trembled with murderous pleasure, with the excitement of saying what could never be retracted; they exulted in wounds inflicted but also in wounds received, and one or the other said at some point, "This is the first time we've spoken the truth since we've known each other!" For even things that came to them more or less on the spur of the moment seemed the most urgent truths that had been hardening for a long time and pushing to get out.

It wasn't so far from laughing to making love, which they did, all with no retraction. Robert made barking noises, as a dog should, and nuzzled Lee in a bruising way, snapping with real appetite at her flesh. Afterward they were enormously and finally sick of each other but no longer disposed to blame.

"There are things I just absolutely and eternally want to forget about," Robert had told Peg. He talked to her about cutting his losses, abandoning old bad habits, old deceptions and self-deceptions, mistaken notions about life, and about himself. He said that he had been an emotional spendthrift, had thrown himself into hopeless and painful entanglements as a way of avoiding anything that had normal possibilities. That was all experiment and posturing, rejection of the ordinary, decent contracts of life. So he said to her. Errors of avoidance, when he had thought he was running risks and getting intense experiences.

"Errors of avoidance that I mistook for errors of passion," he said, then thought that he sounded pretentious when he was actually sweating with sincerity, with the effort and the relief.

In return, Peg gave him facts.

We lived with Dave's parents. There was never enough hot water for the baby's wash. Finally we got out and came to town and we lived beside the car wash. Dave was only with us weekends then. It was very noisy, especially at night. Then Dave got another job, he went up North, and I rented this place.

Errors of avoidance, errors of passion. She didn't say.

Dave had a kidney problem when he was little and he was out of school a whole winter. He read a book about the Arctic. It was probably the only book he ever read that he didn't have to. Anyway, he always dreamed about it; he wanted to go there. So finally he did.

A man doesn't just drive farther and farther away in his trucks until he disappears from his wife's view. Not even if he has always dreamed of the Arctic. Things happen before he goes. Marriage knots aren't going to slip apart painlessly, with the pull of distance. There's got to be some wrenching and slashing. But she didn't say, and he didn't ask, or even think much about that, till now.

He walked very quickly over the snow crust, and when he reached the diner he found that he didn't want to go in yet. He would cross the highway and walk a little farther, then go into the diner to get warmed up on his way home.

By the time he was on his way home, the police car that was parked at the diner ought to be gone. The night constable was there now, taking his break. This was not the same man Robert had seen and listened to when he dropped in on his way home from Keneally. This man would not have seen anything first hand. He hadn't talked to Peg. Nevertheless he would be talking about it; everybody in the diner would be talking about it, going over the same scene and the same questions, the possibilities. No blame to them.

When they saw Robert, they would want to know how Peg was.

There was one thing he was going to ask her, just before Clayton came in. At least, he was turning the question over in his mind, wondering if it would be all right to ask her. A discrepancy, a detail, in the midst of so many abominable details.

And now he knew it wouldn't be all right; it would never be all right. It had nothing to do with him. One discrepancy, one detail—one lie—that would never have anything to do with him.

Walking on this magic surface, he did not grow tired. He grew lighter, if anything. He was taking himself farther and farther away from town, although for a while he didn't realize this. In the clear air, the lights of Gilmore were so bright they seemed only half a field away, instead of half a mile, then a mile and a half, then two miles. Very fine flakes of snow, fine as dust, and glittering, lay on the crust that held him. There was a glitter too around the branches of the trees and bushes that he was getting closer to. It wasn't like the casing around twigs and delicate branches that an ice storm leaves. It was as if the wood itself had altered and begun to sparkle.

This is the very weather in which noses and fingers are frozen. But nothing felt cold.

He was getting quite close to a large woodlot. He was crossing a long slanting shelf of snow, with the trees ahead and to one side of him. Over there, to the side, something caught his eye. There was a new kind of glitter under the trees. A congestion of shapes, with black holes in them, and unmatched arms or petals reaching up to the lower branches of the trees. He headed toward these shapes, but whatever they were did not become clear. They did not look like anything he knew. They did not look like anything, except perhaps a bit like armed giants half collapsed, frozen in combat, or like the jumbled towers of a crazy small-scale city—a space-age, small-scale city. He kept waiting for an explanation, and not getting one, until he got very close. He was so close he could almost have touched one of these monstrosities before he saw that they were just old cars. Old cars and trucks and even a school bus that had been pushed in under the trees and left. Some were completely overturned, and some were tipped over one another at odd angles. They were partly filled, partly covered, with snow. The black holes were their gutted insides. Twisted bits of chrome, fragments of headlights, were glittering.

He thought of himself telling Peg about this—how close he had to get before he saw that what amazed him and bewildered him so was nothing but old wrecks, and how he then felt disappointed, but also like laughing. They needed some new thing to talk about. Now he felt more like going home.

At noon, when the constable in the diner was giving his account, he had described how the force of the shot threw Walter Weeble backward. "It blasted him partways out of the room. His head was laying out in the hall. What was left of it was laying out in the hall."

Not a leg. Not the indicative leg, whole and decent in its trousers, the shod foot. That was not what anybody turning at the top of the stairs would see and would have to step over, step through, in order to go into the bedroom and look at the rest of what was there.

1986

Open Secrets

It was on a Saturday morning
Just as lovely as it could be
Seven girls and their Leader Miss Johnstone
Went camping from the C.G.I.T

"And they almost didn't even go," Frances said. "Because of the downpour Saturday morning. They were waiting half an hour in the United Church basement and she says, Oh, it'll stop—my hikes are never rained out! And now I bet she wishes it had've been. Then it would've been a whole other story."

It did stop raining, they did go, and it got so hot partway out that Miss Johnstone let them stop at a farmhouse, and the woman brought out Coca-Colas and the man let them take the garden hose and spray themselves cool. They were grabbing the hose from each other and doing tricks, and Frances said that Mary Kaye said Heather Bell had been the worst one; the boldest, getting hold of the hose and shooting water on the rest of them in all the bad places.

"They will try to make out she was some poor innocent, but the facts are dead different," Frances said. "It could have been all an arrangement, that she arranged to meet somebody. I mean some man."

Maureen said, "I think that's pretty farfetched."

"Well, I don't believe she drowned," Frances said. "That I don't believe."

The Falls on the Peregrine River were nothing like the waterfalls you see pictures of. They were just water falling over limestone shelves, none of them more than six or seven feet high. There was a breathing spot where you could stand behind the hard-falling curtain of water, and all around in the limestone there were pools, smooth-rimmed and not much bigger than bathtubs, where the water lay trapped and warm. You would have to be very determined to drown in there. But they had looked there—the other girls had run around calling Heather's name and peering into all the pools, and they had even stuck their heads into the dry space behind the curtain of noisy water. They had skipped around on the bare rock and yelled and got themselves soaked, finally, plunging in and out through the curtain. Till Miss Johnstone shouted and made them come back.

There was Betsy and Eva Trowel
And Lucille Chambers as well
There was Ginny Bos and Mary Kaye Trevelyan
And Robin Sands and poor Heather Bell.

"Seven was all she could get," Frances said. "And every one of them, there was a reason. Robin Sands, doctor's daughter. Lucille Chambers, minister's daughter. They can't get out of it. The Trowells—country. Glad to get in on anything. Ginny Bos, the double-jointed monkey—she's along for the swimming and the horsing around. Mary Kaye living next door to Miss Johnstone. Enough said. And Heather Bell new in town. *And* her mother away on the weekend herself—yes, she was taking the opportunity. Getting off on an expedition of her own."

It was about twenty-four hours since Heather Bell had disappeared, on the annual hike of the C.G.I.T.—which stood for Canadian Girls in Training—out to the Falls on the Peregrine River. Mary Johnstone, who was now in her early sixties, had been leading this hike for years, since before the war. There used to be at least a couple of dozen girls heading out the County Road on a Saturday morning in June. They would all be wearing navy-blue shorts and white blouses and red kerchiefs round their necks. Maureen had been one of them, twenty or so years ago.

Miss Johnstone always started them off singing the same thing.

For the Beauty of the Earth,
For the Beauty of the Skies,
For the Love that from our Birth
Over and around us lies—

And you could hear a hum of different words going along, cautiously but determinedly, under the hymn words.

For the sight of Miss Johnstone's bum,
Waddling down the County Road.
We are the morons singing this song—
Doesn't she look just like a toad?

Did anybody else Maureen's age remember these words now? The ones who had stayed in town were mothers—they had girls old enough to go on the hike, and older. They would get into the proper motherly kind of fit about rude language. Having children changed you. It gave you the necessary stake in being grown-up, so that certain parts of you—old parts—could be altogether eliminated and abandoned. Jobs, marriage didn't quite do it—just made you *act* as if you'd forgotten things.

Maureen had no children.

Maureen was sitting with Frances Wall, having coffee and cigarettes at the breakfast table that had been wedged into the old pantry, under the high, glass-fronted cupboards. This was Maureen's house in Carstairs, in 1965. She had been living in the house for eight years, but she still felt as if she got around it on fairly narrow tracks, from one spot where she felt at home to another. She had fixed up this Corner so there was a place to eat other than the dining-room table, and she had put new chintz in the sunroom. It took a long time to work her husband around to changes. The front rooms were full of valuable, heavy furniture, made of oak and walnut, and the curtains were of green-and-mulberry brocade, as in a rich-looking hotel—you could not begin to alter anything there.

Frances worked for Maureen in the house, but she was not like a servant. They were cousins, though Frances was nearly a generation older. She had worked in this house long before Maureen came into it—she had worked for the first wife. Sometimes she called Maureen "Missus." It was a joke, half friendly and half not. How much did you give for those chops, Missus? Oh, they must have seen you coming! And she would tell Maureen she was getting broad in the beam and her hair did not suit her piled and sprayed like an upside-down mixing bowl. This though Frances herself was a dumpling sort of woman with gray hair like brambles all over her head, and a plain, impudent face. Maureen did not think of herself as timid—she had a stately look—and she was certainly not incompetent, having run her husband's law office before she "graduated" (as both she and he would say) to running his house. She sometimes thought she should try for more respect from Frances—but she needed somebody around the house to have spats and jokes with. She could not be a gossip, because of her husband's position, and she didn't think it was her nature, anyway, but she let Frances get away with plenty of mean remarks, and wild, uncharitable, confident speculations.

(For example, what Frances was saying about Heather Bell's mother, and what she said about Mary Johnstone and the hike in general. Frances thought she was an authority on that, because Mary Kaye Trevelyan was her granddaughter.)

Mary Johnstone was a woman you were hardly supposed to mention in Carstairs without attaching the word "wonderful." She had had polio and nearly died of it, at the age of thirteen or fourteen. She was left with short legs, a short, thick body, crooked shoulders, and a slightly twisted neck, which kept her big head a little tilted to one side. She had studied bookkeeping, she had got herself a job in the office at Douds Factory, and she had devoted her spare time to girls, often saying that she had never met a bad one, just some who were confused. Whenever Maureen met Mary Johnstone on the street or in a store, her heart sank. First came that searching smile, the eyes raking yours, the declared delight in any weather—wind or hail or sun or rain, each had something to recommend it—then the laughing question. *So what have you been up to, Mrs. Stephens?* Mary Johnstone always made a point of saying "Mrs. Stephens," but she said it as if it was a play title and she was thinking all the time, It's only Maureen Coulter. (Coulters were just like the Trowells that Frances had remarked on—country. No more, no less.) *What interesting things have you been doing lately, Mrs. Stephens?*

Maureen felt then as if she was being put on the spot and could do nothing about it, as if a challenge was being issued, and it had something to do with her lucky marriage and her tall healthy body, whose only misfortune was a hidden one—her tubes had been tied to make her infertile—and her rosy skin and auburn hair, and the clothes she spent a lot of money and time on. As if she must owe Mary Johnstone something, a never specified compensation. Or as if Mary Johnstone could see more lacking than Maureen herself would face.

Frances didn't care for Mary Johnstone, either, in the pure and simple way she didn't care for anybody who made too much of themselves.

Miss Johnstone had taken them on a half-mile hike before breakfast, as she always did, to climb the Rock—the chunk of limestone that jutted out over the Peregrine River, and was so rare a thing in that part of the country that it was not named anything but the Rock. On Sunday morning you always had to do that hike, dopey as you were from trying to stay awake all night and half sick from smoking smuggled cigarettes. Shivering, too, because the sun wouldn't have reached deep into the woods yet. The path hardly deserved to be called one—you had to climb over rotted tree trunks and wade through ferns and what Miss Johnstone pointed out as Mayapples and wild geraniums, and wild ginger. She would pull it up and nibble it, hardly brushing off the dirt. Look what nature provides us.

I forgot my sweater, Heather said when they were halfway up. Can I go back and get it?

In the old days Miss Johnstone would probably have said no. Get a move on and you'll warm up without it, she would have said. She must have felt uneasy this time, because of the waning popularity of her hikes, which she blamed on television, working mothers, laxity in the home. She said yes.

Yes, but hurry. Hurry and catch up.

Which Heather Bell never did do. At the Rock they looked at the view (Maureen recalled looking around for French safes—did they still call them that?—among the beer bottles and candy wrappers), and Heather had not caught up. On the way back they didn't meet her. She wasn't in the big tent, or in the little tent, where Miss Johnstone had slept, or between the tents. She wasn't in any of the shelters or love nests among the cedars surrounding the campground. Miss Johnstone cut that searching short.

"Pancakes," she called. "Pancakes and coffee! See if the smell of coffee and pancakes won't smoke Miss Mischief out of hiding."

They had to sit and eat—after Miss Johnstone had said grace, thanking God for everything in the woods and at home—and as they ate, Miss Johnstone called out, "Yum-*my*!"

"Doesn't that fresh air give us an appetite?" she said at the top of her voice. "Aren't these the best pancakes you ever did eat? Heather better hurry up or there won't be one left. Heather? Are you listening? Not one left!"

As soon as they were finished, Robin Sands asked if they could go now, could they go and look for Heather?

"Dishes first, my lady," Miss Johnstone said. "Even if you never do pick up a dishrag around home."

Robin nearly burst out crying. Nobody ever spoke to her like that.

After they had cleaned up, Miss Johnstone let them go, and that was when they went back to the Falls. But she brought them back soon enough and made them sit in a semicircle, wet as they were, and she herself sat cross-legged in front of them and called out that anybody listening was welcome to come and join them. "Anybody hiding around here and trying to play tricks is welcome!" Come out now and no questions asked! Otherwise we will just have to get along without you!"

Then she launched into her talk, her Sunday-morning-of-the-hike sermon, without any qualms or worries. She kept going and going, asking a question every now and then, to make sure they were listening. The sun dried their shorts and Heather Bell did not come back. She did not appear out of the trees and still Miss Johnstone did not stop talking. She didn't let go of them until Mr. Trowell drove into the camp in his truck, bringing the ice cream for lunch.

She didn't give them permission then, but they broke loose anyway. They jumped up and ran for the truck. They all started telling him at once. Jupiter, the Trowell's dog, jumped over the tailgate, and Eva Trowell threw her arms about him and started to wail as if he had been the one lost.

Miss Johnstone got to her feet and came over and called out to Mr. Trowell about the girls' clamoring.

"One's taken it into her head to go missing!"

Now the search parties were out. Douds was closed, so that every man who wanted to go could go. Dogs had been added. There was talk of dragging the river downstream from the Falls.

When the constable went to tell Heather Bell's mother, he found her just back from own weekend, wearing a backless sundress and high heels.

"Well, you better find her," she said. "That's your job."

She worked at the hospital—she was a nurse. "Either divorced or never was married in the first place," Frances said. "One for all and all for one, that's her."

Maureen's husband was calling her, and she hurried away to the sunroom. After his stroke two years ago, at the age of sixty-nine, he had given up his law practice, but he still had letters to write and a bit of business to do for old clients who could never get used to anybody else. Maureen typed out all his correspondence and helped him every day with what he called his chores.

"Whaur doing out there?" he said. His speech was sometime slurred, so she had to stay around and interpret for people who did not know him well. Alone with her he made less effort, and his tone could be testy and complaining.

"Talking to Frances," said Maureen.

"Wha'bout?"

"This and that," she said.

"Yeah."

He stretched out the word gloomily, as if to say he well knew what their talk had been about and he did not care for it. Gossip, rumor, the coldhearted thrill of catastrophe. He never went in for much talk, now or in the day when he could talk readily—even his reproofs were brief, a matter of tone and implication. He seemed to call upon a body of belief; on rules known to all decent people and maybe to all people, even those who spent their lives falling short. He seemed to be a little pained, a little embarrassed for all concerned, when he had to do this, and at the same time formidable. His reproofs were extraordinarily effective.

People in Carstairs were just growing out of the habit of calling lawyers Lawyer So-and-So, just as you would always call a doctor by his title. They no longer referred to any of the younger lawyers as Lawyer, but they always called Maureen's husband Lawyer Stephens. Maureen herself often thought of him that way, though she called him Alvin. He dressed every day just as he used to dress to go to his office—in a three-piece gray or brown suit—and his clothes, though they cost enough money, never seemed to fit well or to smooth out his long, lumpy body. Nor did they ever seem to be free of a faint sifting of cigarette ashes, crumbs, maybe even flecks of shed skin. His head wagged downward, his face sagged with preoccupation, his expression was shrewd and absentminded—you could never be sure which. People liked that—they liked that he looked a little unkempt and at a loss and then could flash out with some fearsome detail. He knows the Law, they said. He doesn't have to look it up. He's got it all in his head. His stroke hadn't shaken their faith, and it really hadn't altered his appearance or his manner much, just accentuated what was already there.

Everyone believed he could have been a judge if he had played his cards right. He could have been a senator. But he was too honorable. He wouldn't kowtow. He was a man in a million.

Maureen sat down on the hassock near him to write shorthand. His name for her, in the office, had been the Jewel, because she was intelligent and dependable, in fact quite able to draw up documents and write letters on her own. Even in the household, his wife and the two children, Helena and Gordon, had used that name for her. The children still used it sometimes, though they were grown up and lived away. Helena used it affectionately and provocatively, Gordon with a solemn, self-congratulatory kindness. Helena was an unsettled single woman who came home seldom and got into arguments when she did. Gordon was a teacher at a military college, who liked to bring his wife and children back to Carstairs, making rather a display of the place, and of his father and Maureen, their backwater virtues.

Maureen could still enjoy being the Jewel. Or at least she found it comfortable. Part of her thoughts could slip off on their own. She was thinking now of the way the night's long adventure began, at camp, with Miss Johnstone's abdicating snores, and its objective—staying awake till dawn, and all the strategies and entertainments that were relied on to achieve that, though she had never heard that they were successful. The girls played cards, they told jokes, they smoked cigarettes, and around midnight began the great games of Truth or Dare. Some Dares were: take off your pajama top and show your boobs; eat a cigarette butt; swallow dirt; stick your head in the water pail and try to count to a hundred; go and pee in front of Miss Johnstone's tent. Questions requiring Truth were: Do you hate your mother? Father? Sister? Brother? How many peckers have you seen and whose were they? Have you ever lied? Stolen? Touched anything dead? The sick and dizzy feeling of having smoked too many cigarettes too quickly came back to Maureen, also the smell of the smoke under the heavy canvas that had been soaking up the day's sun, the smell of girls who had swum for hours in the river and run and hidden in the reeds along the banks and had to burn leeches off their legs.

She remembered how noisy she had been then. A shrieker, a daretaker. Just before she hit high school, a giddiness either genuine or faked or half-and-half became available to her. Soon it vanished, her bold body vanished inside this ample one, and she became a studious, shy girl, a blusher. She developed the qualities her husband would see and value when hiring and proposing.

I dare you to run away. Was it possible? There are times when girls are inspired, when they want the risks to go on and on. They want to be heroines, regardless. They want to take a joke beyond where anybody has ever taken it before. To be careless, dauntless, to create havoc—that was the lost hope of girls.

From the chintz-covered hassock at her husband's side she looked out at the old copper-beech trees, seeing behind them not the sunny lawn but the unruly trees along the river—the dense cedars and shiny-leaved oaks and glittery poplars. A ragged sort of wall with hidden doorways, and hidden paths behind it where animals went, and lone humans sometimes, becoming different from what they were outside, charged with different responsibilities, certainties, intentions. She could imagine vanishing. But of course you didn't vanish, and there was always the other person on a path to intersect yours and his head was full of plans for you even before you met.

When she went to the Post Office that afternoon to send off her husband's letters, Maureen heard two new reports. A light-haired young girl had been seen getting into a black car on the Bluewater Highway north of Walley at about one o'clock on Sunday afternoon. She might have been hitchhiking. Or waiting for just one car. That was twenty miles away from the Falls, and it would take about five hours to walk it, across the country. It could be done. Or she could have got a ride in another car.

But some people tidying up family graves in a forsaken country churchyard in the swampy northeastern corner of the country had heard a cry, a scream, in the middle of the afternoon. Who was that? they remembered saying to each other. Not *what* but *who. Who was that?* But later on they thought that it might have been a fox.

Also, the grass was beaten down in a spot close to the camp, and there were fresh cigarette butts lying around. But what did that prove—people were always out there. Lovers. Young boys planning mischief.

And maybe some man did meet her there
That was carrying a gun or a knife
He met her there and he didn't care
He took that young girl's life.

But some will say it wasn't that way
That she met a stranger or a friend
In a big black car she was carried far
And nobody knows the end.

On Tuesday morning, while Frances was getting breakfast and Maureen was helping her husband to finish dressing, there was a knock at the front door; by someone who did not notice or trust the bell. It was not unheard-of for people to drop by this early, but it made difficulties, because Lawyer Stephens was apt to have more trouble with his speech early in the morning, and his mind, too, took a little time to get warmed up.

Through the pebbled glass in the front door Maureen saw the blurry outlines of a man and a woman. Dressed up, at least the woman was—wearing a hat. That meant serious business. But serious business, to the people involved, might still seem humdrum to others. Death threats had been issued over the ownership of a chest of drawers, and a property owner could pop a blood vessel over a six-inch overlap of a driveway. Missing firewood, barking dogs, a nasty letter—all that could fire people up and bring them knocking. *Go and ask Lawyer Stephens. Go and ask about the Law.*

Of course there was a slim chance this pair might be peddling religion.

Not so.

"We've come to see the Lawyer," the woman said.

"Well," said Maureen. "It's early." She did not know who they were right away.

"Sorry, but we got something to tell him," the woman said, and somehow she had stepped into the front hall and Maureen had stepped backward. The man shook his head as if in discomfort or apology, indicating that he had no choice but to follow his wife.

The hall filled up with the smell of shaving soap, paste deodorant, and a cheap drugstore cologne. Lily of the Valley. And now Maureen recognized them.

It was Marian Hubbert. Only, she looked different in a blue suit—which was too heavy for this weather—and her brown cloth gloves, and a brown hat made of feathers. Usually you saw her in town wearing slacks or even what looked like men's work pants. She was a husky woman of about Maureen's age—they had been in high school together, though a year or two apart.

Marian's body was clumsy but quick, and her graying hair was cut short, so that bristles showed on her neck. She had a loud voice, most of the time a rather rambunctious manner. She was toned down now.

The man with her was the man she had married not so long ago. Maybe a couple of years ago. He was tall and boyish-looking, in a cheap, cream-coloured jacket with too much padding in the shoulders. Wavy brown hair, fixed with a wet comb. "Excuse us," he said in a soft voice—perhaps one that his wife was not intended to hear—as Maureen took them into the dining room. Close up, his eyes were not so young—there was a look of strain and dryness, or bewilderment. Perhaps he was not very bright. Maureen remembered now some story about Marian's getting him from an advertisement. *Woman with farm, clear title. Businesswoman with farm*, it could have been, for Marian Hubbert's other name was the Corset Lady. For years and years she had sold made-to-measure corsets and perhaps she still did, to the dwindling number of ladies who wore them. Maureen imagined her taking measurements, prodding like a nurse, bossy and professionally insulting. But she had been kind to her old parents, who lived out on the farm until they were a great age and had any number of things wrong with them. And now another story surfaced, a less malicious one, about her husband. He had driven the bus that took old folks to their therapeutic swimming session, at Walley, in the indoor pool—that was how they had met. Maureen had another picture of him, too—carrying the old father in his arms, into Dr. Sands' office. Marian charging ahead, swinging her purse by its strap, ready to open the door.

She went to tell Frances about breakfast in the dining room, and to ask her to bring extra coffee cups. Then she went to warn her husband.

"It's Marian Hubbert, or she used to be," she said. "And whatever that man's name is that she's married to."

"Slater," her husband said, the way he would dryly bring forth the particulars of a sale or lease that you wouldn't have thought he could know so readily. "Theo."

"You're more up-to-date than I am," Maureen said.

He asked if his porridge was ready. "Eat and listen," he said.

Frances brought in the porridge, and he fell to at once. Slathered with cream and brown sugar, porridge was his favorite food, winter and summer.

When she brought the coffee, Frances tried to hang about, but Marian gave her a steady look that turned her back to the kitchen.

There, thought Maureen. She can manage better than I can.

Marian Hubbert was a woman without one visible advantage. She had a heavy face, a droop to the cheeks—she reminded Maureen of some sort of dog. Not necessarily an ugly dog. Not an ugly face, really. Just a heavy and determined one. But everywhere Marian went, as now in Maureen's dining room, she would present herself as if she had absolute rights. She had to be taken account of.

She had put on a quantity of makeup, and perhaps that was another reason Maureen hadn't immediately recognized her. It was pale and pinkish and unsuited to her olive skin, her black, heavy eyebrows. It made her look odd but not pathetic. It seemed she might have put it on, like the suit and hat, to demonstrate that she could get herself up the way other women did, she knew what was expected. But perhaps she intended to look pretty. Perhaps she saw herself transformed by the pale powder that was hanging on her cheeks, the thick pink lipstick—perhaps she turned when she finished and coyly showed herself to her husband.

Answering for his wife in regard to sugar for her coffee, he almost giggled when he said *lumps*. He said please and thank you as often as possible. He said, "Thank you very much, please. Thank you. The same for me. Thank you."

"Now, we didn't know anything about this girl until after it seems like everybody else knew," Marian was saying. "I mean, we didn't even know anybody was missing or anything. Not until yesterday when we came into town. Yesterday? Monday? Yesterday was Monday. I have got my days all mixed up, because I've been taking painkiller pills."

Marian was not the sort to tell you she had been taking pills and let it go at that. She would tell you what for.

"So I had a terrible big boil on my neck, right there?" She said. She scrunched her head around, trying to show them the dressing on it. "It was giving me pain and I started getting a headache, too, and I think it was something connected. So I was feeling so bad on Sunday I just took a hot cloth and put it to my neck and swallowed a couple of painkillers and I went and laid down. He was off work that day, but now he's working he's always got lots to do when he's home. He's working at the Atomic Energy."

"Douglas Point?" said Lawyer Stephens, with a brief look up from his porridge. There was a certain interest or respect all men showed—even Lawyer

Stephens had to show it—at the mention of the new Atomic Energy Station at Douglas Point.

"That's where he works now," Marian said. Like many country women and Carstairs women, too, she referred to her husband as *he*—it was spoken with a special emphasis—rather than calling him by his name. Maureen had caught herself doing it a few times, but had corrected the habit without anybody's having to point it out to her.

"He had to take the salt out for the cows," Marian said, "and then he went back and worked on the fence. He had to go quarter of a mile, maybe, so he took the truck. But he left Bounder. He went off in the truck without him. Bounder our dog. Bounder won't go any distance unless that he can ride. He left him on guard sort of because he knew I had went and laid down. I had taken a couple of 222s, and I went into a kind of doze more than a regular sleep, and then I heard Bounder barking. It woke me right up. Bounder barking."

She got up then, and she put on her wrapper and went downstairs. She had been lying down just in her underclothing. She looked out the front door, out the lane, and there was nobody. She didn't see Bounder, either, and by that time he had quit his barking. He quit when it was somebody he recognized. Or somebody just going by on the road. But still she wasn't satisfied. She looked out the kitchen windows, which gave on the side yard but not the back. Still nobody. She couldn't see the backyard from the kitchen—to do that, you had to go right out through what they called the back kitchen. It was just a sort of catchall room, like a shed tacked onto the house, all jumbled up with everything. It had a window looking out back, but you couldn't get near that or see out of it because of cardboard boxed piled up and the old couch springs standing on end. You had to go right and open the back door to see out. And now she thought she could hear something at that door like a kind of clawing. Maybe Bounder. Maybe not.

It was so hot in that shut-up back kitchen packed with junk that she could barely breathe. Under her wrapper she was all sticky with sweat. She said to herself, Well, at least you haven't got a fever, you are sweating like a pig.

She was more interested in getting air to breathe than she was scared of what might be out there, so she thrust the door open. It opened outward, pushing the fellow back that was up against it. He staggered back but didn't fall. And she saw who it was. Mr. Siddicup, from town.

Bounder knew him, of course, because he often went by and sometimes cut across the property on his walks and they never stopped him. He came right through the yard, sometimes—it was just because he didn't know any better anymore. She never yelled at him, the way some people did. She had even invited him to sit on the steps and rest if he was tired, she had offered him a cigarette. He would take the cigarette, too. But he would never sit down.

Bounder was just nosing around and fawning on him. Bounder was not particular.

Maureen knew Mr. Siddicup, as everybody did. He used to be the piano tuner at Douds. He used to be a dignified, sarcastic little Englishman, with a pleasant wife. They read books from the library and were noted for their garden, especially strawberries and roses. Then, a few years ago, misfortunes started arriving. Mr. Siddicup had an operation on his throat—it must have been for cancer—and after that he could not talk, just make wheezing and growling noises. He had already retired from Douds—they had some electronic way of tuning pianos now, better than the human ear. His wife died suddenly. Then the changes came in a hurry—he deteriorated from a decent old man into a morose and rather disgusting old urchin, in a matter of months. Dirty whiskers, dribbles on his clothes, a sour smoky smell, and a look in his eyes of constant suspicion, sometimes of loathing. In the grocery store if he could not find what he wanted, or if they had changed the places of things, he would knock canned goods and boxes of cereal over on purpose. He was not welcome anymore in the café, and never went near the library. Women from his wife's church group kept going to see him for a while, bringing a meat dish or some baking. But the smell of the house was dreadful and the disorder perverse—even for a man living alone it was inexcusable—and he was the opposite of grateful. He would toss the remainders of pies and casseroles out on his front walk, breaking the dishes. No woman wanted the joke going round that even Mr. Siddicup wouldn't eat her cooking. So they left him alone. Mostly he just walked the roads. When you were driving along, you might spot him standing still, standing in the ditch, mostly hidden in tall weeds and grass, while cars whizzed by him. You could also run into him in a town miles away from home, and there a strange thing would happen. His face would take on something of its old expression, ready for the genial obligatory surprise, the greeting of people who lived in one place meeting in another. It did look as if he had a hope then that the moment would open out, that words would break through, in fact that perhaps the changes would be wiped out, here in a different place—his voice and his wife and his old stability in life might all be returned to him.

People were not unkind, usually. They were patient up to a point. Marian said she would never have chased him off.

She said he looked pretty wild, this time. Not just as he looked when he was trying to get his meaning out and it would not come, or when he was mad at some kids who were teasing him. His head was bobbing back and forth and his face looked swollen up, like a bawling baby's.

Now then, she said. Now, Mr. Siddicup, what's the matter? What are you trying to tell me? Do you want a cigarette? Are you telling me it's Sunday and you're all out of cigarettes?

Shook his head back and forth, then bobbed it up and down, then shook it back and forth again.

Come on, now. Make up your mind, said Marian.

Ah, ahh was all he said. He put both hands to his head, knocking off his cap. Then he backed farther off and started zigzagging around the yard in between the pump and the clothesline, still making these noises—*ah, ahh*—that would never turn into words.

Here Marian pushed back her chair so abruptly that it almost fell over. She got up and began to show them just what Mr. Siddicup had done. She lurched and crouched and banged her hands to her head, though she did not dislodge her hat. In front of the sideboard, in front of the silver tea service presented to Lawyer Stephens in appreciation of his many years' work for the Law Society, she put on this display. Her husband held his coffee cup in both hands and kept his deferential eyes on her by an effort of will. Something flashed in his face—a tic, a nerve jumping in one cheek. She was watching him in spite of her antics, and her look said, Hold on. Be still.

Lawyer Stephens, as far as Maureen could see, had not glanced up at all.

He did like that, Marian said, reseating herself. He did like that, and because she had not been feeling well herself, she got the idea that perhaps he was in pain.

Mr. Siddicup. Mr. Siddicup. Are you trying to tell me your head hurts? Do you want me to get you a pill? Do you want me to take you to the doctor?

No answer. He wouldn't stop for her. *Ah, ahh.*

In his stumbling around he found himself at the pump. They had running water in the house now, but still used the pump outside and filled Bounder's dish at it. When Mr. Siddicup took note of what it was, he got busy. He went to work on the handle and pumped it up and down like crazy. There wasn't any cup to drink from, like there used to be. But as soon as water came he stuck his head under. It splashed and stopped, because he had quit pumping. Back he went and pumped again, and stuck himself under again, and on like that, pumping and dousing, letting it pour over his head and face and shoulders and chest, soaking himself and still, when he could, making some noise. Bounder was excited and ran around bumping into him and letting out barks and whines in sympathy.

That's enough, you two! Marian yelled at them. Let go that pump! Let go and settle down!

Only Bounder listened to her. Mr. Siddicup had to keep on till he got himself so drenched and blinded he couldn't find the pump handle. Then he stopped. And he lifted one arm up, he lifted and pointed back in the general direction of the bush and the river. He was pointing and making his noises. At the time, that didn't make any sense to her. She didn't think about it till later. Then he quit that and just sat down on the well cover, soaked and shivering, with his head in his hands.

Maybe it's something simple after all, she thought. Complaining because there isn't a cup.

If it's a cup you want, I'll go and get you one. No need to carry on like a baby. You stay there, I'll go get you a cup.

She headed back to the kitchen and got a cup. And she had another idea. She fixed him up some graham crackers, with butter and jam. That was a kid's treat, graham crackers, but it was a thing old people liked, too, she remembered from her mother and daddy.

Back to the door she went and pushed it open with her hands full. But there was no sign of him. Nobody in the yard but Bounder, looking the way he did when he knew he's made a fool of himself.

Where did he go, Bounder? Which way did he go?

Bounder was ashamed and fed up and wouldn't give any sign. He slunk off to his place in the house shade, in the dirt, by the foundations.

Mr. Siddicup! Mr. Siddicup! Come see what I got for you!

All silent as the dead. And her head was pounding. She started eating the crackers herself but she shouldn't have—a couple of bites and wanted to puke.

She took two more pills and went back upstairs. The windows up and blinds down. She wished now they'd bought a fan when the sale was on at Canadian Tire. But she slept without one, and when she woke it was nearly dark. She could hear the mower—*he*, her husband, was out finishing the grass at the side of the house. She went down to the kitchen and saw that he had cut up some cold potatoes and boiled an egg and pulled green onions to make a salad. He was not like some men—a hopeless case in the kitchen waiting for the woman to get out of a sickbed and make him a meal. She picked at the salad but couldn't eat. One more pill and up the stairs and dead to the world till morning.

We better get you to the doctor, he said then. He phoned them up at work. I got to take my wife to the doctor.

Marian said, What if she just boiled a needle and he could lance it? But he could not stand to hurt her, and anyway he was afraid he might do something wrong. So they got in the truck and drove in to see Dr. Sands. Dr. Sands was out, they had to wait. Other people waiting told them the news. Everybody was amazed they didn't know. But they hadn't had the radio on. She was the one who always turned it on and she couldn't stand the noise, the way she felt. And they hadn't noticed any groups of men, anything peculiar, on the road.

Dr. Sands fixed the boil but he didn't lance it. His way of dealing with a boil was to strike it a sharp blow, knock it on the head, when you thought he was just looking at it. There! he said, that's less fuss than the needle and not so painful overall because you didn't have time to get in a sweat. He cleaned it out and put the dressing on and said she'd soon be feeling better.

And so she was, but sleepy. She was so useless and foggy in the head that she went back to bed and slept till her husband came up around four o'clock with a cup of tea. It was then she thought of those girls, coming in with Miss Johnstone on Saturday morning, wanting a drink. She had lots of Coca-Cola and she gave it to them in flowered glasses, with ice cubes. Miss Johnstone would only take water. *He* let them play with the hose, they jumped around and squirted each other and had a great time. They were trying to skip the streams of water, and they were a bit on the wild side when Miss Johnstone wasn't looking. He had to practically wrestle the hose away from them, and give them a few squirts of water to make them behave.

She was trying to picture which girl it was. She knew the minister's daughter and Dr. Sands' daughter and the Trowells—with their little sheep eyes you would know a Trowell anywhere. But which of the others? She recalled one who was very noisy and jumping up trying to get the hose even when he took it away, and one was doing cartwheels and one was a skinny pretty little thing with blond hair. But maybe she was thinking of Robin Sands—Robin had blond hair. She asked her husband that night did he know which one, but he was worse than she was—he didn't know people here and couldn't separate out any of them.

Also she told him about Mr. Siddicup. It all came back to her now. The way he was upset, the pumping, the way he pointed. It bothered her what that could mean. They talked about it and wondered about it and got themselves into a state of wondering so they hardly got any sleep. Until she finally said to him, Well, I know what we have to do. We have to go and talk to Lawyer Stephens.

So they got up and came as soon as they could.

"Police," said Lawyer Stephens now. "Police. Who should gone to see."

The husband spoke. He said, "We didn't know if we should ought to do that or not." He had both hands on the table, fingers spread, pressed down, pulling at the cloth.

"Not accusation," Lawyer Stephens said. "Information."

He had talked in that abbreviated way even before his stroke. And Maureen had noticed, long ago, how just a few words of his, spoken in no very friendly tone—spoken, in fact, in a tone of brusque chastisement—could cheer people up and lift a weight off them.

She had been thinking of the other reason why the women stopped going to visit Mr. Siddicup. They didn't like the clothes. Women's clothes. underwear—old frayed slips and brassières and worn-out underpants and nubbly stockings, hanging from the backs of chairs or from a line about the heater, or just in a heap on the table. All these things must have belonged to his wife, of course, and at first it looked as if he might be washing and drying them and sorting them out, prior to getting rid of them. But they were there week after week, and the women started to wonder: Did he leave them lying around to suggest things? Did he put them on himself next to his skin? Was he a pervert?

Now all that would come out, they'd chalk that up against him.

Pervert. Maybe they were right. Maybe he would lead them to where he'd strangled or beat Heather to death in a sexual fit, or they would find something of hers in his house. And people would say in horrid, hushed voices that no, they weren't surprised. *I wasn't surprised, were you?*

Lawyer Stephens had asked some question about the job at Douglas Point, and Marian said, "He works in Maintenance. Every day when he comes out he's got to go through the check for X-rays, and even the rags he cleans off his boots with, they have to be buried underground."

When Maureen shut the door on the pair of them and saw their shapes wobble away through the pebbled glass, she was not quite satisfied. She climbed three steps to the landing on the stairs, where there was a little arched window. She watched them.

No car was in sight, or truck or whatever they had. They must have left it parked on the main street or in the lot behind the Town Hall. Possibly they did not want it to be seen in front of Lawyer Stephens' house.

The Town Hall was where the Police Office was. They did turn in that direction, but then they crossed the street diagonally and, still within Maureen's sight, they sat down on the low stone wall that ran around the old cemetery and flower plot called Pioneer Park.

Why should they feel a need to sit down after sitting in the dining room for what must have been at least an hour? They didn't talk, or look at each other, but seemed united, as if taking a rest in the midst of hard shared labors.

Lawyer Stephens, when in a reminiscing mood, would talk about how people used to rest on that wall. Farm women who had to walk into town to sell chickens or butter. Country girls on their way to high school, before there was any such thing as a school bus. They would stop and hide their galoshes and retrieve them on the way home.

At other times he had no patience with reminiscing.

"Olden times. Who wants 'em back?"

Now Marian took out some pins and carefully lifted off her hat. So that was it—her hat was hurting her. She set it in her lap, and her husband reached over. He took it away, as if anxious to take away anything that might be a burden to her. He settled it in his lap. He bent over and started to stroke it, in a comforting way. He stroked that hat made of horrible brown feathers as if he were pacifying a little scared hen.

But Marian stopped him. She said something to him, she clamped a hand down on his. The way a mother might interrupt the carrying-on of a simple-minded child—with a burst of abhorrence, a moment's break in her tired-out love.

Maureen felt a shock. She felt a shrinking in her bones.

Her husband came out of the dining room. She didn't want him to catch her looking at them. She turned around the vase of dried grasses that was on the window ledge. She said, "I thought she'd never get done talking."

He hadn't noticed. His mind was on something else.

"Come on down here," he said.

Early in their marriage Maureen's husband had mentioned to her that he and the first Mrs. Stephens gave up sleeping together after Helena, the younger child, was born. "We'd got our boy and our girl," he said, meaning there was no need to try for more. Maureen did not understand then that he might intend some similar cutoff for her. She was in love when she married him. It was true that when he first put his arm around her waist, in the office, she thought he must believe that she was headed for the wrong door and was redirecting her—but that was a conclusion she came to because of his propriety, not because she hadn't longed to feel his arm there. People who thought she was making an advantageous, though kindly, marriage, would have been amazed at how happy she was on her honeymoon—and that was in spite of having to learn to play bridge. She knew his power—the way he used it and the way he held it back. He was attractive to her—never mind his age, ungainliness, nicotine stains on his teeth and fingers. His skin was warm. A couple of years into the marriage she miscarried and bled so heavily that her tubes had been tied, to prevent such a thing from ever happening again. After that that the intimate part of her life with her husband came to an end. It seemed that he had been mostly obliging her, because he felt that it was wrong to deny a woman the chance to have a child.

Sometimes she would pester him a little and he would say, "Now, Maureen. What's all this about?" Or else he would tell her to grow up. "Grow up" was an injunction that he had picked up from his own children, and had continued to use long after they had dropped it, in fact long after they had moved away from home.

His saying that humiliated her, and her eyes would fill with tears. He was a man who detested tears above all things.

And now, she thought, wouldn't it be a relief to have that state of affairs back again! For her husband's appetite had returned—or an entirely new appetite had developed. There was nothing now of the rather clumsy ceremony, the formal fondness, of their early times together. Now his eyes would cloud over and his face would seem weighed down. He would speak to her in a curt and menacing way and sometimes push and prod her, even trying to jam his fingers into her from behind. She did not need any of that to make her hurry—she was anxious to get him into the bedroom as soon as possible, afraid that he might misbehave elsewhere. His old office had been made into a downstairs bedroom with a bathroom adjoining it, so that he would not have to climb the stairs. At least that room had a lock, so Frances could not burst in. But the phone might ring, Frances might have to come looking for them. She might stand outside the door and then she would have to hear the noises—Lawyer Stephens' panting and grunting and bullying, the hiss of disgust with which he would order Maureen to do this or that, his pounding of her right at the end and the command he let out then, a command that perhaps would be incoherent to anybody but Maureen but that would still speak eloquently, like lavatory noises, of his extremity.

"Ta' dirty! Ta' dirty!"

This came from a man who had once shut Helena in her room for calling her brother a shitty bastard.

Maureen knew enough words, but it was difficult for her in her shaken state to call up just which ones might suit, and to utter them in a tone that would be convincing. She did try. She wanted above all else to help him along.

Afterward he fell into the brief sleep that seemed to erase the episode from his memory. Maureen escaped to the bathroom. She did the first cleanup there and then hurried upstairs to replace some clothing. Often at these times she had to hang onto the bannisters, she felt so hollow and feeble. And she had to keep her mouth closed not on any howls of protest but on a long sickening whimper of complaint that would have made her sound like a beaten dog.

Today she managed better than usual. She was able to look into the bathroom mirror, and move her eyebrows, her lips and jaws, around to bring her expression back to normal. So much for that, she seemed to be saying. Even while it was going on she had been able to think of other things. She had thought about making a custard, she thought about whether they had enough milk and eggs. And right through her husband's rampage she thought of the fingers moving in the feathers, the wife's hand laid on top of the husband's, pressing down.

So of Heather Bell we will sing our song,
As we will till our day is done.
In the forest green she was taken from the scene
Though her life had barely begun.

"There is a poem already made up and written down," Frances said. "I've got it here typed out."

"I thought I'd make a custard," said Maureen.

How much had Frances heard of what Marian Hubbert had said? Everything, probably. She sounded breathless with the effort of keeping all that in. She held up the typed lines in front of Maureen's face and Maureen said, "It's too long, I don't have time." She started to separate the eggs.

"It's good," Frances said. "It's good enough to be put to music."

She read it through aloud. Maureen said, "I have to concentrate."

"So I guess I got my marching orders," said Frances, and went to do the sunroom.

Then Maureen had the peace of the kitchen—the old white tiles and high yellowed walls, the bowls and pots and implements familiar and comforting to her, as probably to her predecessor.

What Mary Johnstone told the girls in her talk was always more or less the same thing and most of them knew what to expect. They could even make prepared faces at each other. She told them how Jesus had come and talked to her when she was in the iron lung. She did not mean in a dream, she said, or in a vision, or when she was delirious. She meant that He came and she recognized Him but didn't think anything was strange about it. She recognized Him at once, though he was dressed like a doctor in a white coat. She thought, Well, that's reasonable—otherwise they wouldn't let Him in here. That was how she took it. Lying there in the iron lung, she was sensible and stupid at once, as you are when something like that hits you. (She meant Jesus, not the polio.) Jesus said, "You've got to get back up to bat, Mary." That was all. She was a good softball player, and He used language that He knew she would understand. Then He went away. And she hugged onto Life, the way He had told her to.

There was more to follow, about the uniqueness and specialness of each of their lives and their bodies, which led of course into what Mary Johnstone called "plain talk" about boys and urges. (This was where they did the faces—they were too abashed when she was going on about Jesus.) And about liquor and cigarettes and how one thing can lead to another. They thought she was crazy—and she couldn't even tell that they had smoked themselves sick last night. They reeked and she never mentioned it.

So she was—crazy. But everybody let her talk about Jesus in the hospital because they thought she was entitled to believe that.

But suppose you did see something? Not along the line of Jesus, but something? Maureen has had that happen. Sometimes when she is just going to sleep but not quite asleep, not dreaming yet, she has caught something. Or even in the daytime during what she thinks of as her normal life. She might catch herself sitting on stone steps eating cherries and watching a man coming up the steps carrying a parcel. She had never seen those steps or that man, but for an instant they seem to be part of another life that she is leading, a life just as long and complicated and strange and dull as this one. And she isn't surprised. It's just a fluke, a speedily corrected error, that she knows about both lives at the same time. It seemed so ordinary, she thinks afterward. The cherries. The parcel.

What she sees now isn't in any life of her own. She sees one of those thick-fingered hands that pressed into her tablecloth and that had worked among the feathers, and it is pressed down, unresistingly, but by somebody else's will—it is pressed down on the open burner of the stove where she is stirring the custard in the double boiler, and held there just for a second or two, just long enough to scorch the flesh on the red coil, to scorch but not to maim. In silence this is done, and by agreement—a brief and barbaric and necessary act. So it seems. The punished hand dark as a glove or a hand's shadow, the fingers spread. Still in the same clothes. The cream-colored sleeve, the dull blue.

Maureen hears her husband moving around in the front hall, so she turns off the heat and lays down the spoon and goes in to him. He has tidied himself up. He is ready to go out. She knows without asking where he is going. Down to the Police Office, to find out what has been reported, what is being done.

"Maybe I should drive you," she says. "It's hot out."

He shakes his head, he mutters.

"Or I could walk along with you."

No. He is going on a serious errand and it would diminish him to be accompanied or transported by a wife.

She opens the front door for him and he says, "Thank you," in his stiff, quaintly repentant way. As he goes past, he bends and purses his lips at the air close to her cheek.

They've gone, there's nobody sitting on the wall now.

Heather Bell will not be found. No body, no trace. She has blown away like ashes. Her displayed photograph will fade in public places. Its tight-lipped smile, bitten in at one corner as if suppressing a disrespectful laugh, will seem to be connected with her disappearance rather than her mockery of the school photographer. There will always be a tiny suggestion, in that, of her own free will.

Mr. Siddicup will not be any help. He will alternate between bewilderment and tantrums. They will not find anything when they search his house, unless you count those old underclothes of his wife's, and when they dig up his garden the only bones they will find will be old bones that dogs have buried. Many people will continue to believe that he did something or saw something. *He had something to do with it.* When he is committed to the Provincial Asylum, renamed the Mental Health Centre, there will be letters in the local paper about Preventive Custody, and locking the stable door after the horse is stolen.

There will also be letters in the newspaper from Mary Johnstone, explaining why she behaved as she did, why in all good sense and good faith she behaved as she did that Sunday. Finally the editor will have to let her know that Heather Bell is old news, and not the only thing the town wants to be known for, and if the hikes are to come to an end it won't be the worst thing in the world, and the story can't be rehashed forever.

Maureen is a young woman yet, though she doesn't think so, and she has life ahead of her. First a death—that will come soon—then another marriage, new places and houses. In kitchens hundreds and thousands of miles away, she'll watch the soft skin form on the back of a wooden spoon and her memory will twitch, but it will not quite reveal to her this moment when she seems to be looking into an open secret, something not startling until you think of trying to tell it.

1994

Mordecai Richler

1931–2001

Mordecai Richler was born in the Jewish quarter of Montreal and attended Baron Byng High School and Sir George Williams University (now Concordia University). He left before graduating. He went to Paris in 1951 and began his first novel, *The Acrobats* (1954). He returned to Canada in 1952, worked briefly for the CBC, and left again in 1954 for England, where he lived for the next eighteen years. Supporting himself as a freelance writer, Richler wrote scripts for television and such films as *No Love for Johnny* (1960) and *Life at the Top* (1965). In 1972 he returned to live permanently in Canada. His novels *The Apprenticeship of Duddy Kravitz* (1959) and *St Urbain's Horseman* (1971) are based on his experiences growing up in poverty in Montreal. *Solomon Gursky Was Here* (1989), thought by many to be his best novel, is a satire that takes as its theme the heroic quest to uncover Jewish history and experience in Canada. In 1975 Richler published the first of several books for children, *Jacob Two-Two Meets the Hooded Fang*, which was made into a film, as were two of his other books, *Joshua Then and Now* (1980) and *The Apprenticeship of Duddy Kravitz*. A controversial and prolific journalist, Richler published innumerable articles which he selected and edited in five collections, including *Hunting Tigers under Glass* (1968) and *Home Sweet Home* (1984), in which he waded into discussions about Quebec nationalism and the language laws of his home province. He twice won the Governor General's Award for Fiction, and in 1974 won the Screenwriters Guild of America Award. His last novel, *Barney's Version*, was published in 1997 and won the Giller Prize. *Barney's Version* was made into a film in 2010.

Benny, the War in Europe, and Myerson's Daughter Bella

When Benny was sent overseas in the autumn of 1941 his father, Mr Garber, thought that if he had to give up one son to the army, it might as well be Benny, who was a quiet boy, and who wouldn't push where he shouldn't; and Mrs Garber thought: "My Benny he'll take care, he'll watch out"; and Benny's brother Abe thought "when he comes back, I'll have a garage of my own, you bet, and I'll be able to give him a job." Benny wrote every week, and every week the Garbers sent him parcels full of good things that a Jewish boy should always have, like salami and pickled herring and *shtrudel*. The food parcels were always the same, and the letters—coming from Camp Borden and Aldershot and Normandy and Holland—were always the same too. They began—"I hope you are all well and good"—and ended—"don't worry, all the best to everybody, thank you for the parcel."

When Benny came home from the war in Europe, the Garbers didn't make much of a fuss. They met him at the station, of course, and they had a small dinner for him.

Abe was thrilled to see Benny again. "Atta boy," was what he kept saying all evening, "Atta boy, Benny."

"You shouldn't go back to the factory," Mr Garber said. "You don't need the old job. You can be a help to your brother Abe in his garage."

"Yes," Benny said.

"Let him be, let him rest," Mrs Garber said. "What'll happen if he doesn't work for two weeks?"

"Hey, when Artie Segal came back, Abe said, he said that in Italy there was nothing that a guy couldn't get for a couple of Sweet Caps. Was he shooting me the bull, or what?"

Benny had been discharged and sent home, not because the war was over, but because of the shrapnel in his leg, but he didn't limp too badly and he didn't talk about his wound or the war, so at first nobody noticed that he had changed. Nobody, that is, except Myerson's daughter Bella.

Myerson was the proprietor of Pop's Cigar & Soda, on Laurier Street, and any day of the week, you could find him there seated on a worn, peeling kitchen chair playing poker with the men of the neighbourhood. He had a glass eye and when a player hesitated on a bet, he would take it out and polish it, a gesture that never failed to intimidate. His daughter, Bella, worked behind the counter. She had a club foot and mousy hair and some more hair on her face, and although she was only twenty-six, it was generally supposed that she would end up an old maid. Anyway she was the one—the first one—who noticed that the war in Europe had changed Benny. And, as a matter of fact, the very first time he came into the store after his homecoming she said to him: "What's wrong, Benny? Are you afraid?"

"I'm all right," he said.

Benny was a quiet boy. He was short and skinny with a long narrow face, a pulpy mouth that was somewhat crooked, and soft black eyes. He had big conspicuous hands, which he preferred to keep out of sight in his pockets. In fact, he seemed to want to keep out of sight altogether and whenever possible, he stood behind a chair or in a dim light so that people wouldn't notice him—and, noticing him, chase him away. When he failed the ninth grade at Baron Byng High School, his class-master, a Mr Perkins, had sent him home with a note saying: "Benjamin is not a student, but he has all the makings of a good citizen. He is honest and attentive in class and a hard worker. I recommend that he learn a trade."

And when Mr Garber had read what his son's teacher had written, he had shaken his head and crumpled up the bit of paper and said,—"A trade?"—he had looked at his boy and shaken his head and said—"A trade?"

Mrs Garber had said stoutly, "Haven't you got a trade?"

"Shapiro's boy will be a doctor," Mr Garber had said.

"Shapiro's boy," Mrs Garber said.

And afterwards, Benny had retrieved the note and smoothed out the creases and put it in his pocket, where it had remained. For Benny was sure that one day a policeman, or perhaps even a Mountie, would try to arrest him, and then the paper that Mr Perkins had written so long ago might prove helpful.

Benny figured that he had been lucky, truly lucky, to get away with living for so long. Oh, he had his dreams. He would have liked to have been an aeroplane pilot, or still better, to have been born rich or intelligent. Those kind of people, he had heard, slept in mornings until as late as nine o'clock. But he had been born stupid, people could tell that, just looking at him, and one day they would come to take him away. They would, sure as hell they would.

The day after his return to Montreal, Benny showed up at Abe's garage having decided that he didn't want two weeks off. That pleased Abe a lot. "I can see that you've matured since you've been away," Abe said. "That's good. That counts for you in this world."

Abe worked very hard, he worked night and day, and he believed that having Benny with him would give his business an added kick. "That's my kid brother Benny," Abe used to tell the cabbies. "Four years in the infantry, two of them up front. A tough hombre, let me tell you."

For the first few weeks Abe was very pleased with Benny. "He's slow," he thought, "no genius of a mechanic, but the customers like him and he'll learn." Then Abe began to notice things. When business was slow, Benny—instead of taking advantage of the lull to clean up the shop—used to sit shivering in a dim corner, with his hands folded tight on his lap. The first time Abe noticed his brother behaving like that, he said: 'What's wrong? You got a chill?"

"No. I'm all right."

"You want to go home, or something?"

"No."

Then, when Abe began to notice him sitting like that more and more, he pretended not to see. "He needs time," he thought. But whenever it rained, and it rained often that spring, Benny was not to be found around the garage, and that put Abe in a bad temper. Until one day during a thunder shower, Abe tried the toilet door and found that it was locked. "Benny," he yelled, "come on out, I know you're in there."

Benny didn't answer, so Abe got the key. He found Benny huddled up in a corner with his head buried in his knees, trembling, with sweat running down his face in spite of the cold.

"It's raining," Benny said.

"Benny, get up. What's wrong?"

"Go away," Benny said. "It's raining."

"I'll get a doctor, Benny. I'll . . ."

"Don't—you mustn't. Go away. Please, Abe."

"But Benny . . ."

A terrible chill must have overcome Benny just then for he began to shake violently, just as if an inner whip had been cracked. Then, after it had passed, he looked up at Abe dumbly, his mouth hanging open. "It's raining," he said.

His discovery that afternoon gave Abe a good scare, and the next morning he went to see his father. "It was awful spooky, Pa," Abe said. "I don't know what to do with him."

"The war left him with a bad taste," Mrs Garber said. "It made him something bad."

"Other boys went to war," Abe said.

"Shapiro's boy," Mr Garber said, "was an officer."

"Shapiro's boy," Mrs Garber said. "You give him a vacation, Abe. You insist. He's a good boy. From the best. He'll be all right."

Benny did not know what to do with his vacation so he tried sleeping in late like the rich and the intelligent, but in the late morning hours he dreamed bad dreams and that made him very frightened so he gave up that kind of thing. He did not dare go walking because he was sure people could tell, just looking at him, that he was not working, and he did not want others to think that he was a bum. So he began to do odd jobs for people in the neighbourhood. He repaired bicycles and toasters and lamps. But he did not take any money for his work and that made people a little afraid. "Isn't our money good enough for him? All right, he was wounded, so maybe I was the one who shot him?"

Benny began to hang around Pop's Cigar & Soda.

"I don't like it, Bella," Mr Myerson said, admiring the polish of his glass eye against the light. "I need him here like a cancer."

"Something's wrong with him psychologically," one of the card players said.

But obviously Bella liked having Benny around, and after a while Mr Myerson stopped complaining. "Maybe the boy is serious," he thought, "and what with her club-foot and all that stuff on her face, I can't start picking and choosing. Beside, it's not as if he was a crook!"

Bella and Benny did not talk much when they were together, afraid, perhaps, that whatever it was that was "starting" up between them, was rich in delicacy, and would be soiled by ordinary words. She used to knit, he used to smoke. He would watch silently as she limped about the store, silently, with longing, and burning hope and consternation. The letter from Mr Perkins was in his pocket. He wanted to tell her about the war—about things.

"I was walking with the sergeant. He reached into his pocket to show me a letter from his wife when . . ."

There he would stop. A twitching would start around his eyes and he would swallow hard and stop.

Bella would look up from her knitting, waiting for him the way a mother waits for a child to be reasonable, knowing that it is only a question of time. But Benny would begin to shiver, and, looking down at the floor, grip his hands together until the knuckles went white. Around five in the afternoon he would get up and leave without saying a word. Bella would give him a stack of magazines to take home and at night he would read them all from cover to cover and the next morning he would bring them back as clean as new. Then he would sit with her in the store again, looking down at the floor or at his hands, as though he were in great pain. Time passed, and one day instead of going home around five in the afternoon he went upstairs with her. Mr Myerson, who was watching, smiled happily. He turned to Mr Shub and said: "If I had a boy of my own, I couldn't wish for a better one than Benny."

"Look who's counting his chickens already," Mr Shub said.

Benny's vacation continued for several weeks and every morning he sat down in the store and stared at his hands, as if he expected them to have changed overnight, and every evening he went upstairs with Bella pretending not to have heard the remarks, the good-natured observations that had been made by the card-players as they passed.

Until, one afternoon, she said to him: "I'm going to have a baby."

"All right," Benny said.

"Aren't you even going to say luck or something?"

Benny got up and bit his lower lip and gripped his hands together hard. "If you only knew what I have seen," he said.

They had a very simple wedding without speeches in a small synagogue and after the ceremony was over Abe slapped his younger brother's back and said, "Atta boy, Benny. Atta boy."

"Can I come back to work?"

"Sure, of course you can. You're the old Benny again," Abe said. "I can see that."

And when Mr Garber got home, without much more to expect but getting older, and more tired earlier in the day, he turned to his wife and said: "Shapiro's boy married into the Segals."

"Shapiro's boy," Mrs Garber said.

Benny went back to the garage but this time he settled down to work hard and that pleased Abe a good deal. "That's my kid brother, Benny," Abe used to tell the cabbies, "married six weeks and he's already got one in the oven. A quick worker, I'll tell you."

Benny settled down to work hard and when the baby was born he even laughed a little and began to save money and plan things, but every now and then, usually when there was a slack period at the garage, Benny would shut up tight and sit in a chair in a dark corner and stare at his hands. Bella was good with him. She never raised her voice to say an ugly thing, and when he woke up screaming from a dream about the war in Europe she would stroke his neck and say tender things. He, on the other hand, began to speak to her confidentially.

"Bella?"

"Yes."

"I killed a man."

"What? You what? When did you . . ."

"In the war."

"Oh, in the war. For a moment I—A German you mean . . ."

"Yes, a German."

"If you ask me it's too bad you didn't kill a dozen. Those Germans I . . ."

"I killed him with my hands."

"Go to sleep."

"Bella?"

"Yes."

"Are you ashamed that I . . ."

"Go to sleep."

"I saw babies killed," he said. "What if . . ."

"There won't be another war. Don't worry about our baby."

"But . . ."

"Sleep. Go to sleep."

The baby grew into a fine, husky boy, and whenever there was a parade Benny used to hoist him on his shoulders so that he could see better. He was amazed, truly amazed, that he could have had such a beautiful child. He hardly had nightmares at all any more and he became talkative and somewhat shrewd. One night he came home and said: "Abe is going to open a branch on Mount Royal Street. I'm going to manage it. I'm going to be a partner in it."

So Benny finally threw away the paper that Mr Perkins had written for him so long ago. They bought a car and planned, the following year, to have enough money saved so that Bella could go to a clinic in the United States to have an operation on her club foot. "I can assure you that I'm not going to spend such a fortune to make myself beautiful," Bella said, "and plainly speaking I'm not doing it for you. But I don't want that when the boy is old enough to go to school that he should be teased because his mother is a cripple."

Then, a month before Bella was to go to the clinic, they went to see their first cinemascope film. Now, previous to that evening, Bella had made a point never to take Benny along to see a war film, no matter who was playing in it. So as soon as the newsreel came on—it was that special one about the hydrogen bomb test—she knew that she had made a mistake in bringing Benny with her, cinemascope or no cinemascope. She turned to him quickly. "Don't look," she said.

But Benny was enthralled. He watched the explosion, and he watched as the newsreel showed by means of diagrams what a hydrogen bomb could do to a city the size of New York—never mind Montreal.

Then he got up and left.

When Bella got home that night she found Benny huddled up in a dark corner with his head buried in his knees, trembling, with sweat running down his face. She tried to stroke his neck but he moved away from her.

"Should I send for a doctor?"

"Bella," he said. "Bella, Bella."

"Try to relax," she said. "Try to think about something pretty. Flowers, or something. Try for the boy's sake."

"Bella," he said. "Bella, Bella."

When she woke up the next morning he was still crouching there in the dark corner gripping his hands together tight, and he wouldn't eat or speak—not even to the boy.

The living room was in a mess, papers spilled everywhere, as if he had been searching for something.

Finally—it must have been around noon—he put on his hat and walked out of the house. She knew right then that she should have stopped him. That she shouldn't have let him go. She knew.

Her father came around at five o'clock and she could tell from the expression on his face that she had guessed right. Mr and Mrs Garber were with him.

"He's dead?" Bella asked.

"Shapiro's boy, the doctor," Mr Garber said, "said it was quick."

"Shapiro's boy," Mrs Garber said.

"It wasn't the driver's fault," Mr Myerson said.

"I know," Bella said.

1969

John Updike

1932–2009

A not-so-short story could be made of John Updike's publishing history beginning with his first novel, *The Poorhouse Fair* (1959) and his first collections of stories, *The Same Door* (1959) and *Pigeon Feathers* (1962). If one counts separate volumes (including some limited editions)—novels, poetry, short stories, and collections of essays, but not introductions and other contributions—the total is an astonishing eighty titles. Enumeration is a favourite game in Updike criticism because an economical appraisal of his essential substance is almost impossible and because sheer volume and the tireless professionalism it reflects is inherent to the large, if somewhat hazy, place he occupies in contemporary literature. Whatever form or subject he turns his attention to, the one option Updike never seems to have just under the surface is silence, a sense of the danger, as Don DeLillo articulates it, of the next sentence not making it to the page. It never takes long for a reader or a reviewer to focus on Updike's famous prose style:

its pictorial strength, its compelling rhythm, its lyricism. For most, the style is remarkable; for others, it is facile, but however one gauges Updike's language, it is his trusted mode in registering his compassionate, often humorous pictures of Middle America's particular muddles: sexual, religious, vocational, and, of course, mortal. "My subject," Updike says, "is the American Protestant small-town middle class. I like middles. It is in middles that extremes clash, where ambiguity restlessly rules." Given the centrality to his career of the sequence of novels about "Rabbit" Angstrom, it is easy to forget how adventurous and quirky Updike can—or could—be. At the age of twenty-six, he wrote a novel (*The Poorhouse Fair*) about one fretful day in the lives of people in a nursing home. In *The Centaur* (1963) the vividness of myth and the mundane coalesce with superb grace, and in *The Coup* (1978), far from his own Shillington, Pennsylvania, origins, Updike occupies the consciousness of an exiled African revolutionary leader. Unlike this figure, who attended McCarthy College in Franchise, Wisconsin, Updike graduated from Harvard, then studied art in Oxford at the Ruskin School. From 1955 to 1957 he worked for *The New Yorker*, where many of his stories have appeared. His major awards include the 1988 PEN/Malamud award for excellence in short story writing.

Pigeon Feathers

When they moved to Firetown, things were upset, displaced, rearranged. A red cane-back sofa that had been the chief piece in the living room at Olinger was here banished, too big for the narrow country parlour, to the barn, and shrouded under a tarpaulin. Never again would David lie on its length all afternoon eating raisins and reading mystery novels and science fiction and P.G. Wodehouse. The blue wing chair that had stood for years in the ghostly, immaculate guest bedroom, gazing through the windows curtained with dotted swiss toward the telephone wires and horse-chestnut trees and opposite houses, was here established importantly in front of the smutty little fireplace that supplied, in those first cold April days, their only heat. As a child, David had been afraid of the guest bedroom—it was there that he, lying sick with the measles, had seen a black rod the size of a yardstick jog along at a slight slant beside the edge of the bed and vanish when he screamed—and it was disquieting to have one of the elements of its haunted atmosphere basking by the fire, in the centre of the family, growing sooty with use. The books that at home had gathered dust in the case beside the piano were here hastily stacked, all out of order, in the shelves that the carpenters had built along one wall below the deep-silled windows. David, at fourteen, had been more moved than a mover; like the furniture, he had to find a new place, and on the Saturday of the second week he tried to work off some of his disorientation by arranging the books.

It was a collection obscurely depressing to him, mostly books his mother had acquired when she was young: college anthologies of Greek plays and Romantic poetry, Will Durant's *Story of Philosophy*, a soft-leather set of Shakespeare with string bookmarks sewed to the bindings, *Green Mansions* boxed and illustrated with woodcuts, *I, the Tiger*, by Manuel Komroff, novels by names like Galsworthy and Ellen Glasgow and Irvin S. Cobb and Sinclair Lewis and "Elizabeth." The odour of faded taste made him feel the ominous gap between himself and his parents, the insulting gulf of time that existed before he was born. Suddenly he was tempted to dip into this time. From the heaps of books piled around him on the worn old floorboards, he picked up Volume II of a four-volume set of *The Outline of History*, by H.G. Wells. Once David had read *The Time Machine* in an anthology; this gave him a small grip on the author. The book's red binding had faded to orange-pink on the spine. When he lifted the cover, there was a sweetish, attic-like smell, and his mother's maiden name written in unfamiliar handwriting on the flyleaf—an upright, bold, yet careful signature, bearing a faint relation to the quick scrunched backslant that flowed with marvellous consistency across her shopping lists and budget accounts and Christmas cards to college friends from this same, vaguely menacing long ago.

He leafed through, pausing at drawings, done in an old-fashioned stippled style, of bas-reliefs, masks, Romans without pupils in their eyes, articles of ancient costume, fragments of pottery found in unearthed homes. He knew it would be interesting in a magazine, sandwiched between ads and jokes, but in this undiluted form history was somehow sour. The print was determinedly legible, and smug, like a lesson book. As he bent over the pages, yellow at the edges, they seemed rectangles of dusty glass through which he looked down into unreal and irrelevant worlds. He could see things sluggishly move, and an unpleasant fullness came into his throat. His mother and grandmother fussed in the kitchen; the puppy, which they had just acquired, for "protection in the country," was cowering, with a sporadic panicked scrabble of claws, under the dining table that in their old home had been reserved for special days but that here was used for every meal.

Then, before he could halt his eyes, David slipped into Wells's account of Jesus. He had been an obscure political agitator, a kind of hobo, in a minor colony of the Roman Empire. By an accident impossible to reconstruct, he (the small *h* horrified David) survived his own crucifixion and presumably died a few weeks later. A religion was founded on the freakish incident. The credulous imagination of the times retrospectively assigned miracles and supernatural pretensions to Jesus; a myth grew, and then a church, whose theology at most points was in direct contradiction of the simple, rather communistic teachings of the Galilean.

It was as if a stone that for weeks and even years had been gathering weight in the web of David's nerves snapped them and plunged through the page and a hundred layers of paper underneath. These fantastic falsehoods—plainly untrue; churches stood everywhere, the entire nation was founded "under God"—did not at first frighten him; it was the fact that they had not been permitted to exist in an actual human brain. This was the initial impact—that at a definite spot in time and space a brain black with denial of Christ's divinity had been suffered to exist; that the universe had not spit out this ball of tar but allowed it to continue in its blasphemy, to grow old, win honours, wear a hat, write books that, if true, collapsed everything into a jumble of horror. The world outside the deep-silled windows—a rutted lawn, a whitewashed barn, a walnut tree frothy with fresh green—seemed a haven from which he was forever sealed off. Hot washrags seemed pressed against his cheeks.

He read the account again. He tried to supply out of his ignorance objections that would defeat the complacent march of these black words, and found none. Survivals and misunderstandings more far-fetched were reported daily in the papers. But none of them caused churches to be built in every town. He tried to work backwards through the churches, from their brave high fronts through their shabby, ill-attended interiors back into the events at Jerusalem, and felt himself surrounded by shifting grey shadows, centuries of history, where he knew nothing. The thread dissolved in his hands. Had Christ ever come to him, David Kern, and said, "Here. Feel the wound in My side?" No; but prayers had been answered. What prayers? He had prayed that Rudy Mohn, whom he had purposely tripped so he cracked his head on their radiator, not die, and he had not died. But for all the blood, it was just a cut; Rudy came back the same day, wearing a bandage and repeating the same teasing words. He could never have died. Again, David had prayed for two separate war-effort posters he had sent away for to arrive tomorrow, and though they did not, they did arrive, some days later, together, popping through the clacking letter slot like a rebuke from God's mouth: *I answer your prayers in My way, in My time.* After that, he had made his prayers less definite, less susceptible of being twisted into a scolding. But what a tiny, ridiculous coincidence this was, after all, to throw into battle against H.G. Wells's engines of knowledge! Indeed, it proved the enemy's point: Hope bases vast premises on foolish accidents, and reads a word where in fact only a scribble exists.

His father came home. Though Saturday was a free day for him, he had been working. He taught school in Olinger and spent all his days performing, with a curious air of panic, needless errands. Also, a city boy by birth, he was frightened of the farm and seized any excuse to get away. The farm had been David's mother's birthplace; it had been her idea to buy it back. With an ingenuity and persistence unparalleled in her life, she had gained that end, and moved them all here—her son, her husband, her mother. Granmom, in her prime, had worked these fields alongside her husband, but now she dabbled around the kitchen futilely, her hands waggling with Parkinson's disease. She was always in the way. Strange, out in the country, amid eighty acres, they were crowded together. His father expressed his feelings of discomfort by conducting with Mother an endless argument about organic farming. All through dusk, all through supper, it rattled on.

"Elsie, I know, I *know* from my education, the earth is nothing but chemicals. It's the only damn thing I got out of four years of college, so don't tell me it's not true."

"George, if you'd just walk out on the farm you'd know it's not true. The land has a soul."

"Soil, has, no, soul," he said, enunciating stiffly, as if to a very stupid class. To David he said, "You can't argue with a femme. Your mother's a real femme. That's why I married her, and now I'm suffering for it."

"*This* soil has no soul," she said, "because it's been killed with superphosphate. It's been burned bare by Boyer's tenant farmers." Boyer was the rich man they had bought the farm from. "It used to have a soul, didn't it, Mother? When you and Pop farmed it?"

"Ach, yes; I guess." Granmom was trying to bring a forkful of food to her mouth with her less severely afflicted hand. In her anxiety she brought the other hand up from her lap. The crippled fingers, dull red in the orange light of the kerosene lamp in the centre of the table, were welded by paralysis into one knobbed hook.

"Only human indi-vidu-als have souls," his father went on, in the same mincing, lifeless voice. "Because the Bible tells us so." Done eating, he crossed his legs and dug into his ear with a match miserably; to get at the thing inside his head he tucked in his chin, and his voice came out low-pitched at David. "When God made your mother, He made a real femme."

"George, don't you read the papers? Don't you know that between the chemical fertilizers and the bug sprays we'll all be dead in ten years? Heart attacks are killing every man in the country over forty-five."

He sighed wearily; the yellow skin of his eyelids wrinkled as he hurt himself with the match. "There's no connection," he stated, spacing his words with pained patience, "between the heart—and chemical fertilizers. It's alcohol that's doing it. Alcohol and milk. There is too much—cholesterol—in the tissues of the American heart. Don't tell me about chemistry, Elsie; I majored in the damn stuff for four years."

"Yes and I majored in Greek and I'm not a penny wiser. Mother, put your waggler *away!*" The old woman started, and the food dropped from her fork. For some reason, the sight of her bad hand at the table cruelly irritated her daughter. Granmom's eyes, worn bits of crazed crystal embedded in watery milk, widened behind her cockeyed spectacles. Circles of silver as fine as thread, they clung to the red notches they had carved over the years into her little white beak. In the orange flicker of the kerosene lamp her dazed misery seemed infernal. David's mother began, without noise, to cry. His father did not seem to have eyes at all; just jaundiced sockets of wrinkled skin. The steam of food clouded the scene. It was horrible but the horror was particular and familiar, and distracted David from the formless dread that worked, sticky and sore, within him, like a too large wound trying to heal.

He had to go to the bathroom, and took a flashlight down through the wet grass to the outhouse. For once, his fear of spiders there felt trivial. He set the flashlight, burning, beside him, and an insect alighted on its lens, a tiny insect, a mosquito or flea, made so fine that the weak light projected its X-ray onto the wall boards; the faint rim of its wings, the blurred strokes, magnified, of its long hinged legs, the dark cone at the heart of its anatomy. The tremor must be its heart beating. Without warning, David was visited by an exact vision of death: a long hole in the ground, no wider than your body, down which you are drawn while the white faces above recede. You try to reach them but your arms are pinned. Shovels pour dirt into your face. There you will be forever, in an upright position, blind and silent, and in time no one will remember you, and you will never be called. As strata of rock shift, your fingers elongate, and your teeth are distended sideways in a great underground grimace indistinguishable from a strip of chalk. And the earth tumbles on, and the sun expires, and unaltering darkness reigns where once there were stars.

Sweat broke out on his back. His mind seemed to rebound off a solidness. Such extinction was not another threat, a graver sort of danger, a kind of pain; it was qualitatively different. It was not even a conception that could be voluntarily pictured; it entered him from outside. His protesting nerves swarmed on its surface like lichen on a meteor. The skin of his chest was soaked with the effort of rejection. At the same time that the fear was dense and internal, it was dense and all around him; a tide of clay had swept up to the stars; space was crushed into a mass. When he stood up, automatically hunching his shoulders to keep his head away from the spider webs, it was with a numb sense of being cramped between two huge volumes of rigidity. That he had even this small freedom to move surprised him. In the narrow shelter of that rank shack, adjusting his pants, he felt—his first spark of comfort—too small to be crushed.

But in the open, as the beam of the flashlight skidded with frightened quickness across the remote surfaces of the barn and the grape arbour and the giant pine that stood by the path to the woods, the terror descended. He raced up through the clinging grass pursued, not by one of the wild animals the woods might hold, or one of the goblins his superstitious grandmother had communicated to his childhood, but by spectres out of science fiction, where gigantic cinder moons fill half the turquoise sky. As David ran, a grey planet rolled inches behind his neck. If he looked back, he would be buried. And in the momentum of his terror, hideous possibilities—the dilation of the sun, the triumph of the insects, the crabs on the shore in *The Time Machine*—wheeled out of the vacuum of make-believe and added their weight to his impending oblivion.

He wrenched the door open; the lamps within the house flared. The wicks burning here and there seemed to mirror one another. His mother was washing the dishes in a little pan of heated pump-water; Granmom fluttered near her elbow apprehensive. In the living room—the downstairs of the little square house was two long rooms—his father sat in front of the black fireplace restlessly folding and unfolding a newspaper as he sustained his half of the argument. "Nitrogen, phosphorus, potash: these are the three replaceable constituents of the soil. One crop of corn carries away hundreds of pounds of"—he dropped the paper into his lap and ticked them off on three fingers—"nitrogen, phosphorus, potash."

"Boyer didn't grow corn."

"*Any* crop, Elsie. The human animal—"

"You're killing the *earthworms*, George!"

"The human animal, after thousands and *thousands* of years, learned methods whereby the chemical balance of the soil may be maintained. Don't carry me back to the Dark Ages."

"When we moved to Olinger the ground in the garden was like slate. Just one summer of my cousin's chicken dung and the earthworms came back."

"I'm sure the Dark Ages were a fine place to the poor devils born in them, but I don't want to go there. They give me the creeps." Daddy stared into the cold pit of the fireplace and clung to the rolled newspaper in his lap as if it alone were keeping him from slipping backwards and down, down.

Mother came into the doorway brandishing a fistful of wet forks. "And thanks to your DDT there soon won't be a bee left in the country. When I was a girl here you could eat a peach without washing it."

"It's primitive, Elsie. It's Dark Age stuff."

"Oh what do *you* know about the Dark Ages?"

"I know I don't want to go back to them."

David took from the shelf, where he had placed it this afternoon, the great unabridged Webster's Dictionary that his grandfather had owned. He turned the big thin pages, floppy as cloth, to the entry he wanted, and read

> soul . . . 1. An entity conceived as the essence, substance, animating principle, or actuating cause of life, or of the individual life, esp. of life manifested in psychical activities; the vehicle of individual existence, separate in nature from the body and usually held to be separable in existence.

The definition went on, into Greek and Egyptian conceptions, but David stopped short on the treacherous edge of antiquity. He needed to read no further. The careful overlapping words shingled a temporary shelter for him. "Usually held to be separable in existence"—what could be fairer, more judicious, surer?

His father was saying, "The modern farmer can't go around sweeping up after his cows. The poor devil has *thousands* and thousands of acres on his hands. Your modern farmer uses a scientifically-arrived-at mixture, like five-ten-five, or six-twelve-six, or *three*-twelve-six, and spreads it on with this wonderful machinery which of course we can't afford. Your modern farmer can't *afford* medieval methods."

Mother was quiet in the kitchen; her silence radiated waves of anger.

"No, now Elsie; don't play the femme with me. Let's discuss this calmly like two rational twentieth-century people. Your organic farming nuts aren't attacking five-ten-five; they're attacking the chemical fertilizer crooks. The monster firms."

A cup clinked in the kitchen. Mother's anger touched David's face; his cheeks burned guiltily. Just by being in the living room he was associated with his father. She appeared in the doorway with red hands and tears in her eyes, and said to the two of them, "I knew you didn't want to come here but I didn't know you'd torment me like this. You talked Pop into his grave and now you'll kill me. Go ahead, George, more power to you; at least I'll be buried in good ground." She tried to turn and met an obstacle and screamed, "Mother, stop hanging on my *back*! Why don't you go to *bed*?"

"Let's all go to bed," David's father said, rising from the blue wing chair and slapping his thigh with a newspaper. "This reminds me of death." It was a phrase of his that David had heard so often he never considered its sense.

Upstairs, he seemed to be lifted above his fears. The sheets on his bed were clean. Granmom had ironed them with a pair of flatirons saved from the Olinger attic; she plucked them hot off the stove alternately, with a wooden handle called a goose. It was a wonder, to see how she managed. In the next room, his parents grunted peaceably; they seemed to take their quarrels less seriously than he did. They made comfortable scratching noises as they carried a little lamp back and forth. Their door was open a crack, so he saw the light shift and swing. Surely there would be, in the last five minutes, in the last second, a crack of light, showing the door from the dark room to another, full of light. Thinking of it this vividly frightened him. His own dying, in a specific bed in a specific room, specific walls mottled with wallpaper, the dry whistle of his breathing, the murmuring doctors, the nervous relatives going in and out, but for him no way out but down into the funnel. *Never touch a doorknob again.* A whisper, and his parents' light was blown out. David prayed to be reassured. Though the experiment frightened him, he lifted his hands high into the darkness above his face and begged Christ to touch them. Not hard or long: the faintest, quickest grip would be final for a lifetime. His hands waited in the air, itself a substance, which seemed to move through his fingers; or was it the pressure of his pulse? He returned his hands to beneath the covers uncertain if they had been touched or not. For would not Christ's touch *be* infinitely gentle?

Through all the eddies of its aftermath, David clung to this thought about his revelation of extinction: that there, in the outhouse, he had struck a solidness qualitatively different, a rock of horror firm enough to support any height of construction. All he needed was a little help; a word, a gesture, a nod of certainty, and he would be sealed in, safe. The assurance from the dictionary had melted in the night. Today was Sunday, a hot fair day. Across a mile of clear air the church bells called, *Celebrate, celebrate.* Only Daddy went. He put on a coat over his rolled-up shirtsleeves and got into the little old black Plymouth parked by the barn and went off, with the same pained hurried grimness of all his actions. His churning wheels, as he shifted too hastily into second, raised plumes of red dust on the dirt road. Mother walked to the far field, to see what bushes needed cutting. David, though he usually preferred to stay in the house, went with her. The puppy followed at a distance, whining as it picked its way through the stubble but floundering off timidly if one of them went back to pick it up and carry it. When they reached the crest of the far field, his mother asked, "David, what's troubling you?"

"Nothing. Why?"

She looked at him sharply. The greening woods cross-hatched the space beyond her half-grey hair. Then she showed him her profile, and gestured toward the house, which they had left a half-mile behind them. "See how it sits in the land? They don't know how to build with the land any more. Pop always said the foundations were set with the compass. We must try to get a compass and see. It's supposed to face due south; but south feels a little more *that* way to me." From the side, as she said these things, she seemed handsome and young. The smooth sweep of her hair over her ear seemed white with a purity and calm that made her feel foreign to him. He had never regarded his parents as consolers of his troubles; from the beginning they had seemed to have more troubles than he. Their confusion had flattered him into an illusion of strength; so now on this high clear ridge he jealously guarded the menace all around them, blowing like a breeze on his fingertips, the possibility of all this wide scenery sinking into darkness. The strange fact that though she came to look at the brush she carried no clippers, for she had a fixed prejudice against working on Sundays, was the only consolation he allowed her to offer.

As they walked back, the puppy whimpering after them, the rising dust behind a distant line of trees announced that Daddy was speeding home from church. When they reached the house he was there. He had brought back the Sunday paper and the vehement remark, "Dobson's too intelligent for these farmers. They just sit there with their mouths open and don't hear a thing the poor devil's saying."

"What makes you think farmers are unintelligent? This country was made by farmers. George Washington was a farmer."

"They are, Elsie. They are unintelligent. George Washington's dead. In this day and age only the misfits stay on the farm. The lame, the halt, the blind. The morons with one arm. Human garbage. They remind me of death, sitting there with their mouths open."

"My *father* was a farmer."

"He was a frustrated man, Elsie. He never knew what hit him. The poor devil meant so well, and he never knew which end was up. Your mother'll bear me out. Isn't that right, Mom? Pop never knew what hit him?"

"Ach, I guess not," the old woman quavered, and the ambiguity for the moment silenced both sides.

David hid in the funny papers and sports section until one-thirty. At two, the catechetical class met at the Firetown church. He had transferred from the catechetical class of the Lutheran church in Olinger, a humiliating comedown. In Olinger they met on Wednesday nights, spiffy and spruce, in the atmosphere of a dance. Afterwards, blessed by the brick-faced minister from whose lips the word "Christ" fell like a burning stone, the more daring of them went with their Bibles to a luncheonette and smoked. Here in Firetown, the girls were dull white cows and the boys narrow-faced brown goats in old men's suits, herded on Sunday afternoon into a threadbare church basement that smelled of stale hay. Because his father had taken the car on one of his endless errands to Olinger, David walked, grateful for the open air and the silence. The catechetical class embarrassed him, but today he placed hope in it, as the source of the nod, the gesture, that was all he needed.

Reverend Dobson was a delicate young man with great dark eyes and small white shapely hands that flickered like protesting doves when he preached; he seemed a bit misplaced in the Lutheran ministry. This was his first call. It was a split parish; he served another rural church twelve miles away. His iridescent green Ford, new six months ago, was spattered to the windows with red mud and rattled from bouncing on the rude back roads, where he frequently got lost, to the malicious satisfaction of many. But David's mother liked him, and, more pertinent to his success, the Haiers, the sleek family of feed merchants and inn-keepers and tractor salesmen who dominated the Firetown church, liked him. David liked him, and felt liked in turn; sometimes in class, after some special stupidity, Dobson directed toward him out of those wide black eyes a mild look of disbelief, a look that, though flattering, was also delicately disquieting.

Catechetical instruction consisted of reading aloud from a work booklet answers to problems prepared during the week, problems like, "I am the _______, the _______, and the _______, saith the Lord." Then there was a question period in which no once ever asked any questions. Today's theme was the last third of the Apostles' Creed. When the time came for questions, David blushed and asked, "About the Resurrection of the Body—are we conscious between the time when we die and the Day of Judgment?"

Dobson blinked, and his fine little mouth pursed, suggesting that David was making things more difficult. The faces of the other students went blank, as if an indiscretion had been committed.

"No, I suppose not," Reverend Dobson said.

"Well, where is our soul, then, in this gap?"

The sense grew, in the class, of a naughtiness occurring. Dobson's shy eyes watered, as if he were straining to keep up the formality of attention, and one of the girls, the fattest, simpered toward her twin, who was a little less fat. Their chairs were arranged in a rough circle. The current running around the circle panicked David. Did everybody know something he didn't know?

"I suppose you could say our souls are asleep," Dobson said.

"And then they wake up, and there is the earth like it always is, and all the people who have ever lived? Where will Heaven be?"

Anita Haier giggled. Dobson gazed at David intently, but with an awkward, puzzled flicker of forgiveness, as if there existed a secret between them that David was violating. But David knew of no secret. All he wanted was to hear Dobson repeat the words he said every Sunday morning. This he would not do. As if these words were unworthy of the conversational voice.

"David, you might think of Heaven this way: as the way the goodness Abraham Lincoln did lives after him."

"But is Lincoln conscious of it living on?" He blushed no longer with embarrassment but in anger; he had walked here in good faith and was being made a fool.

"Is he conscious now? I would have to say no; but I don't think it matters." His voice had a coward's firmness; he was hostile now.

"You don't."

"Not in the eyes of God, no." The unction, the stunning impudence, of this reply sprang tears of outrage in David's eyes. He bowed them to his book, where short words like Duty, Love, Obey, Honour, were stacked in the form of a cross.

"Were there any other questions, David?" Dobson asked with renewed gentleness. The others were rustling, collecting their books.

"No." He made his voice firm, though he could not bring up his eyes.

"Did I answer your question fully enough?"

"Yes."

In the minister's silence the shame that should have been his crept over David: the burden and fever of being a fraud were placed upon *him*, who was innocent, and it seemed, he knew, a confession of this guilt that on the way out he was unable to face Dobson's stirred gaze, though he felt it probing the side of his head.

Anita Haier's father gave him a ride down the highway as far as the dirt road. David said he wanted to walk the rest, and figured that his offer was accepted because Mr Haier did not want to dirty his bright blue Buick with dust. This was all right; everything was all right, as long as it was clear. His indignation at being betrayed, at seeing Christianity betrayed, had hardened him. The straight dirt road reflected his hardness. Pink stones thrust up through its packed surface. The April sun beat down from the centre of the afternoon half of the sky; already it had some of summer's heat. Already the fringes of weeds at the edges of the road were bedraggled with dust. From the reviving grass and scuff of the fields he walked between, insects were sending up a monotonous, automatic chant. In the distance a tiny figure in his father's coat was walking along the edge of the woods. His mother. He wondered what joy she found in such walks; to him the brown stretches of slowly rising and falling land expressed only a huge exhaustion.

Flushed with fresh air and happiness, she returned from her walk earlier than he had expected, and surprised him at his grandfather's Bible. It was a stumpy black book, the boards worn thin where the old man's fingers had held them; the spine hung by one weak hinge of fabric. David had been looking for the passage where Jesus says to the one thief on the cross, "Today shalt thou be with me in paradise." He had never tried reading the Bible for himself before. What was so embarrassing about being caught at it, was that he detested the apparatus of piety. Fusty churches, creaking hymns, ugly Sunday-school teachers and their stupid leaflets—he hated everything about them but the promise they held out, a promise that in the most perverse way, as if the homeliest crone in the kingdom were given the Prince's hand, made every good and real thing, ball games and jokes and pert-breasted girls, possible. He couldn't explain this to his mother. There was no time. Her solicitude was upon him.

"David, what are you doing?"

"Nothing."

"What are you doing at Grandpop's Bible?"

"Trying to read it. This is supposed to be a Christian country, isn't it?"

She sat down on the green sofa, which used to be in the sun parlour at Olinger, under the fancy mirror. A little smile still lingered on her face from the walk. "David, I wish you'd talk to me."

"What about?"

"About whatever it is that's troubling you. Your father and I have both noticed it."

"I asked Reverend Dobson about Heaven and he said it was like Abraham Lincoln's goodness living after him."

He waited for the shock to strike her. "Yes?" she said, expecting more.

"That's all."

"And why didn't you like it?"

"Well; don't you see? It amounts to saying there isn't any Heaven at all."

"I don't see that it amounts to that. What do you want Heaven to be?"

"Well, I don't know. I want it to be *some*thing. I thought he'd tell me what it was. I thought that was his job." He was becoming angry, sensing her surprise at him. She had assumed that Heaven had faded from his head years ago. She had imagined that he had already entered, in the secrecy of silence, the conspiracy that he now knew to be all around him.

"David," she asked gently, "don't you ever want to rest?"

"No. Not forever."

"David, you're so young. When you get older, you'll feel differently."

"Grandpa didn't. Look how tattered this book is."

"I never understood your grandfather."

"Well I don't understand ministers who say it's like Lincoln's goodness going on and on. Suppose you're not Lincoln?"

"I think Reverend Dobson made a mistake. You must try to forgive him."

"It's not a *question* of his making a mistake! It's a question of dying and never moving or seeing or hearing anything ever again."

"But"—in exasperation—"darling, it's so *greedy* of you to want more. When God has given us this wonderful April day, and given us this farm, and you have your whole life ahead of you—"

"You think, then, that there is God?"

"Of course I do"—with deep relief, that smoothed her features into a reposeful oval. He had risen and was standing too near her for his comfort. He was afraid she would reach out and touch him.

"He made everything? You feel that?"

"Yes."

"Then who made Him?"

"Why, Man. Man." The happiness of this answer lit up her face radiantly, until she saw his gesture of disgust. She was so simple, so illogical; such a femme.

"Well that amounts to saying there is none."

Her hand reached for his wrist but he backed away. "David, it's a mystery. A miracle. It's a miracle more beautiful than any Reverend Dobson could have told you about. You don't say houses don't exist because Man made them."

"No. God has to be different."

"But, David, you have the *evidence*. Look out the window at the sun; at the fields."

"Mother, good grief. Don't you see"—he rasped away the roughness of his throat—"if when we die there's nothing, all your sun and fields and what not are all, ah, *horror*? It's just an ocean of horror."

"But David, it's not. It's so clearly not that." And she made an urgent opening gesture with her hands that expressed, with its suggestion of a willingness to receive his helplessness, all her grace, her gentleness, her love of beauty, gathered into a passive intensity that made him intensely hate her. He would not be wooed away from the truth. *I am the Way, the Truth . . .*

"No," he told her. "Just let me alone."

He found his tennis ball behind the piano and went outside to throw it against the side of the house. There was a patch high up where the brown stucco that had been laid over the sandstone masonry was crumbling away; he kept trying with the tennis ball to chip more pieces off. Superimposed upon his deep ache was a smaller but more immediate worry; that he had hurt his mother. He heard his father's car rattling on the straightway, and went into the house, to make peace before he arrived. To his relief, she was not giving off the stifling damp heat of her anger, but instead was cool, decisive, maternal. She handed him an old green book, her college text of Plato.

"I want you to read the Parable of the Cave," she said.

"All right," he said, though he knew it would do no good. Some story by a dead Greek just vague enough to please her. "Don't worry about it, Mother."

"I *am* worried. Honestly, David, I'm sure there will be something for us. As you get older, these things seem to matter a great deal less."

"That may be. It's a dismal thought, though."

His father bumped at the door. The locks and jambs stuck here. But before Granmom could totter to the latch and let him in, he had knocked it open. He had been in Olinger dithering with track meet tickets. Although Mother usually kept her talks with David a confidence, a treasure between them, she called instantly, "George, David is worried about death!"

He came to the doorway of the living room, his shirt pocket bristling with pencils, holding in one hand a pint box of melting ice cream and in the other the knife with which he was about to divide it into four sections, their Sunday treat. "Is the kid worried about death? Don't give it a thought, David. I'll be lucky if I live till tomorrow, and I'm not worried. If they'd taken a buckshot gun and shot me in the cradle I'd be better off. The *world'd* be better off. Hell, I think death is a wonderful thing. I look forward to it. Get the garbage out of the way. If I had the man here who invented death, I'd pin a medal on him."

"Hush, George. You'll frighten the child worse than he is."

This was not true; he never frightened David. There was no harm in his father, no harm at all. Indeed, in the man's steep self-disgust the boy felt a kind of ally. A distant ally. He saw his position with a certain strategic coldness. Nowhere in the world of other people would he find the hint, the nod, he needed to begin to build his fortress against death. They none of them believed. He was alone. In that deep hole.

In the months that followed, his position changed little. School was some comfort. All those sexy, perfumed people, wisecracking, chewing gum, all of them doomed to die, and none of them noticing. In their company David felt that they would carry him along into the bright, cheap paradise reserved for them. In any crowd, the fear ebbed a little; he had reasoned that somewhere in the world there must exist a few people who believed what was necessary, and the larger the crowd, the greater the chance that he was near such a soul, within calling distance, if only he was not too ignorant, too ill-equipped, to spot him. The sight of clergymen cheered him; whatever they themselves thought, their collars were still a sign that somewhere, at sometime, someone had recognized that we cannot, *cannot*, submit to death. The sermon topics posted outside churches, the flip, hurried pieties of disc jockeys, the cartoons in magazines showing angels or devils—on such scraps he kept alive the possibility of hope.

For the rest, he tried to drown his hopelessness in clatter and jostle. The pinball machine at the luncheonette was a merciful distraction; as he bent over its buzzing, flashing board of flippers and cushions, the weight and constriction in his chest lightened and loosened. He was grateful for all the time his father wasted in Olinger. Every delay postponed the moment when they must ride together down the dirt road into the heart of the dark farmland, where the only light was the kerosene lamp waiting on the dining-room table, a light that drowned their food in shadow and made it sinister.

He lost his appetite for reading. He was afraid of being ambushed again. In mystery novels people died like dolls being discarded; in science fiction enormities of space and time conspired to crush humans; and even in P.G. Wodehouse he felt a hollowness, a turning away from reality that was implicitly bitter, and became explicit in the comic figures of futile clergymen. All gaiety seemed minced out on the skin of a void. All quiet hours seemed invitations to dread.

Even on weekends, he and his father contrived to escape the farm; and when, some Saturdays, they did stay home, it was to do something destructive—tear down an old henhouse or set huge brush fires that threatened, while Mother shouted and flapped her arms, to spread to the woods. Whenever his father worked, it was with rapt violence; when he chopped kindling, fragments of the old henhouse boards flew like shrapnel and the axe-head was always within a quarter of an inch of flying off the handle. He was exhilarating to watch, sweating and swearing and sucking bits of saliva back into his lips.

School stopped. His father took the car in the opposite direction, to a highway construction job where he had been hired for the summer as a timekeeper, and David was stranded in the middle of acres of heat and greenery and blowing pollen and the strange, mechanical humming that lay invisibly in the weeds and alfalfa and dry orchard grass.

For his fifteenth birthday his parents gave him, with jokes about him being a hillbilly now, a Remington .22. It was somewhat like a pinball machine to take it out to the old kiln in the woods where they dumped their trash, and set up tin cans on the kiln's sandstone shoulder and shoot them off one by one. He'd take the puppy, who had grown long legs and a rich coat of reddish fur—he was part chow. Copper hated the gun but loved the boy enough to accompany him. When the flat acrid crack rang out, he would race in terrified circles that would tighten and tighten until they brought him, shivering, against David's legs. Depending upon his mood, David would shoot again or drop to his knees and comfort the dog. Giving this comfort to a degree returned comfort to him. The dog's ears, laid flat against his skull in fear, were folded so intricately, so—he groped for the concept—*surely*. Where the dull-studded collar made the fur stand up, each hair showed a root of soft white under the length, black-tipped, of the metal-colour that had lent the dog its name. In his agitation Copper panted through nostrils that were elegant slits, like two healed cuts, or like the keyholes of a dainty lock of black, grained wood. His whole whorling, knotted, jointed body was a wealth of such embellishments. And in the smell of the dog's hair David seemed to descend through many finely differentiated layers of earth: mulch, soil, sand, clay, and the glittering mineral base.

But when he returned to the house, and saw the books arranged on the low shelves, fear returned. The four adamant volumes of Wells like four thin bricks, the green Plato that had puzzled him with its queer softness and tangled purity, the dead Galsworthy and "Elizabeth," Grandpa's mammoth dictionary, Grandpa's Bible, the Bible that he himself had received on becoming a member of the Firetown Lutheran Church—at the sight of these, the memory of his fear reawakened and came around him. He had grown stiff and stupid in its embrace. His parents tried to think of ways to entertain him.

"David, I have a job for you to do," his mother said one evening at the table.

"What?"

"If you're going to take that tone perhaps we'd better not talk."

"What tone? I didn't take any tone."

"Your grandmother thinks there are too many pigeons in the barn."

"Why?" David turned to look at his grandmother, but she sat there staring at the burning lamp with her usual expression of bewilderment.

Mother shouted, "Mom, he wants to know why!"

Granmom made a jerky, irritable motion with her bad hand, as if generating the force for utterance, and said, "They foul the furniture."

"That's right," Mother said. "She's afraid for that old Olinger furniture that we'll never use. David, she's been after me for a month about those poor pigeons. She wants you to shoot them."

"I don't want to kill anything especially," David said.

Daddy said, "The kid's like you are, Elsie. He's too good for this world. Kill or be killed, that's my motto."

His mother said loudly, "Mother, he doesn't want to do it."

"Not?" The old lady's eyes distended as if in horror, and her claw descended slowly to her lap.

"Oh, I'll do it, I'll do it tomorrow," David snapped, and a pleasant crisp taste entered his mouth with the decision.

"And I had thought, when Boyer's men made the hay, it would be better if the barn doesn't look like a rookery," his mother added needlessly.

A barn, in day, is a small night. The splinters of light between the dry shingles pierce the high roof like stars, and the rafters and crossbeams and built-in ladders seem, until your eyes adjust, as mysterious as the branches of a haunted forest. David entered silently, the gun in one hand. Copper whined desperately at the door, too frightened to come in with the gun yet unwilling to leave the boy. David stealthily turned, said "Go away," shut the door on the dog, and slipped the bolt across. It was a door within a door; the double door for wagons and tractors was as high and wide as the face of a house.

The smell of old straw scratched his sinuses. The red sofa, half-hidden under its white-splotched tarpaulin, seemed assimilated into this smell, sunk in it, buried. The mouths of empty bins gaped like caves. Rusty oddments of farming—coils of baling wire, some spare tines for a harrow, a handle-less shovel—hung on nails driven here and there in the thick wood. He stood stock-still a minute; it took a while to separate the cooing of the pigeons from the rustling in his ears. When he had focused on the cooing, it flooded the vast interior with its throaty, bubbling outpour: there seemed no other sound. They were up behind the beams. What light there was leaked through the shingles and the dirty glass windows at the far end and the small round holes, about as big as basketballs, high on the opposite stone side walls, under the ridge of the roof.

A pigeon appeared in one of these holes, on the side toward the house. It flew in, with a battering of wings, from the outside, and waited there, silhouetted against its pinched bit of sky, preening and cooing in a throbbing, thrilled, tentative way. David tiptoed four steps to the side, rested his gun against the lowest rung of a ladder pegged between two upright beams, and lowered the gunsight into the bird's tiny, jauntily cocked head. The slap of the report seemed to come off the stone wall behind him, and the pigeon did not fall. Neither did it fly. Instead it stuck in the round hold, pirouetting rapidly and nodding his head as if in frantic agreement. David shot the bolt back and forth and had aimed again before the spent cartridge had stopped jingling on the boards by his feet. He eased the tip of the sight a little lower, into the bird's breast, and took care to squeeze the trigger with perfect evenness. The slow contraction of his hand abruptly sprang the bullet; for a half-second there was doubt, and then the pigeon fell like a handful of rags, skimming down the barn wall into the layer of straw that coated the floor of the mow on this side.

Now others shook loose from the rafters, and whirled in the dim air with a great blurred hurtle of feathers and noise. They would go for the hole; he fixed his sight on the little moon of blue, and when a pigeon came to it, shot him as he was walking the ten inches of stone that would have carried him into the open air. This pigeon lay down in that tunnel of stone, unable to fall either one way or the other, although he was alive enough to lift one wing and cloud the light. It would sink back, and he would suddenly lift it again, the feathers flaring. His body blocked that exit. David raced to the other side of the barn's main aisle, where a similar ladder was symmetrically placed, and rested his gun on the same rung. Three birds came together to this hole; he got one, and two got through. The rest resettled in the rafters.

There was a shallow triangular space behind the cross beams supporting the roof. It was here they roosted and hid. But either the space was too small, or they were curious, for now that his eyes were at home in the dusty gloom David could see little dabs of grey popping in and out. The cooing was shriller now; its apprehensive tremolo made the whole volume of air seem liquid. He noticed one little smudge of a head that was especially persistent in peeking out; he marked the place, and fixed his gun on it, and when the head appeared again, had his finger tightened in advance on the trigger. A parcel of fluff slipped off the beam and fell the barn's height onto a canvas covering some Olinger furniture, and where its head had peaked out there was a fresh prick of light in the shingles.

Standing in the centre of the floor, fully master now, disdaining to steady the barrel with anything but his arm, he killed two more that way. He felt like a beautiful avenger. Out of the shadowy ragged infinity of the vast barn roof these impudent things dared to thrust their heads, presumed to dirty its starred silence with their filthy timorous life, and he cut them off, tucked them back neatly into the silence. He had the sensation of a creator; these little smudges and flickers that he was clever to see and even cleverer to hit in the dim recesses of the rafters—out of each of them he was making a full bird. A tiny peek, probe, dab of life, when he hit it, blossomed into a dead enemy, falling with good, final weight.

The imperfection of the second pigeon he had shot, who was still lifting his wing now and then up in the round hole, nagged him. He put a new clip into the stock. Hugging the gun against his body, he climbed the ladder. The barrel sight scratched his ear; he had a sharp, garish vision, like a colour slide, of shooting himself and being found tumbled on the barn floor among his prey. He locked his arm around the top rung—a fragile, gnawed rod braced between uprights—and shot into the bird's body from a flat angle. The wing folded, but the impact did not, as he had hoped, push the bird out of the hole. He fired again, and again, and still the little body, lighter than air when alive, was too heavy to budge from its high grave. From up here he could see green trees and a brown corner of the house through the hole. Clammy with the cobwebs that gathered between the rungs, he pumped a full clip of eight bullets into the stubborn shadow, with no success. He climbed down, and was struck by the silence in the barn. The remaining pigeons must have escaped out the other hole. That was all right; he was tired of it.

He stepped with his rifle into the light. His mother was coming to meet him, and it tickled him to see her shy away from the carelessly held gun. "You took a chip out of the house," she said. "What were those last shots about?"

"One of them died up in that little round hole and I was trying to shoot it down."

"Copper's hiding behind the piano and won't come out. I had to leave him."

"Well don't blame me. I didn't want to shoot the poor devils."

"Don't smirk. You look like your father. How many did you get?"

"Six."

She went into the barn, and he followed. She listened to the silence. Her hair was scraggly, perhaps from tussling with the dog. "I don't suppose the others will be back," she said wearily. "Indeed, I don't know why I let Mother talk me into it. Their cooing was such a comforting noise." She began to gather up the dead pigeons. Though he didn't want to touch them, David went into the mow and picked up by its tepid, horny, coral-coloured feet the first bird he had killed. Its wings unfolded disconcertingly, as if the creature had been held together by threads that now were slit. It did not weigh much. He retrieved the one on the other side of the barn; his mother got the three in the middle and led the way across the road to the little southern slope of land that went down toward the foundations of the vanished tobacco shed. The ground was too steep to plant and mow; wild strawberries grew in the tangled grass. She put her burden down and said, "We'll have to bury them. The dog will go wild."

He put his two down on her three; the slick feathers let the bodies slide liquidly on one another. He asked, "Shall I get you the shovel?"

"Get it for yourself; *you* bury them. They're your kill. And be sure to make the hole deep enough so he won't dig them up." While he went to the tool shed for the shovel, she went into the house. Unlike her, she did not look up, either at the orchard to the right of her or at the meadow on her left, but instead held her head rigidly, tilted a little, as if listening to the ground.

He dug the hole, in a spot where there were no strawberry plants, before he studied the pigeons. He had never seen a bird this close before. The feathers were more wonderful than dog's hair, for each filament was shaped within the shape of the feather, and the feathers in turn were trimmed to fit a pattern that flowed without error across the bird's body. He lost himself in the geometrical tides as the feathers now broadened and stiffened to make an edge for flight, now softened and constricted to cup warmth around the mute flesh. And across the surface of the infinitely adjusted yet somehow effortless mechanics of the feathers played idle designs of colour, no two alike, designs executed, it seemed, in a controlled rapture, with a joy that hung level in the air above and behind him. Yet these birds bred in the millions and were exterminated as pests. Into the fragrant open earth he dropped one broadly banded in slate shades of blue, and on top of it another, mottled all over in rhythms of lilac and grey. The next was almost wholly white, but for a salmon glaze at its throat. As he fitted the last two, still pliant, on the top, and stood up, crusty coverings were lifted from him, and with a feminine, slipping sensation along his nerves that seemed to give the air hands, he was robed in this certainty: that the God who had lavished such craft upon these worthless birds would not destroy His whole Creation by refusing to let David live forever.

1962

Elena Poniatowska

b. 1933

Born in Paris, the daughter of a French father of Polish ancestry and a Mexican mother, Elena Poniatowska immigrated with her family to Mexico when she was ten years old. She was sent to a British-run school in Mexico and then to a Catholic boarding school in Philadelphia. While speaking French and English within the family, she soon learned Spanish, although until she was twenty she considered herself a foreigner in her adopted country. In 1954 she began working for the Mexico City newspaper *Excélsior*, doing daily interviews with writers, artists, and musicians, and then moved to another paper, *Novedades*. She soon became a well-known journalist and an increasingly vocal critic of political corruption in Mexico. *La noche de Tlatelolco* (1971), translated as *Massacre in Mexico*, exposed the attack by police on a peaceful student protest in Mexico City in 1968, during which 325 unarmed youths were murdered. The influence of journalism on her fiction can be seen in her tendency to base her narratives on actual lives and historical events. *Querido Diego, te abraza Quiela* (1978), translated as *Dear Diego*, is a fictionalized reconstruction of the correspondence between Mexico's foremost painter, Diego Rivera, and the Russian painter, Angelina Beloff, and *Hasta no verte, Jésus mío* (1969), translated as *Here's to you, Jesusa!*, is a first-person account of a poor illiterate woman born in Mexico in 1900. The novel *Tinisima* (1992), which brought her international attention, recounts the life of photographer and militant revolutionary Tina Modotti. Poniatowska's most recent novel, *La piel del cielo* (2001), was awarded a prestigious Spanish prize, the premio Alfaguara.

The Night Visitor

"But, you . . . don't suffer?"

"Me?"

"Yes, you."

"A little, sometimes, like when my shoes are tight. . . ."

"I'm referring to your situation, Mrs Loyden." He stressed the Mrs, letting it fall to the bottom of Hell, Miss-sus, and all it implied. "Don't you suffer because of it?"

"No."

"Wasn't it a lot of trouble to get where you are? Your family went to a good deal of expense?"

The woman shifted in her seat. Her green eyes no longer questioned the Public Ministry agent. She looked at the tips of her shoes. These didn't hurt her. She used them every day.

"Don't you work in an institution that grew out of the Mexican Revolution? Haven't you benefited from it? Don't you enjoy the privileges of a class that yesterday had scarcely arrived from the fields and today receives schooling, medical attention, and social welfare? You've been able to rise, thanks to your work. Oh, I forgot. You have a curious concept of work."

The woman protested in a clear voice, even though its intonations were childish.

"I'm a registered nurse. I can show you my license. Right now, if we go to my house."

"Your house?" said the Public Ministry agent ironically, "Your house? Which of your houses?"

The judge was old, pure worm-eaten wood, painted and repainted, but, strangely, the face of this Public Ministry agent didn't look so old, in spite of his curved shoulders and the shudders that shook them. His voice was old, his intentions old. His gestures were clumsy as was his way of fixing his eyes on her through his glasses and getting irritated like a teacher with a student who hasn't learned his lesson. "Objects contaminate people," she thought. "This man looks like a piece of paper, a drawer, an inkwell. Poor fellow." Behind her in the other armchairs there was no one, just a policeman scratching his crotch near the exit door, which opened to admit a short woman who reached up to the Public Ministry agent's desk and handed him a document. After looking at it, he admonished her in a loud voice, "The crimes must be classified correctly. . . . and at the end, you always forget the 'Effective Suffrage, No Re-Election.' Don't let it happen again, please!"

When they were alone, the accused inquired in her high voice, "Could I call home?"

The judge was about to repeat sharply, "Which one?" But he preferred a negative. He rounded his mouth in such a way that the wrinkles converged like they do on a chicken's ass.

"No."

"Why?"

"Because we-are-in-the-mid-dle-of-an-in-ter-ro-ga-tion. We are making a deposition."

"Oh, and if I have to go to the bathroom, do I have to wait?"

"My God, is this woman mentally retarded, or what? But if she were, how could she have received her diploma?"

He inquired with renewed curiosity, "To whom do you wish to speak?"

"My father."

"Her father . . . her fa-ther," he mocked. "To top it off, you have a father!"

"Yes," she said, swinging her legs, "Yes, my daddy is still alive."

"Really? And does your father know what kind of a daughter he has?"

"I'm very much like him," said the child woman with a smile. "We've always looked alike. Always."

"Really? And when do you see him, if you please?"

"Saturdays and Sundays. I try to spend the weekends with him."

The sweetness of her tone made the policeman stop scratching himself.

"Every Saturday and Sunday?"

"Well, not always. Sometimes an emergency comes up, and I don't go. But I always let him know by phone."

"And the others? Do you let them know?"

"Yes."

"Don't waver, madam. You're in a court of law."

The woman looked with candid eyes at the ten empty chairs behind her, the wooden counter painted grey, and the high file cabinets, government issue. On passing through the rooms on the way to the Public Ministry agent's office, the metal desks almost overwhelmed her. They too were covered with files piled every which way, some with a white card between the pages as a marker. She almost knocked down one of the tall stacks perched dangerously on a corner in front of a fat woman eating her lunch, elbows on her desk. It was obvious that she had previously bitten into a sandwich, and now she was gleefully adding greasy pieces of avocado to the opened bread cut with the paper knife. The floor of the greyish, worn out granite was filthy even though it was mopped daily. Windows that looked out on the street were very small and had thick, closely spaced bars. The dirty panes let through a sad, grime-choked light. It was clear that no one cared about the building, that everyone fled from it as soon as work was finished. No air entered the offices except through the door to the street that closed immediately. The fat lady put the remains of her sandwich that she meant to finish later in a brown paper bag where there also was a banana. The drawer shut with a coiled-spring sound. Then, with greasy hands, she faced her typewriter. All the machines were tall, very old, and the ribbons never returned by themselves. The fat lady put her finger into the carriage—the nail of her little finger—and began to return it. Then she got tired. With an inky finger, she pulled open the middle desk drawer and took out a ballpoint pen that she put in the centre of the ribbon. When she finished—now with her glasses on—she started work without bothering about the defendant in the antechamber reading the accusation: "The witness affirms that he wasn't at home at the time of the events. . . ." The typist stopped to adjust the copies, wetting her thumb and index finger. All the documents were made with ten copies when five would do. That's why there was a great deal of used carbons with government initials in the square grey wastebaskets. "Oh, boy, what a lot of carbon paper! What do they want with so many copies?" Everyone in the tribunal seemed immune to criticism. Some scratched their sides, others their armpits, women fixed a bra strap, grimacing. They grimaced on sitting down, but once seated they got up again to go to another desk to consult whatever it was that made them scratch their noses or pass their tongues several times over their teeth looking for some prodigious milligram. Once they found it, they took it out with their little finger. All in all, if they weren't aware of what they were doing, they weren't aware of the others either.

"Have them send Garcia to take a deposition."

"How many copies will they make?" asked the accused.

Nothing altered the clearness of her gaze, no shadow, no hidden motive on the shining surface.

The Public Ministry agent had to respond, "Ten."

"I knew it!"

"So, how many times have you been arrested?"

"None. This is the first time. I knew it because I noticed when we came in. I'm very observant," she said with a satisfied smile.

"You must be in order to have done what you've done for seven years."

She smiled, a fresh innocent smile, and the judge thought, "It's easy to see. . . ." He almost smiled. "I must keep this impersonal. But how can it be done when this woman seems to be playing, crossing and uncrossing her legs, showing her golden, round, perfectly shaped knees?"

"Let's see . . . your name is . . ."

"Esmeralda Loyden."

"Age?"

"Twenty-seven."

"Place of birth?"

"Mexico City."

"Native?"

"Yes." Esmeralda smiled again.

"Address?"

"27 Mirto, Apartment 3."

"District?"

"Santa Maria la Rivera."

"Postal Zone?"

"Four."

"Occupation?"

"Nurse. Listen, Your Honour, the address I gave you is my father's." She shook her curly head. "You have the other ones."

"All right. Now we're going to look at your declaration. Are you getting this down, Garcia?"

"Yes, Your Honour."

"Catholic?"

"Yes."

"Practising?"

"Yes."

"When?"

"I always go to mass on Sunday, Your Honour."

"Oh, really? And how is your conscience?"

"Fine, your honour. I especially like singing masses."

"And midnight masses? You must like those best," the old man said hoarsely.

"That's only once a year, but I like them, too."

"Oh, really? And who do you go with?"

"My father. I try to spend Christmas with him."

Esmeralda's green eyes, like tender, untrodden grass, got bigger.

"She almost looks like a virgin," thought the agent.

"Let's see, Garcia. We're ready to pronounce sentence in Case 132/6763, Thirtieth Tribunal, Second penal Court on five counts of bigamy."

"Five, your honour?"

"It's five, isn't it?"

"Yes, your honour, but only one accuses her."

"But she's married to five of them, isn't she?"

"Yes, sir."

"Put it down. Then, let's look at the first statement from Queretaro, State of Queretaro. It says, 'United States of Mexico. In the name of the Mexican Republic and as Civil State Judge of this place I make known to those witnesses now present and certify to be true that in the Book titled Marriages of the Civil Registry in my jurisdiction, on page 18, of the year 1948, permission of government 8577, File 351.2/49/82756 of the date June 12, 1948, F.M. at 8:00 p.m., before me appeared the citizens, Pedro Lugo and Miss Esmeralda Loyden with the object of matrimony under the rule of conjugal society.' Are you getting this, Garcia? Like this one, there are four more certificates, all properly certified and sealed. Only the names of the male correspondents change because the female correspondent—horrors—is always the same: Esmeralda Loyden. Here is a document signed in Cuernavaca, Morelos; another in Chilpancingo, Guerrero; another in Los Mochis, Sinaloa; and the fifth in Guadalajara, Jalisco. It appears that, as well as bigamy, you like travelling, madam."

"Not so much, Your Honour. They're the ones that . . . well, you know, for the honeymoon."

"Ah, yes."

"Yes, Your Honour. If it had been up to me, I would have stayed in Mexico City." Her voice was melodious.

The short woman entered again with the folder. The exasperated agent opened it and read aloud, " '. . . with visual inspections and ministerial faith, so much of the injury caused during the course of the above mentioned events in the clause immediately before . . .' Now you can go on from there yourself. It's only a copy. . . . Ah, and look! You forgot the 'Effective Suffrage, No Re-Election' again. Didn't I tell you? Well, watch what you're doing. Don't let it happen again . . . please."

When the dwarf shut the door, the judge hurried to say, "The names of the male parties, Garcia, must appear in the Juridical Edict in strict alphabetical order. Carlos Gonzales, Pedro Lugo, Gabriel Mercado, Livio Martinez, Julio Vallarta . . . one . . . two . . . three . . . four . . . five." The judge counted to himself. . . . "So you're Mrs Esmeralda Loyden Gonzales, Mrs Esmeralda Loyden Lugo, Mrs Esmeralda Loyden Martinez, Mrs Esmeralda Loyden Mercado, Mrs Esmeralda Loyden Vallarta. . . . Hmmm. How does that sound to you, Garcia?"

"Fine."

"What do you mean, fine?"

"The names are all correct, Your Honour, but the only one who's accusing her is Pedro Lugo."

"I'm not asking you that, Garcia. I am pointing out the moral, legal, social, and political implications of the case. They seem to escape you."

"Oh, that, Your Honour!"

"Have you ever encountered, Garcia, in your experience, a case like this?"

"No, Your Honour. Well, not with a woman because with men . . ." Garcia whistled in the air, a long whistle, like a passing train.

"Let's see what the accused has to say. But before that, let me ask you a personal question, Mrs Esmeralda. Didn't you get Julio confused with Livio?"

Esmeralda appeared like a child in front of a marvellous kaleidoscope. She looked through the transparent waters of her eyes. It was a kaleidoscope only she could see. The judge, indignant, repeated his question, and Esmeralda jumped as if the question startled her.

"Get them confused? No, Your Honour. They're all very different!"

"You never had a doubt, a slip up?"

"How could I?" she responded energetically. "I respect them too much."

"Not even in the dark?"

"I don't understand."

She rested a clear, tranquil gaze on the old man, and the agent was taken aback.

"It's incredible," he thought. "Incredible. Now I'm the one who'll have to beg her pardon!"

Then he attacked. "Did she undergo a gynecological exam with the court doctor?"

"Why, no," protested Garcia. "It's not a question of rape."

"Ah, yes, that's true. They're the ones who have to have it," laughed the agent, rubbing his hands together.

The woman also laughed as if it had nothing to do with her. She laughed to be kind, to keep the old man company. This disconcerted him even more.

"So there are five?" He tapped on the grimy wooden table.

"Five of them needed me."

"And you were able to accommodate them?"

"They had a considerable urgency."

"And children? Do you have children?" he asked almost respectfully.

"How could I? They are my children. I take care of them and help them with everything. I wouldn't have time for others."

The judge couldn't go on. Jokes with double meaning, vulgarities, witty comments all went over her head. . . . And Garcia was a hairy beast, an ox. He even appeared to have gone over to her side. That was the limit! He couldn't be thinking of becoming. . . The agent would have to wait until he was at the saloon with his cronies to tell them about this woman who smiled simply because smiling was part of her nature.

"I suppose you met the first one in the park."

"How did you know? Yes, I met Carlos in the Sunken Park. I was there reading Jose Emilio Pacheco's novel, *You Will Die Far Away*."

"So, you like to read?"

"No. He's the only one I've read and that's because I've met him." Esmeralda perked up. "I thought he was a priest. Imagine. We shared the same taxi, and when he got out I said, 'Father, give me your blessing.' He got very nervous and was even sweating. He handed me something black, 'Look. So you'll see I'm not what you think, I'm giving you my book.' "

"Well, what happened with Carlos?"

"Pedro . . . I mean, Carlos sat down on the bench where I was reading and asked me if the book was good. That's how everything started. Oh, no! Then something got in his eye—you know February is the month for dust storms. I offered to get it out for him. His eye was full of tears. I told him I was a nurse and then . . . I got it out. Listen, by the way, I've noticed that your left eye has been watering. Why don't you tell your wife to put some camomile in it, not the kind from a package, but the fresh kind, with a good flower. Tell your wife . . . if I could I would do it for you. You have to make sure the cup is quite clean before boiling a tiny bit of camomile of the good kind. Then you hold yourself like this with your head thrown back. About ten minutes, so it penetrates well. . . . You'll see how it soothes. Pure camomile flower."

"So, you're the kind who offers herself . . . to help."

"Yes, Your Honour. It's my natural reaction. The same thing happened with

Gabriel. He'd burned his arm. You should have seen how awful, one pustule after another. I treated it. It was my job to bandage him as ordered by Dr Carrillo. Then when he was well, he told me—I don't know how many times—that what he loved best in the world—besides me—was his right arm because it was the reason. . . ."

Esmeralda Loyden's five tales were similar. One case followed another with little variation. She related her marriages with shining, confident eyes. Sometimes, she was innocently conceited. "Pedro can't live without me. He doesn't even know where his shirts are." On the Public Ministry agent's lips trembled the words "perversion," "perfidy," "depravity," "absolute shame." But an opportunity never arose to voice them even though they were burning his tongue. With Esmeralda they lost all meaning. Her story was simple, without artifice. Mondays were Pedro's. Tuesdays Carlos's, and so on . . . until the week was complete. Saturdays and Sundays were set aside for washing and ironing clothes and preparing some special dish for Pedro, the most capricious of the five. When an emergency came up, a birthday, a saint's day, an outing, she gave up a Saturday or Sunday. No, no. They accepted everything, as long as they saw her. The only condition she always put was not giving up her nursing career.

"And they were agreeable to only having one day?"

"Sometimes they get an extra day. Besides, they work, too. Carlos is a travelling salesman, but manages to be in the City on Wednesdays. He doesn't miss those. Gabriel sells insurance. He also travels and is so intelligent they've offered him a job with IBM."

"None of them has ever wanted a child?"

"They never said so in so many words. When they talk about it, I tell them we've only been together a few years, that love matures."

"They accept this?"

"Yes, apparently."

"Well, apparently not. Now your game's up because they've denounced you."

"That was Pedro, the most temperamental, the most excitable. But at heart, Your Honour, he's a good fellow. He's generous. You know, like milk that boils over, then settles down. . . . You'll see."

"I'm not going to see anything because you are confined to jail. You've been separated for eight days. Or haven't you noticed, Mrs Loyden? Don't you regret being locked up?"

"Not much. Everyone's very nice. Besides you lose track of time. I've slept at least eight hours a night. I was really tired."

"I imagine so. . . . Then things haven't gone badly for you?"

"No. I've never lost sleep from worrying."

And really, the girl looked good, her skin healthy and clean, her eyes shining with health, all of her a calm smoothness. Ah! Her hair also shone, hair like that of a newborn animal, fine hair that invited caressing, just as her turned up nose invited tweaking. The judge started furiously. He was fed up with so much nonsense.

"Don't you realize you lived in absolute promiscuity? You deceived. You de-ceive. Not only are you immoral, but amoral. You don't have principles. You're pornographic. Yours is a case of mental illness. Your naïveté is a sign of imbecility. Your . . . your . . ."—he began to stutter—"People like you undermine the base of our society. You destroy the family nucleus. You're a social menace! Don't you realize all the wrong you've done with your irresponsible conduct?"

"Wrong to who?" cried Esmeralda.

"The men you've deceived, yourself, society, the principles of the Mexican Revolution!"

"Why? Shared days are happy days! Harmonious. They don't hurt anyone!"

"And the deceit?"

"What deceit? It's one thing not to say anything. It's another to deceive."

"You're crazy. Moreover, the psychiatrist is going to prove it. For sure."

"Really? Then what will happen to me?"

"Ah, hah! Now you're worried! It's the first time you've thought about your fate."

"Yes, Your Honour. I've never been a worrier."

"What kind of woman are you? I don't understand you. Either you're mentally deficient . . . or . . . I don't know . . . a loose woman."

"Loose woman?"—Esmeralda got serious—"Tell Pedro that."

"Pedro, Juan, and the others. When they find out, they're going to think the same thing."

"They won't think the same thing. They're all different. I don't think the same as you, and I couldn't if I wanted to."

"Don't you realize your lack of remorse?"

The agent hit his fist on the table making the age-old dust fly. "You're a wh . . . You act like a pros . . ." (Curiously, he couldn't say the words in front of her. Her smile inhibited him. Looking at her closely . . . he'd never seen such a pretty girl. She wasn't so pretty at first sight, but she grew in healthiness, cleanliness, freshness. She seemed to have just bathed. That was it. What would she smell like? Perhaps like vanilla? A woman with all her teeth. You could see them when she threw her head back to laugh, because the shameless woman laughed.)

"Well, and don't you sometimes see yourself as trash?"

"Me?" she asked, surprised. "Why?"

The agent felt disarmed.

"Garcia, call Lucita to take a statement."

Lucita was the one with the avocado and the banana. She carried her shorthand tablet under her arm, her finger still covered with ink. She sat down grimacing and muttered, "The defendant . . ."

"No, look. Do it directly on the machine. It comes out better. What have you to say in your defence, Mrs Loyden?"

"I don't know legal terms. I wouldn't know how to say it. Why don't you advise me, Your Honour, since you're so knowledgeable?"

"It . . . it . . . it's too much," stuttered the agent, "Now I have to advise her. Read the file, Lucita."

Lucita opened a folder with a white card in the middle and said, "It's not signed."

"If you like," proposed Esmeralda, "I'll sign it."

"You haven't made a statement yet. How are you going to sign it?"

"It doesn't matter. I'll sign beforehand. After all, Gabriel told me that in the courts they write in whatever they want."

"Well, Gabriel's a liar, and I'm going to have the pleasure of sending him a subpoena accusing him of defamation."

"Will I be able to see him?" Esmeralda asked excitedly.

"Gabriel? I doubt very much he'll want to see you."

"But the day he comes, will you send for me?"

(Crazy, ignorant, animal-like, all women are crazy. They are vicious, degenerate, demented, bestial. To think she would get involved with five at a time and awaken fresh as the morning. Because the many nights on duty have not affected this woman at all. She doesn't even hear anything I say, for all I try to make her understand.)

"By that time you'll be behind bars in the Santa Marta Acatitla prison. For desecration of morality, for bigamy, for not being wise"—he thought of various other possible crimes—"for injuries to particular individuals, criminal association, incitement to rebellion, attacks on public property. Yes, yes. Didn't you meet Carlos in the park."

"But, will I be able to see Gabriel?"

"Is he the one you love most?" asked the Public Minister, suddenly intrigued.

"No. I love them all, equally."

"Even Pedro who denounced you?"

"Oh, my sweet Pedro," she said rocking him between her breasts . . . which looked very firm because they stayed erect while she made the rocking gesture.

"That's the last straw!"

Lucita, with a pencil behind her ear, stuck in her greasy hair, crackled something in her hands, a brown paper bag. Perhaps so the agent would notice her or so he would stop shouting. For the past few moments, Lucita had been staring at the accused. In fact, four of five employees weren't missing a word of the confrontation. Carmelita left her *Tears and Laughs*, and Tere put away her photo novel. Carvajal was standing next to Garcia, and Perez and Mantecon were listening intently. In the courtroom, men wore ties, but everyone looked dirty and sweaty. Clothes stuck to them like poultices, their suits shiny and full of lint, and that horrible brown colour, that dark people like to wear. It makes them look like rancid chocolate. Lucita, though, fitted her short stature with screaming colours. A green skirt with a yellow nylon blouse, or was it the opposite? Pure circus combination, but her face was so rapt now that she looked attractive. Interest ennobled them. They had quit scuffing their feet, scratching their bodies, and leaning against the walls. No indolence remained. They had come alive. They remembered they were once men, once young, once totally unattached to the paperwork and marking of cards. Drops of crystalline water shone on their foreheads. Esmeralda bathed them.

"The press is waiting outside," Lucita advised the Public Ministry agent.

He stood up. He wasn't in the habit of making the press wait. It was the fifth power.

Meanwhile, Lucita approached Esmeralda and patted her thigh. "Don't worry, honey. I'm with you. I'm enjoying this because the bastard I married had another woman after a while. He even put her up in a house, and he's got me here working. How terrific that someone like you can get revenge. I'll help on that last interrogation. I swear I'll help. And not only me, but Carmelita, too. That's her desk over there. And Carvajal and Mantecon and Perez and Mr Michael, who's a little old-fashioned, but nice. What can I say? You're better than divine Yesenia for us. Let's see. I'll start the statement, 'the defendant . . .' " (By now, Esmeralda, convicted or not, felt a drowsiness that made her curl up in the chair like a cat whom everyone likes, especially Lucita.)

Lucita's keys flew joyously through the legal terms—written, they're obscure; spoken in a loud voice, they're incomprehensible. Lucita insisted on saying them out loud to Esmeralda to give proof of her loyalty. After typing, "Coordinated Services of Prevention and Social Adaptation," and realizing she got no response, Lucita spoke in Esmeralda's ear. "You're sleepy, honey. We're about done. I'll only need to add something about damages, a notification, and reprehension of the accused. It doesn't all fit. Oh, well, that's in accord with the law. Let'er know her right and the time allowed for appeal. 'Dispatch,' I think it has a 't.' Oh, well. Now the warrants and extra copies. The word 'court' should be capitalized, but I didn't do it the other five times. It's not important. Okay, sweetie, sign it here and . . . listen. D'ya want a cold drink to perk you up? Here are the identifying markers. A formal decree presumes you're guilty and off to prison, but don't pay any attention. We won't let it happen. We need a medical certificate and a corresponding certificate of court appraisal . . . the law's conclusions. They'll all be favourable. You'll see, honey. I'll take care of it. For you, nothing can go wrong."

In her cell, after a good soup with chicken wing and thigh, Esmeralda slept surrounded by sympathetic jailers. The next day, groups came to demonstrate, including feminine sectors of several political parties. Rene Cardona Junior wanted to make a film on the spot. The press had reported events in scandalous form. "Five, Like The Fingers On Her Hand," read the headline across eight columns in the police section. *Ovaciones*, in big black headlines, wrote "Five Winners And The Jockey Is A Woman." Three exclamation marks. An editorial writer sombrely began his column ". . . Once more our primitive nature is confronted and put to the test." He went into detail about low instincts. Another writer, obviously a technician with a state agency, spoke of the multistratification of women; they were treated like objects; domestic work didn't allow them access to the higher realms of culture. There were other dangerous distortions which the readers promised to read later. All in all, it was a tiring day. Among the many visitors appeared two nuns, very excited. That didn't count nuns not wearing habits, progressive ones, usually French. There were many. "Oh, boy," thought Lucita, "What a day for us women! Even though Esmeralda might turn out a scapegoat, she's our rallying flag. Her struggle is ours as well."

The Public Ministry agent took it upon himself, seeing heated spirits, to throw cold water on them.

"The courtroom will be closed to the public."

Lucita disappeared behind the old typewriter with the ribbon she had to rewind by hand.

"In Iztapalapa, Federal District at 10:30 o'clock on the 22nd day, within the period of time specified by Article 19 of the Constitution, proceedings were initiated to resolve the juridical situation of Mrs Esmeralda Loyden Gonzalez Lugo Martinez Mercado Vallarta whom the Public Minister accuses of committing five counts of adultery, considered bigamy, as described by Article 37, Paragraph 1 of the Penal Code of Penal Processes with the writ of damages presented by the accuser who in his civilian state is called Pedro Lugo, who, having sworn and having been warned in terms of the law to conduct himself truthfully, subject to sanctions applied to those who submit false testimony, declared the above to be his name, to be thirty-two years of age, married, Catholic, educated, employed, originally from Coatzacoalcos, state of Veracruz, who in the essential part of his accusation said that on Monday, May 28, when his wife did not arrive as she usually did at 8:00 p.m. on the dot on Mondays at their conjugal dwelling located at 246 Patriotismo, Apartment 16, Colonia San Pedro of the Pines, Postal Zone 13, he went to look for her at the hospital where she said she worked and not finding her, he asked if she would be there the following night and was informed by the receptionist to go see the administration since her name did not appear on the night duty list, that she thought she probably worked during the day, but since she came on with the second shift she was not sure and could not tell him, since she got there la-"—here Lucita just put "la" because "later" didn't fit on the line and she let it go—"and therefore [on the next line] she saw the necessity of sending the plaintiff to the administration to get more information and that in the already mentioned administration the accuser was informed that the one he called his wife never worked the night shift, so the man had to be restrained, putting his hands behind his back, something two attendants had to do after being called by the director, who feared the man wasn't sane. They then saw the accuser leave staggering, beside himself, supporting himself on the walls since he did sustain with the witness sexual relations being her legitimate husband as testified by certificate number 13797, page 18, being the said a pubescent, fecund woman, when he married her seven years ago. Afterward the accuser proceeded to subsequent inquiries adding what remains explained in file number 347597, without the knowledge of the defendant and managed to find out that the other four husbands were in the same situation and whom he proceeded to inform of the 'quintuplicity' of the accused. The presumed penal responsibility of the accused in the commission of the crimes committed with an original and five copies (the original for Pedro Lugo, being he, the first and principal accuser) as charged by the Social Representation, is found accredited to this moment, with the same elements of proof mentioned, in the consideration that precedes, with an emphasis on the direct imputation that the offended party makes and above all, the affidavit concerning the clothes and personal objects of the defendant at the five addresses mentioned as well as the numerous personal details, photographic proofs, inscriptions on photographs, letters and love missives lavishly written by the accused, brought together by the aggrieved and above all, the indisputableness and authenticity of the marriage certificates and the resulting acts derived from the aforesaid. And it can be said according to the five and to the accused herself, the marriages were dutifully and entirely consummated, to the full satisfaction of all, in the physical person of Esmeralda Loyden, so-called nurse by profession. That the defendant emitted declarations that are not supported by any proof that makes them credible, but on the contrary, proven worthless because of the elements which were alluded to [alluded with two "l"s], that the defendant didn't manifest remorse at any moment, neither did she seem to realize that she was charged with five crimes, that she didn't voice any objection except that she was sleepy, that the defendant submits with notable docility to the administering of all tests, allowing all the procedures to be carried out that are necessary for the clarification of the facts, as well as those advanced by the parties, in accordance with the parts III, IV, and V of Article 20 of the Federal Constitution, be it notified and put into effect, the nature and cause of the accusation. On the same date, the Secretary of the Factions Clerk swears that the term for the parties to offer more proof in the present cause begins on this June 20 and concludes on next July 12. I swear this document to be true and valid."

When the Public Ministry Agent was about to put his signature at the bottom of the document, he yelled angrily, "Lucita, what's wrong with you? You forgot the 'Effective Suffrage, No Re-Election' again!"

Afterward, everything was rumour. Some say Esmeralda left with her jailkeepers for the jail wagon, followed by the faithful Lucita, who had prepared her a sandwich for the trip; by Garcia, the scribe, who kissed her hand; and by the affectionate gaze of the Public Ministry agent.

On saying goodbye, the agent again urged as he took her two hands between his own, moving each and everyone with his words: "Esmeralda, look what happens when you get involved in such things. Listen to me. You're young. Get away from all this, Esmeralda. Be respectable. From now on, be proper."

Many spectators made the convicted woman smile when they applauded her gracious manner. Others, on the other hand, saw, in the middle of the crowd behind the grey wooden banister, painted and repainted with an always thinner coat, Pedro Lugo, the accuser, pierce Esmeralda his with intense gaze. On the other side, some saw myopic Julio give her a friendly sign with his hand. Getting into the police wagon, Esmeralda didn't see Carlos, but did notice Livio with his shaved head and eyes filled with tears. She yelled to him, "Why did you cut it? You know I don't like short hair."

The journalists took notes. None of the husbands was missing, not even the travelling salesman. Authoritative voices said the five husbands had tried to stop the trial because they all wanted Esmeralda back. But the sentence was already dictated, and they couldn't appeal to the Supreme Court of Justice. The case had received too much publicity. Each one agreed, in turn, to conjugal visits at Santa Acatitla. Things were nearly the same, "*de facto et in situ*." Before, they had seen her only one night a week. Now they all got together occasionally for Sunday visits. Each one brought a treat. They took a variety of things to please not only Esmeralda, but also Lucita, Carmelita, Tere, Garcia, Carvajal, Perez, Mantecon, and the Public Ministry agent, who from time to time quietly presented himself—he'd grown fond of Esmeralda's responses.

But from these facts a new case couldn't be made. Accusers and accused, judge and litigants, had repented of their haste in bringing the first action, number 479/32/875746, page 68. Everything, though, remained in the so-called book of life which is full of trivia and which preceded the book now used to note the facts. It has an ugly name: computer certification. I swear this document to be true and valid.

Effective Suffrage, No Re-Election

1985
translated by Catherine S. White-House

Austin Clarke

b. 1934

Born in Barbados, Austin Clarke moved to Canada in 1955 to study at the University of Toronto. He started out as a reporter in Timmins and Kirkland Lake, and then joined the CBC, working as a producer and a freelance broadcaster. Between 1968 and 1974 he taught creative writing at various American universities, including Brandeis, Texas, and Yale. In 1974–5 he worked in Caribbean broadcasting and served as an advisor to the prime minister of Barbados. While his first works of fiction dealt with life in Barbados, in 1967 he wrote *The Meeting Point*, the first of a trilogy about the lives of Caribbean immigrants in Toronto, followed by *Storm of Fortune* (1971), and *The Bigger Light* (1975), stinging indictments of the racist hypocrisy in Canadian society. But Clarke's humour laces his fiction, and his portraits, always psychologically astute, give a focus to Black struggle. Often using Caribbean dialect, his dialogue is masterful. He has written numerous stories that document Black immigrant experience. His autobiography, *Growing Up Stupid under the Union Jack* (1980), is not simply a personal memoir, but also examines British colonialism. Clarke was the first Black writer to achieve prominence in Canada and has influenced a generation of young Black writers. In 1999 he was awarded the W.O. Mitchell Prize for his body of work and mentorship of other writers. His recent work includes *The Polished Hoe* (2002), which won the Giller Prize and *They Never Told Me and Other Stories* (2013).

Leaving This Island Place

The faces at the grilled windows of the parish almshouse were looking out, on this hot Saturday afternoon, on a world of grey-flannel and cricket and cream shirts, a different world, as they had looked every afternoon from the long imprisonment of the wards. Something in those faces told me they were all going to die in the almshouse. Standing on the cricket field I searched for the face of my father. I knew he would never live to see the sun of day again.

It is not cricket, it is leaving the island that makes me think about my father. I am leaving the island. And as I walk across the green playing field and into the driveway of the almshouse, its walkway speckled with spots of tar and white pebbles, and walk right up to the white spotless front of the building, I know it is too late now to think of saving him. It is too late to become involved with this dying man.

In the open veranda I could see the men, looking half-alive and half-dead, lying on the smudged canvas cots that were once white and cream as the cricketers' clothes, airing themselves. They have played, perhaps, in too many muddy tournaments, and are now soiled. But I am leaving. But I know before I leave there is some powerful tug which pulls me into this almshouse, grabbing me and almost swallowing me to make me enter these doors and slap me flat on the sore-back canvas cot beside a man in dying health. But I am leaving.

"You wasn't coming to visit this poor man, this poor father o' yourn?" It is Miss Brewster, the head nurse. She knew my father and she knew me. And she knew that I played cricket every Saturday on the field across the world from the almshouse. She is old and haggard. And she looks as if she has looked once too often on the face of death; and now she herself resembles a half-dead, dried-out flying fish, wrapped in the grease-proof paper of her nurse's uniform. "That man having fits and convulsions by the hour! Every day he asking for you. All the time, day in and day out. And you is such a poor-great, high-school educated bastard that you now acting *too proud* to come in here, because it is a almshouse and not a *private ward*, to see your own father! And you didn' even have the presence o' mind to bring along a orange, not even one, or a banana for that man, *your father*!"

She was now leading me through a long dark hallway, through rows of men on their sides, and some on their backs, lying like soldiers on a battlefield. They all looked at me as if I was dying. I tried to avoid their eyes, and I looked instead at their bones and the long fingernails and toenails, the thermometers of their long idle illness. The matted hair and the smell of men overdue for the bed-pan: men too weary now to raise themselves to pass water even in a lonely gutter. They were dying slowly and surely, for the almshouse was crowded and it did not allow its patients to die too quickly. I passed them, miles out of my mind: the rotting clothes and sores, men of all colours, all ages, dressed like women in long blue sailcloth-hard shirts that dropped right down to the scales on their toothpick legs. One face smiled at me, and I wondered whether the smile meant welcome.

"Wait here!" It was Miss Brewster again who had spoken. She opened the door of a room and pushed me inside as you would push a small boy into the headmaster's office for a caning; and straightway the smell of stale urine and of sweat and feces whipped me in the face. When the door closed behind me I was alone with the dead, with the smells of the almshouse.

I am frightened. But I am leaving. I find myself thinking about the trimmed sandwiches and the whisky-and-sodas waiting for me at the farewell party in honour of my leaving. Something inside me is saying I should pay some respect in my thoughts for this man, this dying man. I opened my eyes and thought of Cynthia. I thought of her beautiful face beside my father's face. And I tried to hold her face in the hands of my mind, and I squeezed it close to me and kept myself alive with the living outside world of cricket and cheers and "tea in the pavilion." There is death in this room and I am inside it. And Cynthia's voice is saying to me, Run run run! back through the smells, through the fallen lines of the men, through the front door and out into the green sunlight of the afternoon and the cricket and shouts; out into the applause.

"That's he laying-down there. Your father," the voice said. It was Miss Brewster. She too must have felt the power of death in the room, for she spoke in a whisper.

This is my father: more real than the occasional boundary hit by the cricket bat and the cheers that came with the boundary only. The two large eyeballs in the sunset of this room are my father.

"Boy?" It was the skeleton talking. I am leaving. He held out a hand to touch me. Dirt was under the fingernails like black moons. I saw the hand. A dead hand, a dirty hand, a hand of quarter-moons of dirt under the claws of its nails. ("You want to know something, son?" my godmother told me long ago. "I'll tell you something. That man that your mother tell you to call your father, he isn't your father, in truth. Your mother put the blame of your birth on him because once upon a time, long long ago in this island, that man was a man.")

I do not touch the hand. I am leaving this place.

And then the words, distant and meaningless from this departure of love because they come too late, began to turn the room on a side. Words and words and words. He must have talked this way each time he heard a door open or shut; or a footstep. ". . . is a good thing you going away, son, a good thing. I hear you going away, and that is a good thing . . . because I am going away . . . from this place . . . Miss Brewster, she . . . but I am sorry . . . cannot go with you . . ." (Did my mother hate this man so much to drive him here? Did she drive him to such a stick of love that it broke his heart; and made him do foolish things with his young life on the village green of cricket near his house, that made him the playful enemy of Barrabas the policeman, whose delight, my godmother told me, was to drag my father the captain of the village team away drunk from victory and pleasure to throw him into the crowded jail to make him slip on the cold floor fast as a new cricket pitch with vomit . . . ("And it was then, my child, after all those times in the jail, that your father contract that sickness which nobody in this village don't call by name. It is so horrible a sickness.") . . . and I remember now that even before this time I was told by my mother that my father's name was not to be mentioned in her house which her husband made for me as my stepfather. And she kept her word. For eighteen years. For eighteen years, his name was never mentioned; so he had died before this present visit. And there was not even a spasm of a reminiscence of his name. He was dead before this. But sometimes I would risk the lash of her hand and visit him, in his small shack on the fringe of Rudders Pasture where he lived out the riotous twenty-four years of middle life. ("Your mother never loved that bastard," my godmother said.) But I loved him, in a way. I loved him when he was rich enough to give me two shillings for a visit, for each visit. And although my mother had said he had come "from no family at-all, at-all," had had "no background," yet to me in those laughing days he held a family circle of compassion in his heart. I see him now, lying somewhere on a cot, and I know I am leaving this island. In those days of cricket when I visited him, I visited him in his house: the pin-up girls of the screen, white and naked; and the photographs of black women he had taken with a box camera (because "Your father is some kind o' genius, but in this island we call him a blasted madman, but he may be a real genius"), black women always dressed in their Sunday-best after church, dressed in too much clothes, and above them all, above all those pin-ups and photographs, the photographs of me, caught running in a record time, torn form the island's newspapers. And there was one of me he had framed, when I passed my examinations at Harrison College. And once, because in those days he was my best admirer, I gave him a silver cup which I had won for winning a race in a speed which no boy had done in twenty-five years, at the same school, in the history of the school. And all those women on the walls, and some in real life, looking at me, and whispering under their breath so I might barely hear it, "That's his *son*!"; and some looking at me as if I had entered their bedroom of love at the wrong moment of hectic ecstasy; and he, like a child caught stealing, would hang his father's head in shame and apologize for them in a whisper, and would beg the women in a loud voice, "You don't see I am with *my* son? You can't behave yourself in his presence?" And once, standing in his house alone, when he went to buy a sugar cake for me, I was looking at the photograph of a naked woman on the wall and my eyes became full of mists and I saw coming out of the rainwater of vision my mother's face, and her neck and her shoulders and her breasts and her navel. And I shut my eyes tight, tight, tight and ran into him returning with the sugar cake and ran screaming from his house. That was my last visit. This is my first visit after that. And I am leaving this island place. After that last visit I gave myself headaches wondering if my mother had gone to his shack before she found herself big and heavy with the burden of me in her womb. ("Child, you have no idea what he do to that poor pretty girl, your mother, that she hates his guts even to this day!") . . . and the days at Harrison College when the absence of his surname on my report card would remind me in the eyes of my classmates that I might be the best cricketer and the best runner, but that I was after all, among this cream of best blood and brains, only a bas—) ". . . this island is only a place, one place," his voice was saying. "The only saving thing is to escape." He was a pile of very old rags thrown around a stunted tree. Then he was talking again, in a new way. "Son, do not leave before you get somebody to say a prayer for me . . . somebody like Sister Christopher from the Nazarene Church . . ."

But Sister Christopher is dead. Dead and gone five years now, "When she was shouting at the Lord one night at a revival," my godmother said.

"She's dead."

"*Dead?*"

"Five years."

"But couldn' you still ask her to come, ask Miss Christo, Sister Christopher to come . . ."

There is no point listening to a dying man talk. I am going to leave. No point telling him that Sister Christopher is alive, because he is beyond that, beyond praying for, since he is going to die and he never was a Catholic. And I am going to leave. For I cannot forget the grey-flannel and the cream of the cricket field just because he is dying, and the sharp smell of the massage and the cheers of the men and women at the tape, which I have now made a part of my life. And the Saturday afternoon matinées with the wealthy middle-class girls from Queen's College, wealthy in looks and wealthy in books, with their boyfriends the growing-up leaders of the island. Forget all that? And forget the starched white shirt and the blue-and-gold Harrison College tie? Forget all this because a man is dying and because he tells you he is going to die?

Perhaps I should forget them. They form a part of the accident of my life, a life which—if there were any logic in life—ought to have been spent in the gutters round the Bath Corner, or in some foreign white woman's rose garden, or fielding tennis balls in the Garrison Savannah Tennis Club where those who played tennis could be bad tennis players but had to be white.

Let him die. I am leaving this island place. And let him die with his claim on my life. And let the claim be nailed in the coffin, which the poor authorities for the poor will authorize out of plain dealboard, without a minister or a prayer. And forget Sister Christopher who prefers to testify and shout on God; and call somebody else, perhaps, more in keeping with the grey-flannel and the cream of the cricket field and Saturday afternoon walks in the park and matinées at the Empire Theatre. Call a canon. Call a canon to bury a pauper, call a canon to bury a pauper, ha-ha-haaaa! . . .

Throughout the laughter and the farewell speeches and the drinks that afternoon, all I did hear was the slamming of many heavy oak doors of the rectory when I went to ask the canon to bury the pauper. And I tried to prevent the slamming from telling me what it was telling me: that I was out of place here, that I belonged with the beginning in the almshouse. Each giggle, each toast, each rattle of drunken ice cubes in the whirling glass pointed a finger back to the almshouse. "Man, you not drinking?" a wealthy girl said. "Man, what's wrong with you, at all?" And someone else was saying, "Have any of you remember Freddie?" But Briggs said, "Remember that bitch? The fellar with the girl with the biggest bubbies in the whole Caribbean? And who uses to . . . man, Marcus! Marcus, I calling you! God-blummuh, Marcus we come here to drink rum and you mean to tell me that you selling we *water*, instead o' rum?" And Joan Warton said, "But wait, look this lucky bastard though, saying he going up in Canada to university! Boy, you real lucky, in truth. I hear though that up there they possess some real inferior low-class rum that they does mix with water. Yak-yakyak! From now on you'd be drinking Canadian rum-water, so stop playing the arse and drink this Bajan rum, man. We paying for this, yuh know!" I was leaving. I was thinking of tomorrow, and I was climbing the BOAC gangplank on the plane bound for Canada, for hope, for school, for glory; and the sea and the distance had already eased the pain of conscience; and there was already much sea between me and the cause of conscience . . .

And when the party was over, Cynthia was with me on the sands of Gravesend Beach. And the beach was full of moonlight and love. There was laughter too; and the laughter of crabs scrambling among dead leaves and skeletons of other crabs caught unawares by someone running into the sea. And there was a tourist ship in the outer harbour. "Write! write, write, write, write me every day of the week, every week of the year, and tell me what Canada is like, and think of me always, and don't forget to say nice things in your letters, and pray for me every night. And write poems, love poems like the ones you write in the college magazine; and when you write don't send the letters to the Rectory, because father would, well . . . send them to Auntie's address. You understand? You know how ministers and canons behave and think. I have to tell father, I have to tell him I love you, and that we are getting married when you graduate. And I shall tell him about us . . . when you leave tomorrow." Watching the sea and the moonlight on the sea; and watching to see if the sea was laughing; and the scarecrows of masts on the fishing boats now lifeless and boastless, taking a breather from the depths and the deaths of fishing; and the large incongruous luxury liner drunk-full of tourists. And all the time Cynthia chatting and chattering, ". . . but we should have got married, even secretly and eloped somewhere, even to Trinidad, or even to Tobago. Father won't've known, and won't've liked it, but we would've been married . . . Oh hell, man! this island stifles me, and I wish I was leaving with you. Sometimes I feel like a crab in a crab hole with a pile o' sand in front . . ."

"Remember how we used to build sandcastles on bank holidays?"

"And on Sundays, far far up the beach where nobody came . . ."

"Cynthia?"

"Darling?"

"My Old Man, my Old Man is dying right now . . ."

"You're too philosophical! Anyhow, where? Are you kidding? I didn't even know you had an Old Man." And she laughs.

"I was at the almshouse this afternoon, before the party."

"Is he really in the almshouse?"

"St Michael's almshouse, near . . ."

"You must be joking. You *must* be joking!" She turned her back to me, and her face to the sea. "You aren't pulling my leg, eh?" she said. And before I could tell her more about my father, who he was, how kind a man he was, she was walking from me and we were in her father's Jaguar and speeding away from the beach.

And it is the next day, mid-morning, and I am sitting in the Seawell Airport terminal, waiting to be called to board the plane. I am leaving. My father, is he dead yet? A newspaper is lying on a bench without a man, or woman. Something advises me to look in the obituary column and see if . . . But my mother had said, as she packed my valises, making sure that the fried fish was in my briefcase which Cynthia had brought for me as a going-away present, my mother had said, "Look, boy, leave the dead to live with the blasted dead, do! Leave the dead in this damn islan' place!"

And I am thinking now of Cynthia who promised ("I promise, I promise, I promise. Man, you think I going let you leave this place, *leave Barbados*? and I not going be there at the airport?") to come to wave goodbye, to take a photograph waving goodbye from the terminal and the plane, to get her photograph taken for the social column waving goodbye at the airport, to kiss, to say goodbye and promise return in English, and say "*au revoir*" in French because she was the best student in French at Queen's College.

A man looks at the newspaper, and takes it up, and gives it to a man loaded down as a new-traveller for a souvenir of the island. And the friend wraps two large bottles of Goddards Gold Braid rum in it, smuggling the rum and the newspaper out of the island, in memory of the island. And I know I will never find out how he died. Now there are only the fear and the tears and the handshakes of other people's saying goodbye and the weeping of departure. "Come back real soon again, man!" a fat, sweating man says, "and next time I going take you to some places that going make your head *curl*! Man, I intend to show you the whole islan," and give you some dolphin steaks that is more bigger than the ones we eat down in Nelson Street with the whores last night!" An old woman, who was crying, was saying goodbye to a younger woman who could have been her daughter, or her daughter-in-law, or her niece. "Don't take long to return back, child! Do not tarry too long. Come back again soon . . . and don't forget that you was borned right here, pon this rock, pon this island. This is a good decent island, so return back as soon as you get yuh learning, come back again soon, child . . ."

The plane is ready now. And Cynthia is not coming through the car park in her father's Jaguar. She has not come, she has not come as she promised. And I am leaving the island.

Below me on the ground are the ants of people, standing at an angle, near the terminal. And I can see the architect-models of houses and buildings, and the beautiful quiltwork patches of land under the plough . . . and then there is the sea, and the sea, and then the sea.

1971

Leon Rooke

b. 1934

Born in Roanoke Rapids, North Carolina, Leon Rooke attended Mars Hill College and, in 1955, entered the University of North Carolina to study journalism and drama. Drafted into the US Army, he served two years in Alaska. He returned to the university to study screenwriting but left to take up a job as editor of a North

Carolina newspaper. He returned briefly to the University of North Carolina to serve as writer-in-residence, but soon married and, in 1969, moved with his wife to Vancouver Island where she worked at the University of Victoria while he dedicated his time to writing. Rooke has remained in Canada, serving as writer-in-residence at a number of Canadian schools, including the Universities of Toronto, Western Ontario, and Victoria. He moved to Eden Mills in 1988, and founded the Eden Mills Writers' Festival the following year. He currently resides in Toronto. Rooke is a prolific writer, having published more than two dozen books, including novels, short fiction, plays, and scripts for radio and film. His first collection of stories, *Last One Home Sleeps in the Yellow Bed*, appeared in 1968. His novel *Shakespeare's Dog* (1983) won the Governor General's Award for Fiction. In 2001, a stage adaptation of *Shakespeare's Dog* completed a two-year tour of the Atlantic seaboard by tall ship. His novel *A Good Baby* (1989) was made into a feature film, for which he wrote the screenplay. Rooke's early career as a dramatist influenced him a great deal. His prose has a dramatic edge and his dialogue can be both laconic and electric. He is often described as a "postmodernist" writer because of his willingness to move his narratives to the level of the surreal. Rooke is also a gifted actor as is clear from his parodic performance as a fundamentalist preacher in Michael Ondaatje's short film, *The Love Clinic* (1990).

A Bolt of White Cloth

A man came by our road carrying an enormous bolt of white cloth on his back. Said he was from the East. Said whoever partook of this cloth would come to know true happiness. Innocence without heartbreak, he said, if that person proved worthy. My wife fingered his cloth, having in mind something for new curtains. It was good quality, she said. Beautifully woven, of a fine, light texture, and you certainly couldn't argue with the colour.

"How much is it?" she asked.

"Before I tell you that," the man said, "you must tell me truthfully if you've ever suffered."

"Oh, I've suffered," she said. "I've known suffering of some description every day of my natural life."

I was standing over by the toolshed, with a big smile. My wife is a real joker who likes nothing better than pulling a person's leg. She's known hardships, this and that upheaval, but nothing I would call down-and-out suffering. Mind you, I don't speak for her. I wouldn't pretend to speak for another person.

This man with the bolt of cloth, however, he clearly had no sense of my wife's brand of humour. She didn't get an itch of a smile out of him. He kept the cloth neatly balanced on his shoulder, wincing a little from the weight and from however far he'd had to carry it, staring hard and straight at my wife the whole time she fooled with him, as if he hoped to peer clear through to her soul. His eyes were dark and brooding and hollowed out some. He was like no person either my wife or me had ever seen before.

"Yes," he said, "but suffering of what kind?"

"Worse than I hope forever to carry, I'll tell you that,"my wife said. "But why are you asking me these questions? I like your cloth and if the price is right I mean to buy it."

"You can only buy my cloth with love," he said.

We began right then to understand that he was some kind of oddity. He was not like anybody we'd ever seen and he didn't come from around here. He'd come from a place we'd never heard of, and if that was the East, or wherever, then he was welcome to it.

"Love?" she said. "Love? There's *love* and there's *love*, mister. What kind are talking about?" She hitched a head my way, rolling her eyes, as if to indicate that if it was *passionate* love he was talking about then he'd first have to do something with me. He'd have to get me off my simmer and onto full boil. That's what she was telling him, with this mischief in her eyes.

I put down my pitchfork about here, and strolled nearer. I liked seeing my wife dealing with difficult situations. I didn't want to miss anything. My life with that woman had been packed with the unusual. Unusual circumstances, she calls them. Any time she's ever gone out anywhere without me, whether for a day or an hour or for five minutes, she's come back with whopping good stories about what she's seen and heard and what's happened to her. She's come back with reports on these unusual circumstances, these little adventures in which so many people have done so many extraordinary things or behaved in such fabulous or foolish ways. So what was rare this time, I thought, was that it had come visiting. She hadn't had to go out and find it.

"Hold these," my wife told me. And she put this washtub of clothes in my hands, and went back to hanging wet pieces on the line, which is what she'd been doing when this man with the bolt of cloth ventured up into our yard.

"Love," she told him. "You tell me what kind I need, if I'm to buy that cloth. I got good ears and I'm listening."

The man watched her stick clothespins in her mouth, slap out a good wide sheet, and string it up. He watched her hang two of these, plus a mess of towels, and get her mouth full again before he spoke. He looked about the unhappiest I've ever seen a man look. He didn't have any joy in him. I wondered why he didn't put down that heavy bolt of cloth, and why he didn't step around into a spot of shade. The sun was lick-killing bright in that yard. I was worried he'd faint.

"The ordinary kind," he said. "Your ordinary kind of love will buy this cloth."

My wife flapped her wash and laughed. He was really tickling her. She was having herself a wonderful time.

"What's ordinary?" she said. "I've never known no *ordinary* love."

He jumped right in. He got excited just for a second.

"The kind such as might exist between the closest friends," he said. "The kind such as might exist between a man and his wife or between parents and children or for that matter the love a boy might have for his dog. That kind of love."

"I've got that," she said. "I've had all three. Last year this time I had me a fourth, but it got run over. Up on the road there, by the tall trees, by a man in a car who didn't even stop."

"That would have been your cat," he said. "I don't know much about cats."

I put down the washtub. My wife let her arms drop. We looked at him, wondering how he knew about that cat. Then I laughed, for I figured someone down the road must have told him of my wife's mourning over that cat. She'd dug it a grave under the grapevine and said sweet words over it. She sorely missed that cat.

"What's wrong with loving cats?" she asked him. "Or beasts of the fields? I'm surprised at you."

The man shifted his burden and worked one shoe into the ground. He stared off at the horizon. He looked like he knew he'd said something he shouldn't.

She pushed me out of the way. She wanted to get nearer to him. She had something more to say.

"Now listen to me," she said. "I've loved lots of things in my life. Lots and lots. *Him*!" she said (pointing at me), "*it*" (pointing to our house), "*them*!" (pointing to the flower beds), "*that*" (pointing to the sky), "*those*" (pointing to the woods), "*this*" (pointing to the ground)—"practically *everything*! There isn't any of it I've hated, and not much I've been indifferent to. Including cats. So put that in your pipe and smoke it."

Then swooping up her arms and laughing hard, making it plain she bore no grudge but wasn't just fooling.

Funny thing was, hearing her say it, I felt the same way. *It, them, that, those*—they were all beautiful. I couldn't deny it was love I was feeling.

The man with the cloth had turned each way she'd pointed. He'd staggered a time or two but he'd kept up. In fact, it struck me that he'd got a little ahead of her. That he knew where her arm was next going. Some trickle of pleasure was showing in his face. And something else was happening, something I'd never seen. He had his face lifted up to this burning sun. It was big and orange, that sun, and scorching-hot, but he was staring smack into it. He wasn't blinking or squinting. His eyes were wide open.

Madness or miracle, I couldn't tell which.

He strode over to a parcel of good grass.

"I believe you mean it," he said. "How much could you use?"

He placed the bolt of white cloth down on the grass and pulled out shiny scissors from his back pocket.

"I bet he's blind," I whispered to my wife. "I bet he's got false eyes."

My wife shushed me. She wasn't listening. She had her excitement hat on; her *unusual circumstances* look. He was offering free cloth for love, ordinary love, and she figured she'd go along with the gag.

How much?

"Oh," she said, "maybe eight yards. Maybe ten. It depends on how many windows I end up doing, plus what hang I want, plus the pleating I'm after."

"You mean to make these curtains yourself?" he asked. He was already down on his knees, smoothing the bolt. Getting set to roll it out.

"Why, sure," she said. "I don't know who else would do it for me. I don't know who else I would ask."

He nodded soberly, not thinking about it. "That's so," he said casually. "Mend your own fences first." He was perspiring in the sun, and dishevelled, as though he'd been on the road a long time. His shoes had big holes in them and you could see the blistered soles of his feet, but he had an air of exhilaration now. His hair fell down over his eyes and he shoved the dark locks back. I got the impression that some days he went a long time between customers; that he didn't find cause to give away his cloth every day.

He got a fair bit unrolled. It certainly did look like prime goods, once you saw it spread out on the grass in that long expanse.

"It's so pretty!" My wife said. "Heaven help me, but I think it is *prettier* than grass!"

"It's pretty, all right," he said. "It's a wing-dinger. Just tell me when to stop," he said. "Just shout yoo-hoo."

"Hold up a minute," she said. "I don't want to get greedy. I don't want you rolling off more than we can afford."

"You can afford it," he said.

He kept unrolling. He was up past the well house by now, whipping it off fast, though the bolt didn't appear to be getting any smaller. My wife had both hands up over her mouth. Half of her wanted to run into the house and get her purse so she could pay; the other half wanted to stay and watch this man unfurl his beautiful cloth. She whipped around to me, all agitated.

"I believe he means it," she said. "He means us to have this cloth. What do I do?"

I shook my head. This was her territory. It was the kind of adventure constant to her nature and necessary to her well-being.

"Honey," I said, "you deal with it."

The sun was bright over everything. It was whipping-hot. There wasn't much wind but I could hear the clothes flapping on the line. A woodpecker had himself a pole somewhere and I could hear him pecking. The sky was wavy blue. The trees seemed to be swaying.

He was up by the front porch now, still unrolling. It surprised us both that he could move so fast.

"Yoo-hoo," my wife said. It was no more than a peep, the sound you might make if a butterfly lands on your hand.

"Wait," he said. "One thing. One question I meant to ask. All this talk of love, your *it*, your *those* and *them*, it slipped my mind."

"Let's hear it," my wife said. "Ask away." It seemed to me that she spoke out of a trance. That she was as dazzled as I was.

"You two got no children," he said. "Why is that? You're out here on this nice farm, and no children to your name. Why is that?"

We hadn't expected this query from him. It did something to the light in the yard and how we saw it. It was as if some giant dark bird had fluttered between us and the sun. Without knowing it, we sidled closer to each other. We fumbled for the other's hand. We stared off every which way. No one on our road had asked that question in a long, long time; they hadn't asked it in some years.

"We're not able," we said. Both of us spoke at the same time. It seemed to me that it was my wife's voice which carried; mine was some place down in my chest, and dropping, as if it meant to crawl on the ground.

"We're not able," we said. That time it came out pure, without grief to bind it. It came out the way we long ago learned how to say it.

"Oh," he said. "I see." He mumbled something else. He kicked the ground and took a little walk back and forth. He seemed angry, though not at us. "Wouldn't you know it?" he said. "Wouldn't you know it?"

He swore a time or two. He kicked the ground. He surely didn't like it.

"We're over that now," my wife said. "We're past that caring."

"I bet you are," he said. "You're past that little misfortune."

He took to unrolling his bolt again, working with his back to the sun. Down on his knees, scrambling, smoothing the material. Sweating and huffing. He was past the front porch now, and still going, getting on toward that edge where the high weeds grew.

"About here, do you think?" he asked.

He'd rolled off about fifty yards.

My wife and I slowly shook our heads, not knowing what to think.

"Say the word," he told us. "I can give you more if more is what you want."

"I'd say you were giving us too much," my wife said. "I'd say we don't need nearly that much."

"Never mind that," he said. "I'm feeling generous today."

He nudged the cloth with his fingers and rolled off a few yards more. He would have gone on unwinding his cloth had the weeds not stopped him. He stood and looked back over the great length he had unwound.

"Looks like a long white road, don't it?" he said. "You could walk that road and your feet never get dirty."

My wife clenched my hand; it was what we'd both been thinking.

SnipSnipSnip. He began snipping. His scissors raced over the material. *SnipSnipSnip*. The cloth was sheared clear and clean of his bolt, yet it seemed to me the size of that bolt hadn't lessened any. My wife saw it too.

"He's got cloth for all eternity," she said. "He could unroll that cloth till doomsday."

The man laughed. We were whispering this, but way up by the weeds he heard us. "There's doom and there's doom," he said. "*Which* doomsday?"

I had the notion he'd gone through more than one. That he knew the picture from both sides.

"It *is* smart as grass," he said. "Smarter. It never needs watering." He chuckled at that, spinning both arms. Dancing a little. "You could make *nighties* out of this," he said. "New bedsheets. Transform your whole bedroom."

My wife made a face. She wasn't too pleased, talking *nighties* with another man.

Innocence without heartbreak, I thought. That's what we're coming to.

He nicely rolled up the cloth he'd sheared off and presented it to my wife. "I hope you like it," he said. "No complaints yet. Maybe you can make yourself a nice dress as well. Maybe two or three. Make him some shirts. I think you'll find there's plenty here."

"Goodness, it's light," she said.

"Not if you've been carrying it long as I have," he said. He pulled a blue bandanna from his pocket and wiped his face and neck. He ran his hand through his hair and slicked it back. He looked up at the sky. His dark eyes seemed to have cleared up some. They looked less broody now. "Gets hot," he said, "working in this sun. But a nice day. I'm glad I found you folks home."

"Oh, we're most always home," my wife said.

I had to laugh at that. My wife almost never *is* home. She's forever gallivanting over the countryside, checking up on this person and that, taking them her soups and jams and breads.

"We're homebodies, us two."

She kept fingering the cloth and sighing over it. She held it up against her cheek and with her eyes closed rested herself on it. The man hoisted his own bolt back on his shoulder; he seemed ready to be going. I looked at my wife's closed lids, at the soft look she had.

I got trembly, fearful of what might happen if that cloth didn't work out.

"Now look," I said to him, "what's wrong with this cloth? Is it going to rot inside a week? Tomorrow is some *other* stranger going to knock on our door saying we owe him a hundred or five hundred dollars for this cloth? Mister, I don't understand you," I said.

He hadn't bothered with me before; now he looked me dead in the eye. "I can't help being a stranger," he said. "If you never set eyes on me before, I guess that's what I would have to be. Don't you like strangers? Don't you trust them?"

My wife jumped in. Her face was fiery, like she thought I had wounded him. "We like strangers just fine," she said. "We've helped out many a one. No, I can't say our door has ever been closed to whoever it is comes by. Strangers can sit in our kitchen just the same as our friends."

He smiled at her but kept his stern look for me. "As to your questions," he said, "You're worried about the golden goose, I can see that. Fair enough. No, your cloth will not rot. It will not shred, fade, or tear. Nor will it ever need cleaning, either. This cloth requires no upkeep whatsoever. Though a sound heart helps. A sweet disposition, too. Innocence without heartbreak, as I told you. And your wife, if it's her making the curtains or making herself a dress, she will find it to be an amazingly easy cloth to work with. It will practically do the job itself. No, I don't believe you will ever find you have any reason to complain of the quality of that cloth."

My wife had it up to her face again. She had her face sunk in it.

"Goodness," she said, "it's *soft*! It smells so fresh. It's like someone singing a song to me."

The man laughed. "It is soft," he said. "But it can't sing a note, or has never been known to."

It was my wife singing. She had this little hum under the breath.

"This is the most wonderful cloth in the world," she said.

He nodded. "I can't argue with you on that score," he said. Then he turned again to me. "I believe your wife is satisfied," he said. "But if you have any doubts, if you're worried someone is going to knock on your door tomorrow asking you for a hundred or five hundred dollars, I suppose I could write you up a guarantee. I could give you a PAID IN FULL."

He was making me feel ashamed of myself. They both were. "No, no," I said, "if she's satisfied then I am. And I can see she's tickled pink. No, I beg your pardon. I meant no offence."

"No offence taken," he said.

But his eyes clouded a token. He gazed off at our road and up along the stand of trees and his eyes kept roaming until they snagged the sun. He kept his eyes there, unblinking, open, staring at the sun. I could see the red orbs reflected in his eyes.

"There is one thing," he said.

I caught my breath and felt my wife catch hers. The hitch? A hitch, after all? Coming so late?

He waited.

He shuffled his feet. He brought out his bandanna and wiped his face again. He stared at the ground.

"Should you ever stop loving," he said, "you shall lose this cloth and all else. You shall wake up one morning and it and all else will no longer be where you left it. It will be gone and you will not know where you are. You will not know what to do with yourself. You will wish you'd never been born."

My wife's eyes went saucer-size.

He had us in some kind of spell.

Hocus-pocus, I thought. He is telling us some kind of hocus-pocus. Yet I felt my skin shudder; I felt the goose bumps rise.

"That's it?" my wife said. "That's the only catch?"

He shrugged. "That's it," he said. "Not much, is it? Not a whisper of menace for a pair such as yourselves."

My wife's eyes were gauzed over; there was wetness in them.

"Hold on," she said. "Don't you be leaving yet. Hold this, honey."

She put the cloth in my arms. Then he hastened over to the well, pitched the bucket down, and drew it up running over with fresh water.

"Here," she said, coming back with a good dipperful. "Here's a nice drink of cool water. You need it on a day like this."

The man drank. He held the dipper in both hands, with the tips of his fingers, and drained the dipper dry, then wiped his chin with the back of a hand.

"I did indeed," he said. "That's very tasty water. I thank you."

"That's good water," she said. "That well has been here for a hundred years. You could stay on for supper," she said. "It's getting on toward that time and I have a fine stew on the stove, with plenty to spare."

"That's kind of you," he said back, "and I'm grateful. But I'd best pass on up your road while there's daylight left, and see who else might have need of this cloth."

My wife is not normally a demonstrative woman, not in public. Certainly not with strangers. You could have knocked me over with a feather when she up and kissed him full on the mouth, with a nice hug to boot.

"There's payment," she said, "if our money's no good."

He blushed, trying to hide his pleasure. It seemed to me she had him wrapped around her little finger . . . or the other way around.

"You kiss like a woman," he said. "Like one who knows what kissing is for and can't hardly stop herself."

It was my wife's turn to blush.

I took hold of her hand and held her down to grass, because it seemed to me another kiss or two and she'd fly right away with him.

He walked across the yard and up by the well house, leaving by the same route he had come. Heading for the road. At the turn, he spun around and waved.

"You could try the Hopkins place!" my wife called. "There's a fat woman down that road got a sea of troubles. She could surely use some of that cloth."

He smiled and again waved. Then we saw his head and his bolt of white cloth bobbing along the weeds as he took the dips and rises in the road. Then he went on out of sight.

"There's that man with some horses down that road!" my wife called. "You be careful of him!"

It seemed we heard some sound come back, but whether it was his we couldn't say.

My wife and I stood a long time in the yard, me holding the dipper and watching her while she held her own bolt of cloth in her arms, staring off to where he'd last been.

Then she sighed dreamily and went inside. I went on down to the barn and looked after the animals. Getting my feeding done. I talked a spell to them. Talking to animals is soothing to me, and they like it too. They pretend to stare at the walls or the floor as they're munching their feed down, but I know they listen to me. We had us an *unusual circumstances* chat. "That man with the cloth," I said. "Maybe you can tell me what you make of him."

Thirty minutes later I heard my wife excitedly calling me. She was standing out on the back doorstep, with this incredulous look.

"I've finished," she said. "I've finished the windows. *Nine* windows. It beats me how."

I started up to the house. Her voice was all shaky. Her face flushed, flinging her arms about. Then she got this new look on.

"Wait!" she said. "Stay there! Give me ten minutes!"

And she flung herself back inside, banging the door. I laughed. It always gave me a kick how she ordered me around.

I got the milk pail down under the cow. Before I'd touched and drained all four teats she was calling again.

"*Come look, come look, oh come look!*"

She was standing in the open doorway, with the kitchen to her back. Behind her, through the windows, I could see the streak of a red sunset and how it lit up the swing of trees. But I wasn't looking there. I was looking at her. Looking and swallowing hard and trying to remember how a body produced human speech. I had never thought of white as a colour she could wear. White, it pales her some. It leaves her undefined and washes out what parts I like best. But she looked beautiful now. In her new dress she struck me down to my bootstraps. She made my chest break.

"Do you like it?" she said.

I went running up to her. I was up against her, hugging her and lifting her before she'd even had a chance to get set. I'd never held on so tightly or been so tightly held back.

Truth is, it was the strangest thing. Like we were both so innocent we hadn't yet shot up out of new ground.

"Come see the curtains," she whispered. "Come see the new sheets. Come see what else I've made. You'll see it all. You'll see how our home has been transformed."

I crept inside. There was something holy about it. About it and about us and about those rooms and the whole wide world. Something radiant. Like you had to put your foot down easy and hold it down or you'd float on up.

"That's it," she said. "That's how I feel too."

That night in bed, trying to figure it out, we wondered how Ella Mae down the road had done. How the people all along our road had made out.

"No worry," my wife said. "He'll have found a bonanza around here. There's heaps of decent people in this neck of the woods."

"Wonder where he is now?" we said.

"Wonder where he goes next?"

"Where he gets that cloth?"

"Who he *is*?"

We couldn't get to sleep, wondering about that.

1984

Woody Allen

b. 1935

"I don't want to achieve immortality through my work. I want to achieve it through not dying." The statement is pure Woody Allen in its brilliantly jangled humour, its self-aware whine, and its obsession with mortality. It's what Hamlet might have said if he had been born Jewish and in Brooklyn. Our uncertain, anxiety-ridden, and sometimes scandalous prince was born Allen Stewart Konigsberg, who at age three saw *Snow White and the Seven Dwarfs* and recalls "running" to touch the screen. In 1952 he changed his name and in 1953 enrolled at New York University where he failed the course in motion picture production. According to a later nightclub routine, at NYU he took Death 101 and expected a concerted assault by his household appliances when he returned from class. He survived sufficiently to begin a highly successful part of his career writing for NBC radio, then graduated to the stage as a stand-up comedian. He initiated a long-term attachment to psychoanalysis in 1959, and his extraordinary film work started in 1964 with the screenplay for *What's New, Pussycat?*, followed by a range of creations that have become as entangled with the peculiarities of our "age of narcissism" as those of Allen's beloved Ingmar Bergman. The gloriously funny *Bananas* appeared in 1971, the same year Allen began turning up at Michael's Pub in Manhattan to play jazz clarinet. The film he is still most consistently identified with is *Annie Hall* (1977), which won three Academy Awards, but its comic inventiveness is only one dimension of his genius; a much darker element shapes *Manhattan Murder Mystery* (1993) and, even more so, the thoroughly unnerving *Crimes and Misdemeanors* (1989). He has written successfully for the theatre, and his collections of consciousness-altering stories, *Getting Even* (1971), *Without Feathers* (1975), and *Side Effects* (1980) have virtually reinvented the comic narrative.

The Kugelmass Episode

Kugelmass, a professor of humanities at City College, was unhappily married for the second time. Daphne Kugelmass was an oaf. He also had two dull sons by his first wife, Flo, and was up to his neck in alimony and child support.

"Did I know it would turn out so badly?" Kugelmass whined to his analyst one day. "Daphne had promise. Who suspected she'd let herself go and swell up like a beach ball? Plus she had a few bucks, which is not in itself a healthy reason to marry a person, but it doesn't hurt, with the kind of operating nut I have. You see my point?"

Kugelmass was bald and as hairy as a bear, but he had soul.

"I need to meet a new woman," he went on. "I need to have an affair. I may not look the part, but I'm a man who needs romance. I need softness, I need flirtation. I'm not getting younger, so before it's too late I want to make love in Venice, trade quips at '21,' and exchange coy glances over red wine and candlelight. You see what I'm saying."

Dr Mandel shifted in his chair and said, "An affair will solve nothing. You're so unrealistic. Your problems run much deeper."

"And also this affair must be discreet," Kugelmass continued. "I can't afford a second divorce. Daphne would really sock it to me."

"Mr Kugelmass—"

"But it can't be anyone at City College, because Daphne also works there. Not that anyone on the faculty at CCNY is any great shakes, but some of those coeds . . ."

"Mr Kugelmass—"

"Help me. I had a dream last night. I was skipping through a meadow holding a picnic basket and the basket was marked 'Options.' And then I saw there was a hole in the basket."

"Mr Kugelmass, the worst thing you could do is act out. You must simply express your feelings here, and together we'll analyze them. You have been in treatment long enough to know there is no overnight cure. After all, I'm a analyst, not a magician."

"Then perhaps what I need is a magician," Kugelmass said, rising from his chair. And with that he terminated his therapy.

A couple of weeks later, while Kugelmass and Daphne were moping around in their apartment one night like two pieces of old furniture, the phone rang.

"I'll get it," Kugelmass said. "Hello."

"Kugelmass?" a voice said. "Kugelmass, this is Persky."

"Who?"

"Persky. Or should I say The Great Persky?"

"Pardon me?"

"I hear you're looking all over town for a magician to bring a little exotica into your life? Yes or no?"

"Sh-h-h," Kugelmass whispered. "Don't hang up. Where are you calling from, Persky?"

Early the following afternoon, Kugelmass climbed three flights of stairs in a broken-down apartment house in the Bushwick section of Brooklyn. Peering through the darkness of the hall, he found the door he was looking for and pressed the bell. I'm going to regret this, he thought to himself.

Seconds later, he was greeted by a short, thin, waxy-looking man.

"*You're* Persky the Great?" Kugelmass said.

"The Great Persky. You want a tea?"

"No, I want romance. I want music. I want love and beauty."

"But not tea, eh? Amazing. OK, sit down."

Persky went to the back room, and Kugelmass heard the sounds of boxes and furniture being moved around. Persky reappeared, pushing before him a large object on squeaky roller-skate wheels. He removed some old silk handkerchiefs that were lying on its top and blew away a bit of dust. It was a cheap-looking Chinese cabinet, badly lacquered.

"Persky," Kugelmass said, "what's your scam?"

"Pay attention," Persky said. "This is some beautiful effect. I developed it for a Knights of Pythias date last year, but the booking fell through. Get into the cabinet."

"Why, so you can stick it full of swords or something?"

"You see any swords?"

Kugelmass made a face and, grunting, climbed into the cabinet. He couldn't help noticing a couple of ugly rhinestones glued onto the raw plywood just in front of his face. "If this is a joke," he said.

"Some joke. Now, here's the point. If I throw any novel into this cabinet with you, shut the doors, and tap it three times, you will find yourself projected into that book."

Kugelmass made a grimace of disbelief.

"It's the emess," Persky said. "My hand to God. Not just a novel, either. A short story, a play, a poem. You can meet any of the women created by the world's best writers. Whoever you dreamed of. You could carry on all you like with a real winner. Then when you've had enough you give a yell, and I'll see you're back here in a split second."

"Persky, are you some kind of outpatient?"

"I'm telling you it's on the level," Persky said.

Kugelmass remained skeptical. "What are you telling me—that this cheesy homemade box can take me on a ride like you're describing?"

"For a double sawbuck."

Kugelmass reached for his wallet. "I'll believe this when I see it," he said.

Persky tucked the bills in his pants pocket and turned toward his bookcase. "So who do you want to meet? Sister Carrie? Hester Prynne? Ophelia? Maybe someone by Saul Bellow? Hey, what about Temple Drake? Although for a man your age she'd be a workout."

"French. I want to have an affair with a French lover."

"Nana?"

"I don't want to have to pay for it."

"What about Natasha in *War and Peace*?"

"I said French. I know! What about Emma Bovary? That sounds to me perfect."

"You got it, Kugelmass. Give me a holler when you've had enough." Persky tossed in a paperback copy of Flaubert's novel.

"You sure this is safe?" Kugelmass asked as Persky began shutting the cabinet doors.

"Safe. Is anything safe in this crazy world?" Persky rapped three times on the cabinet and then flung open the doors.

Kugelmass was gone. At the same moment, he appeared in the bedroom of Charles and Emma Bovary's house at Yonville. Before him was a beautiful woman, standing alone with her back turned to him as she folded some linen. I can't believe this, thought Kugelmass, staring at the doctor's ravishing wife. This is uncanny. I'm here. It's her.

Emma turned in surprise. "Goodness, you startled me," she said. "Who are you?" She spoke in the same fine English translation as the paperback.

It's simply devastating, he thought. Then, realizing that it was he whom she had addressed, he said, "Excuse me. I'm Sidney Kugelmass. I'm from City College. A professor of humanities. CCNY? Uptown. I—oh, boy!"

Emma Bovary smiled flirtatiously and said, "Would you like a drink? A glass of wine, perhaps?"

She is beautiful, Kugelmass thought. What a contrast with the troglodyte who shared his bed! He felt a sudden impulse to take this vision into his arms and tell her she was the kind of woman he had dreamed of all his life.

"Yes, some wine," he said hoarsely. "White. No, red. No, white. Make it white."

"Charles is out for the day," Emma said, her voice full of playful implication.

After the wine, they went for a stroll in the lovely French countryside. "I've always dreamed that some mysterious stranger would appear and rescue me from the monotony of this crass rural existence," Emma said, clasping his hand. They passed a small church. "I love what you have on," she murmured. "I've never seen anything like it around here. It's so . . . so modern."

"It's called a leisure suit," he said romantically. "It was marked down." Suddenly he kissed her. For the next hour they reclined under a tree and whispered together and told each other deeply meaningful things with their eyes. Then Kugelmass sat up. He had just remembered he had to meet Daphne at Bloomingdale's. "I must go," he told her. "But don't worry, I'll be back."

"I hope so," Emma said.

He embraced her passionately, and the two walked back to the house. He held Emma's face cupped in his palms, kissed her again, and yelled, "OK, Persky! I got to be at Bloomingdale's by three-thirty."

There was an audible pop, and Kugelmass was back in Brooklyn.

"So? Did I lie?" Persky asked triumphantly.

"Look, Persky, I'm right now late to meet the ball and chain at Lexington Avenue, but when can I go again? Tomorrow?"

"My pleasure. Just bring a twenty. And don't mention this to anybody."

"Yeah. I'm going to call Rupert Murdoch."

Kugelmass hailed a cab and sped off to the city. His heart danced on point. I am in love, he thought, I am the possessor of a wonderful secret. What he didn't realize was that at this very moment students in various classrooms across the country were saying to their teachers, "Who is this character on page 100? A bald Jew is kissing Madame Bovary?" A teacher in Sioux Falls, South Dakota, sighed and thought, Jesus, these kids, with their pot and acid. What goes through their minds!

Daphne Kugelmass was in the bathroom-accessories department at Bloomingdale's when Kugelmass arrived breathlessly. "Where've you been?" she snapped. "It's four-thirty."

"I got held up in traffic," Kugelmass said.

Kugelmass visited Persky the next day, and in a few minutes was again passed magically to Yonville. Emma couldn't hide her excitement at seeing him. The two spent hours together, laughing and talking about their different backgrounds. Before Kugelmass left, they made love. "My God, I'm doing it with Madame Bovary!" Kugelmass whispered to himself. "Me, who failed freshman English."

As the months passed, Kugelmass saw Persky many times and developed a close and passionate relationship with Emma Bovary. "Make sure and always get me into the book before page 120," Kugelmass said to the magician one day. "I always have to meet her before she hooks up with this Rodolphe character."

"Why?" Persky asked. "You can't beat his time?"

"Beat his time. He's landed gentry. Those guys have nothing better to do than flirt and ride horses. To me, he's one of those faces you see in the pages of *Women's Wear Daily*. With the Helmut Berger hairdo. But to her he's hot stuff."

"And her husband suspects nothing?"

"He's out of his depth. He's a lacklustre little paramedic who's thrown in his lot with a jitterbug. He's ready to go to sleep by ten, and she's putting on her dancing shoes. Oh, well . . . See you later."

And once again Kugelmass entered the cabinet and passed instantly to the Bovary estate at Yonville. "How you doing, cupcake?" he said to Emma.

"Oh, Kugelmass," Emma sighed. "What I have to put up with. Last night at dinner, Mr Personality dropped off to sleep in the middle of the dessert course. I'm pouring my heart out about Maxim's and the ballet, and out of the blue I hear snoring."

"It's OK, darling. I'm here now," Kugelmass said, embracing her. I've earned this, he thought, smelling Emma's French perfume and burying his nose in her hair. I've suffered enough. I've paid enough analysts. I've searched till I'm weary. She's young and nubile, and I'm here a few pages after Leon and just before Rodolphe. By showing up during the correct chapters, I've got the situation knocked.

Emma, to be sure, was just as happy as Kugelmass. She had been starved for excitement, and his tales of Broadway night life, of fast cars and Hollywood and TV stars, enthralled the young French beauty.

"Tell me again about O.J. Simpson," she implored that evening, as she and Kugelmass strolled past Abbé Bournisien's church.

"What can I say? The man is great. He sets all kinds of rushing records. Such moves. They can't touch him."

"And the Academy Awards?" Emma said wistfully. "I'd give anything to win one."

"First you've got to be nominated."

"I know. You explained it. But I'm convinced I can act. Of course, I'd want to take a class or two. With Strasberg maybe. Then, if I had the right agent—"

"We'll see, we'll see. I'll speak to Persky."

That night, safely returned to Persky's flat, Kugelmass brought up the idea of having Emma visit him in the big city.

"Let me think about it," Persky said. "Maybe I could work it. Stranger things have happened." Of course, neither of them could think of one.

"Where the hell do you go all the time?" Daphne Kugelmass barked at her husband as he returned home late that evening. "You got a chippie stashed somewhere?"

"Yeah, sure, I'm just the type," Kugelmass said wearily. "I was with Leonard Popkin. We were discussing Socialist agriculture in Poland. You know Popkin. He's a freak on the subject."

"Well, you've been very odd lately," Daphne said. "Distant. Just don't forget about my father's birthday. On Saturday?"

"Oh, sure, sure," Kugelmass said, heading for the bathroom.

"My whole family will be there. We can see the twins. And Cousin Hamish. You should be more polite to Cousin Hamish—he likes you."

"Right, the twins," Kugelmass said, closing the bathroom door and shutting out the sound of his wife's voice. He leaned against it and took a deep breath in. In a few hours, he told himself, he would be back in Yonville again, back with his beloved. And this time, if all went well, he would bring Emma back with him.

At three-fifteen the following afternoon, Persky worked his wizardry again. Kugelmass appeared before Emma, smiling and eager. The two spent a few hours at Yonville with Binet and then remounted the Bovary carriage. Following Persky's instructions, they held each other tightly, closed their eyes, and counted to ten. When they opened them, the carriage was just drawing up at the side door of the Plaza Hotel, where Kugelmass had optimistically reserved a suite earlier in the day.

"I love it! It's everything I dreamed it would be," Emma said as she swirled joyously around the bedroom, surveying the city from their window. "There's F.A.O. Schwarz. And there's Central Park, and the Sherry is which one? Oh, there—I see. It's too divine."

On the bed there were boxes from Halston and Saint Laurent. Emma unwrapped a package and held a pair of black velvet pants against her perfect body.

"The slacks suit is by Ralph Lauren," Kugelmass said. "You'll look like a million bucks in it. Come on, sugar, give us a kiss."

"I've never been so happy!" Emma squealed as she stood before the mirror. "Let's go out on the town. I want to see *Chorus Line* and the Guggenheim and this Jack Nicholson character you always talk about. Are any of his flicks showing?"

"I cannot get my mind around this," a Stanford professor said. "First a strange character named Kugelmass, and now she's gone from the book. Well, I guess the mark of a classic is that you can reread it a thousand times and always find something new."

The lovers passed a blissful weekend. Kugelmass had told Daphne he would be away at a symposium in Boston and would return Monday. Savouring each moment, he and Emma went to the movies, had dinner in Chinatown, passed two hours at a discothèque, and went to bed with a TV movie. They slept till noon on Sunday, visited SoHo, and ogled celebrities at Elaine's. They had caviar and champagne in their suite on Sunday night and talked until dawn. That morning, in the cab taking them to Persky's apartment, Kugelmass thought, It was hectic, but worth it. I can't bring her here too often, but now and then it will be a charming contrast with Yonville.

At Persky's, Emma climbed into the cabinet, arranged her new boxes of clothes neatly around her, and kissed Kugelmass fondly. "My place next time," she said with a wink. Persky rapped three times on the cabinet. Nothing happened.

"Hmmm," Persky said, scratching his head. He rapped again, but still no magic. "Something must be wrong," he mumbled.

"Persky, you're joking!" Kugelmass cried. "How can it not work?"

"Relax, relax. Are you still in the box, Emma?"

"Yes."

Persky rapped again—harder this time.

"I'm still here, Persky."

"I know, darling. Sit tight."

"Persky, we *have* to get her back," Kugelmass whispered. "I'm a married man, and I have a class in three hours. I'm not prepared for anything more than a cautious affair at this point."

"I can't understand it," Persky muttered. "It's such a reliable little trick."

But he could do nothing. "It's going to take a little while," he said to Kugelmass. "I'm going to have to strip it down. I'll call you later."

Kugelmass bundled Emma into a cab and took her back to the Plaza. He barely made it to his class on time. He was on the phone all day, to Persky and to his mistress. The magician told him it might be several days before he got to the bottom of the trouble.

"How was the symposium?" Daphne asked him that night.

"Fine, fine," he said, lighting the filter end of a cigarette.

"What's wrong? You're as tense as a cat."

"Me? Ha, that's a laugh. I'm as calm as a summer night. I'm just going to take a walk." He eased out the door, hailed a cab, and flew to the Plaza.

"This is no good," Emma said. "Charles will miss me."

"Bear with me, sugar," Kugelmass said. He was pale and sweaty. He kissed her again, raced to the elevators, yelled at Persky over a pay phone in the Plaza lobby, and just made it home before midnight.

"According to Popkin, barley prices in Kraków have not been this stable since 1971," he said to Daphne, and smiled wanly as he climbed into bed.

The whole week went like that.

On Friday night, Kugelmass told Daphne there was another symposium he had to catch, this one in Syracuse. He hurried back to the Plaza, but the second weekend there was nothing like the first. "Get me back into the novel or marry me," Emma told Kugelmass. "Meanwhile, I want to get a job or go to class, because watching TV all day is the pits."

"Fine. We can use the money," Kugelmass said. "You consume twice your weight in room service."

"I met an Off Broadway producer in Central Park yesterday, and he said I might be right for a project he's doing," Emma said.

"Who is this clown?" Kugelmass asked.

"He's not a clown. He's sensitive and kind and cute. His name's Jeff Something-or-Other, and he's up for a Tony."

Later that afternoon, Kugelmass showed up at Persky's drunk.

"Relax," Persky told him. "You'll get a coronary."

"Relax. The man says relax. I've got a fictional character stashed in a hotel room, and I think my wife is having me tailed by a private shamus."

"OK, OK. We know there's a problem." Persky crawled under the cabinet and started banging on something with a large wrench.

"I'm like a wild animal," Kugelmass went on. "I'm sneaking around town, and Emma and I have had it up to here with each other. Not to mention a hotel tab that reads like the defence budget."

"So what should I do? This is the world of magic," Persky said. "It's all nuance."

"Nuance, my foot. I'm pouring Dom Pérignon and black eggs into this little mouse, plus her wardrobe, plus she's enrolled at the Neighbourhood Playhouse and suddenly needs professional photos. Also, Persky, Professor Fivish Kopkind, who teaches Comp Lit and who has always been jealous of me, has identified me as the sporadically appearing character in the Flaubert book. He's threatened to go to Daphne. I see ruin and alimony; jail. For adultery with Madame Bovary, my wife will reduce me to beggary."

"What do you want me to say? I'm working on it night and day. As far as your personal anxiety goes, that I can't help you with. I'm a magician, not an analyst."

By Sunday afternoon, Emma had locked herself in the bathroom and refused to respond to Kugelmass's entreaties. Kugelmass stared out the window at the Wollman Rink and contemplated suicide. Too bad this is a low floor, he thought, or I'd do it right now. Maybe if I ran away to Europe and started my life over . . . Maybe I could sell the *International Herald Tribune*, like those young girls used to.

The phone rang. Kugelmass lifted it to his ear mechanically.

"Bring her over," Persky said. "I think I got the bugs out of it."

Kugelmass's heart leaped. "You're serious?" he said. "You got it licked?"

"It was something in the transmission. Go figure."

"Persky, you're a genius. We'll be there in a minute. Less than a minute."

Again the lovers hurried to the magician's apartment, and again Emma Bovary climbed into the cabinet with her boxes. This time there was no kiss. Persky shut the doors, took a deep breath, and tapped the box three times. There was the reassuring popping noise, and when Persky peered inside, the box was empty. Madame Bovary was back in her novel. Kugelmass heaved a great sigh of relief and pumped the magician's hand.

"It's over," he said. "I learned my lesson. I'll never cheat again, I swear it." He pumped Persky's hand again and made a mental note to send him a necktie.

Three weeks later, at the end of a beautiful spring afternoon, Persky answered his doorbell. It was Kugelmass, with a sheepish expression on his face.

"OK, Kugelmass," the magician said. "Where to this time?"

"It's just this once," Kugelmass said. "The weather is so lovely, and I'm not getting any younger. Listen, you've read *Portnoy's Complaint*? Remember The Monkey?"

"The price is now twenty-five dollars, because the cost of living is up, but I'll start you off with one freebie, due to all the trouble I caused you."

"You're good people," Kugelmass said, combing his few remaining hairs as he climbed into the cabinet again. "This'll work all right?"

"I hope. But I haven't tried it much since all that unpleasantness."

"Sex and romance," Kugelmass said from inside the box. "What we go through for a pretty face."

Persky tossed in a copy of *Portnoy's Complaint* and rapped three times on the box. This time, instead of a popping noise there was a dull explosion, followed by a series of crackling noises and a shower of sparks. Persky leaped back, was seized by a heart attack, and dropped dead. The cabinet burst into flames, and eventually the entire house burned down.

Kugelmass, unaware of this catastrophe, had his own problems. He had not been thrust into *Portnoy's Complaint*, or into any other novel, for that matter. He had been projected into an old textbook, *Remedial Spanish*, and was running for his life over a barren, rocky terrain as the word *tener* ("to have")—a large and hairy irregular verb—raced after him on its spindly legs.

1981

Alistair MacLeod

1936–2014

Until the publication of his long-awaited novel, *No Great Mischief* (1999), which won both the Trillium Book Award and the massive IMPAC Dublin Award in 2001, Alistair MacLeod was a writer's writer, his stature emerging from the fourteen stories in *The Lost Salt Gift of Blood* (1976) and, even more, from *As Birds Bring Forth the Sun and Other Stories* (1986). Michael Ondaatje chose to frame his superb collection of Canadian stories, *From Ink Lake* (1990), with pieces from the second volume as a tacit but unmistakable tribute, and other writers would regularly cite MacLeod's work as central to the cultural presence of the short story in Canada. The canonical quality of his work has also fostered some of that puncturing writers have a particular skill for. Aritha Van Herk regards MacLeod's narratives as "overfigured by time," embodiments of the "hauntings" of modernism. A more frequent reading is that his stories are a consummate melding of the realistic and the mythic. Stories of Atlantic Canada, MacLeod's fictions are often devoted, as Jane Urquhart observed in an interview, to the physicality of working men. MacLeod's profound awareness of this physicality began with his family in North Battleford, Saskatchewan, where he was born, and intensified with their reclaimed Maritime life in Cape Breton. But, having worked as a miner, MacLeod chose an academic life, earning a Ph.D. in English from Notre Dame and teaching for over thirty years at the University of Windsor. He retired in 2000. An unexpected revelation about the process of his creativity is that he writes the endings early on, and they become "the lighthouse" toward which the narrative is directed.

As Birds Bring Forth the Sun

Once there was a family with a Highland name who lived beside the sea. And the man had a dog of which he was very fond. She was large and grey, a sort of staghound from another time. And if she jumped up to lick his face, which she loved to do, her paws would jolt against his shoulders with such force that she would come close to knocking him down and he would be forced to take two or three backward steps before he could regain his balance. And he himself was not a small man, being slightly over six feet and perhaps one hundred and eighty pounds.

She had been left, when a pup, at the family's gate in a small handmade box and no one knew where she had come from or that she would eventually grow to such a size. Once, while still a small pup, she had been run over by the steel wheel of a horse-drawn cart which was hauling kelp from the shore to be used as fertilizer. It was in October and the rain had been falling for some weeks and the ground was soft. When the wheel of the cart passed over her, it sunk her body into the wet earth as well as crushing some of her ribs; and apparently the silhouette of her small crushed body was visible in the earth after the man lifted her to his chest while she yelped and screamed. He ran his fingers along her broken bones, ignoring the blood and urine which fell upon his shirt, trying to soothe her bulging eyes and her scrabbling front paws and her desperately licking tongue.

The more practical members of his family, who had seen run-over-dogs before, suggested that her neck be broken by his strong hands or that he grasp her by the hind legs and swing her head against a rock, thus putting an end to her misery. But he would not do it.

Instead, he fashioned a small box and lined it with woollen remnants from a sheep's fleece and one of his old frayed shirts. He placed her within the box and placed the box behind the stove and then warmed some milk in a small saucepan and sweetened it with sugar. And he held open her small and trembling jaws with his left hand while spooning in the sweetened milk with his right, ignoring the needle-like sharpness of her small teeth. She lay in the box most of the remaining fall and into the early winter, watching everything with her large brown eyes.

Although some members of the family complained about her presence and the odour from the box and the waste of time she involved, they gradually adjusted to her; and as the weeks passed by, it became evident that her ribs were knitting together in some form or other and that she was recovering with the resilience of the young. It also became evident that she would grow to a tremendous size, as she outgrew one box and then another and the grey hair began to feather from her huge front paws. In the spring she was outside almost all of the time and followed the man everywhere; and when she came inside during the following months, she had grown so large that she would no longer fit into her accustomed place behind the stove and was forced to lie beside it. She was never given a name but was referred to in Gaelic as *cù mòr glas*, the big grey dog.

By the time she came into her first heat, she had grown to a tremendous height, and although her signs and her odour attracted many panting and highly aroused suitors, none was big enough to mount her and the frenzy of their disappointment and the longing of her unfulfillment were more than the man could stand. He went, so the story goes, to a place where he knew there was a big dog. A dog not as big as she was, but still a big dog, and brought him home with him. And at the proper time he took the *cù mòr glas* and the big dog down to the sea where he knew there was a hollow in the rock which appeared only at low tide. He took some sacking to provide footing for the male dog and he placed the *cù mòr glas* in the hollow of the rock and knelt beside her and steadied her with his left arm under her throat and helped position the male dog above her and guided his blood-engorged penis. He was a man used to working with the breeding of animals, with the guiding of rams and bulls and stallions and often with the funky smell of animal semen heavy on his large and gentle hands.

The winter that followed was a cold one and ice formed on the sea and frequent squalls and blizzards obliterated the offshore islands and caused people to stay near their fires much of the time, mending clothes and nets and harness and waiting for the change of season. The *cù mòr glas* grew heavier and even more large until there was hardly room for her around the stove or even under the table. And then one morning, when it seemed that spring was about to break, she was gone.

The man and even the family, who had become more involved than they cared to admit, waited for her but she did not come. And as the frenzy of spring wore on, they busied themselves with readying their land and their fishing gear and all of the things that so desperately required their attention. And then they were into summer and fall and winter and another spring which saw the birth of the man and his wife's twelfth child. And then it was summer again.

That summer the man and two of his teenaged sons were pulling their herring nets about two miles offshore when the wind began to blow off the land and the water began to roughen. They became afraid that they could not make it safely back to shore, so they pulled in behind one of the offshore islands, knowing that they would be sheltered there and planning to outwait the storm. As the prow of their boat approached the gravelly shore, they heard a sound above them, and looking up they saw the *cù mòr glas* silhouetted on the brow of the hill which was the small island's highest point.

"*M'eudal cù mòr glas*," shouted the man in his happiness—*m'eudal* meaning something like dear or darling; and as he shouted, he jumped over the side of his boat into the waist-deep water, struggling for footing on the rolling gravel as he waded eagerly and awkwardly towards her and the shore. At the same time, the *cù mòr glas* came hurtling down towards him in a shower of small rocks dislodged by her feet; and just as he was emerging from the water, she met him as she used to, rearing up on her hind legs and placing her huge front paws on his shoulders while extending her eager tongue.

The weight and the speed of her momentum met him as he tried to hold his balance on the sloping angle and the water rolling gravel beneath his feet, and he staggered backwards and lost his footing and fell beneath her force. And in that instant again, as the story goes, there appeared over the brow of the hill six more huge grey dogs hurtling down towards the gravelled strand. They had never seen him before; and seeing him stretched prone beneath their mother, they misunderstood, like so many armies, the intention of their leader.

They fell upon him in a fury, slashing his face and tearing aside his lower jaw and ripping out his throat, crazed with blood-lust or duty or perhaps starvation. The *cù mòr glas* turned on them in her own savagery, slashing and snarling and, it seemed, crazed by their mistake; driving them bloodied and yelping before her, back over the brow of the hill where they vanished from sight but could still be heard screaming in the distance. It all took perhaps little more than a minute.

The man's two sons, who were still in the boat and had witnessed it all, ran sobbing through the salt water to where their mauled and mangled father lay; but there was little they could do other than hold his warm and bloodied hands for a few brief moments. Although his eyes "lived" for a small fraction of time, he could not speak to them because his face and throat had been torn away, and of course there was nothing they could do except to hold and be held tightly until that too slipped away and his eyes glazed over and they could not longer feel his hands holding theirs. The storm increased and they could not get home and so they were forced to spend the night huddled beside their father's body. They were afraid to try to carry the body to the rocking boat because he was so heavy and they were afraid that they might lose even what little of him remained and they were afraid also, huddled on the rocks, that the dogs might return. But they did not return at all and there was no sound from them, no sound at all, only the moaning of the wind and the washing of the water on the rocks.

In the morning they debated whether they should try to take his body with them or whether they should leave it and return in the company of older and wiser men. But they were afraid to leave it unattended and felt that the time needed to cover it with protective rocks would be better spent in trying to get across to their home shore. For a while they debated as to whether one should go in the boat and the other remain on the island, but each was afraid to be alone and so in the end they managed to drag and carry and almost float him towards the bobbing boat. They lay him facedown and covered him with what clothes there were and set off across the still-rolling sea. Those who waited on the shore missed the large presence of the man within the boat and some of them waded into the water and others rowed out in skiffs, attempting to hear the tearful messages called out across the rolling waves.

The *cù mòr glas* and her six young dogs were never seen again, or perhaps I should say they were never seen again in the same way. After some weeks, a group of men circled the island tentatively in their boats but they saw no sign. They went again and then again but found nothing. A year later, and grown much braver, they beached their boats and walked the island carefully, looking into the small sea caves and the hollows at the base of the wind-ripped trees, thinking perhaps that if they did not find the dogs, they might at least find their whitened bones; but again they discovered nothing.

The *cù mòr glas*, though, was supposed to be sighted here and there for a number of years. Seen on a hill in one region or silhouetted on a ridge in another or loping across the valleys or glens in the early morning or the shadowy evening. Always in the area of the half perceived. For a while she became rather like the Loch Ness Monster or the Sasquatch on a smaller scale. Seen but not recorded. Seen when there were no cameras. Seen but never taken.

The mystery of where she went became entangled with the mystery of whence she came. There was an increased speculation about the handmade box in which she had been found and much theorizing as to the individual or individuals who might have left it. People went to look for the box but could not find it. It was felt she might have been part of a *buidseachd* or evil spell cast on the man by some mysterious enemy. But no one could go much farther than that. All of his caring for her was recounted over and over again and nobody missed any of the ironies.

What seemed literally known was that she had crossed the winter ice to have her pups and had been unable to get back. No one could remember ever seeing her swim; and in the early months at least, she could not have taken her young pups with her.

The large and gentle man with the smell of animal semen often heavy on his hands was my great-great-great-grandfather, and it may be argued that he died because he was too good at breeding animals or that he cared too much about their fulfillment and well-being. He was no longer there for his own child of the spring who, in turn, became my great-great-grandfather, and he was perhaps too much there in the memory of his older sons who saw him fall beneath the ambiguous force of the *cù mòr glas*. The youngest boy in the boat was haunted and tormented by the awfulness of what he had seen. He would wake at night screaming that he had seen the *cù mòr glas a' bhàis*, the big grey dog of death, and his screams filled the house and the ears and minds of the listeners, bringing home again and again the consequences of their loss. One morning, after a night in which he saw the *cù mòr glas a' bhàis* so vividly that his sheets were drenched with sweat, he walked to the high cliff which faced the island and there he cut his throat with a fish knife and fell into the sea.

The other brother lived to be forty, but, again so the story goes, he found himself in a Glasgow pub one night, perhaps looking for answers, deep and sodden with the whisky which had become his anaesthetic. In the half darkness he saw a large, grey-haired man sitting by himself against the wall and mumbled something to him. Some say he saw the *cù mòr glas a' bhàis* or uttered the name. And perhaps the man heard the phrase through ears equally affected by drink and felt he was being called a dog or a son of a bitch or something of that nature. They rose to meet one another and struggled outside into the cobblestoned passageway behind the pub where, most improbably, there was supposed to be six other large, grey-haired men who beat him to death on the cobblestones, smashing his bloodied head into the stone again and again before vanishing and leaving him to die with his face turned to the sky. The *cù mòr glas a' bhàis* had come again, said his family, as they tried to piece the tale together.

This is how the *cù mòr glas a' bhàis* came into our lives, and it is obvious that all of this happened a long, long time ago. Yet with succeeding generations it seemed the spectre had somehow come to stay and that it had become *ours*—not in the manner of an unwanted skeleton in the closet from a family's ancient past but more in the manner of something close to a genetic possibility. In the deaths of each generation, the grey dog was seen by some—by women who were to die in childbirth; by soldiers who went forth to the many wars but did not return; by those who went forth to feuds or dangerous love affairs; by those who answered mysterious midnight messages; by those who swerved on the highway to avoid the real or imagined grey dog and ended in masses of crumpled steel. And by one professional athlete who, in addition to his ritualized athletic superstitions, carried another fear or belief as well. Many of the man's descendants moved like careful hemophiliacs, fearing that they carried unwanted possibilities deep within them. And others, while they laughed, were like members of families in which there is a recurrence over the generations of repeated cancer or the diabetes which comes to those beyond middle age. The feeling of those who may say little to others but who may say often and quietly to themselves, "It has not happened to me," while adding always the cautionary "*yet*."

I am thinking all of this now as the October rain falls on the city of Toronto and the pleasant, white-clad nurses pad confidently in and out of my father's room. He lies quietly amidst the whiteness, his head and shoulders elevated so that he is in the hospital position of being neither quite prone nor yet sitting. His hair is white upon his pillow and he breathes softly and sometimes unevenly, although it is difficult ever to be sure.

My five grey-haired brothers and I take turns beside his bedside, holding his heavy hands in ours and feeling their response, hoping ambiguously that he will speak to us, although we know that it may tire him. And trying to read his life and ours into his eyes when they are open. He has been with us for a long time, well into our middle age. Unlike those boys in that boat of so long ago, we did not see him taken from us in our youth. And unlike their youngest brother who, in turn, became our great-great-grandfather, we did not grow into a world in which there was no father's touch. We have been lucky to have this large and gentle man so deep into our lives.

No one in this hospital has mentioned the *cù mòr glas a' bhàis*. Yet as my mother said ten years ago, before slipping into her own death as quietly as a grownup child who leaves or enters her parents' house in the early hours, "It is hard to *not* know what you do know."

Even those who are most skeptical, like my oldest brother who had driven here from Montreal, betray themselves by their nervous actions. "I avoided the Greyhound bus stations in both Montreal and Toronto," he smiled upon his arrival, and then added, "Just in case."

He did not realize how ill our father was and has smiled little since then. I watch him turning the diamond ring upon his finger, knowing that he hopes he will not hear the Gaelic phrase he knows too well. Not having the luxury, as he once said, of some who live in Montreal and are able to pretend they do not understand the "other" language. You cannot *not* know what you do know.

Sitting here, taking turns holding the hands of the man who gave us life, we are afraid for him and for ourselves. We are afraid of what he may see and we are afraid to hear the phrase born of the vision. We are aware that it may become confused with what the doctors call "the will to live" and we are aware that some beliefs are what others would dismiss as "garbage." We are aware that there are men who believe the earth is flat and that the birds bring forth the sun.

Bound here in our peculiar mortality, we do not wish to see or see others see that which signifies life's demise. We do not want to hear the voice of our father, as did those other sons, calling down his own particular death upon him.

We would shut our eyes and plug our ears, even as we know such actions to be of no avail. Open still and fearful to the grey hair rising on our necks if and when we hear the scrabble of the paws and the scratching at the door.

1986

Don DeLillo

b. 1936

Prophetic, paranoid, ascetic, ethically ambiguous—these are the dominant words that punctuate notions of Don DeLillo, one of the foremost literary clinicians of contemporary pathologies. Perceptions of him in person, off the page, are images of an almost phantom, philosophical cleric not quite resigned to the world's woeful surprises. His gravitation to fissures in scepticism and faith has increasingly seemed downright eerie, even prescient. He says, "It frequently happens that I begin a novel with just a visual image of something, a vague sense of people in three dimensional space." Before 9/11 the towers of the World Trade Center recur with startling frequency—in *Players*, on the cover of *Underworld*, and in *Mao II*, seen as "standing windowless, two black latex slabs that consumed the available space"—but their presence seems to await their own novel, their own catastrophe. Talking about the fiery shattering of the towers as both literary image and monumental cultural fact, DeLillo says that in writing *Falling Man* (2007) "I wanted to be in the towers and in the planes . . . I've always felt that my subject was living in dangerous times." The dangers he has been drawn to include the Kennedy assassination, the power of crowds, political conspiracies, the fetishistic language devoted to objects, and of course, terrorism. "DeLillo," Martin Amis declares admiringly, "is the laureate of terror." Considering the weightiness of his "dangerous times," it is hardly surprising that DeLillo has published fifteen novels but only one collection of short stories, *The Angel Esmeralda: Nine Stories* (2011), arranged chronologically from 1979 to 2011, in which he proves himself a master of the political story, of stories about "the half-glimpsed lives of others" (Amis). "Baader-Meinhof" (2002) aligns personal terrorism with the political violence implicit in a group of fifteen pictures by Gerhard Richter that appeared at MOMA in 2000 and in a retrospective exhibition there in 2002. DeLillo's story was published in *The New Yorker* on 1 April 2002. His antennae are far more durable than the one on the World Trade Center. Cities within cities, rooms within rooms, and pictures within rooms—these are his prime locations. His early interlocking city was an Italian, working-class section of the Bronx. He grew up more interested in football and baseball than in Proust and Kafka, but went to Fordham, worked at an ad agency, went to a lot of movies, and discovered and continues to discover jazz. Asked about literary influences, DeLillo claims Norman Mailer "largely because [the sort of writer Mailer was] is the last thing I would want to be myself."

Baader-Meinhof

She knew there was someone else in the room. There was no outright noise, just an intimation behind her, a faint displacement of air. She'd been alone for a time, seated on a bench in the middle of the gallery with the paintings set around her, a cycle of fifteen canvases, and this is how it felt to her, that she was sitting as a person does in a mortuary chapel, keeping watch over the body of a relative or a friend.

This was sometimes called the viewing, she believed.

She was looking at Ulrike now, head and upper body, her neck rope-scorched, although she didn't know for certain what kind of implement had been used in the hanging.

She heard the other person walk toward the bench, a man's heavy shuffling stride, and she got up and went to stand before the picture of Ulrike, one of three related images, Ulrike dead in each, lying on the floor of her cell, head in profile. The canvases varied in size. The woman's reality, the head, the neck, the rope burn, the hair, the facial features, were painted, picture to picture, in nuances of obscurity and pall, a detail clearer here than there, the slurred mouth in one painting appearing nearly natural elsewhere, all of it unsystematic.

"Why do you think he did it this way?"

She did not turn to look at him.

"So shadowy. No color."

She said, "I don't know," and went to the next set of images, called *Man Shot Down*. This was Andreas Baader. She thought of him by his full name or surname. She thought of Meinhof, she saw Meinhof as first name only, Ulrike, and the same was the case with Gudrun.

"I'm trying to think what happened to them."

"They committed suicide. Or the state killed them."

He said, "The state." Then he said it again, deep-voiced, in a tone of melodramatic menace, trying out a line reading that might be more suitable.

She wanted to be annoyed but felt instead a vague chagrin. It wasn't like her to use this term—*the state*—in the ironclad context of supreme public power. This was not her vocabulary.

The two paintings of Baader dead in his cell were the same size but addressed the subject somewhat differently, and this is what she did now—she concentrated on the differences, arm, shirt, unknown object at the edge of the frame, the disparity or uncertainty.

"I don't know what happened," she said. "I'm only telling you what people believe. It was twenty-five years ago. I don't know what it was like then, in Germany, with bombings and kidnappings."

"They made an agreement, don't you think?"

"Some people believe they were murdered in their cells."

"A pact. They were terrorists, weren't they? When they're not killing other people, they're killing themselves," he said. She was looking at Andreas Baader, first one painting, then the other, then back again.

"I don't know. Maybe that's even worse in a way. It's so much sadder. There's so much sadness in these pictures."

"There's one that's smiling," he said.

This was Gudrun, in *Confrontation 2*.

"I don't know if that's a smile. It could be a smile."

"It's the clearest image in the room. Maybe the whole museum. She's smiling," he said.

She turned to look at Gudrun across the gallery and saw the man on the bench, half turned her way, wearing a suit with tie unknotted, going prematurely bald. She only glimpsed him. He was looking at her but she was looking past him to the figure of Gudrun in a prison smock, standing against a wall and smiling, most likely, yes, in the middle picture. Three paintings of Gudrun, maybe smiling, smiling and probably not smiling.

"You need special training to look at these pictures. I can't tell the people apart."

"Yes, you can. Just look. You have to look."

She heard a note of slight reprimand in her voice. She went to the far wall to look at the painting of one of the jail cells, with tall bookshelves covering nearly half the canvas and a dark shape, wraithlike, that may have been a coat on a hanger.

"You're a grad student. Or you teach art," he said. "I'm frankly here to pass the time. That's what I do between job interviews."

She didn't want to tell him that she'd been here three straight days. She moved to the adjacent wall, a little closer to his position on the bench. Then she told him.

"Major money," he said. "Unless you're a member."

"I'm not a member."

"Then you teach art."

"I don't teach art."

"You want me to shut up. Shut up, Bob. Only my name's not Bob."

In the painting of the coffins being carried through a large crowd, she didn't know they were coffins at first. It took her a long moment to see the crowd itself. There was the crowd, mostly an ashy blur with a few figures in the center-right foreground discernible as individuals standing with their backs to the viewer, and then there was a break near the top of the canvas, a pale strip of earth or roadway, and then another mass of people or trees, and it took some time to understand that the three whitish objects near the center of the picture were coffins being carried through the crowd or simply propped on biers.

Here were the bodies of Andreas Baader, Gudrun Ensslin and a man whose name she could not recall. He had been shot in his cell. Baader had also been shot. Gudrun had been hanged.

She knew that this had happened about a year and a half after Ulrike. Ulrike dead in May, she knew, of 1976.

Two men entered the gallery, followed by a woman with a cane. All three stood before the display of explanatory material, reading.

The painting of the coffins had something else that wasn't easy to find. She hadn't found it until the second day, yesterday, and it was striking once she'd found it, and inescapable now—an object at the top of the painting, just left of center, a tree perhaps, in the rough shape of a cross.

She went closer to the painting, hearing the woman with the cane move toward the opposite wall.

She knew that these paintings were based on photographs but she hadn't seen them and didn't know whether there was a bare tree, a dead tree beyond the cemetery, in one of the photos, that consisted of a spindly trunk with a single branch remaining, or two branches forming a transverse piece near the top of the trunk.

He was standing next to her now, the man she'd been talking to.

"Tell me what you see. Honestly, I want to know."

A group entered, led by a guide, and she turned for a moment, watching them collect at the first painting in the cycle, the portrait of Ulrike as a much younger woman, a girl, really, distant and wistful, her hand and face half floating in the somber dark around her.

"I realize now that the first day I was only barely looking. I thought I was looking but I was only getting a bare inkling of what's in these paintings. I'm only just starting to look."

They stood looking, together, at the coffins and trees and crowd. The tour guide began speaking to her group.

"And what do you feel when you look?" he said.

"I don't know. It's complicated."

"Because I don't feel anything."

"I think I feel helpless. These paintings make me feel how helpless a person can be."

"Is that why you're here three straight days? To feel helpless?" he said.

"I'm here because I love the paintings. More and more. At first I was confused, and still am, a little. But I know I love the paintings now."

It was a cross. She saw it as a cross and it made her feel, right or wrong, that there was an element of forgiveness in the picture, that the two men and the woman, terrorists, and Ulrike before them, terrorist, were not beyond forgiveness.

But she didn't point out the cross to the man standing next to her. That was not what she wanted, a discussion on the subject. She didn't think she was imagining a cross, seeing a cross in some free strokes of paint, but she didn't want to hear someone raise elementary doubts.

They went to a snack bar and sat on stools arranged along a narrow counter that measured the length of the front window. She watched the crowds on Seventh Avenue, half the world rushing by, and barely tasted what she ate.

"I missed the first-day pop," he said, "where the stock soars like mythically, four hundred percent in a couple of hours. I got there for the aftermarket, which turned out to be weak, then weaker."

When the stools were all occupied, people stood and ate. She wanted to go home and check her phone messages.

"I make appointments now. I shave, I smile. My life is living hell," he said, blandly, chewing as he spoke.

He took up space, a tall broad man with a looseness about him, something offhand and shambling. Someone reached past her to snag a napkin from the dispenser. She had no idea what she was doing here, talking to this man.

He said, "No color. No meaning."

"What they did had meaning. It was wrong but it wasn't blind and empty. I think the painter's searching for this. And how did it end the way it did? I think he's asking this. Everybody dead."

"How else could it end? Tell the truth," he said. "You teach art to handicapped children."

She didn't know whether this was interesting or cruel but saw herself in the window wearing a grudging smile.

"I don't teach art."

"This is fast food that I'm trying to eat slow. I don't have an appointment until three-thirty. Eat slow. And tell me what you teach."

"I don't teach."

She didn't tell him that she was also out of work. She'd grown tired of describing her job, administrative, with an educational publisher, so why make the effort, she thought, now that the job and the company no longer existed.

"Problem is, it's against my nature to eat slow. I have to remind myself. But even then I can't make the adjustment." But that wasn't the reason. She didn't tell him that she was out of work because it would give them a situation in common. She didn't want that, an inflection of mutual sympathy, a comradeship. Let the tone stay scattered.

She drank her apple juice and looked at the crowds moving past, at faces that seemed completely knowable for half a second or so, then were forgotten forever in far less time than that.

He said, "We should have gone to a real restaurant. It's hard to talk here. You're not comfortable."

"No, this is fine. I'm kind of in a rush right now."

He seemed to consider this and then reject it, undiscouraged. She thought of going to the washroom and then thought no. She thought of the dead man's shirt, Andreas Baader's shirt, dirtier or more bloody in one picture than in the other.

"And you have a three o'clock," she said.

"Three-thirty. But that's a long way off. That's another world, where I fix my tie and walk in and tell them who I am." He paused a moment, then looked at her. "You're supposed to say, 'Who are you?'"

She saw herself smile. But she said nothing. She thought that maybe Ulrike's rope burn wasn't a burn but the rope itself, if it was a rope and not a wire or a belt or something else.

He said, "That's your line. 'Who are you?' I set you up beautifully and you totally miss your cue."

They'd finished eating but their paper cups were not empty yet. They talked about rents and leases, parts of town. She didn't want to tell him where she lived. She lived just three blocks away, in a faded brick building whose limitations and malfunctions she'd come to understand as the texture of her life, to be distinguished from a normal day's complaints.

Then she told him. They were talking about places to run and bike, and he told her where he lived and what his jogging route was, and she said that her bike had been stolen from the basement of her building, and when he asked her where she lived she told him, more or less nonchalantly, and he drank his diet soda and looked out the window, or into it, perhaps, at their faint reflections paired on the glass.

When she came out of the bathroom, he was standing at the kitchen window as if waiting for a view to materialize. There was nothing out there but dusty masonry and glass, the rear of the industrial loft building on the next street.

It was a studio apartment, with the kitchen only partly walled off and the bed in a corner of the room, smallish, without posts or headboard, covered in a bright Berber robe, the only object in the room of some slight distinction.

She knew she had to offer him a drink. She felt awkward, unskilled at this, at unexpected guests. Where to sit, what to say, these were matters to consider. She didn't mention the gin she kept in the freezer.

"You've lived here, what?"

"Just under four months. I've been a nomad," she said. "Sublets, staying with friends, always short-term. Ever since the marriage failed."

"The marriage."

He said this in a modified version of the baritone rumble he'd used earlier for "the state."

"I've never been married. Believe that?" he said. "Most of my friends my age. All of them really. Married, children, divorced, children. You want kids someday?"

"When is someday? Yes, I think so."

"I think of kids. It makes me feel selfish, to be so wary of having a family. Never mind do I have a job or not. I'll have a job soon, a good one. That's not it. I'm in awe of raising, basically, someone so tiny and soft."

They drank seltzer with wedges of lemon, seated diagonally at the low wooden table, the coffee table where she ate her meals. The conversation surprised her a little. It was not difficult, even in the pauses. The pauses were unembarrassed and he seemed honest in his remarks.

His cell phone rang. He dug it out of his body and spoke briefly, then sat with the thing in his hand, looking thoughtful.

"I should remember to turn it off. But I think, If I turn it off, what will I miss? Something so incredible."

"The call that changes everything."

"Something so incredible. The total life-altering call. That's why I respect my cell phone."

She wanted to look at the clock.

"That wasn't your interview just now, was it? Canceled?"

He said it wasn't and she sneaked a look at the clock on the wall. She wondered whether she wanted him to miss his interview. That couldn't be what she wanted.

"Maybe you're like me," he said. "You have to find yourself on the verge of something happening before you can begin to prepare for it. That's when you get serious."

"Are we talking about fatherhood?"

"Actually, I canceled the interview myself. When you were in there," he said, nodding toward the bathroom.

She felt an odd panic. He finished his seltzer, tipping his head back until an ice cube slid into his mouth. They sat awhile, letting the ice melt. Then he looked directly at her, fingering one of the dangled ends of his necktie.

"Tell me what you want."

She sat there.

"Because I sense you're not ready and I don't want to do something too soon. But, you know, we're here."

She didn't look at him.

"I'm not one of those controlling men. I don't need to control anyone. Tell me what you want."

"Nothing."

"Conversation, talk, whatever. Affection," he said. "This is not a major moment in the world. It'll come and go. But we're here, so."

"I want you to leave, please."

He shrugged and said, "Whatever." Then he sat there.

"You said, 'Tell me what you want.' I want you to leave."

He sat there. He didn't move. He said, "I canceled the thing for a reason. I don't think this is the reason, this particular conversation. I'm looking at you. I'm saying to myself, You know what she's like? She's like someone convalescing."

"I'm willing to say it was my mistake."

"I mean we're here. How did this happen? There was no mistake. Let's be friends," he said.

"I think we have to stop now."

"Stop what? What are we doing?"

He was trying to speak softly, to take the edge off the moment.

"She's like someone convalescing. Even in the museum, this is what I thought. All right. Fine. But now we're here. This whole day, no matter what we say or do, it'll come and go."

"I don't want to continue this."

"Be friends."

"This is not right."

"No, be friends."

His voice carried an intimacy so false it seemed a little threatening. She didn't know why she was still sitting here. He leaned toward her then, placing a hand lightly on her forearm.

"I don't try to control people. This is not me."

She drew away and stood up and he was all around her then. She tucked her head into her shoulder. He didn't exert pressure or try to caress her breasts or hips but held her in a kind of loose containment. For a moment she seemed to disappear, tucked and still, in breathless hiding. Then she pulled away. He let her do this and looked at her so levelly, with such measuring effect, that she barely recognized him. He was ranking her, marking her in some awful and withering way.

"Be friends," he said.

She found she was shaking her head, trying to disbelieve the moment, to make it reversible, a misunderstanding. He watched her. She was standing near the bed and this was precisely the information contained in his look, these two things, he and the bed. He shrugged as if to say, It's only right. Because what's the point of being here if we don't do what we're here to do? Then he took off his jacket, a set of unhurried movements that seemed to use up the room. In the rumpled white shirt he was bigger than ever, sweating, completely unknown to her. He held the jacket at his side, arm extended.

"See how easy. Now you. Start with the shoes," he said. "First one, then the other."

She went toward the bathroom. She didn't know what to do. She walked along the wall, head down, a person marching blindly, and went into the bathroom. She closed the door but was afraid to lock it. She thought it would make him angry, provoke him to do something, wreck something, worse. She did not slide the bolt. She was determined not to do this unless she heard him approach the bathroom. She didn't think he'd moved. She was certain, nearly certain that he was standing near the coffee table.

She said, "Please leave."

Her voice was unnatural, so fluted and small it scared her further. Then she heard him move. It sounded almost leisurely. It was a saunter, almost, and it took him past the radiator, where the cover rattled slightly, and in the direction of the bed.

"You have to go," she said, louder now.

He was sitting on the bed, unbuckling his belt. This is what she thought she heard, the tip of the belt sliding out of the loop and then a little flick of tongue and clasp. She heard the zipper coming down.

She stood against the bathroom door. After a while she heard him breathing, a sound of concentrated work, nasal and cadenced. She stood there and waited, head down, body on the door. There was nothing she could do but listen and wait.

When he was finished, there was a long pause, then some rustling and shifting. She thought she heard him put on his jacket. He came toward her now. She realized she could have locked the door earlier, when he was on the bed. She stood there and waited. Then she felt him lean against the door, the dead weight of him, and inch away, not pushing but sagging. She slid the bolt into the chamber, quietly. He was pressed there, breathing, sinking into the door.

He said, "Forgive me."

His voice was barely audible, close to a moan. She stood there, and waited.

He said, "I'm sorry. Please. I don't know what to say."

She waited for him to leave. When she heard him cross the room and close the door behind him, finally, she waited a full minute longer. Then she came out of the bathroom and locked the front door.

She saw everything twice now. She was where she wanted to be, and alone, but nothing was the same. Bastard. Nearly everything in the room has a double effect—what it was and the association it carried in her mind. She went out walking and when she came back the connection was still there, on the coffee table, on the bed, in the bathroom. Bastard. She had dinner in a small restaurant nearby and went to bed early.

When she went back to the museum the next morning he was alone in the gallery, seated on the bench in the middle of the room, his back to the entranceway, and he was looking at the last painting in the cycle, the largest by far and maybe most breathtaking, the one with the coffins and cross, called *Funeral*.

2002

Anita Desai

b. 1937

Anita Desai was born in Mussoorie, India. Her father was Bengali and her mother, German. She received her BA from the University of Delhi in 1957 and married Ashvin Desai, a business executive, the following year. Her first novel, *Cry, the Peacock*, was published in 1963. Three of her novels—*Clear Light of Day* (1980), *In Custody* (1984), and *Fasting, Feasting* (1999)—were shortlisted for the Booker Prize. Eschewing the overt politics of earlier Indian fiction, Desai is more interested in how politics impact private lives. She maintains that her primary goal is to discover "the truth that is nine-tenths of the iceberg that lies submerged beneath the one-tenth visible portion we call Reality." Her most remarkable achievement is the lucidity with which she creates characters adrift in a post-colonial world, tragically alienated from the traditions that might give them a sense of home, whether this be the German Baumgartner entrapped in postwar Bombay in *Baumgartner's Bombay* (1988); the rich young Europeans who flee to India in search of spiritual enlightenment in *Journey to Ithaca* (1995); or her Indian characters lost in the exotic world of American culture her collection of stories, *Diamond Dust: Stories* (2000). However, there is always humour in Desai's work, and the collision and melding of cultures does occasionally lead to resolution. An excellent stylist, she has taught creative writing at many US universities, including MIT. Desai currently lives in Massachusetts.

Surface Textures

It was all her own fault, she later knew—but how could she have helped it? When she stood, puckering her lips, before the fruit barrow in the market and, after sullen consideration, at last plucked a rather small but nicely ripened melon out of a heap on display, her only thought had been Is it worth a *rupee* and fifty *paise*? The lychees looked more poetic, in large clusters like some prickly grapes of a charming rose colour, their long stalks and stiff grey leaves tied in a bunch above them—but were expensive. Mangoes were what the children were eagerly waiting for—the boys, she knew, were raiding the mango trees in the school compound daily and their stomach-aches were a result, she told them, of the unripe mangoes they ate and for which they carried paper packets of salt to school in their pockets instead of handkerchiefs—but, leave alone the expense, the ones the fruiterer held up to her enticingly were bound to be sharp and sour for all their parakeet shades of rose and saffron; it was still too early for mangoes. So she put the melon in her string bag, rather angrily—paid the man his one *rupee* and fifty *paise* which altered his expression from one of promise and enticement to that of disappointment and contempt, and trailed off towards the vegetable barrow.

That, she later saw, was the beginning of it all, for if the melon seemed puny to her and boring to the children, from the start her husband regarded it with eyes that seemed newly opened. One would have thought he had never seen a melon before. All through the meal his eyes remained fixed on the plate in the centre of the table with its big button of a yellow melon. He left most of his rice and pulses on his plate, to her indignation. While she scolded, he reached out to touch the melon that so captivated him. With one finger he stroked the coarse grain of its rind, rough with the upraised criss-cross of pale veins. Then he ran his fingers up and down the green streaks that divided it into even quarters as by green silk threads, so tenderly. She was clearing away the plates and did not notice till she came back from the kitchen.

"Aren't you going to cut it for us?" she asked, pushing the knife across to him.

He gave her a reproachful look as he picked up the knife and went about dividing the melon into quarter-moon portions with sighs that showed how it pained him.

"Come on, come on," she said roughly, "the boys have to get back to school."

He handed them their portions and watched them scoop out the icy orange flesh with a fearful expression on his face—as though he were observing cannibals at a feast. She had not the time to pay attention to it then but later described it as horror. And he did not eat his own slice. When the boys rushed away, he bowed his head over his plate and regarded it.

"Are you going to fall asleep?" she cried, a little frightened.

"Oh no," he said, in the low mumble that always exasperated her—it seemed a sign to her of evasiveness and pusillanimity, this mumble—"Oh no, no." Yet he did not object when she seized the plate and carried it off to the kitchen, merely picked up the knife that was left behind and, picking a flat melon seed off its edge where it had remained stuck, he held it between two fingers, fondling it delicately. Continuing to do this, he left the house.

The melon might have been the apple of knowledge for Harish—so deadly its poison that he did not even need to bite into it to imbibe it: that long, devoted look had been enough. As he walked to his office which issued ration cards to the population of their town, he looked about him vaguely but with hunger, his eyes resting not on the things on which people's eyes normally rest—signboards, the traffic, the number of an approaching bus—but on such things, normally considered nondescript and unimportant, as the paving stones on which their feet momentarily pressed, the length of wire in a railing at the side of the road, a pattern of grime on the windowpane of a disused printing press . . . Amongst such things his eyes roved and hunted and, when he was seated at his desk in the office, his eyes continued to slide about—that was Sheila's phrase later: "slide about"—in a musing, calculating way, over the surface of the crowded desk, about the corners of the room, even across the ceiling. He seemed unable to focus them on a file or a card long enough to put to them his signature—they lay unsigned and the people in the queue outside went for another day without rice and sugar and kerosene for their lamps and Janta cookers. Harish searched—slid about, hunted, gazed—and at last found sufficiently interesting a thick book of rules that lay beneath a stack of files. Then his hand reached out—not to pull the book to him or open it, but to run the ball of his thumb across the edge of the pages. In their large number and irregular cut, so closely laid out like some crisp palimpsest, his eyes seemed to find something of riveting interest and his thumb of tactile wonder. All afternoon he massaged the cut edges of the book's seven hundred odd pages—tenderly, wonderingly. All afternoon his eyes gazed upon them with strange devotion. At five o'clock, punctually, the office shut and the queue disintegrated into vociferous grumbles and threats as people went home instead of to the ration shops, empty-handed instead of loaded with those necessary but, to Harish, so dull comestibles.

Although Government service is as hard to depart from as to enter—so many letters to be written, forms to be filled, files to be circulated, petitions to be made that it hardly seems worthwhile—Harish was, after some time, dismissed—time he happily spent judging the difference between white blotting paper and pink (pink is flatter, denser, white spongier) and the texture of blotting paper stained with ink and that which is fresh, that which has been put to melt in a saucer of cold tea and that which has been doused in a pot of ink. Harish was dismissed.

The first few days Sheila stormed and screamed like some shrill, wet hurricane about the house. "How am I to go to market and buy vegetables for dinner? I don't even have enough for that. What am I to feed the boys tonight? No more milk for them. The washerwoman is asking for her bill to be paid. Do you hear? Do you *hear*? And we shall have to leave this flat. Where shall we go?" He listened—or didn't—sitting on a cushion before her mirror, fingering the small silver box in which she kept the red *kum-kum* that daily cut a gash from one end of her scalp to the other after her toilet. It was of dark, almost blackened silver, with a whole forest embossed on it—banana groves, elephants, peacocks and jackals. He rubbed his thumb over its cold, raised surface.

After that, she wept. She lay on her bed in a bath of tears and perspiration, and it was only because of the kindness of their neighbours that they did not starve to death the very first week, for even those who most disliked and distrusted Harish—"Always said he looks like a hungry hyena," said Mr Bhatia who lived below their flat, "not human at all, but like a hungry, hunchbacked hyena hunting along the road"—felt for the distraught wife and the hungry children (who did not really mind as long as there were sour green mangoes to steal and devour) and looked to them. Such delicacies as Harish's family had never known before arrived in stainless steel and brass dishes, with delicate unobtrusiveness. For a while wife and children gorged on sweetmeats made with fresh buffalo milk, on pulses cooked according to grandmother's recipes, on stuffed bread and the first pomegranates of the season. But, although delicious, these offerings came in small quantities and irregularly and soon they were really starving.

"I suppose you want me to take the boys home to my parents," said Sheila bitterly, getting up from the bed. "Any other man would regard that as the worst disgrace of all—but not you. What is my shame to you? I will have to hang my head and crawl home and beg my father to look after us since you won't," and that was what she did. He was sorry, very sorry to see her pack the little silver *kum-kum* box in her black trunk and carry it away.

Soon after, officials of the Ministry of Works, Housing and Land Development came and turned Harish out, cleaned and painted the flat and let in the new tenants who could hardly believe their luck—they had been told so often they couldn't expect a flat in that locality for at least another two years.

The neighbours lost sight of Harish. Once some children reported they had seen him lying under the *pipal* tree at the corner of their school compound, staring fixedly at the red gashes cut into the papery bark and, later, a boy who commuted to school on a suburban train claimed to have seen him on the railway platform, sitting against a railing like some tattered beggar, staring across the criss-cross of shining rails. But next day, when the boy got off the train, he did not see Harish again.

Harish had gone hunting. His slow, silent walk gave him the appearance of sliding rather than walking over the surface of the roads and fields, rather like a snail except that his movement was not as smooth as a snail's but stumbling as if he had only recently become one and was still unused to the pace. Not only his eyes and his hands but even his bare feet seemed to be feeling the earth carefully, in search of an interesting surface. Once he found it, he would pause, his whole body would gently collapse across it and hours—perhaps days—would be devoted to its investigation and worship. Outside the town the land was rocky and bare and this was Harish's especial paradise, each rock having a surface of such exquisite roughness, of such perfection in shape and design, as to keep him occupied and ecstatic for weeks together. Then the river beyond the rock quarries drew him away and there he discovered the joy of fingering silksmooth stalks and reeds, stems and leaves.

Shepherd children, seeing him stumble about the reeds, plunging thigh-deep into the water in order to pull out a water lily with its cool, sinuous stem, fled screaming, not certain whether this was a man or a hairy water snake. Their mothers came, some with stones and some with canes at the ready, but when they saw Harish, his skin parched to a violet shade, sitting on the bank and gazing at the transparent stem of the lotus, they fell back, crying, "Wah!" gathered closer together, advanced, dropped their canes and stones, held their children still by their hair and shoulders, and came to bow to him. Then they hurried back to the village, chattering. They had never had a Swami to themselves, in these arid parts. Nor had they seen a Swami who looked holier, more inhuman than Harish with his matted hair, his blue, starved skin and single-focused eyes. So, in the evening, one brought him a brass vessel of milk, another a little rice. They pushed their children before them and made them drop flowers at his feet. When Harish stooped and felt among the offerings for something his fingers could respond to, they were pleased, they felt accepted. "Swami-ji," they whispered, "speak."

Harish did not speak and his silence made him still holier, safer. So they worshipped him, fed and watched over him, interpreting his moves in their own fashion, and Harish, in turn, watched over their offerings and worshipped.

1978

Robert Stone

b. 1937

Tumultuous and fractured early years—some spent in a New York orphanage which he describes as having had "the social dynamic of a coral reef"—led Robert Stone to an early immersion in narrative, the more expansive and the more rooted in the world's turmoils the better. He briefly attended New York University, received a Stegner Fellowship at Stanford University where, interspersed with his cultural forays as a Merry Prankster with Ken Kesey in the psychedelic sixties, he began writing his first, partly phantasmagoric novel, *A Hall of Mirrors* (1967). Six largely realistic novels have followed. *Damascus Gate* (1998) is uncannily attuned to the brutal quirks of faith in Jerusalem and Gaza, and the most recent novel, *Death of the Black-Haired Girl* (2013), deepens our sense that his portrayals of women are among the most complex in contemporary literature. He has received numerous awards, including the National Book Award for what is still seen as his quintessential work, *Dog Soldiers* (1974), which aligns Vietnam as a bad dream with heroin as malign American promise. Above all, he receives the sometimes overwhelmed devotion of a readership that celebrates him (often while invoking Melville and Conrad) as one of the consummate stylists of the age and even more for his relentless courage in dealing—always skeptically—with loss, violence, and longing, with war as a perpetual state of individual and historical experience. "Miserere" is the opening story in *Bear and His Daughter* (1997) and presents the initial threads in the dense, often frightening tapestry of grace, mercy, and the compulsion of returning to at least an illusion of wholeness that the entire volume weaves. Robert Stone lives with his wife, Janice, his first and constant editor, in New York and Key West.

Miserere

Mary Urquhart had just finished story hour at the library when the muted phone rang at the circulation desk. She had been reading the children *Prince Caspian.*

Camille Innaurato was on the line and as usual she was beside herself.

"Mary, Mary, so listen . . ." Camille began. It sounded almost prayerful. Then Camille began to hyperventilate.

"Oh, Camille," Mrs Urquhart said. "Try to be calm. Are you all right, dear? Do you have your inhaler?"

"I have more!" Camille croaked fiercely at last. The force of the words in her constricted throat made her sound, Mary Urquhart thought, like her counterpart in *Traviata.*

"More?" Although Mary knew at once what Camille meant, she needed the extra moment of freedom.

"More babies!" Camille shouted. She spoke so loudly that even with the receiver as close to her ear as she could bear, Mary Urquhart thought that everyone around the circulation desk must be able to hear her voice on the phone, its unsound passion.

"My brother, he found them!" cried Camille. "And he took them here. So I got them now."

"I see," said Mary Urquhart.

Outside, Mrs Carter, the African-American head librarian, was supervising the reuniting of the story-hour children with their mothers. The children were, without exception, black and Hispanic. The mothers of the black children were mostly West Indian domestics; they were the most scrupulous of the story-hour mothers and they loved their children to have English stories, British stories.

"Mary . . ." Camille gasped over the phone. "Mary?"

Outside the library windows, in the darkening winter afternoon, the children looked lively and happy and well behaved and Mary was proud of them. The mothers were smiling, and Mrs Carter too.

"Easy does it," said Mary Urquhart to her friend Camille. For years after Mary had stopped drinking, she had driven around with a bumper sticker to that effect. Embarrassing to consider now.

"You'll come, Mary? You could come today? Soon? And we could do it?"

The previous year Mrs Urquhart had bought little books of C.S. Lewis tales with her own money for the children to take home. That way at least some might learn to read them. She liked to meet the mothers herself and talk with them. Looking on wistfully, she wished herself out on the sidewalk too, if only to say hello and remind herself of everyone's name. But Mrs Carter was the chief librarian and preempted the privilege of overseeing the dismissal of story hour.

"Yes, dear," Mary said to Camille. "I'll come as soon as we close."

They closed within the hour because the New Jersey city in which Mary worked had scant funds to spare for libraries. It was largely a city of racial minorities, in the late stages of passing from the control of a corrupt white political machine to that of a corrupt black one. Its schools were warrens of pathology and patronage. Its police, still mainly white, were frequently criminals.

Mary Urquhart looked carefully about her as she went out the door into the library parking lot for the walk to her old station wagon. It was nearly night, though a faint stain of the day persisted. At the western horizon, across the river and over the stacks and gables of the former mills, hung a brilliant patch of clear night sky where Venus blazed. Some of the newer street lights around the library's block were broken, their fixtures torn away by junkies for sale to scrap dealers. There were patchy reefs and banks of soiled frozen snow on the ground. Not much had fallen for a week, but the weather was bitter and the northfacing curbs and margins were still partly covered.

"Thou fair-haired angel of the evening," Mary recited silently to the first star. She could not keep the line from her mind.

Temple Street, the road Mary drove toward the strip that led her home, was one of crumbling wooden houses. In some of them, bare lights glowed behind gypsy-coloured bedspreads tacked over the taped windows. About every fifth house was derelict and inside some of these candlelight was already flickering. They were crack houses. Mary had worked as an enumerator in the neighbourhood during the last census and, for all its transience, she knew it fairly well. Many of the houses were in worse condition inside than out. The official census description for all of them was "Dilapidated." A few of her story children lived on the street.

The odd corner had a bodega in a cinderblock building with a faint neon beer sign in its window. The cold had driven the brown-bagging drinkers away from the little strip mall that housed Mashona's Beauty Shoppe, a cheap lamp store and a takeout ribs joint called Floyd's, which kept erratic hours. All the shops closed at dusk and God knew, she thought, where the alcoholics had gone. Maybe out of the bitter wind into the crack houses. Mary knew a lot of the older alcoholics who hung out there by sight and sometimes, in daytime, she stopped for Floyd's ribs, which were not at all bad. Floyd, who always had a smile for her, kept a sign over his register that read CHRIST IS THE ANSWER.

She had an ongoing dialogue with a few of the men. Those who would speak to a middle-aged white woman like herself called her "Mary" and sometimes, in the case of the beat old-timers from down home, "Miss Mary." She had begun by addressing them all as "sir," but she had soon perceived that this offended them as patronizing and was not appropriate to street banter. So, if she did not know them by name, she addressed them as "guy," which amused them. It was how her upper-class Southern husband had addressed his social equals. He had used it long before one heard it commonly; he had been dead for thirteen years.

"I know your story, guy," she would say to a brown-bagging acquaintance as she carried her paper container of ribs to the car. "I'm a juicehead. I'm a boozer."

"But you gotta enjoy your life, Mary," an old man had said to her once. "You ain't got but one, chère?"

And that had stopped her cold.

"But that's it," she had told the man. "You're so right."

He had shaken his head, telling her really, well, she'd never understand. Her life and his? But she'd persisted.

"That's why I don't have my bottle today as you do. Because there was a time, guy. Yes, you best believe it."

Then he'd heard her vestigial Southernness and cocked his head and said, in a distinctly sarcastic but not altogether unfriendly way, "Do it right, Mary. You say so."

"God bless, guy."

"Be right, Mary.

Poor fellow, she'd thought. Who was he? Who might he have become? She wished him grace.

A short distance before Temple Street doglegged into the strip of Route 4, it passed the dangerous side of a city park in which there was a large lake. The cold weather had frozen the lake to a depth that Mary knew must be many feet. After the cold week they'd had, it must be safe for skating. In some towns there would be lights by the lakeside and skating children; not in this one. And for that she could only be grateful, because she did not think she could bear the sight of children skating or lights on the icy surface of a frozen lake. Even after thirteen years.

Along its last quarter mile, Temple Street acquired an aluminum guardrail and some halogen overhead lights, though on these, too, the metal was torn up, unscrewed, pried loose by the locust-junkies.

At the light that marked the intersection with Route 4 stood a large gas station. It was one of a number owned by an immigrant from India. Once the immigrant himself had worked in it, then he'd bought it, then bought another and real estate to go with them. Now he employed other Indian immigrants who worked long shifts, day and night. In the previous twelve months, according to the county newspaper, no fewer than four of the immigrants had been shot dead in holdups and another four wounded.

Mary waited at the light, and it was really easier to think about the poor slaughtered Gujaratis than about the frozen lake. She prayed for them, in her way, eyes focused on the turn signal. It did not suit her to utter repetitions. Rather the words came to her on all the music she had heard, so many settings, that prayer sung over and over since the beginning of music itself.

Agnus Dei, qui tollis peccata mundi,
Miserere nobis.

Then there was Route 4, the American Strip. And this was New Jersey, where she had ended up, its original home and place of incubation, whence it had been nourished to creep out and girdle the world. It had come in time to her own stately corner of North Carolina, looking absolutely the same.

Since her widowhood and recovery, Mary Urquhart had lived in a modest house in what had once been a suburb of this New Jersey city, only a few blocks beyond its formal border. At the suburban end of the street was a hill from which the towers of Manhattan were visible on the clearer mornings. All day and most of the night, planes on a southward descent for Newark passed overhead and, even after so many years, often woke her.

But Mary was not, that afternoon, on her way home. A mile short of the city line, she pulled off Route 4 onto Imperial Avenue. The avenue led to a neighbourhood called Auburn Hill, which had become an Italian enclave in the Spanish-speaking section of the ghetto. Auburn Hill could be relied upon for neat lawns and safe streets, their security reinforced by grim anecdotes of muggers' and housebreakers' summary punishments. Young outlaws nailed to tar rooftops with screwdrivers. Or thrown from an overpass onto the Jersey Central tracks fifty feet below. At Christmastime, the neighbourhood sparkled with cheery lights. Mary had come to know it well and, comprehending both the bitter and the sweet of Auburn Hill, was fond of it.

Camille Innaurato's was like the other houses in that end of town. It was a brick, three-bedroom single-storey with aluminum siding and a narrow awning of the same. It had a small lawn in front, surrounded by a metal fence, and a garden in the back where Camille grew tomatoes and peppers in season.

When Mary pulled into the driveway, she saw Camille's pale, anxious face at the picture window. Camille was mouthing words, clasping her hands. In a moment she opened the door to the winter wind, as Mary emerged from her car and locked it.

"Oh, Mary. I'm thanking God Almighty you could come. Yeah, I'm thanking him."

Camille was one of those women who had grown older in unquestioning service to her aged parents. She had helped raise her younger brother. Later she had shared with her father the care of her sick mother. Then, when he died, she had assumed it all—her mother, the house, everything. Camille worked in a garment-sewing shop that had set itself up on two floors of a former silk mill; she oversaw the Chinese and Salvadoran women employed there.

Her younger brother, August, was technically a policeman, though not an actively corrupt one. In fact, he had no particular constabulary duties. The family had had enough political connections to secure him a clerical job with the department. He was a timid, excitable man, married, with grown children, who lived with his domineering wife in an outer suburb. But as a police insider he knew the secrets of the city.

The Innauratos, brother and sister, had inherited nothing from their parents except the house Camille occupied and their sick mother's tireless piety.

Mary Urquhart stepped inside and took Camille by the shoulders and looked at her.

"Now, Camille, dear, are you all right? Can you breathe?"

She inspected Camille and, satisfied with her friend's condition, checked the house. The living room was neat enough although the television set was off, a sure sign of Camille's preoccupation.

"I gotta show you, Mary. Oh I gotta show you. Yeah I gotta." She sounded as though she were weeping, but the beautiful dark eyes she fixed on Mary were dry. Eyes out of Alexandrian portraiture, Mary thought, sparkling and shimmering with their infernal vision. For a moment it seemed she had returned from some transport. She gathered Mary to her large, soft, barren breast. "You wanna coffee, Mary honey? You wanna *biscote*? A little of wine?"

In her excitement, Camille always offered the wine when there were babies, forgetting Mary could not drink it.

"I'll get you a glass of wine," Mary suggested. "And I'll get myself coffee."

Camille looked after Mary anxiously as she swept past her toward the kitchen.

"Sit down, dear," Mary called to her. "Sit down and I'll bring it out."

Slowly, Camille seated herself on the edge of the sofa and stared at the blank television screen.

In the immaculate kitchen, Mary found an open bottle of sangiovese, unsoured, drinkable. She poured out a glass, then served herself a demitasse of fresh-made espresso from Camille's machine. In the cheerless, spotless living room, they drank side by side on the faded floral sofa, among the lace and the pictures of Camille's family and the portrait photograph of the Pope.

"I used to love sangiovese," Mary said, watching her friend sip. "The wine of the Romagna. Bologna. Urbino."

"It's good," Camille said.

"My husband and I and the children once stayed in a villa outside Urbino. It rained. Yes, every day, but the mountains were grand. And the hill towns down in Umbria. We had great fun."

"You saw the Holy Father?"

Mary laughed. "We were all good Protestants then."

Camille looked at her in wonder, though she had heard the story of Mary's upbringing many times. Then her face clouded.

"You gotta see the babies, Mary."

"Yes," Mary sighed. "But do finish your wine."

When the wine was done they both went back to look at the fetuses. There were four. Camille had laid them on a tarpaulin, under a churchy purple curtain on the floor of an enclosed, unheated back porch, where it was nearly as cold as the night outside. On top of the curtain she had rested one of her wall crucifixes.

Mary lifted the curtain and looked at the little dead things on the floor. They had lobster-claw, unseparated fingers, and one had a face. Its face looked like a Florida Manatee's, Mary thought. It was the only living resemblance she could bring to bear—a manatee, bovine, slope-browed. One was still enveloped in some kind of fibrous membrane that suggested bat wings.

"So sweet," Camille sobbed. "So sad. Who could do such a thing? A murderer!" She bit her thumb. "A murderer, the degenerate fuck, his eyes should be plucked out!" She made the sign of the cross, to ask forgiveness for her outburst.

"Little lamb, who made thee?" Mary Urquhart asked wearily. The things were so disgusting. "Well, to work then."

Camille's brother August had discovered that the scavenger company that handled the county's medical waste also serviced its abortion clinics, which had no incinerators of their own. The fetuses were stored for disposal along with everything else. August had fixed it with the scavengers to report specimens and set them aside. He would pass on the discovery to Camille. Then Camille and a friend—most often Mary—would get to work.

Mary knew a priest named Father Hooke, the pastor of a parish in a wealthy community in the Ramapos. They had known each other for years. Hooke had been, in a somewhat superficial way, Mary's spiritual counsellor. He was much more cultivated than most priests and could be wickedly witty, too. Their conversations about contemporary absurdities, Scripture and the vagaries of the Canon, history and literature had helped her through the last stage of her regained abstinence. She knew of Julian of Norwich through his instruction. He had received her into the Catholic Church and she had been a friend to him. Lately, though, there had been tension between them. She used Camille's telephone to alert him.

"Frank," she said to the priest, "we have some children."

He gave her silence in return.

"Hello, Frank," she said again. "Did you hear me, Father? I said we have some children."

"Yes," said Hooke, in what Mary was coming to think of as his affected tone, "I certainly heard you the first time. Tonight is . . . difficult."

"Yes, it surely is," Mary said. "Difficult and then some. When will you expect us?"

"I've been meaning," Hooke said, "to talk about this before now."

He had quoted Dame Julian to her. "All shall be well, and all shall be well, and all manner of thing shall be well." Those were lines he liked.

"Have you?" she inquired politely. "I see. We can talk after the interment."

"You know, Mary," Father Hooke said with a nervous laugh, "the bishop, that pillar of intellect, our spiritual prince, has been hearing things that trouble him."

Mary Urquhart blushed to hear the priest's lie.

"The bishop," she told him, "is not a problem in any way. You are."

"Me?" He laughed then, genuinely and bitterly. "I'm a problem? Oh, sorry. There are also a few laws . . ."

"What time, Father? Camille works for a living. So do I."

"The thing is," Father Hooke said, "you ought not to come tonight."

"Oh, Frank," Mary said. "Really, really. Don't be a little boy on me. Take up your cross, guy."

"I suppose," Hooke said, "I can't persuade you to pass on this one?"

"Shame on you, Frank Hooke," she said.

The drive to the clean outer suburbs led through subdivisions and parklands, then to thick woods among which colonial houses stood, comfortably lighted against the winter night. Finally there were a few farms, or estates laid out to resemble working farms. The woods were full of frozen lakes and ponds.

The Buick wagon Mary drove was almost fifteen years old, the same one she had owned in the suburbs of Boston as a youngish mother, driving all the motherly routes, taking Charles Junior to soccer practice and Payton to girls' softball and little Emily to playschool.

The fetuses were secured with blind cord in the back of the station wagon, between the tarp and the curtain in which Camille had wrapped them. It was a cargo that did not shift or rattle and they had not tried to put a crucifix on top. More and more, the dark countryside they rode through resembled the town where she had lived with Charles and her children.

"Could you say the poem?" Camille asked. When they went on an interment Camille liked to hear Mary recite poetry for her as they drove. Mary preferred poetry to memorized prayer, and the verse was always new to Camille. It made her cry, and crying herself out on the way to an interment, Mary had observed, best prepared Camille for the work at hand.

"But which poem, Camille?"

Sometimes Mary recited Crashaw's "To the Infant Martyrs," or from his hymn to Saint Teresa. Sometimes she recited Vaughan or Blake.

"The one with the star," Camille said. "The one with the lake."

"Oh," Mary said cheerfully. "Funny, I was thinking about it earlier."

Once, she could not imagine how, Mary had recited Blake's "To the Evening Star" for Camille. It carried such weight of pain for her that she dreaded its every line and trembled when it came to her unsummoned:

Thou fair-hair'd angel of the evening,
Now, whilst the sun rests on the mountains, light
Thy bright torch of love; thy radiant crown
Put on, and smile upon our evening bed!

It has almost killed her to recite it the first time, because that had been her and Charles's secret poem, their prayer for the protection that was not forthcoming. The taste of it in her mouth was of rage unto madness and the lash of grief and above all of whisky to drown it all, whisky to die in and be with them. That night, driving, with the dark dead creatures at their back, she offered up the suffering in it.

Camille wept at the sound of the words. Mary found herself unable to go on for a moment.

"There's more," Camille said.

"Yes," said Mary. She drew upon her role as story lady.

Let thy west wind sleep on
The lake; speak silence with thy glimmering eyes,
And wash the dusk with silver. Soon, full soon,
Dost thou withdraw; then the wolf rages wide,
And the lion glares thro' the dun forest:
The fleeces of our flocks are cover'd with
Thy sacred dew: protect them with thine influence.

Camille sobbed. "Oh Mary," she said. "Yours weren't protected."

"Well, stars . . ." Mary Urquhart said, still cheerfully. "Thin influence. Thin ice."

The parlour lights were lighted in the rectory of Our Lady of Fatima when they pulled off the genteel main street of the foothill town and into the church parking lot. Mary parked the station wagon close to the rectory door, and the two women got out and rang Father Hooke's bell.

Hooke came to the door in a navy cardigan, navy-blue shirt, and chinos. Camille murmured and fairly curtsied in deference. Mary looked the priest up and down. His casual getup seemed like recalcitrance, and unreadiness to officiate. Had he been working himself up to deny them?

"Hello, Frank," said Mary. "Sorry to come so late."

Hooke was alone in the rectory. There was no assistant and he did his own housekeeping, resident rectory biddies being a thing of the past.

"Can I give you coffee?" Father Hooke asked.

"I've had mine," Mary said.

He had a slack, uneasy smile. "Mary," the priest said. "And Miss . . . won't you sit down?"

He had forgotten Camille's name. He was a snob, she thought, a suburban snob. The ethnic, Mariolatrous name of his parish, Our Lady of Fatima, embarrassed him.

"Father," she said, "why don't we just do it?"

He stared at her helplessly. Ashamed for him, she avoided his eye.

"I think," he said, dry-throated, "we should consider from now on."

"Isn't it strange?" she asked Camille. "I had an odd feeling we might have a problem here tonight." She turned on Hooke. "What do you mean? Consider what?"

"All right, all right," he said. A surrender in the pursuit of least resistance. "Where is it?"

"They," Mary said.

"The babies," said Camille. "The poor babies are in Mary's car outside."

But he hung back. "Oh, Mary," said Father Hooke. He seemed childishly afraid.

She burned with rage. Was there such a thing as an adult Catholic? And the race of priests, she thought, these self-indulgent, boneless men.

"Oh, dear," she said. "What can be the matter now? Afraid of how they're going to look?"

"Increasingly . . ." Father Hooke said, "I feel we're doing something wrong."

"Really?" Mary asked. "Is that a fact?" They stood on the edge of the nice red Bolivian rectory carpet, in the posture of setting out for the station wagon. Yet not setting out. There was Haitian art on the wall. No lace curtains here. "What a shame," she said, "we haven't time for an evening of theological discourse."

"We may have to make time," Father Hooke said. "Sit down, girls."

Camille looked to Mary for reassurance and sat with absurd decorousness on the edge of a bare-boned Spanish chair. Mary stood where she was. The priest glanced at her in dread. Having given them an order, he seemed afraid to take a seat himself.

"It isn't just the interments," he told Mary. He ignored Camille. "It's the whole thing. Our whole position." He shuddered and began to pace up and down on the rug, his hands working nervously.

"Our position," Mary repeated tonelessly. "Do you mean *your* position? Are you referring to the Church's teaching?"

"Yes," he said. He looked around as though for help, but as was the case so often with such things, it was not available. "I mean I think we may be wrong."

She let the words reverberate in the rectory's quiet. Then she asked, "Prodded by conscience, are you, Father?"

"I think we're wrong on this," he said with sudden force. "I think women have a right. I do. Sometimes I'm ashamed to wear my collar."

She laughed her pleasant, cultivated laughter. "Ashamed to wear your collar? Poor Frank. Afraid people will think badly of you?"

He summoned anger. "Kindly spare me the ad hominem," he said.

"But Frank," she said, it seemed lightly, "there is only ad hominem."

"I'm afraid I'm not theologian enough," he said, "to follow you there."

"Oh," said Mary, "I'm sorry, Father. What I mean in my crude way is that what is expected of you is expected personally. Expected directly. Of *you*, Frank."

He sulked. A childish resentful silence. Then he said, "I can't believe God wants us to persecute these young women the way you people do. I mean you particularly, Mary, with your so-called counselling."

He meant the lectures she gave the unwed mothers who were referred to her by pamphlet. Mary had attended anti-war and anti-apartheid demonstrations with pride. The abortion clinic demonstrations she undertook as an offered humiliation, standing among the transparent cranks and crazies as a penance and a curb to pride. But surprisingly, when she was done with them in private, over coffee and cake, many pregnant women brought their pregnancies to term.

She watched Father Hooke. He was without gravitas, she thought. The hands, the ineffectual sputter.

"For God's sake," he went on, "look at the neighbourhood where you work! Do you really think the world requires a few million more black, alienated, unwanted children?"

She leaned against one of his antique chests and folded her arms. She was tall and elegant, as much an athlete and a beauty at fifty as she had ever been. Camille sat open-mouthed.

"How contemptible and dishonest of you to pretend an attack of conscience," she told Hooke quietly. "It's respectability you're after. And to talk about what God wants?" She seemed to be politely repressing a fit of genuine mirth. "When you're afraid to go out and look at his living image? Those things in the car, Frank, that poor little you are afraid to see. That's man, guy, those little forked purple beauties. That's God's image, don't you know that? That's what you're scared of."

He took his glasses off and blinked helplessly.

"Your grief . . ." he began. A weakling, she thought, trying for the upper hand. Trying to appear concerned. In a moment he had lost his nerve. "It's made you cruel. . . . Maybe not *cruel*, but . . ."

Mary Urquhart pushed herself upright. "Ah," she said with a flutter of gracious laughter, "the well-worn subject of my grief. Maybe I'm drunk again tonight, eh Father? Who knows?"

Thirteen years before on the lake outside Boston, on the second evening before Christmas, her husband had taken the children skating. First young Charley had wanted to go and Charles had demurred; he'd had a few drinks. Then he had agreed in his shaggy, teasing, slow-spoken way—he was rangy, wry, a Carolina Scot like Mary. It was almost Christmas and the kids were excited and how long would it stay cold enough to skate? Then Payton had demanded to go, and then finally little Emily, because Charles had taught them to snap the whip on ice the day before. And the lake, surrounded by woods, was well lighted and children always skated into the night although there was one end, as it turned out, where the light failed, a lonely bay bordered with dark blue German pine where even then maybe some junkie had come out from Roxbury or Southie or Lowell or God knew where and destroyed the light for the metal around it. And Emily still had her cold and should not have gone.

But they went and Mary waited late, and sometimes, listening to music, having a Wild Turkey, she thought she heard voices sounding strange. She could remember them perfectly now, and the point where she began to doubt, so faintly, that the cries were in fun.

The police said he had clung to the ice for hours, keeping himself alive and the children clinging to him, and many people had heard the calling out but taken it lightly.

She was there when the thing they had been was raised, a blue cluster wrapped in happy seasonal colours, woolly reindeer hats and scarves and mittens, all grasping and limbs intertwined, and it looked, she thought, like a rat king, the tangle of rats trapped together in their own naked tails and flushed from an abandoned hull to float drowned, a raft of solid rat on the swells of the lower Cape Fear River. The dead snarls on their faces, the wild eyes, a paradigm she had seen once as a child she saw again in the model of her family. And near Walden Pond, no less, the west wind slept on the lake, eyes glimmered in the silver dusk, a dusk at morning. She had lost all her pretty ones.

"Because," she said to Father Hooke, "it would appear to me that you are a man—and I know men, I was married to a man—who is a little boy, a little boy-man. A tiny boy-man, afraid to touch the cross or look in God's direction."

He stared at her and swallowed. She smiled as though to reassure him.

"What you should do, Father, is this. Take off the vestments you're afraid to wear. Your mama's dead for whom you became a priest. Become the nice little happy homosexual nonentity you are."

"You are a cruel bitch," Hooke said, pale-faced. "You're a sick and crazy woman."

Camille in her chair began to gasp. Mary bent to attend her. "Camille? Do you have your inhaler?"

Camille had it. Mary helped her adjust it and waited until her friend's breathing was under control. When she stood up, she saw that Father Hooke was in a bad way.

"You dare," Mary said to him, "you wretched tiny man, to speak of black unwanted children? Why, there is not a suffering black child—God bless them all—not a black child in this unhappy foolish country that I would not exalt and nourish on your goddamn watery blood. I would not risk the security of the most doomed, lost, deformed black child for your very life, you worthless pussy!"

Father Hooke had become truly upset. My Lord, she thought, now I've done it. Now I'll see the creature cry. She looked away.

"You were my only friend," Father Hooke told her when he managed to speak again. "Did you know that?"

She sighed. "I'm sorry, Father. I suppose I have my ignorant cracker side and God help me I am sick and I am crazy and cruel. Please accept my sincerest apologies. Pray for me."

Hooke would not be consoled. Kind-hearted Camille, holding her inhaler, took a step toward him as though she might help him somehow go on breathing.

"Get out," he said to them. "Get out before I call the police."

"You have to try to forgive me, Charles." Had she called him Charles? How very strange. Poor old Charles would turn in his grave. "Frank, I mean. You have to try and forgive me, Frank. Ask God to forgive me. I'll ask God to forgive you. We all need it, don't we, Father."

"The police!" he cried, his voice rising. "Because those things, those goddamn things in you car! Don't you understand? People accuse us of violence!" he shouted. "And you are violence!" Then he more or less dissolved.

She went and put a hand on his shoulder as Camille watched in amazement.

"God forgive us, Frank." But he leaned on the back of his leather easy chair and turned from her, weeping. "Oh Frank, you lamb," she said, "what did your poor mama tell you? Did she say that a world with God was easier than one without him?"

She gave Father Hooke a friendly pat and turned to Camille. "Because that would be mistaken, wouldn't it, Camille?"

"Oh, you're right," Camille hastened to say. The tearful priest had moved her too. But still she was dry-eyed, staring, Alexandrian. "You're so right, Mary."

When they were on the road again it was plain Camille Innaurato was exhausted.

"So, Mary," she asked. "So where're we going now, honey?"

"Well," Mary said, "as it happens, I have another fella up my sleeve." She laughed. "Yes, another of these worthies Holy Mother Church provides for our direction. Another selfless man of the cloth."

"I'll miss Mass tomorrow."

"This is Mass," Mary said.

"Right. OK."

This is Mass, she thought, this is the sacrifice nor are we out of it. She reached over and gave Camille a friendly touch.

"You don't work tomorrow, do you, love?"

"Naw, I don't," Camille said. "I don't, but . . ."

"I can take you home. I can get this done myself."

"No," said Camille, a little cranky with fatigue. "No way."

"Well, we'll get these children blessed, dear."

The man Mary had up her sleeve was a priest from central Europe called Monsignor Danilo. It was after ten when Mary telephoned him from a service station, but he hurriedly agreed to do what she required. He was smooth and obsequious and seemed always ready to accommodate her.

His parish, St Macarius, was in an old port town on Newark Bay, and to get there they had to retrace their drive through the country and then travel south past several exits of the Garden State.

It took them nearly an hour, even with the sparse traffic. The church and its rectory were in a waterfront neighbourhood of refineries and wooden tenements little better than the ones around Temple Street. The monsignor had arranged to meet them in the church.

The interior was an Irish-Jansenist nightmare of tarnished marble, white-steepled tabernacles and cream columns. Under a different patron, it had served the Irish dockers of a hundred years before. Its dimensions were too mean and too narrow to support the mass of decoration, and Father Danilo's bunch had piled the space with their icons, vaguely Byzantine Slavic saints and Desert Fathers and celebrity saints in their Slavic aspect.

Candles were flickering as the two women entered. The place smelled of wax, stale wine and the incense of past ceremony. Mary carried the babies under their purple cloth.

Monsignor Danilo waited before the altar, at the end of the main aisle. He wore his empurpled cassock with surplice and a silk stole. His spectacles reflected the candlelight.

Beside him stood a tall, very thin, expressionless young man in cassock and surplus. The young man, in need of a shave, held a paten on which cruets of holy water and chrism and a slice of lemon had been set.

Monsignor Danilo smiled his lupine smile, and when Mary had set the babies down before the altar, he took her hand in his. In the past he had sometimes kissed it; tonight he pressed it to his breast. The intrusion of his flabby body on her senses filled Mary with loathing. He paid no attention to Camille Innaurato and he did not introduce the server.

"Ah," he said, bending to lift the curtain under which the creatures lay, "the little children, no?"

She watched him regard the things with cool compassion, as though he were moved by their beauty, their vestigial humanity, the likeness of their Creator. But perhaps, she thought, he had seen ghastly sights before and smiled on them. Innocent as he might be, she thought, he was the reeking model of every Jew-baiting, clerical fascist murderer who ever took orders east of the Danube. His merry countenance was crass hypocrisy. His hands were huge, thick-knuckled, the hands of a brute, as his face was the face of a smiling Cain.

"So beautiful," he said. Then he said something in his native language to the slovenly young man, who looked at Mary with a smirk and shrugged and smiled in a vulgar manner. She did not let her gaze linger.

Afterward, she would have to hear about Danilo's mother and her trip to behold the apparition of the Virgin in some Bessarabian or Balkan hamlet and the singular misfortunes, historically unique, of Danilo's native land. And she would have to give him at least seventy-five dollars or there would be squeals and a disappointed face. And now something extra for the young man, no doubt an illegal alien, jumped-ship and saving his pennies.

Camille Innaurato breathed through her inhaler. Father Danilo took a cruet from the paten and with his thick fingers sprinkled a blessing on the lifeless things. Then they all faced the altar and the Eastern crucifix that hung suspended there. They prayed together in the Latin each knew:

Agnus Dei, qui tollis peccata mundi,
Miserere nobis.

Finally, she was alone with the ancient Thing before whose will she still stood amazed, whose shadow and line and light they all were: the bad priest and the questionable young man and Camille Innaurato, she herself and the unleavened flesh fouling the floor. Adoring, defiant, in the crack-house flicker of that hideous, consecrated half-darkness, she offered It Its due, by old command.

> Lamb of God, who takest away the sins of the world,
> Have mercy on us.

1997

Jack Hodgins

b. 1938

Born in the Comox Valley on Vancouver Island, Jack Hodgins grew up in the logging and farming community of Merville. After graduating from the University of British Columbia in 1961, he moved to Nanaimo, where he taught English at the Nanaimo District Senior Secondary School until 1979. He served as writer-in-residence at Simon Fraser University and the University of Ottawa and, in 1983, accepted a position teaching creative writing at the University of Victoria. He is married and has three children. His first collection of stories, *Spit Delaney's Island* (1976), used Vancouver Island as the locus of all the stories. Hodgins speaks of the Island as a geography where cultural escapees end up, making it a place of eccentric narratives. He always uses local venues—logging camps, pulp mills, stump ranches, or outback farms—as well as local history, to texture his fiction. In *The Invention of the World* (1977), a novel credited with introducing magic realism into Canadian fiction, Hodgins uses a real-life figure—Brother Twelve, a 1920s cult leader, and the community he founded near Nanaimo, BC—as the jumping-off point for a tale of a bizarre evangelist who beguiled an entire Irish village into coming to Vancouver Island to set up the Revelations Colony of Truth. *Broken Ground* (1998) is set in Merville in 1922 in a soldiers' settlement called Portuguese Creek. On land grants from a grateful nation, World War I veterans set out tents and attempt to clear the land. A fire that ravages the new settlement conjures the remembered horror of the war. The novel *The Resurrection of Joseph Bourne* (1979) won the Governor General's Award for Fiction. Among Hodgins's books are a half-dozen novels, two collections of stories, and the writing guide *A Passion for Narrative: A Guide for Writing Fiction* (1994).

Separating

People driving by don't notice Spit Delaney. His old gas station is nearly hidden now behind the firs he's let grow up along the road, and he doesn't bother to whitewash the scalloped row of half-tires someone planted once instead of a fence. And rushing by on the Island highway today, heading north or south, there's little chance that anyone will notice Spit Delaney seated on the big rock at the side of his road-end, scratching at his narrow chest, or hear him muttering to the flat grey highway and to the scrubby firs and to the useless old ears of his neighbour's dog that he'll be damned if he can figure out what it is that is happening to him.

Hitchhikers do notice, however; they can hear his muttering. Walking past the sheep sorrel and buttercup on the gravel shoulder, they see him suddenly, they turn alarmed eyes his way. Nodding, half smiling at this long-necked man with the striped engineer's cap, they move through the shade-stripes of trees, their own narrow shadows like knives shaving the pavement beside them. And all he gives back, all they can take away with them, is a side-tilted look they have seen a hundred times in family snapshots, in the eyes of people out at the edge of group photos unsure they belong. Deference. *Look at the camera, son, this is all being done for you, it has nothing to do with me.* He does not accept their attention, he admits only to being a figure on the edge of whatever it is they are really looking at: his gas station perhaps, or his rusty old tow truck, or his wife piling suitcases into the trunk of her car. He relocates his cap, farther back on his head; his Adam's apple slides up his long throat like a bubble in a tube, then pushes down.

Spit Delaney cannot remember a time when he was not fascinated by the hitchhikers. His property is close to a highway junction where they are often dropped off by the first ride that picked them up back near the ferry terminal. On these late-summer days, they line up across the front of his place like a lot of shabby refugees to wait for their second ride. Some walk past to get right out beyond the others, but most space themselves along the gravel, motionless, expressionless, collapsed. In pairs or clusters they drape themselves over their canvas packsacks and their sleeping bags. Some stretch out level on the ground, using their gear as headrests with only an arm and an upright thumb to show that they're awake, or alive. They are heading for the west coast of the Island, he knows, the Pacific, where they have heard it is still possible to live right down on the beach under driftwood shelters and go everywhere naked from morning until night. The clothes they are so eager to shed are patched jeans and wide braces and shirts made to look like flags and big floppy hats. There is a skinny boy with a panting St Bernard tied to his pack with a length of clothes line; there is a young frizzy-haired couple with a whining baby they pass back and forth; there is a grizzled old man, a hunched-over man with a stained-yellow beard, who must be at least in his seventies though he is dressed the same as the others. Stupid old fool, thinks Spit Delaney, and grins. Sitting on his rock, at the foot of the old paint-peeled sign saying B/A, he isn't afraid to envy.

There are ninety miles of road, of this road and another, between the rock at his road-end and the west-coast beaches they are heading for. It runs greysilver over hills and along bays and through villages and around mountains and along river banks, and is alive already with traffic: tourists set loose from a ferry and racing for campsites, salesmen released from motels and rushing for appointments. Beginnings are hard, and endings, but the long grey ribbon that joins them runs smooth and mindless along the surface of things. In his head Spit Delaney can follow it, can see every turn, can feel himself coming over the last hill to find the ocean laid out in the wide blue haze beneath him. The long curving line of sand that separates island from sea and man from whale is alive with the quick flashing movements of people.

Behind him the trunk lid slams shut. His wife's footsteps crunch down the gravel towards him. He can tell without looking that she is wearing the crepesoled shoes she bought in a fire sale and tried to return the next day. Spit Delaney's heavy brows sink, as if he is straining to see something forty miles across the road, deep into brush. He dispatches a wad of throat-phlegm in a clean arc out onto a stalk of dog daisy, and doesn't bother watching it slide to the ground.

She stops a few feet behind. "There's enough in the fridge to last you a week," she says.

He ducks his head, to study the wild sweet pea that twists in the grass between his boots.

She is going, now.

That is what they have agreed on.

"Sit down when you eat," she says. "Don't go standing up at the counter, the way you will."

The boy with the St Bernard gets a ride at this moment, a green GMC pickup. They leap into the back, dog and boy, and scramble up close to the cab. Then the boy slaps his hand on the roof, signal to start, and settles back with an arm around the dog's neck, laughing. For a moment his eyes meet Spit's, the laugh dies; they watch each other until the pickup has gone on past the other hitchhikers, on up the road out of sight behind trees.

I am a wifeless man, Spit tells the disappeared youth. This is the day of our separation. I am a wifeless man.

In his fortieth year Spit Delaney was sure he'd escaped all the pitfalls that seemed to catch everyone else in their thirties. He was a survivor.

"This here's one bugger you don't catch with his eyes shut," was his way of putting it.

And wasn't it obvious? While all his friends were getting sick of the jobs they'd worked at ever since they quit high school and were starting to hop around from one new job to another, Spit Delaney was still doing the same thing he'd been doing for twenty years, the thing he loved: operating Old Number One steam locomotive in the paper mill, shunting up and down the tracks, pushing flatcars and boxcars and tankcars off and onto barges. "Spit and Old Number One, a marriage made in heaven," people joked. "Him and that machine was made for each other, a kid and his toy. That train means more to him than any other human could hope to." Only it wasn't a joke, it was true, he was glad to admit it. Who else in all that mill got out of bed at four o'clock in the morning to fire up a head of steam for the day's work? Who else hung around after the shift was over, cleaning and polishing? Roy Rogers and Trigger, that's what they were. Spit and Old Number One. He couldn't name another person whose job was so much a part of himself, who was so totally committed to what he did for a living.

In the family department, too, he was a survivor. While everyone else's kids in their teens seemed to be smashing up the old man's car or getting caught at pot parties or treating their parents like slaves or having quiet abortions on the mainland, Jon and Cora looked as if they were going to sail right through their adolescence without a hitch: Cora would rather watch television and eat chocolate cake than fool around with boys or go to parties; Jon would rather read a book than do anything else at all. The two of them looked safe enough. It was a sign that they respected their father, Spit would say, though he admitted some of the credit had to go to his wife.

Stella. That was one more thing. All through his thirties it seemed as if every time he turned around someone else was splitting up. Everybody except him and Stella. Friends broke up, divorced, couples fell apart and regrouped into new couples. The day came when Stella Delaney looked at him out of her flat, nearly colourless eyes and said, "You and me are just about the only people we know still married." You couldn't count on the world being the same two weekends in a row. It was a hazard of their age, boredom was doing it, Stella told him, boredom and the new morality. People suddenly realized what they didn't have to put up with. There was no sense inviting anybody over for Saturday night, she said, they could be separated by then. But, miraculously, by the time Spit reached his fortieth year, he and Stella were still married, still together. However, if they intended to continue with their marriage, she told him, they'd have to make some new friends. Everybody else their age was newly single or newly remarried or shacking up with people half their age; what would they have in common?

The secret of his successful marriage, Spit insisted, was the way it started. Stella was a long-legged bony-faced woman of twenty-two, already engaged to some flat-assed logger from Tahsis, when Spit came into the kitchen at the back of her father's store. She was doing peach preserves for her first married winter, and admiring the logger's dinky little diamond ring up on the windowsill in front of her. Her big hands, in the orange mess of peel and juice and carved-out bruises, reminded him of the hands of a fisherman gouging out fish guts. The back of her cotton dress dipped up at the hem, to show the tiny blue veins behind her knees and the pink patches of skin where she'd pressed one leg to the other. He touched. She told him "Get lost mister, I got work to do," and he said "That logger musta been bushed and desperate is all I can say" but stayed to win her anyway, and to rush her off to a preacher's house on the day before her intended wedding. With a start like that, he said, how could anything go wrong?

It couldn't. He was sure of it. Things that were important to him, things that were real—his job, his family, his marriage—these things were surely destined to survive even the treacherous thirties.

But before he had time to congratulate himself, things began to fall apart. He insisted later that it was all because the stupidest goddamned question he ever heard just popped into his head all of a sudden. He didn't look for it, he didn't ask for it, it just came.

He'd driven over with the family to the west coast for the weekend, had parked the camper up in the trees above the high tide line. Stella was lying beside him on her giant towel, reading a magazine, oiled and gleaming like a beached eel. The question just popped into his head, all of a sudden: *Where is the dividing line?*

He was so surprised that he answered out loud. "Between what and what?"

Stella turned a page and folded it back. Most of the new page was taken up with a photograph of a women who'd increased her bust measurement in a matter of days and wanted to show Stella how to do the same.

"Wha'd you say?"

"Nothing," he said, and rolled over onto his side to face away from her. Between what and what? he asked himself. Maybe he was beginning to crack up. He'd heard of the things that happened to some men at his age.

Between what is and what isn't.

Spit sat up, cursing.

Stella slid her dark glasses down her nose and peered at him. "What's the matter with you?"

"Nothing," he said. *Where is the dividing line?* When the words hit him again like that he jumped to his feet and shook his head, like a cow shaking off flies.

"Sand fleas?" she said.

"It's nothing," he said, and stomped around to shake the sand out of the hair on his legs.

"Too much sun," she said, and pushed herself up. "We better move up into shade."

But when they settled down by a log, cool in the shade of the wind-crippled spruce, she told him it might just be this beach that was spooking him. "This Indian Lady at Lodge," she said, "told me her people get uneasy along this beach." Spit knew Sophie Jim by name, but Stella always referred to her as This Indian Lady at Lodge. It was some kind of triumph, apparently, when Sophie was finally persuaded to join the Daughters, their first native. "She said there's a story that some kind of Sea-Wolf monster used to come whanging up out of the Pacific here to gobble up people. It came up to sire wolves for the land too, but went back into the sea to live. She says they're all just a little nervous of this place."

Spit's brain itched from the slap of the sudden question. He wanted to go home, but the kids were far out on the sand at the water's edge and he could holler at them till he was blue in the face without being heard above the roar of the waves.

"She said all up and down the coast there are stories. About monsters that come out and change people into things. To hear her tell it there must've been a whole lot of traffic back and forth between sea and land."

"A whole lot of bull," he said, and put on his shirt. It was cold up here, and what did he care about a lot of Indian stuff? He knew Indians. When he was a boy the people up the road adopted a little Indian kid, a girl, and told it around that nobody, *nobody* was to dare tell her what she was. When she was ten years old she still hadn't figured out that she wasn't the same as everybody else, so Spit sat her down on the step and told her. He had to tell her three times before she believed him and then she started to howl and cry and throw herself around. But she dried out eventually and went Indian with a vengeance, to make up for lost time. He couldn't go near her without having to listen to a whole lot of stuff she'd got soaked up into her brain from hanging around the Reserve. So he knew all about Wasgo, Stella couldn't tell him anything new about that guy. He knew about Kanikiluk too, which was worse. That son of a bitch would think nothing of stepping out of the ocean and turning a man into a fish or making a piece of seaweed think it was human. He knew all about the kind of traffic she meant.

"They say we crawled up out of there ourselves," she said. "Millions of years ago."

"Let's go home," he said. "Let's get out of here."

Within fifteen minutes they had Cora and Jon herded up off that beach and pushed into the back of the camper and had started on their way across the island to their little house behind the gas station. It wasn't really a gas station any more, though he had never bothered to pull the pumps out; the shed was a good place to store the car parts and engine pieces he kept against the day they would be needed, and the roof out over the pumps was a good place to park the tow truck. Nor was it a real business—his job at the paper mill was enough for anyone to handle—but he'd fixed up the tow truck himself out of parts and used it to pull people out of snowbanks in winter or to help friends when they got their tractors mired in swamp.

When he got home from the coast he did not go into the gas station to brood, as he might have done, nor did he sit behind the wheel of his tow truck. This was too serious for that. He drove all the way down to the paper mill, punched himself in at the gate, and climbed up into the cab of Old Number One. He knew even then that something was starting to go wrong. *Where is the dividing line?* He sat there with his hands on the levers deep into night, all the way through the early morning when it was time to fire up her boilers and start getting ready for the day's work ahead. *And what does it take to see it?*

And, naturally, that was the day the company picked to tell him what they'd done with Old Number One.

Sold her to the National Museum in Ottawa.

For tourists to gawk at.

Sons of bitches. They might as well have lopped off half of his brain. Why didn't they sell the government his right arm too, while they were at it?

The hundred-and-thirty-ton diesel-electric they offered was no consolation. "A dummy could run that rig!" he shouted. "It takes a man to put life into Old Number One!"

He ought to be glad, they told him. That shay was long past her usefulness, the world had changed, the alternative was the junkyard. You can't expect *things* to last for ever.

But this was one uncoupling that would not be soon forgiven.

First he hired a painter to come into the mill and do a four-foot oil of her to hang over the fireplace. And unscrewed the big silver 1 from the nose to hang on the bedroom door. And bought himself a good-quality portable recorder to get the locomotive's sounds immortalized on tape. While there was some small comfort in knowing the old girl at least wasn't headed for the scrapyard, it was no easy thing when he had to bring her out on that last day, sandblasted and repainted a gleaming black, to be taken apart and shipped off in a boxcar. But at least he knew that while strangers four thousand miles away were staring at her, static and soundless as a stuffed grizzly, he would be able to sit back, close his eyes, and let the sounds of her soul shake through him full-blast just whenever he felt like it.

Stella allowed him to move her Tom Thomson print to the side wall to make room for the new painting; she permitted him to hang the big number 1 on the bedroom door; but she forbade him to play his tape when she was in the house. Enough is enough, she said. Wives who only had infidelity to worry about didn't know how lucky they were.

She was president of her Lodge, and knew more than she could ever tell of the things women had to put up with.

"Infidelity?" he said. It had never occurred to him. He rolled his eyes to show it was something he was tempted to think about, now that she'd brought it up, then kissed the top of her head to show he was joking.

"A woman my age," she said, "starts to ask what has she got and where is she headed."

"What you need is some fun out of life," he said, and gathered the family together. How did a world tour sound?

It sounded silly, they said.

It wounded like a waste of good money.

Good money or bad, he said, who'd been the one to go out and earn it? Him and Old Number One, that's who. Hadn't he got up a four o'clock every damn morning to get the old girl fired up, and probably earned more overtime that way than anybody else on this island? Well, was there a better way to spend money than taking his family to Europe at least?

They left her mother behind to keep an eye on the house. An old woman who had gone on past movement and caring and even speech, she could spend the time primly waiting in an armchair, her face in the only expression she seemed to have left: dark brows lowered in a scowl, eyes bulging as if in behind them she was planning to push until they popped out and rolled on the floor. Watching was the one thing she did well, she looked as if she was trying with the sheer force of those eyes to make things stay put. With her in the house it was safe to leave everything behind.

If they thought he'd left Old Number One behind him, however, if they thought he'd abandoned his brooding, they were very much mistaken; but they got all the way through Spain and Italy and Greece before they found it out. They might have suspected if they'd been more observant; they might have noticed the preoccupied, desperate look in his eyes. But they were in Egypt before that desperation became intense enough to risk discovery.

They were with a group of tourists, standing in desert, looking at a pyramid. Cora whined about the heat, and the taste of dry sand in the air.

"It's supposed to be hot, stupid," Jon said. "This is Egypt." He spent most of the trip reading books about the countries they were passing through, and rarely had time for the real thing. It was obvious to Spit that his son was cut out for a university professor.

And Cora, who hated everything, would get married. "I can't see why they don't just tear it down. A lot of hot stone."

Jon sniffed his contempt. "It's a monument. Its something they can look at to remind them of their past.

"Then they ought to drag it into a museum somewhere under a roof. With air conditioning."

Stella said, "Where's Daddy?"

He wasn't anywhere amongst the tourists. No one in the family had seen him leave.

"Maybe he got caught short," Jon said, and sniggered.

Cora stretched her fat neck, to peer. "And he's not in the bus."

The other tourists, too, appeared uneasy. Clearly something was sensed, something was wrong. They shifted, frowned, looked where there was nothing to see. Stella was the first to identify it: somewhere out there, somewhere out on that flat hot sand, that desert, a train was chugging, my God a steam engine was chugging and hissing. People frowned at one another, craned to see. Uneasy feet shifted. Where in all that desert was there a train?

But invisible or not it got closer, louder. Slowing. *Hunph hunph hunph hunph.* Then speeding up, clattering, hissing. When it could have been on top of them all, cutting their limbs off on invisible tracks, the whistle blew like a long clarion howl summoning them to death.

Stella screamed. "Spit! Spit!" She ran across sand into the noise, forgetting to keep arms clamped down against the circles of sweat.

She found him where in the shrill moment of the whistle she'd realized he would be, at the far side of the pyramid, leaning back against the dusty base with his eyes closed. The tape recorder was clutched with both hands against his chest. Old Number One rattled through him like a fever.

When it was over, when he'd turned the machine off, he raised his eyes to her angry face.

"Where is the line?" he said, and raised an eyebrow.

"You're crazy," she said. "Get a hold of yourself." Her eyes banged around in her bony head as if they'd gone out of control. There were witnesses all over this desert, she appeared to be saying, who knew what kind of a fool she had to put up with. He expected her to kick at him like someone trying to rout a dog. Her mouth gulped at the hot air; her throat pumped like desperate gills. Lord, you're an ugly woman, he thought.

The children, of course, refused to speak to him through Israel, Turkey, and France. They passed messages through their mother—"We're starved, let's eat" or "I'm sick of this place"—but they kept their faces turned from him and pretended, in crowds, that they had come alone, without parents. Cora cried a great deal, out of shame. And Jon read a complete six-volume history of Europe. Stella could not waste her anxiety on grudges, for while the others brooded over the memory of his foolishness she saw the same symptoms building up again in his face. She only hoped that this time he would choose some place private.

He chose Anne Hathaway's Cottage in Stratford. They wouldn't have gone there at all if it hadn't been for Jon, who'd read a book on Shakespeare and insisted on seeing the place. "You've dragged me from one rotten dump to another," he said, "now let me see one thing I want to see. She was twenty-six and Shakespeare was only my age when he got her pregnant. That's probably the only reason he married her. Why else would a genius marry an old woman?" Spit bumped his head on the low doorway and said he'd rather stay outside. He couldn't see any point in a monument to a woman like that, anyway. The rest of them were upstairs in the bedroom, looking at the underside of the thatched roof, when Old Number One started chugging her way towards them from somewhere out in the garden.

By the time they got to Ireland, where they would spend the next two weeks with one of her distant cousins, Stella Delaney was beginning to suffer from what she called a case of nerves. She had had all she could take of riding in foreign trains, she said, she was sure she'd been on every crate that ran on tracks in every country of Europe and northern Africa; and now she insisted that they rent a car in Dublin for the drive down to her cousin's, who lived about as far as you get on that island, way out at the end of one of those southwestern peninsulas. "For a change let's ride in style," she said, and pulled her chin to show she meant business. She was missing an important Lodge convention for this. The least he could do, she said, was make it comfortable.

The cousin, a farmer's wife on a mountain slope above Ballinskelligs Bay, agreed. "'Tis a mad life you've been living, sure. Is it some kind of race you're in?"

"It is," Stella said. "But I haven't the foggiest idea who or what we're racing against. Or what is chasing us."

"Ah well," said the cousin, wringing her hands. "God is good. That is one thing you can be certain of. Put your feet up and relax so."

She knew about American men, the cousin told them. You had to watch them when they lost their playthings, or their jobs, they just shrivelled up and died.

Stella looked frightened.

Oh yes, the cousin said. She knew. She'd been to America once as a girl, to New York, and saw all she needed to see of American men.

Spit Delaney thought he would go mad. He saw soon enough that he could stare out this farmhouse window all he wanted and never find what he needed. He could look at sheep grazing in their little, hedged-in patches, and donkey carts passing by, and clumps of furze moving in the wind, he could look at the sloping farms and the miles and miles of flat green bog with its brown carved out gleaming beds and piled-up bricks of turf and at the deep curved bay of Atlantic ocean with spray standing up around the jagged rocks until he was blind from looking, but he'd never see a train of any kind. Nor find an answer. Old Number One was in Ottawa by now, being polished and dusted by some uniformed pimple-faced kid who wouldn't know a piston from a lever.

"We'd've been better off spending the money on a swimming pool," Stella told her cousin. "We might as well have flushed it down the toilet."

"That's dumb," Cora said. She buttered a piece of soda bread and, scooped out a big spoonful of gooseberry jam.

"Feeding your pimples," Jon said. He had clear skin, not a single adolescent blemish, nor any sign of a whisker. Sexually he was a late developer, he explained, and left you to conclude the obvious: he was a genius. Brilliant people didn't have time for a messy adolescence. They were too busy thinking.

"Don't pick on your sister," Stella said. "And be careful or you'll get a prissy mouth. There's nothing worse on a man."

A hollow ache sat in Spit's gut. He couldn't believe these people belonged to him. This family he'd been dragging around all over the face of the earth was as foreign to him as the little old couple who lived in this house. What did the prim sneery boy have to do with him? Or that fat girl. And Stella: behind those red swollen eyes she was as much a stranger to him now as she was on the day he met her. If he walked up behind her and touched her leg, he could expect her to say Get lost mister I got work to do, just as she had then. They hadn't moved a single step closer.

I don't know what's going on, he thought, but something's happening. If we can't touch, in our minds, how can I know you are there? How can I know who you are? If two people can't overlap, just a little, how the hell can they be sure of a goddamn thing?

The next day they asked him to drive in to Cahirciveen, the nearest village, so Jon could have a look around the library and Stella could try on sweaters, which she said were bound to be cheaper since the sheep were so close at hand. Waiting for them, sitting in the little rented car, he watched the people on the narrow crooked street. Fat red-faced women chatted outside shop doors; old men in dark suits stood side by side in front of a bar window looking into space; a tall woman in a black shawl threaded her way down the sidewalk; a fish woman with a cigarette stuck in the middle of her mouth sat with her knees locked around a box of dried mackerel; beside the car a cripple sat right on the concrete with his back to the storefront wall and his head bobbing over a box for tossed coins.

The temptation was too much to resist. He leaned back and closed his eyes, pressed the button, and turned the volume up full. Old Number One came alive again, throbbed through him, swelled to become the whole world. His hand shifted levers, his foot kicked back from a back-spray of steam, his fingers itched to yank the whistle-cord. Then, when it blew, when the old steam whistle cut right through his core, he could have died happily.

But he didn't die. Stella was at the window, screaming at him, clawing at the recorder against his chest. A finger caught at the strap and it went flying out onto the street. The whistle died abruptly, all sound stopped. Her face, horrified, glowing red, appeared to be magnified a hundred times. Other faces, creased and toothless, whiskered, stared through glass. It appeared that the whole street had come running to see him, this maniac.

Stella, blushing, tried to be pleasant, dipped apologies, smiled grimly as she went around to her side of the car.

If her Lodge should hear of this. Or her mother.

The chin, tucked back, was ready to quiver. She would cry this time, and that would be the worst of all. Stella, crying, was unbearable.

But she didn't cry. She was furious. "You stupid stupid man," she said, as soon as she'd slammed the door. "You stupid stupid man."

He got out to rescue his recorder, which had skidded across the sidewalk almost to the feet of the bobbing cripple. When he bent to pick it up, the little man's eyes met his, dully, for a moment, then shifted away.

Jon refused to ride home with them. He stuck his nose in the air, swung his narrow shoulders, and headed down the street with a book shoved into his armpit. He'd walk the whole way back to the cousin's, he said, before he'd ride with them.

She sat silent and bristling while he drove out past the last grey buildings and the Co-op dairy and the first few stony farms. She scratched scales of skin off the dry eczema patches that were spreading on her hands. Then, when they were rushing down between rows of high blooming fuchsia bushes, she asked him what he thought she was supposed to be getting out of this trip.

"Tomorrow," he said. "Tomorrow we go home."

Spit Delaney had never travelled off the Island more than twice before in his life, both those times to see a doctor on the mainland about the cast in his eye. Something told him a once-in-a-lifetime trip to Europe ought to have been more than it was. Something told him he'd been cheated. Cheated in a single summer out of Old Number One, his saved-up overtime money, the tourist's rightfully expected fun, and now out of wife as well. For the first thing she told him when the plane landed on home territory was this: "Maybe we ought to start thinking about a separation. This is no marriage at all anymore."

He stopped at the house only long enough to drop them off, then fled for the coast, his ears refusing the sounds of her words.

But it was a wet day, and the beach was almost deserted. A few seagulls slapped around on the sand, or hovered by tide pools. Trees, already distorted and one-sided from a lifetime of assaults, bent even farther away from the wind. A row of yellowish seaweed, rolled and tangled with pieces of bark and chunks of wood, lay like a continuous windrow along the uneven line of last night's highest tide. Far out on the sand an old couple walked, leaning on each other, bundled up in toques and Cowichan sweaters and gum boots. The ocean was first a low lacy line on sand, then sharp chopped waves like ploughed furrows, then nothing but haze and mist, a thick blending with uncertain sky.

There was no magic here. No traffic, no transformations. No Kanikiluk in sight. He'd put ninety miles on the camper for nothing. He might as well have curled up in a corner of the old gas station, amongst the car parts, or sat in behind the wheel of his tow truck to brood. The world was out to cheat him wherever he turned.

Still, he walked out, all the way out in the cold wind to the edge of the sea, and met a naked youth coming up out of the waves to greet him.

"Swimming?" Spit said, and frowned. "Don't you tell me it's warm when you get used to it, boy, I can see by the way you're all shrivelled up that you're nearly froze."

The youth denied nothing. He raised both arms to the sky as if expecting to ascend, water streaming from his long hair and beard and his crotch, forming in beads in the hairs, shining on goose-bumped skin. Then he tilted his head.

"Don't I know you?".

"Not me," Spit said. "I don't live here."

"Me neither," the youth said. "Me and some other guys been camping around that point over there all summer, I go swimming twice a day."

Spit put both hands in his pockets, planted his feet apart, and stretched his long neck. He kept his gaze far out to sea, attempting to bore through that mist. "I just come down for a look at this here ocean."

"Sure, man," the youth said. "I *do* know you. You let me use your can."

"What? What's that?" Why couldn't the kid just move on? You had to be alone sometimes, other people only complicated things.

"I was waiting for a ride, to come up here, and I come to your house to use the can. Hell, man, you gave me a beer and sat me down and told me your whole life story. When I came out my friend had gone without me."

Spit looked at the youth's face. He remembered someone, he remembered the youth on that hot day, but there was nothing in his face that he recognized. It was as if when he'd stripped off his clothes he'd also stripped off whatever it was that would make his face different from a thousand others.

"You know what they found out there, don't you?" the youth said. He turned to face the ocean with Spit. "Out there they found this crack that runs all around the ocean floor. Sure, man, they say it's squeezing lava out like toothpaste all the time. Runs all the way around the outside edge of this ocean."

"What?" Spit said. "What are you talking about?"

"Squirting lava up out of the centre of the earth! Pushing the continents farther and farther apart! Don't that blow your mind?"

"Look," Spit said. But he lost the thought that had occurred.

"Pushing and pushing. Dividing the waters. Like that what-was-it right back there at the beginning of things. And there it is, right out there somewhere, a bloody big seam. Spreading and pushing."

"You can't believe them scientists," Spit said. "They like to scare you."

"I thought I recognized you. You pulled two beer out of the fridge, snapped off the caps, and put them on the table. Use the can, you said, and when you come out this'll wash the dust from your throat. You must've kept me there the whole afternoon, talking."

"Well, nobody's stopping you now. Nobody's forcing you to stay. Go on up and get dressed." If all he came up out of that ocean to tell about was a crack, he might as well go back in.

Which he did, on the run.

Straight back through ankle-foam, into breakers, out into waves. A black head, bobbing; he could be a seal, watching the shore.

Go looking for your crack, he wanted to shout. Go help push the continents apart. Help split the goddamned world in two.

"There's no reason why we can't do this in a friendly fashion," Stella said when he got home. "It's not as if we hate each other. We simply want to make a convenient arrangement. I phoned a lawyer while you were out."

She came down the staircase backwards, on her hands and knees, scrubbing, her rear end swinging to the rhythm of her arm. Stella was death on dirt, especially when she was upset.

"Don't be ridiculous," Spit said. "This isn't Hollywood, this is *us*. We survived all that crap."

She turned on the bottom step, sat back, and pushed her hair away from her eyes. "Not quite survived. It just waited until we were off guard, until we thought we were home-safe."

He could puke.

Or hit her.

"But there isn't any home-safe, Spit. And this *is* Hollywood, the world has shrunk, it's changed, even here." She tapped the pointed wooden scrub brush on the step, to show where here was.

Spit fingered the cassette in his pocket. She'd smashed his machine. He'd have to buy a new one, or go without.

"Lady," he said, "that flat-assed logger don't know what a close call he had. If he'd've known he'd be thanking me every day of his life."

Though he didn't mean it.

Prying him loose from Stella would be like prying off his arm. He'd got used to her, and couldn't imagine how he'd live without her.

Her mother sat in her flowered armchair and scowled out over her bulging eyeballs at him as if she were trying to see straight to his centre and burn what she found. Her mouth chewed on unintelligible sounds.

"This is my bad year," he said. "First they take away Old Number One, and now this. The only things that mattered to me. Real things."

"Real!" the old woman screeched, threw up her hands, and slapped them down again on her skinny thighs. She laughed, squinted her eyes at the joke, then blinked them open again, bulged them out, and pursed her lips. Well, have we got news for you, she seemed to be saying. She could hardly wait for Stella's answer.

"The only things you can say that about," Stella said, "are the things that people can't touch, or wreck. Truth is like that, I imagine, if there is such a thing."

The old woman nodded, nodded: That'll show you, that'll put you in your place. Spit could wring her scrawny neck.

"You!" he said. "What do you know about anything?"

The old woman pulled back, alarmed. Her big eyes filled with tears, her hand dug into the folds of her dress. The lips moved, muttered, mumbled things at the window, at the door, at her own pointed knees. Then suddenly she leaned ahead again, seared a scowl into him. "All a mirage!" she shrieked, and looked frightened by her own words. She drew back, swallowed, gathered courage again. "Blink your eyes and it's gone, or moved!"

Spit and Stella looked at each other. Stella raised an eyebrow. "That's enough, Mother," she said. Gently.

"Everybody said we had a good marriage," he said. "Spit and Stella, solid as rocks."

"If you had a good marriage," the old woman accused, "it was with your train, not a woman." And looked away, pointed her chin elsewhere.

Stella leapt up, snorting, and hurried out of the room with her bucket of soapy water.

Spit felt, he said, like he'd been dragged under the house by a couple of dogs and fought over. He had to lie down. And, lying down, he had to face up to what was happening. She came into the bedroom and stood at the foot of her bed. She puffed up her cheeks like a blowfish and fixed her eyes on him.

"I told the lawyer there was no fighting involved. I told him it was a friendly separation. But he said one of us better get out of the house all the same, live in a motel or something until it's arranged. He said you."

"Not me," he said. "I'll stay put, thank you."

"Then I'll go." Her face floated back, wavered in his watery vision, then came ahead again.

"I'd call that desertion," he said.

"You wouldn't dare."

And of course he wouldn't. It was no more and no less then what he'd expected, after everything else, if he thought about it.

All he wanted to do was put his cassette tape into a machine, lie back, close his eyes, and let the sounds of Old Number One rattle through him. That was all he wanted. When she'd gone he would drive into town and buy a new machine.

"I'll leave the place clean," she said. "I'll leave food in the fridge when I go, in a few days. Do you think you can learn how to cook?"

"I don't know," he said. "How should I know? I don't even believe this is happening. I can't even think what it's going to be like."

"You'll get used to it. You've had twenty years of one kind of life, you'll get used to another."

Spit put his head back on the pillow. There wasn't a thing he could reach out and touch and be sure of.

At the foot of his obsolete B/A sign, Spit on his rock watches the hitchhikers spread out along the roadside like a pack of ragged refugees. Between him and them there is a ditch clogged with dry podded broom and a wild tangle of honeysuckle and blackberry vines. They perch on their packs, lean against the telephone pole, lie out flat on the gravel; every one of them indifferent to the sun, the traffic, to one another. We have all day, their postures say, we have forever. If you won't pick us up, someone else just as good will do it, nobody needs you.

Spit can remember a time when he tried to have a pleading look on his face whenever he was out on the road. A look that said Please pick me up I may die if I don't get where I'm going on time. And made obscene gestures at every driver that passed him by. Sometimes hollered insults. These people, though, don't care enough to look hopeful. It doesn't matter to them if they get picked up or not, because they think where they're going isn't the slightest bit different from where they are now. Like bits of dry leaves, letting the wind blow them whatever way it wants.

The old bearded man notices Spit, raises a hand to his forehead in greeting. His gaze runs up the pole, flickers over the weathered sign, and runs down again. He gives Spit a grin, a slight shake of his head, turns away. Old fool, Spit thinks. At your age. And lifts his engineer cap to settle it farther back.

Spit cannot bear to think where these people are going, where their rides will take them. His mind touches, slides away from the boy with the St Bernard, sitting up against the back of that green pickup cab. He could follow them, in his mind he could go the whole distance with them, but he refuses, slides back from it, holds onto the things that are happening here and now.

The sound of Stella's shoes shifting in gravel. The scent of the pines, leaking pitch. The hot smell of sun on the rusted pole.

"I've left my phone number on the memo pad, on the counter."

The feel of the small pebbles under his boots.

"Jon and Cora'll take turns, on the weekends. Don't be scared to make Cora do your shopping when she's here. She knows how to look for things, you'll only get yourself cheated."

He'd yell *Okay*!

He holds on. He thinks of tourists filing through the National Museum, looking at Old Number One. People he'll never see, from Ottawa and Toronto and New York and for all he knows from Africa and Russia, standing around Old Number One, talking about her, pointing, admiring the black shine of her finish. Kids wondering what it would be like to ride in her, feel the thudding of her pistons under you.

He'd stand at the edge of the water and yell *Okay you son of a bitch, okay*!

"It don't look like there's going to be any complications. My lawyer can hardly believe how friendly all this's been. It'll all go by smooth as sailing."

Spit Delaney sees himself get up into the pickup with the youth and the St Bernard, sees himself slide his ass right up against the cab, slam his hand in a signal on the hot metal roof. Sees himself going down that silver-grey road, heading west. Sees himself laughing.

He says, "My lawyer says if it's all so goddamned friendly how come you two are splitting up."

"That's just it," she says. "Friends are one thing. You don't have to be married to be a friend."

"I don't know what you're talking about," Spit says. It occurs to him that he has come home from a trip through Europe and northern Africa and can't remember a thing. Something happened there, but what was it?

He sees himself riding in that pickup all up through the valley farmlands, over the mountains in the centre of the island, down along the lakes and rivers, snaking across towards the Pacific. Singing, maybe, with that boy. Throwing his arm around the floppy dog's ugly neck. Feeling the air change gradually to damp, and colder. Straining his neck to see.

"I got my Lodge tonight, so I better get going, it'll give me the day to get settled in, it takes time to unpack. You'll be all right?"

Sees himself hopping off the green pickup, amongst the distorted combed-back spruce, the giant salal, sees himself touching the boy goodbye, patting the dog. Sees himself go down through the logs, through the white dry sand, over the damp brown sand and the seaweed. Sees himself at the water's edge on his long bony legs like someone who's just grown them, unsteady, shouting.

Shouting into the blind heavy roar.

Okay!

Okay you son of a bitch!

I'm stripped now, okay, now where is that goddamned line?

1976

Margaret Atwood

b. 1939

Born in Ottawa, Margaret Atwood moved with her family to Sault Ste Marie in 1945 and to Toronto a year later. She was educated at the University of Toronto, Radcliffe College, and Harvard University. A prolific author in every genre, she has written fourteen novels, more than a dozen collections of poetry, five volumes of short fiction, and three of criticism, as well as scripts, libretti, and books for children. Two of her novels, *Surfacing* (1972) and *The Handmaid's Tale* (1985), have been made into films. She has received numerous awards, including the Governor General's Award (twice) and the Molson Prize. Her novel *Alias Grace* (1996) was awarded the Giller Prize for Fiction, and *The Blind Assassin* (2000) won the Booker Prize. The daughter of an entomologist who specialized in forest insects, she spent much of her childhood in the bush country of northern Ontario and Quebec. "Death By Landscape" from the collection *Wilderness Tips* (1991), speaks to her intensely informed knowledge of the Canadian landscape. The experience of working as a summer camp counsellor, first on Georgian Bay and later in the Haliburton region of Ontario, provided background detail for her stories, including an incident of a child drowning. Atwood's ability to turn landscape into symbol is evident in her foreword to *Charles Pachter*, a collection of the painter's work. She writes: "The recognition of the gap between smooth presentation and dangerous, complex reality is not, of course, unique to Pachter. . . . This is the environment in which Pachter grew up, then: a Canada noted for its niceness, a bland surface which concealed a wildness, a Gothic weirdness, even a menace. Any Canadian . . . knows that under the surface of the lake there's someone drowning." Atwood and her husband, novelist Graeme Gibson, were among the founders of the Writers' Union of Canada and the Canadian Centre (English speaking) of International PEN.

Death by Landscape

Now that the boys are grown up and Rob is dead, Lois has moved to a condominium apartment in one of the newer waterfront developments. She is relieved not to have to worry about the lawn, or about the ivy pushing its muscular little suckers into the brickwork, or the squirrels gnawing their way into the attic and eating the insulation off the wiring, or about strange noises. This building has a security system, and the only plant life is in pots in the solarium.

Lois is glad she's been able to find an apartment big enough for her pictures. They are more crowded together than they were in the house, but this arrangement gives the walls a European look: blocks of pictures, above and beside one another, rather than one over the chesterfield, one over the fireplace, one in the front hall, in the old acceptable manner of sprinkling art around so it does not get too intrusive. This way has more of an impact. You know it's not supposed to be furniture.

None of the pictures is very large, which doesn't mean they aren't valuable. They are paintings, or sketches and drawings, by artists who were not nearly as well known when Lois began to buy them as they are now. Their work later turned up on stamps, or as silk-screen reproductions hung in the principals' offices of high schools, or as jigsaw puzzles, or on beautifully printed calendars sent out by corporations as Christmas gifts, to their less important clients. These artists painted mostly in the twenties and thirties and forties; they painted landscapes. Lois has two Tom Thomsons, three A.Y. Jacksons, a Lawren Harris. She has an Arthur Lismer, she has a J.E.H. MacDonald. She has a David Milne. They are pictures of convoluted tree trunks on an island of pink wave-smoothed stone, with more islands behind; of a lake with rough, bright, sparsely wooded cliffs; of a vivid river shore with a tangle of bush and two beached canoes, one red, one grey; of a yellow autumn woods with the ice-blue gleam of a pond half-seen through the interlaced branches.

It was Lois who'd chosen them. Rob had no interest in art, although he could see the necessity of having something on the walls. He left all the decorating decisions to her, while providing the money, of course. Because of this collection of hers, Lois's friends—especially the men—have given her the reputation of having a good nose for art investments.

But this is not why she bought the pictures, way back then. She bought them because she wanted them. She wanted something that was in them, although she could not have said at the time what it was. It was not peace: she does not find them peaceful in the least. Looking at them fills her with a wordless unease. Despite the fact that there are no people in them or even animals, it's as if there is something, or someone, looking back out.

⟜○⟝

When she was thirteen, Lois went on a canoe trip. She'd only been on overnights before. This was to be a long one, into the trackless wilderness, as Cappie put it. It was Lois's first canoe trip, and her last.

Cappie was the head of the summer camp to which Lois had been sent ever since she was nine. Camp Manitou, it was called; it was one of the better ones, for girls, though not the best. Girls of her age whose parents could afford it were routinely packed off to such camps, which bore a generic resemblance to one another. They favoured Indian names and had hearty, energetic leaders, who were called Cappie or Skip or Scottie. At these camps you learned to swim well and sail, and paddle a canoe, and perhaps ride a horse or play tennis. When you weren't doing these things you could do Arts and Crafts and turn out dingy, lumpish clay ashtrays for your mother—mothers smoked more, then—or bracelets made of coloured braided string.

⊸o⊷

Cheerfulness was required at all times, even at breakfast. Loud shouting and the banging of spoons on the tables were allowed, and even encouraged, at ritual intervals. Chocolate bars were rationed, to control tooth decay and pimples. At night, after supper, in the dining hall or outside around a mosquito-infested campfire ring for special treats, there were singsongs. Lois can still remember all the words to "My Darling Clementine," and to "My Bonnie Lies Over the Ocean," with acting-out gestures: a rippling of the hands for "the ocean," two hands together under the cheek for "lies." She will never be able to forget them, which is a sad thought.

Lois thinks she can recognize women who went to these camps, and were good at it. They have a hardness to their handshakes, even now; a way of standing, legs planted firmly and farther apart than usual; a way of sizing you up, to see if you'd be any good in a canoe—the front, not the back. They themselves would be in the back. They would call it the stern.

She knows that such camps still exist, although Camp Manitou does not. They are one of the few things that haven't changed much. They now offer copper enamelling, and functionless pieces of stained glass baked in electric ovens, though judging from the productions of her friends' grandchildren the artistic standards have not improved.

To Lois, encountering it in the first year after the war, Camp Manitou seemed ancient. Its log-sided buildings with the white cement in between the half-logs, its flagpole ringed with whitewashed stones, its weathered grey dock jutting out into Lake Prospect, with its woven rope bumpers and its rusty rings for tying up, its prim round flowerbed of petunias near the office door, must surely have been there always. In truth it dated only from the first decade of the century; it had been founded by Cappie's parents, who'd thought of camping as bracing to the character, like cold showers, and had been passed along to her as an inheritance, and an obligation.

Lois realized, later, that it must have been a struggle for Cappie to keep Camp Manitou going, during the Depression and then the war, when money did not flow freely. If it had been a camp for the very rich, instead of the merely well off, there would have been fewer problems. But there must have been enough Old Girls, ones with daughters, to keep the thing in operation, though not entirely shipshape: furniture was battered, painted trim was peeling, roofs leaked. There were dim photographs of these Old Girls dotted around the dining hall, wearing ample woollen bathing suits and showing their fat, dimpled legs, or standing, arms twined, in odd tennis outfits with baggy skirts.

In the dining hall, over the stone fireplace that was never used, there was a huge moulting stuffed moose head, which looked somehow carnivorous. It was a sort of mascot; its name was Monty Manitou. The older campers spread the story that it was haunted, and came to life in the dark, when the feeble and undependable lights had been turned off or, due to yet another generator failure, had gone out. Lois was afraid of it at first, but not after she got used to it.

Cappie was the same: you had to get used to her. Possibly she was forty, or thirty-five, or fifty. She had fawn-coloured hair that looked as if it was cut with a bowl. Her head jutted forward, jigging like a chicken's as she strode around the camp, clutching notebooks and checking things off in them. She was like their minister in church: both of them smiled a lot and were anxious because they wanted things to go well; they both had the same overwashed skins and stringy necks. But all this disappeared when Cappie was leading a singsong, or otherwise leading. Then she was happy, sure of herself, her plain face almost luminous. She wanted to cause joy. At these times she was loved, at others merely trusted.

There were many things Lois didn't like about Camp Manitou, at first. She hated the noisy chaos and spoon-banging of the dining hall, the rowdy singsongs at which you were expected to yell in order to show that you were enjoying yourself. Hers was not a household that encouraged yelling. She hated the necessity of having to write dutiful letters to her parents claiming she was having fun. She could not complain, because camp cost so much money.

She didn't much like having to undress in a roomful of other girls, even in the dim light, although nobody paid any attention, or sleeping in a cabin with seven other girls: some of whom snored because they had adenoids or colds, some of whom had nightmares, or wet their beds and cried about it. Bottom bunks made her feel closed in, and she was afraid of falling out of top ones; she was afraid of heights. She got homesick, and suspected her parents of having a better time when she wasn't there than when she was, although her mother wrote to her every week saying how much they missed her. All this was when she was nine. By the time she was thirteen she liked it. She was an old hand by then.

⁂

Lucy was her best friend at camp. Lois had other friends in winter, when there was school and itchy woollen clothing and darkness in the afternoons, but Lucy was her summer friend.

She turned up the second year, when Lois was ten, and a Bluejay. (Chickadees, Bluejays, Ravens, and Kingfishers—these were the names Camp Manitou assigned to the different age groups, a sort of totemic clan system. In those days, thinks Lois, it was birds for girls, animals for boys: wolves, and so forth. Though some animals and birds were suitable and some were not. Never vultures, for instance; never skunks, or rats.)

Lois helped Lucy to unpack her tin trunk and place the folded clothes on the wooden shelves, and to make up her bed. She put her in the top bunk right above her, where she could keep an eye on her. Already she knew that Lucy was an exception, to a good many rules; already she felt proprietorial.

Lucy was from the United States, where the comic books came from, and the movies. She wasn't from New York or Hollywood or Buffalo, the only American cities Lois knew the names of, but from Chicago. Her house was on the lakeshore and had gates to it, and grounds. They had a maid, all of the time. Lois's family only had a cleaning lady twice a week.

The only reason Lucy was being sent to *this* camp (she cast a look of minor scorn around the cabin, diminishing it and also offending Lois, while at the same time daunting her) was that her mother had been a camper here. Her mother had been a Canadian once, but had married her father, who had a patch over one eye, like a pirate. She showed Lois the pictures of him in her wallet. He got the patch in the war. "Shrapnel," said Lucy. Lois, who was unsure about shrapnel, was so impressed she could only grunt. Her own two-eyed, unwounded father was tame by comparison.

"My father plays golf," she ventured at last.

"*Everyone* plays golf," said Lucy. "My *mother* plays golf."

Lois's mother did not. Lois took Lucy to see the outhouses and the swimming dock and the dining hall with Monty Manitou's baleful head, knowing in advance they would not measure up.

This was a bad beginning; but Lucy was good-natured, and accepted Camp Manitou with the same casual shrug with which she seemed to accept everything. She would make the best of it, without letting Lois forget that this was what she was doing.

However, there were things Lois knew that Lucy did not. Lucy scratched the tops off all her mosquito bites and had to be taken to the infirmary to be daubed with Ozonol. She took her T-shirt off while sailing, and although the counsellor spotted her after a while and made her put it back on, she burnt spectacularly, bright red, with the X of her bathing-suit straps standing out in alarming white; she let Lois peel the sheets of whispery-thin burned skin off her shoulders. When they sang "Alouette" around the campfire, she did not know any of the French words. The difference was that Lucy did not care about the things she didn't know, whereas Lois did.

During the next winter, and subsequent winters, Lucy and Lois wrote to each other. They were both only children, at a time when this was thought to be a disadvantage, so in their letters they pretended to be sisters, or even twins. Lois had to strain a little over this, because Lucy was so blond, with translucent skin and large blue eyes like a doll's, and Lois was nothing out of the ordinary—just a tallish, thinnish, brownish person with freckles. They signed their letters LL, with the L's entwined together like the monograms on a towel. (Lois and Lucy, thinks Lois. How our names date us. Lois Lane, Superman's girlfriend, enterprising female reporter; "I Love Lucy." Now we are obsolete, and it's little Jennifers, little Emilys, little Alexandras and Carolines and Tiffanys.)

They were more effusive in their letters than they ever were in person. They bordered their pages with X's and O's, but when they met again in the summers it was always a shock. They had changed so much, or Lucy had. It was like watching someone grow up in jolts. At first it would be hard to think up things to say.

But Lucy always had a surprise or two, something to show, some marvel to reveal. The first year she had a picture of herself in a tutu, her hair in a ballerina's knot on the top of her head; she pirouetted around the swimming dock, to show Lois how it was done, and almost fell off. The next year she had given that up and was taking horseback riding. (Camp Manitou did not have horses.) The next year her mother and father had been divorced, and she had a new stepfather, one with both eyes, and a new house, although the maid was the same. The next year, when they had graduated from Bluejays and entered Ravens, she got her period, right in the first week of camp. The two of them snitched some matches from their counsellor, who smoked illegally, and made a small fire out behind the farthest outhouse, at dusk, using their flashlights. They could set all kinds of fires by now; they had learned how in Campcraft. On this fire they burned one of Lucy's used sanitary napkins. Lois is not sure why they did this, or whose idea it was. But she can remember the feeling of deep satisfaction it gave her as the white fluff singed and the blood sizzled, as if some wordless ritual had been fulfilled.

They did not get caught, but then they rarely got caught at any of their camp transgressions. Lucy had such large eyes, and was such an accomplished liar.

This year Lucy is different again: slower, more languorous. She is no longer interested in sneaking around after dark, purloining cigarettes from the counsellor, dealing in black-market candy bars. She is pensive, and hard to wake in the mornings. She doesn't like her stepfather, but she doesn't want to live with her real father either, who has a new wife. She thinks her mother may be having a love affair with a doctor; she doesn't know for sure, but she's seen them smooching in his car, out on the driveway, when her stepfather wasn't there. It serves him right. She hates her private school. She has a boyfriend, who is sixteen and works as a gardener's assistant. This is how she met him: in the garden. She describes to Lois what it is like when he kisses her—rubbery at first, but then your knees go limp. She has been forbidden to see him, and threatened with boarding school. She wants to run away from home.

Lois has little to offer in return. Her own life is placid and satisfactory, but there is nothing much that can be said about happiness. "You're so lucky," Lucy tells her, a little smugly. She might as well say *boring* because this is how it makes Lois feel.

Lucy is apathetic about the canoe trip, so Lois has to disguise her own excitement. The evening before they are to leave, she slouches into the campfire ring as if coerced, and sits down with a sigh of endurance, just as Lucy does.

Every canoe trip that went out of camp was given a special send-off by Cappie and the section leader and counsellors, with the whole section in attendance. Cappie painted three streaks of red across each of her cheeks with a lipstick. They looked like three-fingered claw marks. She put a blue circle on her forehead with fountain-pen ink, and tied a twisted bandanna around her head and struck a row of frazzle-ended feathers around it, and wrapped herself in a red-and-black Hudson's Bay blanket. The counsellors, also in blankets but with only two streaks of red, beat on tom-toms made of round wooden cheese boxes with leather stretched over the top and nailed in place. Cappie was Chief Cappeosota. They all had to say "How!" when she walked into the circle and stood there with one hand raised.

Looking back on this, Lois finds it disquieting. She knows too much about Indians: this is why. She knows, for instance, that they should not even be called Indians, and that they have enough worries without other people taking their names and dressing up as them. It has all been a form of stealing.

But she remembers too, that she was once ignorant of this. Once she loved the campfire, the flickering of light on the ring of faces, the sound of the fake tom-toms, heavy and fast like a scared heartbeat; she loved Cappie in a red blanket and feathers, solemn, as a chief should be, raising her hand and saying, "Greetings, my Ravens." It was not funny, it was not making fun. She wanted to be an Indian. She wanted to be adventurous and pure, and aboriginal.

"You go on big water," says Cappie. This is her idea—all their ideas—of how Indians talk. "You go where no man has ever trod. You go many moons." This is not true. They are only going for a week, not many moons. The canoe route is clearly marked, they have gone over it on a map, and there are prepared campsites with names which are used year after year. But when Cappie says this—and despite the way Lucy rolls up her eyes—Lois can feel the water stretching out, with the shores twisting away on either side, immense and a little frightening.

"You bring back much wampum," says Cappie. "Do good in war, my braves, and capture many scalps." This is another of her pretences: that they are boys, and bloodthirsty. But such a game cannot be played by substituting the word "squaw." It would not work at all.

Each of them has to stand up and step forward and have a red line drawn across her cheeks by Cappie. She tells them they must follow the paths of their ancestors (who most certainly, thinks Lois, looking out the window of her apartment and remembering the family stash of daguerreotypes and sepia-coloured portraits on her mother's dressing table, the stiff-shirted, black-coated, grim-faced men and the beflounced women with their severe hair and their corseted respectability, would never have considered heading off onto an open lake, in a canoe, just for fun).

At the end of the ceremony they all stood and held hands around the circle, and sang taps. This did not sound very Indian, thinks Lois. It sounded like a bugle call at a military post, in a movie. But Cappie was never one to be much concerned with consistency, or with archaeology.

After breakfast the next morning they set out from the main dock, in four canoes, three in each. The lipstick stripes have not come off completely, and still show faintly pink, like healing burns. They wear their white denim sailing hats, because of the sun, and thin-striped T-shirts, and pale baggy shorts with the cuffs rolled up. The middle one kneels, propping her rear end against the rolled sleeping bags. The counsellors going with them are Pat and Kip. Kip is no-nonsense; Pat is easier to wheedle, or fool.

There are puffy clouds and a small breeze. Glints come from the little waves. Lois is in the bow of Kip's canoe. She still can't do a J-stroke very well, and she will have to be in the bow or the middle for the whole trip. Lucy is behind her; her own J-stroke is even worse. She splashes Lois with her paddle, quite a big splash.

"I'll get you back," says Lois.

"There was a stable fly on your shoulder," Lucy says.

Lois turns to look at her, to see if she's grinning. They're in the habit of splashing each other. Back there, the camp has vanished behind the first long point of rock and rough trees. Lois feels as if an invisible rope has been broken. They're floating free, on their own, cut loose. Beneath the canoe the lake goes down deeper and colder than it was a minute before.

"No horsing around in the canoe," says Kip. She's rolled her T-shirt sleeves up to the shoulder; her arms are brown and sinewy, her jaw determined, her stroke perfect. She looks as if she knows exactly what she is doing.

The four canoes keep close together. They sing, raucously and with defiance; they sing "The Quartermaster's Store," and "Clementine," and "Alouette." It is more like bellowing than singing.

After that the wind grows much stronger, blowing slantwise against the bows, and they have to put all their energy into shoving themselves through the water.

Was there anything important, anything that would provide some sort of reason or clue to what happened next? Lois can remember everything, every detail; but it does her no good.

They stopped at noon for a swim and lunch, and went on in the afternoon. At last they reached Little Birch, which was the first campsite for overnight. Lois and Lucy made the fire, while the others pitched the heavy canvas tents. The fireplace was already there, flat stones piled into a U. A burned tin can and a beer bottle had been left in it. Their fire went out, and they had to restart it. "Hustle your bustle," said Kip. "We're starving."

The sun went down, and in the pink sunset light they brushed their teeth and spat the toothpaste froth into the lake. Kip and Pat put all the food that wasn't in cans into a packsack and slung it into a tree, in case of bears.

Lois and Lucy weren't sleeping in a tent. They'd begged to be allowed to sleep out; that way they could talk without the others hearing. If it rained, they told Kip, they promised not to crawl dripping into the tent over everyone's legs: they would get under the canoes. So they were out on the point.

Lois tried to get comfortable inside her sleeping bag, which smelled of musty storage and of earlier campers, a stale salty sweetness. She curled herself up, with her sweater rolled up under her head for a pillow and her flashlight inside her sleeping bag so it wouldn't roll away. The muscles of her sore arms were making small pings, like rubber bands breaking.

Beside her Lucy was rustling around. Lois could see the glimmering oval of her white face.

"I've got a rock poking into my back," said Lucy.

"So do I," said Lois. "You want to go into the tent?" She herself didn't, but it was right to ask.

"No," said Lucy. She subsided into her sleeping bag. After a moment she said. "It would be nice not to go back."

"To camp?" said Lois.

"To Chicago," said Lucy. "I hate it there."

"What about your boyfriend?" said Lois. Lucy didn't answer. She was either asleep or pretending to be.

There was a moon, and a movement of the trees. In the sky there were stars, layers of stars that went down and down. Kip said that when the stars were bright like that instead of hazy it meant bad weather later on. Out on the lake there were two loons, calling to each other in their insane, mournful voices. At the time it did not sound like grief. It was just background.

The lake in the morning was flat calm. They skimmed along over the glassy surface, leaving V-shaped trails behind them; it felt like flying. As the sun rose higher it got hot, almost too hot. There were stable flies in the canoes, landing on a bare arm or leg for a quick sting. Lois hoped for wind.

They stopped for lunch at the next of the named campsites, Lookout Point. It was called this because, although the site itself was down near the water on a flat shelf of rock, there was a sheer cliff nearby and a trail that led up to the top. The top was the lookout, although what you were supposed to see from there was not clear. Kip said it was just a view.

Lois and Lucy decided to make the climb anyway. They didn't want to hang around waiting for lunch. It wasn't their turn to cook, though they hadn't avoided much by not doing it, because cooking lunch was no big deal, it was just unwrapping the cheese and getting out the bread and peanut butter, but Pat and Kip always had to do their woodsy act and boil up a billy tin for their own tea.

They told Kip where they were going. You had to tell Kip where you were going, even if it was only a little way into the woods to get dry twigs for kindling. You could never go anywhere without a buddy.

"Sure," said Kip, who was crouching over the fire, feeding driftwood into it. "Fifteen minutes to lunch."

"Where are they off to?" said Pat. She was bringing their billy tin of water from the lake.

"Lookout," said Kip.

"Be careful," said Pat. She said it as an afterthought, because it was what she always said.

"They're old hands," Kip said.

Lois looks at her watch: it's ten to twelve. She is the watch-minder; Lucy is careless of time. They walk up the path, which is dry earth and rocks, big rounded pinky-grey boulders or split-open ones with jagged edges. Spindly balsam and spruce trees grow to either side, the lake is blue fragments to the left. The sun is right overhead; there are no shadows anywhere. The heat comes up at them as well as down. The forest is dry and crackly.

It isn't far, but it's a steep climb and they're sweating when they reach the top. They wipe their faces with their bare arms, sit gingerly down on a scorching-hot rock, five feet from the edge but too close for Lois. It's a lookout all right, a sheer drop to the lake and a long view over the water, back the way they've come. It's amazing to Lois that they've travelled so far, over all that water, with nothing to propel them but their own arms. It makes her feel strong. There are all kinds of things she is capable of doing.

"It would be quite a dive off here," says Lucy.

"You'd have to be nuts," says Lois.

"Why?" says Lucy. "It's really deep. It goes straight down." She stands up and takes a step nearer the edge. Lois gets a stab in her midriff, the kind she gets when a car goes too fast over a bump. "Don't," she says.

"Don't what?" says Lucy, glancing around at her mischievously. She knows how Lois feels about heights. But she turns back. "I really have to pee," she says.

"You have toilet paper?" says Lois, who is never without it. She digs in her shorts pocket.

"Thanks," says Lucy.

They are both adept at peeing in the woods: doing it fast so the mosquitoes don't get you, the underwear pulled up between the knees, the squat with the feet apart so you don't wet your legs, facing downhill. The exposed feeling of your bum, as if someone is looking at you from behind. The etiquette when you're with someone else is not to look. Lois stands up and starts to walk back down the path, to be out of sight.

"Wait for me?" says Lucy.

Lois climbed down, over and around the boulders, until she could not see Lucy; she waited. She could hear the voices of the others, talking and laughing, down near the shore. One voice was yelling, "Ants! Ants!" Someone must have sat on an ant hill. Off to the side, in the woods, a raven was croaking, a hoarse single note.

She looked at her watch: it was noon. This is when she heard the shout.

She has gone over and over it in her mind since, so many times that the first, real shout has been obliterated, like a footprint trampled by other footprints. But she is sure (she is almost positive, she is nearly certain) that it was not a shout of fear. Not a scream. More like a cry of surprise, cut off too soon. Short, like a dog's bark.

"Lucy?" Lois said. Then she called "Lucy!" By now she was clambering back up, over the stones of the path. Lucy was not up there. Or she was not in sight.

"Stop fooling around," Lois said. "It's lunchtime." But Lucy did not rise from behind the rock or step out, smiling, from behind a tree. The sunlight was all around; the rocks looked white. "This isn't funny!" Lois said, and it wasn't, panic was rising in her, the panic of a small child who does not know where the bigger ones are hidden. She could hear her own heart. She looked quickly around; she lay down on the ground and looked over the edge of the cliff. It made her feel cold. There was nothing.

She went back down the path, stumbling; she was breathing too quickly; she was too frightened to cry. She felt terrible—guilty and dismayed, as if she had done something very bad, by mistake. Something that could never be repaired. "Lucy's gone," she told Kip.

Kip looked up from her fire, annoyed. The water in the billy can was boiling. "What do you mean, gone?" she said. "Where did she go?"

"I don't know," said Lois. "She's just gone."

No one had heard the shout, but then no one had heard Lois calling, either. They had been talking among themselves, by the water.

Kip and Pat went up to the lookout and searched and called, and blew their whistles. Nothing answered.

Then they came back down, and Lois had to tell exactly what had happened. The other girls all sat in a circle and listened to her. Nobody said anything. They all looked frightened, especially Pat and Kip. They were leaders. You did not just lose a camper like this, for no reason at all.

"Why did you leave her alone?" said Kip.

"I was just down the path," said Lois. "I told you. She had to go to the bathroom." She did not say *pee* in front of people older than herself.

Kip looked disgusted.

"Maybe she just walked off into the woods and got turned around," said one of the girls.

"Maybe she's doing it on purpose," said another.

Nobody believed either of these theories.

They took the canoes and searched around the base of the cliff, and peered down into the water. But there had been no sound of falling rock; there had been no splash. There was no clue, nothing at all. Lucy had simply vanished.

That was the end of the canoe trip. It took them the same two days to go back that it had taken coming in, even though they were short a paddler. They did not sing.

After that, the police went in a motorboat, with dogs; they were the Mounties and the dogs were German shepherds, trained to follow trails in the woods. But it had rained since, and they could find nothing.

Lois is sitting in Cappie's office. Her face is bloated with crying, she's seen that in the mirror. By now she feels numbed; she feels as if she has drowned. She can't stay here. It has been too much of a shock. Tomorrow her parents are coming to take her away. Several of the other girls who were on the canoe trip are also being collected. The others will have to stay, because their parents are in Europe, or cannot be reached.

Cappie is grim. They've tried to hush it up, but of course everyone in camp knows. Soon the papers will know too. You can't keep it quiet, but what can be said? What can be said that makes any sense? "Girl vanishes in broad daylight, without a trace." It can't be believed. Other things, worse things, will be suspected. Negligence, at the very least. But they have always taken such care. Bad luck will gather around Camp Manitou like a fog; parents will avoid it, in favour of other, luckier places. Lois can see Cappie thinking all this, even through her numbness. It's what anyone would think.

Lois sits on the hard wooden chair in Cappie's office, beside the old wooden desk, over which hangs the thumbtacked bulletin board of normal camp routine, and gazes at Cappie through her puffy eyelids. Cappie is now smiling what is supposed to be a reassuring smile. Her manner is too casual: she's after something. Lois has seen this look on Cappie's face when she's been sniffing out contraband chocolate bars, hunting down those rumoured to have snuck out of their cabins at night.

"Tell me again," says Cappie, "from the beginning."

Lois has told her story so many times by now, to Pat and Kip, to Cappie, to the police, that she knows it word for word for word. She knows it, but she no longer believes it. It has become a story. "I told you," she said. "She wanted to go to the bathroom. I gave her my toilet paper. I went down the path, I waited for her. I heard this kind of shout . . ."

"Yes," says Cappie, smiling confidingly, "but before that. What did you say to one another?"

Lois thinks. Nobody has asked her this before. "She said you could dive off there. She said it went straight down."

"And what did you say?"

"I said you'd have to be nuts."

"Were you mad at Lucy?" says Cappie, in an encouraging voice.

"No," says Lois. "Why would I be mad at Lucy? I wasn't ever mad at Lucy." She feels like crying again. The times when she has in fact been mad at Lucy have been erased already. Lucy was always perfect.

"Sometimes we're angry when we don't know we're angry," says Cappie, as if to herself. "Sometimes we get really mad and we don't even know it. Sometimes we might do a thing without meaning to, or without knowing what will happen. We lose our tempers."

Lois is only thirteen, but it doesn't take her long to figure out that Cappie is not including herself in any of this. By *we* she means Lois. She is accusing Lois of pushing Lucy off the cliff. The unfairness of this hits her like a slap. "I didn't!" she says.

"Didn't what?" says Cappie softly. "Didn't what, Lois?"

Lois does the worst thing, she begins to cry. Cappie gives her a look like a pounce. She's got what she wanted.

Later when she was grown up, Lois was able to understand what this interview had been about. She could see Cappie's desperation, her need for a story, a real story with a reason in it; anything but the senseless vacancy Lucy had left for her to deal with. Cappie wanted Lois to supply the reason, to be the reason. It wasn't even for the newspapers or the parents, because she could never make such an accusation without proof. It was for herself: something to explain the loss of Camp Manitou and of all she had worked for, the years of entertaining spoiled children and buttering up parents and making a fool of herself with feathers stuck in her hair. Camp Manitou was in fact lost. It did not survive.

Lois worked all this out, twenty years later. But it was far too late. It was too late even ten minutes afterwards, when she'd left Cappie's office and was walking slowly back to her cabin to pack. Lucy's clothes were still there, folded on the shelves, as if waiting. She felt the other girls in the cabin watching her with speculation in their eyes. *Could she have done it? She must have done it.* For the rest of her life, she has caught people watching her in this way.

Maybe they weren't thinking this. Maybe they were merely sorry for her. But she felt she had been tried and sentenced, and this is what has stayed with her: the knowledge that she had been singled out, condemned for something that was not her fault.

Lois sits in the living room of her apartment, drinking a cup of tea. Through the knee-to-ceiling window she has a wide view of Lake Ontario, with its skin of wrinkled blue-grey light, and of the willows of Centre Island shaken by a wind, which is silent at this distance, and on this side of the glass. When there isn't too much pollution she can see the far shore, the foreign shore; though today it is obscured.

Possibly she could go out, go downstairs, do some shopping; there isn't much in the refrigerator. The boys say she doesn't get out enough. But she isn't hungry, and moving, stirring from this space, is increasingly an effort.

She can hardly remember, now, having her two boys in the hospital, nursing them as babies; she can hardly remember getting married, or what Rob looked like. Even at the time she never felt she was paying full attention. She was tired a lot, as if she was living not one life but two: her own, and another, shadowy life that hovered around her and would not let itself be realized—the life of what would have happened if Lucy had not stepped sideways, and disappeared from time.

She would never go up north, to Rob's family cottage or to any place with wild lakes and wild trees and the calls of loons. She would never go anywhere near. Still, it was as if she was listening for another voice, the voice of a person who should have been there but was not. An echo.

While Rob was alive, while the boys were growing up, she could pretend she didn't hear it, this empty space in sound. But now there is nothing much left to distract her.

She turns away from the window and looks at her pictures. There is the pinkish island, in the lake, with the intertwisted trees. It's the same landscape they paddled through, that distant summer. She's seen travelogues of this country, aerial photographs; it looks different from above, bigger, more hopeless: lake after lake, random blue puddles in dark green bush, the trees like bristles.

How could you ever find anything there, once it was lost? Maybe if they cut it all down, drained it all away, they might find Lucy's bones, some time, wherever they are hidden. A few bones, some buttons, the buckle from her shorts.

But a dead person is a body; a body occupies space, it exists somewhere. You can see it; you put it in a box and bury it in the ground, and then it's in a box in the ground. But Lucy is not in a box, or in the ground. Because she is nowhere definite, she could be anywhere.

And these paintings are not landscape paintings. Because there aren't any landscapes up there, not in the old, tidy European sense, with a gentle hill, a curving river, a cottage, a mountain in the background, a golden evening sky. Instead there's a tangle, a receding maze, in which you can become lost almost as soon as you step off the path. There are no backgrounds in any of these paintings, no vistas; only a great deal of foreground that goes back and back, endlessly, involving you in its twists and turns of tree and branch and rock. No matter how far back in you go, there will be more. And the trees themselves are hardly trees; they are currents of energy, charged with violent colour.

Who knows how many trees there were on the cliff just before Lucy disappeared? Who counted? Maybe there was one more, afterwards.

Lois sits in her chair and does not move. Her hand with the cup is raised halfway to her mouth. She hears something, almost hears it: a shout of recognition, or of joy.

She looks at the paintings, she looks into them. Every one of them is a picture of Lucy. You can't see her exactly, but she's there, in behind the pink stone island or the one behind that. In the picture of the cliff she is hidden by the clutch of fallen rocks towards the bottom, in the one of the river shore she is crouching beneath the overturned canoe. In the yellow autumn woods she's behind the tree that cannot be seen because of other trees, over beside the blue sliver of pond; but if you walked into the picture and found the tree, it would be the wrong one, because the right one would be farther on.

Everyone has to be somewhere, and this is where Lucy is. She is in Lois's apartment, in the holes that open inwards on the wall, not like windows but like doors. She is here. She is entirely alive.

1991

Marie-Claire Blais

b. 1939

Marie-Claire Blais was born the eldest of five children in Quebec City. From childhood she was obsessed with writing; by the time she published her first novel at the age of twenty, she had written over 200 poems, four novels, and twelve plays. Because of financial difficulties, she was compelled to leave convent school at the age of fifteen to work in a shoe factory. Her family objected to her writing; her mother was once so horrified by one of her stories that she threw it in the fire. At the insistence of friends, Blais took her manuscripts to Father Georges-Henri Lévesque of the Université de Laval and, with his encouragement, she wrote *La belle bête* in fifteen days. The priest took the novel to the Institut Littéraire de Québec where it was published. It caused a literary storm, going through two editions in six weeks, and attracted the attention of the American critic Edmund Wilson, through whose influence Blais won a Guggenheim Fellowship. She moved to Cape Cod and then to Paris before returning to live permanently in Montreal. She has published over twenty books in France and Quebec—most of which have been translated into English—including novels, plays, and several collections of poetry. She has won the Prix Medicis, the Prix Belgo-Canadien, the Prix France-Québec, and is a three-time winner of the Governor General's Award for Fiction.

The Forsaken

She was just an ordinary person. There were, far away, individuals, tragic events, but that was far off in countries bathed in blood, while here, in this part of the world where she had been tucked away since the day she was born, one met nothing but ordinary people and, without being happy, never had to suffer a single tragic event. Sometimes she wondered whether she really existed, or whether through some blind act of cruelty whoever it was that had placed her here, said to be God, had not insidiously abandoned her inside this body that resembled so many others, even though she constantly doubted the reality of her earthly existence. Like everyone else who had not reached the age of discretion and whose lives, plagued by monotony, she could see close at hand, she was just as much a monster on a small scale, fond of games and skirmishes, as ready as the next one to take part in those sly applications of fingernails to skin and, when she was less bored, in their greedy buzzing around the life of the senses. The days followed one upon the other, the seasons too, and not one catastrophe came along to alter her miserable fate of being nobody, always nobody, of being held captive in this body, inside this ordinary person. The only things she could feel were: the burden of her alien existence, which was silently growing; the skin of those she approached, touched in hopes of breaking through the haze that separated her from herself, which was by turns oily, sweaty, or hot, and if they were old, often insensible to her caresses. She would kiss them or hug them, aware that they too were oppressed, uncommunicative creatures, and whatever soul or existence they had was devoid of calamity because they had also been forsaken within their lives, those cramped cells of flesh where they had been condemned to feel that nothing every happened, where there was never anything to fear, not even the fear itself of a great misfortune.

In winter there was the stale odour of snow, or perhaps there was no odour at all. The warlike contraptions she kept seeing in her dreams would be used here for nothing but clearing the streets and sidewalks of the mountains of grimy snow, underneath which it was forbidden to lie down and go to sleep, calm and breathless. Those machines had ground the featureless lives of her friends to bits, and nothing of them had been recovered but bloody fragments, a foot, a hand—they had died in pieces, just as others were dying in far off places, mowed down by ghastly machines. But here one did not perish gloriously in the carnage of a war, one died in solitude, without anyone knowing, a death already submitted to and lacking all hope of resurrection in memories or hearts.

In summer one gulped down the dust from the streets while running, a heady feeling, voluptuous, even for an ordinary person. Life would suddenly catch at you, like the pernicious spikes that run along the fences around buildings: she stopped running, looked at the sun that seemed to want to obliterate everything, and remembered that she was merely a drab creature that had been overlooked here on the sidewalk, under the vast white sky that glittered and offended her sight. Could it be that she was more miserable than the real wretches who were dying in distant places under the bombs, and, if she did resemble, without knowing them, those creatures who were subjected to genuine suffering—out there—what was she doing here, in this body that pretended to breathe, play, live, like all the others? She would have done better to leave, like the victims, carrying her few belongings in a wheelbarrow. But in the midst of all those mortals who had no personal destiny other than the common fate of being people to whom nothing would happen, she diverted her numbed spirits by going through the same motions each day, sleeping at night, rising in the morning, eating with no appetite, fingering the hollows created by hunger in this body that could shudder without existing and that had never known the evils of famine and death, the unending curse that, right now, in some other place, was weighing upon all those whom misfortune had not forsaken.

One morning, while lounging against a red brick wall that bruised her hands and elbows, a wall whose bricks were hot under a sky that was setting fire with its dull flame to the whole world, she had the temerity to think she, too, would leave. She did not yet know where it was that she would be going, but she would follow the lead of those who headed out towards distant parts with a wheelbarrow, a few objects, a bit of clothing and food, for one did not sleep, did not eat on such a journey, there was time only to flee, under the bombs, in the whirlwind of an avenging sky. She had to leave this red brick wall because, by leaning her sweat-soaked back, her elbows, the palms of her hands against it too hard, was she not running a risk of imprinting into the rough substance, which was about to melt in the sun, the outline of this body that she was not sure she inhabited? Her heart was pounding deep inside her chest as if it had been left by itself with its persistent beating motion inside a subterranean passage. Now, she was leaving. The sky was white and harsh, her wheelbarrow, which she dragged clumsily behind her, held the spade and the knife for the rats that might swarm over the stone or concrete walls; but the rats themselves were drowsy from the heat and did not venture out of their thornbushes, and the lecherous drunkards, whom she feared as much as the rat-bites, also seemed to be asleep in their shacks, with the blinds down. The sky was silent, white and still, with its unblinking sun overhead. The sun, to some extent, illuminated the way through the dust; she had by now walked for so long that her hair was sticking to her temples. From time to time she would pause before a landscape that she had never seen before this day, a lush part of the world, and spend hours there, waiting for the tragic event that was not taking place, for no threat of any kind erupted from the heavens. She ran through the tall, cool grass, telling herself that the far-off war had perhaps come to an end, she would soon be able, she thought, to inhabit her body, to live, breathe, like everyone else. They would very likely come looking for her during the night, and would tell her again not to run away—because she was only an ordinary person—but here, in this fresh patch of green that was a new landscape, a new vision of a world to come, with her face lifted towards the sun, she had felt that it was time for her to make her peace with all those dead people who passed through her dreams at night, and with the living ones who preyed on her mind during the day, those whom misfortune had forgotten.

1984
translated by Patricia Sillers

Angela Carter

1940–1992

Born in Eastbourne, Sussex, in the United Kingdom, Angela Carter, the daughter of a journalist, married at the age of twenty. As a teenager she worked for the Croydon *Advertiser*, writing features and reviews. She studied English at the University of Bristol. She published her first novel, *Shadow Dance* (1965), at the age of twenty-five. In a career shortened by cancer, she was prolific, publishing more than two dozen books, including novels, short story collections, drama, and criticism. Trying to locate her work, critics called it magic realism, to which she often added elements of Gothic eroticism and violence. She was interested in the genre of fantasy fiction, as is evident in the title of her 1972 novel *The Infernal Desire Machines of Doctor Hoffman*. Carter's enduring fascination with fairy tales led to her translation of *The Fairy Tales of Charles Perrault* (1979) and her two-volume edition of *The Virago Book of Fairy Tales* (1990, 1992). Her interest in postmodern and feminist theory also defines her work and led to her critical study *The Sadeian Woman: An Exercise in Cultural History* (1979). Though she will be remembered for her short stories, her novels—in particular *Black Venus* (1985), *Wise Children* (1991), and *The Magic Toyshop* (1996)—are highly regarded. Her story "The Company of Wolves" was made into a film in 1984, directed by Neil Jordan.

The Company of Wolves

One beast and only one howls in the woods by night.

The wolf is carnivore incarnate and he's as cunning as he is ferocious; once he's had a taste of flesh then nothing else will do.

At night, the eyes of wolves shine like candle flames, yellowish, reddish, but that is because the pupils of their eyes fatten on darkness and catch the light from your lantern to flash it back to you—red for danger; if a wolf's eyes reflect only moonlight, then they gleam a cold and unnatural green, a mineral, a piercing colour. If the benighted traveller spies those luminous, terrible sequins stitched suddenly on the black thickets, then he knows he must run, if fear has not struck him stock-still.

But those eyes are all you will be able to glimpse of the forest assassins as they cluster invisibly round your smell of meat as you go through the wood unwisely late. They will be like shadows, they will be like wraiths, grey members of a congregation of nightmare; hark! his long, wavering howl . . . an aria of fear made audible.

The wolfsong is the sound of the rending you will suffer, in itself a murdering.

It is winter and cold weather. In this region of mountain and forest, there is now nothing for the wolves to eat. Goats and sheep are locked up in the byre, the deer departed for the remaining pasturage on the southern slopes—wolves grow lean and famished. There is so little flesh on them that you could count the starveling ribs through their pelts, if they gave you time before they pounced. Those slavering jaws; the lolling tongue; the rime of saliva on the grizzled chops—of all the teeming perils of the night and the forest, ghosts, hobgoblins, ogres that grill babies upon gridirons, witches that fatten their captives in cages for cannibal tables, the wolf is worst for he cannot listen to reason.

You are always in danger in the forest, where no people are. Step between the portals of the great pines where the shaggy branches tangle about you, trapping the unwary traveller in nets as if the vegetation itself were in a plot with the wolves who live there, as though the wicked trees go fishing on behalf of their friends—step between the gateposts of the forest with the greatest trepidation and infinite precautions, for if you stray from the path for one instant, the wolves will eat you. They are grey as famine, they are as unkind as plague.

The grave-eyed children of the sparse villages always carry knives with them when they go to tend the little flocks of goats that provide the homesteads with acrid milk and rank, maggoty cheese. Their knives are half as big as they are, the blades are sharpened daily.

But the wolves have ways of arriving at your own hearthside. We try and try but sometimes we cannot keep them out. There is no winter's night the cottager does not fear to see a lean, grey, famished snout questing under the door, and there was a woman once bitten in her own kitchen as she was straining the macaroni.

Fear and flee the wolf; for, worst of all, the wolf may be more than he seems.

There was a hunter once, near here, that trapped a wolf in a pit. This wolf had massacred the sheep and goats; eaten up a mad old man who used to live by himself in a hut halfway up the mountain and sing to Jesus all day; pounced on a girl looking after the sheep, but she made such a commotion that men came with rifles and scared him away and tried to track him to the forest but he was cunning and easily gave them the slip. So this hunter dug a pit and put a duck in it, for bait, all alive-oh; and he covered the pit with straw smeared with wolf dung. Quack, quack! went the duck and a wolf came slinking out of the forest, a big one, a heavy one, he weighed as much as a grown man and the straw gave way beneath him—into the pit he tumbled. The hunter jumped down after him, slit his throat, cut off all his paws for a trophy.

And then no wolf at all lay in front of the hunter but the bloody trunk of a man, headless, footless, dying, dead.

A witch from up the valley once turned an entire wedding party into wolves because the groom had settled on another girl. She used to order them to visit her, at night, from spite, and they would sit and howl around her cottage for her, serenading her with their misery.

Not so very long ago, a young woman in our village married a man who vanished clean away on her wedding night. The bed was made with new sheets and the bride lay down in it; the groom said, he was going out to relieve himself, insisted on it, for the sake of decency, and she drew the coverlet up to her chin and lay there. And she waited and she waited and then she waited again—surely he's been gone a long time? Until she jumps up in bed and shrieks to hear a howling, coming on the wind from the forest.

That long-drawn, wavering howl has, for all its fearful resonance, some inherent sadness in it, as if the beasts would love to be less beastly if only they knew how and never cease to mourn their own condition. There is a vast melancholy in the canticles of the wolves, melancholy infinite as the forest, endless as these long nights of winter and yet that ghastly sadness, that mourning for their own, irremediable appetites, can never move the heart for not one phrase in it hints at the possibility of redemption; grace could not come to the wolf from its own despair, only through some external mediator, so that, sometimes, the beast will look as if he half welcomes the knife that dispatches him.

The young woman's brothers searched the outhouses and the haystacks but never found any remains so the sensible girl dried her eyes and found herself another husband not too shy to piss into a pot who spent the nights indoors. She gave him a pair of bonny babies and all went right as a trivet until, one freezing night, the night of the solstice, the hinge of the year when things do not fit together as well as they should, the longest night, her first good man came home again.

A great thump on the door announced him as she was stirring the soup for the father of her children and she knew him the moment she lifted the latch to him although it was years since she'd worn black for him and now he was in rags and his hair hung down his back and never saw a comb, alive with lice.

"Here I am again, missus," he said. "Get me my bowl of cabbage and be quick about it."

Then her second husband came in with wood for the fire and when the first one saw she'd slept with another man and, worse, clapped his red eyes on her little children who'd crept into the kitchen to see what all the din was about, he shouted: "I wish I were a wolf again, to teach this whore a lesson!" So a wolf he instantly became and tore off the eldest boy's left foot before he was chopped by the hatchet they used for chopping logs. But when the wolf lay bleeding and gasping its last, the pelt peeled off again and he was just as he had been, years ago, when he ran away from his marriage bed, so that she wept and her second husband beat her.

They say there's an ointment the Devil gives you that turns you into a wolf the minute you rub it on. Or, that he was born feet first and had a wolf for his father and his torso is a man's but his legs and genitals are a wolf's. And he has a wolf's heart.

Seven years is a werewolf's natural span but if you burn his human clothes you condemn him to wolfishness for the rest of his life, so old wives hereabouts think it some protection to throw a hat or an apron at the werewolf, as if clothes made the man. Yet by the eyes, those phosphorescent eyes, you know him in all his shapes; the eyes alone unchanged by metamorphosis.

Before he can become a wolf, the lycanthrope strips stark naked. If you spy a naked man among the pines, you must run as if the Devil were after you.

It is midwinter and the robin, the friend of man, sits on the handle of the gardener's spade and sings. It is the worst time in all the year for wolves but this strong-minded child insists she will go off through the wood. She is quite sure the wild beasts cannot harm her although, well-warned, she lays a carving knife in the basket her mother has packed with cheeses. There is a bottle of harsh liquor distilled from brambles; a batch of flat oatcakes baked on the heathstone; a pot or two of jam. The girl will take these delicious gifts to a reclusive grandmother so old the burden of her years is crushing her to death. Granny lives two hours' trudge through the winter woods; the child wraps herself up in her thick shawl, draws it over her head. She steps into her stout wooden shoes; she is dressed and ready and it is Christmas Eve. The malign door of the solstice still swings upon its hinges but she has been too much loved ever to feel scared.

Children do not stay young for long in this savage country. There are no toys for them to play with so they work hard and grow wise but this one, so pretty and the youngest of her family, a little latecomer, had been indulged by her mother and the grandmother who'd knitted her the red shawl that, today, has the ominous if brilliant look of blood on snow. Her breasts have just begun to swell; her hair is like lint, so fair it hardly makes a shadow on her pale forehead; her cheeks are an emblematic scarlet and white and she has just started her woman's bleeding, the clock inside her that will strike, henceforward, once a month.

She stands and moves within the invisible pentacle of her own virginity. She is an unbroken egg; she is a sealed vessel; she has inside her a magic space the entrance to which is shut tight with a plug of membrane; she is a closed system; she does not know how to shiver. She has her knife and she is afraid of nothing.

Her father might forbid her, if he were home, but he is away in the forest, gathering wood, and her mother cannot deny her.

The forest closed upon her like a pair of jaws.

There is always something to look at in the forest, even in the middle of winter—the huddled mounds of birds, succumbed to the lethargy of the season, heaped on the creaking boughs and too forlorn to sing; the bright frills of the winter fungi on the blotched trunks of the trees; the cuneiform slots of rabbits and deer, the herringbone tracks of the birds, a hare as lean as a rasher of bacon streaking across the path where the thin sunlight dapples the russet brakes of last year's bracken.

When she heard the freezing howl of a distant wolf, her practised hand sprang to the handle of the knife, but she saw no sign of a wolf at all, nor of a naked man, neither, but then she heard a clattering among the brushwood and there sprang on to the path a fully clothed one, a very handsome young one, in the green coat and wideawake hat of a hunter, laden with carcasses of game birds. She had her hand on her knife at the first rustle of twigs but he laughed with a flash of white teeth when he saw her and made her a comic yet flattering little bow; she'd never seen such a fine fellow before, not among the rustic clowns of her native village. So on they went, through the thickening light of the afternoon.

Soon they were laughing and joking like old friends. When he offered to carry her basket, she gave it to him although her knife was in it because he told her his rifle would protect them. As the day darkened, it began to snow again; she felt the first flakes settle on her eyelashes but now there was only half a mile to go and there would be a fire, and hot tea, and a welcome, a warm one surely, for the dashing huntsman as well as for herself.

This young man had a remarkable object in his pocket. It was a compass. She looked at the little round glassface in the palm of his hand and watched the wavering needle with a vague wonder. He assured her this compass had taken him safely through the wood on his hunting trip because the needle always told him with perfect accuracy where the north was. She did not believe it; she knew she should never leave the path on the way through the wood or else she would be lost instantly. He laughed at her again; gleaming trails of spittle clung to his teeth. He said, if he plunged off the path into the forest that surrounded them, he would guarantee to arrive at her grandmother's house a good quarter of an hour before she did, plotting his way through the undergrowth with his compass, while she trudged the long way, along the winding path.

I don't believe you. Besides, aren't you afraid of the wolves?

He only tapped the gleaming butt of his rifle and grinned.

Is it a bet? he asked her. Shall we make a game out of it? What will you give me if I get to your grandmother's house before you?

What would you like? she asked disingenuously.

A kiss.

Commonplaces of a rustic seduction; she lowered her eyes and blushed.

He went through the undergrowth and took her basket with him but she forgot to be afraid of the beasts, although now the moon was rising, for she wanted to dawdle on her way to make sure the handsome gentleman would win his wager.

Grandmother's house stood by itself a little way out of the village. The freshly falling snow blew in eddies about the kitchen garden and the young man stepped delicately up the snowy path to the door as if he were reluctant to get his feet wet, swinging his bundle of game and the girl's basket and humming a little tune to himself.

There is a faint trace of blood on his chin; he has been snacking on his catch.

He rapped upon the panels with his knuckles.

Aged and frail, granny is three-quarters succumbed to the mortality the ache in her bones promises her and almost ready to give in entirely. A boy came out from the village to build up her hearth for the night an hour ago and the kitchen crackles with busy firelight. She has her Bible for company, she is a pious old woman. She is propped up on several pillows in the bed set into the wall peasant-fashion, wrapped up in the patchwork quilt she made before she was married, more years ago than she cares to remember. Two china spaniels with liver-coloured blotches on their coats and black noses sit on either side of the fireplace. There is a bright rug of woven rags on the pantiles. The grandfather clock ticks away her eroding time.

We keep the wolves outside by living well.

He rapped upon the panels with his hairy knuckles.

It is your granddaughter, he mimicked in a high soprano.

Lift up the latch and walk in, my darling.

You can tell them by their eyes, eyes of a beast of prey, nocturnal, devastating eyes as red as a wound; you can hurl your Bible at him and your apron after, granny, you thought that was a sure prophylactic against these infernal vermin . . . now call on Christ and his mother and all the angels in heaven to protect you but it won't do you any good.

His feral muzzle is sharp as a knife; he drops his golden burden of gnawed pheasants on the table and puts down your dear girl's basket, too. Oh, my God, what have you done with her?

Off with his disguise, that coat of forest-coloured cloth, the hat with the feather tucked into the ribbon; his matted hair streams down his white shirt and she can see the lice moving in it. The sticks in the hearth shift and hiss; night and the forest has come into the kitchen with darkness tangled in its hair.

He strips off his shirt. His skin is the colour and texture of vellum. A crisp stripe of hair runs down his belly, his nipples are ripe and dark as poison fruit but he's so thin you count his ribs under his skin if only he gave you the time. He strips off his trousers and she can see how hairy his legs are. His genitals, huge. Ah! huge.

The last thing the old lady saw in all this world was a young man, eyes like cinders, naked as stone, approaching her bed.

The wolf is carnivore incarnate.

When he had finished with her, he licked his chops and quickly dressed himself again, until he was just as he had been when he came through her door. He burned the inedible hair in the fireplace and wrapped the bones up in a napkin that he hid away under the bed in the wooden chest in which he found a clean pair of sheets. These he carefully put on the bed instead of the telltale stained ones he stowed away in the laundry basket. He plumped up the pillows and shook out the patchwork quilt, he picked up the Bible from the floor, closed it and laid it on the table. All was as it had been before except that grandmother was gone. The sticks twitched in the grate, the clock ticked and the young man sat patiently, deceitfully beside the bed in granny's nightcap.

Rat-a-tap-tap.

Who's there, he quavers in granny's antique falsetto.

Only your granddaughter.

So she came in, bringing with her a flurry of snow that melted in tears on the tiles, and perhaps she was a little disappointed to see only her grandmother sitting beside the fire. But then he flung off the blanket and sprang to the door, pressing his back against it so that she could not get out again.

The girl looked around the room and saw there was not even the indentation of a head on the smooth cheek of the pillow and how, for the first time she'd seen it so, the Bible lay closed on the table. The tick of the clock cracked like a whip. She wanted her knife from her basket but she did not dare reach for it because his eyes were fixed upon her—huge eyes that now seemed to shine with a unique, interior light, eyes the size of saucers, saucers full of Greek fire, diabolic phosphorescence.

What big eyes you have.

All the better to see you with.

No trace at all of the old woman except for a tuft of white hair that had caught in the bark of an unburned log. When the girl saw that, she knew she was in danger of death.

Where is my grandmother?

There's nobody here but we two, my darling.

Now a great howling rose up all around them, near, very near as close as the kitchen garden, the howling of a multitude of wolves; she knew the worst wolves are hairy on the inside and she shivered, in spite of the scarlet shawl she pulled more closely round herself as if it could protect her although it was as red as the blood she must spill.

Who has come to sing us carols, she said.

Those are the voices of my brothers, darling; I love the company of wolves. Look out of the window and you'll see them.

Snow half-caked the lattice and she opened it to look into the garden. It was a white night of moon and snow; the blizzard whirled round the gaunt, grey beasts who squatted on their haunches among the rows of winter cabbage, pointing their sharp snouts to the moon and howling as if their hearts would break. Ten wolves; twenty wolves—so many wolves she could not count them, howling in concert as if demented or deranged. Their eyes reflected the light from the kitchen and shone like a hundred candles.

It is very cold, poor things, she said; no wonder they howl so.

She closed the window on the wolves' threnody and took off her scarlet shawl, the colour of poppies, the colour of sacrifices, the colour of her menses, and, since her fear did her no good, she ceased to be afraid.

What shall I do with my shawl?

Throw it on the fire, dear one. You won't need it again.

She bundled up her shawl and threw it on the blaze, which instantly consumed it. Then she drew her blouse over her head; her small breasts gleamed as if the snow had invaded the room.

What shall I do with my blouse?

Into the fire with it, too, my pet.

The thin muslin went flaring up the chimney like a magic bird and now off came her skirt, her woollen stockings, her shoes, and on to the fire they went, too, and were gone for good. The firelight shone through the edges of her skin; now she was clothed only in her untouched integument of flesh. This dazzling, naked she combed out her hair with her fingers; her hair looked white as the snow outside. Then went directly to the man with red eyes in whose unkempt mane the lice moved; she stood up on tiptoe and unbuttoned the collar of his shirt.

What big arms you have.

All the better to hug you with.

Every wolf in the world now howled a prothalamion outside the window as she freely gave him the kiss she owed him.

What big teeth you have!

She saw how his jaw began to slaver and the room was full of the clamour of the forest's *Liebestod* but the wise child never flinched, even as he answered: All the better to eat you with.

The girl burst out laughing; she knew she was nobody's meat. She laughed at him full in the face, she ripped off his shirt for him and flung it into the fire, in the fiery wake of her own discarded clothing. The flames danced like dead souls on Walpursignacht and the old bones under the bed set up a terrible clattering but she did not pay them any heed.

Carnivore incarnate, only immaculate flesh appeases him.

She will lay his fearful head on her lap and she will pick out the lice from his pelt and perhaps she will put the lice into her mouth and eat them, as he will bid her, as she would do in a savage marriage ceremony.

The blizzard will die down.

The blizzard died down, leaving the mountains as randomly covered with snow as if a blind woman had thrown a sheet over them, the upper branches of the forest pines limed, creaking, swollen with the fall.

Snowlight, moonlight, a confusion of paw-prints.

All silent, all silent.

Midnight; and the clock strikes. It is Christmas day, the werewolves' birthday, the door of the solstice stands wide open; let them all sink through.

See! sweet and sound she sleeps in granny's bed, between the paws of the tender wolf.

1979

Maxine Hong Kingston

b. 1940

Maxine Hong Kingston was born in Stockton, California, the eldest of six American-born children. Two older siblings had died previously in China. A scholar, poet, and teacher in China, her father worked in a Chinese laundry after immigrating to the

United States in 1924. Her mother joined him in New York City in 1939; trained as a midwife in China, she also initially worked in a laundry and as a field hand. The family moved to California when Kingston's father was offered work in a gambling house. Eventually he started his own laundry. Surrounded in childhood by other immigrants from her father's village, Kingston instinctively collected the stories that would provide fertile material for her writing. A scholarship student at the University of California at Berkeley, she graduated with a BA in 1962, the year she married actor Earl Kingston; their son was born two years later. In 1967 the couple moved to Hawaii where Kingston began her career as a high school teacher at the Mid-Pacific Institute in Honolulu. In 1976 she published *The Woman Warrior: Memoirs of a Girlhood among Ghosts*. Though called non-fiction and offered as a memoir of growing up female and Chinese-American in a California laundry, the book is really an amalgam of autobiography, mythology, fiction, and ancestral history. It was an immediate success, winning the National Book Critics Circle Award for non-fiction, and it has become a seminal work in Asian-American cultural studies. Kingston remarked: "This was a book that I started to write when I was ten years old, but I didn't have the words. Twenty-five years later I was able to do it. . . . At first I thought I could do it all in one volume, the men and the women, but the men's stories didn't fit in with the women's stories. The mythology is so different." *China Men* (1980) is meant as a companion volume to *The Woman Warrior*. Woven from memory, myth, and fact, it begins with Kingston's grandfather's generation and describes the lives of the men who came to "Gold Mountain," as the Chinese called America. Resisting generic classification, Kingston's books are, in her own description, "biographies of a people's imagination." In 1989 she published her first novel, *Tripmaster Monkey: His Fake Book*, a surrealistic satire whose protagonist, Wittman Ah Sing, a fifth-generation Chinese-American hippie living in 1960s San Francisco, is attempting to write the great Chinese-American play. In 2000, Kingston was invited to give the William Massey lectures at Harvard. *To Be a Poet* (2002), an expanded version of the lectures, is a meditation, mostly in verse, on writing poetry.

On Mortality

As you know, any plain person you chance to meet can prove to be a powerful immortal in disguise come to test you.

Li Fu-yen told a story about Tu Tzu-chun, who lived from AD 558 to 618, during the Northern Chou and Sui Dynasties. Tu's examiner was a Taoist monk, who made him rich twice, and twice Tu squandered his fortune though it took him two lifetimes to do so. The third time the Taoist gave him money, he bought a thousand li of good land, plowed it himself, seeded it, built houses, roads, and bridges, then welcomed widows and orphans to live on it. With the leftover money, he found a husband for each spinster and a wife for every bachelor in his family, and also paid for the weddings. When he met the Taoist again, he said, "I've used up all your money on the unfortunates I've come across."

"You'll have to repay me by working for me," said the Taoist monk. "I need your help on an important difficult task." He gave Tu three white pills. "Swallow these," he said, pouring him a cup of wine. "All that you'll see and feel will be illusions. No matter what happens, don't speak; don't scream. Remember the saying 'Hide your broken arms in your sleeves.' "

"How easy," said Tu as he swallowed the pills in three gulps of wine. "Why should I scream if I know they're illusions?"

Level by level he descended into the nine hells. At first he saw oxheads, horsefaces, and the heads of generals decapitated in war. Illusions. Only illusions, harmless. He laughed at the heads. He had seen heads before. Soon fewer heads whizzed through the dark until he saw no more of them.

Suddenly his wife was being tortured. Demons were cutting her up into pieces, starting with her toes. He heard her scream; he heard her bones crack. He reminded himself that she was an illusion. *Illusion*, he thought. She was ground into bloodmeal.

Then the tortures on his own body began. Demons poured bronze down his throat and beat him with iron clubs and chains. They mortar-and-pestled and packed him into a pill.

He had to walk over mountains of knives and through fields of knives and forests of swords. He was killed, his head chopped off, rolling into other people's nightmares.

He heard gods and goddesses talking about him, "This man is too wicked to be reborn a man. Let him be born a woman." He saw the entrance of a black tunnel and felt tired. He would have to squeeze his head and shoulders down into that enclosure and travel a long distance. He pushed headfirst through the entrance, only the beginning. A god kicked him in the butt to give him a move on. (This kick is the reason many Chinese babies have a blue-grey spot on their butts or lower backs, the "Mongolian spot.") Sometimes stuck in the tunnel, sometimes shooting helplessly through it, he emerged again into light with many urgent things to do, many messages to deliver, but his hands were useless baby's hands, his legs wobbly baby's legs, his voice a wordless baby's cries. Years had to pass before he could regain adult powers; he howled as he began to forget the cosmos, his attention taken up with mastering how to crawl, how to stand, how to walk, how to control his bowel movements.

He discovered that he had been reborn a deaf-mute female named Tu. When she became a woman, her parents married her to a man named Lu, who at first did not mind. "Why does she need to talk," said Lu, "to be a good wife. Let her set an example for women." They had a child. But years later, Lu tired of Tu's dumbness. "You're just being stubborn," he said, and lifted their child by the feet. "Talk, or I'll dash its head against the rocks." The poor mother held her hand to her mouth. Lu swung the child, broke its head against the wall.

Tu shouted out, "Oh! Oh!"—and he was back with the Taoist, who sadly told him that at the moment when she had said, "Oh! Oh!" the Taoist was about to complete the last step in making the elixir for immortality. Now that Tu had broken his silence, the formula was spoiled, no immortality for the human race.

"You overcame joy and sorrow, anger, fear, and evil desire, but not love," said the Taoist, and went on his way.

1980

Emma Lee Warrior

b. 1941

A member of the North Peigan (Blackfoot) band, Emma Lee Warrior was born in Brocket and grew up on the Peigan Reserve in southern Alberta. She attended boarding school there, and it took a great effort to overcome that early repression. Writing, she explains, was "a great freedom" after the school's rules and restrictions. She went on to complete a Master of Fine Arts degree from the University of Washington. She is employed on the Blackfoot Reserve in Alberta. Her stories and poems have been published in *Wicazo Sa*, *Canadian Fiction Magazine*, *A Gathering of Spirit*, *Harper's Anthology of Twentieth Century Native American Poetry*, and *An Anthology of Canadian Native Literature in English*.

Compatriots

Lucy heard the car's motor wind down before it turned off the gravel road a quarter of a mile west of the house. Maybe it was Bunky. She hurried and left the outhouse. She couldn't run if she wanted to. It would be such a relief to have this pregnancy over with. She couldn't see the colour of the vehicle, for the slab fence was between the house and the road. That was just as well. She'd been caught in the outhouse a few times, and it still embarrassed her to have a car approach while she was in there.

She got inside the house just as the car came into view. It was her aunt, Flora. Lucy looked at the clock. It was seven-thirty. She wondered what was going on so early in the morning. Flora and a young white woman approached the house. Bob barked furiously at them. Lucy opened the door and yelled at him. "I don't know what's wrong with Bob; he never barks at me," said Flora.

"He's probably barking at her," explained Lucy. "Not many whites come here."

"Oh, this is Hilda Afflerbach. She's from Germany," began Flora. "Remember? I told you I met her at the Calgary Stampede? Well, she got off the seven o'clock bus, and I don't have time to drive her all the way down to my house. I took her over to my mother's, but she's getting ready to go to Lethbridge. Can she stay with you till I get off work?"

Lucy smiled. She knew she was boxed in. "Yeah, but I've got no running water in the house. You have to go outside to use the toilet," she said, looking at Hilda.

"Oh, that's okay," her aunt answered. "She's studying about Indians, anyway. Might as well get the true picture, right? Oh, Hilda, this is my niece, Lucy." Flora lowered her voice and asked, "Where's Bunky?"

"He never came home last night. I was hoping it was him coming home. He's not supposed to miss any more work. I've got his lunch fixed in case he shows up." Lucy poured some water from a blue plastic water jug into a white enamel basin and washed her hands and face. "I haven't even had time to make coffee. I couldn't sleep waiting for him to come home." She poured water into a coffeemaker and measured out the coffee into the paper filter.

"I'd have some coffee if it was ready, but I think I'd better get to work. We have to punch in now; it's a new rule. Can't travel on Indian time any more," said Flora. She opened the door and stepped out, then turned to say, "I think the lost has returned," and continued down the steps.

The squeak of the dusty truck's brakes signalled Bunky's arrival. He strode toward the door, barely acknowledging Flora's presence. He came in and took the lunch pail Lucy had. "I stayed at Herbie's," was all he said before he turned and went out. He started the truck and beeped the horn.

"I'll go see what he wants." She motioned Flora to wait.

When Bunky left, she went to Flora: "Maybe it's a good thing you came here. Bunky didn't want to go to work 'cause he had a hangover. When he found out Hilda was going to be here all day, he decided he'd rather go to work."

"If I don't have to leave the office this afternoon, I'll bring the car over and you can drive Hilda around to look at the reserve, okay."

"Sure, that'll be good. I can go and do my laundry in Spitzee." She surveyed the distant horizon. The Rockies were spectacular, blue and distinct. It would be a nice day for a drive. She hoped it would be a repeat of yesterday, not too hot, but, as she stood there, she noticed tiny heat waves over the wheat fields. Well, maybe it won't be a repeat, she thought. Her baby kicked inside of her, and she said, "Okay, I'd better go tend to the guest." She didn't relish having a white visitor, but Flora had done her a lot of favours and Hilda seemed nice.

And she was. Hilda made friends with the kids, Jason and Melissa, answering their many questions about Germany as Lucy cooked. She ate heartily, complimenting Lucy on her cooking even though it was only the usual scrambled eggs and fried potatoes with toast and coffee. After payday, there'd be sausages or ham, but payday was Friday and today was only Tuesday.

"Have you heard of Helmut Walking Eagle?" Hilda wanted to know.

"Yeah, well, I really don't know him to talk to him, but I know what he looks like. He's from Germany, too. I always see him at Indian dances. He dresses up like an Indian." She had an urge to tell her that most of the Indians wished Helmut would disappear.

"I want to see him," Hilda said. "I heard about him and I read a book he wrote. He seems to know a lot about the Indians, and he's been accepted into their religious society. I hope he can tell me things I can take home. People in Germany are really interested in Indians. They even have clubs."

Lucy's baby kicked, and she held her hand over the spot. "My baby kicks if I sit too long. I guess he wants to do the dishes."

Hilda got up quickly and said, "Let me do the dishes. You can take care of the laundry."

"No, you're the visitor. I can do them," Lucy countered. But Hilda was persistent, and Lucy gave in.

Flora showed up just after twelve with the information that there was a sun-dance going on on the north side of the reserve. "They're already camping. Let's go there after work. Pick me up around four."

"I can't wait to got to the sun-dance! Do you go to them often?" Hilda asked Lucy.

"No, I never have. I don't know much about them," Lucy said.

"But why? Don't you believe in it? It's your culture!" Hilda's face showed concern.

"Well, they never had sun-dances here—in my whole life there's never been a sun-dance here."

"Really, is that true? But I thought you have them every year here."

"Not here. Over on the Blood Reserve they do and some places in the States, but not here."

"But don't you want to go to a sun-dance? I think it's so exciting!" Hilda moved forward in her seat and looked hopefully at Lucy.

Lucy smiled at her eagerness. "No, I don't care to go. It's mostly those mixed-up people who are in it. You see, Indian religion just came back here on the reserve a little while ago, and there are different groups who all quarrel over which way to practise it. Some use Sioux ways, and others use Cree. It's just a big mess," she said, shaking her head.

Hilda looked at Lucy, and Lucy got the feeling she was telling her things she didn't want to hear.

Lucy had chosen this time of day to do her wash. The Happy Suds Laundromat would be empty. As a rule, the Indians didn't show up till after lunch with their endless garbage bags of laundry.

After they had deposited their laundry in the machines, Lucy, Hilda, and the kids sauntered down the main street to a café for lunch. An unkempt Indian man dogged them, talking in Blackfoot.

"Do you know what he's saying?" asked Hilda.

"He wants money. He's related to my husband. Don't pay any attention to him. He always does this," said Lucy. "I used to give him money, but he just drinks it up."

The café was a cool respite from the heat outside, and the cushioned seats in the booth felt good. They sat by the window and ordered hamburgers, fries, and lemonade. The waitress brought tall, frosted glasses, and beads of water dripped from them.

"Hello, Lucy," a man's shaky voice said, just when they were really enjoying their lunch. They turned to look at the Indian standing behind Hilda. He was definitely ill. His eyes held pain, and he looked as though he might collapse from whatever ailed him. His hands shook, perspiration covered his face, and his eyes roamed the room constantly.

Lucy moved over to make room for him, but he kept standing and asked her, "Could you give me a ride down to Badger? The cops said I have to leave town. I don't want to stay 'cause they might beat me up."

"Yeah, we're doing laundry. I've got Flora's car. This is her friend, Hilda. She's from Germany."

The sick man barely nodded at her, then, turning back to Lucy, he asked her, "Do you have enough to get me some soup. I'm really hungry."

Lucy nodded and the man said, "I'll just sit in the next booth."

"He's my uncle," Lucy explained to Hilda as she motioned to the waitress. "His name is Sonny."

"Order some clear soup or you'll get sick," Lucy suggested to her uncle.

He nodded, as he pulled some paper napkins out of a chrome container on the table and wiped his face.

The women and children left Sonny with his broth and returned to the laundromat. As they were folding the clothes, he came in. "Here, I'll take these," he said, taking the bags from Lucy. His hands shook, and the effort of lifting the bags was clearly too much for him. "That's okay," protested Lucy, attempting to take them from him, "they're not that heavy. Clothes are always lighter after they've been washed."

"Hey, Lucy, I can manage. You're not supposed to be carrying big things around in your condition." Lucy let him take the plastic bags, which he dropped several times before he got to the car. The cops had probably tired of putting him in jail and sending him out each morning. She believed the cops did beat up Indians, although none was ever brought to court over it. She'd take Sonny home, and he's straighten out for a few weeks till he got thirsty again, and he'd disappear as soon as he got money. It was no use to hope he'd stop drinking. Sonny wouldn't quit drinking till he quit living.

As they were pulling out of town, Lucy remembered she had to get some Kool-Aid and turned the car in the Stop-n-Go Mart. Hilda got out with her and noticed the man who had followed them through the street sitting in the shade of a stack of old tires.

"Hey, tamohpomaat sikaohki," he told Lucy on her way into the store.

"What did he say? Sikaohki?" queried Hilda.

The Kool-Aid was next to the cash register and she picked up a few packages, and laid them on the counter with the money. When the cashier turned to the register, Lucy poked Hilda with her elbow and nodded her head toward the sign behind the counter. Scrawled unevenly in big, black letters, it said, "Ask for Lysol, vanilla, and shaving lotion at the counter."

They ignored the man on the way to the car. "That's what he wants; he's not allowed to go into the stores 'cause he steals it. He wanted vanilla. The Indians call it 'sikaohki'; it means 'black water.' "

Although the car didn't have air-conditioning, Lucy hurried toward it to escape the blistering heat. When she got on the highway, she asked her uncle. "Did you hear anything about a sun-dance?"

At first he grunted a negative "Huh-uh," then, "Oh, yeah, it's across the river, but I don't know where. George Many Robes is camping there. Saw him this morning. Are you going there?"

"Flora and Hilda are. Hilda wants to meet that German guy, Helmut Walking Eagle. You know, that guy who turned Indian?"

"Oh yeah, is he here?" he said indifferently, closing his eyes.

"Probably. He's always in the middle of Indian doings," said Lucy.

"Shit, that guy's just a phony. How could anybody turn into something else? Huh? I don't think I could turn into a white man if I tried all my life. They wouldn't let me, so how does that German think he can turn into an Indian. White people think they can do anything—turn Chinese or Indian—they're crazy!"

Sonny laid his head back on the seat and didn't say another word. Lucy felt embarrassed, but she had to agree with him; it seemed that Indians had come into focus lately. She'd read in the papers how some white woman in Hollywood became a medicine woman. She was selling her book on her life as a medicine woman. Maybe some white person or other person who wasn't Indian would get fooled by that book, but not an Indian. She herself didn't practise Indian religion, but she knew enough about it to know that one didn't just join an Indian religious group if one were not raised with it. That was a lot of the conflict going on among those people who were involved in it. They used sacred practices from other tribes, Navajo and Sioux, or whatever pleased them.

The heat of the day had reached its peak, and trails of dust hung suspended in the air wherever cars or trucks travelled the gravel roads on the reserve. Sonny fashioned a shade behind the house underneath the clothesline in the deep grass, spread a blanket, and filled a gallon jar from the pump. He covered the water with some old coats, lay down, and began to sweat the booze out.

The heat waves from this morning's forecast were accurate. It was just too hot. "Lordy, it's hot," exclaimed Lucy to Hilda as they brought the laundry in. "It must be close to ninety-five or one hundred. Let's go up to Badger to my other aunt's house. She's got a tap by her house and the kids can cool off in her sprinkler. Come on, you kids. Do you want to run in the sprinkler?"

The women covered the windows on the west side where the sun would shine. "I'm going to leave all the windows open to let the air in," said Lucy, as she walked around the house pushing them up.

Lucy's aunt's house sat amongst a clutter of junk. "Excuse the mess," she smiled at Hilda, waving her arm over her yard. "Don't wanna throw it away, it might come in handy." There were thick grass and weeds crisscrossed with paths to and from the clothesline, the outhouse, the woodstove. Lucy's aunt led them to an arbour shaded with huge spruce branches.

"This is nice," cooed Hilda, admiring the branches. Lucy's aunt beamed, "Yes, I told my old man, 'Henry, you get me some branches that's not gonna dry up and blow away,' and he did. He knows what's good for him. You sit down right here, and I'll get us some drinks." She disappeared and soon returned with a large thermos and some plastic tumblers.

They spent the afternoon hearing about Henry, as they watched the kids run through the sprinkler that sprayed the water back and forth. Once in a while, a suggestion of a breeze would touch the women, but it was more as if they imagined it.

Before four, they left to pick Flora up and headed back to Lucy's. "It's so hot after being in the cool cement building all day!" exclaimed Flora, as she settled herself into the car's stifling interior. "One thing for sure, I'm not going home to cook anything. Lucy, do you think Bunky would mind if you came with us? I'll get us some Kentucky Fried Chicken and stuff in town so you don't have to cook. It's too hot to cook, anyway." She rolled up a newspaper and fanned her face, which was already beginning to flush.

"No, he won't care. He'll probably want to sleep. We picked Sonny up in town. Both of them can lie around and get better. The kids would bother them if we were there."

It was a long ride across the Napi River toward the Porcupine Hills. A few miles from the Hills, they veered off until they were almost by the river. "Let's get off," said Flora.

Hilda gasped at what she saw before her. There was a circle of teepees and tents with a large open area in the middle. Exactly in the centre of the opening was a circular structure covered with branches around the sides. Next to this was a solitary unpainted teepee. Some of the teepees were painted with lines around the bottom; others had orbs bordering them, and yet others had animal figures painted on them. Smoke rose from stoves outside the teepees as people prepared their evening meals. Groups of horses stood languidly in the waning heat of the day, their heads resting on one another's backs and their tails occasionally flicking insect away. The sound of bantering children and yapping dogs carried to where they stood.

"Let's eat here," the kids said, poking their heads to look in the bags of food. Flora and Lucy spread a blanket on the ground, while Hilda continued to stand where she was, surveying the encampment. Flora pointed out the central leafy structure as the sacred area of prayer and dance.

"The teepee next to it is the sacred teepee. That's where the holy woman who is putting up the sun-dance stays the entire time. That's where they have the ceremonies."

"How many sun-dances have you been to?" asked Hilda.

"This is my first time, but I know all about this from books," said Flora. "Helmut Walking Eagle wrote a book about it, too. I could try to get you one. He sells them cheaper to Indians."

Hilda didn't eat much and kept looking at the camp. "It's really beautiful," she said, as if to herself.

"Well, you better eat something before you get left out," advised Lucy. "These kids don't know when to stop eating chicken."

"Yeah," agreed Flora. "Then we can go down and see who's all there." Hilda had something to eat, and then they got back into the car and headed down toward the encampment. They drove around the edge of the camp and stopped by Flora's cousin's tent. "Hi, Delphine," said Flora, "I didn't know you were camping here."

Lucy knew Flora and Delphine were not especially close. Their fathers were half-brothers, which made them half-cousins. Delphine had grown up Mormon and had recently turned to Indian religion, just as Flora had grown up Catholic and was now exploring traditional beliefs. The same could be said about many of the people here. To top things off, there was some bad feeling between the cousins about a man, some guy they both had been involved with in the past.

"Can anybody camp here? I've got a teepee. How about if I camp next to you."

Delphine bridled. "You're supposed to camp with your own clan."

Flora looked around the camp. "I wonder who's my clan. Say, there's George Many Robes, he's my relation, on my dad's side. Maybe I'll ask him if I can camp next to him."

Delphine didn't say anything but busied herself with splitting kindling from a box of sawn wood she kept hidden underneath a piece of tarp. Jason spied a thermos under the tarp and asked for a drink of water.

"I have to haul water, and nobody pays for my gas," grumbled Delphine, as she filled a cup halfway with water.

"Oh, say," inquired Flora, "do you know if Helmut Walking Eagle is coming here? This girl is from Germany, and she wants to see him."

"Over there, that big teepee with a Winnebago beside it. That's his camp," Delpine answered, without looking at them.

"Is she mad at you?" Jason asked Flora.

"Yeah, it must be the heat," Flora told him with a little laugh.

Elsie Walking Eagle was cooking the evening meal on a camp stove outside the teepee. She had some folding chairs that Lucy would've liked to sit down in, but Elsie didn't ask any of them to sit down though she was friendly enough.

"Is your husband here?" asked Flora.

"No, he's over in the sacred teepee," answered Elsie.

"How long is he going to take?"

"Oh, he should be home pretty soon," Elsie said, tending her cooking.

"Do you mind if we just wait? I brought this girl to see him. She's from Germany, too," Flora said.

Lucy had never seen Helmut in anything other than Indian regalia. He was a smallish man with blond hair, a broad face, and a large thin nose. He wore his hair in braids and always wore round, pink shell earrings. Whenever Lucy saw him, she was reminded of the Plains Indian Museum across the line.

Helmut didn't even glance at the company but went directly inside the teepee. Flora asked Elsie, "Would you tell him we'd like to see him?"

"Just wait here, I'll go talk to him," Elsie said, and followed her husband inside. Finally, she came out and invited them in. "He doesn't have much time to talk with you, so . . ." Her voice trailed off.

The inside of the teepee was stunning. It was roomy, and the floor was covered with buffalo hides. Backrests, wall hangings, parfleche bags, and numerous artifacts were magnificently displayed. Helmut Walking Eagle sat resplendent amidst his wealth. The women were dazzled. Lucy felt herself gaping and had to shush her children from asking any questions.

Helmut looked at them intently and rested his gaze on Hilda. Hilda walked toward him, her hand extended in greeting, but Helmut ignored it. Helmut turned to his wife and asked in Blackfoot, "Who is this?"

"She says she's from Germany," was all Elsie said, before making a quick move toward the door.

"Wait!" he barked in Blackfoot, and Elsie stopped where she was.

"I only wanted to know if you're familiar with my home town Weisbaden?" said Hilda.

"Do you know what she's talking about?" Helmut asked Elsie in Blackfoot. Elsie shook her head in a shamed manner.

"Why don't you ask *her* questions about Germany?" He hurled the words at Hilda, then, looking meanly at his wife, he added, "She's been there." Elsie flinched, and, forcing a smile, waved weakly at the intruders and asked them in a kind voice to come outside. As Lucy waited to leave, she looked at Helmut whose jaw twitched with resentment. His anger seemed to be tangibly reaching out to them.

"Wow!" whispered Hilda in Lucy's ear.

Outside, Flora touched a book on the fold-out table. Its title read *Indian Medicine* and in smaller letters, *A Revival of Ancient Cures and Ceremonies*. There was a picture of Helmut and Elsie on the cover. Flora asked, "Is this for sale?"

"No, that one's for someone here at camp, but you can get them in the bookstores."

"How much are they?" Flora asked, turning the book over.

"They're twenty-seven dollars. A lot of work went into it," Elsie replied.

Helmut, in Blackfoot, called out his wife's name, and Elsie said to her unwelcome callers, "I don't have time to visit. We have a lot of things to do." She left them and went to her husband.

"Do you think she wrote that book?" Lucy asked Flora.

"He's the brains; she's the source," Flora said. "Let's go. My kids are probably wondering what happened to me."

"I'm sorry I upset her husband. I didn't mean to," said Hilda. "I thought he would be willing to teach me something, because we're both German."

"Maybe you could buy his book," suggested Lucy.

"Look," said Flora, "if you're going to be around for a while, I'm going to a sun-dance this next weekend. I'm taking a few days off work. I have a friend up north who can teach you about Indian religion. She's a medicine woman. She's been to Germany. Maybe she even went to your home town."

"Oh, really!" gushed Hilda. "Of course, I'll be around. I'd love to go with you and meet your friends."

"You can come into the sweat with us. First, you'll need to buy four square yards of cotton . . ." began Flora.

But Hilda wasn't really listening to her. She looked as if she were already miles and miles away in the north country. Now, a sweat, she thought, would be real Indian.

1990

Sandra Birdsell

b. 1942

Sandra Birdsell was born in Hamiota and raised in Morris, Manitoba. Her first book, *Night Travellers* (1982), a collection of stories set in the fictional town of Agassiz, won the Gerald Lampert Memorial Award. It was followed by *Ladies of the House* (1984), stories linked to the first collection through interrelated storylines about the Lafrenière family; in 1987 the two collections were reissued in one volume as *Agassiz Stories*. Birdsell has published three novels: *The Missing Child* (1989), which won the W.H. Smith/Books in Canada First Novel Award; *The Chrome Suite* (1992), which won the Manitoba Book of the Year Award; and *The Russländer* (2001), which won the Saskatchewan Book of the Year, and was nominated for the Giller Prize. Evidence of her enduring obsession with the Mennonite community, this last novel chronicles the lives of a family called Vogt in the years leading up to the First World War and the Russian Revolution, and the family's eventual emigration to Canada. Birdsell won the Marian Engel Award in 1993.

The Wednesday Circle

Betty crosses the double planks that span the ditch in front of Joys' yard. Most people have only one plank. But Mrs Joy needs two. Mrs Joy is a possible candidate for the circus. Like sleeping with an elephant, Betty's father says often. But Mr and Mrs Joy, the egg people, don't sleep together. Betty knows this even though she's never gone further than inside their stale smelling kitchen.

The highway is a smeltering strip of gunmetal grey at her back. It leads to another town like the one she lives in. If you kept on going south, you would get to a place called Pembina in the States and a small dark tavern where a woman will serve under-age kids beer. Laurence, Betty's friend, knows about this. But if you turn from the highway and go west, there are dozens of villages and then the Pembina Hills which Betty has seen on one occasion, a school trip to the man-made lake at Morden. Home of the rich and the godly, Betty's father calls these villages. Wish the godly would stay home. Can't get a seat in the parlour on Friday nights.

Beyond her lies a field in summer fallow and a dirt road rising to a slight incline and then falling as it meets the highway. Before her is the Joys' crumbling yellow cottage, flanked on all sides by greying bales of straw which have swollen and broken free from their bindings and are scattered about the yard. Behind the cottage is the machine shed. Behind the machine shed and bumping up against the prairie is the chicken coop.

Because Mika, Betty's mother, sends her for the eggs instead of having them delivered by Mr Joy, she gets them cheaper.

Betty balances the egg cartons beneath her chin and pushes open the gate. It shrieks on its rusty hinges. The noise doesn't affect her as it usually does. Usually, the noise is like a door opening into a dark room and she is filled with dread. Today, she is prepared for it. Today is the day for the Wednesday Circle. The church ladies are meeting at her home. Even now, they're there in the dining room, sitting in a circle with their Bibles on their laps. It's like women and children in the centre. And arrows flying. Wagons are going up in flames and smoke. The goodness and matronly wisdom of the Wednesday Circle is a newly discovered thing. She belongs with them now. They can reach out to protect her even here, by just being what they are. And although she wants nothing to happen today, she is prepared for the worst.

"Come on in," Mrs Joy calls from the kitchen.

Betty sets the egg cartons down on the steps and enters the house. Mrs Joy's kitchen resembles a Woolworth store. There are porcelain dogs and cats in every corner on knick-knack shelves. Once upon a time, she used to love looking at those figurines but now she thinks they're ugly.

The woman sits in her specially made chair which is two chairs wired together. Her legs are stretched out in front resting up on another chair. Out of habit, Betty's heart constricts because she knows the signs. Mrs Joy is not up to walking back to the chicken coop with her. And that's how it all began.

"Lo, I am with you always even unto the end of the world," her mind recites.

These verses rise unbidden. She has memorized one hundred of them and won a trip to a summer Bible camp at Lake Winnipeg. She has for the first time seen the ocean on the prairie and tried to walk on water. The waves have lifted and pulled her out where her feet couldn't touch the sandy bottom and she has been swept beneath that mighty sea and heard the roaring of the waves in her head and felt the sting of fish water in her nostrils. Like a bubble of froth she is swept beneath the water, back and forth by the motion of the waves. She is drowning. What happens is just as she's heard. Her whole life flashes by. Her head becomes a movie screen playing back every lie and swearing, malicious and unkind deeds, thoughts, words. There is not one thing that makes her look justified for having done or said them. And then her foot touches a rock and she pushes herself forward in desperation, hoping it's the right direction.

Miraculously, it is. She bounces forward from the depths to where she can tip-toe to safety, keeping her nose above the waves. She runs panting with fear to her cabin. She pulls the blankets over her. She tells no one. But that evening in the chapel during devotions, the rustling wind in the poplars against the screen causes her to think of God. When they all sing, "Love Lifted Me," the sunset parts the clouds above the water so there is a crack of gold where angels hover, watching. So she goes forward to the altar with several others and has her name written in the Book of Life. They tell her the angels are clapping and she thinks she can hear them there at that crack of gold which is the door to heaven. She confesses every sin she's been shown in the water except for one. For some reason, it wasn't there in the movie. And they are such gentle, smiling nice people who have never done what she's done. So she can't bring herself to tell them that Mr Joy puts his hands in her pants.

"Rainin' today, ain't it child?" Mrs Joy asks.

"No, not yet," Betty says. 'It's very muggy."

"Don't I know it," she says.

"Are your legs sore?" Betty asks.

"Oh Lord, yes, how they ache," Mrs Joy says and rolls her eyes back into her head. Her jersey dress is a tent stretched across her knees. She cradles a cookie tin in her lap.

"That's too bad," Betty says.

A chuckle comes from deep inside her mammoth chest. "You sound just like your mother," she says. "And you're looking more and more like her each time I see you. You're just like an opal, always changing."

God's precious jewels, Mrs Joy calls them when she visits Mika. She lines them up verbally, Betty and her sisters and brothers, comparing chins, noses. This one here, she says about Betty, she's an opal. You oughta keep a watch over that one. Always changing. But it just goes to show, His mysteries does He perform. Not one of them the same.

"Thank you," Betty says, but she hates being told she looks like her mother. Mika has hazel eyes and brown hair. She is blonde and blue-eyed like her Aunt Elizabeth.

"Well, you know where the egg pail is," Mrs Joy says, dismissing her with a flutter of her pudgy hand.

"Aren't you coming?" Betty asks.

"Not today, girl. It aches me so to walk. You collect the eggs and then you jest find Mr Joy and you pay him. He gets it in the end anyhow."

Betty looks around the kitchen. His jacket is missing from its hook on the wall. She goes over to the corner by the window and feigns interest in the porcelain figures. She picks one up, sets it down. His truck is not in the yard.

"Where is he?"

"Went to town for something," Mrs Joy says. "But I thought he'd be back by now. Doesn't matter though, jest leave the money in the back porch."

The egg pail thumps against her leg as she crosses the yard to the chicken coop. She walks toward the cluttered wire enclosure, past the machine shed. The doors are open wide. The hens scratch and dip their heads in her direction as she approaches. Hope rises like an erratic kite as she passes the shed and there are no sounds coming from it. She stamps her feet and the hens scatter before her, then circle around and approach her from behind, silently. She quickly gathers three dozen of the warm, straw-flecked eggs, and then steps free of the stifling smelly coop out into the fresh moist air. She is almost home-free. She won't have to face anything today. It has begun to rain. Large spatters spot her white blouse, feel cool on her back. She sets the pail down on the ground beside the egg cartons and begins to transfer the eggs.

"Here, you don't have to do that outside." His sudden voice, as she fills the egg cartons, brings blood to her face, threatens to pitch her forward over the pail.

He strides across the yard from the shed. "Haven't got enough sense to come in out of the rain," he says. "Don't you know you'll melt? Be nothing left of you but a puddle."

He carries the pail, she carries the cartons. He has told her: Mrs Joy is fat and lazy, you are my sunshine, my only sunshine. I would like six little ones running around my place too, but Mrs Joy is fat and lazy. His thin hand has gone from patting her on the head with affection, to playfully slapping her on the behind, graduated then to tickling her armpits and ribs and twice now, his hands have been inside her underpants.

"Be not afraid," a verse leaps into her head. "For I am with you." She will put her plan into action. The Wednesday Circle women are strong and mighty. She knows them all, they're her mother's friends. She'll just go to them and say, Mr Joy feels me up, and that will be the end of it.

She walks behind him, her heart pounding. He has an oil rag hanging from his back pocket and his boots are caked with clay, adding inches to his height.

"I'm waiting for my parts," he says over his shoulder. "Can't do anything until I get that truck fixed." Sometimes he talks to her as though she were an adult. Sometimes as though she were ten again and just coming for the eggs for the first time. How old are you, he'd asked the last time and was surprised when she said, fourteen. My sunshine has grown up.

They enter the machine shed and he slides the doors closed behind them, first one and then the other, leaving a sliver of daylight beaming through where the doors join. A single light bulb dangles from the wire, shedding a circle of weak yellow light above the truck, not enough to clear the darkness from the corners.

"Okay-dokey," he says and puts the pail of eggs on the workbench. "You can work here. I've got things to do." He goes over to the truck, disappears beneath its raised hood.

Then he's back at the workbench, searching through his tool box. "Seen you with your boyfriend the other day," he says. "That Anderson boy."

"He's not my boyfriend," she says.

"I saw you," he says. His usual bantering tone is missing. "The two of you were in the coulee." Then his breath is warm on the side of her face as he reaches across her. His arms knock against her breast, sending pain shooting through her chest. I need a bra, she has told Mika. Whatever for? Wear an undershirt if you think you really need to.

"Do you think it's a good idea to hang around in the coulee with your boyfriend?"

"He's not my boyfriend," she says. "I told you."

He sees her flushed cheeks, senses her discomfort. "Aha," he says. "So he is. You can't fool me."

She moves away from him. Begins to stack cartons up against her chest, protection against his nudgings. Why is it that everyone but her own mother notices that she has breasts now?

"Don't rush off," he says. "Wait until the rain passes." The sound of it on the tin roof is like small pebbles being dropped one by one.

He takes the cartons from her and sets them back on the workbench. He smiles and she can see that perfect decayed circle between his front teeth. His hair is completely grey even though he's not as old as her father. He starts to walk past her, back towards the truck and then suddenly he grasps her about the waist and begins to tickle her ribs. She is slammed up against him and gasping for breath. His whiskers prickle against her neck. She tastes the bitterness of his flannel shirt.

She pushes away. "Stop."

He holds her tighter. "You're so pretty," he says. "No wonder the boys are chasing you. When I'm working in here, know what I'm thinking all the time?"

"Let me go." She continues to push against his bony arms.

"I'm thinking about all the things I could do to you."

Against her will, she has been curious to know. She feels desire rising when he speaks of what he would like to do. He has drawn vivid word-pictures that she likes to reconstruct until her face burns. Only it isn't Mr Joy in the pictures, it's Laurence. It's what made her pull aside her underpants so he could fumble inside her moist crevice with his grease-stained fingers.

"Show me your tits," he whispers into her neck. "I'll give you a dollar if you do."

She knows the only way out of this is to tell. When the whole thing is laid out before the Wednesday Circle, she will become whiter than snow. "No," she says.

"What do you mean, no," he says, jabbing her in the ribs once again.

"I'm going to tell," she says. "You can't make me do anything anymore because I'm going to tell on you." She feels as though a rock has been taken from her stomach. He is ugly. He is like a salamander dropping from the sky after a rainstorm into a mincemeat pail. She doesn't know how she could ever have liked him.

"Make you?" he says. "Make you? Listen here, girlie, I've only done what you wanted me to do."

She knows this to be true and not true. She isn't certain how she has come to accept and even expect his fondling. It has happened over the course of four years, gradually, like growing.

She walks to the double doors where the light shines through. "Open them, please," she says.

"Open them yourself," he says. She can feel the presence of the Wednesday Circle. The promise of their womanly strength is like a lamp unto her feet. They will surround her and protect her. Freedom from his word-pictures will make her a new person.

"You say anything," he says. "You say one thing and I'll have some pretty stories to tell about you. You betcha."

"That woman," Mika is saying to the Wednesday Circle as Betty enters the dining room. "That woman. She has absolutely no knowledge of the scriptures. She takes everything out of context." Mika is standing at the buffet with a china tea cup in her hand. Betty steps into the circle of chairs and sits down in Mika's empty one. Mika stops talking, throws her a look of surprise and question. The other women greet her with smiles, nods.

"Did you get the eggs?" Mika asks.

Betty feels her mouth stretching, moving of its own accord into a silly smile. She knows the smile irritates Mika but she can't help it. At times like these, her face moves on its own. She can hear her own heartbeat in her ears, like the ocean, roaring.

"What now?" Mika asks, worried.

"What do you mean, she takes everything out of context?" Mrs Brawn asks, ignoring Betty. It's her circle. She started it off, arranging for the church women to meet in each others' homes twice a month to read scripture and sew things which they send to a place in the city where they are distributed to the poor. The women are like the smell of coffee to Betty and at the same time, they are like the cool opaque squares of Mika's lemon slice which is arranged on bread and butter plates on the table. They are also like the sturdy varnished chairs they sit on. To be with them now is the same as when she was a child and thought that if you could always be near an adult when you were ill, you wouldn't die.

"My, my," Mika mimics someone to demonstrate to Mrs Brawn what she means. She places her free hand over her chest in a dramatic gesture. "They are different, ain't they? God's precious jewels. Just goes to show, His mysteries does He perform."

Betty realizes with a sudden shock that her mother is imitating Mrs Joy.

Mrs Brawn takes in Mika's pose with a stern expression and immediately Mika looks guilty, drops her hand from her breast and begins to fill cups with coffee.

"I suppose that we really can't expect much from Mrs Joy," Mika says with her back to them. Betty hears the slight mocking tone in her voice that passes them by.

Heads bent over needlework nod their understanding. The women's stitches form thumbs, forest-green fingers; except for the woman who sits beside Betty. With a hook she shapes intricate spidery patterns to lay across varnished surfaces, the backs of chairs. What the poor would want with those, I'll never know, Mika has said privately. But they include the doilies in their parcels anyway because they have an understanding. They whisper that this whitehaired woman has known suffering.

She works swiftly. It seems to Betty as though the threads come from the ends of her fingers, white strings with a spot of red every few inches. It looks as though she's cut her finger and secretly bleeds the colour into the lacy scallops. The women all unravel and knit and check closely for evenness of tension.

Mika enters the circle of chairs then, carrying the tray of coffee, and begins to make her way around it. She continues to speak of Mrs Joy.

"Are you looking forward to school?" the white-haired woman asks Betty. Her voice is almost a whisper, a knife peeling skin from a taut apple. Betty senses that it has been difficult for her to speak, feels privileged that she has.

"Yes, I miss school."

The woman blinks as she examines a knot in her yarn. She scrapes at it with her large square thumbnail which is flecked oddly with white fish-hook-shaped marks. "Your mother tells us you were at camp," she says. "What did you do there?"

Mika approaches them with the tray of coffee. "I just wish she hadn't picked me out, that's all," Mika says. "She insists on coming over here in the morning and it's impossible to work with her here. And Mr Joy is just as bad. I send Betty for the eggs now because he used to keep me at the door talking."

Mr Joy is just as bad. Mr Joy makes me ashamed of myself and I let him do it. The woman shakes loose the doily; it unfolds into the shape of a star as she holds it up.

"You like it?" the white-haired woman asks Betty.

"It's pretty."

"Maybe I give it to you."

"Ah, Mika," a woman across the circle says, "she just knows where she can find the best baking in town."

Then they all laugh; even the quiet woman beside Betty has a dry chuckle over the comment, only Mrs Brawn doesn't smile. She stirs her coffee with more force than necessary and sets the spoon alongside it with a clang.

"Obesity is no laughing matter," she says. "Mrs Joy is a glutton and that's to be pitied. We don't laugh at sin, the wages of sin is death."

"But the gift of God is eternal life through Jesus Christ our Lord," the woman says so softly, the words are nail filings dropping into her lap. If Betty hadn't seen her lips moving, she wouldn't have heard it. "God forgives," the woman says then, louder. She is an odd combination of young and old. Her voice and breasts are young but her hair is white.

Mika stands before them with a the tray of coffee. "Not always," Mika says. "There's the unpardonable sin, don't forget about that." She seems pleased to have remembered this.

"Which is?" the woman asks.

"Well, suicide," Mika says. "It has to be, because when you think of it, it's something you can't repent of once the deed is done." Mika smiles around the circle as if to say to them, see, I'm being patient with this woman who has known suffering.

"Perhaps there is no need to repent," the woman says.

"Pardon?"

"In Russia," the woman begins and then stops to set her thread down into her lap. She folds her hands one on top of the other and closes her eyes. The others, sensing a story, fall silent.

"During the revolution in Russia, there was once a young girl who was caught by nine soldiers and was their prisoner for two weeks. She was only thirteen. These men had their way with her many times, each one taking their turn, every single night. In the end, she shot herself. What about her?"

"I've never heard of such a case," Mika says. She sounds as though she resents hearing of it now.

"There are always such cases," the woman says. "If God knows the falling of a single sparrow, He is also merciful. He knows we're only human."

Mrs Brawn sets her knitting down on the floor in front of her chair, leans forward slightly. "Oh, He knows," she says. "But He never gives us more than we can bear. When temptation arises, He gives us strength to resist." She closes her statement with her hands, like a conductor pinching closed the last sound.

Betty watches as the white-haired woman twists and untwists her yarn into a tight ring around her finger. "I don't believe for one moment," she says finally, "that God would condemn such a person to hell. Jesus walked the earth and so He knows."

"No, no," Mika says from the Buffet. "He doesn't condemn us, don't you see? That's where you're wrong. We condemn ourselves. We make that choice."

"And what choice did that young girl have?" the woman asks. "It was her means of escape. God provided the gun."

Mika holds the tray of lemon squares up before her as though she were offering them to the sun. She looks stricken. Deep lines cut a sharp V above her nose. "You don't mean that," she says. "Suicide is unpardonable. I'm sure of it. Knowing that keeps me going. Otherwise, I would have done it myself long ago."

There is shocked silence and a rapid exchange of glances around the circle, at Betty, to see if she's heard.

"You shouldn't say such things," Mrs Brawn says quietly. "For shame. You have no reason to say that."

The white-haired woman speaks with a gaunt smile. "Occasionally," she says, "in this room, someone dares to speak the truth."

"What do you mean?" asks Mrs Brawn.

"Look at us," the woman says. "We're like filthy rags to Him in our self-righteousness. We obey because we fear punishment, not because we love."

Betty sees the grease spot on her blouse where his arm has brushed against her breast. Her whole body is covered with handprints. The stone is back in her stomach. She feels betrayed. For a moment the women are lost inside their own thoughts and they don't notice as she rises from her chair and sidles over to the door. Then, as if on some signal, their conversation resumes its usual level, each one waiting impatiently for the other to be finished so they can speak their words. Their laughter and goodwill have a feeling of urgency, of desperation.

Betty stands at the door; a backward glance and she sees the white-haired woman bending over her work again, eyes blinking rapidly, her fingers moving swiftly and the doily, its flecked pattern spreading like a web across her lap.

1982

Thomas King

b. 1943

Thomas King was born in Sacramento, California. His mother is of Greek and German descent and his father Cherokee. He obtained his Ph.D. from the University of Utah in 1986 and was director of the Native Studies program there. He also taught at the Universities of California and Minnesota. Choosing to identify himself as Native and North American, he also acknowledges his European ethnicity, and says "I don't want people to get the mistaken idea that I am an 'authentic Indian.'" Indeed, King explores notions of racial "authenticity" in his writing, and explodes the concept of a coherent and monolithic Native identity. King taught Native Studies for ten years at the University of Lethbridge, and began to write his own fiction. He currently teaches at Guelph University. His first novel, *Medicine River* (1990), was runner-up for the Commonwealth Literature Prize and was made into a CBC-TV movie. His second novel, *Green Grass, Running Water* (1993), which was short-listed for the Governor General's Award, established his reputation. Using the ancient mythological trickster figure Coyote to retell the story of creation, and using this story as a frame for the book, King explores issues of domestic life and political resistance. His technique draws on the oral traditions of Native cultures and enables him to create an original, laconic spoken language. His short fiction collection *One Good Story, That One* came out in 1993, and his third novel, *Truth and Bright Water*, in 1999. His anthology *All My Relations: An Anthology of Contemporary Canadian Native Fiction* (1990) was an important book, breaking the stereotypes about Native writing by the variety and complexities of its styles and concerns. King is most noted for his off-kilter humour, very evident in his twice-weekly CBC Radio comedy serial *Dead Dog Café* (1996–2001), which poked fun at Aboriginal affairs from an Aboriginal perspective. In 2002, writing under the name Hartley GoodWeather, King published the first in a planned series of comic mysteries, *Dreadful Water Shows Up*.

The One about Coyote Going West

This one is about Coyote. She was going west. Visiting her relations. That's what she said. You got to watch that one. Tricky one. Full of bad business. No, no, no, no, that one says. I'm just visiting.

Going to see Raven.

Boy, I says. That's another tricky one.

Coyote comes by my place. She wag her tail. Make them happy noises. Sit on my porch. Look around. With them teeth. With that smile. Coyote put her nose in my tea. My good tea. Get that nose out of my tea, I says.

I'm going to see my friends, she says. Tell those stories. Fix this world. Straighten them up.

Oh boy, pretty scary that, Coyote fix the world, again.

Sit down, I says. Eat some food. Hard work that fix up the world. Maybe you have a song. Maybe you have a good joke.

Sure, says Coyote. That one wink her ears. Lick her whiskers.

I tuck my feet under that chair. Got to hide my toes. Sometimes that tricky one leave her skin sit in that chair. Coyote skin. No Coyote. Sneak around. Bite them toes. Make you jump.

I been reading those books, she says.

You must be one smart Coyote, I says.

You bet, she says.

Maybe you got a good story for me, I says.

I been reading about that history, says Coyote. She sticks that nose back in my tea. All about who found us Indians.

Ho, I says. I like those old ones. Them ones are the best. You tell me your story, I says. Maybe some biscuits will visit us. Maybe some moose-meat stew come along, listen to your story.

Okay, she says and she sings her story song.

Snow's on the ground the snakes are asleep.
Snow's on the ground my voice is strong.
Snow's on the ground the snakes are asleep.
Snow's on the ground my voice is strong.

She sings like that. With that tail, wagging. With that smile. Sitting there.

Maybe I tell you the one about Eric the Lucky and the Vikings play hockey for the Old-timers, find us Indians in Newfoundland, she says.

Maybe I tell you the one about Christopher Cartier looking for something good to eat. Find us Indians in a restaurant in Montreal.

Maybe I tell you the one about Jacques Columbus come along that river, Indians waiting for him. We all wave and say, here we are, here we are.

Everyone knows those stories, I says. White man stories. Baby stories you got in your mouth.

No, no, no, no, says that Coyote. I read these ones in that old book.

Ho, I says. You are trying to bite my toes. Everyone knows who found us Indians. Eric the Lucky and that Christopher Cartier and that Jacques Columbus come along later. Those ones get lost. Float about. Walk around. Get mixed up. Ho, ho, ho, those ones cry, we are lost. So we got to find them. Help them out. Feed them. Show them around.

Boy, I says. Bad mistake that one.

You are very wise, grandmother, says Coyote, bring her eyes down. Like she is sleepy. Maybe you know who discovered Indians.

Sure, I says. Everyone knows that. It was Coyote. She was the one.

Oh, grandfather, that Coyote says. Tell me that story. I love those stories about that sneaky one. I don't think I know that story, she says.

All right, I says. Pay attention.

Coyote was heading west. That's how I always start this story. There was nothing else in the world. Just Coyote. She could see all the way, too. No mountains then. No rivers. No forests then. Pretty flat then. So she starts to make things. So she starts to fix this world.

This is exciting, says Coyote, and she takes her nose out of my tea.

Yes, I says. Just the beginning, too. Coyote got a lot of things to make.

Tell me, grandmother, says Coyote. What does the clever one make first?

Well, I says. Maybe she makes that tree grows by the river. Maybe she makes that buffalo. Maybe she makes that mountain. Maybe she makes them clouds.

Maybe she makes that beautiful rainbow, says Coyote.

No, I says. She don't make that thing. Mink makes that.

Maybe she makes that beautiful moon, says Coyote.

No, I says. She don't do that either. Otter finds that moon in a pond later on.

Maybe she makes the oceans with that blue water, says Coyote.

No, I says. Ocean are already here. She don't do any of that. The first thing Coyote makes, I tell Coyote, is a mistake.

Boy, Coyote sit up straight. Them eyes pop open. That tail stop wagging. That one swallow that smile.

Big one, too, I says. Coyote is going west thinking of things to make. That one is trying to think of everything to make at once. So she don't see that hole. So she falls in that hole. Then those thoughts bump around. They run into each other. Those ones fall out of Coyote's ears. In that hole. Ho, that Coyote cries. I have fallen into a hole. I must have made a mistake. And she did.

So, there is that hole. And there is that Coyote in that hole. And there is that big mistake in that hole with Coyote. Ho, says that mistake. You must be Coyote.

That mistake is real big and that hole is small. Not much room. I don't want to tell you what that mistake looks like. First mistake in the world. Pretty scary. Boy, I can't look. I got to close my eyes. You better close your eyes, too, I tell Coyote.

Okay, I'll do that, she says, and she puts her hands over her eyes. But she don't fool me. I can see she's peeking.

Don't peek, I says.

Okay, she says. I won't do that.

Well, you know, that Coyote thinks about the hole. And she thinks about how she's going to get out of that hole. She thinks how she's going to get that big mistake back in her head.

Say, says that mistake. What is it that you're thinking about?

I'm thinking of a song, says Coyote. I'm thinking of a song to make this hole bigger.

That's a good idea, says that mistake. Let me hear your hole song.

But that's not what Coyote sings. She sings a song to make the mistake smaller. But that mistake hears her. And that mistake grabs Coyote's nose. And that one pulls off her mouth so she can't sing. And that one jumps up and down on Coyote until she is flat. Then that one leaps out of that hole, wanders around looking for things to do.

Well, Coyote is feeling pretty bad, all flat her nice fur coat full of stomp holes. So she thinks hard, and she think about a healing song. And she tries to sing a healing song, but her mouth is in other places. So she thinks harder and tries to sing that song through her nose. But that nose don't make any sound, just drip a lot. She tries to sing that song out her ears, but those ears don't hear anything.

So, that silly one thinks real hard and tries to sing out her butt-hole. Pssst! Pssst! That is what that butt-hole says, and right away things don't smell so good in that hole. Pssst.

Boy, Coyote thinks. Something smells.

That Coyote lies there flat and practise and practise. Pretty soon, maybe two days, maybe one year, she teach that butt-hole to sing. That song. That healing song. So that butt-hole sings that song. And Coyote begins to feel better. And Coyote don't feel so flat anymore. Pssst! Pssst! Things still smell pretty bad, but Coyote is okay.

That one look around in that hole. Find her mouth. Put that mouth back. So, she says to that butt-hole. Okay, you can stop singing now. You can stop making them smells now. But, you know, that butt-hole is liking all that singing, and so that butt-hole keeps on singing.

Stop that, says Coyote. You going to stink up the whole world. But it don't. So Coyote jumps out of that hole and runs across the prairies real fast. But that butt-hole follows her. Pssst. Pssst. Coyote jumps into a lake, but that butt-hole don't drown. It just keeps on singing.

Hey, who is doing all that singing, someone says.

Yes, and who is making that bad smell, says another voice.

It must be Coyote, says a third voice.

Yes, says a fourth voice. I believe it is Coyote.

That Coyote sit in my chair, put her nose in my tea, say, I know who that voice is. It is that big mistake playing a trick. Nothing else is made yet.

No, I says. That mistake is doing other things.

Then those voices are spirits, says Coyote.

No, I says. Them voices belong to them ducks.

Coyote stand up on my chair. Hey, she says, where did them ducks come from?

Calm down, I says. This story is going to be okay. This story is doing just fine. This story knows where it is going. Sit down. Keep your skin on.

So.

Coyote look around, and she see them four ducks. In that lake. Ho, she says. Where did you ducks come from? I didn't make you yet.

Yes, says them ducks. We were waiting around, but you didn't come. So we got tired of waiting. So we did it ourselves.

I was in a hole, says Coyote.

Pssst. Pssst.

What's that noise, says them ducks. What's that bad smell?

Never mind, says Coyote. Maybe you've seen something go by. Maybe you can help me find something I lost. Maybe you can help me get it back.

Those ducks swim around and talk to themselves. Was it something awful to look at? Yes, says Coyote, it certainly was. Was it somethings with ugly fur? Yes, says Coyote, I think it had that, too. Was it something that made a lot of noise? ask them ducks. Yes, it was pretty noisy, says Coyote. Did it smell bad, them ducks want to know. Yes, says Coyote. I guess you ducks have seen my something.

Yes, says them ducks. It is right there behind you.

So that Coyote turn around, and there is nothing there.

It's still behind you, says those ducks.

So Coyote turn around again but she don't see anything.

Pssst! Pssst!

Boy, says those ducks. What a noise! What a smell! They say that, too. What an ugly thing with all that fur!

Never mind, says that Coyote, again. That is not what I'm looking for. I'm looking for something else.

Maybe you're looking for Indians, says those ducks.

Well, that Coyote is real surprised because she hasn't created Indians, either. Boy, says that one, mischief is everywhere. This world is getting bent.

All right.

So Coyote and those ducks are talking, and pretty soon they hear a noise. And pretty soon there is something coming. And those ducks says, oh, oh, oh, oh. They say that like they see trouble, but it is not trouble. What comes along is a river.

Hello, says that river. Nice day. Maybe you want to take a swim. But Coyote don't want to swim, and she looks at that river and she looks at that river again. Something's not right here, she says. Where are those rocks? Where are those rapids? What did you do with them waterfalls? How come you're so straight?

And Coyote is right. That river is nice and straight and smooth without any bumps or twists. It runs both ways, too, not like a modern river.

We got to fix this, says Coyote, and she does. She puts some rocks in that river, and she fixes it so it only runs one way. She puts a couple of waterfalls in and makes a bunch of rapids where things get shallow fast.

Coyote is tired with all this work, and those ducks are tired just watching. So that Coyote sits down. So she closes her eyes. So she puts her nose in her tail. So those ducks shout, wake up, wake up! Something big is heading this way! And they were right.

Mountain comes sliding along, whistling. Real happy mountain. Nice and round. This mountain is full of grapes and other good things to eat. Apples, peaches, cherries. Howdy-do, says the polite mountain, nice day for whistling.

Coyote looks at that mountain, and that one shakes her head. Oh, no, she says, this mountain is all wrong. How come you're so nice and round? Where are those craggy peaks? Where are all them cliffs? What happened to all that snow? Boy, we got to fix this thing, too. So she does.

Grandfather, grandfather, says that Coyote, sit in my chair, put her nose in my tea. Why is that Coyote changing all those good things?

That is a real sly one, ask me that question. I look at those eyes. Grab them ears. Squeeze that nose. Hey, let go my nose, that Coyote says.

Okay, I says. Coyote still in Coyote skin. I bet you know why Coyote change that happy river. Why she change that mountain sliding along whistling.

No, says that Coyote, look around my house, lick her lips, make them baby noises.

Maybe it's because she is mean, I says.

Oh, no, says Coyote. That one is sweet and kind.

Maybe it's because that one is not too smart.

Oh, no, says Coyote. That Coyote is very wise.

Maybe it's because she made a mistake.

Oh, no, says Coyote. She made one of those already.

All right, I says. The Coyote must be doing the right thing. She must be fixing up the world so it is perfect.

Yes, says Coyote. That must be it. What does that brilliant one do next?

Everyone knows what Coyote does next, I says. Little babies know what Coyote does next.

Oh no, says Coyote. I have never heard this story. You are wonderful storyteller. You tell me your good Coyote story.

Boy, you got to watch that one all the time. Hide them toes.

Well, I says. Coyote thinks about that river. And she thinks about that mountain. And she thinks somebody is fooling around. So she goes looking around. She goes looking for that one who is messing up the world.

She goes to the north, and there is nothing. She goes to the south, and there is nothing there, either. She goes to the east, and there is still nothing there. She goes to the west, and there is a pile of snow tires.

And there is some televisions. And there is some vacuum cleaners. And there is a bunch of pastel sheets. And there is an air humidifier. And there is a big mistake sitting on a portable gas barbecue reading a book. Big book. Department store catalogue.

Hello, says that mistake. Maybe you want a hydraulic jack.

No, says that Coyote. I don't want one of them. But she don't tell that mistake what she want because she don't want to miss her mouth again. But when she thinks about being flat and full of stomp holes, that butt-hole wakes up and begins to sing. Pssst. Pssst.

What's that noise? says that big mistake.

I'm looking for Indians, says that Coyote, real quick. Have you seen any?

What's that bad smell?

Never mind, says Coyote. Maybe you have some Indians around here.

I got some toaster ovens, says that mistake.

We don't need that stuff, says Coyote. You got to stop making all those things. You're going to fill up this world.

Maybe you want a computer with a colour monitor. That mistake keeps looking through that book and those things keep landing in piles all around Coyote.

Stop, stop, cries Coyote. Golf cart lands on her foot. Golf balls bounce off her head. You got to give me that book before the world gets lopsided.

These are good things, says that mistake. We need these things to make up the world. Indians are going to need this stuff.

We don't have any Indians, says Coyote.

And that mistake can see that that's right. Maybe we better make some Indians, says that mistake. So that one looks in that catalogue, but it don't have any Indians. And Coyote don't know how to do that, either. She has already made four things.

I've made four things already, she says. I got to have help.

We can help, says some voices and it is those ducks come swimming along. We can help you make Indians, says the white duck. Yes, we can do that, says the green duck. We have been thinking about this, says that blue duck. We have a plan, says the red duck.

Well, that Coyote don't know what to do. So she tells them ducks to go ahead because this story is pretty long and it's getting late and everyone want to go home.

You still awake, I says to Coyote. You still here?

Oh yes, grandmother, says Coyote. What do those clever ducks do?

So I tell Coyote that those ducks lay some eggs. Ducks do that, you know. That white duck lay an egg, and it is blue. That red duck lay an egg, and it is green. That blue duck lay an egg, and it is red. That green duck lay an egg, and it is white.

Come on, says those ducks. We got to sing a song. We got to do a dance. So they do. Coyote and that big mistake and those four ducks dance around the eggs. So they dance and sing for a long time, and pretty soon Coyote gets hungry.

I know this dance, she says, but you got to close your eyes when you do it or nothing will happen. You got to close your eyes tight. Okay, says those ducks. We can do that. And they do. And that big mistake closes its eyes, too.

But Coyote, she don't close her eyes, and all of them start dancing again, and Coyote dances up close to that white duck, and she grabs that white duck by her neck.

When Coyote grabs that duck, that duck flaps her wings, and that big mistake hears the noise and opens them eyes. Say, says that big mistake, that's not the way the dance goes.

By golly, you're right, says Coyote, and she lets that duck go. I am getting it mixed up with another dance.

So they start to dance again. And Coyote is very hungry, and she grabs that blue duck, and she grabs his wings, too. But Coyote's stomach starts to make hungry noises, and that mistake opens them eyes and see Coyote with the blue duck. Hey, says that mistake, you got yourself mixed up again.

That's right, says Coyote, and she drops that duck and straightens out that neck. It sure is good you're around to help me with this dance.

They all start that dance again, and, this time, Coyote grabs the green duck real quick and tries to stuff it down that greedy throat, and there is nothing hanging out but them yellow duck feet. But those feet are flapping in Coyote's eyes, and she can't see where she is going, and she bumps into the big mistake and the mistake turns around to see what has happened.

Ho, says that big mistake, you can't see where you're going with them yellow duck feet flapping in your eyes, and that mistake pulls that green duck out of Coyote's throat. You could hurt yourself dancing like that.

You are one good friend, look after me like that, says Coyote.

Those ducks start to dance again, and Coyote dances with them, but that red duck says, we better dance with one eye open, so we can help Coyote with this dance. So they dance some more, and, then, those eggs begin to move around, and those eggs crack open. And if you look hard, you can see something inside those eggs.

I know, I know, says that Coyote, jump up and down on my chair, shake up my good tea. Indians come out of those eggs. I remember this story, now. Inside those eggs are the Indians Coyote's been looking for.

No, I says. You are one crazy Coyote. What comes out of those duck eggs are baby ducks. You better sit down, I says. You may fall and hurt yourself. You may spill my tea. You may fall on top of this story and make it flat.

Where are the Indians? says that Coyote. This story was about how Coyote found the Indians. Maybe the Indians are in the eggs with the baby ducks.

No, I says, nothing in those eggs but little ducks. Indians will be along in a while. Don't lose your skin.

So.

When those ducks see what has come out of the eggs, they says, boy, we didn't get that quite right. We better try again. So they do. They lay them eggs. They dance that dance. They sing that song. Those eggs crack open and out comes some more baby ducks. They do this seven times and each time, they get more ducks.

By golly, says those four ducks. We got more ducks than we need. I guess we got to be the Indians. And so they do that. Before Coyote or that big mistake can mess things up, those four ducks turn into Indians, two women and two men. Good-looking Indians, too. They don't look at all like ducks any more.

But those duck-Indians aren't happy. They look at each other and they begin to cry. This is pretty disgusting, they says. All this ugly skin. All these bumpy bones. All this awful black hair. Where are our nice soft feathers? Where are our beautiful feet? What happened to our wonderful wings? It's probably all that Coyote's fault because she didn't do the dance right, and those four duck-Indians come over and stomp all over Coyote until she is flat like before. Then they leave. That big mistake leave, too. And that Coyote, she starts to think about a healing song.

Pssst. Pssst.

That's it, I says. It is done.

But what happens to Coyote, says Coyote. That wonderful one is still flat.

Some of these stories are flat, I says. That's what happens when you try to fix this world. This world is pretty good all by itself. Best to leave it alone. Stop messing around with it.

I better get going, says Coyote. I will tell Raven your good story. We going to fix this world for sure. We know how to do it now. We know to do it right.

So, Coyote drinks my tea and that one leave. And I can't talk any more because I got to watch the sky. Got to watch out for falling things that land in piles. When that Coyote's wandering around looking to fix things, nobody in this world is safe.

1989

Richard Ford

b. 1944

Richard Ford was born in Jackson, Mississippi, and was shuttled between Jackson and Little Rock, Arkansas, where his grandfather managed a hotel, after his father, a travelling salesman, had a heart attack. A fascination with itinerancy and travel is central to his fiction. "Nothing ever got stale," Ford remarks about his early life. He attended Michigan State University and signed up for the Marines—a case of hepatitis promptly led to a medical discharge. Though he suffered from mild dyslexia as a child, he turned to literature: "Being a slow reader admitted me to books at a very basic level—word by word. That doesn't seem like bad preparation to me, if writers are people who essentially live in sentences." He taught high school and coached baseball in Flint, Michigan, then moved to New York and worked as an editor. At the age of twenty-three he rejected a job at the CIA, and then, "purely on instinct and whimsy" as he claimed, turned to writing. He went to graduate school at the University of California in Irvine, where he was taught by E.L Doctorow and Oakley Hall. His first novel, *A Piece of My Heart* (1976), is the only one of his novels set in the South; however, critics frequently identify him as a Southern writer and as part of that literary tradition. But Ford is unwilling to be tagged as a Southern writer: "I always wanted my books to exist outside the limits of so-called Southern writing." He set his next novel, *The Ultimate Good Luck* (1981), about a Vietnam veteran, in Mexico. When his novels failed to sell, Ford turned to a career as a sportswriter for a magazine called *Inside Sports*, which became the basis for his novel *The Sportswriter* (1986). The story collection *Rock Springs* (1987) solidified Ford's reputation as one of the best contemporary American writers. *Independence*

Day (1995), a sequel to *The Sportswriter*, where the main character has become a real estate salesman, was awarded the Pulitzer Prize and the PEN/Faulkner Award for Fiction. Among Ford's recent work is the marvellous *Canada* (2012).

Rock Springs

Edna and I had started down from Kalispell, heading for Tampa-St Pete where I still had some friends from the old glory days who wouldn't turn me in to the police. I had managed to scrape with the law in Kalispell over several bad cheques—which is a prison crime in Montana. And I knew Edna was already looking at her cards and thinking about a move, since it wasn't the first time I'd been in law scrapes in my life. She herself had already had her own troubles, losing her kids and keeping her ex-husband, Danny, from breaking in her house and stealing her things while she was at work, which was really why I had moved in in the first place, that and needing to give my little daughter, Cheryl, a better shake at things.

I don't know what was between Edna and me, just beached by the same tides when you got down to it. Though love has been built on frailer ground than that, as I well know. And when I came in the house that afternoon, I just asked her if she wanted to go to Florida with me, leave things where they sat, and she said, "Why not? My datebook's not that full."

Edna and I had been a pair eight months, more or less man and wife, some of which time I had been out of work, and some when I'd worked at the dog track as a lead-out and could help with the rent and talk sense to Danny when he came around. Danny was afraid of me because Edna had told him I'd been in prison in Florida for killing a man, though that wasn't true. I had once been in jail in Tallahassee for stealing tires and had gotten into a fight on the county farm where a man had lost his eye. But I hadn't done the hurting, and Edna just wanted the story worse than it was so Danny wouldn't act crazy and make her have to take her kids back, since she had made a good adjustment to not having them, and I already had Cheryl with me. I'm not a violent person and would never put a man's eye out, much less kill someone. My former wife, Helen, would come all the way from Waikiki Beach to testify to that. We never had violence, and I believe in crossing the street to stay out of trouble's way. Though Danny didn't know that.

But we were half down through Wyoming, going towards I-80 and feeling good about things, when the oil light flashed on in the car I'd stolen, a sign I knew to be a bad one.

I'd gotten us a good car, a cranberry Mercedes I'd stolen out of an ophthalmologist's lot in Whitefish, Montana. I stole it because I thought it would be comfortable over a long haul, because I thought it got good mileage, which it didn't, and because I'd never had a good car in my life, just old Chevy junkers and used trucks back from when I was a kid swamping citrus with Cubans.

The car made us all high that day. I ran the windows up and down, and Edna told us some jokes and made faces. She could be lively. Her features would light up like a beacon and you could see her beauty, which wasn't ordinary. It all made me giddy, and I drove clear down to Bozeman, then straight on through the park to Jackson Hole. I rented us the bridal suite in the Quality Court in Jackson and left Cheryl and her little dog, Duke, sleeping while Edna and I drove to a rib barn and drank beer and laughed till after midnight.

It felt like a whole new beginning for us, bad memories left behind and a new horizon to build on. I got so worked up, I had a tattoo done on my arm that said FAMOUS TIMES, and Edna bought a Bailey hat with an Indian feather band and a little turquoise-and-silver bracelet for Cheryl, and we made love on the seat of the car in the Quality Court parking lot just as the sun was burning up on the Snake River, and everything seemed then like the end of the rainbow.

It was that very enthusiasm, in fact, that made me keep the car one day longer instead of driving it into the river and stealing another one, like I should've done and had done before.

Where the car went bad there wasn't a town in sight or even a house, just some low mountains maybe fifty miles away or maybe a hundred, a barbed-wire fence in both directions, hardpan prairie, and some hawks riding the evening air seizing insects.

I got out to look at the motor, and Edna got out with Cheryl and the dog to let them have a pee by the car. I checked the water and checked the oil stick, and both of them said perfect.

"What's that light mean, Earl?" Edna said. She had come and stood by the car with her hat on. She was just sizing things up for herself.

"We shouldn't run it," I said. "Something's not right in the oil."

She looked around at Cheryl and Little Duke, who were peeing on the hardtop side-by-side like two little dolls, then out at the mountains, which were becoming black and lost in the distance. "What're we doing?" she said. She wasn't worried yet, but she wanted to know what I was thinking about.

"Let me try it again."

"That's a good idea," she said, and we all got back in the car.

When I turned the motor over, it started right away and the red light stayed off and there weren't any noises to make you think something was wrong. I let it idle a minute, then pushed the accelerator down and watched the red bulb. But there wasn't any light on, and I started wondering if maybe I hadn't dreamed I saw it, or that it had been the sun catching an angle off the window chrome, or maybe I was scared of something and didn't know it.

"What's the matter with it, Daddy?" Cheryl said from the backseat. I looked back at her, and she had on her turquoise bracelet and Edna's hat set back on the back of her head and that little black-and-white Heinz dog on her lap. She looked like a little cowgirl in the movies.

"Nothing, honey, everything's fine now," I said.

"Little Duke tinkled where I tinkled," Cheryl said, and laughed.

"You're two of a kind," Edna said, not looking back. Edna was usually good with Cheryl, but I knew she was tired now. We hadn't had much sleep, and she had a tendency to get cranky when she didn't sleep. "We oughta ditch this damn car first chance we get," she said.

"What's the first chance we got?" I asked, because I knew she'd been at the map.

"Rock Springs, Wyoming," Edna said with conviction. "Thirty miles down this road." She pointed out ahead.

I had wanted all along to drive the car into Florida like a big success story. But I knew Edna was right about it, that we shouldn't take crazy chances. I had kept thinking of it as my car and not the ophthalmologist's, and that was how you got caught in these things.

"Then my belief is we ought to go to Rock Springs and negotiate ourselves a new car," I said. I wanted to stay upbeat, like everything was panning out right.

"That's a great idea," Edna said, and she leaned over and kissed me hard on the mouth.

"That's a great idea," Cheryl said. "Let's pull on out of here right now."

The sunset that day I remember as being the prettiest I'd ever seen. Just as it touched the rim of the horizon, it all at once fired the air into jewels and red sequins the precise likes of which I had never seen before and haven't seen since. The West has it all over everywhere for sunsets, even Florida, where it's supposedly flat but where half the time trees block your view.

"It's cocktail hour," Edna said after we'd driven a while. "We ought to have a drink and celebrate something." She felt better thinking we were going to get rid of the car. It certainly had dark troubles and was something you'd want to put behind you.

Edna had out a whisky bottle and some plastic cups and was measuring levels on the glove-box lid. She liked drinking, and she liked drinking in the car, which was something you got used to in Montana, where it wasn't against the law, but where, strangely enough, a bad cheque would land you in Deer Lodge Prison for a year.

"Did I ever tell you I once had a monkey?" Edna said, setting my drink on the dashboard where I could reach it when I was ready. Her spirits were already picked up. She was like that, up one minute and down the next.

"I don't think you ever did tell me that," I said. "Where were you then?"

"Missoula," she said. She put her bare feet on the dash and rested the cup on her breasts. "I was waitressing at the AmVets. This was before I met you. Some guy came in one day with a monkey. A spider monkey. And I said, just to be joking, 'I'll roll you for that monkey.' And the guy said, 'Just one roll?' And I said, 'Sure.' He put the monkey down on the bar, picked up a cup, and rolled out boxcars. I picked it up and rolled out three fives. And I just stood there looking at the guy. He was just some guy passing through, I guess a vet. He got a strange look on his face—I'm sure not as strange as the one I had—but he looked kind of sad and surprised and satisfied all at once. I said, 'We can roll again.' But he said, 'No, I never roll twice for anything.' And he sat and drank a beer and talked about one thing and another for a while, about nuclear war and building a stronghold somewhere up in the Bitterroot, whatever it was, while I just watched the monkey, wondering what I was going to do with it when the guy left. And pretty soon he got up and said, 'Well, good-bye, Chipper'—that was this monkey's name, of course. And then he left before I could say anything. And the monkey just sat on the bar all that night. I don't know what made me think of that, Earl. Just something weird. I'm letting my mind wander."

"That's perfectly fine," I said. I took a drink of my drink. "I'd never own a monkey," I said after a minute. "They're too nasty. I'm sure Cheryl would like a monkey, though, wouldn't you, honey?" Cheryl was down on the seat playing with Little Duke. She used to talk about monkeys all the time then. "What'd you ever do with that monkey?" I said, watching the speedometer. We were having to go slower now because the red light kept fluttering on. And all I could do to keep it off was go slower. We were going maybe thirty-five and it was an hour before dark, and I was hoping Rock Springs wasn't far away.

"You really want to know?" Edna said. She gave me a quick glance, then looked back at the empty desert as if she was brooding over it.

"Sure," I said. I was still upbeat. I figured I could worry about breaking down and let other people be happy for a change.

"I kept it a week." And she seemed gloomy all of a sudden, as if she saw some aspect of the story she had never seen before. "I took it home and back and forth to the AmVets on my shifts. And it didn't cause any trouble. I fixed a chair up for it to sit on, back of the bar, and people liked it. It made a nice little clicking noise. We changed its name to Mary because the bartender figured out it was a girl. Though I was never really comfortable with it at home. I felt like it watched me too much. Then one day a guy came in, some guy who'd been in Vietnam, still wore a fatigue coat. And he said to me, 'Don't you know that a monkey'll kill you? It's got more strength in its fingers than you got in your whole body.' He said people had been killed in Vietnam by monkeys, bunches of them marauding while you were asleep, killing you and covering you with leaves. I didn't believe a word of it, except that when I got home and got undressed I started looking over across the room at Mary on her chair in the dark watching me. And I got the creeps. And after a while I got up and went out to the car, got a length of clothesline wire, and came back in and wired her to the doorknob through her little silver collar, then went back and tried to sleep. And I guess I must've slept the sleep of the dead—though I don't remember it—because when I got up I found Mary had tipped off her chair-back and hanged herself on the wire line. I'd made it too short."

Edna seemed badly affected by that story and slid low in the seat so she couldn't see out over the dash. "Isn't that a shameful story, Earl, what happened to that poor little monkey?"

"I see a town! I see a town!" Cheryl started yelling from the back seat, and right up Little Duke started yapping and the whole car fell into a racket. And sure enough she had seen something I hadn't, which was Rock Springs,

Wyoming, at the bottom of a long hill, a little glowing jewel in the desert with I-80 running on the north side and the black desert spread out behind.

"That's it, honey," I said. "That's where we're going. You saw it first."

"We're hungry," Cheryl said. "Little Duke wants some fish, and I want spaghetti." She put her arms around my neck and hugged me.

"Then you'll just get it," I said. "You can have anything you want. And so can Edna and so can Little Duke." I looked over at Edna, smiling, but she was staring at me with eyes that were fierce with anger. "What's wrong?" I said.

"Don't you care anything about that awful thing that happened to me?" Her mouth was drawn tight, and her eyes kept cutting back at Cheryl and Little Duke, as if they had been tormenting her.

"Of course I do," I said. "I thought that was an awful thing." I didn't want her to be unhappy. We were almost there, and pretty soon we could sit down and have a real meal without thinking somebody might be hurting us.

"You want to know what I did with that monkey?" Edna said.

"Sure I do," I said.

"I put her in a green garbage bag, put it in the trunk of my car, drove to the dump, and threw her in the trash." She was staring at me darkly, as if the story meant something to her that was real important but that only she could see and that the rest of the world was a fool for.

"Well, that's horrible," I said. "But I don't see what else you could do. You didn't mean to kill her. You'd have done it differently if you had. And then you had to get rid of it, and I don't know what else you could have done. Throwing it away might seem unsympathetic to somebody, probably, but not to me. Sometimes that's all you can do, and you can't worry about what somebody else thinks." I tried to smile at her, but the red light was staying on if I pushed the accelerator at all, and I was trying to gauge if we could coast to Rock Springs before the car gave out completely. I looked at Edna again. "What else can I say?" I said.

"Nothing," she said, and stared back at the dark highway. "I should've known that's what you'd think. You've got a character that leaves something out, Earl. I've known that a long time."

"And yet here you are," I said. "And you're not doing so bad. Things could be a lot worse. At least we're all together here."

"Things could always be worse," Edna said. "You could go to the electric chair tomorrow."

"That's right," I said. "And somewhere somebody probably will. Only it won't be you."

"I'm hungry," said Cheryl. "When're we gonna eat? Let's find a motel. I'm tired of this. Little Duke's tired of it too."

Where the car stopped rolling was some distance from the town, though you could see the clear outline of the interstate in the dark with Rock Springs lighting up the sky behind. You could hear the big tractors hitting the spacers in the overpass, revving up for the climb to the mountains.

I shut off the lights.

"What're we going to do now?" Edna said irritably, giving me a bitter look.

"I'm figuring it," I said. "It won't be hard, whatever it is. You won't have to do anything."

"I'd hope not," she said and looked the other way.

Across the road and across a dry wash a hundred yards was what looked like a huge mobile-home town, with a factory or a refinery of some kind lit up behind it and in full swing. There were lights on in a lot of the mobile homes, and there were cars moving along an access road that ended near the freeway overpass a mile the other way. The lights in the mobile homes seemed friendly to me, and I knew right then what I should do.

"Get out," I said, opening my door.

"Are we walking?" Edna said.

"We're pushing."

"I'm not pushing." Edna reached up and locked her door.

"All right," I said. "Then you just steer."

"You're pushing us to Rock Springs, are you, Earl? It doesn't look like it's more than about three miles."

"I'll push," Cheryl said from the back.

"No, hon. Daddy'll push. You just get out with Little Duke and move out of the way."

Edna gave me a threatening look, just as if I'd tried to hit her. But when I got out she slid into my seat and took the wheel, staring angrily ahead straight into the cottonwood scrub.

"Edna can't drive that car," Cheryl said from out in the dark. "She'll run it in the ditch."

"Yes, she can, hon. Edna can drive it as good as I can. Probably better."

"No she can't," Cheryl said. "No she can't either." And I thought she was about to cry, but she didn't.

I told Edna to keep the ignition on so it wouldn't lock up and to steer into the cottonwoods with the parking lights on so she could see. And when I started, she steered it straight off into the trees, and I kept pushing until we were twenty yards into the cover and the tires sank in the soft sand and nothing at all could be seen from the road.

"Now where are we?" she said, sitting at the wheel. Her voice was tired and hard, and I knew she could have put a good meal to use. She had a sweet nature, and I recognized that this wasn't her fault but mine. Only I wished she could be more hopeful.

"You stay right here, and I'll go over to that trailer park and call us a cab," I said.

"What cab?" Edna, her mouth wrinkled as if she'd never heard anything like that in her life.

"There'll be cabs," I said, and tried to smile at her. "There's cabs everywhere."

"What're you going to tell him when he gets here? Our stolen car broke down and we need a ride to where we can steal another one? That'll be a big hit, Earl."

"I'll talk," I said. "You just listen to the radio for ten minutes and then walk on out to the shoulder like nothing was suspicious. And you and Cheryl act nice. She doesn't need to know about this car."

"Like we're not suspicious enough already, right?" Edna looked up at me out of the lighted car. "You don't think right, did you know that, Earl? You think the world's stupid and you're smart. But that's not how it is. I feel sorry for you. You might've *been* something, but things just went crazy someplace."

I had a thought about poor Danny. He was a vet and crazy as a shit-house mouse, and I was glad he wasn't in for all this. "Just get the baby in the car," I said, trying to be patient. "I'm hungry like you are."

"I'm tired of this," Edna said. "I wish I stayed in Montana."

"Then you can go back in the morning," I said. "I'll buy the ticket and put you on the bus. But not till then."

"Just get on with it, Earl." She slumped down in the seat, turning off the parking lights with one foot and the radio with the other.

The mobile-home community was as big as any I'd ever seen. It was attached in some way to the plant that was lighted up behind it, because I could see a car once in a while leave one of the trailer streets, turn in the direction of the plant, then go slowly into it. Everything in the plant was white, and you could see that all the trailers were painted and looked exactly alike. A deep hum came out of the plant, and I thought as I got closer that it wouldn't be a location I'd ever want to work in.

I went right to the first trailer where there was a light, and knocked on the metal door. Kids' toys were lying in the gravel around the little wood steps, and I could hear talking on TV that suddenly went off. I heard a woman's voice talking, and then the door opened wide.

A large Negro woman with a wide, friendly face stood in the doorway. She smiled at me and moved forward as if she was going to come out, but she stopped at the top step. There was a little Negro boy behind her peeping out from behind her legs, watching me with his eyes half closed. The trailer had that feeling that no one else was inside, which was a feeling I knew something about.

"I'm sorry to intrude," I said. "But I've run up on a little bad luck tonight. My name's Earl Middleton."

The woman looked at me, then out into the night toward the freeway as if what I had said was something she was going to be able to see. "What kind of bad luck?" she said, looking down at me again.

"My car broke down out on the highway," I said. "I can't fix it myself, and I wondered if I could use your phone to call for help."

The woman smiled down at me knowingly. "We can't live without cars, can we?"

"That's the honest truth," I said.

"They're like our hearts," she said, her face shining in the little bulb of light that burned beside the door. "Where's your car situated?"

I turned and looked over into the dark, but I couldn't see anything because of where we'd put it. "It's over there," I said. "You can't see it in the dark."

"Who all's with you now?" the woman said. "Have you got your wife with you?"

"She's with my little girl and our dog in the car," I said. "My daughter's asleep or I would have brought them."

"They shouldn't be left in the dark by themselves," the woman said and frowned. "There's too much unsavouriness out there."

"The best I can do is hurry back." I tried to look sincere, since everything except Cheryl being asleep and Edna being my wife was the truth. The truth is meant to serve you if you'll let it, and I wanted it to serve me. "I'll pay for the phone call," I said. "If you'll bring the phone to the door I'll call from right here."

The woman looked at me again as if searching for a truth of her own, then back out into the night. She was maybe in her sixties, but I couldn't say for sure. "You're not going to rob me, are you, Mr Middleton?" She smiled like it was a joke between us.

"Not tonight," I said, and smiled a genuine smile. "I'm not up to it tonight. Maybe another time."

"Then I guess Terrel and I can let you use our phone with Daddy not here, can't we, Terrel? This is my grandson, Terrel Junior, Mr Middleton." She put her hand on the boy's head and looked down at him. "Terrel won't talk. Though if he did he'd tell you to use our phone. He's a sweet boy." She opened the screen for me to come in.

The trailer was a big one with a new rug and a new couch and a living room that expanded to give the space of a real house. Something good and sweet was cooking in the kitchen, and the trailer felt like it was somebody's comfortable new home instead of just temporary. I've lived in trailers, but they were just snailbacks with one room and no toilet, and they always felt cramped and unhappy—though I've thought maybe it might've been me that was unhappy in them.

There was a big Sony TV and a lot of kids' toys scattered on the floor. I recognized a Greyhound bus I'd gotten for Cheryl. The phone was beside a new leather recliner, and the Negro woman pointed for me to sit down and call and gave me the phone book. Terrel began fingering his toys and the woman sat on the couch while I called, watching me and smiling.

There were three listings for cab companies, all with one number different. I called the numbers in order and didn't get an answer until the last one, which answered with the name of the second company. I said I was on the highway beyond the interstate and that my wife and family needed to be taken to town and I would arrange for a tow later. While I was giving the location. I looked up the name of a tow service to tell the driver in case he asked.

When I hung up, the Negro woman was sitting looking at me with the same look she had been staring with into the dark, a look that seemed to want truth. She was smiling, though. Something pleased her and I reminded her of it.

"This is a very nice home," I said, resting in the recliner, which felt like the driver's seat of the Mercedes, and where I'd have been happy to stay.

"This isn't *our* house, Mr Middleton," the Negro woman said. "The company owns these. They give them to us for nothing. We have our own home in Rockford, Illinois."

"That's wonderful," I said.

"It's never wonderful when you have to be away from home, Mr Middleton, though we're only here three months, and it'll be easier when Terrel Junior begins his special school. You see, our son was killed in the war, and his wife ran off without Terrel Junior. Though you shouldn't worry. He can't understand us. His little feelings can't be hurt." The woman folded her hands in her lap and smiled in a satisfied way. She was an attractive woman, and had on a blue-and pink floral dress that made her seem bigger than she could've been, just the right woman to sit on the couch she was sitting on. She was good nature's picture, and I was glad she could be, with her little brain-damaged boy, living in a place where no one in his right mind would want to live a minute. "Where do *you* live, Mr Middleton?" she said politely, smiling in the same sympathetic way.

"My family and I are in transit," I said. "I'm an ophthalmologist, and we're moving back to Florida, where I'm from. I'm setting up practice in some little town where it's warm year-round. I haven't decided where."

"Florida's a wonderful place," the woman said. "I think Terrel would like it there."

"Could I ask you something?" I said.

"You certainly may," the woman said. Terrel had begun pushing his Greyhound across the front of the TV screen, making a scratch that no one watching the set could miss. "Stop that, Terrel Junior," the woman said quietly. But Terrell kept pushing his bus on the glass, and she smiled at me again as if we both understood something sad. Except I knew Cheryl would never damage a television set. She had respect for nice things, and I was sorry for the lady that Terrel didn't. "What did you want to ask?" the woman said.

"What goes on in that plant or whatever it is back there beyond these trailers, where all the lights are on?"

"Gold," the woman said and smiled.

"It's what?" I said.

"Gold," the Negro woman said, smiling as she had for almost all the time I'd been there. "It's a gold mine."

"They're mining gold back there?" I said, pointing.

"Every night and every day." She smiled in a pleased way.

"Does your husband work there?" I said.

"He's the assayer," she said. "He controls the quality. He works three months a year, and we live the rest of the time at home in Rockford. We've waited a long time for this. We've been happy to have our grandson, but I won't say I'll be sorry to have him go. We're ready to start our lives over." She smiled broadly at me and then at Terrel, who was giving her a spiteful look from the floor. "You said you had a daughter," the Negro woman said. "And what's her name?"

"Irma Cheryl," I said. "She's named for my mother."

"That's nice. And she's healthy, too. I can see it in your face." She looked at Terrel Junior with pity.

"I guess I'm lucky," I said.

"So far you are. But children bring you grief, the same way they bring you joy. We were unhappy for a long time before my husband got his job in the gold mine. Now, when Terrel starts going to school, we'll be kids again." She stood up. "You might miss your cab, Mr Middleton," she said, walking toward the door, though not to be forcing me out. She was too polite. "If *we* can't see your car, the cab surely won't be able to."

"That's true." I got up off the recliner, where I'd been so comfortable. "None of us have eaten yet, and your food makes me know how hungry we probably all are."

"There are fine restaurants in town, and you'll find them," the Negro woman said. "I'm sorry you didn't meet my husband. He's a wonderful man. He's everything to me."

"Tell him I appreciate the phone," I said. "You saved me."

"You weren't hard to save," the woman said. "Saving people is what we were all put on earth to do. I just passed you on to whatever's coming to you."

"Let's hope it's good," I said, stepping back into the dark.

"I'll be hoping, Mr Middleton. Terrel and I will both be hoping."

I waved to her as I walked out into the darkness toward the car where it was hidden in the night.

The cab had already arrived when I got there. I could see its little red-and-green roof lights all the way across the dry wash, and it made me worry that Edna was already saying something to get us in trouble, something about the car or where we'd come from, something that would cast suspicion on us. I thought, then, how I never planned things well enough. There was always a gap between my plan and what happened, and I only responded to things as they came along and hoped I wouldn't get in trouble. I was an offender in the law's eyes. But I always *thought* differently, as if I weren't an offender and had no intention of being one, which was the truth. But as I read on a napkin once, between the idea and the act a whole kingdom lies. And I had a hard time with my acts, which were oftentimes offender's acts, and my ideas, which were as good as the gold they mined there where the bright lights were blazing.

"We're waiting for you, Daddy," Cheryl said when I crossed the road. "The taxicab's already here."

"I see, hon," I said, and gave Cheryl a big hug. The cabdriver was sitting in the driver's seat having a smoke with the lights on inside. Edna was leaning against the back of the cab between the taillights, wearing her Bailey hat. "What'd you tell him?" I said when I got close.

"Nothing," she said. "What's there to tell?"

"Did he see the car?"

She glanced over in the direction of the trees where we had hid the Mercedes. Nothing was visible in the darkness, though I could hear Little Duke combing around in the underbrush tracking something, his little collar tinkling. "Where're we going?" she said. "I'm so hungry I could pass out."

"Edna's in a terrible mood," Cheryl said. "She already snapped at me."

"We're tired, honey," I said. "So try to be nicer."

"She's never nice," Cheryl said.

"Run go get Little Duke," I said. "And hurry back."

"I guess *my* questions come last here, right?" Edna said.

I put my arm around her. "That's not true."

"Did you find somebody over there in the trailers you'd rather stay with? You were gone long enough."

"That's not a thing to say," I said. "I was just trying to make things look right, so we don't get put in jail."

"So *you* don't, you mean." Edna laughed a little laugh I didn't like hearing.

"That's right. So I don't," I said. "I'd be the one in Dutch." I stared out at the big, lighted assemblage of white buildings and white lights beyond the trailer community, plumes of white smoke escaping up into the heartless Wyoming sky, the whole company of buildings looking like some unbelievable castle, humming away in a distorted dream. "You know what all those buildings are there?" I said to Edna, who hadn't moved and who didn't really seem to care if she ever moved anymore ever.

"No. But I can't say it matters, because it isn't a motel and it isn't a restaurant."

"It's a gold mine," I said, staring at the gold mine, which, I knew now, was a greater distance from us than it seemed, though it seemed huge and near, up against the cold sky. I thought there should've been a wall around it with guards instead of just the lights and no fence. It seemed as if anyone could go in and take what they wanted, just the way I had gone up to that woman's trailer and used the telephone, though that obviously wasn't true.

Edna began to laugh then. Not the mean laugh I didn't like, but a laugh that had something caring behind it, a full laugh that enjoyed a joke, a laugh she was laughing the first time I laid eyes on her, in Missoula in the East Gate Bar in 1979, a laugh we used to laugh together when Cheryl was still with her mother and I was working steady at the track and not stealing cars or passing bogus cheques to merchants. A better time all around. And for some reason it made me laugh just hearing her, and we both stood there behind the cab in the dark, laughing at the gold mine in the desert, me with my arm around her and Cheryl out rustling up Little Duke and the cabdriver smoking in the cab and our stolen Mercedes-Benz, which I'd had such hopes for in Florida, stuck up to its axle in sand, where I'd never get to see it again.

"I always wondered what a gold mine would look like when I saw it," Edna said, still laughing, wiping a tear from her eye.

"Me too," I said. "I was always curious about it."

"We're a couple of fools, aren't we, Earl?" she said, unable to quit laughing completely. "We're two of a kind."

"It might be a good sign, though," I said.

"How could it be? It's not our gold mine. There aren't any drive-up windows." She was still laughing.

"We've seen it," I said, pointing. "That's it right there. It may mean we're getting closer. Some people never see it at all."

"In a pig's eye, Earl," she said. "You and me see it in a pig's eye."

And she turned and got into the cab to go.

The cabdriver didn't ask anything about our car or where it was, to mean he'd noticed something queer. All of which made me feel like we had made a clean break from the car and couldn't be concerned with it until it was too late, if ever. The driver told us a lot about Rock Springs while he drove, that because of the gold mine a lot of people had moved there in just six months, people from all over, including New York, and that most of them lived out in the trailers. Prostitutes from New York City, who he called "B-girls," had come into town, he said, on the prosperity tide, and Cadillacs with New York plates cruised the little streets every night, full of Negroes with big hats who ran the women. He told us that everybody who got in his cab now wanted to know where the women were, and when he got our call he almost didn't come because some of the trailers were brothels operated by the mine for engineers and computer people away from home. He said he got tired of running back and forth out there just for vile business. He said that *60 Minutes* had even done a program about Rock Springs and that a blow-up had resulted in Cheyenne, though nothing could be done unless the boom left town. "It's prosperity's fruit," the driver said. "I'd rather be poor, which is lucky for me."

He said all the motels were sky-high, but since we were family he could show us a nice one that was affordable. But I told him we wanted a first-rate place where they took animals, and the money didn't matter because we had had a hard day and wanted to finish on a high note. I also knew that it was in the little nowhere places that the police would look for you and find you. People I'd known were always being arrested in cheap hotels and tourist courts with names you'd never heard of before. Never in Holiday Inns or TraveLodges.

I asked him to drive us to the middle of town and back out again so Cheryl could see the train station, and while we were there I saw a pink Cadillac with New York plates and a TV aerial being driven slowly by a Negro in a big hat down a narrow street where there were just bars and a Chinese restaurant. It was an odd sight, nothing you could ever expect.

"There's your pure criminal element," the cabdriver said and seemed sad. "I'm sorry for people like you to see a thing like that. We've got a nice town here, but there's some that want to ruin it for everybody. There used to be a way to deal with trash and criminals, but those days are gone forever."

"You said it," Edna said.

"You shouldn't let it get *you* down," I said to him. "There's more of you than them. And there always will be. You're the best advertisement this town has. I know Cheryl will remember you and not *that* man, won't you, honey?" But Cheryl was asleep by then, holding Little Duke in her arms on the taxi seat.

The driver took us to the Ramada Inn on the interstate, not far from where we'd broken down. I had a small pain of regret as we drove under the Ramada awning that we hadn't driven up in a cranberry-coloured Mercedes but instead a beat-up old Chrysler taxi driven by an old man full of complaints. Though I knew it was for the best. We were better off without the car; better, really, in any other car but that one, where the signs had turned bad.

I registered under another name and paid for the room in cash so there wouldn't be any questions. On the line where it said "Representing" I wrote "Ophthalmologist" and put "MD" after the name. It had a nice look to it, even though it wasn't my name.

When we got to the room, which was in the back where I'd asked for it, I put Cheryl on one of the beds and Little Duke beside her so they'd sleep. She'd missed dinner, but it only meant she'd be hungry in the morning, when she could have anything she wanted. A few missed meals don't make a kid bad. I'd missed a lot of them myself and haven't turned out completely bad.

"Let's have some fried chicken," I said to Edna when she came out of the bathroom. "They have good fried chicken at Ramadas, and I noticed the buffet was still up. Cheryl can stay right here, where it's safe, till we're back."

"I guess I'm not hungry anymore," Edna said. She stood at the window staring out into the dark. I could see out the window past her some yellowish foggy glow in the sky. For a moment I thought it was the gold mine out in the distance lighting the night, though it was only the interstate.

"We could order up," I said. "Whatever you want. There's a menu on the phone book. You could just have a salad."

"You go ahead," she said. "I've lost my hungry spirit." She sat on the bed beside Cheryl and Little Duke and looked at them in a sweet way and put her hand on Cheryl's cheek just as if she'd had a fever. "Sweet little girl," she said. "Everybody loves you."

"What do you want to do?" I said. "I'd like to eat. Maybe *I'll* order up some chicken."

"Why don't you do that?" She said. "It's your favourite." And she smiled at me from the bed.

I sat on the other bed and dialed room service. I asked for chicken, garden salad, potato, and a roll, plus a piece of hot apple pie and iced tea. I realized I hadn't eaten all day. When I put down the phone I saw that Edna was watching me, not in a hateful way or a loving way, just in a way that seemed to say she didn't understand something and was going to ask me about it.

"When did watching me get so entertaining?" I said and smiled at her. I was trying to be friendly. I knew how tired she must be. It was after nine o'clock.

"I was just thinking how much I hated being in a motel without a car that was mine to drive. Isn't that funny? I started feeling like that last night when that purple car wasn't mine. That purple car just gave me the willies, I guess, Earl."

"One of those cars *outside* is yours," I said. "Just stand right there and pick it out."

"I know," she said. "But that's different, isn't it?" She reached and got her blue Bailey hat, put it on her head, and set it way back like Dale Evans. She looked sweet. "I used to like to go to motels, you know," she said. "There's something secret about them and free—I was never paying, of course. But you felt safe from everything and free to do what you wanted because you'd made the decision to be there and paid that price, and all the rest was the good part. Fucking and everything, you know." She smiled at me in a good-natured way.

"Isn't that the way this is?" I was sitting on the bed, watching her, not knowing what to expect her to say next.

"I don't guess it is, Earl," she said and stared out the window. "I'm thirty-two and I'm going to have to give up on motels. I can't keep that fantasy going anymore."

"Don't you like this place?" I said and looked around at the room. I appreciated the modern paintings and the lowboy bureau and the big TV. It seemed like a plenty nice enough place to me, considering where we'd been.

"No, I don't," Edna said with real conviction. "There's no use in my getting mad at you about it. It isn't your fault. You do the best you can for everybody. But every trip teaches you something. And I've learned I need to give up on motels before some bad thing happens to me. I'm sorry."

"What does that mean?" I said, because I really didn't know what she had in mind to do, though I should've guessed.

"I guess I'll take that ticket you mentioned," she said, and got up and faced the window. "Tomorrow's soon enough. We haven't got a car to take me anyhow."

"Well, that's a fine thing," I said, sitting on the bed, feeling like I was in shock. I wanted to say something to her, to argue with her, but I couldn't think what to say that seemed right. I didn't want to be mad at her, but it made me mad.

"You've got a right to be mad at me, Earl," she said, "but I don't think you can really blame me." She turned around and faced me and sat on the windowsill, her hands on her knees. Someone knocked on the door, and I just yelled for them to set the tray down and put it on the bill.

"I guess I *do* blame you," I said, and I was angry. I thought about how I could've disappeared into that trailer community and hadn't, had come back to keep things going, had tried to take control of things for everybody when they looked bad.

"Don't. I wish you wouldn't," Edna said and smiled at me like she wanted me to hug her. "Anybody ought to have their choice in things if they can. Don't you believe that, Earl? Here I am out here in the desert where I don't know anything, in a stolen car, in a motel room under an assumed name, with no money of my own, a kid that's not mine, and the law after me. And I have a choice to get out of all of it by getting on a bus. What would you do? I know exactly what you'd do."

"You think you do," I said. But I didn't want to get into an argument about it and tell her all I could've done and didn't do. Because it wouldn't have done any good. When you get to the point of arguing, you're past the point of changing anybody's mind, even though it's supposed to be the other way, and maybe for some classes of people it is, just never mine.

Edna smiled at me and came across the room and put her arms around me where I was sitting on the bed. Cheryl rolled over and looked at us and smiled, then closed her eyes, and the room was quiet. I was beginning to think of Rock Springs in a way I knew I would always think of it, a lowdown city full of crimes and whores and disappointments, a place where a woman left me, instead of a place where I got things on the straight track once and for all, a place I saw a gold mine.

"Eat your chicken, Earl," Edna said. "Then we can go to bed. I'm tired, but I'd like to make love to you anyway. None of this is a matter of not loving you, you know that."

Sometime late in the night, after Edna was asleep, I got up and walked outside into the parking lot. It could've been anytime because there was still the light from the interstate frosting the low sky and the big red Ramada sign humming motionlessly in the night and no light at all in the east to indicate it might be morning. The lot was full of cars all nosed in, a couple of them with suitcases strapped to their roofs and their trunks weighed down with belongings the people were taking someplace, to a new home or a vacation resort in the mountains. I had laid in bed a long time after Edna was asleep, watching the Atlanta Braves on television, trying to get my mind off how I'd feel when I saw that bus pull away the next day, and how I'd feel when I turned around and there stood Cheryl and Little Duke and no one to see about them but me alone, and that the first thing I had to do was get hold of some automobile and get the plates switched, then get them some breakfast and get us all on the road to Florida, all in the space of probably two hours, since that Mercedes would certainly look less hid in the daytime than the night, and word travels fast. I've always taken care of Cheryl myself as long as I've had her with me. None of the women ever did. Most of them didn't even seem to like her, though they took care of me in a way so that I could take care of her. And I knew that once Edna left, all that was going to get harder. Though what I wanted most to do was not think about it just for a while, try to let my mind go limp so it could be strong for the rest of what there was. I thought that the difference between a successful life and an unsuccessful one, between me at that moment and all the people who owned the cars that were nosed into their proper places in the lot, maybe between me and that woman out in the trailers by the gold mine, was how well you were able to put things like this out of your mind and not be bothered by them, and maybe, too, by how many troubles like this one you had to face in a lifetime. Through luck or design they had all faced fewer troubles, and by their own characters, they forgot them faster. And that's what I wanted for me. Fewer troubles, fewer memories of trouble.

I walked over to a car, a Pontiac with Ohio tags, one of the ones with bundles and suitcases strapped to the top and a lot more in the trunk, by the way it was riding. I looked inside the driver's window. There were maps and paperback books and sunglasses and the little plastic holders for cans that hang on the window wells. And in the back there were kid's toys and some pillows and a cat box with a cat sitting in it staring up at me like I was the face of the moon. It all looked familiar to me, the very same things I would have in my car if I had a car. Nothing seemed surprising, nothing different. Though I had a funny sensation at that moment and turned and looked up at the windows along the back of the motel. All were dark except two. Mine and another one. And I wondered, because it seemed funny, what would you think a man was doing if you saw him in the middle of the night looking in the windows of cars in the parking lot of the Ramada Inn? Would you think he was trying to get his head cleared? Would you think he was trying to get ready for a day when trouble would come down on him? Would you think his girlfriend was leaving him? Would you think he had a daughter? Would you think he was anybody like you?

1987

Keath Fraser

b. 1944

Keath Fraser should be much better known than he is. He has published comparatively few books and keeps a low literary profile. But he has achieved almost a cult status, the sort that emerges from both rumour and actual reading of his fine, eccentric work. He has remained in his birthplace, Vancouver, and from there has explored the complexities of time, place, and narrative form. He is a director of Canada India Village Aid, and the author of three short story collections—*Taking Cover* (1982), *Foreign Affairs* (1985) (which was shortlisted for the Governor General's Fiction Award), and *Telling My Love Lies* (1996)—as well as a memoir of Sinclair Ross. His one novel, the prize-winning *Popular Anatomy* (1995), plays dramatically on sweeps of historical and imaginative time. In "Notes toward a Supreme Fiction," published in *Canadian Literature*, Fraser claims that "true innovation is inseparable from content. And the content of Supreme Fiction is subversive. I am talking about fiction that overturns expectation by juxtaposition, nexus, dislocation." Aritha van Herk pays tribute to the success of his subversiveness, his resistance to "the canonical trend" of the Munro-dominated Canadian story. "Roget's Thesaurus" is "an enormous bend in the road of determinedly elucidative fiction." Subversive as the story may be, it is also "classical" in pointing to the disparity between abbreviated narrative space and the implied elongation of human experience.

Roget's Thesaurus

I had begun my lists. Mother was always saying, "Peter, why not play outside like other boys?" Her patience with collectors was not prodigal; she didn't understand my obsession. I wanted to polish words like shells, before I let them in. Sometimes I tied on bits of string to watch them sway, bump maybe, like chestnuts. They were treasures these words. I could have eaten them had the idiom not existed, even then, to mean remorse. I loved the way they smelled, their inky scent of coal. Sniffing their penny notebook made me think of fire. (See FERVOUR.)

I fiddled with sounds and significations. No words could exist, even in their thousands, until I made them objects on paper: hairpins, lapis lazuli, teeth, fish hooks, dead bees . . . Later on my study became a museum for the old weapons poets had used. Mother would have died. By then, of course, she had; pleased I had grown up to become what she approved, a doctor.

My young wife died of tumours the size of apples. That I was a practitioner of healing seemed absurd. It smothered me like fog, her dying, her breath in the end so moist. When his wife died my uncle took a razor to his throat. (See DESPAIR, see INSANITY, see OMEGA.) He died disbelieving in the antidote of language. Oh, my wife, I have only words to play with.

When I retired it was because of deafness. My passion for travel spent, my sense of duty to the poor used up, I remembered listening for words everywhere. At the Athenaeum, among the dying in Millbank Penitentiary, after concerts, at the Royal Society, during sermons in St Pancras. I started to consolidate. At last I could describe—not prescribe. After fifty years I concluded synonyms were reductive, did not exist, were only analogous words. Unlike Dr Johnson I was no poet. My book would be a philosopher's tool, my sobriquet a thesaurus.

My contribution was to relationships. I created families out of ideas like Space and Matter and Affections. I grouped words in precisely a thousand ways: reacquainted siblings, introduced cousins, befriended black sheep, mediated between enemies. I printed place names and organized a banquet.

London had never seen anything quite like it. Recalcitrant louts, my words, they scented taxonomy and grew inebrious. Mother was well out of it.

She knew me for my polite accomplishments, my papers on optics, comparative anatomy, the poor, zoology, human aging, mathematics, the deaf and dumb. I was a Renaissance man for I chewed what I bit off. Still, I was no more satisfied with my Bridgewater Treatise on the design of all natural history than with my report for the Water Commission on pollution in the Thames. Only less pessimistic. By the time Asiatic cholera broke out, and people were vomiting and diarrhetic, my work had been forgotten. Not until I fathered my *Thesaurus* did I dream of prinking. Who knew, perhaps crazy poets would become Roget's trollops, when they discovered his interest in truth not eloquence.

My book appeared the same year as volumes by Dickens, Hawthorne, Melville—fabulators, all of us. (See FICTION.) I too dreamed of the unity of man's existence, and offered a tool for attacking false logic, truisms, jargon, sophism. Though any fretless voice can sing if words are as precise as notes, men in power often sound discordant. Music isn't accident, nor memory history. Language (like the violin) so long to learn.

There is no language, I used to say to Mother, like our own. Look how nations that we oppress trust it. It's the bridge we use to bring back silks and spices, tobacco leaves and cinnamon. Yet all one reviewer wrote of my work was it "made eloquence too easy for the lazy and ignorant." Eloquence I have always distrusted. Maybe this is why my *Thesaurus* has gone through twenty-eight editions.

Men are odd animals. I have never felt as at home around *them* as around their words; without these they're monkeys. (See TRUISM.) The other day I was going through my book and it struck me I have more words for Disapprobation than Approbation. Why is this?

So I spend my last days at West Malvern in my ninety-first year. I no longer walk in parks. I'm pleased I fear death, it makes me feel younger. Death is a poet's idiom to take the mind off complacency. (See SWAN SONG, see CROSSING THE BAR, see THE GREAT ADVENTURE.) I have never thought of death but that it has refurbished me.

1982

Tobias Wolff

b. 1945

Tobias Wolff's geographic origins are as various as the tones of his writing. Born in Alabama, he grew up near Seattle (Carver country), a period chronicled in his memoir, *This Boy's Life*, which in 1993 was turned into a finely textured film of the same name. Although he taught at the University of Syracuse for seventeen years, in 1997 he returned to California and Stanford University, where he had started his writing life as a Stegner Fellow in 1975. Punctuating these movements were stints in Oxford (as a student of English literature) and Vietnam (as a Green Beret). The author of one of the finest recollections of the war, *In Pharoah's Army: Memories of the Lost War* (1994), he has also published a novel, *Ugly Rumours* (1975), and four volumes of short fiction. Associated by literary historians with "dirty realism," a.k.a. "K-mart realism," Wolff's prose is far richer and more fluid than these designations suggest. It is indeed devoted to the textures of ordinary life, but the shadings of human response are remarkably subtle and often unexpected. There is a rare and humane delicacy even to the violent experiences that are never far from the centre of his fiction, and a quiet pleasure in the sudden shifts of perspective that open a story just as it ends. The astonishing conclusion of "Casualty" is an instance of Wolff's imaginative bravery and compassion. His most recent collection is *Our Story Begins: New and Selected Stories* (2008).

Casualty

B.D. carried certain objects. He observed in his dispositions and arrangements a certain order, and became irritable and fearful whenever that order was disrupted. There were certain words he said to himself at certain moments, power words. Sometimes he really believed in all of this; other times he believed in nothing. But he was alive, and he gave honour to all possible causes.

His name was Benjamin Delano Sears, B.D. for short, but his friends in the unit had taken to calling him Biddy because of his fussiness and the hennish way he brooded over them. He always had to know where they were. He bugged them about taking their malaria pills and their salt tablets. When they were out in the bush he drove them crazy with equipment checks. He acted like a squad leader, which he wasn't and never would be, because Sergeant Holmes refused to consider him for the job. Sergeant Holmes had a number of sergeant-like sayings. One of them was "If you don't got what it takes, it'll take what you gots." He had decided that B.D. didn't have what it took, and B.D. didn't argue; he knew even better than Sergeant Holmes how scared he was. He just wanted to get himself home, himself and his friends.

Most of them did get home. The unit had light casualties during B.D.'s tour, mainly through dumb luck. One by one B.D.'s friends rotated stateside, and finally Ryan was the only one left. B.D. and Ryan had arrived the same week. They knew the same stories. The names of absent men and past operations and nowhere places had meaning for them, and those who came later began to regard the pair of them as some kind of cultish remnant. And that was pretty much how B.D. and Ryan saw themselves.

They hadn't started off as friends. Ryan was a lip, a bigmouth. He narrated whatever was happening, like a sportscaster, but the narration never fit what was going on. He'd complain when operations got cancelled, go into fey French-accented ecstasies over cold C-rats, offer elaborate professions of admiration for orders of the most transparent stupidity. At first B.D. thought he was a pain in the ass. Then one morning he woke up laughing at something Ryan had said the night before. They'd been setting out claymores. Sergeant Holmes got exasperated fiddling with one of them and said, "Any of you boys gots a screwdriver?" and Ryan said, instantly, "What size?" This was regulation blab, but it worked on B.D. He kept hearing Ryan's voice, its crispness and competence, its almost perfect imitation of sanity.

What size?

Ryan and B.D. had about six weeks left to go when Lieutenant Puchinsky, their commanding officer, got transferred to battalion headquarters. Pinch Puchinsky saw himself as a star—he'd been a quarterback at Penn State, spoiled, coddled, illegally subsidized—and he took it for granted that other men would see him the same way. And they did. He never had to insist on an order and never thought to insist, because he couldn't imagine anyone refusing. He couldn't imagine anything disagreeable, in fact, and carried himself through every danger as if it had nothing to do with him. Because hardly any of his men got hurt, they held him in reverence.

So it was in the nature of things that his replacement, Lieutenant Dixon, should be despised, though he was not despicable. He was a proud, thoughtful man who had been wounded twice already and now found himself among soldiers whose laxity seemed perfectly calculated to finish him off. The men didn't maintain their weapons properly. They had no concept of radio discipline. On patrol they were careless and noisy and slow to react. Lieutenant Dixon took it upon himself to whip them into shape.

This proved hard going. He owned no patience or humour, no ease of command. He was short and balding; when he got worked up his face turned red and his voice broke into falsetto. Therefore the men called him Fudd. Ryan mimicked him relentlessly and with terrible precision. That Lieutenant Dixon should overhear him was inevitable, and it finally happened while Ryan and B.D. and some new guys were sandbagging the interior walls of a bunker. Ryan was holding forth in Lieutenant Dixon's voice when Lieutenant Dixon's head appeared in the doorway. Everyone saw him. But instead of shutting up, Ryan carried on as if he weren't there. B.D. kept his head down and his hands busy. At no time was he tempted to laugh.

"Ryan," Lieutenant Dixon said, "just what do you think you're doing?"

Still in the Lieutenant's voice, Ryan said, "Packing sandbags, sir."

Lieutenant Dixon watched him. He said, "Ryan, is this your idea of a j-joke?"

"No, sir. My idea of a j-joke is a four-inch dick on a two-inch lieutenant."

B.D. closed his eyes, and when he opened them Lieutenant Dixon was gone. He straightened up. "Suave," he said to Ryan.

Ryan pushed his shovel into the dirt and leaned against it. He untied the bandana from his forehead and wiped the sweat from his face, from his thin shoulders and chest. His ribs showed. His skin was dead white, all but his hands and neck and face, which were densely freckled, almost black in the dimness of the bunker. "I just can't help it," he said.

Three nights later Lieutenant Dixon sent Ryan out on ambush with a bunch of new guys. This was strictly contrary to the arrangement observed by Lieutenant Puchinsky, whereby the shorter you got the less you had to do. You weren't supposed to get stuck with this kind of duty when you had less than two months to go. Lieutenant Dixon did not exactly order Ryan out. What he did instead was turn to him during the noon formation and ask if he'd like to volunteer. Ryan said that he would *love* to volunteer, that he'd been just *dying* to be asked. Lieutenant Dixon put his name down.

B.D. watched the detail go out that night. With blackened faces they moved silently through the perimeter, weaving a loopy path between mines and trip-flares, and crossed the desolate ground beyond the wire into the darkness of the trees. The sky was a lilac haze.

B.D. went back to his bunk and sat there with his hands on his knees, staring at the mess on Ryan's bunk: shaving gear, cigarettes, dirty clothes, sandals, a high-school yearbook that Ryan liked to browse in. B.D. lifted the mosquito netting and picked up the yearbook. *The Aloysian*, it was called. There was a formal portrait of Ryan in the senior class gallery. He looked solemn, almost mournful. His hair was long. The photographer had airbrushed the freckles out and used backlights to brighten the outline of his head and shoulders. B.D. wouldn't have known him without the name. Below Ryan's picture was the line, "O for a beakerful of the warm South!"

Now what the hell was that supposed to mean?

He found Ryan in a few group pictures. In one, taken in metal shop, Ryan was standing with some other boys behind the teacher, holding a tangle of antlerish rods above the teacher's head.

B.D. studied the picture. He was familiar with this expression, the plausible blandness worn like a mask over cunning and mockery. It made B.D. want to catch Ryan's eye and let him know that he saw what was going on. He put the book back on Ryan's bed.

His stomach hurt. It was a new pain, not sharp but steady, and so diffuse that B.D. had to probe with his fingers to find its source. When he bent over the pain got worse, then eased up when he stood and walked back and forth in front of his bunk. One of the new guys, a big Hawaiian, said, "Hey, Biddy, you okay?" B.D. stopped pacing. He had forgotten there was anyone else in the room. This Hawaiian and a guy with a green eyeshade and a bunch of others were playing cards. They were all watching him.

B.D. said, "Haven't you read the surgeon-general's warning?"

The Hawaiian looked down at his cigarette.

"Fuckin' Biddy," said the man with the eyeshade, as if B.D. wasn't there. "Eight months I've been in this shithole and he's still calling me *new guy*."

"Ryan calls me Tonto," the Hawaiian said. "Do I look like an Indian? Seriously, man, do I look like an Indian?"

"You don't exactly look like a white man."

"Yeah? Well I don't *even* look like an Indian, okay?"

"Call him Kemo Sabe. See how he likes that."

"Ryan? He'd love it."

B.D. walked toward Sergeant Holmes's hooch. The sky was low and heavy. They'd had hamburgers that night for dinner, "ratburgers," Ryan called them *(Hey, Cookie, how about tucking in the tail on this one?)*, and the air still smelled of grease. B.D. felt a sudden coldness on his back and dropped to a crouch, waiting for something; he didn't know what. He heard the chugging of generators, crumple and thud of distant artillery, the uproarious din of insects. B.D. huddled there. Then he stood and looked around and went on his way.

Sergeant Holmes was stretched out on his bunk, listening to a big reel-to-reel through a set of earphones that covered his head like a helmet. He had on red Bermuda shorts. His eyes were closed, his long spidery fingers waving languorously over his sunken belly. He had the blackest skin B.D. had ever seen on anyone. B.D. sat down beside him and shook his foot. "Hey," he said. "Hey, Russ."

Sergeant Holmes opened his eyes, then slowly pulled the earphones off.

"Dixon has no business sending Ryan out on ambush."

Sergeant Holmes sat up and put the earphones on the floor. "You wrong about that. That's what the man's business is, is sending people out."

"Ryan's been out. Plenty. He's under two months now."

"Same-same you, right?"

B.D. nodded.

"I see why you worried."

"Fuck you," B.D. said.

Sergeant Holmes grinned. It was an event in that black face.

"This goes against the deal, Russ."

"Deal? What's this deal shit? You got something on paper?"

"It was understood."

"Eltee Pinch gone, Biddy. Eltee Dixon head rat-catcher now, and he got his own different philosophy."

"Philosophy," B.D. said.

"That's how it is," Sergeant Holmes said.

B.D. sat there, looking at the floor, rubbing his knuckles. "What do you think?"

"I think Lieutenant Dixon in charge now."

"The new guys can take care of themselves. *We* did."

"You did shit, Biddy. You been duckin' ever since you got here, you and Ryan both."

"We took our chances."

"Hey, that's how it is, Biddy. You don't like it, talk to the Eltee." He pulled his earphone on, lay back on the bunk, and closed his eyes. His fingers waved in the air like seaweed.

A few days later Lieutenant Dixon put together another ambush patrol. Before reading off the names he asked if one of the short-timers would like to volunteer. Nobody answered. Everyone was quiet, waiting. Lieutenant Dixon studied his clipboard, wrote something, and looked up. "Right. So who's going?" When no one spoke he said, "Come on, it isn't all that bad. Is it, Ryan?"

B.D. was standing next to him. "Don't answer," he whispered.

"It's just great!" Ryan said. "Nothing like it, sir. You've got your stars twinkling up there in God's heaven—"

"Thanks," Lieutenant Dixon said.

"The trees for company—"

"Shut up," B.D. said.

But Ryan kept at it until Lieutenant Dixon got impatient and cut him off. "That's fine," he said, then added, "I'm glad to hear you like it so much."

"Can't get enough of it, sir."

Lieutenant Dixon slapped the clipboard against his leg. He did it again. "So I guess you wouldn't mind having another crack at it."

"Really, sir? Can I?"

"I think it can be arranged."

B.D. followed Ryan to their quarters after lunch. Ryan was laying out his gear. "I know, I know," he said. "I just can't help it."

"You can keep your mouth shut. You can stop hard-assing the little fuck."

"The thing is, I can't. I try to but I can't."

"Bullshit," B.D. said, but he saw that Ryan meant it, and the knowledge made him tired. He lowered himself onto his bunk and lay back and stared up at the canvas roof. Sunlight spangled in a thousand little holes.

"He's such an asshole," Ryan said. "Somebody's got to brief him on that, because he just doesn't get the picture. He doesn't have *any* hard intelligence on what an asshole he is. Somebody around here's got to take responsibility."

"Nobody assigned you," B.D. said.

"Individual initiative," Ryan said. He sat down on his footlocker and began tinkering with the straps of his helmet.

B.D. closed his eyes. The air was hot and pressing and smelled of the canvas overhead, a smell that reminded him of summer camp.

"But that's not really it," Ryan said. "I'd just as soon let it drop. I think I've made my point."

"Affirmative. Rest assured."

"It's like I'm allergic—you know, like some people are with cats? I get near him and boom! my heart starts pumping like crazy and all this stuff starts coming out. I'm just standing there, watching it happen. Strange, huh? Strange but true."

"All you have to do," B.D. said hopelessly, "is keep quiet."

The power of an M-26 fragmentation grenade, sufficient by itself to lift the roof off a small house, could be "exponentially enhanced," according to a leaflet issued by the base commander, "by detonating it in the context of volatile substances." This absurdly overwritten leaflet, intended as a warning against the enemy practice of slipping delay-rigged grenades into the gas tanks of unattended jeeps and trucks, was incomprehensible to half the men in the division. But B.D. had understood it, and he'd kept it in mind.

His idea was to pick up a five-gallon can of gasoline from one of the generators and leave it beside the tent where Lieutenant Dixon did his paperwork at night. He would tape down the handle of a grenade, pull the pin, and drop the grenade in the can. By the time the gas ate through the tape he'd be in his bunk.

B.D. didn't think he had killed anyone yet. His company had been ambushed three times and B.D. had fired back with everyone else, but always hysterically and in a kind of fog. Something happened to his vision; it turned yellow and blurry and he saw everything in a series of stuttering frames that he could never afterward remember clearly. He couldn't be sure what had happened. But he thought he'd know if he had killed somebody, even if it was in darkness or behind cover where he couldn't see the man go down. He was sure that he would know.

Only once did he remember having someone actually in his sights. This was during a sweep through an area that had been cleared of its population and declared a free-fire zone. Nobody was supposed to be there. All morning they worked their way upriver, searching empty hamlets along the bank. Nothing. Negative booby traps, negative snipers, negative mines. Zilch. But then, while they were eating lunch, B.D. saw something. He was on guard in the rear of the company when a man came out of the trees into an expanse of overgrown paddies. The man had a stick that he swung in front of him as he made his way with slow, halting steps toward the opposite treeline. B.D. kept still and watched him. The sun was warm on his back. The breeze blew across the paddies, bending the grass, rippling the water. Finally he raised his rifle and drew a bead on the man. He held him in his sights. He could have dropped him, easy as pie, but he decided that the man was blind. He let him go and said nothing about it. But later he wondered: What if he wasn't blind? What if he was just a guy with a stick, taking his time? Either way, he had no business being there. B.D. felt funny about the whole thing. What if he was actually VC, what if he killed a bunch of Americans afterward? He could be VC even if he was blind; he could be cadre, infrastructure, some high official . . .

Blind people could do all kinds of things.

Once it got dark B.D.walked across the compound to one of the guard bunkers and palmed a grenade from an open crate while pretending to look for a man named Walcott.

He was about to leave when pumpkin-headed Captain Kroll appeared wheezing in the doorway. He had a normal enough body, maybe a little plump but nothing freakish, and then this incredible head. His head was so big that everyone in camp knew who he was and generally treated him with a tolerance he might not have enjoyed if his head had been a little smaller. "Captain Head," they called him, or just "The Head." He worked in battalion intelligence, which was good for a few laughs, and didn't seem to realize just how big his head really was.

Captain Kroll crouched on the floor and had everyone bunch up around him; it was like a football huddle. B.D. saw no choice but to join in. Captain Kroll looked into each of their faces, and in a hushed voice he said that their reconnaissance patrols were reporting *beaucoup* troop movements all through the valley. They should maintain an extreme degree of alertness, he said. Mister Charles needed some scalps to show off in Paris. Mister Charles was looking for a party.

"Rock and roll!" said the guy behind B.D.

It was a dumbfuck thing to say. Nobody else said a word.

"Any questions?"

No questions.

Captain Kroll rolled his big head from side to side. "Get some," he said.

Everyone broke out laughing.

Captain Kroll rocked back as if he'd been slapped, then stood and left the bunker. B.D. followed him outside and struck off in the opposite direction. The grenade knocked against his hip as he wandered, dull and thoughtless, across the compound. He didn't know where he was going until he got there.

Lieutenant Puchinsky was drinking beer with a couple of other officers. B.D. stood in the doorway of the hooch. "Sir, it's Biddy," he said. "Biddy Sears."

"Biddy?" Lieutenant Puchinsky leaned forward and squinted at him. "Christ. Biddy." He put his can down.

They walked a little ways. Lieutenant Puchinsky gave off a certain ripeness, distinct but not rank, that B.D. had forgotten and now remembered and breathed in, taking comfort from it as he took comfort from the man's bulk, the great looming mass of him.

Lieutenant Puchinsky stopped beside a cyclone fence enclosing a pit filled with crates. "You must be getting pretty short," he said.

"Thirty-four and a wake-up."

"I'm down to twenty."

"Twenty. Jesus, sir. That's all right. I could handle twenty."

A flare burst over the dead space outside the wire. Both men shrank from the sudden brightness. The flare drifted slowly down, hissing as it fell, covering the camp with a cold green light in which everything took on a helpless, cringing aspect. They didn't speak until it came to ground.

"Ours," Lieutenant Puchinsky said.

"Yes, sir," B.D. said, though he knew this might not be true.

Lieutenant Puchinsky shifted from foot to foot.

"It's about Lieutenant Dixon, sir."

"Oh, Christ. You're *not* going to tell me you're having trouble with Lieutenant Dixon."

"Yes, sir."

When Lieutenant Puchinsky asked if he'd gone through channels, B.D. knew he'd already lost his case. He tried to explain the situation but couldn't find the right words, and Lieutenant Puchinsky kept interrupting to say that it wasn't his outfit anymore. He wouldn't even admit that an injustice had been done since Ryan had, after all, volunteered.

"Lieutenant Dixon made him," B.D. said.

"How is that?"

"I can't explain, sir. He has a way."

Lieutenant Puchinsky didn't say anything.

"We did what you wanted," B.D. said. "We kept our part of the deal."

"There weren't any deals," Lieutenant Puchinsky said. "It sounds to me like you've got a personal problem, soldier. If your mission requires personal problems, we'll issue them to you. Is that clear?"

"Yes, sir."

"If you're so worried about him, why don't *you* volunteer?"

B.D. came to attention, snapped a furiously correct salute, and turned away.

"Hold up, Biddy." Lieutenant Puchinsky walked over to him. "What do you expect me to do? Put yourself in my place—what am I supposed to do?"

"You could talk to him."

"It won't do any good, I can guarantee you that." When B.D. didn't answer, he said, "All right. If it makes you feel any better, I'll talk to him."

B.D. did feel better, but not for long.

He had trouble sleeping that night, and as he lay in the darkness, eyes open, a rusty taste in his mouth, the extent of his failure became clear to him. He knew exactly what would happen. Lieutenant Puchinsky thought he was going to talk to Lieutenant Dixon, and he would be loyal to this intention for maybe an hour or two, maybe even the rest of the night, and in the morning he'd forget it. He was an officer. Officers could look like men and talk like men, but when you drew the line they always went over to the officer side because that was what they were. Lieutenant Puchinsky had already decided that speaking to Lieutenant Dixon wouldn't make any difference. And he was right. B.D. knew that. He understood that he had known it all along, that he'd gone to Lieutenant Puchinsky so he wouldn't be able to deal with Lieutenant Dixon afterward. He'd tipped his hand because he was afraid to play it, and now the chance was gone. In another four or five days, the next time battalion sent down for an ambush party, Lieutenant Dixon would be out there asking for a volunteer, and Ryan would shoot off his mouth again.

And Lieutenant Puchinsky thought that he, B.D., should go out instead.

B.D. lay on his back for a while, then turned on his side. It was hot. Finally he got up and went to the doorway of the hooch. A new guy was sitting there in his boxer shorts, smoking a pipe. He nodded at B.D. but didn't say anything. There was no breeze. B.D. stood in the doorway, then went back inside and sat on his bunk.

B.D. wasn't brave. He knew that, as he knew other things about himself that he would not have believed a year ago. He would not have believed that he could walk past begging children and feel nothing. He would not have believed that he could become a frequenter of prostitutes. He would not have believed that he could become a whiner or a shirker. He had been forced to surrender certain pictures of himself that had once given him pride and a serene sense of entitlement to his existence, but the one picture he had not given up, and which had become essential to him, was the picture of himself as a man who would do anything for a friend.

Anything meant anything. It could mean getting himself hurt or even killed. B.D. had some ideas as to how this might happen, acts of impulse like going after a wounded man, jumping on a grenade, other things he'd heard and read about, and in which he thought he recognized the possibilities of his own nature. But this was different.

In fact, B.D. could see a big difference. It was one thing to do something in the heat of the moment, another to think about it, accept it in advance. Anything meant anything, but B.D. never thought it would mean volunteering for an ambush party. He'd pulled that duty and hated it worse than anything. You had to lie out there all night without moving. When you thought a couple of hours had gone by, it turned out to be fifteen minutes. You couldn't see a thing. You had to figure it all out with your ears, and every sound made you want to blow the whole place apart, but you couldn't because then they'd know where you were. Then they had you. Or else some friendly unit heard the firing and got spooked and called down artillery. That happened once when B.D. was out; some guys freaked and shot the shit out of some bushes, and it wasn't three minutes before the artillery started coming in. B.D. had been mortared but he'd never been under artillery before. Artillery was something else. Artillery was like the end of the world. It was a miracle he hadn't gotten killed—a miracle. He didn't know if he was up for that again. He just didn't know.

B.D. rummaged in Ryan's stuff for some cigarettes. He lit one and puffed it without inhaling, blowing the smoke over his head; he hated the smell of it. The men around him slept on, their bodies pale and vague under the mosquito netting. B.D. ground the cigarette out and lay down again.

He didn't know Ryan all that well, when you came right down to it. The things he knew about Ryan he could count on his fingers. Ryan was nineteen. He had four older sisters, no brothers, a girlfriend he never talked about. What he did like to talk about was driving up to New Hampshire with his buddies and fishing for trout. He was clumsy. He talked too much. He could eat anything, even gook food. He called the black guys Zulus but got along with them better than B.D., who claimed to be colour-blind. His mother was dead. His father ran a hardware store and picked up the odd dollar singing nostalgic Irish songs at weddings and wakes. Ryan could do an imitation of his father singing that put B.D. right on the floor, every time. It was something he did with his eyebrows. Just thinking of it made B.D. laugh silently in the darkness.

Ryan was on a supply detail that weekend, completely routine, carrying ammunition forward from a dump in the rear, when a machine gun opened fire from a low hill that was supposed to be secure. It caught Ryan and several other men as they were humping crates across a mudfield. The whole area went on alert. Perimeter guards were blasting away at the hill. Officers kept running by, shouting different orders.

When B.D. heard about Ryan he left his position and took off running toward the LZ. There were two wounded men there, walking wounded, and a corpse in a bag, but Ryan was gone. He'd been lifted out with the other criticals a few minutes earlier. The medic on duty said that Ryan had taken a round just above the left eye, or maybe it was the right. He didn't know how serious it was, whether the bullet had hit him straight on or from the side.

B.D. looked up at the sky, at the dark, low, eddying clouds. He was conscious of the other men, and he clenched his jaw to show that he was keeping a tight lid on his feelings, as he was. Years later he told all this to the woman he lived with and would later marry, offering it to her as something important to know about him—how this great friend of his, Ryan, had gotten hit, and how he'd run to be with him and found him gone. He described the scene in the clearing, the wounded men sitting on tree stumps, muddy, dumb with shock, and the dead man in his bag, not stretched out like someone asleep but all balled up in the middle. A big lump. He described the churned-up ground, the jumble of boxes and canisters. The dark sky. And Ryan gone, just like that. His best friend.

This story did not come easily to B.D. He hardly ever talked about the war except in generalities, and then in a grudging, edgy way. He didn't want to sound like other men when they got on the subject, pulling a long face or laughing it off—striking a pose. He did not want to imply that he'd done more than he had done, or to say, as he believed, that he hadn't done enough; that all he had done was stay alive. When he thought about those days, the life he'd led since—working his way through school, starting a business, being a good friend to his friends, nursing his mother for three months while she died of cancer—all this dropped away as if it were nothing, and he felt as he had felt then, weak, corrupt, and afraid.

So B.D. avoided the subject.

Still, he knew that his silence had become its own kind of pose, and that was why he told his girlfriend about Ryan. He wanted to be truthful with her. What a surprise, then, to have it all come out sounding like a lie. He couldn't get it right, couldn't put across what he had felt. He used the wrong words, words that somehow rang false, in sentimental cadences. The details sounded artful. His voice was halting and grave, self-aware, phony. It embarrassed him and he could see that it was embarrassing her, so he stopped. B.D. concluded that grief was impossible to describe.

But that was not why he failed. He failed because he had not felt grief that day, finding Ryan gone. He had felt delivered—set free. He couldn't recognize it, let alone admit it, but that's what it was, a strong, almost disabling sense of release. It took him by surprise but he fought it down, mastered it before he knew what it was, thinking it must be something else. He took charge of himself as necessity decreed. When the next chopper came in, B.D. helped the medic put the corpse and the wounded men on board, and then he went back to his position. It was starting to rain.

A doctor in Qui Nhon did what he could for Ryan and then tagged him for shipment to Japan. That night they loaded him onto a C-141 med evac bound for Yokota, from there to be taken to the hospital at Zama. The ride was rough at first because of driving winds and the steep, almost corkscrew turns the pilot had to make to avoid groundfire from around the airfield. The nurses crouched in the aisle, gripping the frames of the berths as the plane pitched and yawed. The lights flickered. IV bags swung from their hooks. Men cried out. In this way they spiraled upward until they gained the thin, cold, untroubled heights, and then the pilot set his course, and the men mostly quieted down, and the nurses went about their business.

One heard Ryan say something as she passed his cot. She knelt beside him and he said it again, a word she couldn't make out. She took his pulse, monitored his breathing: shallow but regular. The dressing across his forehead and face was soaked through. She changed it, but had to leave the seeping compress on the wound; the orders on the chart specified that no one should touch it until he reached a certain team of doctors in Zama. When she'd finished with the dressing the nurse began to wipe his face. "Come on in," Ryan said, and seized her hand.

It gave her a start. "What?" she said.

He didn't speak again. She let him hold her hand until his grasp loosened, but when she tried to pull away he clamped down again. His lips moved soundlessly.

In the berth next to Ryan's was a boy who'd had both feet blown off. He was asleep, or unconscious; she could see the rise and fall of his chest. His near hand was resting on the deck. She picked it up by the wrist, and when Ryan relaxed his grip again she gave him his neighbour's hand and withdrew her own. He didn't seem to know the difference. She wiped his face once more and went to help another nurse with a patient who kept trying to get up.

She wasn't sure exactly when Ryan died. He was alive at one moment, and when she stopped by again, not so long afterward, he was gone. He still had the other boy's hand. She stood there and looked at them. She couldn't think what to do. Finally she went over to another nurse and took her aside. "I'm going to need a little something after all," she said.

The other nurse looked around. "I don't have any."

"Beth," she said. "Please."

"Don't ask, okay? You made me promise."

"Look," she said, "just this trip. It's all right—really, Beth, I mean it. It's all right."

During a lull later on she stopped and leaned her forehead against a porthole. The sun was just above the horizon. The sky was clear, no clouds between her and the sea below, whose name she loved to hear the pilots say—the East China Sea. Through the crazed Plexiglas she could make out some small islands and the white glint of a ship in the apex of its wake. Someday she was going to take passage on one of those ships, by herself or maybe with some friends. Lie in the sun. Breathe the good air. Do nothing all day but eat and sleep and be clean, throw crumbs to the gulls and watch the dolphins play alongside, diving and then leaping high to show off for the people at the rail, for her and her friends. She could see the whole thing. When she closed her eyes she could see the whole thing, perfectly.

1996

Lydia Davis

b. 1947

Lydia Davis has more than maintained her parents' academic and literary legacy, one a literary critic, the other a short-story writer. Her immense talent has been gauged by her MacArthur Fellowship and by her devoted readers who, until the Man Booker International Prize of 2013, felt in possession of a wonderful secret. In fact, Davis has expanded her legacy by contracting the form in which she primarily works. Her stories tend to be unusually short, sometimes almost two (short) pages, sometimes a brief paragraph. In response to the publication of her *Collected Stories* in 2009, Craig Morgan Teicher helped clarify perceptions of her writing: Davis is "the master of a literary form of her own invention." The complex pleasure of reading her work is often mixed with an almost gleeful attempt at identifying what her fictions should be called. "Aphoristic parable" (Christopher Tyler) is a good shot, prose poem (much) less so. Because her intelligence is as ranging as her stories are elliptical and cryptic, Davis has deflated the potential bloat of generic categorization. "Even if the thing is only a line or two, there is always a little fragment of narrative in there, or the reader can turn away and imagine a larger narrative . . . I can get away with calling them stories." An expansion of being content with "story" is her terse and powerful description of the form as "isolated events in a context of mystery with which, I and my characters, are quite comfortable." She acknowledges that to some extent her miniaturist style "was a reaction to Proust's very long sentences." Translating Proust with great success is Davis's day—or night—job. Compare the shelf space occupied by Proust with Davis's *Collected Stories.* Even the design of the book reflects a devotion to concision. It is about three-fifths the size of most volumes of selected stories. Davis is far from the first writer to work magic in extreme brevity. Kafka and Hemingway were masters of the two-page story. But in his "challenge" to her "intelligence," his comic instinct, and the construction of his sentences, Beckett is likely the major presence in Davis's creative ancestry. Less immediately apparent is how closely her most honed stories resemble Roman epigrams, particularly Martial's. The striking difference between her stories and modernist miniatures is the lack of metaphor, of charged, propulsive language. There's a bone here, a mandolin there, some bottles of wine. Ostensibly abstract, even clinical, her stories possess great affective power. Emotions peer out from the edges of sentences and their sharp physical details; emotions peer out, too, from the absences so dominant in Davis's stories, absences that connect her with her more narratively expansive peers, Joyce and Munro.

The Bone

Many years ago, my husband and I were living in Paris and translating art books. Whatever money we made we spent on movies and food. We went mostly to old American movies, which were very popular there, and we ate out a lot of the time because restaurant meals were cheap then and neither of us knew how to cook very well.

One night, though, I cooked some fillets of fish for dinner. These fillets were not supposed to contain bones, and yet there must have been a small bone in one of them because my husband swallowed it and it got caught in his throat. This had never happened to either of us before, though we had always worried about it. I gave him bread to eat, and he drank many glasses of water, but the bone was really stuck, and didn't move.

After several hours in which the pain intensified and my husband and I grew more and more uneasy, we left the apartment and walked out into the dark streets of Paris to look for help. We were first directed to the ground-floor apartment of a nurse who lived not far away, and she then directed us to a hospital. We walked on some way and found the hospital in the rue de Vaugirard. It was old and quite dark, as though it didn't do much business anymore.

Inside, I waited on a folding chair in a wide hallway near the front entrance while my husband sat behind a closed door nearby in the company of several nurses who wanted to help him but could not do more than spray his throat and then stand back and laugh, and he would laugh too, as best he could. I didn't know what they were all laughing about.

Finally a young doctor came and took my husband and me down several long, deserted corridors and around two sides of the dark hospital grounds to an empty wing containing another examining room in which he kept his special instruments. Each instrument had a different angle of curvature but they all ended in some sort of a hook. Under a single pool of light, in the darkened room, he inserted one instrument after another down my husband's throat, working with fierce interest and enthusiasm. Every time he inserted another instrument my husband gagged and waved his hands in the air.

At last the doctor drew out the little fish bone and showed it around proudly. The three of us smiled and congratulated one another.

The doctor took us back down the empty corridors and out under the vaulted entryway that had been built to accommodate horse-drawn carriages. We stood there and talked a little, looking around at the empty streets of the neighborhood, and then we shook hands and my husband and I walked home.

More than ten years have passed since then, and my husband and I have gone our separate ways, but every now and then, when we are together, we remember that young doctor. "A great Jewish doctor," says my husband, who is also Jewish.

2009

A Few Things Wrong with Me

He said there were things about me that he hadn't liked from the very beginning. He didn't say this unkindly. He's not an unkind person, at least not intentionally. He said it because I was trying to get him to explain why he changed his mind about me so suddenly.

I may ask his friends what they think about this, because they know him better than I do. They've known him for more than fifteen years, whereas I've known him for only about ten months. I like them, and they seem to like me, though we don't know each other very well. What I want to do is to have a meal or a drink with at least two of them and talk about him until I begin to get a better picture of him.

It's easy to come to the wrong conclusions about people. I see now that all these past months I kept coming to the wrong conclusions about him. For example, when I thought he would be unkind to me, he was kind. Then when I thought he would be effusive he was merely polite. When I thought he would be annoyed to hear my voice on the telephone he was pleased. When I thought he would turn against me because I had treated him rather coldly, he was more anxious than ever to be with me and went to great trouble and expense so that we could spend a little time together. Then when I made up my mind that he was the man for me, he suddenly called the whole thing off.

It seemed sudden to me even though for the last month I could feel him drawing away. For instance, he didn't write as often as he had before, and then when we were together he said more unkind things to me than he ever had before. When he left, I knew he was thinking it over. He took a month to think it over, and I knew it was fifty-fifty he would come to the point of saying what he did.

I suppose it seemed sudden because of the hopes I had for him and me by then, and the dreams I had about us—some of the usual dreams about a nice house and nice babies and the two of us together in the house working in the evening while the babies were asleep, and then some other dreams, about how we would travel together, and about how I would learn to play the banjo or the mandolin so that I could play with him, because he has a lovely tenor voice. Now, when I picture myself playing the banjo or the mandolin, the idea seems silly.

The way it all ended was that he called me up on a day he didn't usually call me and said he had finally come to a decision. Then he said that because he had had trouble figuring all this out, he had made some notes about what he was going to say and he asked me if I would mind if he read them. I said I would mind very much. He said he would at least have to look at them now and then as he talked.

Then he talked in a very reasonable way about how bad the chances were for us to be happy together, and about changing over to a friendship now before it was too late. I said he was talking about me as though I were an old tire that might blowout on the highway. He thought that was funny.

We talked about how he had felt about me at various times, and how I had felt about him at various times, and it seemed that these feelings hadn't matched very well. Then, when I wanted to know exactly how he had felt about me from the very beginning, trying to find out, really, what was the most he had ever felt, he made this very plain statement about how there were things about me that he hadn't liked from the very beginning. He wasn't trying to be unkind, but just very clear. I told him I wouldn't ask him what these things were but I knew I would have to go and think about it.

I didn't like hearing there were things about me that bothered him. It was shocking to hear that someone I loved had never liked certain things about me. Of course there were a few things I didn't like about him too, for instance an affectation in his manner involving the introduction of foreign phrases into his conversation, but although I had noticed these things, I had never said it to him in quite this way. But if I try to be logical, I have to think that after all there may be a few things wrong with me. Then the problem is to figure out what these things are.

For several days, after we talked, I tried to think about this, and I came up with some possibilities. Maybe I didn't talk enough. He likes to talk a lot and he likes other people to talk a lot. I'm not very talkative, or at least not in the way he probably likes. I have some good ideas from time to time, but not much information. I can talk for a long time only when it's about something boring. Maybe I talked too much about which foods he should be eating. I worry about the way people eat and tell them what they should eat, which is a tiresome thing to do, something my ex-husband never liked either. Maybe I mentioned my ex-husband too often, so that he thought my ex-husband was still on my mind, which wasn't true. He might have been irritated by the fact that he couldn't kiss me in the street for fear of getting poked in the eye by my glasses—or maybe he didn't even like being with a woman who wore glasses, maybe he didn't like always having to look at my eyes through this blue-tinted glass. Or maybe he doesn't like people who write things on index cards, diet plans on little index cards and plot summaries on big index cards. I don't like it much myself, and I don't do it all the time. It's just a way I have of trying to get my life in order. But he might have come across some of those index cards.

I couldn't think of much else that would have bothered him from the very beginning. Then I decided I would never be able to think of the things about me that bothered him. Whatever I thought of would probably not be the same things. And anyway, I wasn't going to go on trying to identify these things, because even if I knew what they were I wouldn't be able to do anything about them.

Late in the conversation, he tried to tell me how excited he was about his new plan for the summer. Now that he wasn't going to be with me, he thought he would travel down to Venezuela, to visit some friends who were doing anthropological work in the jungle. I told him I didn't want to hear about that.

While we talked on the phone, I was drinking some wine left over from a large party I had given. After we hung up I immediately picked up the phone again and made a series of phone calls, and while I talked, I finished one of the leftover bottles of wine and started on another that was sweeter than the first, and then finished that one too. First I called a few people here in the city, then when it got too late for that I called a few people in California, and when it got too late to go on calling California, I called someone in England who had just woken up and was not in a very good mood.

Between one phone call and the next I would sometimes walk by the window and look up at the moon, which was in its first quarter but remarkably bright, and think of him and then wonder when I would stop thinking of him every time I saw the moon. The reason I thought of him when I saw the moon was that during the five days and four nights he and I were first together, the moon was waxing and then full, the nights were clear, we were in the country, where you notice the sky more, and every night, early or late, we would walk outdoors together, partly to get away from the various members of our families who were in the house and partly just to take pleasure in the meadows and the woods under the moonlight. The dirt road that sloped up away from the house into the woods was full of ruts and rocks, so that we kept stumbling against each other and more tightly into each other's arms. We talked about how nice it would be to bring a bed out into the meadow and lie down on it in the moonlight.

The next time the moon was full, I was back in the city, and I saw it out the window of a new apartment. I thought to myself that a month had passed since he and I were together, and that it had passed very slowly. After that, every time the moon was full, shining on the leafy, tall trees in the backyards here, and on the flat tar roofs, and then on the bare trees and snowy ground in the winter, I would think to myself that another month had passed, sometimes quickly and sometimes slowly. I liked counting the months that way.

He and I always seemed to be counting the time as it passed and waiting for it to pass so that the day would come when we would be together again. That was one reason he said he couldn't go on with it. And maybe he's right, it isn't too late, we will change over to a friendship, and he will talk to me now and then long distance, mostly about his work or my work, and give me good advice or a plan of action when I need one, then call himself something like my "éminence grise."

When I stopped making my phone calls, I was too dizzy to go to sleep, because of the wine, so I turned on the television and watched some police dramas, some old situation comedies, and finally a show about unusual people across the country. I turned the set off at five in the morning when the sky was light, and I fell asleep right away.

It's true that by the time the night was over I wasn't worrying anymore about what was wrong with me. At that hour of the morning I can usually get myself out to the end of something like a long dock with water all around where I'm not touched by such worries. But there will always come a time later that day or a day or two after when I ask myself that difficult question once, or over and over again, a useless question, really, since I'm not the one who can answer it and anyone else who tries will come up with a different answer, though of course all the answers together may add up to the right one, if there is such a thing as a right answer to a question like that.

2009

Jane Urquhart

b. 1949

Jane Urquhart was born in the small northern Ontario mining community of Little Long Lac (near Geraldton) and spent her later childhood and adolescence in Toronto. She began her writing career as a poet, publishing two books of poetry, *I'm Walking in the Garden of His Imaginary Palace* and *False Shuffles*, in 1982, followed by *The Little Flowers of Madame de Montespan* (1984). Her first novel, *The Whirlpool* (1986), an immediate critical success, was the first Canadian book to win France's prestigious Prix du Meilleur Livre Étranger in 1992. Urquhart's second novel, *Changing Heaven* (1990), intertwines the histories of a contemporary Brontë scholar, a nineteenth-century balloonist, and the ghost of Emily Brontë. *Away* (1993), which Timothy Findley described as a "great romantic tale . . . with language worthy of Emily Brontë and Thomas Hardy," remained on the *Globe and Mail*'s National Bestseller list for 132 weeks (the longest of any Canadian book), and won the 1994 Trillium Book Award. *The Underpainter* (1997), Urquhart's deliberate experiment in writing from a male point of view, is a meditation on the relation between art and life, a favourite Urquhart theme. The novel offers a portrait of an aging American minimalist painter who has denied himself a private life for the sake of his art, only to discover his art is cold and lifeless as a consequence. The novel won the Governor General's Award. Her novel, *The Stone Carvers* (2001), about the carving of Walter Allward's war memorial at Vimy, France, takes as its theme what Urquhart calls "the redemptive nature of making art." Her most recent fiction is Sanctuary Line (2010). She has been writer-in-residence at the Universities of Ottawa and Toronto, and at Memorial University in Newfoundland. In 1994 she received the Marian Engel Award, and in 1996 she was named to France's Order of Arts and Letters as a Chevalier.

The Death of Robert Browning

In December of 1889, as he was returning by gondola from the general vicinity of the Palazzo Manzoni, it occurred to Robert Browning that he was more than likely going to die soon. This revelation had nothing to do with either his advanced years or the state of his health. He was seventy-seven, a reasonably advanced age, but his physical condition was described by most of his acquaintances as vigorous and robust. He took a cold bath each morning and every afternoon insisted on a three-mile walk during which he performed small errands from a list his sister had made earlier in the day. He drank moderately and ate well. His mind was as quick and alert as ever.

Nevertheless, he knew he was going to die. He also had to admit that the idea had been with him for some time—two or three months at least. He was not a man to ignore symbols, especially when they carried personal messages. Now he had to acknowledge that the symbols were in the air as surely as winter. Perhaps, he speculated, a man carried the seeds of his death with him always, somewhere buried in the brain, like the face of a woman he is going to love. He leaned to one side, looked into the deep waters of the canal, and saw his own face reflected there. As broad and distinguished and cheerful as ever, health shining vigorously, robustly from his eyes—even in such a dark mirror.

Empty Gothic and Renaissance palaces floated on either side of him like soiled pink dreams. Like sunsets with dirty faces, he mused, and then, pleased with the phrase, he reached into his jacket for his notebook, ink pot, and pen. He had trouble recording the words, however, as the chill in the air had numbed his hands. Even the ink seemed affected by the cold, not flowing as smoothly as usual. He wrote slowly and deliberately, making sure to add the exact time and the location. Then he closed the book and returned it with the pen and pot to his pocket, where he curled and uncurled his right hand for some minutes until he felt the circulation return to normal. The celebrated Venetian dampness was much worse in winter, and Browning began to look forward to the fire at his son's palazzo where they would be beginning to serve afternoon tea, perhaps, for his benefit, laced with rum.

A sudden wind scalloped the surface of the canal. Browning instinctively looked upwards. Some blue patches edged by ragged white clouds, behind them wisps of grey and then the solid dark strip of a storm front moving slowly up on the horizon. Such a disordered sky in this season. No solid, predictable blocks of weather with definite beginnings, definite endings. Every change in the atmosphere seemed an emotional response to something that had gone before. The light, too, harsh and metallic, not at all like the golden Venice summer. There was something broken about all of it, torn. The sky, for instance, was like a damaged canvas. Pleased again by his own metaphorical thoughts, Browning considered reaching for the notebook. But the cold forced him to reject the idea before it had fully formed in his mind.

Instead, his thoughts moved lazily back to the place they had been when the notion of death so rudely interrupted them; back to the building he had just visited. Palazzo Manzoni. *Bello, bello* Palazzo Manzoni! The colourful marble medallions rolled across Browning's inner eye, detached from their home on the Renaissance façade, and he began, at once, to reconstruct for the thousandth time the imaginary windows and balconies he had planned for the building's restoration. In his daydreams the old poet had walked over the palace's swollen marble floors and slept beneath its frescoed ceilings, lit fires underneath its sculptured mantels and entertained guests by the light of its chandeliers. Surrounded by a small crowd of admirers he had read poetry aloud in the evenings, his voice echoing through the halls. *No R.B. tonight*, he had said to them, winking, *Let's have some real poetry*. Then, moving modestly into the palace's impressive library, he had selected a volume of Dante or Donne.

But they had all discouraged him and it had never come to pass. Some of them said that the façade was seriously cracked and the foundations were far from sound. Others told him that the absentee owner would never part with it for anything resembling a fair price. Eventually, friends and family wore him down with their disapproval and, on their advice, he abandoned his daydream though he still made an effort to visit it, despite the fact that it was now damaged and empty and the glass in its windows was broken.

It was the same kind of frustration and melancholy that he associated with his night dreams of Asolo, the little hill town he had first seen (and then only at a distance), when he was twenty-six years old. Since that time, and for no rational reason, it had appeared over and over in the poet's dreams as a destination on the horizon, one that, due to a variety of circumstances, he was never able to reach. Either his companions in the dream would persuade him to take an alternate route, or the road would be impassable, or he would awaken just as the town gate came into view, frustrated and out of sorts. "I've had my old Asolo dream again," he would tell his sister at breakfast, "and it has no doubt ruined my work for the whole day."

Then, just last summer, he had spent several months there at the home of a friend. The house was charming and the view of the valley delighted him. But, although he never once broke the well-established order that ruled the days of his life, a sense of unreality clouded his perceptions. He was visiting the memory of a dream with a major and important difference. He had reached the previously elusive hill town with practically no effort. Everything had proceeded according to plan. Thinking about this, under the December sky in Venice, Browning realized that he had known since then that it was only going to be a matter of time.

The gondola bumped against the steps of his son's palazzo.

Robert Browning climbed onto the terrace, paid the gondolier, and walked briskly inside.

Lying on the magnificent carved bed in his room, trying unsuccessfully to surrender himself to his regular pre-dinner nap, Robert Browning examined his knowledge like a stolen jewel he had coveted for years; turning it first this way, then that, imagining the reactions of his friends, what his future biographers would have to say about it all. He was pleased that he had prudently written his death poem at Asolo in direct response to having received a copy of Tennyson's "Crossing the Bar" in the mail. How he detested that poem! What *could* Alfred have been thinking of when he wrote it? He had to admit, none the less, that to suggest that mourners restrain their sorrow, as Tennyson had, guarantees the floodgates of female tears will eventually burst open. His poem had, therefore, included similar sentiments, but without, he hoped, such obvious sentimentality. It was the final poem of his last manuscript which was now, mercifully, at the printers.

Something for the biographers and for the weeping maidens; those who had wept so copiously for his dear departed, though soon to be reinstated wife. Surely it was not too much to ask that they might shed a few tears for him as well, even if it was a more ordinary death, following, he winced to have to add, a fairly conventional life.

How had it all happened? He had placed himself in the centre of some of the world's most exotic scenery and had then lived his life there with the regularity of a copy clerk. A time for everything, everything in its time. Even when hunting for lizards in Asolo, an occupation he considered slightly exotic, he found he could predict the moment of their appearance; as if they knew he was searching for them and assembled their modest population at the sound of his footsteps. Even so, he was able to flush out only six or seven from a hedge of considerable length and these were, more often than not, of the same type. Once he thought he had seen a particularly strange lizard, large and lumpy, but it had turned out to be merely two of the ordinary sort, copulating.

Copulation. What sad dirge-like associations the word dredged up from the poet's unconscious. All those Italians; those minstrels, dukes, princes, artists, and questionable monks whose voices had droned through Browning's pen over the years. Why had they all been so endlessly obsessed with the subject? He could never understand or control it. And even now, one of them had appeared in full period costume in his imagination. A duke, no doubt, by the look of the yards of velvet which covered his person. He was reading a letter that was causing him a great deal of pain. Was it a letter from his mistress? A draught of poison waited on an intricately tooled small table to his left. Perhaps a pistol or a dagger as well, but in this light Browning could not quite tell. The man paced, paused, looked wistfully out the window as if waiting for someone he knew would never, ever appear. Very, very soon now he would begin to speak, to tell his story. His right hand passed nervously across his eyes. He turned to look directly at Robert Browning who, as always, was beginning to feel somewhat embarrassed. Then the duke began:

At last to leave these darkening moments
These rooms, these halls where once
We stirred love's poisoned potions
The deepest of all slumbers,
After this astounds the mummers
I cannot express the smile that circled
Round and round the week
This room and all our days when morning
Entered, soft, across her cheek.
She was my medallion, my caged dove,
A trinket, a coin I carried warm,
Against the skin inside my glove
My favourite artwork was a kind of jail
Our portrait permanent, imprinted by the moon
Upon the ancient face of the canal.

The man began to fade. Browning, who had not invited him into the room in the first place, was already bored. He therefore dismissed the crimson costume, the table, the potion housed in its delicate goblet of fine Venetian glass and began, quite inexplicably, to think about Percy Bysshe Shelley; about his life, and under the circumstances, more importantly, about his death.

Dinner over, sister, son and daughter-in-law, and friend all chatted with and later read to, Browning returned to his room with Shelley's death hovering around him like an annoying, directionless wind. He doubted, as he put on his nightgown, that Shelly had ever worn one, particularly in those dramatic days preceding his early demise. In his night-cap he felt as ridiculous as a humorous political drawing for *Punch* magazine. And, as he lumbered into bed alone, he remembered that Shelley would have had Mary beside him and possibly Clare as well, their minds buzzing with nameless Gothic terrors. For a desperate moment or two Browning tried to conjure a Gothic terror but discovered, to his great disappointment, that the vague shape taking form in his mind was only his dreary Italian duke coming, predictably, once again into focus.

Outside the ever calm water of the canal licked the edge of the terrace in a rhythmic, sleep-inducing manner; a restful sound guaranteeing peace of mind. Browning knew, however, that during Shelley's last days at Lerici, giant waves had crashed into the ground floor of Casa Magni, prefiguring the young poet's violent death and causing his sleep to be riddled with wonderful nightmares. Therefore, the very lack of activity on the part of the water below irritated the old man. He began to pad around the room in his bare feet, oblivious to the cold marble floor and the dying embers in the fireplace. He peered through the windows into the night, hoping that he, like Shelley, might at least see his double there, or possibly Elizabeth's ghost beckoning to him from the centre of the canal. He cursed softly as the night gazed back at him, serene and cold and entirely lacking in events—mysterious or otherwise.

He returned to the bed and knelt by its edge in order to say his evening prayers. But he was completely unable to concentrate. Shelley's last days were trapped in his brain like fish in a tank. He saw him surrounded by the sublime scenery of the Ligurian coast, searching the horizon for the boat that was to be his coffin. Then he saw him clinging desperately to the mast of that boat while lightning tore the sky in half and the ocean spilled across the hull. Finally, he saw Shelley's horrifying corpse rolling on the shoreline, practically unidentifiable except for the copy of Keats' poems housed in his breast pocket. *Next to his heart*, Byron had commented, just before he got to work on the funeral pyre.

Browning abandoned God for the moment and climbed beneath the blankets.

"I might at least have a nightmare," he said petulantly to himself. Then he fell into a deep and dreamless sleep.

Browning awakened the next morning with an itchy feeling in his throat and lines from Shelley's *Prometheus Unbound* dancing in his head.

"Oh, God," he groaned inwardly, "now this. And I don't even *like* Shelley's poetry anymore. Now I suppose I'm going to be plagued with it, day in, day out, until the instant of my imminent death."

How he wished he had never, ever, been fond of Shelley's poems. Then, in his youth, he might have had the common sense not to read them compulsively to the point of total recall. But how could he have known in those early days that even though he would later come to reject both Shelley's life and work as being too impossibly self-absorbed and emotional, some far corner of his brain would still retain every syllable the young man had committed to paper. He had memorized his life's work. Shortly after Browning's memory recited *The crawling glaciers pierce me with spears / Of their moon freezing crystals, the bright chains / Eat with their burning cold into my bones*, he began to cough, a spasm that lasted until his sister knocked discreetly on the door to announce that, since he had not appeared downstairs, his breakfast was waiting on a tray in the hall.

While he was drinking his tea, the poem "Ozymandias" repeated itself four times in his mind except that, to his great annoyance, he found that he could not remember the last three lines and kept ending with *Look on my works, ye Mighty, and despair.* He knew for certain that there were three more lines, but he was damned if he could recall even one of them. He thought of asking his sister but soon realized that, since she was familiar with his views on Shelley, he would be forced to answer a series of embarrassing questions about why he was thinking about the poem at all. Finally, he decided that *Look on my works, ye Mighty, and despair* was a much more fitting ending to the poem and attributed his lack of recall to the supposition that the last three lines were either unsuitable or completely unimportant. That settled, he wolfed down his roll, donned his hat and coat, and departed for the streets in hopes that something, anything, might happen.

Even years later, Browning's sister and son could still be counted upon to spend a full evening discussing what he might have done that day. The possibilities were endless. He might have gone off hunting for a suitable setting for a new poem, or for the physical characteristics of a duke by examining handsome northern Italian workmen. He might have gone, again, to visit his beloved Palazzo Manzoni, to gaze wistfully at its marble medallions. He might have gone to visit a Venetian builder, to discuss plans for the beautiful tower he had talked about building at Asolo, or out to Murano to watch men mould their delicate bubbles of glass. His sister was convinced that he had gone to the Church of S.S. Giovanni e Paolo to gaze at his favourite equestrian statue. His pious son, on the other hand, liked to believe that his father had spent the day in one of the few English churches in Venice, praying for the redemption of his soul. But all of their speculations assumed a sense of purpose on the poet's part, that he had left the house with a definite destination in mind, because as long as they could remember, he had never acted without a predetermined plan.

Without a plan, Robert Browning faced the Grand Canal with very little knowledge of what, in fact, he was going to do. He looked to the left, and then to the right, and then, waving aside an expectant gondolier, he turned abruptly and entered the thick of the city behind him. There he wandered aimlessly through a labyrinth of narrow streets, noting details; *putti* wafting stone garlands over windows, door knockers in the shape of gargoyles' heads, painted windows that fooled the eye, items that two weeks earlier would have delighted him but now seemed used and lifeless. Statues appeared to leak and ooze damp soot, window-glass was fogged with moisture, steps that led him over canals were slippery, covered with an unhealthy slime. He became peculiarly aware of smells he had previously ignored in favour of the more pleasant sensations the city had to offer. But now even the small roof gardens seemed to grow as if in stagnant water, winter chrysanthemums emitting a putrid odour, which spoke less of blossom than decay. With a kind of slow horror, Browning realized that he was seeing his beloved city through Shelley's eyes and immediately his inner voice began again: *Sepulchres where human forms / Like pollution nourished worms / To the corpse of greatness cling / Murdered and now mouldering.*

He quickened his steps, hoping that if he concentrated on physical activity his mind would not subject him to the complete version of Shelley's "Lines Written Among the Euganean Hills." But he was not to be spared. The poem had been one of his favourites in his youth and, as a result, his mind was now capable of reciting it to him, word by word, with appropriate emotional inflections, followed by a particularly moving rendition of "Julian and Maddalo" accompanied by mental pictures of Shelley and Byron galloping along the beach at the Lido.

When at last the recitation ceased, Browning had walked as far as possible and now found himself at the edge of the Fondamente Nuove with only the wide flat expanse of the Laguna Morta in front of him.

He surveyed his surroundings and began, almost unconsciously, and certainly against his will, to search for the islanded madhouse that Shelley had described in "Julian and Maddalo": *A building on an island; such a one / As age to age might add, for uses vile / A windowless, deformed and dreary pile.* Then he remembered, again against his will, that it was on the other side, near the Lido. Instead, his eyes came to rest on the cemetery island of San Michele whose neat white mausoleums and tidy cypresses looked fresher, less sepulchral than any portion of the city he had passed through. Although he had never been there, he could tell, even from this distance, that its paths would be raked and its marble scrubbed in a way that the rest of Venice never was. Like a disease that cannot cross the water, the rot and mould of the city had never reached the cemetery's shore.

It pleased Browning, now, to think of the island's clean-boned inhabitants sleeping in their white-washed houses. Then, his mood abruptly changing, he thought with disgust of Shelley, of his bloated corpse upon the sands, how his flesh had been saturated by water, then burned away by fire, and how his heart had refused to burn, as if it had not been made of flesh at all.

Browning felt the congestion in his chest take hold, making his breathing shallow and laboured, and he turned back into the city, attempting to determine the direction of his son's palazzo. Pausing now and then to catch his breath, he made his way slowly through the streets that make up the Fondamente Nuove, an area with which he was completely unfamiliar. This was Venice at its most squalid. What little elegance had originally existed in this section had now faded so dramatically that it had all but disappeared. Scrawny children screamed and giggled on every narrow walkway and tattered washing hung from most windows. In doorways, sullen elderly widows stared insolently and with increasing hostility at this obvious foreigner who had invaded their territory. A dull panic began to overcome him as he realized he was lost. The disease meanwhile had weakened his legs, and he stumbled awkwardly under the communal gaze of these women who were like black angels marking his path. Eager to be rid of their judgmental stares, he turned into an alley, smaller than the last, and found to his relief that it was deserted and graced with a small fountain and a stone bench.

The alley, of course, was blind, went nowhere, but it was peaceful and Browning was in need of a rest. He leaned back against the stone wall and closed his eyes. The fountain murmured *Bysshe, Bysshe, Bysshe* until the sound finally became soothing to Browning and he dozed, on and off, while fragments of Shelley's poetry moved in and out of his consciousness.

Then, waking suddenly from one of these moments of semi-slumber, he began to feel again that he was being watched. He searched the upper windows and the doorways around him for old women and found none. Instinctively, he looked at an archway which was just a fraction to the left of his line of vision. There, staring directly into his own, was the face of Percy Bysshe Shelley, as young and sad and powerful as Browning had ever known it would be. The visage gained flesh and expression for a glorious thirty seconds before returning to the marble that it really was. With a sickening and familiar sense of loss, Browning recognized the carving of Dionysus, or Pan, or Adonis, that often graced the tops of Venetian doorways. The sick old man walked towards it and, reaching up, placed his fingers on the soiled cheek. "Suntreader," he mumbled, then he moved out of the alley, past the black, disapproving women, into the streets towards a sizeable canal. There, bent over his walking stick, coughing spasmodically, he was able to hail a gondola.

All the way back across the city he murmured, "Where have you been, where have you been, where did you go?"

Robert Browning lay dying in his son's Venetian palazzo. Half of his face was shaded by a large velvet curtain which was gathered by his shoulder, the other half lay exposed to the weak winter light. His sister, son, and daughter-in-law stood at the foot of the bed nervously awaiting words or signs from the old man. They spoke to each other silently by means of glances and gestures, hoping they would not miss any kind of signal from his body, mountain-like under the bedclothes. But for hours now nothing had happened. Browning's large chest moved up and down in a slow and rhythmic fashion, not unlike an artificially manipulated bellows. He appeared to be unconscious.

But Browning was not unconscious. Rather, he had used the last remnants of his free will to make a final decision. There were to be no last words. How inadequate his words seemed now compared to Shelley's experience, how silly this monotonous bedridden death. He did not intend to further add to the absurdity by pontificating. He now knew that he had said too much. At this very moment, in London, a volume of superfluous words was coming off the press. All this chatter filling up the space of Shelley's more important silence. He now knew that when Shelley had spoken it was by choice and not by habit, that the young man's words had been a response and not a fabrication.

He opened his eyes a crack and found himself staring at the ceiling. The fresco there moved and changed and finally evolved into Shelley's iconography—an eagle struggling with a serpent. *Suntreader.* The clouds, the white foam of the clouds, like water, the feathers of the great wings becoming lost in this. *Half angel, half bird.* And the blue of the sky, opening now, erasing the ceiling, limitless so that the bird's wing seemed to vaporize. *A moulted feather, an eagle feather.* Such untravelled distance in which light arrived and disappeared leaving behind something that was not darkness. *His radiant form becoming less radiant.* Leaving its own natural absence with the strength and the suck of a vacuum. No alternate atmosphere to fill the place abandoned. *Suntreader.*

And now Browning understood. It was Shelley's absence he had carried with him all these years until it had passed beyond his understanding. *Soft star.* Shelley's emotions so absent from the old poet's life, his work, leaving him unanswered, speaking through the mouths of others, until he had to turn away from Shelley altogether in anger and disgust. The drowned spirit had outdistanced him wherever he sought it. *Lone and sunny idleness of heaven.* The anger, the disgust, the evaporation. *Suntreader, soft star.* The formless form he never possessed and was never possessed by.

Too weak for anger now, Robert Browning closed his eyes and relaxed his fists, allowing Shelley's corpse to enter the place in his imagination where once there had been only absence. It floated through the sea of Browning's mind, its muscles soft under the constant pressure of the ocean. Limp and drifting, the drowned man looked as supple as a mermaid, arms swaying in the current, hair and clothing tossed as if in a slow, slow wind. His body was losing colour, turning from pastel to opaque, the open eyes staring, pale, as if frozen by an image of the moon. Joints unlocked by moisture, limbs swung easy on their threads of tendon, the spine undulating and relaxed. The absolute grace of this death, that life caught there moving in the arms of the sea. Responding, always responding to the elements.

Now the drowned poet began to move into a kind of Atlantis consisting of Browning's dream architecture; the unobtainable and the unconstructed. In complete silence the young man swam through the rooms of the Palazzo Manzoni, slipping up and down the staircase, gliding down halls, in and out of fireplaces. He appeared briefly in mirrors. He drifted past balconies to the tower Browning had thought of building at Asolo. He wavered for a few minutes near its crenellated peak before moving in a slow spiral down along its edges to its base.

Browning had just enough time to wish for the drama and the luxury of a death by water. Then his fading attention was caught by the rhythmic bump of a moored gondola against the terrace below. The boat was waiting, he knew, to take his body to the cemetery at San Michele when the afternoon had passed. Shelly had said somewhere that a gondola was a butterfly of which the coffin was a chrysalis.

Suntreader. Still beyond his grasp. The eagle on the ceiling lost in unfocused fog. *A moulted feather, an eagle feather, well I forget the rest.* The drowned man's body separated into parts and moved slowly out of Browning's mind. The old poet contented himself with the thought of one last journey by water. The coffin boat, the chrysalis. Across the Laguna Morta to San Michele. All that cool white marble in exchange for the shifting sands of Lerici.

1987

Barbara Gowdy

b. 1950

Barbara Gowdy was born in Windsor, Ontario, and grew up in the Toronto suburb of Don Mills. After graduating from high school in the late 1960s, she studied at York University and at the Royal Conservatory of Music. Before dedicating herself to writing, Gowdy tried several careers, including working in musical theatre, in the securities industry, and, from 1974 to 1979, with the publishing firm Lester & Orpen Dennys, eventually becoming managing editor. With her 1992 collection, *We So Seldom Look on Love*, which features stories about transvestism, exhibitionism, and necrophilia. Gowdy became known as a black humorist who looks with a slightly skewed vision at many aspects of sexual deviation, monstrosity, illness, and exhibitionism—a kind of Diane Arbus in prose rather than photography. But while her stories are sometimes shocking and even sensational, they are brilliantly crafted and driven by an imperative to resist sentimentality and to confront the crisis in values in consumer culture. In her scrupulously researched novel *The White Bone* (1998), she expands her fascination with other mentalities to include animals, examining the life of a community of elephants. The book is an elegy for the animal kingdom, desecrated by human cruelty and greed. Gowdy has taught creative writing at a number of universities, including Ryerson and the University of Toronto. Her story "We so Seldom Look on Love" was made into the successful film *Kissed* (1997).

We So Seldom Look on Love

When you die, and your earthly self begins turning into your disintegrated self, you radiate an intense current of energy. There is always energy given off when a thing turns into its opposite, when love, for instance, turns into hate. There are always sparks at those extreme points. But life turning into death is the most extreme of extreme points. So just after you die, the sparks are really stupendous. Really magical and explosive.

I've seen cadavers shining like stars. I'm the only person I've ever heard of who has. Almost everyone senses something, though, some vitality. That's why you get resistance to the idea of cremation or organ donation. "I want to be in one piece," people say. Even Matt, who claimed there was no soul and no afterlife, wrote a P.S. in his suicide note that he be buried intact.

As if it would have made any difference to his energy emission. No matter what you do—slice open the flesh, dissect everything, burn everything—you're in the path of a power way beyond your little interferences.

I grew up in a nice, normal, happy family outside a small town in New Jersey. My parents and my brothers are still living there. My dad owned a flower store. Now my brother owns it. My brother is three years older than I am, a serious, remote man. But loyal. When I made the headlines he phoned to say that if

I needed money for a lawyer, he would give it to me. I was really touched. Especially as he was standing up to Carol, his wife. She got on the extension and screamed, "You're sick! You should be put away!"

She'd been wanting to tell me that since we were thirteen years old.

I had an animal cemetery back then. Our house was beside a woods and we had three outdoor cats, great hunters who tended to leave their kills in one piece. Whenever I found a body, usually a mouse or a bird, I took it into my bedroom and hid it until midnight. I didn't know anything about the ritual significance of the midnight hour. My burials took place then because that's when I woke up. It no longer happens, but I was such a sensitive child that I think I must have been aroused by the energy given off as day clicked over into the dead of night and, simultaneously, as the dead of night clicked over into the next day.

In any case, I'd be wide awake. I'd get up and go to the bathroom to wrap the body in toilet paper. I felt compelled to be so careful, so respectful. I whispered a chant. At each step of the burial I chanted. "I shroud the body, shroud the body, shroud little sparrow with broken wing." Or "I lower the body, lower the body . . ." And so on.

Climbing out the bathroom window was accompanied by: "I enter the night, enter the night . . ." At my cemetery I set the body down on a special flat rock and took my pyjamas off. I was behaving out of pure inclination. I dug up four or five graves and unwrapped the animals from their shrouds. The rotting smell was crucial. So was the cool air. Normally I'd be so keyed up at this point that I'd burst into a dance.

I used to dance for dead men, too. Before I climbed on top of them, I'd dance all around the prep room. When I told Matt about this he said that I was shaking my personality out of my body so that the sensation of participating in the cadaver's energy eruption would be intensified. "You're trying to imitate the disintegration process," he said.

Maybe—on an unconscious level. But what I was aware of was the heat, the heat of my danced-out body, which I cooled by lying on top of the cadaver. As a child I'd gently wipe my skin with two of the animals I'd just unwrapped. When I was covered all over with their scent, I put them aside, unwrapped the new corpse and did the same with it. I called this the Anointment. I can't describe how it felt. The high, high rapture. The electricity that shot through me.

The rest, wrapping the bodies back up and burying them, was pretty much what you'd expect.

It astonishes me now to think how naive I was. I thought I had discovered something that certain other people, if they weren't afraid to give it a try, would find just as fantastic as I did. It was a dark and forbidden thing, yes, but so was sex. I really had no idea I was jumping across a vast behavioural gulf. In fact, I couldn't see that I was doing anything wrong. I still can't, and I'm including what happened with Matt. Carol said I should have been put away, but I'm not bad-looking, so if offering my body to dead men is a crime, I'd like to know who the victim is.

Carol has always been jealous of me. She's fat and has a wandering eye. Her eye gives her a dreamy, distracted quality that I fell for (as I suppose my brother would eventually do) one day at a friend's thirteenth birthday party. It was the beginning of the summer holidays, and I was yearning for a kindred spirit, someone to share my secret life with. I saw Carol standing alone, looking everywhere at once, and I chose her.

I knew to take it easy, though. I knew not to push anything. We'd search for dead animals and birds, we'd chant and swaddle the bodies, dig graves, make popsicle-stick crosses. All by daylight. At midnight I'd go out and dig up the grave and conduct a proper burial.

There must have been some chipmunk sickness that summer. Carol and I found an incredible number of chipmunks, and a lot of them had no blood on them, no sign of cat. One day we found a chipmunk that evacuated a string of fetuses when I picked it up. The fetuses were still alive, but there was no saving them, so I took them into the house and flushed them down the toilet.

A mighty force was coming from the mother chipmunk. It was as if, along with her own energy, she was discharging all the energy of her dead brood. When Carol and I began to dance for her, we both went a little crazy. We stripped down to our underwear, screamed, spun in circles, threw dirt up into the air. Carol has always denied it, but she took off her bra and began whipping trees with it. I'm sure the sight of her doing this is what inspired me to take off my undershirt and underpants and to perform the Anointment.

Carol stopped dancing. I looked at her, and the expression on her face stopped me dancing, too. I looked down at the chipmunk in my hand. It was bloody. There were streaks of blood all over my body. I was horrified. I thought I'd squeezed the chipmunk too hard.

But what had happened was, I'd begun my period. I figured this out a few minutes after Carol ran off. I wrapped the chipmunk in its shroud and buried it. Then I got dressed and lay down on the grass. A little while later my mother appeared over me.

"Carol's mother phoned," she said. "Carol is very upset. She says you made her perform some disgusting witchcraft dance. You made her take her clothes off, and you attacked her with a bloody chipmunk."

"That's a lie," I said. "I'm menstruating."

After my mother had fixed me up with a sanitary napkin, she told me she didn't think I should play with Carol any more. "There's a screw loose in there somewhere," she said.

I had no intention of playing with Carol any more, but I cried at what seemed like a cruel loss. I think I knew that it was all loneliness from that moment on. Even though I was only thirteen, I was cutting any lines that still drifted out toward normal eroticism. Bosom friends, crushes, pyjama-party intimacy, I was cutting all those lines off.

A month or so after becoming a woman I developed a craving to perform autopsies. I resisted doing it for almost a year, though. I was frightened. Violating the intactness of the animal seemed sacrilegious and dangerous. Also unimaginable—I couldn't imagine what would happen.

Nothing. Nothing would happen, as I found out. I've read that necrophiles are frightened of getting hurt by normal sexual relationships, and maybe there's some truth in that (although my heart's been broken plenty of times by cadavers, and not once by a live man), but I think that my attraction to cadavers isn't driven by fear, it's driven by excitement, and that one of the most exciting things about a cadaver is how dedicated it is to dying. Its will is all directed to a single intention, like a huge wave heading for shore, and you can ride along on the wave if you want to, because no matter what you do, because with you or without you, that wave is going to hit the beach.

I felt this impetus the first time I worked up enough nerve to cut open a mouse. Like anyone else, I balked a little at slicing into the flesh, and I was repelled for a few seconds when I saw the insides. But something drove me to go through these compunctions. It was as if I were acting solely on instinct and curiosity, and anything I did was all right, provided it didn't kill me.

After the first few times, I started sticking my tongue into the incision. I don't know why. I thought about it, I did it, and I kept on doing it. One day I removed the organs and cleaned them with water, then put them back in, and I kept on doing that, too. Again, I couldn't tell you why except to say that any provocative thought, if you act upon it, seems to set you on a trajectory.

By the time I was sixteen I wanted human corpses. Men. (That way I'm straight.) I got my chauffeur's licence, but I had to wait until I was finished high school before Mr Wallis would hire me as a hearse driver at the funeral home.

Mr Wallis knew me because he bought bereavement flowers at my father's store. Now *there* was a weird man. He would take a trocar, which is the big needle you use to draw out a cadaver's fluids, and he would push it up the penises of dead men to make them look semi-erect, and then he'd sodomize them. I caught him at it once, and he tried to tell me that he'd been urinating in the hopper. I pretended to believe him. I was upset though, because I knew that dead men were just dead flesh to him. One minute he'd be locked up with a young male corpse, having his way with him, and the next minute he'd be embalming him as if nothing had happened, and making sick jokes about him, pretending to find evidence of rampant homosexuality—colons stalagmite with dried semen, and so on.

None of this joking ever happened in front of me. I heard about it from the crazy old man who did the mopping up. He was also a necrophile, I'm almost certain, but no longer active. He called dead women Madonnas. He rhapsodized about the beautiful Madonnas he'd had the privilege of seeing in the 1940s, about how much more womanly and feminine the Madonnas were twenty years before.

I just listened. I never let on what I was feeling, and I don't think anyone suspected. Necrophiles aren't supposed to be blond and pretty, let alone female. When I'd been working at the funeral home for about a year, a committee from the town council tried to get me to enter the Milk Marketer's Beauty Pageant. They knew about my job, and they knew I was studying embalming at night, but I had told people I was preparing myself for medical school, and I guess the council believed me.

For fifteen years, ever since Matt died, people have been asking me how a woman makes love to a corpse.

Matt was the only person who figured it out. He was a medical student, so he knew that if you apply pressure to the chest of certain fresh corpses, they purge blood out of their mouths.

Matt was smart. I wish I could have loved him with more than sisterly love. He was tall and thin. My type. We met at the doughnut shop across from the medical library, got to talking, and liked each other immediately, an unusual experience for both of us. After about an hour I knew that he loved me and that his love was unconditional. When I told him where I worked and what I was studying, he asked why.

"Because I'm a necrophile," I said.

He lifted his head and stared at me. He had eyes like high-resolution monitors. Almost too vivid. Normally I don't like looking people in the eye, but I found myself staring back. I could see that he believed me.

"I've never told anyone else," I said.

"With men or women?" he asked.

"Men. Young men."

"How?"

"Cunnilingus."

"Fresh corpses?"

"If I can get them."

"What do you do, climb on top of them?"

"Yes."

"You're turned on by blood."

"It's a lubricant." I said. "It's colourful. Stimulating. It's the ultimate bodily fluid."

"Yes," he said, nodding. "When you think about it. Sperm propagates life. But blood sustains it. Blood is primary."

He kept asking questions, and I answered them as truthfully as I could. Having confessed what I was, I felt myself driven to testing his intellectual rigour and the strength of his love at first sight. Throwing rocks at him without any expectation that he'd stay standing. He did, though. He caught the whole arsenal and asked for more. It began to excite me.

We went back to his place. He had a basement apartment in an old rundown building. There were books in orange-crate shelves, in piles on the floor, all over the bed. On the wall above his desk was a poster of Doris Day in the movie *Tea for Two*. Matt said she looked like me.

"Do you want to dance first?" he asked, heading for his record player. I'd told him about how I danced before climbing on corpses.

"No."

He swept the books off the bed. Then he undressed me. He had an erection until I told him I was a virgin. "Don't worry," he said, sliding his head down my stomach. "Lie still."

The next morning he phoned me at work. I was hungover and blue from the night before. After leaving his place I'd gone straight to the funeral home and made love to an autopsy case. Then I'd got drunk in a seedy country-and-western bar and debated going back to the funeral home and suctioning out my own blood until I lost consciousness.

It had finally hit me that I was incapable of falling in love with a man who wasn't dead. I kept thinking, "I'm not normal." I'd never faced this before. Obviously, making love to corpses isn't normal, but while I was still a virgin I must have been assuming that I could give it up any time I liked. Get married, have babies. I must have been banking on a future that I didn't even want, let alone have access to.

Matt was phoning to get me to come around again after work.

"I don't know," I said.

"You had a good time. Didn't you?"

"Sure, I guess."

"I think you're fascinating," he said.

I sighed.

"Please," he said. "Please."

A few nights later I went to his apartment. From then on we started to meet every Tuesday and Thursday evening after my embalming class, and as soon as I left his place, if I knew there was a corpse at the mortuary—any male corpse, young or old—I went straight there and climbed in a basement window.

Entering the prep room, especially at night when there was nobody else around, was like diving into a lake. Sudden cold and silence, and the sensation of penetrating a new element where the rules of other elements don't apply. Being with Matt was like lying on the beach of the lake. Matt had warm, dry skin. His apartment was overheated and noisy. I lay on Matt's bed and soaked him up, but only to make the moment when I entered the prep room even more overpowering.

If the cadaver was freshly embalmed, I could usually smell him from the basement. The smell is like a hospital and old cheese. For me, it's the smell of danger and permission, it used to key me up like amphetamine, so that by the time I reached the prep room, tremors were running up and down my legs. I locked the door behind me and broke into a wild dance, tearing my clothes off, spinning around, pulling at my hair. I'm not sure what this was all about, whether or not I was trying to take part in the chaos of the corpse's disintegration, as Matt suggested. Maybe I was prostrating myself, I don't know.

Once the dancing was over I was always very calm, almost entranced. I drew back the sheet. This was the most exquisite moment. I felt as if I were being blasted by white light. Almost blinded, I climbed onto the table and straddled the corpse. I ran my hands over his skin. My hands and the insides of my thighs burned as if I were touching dry ice. After a few minutes I lay down and pulled the sheet up over my head. I began to kiss his mouth. By now he might be drooling blood. A corpse's blood is thick, cool and sweet. My head roared.

I was no longer depressed. Far from it, I felt better, more confident, than I had ever felt in my life. I had discovered myself to be irredeemably abnormal. I could either slit my throat or surrender—wholeheartedly now—to my obsession. I surrendered. And what happened was that obsession began to storm through me, as if I were a tunnel. I became the medium of obsession as well as both ends of it. With Matt, when we made love, I was the receiving end, I was the cadaver. When I left him and went to the funeral home, I was the lover. Through me Matt's love poured into the cadavers at the funeral home, and through me the cadavers filled Matt with explosive energy.

He quickly got addicted to this energy. The minute I arrived at his apartment, he had to hear every detail about the last corpse I'd been with. For a month or so I had him pegged as a latent homosexual necrophile voyeur, but then I began to see that it wasn't the corpses themselves that excited him, it was my passion for them. It was the power that went into that passion and that came back, doubled, for his pleasure. He kept asking. "How did you feel? Why do you think you felt that way?" And then, because the source of all this power disturbed him, he'd try to prove that my feelings were delusory.

"A corpse shows simultaneous extremes of character," I told him. "Wisdom and innocence, happiness and grief, and so on."

"Therefore all corpses are alike," he said. "Once you've had one you've had them all."

"No, no. They're all different. Each corpse contains his own extremes. Each corpse is only as wise and as innocent as the living person could have been."

He said, "You're drafting personalities onto corpses in order to have power over them."

"In that case," I said, "I'm pretty imaginative, since I've never met two corpses who were alike."

"You *could* be that imaginative," he argued. "Schizophrenics are capable of manufacturing dozens of complex personalities."

I didn't mind these attacks. There was no malice in them, and there was no way they could touch me, either. It was as if I were luxuriously pouring my heart out to a very clever, very concerned, very tormented analyst. I felt sorry for him. I understood his twisted desire to turn me into somebody else (somebody who might love him). I used to fall madly in love with cadavers and then cry because they were dead. The difference between Matt and me was that I had become philosophical. I was all right.

I thought that he was, too. He was in pain, yes, but he seemed confident that what he was going through was temporary and not unnatural. "I am excessively curious," he said. "My fascination is any curious man's fascination with the unusual." He said that by feeding his lust through mine, he would eventually saturate it, then turn it to disgust.

I told him to go ahead, give it a try. So he began to scour the newspapers for my cadavers' obituaries and to go to their funerals and memorial services. He made charts of my preferences and the frequency of my morgue encounters. He followed me to the morgue at night and waited outside so that he could get a replay while I was still in an erotic haze. He sniffed my skin. He pulled me over to streetlights and examined the blood on my face and hands.

I suppose I shouldn't have encouraged him. I can't really say why I did, except that in the beginning I saw his obsession as the outer edge of my own obsession, a place I didn't have to visit as long as he was there. And then later, and despite his increasingly erratic behaviour, I started to have doubts about an obsession that could come on so suddenly and that could come through me.

One night he announced that he might as well face it, he was going to have to make love to corpses, male corpses. The idea nauseated him, he said, but he said that secretly, deep down, unknown even to himself, making love to male corpses was clearly the target of his desire. I blew up. I told him that necrophilia wasn't something you forced yourself to do. You longed to do it, you needed to do it. You were born to do it.

He wasn't listening. He was glued to the dresser mirror. In the last weeks of his life he stared at himself in the mirror without the least self-consciousness. He focused on his face, even though what was going on from the neck down was the arresting part. He had begun to wear incredibly weird outfits. Velvet capes, pantaloons, high-heeled red boots. When we made love, he kept these outfits on. He stared into my eyes, riveted (it later occurred to me) by his own reflection. Matt committed suicide, there was never any doubt about that. As for the necrophilia, it wasn't a crime, not fifteen years ago. So even though I was caught in the act, naked and straddling an unmistakably dead body, even though the newspapers found out about it and made it front-page news, there was nothing the police could charge me with.

In spite of which I made a full confession. It was crucial to me that the official report contain more than the detective's bleak observations. I wanted two things on record: one, that Matt was ravished by a reverential expert; two, that his cadaver blasted the energy of a star.

"Did this energy blast happen before or after he died?" the detective asked.

"After," I said, adding quickly that I couldn't have foreseen such a blast. The one tricky area was why I hadn't stopped the suicide. Why I hadn't talked, or cut, Matt down.

I lied. I said that as soon as I entered Matt's room, he kicked away the ladder. Nobody could prove otherwise. But I've often wondered how much time actually passed between when I opened the door and when his neck broke. In crises, a minute isn't a minute. There's the same chaos you get at the instant of death, with time and form breaking free, and everything magnifying and coming apart.

Matt must have been in a state of crisis for days, maybe weeks before he died. All that staring in mirrors, thinking, "Is this my face?" Watching as his face separated into its infinitesimal particles and reassembled into a strange new face. The night before he died, he had a mask on. A Dracula mask, but he wasn't joking. He wanted to wear the mask while I made love to him as if he were a cadaver. No way, I said. The whole point, I reminded him, was that *I* played the cadaver. He begged me, and I laughed because of the mask and with relief. If he wanted to turn the game around, then it was over between us, and I was suddenly aware of how much I liked that idea.

The next night he phoned me at my parents' and said, "I love you," then hung up.

I don't know how I knew, but I did. A gun, I thought. Men always use guns. And then I thought, no, poison, cyanide. He was a medical student and had access to drugs. When I arrived at his apartment, the door was open. Across from the door, taped to the wall, was a note: "DEAD PERSON IN BEDROOM."

But he wasn't dead. He was standing on a stepladder. He was naked. An impressively knotted noose, attached to a pipe that ran across the ceiling, was looped around his neck.

He smiled tenderly. "I knew you'd come," he said.

"So why the note?" I demanded.

"Pull away the ladder," he crooned. "My beloved."

"Come on. This is stupid. Get down." I went up to him and punched his leg.

"All you have to do," he said, "is pull away the ladder."

His eyes were even darker and more expressive than usual. His cheekbones appeared to be highlighted. (I discovered minutes later he had makeup on.) I glanced around the room for a chair or a table that I could bring over and stand on. I was going to take the noose off him myself.

"If you leave," he said, "if you take a step back, if you do anything other than pull away the ladder, I'll kick it away."

"I love you," I said. "Okay?"

"No, you don't," he said.

"I do!" To sound like I meant it I stared at his legs and imagined them lifeless. "I do!"

"No, you don't," he said softly. "But," he said, "you will."

I was gripping the ladder. I remember thinking that if I held tight to the ladder, he wouldn't be able to kick it away. I was gripping the ladder, and then it was by the wall, tipped over. I have no memory of transition between these two events. There was a loud crack, and gushing of water. Matt dropped gracefully, like a girl fainting. Water poured on him from the broken pipe. There was a smell of excrement. I dragged him by the noose.

In the living room I pulled him onto the green shag carpet. I took my clothes off. I knelt over him. I kissed the blood at the corner of his mouth.

True obsession depends on the object's absolute unresponsiveness. When I used to fall for a particular cadaver, I would feel as if I were a hollow instrument, a bell or a flute. I'd empty out. I would clear out (it was involuntary) until I was an instrument for the cadaver to swell into and be amplified. As the object of Matt's obsession how could I be, other than impassive, while he was alive?

He was playing with fire, playing with me. Not just because I couldn't love him, but because I was irradiated. The whole time that I was involved with Matt, I was making love to corpses, absorbing their energy, blazing it back out. Since that energy came from the act of life alchemizing into death, there's a possibility that it was alchemical itself. Even if it wasn't, I'm sure it gave Matt the impression that I had the power to change him in some huge and dangerous way.

I now believe that his addiction to my energy was really a craving for such a transformation. In fact, I think that all desire is desire for transformation, and that all transformation—all movement, all process—happens because life turns into death.

I am still a necrophile, occasionally and recklessly. I have found no replacement for the torrid serenity of a cadaver.

1992

Elizabeth Hay

b. 1951

Elizabeth Hay was born and raised in Owen Sound, Ontario, on Georgian Bay. After attending Victoria College, University of Toronto, she worked for CBC Radio in Yellowknife (1974–8); in Winnipeg (1979); and in Toronto for *Sunday Morning* as host, interviewer, and documentary producer until 1982. She lived in Mexico for a year and a half, working as a freelance journalist. There she met her American-born husband. They moved to Brooklyn, and she taught creative writing at New York University, eventually returning to Canada in 1992. She now lives in Ottawa with her husband—a translator—and their two children. Her novel *A Student of Weather* (2000), set in Saskatchewan during the Depression, focuses on two sisters whose lives are altered by the arrival of a stranger, Maurice Dove, who is a "student of weather." The novel has an archetypal fairy-tale quality to its plot and is elegant and spare in its prose. "What I like," says Hay, "is weather as a visual event. Weather as a force of history that moves groups of people from one place to another. Weather as superstition." Hay published her first collection of stories, *Crossing the Snow Line*, in 1989. Her second collection, *Small Change* (1997), was nominated for a Governor General's Award and the Trillium Book Award. Hay's third novel, *Late Nights on Air*, won the Giller Prize (2007).

The Friend

She was thirty, a pale beautiful woman with long blond hair and high cheekbones, small eyes, sensuous mouth, an air of serenity and loftiness—superiority—and under that, nervousness, insecurity, disappointment. She was tired. There was the young child who woke several times a night. There was Danny who painted till two in the morning, then slid in beside her and coaxed her awake. There was her own passivity. She was always willing, even though she had to get up early, and always resentful, but never out loud. She complied. In conversation she was direct and Danny often took part, but in bed, apparently, she said nothing. She felt him slide against her, his hand between her legs, its motion the reverse of a woman wiping herself, back to front instead of front to back. She smelled paint—the air of the poorly ventilated attic where he worked—and felt his energetic weariness and responded with a weary energy of her own.

He didn't speak. He didn't call her by any name (during the day he called her Moe more often than Maureen). He reached across her and with practised efficiency found the Vaseline in the bedside drawer.

I met her one afternoon on the sidewalk outside the neighbourhood grocery store. It was sunny and it must have been warm—a Saturday in early June. Our section of New York was poor and Italian, and we looked very different from the dark women around us. The friendship began with that shorthand—shortcut to each other—an understanding that goes without saying. I had a small child too.

A week later, at her invitation, I walked the three blocks to her house and knocked on the front door. She opened a side door and called my name. "Beth," she said, "this way." She was dressed in a loose and colourful quilted top and linen pants. She looked composed and bohemian and from another class.

Inside there was very little furniture: a sofa, a chest, a rug, Danny's paintings on the wall. He was there. A small man with Fred Astaire's face and an ingratiating smile. Once he started to talk, she splashed into the conversation, commenting on everything he said and making it convoluted out of what I supposed was a desire to be included. Only later did I realize how much she insisted on being the centre of attention, and how successfully she became the centre of mine.

We used to take our kids to the only playground within walking distance. It was part of a school yard that marked the border between our neighbourhood and the next. The pavement shimmered with broken glass, the kids were wild and unattended. We pushed our two on the swings and kept each other company. She said she would be so mad if Danny got AIDS, and I thought about her choice of words—"so mad"—struck by the understatement.

I learned about sex from her the way girls learn about sex from each other. In this case the information came not in whispered conversations behind a hedge, but more directly and personally than anything I might have imagined at the age of twelve. In those days the hedge was high and green and the soil below it dark, a setting at once private, natural, and fenced off. This time everything was in the open. I was the audience, the friend with stroller, the mild-mannered wide-eyed listener who learned that breastfeeding brought her to the point of orgasm, that childbirth had made her vagina sloppy and loose, that anal sex hurt so much she would sit on the toilet afterwards, bracing herself against the stabs of pain.

We were in the playground (that sour, overused, wrongly used, hardly playful patch of pavement) and she said she was sore and told me why. When I protested on her behalf she said, "But I might have wanted it. I don't know. I think I did want it in some way."

I can't remember her hands, not here in this small cool room in another country and several years after the fact. I remember watching her do many things with her hands; yet I can't remember what they looked like. They must have been long, slender, pale unless tanned. But they don't come to mind the way a man's might and I suppose that's because she didn't touch me. Or is it because I became so adept at holding her at bay? I remember her lips, those dry thin Rock Hudson lips.

One evening we stood on the corner and she smiled her fleeting meaningful smiles, looking at me with what she called her northern eyes (they were blue and she cried easily) while her heartbreak of a husband put his arm around her. What will become of her, I wondered, even after I found out.

She was standing next to the stove and I saw her go up in flames: the open gas jets, the tininess of the room, the proximity of the children—standing on chairs by the stove—and her hair. It slid down her front and fell down her back. She was making pancakes that were obviously raw. She knew they were raw, predicted they would be, yet did nothing about it. Nor did I. I just poured on lots of syrup and said they were good.

I saw her go up in flames, or did I wish it?

In the beginning we saw each other almost every day and couldn't believe how much the friendship had improved our lives. A close, easy intensity which lasted in that phase of its life for several months. My husband talked of moving—an apartment had come open in a building where we had friends—but I couldn't imagine moving away from Maureen.

It was a throwback to girlhood, the sort of miracle that occurs when you find a friend with whom you can talk about everything.

Maureen had grown up rich and poor. Her family was poor, but she was gifted enough to receive scholarships to private schools. It was the private school look she had fixed on me the first time we met, and the poor background she offered later. As a child she received nothing but praise, she said, from parents astonished by their good fortune: They had produced a beautiful and brilliant daughter while everything else went wrong: car accidents, sudden deaths, mental illness.

Danny's private school adjoined hers. They met when they were twelve and he never tried to hide his various obsessions. She could never say that she had never known.

In the spring her mother came to visit. The street was torn up for repairs, the weather prematurely hot, the air thick with dust. Maureen had spread a green cloth over the table and set a vase of cherry blossoms in the middle. I remember the shade of green and the lushness of the blossoms because the sight was so out of character: everything about Maureen was usually in scattered disarray.

Her mother was tall, and more attractive in photographs than in person. In photographs she was still, in person she darted about, high-strung, high-pitched, erratic. Her rapid murmur left the same impression: startling in its abnormality, yet apparently normal. After years of endless talking about the same thing she now made the sounds that people heard: they had stopped up their ears long ago.

She talked about Maureen. How precocious she had been as a child, reading by the age of four and by the age of five memorizing whole books.

"I remember her reading a page, and I told her to go and read it to Daddy. She said, "With or without the paper?" Lots of children can read at five, even her sister was reading at five, but few have Maureen's stamina. She could read for hours, and adult books. I had to put Taylor Caldwell on the top shelf."

A photograph of the child was tacked to the wall in Danny's studio. She was seated in a chair wearing one of those very short summer dresses we used to wear that ended up well above bare round knees. Her face was unforgettable. It was more than beautiful. It had a direct, knowing, almost luminous look produced by astonishingly clear eyes and fair, fair skin. Already she knew enough not to smile.

"That's her," said Danny. "There she is."

The beautiful kernel of the beautiful woman.

She had always imagined bodies firmer than hers but not substantially different. She had always imagined Danny with a boy.

I met the lover without realizing it. It was late summer, we were at their house in the country, a shaded house beside a stream—cool, green, quiet—the physical manifestation of the serenity I once thought she possessed. A phrase in a movie review: her wealth so old it had a patina. Maureen's tension so polished it had a fine sheen.

All weekend I picked her long hairs off my daughter's sweater and off my own. I picked them off the sheet on the bed. I picked blackberries, which left hair-like scratches on my hands.

My hands felt like hers. I looked down at my stained fingers and they seemed longer. I felt the places where her hands had been, changing diapers, buttoning shirts, deep in tofu and tahini, closing in on frogs which she caught with gusto. Swimming, no matter how cold.

I washed my hands and lost that feeling of being in contact with many things. Yet the landscape continued—the scratches if not the smells, the sight of her hands and hair.

An old painter came to visit. He parked his station wagon next to the house and followed Danny into his studio in the barn. Maureen and I went off with the kids to pick berries. It was hot and humid. There would be rain in the night and again in the morning. We followed a path through the woods to a stream where the kids splashed about while Maureen and I dangled our feet over the bank. Her feet were long and slender, mine were wide and short. We sent ripples of water towards the kids.

She told me that Henry—the painter's name was Henry—was Danny's mentor, they had known each other for years and he was a terrible alcoholic. Then she leaned so close her shoulder touched mine. One night last summer Danny had come back from Henry's studio and confessed—confided—that he had let the old man blow him. Can you believe it? And she laughed—giddy—flushed—excited—and eager, it seemed, to impress me with her sexual openness and to console herself with the thought that she had impressed me. A warm breeze blew a strand of her hair into my face. I brushed it away and it came back—ticklish, intimate, warm and animal-like. I didn't find it unpleasant, not at the time.

We brought the berries back to the house, and late in the afternoon the two men emerged to sit with us on the veranda. Henry was whiskery, gallant, shy. Maureen talked a great deal and laughed even more. Before dark, Henry drove away.

She knew. It all came out the next spring and she pretended to be horrified, but she knew.

That night sounds woke me: Danny's low murmur, Maureen's uninhibited cries. I listened for a long time. It must have occurred to me then that the more gay he was, the more she was aroused.

I thought it was someone come to visit. But the second time I realized it was ice falling. At midday, icicles fall from the eavestrough into the deep snow below.

And the floor which I keep sweeping for crumbs? There are no crumbs. The sound comes from the old linoleum itself. It crackles in the cold.

Often I wake at two in the morning, overheated from the hot water bottle, the three blankets, the open sleeping bag spread on top. In my dreams I take an exam over and over again.

In the morning I go down in the socks I've worn all night to turn up the heat and raise the thin bamboo blind through which everyone can see us anyway. I make coffee, then scald milk in a hand-beaten copper pot with a long handle. Quebec has an expression for beating up egg whites: *monter en neige*. Milk foams up and snow rises.

Under the old linoleum old newspapers advertise an "equipped one bedroom at Lorne near Albert" for $175. Beside the porch door the linoleum has broken away and you can read mildew, dust, grit. *Ottawa Citizen*, May 1, 1979. The floor is a pattern of squares inset with triangles and curlicues in wheat shades of immature to ripe. Upstairs the colours are similar but faded; and flowers, petals.

During the eclipse last month I saw Maureen when I saw the moon. I saw my thumb inch across her pale white face.

I have no regrets about this. But I have many thoughts.

We pushed swings in the playground while late afternoon light licked at the broken glass on the pavement. New York's dangers were all around us, as was Maureen's fake laugh. She pushed William high in the swing, then let out a little trill each time he came swooping back.

It was the time of Hedda Nussbaum. We cut out the stories in the newspaper and passed them back and forth, photographs of Hedda's beaten face, robust husband, abused and dead daughter. It had been going on for so long. Hedda had been beaten for thirteen years, the child was seven years old.

In the playground, light licked at the broken glass and then the light died and we headed home. Often we stopped for tea at Maureen's. Her house always had a loose and welcoming atmosphere which hid the sharp edge of need against which I rubbed.

She began to call before breakfast, dressing me with her voice, her worries, her anger, her malleability. Usually she was angry with Danny for staying up so late that he was useless all day, of no help in looking after William, while she continued to work to support them, to look after the little boy in the morning and evening, to have no time for herself. But when I expressed anger on her behalf she defended him . . .

Similarly with the stomach pains. An ulcer, she suggested, then made light of the possibility when I took it seriously.

She would ask, "Is this all? Is this going to be my contribution?" She was referring to her brilliant past and her sorry present: her pedestrian job, the poor neighbourhood, her high-maintenance husband when there were any number of men she could have married, any number she said. Motherhood gave her something to excel at. She did everything for her son—dressed him, fed him, directed every moment of play. "Is this all right, sweetie? Is this? What about this? Then, sweetie pie, what do you want?"

Sweetie pie wanted what he got. His mother all to himself for a passionately abusive hour, then peace, affection. During a tantrum she would hold him in her lap behind a closed door, then emerge half an hour later with a small smile. "That was a short one. You should see what they're like sometimes."

Even when Danny offered to look after him, even when he urged her to take a long walk, she refused. Walked, but briefly, back and forth on the same sidewalk, or up and down the same driveway. Then returned out of a sense of responsibility to the child. But the child was fine.

At two years he still nursed four or five times a night and her nipples were covered with scabs. "But the skin there heals so quickly," she said.

We moved to the other side of the city and the full force of it hit me. I remember bending down under the sink of our new apartment, still swallowing a mouthful of peanut butter, to cram SOS pads into the hole—against the mouse, taste of it, peanut butter in the trap. Feel of it, dry and coarse under my fingers. Look of it, out of the corner of my eye a small dark slipper. Her hair always in her face, and the way I was ratting on her.

It got to the point where I knew the phone was going to ring before it rang. Instead of answering, I stood there counting. Thirty rings. Forty. Once I told her I thought she had called earlier, I was in the bathroom and the phone rang forever. Oh, she said, I'm sorry, I wasn't even paying attention. The I saw the two of us: Maureen mesmerized by the act of picking up a phone and holding it for a time; and me, frantic with resentment at being swallowed whole.

"Why is she so exhausting?" I asked my husband. Then answered my own question. "She never stops talking and she always talks about the same thing."

But I wasn't satisfied with my answer. "She doesn't want solutions to her problems. That's what is so exhausting."

And yet that old wish—a real wish—to get along. I went to bed thinking about her, and something different, yet related, the two mixed together in a single emotion. I had taken my daughter to play with her friend Joyce, another girl was already there and they didn't want Annie to join them. I woke up thinking of my daughter's rejection, my own various rejections, and Maureen.

It seemed inevitable that he would leave her—clear that he was gay and therefore inevitable that he would leave her. He was an artist. To further his art he would pursue his sexuality. But I was wrong; he didn't leave her. And neither did I.

Every six months he had another gay attack and talked, thought, drew penises. Every six months she reacted predictably and never tired of her reactions, her persistence taking on huge, saintly proportions. As for me, I never initiated a visit or a call, but I didn't make a break. As yielding as she was, and she seemed to be all give, Danny and I were even more so.

Tensions accumulated—the panic as she continued to call and I continued to come when called, though each visit became more abrasive, more insulting, as though staged to show who cared least: You haven't called me, you never call me, you think you can make up for your inattention with this visit but I'll show you that I don't care either: the only reason I'm here is so that my son can play with your daughter.

We walked along the river near her country place. William was on the good tricycle, my daughter on the one that didn't work. Maureen said, "I don't think the children should be forced to share. Do you? I think kids should share when they want to share."

Her son would not give my daughter a turn the whole long two-hour walk beside the river—with me pointing out what? Honeysuckle. Yes, honeysuckle. Swathes of it among the rocks. And fishermen with strings of perch. I stared out over the river, unable to look at Maureen and not arguing; I couldn't find the words.

With each visit there was the memory of an earlier intimacy, and no interest in resurrecting it. Better than nothing. Better than too much. And so it continued until it spun lower.

We were sitting on the mattress on the floor of Danny's studio in front of a wall-sized mirror. Around us were his small successful paintings and his huge failures. He insisted on painting big, she said, because he was so small. "I really think so. It's just machismo."

How clear-eyed she was.

I rested my back against the mirror, Maureen faced it. She glanced at me, then the mirror, and each time she looked in the mirror she smiled slightly. Her son was there. He wandered off and then it became clear that she was watching herself.

She told me she was pregnant again. It took two years to persuade Danny, "and now he's even more eager than I am," smiling at herself in the mirror.

Danny got sick. I suppose he had been sick for months, but I heard about it in the spring. Maureen called in tears. "The shoe has dropped," she said.

He was so sick that he had confessed to the doctors that he and Henry—old dissipated Henry whose cock had slipped into who knows what—had been screwing for the last five years. Maureen talked and wept for thirty minutes before I realized that she had no intention of leaving him, or he of leaving her. They would go on. The only change, and this wasn't certain, was that they wouldn't sleep together. They would go to their country place in June and stay all summer.

I felt cheated, set up, used. "Look, you should *do* something," I said. "Make some change."

She said, "I know. But I don't want to precipitate anything. Now isn't the time."

She said it wasn't AIDS.

Her lips dried out like tangerine sections separated in the morning and left out all day. She nursed her children so long that her breasts turned into small apricots, and now I cannot hold an apricot in my hand and feel its soft loose skin, its soft non-weight, without thinking of small spent breasts—little dugs.

She caught hold of me, a silk scarf against an uneven wall, and clung.

Two years later I snuck away. In the weeks leading up to the move, I thought I might write to her afterwards, but in the days immediately before, I knew I would not. One night in late August when the weather was cool and the evenings still long, we finished packing at nine and pulled away in the dark.

We turned right on Broadway and rode the traffic in dark slow motion out of the city, north along the Hudson, and home.

In Canada I thought about old friends who were new friends because I hadn't seen them for such a long time. And newer friends who were old friends because I'd left them behind in the other place. And what I noticed was that I had no landscape in which to set them. They were portraits in my mind (not satisfying portraits either, because I couldn't remember parts of their bodies; their hands, for instance, wouldn't come to mind). They were emotion and episode divorced from time and place. Yet there was a time—the recent past, and a place—a big city across the border.

And here was I, where I had wanted to be for as long as I had been away from it—home—and it didn't register either. In other words, I discovered that I wasn't in a place. I was the place. I felt populated by old friends. They lived in my head amid my various broodings. Here they met again, going through the same motions and different ones. Here they coupled in ways that hadn't occurred really. And here was I, disloyal but faithful, occupied by people I didn't want to see and didn't want to lose.

September came and went, October came and went, winter didn't come. It rained in November, it rained again in December. In January a little snow fell, then more rain.

Winter came when I was asleep. One morning I looked out at frozen puddles dusted with snow. It was very cold. I stepped carefully into the street and this is what I saw. I saw the landscape of friendship. I saw Sunday at four in the afternoon. I saw childhood panic. People looked familiar to me, yet they didn't say hello. I saw two people I hadn't seen in fifteen years, one seated in a restaurant, the other skating by. I looked at them keenly, waiting for recognition to burst upon them, but it didn't.

Strangers claimed to recognize me. They said they had seen me before, some said precisely where. "It was at a conference two years ago." Or, "I saw you walk by every day with your husband last summer. You were walking quickly."

But last summer Ted and I had been somewhere else.

The connections were wistful, intangible, maddening. Memory tantalized before it finally failed. Yet as much as memory failed, those odd, unhinged conjunctures helped. Strange glimmerings and intense looks were better than nothing.

The last time I saw Maureen, she was wearing a black-and-white summer dress and her teeth were chattering. "Look at me," she said, her mouth barely able to form the words, her lower jaw shaking. "It's not that cold."

We were in the old neighbourhood. The street was dark and narrow with shops on either side, and many people. I was asking my usual questions, she was doing her best to answer them.

"Look," she said again, pointing to her lips which were shaking uncontrollably.

I nodded, drew my jacket tight, mentioned how much warmer it had been on the way to the café, my voice friendly enough but without the intonations of affection and interest, the rhythms of sympathy, the animation of friendship. In the subway we felt warm again. She waited for my train to come, trying to redeem and at the same time distance herself. I asked about Danny and she answered. She talked about his job, her job, how little time each of them had for themselves. She went on and on. Before she finished I asked about her children. Again she talked.

"I don't mean to brag," she said, helpless against the desire to brag, "but Victoria is so verbal."

Doing to her children and for herself what her mother had done to her and for herself.

"So verbal, so precocious. I don't say this to everyone," listing the words that Victoria already knew.

She still shivered occasionally. She must have known why I didn't call anymore, aware of the reasons while inventing others in a self-defence that was both pathetic and dignified. She never asked what went wrong. Never begged for explanations (dignified even in her begging: her persistence as she continued to call and extend invitations).

We stood in the subway station—one in a black-and-white dress, the other in a warm jacket—one hurt and pale, the other triumphant in the indifference which had taken so long to acquire. We appeared to be friends. But a close observer would have seen how static we were, rooted in a determination not to have a scene, not to allow the other to cause hurt. Standing, waiting for my train to come in.

1997

Dionne Brand

b. 1953

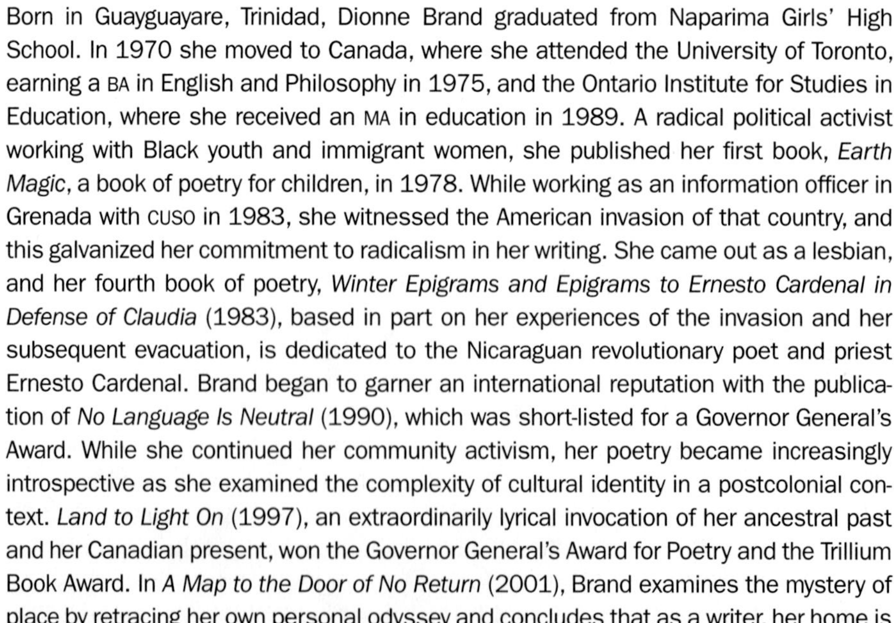

Born in Guayguayare, Trinidad, Dionne Brand graduated from Naparima Girls' High School. In 1970 she moved to Canada, where she attended the University of Toronto, earning a BA in English and Philosophy in 1975, and the Ontario Institute for Studies in Education, where she received an MA in education in 1989. A radical political activist working with Black youth and immigrant women, she published her first book, *Earth Magic*, a book of poetry for children, in 1978. While working as an information officer in Grenada with CUSO in 1983, she witnessed the American invasion of that country, and this galvanized her commitment to radicalism in her writing. She came out as a lesbian, and her fourth book of poetry, *Winter Epigrams and Epigrams to Ernesto Cardenal in Defense of Claudia* (1983), based in part on her experiences of the invasion and her subsequent evacuation, is dedicated to the Nicaraguan revolutionary poet and priest Ernesto Cardenal. Brand began to garner an international reputation with the publication of *No Language Is Neutral* (1990), which was short-listed for a Governor General's Award. While she continued her community activism, her poetry became increasingly introspective as she examined the complexity of cultural identity in a postcolonial context. *Land to Light On* (1997), an extraordinarily lyrical invocation of her ancestral past and her Canadian present, won the Governor General's Award for Poetry and the Trillium Book Award. In *A Map to the Door of No Return* (2001), Brand examines the mystery of place by retracing her own personal odyssey and concludes that as a writer, her home is neither the Caribbean nor Canada, but poetry. Brand has written fiction, including *Sans Souci and Other Stories* (1988) and *In Another Place, Not Here* (1996), which was shortlisted for the Chapters/Books in Canada First Novel Award. Her novel, *At the Full and Change of the Moon* (1999), examines the life of a nineteenth-century Caribbean slave, Marie-Ursule, and her modern descendents, who are scattered all over the world. Brand has directed a number of documentary films, including *Sisters in the Struggle* (1991), which profiles five Black women activists in their battles against racism and sexism, and *Listening for Something: Adrienne Rich and Dionne Brand in Conversation* (1996). Her most recent fiction is *What We All Long For* (2005). She has taught at schools and universities in Halifax, Vancouver, Guelph, and Toronto.

Photograph

My grandmother has left no trace, no sign of her self. There is no photograph, except one which she took with much trouble for her identity card. I remember the day that she had to take it. It was for voting, when we got Independence; and my grandmother, with fear in her eyes, woke up that morning, got dressed, put on her hat, and left. It was the small beige hat with the lace piece for the face. There was apprehension in the house. My grandmother, on these occasions, the rare ones when she left the house, patted her temples with limacol. Her smelling salts were placed in her purse. The little bottle with the green crystals and liquid had a pungent odour and a powerful aura for me until I was much older. She never let us touch it. She kept it in her purse, now held tightly in one hand, the same hand which held her one embroidered handkerchief.

That morning we all woke up and were put to work getting my grandmother ready to go to the identity card place.

One of us put the water to boil for my grandmother's bath; my big sister combed her hair and the rest of us were dispatched to get shoes, petticoat, or stockings. My grandmother's mouth moved nervously as these events took place and her fingers hardened over ours each time our clumsy efforts crinkled a pleat or spilled scent.

We were an ever growing bunch of cousins, sisters, and brothers. My grandmother's grandchildren. Children of my grandmother's daughters. We were seven in all, from time to time more, given to my grandmother for safekeeping. Eula, Kat, Ava, and I were sisters. Eula was the oldest. Genevieve, Wil, and Dri were sister and brothers and our cousins. Our mothers were away. Away-away or in the country-away. That's all we knew of them except for their photographs which we used tauntingly in our battles about whose mother was prettier.

Like the bottle of smelling salts, all my grandmother's things had that same aura. We would wait until she was out of sight, which only meant that she was in the kitchen since she never left the house, and then we would try on her dresses or her hat, or open the bottom drawer of the wardrobe where she kept sheets, pillowcases and underwear, candles and candlesticks, boxes of matches, pieces of cloth for headties and dresses and curtains, black cake and wafers, rice and sweetbread, in pillow cases, just in case of an emergency. We would unpack my grandmother's things down to the bottom of the drawer, where she kept camphor balls, and touch them over and over again. We would wrap ourselves in pieces of cloth, pretending we were African queens; we would put on my grandmother's gold chain, pretending we were rich. We would pinch her black cakes until they were down to nothing and then we would swear that we never touched them and never saw who did. Often, she caught us and beat us, but we were always on the lookout for the next chance to interfere in my grandmother's sacred things. There was always something new there. Once, just before Christmas, we found a black doll. It caused a commotion and rare dissension among us. All of us wanted it so, of course, my grandmother discovered us. None of us, my grandmother said, deserved it and on top of that she threatened that there would be no Santa Claus for us. She kept the doll at the head of her bed until she relented and gave it to Kat, who was the littlest.

We never knew how anything got into the drawer, because we never saw things enter the house. Everything in the drawer was pressed and ironed and smelled of starch and ironing and newness and oldness. My grandmother guarded them often more like burden than treasure. Their depletion would make her anxious; their addition would pose problems of space in our tiny house.

As she rarely left the house, my grandmother felt that everyone on the street where we lived would be looking at her, going to take her picture for her identity card. We felt the same too and worried as she left, stepping heavily, yet shakily down the short hill that lead to the savannah, at the far end of which was the community centre. My big sister held her hand. We could see the curtains moving discreetly in the houses next to ours, as my grandmother walked, head up, face hidden behind her veil. We prayed that she would not fall. She had warned us not to hang out of the windows looking at her. We, nevertheless, hung out of the windows gawking at her, along with the woman who lived across the street, whom my grandmother thought lived a scandalous life and had scandalous children and a scandalous laugh which could be heard all the way up the street when the woman sat old blagging with her friends on her veranda. We now hung out of the windows keeping company with "Tante," as she was called, standing with her hands on her massive hips looking and praying for my grandmother. She did not stop, nor did she turn back to give us her look; but we knew that the minute she returned our ears would be burning, because we had joined Tante in disgracing my grandmother.

The photograph from that outing is the only one we have of grandmother and it is all wrinkled and chewed up, even after my grandmother hid it from us and warned us not to touch it. Someone retrieved it when my grandmother was taken to the hospital. The laminate was now dull and my grandmother's picture was grey and creased and distant.

As my grandmother turned the corner with my sister, the rest of us turned to lawlessness, eating sugar from the kitchen and opening the new refrigerator as often as we wanted and rummaging through my grandmother's things. Dressed up in my grandmother's clothes and splashing each other with her limacol, we paraded outside the house where she had distinctly told us not to go. We waved at Tante, mincing along in my grandmother's shoes. After a while, we grew tired and querulous; assessing the damage we had done to the kitchen, the sugar bowl, and my grandmother's wardrobe, we began assigning blame. We all decided to tell on each other. Who had more sugar than whom and who was the first to open the cabinet drawer where my grandmother kept our birth certificates.

We liked to smell our birth certificates, their musty smell and yellowing water-marked coarse paper was proof that my grandmother owned us. She had made such a fuss to get them from our mothers.

A glum silence descended when we realized that it was useless quarrelling. We were all implicated and my grandmother always beat everyone, no matter who committed the crime.

When my grandmother returned we were too chastened to protest her beating. We began to cry as soon as we saw her coming around the corner with my sister. By the time she hit the doorstep we were weeping buckets and the noise we made sounded like a wake, groaning in unison and holding onto each other. My grandmother, too tired from her ordeal at the identity card place, looked at us scornfully and sat down. There was a weakness in her eyes which we recognized. It meant that our beating would be postponed for hours, maybe days, until she could regain her strength. She had been what seemed like hours at the identity card place. My grandmother had to wait, leaning on my sister and having people stare at her, she said. All that indignity and the pain which always appeared in her back at these moments, had made her barely able to walk back to the house. We, too, had been so distraught that we did not even stand outside the house jumping up and down and shouting that she was coming. So at least she was spared that embarrassment. For the rest of the day we quietly went about our chores, without being told to do them and walked lightly past my grandmother's room, where she lay resting in a mound, under the pink chenille.

We had always lived with my grandmother. None of us could recollect our mothers, except as letters from England or occasional visits from women who came on weekends and made plans to take us, eventfully, to live with them. The letters from England came every two weeks and at Christmas with a brown box full of foreign-smelling clothes. The clothes smelled of a good life in a country where white people lived and where bad-behaved children like us would not be tolerated. All this my grandmother said. There, children had manners and didn't play in mud and didn't dirty everything and didn't cry if there wasn't any food and didn't run under the mango trees, grabbing mangoes when the wind blew them down and walked and did not run through the house like warrahoons and did not act like little old niggers. Eula, my big sister, would read the letters to my grandmother who, from time to time, would let us listen. Then my grandmother would urge us to grow up and go away too and live well. When she came to the part about going away, we would feel half-proud and half-nervous. The occasional visits made us feel as precarious as the letters. When we misbehaved, my grandmother often threatened to send us away-away, where white men ate Black children, or to quite-to-quite in the country.

Passing by my grandmother's room, bunched up under the spread, with her face tight and hollow-cheeked, her mouth set against us, the spectre of quite-to-quite and white cannibals loomed brightly. It was useless trying to "dog back" to her she said, when one of my cousins sat close to her bed, inquiring if she would like us to pick her grey hairs out. That was how serious the incident was. Because my grandmother loved us to pick her grey hairs from her head. She would promise us a penny for every ten which we could get by the root. If we broke a hair, that would not count, she said. And, if we threw the little balls of her hair out into the yard for the wind, my grandmother became quite upset since that meant that birds would fly off with her hair and send her mad, send her mind to the four corners of the earth, or they would build a nest with her hair and steal her brain. We never threw hair in the yard for the wind, at least not my grandmother's hair and we took on her indignant look when we chastised each other for doing it with our own hair. My cousin Genevieve didn't mind though. She chewed her long front plait when she sucked on her thumb and saved balls of hair to throw to the birds. Genevieve made mudpies under the house, which we bought with leaf money. You could get yellow mudpies or brown mudpies or red mudpies, this depended on the depth of the hole under the house and the wash water which my grandmother threw there on Saturdays. We took my grandmother's word that having to search the four corners of the earth for your mind was not an easy task, but Genevieve wondered what it would be like.

There's a photograph of Genevieve and me and two of my sisters someplace. We took it to send to England. My grandmother dressed us up, put my big sister in charge of us, giving her 50 cents tied up in a handkerchief and pinned to the waistband of her dress, and warned us not to give her any trouble. We marched to Wong's Studio on the Coffee, the main road in our town, and fidgeted as Mr Wong fixed us in front of a promenade scene to take our picture. My little sister cried through it all and sucked her fingers. Nobody knows that it's me in the photograph, but my sisters and Genevieve look like themselves.

Banishment from my grandmother's room was torture. It was her room, even though three of us slept beside her each night. It was a small room with two windows kept shut most of the time, except every afternoon when my grandmother would look out of the front window, her head resting on her big arms, waiting for us to return from school. There was a bed in the room with a headboard where she kept the bible, a bureau with a round mirror, and a washstand with a jug and basin. She spent much of her time here. We too, sitting on the polished floor under the front window talking to her or against the foot of the bed, if we were trying to get back into her favour or beg her for money. We knew the smell of the brown varnished wood of her bed intimately.

My grandmother's room was rescue from pursuit. Anyone trying to catch anyone would pull up straight and quiet, if you ducked into her room. We read under my grandmother's bed and, playing catch, we hid from each other behind the bulk of her body.

We never received that licking for the photograph day, but my grandmother could keep a silence that was punishment enough. The photograph now does not look like her. It is grey and pained. In real, she was round and comfortable. When we knew her she had a full lap and beautiful arms, her cocoa brown skin smelled of wood smoke and familiar.

My grandmother never thought that people should sleep on Saturdays. She woke us up "peepee au jour" as she called it, which meant before it was light outside, and set us to work. My grandmother said that she couldn't stand a lazy house, full of lazy children. The washing had to be done and dried before three o'clock on Saturday when the baking would begin and continue until evening. My big sister and my grandmother did the washing, leaning over the scrubbing board and the tub and when we others grew older we scrubbed the clothes out, under the eyes of my grandmother. We had to lay the soap-scrubbed clothes out on the square pile of stones so that the sun would bleach them clean, then pick them up and rinse and hang them to dry. We all learned to bake from the time that our chins could reach the table and we washed dishes standing on the bench in front of the sink. In the rainy season, the washing was done on the sunniest days. A sudden shower of rain and my grandmother would send us flying to collect the washing off the lines. We would sit for hours watching the rain gush through the drains which we had dug in anticipation around the flower garden in front of the house. The yellow brown water lumbered unsteadily through the drains rebuilding the mud and forming a lake at the place where our efforts were frustrated by a large stone.

In the rainy season, my big sister planted corn and pigeon peas on the right side of the house. Just at the tail end of the season, we planted the flower garden. Zinnias and jump-up-and-kiss-me, which grew easily, and xora and roses which we could never get to grow. Only the soil on one side of the front yard was good for growing flowers or food. On the other side a sour-sop tree and an almond tree sucked the soil of everything, leaving the ground sandy and thin, and pushed up their roots, ridging the yard, into a hill. The almond tree, under the front window, fed a nest of ants which lived in one pillar of our house. A line of red ants could be seen making their way from pillar to almond tree, carrying bits of leaves and bark.

One Saturday evening, I tried to stay outside playing longer than allowed by my grandmother, leaning on the almond tree and ignoring her calls. "Laugh and cry live in the same house," my grandmother warned, threatening to beat me when I finally came inside. At first I only felt the bite of one ant on my leg but, no sooner, my whole body was invaded by thousands of little red ants biting my skin blue crimson. My sisters and cousins laughed, my grandmother, looking at me pitiably, sent me to the shower; but the itching did not stop and the pains did not subside until the next day.

I often polished the floor on Saturdays. At first, I hated the brown polish-dried rag with which I had to rub the floors, creeping on my hands and knees. I hated the corners of the room which collected fluff and dust. If we tried to polish the floor without first scrubbing it, my grandmother would make us start all over again. My grandmother supervised all these activities when she was ill, sitting on the bed. She saw my distaste for the rag and therefore insisted that I polish over and over again some spot which I was sure that I had gone over. I learned to look at the rag, to notice its layers of brown polish, its waxy shines in some places, its wetness when my grandmother made me mix the polish with kerosene to stretch its use. It became a rich object, all full of continuous rubbing and working, which my grandmother insisted that I do with my hands and no shortcuts of standing and doing with the heel of my foot. We poor people had to get used to work, my grandmother said. After polishing, we would shine the floor with more rags. Up and down, until my grandmother was satisfied. Then the morris chairs, whose slats fell off every once in a while with our jumping, had to be polished and shined, and the cabinet, and all put back in their place.

She wasted nothing. Everything turned into something else when it was too old to be everything. Dresses turned into skirts and then into underwear. Shoes turned into slippers. Corn, too hard for eating, turned into meal. My grandmother herself never wore anything new, except when she went out. She had two dresses and a petticoat hanging in the wardrobe for those times. At home, she dressed in layers of old clothing, half-slip over dress, old socks, because her feet were always cold, and slippers, cut out of old shoes. A safety pin or two, anchored to the front of her dress or the hem of her skirt, to pin up our falling underwear or ruined zippers.

My grandmother didn't like it when we changed the furniture around. She said that changing the furniture around was a sign to people that we didn't have any money. Only people with no money changed their furniture around and around all the time. My grandmother had various lectures on money, to protect us from the knowledge that we had little or none. At night, we could not drop pennies on the floor, for thieves may be passing and think that we did have money and come to rob us.

My grandmother always said that money ran through your hands like water, especially when you had so many mouths to feed. Every two or three weeks money would run out of my grandmother's hands. These times were as routine as our chores or going to school or the games which we played. My grandmother had stretched it over stewed chicken, rice, provisions and macaroni pie on Sundays, split peas soup on Mondays, fish and bake on Tuesdays, corn meal dumplings and salt cod on Wednesdays, okra and rice on Thursdays, split peas, salt cod, and rice on Fridays, and pelau on Saturdays. By the time the third week of the month came around my grandmother's stretching would become apparent. She carried a worried look on her face and was more silent than usual. We understood this to be a sign of lean times and times when we could not bother my grandmother or else we would get one of her painful explanations across our ears. Besides it really hurt my grandmother not to give us what we needed, as we all settled with her into a depressive hungry silence.

At times we couldn't help but look accusingly at her. Who else could we blame for the gnawing pain in our stomachs and the dry corners of our mouths. We stared at my grandmother hungrily, while she avoided our eyes. We would all gather around her as she lay in bed, leaning against her or sitting on the floor beside the bed, all in silence. We devoted these silences to hope—hope that something would appear to deliver us, perhaps my grandfather, with provisions from the country—and to wild imagination that we would be rich some day and be able to buy pounds of sugar and milk. But sweet water, a thin mixture of water and sugar, was all the balm for our hunger. When even that did not show itself in abundance, our silences were even deeper. We drank water, until our stomachs became distended and nautical.

My little sister, who came along a few years after we had grown accustomed to the routine of hunger and silence, could never grasp the importance of these moments. We made her swear not to cry for food when there wasn't any and, to give her credit, she did mean it when she promised. But the moment the hungry silence set in, she began to cry, begging my grandmother for sweet water. She probably cried out of fear that we would never eat again, and admittedly our silences were somewhat awesome, mixtures of despair and grief, made potent by the weakness which the heavy hot sun brought on in our bodies.

We resented my little sister for these indiscretions. She reminded us that we were hungry, a thought we had been transcending in our growing asceticism, and we felt sorry for my grandmother having to answer her cries. Because it was only then that my grandmother relented and sent one of us to borrow a cup of sugar from the woman across the street, Tante. One of us suffered the indignity of crossing the road and repeating haltingly whatever words my grandmother had told her to say.

My grandmother always sent us to Tante, never to Mrs Sommard who was a religious woman and our next door neighbour, nor to Mrs Benjamin who had money and was our other next door neighbour. Mrs Sommard only had prayers to give and Mrs Benjamin, scorn. But Tante, with nothing, like us, would give whatever she could manage. Mrs Sommard was a Seventh Day Adventist and the only time my grandmother sent one of us to beg a cup of something, Mrs Sommard sent back a message to pray. My grandmother took it quietly and never sent us there again and told us to have respect for Mrs Sommard because she was a religious woman and believed that God would provide.

Mrs Sommard's husband, Mr Sommard, took two years to die. For the two years that he took to die the house was always brightly lit. Mr Sommard was so afraid of dying that he could not sleep and didn't like it when darkness fell. He stayed awake all night and all day for two years and kept his wife and daughter awake too. My grandmother said he pinched them if they fell asleep and told them that if he couldn't sleep, they shouldn't sleep either. How this ordeal squared with Mrs Sommard's religiousness, my grandmother was of two minds about. Either the Lord was trying Mrs Sommard's faith or Mrs Sommard had done some wickedness that the Lord was punishing her for.

The Benjamins, on the other side, we didn't know where they got their money from, but they seemed to have a lot of it. For Mrs Benjamin sometimes told our friend Patsy not to play with us. Patsy lived with Mrs Bengamin, her grandmother; Miss Lena, her aunt and her grandfather, Mr Benjamin. We could always smell chicken that Miss Lena was cooking from their pot, even when our house fell into silence.

The Benjamins were the reason that my grandmother didn't like us running down into the backyard to pick up mangoes when the wind blew them down. She felt ashamed that we would show such hunger in the eyes of people who had plenty. The next thing was that the Benjamins' rose mango tree was so huge, it spread half its body over the fence into our yard. We felt that this meant that any mangoes that dropped on our side belonged to us and Patsy Benjamin and her family thought that it belonged to them. My grandmother took their side, not because she thought that they were right, but she thought that if they were such greedy people, they should have the mangoes. Let them kill themselves on it, she said. So she made us call to Mrs Benjamin and give them all the rose mangoes that fell in our yard. Mrs Benjamin thought that we were doing this out of respect for their status and so she would often tell us with superiority to keep the mangoes, but my grandmother would decline. We, grudgingly, had to do the same and, as my grandmother warned us, without a sad look on our faces. From time to time, we undermined my grandmother's pride, by pretending not to find any rose mangoes on the ground, and hid them in a stash under the house or deep in the backyard under leaves. Since my grandmother never ventured from the cover and secrecy of the walls of the house, or that area in the yard hidden by the walls, she was never likely to discover our lie.

Deep in the backyard, over the drain which we called the canal, we were out of range of my grandmother's voice, since she refused to shout, and the palms of her hands, but not her eyes. We were out of reach of her broomstick which she flung at our fleeing backs or up into one of the mango trees where one of us was perched, escaping her beatings.

Deep in the back of the yard, we smoked sponge wood and danced in risqué fashion and uttered the few cuss words that we knew and made up calypsos. There, we pretended to be big people with children. We put our hands on our hips and shook our heads, as we had seen big people do, and complained about having so much children, children, children to feed.

My grandmother showed us how to kill a chicken, holding its body in the tub and placing the scrubbing board over it leaving the neck exposed, then with a sharp knife quickly cut the neck, leaving the scrubbing board over the tub. Few of us became expert at killing a chicken. The beating of the dying fowl would frighten us and the scrubbing board would slip whereupon the headless bird would escape, its warm blood still gushing, propelling its body around and around the house. My grandmother would order us to go get the chicken, which was impossible since the direction that the chicken took and the speed with which it ran were indeterminate. She didn't like us making our faces up in distaste at anything that had to do with eating or cleaning or washing. So, whoever let the chicken escape or whoever refused to go get it would have to stand holding it for five minutes until my grandmother made a few turns in the house, then they would have to pluck it and gut it and wrap the feathers and innards in newspaper, throwing it in the garbage. That person may well have to take the garbage out for a week. If you can eat, my grandmother would say, you can clean and you shouldn't scorn a life.

One day we found a huge balloon down in the backyard. It was the biggest balloon we'd ever had and it wasn't even around Christmas time. Patsy Benjamin, who played through her fence with us, hidden by the rose mango tree from her aunt Lena, forgot herself and started shouting that it was hers. She began crying and ran complaining to her aunt that we had stolen her balloon. Her aunt dragged her inside and we ran around our house fighting and pulling at each other, swearing that the balloon belonged to this one or that one. My grandmother grabbed one of us on the fourth or fifth round and snatched the balloon away. We never understood the cause for this, since it was such a find and never quite understood my grandmother muttering something about Tante's son leaving his "nastiness" everywhere. Tante herself had been trying to get our attention, as we raced round and round the house. This was our first brush with what was called "doing rudeness." Later, when my big sister began to menstruate and stopped hanging around with us, we heard from our classmates that men menstruated too and so we put two and two together and figured that Tante's son's nastiness must have to do with his menstruation.

On our way home from school one day, a rumour blazed its way through all the children just let out from school that there was a male sanitary napkin at the side of the road near the pharmacy on Royal Road. It was someone from the Catholic girl's school who started it and troupe after troupe of school children hurried to the scene, to see it. The rumour spread back and forth, along the Coffee, with school children corroborating and testifying that they had actually seen it. By the time we got there, we only saw an empty brown box which we skirted, a little frightened at first, then pressed in for a better view. There really wasn't very much more to see and we figured that someone must have removed it before we got there. Nevertheless, we swore that we had seen and continued to spread the rumour along the way, until we got home, picking up the chant which was building as all the girls whipped their fingers at the boys on the street singing, "Boys have periods TOOOOO!" We couldn't ask my grandmother if men had periods, but it was the source of weeks of arguing back and forth.

When my period came, it was my big sister who told me what to do. My grandmother was not there. By then, my mother had returned from England and an unease had fallen over us. Anyway, when I showed my big sister, she shoved a sanitary napkin and two pins at me and told me not to play with boys anymore and that I couldn't climb the mango tree anymore and that I shouldn't fly around the yard anymore either. I swore everyone not to tell my mother when she got home from work but they all did anyway and my mother with her air, which I could never determine since I never looked her in the face, said nothing.

My mother had returned. We had anticipated her arrival with a mixture of pride and fear. These added to an uncomfortable sense that things would not be the same, because in the weeks preceding her arrival my grandmother revved up the old warning about us not being able to be rude or disobey anymore, that we would have to be on our best behaviour to be deserving of this woman who had been to England, where children were not like us. She was my grandmother's favourite daughter too, so my grandmother was quite proud of her. When she arrived, some of us hung back behind my grandmother's skirt, embarrassing her before my mother who, my grandmother said, was expecting to meet well brought up children who weren't afraid of people.

To tell the truth, we were expecting a white woman to come through the door, the way my grandmother had described my mother and the way the whole street that we lived on treated the news of my mother's return, as if we were about to ascend in their respect. The more my grandmother pushed us forward to say hello to my mother, the more we clung to her skirts until she finally had to order us to say hello. In the succeeding months, my grandmother tried to push us toward my mother. She looked at us with reproach in her eyes that we did not acknowledge my mother's presence and her power. My mother brought us wieners and fried eggs and mashed potatoes, which we had never had before, and said that she longed for kippers, which we did not know. We enjoyed her strangeness but we were uncomfortable under her eyes. Her suitcase smelled strange and foreign and for weeks despite our halting welcome of her, we showed off in the neighbourhood that we had someone from away.

Then she began ordering us about and the wars began.

Those winters in England, when she must have bicycled to Hampstead General Hospital from which we once received a letter and a postcard with her smiling to us astride a bicycle, must have hardened the smile which my grandmother said that she had and which was dimly recognizable from the photograph. These winters, which she wrote about and which we envied as my sister read them to us, she must have hated. And the thought of four ungrateful children who deprived her of a new dress or stockings to travel London, made my mother unmerciful on her return.

We would run to my grandmother, hiding behind her skirt, or dive for the sanctuary of my grandmother's room. She would enter, accusing my grandmother of interfering in how she chose to discipline "her" children. We were shocked. Where my mother acquired this authority we could not imagine. At first my grandmother let her hit us, but finally she could not but intervene and ask my mother if she thought she was beating animals. Then my mother would reply that my grandmother had brought us up as animals. This insult would galvanize us all against my mother. A back answer would fly from the child in question who would, in turn, receive a slap from my grandmother, whereupon my grandmother would turn on my mother with the length of her tongue. When my grandmother gave someone the length of her tongue, it was given in a low, intense, and damning tone, punctuated by chest beating and the biblical, "I have nurtured a viper in my bosom."

My mother often became hysterical and left the house, crying what my grandmother said were crocodile tears. We had never seen an adult cry in a rage before. The sound in her throat was a gagging yet raging sound, which frightened us, but it was the sight of her tall threatening figure which cowed us. Later, she lost hope that we would ever come around to her and she began to think and accuse my grandmother of setting her children against her. I recall her shoes mostly, white and thick, striding across the tiny house.

These accusations increased and my grandmother began to talk of dying and leaving us. Once or twice, my mother tried to intervene on behalf of one or the other of us in a dispute with my grandmother. There would be silence from both my grandmother and us, as to the strangeness of this intervention. It would immediately bring us on side to my grandmother's point of view and my mother would find herself in the company of an old woman and some children who had a life of their own—who understood their plays, their dances, gestures, and signals, who were already intent on one another. My mother would find herself standing outside these gestures into which her inroads were abrupt and incautious. Each foray made our dances more secretive, our gestures subterranean.

Our life stopped when she entered the door of the house, conversations closed in mid-sentence and elegant gestures with each other turned to sharp asexual movements.

My mother sensed these closures since, at first, we could not hide these scenes fast enough to escape her jealous glance. In the end, we closed our scenes ostentatiously in her presence. My grandmother's tongue lapping over a new story or embellishing an old one would become brusque in, "Tell your mother good evening." We, telling my grandmother a story or receiving her assurance that when we get rich, we would buy a this or a that, while picking out her grey hairs, would fall silent. We longed for when my mother stayed away. Most of all we longed for when she worked nights. Then we could sit all evening in the grand darkness of my grandmother's stories.

When the electricity went out and my grandmother sat in the rocking chair, the wicker seat bursting from the weight of her hips, the stories she spun, no matter how often we heard them, languished over the darkness whose thickness we felt, rolling in and out of the veranda. Some nights the darkness, billowing about us would be suffused by the perfume of lady-of-the-night, a white, velvet, yellow, orchid-like flower which grew up the street in a neighbour's yard. My grandmother's voice, brown and melodic, about how my grandfather, "Yuh Papa, one dark night, was walking from Ortoire to Guayaguayare . . ."

The road was dark and my grandfather walked alone with his torch light pointed toward his feet. He came to a spot in the road, which suddenly chilled him. Then, a few yards later, he came to a hot spot in the road, which made him feel for a shower of rain. Then, up ahead, he saw a figure and behind him he heard its footsteps. He kept walking, the footsteps pursued him dragging a chain, its figure ahead of him. If he had stopped, the figure, which my grandfather knew to be a legahoo, would take his soul; so my grandfather walked steadily, shining his torch light at his feet and repeating psalm twenty-three, until he passed the bridge by the sea wall and passed the savannah, until he arrived at St Mary's, where he lived with my grandmother.

It was in the darkness on the veranda, in the honey chuckle back of my grandmother's throat, that we learned how to catch a soucouyant and a lajabless and not to answer to the "hoop! hoop! hoop!" of duennes, the souls of dead children who were not baptized, come to call living children to play with them. To catch a soucouyant, you had to either find the barrel of rain water where she had left her skin and throw pepper in it or sprinkle salt or rice on your doorstep so that when she tried to enter the house to take your blood, she would have to count every grain of salt or rice before entering. If she dropped just one grain or miscounted, she would have to start all over again her impossible task and in the mornings she would be discovered, distraught and without her skin on the doorstep.

When we lived in the country before moving to the street, my grandmother had shown us, walking along the beach in back of the house, how to identify a duenne foot. She made it with her heel in the sand and then, without laying the ball of foot down, imprinted her toes in the front of the heel print.

Back in the country, my grandmother walked outside and up and down the beach and cut coconut with a cutlass and dug, chip-chip, on the beach and slammed the kitchen window one night just as a mad man leapt to it to try to get into the house. My grandmother said that, as a child in the country, my mother had fallen and hit her head, ever since which she had been pampered and given the best food to eat and so up to this day she was very moody and could go off her head at the slightest. My mother took this liberty whenever she returned home, skewing the order of our routines in my grandmother.

It seemed that my grandmother had raised more mad children than usual, for my uncle was also mad and one time he held up a gas station which was only the second time that my grandmother had to leave the house, again on the arm of my big sister. We readied my grandmother then and she and my big sister and I went to the courthouse on the Promenade to hear my uncle's case. They didn't allow children in, but they allowed my big sister as my grandmother had to lean on her. My uncle's case was not heard that morning, so we left the court and walked up to the Promenade. We had only gone a few steps when my grandmother felt faint. My sister had the smelling salts at her nostrils, as we slowly made our way as inconspicuously as we could to a bench near the bandstand. My grandmother cried, mopping her eyes with her handkerchief and talked about the trouble her children had caused her. We, all three, sat on the bench on the Promenade near the bandstand, feeling stiff and uncomfortable. My grandmother said my uncle had allowed the public to wash their mouth in our family business. She was tired by then and she prayed that my mother would return and take care of us, so that she would be able to die in peace.

Soon after, someone must have written my mother to come home, for we received a letter saying that she was finally coming.

We had debated what to call my mother over and over again and came to no conclusions. Some of the words sounded insincere and disloyal, since they really belonged to my grandmother, although we never called her by those names. But when we tried them out for my mother, they hung so cold in the throat that we were discouraged immediately. Calling my mother by her given name was too presumptuous, even though we had always called all our aunts and uncles by theirs. Unable to come to a decision we abandoned each other to individual choices. In the end, after our vain attempts to form some word, we never called my mother by any name. If we needed to address her we stood about until she noticed that we were there and then we spoke. Finally, we never called my mother.

All of the words which we knew belonged to my grandmother. All of them, a voluptuous body of endearment, dependence, comfort, and infinite knowing. We were all full of my grandmother, she had left us full and empty of her. We dreamed in my grandmother and we woke up in her, bleary-eyed and gesturing for her arm, her elbows, her smell. We jockeyed with each other, lied to each other, quarrelled with each other and with her for the boon of lying close to her, sculpting ourselves around the roundness of her back. Braiding her hair and oiling her feet. We dreamed in my grandmother and we woke up in her, bleary-eyed and gesturing for her lap, her arms, her elbows, her smell, the flat flesh of her arms. We fought, tricked each other for the crook between her thighs and calves. We anticipated where she would sit and got there before her. We brought her achar and paradise plums.

My mother had walked the streets of London, as the legend went, with one dress on her back for years, in order to send those brown envelopes, the stamps from which I saved in an old album. But her years of estrangement had left her angry and us cold to her sacrifice. She settled into fits of fury. Rage which raised welts on our backs, faces, and thin legs. When my grandmother had turned away, laughing from us, saying there was no place to beat, my mother found room.

Our silences which once warded off hunger now warded off her blows. She took this to mean impudence and her rages whipped around our silences more furiously than before. I, the most ascetic of us all, sustained the most terrible moments of her rage. The more enraged she grew, the more silent I became, the harder she hit, the more wooden, I. I refined this silence into a jewel of the most sacred sandalwood, finely grained, perfumed, mournful yet stoic. I became the only inhabitant of a cloistered place carrying my jewel of fullness and emptiness, voluptuousness and scarcity. But she altered the silences profoundly.

Before, with my grandmother, the silences had company, were peopled by our hope. Now, they were desolate.

She had left us full and empty of her. When someone took the time to check, there was no photograph of my grandmother, no figure of my grandmother in layers of clothing and odd-sided socks, no finger stroking the air in reprimand, no arm under her chin at the front window or crossed over her breasts waiting for us.

My grandmother had never been away from home for more than a couple of hours and only three times that I could remember. So her absence was lonely. We visited her in the hospital every evening. They had put her in a room with eleven other people. The room was bare. You could see underneath all the beds from the doorway and the floors were always scrubbed with that hospital smelling antiseptic which reeked its own sickliness and which I detested for years after. My grandmother lay in one of the beds nearest the door and I remember my big sister remarking to my grandmother that she should have a better room, but my grandmother hushed her saying that it was alright and anyway she wouldn't be there for long and the nurses were nice to her. From the chair beside my grandmother's bed in the hospital you could see the parking lot on Chancery Lane. I would sit with my grandmother, looking out the window and describing the scene to her. You could also see part of the wharf and the gulf of Paria which was murky where it held to the wharf. And St Paul's Church, where I was confirmed, even though I did not know the catechism and only mumbled when Canon Farquar drilled us in it.

Through our talks at the window my grandmother made me swear that I would behave for my mother. We planned, when I grew up and went away, that I would send for my grandmother and that I would grow up to be something good, that she and I and Eula and Ava and Kat and Genevieve would go to Guayaguayare and live there forever. I made her promise that she would not leave me with my mother.

It was a Sunday afternoon, the last time I spoke with my grandmother. I was describing a bicycle rider in the parking lot and my grandmother promised to buy one for me when she got out of hospital.

My big sister cried and curled herself up beneath the radio when my grandmother died. Genevieve's face was wet with tears, her front braid pulled over her nose, she, sucking her thumb.

When they brought my grandmother home, it was after weeks in the white twelve-storey hospital. We took the curtains down, leaving all the windows and doors bare, in respect for the dead. The ornaments, doilies, and plastic flowers were removed and the mirrors and furniture covered with white sheets. We stayed inside the house and did not go out to play. We kept the house clean and we fell into our routine of silence when faced with hunger. We felt alone. We did not believe. We thought that it was untrue. In disbelief, we said of my grandmother, "Mama can't be serious!"

The night of the wake, the house was full of strangers. My grandmother would never allow this. Strangers, sitting and talking everywhere, even in my grandmother's room. Someone, a great aunt, a sister of my grandmother, whom we had never seen before, turned to me sitting on the sewing machine and ordered me in a stern voice to get down. I left the room, slinking away, feeling abandoned by my grandmother to strangers.

I never cried in public for my grandmother. I locked myself in the bathroom or hid deep in the backyard and wept. I had learned as my grandmother had taught me, never to show people your private business.

When they brought my grandmother home the next day, we all made a line to kiss her goodbye. My little sister was afraid; the others smiled for my grandmother. I kissed my grandmother's face hoping that it was warm.

1988

Louise Erdrich

b. 1954

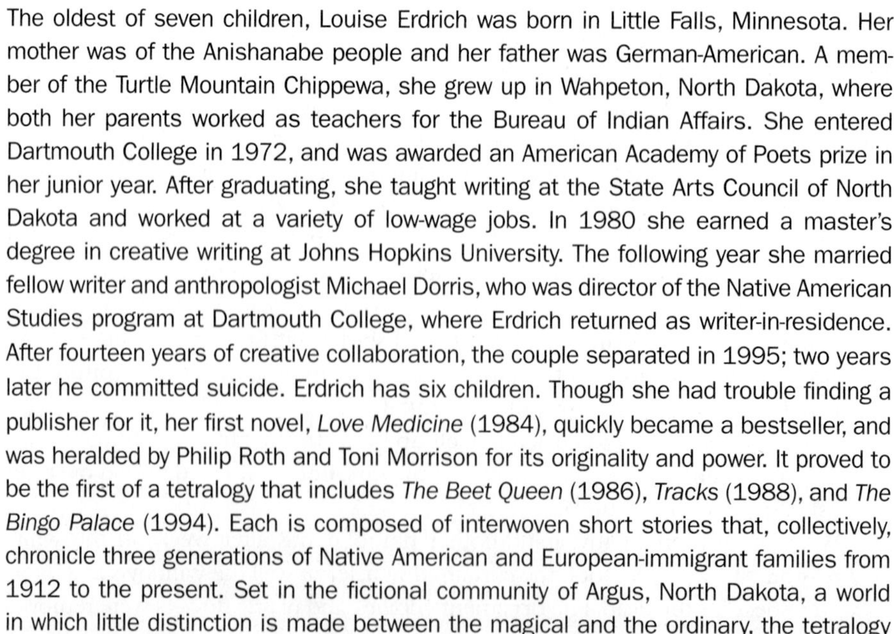

The oldest of seven children, Louise Erdrich was born in Little Falls, Minnesota. Her mother was of the Anishanabe people and her father was German-American. A member of the Turtle Mountain Chippewa, she grew up in Wahpeton, North Dakota, where both her parents worked as teachers for the Bureau of Indian Affairs. She entered Dartmouth College in 1972, and was awarded an American Academy of Poets prize in her junior year. After graduating, she taught writing at the State Arts Council of North Dakota and worked at a variety of low-wage jobs. In 1980 she earned a master's degree in creative writing at Johns Hopkins University. The following year she married fellow writer and anthropologist Michael Dorris, who was director of the Native American Studies program at Dartmouth College, where Erdrich returned as writer-in-residence. After fourteen years of creative collaboration, the couple separated in 1995; two years later he committed suicide. Erdrich has six children. Though she had trouble finding a publisher for it, her first novel, *Love Medicine* (1984), quickly became a bestseller, and was heralded by Philip Roth and Toni Morrison for its originality and power. It proved to be the first of a tetralogy that includes *The Beet Queen* (1986), *Tracks* (1988), and *The Bingo Palace* (1994). Each is composed of interwoven short stories that, collectively, chronicle three generations of Native American and European-immigrant families from 1912 to the present. Set in the fictional community of Argus, North Dakota, a world in which little distinction is made between the magical and the ordinary, the tetralogy has been called a major epic of Native American life. Erdrich claims her penchant for turning life into stories is characteristic of Native people, who "love to tell a good story. People just sit and the stories start coming, one after another. . . . I suppose that when you grow up constantly hearing the stories rise, break, and fall, it gets into you somehow." A prolific writer, Erdrich has also published *Tales of Burning Love* (1996), *The Antelope Wife* (1998), and *The Last Report on the Miracles at Little No Horse* (2001). She co-wrote the novel *The Crown of Columbus* (1991) with her husband; it marks the quincentennial anniversary of the Spanish explorer's voyage in a decidedly critical light. She has also published two books of poetry and has written children's fiction.

Fleur

The first time she drowned in the cold and glassy waters of Lake Turcot, Fleur Pillager was only a girl. Two men saw the boat tip, saw her struggle in the waves. They rowed over to the place she went down, and jumped in. When they dragged her over the gunwales, she was cold to the touch and stiff, so they slapped her face, shook her by the heels, worked her arms back and forth, and pounded her back until she coughed up lake water. She shivered all over like a dog, then took a breath. But it wasn't long afterward that those two men disappeared. The first wandered off, and the other, Jean Hat, got himself run over by a cart.

It went to show, my grandma said. It figured to her, all right. By saving Fleur Pillager, those two men had lost themselves.

The next time she fell in the lake, Fleur Pillager was twenty years old and no one touched her. She washed onshore, her skin a dull grey, but when George Many Women bent to look closer, he saw her chest move. Then her eyes spun open, sharp black riprock, and she looked at him. "You'll take my place," she hissed. Everybody scattered and left her there, so no one knows how she dragged herself home. Soon after that we noticed Many Women changed, grew afraid, wouldn't leave his house, and would not be forced to go near water. For his caution, he lived until the day that his sons brought him a new tin bathtub. Then the first time he used the tub he slipped, got knocked out, and breathed water while his wife stood in the other room frying breakfast.

Men stayed clear of Fleur Pillager after the second drowning. Even though she was good-looking, nobody dared to court her because it was clear that Misshepeshu, the waterman, the monster, wanted her for himself. He's a devil, that one, love-hungry with desire and maddened for the touch of young girls, the strong and daring especially, the ones like Fleur.

Our mothers warn us that we'll think he's handsome, for he appears with green eyes, copper skin, a mouth tender as a child's. But if you fall into his arms, he sprouts horns, fangs, claws, fins. His feet are joined as one and his skin, brass scales, rings to the touch. You're fascinated, cannot move. He casts a shell necklace at your feet, weeps gleaming chips that harden into mica on your breasts. He holds you under. Then he takes the body of a lion or a fat brown worm. He's made of gold. He's made of beach moss. He's a thing of dry foam, a thing of death by drowning, the death a Chippewa cannot survive.

Unless you are Fleur Pillager. We all knew she couldn't swim. After the first time, we thought she'd never go back to Lake Turcot. We thought she'd keep to herself, live quiet, stop killing men off by drowning in the lake. After the first time, we thought she'd keep the good ways. But then, after the second drowning, we knew that we were dealing with something much more serious. She was haywire, out of control. She messed with evil, laughed at the old women's advice, and dressed like a man. She got herself into some half-forgotten medicine, studied ways we shouldn't talk about. Some say she kept the finger of a child in her pocket and a powder of unborn rabbits in a leather thong around her neck. She laid the heart of an owl on her tongue so she could see at night, and went out, hunting, not even in her own body. We know for sure because the next morning, in the snow or dust, we followed the tracks of her bare feet and saw where they changed, where the claws sprang out, the pad broadened and pressed into the dirt. By night we heard her chuffing cough, the bear cough. By day her silence and the wide grin she threw to bring down our guard made us frightened. Some thought that Fleur Pillager should be driven off the reservation, but not a single person who spoke like this had the nerve. And finally, when people were just about to get together and throw her out, she left on her own and didn't come back all summer. That's what this story is about.

During the summer, when she lived a few miles south in Argus, things happened. She almost destroyed a town.

When she got down to Argus in the year 1920, it was just a small grid of six streets on either side of the railroad depot. There were two elevators, one central, the other a few miles west. Two stores competed for the trade of the three hundred citizens, and three churches quarrelled with one another for their souls. There was a frame building for Lutherans, a heavy brick one for Episcopalians, and a long narrow shingled Catholic church. This last had a tall slender steeple, twice as high as any building or tree.

No doubt, across the low, flat wheat, watching from the road as she came near Argus on foot, Fleur saw that steeple rise, a shadow thin as a needle. Maybe in that raw space it drew her the way a lone tree draws lightning. Maybe, in the end, the Catholics are to blame. For if she hadn't seen that sign of pride, that slim prayer, that marker, maybe she would have kept walking.

But Fleur Pillager turned, and the first place she went once she came into town was to the back door of the priest's residence attached to the landmark church. She didn't go there for a handout, although she got that, but to ask for work. She got that too, or the town got her. It's hard to tell which came out worse, her or the men or the town, although the upshot of it all was that Fleur lived.

The four men who worked at the butcher's had carved up about a thousand carcasses between them, maybe half of that steers and the other half pigs, sheep, and game animals like deer, elk, and bear. That's not even mentioning the chickens, which were beyond counting. Pete Kozka owned the place, and employed Lily Veddar, Tor Grunewald, and my stepfather, Dutch James, who had brought my mother down from the reservation the year before she disappointed him by dying. Dutch took me out of school to take her place. I kept house half the time and worked the other in the butcher shop, sweeping floors, putting sawdust down, running a hambone across the street to a customer's bean pot or a package of sausage to the corner. I was a good one to have around because until they needed me, I was invisible. I blended into the stained brown wall, a skinny, big-nosed girl with staring eyes. Because I could fade into a corner or squeeze beneath a shelf, I knew everything, what the men said when no one was around, and what they did to Fleur.

Kozka's Meats served farmers for a fifty-mile area, both to slaughter, for it had a stock pen and chute, and to cure the meat by smoking it or spicing it in sausage. The storage locker was a marvel, made of many thicknesses of brick, earth insulation, and Minnesota timber, lined inside with sawdust and vast blocks of ice cut from Lake Turcot, hauled down from home each winter by horse and sledge.

A ramshackle board building, part slaughterhouse, part store, was fixed to the low, thick square of the lockers. That's where Fleur worked. Kozka hired her for her strength. She could lift a haunch or carry a pole of sausages without stumbling, and she soon learned cutting from Pete's wife, a string-thin blonde who chain-smoked and handled the razor-sharp knives with nerveless precision, slicing close to her stained fingers. Fleur and Fritzie Kozka worked afternoons, wrapping their cuts in paper, and Fleur hauled the packages to the lockers. The meat was left outside the heavy oak doors that were only opened at 5:00 each afternoon, before the men ate supper.

Sometimes Dutch, Tor, and Lily ate at the lockers, and when they did I stayed too, cleaned floors, restoked the fires in the front smokehouse, while the men sat around the squat cast-iron stove spearing slats of herring onto hardtack bread. They played long games of poker or cribbage on a board made from the planed end of a salt crate. They talked and I listened, although there wasn't much to hear since almost nothing ever happened in Argus. Tor was married, Dutch had lost my mother, and Lily read circulars. They mainly discussed about the auctions to come, equipment, or women.

Every so often, Pete Kozka came out front to make a whist, leaving Fritzie to smoke cigarettes and fry raised doughnuts in the back room. He sat and played a few rounds but kept his thoughts to himself. Fritzie did not tolerate him talking behind her back, and the one book he read was the New Testament. If he said something, it concerned weather or a surplus of sheep stomachs, a ham that smoked green or the markets for corn and wheat. He had a good-luck talisman, the opal-white lens of a cow's eye. Playing cards, he rubbed it between his fingers. That soft sound and the slap of cards was about the only conversation.

Fleur finally gave them a subject.

Her cheeks were wide and flat, her hands large, chapped, muscular. Fleur's shoulders were broad as beams, her hips fishlike, slippery, narrow. An old green dress clung to her waist, worn thin where she sat. Her braids were thick like the tails of animals, and swung against her when she moved, deliberately, slowly in her work, held in and half-tamed, but only half. I could tell, but the others never saw. They never looked into her sly brown eyes or noticed her teeth, strong and curved and very white. Her legs were bare, and since she padded around in beadwork moccasins they never saw that her fifth toes were missing. They never knew she'd drowned. They were blinded, they were stupid, they only saw her in the flesh.

And yet it wasn't just that she was a Chippewa, or even that she was a woman, it wasn't that she was good-looking or even that she was alone that made their brains hum. It was how she played cards.

Women didn't usually play with men, so the evening that Fleur drew a chair up to the men's table without being so much as asked, there was a shock of surprise.

"What's this," said Lily. He was fat with a snake's cold pale eyes and precious skin, smooth and lily-white, which is how he got his name. Lily had a dog, a stumpy mean little bull of a thing with a belly drum-tight from eating pork rinds. The dog liked to play cards just like Lily, and straddled his barrel thighs through games of stud, rum poker, vingt-un. The dog snapped at Fleur's arm that first night, but cringed back, its snarl frozen, when she took her place.

"I thought," she said, her voice was soft and stroking, "you might deal me in."

There was a space between the heavy bin of spiced flour and the wall where I just fit. I hunkered down there, kept my eyes open, saw her black hair swing over the chair, her feet solid on the wood floor. I couldn't see up on the table where the cards slapped down, so after they were deep in their game I raised myself up in the shadows, and crouched on a sill of wood.

I watched Fleur's hands stack and ruffle, divide the cards, spill them to each player in a blur, rake them up and shuffle again. Tor, short and scrappy, shut one eye and squinted the other at Fleur. Dutch screwed his lips around a wet cigar.

"Gotta see a man," he mumbled, getting up to go out back to the privy. The others broke, put their cards down, and Fleur sat alone in the lamplight that glowed in a sheen across the push of her breasts. I watched her closely, then she paid me a beam of notice for the first time. She turned, looked straight at me, and grinned the white wolf grin a Pillager turns on its victims, except that she wasn't after me.

"Pauline there," she said, "how much money you got?"

We'd all been paid for the week that day. Eight cents was in my pocket.

"Stake me," she said, holding out her long fingers. I put the coins in her palm and then I melted back to nothing, part of the walls and tables. It was a long time before I understood that the men would not have seen me no matter what I did, how I moved. I wasn't anything like Fleur. My dress hung loose and my back was already curved, an old woman's. Work had roughened me, reading made my eyes sore, caring for my mother before she died had hardened my face. I was not much to look at, so they never saw me.

When the men came back and sat around the table, they had drawn together. They shot each other small glances, stuck their tongues in their cheeks, burst out laughing at odd moments, to rattle Fleur. But she never minded. They played their vingt-un, staying even as Fleur slowly gained. Those pennies I had given her drew nickels and attracted dimes until there was a small pile in front of her.

Then she hooked them with five-card draw, nothing wild. She dealt, discarded, drew, and then she sighed and her cards gave a little shiver. Tor's eye gleamed, and Dutch straightened in his seat.

"I'll pay to see that hand," said Lily Veddar.

Fleur showed, and she had nothing there, nothing at all.

Tor's thin smile cracked open, and he threw his hand in too.

"Well, we know one thing," he said, leaning back in his chair, "the squaw can't bluff."

With that I lowered myself into a mound of swept sawdust and slept. I woke up during the night, but none of them had moved yet, so I couldn't either. Still later, the men must have gone out again, or Fritzie come out to break the game, because I was lifted, soothed, cradled in a woman's arms and rocked so quiet that I kept my eyes shut while Fleur rolled me into a closet of grimy ledgers, oiled paper, balls of string, and thick files that fit beneath me like a mattress.

The game went on after work the next evening. I got my eight cents back five times over, and Fleur kept the rest of the dollar she'd won for a stake. This time they didn't play so late, but they played regular, and then kept going at it night after night. They played poker now, or variations, for one week straight, and each time Fleur won exactly one dollar, no more and no less, too consistent for luck.

By this time, Lily and the other men were so lit with suspense that they got Pete to join the game with them. They concentrated, the fat dog sitting tense in Lily Veddar's lap, Tor suspicious, Dutch stroking his huge square brow, Pete steady. It wasn't that Fleur won that hooked them in so, because she lost hands too. It was rather that she never had a freak hand or even anything above a straight. She only took on her low cards, which didn't sit right. By chance, Fleur should have gotten a full or flush by now. The irritating thing was she beat with pairs and never bluffed, because she couldn't, and still she ended up each night with exactly one dollar. Lily couldn't believe, first of all, that a woman could be smart enough to play cards, but even if she was, that she would then be stupid enough to cheat for a dollar at night. By day I watched him turn the problem over, his hard white face dull, small fingers probing at his knuckles, until he finally thought he had Fleur figured out as a bit-time player, caution her game. Raising the stakes would throw her.

More than anything now, he wanted Fleur to come away with something but a dollar. Two bits less or ten more, the sum didn't matter, just so he broke her streak.

Night after night she played, won her dollar, and left to stay in a place that just Fritzie and I knew about. Fleur bathed in the slaughtering tub, then slept in the unused brick smokehouse behind the lockers, a windowless place tarred on the inside with scorched fats. When I brushed against her skin I noticed that she smelled of the walls, rich and woody, slightly burnt. Since that night she put me in the closet I was no longer afraid of her, but followed her close, stayed with her, became her moving shadow that the men never noticed, the shadow that could have saved her.

August, the month that bears fruit, closed around the shop, and Pete and Fritzie left for Minnesota to escape the heat. Night by night, running, Fleur had won thirty dollars, and only Pete's presence had kept Lily at bay. But Pete was gone now, and one payday, with the heat so bad no one could move but Fleur, the men sat and played and waited while she finished work. The cards sweat, limp in their fingers, the table was slick with grease, and even the walls were warm to the touch. The air was motionless. Fleur was in the next room boiling heads.

Her green dress, drenched, wrapped her like a transparent sheet. A skin of lakeweed. Black snarls of veining clung to her arms. Her braids were loose, half unravelled, tied behind her neck in a thick loop. She stood in steam, turning skulls through a vat with a wooden paddle. When scraps boiled to the surface, she bent with a round tin sieve and scooped them out. She'd filled two dishpans.

"Ain't that enough now?" called Lily. "We're waiting." The stump of a dog trembled in his lap, alive with rage. It never smelled me or noticed me above Fleur's smoky skin. The air was heavy in my corner, and pressed me down. Fleur sat with them.

"Now what do you say?" Lily asked the dog. It barked. That was the signal for the real game to start.

"Let's up the ante," said Lily, who had been stalking this night all month. He had a roll of money in his pocket. Fleur had five bills in her dress. The men had each saved their full pay.

"Ante a dollar then," said Fleur, and pitched hers in. She lost, but they let her scrape along, cent by cent. And then she won some. She played unevenly, as if chance was all she had. She reeled them in. The game went on. The dog was stiff now, poised on Lily's knees, a ball of vicious muscle with its yellow eyes slit in concentration. It gave advice, seemed to sniff the lay of Fleur's cards, twitched and nudged. Fleur was up, then down, saved by a scratch. Tor dealt seven cards, three down. The pot grew, round by round, until it held all the money. Nobody folded. Then it all rode on one last card and they went silent. Fleur picked hers up and blew a long breath. The heat lowered like a bell. Her card shook, but she stayed in.

Lily smiled and took the dog's head tenderly between his palms.

"Say, Fatso," he said, crooning the words, "you reckon that girl's bluffing?"

The dog whined and Lily laughed. "Me too," he said, "let's show." He swept his bills and coins into the pot and then they turned their cards over.

Lily looked once, looked again, then he squeezed the dog up like a fist of dough and slammed it on the table.

Fleur threw her arms out and drew the money over, grinning that same wolf grin that she'd used on me, the grin that had them. She jammed the bills in her dress, scooped the coins up in a waxed white paper that she tied with string.

"Let's go another round," said Lily, his voice choked with burrs. But Fleur opened her mouth and yawned, then walked out back to gather slops for the one big hog that was waiting in the stock pen to be killed.

The men sat still as rocks, their hands spread on the oiled wood table. Dutch had chewed his cigar to damp shreds, Tor's eye was dull. Lily's gaze was the only one to follow Fleur. I didn't move. I felt them gathering, saw my stepfather's veins, the ones in his forehead that stood out in anger. The dog had rolled off the table and curled in a knot below the counter, where none of the men could touch it.

Lily rose and stepped out back to the closet of ledgers where Pete kept his private stock. He brought back a bottle, uncorked and tipped it between his fingers. The lump in his throat moved, then he passed it on. They drank, quickly felt the whisky's fire, and planned with their eyes things they couldn't say out loud.

When they left, I followed. I hid out back in the clutter of broken boards and chicken crates beside the stock pen, where they waited. Fleur could not be seen at first, and then the moon broke and showed her, slipping cautiously along the rough board chute with a bucket in her hand. Her hair fell, wild and coarse, to her waist, and her dress was a floating patch in the dark. She made a pig-calling sound, rang the tin pail lightly against the wood, froze suspiciously. But too late. In the sound of the ring Lily moved, fat and nimble, stepped right behind Fleur and put out his creamy hands. At his first touch, she whirled and doused him with the bucket of sour slops. He pushed her against the big fence and the package of coins split, went clinking and jumping, winked against the wood. Fleur rolled over once and vanished in the yard.

The moon fell behind a curtain of ragged clouds, and Lily followed into the dark muck. But he tripped, pitched over the huge flank of the pig, who lay mired to the snout, heavily snoring. I sprang out of the weeds and climbed the side of the pen, stuck like glue. I saw the sow rise to her neat, knobby knees, gain her balance, and sway, curious, as Lily stumbled forward. Fleur had backed into the angle of rough wood just beyond, and when Lily tried to jostle past, the sow tipped up on her hind legs and struck, quick and hard as a snake. She plunged her head into Lily's thick side and snatched a mouthful of his shirt. She lunged again, caught him lower, so that he grunted in pained surprise. He seemed to ponder, breathing deep. Then he launched his huge body in a swimmer's dive.

The sow screamed as his body smacked over hers. She rolled, striking out with her knife-sharp hooves, and Lily gathered himself upon her, took her foot-long face by the ears and scraped her snout and cheeks against the trestle of the pen. He hurled the sow's tight skull against an iron post, but instead of knocking her dead, he merely woke her from her dream.

She reared, shrieked, drew him with her so that they posed standing upright. They bowed jerkily to each other, as if to begin. Then his arms swung and flailed. She sank her black fangs into his shoulder, clasping him, dancing him forward and backward through the pen. Their steps picked up pace, went wild. The two dipped as one, box-stepped, tripped each other. She ran her split foot through his hair. He grabbed her kinked tail. They went down and came up, the same shape and then the same colour, until the men couldn't tell one from the other in that light and Fleur was able to launch herself over the gates, swing down, hit gravel.

The men saw, yelled, and chased her at a dead run to the smokehouse. And Lily too, once the sow gave up in disgust and freed him. That is where I should have gone to Fleur, saved her, thrown myself on Dutch. But I went stiff with fear and couldn't unlatch myself from the trestles or move at all. I closed my eyes and put my head in my arms, tried to hide, so there is nothing to describe but what I couldn't block out, Fleur's hoarse breath, so loud it filled me, her cry in the old language, and my name repeated over and over among the words.

The heat was still dense the next morning when I came back to work. Fleur was gone but the men were there, slack-faced, hungover. Lily was paler and softer than ever, as if his flesh had steamed on his bones. They smoked, took pulls off a bottle. It wasn't noon yet. I worked awhile, waiting shop and sharpening steel. But I was sick,

I was smothered, I was sweating so hard that my hands slipped on the knives, and I wiped my fingers clean of the greasy touch of the customers' coins. Lily opened his mouth and roared once, not in anger. There was no meaning to the sound. His boxer dog, sprawled limp beside his foot, never lifted its head. Nor did the other men.

They didn't notice when I stepped outside, hoping for a clear breath. And then I forgot them because I knew that we were all balanced, ready to tip, to fly, to be crushed as soon as the weather broke. The sky was so low that I felt the weight of it like a yoke. Clouds hung down, witch teats, a tornado's greenbrown cones, and as I watched one flicked out and became a delicate probing thumb. Even as I picked up my heels and ran back inside, the wind blew suddenly, cold, and then came rain.

Inside, the men had disappeared already and the whole place was trembling as if a huge hand was pinched at the rafters, shaking it. I ran straight through, screaming for Dutch or for any of them, and then I stopped at the heavy doors of the lockers, where they had surely taken shelter. I stood there a moment. Everything went still. Then I heard a cry building in the wind, faint at first, a whistle and then a shrill scream that tore through the walls and gathered around me, spoke plain so I understood that I should move, put my arms out, and slam down the great iron bar that fit across the hasp and lock.

Outside, the wind was stronger, like a hand held against me. I struggled forward. The bushes tossed, the awnings flapped off storefronts, the rails of porches rattled. The odd cloud became a fat snout that nosed along the earth and sniffled, jabbed, picked at things, sucked them up, blew them apart, rooted around as if it was following a certain scent, then stopped behind me at the butcher shop and bored down like a drill.

I went flying, landed somewhere in a ball. When I opened my eyes and looked, stranger things were happening.

A herd of cattle flew through the air like giant birds, dropping their dung, their mouths open in stunned bellows. A candle, still lighted, blew past, and tables, napkins, garden tools, a whole school of drifting eyeglasses, jackets on hangers, hams, a checkerboard, a lampshade, and at last the sow from behind the lockers, on the run, her hooves a blur, set free, swooping, diving, screaming as everything in Argus fell apart and got turned upside down, smashed, and thoroughly wrecked.

Days passed before the town went looking for the men. They were bachelors, after all, except for Tor, whose wife had suffered a blow to the head that made her forgetful. Everyone was occupied with digging out, in high relief because even though the Catholic steeple had been torn off like a peaked cap and sent across five fields, those huddled in the cellar were unhurt. Walls had fallen, windows were demolished, but the stores were intact and so were the bankers and shop owners who had taken refuge in their safes or beneath their cash registers. It was a fair-minded disaster, no one could be said to have suffered much more than the next, at least not until Fritzie and Pete came home.

Of all the businesses in Argus, Kozka's Meats had suffered worst. The boards of the front building had been split to kindling, piled in a huge pyramid, and the shop equipment was blasted far and wide. Pete paced off the distance the iron bathtub had been flung—a hundred feet. The glass candy case went fifty, and landed without so much as a cracked pane. There were other surprises as well, for the back rooms where Fritzie and Pete lived were undisturbed. Fritzie said the dust still coated her china figures, and upon her kitchen table, in the ashtray, perched the last cigarette she'd put out in haste. She lit it up and finished it, looking through the window. From there, she could see that the old smokehouse Fleur had slept in was crushed to a reddish sand and the stockpens were completely torn apart, the rails stacked helter-skelter. Fritzie asked for Fleur. People shrugged. Then she asked about the others and, suddenly, the town understood that three men were missing.

There was a rally of help, a gathering of shovels and volunteers. We passed boards from hand to hand, stacked them, uncovered what lay beneath the pile of jagged splinters. The lockers, full of the meat that was Pete and Fritzie's investment, slowly came into sight, still intact. When enough room was made for a man to stand on the roof, there were calls, a general urge to hack through and see what lay below. But Fritzie shouted that she wouldn't allow it because the meat would spoil. And so the work continued, board by board, until at last the heavy oak doors of the freezer were revealed and people pressed to the entry. Everyone wanted to be the first, but since it was my stepfather lost, I was let go in when Pete and Fritzie wedged through into the sudden icy air.

Pete scraped a match to his boot, lit the lamp Fritzie held, and then the three of us stood still in its circle. Light glared off the skinned and hanging carcasses, the crates of wrapped sausages, the bright and cloudy blocks of lake ice, pure as winter. The cold bit into us, pleasant at first, then numbing. We must have stood there a couple of minutes before we saw the men, or more rightly, the humps of fur, the iced and shaggy hides they wore, the bearskins they had taken down and wrapped around themselves. We stepped closer and tilted the lantern beneath the flaps of fur into their faces. The dog was there, perched among them, heavy as a doorstop. The three had hunched around a barrel where the game was still laid out, and a dead lantern and an empty bottle, too. But they had thrown down their last hands and hunkered tight, clutching one another, knuckles raw from beating at the door they had also attacked with hooks. Frost stars gleamed off their eyelashes and the stubble of their beards. Their faces were set in concentration, mouths open as if to speak some careful thought, some agreement they'd come to in each other's arms.

Power travels in the bloodlines, handed out before birth. It comes down through the hands, which in the Pillagers were strong and knotted, big, spidery, and rough, with sensitive fingertips good at dealing cards. It comes through the eyes, too, belligerent, darkest brown, the eyes of those in the bear clan, impolite as they gaze directly at a person.

In my dreams, I look straight back at Fleur, at the men. I am no longer the watcher on the dark sill, the skinny girl.

The blood draws us back, as if it runs through a vein of earth. I've come home and, except for talking to my cousins, live a quiet life. Fleur lives quiet too, down on Lake Turcot with her boat. Some say she's married to the waterman, Misshepeshu, or that she's living in shame with white men or windigos, or that she's killed them all. I'm about the only one here who ever goes to visit her. Last winter, I went to help out in her cabin when she bore a child, whose green eyes and skin the colour of an old penny made more talk, as no one could decide if the child was mixed blood or what, fathered in a smokehouse, or by a man with brass scales, or by the lake. The girl is bold, smiling in her sleep, as if she knows what people wonder, as if she hears the old men talk, turning the story over. It comes up different every time and has no ending, no beginning. They get the middle wrong too. They only know that they don't know anything.

1986

Lorrie Moore

b. 1957

"Wry," "mordant," "compassionate," "scalpel-like," "caustic," "odd"—these are the words that recur in responses to Lorrie Moore's work, her three collections of stories and two novels. Probing the various agonies of contemporary American life (marriage, illness, expectation, children, the lack of children, pets, the death of pets), Moore has created that very kind of rare narrative, the comic story. The Irish writer Frank O'Connor spoke of the hospitality of the short story to a sense of loneliness; Moore brings loneliness together with astonishing levels of jokes and turns of phrase that take everyone by surprise, except the characters who say or hear them. Picked in one of those literary anointments by *Granta* as among "the best of young American novelists," Moore has been unusually consistent in her success. By the time she was twenty-six she had won a number of awards, the first when she was nineteen, the second when she was twenty-one. She wrote her first volume of stories, *Self-Help* (1985), while completing an MFA at Cornell. Written as a second-person how-to book, it anticipates the bestselling *Birds of America* (1998) and its unusual organization. In a wide-ranging appraisal of the American short story (1999), Vince Passaro praises Moore (together with Denis Johnson, Mary Gaitskill, and Rick Moody, for regenerating the form through urbane irony and innovativeness. Her *Collected Stories* appeared in 2008 and another volume, *Bark*, in 2014. Moore taught English at the University of Wisconsin, an experience she describes as a source of comedy.

Agnes of Iowa

Her mother had given her the name Agnes, believing that a good-looking woman was even more striking when her name was a homely one. Her mother was named Cyrena, and was beautiful to match, but had always imagined her life would have been more interesting, that she herself would have had a more dramatic, arresting effect on the world and not ended up in Cassell, Iowa, if she had been named Enid or Hagar or Maude. And so she named her first daughter Agnes, and when Agnes turned out not to be attractive at all, but puffy and prone to a rash between her eyebrows, her hair a flat and bilious hue, her mother backpedalled and named her second daughter Linnea Elise (who turned out to be a lovely, sleepy child with excellent bones, a sweet mouth, and a rubbery mole above her lip that later in life could be removed without difficulty, everyone was sure).

Agnes herself had always been a bit at odds with her name. There was a brief period in her life, in her mid-twenties, when she had tried to pass it off as French—she had put in the accent grave and encouraged people to call her "On-yez." This was when she was living in New York City, and often getting together with her cousin, a painter who took her to parties in TriBeCa lofts or at beach houses or at mansions on lakes upstate. She would meet a lot of not very bright rich people who found the pronunciation of her name intriguing. It was the rest of her they were unclear on. "On-yez, where are you from, dear?" asked a black-slacked, frosted-haired woman whose skin was papery and melanomic with suntan. "Originally." She eyed Agnes's outfit as if it might be what in fact it was: a couple of blue things purchased in a department store in Cedar Rapids.

"Where am I from?" Agnes said it softly. "Iowa." She had a tendency not to speak up.

"*Where?*" The woman scowled, bewildered.

"Iowa," Agnes repeated loudly.

The woman in black touched Agnes's wrist and leaned in confidentially. She moved her mouth in a concerned and exaggerated way, like a facial exercise. "No, dear," she said. "*Here* we say *O-hi-o.*"

That had been in Agnes's mishmash decade, after college. She had lived improvisationally then, getting this job or that, in restaurants or offices, taking a class or two, not thinking too far ahead, negotiating the precariousness and subway flus and scrimping for an occasional manicure or a play. Such a life required much exaggerated self-esteem. It engaged gross quantities of hope and despair and set them wildly side by side, like a Third World country of the heart. Her days grew messy with contradictions. When she went for walks, for her health, cinders would spot her cheeks and soot would settle in the furled leaf of each ear. Her shoes became unspeakable. Her blouses darkened in a breeze, and a blast of bus exhaust might linger in her hair for hours. Finally, her old asthma returned and, with a hacking, incessant cough, she gave up. "I feel like I've got five years to live," she told people, "so I'm moving back to Iowa so that it'll feel like fifty."

When she packed up to leave, she knew she was saying good-bye to something important, which was not that bad, in a way, because it meant that at least you had said hello to it to begin with, which most people in Cassell, Iowa, she felt, could not claim to have done.

A year and a half later, she married a boyish man twelve years her senior, a Cassell realtor named Joe, and together they bought a house on a little street called Birch Court. She taught a night class at the Arts Hall and did volunteer work on the Transportation Commission in town. It was life like a glass of water: half-empty, half-full. Half-full. Half-full. Oops: half-empty. Over the years, she and Joe tried to have a baby, but one night at dinner, looking at each other in a lonely way over the meat loaf, they realized with a shock that they probably never would. Nonetheless, after six years, they still tried, vandalizing what romance was left in their marriage.

"Honey," she would whisper at night when he was reading under the reading lamp and she had already put her book away and curled toward him, wanting to place the red scarf over the lamp shade but knowing it would annoy him and so not doing it. "Do you want to make love? It would be a good time of the month."

And Joe would groan. Or he would yawn. Or he would already be asleep. Once, after a long, hard day, he said, "I'm sorry, Agnes. I guess I'm just not in the mood."

She grew exasperated. "You think *I'm* in the mood?" she said. "I don't want to do this any more than you do," and he looked at her in a disgusted way, and it was two weeks after that that they had the sad dawning over the meat loaf.

At the Arts Hall, formerly the Grange Hall, Agnes taught the Great Books class, but taught it loosely, with cookies. She let her students turn in poems and plays and stories that they themselves had written; she let them use the class as their own little time to be creative. Someone once even brought in a sculpture: an electric one with blinking lights.

After class, she sometimes met with students individually. She recommended things for them to write about or read or consider in their next project. She smiled and asked if things were going well in their lives. She took an interest.

"You should be stricter," said Willard Stauffbacher, the head of the Instruction Department; he was a short, balding musician who liked to tape on his door pictures of famous people he thought he looked like. Every third Monday, he conducted the monthly departmental meeting—aptly named, Agnes liked to joke, since she did indeed depart mental. "Just because it's a night course doesn't mean you shouldn't impart standards," Stauffbacher said in a scolding way. "If it's piffle, use the word *piffle*. If it's meaningless, write *meaningless* across the top of every page." He had once taught at an elementary school and once at a prison. "I feel like I do all the real work around here," he added. He had posted near his office a sign that read RULES FOR THE MUSIC ROOM:

I will stay in my seat unless [*sic*] permission to move.
I will sit up straight.
I will listen to directions.
I will not bother my neighbour.
I will not talk when Mr Stauffbacher is talking.
I will be polite to others.
I will sing as well as I can.

Agnes stayed after one night with Christa, the only black student in her class. She liked Christa a lot—Christa was smart and funny, and Agnes sometimes liked to stay after with her to chat. Tonight, Agnes had decided to talk Christa out of writing about vampires all the time.

"Why don't you write about that thing you told me about that time?" Agnes suggested.

Christa looked at her skeptically. "What thing?"

"The time in your childhood, during the Chicago riots, walking with your mother through the police barricades."

"Man, I lived that. Why should I want to write about it?"

Agnes sighed. Maybe Christa had a point. "It's just that I'm no help to you with this vampire stuff," Agnes said. "It's formulaic, genre fiction."

"You would be of more help to me with *my childhood*?"

"Well, with more serious stories, yes."

Christa stood up, perturbed. She grabbed back her vampire story. "You with all your Alice Walker and Zora Hurston. I'm just not interested in that anymore. I've done that already. I read those books years ago."

"Christa, please don't be annoyed." *Please do not talk when Mr Stauffbacher is talking.*

"You've got this agenda for me."

"Really, I don't at all," said Agnes. "It's just that—you know what it is? It's that I'm just sick of these vampires. They're so roaming and repeating."

"If you were black, what you're saying might have a different spin. But the fact is, you're not," Christa said, and picked up her coat and strode out—though ten seconds later, she gamely stuck her head back in and said, "See you next week."

"We need a visiting writer who's black," Agnes said in the next departmental meeting. "We've never had one." They were looking at their budget, and the readings this year were pitted against Dance Instruction, a program headed up by a redhead named Evergreen.

"The Joffrey is just so much central casting," said Evergreen, apropos of nothing. As a vacuum cleaner can start to pull up the actual thread of a carpet, her brains had been sucked dry by too much yoga. No one paid much attention to her.

"Perhaps we can get Harold Raferson in Chicago," Agnes suggested.

"We've already got somebody for the visiting writer slot," said Stauffbacher coyly. "An Afrikaner from Johannesburg."

"What?" said Agnes. Was he serious? Even Evergreen barked out a laugh.

"W.S. Beyerbach. The university's bringing him in. We pay our five hundred dollars and we get him out here for a day and a half."

"Who?" asked Evergreen.

"This has already been decided?" asked Agnes.

"Yup." Stauffbacher looked accusingly at Agnes. "I've done a lot of work to arrange for this. *I've* done all the work!"

"Do less," said Evergreen.

When Agnes first met Joe, they'd fallen madly upon each other. They'd kissed in restaurants; they'd groped, under coats, at the movies. At his little house, they'd made love on the porch, or the landing of the staircase, against the wall in the hall by the door to the attic, filled with too much desire to make their way to a real room.

Now they struggled self-consciously for atmosphere, something they'd never needed before. She prepared the bedroom carefully. She played quiet music and concentrated. She lit candles—as if she were in church, praying for the deceased. She donned a filmy gown. She took hot baths and entered the bedroom in nothing but a towel, a wild fishlike creature of moist, perfumed heat. In the nightstand drawer she still kept the charts a doctor once told her to keep, still placed an X on any date she and Joe actually had sex. But she could never show these to her doctor; not now. It pained Agnes to see them. She and Joe looked like worse than bad shots. She and Joe looked like idiots. She and Joe looked dead.

Frantic candlelight flickered on the ceiling like a puppet show. While she waited for Joe to come out of the bathroom, Agnes lay back on the bed and thought about her week, the bloody politics of it, how she was not very good at politics. Once, before he was elected, she had gone to a rally for Bill Clinton, but when he was late and had kept the crowd waiting for over an hour, and when the sun got hot and bees began landing on people's heads, when everyone's feet hurt and tiny children began to cry and a state assemblyman stepped forward to announce that Clinton had stopped at a Dairy Queen in Des Moines and that was why he was late—Dairy Queen!—she had grown angry and resentful and apolitical in her own sweet-starved thirst and she'd joined in with some other people who had started to chant, "Do us a favour, tell us the flavour."

Through college she had been a feminist—basically: she shaved her legs, *but just not often enough*, she liked to say. She signed daycare petitions, and petitions for Planned Parenthood. And although she had never been very aggressive with men, she felt strongly that she knew the difference between feminism and Sadie Hawkins Day—which some people, she believed, did not.

"Agnes, are we out of toothpaste or is this it—oh, okay, I see."

And once, in New York, she had quixotically organized the ladies' room line at the Brooks Atkinson Theatre. Because the play was going to start any minute and the line was still twenty women long, she had gotten six women to walk across the lobby with her to the men's room. "Everybody out of there?" she'd called in timidly, allowing the men to finish up first, which took awhile, especially with other men coming up impatiently and cutting ahead in line. Later, at intermission, she saw how it should have been done. Two elderly black women, with greater expertise in civil rights, stepped very confidently into the men's room and called out, "Don't mind us, boys. We're coming on in. Don't mind us."

"Are you okay?" asked Joe, smiling. He was already beside her. He smelled sweet, of soap and minty teeth, like a child.

"I think so," she said, and turned toward him in the bordello light of their room. He had never acquired the look of maturity anchored in sorrow that burnished so many men's faces. His own sadness in life—a childhood of beatings, a dying mother—was like quicksand, and he had to stay away from it entirely. He permitted no unhappy memories spoken aloud. He stuck with the same mild cheerfulness he'd honed successfully as a boy, and it made him seem fatuous—even, she knew, to himself. Probably it hurt his business a little.

"Your mind's wandering," he said, letting his own eyes close.

"I know." She yawned, moved her legs onto his for warmth, and in this way, with the candles burning into their tins, she and Joe fell asleep.

The spring arrived cool and humid. Bulbs cracked and sprouted, shot up their green periscopes, and on April first, the Arts Hall offered a joke lecture by T.S. Eliot, visiting scholar. "The Cruellest Month," it was called. "You don't find that funny?" asked Stauffbacher.

April fourth was the reception for W.S. Beyerbach. There was to be a dinner afterward, and then Beyerbach was to visit Agnes's Great Books class. She had assigned his second collection of sonnets, spare and elegant things with sighing and diaphanous politics. The next afternoon there was to be a reading.

Agnes had not been invited to the dinner, and when she asked about this, in a mildly forlorn way, Stauffbacher shrugged, as if it were totally out of his hands. I'm a *published poet*, Agnes wanted to say. She *had* published a poem once—in *The Gizzard Review*, but still!

"It was Edie Canterton's list," Stauffbacher said. "I had nothing to do with it."

She went to the reception anyway, annoyed, and when she planted herself like a splayed and storm-torn tree near the cheese, she could actually feel the crackers she was eating forming a bad paste in her mouth and she became afraid to smile. When she finally introduced herself to W.S. Beyerbach, she stumbled on her own name and actually pronounced it "On-yez."

"On-yez," repeated Beyerbach in a quiet Englishy voice. Condescending, she thought. His hair was blond and white, like a palomino, and his eyes were blue and scornful as mints. She could see he was a *withheld* man; although some might say shy, she decided it was withheld: a lack of generosity. Passive aggressive. It was causing the people around him to squirm and blurt things nervously. He would simply nod, the smile on his face faint and vaguely pharmaceutical. Everything about him was tight and coiled as a door spring. From living in *that country*, thought Agnes. How could he live in that country?

Stauffbacher was trying to talk heartily about the mayor. Something about his old progressive ideas, and the forthcoming convention centre. Agnes thought of her own meetings on the Transportation Commission, of the mayor's leash law for cats, of his new squadron of meter maids and bicycle police, of a councilman the mayor once slugged in a bar. "Now, of course, the mayor's become a fascist," said Agnes in a voice that sounded strangely loud, bright with anger.

Silence fell all around. Edie Canterton stopped stirring the punch. Agnes looked about her. "Oh," she said. "Are we not supposed to use *that word* in this room?" Beyerbach's expression went blank. Agnes's face burned in confusion.

Stauffbacher appeared pained, then stricken. "More cheese, anyone?" he asked, holding up the silver tray.

After everyone left for dinner, she went by herself to the Dunk 'N' Dine across the street. She ordered the California BLT and a cup of coffee, and looked over Beyerbach's work again: dozens of images of broken, rotten bodies, of the body's mutinies and betrayals, of the body's strange housekeeping and illicit pets. At the front of the book was a dedication—*To DFB (1970–1989).* Who could that be? A political activist, maybe. Perhaps it was the young woman referred to often in his poems, "a woman who had thrown aside the unreasonable dress of hope," only to look for it again "in the blood-blooming shrubs." Perhaps if Agnes got a chance, she would ask him. Why not? A book was a public thing, and its dedication was part of it. If it was too personal a question for him, *tough.* She would find the right time, she decided. She paid the check, put on her jacket, and crossed the street to the Arts Hall, to meet Beyerbach by the front door. She would wait for the moment, then seize it.

He was already at the front door when she arrived. He greeted her with a stiff smile and a soft "Hello, Onyez," an accent that made her own voice ring coarse and country-western.

She smiled and then blurted, "I have a question to ask you." To her own ears, she sounded like Johnny Cash.

Beyerbach said nothing, only held the door open for her and then followed her into the building.

She continued as they stepped slowly up the stairs. "May I ask to whom your book is dedicated?"

At the top of the stairs, they turned left down the long corridor. She could feel his steely reserve, his lip-biting, his shyness no doubt garbed and rationalized with snobbery, but so much snobbery to handle all that shyness, he could not possibly be a meaningful critic of his country. She was angry with him. *How can you live in that country?* she again wanted to say, although she remembered when someone had once said that to her—a Danish man on Agnes's senior trip abroad to Copenhagen. It had been during the Vietnam War and the man had stared meanly, righteously. "The United States—how can you live in that country?" the man had asked. Agnes shrugged. "A lot of my stuff is there," she'd said, and it was then that she first felt all the dark love and shame that came from the pure accident of home, the deep and arbitrary place that happened to be yours.

"It's dedicated to my son," Beyerbach said finally.

He would not look at her, but stared straight ahead along the corridor floor. Now Agnes's shoes sounded very loud.

"You lost a son," she said.

"Yes," he said. He looked away, at the passing wall, past Stauffbacher's bulletin board, past the men's room, the women's room, some sternness in him broken, and when he turned back, she could see his eyes filling with water, his face a plethora, reddened with unbearable pressure.

"I'm so sorry," Agnes said.

Side by side now, their footsteps echoed down the corridor toward her classroom; all the anxieties she felt with this mournful quiet man now mimicked the anxieties of love. What should she say? It must be the most unendurable thing to lose a child. Shouldn't he say something of this? It was his turn to say something.

But he would not. And when they finally reached her classroom, she turned to him in the doorway and, taking a package from her purse, said simply, in a reassuring way, "We always have cookies in class."

Now he beamed at her with such relief that she knew she had for once said the right thing. It filled her with affection for him. Perhaps, she thought, that was where affection began: in an unlikely phrase, in a moment of someone's having unexpectedly but at last said the right thing. *We always have cookies in class.*

She introduced him with a bit of flourish and biography. Positions held, universities attended. The students raised their hands and asked him about apartheid, about shantytowns and homelands, and he answered succinctly, after long sniffs and pauses, only once referring to a question as "unanswerably fey," causing the student to squirm and fish around in her purse for something, nothing, Kleenex perhaps. Beyerbach did not seem to notice. He went on, spoke of censorship, how a person must work hard not to internalize a government's program of censorship, since that is what a government would like best, for *you* to do it *yourself*, and how he was not sure he had not succumbed. Afterward, a few students stayed and shook his hand, formally, awkwardly, then left. Christa was the last. She, too, shook his hand and then started chatting amiably. They knew someone in common—Harold Raferson in Chicago!—and as Agnes quickly wiped the seminar table to clear it of cookie crumbs, she tried to listen, but couldn't really hear. She made a small pile of crumbs and swept them into one hand.

"Good night" sang out Christa when she left.

"Good night, Christa," said Agnes, brushing the crumbs into the wastebasket.

Now she stood with Beyerbach in the empty classroom. "Thank you so much," she said in a hushed way. "I'm sure they all got quite a lot out of that. I'm very sure they did."

He said nothing, but smiled at her gently.

She shifted her weight from one leg to the other. "Would you like to go somewhere and get a drink?" she asked. She was standing close to him, looking up into his face. He was tall, she saw now. His shoulders weren't broad, but he had a youthful straightness to his carriage. She briefly touched his sleeve. His suitcoat was corduroy and bore the faint odour of clove. This was the first time in her life that she had ever asked a man out for a drink.

He made no move to step away from her, but actually seemed to lean toward her a bit. She could feel his dry breath, see up close the variously hued spokes of his irises, the greys and yellows in the blue. There was a sprinkling of small freckles near his hairline. He smiled, then looked at the clock on the wall. "I would love to, really, but I have to get back to the hotel to make a phone call at ten-fifteen." He looked a little disappointed—not a lot, thought Agnes, but certainly a little.

"Oh, well," she said. She flicked off the lights and in the dark he carefully helped her on with her jacket. They stepped out of the room and walked together in silence, back down the corridor to the front entrance of the hall. Outside on the steps, the night was balmy and scented with rain. "Will you be all right walking back to your hotel?" she asked. "Or—"

"Oh, yes, thank you. It's just around the corner."

"Right. That's right. Well, my car's parked way over there. So I guess I'll see you tomorrow afternoon at your reading."

"Yes," he said. "I shall look forward to that."

"Yes," she said. "So shall I."

The reading was in the large meeting room at the Arts Hall and was from the sonnet book she had already read, but it was nice to hear the poems again, in his hushed, pained tenor. She sat in the back row, her green raincoat sprawled beneath her on the seat like a leaf. She leaned forward, onto the seat ahead of her, her back an angled stem, her chin on double fists, and she listened like that for some time. At one point, she closed her eyes, but the image of him before her, standing straight as a compass needle, remained caught there beneath her lids, like a burn or a speck or a message from the mind.

Afterward, moving away from the lectern, Beyerbach spotted her and waved, but Stauffbacher, like a tugboat with a task, took his arm and steered him elsewhere, over toward the side table with the little plastic cups of warm Pepsi. We are both men, the gesture seemed to say. We both have *bach* in our names. Agnes put on her green coat. She went over toward the Pepsi table and stood. She drank a warm Pepsi, then placed the empty cup back on the table. Beyerbach finally turned toward her and smiled familiarly. She thrust out her hand. "It was a wonderful reading," she said. "I'm very glad I got the chance to meet you." She gripped his long, slender palm and locked thumbs. She could feel the bones in him.

"Thank you," he said. He looked at her coat in a worried way. "You're leaving?"

She looked down at her coat. "I'm afraid I have to get going home." She wasn't sure whether she really had to or not. But she'd put on the coat, and it now seemed an awkward thing to take off.

"Oh," he murmured, gazing at her intently. "Well, all best wishes to you, Onyez."

"Excuse me?" There was some clattering near the lectern.

"All best to you," he said, something retreating in his expression.

Stauffbacher suddenly appeared at her side, scowling at her green coat, as if it were incomprehensible.

"Yes," said Agnes, stepping backward, then forward again to shake Beyerbach's hand once more; it was a beautiful hand, like an old and expensive piece of wood. "Same to you," she said. Then she turned and fled.

For several nights, she did not sleep well. She placed her face directly into her pillow, then turned it some for air, then flipped over to her back and opened her eyes, staring at the far end of the room through the stark angle of the door frame toward the tiny light from the bathroom which illuminated the hallway, faintly, as if someone had just been there.

For several days, she thought perhaps he might have left her a note with the secretary, or that he might send her one from an airport somewhere. She thought that the inadequacy of their goodbye would haunt him, too, and that he might send her a postcard as elaboration.

But he did not. Briefly, she thought about writing him a letter, on Arts Hall stationery, which for money reasons was no longer the stationery, but photocopies of the stationery. She knew he had flown to the West Coast, then off to Tokyo, then Sydney, then back to Johannesburg, and if she posted it now, perhaps he would receive it when he arrived. She could tell him once more how interesting it had been to meet him. She could enclose her poem from *The*

Gizzard Review. She had read in the newspaper an article about bereavement—and if she were her own mother, she could send him that, too.

Thank God, thank God, she was not her mother.

Spring settled firmly in Cassell with a spate of thundershowers. The perennials—the myrtle and grape hyacinths—blossomed around town in a kind of civic blue, and the warming air brought forth an occasional mosquito or fly. The Transportation Commission meetings were dreary and long, too often held over the dinner hour, and when Agnes got home, she would replay them for Joe, sometimes bursting into tears over the parts about the photoradar or the widening interstate.

When her mother called, Agnes got off the phone fast. When her sister called about her mother, Agnes got off the phone even faster. Joe rubbed her shoulders and spoke to her of carports, of curb appeal, of asbestos-wrapped pipes.

At the Arts Hall, she taught and fretted and continued to receive the usual memos from the secretary, written on the usual scrap paper—except that the scrap paper this time, for a while, consisted of the extra posters for the Beyerbach reading. She would get a long disquisition on policies and procedures concerning summer registration, and she would turn it over and there would be his face—sad and pompous in the photograph. She would get a simple phone message—"Your husband called. Please phone him at the office"—and on the back would be the ripped centre of Beyerbach's nose, one minty eye, an elbowish chin. Eventually, there were no more, and the scrap paper moved on to old contest announcements, grant deadlines, Easter concert notices.

At night, she and Joe did yoga to a yoga show on TV. It was part of their effort not to become their parents, though marriage, they knew, held that hazard. The functional disenchantment, the sweet habit of each other had begun to put lines around her mouth, lines that looked like quotation marks—as if everything she said had already been said before. Sometimes their old cat, Madeline, a fat and pampered calico reaping the benefits of life with a childless couple during their childbearing years, came and plopped herself down with them, between them. She was accustomed to much nestling and appreciation and drips from the faucet, though sometimes she would vanish outside, and they would not see her for days, only to spy her later, in the yard, dirty and matted, chomping a vole or eating old snow.

For Memorial Day weekend, Agnes flew with Joe to New York, to show him the city for the first time. "A place," she said, "where if you're not white and not born there, you're not automatically a story." She had grown annoyed with Iowa, the pathetic thirdhand manner in which the large issues and conversations of the world were encountered, the oblique and tired way history situated itself there—if ever. She longed to be a citizen of the globe!

They rollerskated in Central Park. They looked in the Lord & Taylor windows. They went to the Joffrey. They went to a hair salon on Fifty-seventh Street and there she had her hair dyed red. They sat in the window booths of coffee shops and got coffee refills and ate apple pie.

"So much seems the same," she said to Joe. "When I lived here, everyone was hustling for money. The rich were. The poor were. But everyone tried hard to be funny. Everywhere you went—a store, a manicure place—someone was telling a joke. A *good* one." She remembered it had made any given day seem bearable, that impulse toward a joke. It had been a determined sort of humour, an intensity mirroring the intensity of the city, and it seemed to embrace and alleviate the hard sadness of people having used one another and marred the earth the way they had. "It was like brains having sex. It was like every brain was a sex maniac." She looked down at her pie. "People really worked at it, the laughing," she said. "People need to laugh."

"They do," said Joe. He took a swig of coffee, his lips out over the cup in a fleshy flower. He was afraid she might cry—she was getting that look again—and if she did, he would feel guilty and lost and sorry for her that her life was not here anymore, but in a far and boring place now with him. He set the cup down and tried to smile. "They sure do," he said. And he looked out the window at the rickety taxis, the oystery garbage and tubercular air, seven pounds of chicken giblets dumped on the curb in front of the restaurant where they were. He turned back to her and made the face of a clown.

"What are you doing?" she asked.

"It's a clown face."

"What do you mean, 'a clown face'?" Someone behind her was singing "I Love New York," and for the first time she noticed the strange irresolution of the tune.

"A regular clown face is what I mean."

"It didn't look like that."

"No? What did it look like?"

"You want me to do the face?"

"Yeah, do the face."

She looked at Joe. Every arrangement in life carried with it the sadness, the sentimental shadow, of its not being something else, but only itself: she attempted the face—a look of such monstrous emptiness and stupidity that Joe burst out in a howling sort of laughter, like a dog, and then so did she, air exploding through her nose in a snort, her head thrown forward, then back, then forward again, setting loose a fit of coughing.

"Are you okay?" asked Joe, and she nodded. Out of politeness, he looked away, outside, where it had suddenly started to rain. Across the street, two people had planted themselves under the window ledge of a Gap store, trying to stay dry, waiting out the downpour, their figures dark and scarecrowish against the lit window display. When he turned back to his wife—his sad young wife—to point this out to her, to show her what was funny to a man firmly in the grip of middle age, she was still bent sideways in her seat, so that her face fell below the line of the table, and he could only see the curve of her heaving back, the fuzzy penumbra of her thin spring sweater, and the garish top of her bright, new, and terrible hair.

1999

George Saunders

b. 1958

The title of George Saunders's most recent and justly celebrated collection, *Tenth of December*, may be a joke, a distinctively Saunders joke melding zaniness with the utmost gravity. He loves the play of words, the more ludic the spin the better, and he has a whimsical-serious take on the special challenges of writing short stories. "The land of the short story . . . is a brutal land, a land very similar, in its strictness, to the land of the joke." *Tenth of December* seems to play off the much more weighty and even more celebrated pronouncement, the christening of modernism by Virginia Woolf, "On or about December 1910, human character changed." In so many of his comments about the collection, the very forthcoming Saunders keeps returning to a change in what he perceives as human, that is, his human characters—a perilous change but real enough (he also speaks of the volume as generally more realistic than his others). "I found my eye being drawn to the moments when things don't go down the shitter, and asking, well, how does that happen?" For once "the most interesting aesthetic motion—the plot twist, if you will—was the one that swerved away from the habitually catastrophic." With a distinct sense of relief, Michiko Kakutani, a hardened reviewer of contemporary fiction, notes that for all their "loneliness" and "disappointment," these stories often allow "the possibility of rescue or hope." One may even suggest that in *Tenth of December*, there is a note of grace, theologically uncertain but humanly compelling and imminent, a note more in keeping with Woolf's modernists than with the postmodernists whose technical flourishes formed much of Saunders's literary education. He remains enchanted, however, with modes of telling, with possibilities in the nature of both reflection and dialogue, the clipped telegraphic style reminiscent of John Dos Passos, particularly The Camera Eye and Newsreel units of *U.S.A.* (1938). The almost benign creepiness of "The Semplica Girl Diaries" arises from its bizarre form as a sci-fi suburban fantasy, and as in Saunders's earlier work, we are rarely far from the "cartoonish." Archie and Veronica meet Kierkegaard. Yet in his play with cartoons, Saunders is compassionate, not contemptuous, a quality that spills over into readers' reverential tones. Because of the generosity that inflects his work and because in public Saunders seems so little taken with self-love, "he has become," in Joel Lovell's words, "a kind of superhero."

Victory Lap

Three days shy of her fifteenth birthday, Alison Pope paused at the top of the stairs.

Say the staircase was marble. Say she descended and all heads turned. Where was {special one}? Approaching now, bowing slightly, he exclaimed, How can so much grace be contained in one small package? Oops. Had he said *small package?* And just stood there? Broad princelike face totally bland of expression? Poor thing! Sorry, no way, down he went, he was definitely not {special one}.

What about this guy, behind Mr. Small Package, standing near the home entertainment center? With a thick neck of farmer integrity yet tender ample lips, who, placing one hand on the small of her back, whispered, Dreadfully sorry you had to endure that bit about the small package just now. Let us go stand on the moon. Or, uh, in the moon. In the moonlight.

Had he said, *Let us go stand on the moon?* If so, she would have to be like, {eyebrows up}. And if no wry acknowledgment was forthcoming, be like, Uh, I am not exactly dressed for standing on the moon, which, as I understand it, is super-cold?

Come on, guys, she couldn't keep treading gracefully on this marble stairwell in her mind forever! That dear old white-hair in the tiara was getting all like, *Why are those supposed princes making that darling girl march in place ad nausea?* Plus she had a recital tonight and had to go fetch her tights from the dryer.

Egads! One found oneself still standing at the top of the stairs.

Do the thing where, facing upstairs, hand on railing, you hop down the stairs one at a time, which was getting a lot harder lately, due to, someone's feet were getting longer every day, seemed like.

Pas de chat, pas de chat.

Changement, changement.

Hop over thin metal thingie separating hallway tile from living-room rug.

Curtsy to self in entryway mirror.

Come on, Mom, get here. We do not wish to be castrigated by Ms. Callow again in the wings.

Although actually she loved Ms. C. So strict! Also loved the other girls in class. And the girls from school. *Loved* them. Everyone was so nice. Plus the boys at her school. Plus the teachers at her school. All of them were doing their best. Actually, she loved her whole town. That adorable grocer, spraying his lettuce! Pastor Carol, with her large comfortable butt! The chubby postman, gesticulating with his padded envelopes! It had once been a mill town. Wasn't that crazy? What did that even mean?

Also she loved her house. Across the creek was the Russian church. So ethnic! That onion dome had loomed in her window since her Pooh footie days. Also loved Gladsong Drive. Every house on Gladsong was a Corona del Mar. That was amazing! If you had a friend on Gladsong, you already knew where everything was in his or her home.

Jeté, jeté, rond de jambe.

Pas de bourrée.

On a happy whim, do front roll, hop to your feet, kiss the picture of Mom and Dad taken at Penney's back in the Stone Ages, when you were that little cutie right there {kiss} with a hair bow bigger than all outdoors.

Sometimes, feeling happy like this, she imagined a baby deer trembling in the woods.

Where's your mama, little guy?

I don't know, the deer said in the voice of Heather's little sister Becca.

Are you afraid? she asked it. Are you hungry? Do you want me to hold you?

Okay, the baby deer said.

Here came the hunter now, dragging the deer's mother by the antlers. Her guts were completely splayed. Jeez, that was nice! She covered the baby's eyes and was like, Don't you have anything better to do, dank hunter, than kill this baby's mom? You seem like a nice enough guy.

Is my mom killed? the baby said in Becca's voice.

No, no, she said. This gentleman was just leaving.

The hunter, captivated by her beauty, toffed or doffed his cap, and, going down on one knee, said, If I could will life back into this fawn, I would do so, in hopes you might defer one tender kiss upon our elderly forehead.

Go, she said. Only, for your task of penance, do not eat her. Lay her out in a field of clover, with roses strewn about her. And bestow a choir, to softly sing of her foul end.

Lay who out? the baby deer said.

No one, she said. Never mind. Stop asking so many questions.

Pas de chat, pas de chat.

Changement, changement.

She felt hopeful that {special one} would hail from far away. The local boys possessed a certain *je ne sais quoi,* which, tell the truth, she was not *très* crazy about, such as: actually named their own nuts. She had overheard that! And aspired to work for CountyPower because the work shirts were awesome and you got them free.

So ixnay on the local boys. A special ixnay on Matt Drey, owner of the largest mouth in the land. Kissing him last night at the pep rally had been like kissing an underpass.

Scary! Kissing Matt was like suddenly this cow in a sweater is bearing down on you, who will not take no for an answer, and his huge cow head is being flooded by chemicals that are drowning out what little powers of reason Matt actually did have.

What she liked was being in charge of her. Her body, her mind. Her thoughts, her career, her future.

That was what she liked.

So be it.

We might have a slight snack.

Un petit repas.

Was she special? Did she consider herself special? Oh, gosh, she didn't know. In the history of the world, many had been more special than her. Helen Keller had been awesome; Mother Teresa was amazing; Mrs. Roosevelt was quite chipper in spite of her husband, who was handicapped, which, in addition, she had been gay, with those big old teeth, long before such time as being gay and First Lady was even conceptual. She, Alison, could not hope to compete in the category of those ladies. Not yet, anyway!

There was so much she didn't know! Like how to change the oil. Or even check the oil. How to open the hood. How to bake brownies. That was embarrassing, actually, being a girl and all. And what was a mortgage? Did it come with the house? When you breast-fed, did you have to like push the milk out?

Egads. Who was this wan figure, visible through the living-room window, trotting up Gladsong Drive? Kyle Boot, palest kid in all the land? Still dressed in his weird cross-country toggles?

Poor thing. He looked like a skeleton with a mullet. Were those cross-country shorts from the like *Charlie's Angels* days or *quoi?* How could he run so well when he seemed to have literally no muscles? Every day he ran home like this, shirtless with his backpack on, then hit the remote from down by the Fungs' and scooted into his garage without breaking stride.

You almost had to admire the poor goof.

They'd grown up together, been little beaners in that mutual sandbox down by the creek. Hadn't they bathed together when wee or some such crud? She hoped that never got out. Because in terms of friends, Kyle was basically down to Feddy Slavko, who walked leaning way backward and was always retrieving things from between his teeth, announcing the name of the retrieved thing in Greek, then re-eating it. Kyle's mom and dad didn't let him do squat. He had to call home if the movie in World Culture might show bare boobs. Each of the items in his lunch box was clearly labeled.

Pas de bourrée.

And curtsy.

Pour quantity of Cheez Doodles into compartmentalized old-school Tupperware dealie.

Thanks, Mom, thanks, Dad. Your kitchen *rocks.*

Shake Tupperware dealie back and forth like panning for gold, then offer to some imaginary poor gathered round.

Please enjoy. Is there anything else I can do for you folks?

You have already done enough, Alison, by even deigning to speak to us.

That is so not true! Don't you understand, all people deserve respect? Each of us is a rainbow.

Uh, really? Look at this big open sore on my poor shriveled flank.

Allow me to fetch you some Vaseline.

That would be much appreciated. This thing kills.

But as far as that rainbow idea? She believed that. People were amazing. Mom was awesome, Dad was awesome, her teachers worked so hard and had kids of their own, and some were even getting divorced, such as Mrs. Dees, but still always took time for their students. What she found especially inspiring about Mrs. Dees was that, even though Mr. Dees was cheating on Mrs. Dees with the lady who ran the bowling alley, Mrs. Dees was still teaching the best course ever in Ethics, posing such questions as: Can goodness win? Or do good people always get shafted, evil being more reckless? That last bit seemed to be Mrs. Dees taking a shot at the bowling-alley gal. But seriously! Is life fun or scary? Are people good or bad? On the one hand, that clip of those gauntish pale bodies being steam rolled while fat German ladies looked on chomping gum. On the other hand, sometimes rural folks, even if their particular farms were on hills, stayed up late filling sandbags.

In their straw poll she had voted for people being good and life being fun, with Mrs. Dees giving her a pitying glance as she stated her views: To do good, you just have to decide to do good. You have to be brave. You have to stand up for what's right. At that last, Mrs. Dees had made this kind of groan. Which was fine. Mrs. Dees had a lot of pain in her life, yet, interestingly? Still obviously found something fun about life and good about people, because otherwise why sometimes stay up so late grading you come in next day all exhausted, blouse on backward, having messed it up in the early-morning dark, you dear discombobulated thing?

Here came a knock on the door. Back door. In-ter-est-ing. Who could it be? Father Dmitri from across the way? UPS? FedEx? With *un petit* check *pour Papa?*

Jeté, jeté, rond de jambe.

Pas de bourrée.

Open door, and—

Here was a man she did not know. Quite huge fellow, in one of those meter-reader vests.

Something told her to step back in, slam the door. But that seemed rude.

Instead she froze, smiled, did {eyebrow raise} to indicate: May I help you?

Kyle Boot dashed through the garage, into the living area, where the big clock-like wooden indicator was set at All Out. Other choices included: Mom & Dad Out; Mom Out; Dad Out; Kyle Out; Mom & Kyle Out; Dad & Kyle Out; and All In.

Why did they even need All In? Wouldn't they know it when they were All In? Would he like to ask Dad that? Who, in his excellent totally silent downstairs woodshop, had designed and built the Family Status Indicator?

Ha.

Ha ha.

On the kitchen island was a Work Notice.

> *Scout: New geode on deck. Place in yard per included drawing. No goofing. Rake areas first, put down plastic as I have shown you. Then lay in white rock.* THIS GEODE EXPENSIVE. *Pls take seriously. No reason this should not be done by time I get home. This = five (5) Work Points.*

Gar, Dad, do you honestly feel it fair that I should have to slave in the yard until dark after a rigorous cross-country practice that included sixteen 440s, eight 880s, a mile-for-time, a kajillion Drake sprints, and a five-mile Indian relay?

Shoes off, mister.

Yoinks, too late. He was already at the TV. And had left an incriminating trail of microclods. Way verboten. Could the microclods be hand-plucked? Although, problem: if he went back to hand-pluck the microclods, he'd leave an incriminating new trail of microclods.

He took off his shoes and stood mentally rehearsing a little show he liked to call WHAT IF . . . RIGHT NOW?

WHAT IF they came home RIGHT NOW?

It's a funny story, Dad! I came in thoughtlessly! Then realized what I'd done! I guess, when I think about it, what I'm happy about? Is how quickly I self-corrected! The reason I came in so thoughtlessly was, I wanted to get right to work, Dad, per your note!

He raced in his socks to the garage, threw his shoes into the garage, ran for the vacuum, vacuumed up the microclods, then realized, holy golly, he had thrown his shoes into the garage rather than placing them on the Shoe Sheet as required, toes facing away from the door for ease of donnage later.

He stepped into the garage, placed his shoes on the Shoe Sheet, stepped back inside.

Scout, Dad said in his head, has anyone ever told you that even the most neatly maintained garage is going to have some oil on its floor, which is now on your socks, being tracked all over the tan Berber?

Oh gar, his ass was grass.

But no—*celebrate good times, come on*— no oil stain on rug.

He tore off his socks. It was absolutely verboten for him to be in the main living area barefoot. Mom and Dad coming home to find him Tarzaning around like some sort of white trasher would not be the least fucking bit—

Swearing in your head? Dad said in his head. Step up, Scout, be a man. If you want to swear, swear aloud.

I don't want to swear aloud.

Then don't swear in your head.

Mom and Dad would be heartsick if they could hear the swearing he sometimes did in his head, such as crap-cunt shit-turd dick-in-the-ear butt-creamery. Why couldn't he stop doing that? They thought so highly of him, sending weekly braggy emails to both sets of grandparents, such as: Kyle's been super-busy keeping up his grades while running varsity cross-country though still a sophomore, while setting aside a little time each day to manufacture such humdingers as cunt-swoggle rear-fuck—

What was wrong with him? Why couldn't he be grateful for all that Mom and Dad did for him, instead of—

Cornhole the ear-cunt.

Flake-fuck the pale vestige with a proddering dick-knee.

You could always clear the mind with a hard pinch on your own minimal love handle.

Ouch.

Hey, today was Tuesday, a Major Treat day. The five (5) new Work Points for placing the geode, plus his existing two (2) Work Points, totaled seven (7) Work Points, which, added to his eight (8) accrued Usual Chore Points, made fifteen (15) Total Treat Points, which could garner him a Major Treat (for example, two handfuls of yogurt-covered raisins) plus twenty free-choice TV minutes, although the particular show would have to be negotiated with Dad at time of cash-in.

One thing you will not be watching, Scout, is *America's Most Outspoken Dirt Bikers.*

Whatever.

Whatever, Dad.

Really, Scout? "Whatever"? Will it be "whatever" when I take away all your Treat Points and force you to quit cross-country, as I have several times threatened to do if a little more cheerful obedience wasn't forthcoming?

No, no, no. I don't want to quit, Dad. Please. I'm good at it. You'll see, first meet. Even Matt Drey said—

Who is Matt Drey? Some ape on the football team?

Yes.

Is his word law?

No.

What did he say?

Little shit can run.

Nice talk, Scout. Ape talk. Anyway, you may not make it to the first meet. Your ego seems to be overflowing its banks. And why? Because you can jog? Anyone can jog. Beasts of the field can jog.

I'm not quitting! Anal-cock shit-bird rectum-fritz! Please, I'm begging you, it's the only thing I'm decent at! Mom, if he makes me quit I swear to God I'll—

Drama doesn't suit you, Beloved Only.

If you want the privilege of competing in a team sport, Scout, show us that you can live within our perfectly reasonable system of directives designed to benefit you.

Hello.

A van had just pulled up in the St. Mikhail's parking lot.

Kyle walked in a controlled, gentlemanly manner to the kitchen counter. On the counter was Kyle's Traffic Log, which served the dual purpose of (1) buttressing Dad's argument that Father Dmitri should build a soundproof retaining wall and (2) constituting a data set for a possible Science Fair project for him, Kyle, entitled, by Dad, "Correlation of Church Parking Lot Volume vs. Day of Week, with Ancillary Investigation of Sunday Volume Throughout Year."

Smiling agreeably as if he enjoyed filling out the Log, Kyle very legibly filled out the Log:

Vehicle: VAN.
Color: GRAY.
Make: CHEVY.
Year: UNKNOWN.

A guy got out of the van. One of the usual Rooskies. "Rooskie" was an allowed slang. Also "dang it." Also "holy golly." Also "crapper." The Rooskie was wearing a jean jacket over a hoodie, which, in Kyle's experience, was not unusual church-wear for the Rooskies, who sometimes came directly over from Jiffy Lube still wearing coveralls.

Under "Vehicle Driver" he wrote, PROBABLE PARISHIONER.

That sucked. Stank, rather. The guy being a stranger, he, Kyle, now had to stay inside until the stranger left the neighborhood. Which totally futzed up his geode placing. He'd be out there until midnight. What a detriment!

The guy put on a Day Glo-vest. Ah, dude was a meter reader.

The meter reader looked left, then right, leaped across the creek, entered the Pope backyard, passed between the soccer-ball rebounder and the in-ground pool, then knocked on the Pope door.

Good leap there, Boris.

The door swung open.

Alison.

Kyle's heart was singing. He'd always thought that was just a phrase. Alison was like a national treasure. In the dictionary under "beauty" there should be a picture of her in that jean skort. Although lately she didn't seem to like him all that much.

Now she stepped across her deck so the meter reader could show her something. Something electrical wrong on the roof? The guy seemed eager to show her. Actually, he had her by the wrist. And was like tugging.

That was weird. Wasn't it? Something had never been weird around here before. So probably it was fine. Probably the guy was just a really new meter reader?

Somehow Kyle felt like stepping out onto the deck. He stepped out. The guy froze. Alison's eyes were scared-horse eyes. The guy cleared his throat, turned slightly to let Kyle see something.

A knife.

The meter reader had a knife.

Here's what you're doing, the guy said. Standing right there until we leave. Move a muscle, I knife her in the heart. Swear to God. Got it?

Kyle's mouth was so spitless all he could do was make his mouth do the shape it normally did when saying Yes.

Now they were crossing the yard. Alison threw herself to the ground. The guy hauled her up. She threw herself down. He hauled her up. It was odd seeing Alison tossed like a rag doll in the sanctuary of the perfect yard her dad had made for her. She threw herself down.

The guy hissed something and she rose, suddenly docile.

In his chest Kyle felt the many directives, Major and Minor, he was right now violating. He was on the deck shoeless, on the deck shirtless, was outside when a stranger was near, had engaged with that stranger.

Last week Sean Ball had brought a wig to school to more effectively mimic the way Bev Mirren chewed her hair when nervous. Kyle had briefly considered intervening. At Evening Meeting, Mom had said that she considered Kyle's decision not to intervene judicious. Dad had said, That was none of your business. You could have been badly hurt. Mom had said, Think of all the resources we've invested in you, Beloved Only. Dad had said, I know we sometimes strike you as strict but you are literally all we have.

They were at the soccer-ball rebounder now, Alison's arm up behind her back. She was making a low repetitive sound of denial, like she was trying to invent a noise that would adequately communicate her feelings about what she'd just this instant realized was going to happen to her.

He was just a kid. There was nothing he could do. In his chest he felt the lush release of pressure that always resulted when he submitted to a directive. There at his feet was the geode. He should just look at that until they left. It was a great one. Maybe the greatest one ever. The crystals at the cutaway glistened in the sun. It would look nice in the yard. Once he placed it. He'd place it once they were gone. Dad would be impressed that even after what had occurred he'd remembered to place the geode.

That's the ticket, Scout.
We are well pleased, Beloved Only.
Super job, Scout.

Holy crap. It was happening. She was marching along all meek like the trouper he'd known she'd be. He'd had her in mind since the baptism of what's-his-name. Sergei's kid. At the Russian church. She'd been standing in her yard, her dad or some such taking her picture.

He'd been like, Hello, Betty.

Kenny had been like, Little young, bro.

He'd been like, For you, grandpa.

When you studied history, the history of cultures, you saw your own individual time as hidebound. There were various theories of acquiescence. In Bible days a king might ride through a field and go: That one. And she would be brought unto him. And they would duly be betrothed and if she gave birth unto a son, super, bring out the streamers, she was a keeper. Was she, that first night, digging it? Probably not. Was she shaking like a leaf? Didn't matter. What mattered was offspring and the furtherance of the lineage. Plus the exaltation of the king, which resulted in righteous kingly power.

Here was the creek.

He marched her through.

The following bullet points remained in the decision matrix: take to side van door, shove in, follow in, tape wrists mouth, hook to chain, make speech. He had the speech down cold. Had practiced it both in his head and on the recorder: *Calm your heart, darling, I know you're scared because you don't know me yet and didn't expect this today but give me a chance and you will see we will fly high. See I am putting the knife right over here and I don't expect I'll have to use it, right?*

If she wouldn't get in the van, punch hard in gut. Then pick up, carry to side van door, throw in, tape wrists/mouth, hook to chain, make speech, etc., etc.

Stop, pause, he said.

Gal stopped.

Fucksake. Side door of the van was locked. How undisciplined was that. Ensuring that the door was unlocked was clearly indicated on the pre-mission matrix. Melvin appeared in his mind. On Melvin's face was the look of hot disappointment that had always preceded an ass whooping, which had always preceded the other thing. Put up your hands, Melvin said, defend yourself.

True, true. Little error there. Should have double-checked the pre-mission matrix.

No biggie.

Joy not fear.

Melvin was dead fifteen years. Mom dead twelve.

Little bitch was turned around now, looking back at the house. That willfulness wouldn't stand. That was going to get nipped in the bud. He'd have to remember to hurt her early, establish a baseline.

Turn the fuck around, he said.

She turned around.

He unlocked the door, swung it open. Moment of truth. If she got in, let him use the tape, they were home free. He'd picked out a place in Sackett, big-ass cornfield, dirt road leading in. If fuckwise it went good they'd pick up the freeway from there. Basically steal the van. It was Kenny's van. He'd borrowed it for the day. Screw Kenny. Kenny had once called him stupid. Too bad, Kenny, that remark just cost you one van. If fuckwise it went bad, she didn't properly arouse him, he'd abort the activity, truncate the subject, heave the thing out, clean van as necessary, go buy corn, return van to Kenny, say, Hey, bro, here's a shitload of corn, thanks for the van, I never could've bought a suitable quantity of corn in my car. Then lay low, watch the papers like he'd done with the nonarousing redhead out in—

Gal gave him an imploring look, like, Please don't.

Was this a good time? To give her one in the gut, knock the wind out of her sails?

It was.

He did.

The geode was beautiful. What a beautiful geode. What made it beautiful? What were the principal characteristics of a beautiful geode? Come on, think. Come on, concentrate.

She'll recover in time, Beloved Only.

None of our affair, Scout.

We're amazed by your good judgment, Beloved Only.

Dimly he noted that Alison had been punched. Eyes on the geode, he heard the little *oof.*

His heart dropped at the thought of what he was letting happen. They'd used goldfish snacks as coins. They'd made bridges out of rocks. Down by the creek. Back in the day. Oh God. He should've never stepped outside. Once they were gone he'd just go back inside, pretend he'd never stepped out, make the model-railroad town, still be making it when Mom and Dad got home. When eventually someone told him about it? He'd make a certain face. Already on his face he could feel the face he would make, like, What? Alison? Raped? Killed? Oh God. Raped and killed while I innocently made my railroad town, sitting cross-legged and unaware on the floor like a tiny little—

No. No, no, no. They'd be gone soon. Then he could go inside. Call 911. Although then everyone would know he'd done nothing. All his future life would be bad. Forever he'd be the guy who'd done nothing. Besides, calling wouldn't do any good. They'd be long gone. The parkway was just across Featherstone, with like a million arteries and cloverleafs or whatever spouting out of it. So that was that. In he'd go. As soon as they left. Leave, leave, leave, he thought, so I can go inside, forget this ever—

Then he was running. Across the lawn. Oh God! What was he doing, what was he doing? Jesus, shit, the directives he was violating! Running in the yard (bad for the sod); transporting a geode without its protective wrapping; hopping the fence, which stressed the fence, which had cost a pretty penny; leaving the yard;

leaving the yard barefoot; entering the Secondary Area without permission; entering the creek barefoot (broken glass, dangerous microorganisms), and, not only that, oh God, suddenly he saw what this giddy part of himself intended, which was to violate a directive so Major and absolute that it wasn't even a directive, since you didn't need a directive to know how totally verboten it was to—

He burst out of the creek, the guy still not turning, and let the geode fly into his head, which seemed to emit a weird edge-seep of blood even before the skull visibly indented and the guy sat right on his ass.

Yes! Score! It was fun! Fun dominating a grown-up! Fun using the most dazzling gazelle-like leg speed ever seen in the history of mankind to dash soundlessly across space and master this huge galoot, who otherwise, right now, would be—

What if he hadn't?

God, what if he hadn't?

He imagined the guy bending Alison in two like a pale garment bag while pulling her hair and thrusting bluntly, as he, Kyle, sat cowed and obedient, tiny railroad viaduct grasped in his pathetic babyish—

Jesus! He skipped over and hurled the geode through the windshield of the van, which imploded, producing an inward rain of glass shards that made the sound of thousands of tiny bamboo wind chimes.

He scrambled up the hood of the van, retrieved the geode.

Really? Really? You were going to ruin her life, ruin my life, you cunt-probe dick-munch ass-gashing Animal? Who's bossing who now? Gash-ass, jizz-lips, turd-munch—

He'd never felt so strong/angry/wild. Who's the man? Who's your daddy? What else must he do? To ensure that Animal did no further harm? You still moving, freak? Got a plan, stroke-dick? Want a skull gash on top of your existing skull gash, big man? You think I won't? You think I—

Easy, Scout, you're out of control.

Slow your motor down, Beloved Only.

Quiet. I'm the boss of me.

FUCK!

What the hell? What was he doing on the ground? Had he tripped? Did someone wonk him? Did a branch fall? God damn. He touched his head. His hand came away bloody.

The beanpole kid was bending. To pick something up. A rock. Why was that kid off the porch? Where was the knife?

Where was the gal?

Crab-crawling toward the creek.

Flying across her yard.

Going into her house.

Fuck it, everything was fucked. Better hit the road. With what, his good looks? He had like eight bucks total.

Ah Christ! The kid had smashed the windshield! With the rock! Kenny was not going to like that one bit.

He tried to stand but couldn't. The blood was just pouring out. He was not going to jail again. No way. He'd slit his wrists. Where was the knife? He'd stab himself in the chest. That had nobility. Then the people would know his name. Which of them had the balls to samurai themselves with a knife in the chest?

None.

Nobody.

Go ahead, pussy. Do it.

No. The king does not take his own life. The superior man silently accepts the mindless rebuke of the rabble. Waits to rise and fight anew. Plus he had no idea where the knife was. Well, he didn't need it. He'd crawl into the woods, kill something with his bare hands. Or make a trap from some grass. Ugh. Was he going to barf? There, he had. Right on his lap.

Figures you'd blow the simplest thing, Melvin said.

Melvin, God, can't you see my head is bleeding so bad?

A kid did it to you. You're a joke. You got fucked by a kid.

Oh, sirens, perfect.

Well, it was a sad day for the cops. He'd fight them hand to hand. He'd sit until the last moment, watching them draw near, doing a silent death mantra that would centralize all his life power in his fists.

He sat thinking about his fists. They were huge granite boulders. They were a pit bull each. He tried to get up. Somehow his legs weren't working. He hoped the cops would get here soon. His head really hurt. When he touched up there, things moved. It was like he was wearing a gore cap. He was going to need a bunch of stitches. He hoped it wouldn't hurt too much. Probably it would, though.

Where was that beanpole kid?

Oh, here he was.

Looming over him, blocking out the sun, rock held high, yelling something, but he couldn't tell what, because of the ringing in his ears.

Then he saw that the kid was going to bring the rock down. He closed his eyes and waited and was not at peace at all but instead felt the beginnings of a terrible dread welling up inside him, and if that dread kept growing at the current rate, he realized in a flash of insight, there was a name for the place he would be then, and it was Hell.

Alison stood at the kitchen window. She'd peed herself. Which was fine. People did that. When super-scared. She'd noticed it while making the call. Her hands had been shaking so bad. They still were. One leg was doing that Thumper thing. God, the stuff he'd said to her. He'd punched her. He'd pinched her. There was a big blue mark on her arm. How could Kyle still be out there? But there he was, in those comical shorts, so confident he was goofing around, hands clenched over his head like a boxer from some cute alt universe where a kid that skinny could actually win a fight against a guy with a knife.

Wait.

His hands weren't clenched. He was holding the rock, shouting something down at the guy, who was on his knees, like the blindfolded prisoner in that video they'd seen in History, about to get sword-killed by a formal dude in a helmet.

Kyle, don't, she whispered.

For months afterward she had nightmares in which Kyle brought the rock down. She was on the deck trying to scream his name but nothing was coming out. Down came the rock. Then the guy had no head. The blow just literally dissolved his head. Then his body tumped over and Kyle turned to her with this heartbroken look of, My life is over. I killed a guy.

Why was it, she sometimes wondered, that in dreams we can't do the simplest things? Like a crying puppy is standing on some broken glass and you want to pick it up and brush the shards off its pads but you can't because you're balancing a ball on your head. Or you're driving and there's this old guy on crutches, and you go, to Mr. Feder, your Driver's Ed teacher, Should I swerve? And he's like, Uh, probably. But then you hear this big clunk and Feder makes a negative mark in his book.

Sometimes she'd wake up crying from the dream about Kyle. The last time, Mom and Dad were already there, going, That's not how it was. Remember, Allie? How did it happen? Say it. Say it out loud. Allie, can you tell Mommy and Daddy how it really happened?

I ran outside, she said. I shouted.

That's right, Dad said. You shouted. Shouted like a champ.

And what did Kyle do? Mom said.

Put down the rock, she said.

A bad thing happened to you kids, Dad said. But it could have been worse.

So much worse, Mom said.

But because of you kids, Dad said, it wasn't.

You did so good, Mom said.

Did beautiful, Dad said.

2013

Ben Okri

b. 1959

Ben Okri, a member of the Urhobo people, was born in Lagos, Nigeria, and spent his early childhood in London, United Kingdom, where his father pursued a law degree. When he was seven the family returned to Lagos, then in the midst of a brutal civil war. He was educated at Urhobo College, Warri, and then returned to the UK to study comparative literature at the University of Essex. He wrote his first novel, *Flowers and Shadows*, at the age of nineteen—though it didn't find a publisher until 1980. In his mid-twenties he worked as a broadcaster with the BBC World Service and was poetry editor of *West*

Africa before becoming a full-time writer and a freelance reviewer for *The Guardian*, *The Observer*, and the *New Statesman*. It was when he was outside Nigeria that Okri discovered his subject matter was the tales of his own African landscape. "All human beings have their signatures stamped in the stories they tell themselves in dreams, the stories that are embedded in their childhood," he has remarked. His third novel, *The Famished Road* (1991), which brought him to international attention and won the Booker Prize, draws on a Nigerian belief in "spirit children" who constantly die and are reborn. The novel's protagonist, Azaro, refuses to return to the benign spirit realm, choosing instead to remain in a human world fraught with violence and poverty because he wishes to explore the mysteries of love and human survival. Azaro's narrative is continued in two other novels, *Songs of Enchantment* (1994) and *Infinite Riches* (1998). A prolific author, Okri has written several other novels, collections of short stories, volumes of poetry including *An African Elegy* (1992), and *Mental Fight* (1999). *A Way of Being Free* (1997), a collection of ten essays, offers, among other subjects, a meditation on the role of the poet, suggesting that true creativity is a form of prayer. His vision of the social and political responsibilities of the writer carries on the tradition of fellow Nigerian Wole Soyinka. His recent work includes a collection of stories, *Tales of Freedom* (2009).

Laughter Beneath the Bridge

Those were long days as we lay pressed to the prickly grass waiting for the bombs to fall. The civil war broke out before mid-term and the boarding school emptied fast. Teachers disappeared; the English headmaster was rumoured to have flown home; and the entire kitchen staff fled before the first planes went past overhead. At the earliest sign of trouble in the country parents appeared and secreted away their children. Three of us were left behind. We all hoped someone would turn up to collect us. We were silent most of the time.

Vultures showed up in the sky. They circled the school campus for a few days and then settled on the watchnight's shed. In the evenings we watched as some religious maniacs roamed the empty school compound screaming about the end of the world and then as a wild bunch of people from the city scattered through searching for those of the rebel tribe. They broke doors and they looted the chapel of its icons, statuaries and velvet drapes; they took the large vivid painting of the agony of Christ. In the morning we saw the Irish priest riding furiously away from town on his Raleigh bicycle. After he left, ghosts flitted through the chapel and rattled the roof. One night we heard the altar fall. The next day we saw lizards nodding on the chapel walls.

We stayed on in the dormitories. We rooted for food in the vegetable field. We stole the wine of tapsters at the foot of palm trees. We broke into the kitchen and raided the store of baked beans, sardines and stale bread. In the daytime we waited at the school gate, pressed to the grass, watching out for our parents. Sometimes we went to town to forage. We talked about the bombings in the country whispered to us from the fields. One day, after having stolen bread from the only bakery in town, we got to the dormitory and found the lizards there. They were under the double-decked beds and on the cupboards, in such great numbers, in such relaxed occupation, that we couldn't bear to sleep there any more. All through the days we waited for the bombs to fall. And all through that time it was Monica I thought about.

She was a little girl when I learned how to piss straight. When I learned how to cover my nakedness she developed long legs and a pert behind and took to moving round our town like a wild and beautiful cat. She became famous for causing havoc at the barbers' shops, the bukkas, pool offices. She nearly drowned once trying to outswim the other boys across our town's river, which was said to like young girls. I watched them dragging her through the muddied water: her face was pale, she looked as though she had taken a long journey from her body. After that she took to going around with Egunguns, brandishing a whip, tugging the masked figure, abusing the masquerade for not dancing well enough. That was a time indeed when she broke our sexual taboos and began dancing our street's Egungun round town, fooling all the men. She danced so well that we got coins from the stingiest dressmakers, the meanest pool-shop owners. I remember waking up one night during the holidays to go out and ease myself at the backyard. I saw her bathing near the shrubs of hibiscus and there was a moon out. I dreamed of her new-formed breasts when the lizards chased us from the dormitories, and when the noise of fighter planes drove us to the forests.

I remember it as a beautiful time. I don't know how Sirens and fire engines made it seem like there was an insane feast going on somewhere in the country. In town we saw a man set upon by a mob they beat him up in a riot of vengeance, they broke sticks and bottles on his head. So much blood came from him. Maybe it seemed like a beautiful time because we often sat in the school field, staring at the seven hills that were like pilings of verdigris in the distance: and because none of us cried. We were returning from a search for food one day when we saw someone standing like a scarecrow in the middle of the field. We drew closer. The figure stayed still. It was mother. She looked at us a long time and she didn't recognize me. Fear makes people go stiff. When she finally recognized me she held all three of us together like we were family.

"Can't take your friends," mother said, after we had all been given something to eat.

"I'm not a wicked person to leave behind children who are stranded," mother said, her face bony, "but how will I rest in my grave if the soldiers we meet hold them, because of me?"

I didn't understand. I began to say a prayer for my friends.

"You will have to wait for your parents, or both of you go with the first parent that turns up. Can you manage?" mother asked them. They nodded. She looked at them for a long time and then cried.

Mother left them some money and all the food she brought. She took off two of her three wrappers for them to cover themselves with in the cold winds of the night. I felt sad at having to leave them behind. Mother prayed for them and I tried not to think of them as we walked the long distance to the garage. I tried not to see both of them in the empty fields as we struggled to catch a bus in the garage. Then the commotion of revving lorries, wheezing buses, the convulsion of people running home to their villages, women weeping, children bawling, soldiers everywhere in battle-dress and camouflage helmets, their guns stiff and strange, the whole infernal commotion simply wiped my two friends from my mind. After several hours we finally caught a lorry that could take us home. Then afterwards I tried to think only of Monica.

The lorry we caught was old and slow. It had an enduring, asthmatic engine. The driver was very talkative and boastful. There were all kinds of cupboards and long brooms and things in sacks strapped to its roof. As we fought to clamber in, I caught a glimpse of the legend painted on the old wooden bodywork. It read: THE YOUNG SHALL GROW.

There was absolutely no space in the lorry to move because most of the passengers had brought with them as many of the acquisitions of their lives in the city as they could carry. We sat on wooden benches and all about us were buckets, sewing machines, mattresses, calabashes, mats, clothes, ropes, pots, blackened pans, machetes. Even those with household jujus could not hide them and we stared at the strange things they worshipped. It was so uncomfortable and airless in the lorry that I nodded in and out of sleep, the only relief.

That was a long journey indeed. The road seemed to have no end. The leaves of the trees and bushes were covered with dust. There were a hundred checkpoints. The soldiers at every one of them seemed possessed of a belligerent vitality. They stopped every vehicle, searched all nooks and crannies, emptied every bag and sack, dug their guns in our behinds, barked a thousand questions. We passed stretches of forest and saw numerous corpses along the road. We saw whole families trudging along the empty wastes, children straggling behind, weeping without the possibility of consolation.

I was asleep when mother woke me up. It was another checkpoint. There were many soldiers around, all shouting and barking orders at the same time. There was a barricade across the road. There was a pit not far from the barricade. The bodies of three grown men lay bundled in the pit. One of them had been shot through the teeth. Another one was punctured with gunshots and his face was so contorted it seemed he had died from too much laughing.

The soldiers shouted that we should all jump down. It would begin all over again: unpacking the entire lorry, unstrapping the load at the top, being subjected to a thorough and leisurely search. Then we would wait for one or two who couldn't prove they were not of the rebel tribe, sometimes being made to leave without them.

"Come down, all of you! Jump down now!" shouted the soldiers. We all tramped down. They lined us up along the road. Evening was approaching and the sun had that ripe, insistent burn. The forest was riotous with insects. Many of the soldiers had their fingers on the triggers. As they searched the lorry, one of the soldiers kept blowing his nose, covering the lemon-grass with snot. They questioned the driver, who shivered in servility. They took us aside, into the bush, one by one, to be questioned. I stood there beneath the mature burning sun, starving, bored, and thinking of Monica. Occasionally I heard one of the women burst into crying. I heard the butt of a gun crash on someone's head. I didn't hear them cry out.

They searched and questioned us a long time. The sun turned from ripe, blazing red to dull orange. I blew my nose on the lemon-grass, thinking of Monica. The soldiers who had also been blowing his nose came over to me.

"You dey crase?" he shouted at me.

I didn't know what he was talking about so he cracked me across the head. I saw one of Monica's masks in the stars.

"Are you mad?" he shouted at me again.

I still didn't know what he was talking about. He whacked me harder, with the back of his hand, and sent me flying into the cluster of yellowing lemongrass. Mother screamed at him, dived for his eyes, and he pushed her so hard that she landed near me. She picked herself up, snot drooling from the back of her wrapper; her wig had fallen into the pit. I lay on the lemon-grass and refused to get up. My head hurt. Behind me another soldier was knocking a woman about in the bushes. The soldier who had hit me came over to where I lay. His gun pointed at me from the hip. Mother, who feared guns, cowered behind him. Someone called to the soldier.

"Frank O'Nero," the voice said, "leave the poor boy alone now, ah ah."

Frank O'Nero turned to the voice, swinging the gun in its direction, then swinging back to me. His eyes were raw. I was afraid that he was mad.

"All you children of rich men. You think because you go to school you can behave anyhow you want? Don't you know this is a war? Goat! Small goat!"

Mother, in a weak voice, said: "Leave my son alone, you hear. God didn't give me many of them."

Frank O'Nero looked at her, then at me. He turned with a swagger and went to the bush were they were questioning the passengers. They called us next.

Behind the bushes three soldiers smoked marijuana. Half-screened, a short way up, two soldiers struggled with a light-complexioned woman. The soldiers smoking marijuana asked mother questions and I never heard her answers because I was fascinated with what the soldiers a short way up were doing. The soldiers asked mother where she came from in the country and I thought of Monica as the soldiers, a short way up, struggled with and finally subdued the woman. They shouted to mother to recite the paternoster in the language of the place she claimed to come from: and mother hesitated as the woman's legs were forced apart. Then mother recited the paternoster fluently in father's language. She was of the rebel tribe but father had long ago forced her to master his language. Mother could tell that the interpreter who was supposed to check on the language didn't know it too well: so she extended the prayer, went deeper into idiom, abusing their mothers and fathers, cursing the suppurating vaginas that must have shat them out in their wickedness, swearing at the rotten pricks that dug up the maggoty entrails of their mothers—and the soldiers half-screened by the bushes rode the woman furiously till the sun started its slow climb into your eyes, Monica. The soldiers listened to mother's recitation with some satisfaction. Then they turned to me and asked me to recite the Hail Mary. The soldier in the bush had finished wrecking his manhood on the woman and was cleaning himself with leaves. I told the soldier interrogating me that I couldn't speak our language that well.

"Why not?" he asked, his voice thundering.

I heard the question but I couldn't find an answer. The woman on the floor in the bush was silent: her face was contorted, she was covered in a foam of sweat.

"I'm talking to you! Idiot!" he shouted. "If you don't speak your language you're not going with your mother, you hear?"

I nodded. Their marijuana smoke was beginning to tickle me. Mother came in quickly and explained that I hadn't grown up at home. The woman on the ground began to wail tonelessly. Mother turned on me, pinched me, hit my head, urged me to speak the language of my father, gave me hints of children's songs, the beginnings of stories. I couldn't at that moment remember a word: it had all simply vanished from my head. Besides, I was suddenly overcome with the desire to laugh.

It was partly the interrogator's fault. He said: "If he can't speak a word of your language then he can't be your son."

I burst out laughing and not even mother's pincerous fingernails, nor the growing fury of the soldiers, could stop me. I soon found myself being dragged deep into the forest by Frank O'Nero. Mother wailed a dirge, her hair all scattered. The woman on the ground made inhuman noises. Fear overcame me and I shouted the oldest word I knew and mother seized on it, screaming, the boy has spoken, he has just said that he wants to shit. Frank O'Nero stopped, his fingers like steel round my wrists. He looked at the other soldiers; then at mother, and me. Then he completely surprised, and scared, me with the rough sound that came from his throat. Mother wasted no time rushing to me, pushing me towards the lorry. The soldiers passed the joke all the way round the barricade. In the lorry, we waited for the others to prove they were not the enemy. The woman on the ground was obscured from view, but I could still hear her wailing. The sky was darkening when we pulled away. We were forced to leave without her.

Mother never stopped chastising me. They shoot people who can't speak their language, she said. As she chastised me, I thought about Monica, who did only what she wanted. I wondered if she would have long enough to say a word when they came for her.

The rest of the journey was not peaceful either. The faces of war leapt up from the tarmac, shimmering illusions in my drowsiness. Armoured trucks, camouflaged with burr, thundered up and down the roads. Planes roared overhead. From time to time a frenzy seized the driver: he would suddenly stop the lorry in the middle of the road and dive for the bushes. Sometimes it took a while to convince him to come out, that we were safe.

"I'm never going to drive again in this madness," he kept saying.

The taste of madness like the water of potent springs, the laughter of war: that is perhaps why I remember it as a beautiful time. And because in the lorry, with corpses drifting past along the road and soldiers noisy in their jeeps, we were all silent. The weight of our silence was enormous. When we finally arrived I felt like I had seen several lifetimes go past.

Loud cheering and hooting broke out as our lorry swung into the town's garage. People rushed to us from all the silent houses. Children ran with them, cheering and not knowing why. We came down and were thronged by people who wanted to know how the war was doing, how many dead bodies we saw. The driver told them all the stories they wanted to hear.

Mother didn't like the bicycle taxis, which were the only taxis in operation, so she made us walk home. There were soldiers everywhere. Hysteria blew along the streets, breathed over the buildings and huts.

When father saw us coming up the street I heard him shout that the chicken should be caught. It turned out to be an unruly little chicken with a red cloth tied to its leg, one that had been bought expensively and saved up during that time of food shortage. We had been expected for some time and father was afraid something bad had happened. They had all grown a little fond of the chicken. Father opened a bottle of Ogogoro and made profuse libations to our ancestors, thanking them for allowing our safe passage home. Father made me bathe in herbal water, to wash the bad things of the journey off me. Then the chicken was killed and cooked and served with Portuguese sardines, boiled cassava, little green tomatoes and some yam.

And then I started looking out of our window, stirring as I looked, down our street, past the yellowing leaves of the guava tree and the orange tree, with its mottled trunk, that was planted the year before I was born, past the cluster of hibiscus and passion plants, looking at the house which was really a squat bungalow, where she lived with her family, ten in all, in one room. And with a small part of my mind I heard the old ones in the sitting-room, their voices cracked by the searing alcohol, as they talked in undertones about the occupation of the town, about the ones who had died, or gone mad, or the ones who had joined the army and promised good things and turned in the heat of battle and fired at their own men.

When mother came to urge me to sleep, I asked, as though it were her responsibility:

"Where's Monica?"

"Why are you asking me? Haven't we both just come from a journey?"

"Where is she?"

Mother sighed.

"How would I know? Before I left she was staying with us. The townspeople pursued them from their house and the family are scattered in the forests. They killed her brother."

"Which one?"

"Ugo."

I felt sick.

"So where is she then?"

"What sort of question is that? Nobody in the house knows where Monica is. Sometimes she comes back to the house to eat and then she disappears for several days and then she come back again. You know how stubborn she is. The day before I came to collect you she went to the market and got into some trouble with a soldier. The soldier nearly shot her. It was your father's good name which saved her."

I wanted to go out, to find her.

"We are thinking of sending her to the village. The way she is behaving they will kill her before the war is over. You always liked her. When she comes back, talk to her. You will soon be a man, you know."

Flattered by the last thing she said, for I was only ten, I got up.

As I went out through the door, father said: "Don't go far-o! There's a curfew. This is not a holiday, you hear?"

At the backyard the other kids said they hadn't seen her all day. I went to the town's market, which sprawled along the length of the main road all the way to the bridge. Couldn't find her. I went round all the empty stalls of the butchers, where she sometimes went to collect offal, which she had a talent for cooking. Couldn't find her. I went to the record shop that overlooked an abattoir of cow and sheep bones. Went to the palm wine bars where she sometimes sold wine to the hungry bachelors and old men of the town: they were now full of soldiers. I went from one rubber plantation to another, walking through tracts of forest sizzling with insects, listening to the rubber pods explode through tangles of branches and crash on the ground. Still couldn't find her.

When I got home father was in a furious temper. Monica stood by the door, her head drooping, staring mulishly at the floor. Father shouted that he didn't want to be responsible for anyone's death, that this was a war, and so on. Father finished shouting at her and she rushed out and went and stood beneath the mango tree, scratching herself, slapping at mosquitoes. It was getting dark. The fragrance of mango fruit was on the wind.

"Monica!" I called.

"Get away!" she screamed at me.

"Where have you been? I've been looking every . . ."

"Get away from here!" she screamed even louder. I went away, up the street. I walked past the post office and came back. She was still leaning against the tree, her eyes hard. I went on into the sitting-room, where I slept at night on a mat on the floor. Later she tapped on the window with a mango branch. I opened the window and she climbed in.

"Let's go out," she whispered. She saw father's Ogogoro bottle and took a swig of the alcohol.

"Get away!"

"Let's go out," she said again.

"Where were you today? I searched for you all over town."

"Look at your big nose," she said, "full of pimples."

"Leave my nose alone."

She always had such a peppery mouth. She went on abusing me.

"Your head like a bullet," she said. "You no tall, you no short, you be like Hausa dagger."

"What about you? Anyway, where have you been that no one can find you?"

"You're such a fool," she whispered.

Then she went quiet. She seemed to travel away from her body a little bit and then she came back. All that time I had been telling her about our journey and the soldiers and the lizards. She sort of looked at me with strange eyes and I wanted to draw close to her, to hold her, wrestle with her.

But she said: "Let's go out."

"Where?"

"I won't tell you."

"What about the curfew?"

"What about it?"

"What about the soldiers?"

"What about them?" she asked, taking another swig, the alcohol dripping down her mouth on to her lap. She coughed and her eyes reddened.

"I'm not going. I'm sleepy. They are killing people, you know!"

"So you are afraid of them?"

"No, I'm not."

"You are a fool."

She looked me up and down. She pouted her lips. She climbed back out of the window. And I followed.

There was a moon coming over the mango tree.

She went out of the compound and up the street and then turned into another compound. I got there and found a group of kids standing beneath a hedge of hibiscus. Two of them carried great wads of raffia trailings. One of them held a big and ugly mask. Another had little drums surrounding him.

I felt left out.

"Who's building an Egungun?" I asked in as big a voice as I could muster.

"Why do you want to know?" came from, of all people, Monica.

"I want to dance the Egungun. I have not danced it for a long time."

"Why don't you go and build your own?"

I ignored her and went to the other kids and tried to rough them up a little. None of them said anything. There was a long silence and I listened to the wind moaning underneath the moon. I watched the kids as they went on building the Egungun, sticking raffia trailings to the mask. They strung threads through the corals, which would eventually become bracelets and anklets and make joyous cackles when dancing. The drummer tapped on one of the drums. He got a little carried away. Someone opened a window and shouted at us to stop making noise. One of the boys tried on the mask and shook around. I tried to snatch it from him and Monica said: "Don't do that. You know you're not allowed to take off an Egungun's mask. You'll die if you do."

"It's an ugly mask, anyway," I said, going out from the compound and up the street towards the main road. There were a few bicyclists around, furtively looking out for passengers. The moon was big and clear. I heard footsteps. Monica was coming behind me. Two other kids from the group were behind her: ragged companions. I could hear them talking about running away from home to join the army. I suddenly had a vision of my two friends at school, standing in the expanse of fields, surrounded by lizards. I said a prayer for them.

We walked alongside the market. Its arcade of rusted zinc roofing was totally dark underneath: but above it was bright with the moon. The piles of refuse continued all the way past the market.

In the moonlight we could see that there was a roadblock just after the bridge. Mosquitoes were madly whining. Soldiers sat around on metal chairs, smoking intensely in the dark. Their armoured truck, a solitary bulk, covered the road. The other two kids said they were going back, that their parents would be worried about them. I wanted to go back too. I didn't like the way the soldiers smoked their cigarettes. I didn't like the sound of the laughter that came from the truck.

But Monica was determined to go past them.

The other kids stopped and said they were going to improve on the Egungun. They didn't look too happy about going back. They turned and went sadly alongside the dark and empty market. I looked for Monica and found that she was already over the bridge. I had to run and catch up with her before she got to the soldiers.

They stopped us as we went past.

"Where do you think you are going?"

"Our father sent us a message," Monica said.

The soldier who had spoken got up from the metal chair. Then he sat down again.

"What message? What message? Is your father mad? Doesn't he know we are fighting a war? Does he think that killing Biafrans is a small thing? Is he mad?"

Monica fidgeted with her toes on the asphalt. The other soldiers smoked stolidly in the dark, taking a mild interest in us. The soldier who had been shouting asked us to move closer. We did. He was a stocky man with an ill-fitting uniform. He had bulging cheeks and a paunch. He looked at Monica in a funny way. He looked at her breasts and then at her neck.

He said: "Come closer."

"Who? Me?" I asked.

"Shut up!" he said. Then to Monica: "I said, come closer."

Monica moved backwards.

The soldier stood up suddenly and his rifle fell from his lap and clattered on the road. I ducked, half-expecting it to fire. He scooped it up angrily and, to Monica, said: "You be Yamarin?"

Monica stiffened.

"We're from this town," I said haltingly, in our language.

The soldier looked at me as though I had just stepped in from the darkness.

"Who is your father?"

"The District Commissioner," I said, lying.

He eyed Monica, stared at her legs. He scratched his nose, fingered his gun, and pulled his sagging military pants all the way up his paunch. He looked as though he was confronted with the biggest temptation of his adult life. Then he touched her. On the shoulder. Monica stepped back, pulled me by my shirt sleeve, urged us to hurry. Soon Monica was in front and her buttocks moved in a manner I hadn't noticed before. We turned and went down the bank of reeds alongside the stream. We sat under a tree and soon a terrible smell came from the water and it stayed a long time and after a while I didn't notice it.

Monica was restless. I had an amazing sense of inevitability. The last time I tried something on Monica she swiped me viciously on the head. Blooming had the effect of making her go around with an exaggerated sense of herself. She always believed she'd marry a prince.

She said: "I feel like going to war."

"As what?"

"A soldier. I want to carry a gun. Shoot. Fire."

"Shut up."

She was quiet for a moment.

"You know they killed Ugo?"

I nodded. Her eyes were very bright. I had this feeling that she had been changed into something strange: I looked at her face and it seemed to elude me. The moon was in her eyes.

"This is where they dumped his body. It's floated away now."

She was crying.

"Shoot a few people. Fire. Shoot," she said. Then she got up and tried to climb the gnarled trunk of the iroko tree. Couldn't do it. She stopped trying to climb and then stood staring at the stream. The soldiers were laughing above the bridge, their boots occasionally crunching the gravel. I went to Monica and she pushed me away. I went to her again and she shoved me away so hard that I fell. I lay down and watched her.

"This is where I've been. All day I sit here and think."

I went to her and held her around the waist and she didn't do anything. I could smell her armpit, a new smell to me. Above on the bridge, one of the soldiers laughed so hard he had to cough and spit at the end of it.

"So you see the stream?" she asked me, in a new voice.

"Yes."

"What do you see?"

"I see the stream with the moonlight on the rubbish."

"Is that all?"

"Yes."

"Look. Look. That's where Ugo was. I measured the place with this tree."

Then something shifted in my eyes. The things on the water suddenly looked different, transformed. The moment I saw them as they were I left her and ran up the bank. The stream was full of corpses that had swollen, huge massive bodies with enormous eyes and bloated cheeks. They were humped along on the top of the water. The bridge was all clogged up underneath with waterweeds and old engines and vegetable waste from the market.

"Monica!"

She was silent. The smell from the stream got terrible again.

"Monica!"

Then she started to laugh. I had never heard that sort of twisted laughter before. After a while I couldn't see her clearly and I called her and she laughed and then I thought it was all the swollen corpses that were laughing.

"Monica! I am going home-o!"

One of the soldiers fired a shot into the air. I rushed down and grabbed Monica. She was shivering. Her mouth poured with saliva, her face was wet. I held her close as we passed the armoured truck. She was jabbering away and I had to cover her mouth with my palm. We didn't look at the soldiers. I could smell their sweat.

When we got home we both came down with a fever.

By Saturday the town had begun to smell. All the time I lay in bed, feverish and weak, the other kids brought me stories of what was happening. They said that at night swollen ghosts with large eyes clanked over the bridge. They said the soldiers had to move from the bridge because the smell of the stream got too strong for them.

I saw very little of Monica. It seemed she recovered faster than I did. When I saw her again she looked very thin and her eyes were mad. There was a lot more talk of sending her to the village. I learnt that in the bungalow behind the hibiscus hedge they were building a mighty Egungun—one that would dwarf even the one with which ja-ja johnny walked over the River Niger, long ago before the world came to be like this. I asked who would ride the Egungun and the others still wouldn't say. On Saturday afternoon I was just strong enough to go and see this new masquerade for myself. The town stank. It was true: the boys had built this wonderful Egungun with a grotesque laughing mask. The mask had been broken—they say Monica's temper was responsible—but it was gummed back together.

In my loudest voice I said: "I will dance the Egungun."

They stared at me and then fled, as though they had seen another spirit.

How could it have been a beautiful time when that afternoon the smell got so strong that gas masks and wooden poles had to be distributed to respectable and proven citizens of the town so that they could prod the bodies and clear the rubbish to enable the corpses to flow away beneath the bridge? We saw these respectable citizens marching down our street. They were doctors, civil servants, businessmen, police constables. Their pot-bellies wobbled as they marched. They had the gas masks on. Mother spat when they passed us. The kids in the street jeered at them.

When they had gone I went to the building-place of the Egungun and found that the group was ready to dance along the market and all the way round town. Two small Egunguns warmed up and shook their feet while they waited for the main one. Then we heard a flourish of drums from the backyard and the main Egungun came dancing vigorously towards us. We cheered. Too weak to do anything else, I ended up getting a rope that controlled the main one.

We danced up the street and down the market road. The drumming was strong. The masquerade danced with a wild frenzy, the bracelets and anklets contributing to the rough music. Occasionally the Egungun tore away from my grip and the others blamed me and I had to run and catch the rope and restrain its ferocity. We shouldered bicyclists from the road, danced round old men and women, rattling the castanets made out of Bournvita cans and bird-seeds. When we got to the empty market the spirit of Egunguns entered us. As we danced round the stalls, in the mud of rotting vegetables and meat, we were suddenly confronted by a group of big huge spirits. They were tall, their heads reached the top of the zinc roofing. They had long faces and big eyes. We ran, screaming, and regrouped outside the market. We went towards the bridge.

The Egungun didn't want to cross the bridge. The small ones were dancing over and we were beating our drums across and singing new songs and we turned and found the main Egungun still behind, refusing to come with us. We went back and flogged it and pulled and pushed; but it didn't want to go. The other boys suggested we stone the Egungun. I suggested that we drown it. Then finally the Egungun turned round and we followed, singing ja-ja johnny to the ground, hitting the drums, beating the castanets on our thighs. We danced past the shop of the only tailor in town, whose sign read: TRAINED IN LONDON; and the barber's shed that bore the legend: NO JUSTICE IN THIS WORLD; and past the painter of signboards (who had all sorts of contradictory legends nailed round his shed). We bobbed in front of the houses of the town that were built with the hope that they would, at least, be better than their neighbours. Nobody threw us any coins. None of the grown-ups liked us dancing at that time and they drove us away and abused us. We danced our way back up town again. At the market we saw a confusion of several other Egunguns. We didn't know where they had sprung from. They rattled tin castanets, beat drums, brandished whips.

We clashed with them. We fought and whipped one another under the blazing sun. We toppled stalls and threw stones and spat and cursed, sending a wild clamour through the market. The drummers went completely mad competing amongst themselves. We fought and the commotion increased till some soldiers ran over from the bridge and shouted at us. When we heard the soldiers we took cover behind the fallen stalls. Only our Egungun—an insane laughing mask split in the middle of the face—went on as if nothing had happened. It danced round the stalls, provocatively shaking its buttocks, uttering its possessed language, defying the soldiers.

"Stop dancing! Stop dancing!" one of them thundered. Our Egungun seemed to derive more frenzy from the order. Then one of the soldiers stepped forward, tore the mask off the Egungun's face, and slapped Monica so hard that I felt the sound. Then suddenly her eyes grew large as a mango and her eyelids kept twitching.

"Speak your language!" the soldier shouted, as her thighs quivered. "Speak your language!" he screamed, as she urinated down her thighs and shivered in her own puddle. She wailed. Then she jabbered. In her language.

There was a terrible silence. Nobody moved. The soldiers dragged Monica towards the bridge and on to the back of a jeep. When the jeep sped off, raising dust in its read, there was a burst of agitation and wailing and everybody began to mutter and curse at once and the spirits in the market were talking too, incoherently and in feverish accents. I ran home to tell father what had happened. He rushed out in a very bad temper and I didn't hear what abuse he came out with because when we got to the market a cry of exultation from the men in gas masks told us that the stream had been cleared. The rubbish had gone.

Father rushed on angrily to the army barracks. We passed the bridge and I saw the great swollen bodies as they flowed reluctantly down the narrow stream. I never saw Monica again. The young shall grow.

1986

Anne Enright

b. 1962

Born in Dublin, Anne Enright's education was initiated by "a funny school in Canada" (Lester B. Pearson College in Victoria, BC), an adventure which also fostered her longtime interest in and skepticism about the virtue of travel. Whether Trinity College, Dublin, where she delved into English and Philosophy, was also "a funny school" is undocumented, but given her deep and early attachment to irony and mischief, it probably was. Subsequently, she pursued an MA in Creative Writing at the University of East Anglia, where she was mentored by the famed and fated Angela Carter. But Enright did not take a direct route into a life of writing fiction. She was an RTE television producer and partly responsible for the successful program *Nighthawks*. Once committed to her writing, Enright was a local prize, admired for the play of somberness and humour in her narratives of mainly personal experience. In 2007, the Man Booker award for *The Gathering*, her narrative about the aftermath of a suicide, its bleakness punctuated by the necessity of comedy, transformed local appeal to worldwide readership. She seems to alternate between short stories and novels, and has written something like a memoir, the startling reflection on gender and birth, *Making Babies: Stumbling into Motherhood* (2004). Enright undermines everything ethereal and sanctimonious about motherhood. "There is a part of me, I have realized, that wants to nurse the stranger on the bus. Or perhaps it wants to nurse the bus itself." A vexed mother, she is equally complicated in her perspectives on Irish writing, especially the Irish short story. "But though I am not a romantic, I am quite passionate about the whole business of being an Irish writer . . . We write against our own foolishness, not anyone else's. In which case the short story is as good a place as any other to keep things real." Much of her introduction to *The Granta Book of the Irish Short Story* is devoted to a reflection on Frank O'Connor's thought (quoted in the introduction to this volume) that "an intense awareness of human loneliness" is endemic to the short story, but much less so in the novel. "Not sure" that this perception is true, Enright is certain, however, that "connection and the lack of it is one of the great themes of the short story." From this statement to Enright's own stories is a very short transition. A writer with a deeply rooted instinct for the fluidities of realism, Enright takes the temperatures of personal relationships. Leavened by her unyielding generosity, her stories deal with the inevitabilities of connections and lesions between people: husbands and wives, former and current selves, mothers and children. "'Why should he be unhappy?' she wanted to say. 'He has had so few days in this world. Why should the unhappiness start here?'"

Yesterday's Weather

Hazel didn't want to eat outside—the amount of suncream you had to put on a baby and the way he kept shaking the little hat off his head. Also there were flies, and her sister-in-law Margaret didn't have a steriliser—why should she?—so Hazel would be boiling bottles and cups and spoons to beat the band. Then John would mooch up to her at the cooker and tell her to calm down—so not only would she have to do all the work, she would also have to apologise for doing all the work when she should be having a good time, sitting outside and watching blue-bottles put their shitty feet on the teat of the baby's bottle while everyone else got drunk in the sun.

She remembered a man in the hotel foyer, very tall, he handled his baby like a newborn lamb; setting it down on its stomach to swim its way across the carpet. And Hazel had, briefly, wanted to be married to him instead.

Now she grabbed a bowl of potato salad with the arm that held the baby and a party pack of crisps with the other, hoofed the sliding door open and stepped over the chrome lip on to the garden step. The baby buried his face in her shoulder and wiped his nose on her T-shirt. He had a summer cold, so Hazel's navy top was criss-crossed with what looked like slug trails. There was something utterly depressing about being covered in snot. It was just not something she had ever anticipated. She would go and change but the baby would not be put down and John, when she looked for him, was playing rounders with his niece and nephews under the apple trees. He saw her and waved. She put down the bowl and the crisps on the garden table, and shielded the baby's head against the hard ball.

The baby's skin, under the downy hair, breathed a sweat so fine it was lost as soon as she lifted her hand. Women don't even know they miss this until they get it, this smoothness, seeing as men were so abrasive or—what were they like? She tried to remember the comfort of John's belly with the hair stroked all one way, or the shocking silk of his dick, even, bobbing up under her hand, but he was so lumbering and large, these days, and it was always too long since he had shaved.

"Grrrr . . ." said Margaret, beside her, rummaging a bag of crisps from out of the party pack. This is what happens when you have kids, Hazel thought, you eat all their food—while Margaret's children, as far as she could see, ate nothing at all. They ate nothing whatsoever. Even so, everyone was fat.

"Come and eat," Margaret shouted down the garden, while Hazel turned the baby away from the sudden noise.

"Boys! Steffie! Please! Come and eat."

Her voice was solid in the air, you could almost feel it hitting the side of the baby's head. But her children ignored her—John too. He had lost his manners since coming home. He pretended his sister did not exist, or only barely existed.

"How's the job coming?" she might say and he'd say, ". . . Fine," like, *What a stupid question.*

It made Hazel panic, slightly. Though he was not like that with her. At least, not yet. And he lavished affection on his sister's three little children, he threw them up in the air, and he caught them, coming down. Still, Hazel found it hard to get her breath; she felt as though the baby was still inside her, pushing up against her lungs, making everything tight.

But the baby was not inside her. The baby was in her arms.

"Come and eat!" shouted Margaret again. "Come on!"

Still, no one found it necessary to hear. Hazel would shout herself, but that would definitely make the baby cry. She stood by the white wrought-iron table, set with salads and fizzy orange and cut ham, and she watched this perfect picture of a family at play, while beside her Margaret said, "God between me and prawn-flavoured Skips," ripping open one of the crinkly packets and diving in.

The ball thumped past Hazel's foot. John looked up the length of the garden at her.

"Hey!" he called.

"What?"

"The ball."

"Sorry?"

"The ball!"

It seemed to Hazel that she could not hear him, even though his words were quite clear to her. Or that she could not be heard, even though she was saying nothing at all. She found herself walking down the garden, and she did not know why until she was standing in front of him, with the baby thrust out at arms' length.

"Take him," she said.

"What?"

"Take the baby."

"What?"

"Take the fucking baby!"

The baby dangled between them, so shocked that when John fumbled it into his arms, the sound of wailing was a relief—at least it turned the volume in her head back on. But Hazel was already walking back up to the ball. She picked it up and slung it low towards the apple trees.

"Now. There's your ball." Then she turned to go inside.

John's father was at the sliding door; his stick clutched high against his chest, as he managed his way down the small step. He looked at her and smiled so sweetly that Hazel knew he had just witnessed the scene on the lawn. Also that he forgave her. And this was so unbearable to her—that a complete stranger should be able to forgive her most intimate dealings in this way—that Hazel swung past the tiny old man as she went inside, nearly pushing him against the glass.

John found her hunkered on the floor in the living room searching through the nappy bag. She looked up. He was not carrying the baby.

"Where's the baby?" she said.

"What's wrong with you?" he said.

"I have to change my top. What did you do with the baby?"

"What's wrong with your top?"

Snots. Hazel could not bring herself to say the word; it would make her cry, and then they would both laugh.

But there was no clean T-shirt in the bag. They were staying in a hotel, because Hazel had thought it would be easier to get the baby asleep away from all the noise. But there was always a teething ring left in the cool of the mini-bar, or a vital plastic spoon in the hotel sink, and so of course there was no T-shirt in the bag. And anyway, John would not let her bring the baby back to the hotel for a nap.

"He's fine. He's fine," he kept saying as the baby became ever more cranky and bewildered; screaming in terror if she tried to put him down.

"Why should he be unhappy?" she wanted to say. "He has had so few days in this world. Why should the unhappiness start here?"

Instead she kept her head down, and rummaged for nothing in the nappy bag.

"Go and get the baby," she said.

"He's with Margaret, he's fine."

Hazel had a sudden image of the baby choking on a prawn-flavoured Skip—but she couldn't say this, of course, because if she said this, then she would sound like a snob. It seemed that, ever since they had arrived in Clonmel, there was a reason not to say every single thought that came into her head.

"I hate this," she said, eventually, sinking back from the bag.

"What?"

"All of it."

"Hazel," he said. "We are just having a good time. This is what people do when they have a good time."

And she would have cried then, for being such a wrongheaded, miserable bitch, were it not for a quiet thought that crossed her mind. She looked up at him.

"No, you're not," she said.

"What?"

"You are not having a good time."

"Sure," he said. "Right. Whatever you say," and turned to go.

Margaret hadn't, in fact, asked the baby to suck a prawn-flavoured Skip. She had transformed the baby into a gurgling stranger, sitting on the brink of her knee and getting its hands clapped. The baby's brown eyes were dark with delight, and his mouth was fizzing with smiles and spit. At least it was, until he heard Hazel's voice, when he turned, and remembered who his mother was, and started to howl.

"Well, don't say you didn't like it," said Hazel, taking him on to her shoulder, feeling betrayed.

"Sorry," said Margaret, "I was dying to have a go."

"Oh, any time," said Hazel, archly. "You can keep him if you like," listening already to her housewife's camp.

Why not? She sat down at the table and threw a white baby cloth over the worst of the slug trails on her chest and lifted her face to the weak Easter sun.

"How's the new house?" said Margaret.

"Oh, I don't know," said Hazel. "You can't get anything done."

"Five years," said Margaret. "Five years I have been trying to get carpet for the back bedrooms."

"I know what you mean."

"I mean, five years I've been trying to get to the shop to look at the carpet books to start thinking about carpet for the back bedrooms."

"What did you used to have?" said Hazel, then realised she shouldn't ask this, because it was John's parents' house, and talking about the old carpet was talking about his dead mother, and God knows what else.

"I mean, did you have lino or boards, or what?"

"I couldn't look at them," said Margaret. "I got down on my hands and knees and I got—you know—a claw hammer, and I prised them up."

Hazel looked at the laughing children running after John, who was also laughing.

"The dirt," said Margaret.

"John!" said Hazel. "Tea-time. Now please." Then she said to her sister-in-law, "A friend of mine found amazing stuff on the Internet. Stripes and picture rugs, and I don't know what else."

"Really," said Margaret, and started to butter a round of bread.

⊰o⊱

John's father turned to them, and either shook his fist, or just lifted his hand—he had such a bad tremor, it was hard to tell. And this was another thing that Hazel could not figure out: what part of him was affected by the Parkinson's, or was it Parkinson's at all? Was his speech funny? Truth be told, she never understood a word he said.

"Hffash en silla?"

"Well, they're kids, Daddy," said Margaret without a blink—so maybe it was just her, after all. They watched him for a while, poking at the flower bed with his stick.

"He used to love his sweet pea along that wall," Margaret said, like the man was already dead.

Hazel said nothing.

"Will you take a bite to eat, Daddy, pet?" but he ignored her, like all the rest.

Hazel had a sudden pang for her little garden in Lucan. The seeded grass was sprouting, and the tulips were about to bloom. She had planted the bulbs the week they got the keys: kneeling on the front path, seven months pregnant, digging with the little shovel from the fire-irons; a straight line from the gate to the door of fat, red tulips, the type you get in a park—"a bit municipal," as her mother had said, squinting at the pack—that were now flaming red at the tips, like little cups of green fire.

"That's what I love about this place," she said. "This wonderful stretch of garden."

"Yes," said Margaret, carefully.

"John. Divorce! Now," shouted Hazel, and he finally brought the laughing children to the tableside.

The baby didn't cry when she shouted. That was something she hadn't known, that the baby didn't actually mind shouting. Or maybe he just didn't mind her shouting.

Still, it was an advance.

"Who wants ham?" Hazel said to the kids; loading it on to the bread, helping out.

"I don't like ham," said Stephanie, who was nearly four.

"No?"

"No, I don't like it."

"I don't like ham." They were all saying it now, the big brother and the little brother. "I don't like ham." It was all a bit intense, Hazel thought, and accusatory.

"I think you are confusing me with someone who gives a fuck," she said—changing at the last moment, of course, to, "Someone who cares whether, or not, you like ham."

John gave her a quick glance. The child, Stephanie, gazed at her with blank and sophisticated eyes.

"Maybe a little bit of ham?" said Hazel.

"I don't think so," said Stephanie.

"Right."

John picked an apple out of the pile on the table.

"A is for?" he said, holding it high.

"Answer," said Stephanie. "A is for A-A-Answer," and the children laughed, even though they didn't quite know what the joke was. They laughed on and on, and then they laughed at the sound of their own laughter, for a little while more.

"How do you spell 'wrong'?" said Kenneth, the eldest.

"W-R-O-N-G," said Hazel.

"W is for Wrong," he said. "W is for Wrong Answer," and they were off again; this amazing, endless, senseless sound—and this time the baby joined in, too.

He was asleep before they reached the hotel. The weather had changed and they carried him through a wind-whipped car park that did not even make him stir. Nor did he wake up in the room, when Hazel prised him out of the car seat—so she lay him on the bed as he was, profoundly asleep, in a dirty nappy and milk-encrusted babygro.

"He'll wake up in a minute," she said. "He needs a feed." But he still didn't wake up: not for his feed, not when John went down to the bar for drinks. He slept through the remains of a film on the telly and another round of drinks, and he slept through the sound of his parents screaming at each other from either side of the bed where he lay. It blew up from nowhere.

"And you can tell your fucking sister that I don't want her fucking house."

"No one says you want it."

"Jesus, sometimes I think you're just pretending to be thick and sometimes I think you actually are thick. You can't talk about the carpets without her thinking what you'd put down on the floors if you got her out of there when the old man died."

"Oh, you are," he said, with his voice quite trembly. "Oh, you really are . . ."

"You fucking bet I am."

"No, well done. Well done."

"Oh, shut up."

"Carpet, is it? I thought you were talking about my father."

"Whatever."

"I thought you were talking about my father, there, for a minute."

"Well, I am not talking about your father. That is exactly what I am not talking about. You are the one who is talking about your father. Actually. Or not talking about him. Or whatever passes in your fucking family for talking."

"You are such an uppity cunt, you know that?"

"Yes, I am. Yes, I fucking am. And I don't want your fat sister's fat house."

"Well, actually, it's not her house."

"Actually, if you don't mind, I don't want to talk about whose house it is. We can get our own house."

"We have our own house."

"A proper fucking house!!!"

Hazel was so angry she thought she might pop something, or have some style of a prolapse; her body, after the baby, being a much less reliable place. Meanwhile, the reason they needed a house in the first place slept on. His blissful flesh rose and fell. His mouth smiled.

The baby slept like he knew just what he was doing. The baby slept like he was eating sleep; his front stiff with old food and his back soft with shit. He slept through the roaring and the thrown hairbrush, and the storming of his father off to the residents' bar. He slept through the return of his father twenty seconds later to say something very level and very telling, and the double-fisted assault as his mother pushed him back out to the corridor crying that he could sleep in the fucking bar. He slept through his mother's anguished weeping, the roar of the taps, and the sad slosh and drip of her body shifting in the bath. It was, in fact, only when Hazel had fallen asleep, crawling for a moment in under the covers, that the baby decided to wake up and scream. Maybe it was the silence that woke him. Mind you, his screaming sounded the same as every other night's screaming, she thought, so it was impossible to know how much he had been damaged by it all; by the total collapse of the love that made him. Could anger hurt him, when he had never heard it before?

Hazel plugged his roars with the bottle that was still floating, forgotten, in the hotel kettle. She undid the poppers on his babygro, as he sucked, and extracted him from it, one limb at a time. She reached between his soft legs to undo the poppers of his vest, which had a wet brown stain across the back, and she rolled the vest carefully under itself to keep the shit on the inside. When the vest was finally off, she pushed two baby wipes down into the nappy to stop the leak. All of this while the baby sat in her naked lap, with her left hand propping up the bottle and his eyes on hers.

The baby was huge. Maybe it was because she had no clothes on, but he seemed twice as big as the last time she had him in her arms. Hazel felt like she kept losing this baby, and getting someone new. She thought that she would fall in love with the baby if only it would stay still, just for a minute, but the baby never did stay still. Sometimes it seemed like it was all around her, as though there was nothing in her world except the baby, but every time she looked straight at the baby, or tried to look straight at the baby . . . whatever it was, just wasn't there.

She was looking at him now.

But she still clung to it, whatever it was. She still hoped and hung on. Was this enough? Was this the way you loved a baby?

The line of milk pulsed and bubbled as it sank down into the teat, and the baby started to suck air. Hazel pulled the empty bottle out with a pop and set him on her shoulder, holding him with her forearms now, because she thought there might be shit on her hands.

The baby was full, his belly taut. She would get some wind out of him, and then clean up. Meanwhile, the feel of his bare skin against her own made Hazel vague with pleasure. She brushed her cheek against his fine hair, and the baby belched fantastically down the skin of her back.

"Oh! so clever," she said, dipping and turning around. "Oh! so clever," dipping and turning back again. She did it a few more times, just to get the weight and poise of it, with the fat baby against her fat chest, and her crossed hands dangling beneath his bum. Dip and turn, dip and turn. The baby's cheek a millimetre away from her own cheek—a hair's breadth, that is what that was called. A hair's breath.

Outside, the wind had picked up.

Rock a bye baby, she sang in a whisper, On the tree top.

She was nearly out of wipes. She did not have the courage to put him in a slippery bath. She would dunk a hotel towel in the sink and use that, no matter who had to pick it up, or use it afterwards. God, this baby business brought you very low, she thought, and turned with a smile to the opening door.

They were shattered when they got home.

John drove as though the road could feel his tyres; the tyres could feel the road. The whole world seemed as tender as they were. At Monasterevin, he reached his hand to touch her cheek, and she held it there with the flat of her own hand while, in the back of the car, the baby still slept.

When they pulled into the driveway, Hazel saw that her tulips had been blown down—at least, the ones that had opened first. She wondered if the storm had hit here too, and how strong was that wind anyway—was it a usual sort of wind? What would she be able to grow, here? She tried to think of a number she could ring, or a site online, but there was nowhere she could find out what she needed to know. It was all about tomorrow: warm fronts, cold snaps, showers expected. No one ever stopped to describe yesterday's weather.

1989

Sherman Alexie

b. 1966

Sherman Alexie has both defied expectations and created monumental ones. Born into an alcoholic family on the Spokane reservation near Seattle, he was diagnosed with hydrocephalus and after surgery was expected to be severely disabled. Instead, he vaulted through his adolescence at a white high school, then attended Washington State University, and soon after graduation began to publish at a great rate the poems and stories that have made him one of the most fascinating young writers in contemporary America. *The Lone Ranger and Tonto Fistfight in Heaven* (1993) was shortlisted for a PEN/Hemingway award; the story included here became the basis for the film *Smoke Signals* (1998), which Alexie co-produced and scripted. Since then he has published the unnervingly violent *Indian Killer* (1996) and *The Toughest Indian in the World* (2000). Ambitious both for himself and for his community, Alexie seems immune to modesty or detachment. "I'm a good writer who may be a great writer one day," he has pronounced, and has encountered little disagreement. He is very much attuned to current media, recognizes the power of the rock star and the film screen, and has perfected a comic, speedy performance manner that is both passionate and political. "I'm not trying to speak for everybody. I'm one individual heavily influenced by my tribe. And good art doesn't come out of assimilation—it comes out of tribalism." Among his other triumphs, in 1998 Alexie wrested the annual World Championship Poetry title away from Albuquerque writer Jimmy Santiago Baca.

This Is What It Means to Say Phoenix, Arizona

Just after Victor lost his job at the Bureau of Indian Affairs, he also found out that his father had died of a heart attack in Phoenix, Arizona. Victor hadn't seen his father in a few years, had only talked to him on the telephone once or twice, but there still was a genetic pain, which was as real and immediate as a broken bone. Victor didn't have any money. Who does have money on a reservation, except the cigarette and fireworks salespeople? His father had a savings account waiting to be claimed, but Victor needed to find a way to get from Spokane to Phoenix. Victor's mother was just as poor as he was, and the rest of his family didn't have any use at all for him. So Victor called the tribal council.

"Listen," Victor said. "My father just died. I need some money to get to Phoenix to make arrangements."

"Now, Victor," the council said, "you know we're having a difficult time financially."

"But I thought the council had special funds set aside for stuff like this."

"Now, Victor, we do have some money available for the proper return of tribal members' bodies. But I don't think we have enough to bring your father all the way back from Phoenix."

"Well," Victor said. "It ain't going to cost all that much. He had to be cremated. Things were kind of ugly. He died of a heart attack in his trailer and nobody found him for a week. It was really hot, too. You get the picture."

"Now, Victor, we're sorry for your loss and the circumstances. But we can really only afford to give you one hundred dollars."

"That's not even enough for a plane ticket."

"Well, you might consider driving down to Phoenix."

"I don't have a car. Besides, I was going to drive my father's pickup back up here."

"Now, Victor," the council said, "we're sure there is somebody who could drive you to Phoenix. Or could anybody lend you the rest of the money?"

"You know there ain't nobody around with that kind of money."

"Well, we're sorry, Victor, but that's the best we can do."

Victor accepted the tribal council's offer. What else could he do? So he signed the proper papers, picked up his cheque, and walked over to the Trading Post to cash it.

While Victor stood in line, he watched Thomas Builds-the-Fire standing near the magazine rack talking to himself. Like he always did. Thomas was a storyteller whom nobody wanted to listen to. That's like being a dentist in a town where everybody has false teeth.

Victor and Thomas Builds-the-Fire were the same age, had grown up and played in the dirt together. Ever since Victor could remember, it was Thomas who had always had something to say.

Once, when they were seven years old, when Victor's father still lived with the family, Thomas closed his eyes and told Victor this story: "Your father's heart is weak. He is afraid of his own family. He is afraid of you. Late at night, he sits in the dark. Watches the television until there's nothing but that white noise. Sometimes he feels like he wants to buy a motorcycle and ride away. He wants to run and hide. He doesn't want to be found."

Thomas Builds-the-Fire had known that Victor's father was going to leave, known it before anyone. Now Victor stood in the Trading Post with a one-hundred-dollar cheque in his hand, wondering if Thomas knew that Victor's father was dead, if he knew what was going to happen next.

Just then, Thomas looked at Victor, smiled, and walked over to him.

"Victor, I'm sorry about your father," Thomas said.

"How did you know about it?" Victor asked.

"I heard it on the wind. I heard it from the birds. I felt it in the sunlight. Also, your mother was just in here crying."

"Oh," Victor said and looked around the Trading Post. All the other Indians stared, surprised that Victor was even talking to Thomas. Nobody talked to Thomas anymore because he told the same damn stories over and over again. Victor was embarrassed, but he thought that Thomas might be able to help him. Victor felt a sudden need for tradition.

"I can lend you the money you need," Thomas said suddenly. "But you have to take me with you."

"I can't take your money," Victor said. "I mean, I haven't hardly talked to you in years. We're not really friends anymore.

"I didn't say we were friends. I said you had to take me with you."

"Let me think about it."

Victor went home with his one hundred dollars and sat at the kitchen table. He held his head in his hands and thought about Thomas Builds-the-Fire, remembered little details, tears and scars, the bicycle they shared for a summer, so many stories.

Thomas Builds-the-Fire sat on the bicycle, waiting in Victor's yard. He was ten years old and skinny. His hair was dirty because it was the Fourth of July.

"Victor," Thomas yelled. "Hurry up. We're going to miss the fireworks."

After a few minutes, Victor ran out of his family's house, vaulted over the porch railing, and landed gracefully on the sidewalk.

Thomas gave him the bike and they headed for the fireworks. It was nearly dark and the fireworks were about to start.

"You know," Thomas said, "it's strange how us Indians celebrate the Fourth of July. It ain't like it was our independence everybody was fighting for."

"You think about things too much," Victor said. "It's just supposed to be fun. Maybe Junior will be there."

"Which Junior? Everybody on this reservation is named Junior."

The fireworks were small, hardly more than a few bottle rockets and a fountain. But it was enough for two Indian boys. Years later, they would need much more.

Afterward, sitting in the dark, fighting off mosquitoes, Victor turned to Thomas Builds-the-Fire.

"Hey," Victor said. "Tell me a story."

Thomas closed his eyes and told this story: "There were these two Indian boys who wanted to be warriors. But it was too late to be warriors in the old way. All the horses were gone. So the two Indian boys stole a car and drove to the city. They parked the stolen car in the front of the police station and then hitchhiked back home to the reservation. When they got back, all their friends cheered and their parents' eyes shone with pride. 'You were very brave,' everybody said to the two Indian boys. 'Very brave.' "

"Ya-hey," Victor said. "That's a good one. I wish I could be a warrior."

"Me too," Thomas said.

Victor sat at his kitchen table. He counted his one hundred dollars again and again. He knew he needed more to make it to Phoenix and back. He knew he needed Thomas Builds-the-Fire. So he put his money in his wallet and opened the front door to find Thomas on the porch.

"Ya-hey, Victor," Thomas said. "I knew you'd call me."

Thomas walked into the living room and sat down in Victor's favorite chair.

"I've got some money saved up," Thomas said. "It's enough to get us down there, but you have to get us back."

"I've got this hundred dollars," Victor said. "And my dad had a savings account I'm going to claim."

"How much in your dad's account?"

"Enough. A few hundred."

"Sounds good. When we leaving?"

When they were fifteen and had long since stopped being friends, Victor and Thomas got into a fistfight. That is, Victor was really drunk and beat Thomas up for no reason at all. All the other Indian boys stood around and watched it happen. Junior was there and so were Lester, Seymour, and a lot of others.

The beating might have gone on until Thomas was dead if Norma Many Horses hadn't come along and stopped it.

"Hey, you boys," Norma yelled and jumped out of her car. "Leave him alone."

If it had been someone else, even another man, the Indians boys would've just ignored the warnings. But Norma was a warrior. She was powerful. She could have picked up any two of the boys and smashed their skulls together. But worse than that, she would have dragged them all over to some tepee and made them listen to some elder tell a dusty old story.

The Indian boys scattered, and Norma walked over to Thomas and picked him up.

"Hey, little man, are you OK?" she asked.

Thomas gave her a thumbs-up.

"Why they always picking on you?"

Thomas shook his head, closed his eyes, but no stories came to him, no words or music. He just wanted to go home, to lie in his bed and let his dreams tell the stories for him.

Thomas Builds-the-Fire and Victor sat next to each other in the airplane coach section. A tiny white woman had the window seat. She was busy twisting her body into pretzels. She was flexible.

"I have to ask," Thomas said, and Victor closed his eyes in embarrassment.

"Don't," Victor said.

"Excuse me, miss," Thomas asked. "Are you a gymnast or something?"

"There's no something about it," she said. "I was first alternate on the 1980 Olympic team."

"Really?" Thomas asked.

"Really."

"I mean, you used to be a world-class athlete?" Thomas asked.

"My husband thinks I still am."

Thomas Builds-the-Fire smiled. She was a mental gymnast too. She pulled her leg straight up against her body so that she could've kissed her kneecap.

"I wish I could do that," Thomas said.

Victor was ready to jump out of the plane. Thomas, that crazy Indian storyteller with ratty old braids and broken teeth, was flirting with a beautiful Olympic gymnast. Nobody back home on the reservation would ever believe it.

"Well," the gymnast said. "It's easy. Try it."

Thomas grabbed at his leg and tried to pull it up into the same position as the gymnast's. He couldn't even come close, which made Victor and the gymnast laugh.

"Hey," she asked. "You two are Indian, right?"

"Full-blood," Victor said.

"Not me," Thomas said. "I'm half magician on my mother's side and half clown on my father's."

They all laughed.

"What are your names?" she asked.

"Victor and Thomas."

"Mine is Cathy. Pleased to meet you all."

The three of them talked for the duration of the flight. Cathy the gymnast complained about the government, how they screwed the 1980 Olympic team by boycotting the games.

"Sounds like you all got a lot in common with Indians," Thomas said.

Nobody laughed.

After the plane landed in Phoenix and they had found their way to the terminal, Cathy the gymnast smiled and waved goodbye.

"She was really nice," Thomas said.

"Yeah, but everybody talks to everybody on airplanes," Victor said.

"You always used to tell me I think too much," Thomas said. "Now it sounds like you do."

"Maybe I caught it from you."

"Yeah."

Thomas and Victor rode in a taxi to the trailer where Victor's father had died.

"Listen," Victor said as they stopped in front of the trailer. "I never told you I was sorry for beating you up that time."

"Oh, it was nothing. We were just kids and you were drunk."

"Yeah, but I'm sorry."

"That's all right."

Victor paid for the taxi, and the two of them stood in the hot Phoenix summer. They could smell the trailer.

"This ain't going to be nice," Victor said. "You don't have to go in."

"You're going to need help."

Victor walked to the front and opened it. The stink rolled out and made them both gag. Victor's father had lain in that trailer for a week in hundred-degree temperatures before anyone had found him. And the only reason anyone found him was the smell. They needed dental records to identify him. That's exactly what the coroner said. They needed dental records.

"Oh, man," Victor said. "I don't know if I can do this."

"Well, then don't."

"But there might be something valuable in there."

"I thought his money was in the bank."

"It is. I was talking about pictures and letters and stuff like that."

"Oh," Thomas said as he held his breath and followed Victor into the trailer.

⊸○⊷

When Victor was twelve, he stepped into an underground wasps' nest. His foot was caught in the hole and no matter how hard he struggled, Victor couldn't pull free. He might have died there, stung a thousand times, if Thomas Builds-the-Fire had not come by.

"Run," Thomas yelled and pulled Victor's foot from the hole. They ran then, hard as they ever had, faster than Billy Mills, faster than Jim Thorpe, faster than the wasps could fly.

Victor and Thomas ran until they couldn't breathe, ran until it was cold and dark outside, ran until they were lost and it took hours to find their way home. All the way back, Victor counted his stings.

"Seven," Victor said. "My lucky number."

Victor didn't find much to keep in the trailer. Only a photo album and stereo. Everything else had that smell stuck in it or was useless anyway. "I guess this is all," Victor said. "It ain't much."

"Better than nothing," Thomas said.

"Yeah, and I do have the pickup."

"Yeah," Thomas said. "It's in good shape."

"Dad was good about that stuff."

"Yeah, I remember your dad."

"Really?" Victor asked. "What do you remember?"

Thomas Builds-the-Fire closed his eyes and told this story: "I remember when I had this dream that told me to go to Spokane, to stand by the falls in the middle of the city and wait for a sign. I knew I had to go there but I didn't have a car. Didn't have a license. I was only thirteen. So I walked all the way, took me all day, and I finally made it to the falls. I stood there for an hour waiting. Then your dad came walking up. 'What the hell are you doing here?' he asked me. I said, 'Waiting for a vision.' Then your father said, 'All you're going to get here is mugged.' So he drove me over to Denny's, bought me dinner, and then drove me home to the reservation. For a long time, I was mad because I thought my dreams had lied to me. But they hadn't. Your dad was my vision. *Take care of each other* is what my dreams were saying. *Take care of each other.*"

Victor was quiet for a long time. He searched his mind for memories of his father, found the good ones, found a few bad ones, added it all up, and smiled.

"My father never told me about finding you in Spokane," Victor said.

"He said he wouldn't tell anybody. Didn't want me to get in trouble. But he said I had to watch out for you as part of the deal."

"Really?"

"Really. Your father said you would need the help. He was right."

"That's why you came down here with me, isn't it?" Victor asked.

"I came because of your father."

Victor and Thomas climbed into the pickup, drove over to the bank, and claimed the three hundred dollars in the savings account.

Thomas Builds-the-Fire could fly.

Once, he jumped off the roof of the tribal school and flapped his arms like a crazy eagle. And he flew. For a second he hovered, suspended above all the other Indian boys, who were too smart or too scared to jump too.

"He's flying," Junior yelled, and Seymour was busy looking for the trick wires or mirrors. But it was real. As real as the dirt when Thomas lost altitude and crashed to the ground.

He broke his arm in two places.

"He broke his wing, he broke his wing, he broke his wing," all the Indian boys chanted as they ran off, flapping their wings, wishing they could fly too. They hated Thomas for his courage, his brief moment as a bird. Everybody has dreams about flying. Thomas flew.

One of his dream came true for just a second, just enough to make it real.

Victor's father, his ashes, fit in one wooden box with enough left over to fill a cardboard box.

"He always was a big man," Thomas said.

Victor carried part of his father out to the pickup, and Thomas carried the rest. They set him down carefully behind the seats, put a cowboy hat on the wooden box and a Dodgers cap on the cardboard box. That was the way it was supposed to be.

"Ready to head back home?" Victor asked.

"It's going to be a long drive."

"Yeah, take a couple days, maybe."

"We can take turns," Thomas said.

"OK," Victor said, but they didn't take turns. Victor drove for sixteen hours straight north, made it halfway up Nevada toward home before he finally pulled over.

"Hey, Thomas," Victor said. "You got to drive for a while."

"OK."

Thomas Builds-the-Fire slid behind the wheel and started off down the road. All through Nevada, Thomas and Victor had been amazed at the lack of animal life, at the absence of water, of movement.

"Where is everything?" Victor had asked more than once.

Now, when Thomas was finally driving, they saw the first animal, maybe the only animal in Nevada. It was a long-eared jackrabbit.

"Look," Victor yelled. "It's alive."

Thomas and Victor were busy congratulating themselves on their discovery when the jackrabbit darted out into the road and under the wheel of the pickup.

"Stop the goddamn car," Victor yelled, and Thomas did stop and backed the pickup to the dead jackrabbit.

"Oh, man, he's dead," Victor said as he looked at the squashed animal.

"Really dead."

"The only thing alive in this whole state and we just killed it."

"I don't know," Thomas said. "I think it was suicide."

Victor looked around the desert, sniffed the air, felt the emptiness and loneliness, and nodded his head.

"Yeah," Victor said. "It had to be suicide."

"I can't believe this," Thomas said. "You drive for a thousand miles and there ain't even any bugs smashed on the windshield. I drive for ten seconds and kill the only living thing in Nevada."

"Yeah," Victor said. "Maybe I should drive."

"Maybe you should."

Thomas Builds-the-Fire walked through the corridors of the tribal school by himself. Nobody wanted to be anywhere near him because of all those stories. Story after story.

Thomas closed his eyes and this story came to him: "We are all given one thing by which our lives are measured, one determination. Mine are the stories that can change or not change the world. It doesn't matter which, as long as I continue to tell the stories. My father, he died on Okinawa in World War II, died fighting for his country, which had tried to kill him for years. My mother, she died giving birth to me, died while I was still inside her: She pushed me out into the world with her last breath. I have no brothers or sisters. I have only my stories, which came to me before I even had the words to speak. I learned a thousand stories before I took my first thousand steps. They are all I have. It's all I can do."

Thomas Builds-the-Fire told his stories to all those who would stop and listen. He kept telling them long after people stopped listening.

Victor and Thomas made it back to the reservation just as the sun was rising. It was the beginning of a new day on earth, but the same old shit on the reservation.

"Good morning," Thomas said.

"Good morning."

The tribe was waking up, ready for work, eating breakfast, reading the newspaper, just like everybody else does. Willene LeBret was out in her garden, wearing a bathrobe. She waved when Thomas and Victor drove by.

"Crazy Indians made it," she said to herself and went back to her roses.

Victor stopped the pickup in front of Thomas Builds-the-Fire's HUD house. They both yawned, stretched a little, shook dust from their bodies.

"I'm tired," Victor said.

"Of everything," Thomas added.

They both searched for words to end the journey. Victor needed to thank Thomas for his help and for the money, and to make the promise to pay it all back.

"Don't worry about the money," Thomas said. "It don't make any difference anyhow."

"Probably not, enit?"

"Nope."

Victor knew that Thomas would remain the crazy storyteller who talked to dogs and cars, who listened to the wind and pine trees. Victor knew that he couldn't really be friends with Thomas, even after all that had happened. It was cruel but it was real. As real as the ash, as Victor's father, sitting behind the seats.

"I know how it is," Thomas said. "I know you ain't going to treat me any better than you did before. I know your friends would give you too much shit about it."

Victor was ashamed of himself. Whatever happened to the tribal ties, the sense of community? The only real thing he shared with anybody was a bottle and broken dreams. He owed Thomas something, anything.

"Listen," Victor said and handed Thomas the cardboard box that contained half of his father. "I want you to have this."

Thomas took the ashes and smiled, closed his eyes, and told this story: "I'm going to travel to Spokane Falls one last time and toss these ashes into the water. And your father will rise like a salmon, leap over the bridge, over me, and find his way home. It will be beautiful. His teeth will shine like silver, like a rainbow. He will rise, Victor, he will rise."

Victor smiled.

"I was planning on doing the same thing with my half," Victor said. "But I didn't imagine my father looking anything like a salmon. I thought it'd be like cleaning the attic or something. Like letting things go after they've stopped having any use."

"Nothing stops, cousin," Thomas said. "Nothing stops."

Thomas Builds-the-Fire got out of the pickup and walked up his driveway. Victor started the pickup and began to drive home.

"Wait," Thomas yelled suddenly from his porch. "I just got to ask one favour."

Victor stopped the pickup, leaned out the window, and shouted back.

"What do you want?" he asked.

"Just one time when I'm telling a story somewhere, why don't you stop and listen?" Thomas asked.

"Just once?"

"Just once."

Victor waved his arms to let Thomas know that the deal was good. It was a fair trade. That's all Thomas had ever wanted from his while life. So Victor drove his father's pickup toward home while Thomas went into his house, closed the door behind him, and heard a new story come to him in the silence afterward.

1993

Edwidge Danticat

b. 1969

"My own parents left Haiti to work in New York while I stayed behind. I didn't grow up in an orphanage, but I grew up in my uncle's house with a lot of kids like me, whose parents were abroad working." In 1981 she joined them in Brooklyn, the feeling of exile accentuated by the uncertainty of her English. Fifteen years later, in 1996, Danticat had a place in *Granta's The Best of Young American Novelists*. In 2009 she was awarded one of the rare MacArthur Grants in recognition of work done and faith in work to come. If anything, these acknowledgements deepened her already intricate and intimate ties with Haitian life. While still a child in Port-au-Prince and speaking Creole, she initially took on writing through the stories of her grandmothers and aunt. She created her "own little books with folded paper," and in the United States at age fourteen, wrote for high school newspapers. She studied French literature at Barnard and creative writing at Brown. Her MFA thesis there became her first novel, *Breath, Eyes, Memory* (1994), a novel, to judge from her generous interviews, that propelled the transmutation of Creole in the mysteries of her creativity: "Creole, more than French, is always behind the English I am writing. My characters are speaking in Creole and in my mind I do a simultaneous translation as I am writing." The intimacy between her writing and the layers of her private and public Haitian lives was particularly striking when, four months after the call from the MacArthur Foundation, the catastrophic earthquake occurred in Haiti.

"That money," she says quietly, "touched so many people's lives." Since then, she has been as tireless in her support of Haitian culture and political rejuvenation as she has been devoted to the many forms of her writing life. But for all their range, Danticat's short stories and the genre of the short story collection have a special appeal for her readers and, it seems, for her. "I love how that kind of freedom in narration echoes back to the old traditions of storytelling." Asked about Alice Munro's Nobel Prize, Danticat replies: "The short story is like an exquisite painting and you might, when looking at this painting, be wondering what came before or after, but you are fully absorbed in what you're seeing. Your gaze is fixed, and you're fully engaged. That's the beauty of the short story."

Between the Pool and the Gardenias

She was very pretty. Bright shiny hair and dark brown skin like mahogany cocoa. Her lips were wide and purple, like those African dolls you see in tourist store windows but could never afford to buy.

I thought she was a gift from Heaven when I saw her on the dusty curb, wrapped in a small pink blanket, a few inches away from a sewer as open as a hungry child's yawn. She was like Baby Moses in the Bible stories they read to us at the Baptist Literary Class. Or Baby Jesus, who was born in a barn and died on a cross, with nobody's lips to kiss before he went. She was just like that. Her still round face. Her eyes closed as though she was dreaming of a far other place.

Her hands were bony, and there were veins so close to the surface that it looked like you could rupture her skin if you touched her too hard. She probably belonged to someone, but the street had no one in it. There was no one there to claim her.

At first I was afraid to touch her. Lest I might disturb the early-morning sun rays streaming across her forehead. She might have been some kind of *wanga*, a charm sent to trap me. My enemies were many and crafty. The girls who slept with my husband while I was still grieving over my miscarriages. They might have sent that vision of loveliness to blind me so that I would never find my way back to the place that I yanked out my head when I got on that broken down minibus and left my village months ago.

The child was wearing an embroidered little blue dress with the letters *R-O-S-E* on a butterfly collar. She looked the way that I had imagined all my little girls would look. The ones my body could never hold. The ones that somehow got suffocated inside me and made my husband wonder if I was killing them on purpose.

I called out all the names I wanted to give them: Eveline, Josephine, Jacqueline, Hermine, Marie Magdalene, Célianne. I could give her all the clothes that I had sewn for them. All these little dresses that went unused.

At night, I could rock her alone in the hush of my room, rest her on my belly, and wish she were inside.

When I had just come to the city, I saw on Madame's television that a lot of poor city women throw out their babies because they can't afford to feed them. Back in Ville Rose you cannot even throw out the bloody crumps that shoot out of your body after your child is born. It is a crime, they say, and your whole family would consider you wicked if you did it. You have to save every piece of flesh and give it a name and bury it near the roots of a tree to that the world won't fall apart around you.

In the city, I hear they throw out whole entire children. They throw them out anywhere: on doorsteps, in garbage cans, at gas pumps, sidewalks. In the time that I had been in Port-au-Prince, I had never seen such a child until now.

But Rose. My, she was so clean and warm. Like a tiny angel, a little cherub, sleeping after the wind had blown a lullaby into her little ears.

I picked her up and pressed her cheek against mine.

I whispered to her, "Little Rose, my child," as though that name was a secret.

She was like the palatable little dolls we played with as children—mango seeds that we drew faces on and then called by our nicknames. We christened them with prayers and invited all our little boy and girls friends for colas and cassavas and—when we could get them—some nice butter cookies.

Rose didn't stir or cry. She was like something that was thrown aside after she became useless to someone cruel. When I pressed her face against my heart, she smelled like the scented powders in Madame's cabinet, the mixed scent of gardenias and fish that Madame always had on her when she stepped out of her pool.

⊰o⊱

I have always said my mother's prayers at dawn. I welcomed the years that were slowing bringing me closer to her. For no matter how much distance death tried to put between us, my mother would often come to visit me. Sometimes in the short sighs and whispers of somebody else's voice. Sometimes in somebody else's face. Other times in brief moments in my dreams.

There were many nights when I saw some old women leaning over my bed.

"That there is Marie," my mother would say. "She is now the last one of us left."

Mama had to introduce me to them, because they had all died before I was born. There was my great grandmother Eveline who was killed by Dominican soldiers at the Massacre River. My grandmother Défilé who died with a bald head in a prison, because God had given her wings. My godmother Lili who killed herself in old age because her husband had jumped out of a flying balloon and her grown son left her to go to Miami.

We all salute you Mary, Mother of God. Pray for us poor sinners, from now until the hour of death. Amen.

I always knew they would come back and claim me to do some good for somebody. Maybe I was to do some good for this child.

I carried Rose with me to the outdoor market in Croix-Bossale. I swayed her in my arms like she was and had always been mine.

In the city, even people who come from your own village don't know you or care about you. They didn't notice that I had come the day before with no child. Suddenly, I had one, and nobody asked a thing.

⊰o⊱

In the maid's room, at the house in Pétion-Ville, I laid Rose on my mat and rushed to prepare lunch. Monsieur and Madame sat on their terrace and welcomed the coming afternoon by sipping the sweet out of my sour-sop juice.

They liked that I went all the way to the market every day before dawn to get them a taste of the outside country, away from their protected bourgeois life.

"She is probably one of those *manbos*," they say when my back is turned. "She's probably one of those stupid people who think that they have to spell to make themselves invisible and hurt other people. Why can't none of them get a spell to make themselves rich? It's that voodoo nonsense that's holding us Haitians back."

I lay Rose down on the kitchen table as I dried the dishes. I had a sudden desire to explain to her my life.

"You see, young one, I loved that man at one point. He was very nice to me. He made me feel proper. The next thing I know, it's ten years with him. I'm old like a piece of dirty paper people used to wipe their behinds, and he's got ten different babies with ten different women. I just had to run."

I pretended that it was all mine. The terrace with that sight of the private pool and the holiday ships cruising in the distance. The large television system and all those French love songs and *rara* records, with the talking drums and conch shell sounds in them. The bright paintings with white winged horses and snakes as long and wide as lakes. The pool that the sweaty Dominican man cleaned three times a week. I pretended that it belonged to us: him, Rose, and me.

The Dominican and I made love on the grass once, but he never spoke to me again. Rose listened with her eyes closed even though I was telling her things that were much too strong for a child's ears.

I wrapped her around me with my apron as I fried some plantains for the evening meal. It's so easy to love somebody, I tell you, when there's nothing else around.

Her head fell back like any other infant's. I held out my hand and let her three matted braids tickle the life-lines in my hand.

"I am glad you are not one of those babies that cry all day long," I told her. "All little children should be like you. I am glad you don't cry and make a lot of noise. You're just a perfect child, aren't you?"

I put her back in my room when Monsieur and Madame came home for their supper. As soon as they went to sleep, I took her out by the pool so we could talk some more.

You don't just join a family not knowing what you're getting into. You have to know some of the history. You have to know that they pray to Erzulie, who loves men like men love her, because she's mulatto and some Haitian men seem to love her kind. You have to look into your looking glass on the day of the dead because you might see faces there that knew you even before you ever came into this world.

I fell asleep rocking her in a chair that wasn't mine. I knew she was real when I woke up the next day and she was still in my arms. She looked the same as she did when I found her. She continued to look like that for three days. After that, I had to bathe her constantly to keep down the smell.

I once had an uncle who bought pigs' intestines in Ville Rose to sell at the market in the city. Rose began to smell like the intestines after they hadn't sold for a few days.

I bathed her more and more often, sometimes three or four times a day in the pool. I used some of Madame's perfume, but it was not helping. I wanted to take her back to the street where I had found her, but I'd already disturbed her rest and had taken on her soul as my own personal responsibility.

I left her in a shack behind the house, where the Dominican kept his tools. Three times a day, I visited her with my hand over my nose. I watched her skin grow moist, cracked, and sunken in some places, then ashy and dry in others. It seemed like she had aged in four days as many years as there were between me and my dead aunts and grandmothers.

I knew I had to act with her because she was attracting flies and I was keeping her spirit from moving on.

I gave her one last bath and slipped on a little yellow dress that I had sewn while praying that one of my little girls would come along further than three months.

I took Rose down to a spot in the sun behind the big house. I dug a hole in the garden among the gardenias. I wrapped her in the little pink blanket that

I had found her in, covering everything but her face. She smelled so bad that I couldn't even bring myself to kiss her without chocking on my breath.

I felt a grip on my shoulder as I lowered her into the small hole in the ground. At first I thought it was Monsieur or Madame, and I was real afraid that Madame would be angry with me for having used a whole bottle of her perfume without asking.

Rose slipped and fell out of my hands as my body was forced to turn around.

"What are you doing?" the Dominican asked.

His face was a deep Indian brown but his hands were bleached and wrinkled from the chemicals in the pool. He looked down at the baby lying in the dust. She was already sprinkled with some soil that I had dug up.

"You see, I saw these faces standing over me in my dreams—"

I could have started my explanation in a million of ways.

"Where did you take this child from?" he asked me in his Spanish Creole.

He did not give me a chance to give my answer.

"I go already." I thought I heard a little *méringue* in the sway of his voice. "I call the gendarmes. They are coming. I smell that rotten flesh. I know you kill the child and keep it with you for evil."

"You acted too soon," I said.

"You kill the child and keep it in your room."

"You know me," I said. "We've been together."

"I don't know you from the fly on a pile of cow manure," he said. "You eat little children who haven't even had time to earn their souls."

He only kept his hands on me because he was afraid that I would run away and escape.

I looked down at Rose. In my mind I saw what I had seen for all my other girls. I imagined her teething, crawling, crying, fussing, and just misbehaving herself.

Over her little corpse, we stood, a country maid and a Spaniard grounds man. I should have asked his name before I offered him my body.

We made a pretty picture standing there. Rose, me, and him. Between the pool at the gardenias, waiting for the law.

1995

Sarah Hall

b. 1974

Born in the United Kingdom—Carlisle, in England's northern Cumbria region—Sarah Hall, who joined the *Granta Best of Young British Novelists* in 2013, studied English and Art History at Aberystwyth University in Wales. She returned north to pursue an MLitt in Creative Writing at St Andrews University. She lives in Norwich and for a spell was in North Carolina. She reports that she "quickly bailed from the world of poetry, sensibly."

But her perseverance writing short stories (novels seemed to come more handily) has and is likely to remain long term. Her study of the short story at St Andrews produced pieces that were "dreadful. I knew they were dreadful. They were squibs. They lacked shape, concentration, and metaphysics." Over fifteen years, these qualities, "shape, concentration, and metaphysics"—registered through "a gorgeously dispassionate prose" (Justine Jordan)—have become marks of her immense talent. In 2013, in the same week when Alice Munro was awarded the Nobel Prize for Literature, Hall's story "Mrs. Fox" received the BBC National Short Story Award. Although their work goes in different directions, Munro and Hall have some essential qualities in common: a deeply free inventiveness, a mastery of absences, and nerves of steel. "Disquiet," "menace," "unease" are common repetitions in readings of *The Beautiful Indifference* (2011). The Cumbrian landscape and its tribal legacies persist in Hall's imagination, which is drawn to the beautiful and frightening overlaps of human and natural—that is, non-human—worlds. Cumbria does not seem to be terribly far from a Finnish lake or an African coastal jungle, territories where, in two stories, the separations between people occur and passions become ghosts less distinct than the forest corridors and colours of the sky-reflecting waters. In "The Nightlong River," the dead "vanish from this earth and vanish from the air. What remains are moors and mountains, the solid world upon which we find ourselves, and in which we reign. We are the wolves. We are the lions." In the story included here, the protagonist, pursued through the jungle by something, feels her feet to be "narrow, hoof-like," and herself to be "all meat, all scent," which leads to an intersection of worlds lateral to the one she dreads. Reflecting on the nature of short stories, Hall has said that "the best provoke potent sensations in the reader—discomfort, arousal, exhilaration, fear." If we add to this a protean beauty tilting toward a vanishing, the description captures the power of her own work.

She Murdered Mortal He

When the fight was over she left the salon tent and walked towards the beach. The way through the jungle was signposted. It was not yet dark. She was not sure what to do. Everything was out of control. She wanted to think clearly, get her bearings. She wanted not to feel so lost, or to feel so lost that nothing more could be taken. Mostly she just wanted to leave their room. She followed the path through the bowed and necking trees. The air was heavy, greenly perfumed, and the avian calls were loud and greasy. The dust felt cool against her feet. She turned left, then right. They had walked this way earlier, after arriving in the complex, to get to the town a mile up the coast, and they'd been surprised by the sudden vertiginous drop. The jungle ended abruptly and the dunes were incredibly steep. There was no gradation. The dark canopy, with its humidity and silicone music, gave way to a long corrugated ramp, ionic sea wind, vast space—two utterly different realms. The path wove through the brush. She stooped under low branches, careful, despite the surging recklessness, where she trod, not wanting to disturb snakes coiled under the leaves.

What's wrong, she had asked him, as they lay on the bed after their trip into town, stroking his back. You seem distracted.

Nothing, he had said a few times.

But she had persisted. What? What is it?

After a while he had turned.

Something feels different, he had said. Don't you think so?

They had been together a year. He had said nothing like this before. She had knelt upright at the corner of the bed, and put her arms round herself. He had begun breathing hard, blowing out, as if what he was saying, or was about to say, was heavy labour.

Something feels wrong between us. We should talk about it.

Then, with such terrible ease, it had all begun to unravel. Their meeting at the Hallowe'en party, and his ridiculous bloody stump. Their conversation about Flaubert, the shared cigarette. The kiss, in his terrible heatless flat. The late-night texts. Their first dinner party with its triumphant co-concocted fish soup. The formative moments, winding away, as if they had never been safe.

She picked her way through the foliage, through muggy, scented chambers. Now the birds around her sounded electrical, like mobile phones. Every time she heard a melodic stammer she thought she would come upon someone talking. But there was no one on the path—the lodge was almost deserted, the other salon tents were empty. And there was no phone signal here. An occasional bar crept up on the display, then disappeared, a faint or false satellite. She stopped. All around were intimately knotted branches. The pulp inside the peeling bark was an extraordinary garish orange. There were leopards in here, they had been told by their driver—elusive, flaxen-eyed creatures that were almost never seen. Or seen too late. They were gradually coming back after years of being hunted. And the thought occurred to her, that if one of them were to take her now, powerfully by the neck, and drag her up into the crux of a tree, what then? Nothing then. She began walking again.

⊸○⊷

The tide was on the way out. She knew this even before coming upon the beach. She could hear its retreat, the sonorous hiss at the back of its throat. The trees finished. The air thinned. She saw the ocean for the second time that day, and drew a breath. How had she forgotten its scale, its grandeur? The water was a literal blue. All blues. For a moment the scene looked like one of the cheap plasticised paintings of the Mediterranean on sale in the harbours of southern Europe. But this was not the Mediterranean. This was a body of water so prodigious it looked almost solid, except for the ragged crests, the series of spraying breakers that came from far out and swept up the shore, driving sand high into the jungle. This ocean generated its own wind. It bellowed. Its inhabitants were huge breaching creatures that were of no consequence. After an aborted attempt earlier that day they had not swum. Even knee-deep the undertow had been too strong, dragging their feet down into trenches, making them flap their arms, squat forward and wade against the pull.

The holiday had been her idea. She had read an article in the travel section of the *Guardian*. The writer had urged people to come before the character of the place changed irreversibly. She'd pitched the idea, of being more intrepid, of a different kind of trip, and after a week or two he'd agreed. They had left the hire car at the South African border and been brought to the tiny, fledgling resort in an old white Land Rover with an insecure driver's door that kept swinging open. The driver's name was Breck. He was from Richards Bay, but had come north because the opportunities for new tourism were exciting. He taught scuba and arranged whale-watching during migration season. As he drove down the unmade roads he waved to the women carrying canisters and baskets on their hips and heads, and to the children. There were children everywhere. When they passed a man with no hands sitting on an oil drum he said, Look. Long sleeves, I reckon. He's from Zimbabwe. A few have come here. It used to be the other way round. What do you do? he'd asked them.

I'm a lawyer.

Ah. Right. Clever guy. And you?

I manage a company that arranges ghost tours.

Oh, what, to see ghosts?

Places where people have seen ghosts, in London. There are lots of places.

But not the ghosts?

No.

That's good. Then they can't ask for their money back.

Not really, no.

Though an American woman had fainted in Whitechapel the previous week and had made an official complaint. She had not realised the tour would include spots where victims of the Ripper had been found, she said. She just wanted to see queens and princes. Breck had worked hard to sell the area to them, playing up the economic recovery, making claims about the restoration of wildlife.

The transit vehicle needed to be booked in advance. The border checkpoint closed at 5 p.m. Though she did not want to stay at the lodge that night, though she could not face seeing him after what had been said, or half said, her window to leave was gone.

She waded down the steep sand bank, leaning back, sinking up to her calves. The beach levelled off and she began to walk towards the headland with the cliff path that could be taken into town. Crabs were working the tideline, scissoring pieces of blue jellyfish, dragging the dissections backwards into their burrows. The sun was setting on the other side of the dunes. She could not see any red display, just a dull luminescence above the treetops. She turned and looked behind. The beach was misty with spray and deserted, a long alluvial corridor. He was not following. He would not follow; she knew that. She had refused to let him comfort her after she'd begun crying. He would adhere to this preference, even if she did not.

She continued on. She replayed the argument in her head, accurately or inaccurately; it did not matter. By the end of the conversation a reptilian dullness had crept into his eyes. It was as if he was persuading himself of his own point of view, of mutual failure.

I used to think you were strange and amazing, he had said. But I wonder how much we have in common. We seem to want different things. Why are we here?

She had stopped crying now, and did not feel sick with panic any more. She felt tender and very alert, as if having risen from a fever, as if driving a new body.

There was the reek of kelp all about. Though she was profoundly alone, she felt self-conscious. Observed. To her left, at the top of the rise, the jungle was greenish-brown, oily and complicated, immune to the salt air. It was like a mouth, or many mouths, spitting out the sand that it was relentlessly fed. Now that she was looking up at it, the entity seemed superior to the ocean. The uppermost branches shifted and rustled. Nothing flew above. Nothing flitted in or out. Everything inside was hidden. What was he doing back in their room, she wondered. Repacking his bag, perhaps? Reading a book? Or maybe he was asleep; oblivious to everything, making use of that shut-off mechanism men could rely upon in such situations.

She walked on. The ocean wind was strong. Grains of airborne sand stung her arms and face. Her dress fluttered. Perhaps he was right. Perhaps they were not in step. Why had she wanted to come here, to a place like this, with its memory of recent troubles? Sub-Saharan gothic, he had joked, a busman's holiday. He had booked two weeks off work, which meant handing an important case over to a colleague. They had flown into Johannesburg, visited a few game parks, photographed giraffe and zebra, then come north. They had arrived at midday and the staff had been friendly. The receptionist had kissed them both three times. They had lain on towels and applied sun-lotion, and had eaten lunch in a cafe in town. They had talked about going up to the ruined lighthouse on the highest dune to see the sunset. But the sense of this being a holiday was somehow absent. There were still signs of the war—abandoned farms, ruins. Now, separate from him, any meaningful frame for being here was gone. She was anomic. The sand was difficult to tread. Her ankle kept turning. She began to feel foolish.

After a while she turned and looked behind again. There was a white form a few hundred metres back down the beach, where the path to the lodge began His white linen shirt. Briefly, a sense of elation possessed her. He was looking for her, which meant he was worried. It meant a reversal, perhaps. Should she wait for him or walk on and let him make up the distance? Should she make it easy? She lingered a moment. No. This was his doing. He had instigated their division. He would have to catch up with her. She turned and walked on, not with haste, but purposefully, her steps widening over the dry reefs, the flats of her sandals slapping the soles of her feet. Crabs scattered towards the water. She went about thirty paces. Then she slowed. Perhaps he would not see her so far away. Her dress was pale; she might be indistinguishable against the sand. And she did want to be seen, didn't she? She paused, looked behind again. The white shape was in the same position, perhaps a little closer. She squinted. The surf was creating an illusory fog; the light was thickening. It was difficult to gain focus. She bridged her hands over her eyes.

The shape was low to the ground, and was not particularly large, not elongated like a man. It was not him. Her disappointment was simply confirmation. She knew he would not come. Still, she was annoyed to have hoped, to have permitted the minor fantasy. The white object was not large, but it was too big to be a seabird. Something mid-sized, then. It was definitely moving; it had velocity, a gait, but she could not tell in which direction it was heading, towards her or away. She peered along the corridor of sand. Towards her. It was coming towards her. She could make out a rocking motion, forwards and backwards, side to side. A creature loping, or running. A spark of alarm fired across her chest. Suddenly there was no air to breathe, though the beach was a cathedral of air. She stood still, lifted a hand to her mouth. A creature running towards her. A creature running towards her. She couldn't move, couldn't make a clear assessment.

There were many dangers here; all outlined in the literature she had received from her health centre. Since arriving on the continent she had retained a prudent fear of the environment. The disease. The bacteria. The wildlife. Not all of it could be washed away, contained, or immunised against. On the way to one of the game parks they had passed an iron-roofed clinic. Outside there had been a long queue of patients. A white doctor was leaning against the clinic wall taking enormous rushed bites out of a sandwich. On the road to the border the traffic had suddenly stopped. After a minute or two the cars ahead had pulled away and driven on, cautiously. A rhino was on the carriageway. It was grazing unspectacularly on the verge as they crawled past. Its plated torso was earth-coloured. Its eye was a tiny dark recess. Twenty miles later they had passed a woman in the middle of the road, waving her arms up and down. Then they'd seen the body, splayed, folded over itself, made boneless by the impact. A young man, walking to work, perhaps. The debris of his briefcase lay in the oncoming lane.

It was everywhere, close to the surface, or rupturing through.

She turned and walked on, quicker than before. She lengthened her stride. Whatever was behind her might simply have strayed onto the beach, and would cut up into the brush again, leaving her alone. If it was following without motive, or through curiosity, she could probably make it to the headland pass before it came too close. Just walk, she thought. Walk. Don't run.

The drifts were hard going. The dry crust seemed to support her whole weight for a moment then became slack and collapsed and her heels submerged. Sand worked its way between her toes. She walked closer to the shoreline, where the ground was firmer and less abrasive, but still her feet seemed poorly designed for the task. They were narrow, hoof-like. Her shins ached. The glow on the other side of the trees was fading. Soon even the dusk light would be extinguished. There were no long twilights like at home. Here the shift came swiftly. She walked on. The crabs scuttled away as she approached, or circled about her feet, their claws held aloft. She did not want to look behind again. Nor did she want to imagine what was there. The latter option was worse. The dress she was wearing was low-backed. Her flesh felt exposed. She was all meat, all scent. Had whatever it was gained? Had it materialised properly? A thing born from the jungle: acute and mindless in its predation, glistening-jawed. Her nails dug into her palms as she paced. It might be a breath away from her. Or it might be gone. Turn, she thought. Turn now.

She stopped and turned and the white shape was coming faster, on all fours. A clean bolt of panic struck against her sternum. She wheeled round. Not far ahead volcanic cliffs rose and an uneven stage of rocks began. She began to run; heavy, stumbling steps. It would be the only way she could make the headland, so she could clamber up to a higher, safer place. But it was like running in a dream. The turgid ground, the dreadful incapacity. She pulled herself forward. She fought the sand. Her thighs burnt, began to seize. Stop, she thought. You have to stop. Showing fear means accepting you are prey. She stopped. She turned and looked back.

It was a dog. A big white dog was coming after her; paws skimming the sand, head held low. It was tracking her. It was engaged in the act, but not at full speed, not in pursuit. She drew herself in, filled her lungs. OK. A dog. A dog was not the worst possibility, even if wild. She'd had the shots, painfully and expensively in the upper arm, there was still a hard lump under the surface, as if a coin had been inserted. And she could recall no reports in the news of tourists set upon and killed by dogs; such a thing must be uncommon. It was war or malaria or road accidents that spawned tragedy. Though she could recall now, luridly, and out of nowhere, the face of that little girl from the north-east, from Sunderland, who had been mauled by the family bull terrier earlier in the year. She could recall her face and neck in the photographs: a grotesque map of welts, flaps and bruises, crescents of black stitches. Then the later pictures: her skull bone grafted over, her nose rebuilt, less striking, surgical disfigurements.

She put her shoulders back, stood her ground, waited for the thing to catch up. When it was within close range the dog lifted its head and veered to the side, then came into line with her, higher up on the ramp of sand. It stopped. The dog looked down at her. Its eyes were dark, bright. Big paws. It was part Labrador, perhaps, blunt-headed, its fur dirty. There was no collar. Its tongue spooned from its jaw. It looked at her. Its eyes were very, very bright. Under the muddy coat was a distended belly and long black teats. It did not appear emaciated.

She was not usually afraid of dogs. She had had a dog as a child.

Come here, she said Come. Come here.

The dog dropped its head and came and stood next to her, its warm body pressing against her leg. She put out a hand and let it sniff between her fingers, then she stroked its head, carefully. The fur was damp and gummy. There were lumps on the ears. A stray. But it had once been tame, and it was still tame. Not wild. Not rabid. Biddable. The relief was like stepping into a warm bath. Something within her let go. Her muscles relaxed. She began crying again, though gently, not as she had after the fight. The dog nudged her hand with its head. She petted the dog with the tips of her fingers, combing the sticky fur. It continued to lean warmly against her leg. After a minute she wiped her eyes and walked on again. The dog held back for a moment then followed and fell in beside her.

You gave me a scare, she said. Listen, I'm not going to keep you.

She continued down the beach with the dog as her companion. She walked slowly. Now and then the dog brushed past and went ahead, then came back to her side. A couple of times it chased after crabs, bounding towards them, knocking clods of wet sand up with its paws and snapping at the angry, fencing creatures. Then it came to her side again, as if demonstrating obedience.

You know where you're going? she asked. Well, you seem to.

She watched the dog. It was nice to watch. It moved deliberately, in accordance with its proclivities. It sniffed seaweed and chased crabs. Then it wanted to be at her side. For no real reason its presence made her feel better. At the headland rocks they both paused and then picked their way along the puddled outcrop. There were pools the shape of hexagons, strange geological structures. At the edge of the headland the ocean washed over them. As they began to round the cliff, the jungle disappeared from sight. The dog stepped through the shallower pools. It lapped some of the water.

Hey, don't drink that.

She thought perhaps the dog would not come up the cliff path but as she began the ascent it followed, bounding up off its back legs onto the boulders. It squeezed past her where the path was almost too narrow for them both, then wanted to lead. The dog trotted ahead confidently, piloting. Perhaps it belonged to someone in the town, she thought, and had just ranged out. In places she had to bend and scrape through bushes. She brushed her shoulders down afterwards, shook out her dress. The rock was volcanic, sculpted into minuscule peaks. Not far below the ocean hawked in and out of eroded gullies. With the sun off it, the water was no longer the intense blue, but colourless.

It took five minutes to round the headland, and then the settlement came into view, the green-roofed cabins on stilts, thatched huts, the seafood bar, and the little blue Portuguese church with its naïve Madonna painted on the gable, her figure and head undulating like an expressionist portrait. There were steps carved into the rocks. She walked down them with the dog and walked along the bay to the launching stage, past a few fishermen who nodded at her, and when she arrived at the edge of the town she stopped.

OK. Go home, she said to the dog. Go on.

The dog sat and faced her. Its teats hung from its black belly. Its claws were long and curved and the webs between looked sore. It cocked its head and looked as if it did not understand the command, or as if she might issue another, preferable instruction. In the failing light its eyes were huge. She made her tone firmer.

Go home. Go. Home.

She clapped her hands in front of its face. The dog got to its feet but did not move. She turned her back and walked away. She glanced back. The dog was not following. It was standing in the same spot on the beach, its ears knuckled upwards, watching her. She continued to walk. When she looked back properly the dog was trotting down to the edge of the water, chasing crabs again.

—o—

She did not really know what she was doing, coming into the town. Acting out of anger, but her anger had ebbed now. Though she knew it was relatively safe—Breck, the driver, had vouched for that—she was nervous. She did not want to go back yet. She could not bear the idea of taking up where they had left off. She could not bear seeing him in an altered state, unmoved by her, his eyes blank. She wanted to sit and have a drink, sit and think. She had to get her mind round the situation, had to assimilate it. She'd probably be able to get a ride back to the lodge complex later; locals seemed amenable to casual work. Or she could walk back along the beach. It would be a clear night by the look of the sky. Let him wonder where she had gone. Let him think about things too, what it was he had said, or tried to say, what it was he might be giving up. He was as trapped here as she was, at least until tomorrow when the Land Rover could be booked. If there was a lover he had not yet admitted to—and she had asked, she had demanded to know—he would not be able to reach her by phone to say, yes, he had begun to break things off. No more than she could reach a friend, or member of her family, to be consoled.

She still did not really understand what was going on. He had said nothing about feeling unhappy previously. Why had she asked him, again and again, what was wrong, instead of taking a nap with him on the bed before dinner? Had her asking created a situation that would not otherwise have existed? If she had not asked him, if she had rested her cheek on his back and her hand on his stomach, and had slept for an hour against his side, would the argument never have taken place? Would they still be together? They had had sex that morning, in a different bed, in a game lodge further south. The sex had been good; he had initiated it, and when she had taken him into her mouth he had said her name with surprise, as if at a loss, as if helpless, and he had been desperate to be inside her and they had both moved well, automatically, uniformly, and when she had come he had too. He had seemed moved, looking down at her. Did he know then that later in the day he would be saying such damaging things?

What about this morning, she had said during the argument. You felt something for me then, didn't you?

Yes, he said, something. But that's unfair. It's different. Sex is not rational.

They had bickered on the drive up, about nothing important, when to make a rest-stop, whether to buy more bottled water. They had disagreed about whether tourism was a good or bad thing for countries such as this. But the true argument had seemingly come out of nowhere. As if with her arch invitation to speak his mind, she had conjured from a void the means to destroy everything. As if he had suddenly decided it could end. Like deciding he wanted her phone number. Like deciding to get a spare door key cut for her. How easily inverted the world could be. How dual it was.

She made her way along the dirt road towards the cafe. Lights outside the bars were coming on. The evening was still warm. People were sitting drinking beer on the concrete groyne. Three surfers were loading their boards into rusting pick-up trucks. There were locals still trying to sell cashews and carvings. The last of the vendors watched her as she passed by but did not approach. Earlier that day they had made good pitches to them both as they lay on towels reading.

Buy these nuts; they are delicious. Just try one for free and then decide.

Perhaps they could witness the recent distress in her, like looking at a dishevelled tract of land a storm has lately passed through. She walked past the oil drum where the handless man had been sitting. She went into the cafe that they had been in earlier, feeling safer for the vague familiarity. She sat at an empty table and the same waiter approached her, a young man, in his twenties, wearing a yellow and green T-shirt.

Hello again.

Hello.

He greeted her pleasantly, but she could see that he was confused. He kept looking at the door. This was not a resort, if it could yet be called a resort—locked in by sand roads, and visited by only a few dozen tourists a week—where a woman would drink alone. She had three hundred rand in the pocket of her dress. She ordered a beer. The waiter nodded and went to the refrigerator and brought one over. He set it down on the table with great care, positioning a glass next to the bottle. She thanked him.

Obrigada.

And to eat?

She shook her head. He nodded and withdrew.

She sipped the beer. She thought about him, and what her life might be like without him. They lived in the same city and saw each other regularly, socialised with each other's friends. Most nights they spent together. They had taken a few trips. This was the most exotic—a twelve-hour flight, prophylaxis and rehydration tablets. They had been getting along fine, she thought. She tried to find any recent tells. Perhaps he had been moody these past few weeks, a little indifferent, stressed at work. He had been curt with her when she said, again, that she wanted to change jobs, that the tours were not what she really wanted to do. But nothing had seemed worrying. She was thirty-one. The thought of going back out, on dates, to parties and clubs, looking for someone, having to generate that intellectual and sexual optimism, made her feel tired. She remembered their first night together. He had taken her for a walk in the park by his house, and out for dinner. They had undressed in the living room of his cold flat and had moved to the bedroom only when his flatmate's door had opened. They had barely slept. They were astonished by each other. The next day they had eaten a late breakfast, gone to the cinema, and come back to the flat to collect her necklace. They had had sex again, better, quick and inconsiderate, her underwear taken off, her skirt left on, and then she had gone to work. She had felt extreme happiness. There had been nothing to lose.

She finished the beer and ordered another. The waiter's politeness increased as he took her order. She knew she was making him nervous. But she wanted the anaesthesia, the insulation. She wanted to go back and not to care about losing him. Part of her thought she should stay out, stubbornly, sleep on the beach, or try to make other arrangements, but she did not have the resolve. She had been gone a few hours; that was enough. If it was over, it was over. She took a few more sips, then pushed the bottle away. She put the rand on the table and stood and left the bar.

OK, the waiter called after her. OK. OK, now.

She felt soft at the edges as she moved, and lesser. Outside the sky was dark, full of different stars. The world seemed overturned but balanced.

A few men called out to her as she walked back towards the beach, not in a threatening way. She did not understand the language and it did not matter what they said. The worst had already happened tonight. In a way she was immune, even from the chill that was beginning. She walked along the beach. It was easier to walk when she felt soft. She was more flexible, more adaptable. There was a quarter moon, brilliantly cut. She could see the shape of the headland and the pale drape of sand leading up to it. The tide had receded. The waves sounded smaller. The crests looked thinner. She could probably walk around the lower section of the cliff now. Beneath everything disastrous, everything menacing, there was honesty. It was beautiful here. She had known it would be. Perhaps that's why she had wanted to come.

As she was walking something loomed up at her side and pushed against her leg. She flinched and stopped moving, then relaxed.

You again.

She petted the dog's head.

Have you been waiting? Look, you're not mine.

The dog was leaning against her, warmly, familiarly. Its coat in the near darkness seemed cleansed. The dog pressed against her and she put a hand on its back. She had avoided touching it properly before, worried about grime and germs. Now she crouched down and took hold of the dog's ears, then under its jaw, and rubbed.

Is that nice?

There was a fusty smell to the animal. The muzzle was wet and when she lifted it up to look underneath she could see it was dark and shiny,

Hey. What have you had your face in, stupid?

Something viscous and warm. When she took her hands away they were tacky. She knew, before the thought really registered, that it was blood.

Oh no, she said. What have you done? What have you done to yourself?

The dog shook its head. Its jowls slopped about. She wiped her face on her inner arm. Perhaps it had gone off and fought with another dog over some scraps while she was in the bar. Or one of the crabs it had been chasing had pinched it. She took hold of the dog's head again and moved it around to try to find a wound, but it was too dark to see properly. The animal was compliant, twitching a little but not pulling back from her grip. It did not seem to be in pain.

She stood up and walked to the edge of the water. She took off her sandals and stepped in. A wave came and soaked the hem of her dress. She stumbled, widened her stance. She slapped her thighs and tried to get the dog to come into the surf, but the dog stood on the beach, watching her, and then it began to whine. After a few attempts she came back out.

OK, she said. You're fine. Let's go.

They walked towards the headland and when they reached the rocks they stayed low and began to pick their way around the pools and gullies. This time the dog did not pilot. It kept close, nudging against her legs. When she looked down she could make out a dark smear on her dress. Where the outcrop became more uneven she bent and felt her way using her hands and was careful where she put her feet. The largest waves washed over the apron of rock against her shins. Towards the end of the headland, water was breaking against the base of the cliff. She timed her move and went quickly, stepping across the geometric stones. A wave came in and she heard it coming and held tightly to the rock face as it dashed upwards, wetting her dress to the waist. She gasped. Her body was forced against the rock. She felt one of her sandals come off. Water exploded around her and rushed away. The haul of the ocean was so great she was sure she'd be taken. She clung to the cliff. Every atom felt dragged. Then the grip released. She lurched around the pillar onto the flat ground, grazing her ankle as she landed. She winced and flexed her foot. She took off the remaining sandal and held it for a moment. Then she threw it away. She wrung out the bottom of her dress. She looked back. The white dog was standing on the other side of the rocky spur, its head hanging low.

Come on, she called. Come on.

It did not move.

Come on, she said. Come on.

The dog stayed on the rocks for a moment and then turned and she could see it was going back the way they had come.

She watched its white body moving. It floated. There seemed to be nothing holding it up. When the shape disappeared she turned and faced the long steep stretch of beach. The ramp of sand disappeared into the black jungle. The white tideline disappeared into the dark body of the ocean. Only the pale boundary was visible. Tideline meeting sand. She began to walk. She could not remember exactly where the hotel path was, about a mile away, but there was a signpost right by it, she knew that. She walked for a long time, feeling nothing but sand grinding the soles of her feet and chafing her ankles, salt tightening on her skin. She prepared herself. She could accept the end now. She could embrace it. No one was irreplaceable. No one. He could go. She would let him go. She did not like his friends, the smug barristers, the university clique, because they did not like her, because she was not their sort. She did not like his reticence or his conservatism, the way he drove, the way he danced. She would miss the sex, the companionship, until she found someone else. And she would find someone else. Let him join the men of the past. Her old lovers were ghosts. None of them had survived; none were missed.

After a while she stopped. She had come too far. She must have missed the let-out. She doubled back and after a time she saw the small skewed signpost at the top of the dune. She leaned forward and climbed up the bank towards it. Sand spilled backwards, skittering down the slope as she moved. Her legs ached. She felt exhausted. All she wanted to do was lie down and sleep. She sat for a moment at the top of the rise and looked at the ocean—a relentless dark mass. Tomorrow she would probably not see it. Then she stood.

—o—

The entrance of the path was nothing but a void in the jungle. There was still some warmth inside the foliage as she entered. She bent over and felt her way along, through the trees, to the wooden steps and up. She trod carefully. Occasionally she stamped a foot and the noise echoed dully. Under her feet the fine drifts of dust were cold. There was no light, no reflection. She felt invisible. She felt absent. She made her way through the trees, holding her hands out before her and feeling for low-hanging branches. Her eyes adjusted but the darkness continually bled back into their sockets and she had to fight blindness. The birds and the insects were silent. Then, the low-wattage lights of the outer salon tents.

Before she reached the complex she heard aggravated voices. She could not make out the words. She wondered whether he had raised the alarm. She was embarrassed by the thought, by the idea that people might know she had acted rashly, and why. As she came into the clearing where the main lodge was she could see in the external light a group of people standing together. He was not among them. Some of the staff were there, speaking earnestly to each other in Portuguese and an African language. One of them, the woman who had given them their key earlier that day when they checked in, had her arms wrapped around herself and she was rocking slightly. The fuss was embarrassing.

She thought about slipping back to the tent, unseen. She held back for a moment, and then she approached. They turned to look at her. No one spoke. Then the receptionist cried out, came towards her, gripped her painfully by the arms, and looked towards the men.

Ela está aqui! Ela está aqui!

I went for a walk. On the beach.

The woman released her and took a step backwards and raised her hand as if she might be about to strike her. Then she shook her hand and flicked her fingers.

Você não está morta?

I just went for a walk, she said again. What's happening? I'm alright.

There was a period of confusion. The discussion resumed and broke down. The receptionist shook her hands and walked away, in the shadows. She wanted to leave too, go back to the salon tent, face what she must and then sleep, but the intensity of the situation held her. Something was wrong. Her arrival back at the complex had not lessened their distress. One of the men in the group, the sub-manager, stepped forward. He gestured for her to follow. She walked with him to the entrance of the main lodge. By the doorway, on the ground, there was a bundle of cloths. They were knotted and blood-stained. The man pushed them aside with his foot, into the corner of the wooden porch. She began to feel dizzy. Heat bloomed up her neck.

What is it? she asked. Has there been an accident?

Ok, he said. Ok. Come inside.

He went through the door. She followed him into the bar and the man gestured for her to sit at a stool and she sat. His face was damp. He was scratching his arm. She heard others from the group entering the bar behind them.

Ah, he said. Ok. Your husband. He was looking around for you. He went to find you. He was very worried. He was . . . there was an attack, you see.

He was attacked? By who?

No. Not a fight. We don't really know how it happened. He was found by George one hour ago. Outside, in the dunes. But he was not conscious. There was a lot of blood. The wound is . . .

He called over to the ground of men by the door.

Ei, como você diz tendão?

Tendon.

Yes. The bite is in the tendon of his leg. It's very deep. And a lot of blood is gone. Breck is taking him to the hospital. They will probably have to go to Maputo in the ambulance.

She brought her hands to her face.

Oh my God, she said. Oh my God. I didn't think he would come after me.

Her palms smelled musty, like old meat, like a sick animal. She took them away from her mouth and looked up at the man. He was watching her, nervously. His eyes kept flicking away and back towards her, as if she might react dangerously, as if she might faint or bolt. She shook her head.

What was it? Was it a leopard?

No, he said. No. No. There are no leopards.

2011

Karen Russell

b. 1981

Karen Russell, by all accounts a new and unparalleled force in American literature, is in her early thirties. There is so little biographical detail about her that sketches are forced to include her Miami high school (Coral Gables, graduated 1999), after which she received a BA in Spanish from Northwestern University in 2003 and graduated from the MFA program at Columbia University in 2006. Along with a stint at the American Academy in Berlin, she has taught at Columbia, Bard, and Bryn Mawr. Notable as these facts are, we do not know how long she spent (and what that time was like) with alligator wrestlers in the Florida Everglades in the writing of her first novel and second book, the zany, bizarre and profoundly serious family saga, *Swamplandia!* (2011). But her literary profile is building with astonishing rapidity. In 2013, along with the publication—to a rare degree of celebration—of *Vampires in the Lemon Grove,* she was awarded a MacArthur Fellowship, fondly and jealously known as the "genius grant." Russell's writing life has not so much evolved as it has burst forth in cascades of language and narrative adventures, often through children and adolescents in magically imagined terrains: in "St. Lucy's Home for Girls Raised by Wolves," werewolf offspring are (more or less) taught ladylike behaviour; in "The New Veterans," a massage therapist transmutes a veteran's mural-like tattoo on his back of a dreadful day in Iraq; in the lemon grove, monogamous vampires meet in hemophilic harmony: "We bared our fangs over a tombstone and recognized each other. There is a loneliness that must be particular to monsters." As excited, truly awed, as they are by Russell's creation of story, readers seem almost content to list phrases and sentences, totemic evidence of an unusual talent at work (or "play," since Russell is a writer who has absorbed the deepest meaning of "play"). Loving to work at the "level of the sentence" is likely a factor in Russell's gravitation to the short story. "A story collection" she says, "simultaneously 'narrow and deep,'" also allows her to "come at some of the same themes and preoccupations from different angles . . . And then you can hop bodies and continents, so there's sort of this pinwheeling freedom."

Vampires in the Lemon Grove

In October, the men and women of Sorrento harvest the *primofiore*, or "first flowering fruit," the most succulent lemons; in March, the yellow *bianchetti* ripen, followed in June by the green *verdelli*. In every season you can find me sitting at my bench, watching them fall. Only one or two lemons tumble from the branches each hour, but I've been sitting here so long their falls seem contiguous, close as raindrops. My wife has no patience for this sort of meditation. "Jesus Christ, Clyde," she says. "You need a hobby."

Most people mistake me for a small, kindly Italian grandfather, a *nonno*. I have an old *nonno*'s coloring, the dark walnut stain peculiar to southern Italians, a tan that won't fade until I die (which I never will). I wear a neat periwinkle shirt, a canvas sunhat, black suspenders that sag at my chest. My loafers are battered but always polished. The few visitors to the lemon grove who notice me smile blankly into my raisin face and catch the whiff of some sort of tragedy; they whisper that I am a widower, or an old man who has survived his children. They never guess that I am a vampire.

Santa Francesca's Lemon Grove, where I spend my days and nights, was part of a Jesuit convent in the 1800s. Today it's privately owned by the Alberti family, the prices are excessive, and the locals know to buy their lemons elsewhere. In summers a teenage girl named Fila mans a wooden stall at the back of the grove. She's painfully thin, with heavy black bangs. I can tell by the careful way she saves the best lemons for me, slyly kicking them under my bench, that she knows I am a monster. Sometimes she'll smile vacantly in my direction, but she never gives me any trouble. And because of her benevolent indifference to me, I feel a swell of love for the girl.

Fila makes the lemonade and monitors the hot dog machine, watching the meat rotate on wire spigots. I'm fascinated by this machine. The Italian name for it translates as "carousel of beef." Who would have guessed at such a device two hundred years ago? Back then we were all preoccupied with visions of apocalypse; Santa Francesca, the foundress of this very grove, gouged out her eyes while dictating premonitions of fire. What a shame, I often think, that she foresaw only the end times, never hot dogs.

A sign posted just outside the grove reads:

> CIGERETTE PIE
> HEAT DOGS
> GRANITE DRINKS
> *Santa Francesca's Limonata—*
> THE MOST REFRISHING DRANK ON THE PLENET!!

Every day, tourists from Wales and Germany and America are ferried over from cruise ships to the base of these cliffs. They ride the funicular up here to visit the grove, to eat "heat dogs" with speckly brown mustard and sip lemon ices. They snap photographs of the Alberti brothers, Benny and Luciano, teenage twins who cling to the trees' wooden supports and make a grudging show of harvesting lemons, who spear each other with trowels and refer to the tourist women as "vaginas" in Italian slang. "*Buona sera*, vaginas!" they cry from the trees. I think the tourists are getting stupider. None of them speak Italian anymore, and these new women seem deaf to aggression. Often I fantasize about flashing my fangs at the brothers, just to keep them in line.

As I said, the tourists usually ignore me; perhaps it's the dominoes. A few years back, I bought a battered red set from Benny, a prop piece, and this makes me invisible, sufficiently banal to be hidden in plain sight. I have no real interest in the game; I mostly stack the pieces into little houses and corrals.

At sunset, the tourists all around begin to shout. "Look! Up there!" It's time for the path of *I Pipistrelli Impazziti*—the descent of the bats.

They flow from cliffs that glow like pale chalk, expelled from caves in the seeming billions. Their drop is steep and vertical, a black hail. Sometimes a change in weather sucks a bat beyond the lemon trees and into the turquoise sea. It's three hundred feet to the lemon grove, six hundred feet to the churning foam of the Tyrrhenian. At the precipice, they soar upward and crash around the green tops of the trees.

"Oh!" the tourists shriek, delighted, ducking their heads.

Up close, the bats' spread wings are alien membranes—fragile, like something internal flipped out. The waning sun washes their bodies a dusky red. They have wrinkled black faces, these bats, tiny, like gargoyles or angry grandfathers. They have teeth like mine.

Tonight, one of the tourists, a Texan lady with a big strawberry red updo, has successfully captured a bat in her hair, simultaneously crying real tears and howling: "TAKE THE GODDAMN PICTURE, Sarah!"

I stare ahead at a fixed point above the trees and light a cigarette. My bent spine goes rigid. Mortal terror always trips some old wire that leaves me sad and irritable. It will be whole minutes now before everybody stops screaming.

The moon is a muted shade of orange. Twin disks of light burn in the sky and the sea. I scan the darker indents in the skyline, the cloudless spots that I know to be caves. I check my watch again. It's eight o'clock, and all the bats have disappeared into the interior branches. Where is Magreb? My fangs are throbbing, but I won't start without her.

I once pictured time as a black magnifying glass and myself as a microscopic flightless insect trapped in that circle of night. But then Magreb came along, and eternity ceased to frighten me. Suddenly each moment followed its antecedent in a neat chain, moments we filled with each other.

I watch a single bat falling from the cliffs, dropping like a stone: headfirst, motionless, dizzying to witness.

Pull up.

I close my eyes. I press my palms flat against the picnic table and tense the muscles of my neck.

Pull UP. I tense until my temples pulse, until little black-and-red stars flutter behind my eyelids.

"You can look now."

Magreb is sitting on the bench, blinking her bright pumpkin eyes. "You weren't even *watching*. If you saw me coming down, you'd know you have nothing to worry about." I try to smile at her and find I can't. My own eyes feel like ice cubes.

"It's stupid to go so fast." I don't look at her. "That easterly could knock you over the rocks."

"Don't be ridiculous. I'm an excellent flier."

She's right. Magreb can shape-shift midair, much more smoothly than I ever could. Even back in the 1850s, when I used to transmute into a bat two, three times a night, my metamorphosis was a shy, halting process.

"Look!" she says, triumphant, mocking. "You're still trembling!"

I look down at my hands, angry to realize it's true.

Magreb roots through the tall, black blades of grass. "It's late, Clyde; where's my lemon?"

I pluck a soft, round lemon from the grass, a summer moon, and hand it to her. The *verdelli* I have chosen is perfect, flawless. She looks at it with distaste and makes a big show of brushing off a marching ribbon of ants.

"A toast!" I say.

"A toast," Magreb replies, with the rote enthusiasm of a Christian saying grace. We lift the lemons and swing them to our faces. We plunge our fangs, piercing the skin, and emit a long, united hiss: "*Aaah!*"

Over the years, Magreb and I have tried everything—fangs in apples, fangs in rubber balls. We have lived everywhere: Tunis, Laos, Cincinnati, Salamanca. We spent our honeymoon hopping continents, hunting liquid chimeras: mint tea in Fez, coconut slurries in Oahu, jet-black coffee in Bogotá, jackal's milk in Dakar, Cherry Coke floats in rural Alabama, a thousand beverages purported to have magical quenching properties. We went thirsty in every region of the globe before finding our oasis here, in the blue boot of Italy, at this dead nun's lemonade stand. It's only these lemons that give us any relief.

When we first landed in Sorrento I was skeptical. The pitcher of lemonade we ordered looked cloudy and adulterated. Sugar clumped at the bottom. I took a gulp, and a whole small lemon lodged in my mouth; there is no word sufficiently lovely for the first taste, the first feeling of my fangs in that lemon. It was bracingly sour, with a delicate hint of ocean salt. After an initial prickling—a sort of chemical effervescence along my gums—a soothing blankness traveled from the tip of each fang to my fevered brain. These lemons are a vampire's analgesic. If you have been thirsty for a long time, if you have been suffering, then the absence of those two feelings—however brief—becomes a kind of heaven. I breathed deeply through my nostrils. My throbbing fangs were still.

By daybreak, the numbness had begun to wear off. The lemons relieve our thirst without ending it, like a drink we can hold in our mouths but never swallow. Eventually the original hunger returns. I have tried to be very good, very correct and conscientious about not confusing this original hunger with the thing I feel for Magreb.

Can't joke about my early years on the blood, can't even think about them without guilt and acidic embarrassment. Unlike Magreb, who has never had a sip of the stuff, I listened to the village gossips and believed every rumor, internalized every report of corrupted bodies and boiled blood. Vampires were the favorite undead of the Enlightenment, and as a young boy I aped the diction and mannerisms I read about in books: Vlad the Impaler, Count Heinrich the Despoiler, Goethe's bloodsucking bride of Corinth. I eavesdropped on the terrified prayers of an old woman in a cemetery, begging God to protect her from . . . me. I felt a dislocation then, a spreading numbness, as if I were invisible or already dead. After that, I did only what the stories suggested, beginning with that old woman's blood. I slept in coffins, in black cedar boxes, and woke every night with a fierce headache. I was famished, perennially dizzy. I had unspeakable dreams about the sun.

In practice I was no suave viscount, just a teenager in a red velvet cape, awkward and voracious. I wanted to touch the edges of my life—the same instinct, I think, that inspires young mortals to flip tractors and enlist in foreign wars. One night I skulked into a late Mass with some vague plan to defeat eternity. At the back of the nave, I tossed my mousy curls, rolled my eyes heavenward, and then plunged my entire arm into the bronze pail of holy water. Death would be painful, probably, but I didn't care about pain. I wanted to overturn my sentence. It was working; I could feel the burn beginning to spread. Actually, it was more like an itch, but I was sure the burning would start any second. I slid into a pew, snug in my misery, and waited for my body to turn to ash.

By sunrise, I'd developed a rash between my eyebrows, a little late-flowering acne, but was otherwise fine, and I understood I truly was immortal. At that moment I yielded all discrimination; I bit anyone kind or slow enough to let me get close: men, women, even some older boys and girls. The littlest children I left alone, very proud at the time of this one scruple. I'd read stories about Hungarian *vampirs* who drank the blood of orphan girls, and mentioned this to Magreb early on, hoping to impress her with my decency. *Not children!* she wept.

She wept for a day and a half.

Our first date was in Cementerio de Colón, if I can call a chance meeting between headstones a date. I had been stalking her, following her swishing hips as she took a shortcut through the cemetery grass. She wore her hair in a low, snaky braid that was coming unraveled. When I was near enough to touch her trailing ribbon she whipped around. "Are you following me?" she asked, annoyed, not scared. She regarded my face with the contempt of a woman confronting the town drunk. "Oh," she said, "your teeth . . ."

And then she grinned. Magreb was the first and only other vampire I'd ever met. We bared our fangs over a tombstone and recognized each other. There is a loneliness that must be particular to monsters, I think, the feeling that each is the only child of a species. And now that loneliness was over.

Our first date lasted all night. Magreb's talk seemed to lunge forward like a train without a conductor; I suspect even she didn't know what she was saying. I certainly wasn't paying attention, staring dopily at her fangs, and then I heard her ask: "So, when did you figure out that the blood does nothing?"

At the time of this conversation, I was edging on 130. I had never gone a day since early childhood without drinking several pints of blood. *The blood does nothing?* My forehead burned and burned.

"Didn't you think it suspicious that you had a heartbeat?" she asked me. "That you had a reflection in water?"

When I didn't answer, Magreb went on, "Every time I saw my own face in a mirror, I knew I wasn't any of those ridiculous things, a bloodsucker, a *sanguina*. You know?"

"Sure," I said, nodding. For me, mirrors had the opposite effect: I saw a mouth ringed in black blood. I saw the pale son of the villagers' fears.

Those initial days with Magreb nearly undid me. At first my euphoria was sharp and blinding, all my thoughts spooling into a single blue thread of relief—*The blood does nothing! I don't have to drink the blood!*—but when that subsided, I found I had nothing left. If we didn't have to drink the blood, then what on earth were these fangs for?

Sometimes I think she preferred me then: I was like her own child, raw and amazed. We smashed my coffin with an ax and spent the night at a hotel. I lay there wide-eyed in the big bed, my heart thudding like a fish tail against the floor of a boat.

"You're really sure?" I whispered to her. "I don't have to sleep in a coffin? I don't have to sleep through the day?" She had already drifted off.

A few months later, she suggested a picnic.

"But the sun."

Magreb shook her head. "You poor thing, believing all that garbage."

By this time we'd found a dirt cellar in which to live in Western Australia, where the sun burned through the clouds like dining lace. That sun ate lakes, rising out of dead volcanoes at dawn, triple the size of a harvest moon and skull-white, a grass-scorcher. Go ahead, try to walk into that sun when you've been told your bones are tinder.

I stared at the warped planks of the trapdoor above us, the copper ladder that led rung by rung to the bright world beyond. Time fell away from me and I was a child again, afraid, afraid. Magreb rested her hand on the small of my back. "You can do it," she said, nudging me gently. I took a deep breath and hunched my shoulders, my scalp grazing the cellar door, my hair soaked through with sweat. I focused my thoughts to still the tremors, lest my fangs slice the inside of my mouth, and turned my face away from Magreb.

"Go on."

I pushed up and felt the wood give way. Light exploded through the cellar. My pupils shrank to dots.

Outside, the whole world was on fire. Mute explosions rocked the scrubby forest, motes of light burning like silent rockets. The sun fell through the eucalyptus and Australian pines in bright red bars. I pulled myself out onto my belly, balled up in the soil, and screamed for mercy until I'd exhausted myself. Then I opened one watery eye and took a long look around. The sun wasn't fatal! It was just uncomfortable, making my eyes itch and water and inducing a sneezing attack.

After that, and for the whole of our next thirty years together, I watched the auroral colors and waited to feel anything but terror. Fingers of light spread across the gray sea toward me, and I couldn't see these colors as beautiful. The sky I lived under was a hideous, lethal mix of orange and pink, a physical deformity. By the 1950s we were living in a Cincinnati suburb; and as the day's first light hit the kitchen windows, I'd press my face against the linoleum and gibber my terror into the cracks.

"Sooo," Magreb would say, "I can tell you're not a morning person." Then she'd sit on the porch swing and rock with me, patting my hand.

"What's wrong, Clyde?"

I shook my head. This was a new sadness, difficult to express. My bloodlust was undiminished but now the blood wouldn't fix it.

"It never fixed it," Magreb reminded me, and I wished she would please stop talking.

That cluster of years was a very confusing period. Mostly I felt grateful, aboveground feelings. I was in love. For a vampire, my life was very normal. Instead of stalking prostitutes, I went on long bicycle rides with Magreb. We visited botanical gardens and rowed in boats. In a short time, my face had gone from lithium white to the color of milky coffee. Yet sometimes, especially at high noon, I'd study Magreb's face with a hot, illogical hatred, each pore opening up to swallow me. *You've ruined my life*, I'd think. To correct for her power over my mind I tried to fantasize about mortal women, their wild eyes and bare swan necks; I couldn't do it, not anymore—an eternity of vague female smiles eclipsed by Magreb's tiny razor fangs. Two gray tabs against her lower lip.

But like I said, I was mostly happy. I was making a kind of progress.

One night, children wearing necklaces of garlic bulbs arrived giggling at our door. It was Halloween; they were vampire hunters. The smell of garlic blasted through the mail slot, along with their voices: "Trick or treat!" In the old days, I would have cowered from these children. I would have run downstairs to barricade myself in my coffin. But that night, I pulled on an undershirt and opened the door. I stood in a square of green light in my boxer shorts hefting a bag of Tootsie Pops, a small victory over the old fear.

"Mister, you okay?"

I blinked down at a little blond child and then saw that my two hands were shaking violently, soundlessly, like old friends wishing not to burden me with their troubles. I dropped the candies into the children's bags, thinking: *You small mortals don't realize the power of your stories.*

We were downing strawberry velvet cocktails on the Seine when something inside me changed. Thirty years. Eleven thousand dawns. That's how long it took for me to believe the sun wouldn't kill me.

"Want to go see a museum or something? We're in Paris, after all."

"Okay."

We walked over a busy pedestrian bridge in a flood of light, and my heart was in my throat. Without any discussion, I understood that Magreb was my wife.

Because I love her, my hunger pangs have gradually mellowed into a comfortable despair. Sometimes I think of us as two holes cleaved together, two twin hungers. Our bellies growl at each other like companionable dogs. I love the sound, assuring me we're equals in our thirst. We bump our fangs and feel like we're coming up against the same hard truth.

Human marriages amuse me: the brevity of the commitment and all the ceremony that surrounds it, the calla lilies, the veiled mother-in-laws like lilac spiders, the tears and earnest toasts. Till death do us part! Easy. These mortal couples need only keep each other in sight for fifty, sixty years.

Often I wonder to what extent a mortal's love grows from the bedrock of his or her foreknowledge of death, love coiling like a green stem out of that blankness in a way I'll never quite understand. And lately I've been having a terrible thought: *Our love affair will end before the world does.*

One day, without any preamble, Magreb flew up to the caves. She called over her furry, muscled shoulder that she just wanted to sleep for a while.

"What? Wait! What's wrong?"

I'd caught her mid-shift, halfway between a wife and a bat.

"Don't be so sensitive, Clyde! I'm just tired of this century, so very tired, maybe it's the heat? I think I need a little rest . . ."

I assumed this was an experiment, like my cape, an old habit to which she was returning, and from the clumsy, ambivalent way she crashed around on the wind I understood I was supposed to follow her. Well, too bad. Magreb likes to say she freed me, disabused me of the old stories, but I gave up more than I intended: I can't shudder myself out of this old man's body. I can't fly anymore.

Fila and I are alone. I press my dry lips together and shove dominoes around the table; they buckle like the cars of a tiny train.

"More lemonade, *nonno*?" She smiles. She leans from her waist and boldly touches my right fang, a thin string of hanging drool. "Looks like you're thirsty."

"Please," I gesture at the bench. "Have a seat."

Fila is seventeen now and has known about me for some time. She's toying with the idea of telling her boss, weighing the sentence within her like a bullet in a gun: *There is a vampire in our grove.*

"You don't believe me, Signore Alberti?" she'll say, before taking him by the wrist and leading him to this bench, and I'll choose that moment to rise up and bite him in his hog-thick neck. "Right through his stupid tie!" she says with a grin.

But this is just idle fantasy, she assures me. Fila is content to let me alone. "You remind me of my *nonno*," she says approvingly, "you look very Italian."

In fact, she wants to help me hide here. It gives her a warm feeling to do so, like helping her own fierce *nonno* do up the small buttons of his trousers, now too intricate a maneuver for his palsied hands. She worries about me, too. And she should: lately I've gotten sloppy, incontinent about my secrets. I've stopped polishing my shoes; I let the tip of one fang hang over my pink lip. "You must be more careful," she reprimands. "There are tourists *everywhere*."

I study her neck as she says this, her head rolling with the natural expressiveness of a girl. She checks to see if I am watching her collarbone, and I let her see that I am. I feel like a threat again.

Last night I went on a rampage. On my seventh lemon I found with a sort of drowsy despair that I couldn't stop. I crawled around on all fours looking for the last *bianchettis* in the dewy grass: soft with rot, mildewed, sun-shriveled, blackened. Lemon skin bulging with tiny cellophane-green worms. Dirt smells, rain smells, all swirled through with the tart sting of decay.

In the morning, Magreb steps around the wreckage and doesn't say a word.

"I came up with a new name," I say, hoping to distract her. "*Brandolino.* What do you think?"

I have spent the last several years trying to choose an Italian name, and every day that I remain Clyde feels like a defeat. Our names are relics of the places we've been. "Clyde" is a souvenir from the California Gold Rush. I was callow and blood-crazed back then, and I saw my echo in the freckly youths panning along the Sacramento River. I used the name as a kind of bait. "Clyde" sounded innocuous, like someone a boy might get a malt beer with or follow into the woods.

Magreb chose her name in the Atlas Mountains for its etymology, the root word *ghuroob,* which means "to set" or "to be hidden." "That's what we're looking for," she tells me. "The setting place. Some final answer." She won't change her name until we find it.

She takes a lemon from her mouth, slides it down the length of her fangs, and places its shriveled core on the picnic table. When she finally speaks, her voice is so low the words are almost unintelligible.

"The lemons aren't working, Clyde."

But the lemons have never worked. At best, they give us eight hours of peace. We aren't talking about the lemons.

"How long?"

"Longer than I've let on. I'm sorry."

"Well, maybe it's this crop. Those Alberti boys haven't been fertilizing properly, maybe the *primofiore* will turn out better."

Magreb fixes me with one fish-bright eye. "Clyde, I think it's time for us to go."

Wind blows the leaves apart. Lemons wink like a firmament of yellow stars, slowly ripening, and I can see the other, truer night behind them.

"Go where?" Our marriage, as I conceive it, is a commitment to starve together.

"We've been resting here for decades. I think it's time . . . what is that thing?"

I have been preparing a present for Magreb, for our anniversary, a "cave" of scavenged materials—newspaper and bottle glass and wooden beams from the lemon tree supports—so that she can sleep down here with me. I've smashed dozens of bottles of fruity beer to make stalactites. Looking at it now, though, I see the cave is very small. It looks like an umbrella mauled by a dog.

"That thing?" I say. "That's nothing. I think it's part of the hot dog machine."

"Jesus. Did it catch on fire?"

"Yes. The girl threw it out yesterday."

"Clyde." Magreb shakes her head. "We never meant to stay here forever, did we? That was never the plan."

"I didn't know we had a plan," I snap. "What if we've outlived our food supply? What if there's nothing left for us to find?"

"You don't really believe that."

"Why can't you just be grateful? Why can't you be happy and admit defeat? Look at what we've found here!" I grab a lemon and wave it in her face.

"Good night, Clyde."

I watch my wife fly up into the watery dawn, and again I feel the awful tension. In the flats of my feet, in my knobbed spine. Love has infected me with a muscular superstition that one body can do the work of another.

I consider taking the funicular, the ultimate degradation—worse than the dominoes, worse than an eternity of sucking cut lemons. All day I watch the cars ascend, and I'm reminded of those American fools who accompany their wives to the beach but refuse to wear bathing suits. I've seen them by the harbor, sulking in their trousers, panting through menthol cigarettes and pacing the dock while the women sea-bathe. They pretend they don't mind when sweat darkens the armpits of their suits. When their wives swim out and leave them. When their wives are just a splash in the distance.

Tickets for the funicular are twenty lire. I sit at the bench and count as the cars go by.

That evening, I take Magreb on a date. I haven't left the lemon grove in upward of two years, and blood roars in my ears as I stand and clutch at her like an old man. We're going to the Thursday night show at an antique theater in a castle in the center of town. I want her to see that I'm happy to travel with her, so long as our destination is within walking distance.

A teenage usher in a vintage red jacket with puffed sleeves escorts us to our seats, his biceps manacled in clouds, threads loosening from the badge on his chest. I am jealous of the name there: GUGLIELMO.

The movie's title is already scrolling across the black screen: SOMETHING CLANDESTINE IS HAPPENING IN THE CORN!

Magreb snorts. "That's a pretty lousy name for a horror movie. It sounds like a student film."

"Here's your ticket," I say. "I didn't make the title up."

It's a vampire movie set in the Dust Bowl. Magreb expects a comedy, but the Dracula actor fills me with the sadness of an old photo album. An Okie has unwittingly fallen in love with the monster, whom she's mistaken for a rich European creditor eager to pay off the mortgage on her family's farm.

"That Okie," says Magreb, "is an idiot."

I turn my head miserably and there's Fila, sitting two rows in front of us with a greasy young man. Benny Alberti. Her white neck is bent to the left, Benny's lips affixed to it as she impassively sips a soda.

"Poor thing," Magreb whispers, indicating the pigtailed actress. "She thinks he's going to save her."

Dracula shows his fangs, and the Okie flees through a cornfield. Cornstalks smack her face. "Help!" she screams to a sky full of crows. "He's not actually from Europe!"

There is no music, only the girl's breath and the *fwap-fwap-fwap* of the off-screen fan blades. Dracula's mouth hangs wide as a sewer grate. His cape is curiously still.

The movie picture is frozen. The *fwapping* is emanating from the projection booth; it rises to a grinding *r-r-r*, followed by lyrical Italian cussing and silence and finally a tidal sigh. Magreb shifts in her seat.

"Let's wait," I say, seized with empathy for these two still figures on the screen, mutely pleading for repair. "They'll fix it."

People begin to file out of the theater, first in twos and threes and then in droves. "I'm tired, Clyde."

"Don't you want to know what happens?" My voice is more frantic than I intend.

"I already know what happens."

"Don't you leave now, Magreb. I'm telling you, they're going to fix it. If you leave now, that's it for us, I'll never . . ."

Her voice is beautiful, like gravel underfoot: "I'm going to the caves."

I'm alone in the theater. When I turn to exit, the picture is still frozen, the Okie's blue dress floating over windless corn, Dracula's mouth a hole in his white greasepaint.

Outside I see Fila standing in a clot of her friends, lit by the marquee. These kids wear too much makeup and clothes that move like colored oils. They all look rained on. I scowl at them and they scowl back, and then Fila crosses to me.

"Hey, you," she says, grinning, breathless, so very close to my face. "Are you stalking somebody?"

My throat tightens.

"Guys!" Her eyes gleam. "Guys, come over and meet the *vampire*."

But the kids are gone.

"Well! Some friends," she says, then winks. "Leaving me alone, defenseless . . ."

"You want the old vampire to bite you, eh?" I hiss. "You want a story for your friends?"

Fila laughs. Her horror is a round, genuine thing, bouncing in both her black eyes. She smells like hard water and glycerin. The hum of her young life all around me makes it difficult to think. A bat filters my thoughts, opens its trembling lampshade wings.

Magreb. She'll want to hear about this. How ridiculous, at my age, to find myself down this alley with a young girl: Fila powdering her neck, doing her hair up with little temptress pins, yanking me behind this Dumpster. "Can you imagine"—Magreb will laugh—"a teenager goading you to attack her! You're still a menace, Clyde."

I stare vacantly at a pale mole above the girl's collarbone. *Magreb*, I think again, and I smile, and the smile feels like a muzzle stretched taut against my teeth. It seems my hand has tightened on the girl's wrist, and I realize with surprise, as if from a great distance, that she is twisting away.

"Hey, *nonno*, come on now, what are you—"

The girl's head lolls against my shoulder like a sleepy child's, then swings forward in a rag-doll circle. The starlight is white mercury compared to her blotted-out eyes. There's a dark stain on my periwinkle shirt, and one suspender has snapped. I sit Fila's body against the alley wall, watch it dim and stiffen. Spidery graffiti weaves over the brick behind her, and I scan for some answer contained there: GIOVANNA & FABIANO. VAFFANCULO! VAI IN CULO.

A scabby-furred creature, our only witness, arches its orange back against the Dumpster. If not for the lock I would ease the girl inside. I would climb in with her and let the red stench fill my nostrils, let the flies crawl into the red corners of my eyes. I am a monster again.

I ransack Fila's pockets and find the key to the funicular office, careful not to look at her face. Then I'm walking, running for the lemon grove. I jimmy my way into the control room and turn the silver key, relieved to hear the engine roar to life. Locked, locked, every funicular car is locked, but then I find one with thick tape in Xs over a busted door. I dash after it and pull myself onto the cushion, quickly, because the cars are already moving. Even now, after what I've done, I am still unable to fly, still imprisoned in my wretched *nonno*'s body, reduced to using the mortals' machinery to carry me up to find my wife. The box jounces and trembles. The chain pulls me into the heavens link by link.

My lips are soon chapped; I stare through a crack in the glass window. The box swings wildly in the wind. The sky is a deep blue vacuum. I can still smell the girl in the folds of my clothes.

The cave system at the top of the cliffs is vaster than I expected; and with their grandfather faces tucked away, the bats are anonymous as stones.

I walk beneath a chandelier of furry bodies, heartbeats wrapped in wings the color of rose petals or corn silk. Breath ripples through each of them, a tiny life in its translucent envelope.

"Magreb?"

Is she up here?

Has she left me?

(I will never find another vampire.)

I double back to the moonlit entrance that leads to the open air of the cliffs, the funicular cars. When I find Magreb, I'll beg her to tell me what she dreams up here. I'll tell her my waking dreams in the lemon grove: The mortal men and women floating serenely by in balloons freighted with the ballast of their deaths. Millions of balloons ride over a wide ocean, lives darkening the sky. Death is a dense powder cinched inside tiny sandbags, and in the dream I am given to understand that instead of a sandbag I have Magreb.

I make the bats' descent in a cable car with no wings to spread, knocked around by the wind with a force that feels personal. I struggle to hold the door shut and look for the green speck of our grove.

The box is plunging now, far too quickly. It swings wide, and the igneous surface of the mountain fills the left window. The tufa shines like water, like a black, heat-bubbled river. For a dizzying instant I expect the rock to seep through the glass.

Each swing takes me higher than the last, a grinding pendulum that approaches a full revolution around the cable. I'm on my hands and knees on the car floor, sea-sick in the high air, pressing my face against the floor grate. I can see stars or boats burning there, and also a ribbon of white, a widening fissure. Air gushes through the cracks in the glass box. With a lurch of surprise, I realize that I could die.

What does Magreb see, if she is watching? Is she waking from a nightmare to see the line snap, the glass box plummet? From her inverted vantage, dangling from the roof of the cave, does the car seem to be sucked upward, rushing not toward the sea but into another sort of sky? To a black mouth open and foaming with stars?

I like to picture my wife like this: Magreb shuts her thin eyelids tighter. She digs her claws into the rock. Little clouds of dust plume around her toes as she swings upside down. She feels something growing inside her, a dreadful suspicion. It is solid, this new thing, it is the opposite of hunger. She's emerging from a dream of distant thunder, rumbling and loose. Something has happened tonight that she thought impossible. In the morning, she will want to tell me about it.

2013

Acknowledgements

CHINUA ACHEBE. "Civil Peace" from *Girls at War and Other Stories* by Chinua Achebe. Copyright © 1972, 1973 by Chinua Achebe, used by permission of the Wylie Agency LLC.

SHERMAN ALEXIE. "This Is What It Means to Say Phoenix, Arizona" from *The Lone Ranger and Tonto Fistfight in Heaven* © 1993 by Sherman Alexie. Used by permission of Grove/Atlantic, Inc. Any third party use of this material, outside this publication, is prohibited.

WOODY ALLEN. "The Kugelmass Episode", copyright © 1977 by Woody Allen, from *Side Effects* by Woody Allen. Used by permission of Random House, an imprint and division of Random House LLC. All rights reserved.

MARGARET ATWOOD. "Death by Landscape" excerpted from *Wilderness Tips* by Margaret Atwood. Copyright © 1991 O.W. Toad Ltd. Reprinted by permission of McClelland & Stewart, a division of Random House of Canada Limited, a Penguin Random House Company.

SAMUEL BECKETT. "Imagination Dead Imagine" from *First Love, & Other Shorts*, copyright © 1957, 1965, 1966, 1969, 1970, 1973, 1974 by Samuel Beckett, copyright © this collection 1974 by Grove Press, Inc. Used by permission of Grove/Atlantic, Inc. Any third party use of this material, outside of this publication, is prohibited.

JOHN BERGER. "Islington" © 2005 by John Berger.

SANDRA BIRDSELL. "The Wednesday Circle" excerpted from *Agassiz Stories* by Sandra Birdsell. *Night Travellers* Copyright © 1982 Sandra Birdsell. Copyright © 2002 Sandra Birdsell. Reprinted by permission of Emblem/McClelland & Stewart, a division of Random House of Canada Limited, a Penguin Random House Company.

MARIE-CLAIRE BLAIS. "The Forsaken" © Marie-Claire Blais. Reprinted by permission of the author. English translation © Patricia Sillers. Reprinted by permission.

JORGE LUIS BORGES. "The Library of Babel", from *Collection Fictions* by Jorge Luis Borges. Copyright © Maria Kodama, 1998. Translation and notes copyright © Penguin Putnam Inc., 1998. Reprinted by permission of Penguin Canada Books Inc.

DIONNE BRAND. "Photograph" from *Sans Souci and Other Stories*. Copyright © 1989 by Dionne Brand. Published 1994 by Three O'Clock Press. Reprinted by permission of the publisher.

ALBERT CAMUS. "The Guest" from *Exile and the Kingdom* by Albert Camus and translated by Justin O'Brien, copyright © 1957, 1958 by Alfred A. Knopf, a division of Random House LLC. Used by permission of Alfred A. Knopf, an imprint of the Knopf Doubleday Publishing Group, a division of Random House LLC. All rights reserved.

ANGELA CARTER. "The Company of Wolves" Copyright © Angela Carter 1995. Reproduced by permission of the author c/o Rogers, Coleridge & White Ltd., 20 Powis Mews, London W11 1JN.

RAYMOND CARVER. "Errand" from *Where I'm Calling From* © 1988 by Raymond Carver. Used by permission of Grove/Atlantic, Inc. Any third party use of this material, outside of this publication, is prohibited.

AUSTIN CLARKE. "Leaving This Island Place" by Austin Clarke, originally appeared in *Choosing His Coffin: The Best Stories of Austin Clarke*, (Thomas Allen Publishers, 2003) by permission of Dundurn Press Limited.

EDWIDGE DANTICAT. "Between the Pool and the Gardenias" from *Krik? Krak!*, copyright © 1991, 1995 by Edwidge Danticat, reprinted by permission of Soho Press, Inc. All rights reserved.

LYDIA DAVIS. "The Bone" and "A Few Things Wrong with Me" from *The Collected Stories of Lydia Davis* by Lydia Davis. Copyright © 2009 by Lydia Davis. Reprinted by permission of Farrar, Straus and Giroux, LLC.

DON DELILLO. "Baader-Meinhof" reprinted with the permission of Scribner Publishing Group, a division of Simon & Schuster, Inc. from *The Angel Esmeralda: Nine Stories* by Don DeLillo. Copyright © 2011 by Don DeLillo. All rights reserved.

ANITA DESAI. "Surface Textures" copyright © Anita Desai 1978. Reproduced by permission of Rogers, Coleridge & White Ltd., 20 Powis Mews, London W11 1JN.

ANNE ENRIGHT. "Yesterday's Weather" excerpted from *Yesterday's Weather* by Anne Enright. Copyright © 1989, 1991, 2008 Anne Enright. Reprinted by permission of McClelland & Stewart, a division of Random House of Canada Limited, a Penguin Random House Company.

LOUISE ERDRICH. "Fleur" from *Tracks* by Louise Erdrich. Copyright © 1988 by Louise Erdrich, used by permission of The Wylie Agency LLC.

RICHARD FORD. "Rock Springs" from *Rock Springs*, copyright © 1987 by Richard Ford. Used by permission of Grove/Atlantic, Inc. Any third party use of this material, outside of this publication, is prohibited.

KEATH FRASER. "Roget's Thesaurus" from *Taking Cover* by Keath Fraser. © 1982. Reprinted by permission of the author.

MAVIS GALLANT. "In Youth is Pleasure" and "Voices Lost in Snow" from *Home Truths* by Mavis Gallant. Copyright © 1956, 1959, 1963, 1954, 1968, 1971, 1975, 1976, 1977, 1978, 1981 by Mavis Gallant. Reprinted by permission of Georges Borchardt, Inc., on behalf of the author.

GABRIEL GARCÍA MÁRQUEZ. All pages from "The Handsomest Drowned Man in the World" from *Leaf Storm and Other Stories* by Gabriel García Márquez. Copyright © 1971 by Gabriel García Márquez. Reprinted by permission of HarperCollins Publishers.

NADINE GORDIMER. "Is There Nowhere Else We Can Meet?" from *The Soft Voice of the Serpent and Other Stories*. Reprinted by the permission of Russell & Volkening as agents for the author. Copyright © 1952 by Nadine Gordimer, renewed in 1980 by Nadine Gordimer.

BARBARA GOWDY. "We So Seldom Look on Love" from *We So Seldom Look on Love* by Barbara Gowdy (Somerville House Publishing, 1992). Copyright © 1992 Barbara Gowdy. With permission of the author.

SARAH HALL. "She Murdered Mortal He" from *The Beautiful Indifference*. © Sarah Hall and reprinted by permission of Faber and Faber Ltd.

ELIZABETH HAY. "The Friend" excerpted from *Small Change* by Elizabeth Hay. Copyright © 1997 Elizabeth Hay. Reprinted by permission of Emblem/McClelland & Stewart, a division of Random House of Canada Limited, a Penguin Random House Company.

ERNEST HEMINGWAY. "A Clean, Well-Lighted Place" reprinted with the permission of Scribner Publishing Group, a division of Simon & Schuster, Inc. from *Winner Take Nothing* by Ernest Hemingway. Copyright © 1933 by Charles Scribner's Sons. Copyright renewed © 1961 by Mary Hemingway. All rights reserved.

JACK HODGINS. "Separating" from *Spit Delaney's Island: Selected Stories* by Jack Hodgins (Macmillan, 1976). Copyright © 1976 Jack Hodgins. With permission of the author.

FRANZ KAFKA. "Before the Law" from *The Complete Stories* by Franz Kafka, copyright © 1946, 1947, 1948, 1949, 1954, 1958, 1971 by Schocken Books, an imprint of the Knopf Doubleday Group, a division of Random House LLC. Used by permission of Schocken Books, an imprint of the Knopf Doubleday Publishing Group, a division of Random House LLC. All rights reserved.

THOMAS KING. "The One About Coyote Going West" from *One Good Story, That One* by Thomas King (HarperCollins Canada, 1993). Copyright © 1993 Thomas King. With permission of the author.

MAXINE HONG KINGSTON. "On Mortality" from *China Men* by Maxine Hong Kingston, copyright © 1977, 1978, 1979, 1980 by Maxine Hong Kingston. Used by permission of Alfred A. Knopf, an imprint of the Knopf Doubleday Publishing Group, a division of Random House LLC. All rights reserved.

DORIS LESSING. "A Man and Two Women" from *A Man and Two Women*. Copyright © 1963 Doris Lessing. Reprinted by kind permission of Jonathan Clowes Ltd., London, on behalf of Doris Lessing.

ALISTAIR MACLEOD. "Vision" excerpted from *Island: The Collected Stories of Alistair MacLeod* by Alistair MacLeod. Copyright © 2000 Alistair MacLeod. Reprinted by permission of McClelland & Stewart, a division of Random House of Canada Limited, a Penguin Random House Company.

LORRIE MOORE. "Agnes of Iowa" from *Birds of America: Stories* by Lorrie Moore, copyright © 1998 by Lorrie Moore. Used by permission of Alfred A. Knopf, an imprint of the Knopf Doubleday Publishing Group, a division of Random House LLC. All rights reserved.

TONI MORRISON. "Recicatif" © 1993 by Toni Morrison. Used by Permission. All rights reserved.

ALICE MUNRO. "Fits" excerpted from *The Progress of Love* by Alice Munro. Copyright © 1986 Alice Munro. Reprinted by permission of McClelland & Stewart, a division of Random House of Canada Limited, a Penguin Random House Company.

ALICE MUNRO. "Open Secrets" excerpted from *Open Secrets* by Alice Munro. Copyright © 1994 Alice Munro. Reprinted by permission of McClelland & Stewart, a division of Random House of Canada Limited, a Penguin Random House Company.

BEN OKRI. Extract from *From Incidents at the Shrine* by Ben Okri. Published by Jonathan Cape. Reprinted by permission of The Random House Group Limited.

TILLIE OLSEN. "I Stand Here Ironing" reprinted from *Tell Me a Riddle, Requa I, and Other Works* by Tillie Olsen by permission of the University of Nebraska Press. Copyright 1961 by Tillie Olsen.

ELENA PONIATOWSKA. "The Night Visitor", translated by Catherine S. White-House, from *Other Fires: Short Fiction by Latin-American Women* edited by Alberto Manguel. Toronto: Lester & Orpen Dennys, 1986. Reprinted by permission of Elena Poniatowska, author of *Massacre in Mexico, Dear Diego, Here's To You Jésusa!*, and *Tinisima*.

MORDECAI RICHLER. "Benny, the War in Europe, and Myerson's Daughter Bella" excerpted from *The Street* by Mordecai Richler. Copyright © 1969 Mordecai Richler. Copyright © 2002 Mordecai Richler Productions Inc. Reprinted by permission of McClelland & Stewart, a division of Random House of Canada Limited, a Penguin Random House Company.

LEON ROOKE. "A Bolt of White Cloth" reprinted by permission of the author.

KAREN RUSSELL. "Vampires in the Lemon Grove" from *Vampires in the Lemon Grove: Stories* by Karen Russell, copyright © 2013. Used by permission of Alfred A. Knopf, an imprint of the Doubleday Publishing Group, a division of Random House LLC. All rights reserved.

GEORGE SAUNDERS. "Victory Lap" from *Tenth of December: Stories* by George Saunder, copyright © 2013 by George Saunders. Used by permission of Random House, and imprint and division of Random House LLC. All rights reserved.

BRUNO SCHULZ. "Sanitorium Under the Sign of the Hourglass" © Bruno Schulz, 1937, 1978 *Sanitorium Under the Sign of the Hourglass,* trans. Celina Wieniewska, Walker Books, an imprint of Bloomsbury Publishing Inc.

SINCLAIR ROSS. "The Painted Door" excerpted from *The Lamp at Noon and Other Stories* by Sinclair Ross. Copyright © 1968 Sinclair Ross. Reprinted by permission of McClelland & Stewart, a division of Random House of Canada Limited, a Penguin Random House Company.

JOSEF ŠKVORECKÝ. "panta rei" excerpted from *Headed for the Blues: A Memoir with Ten Stories* by Josef Škvorecký. Copyright © 1997 Josef Škvorecký. Reprinted by permission of Alfred A. Knopf Canada, a division of Random House of Canada Limited, a Penguin Random House Company.

ROBERT STONE. "Miserere" from *Bear and His Daughter: Stories* by Robert Stone. Copyright © 1997 by Robert Stone. Reprinted by permission of Houghton

Mifflin Harcourt Publishing Company. All rights reserved.

WILLIAM TREVOR. "The Piano Tuner's Wives" from *After Rain*. Reprinted by permission of SLL/Sterling Lord Literistic, Inc. Copyright by William Trevor.

JOHN UPDIKE. "Pigeon Feathers" from *Pigeon Feathers and Other Stories* by John Updike, copyright © 1962, copyright renewed 1990 by Jonh Updike. Used by permisson of Alfred A. Knopf, an imprint of the Knopf Doubleday Publishing Group, a division of Random House LLC. All rights reserved.

JANE URQUHART. "The Death of Robert Browning" excerpted from *Storm Glass* by Jane Urquhart. Copyright © 1987 Jane Urquhart. Reprinted by permission of McClelland & Stewart, a division of Random House of Canada Limited, a Penguin Random House Company.

EMMA LEE WARRIOR. "Compatriots" from *All My Relations: An Anthology of Contemporary Canadian Native Fiction.* Toronto: McClelland & Stewart, 1990. Reprinted by the author.

SHEILA WATSON. "Antigone" from *Four Stories* by Sheila Watson, Coach House Press, 1979. Reprinted by permission of the Estate of Sheila Watson.

TOBIAS WOLFF. "Casualty" from *The Night in Question: Stories* by Tobias Wolff, copyright © 1996 by Tobias Wolff. Used by permission of Alfred A. Knopf, an imprint of the Knopf Doubleday Publishing Group, a division of Random House LLC. All rights reserved.

RICHARD WRIGHT. "The Man Who Was Almost a Man" [pp. 3–18] from *Eight Men* by Richard Wright. Copyright © 1940, 1961, by Richard Wright; renewed © 1989 by Ellen Wright. Introduction copyright © 1996 by Paul Gilroy. Reprinted by permission of HarperCollins Publishers.

Index